THE LOCKED-ROOM MYSTERIES

ALSO EDITED BY OTTO PENZLER

First published in the United States in 2014 by Vintage Books, a division of Random House LLC, New York and in Canada by Random House of Canada Limited, Toronto, Penguin Random House companies.

Published in e-book in 2014 and trade paperback in Great Britain in 2015 by Corvus, an imprint of Atlantic Books Ltd.

10 9 8 7 6 5 4 3 2 1

A CIP catalogue record for this book is available from the British Library.

Trade paperback ISBN: 978 0 857 89892 0
E-book ISBN: 978 1 782 39029 9

Printed in Great Britain by TJ International Ltd. Padstow Cornwall

Corvus
An imprint of Atlantic Books Ltd
Ormond House
26–27 Boswell Street
London
WC1N 3JZ

www.corvus-books.co.uk

THE LOCKED-ROOM MYSTERIES

EDITED AND WITH AN INTRODUCTION BY *Otto Penzler*

CORVUS

For Anthony Cheetham
Gentleman, scholar, loyal friend

CONTENTS

FOOTPRINTS IN THE SANDS OF TIME

*(Is there a more baffling scenario than to find a body in
smooth sand or snow with no footprints leading to or from the victim?)*

AND WE MISSED IT, LOST FOREVER

*(It is a fantasy for many people to disappear from their present lives. Some people
disappear because they want to; others disappear because someone else wants them
to. And objects—large objects—sometimes disappear in the same manner.)*

HOW EASILY IS MURDER DISCOVERED

(There are so many ways for the creative killer to accomplish the act.)

SHOOT IF YOU MUST

(It may not be terribly original, but shooting someone tends to be pretty effective.)

STOLEN SWEETS ARE BEST

*(How does a thief remove valuables from
a closely guarded room? It seems impossible, but . . .)*

ONE MAN'S POISON, SIGNOR, IS ANOTHER'S MEAT

*(Often described as a woman's murder weapon,
poison doesn't really care who administers it.)*

OUR FINAL HOPE IS FLAT DESPAIR

(Some stories simply can't be categorized.)

INTRODUCTION

OTTO PENZLER

AMONG AFICIONADOS of detective fiction, the term "locked-room mystery" has become an inaccurate but useful catchall phrase meaning the telling of a crime that appears to be impossible. The story does not require a hermetically sealed chamber so much as a location with an utterly inaccessible murder victim. A bludgeoned, stabbed, or strangled body in the center of pristine snow or sand is just as baffling as a lone figure on a boat at sea or aboard a solo airplane or in the classic locked room.

Like so much else in the world of mystery fiction, readers are indebted to Edgar Allan Poe for the invention of the locked-room mystery, which happened to be the startling core of the first pure detective story ever written, "The Murders in the Rue Morgue," initially published in the April 1841 issue of *Graham's Magazine*. In this groundbreaking tale, two women are heard to be screaming and a group of neighbors race up the stairs to the women's apartment. They break down the locked door, the key still in the lock on the inside, to find the savagely murdered mother and daughter. The windows are closed and fastened, egress through the fireplace chimney is impassable, and there are no loose floorboards or secret passages. Of course, the police are baffled (just as readers were then, and continue to be today, one hundred seventy years after the story's original appearance). Only the detective, C. Auguste Dupin, sees the solution, establishing another of the mainstays of the detective story: the brilliant amateur (often replaced in later stories by the private eye) who is smarter than both the criminal and the official police.

The locked-room mystery, or impossible-crime story, is the ultimate manifestation of the cerebral detective story. It fascinates the reader in precisely the same way that a magician is able to bring wonderment to his audience. What he demonstrates appears to be impossible. After all, young ladies, no matter how attractive and scantily clad, don't just disappear, or turn into tigers, or get sawed in half. Yet we have just seen it happen, right before our very focused eyes.

Be warned. As you read these astoundingly inventive stories, you will inevitably be disappointed, just as explanations of stage illusions exterminate the spell of magic that we experience as we watch the impossible occur. Impossible crimes cannot be impossible, as the detective will quickly point out, because they have happened. Treasure has been stolen from a locked and guarded room or museum or library, in spite of the constant surveillance by trained policemen. A frightened victim-to-be has locked, bolted, and sealed his home because the murderer has warned him that he will die at midnight, and a brigade of officers in a cordon surrounding the house cannot prevent it.

If the mind of a diabolical genius can invent a method of robbery or murder that appears to be insoluble, then surely there must be a mind of equal brilliance that is able to penetrate the scheme and explain its every nuance. That is the detective's role and, although he appears to be explaining it all to the police and other interested parties, he is, of course, describing the scenario to the reader. The curtain that has masked the magic, that has screened the illusion, is raised, and all returns to ordinary mechanics, physics, and psychology—the stuff of everyday life.

Therefore, if you want to maintain the beauty of a magic show, refuse to listen to a magician who is willing to explain how he performed his illusion. Similarly, if the situations in these locked-room mysteries have provided a delicious frisson of wonder, stop reading them as soon as you reach the denouement.

No, of course you can't do that. It is human nature to want to *know*, and the moment of clarity, when all is revealed, brings a different kind of satisfaction. Admiration replaces awe. The legerdemain achieved by the authors of the stories in this volume is, to use a word that has sadly become cheapened by overuse, awesome.

While it is true that Poe invented the locked-room story (although Robert Adey, in the introduction to his monumental bibliography, *Locked Room Murders*, gives credit to a pioneering effort by the great Irish novelist Sheridan Le Fanu, claiming the honor of first story for "A Passage in the Secret History of an Irish Countess," which appeared in the November 1838 issue of *Dublin University Magazine* and was later reprinted in the posthumously published *The Purcell Papers* in 1880), there can be no argument that the greatest practitioner of this demanding form was John Dickson Carr.

Not only did Carr produce one hundred twenty-six novels, short stories, and radio plays under his own name and as Carter Dickson, but the range of seemingly impossible murder methods he created was so broad and varied that it simply freezes the brain to contemplate. In perhaps the most arrogant display of his command of the locked-room mystery, in his 1935 novel *The Three Coffins* (published in England as *The Hollow Man*), he has his series detective, Dr. Gideon Fell, deliver a lecture to a captivated audience. In this display of erudition, Fell spends fifteen pages enumerating all the ways in which a locked room does not turn out to be impenetrable after all, and in which the impossible is clearly explained. He offers scores of ideas for solutions to the most challenging puzzles in the mystery genre, tossing off in rapid succession a greater cornucopia of invention than most mystery writers will conceive in a lifetime. When he has concluded his seemingly comprehensive tutorial, he informs the attendees that none of these explanations are pertinent to the present case and heads off to conclude the investigation.

Many solutions to the feats of prestidigitation in this collection will have been covered in Fell's lecture, but the sheer inventive genius of many of the contributors will have exceeded even Carr's tour de force. In his brilliant history of the mystery genre, *Murder for Pleasure* (1941), Howard Haycraft warned writers of detective fiction to stay away from the locked-room puzzle because "only a genius can invest it with novelty or interest today." It should be pointed out that, however well-intentioned the admonition, nearly half the stories in this volume were written after the publication date of that cornerstone history and appreciation of the literature of crime.

The locked-room mystery reached its pinnacle of popularity during the Golden Age of detective fiction between the two world wars. This is when Agatha Christie flourished, and so did Dorothy L. Sayers, Ellery Queen, Clayton Rawson, R. Austin Freeman, Margery Allingham, and, of course, Carr. In those years, the emphasis, particularly in England, was on the creation and solution of a puzzle. Readers were more interested in *who* dunnit, and *how* dunnit, whereas in the more modern era a greater focus has been placed on *why* dunnit. Murder—the taking of another person's life—was a private affair and its solution demanded a ritual that was largely followed by most writers. The book or short story generally began with a fairly tranquil community (even if that community was in a big city such as London or New York) in which all the participants knew each other. A terrible crime, usually murder, occurred, rending the social fabric. The police came to investigate, usually a single detective rather than an entire team of forensic experts, and either he (there were precious few female police officers in the detective stories of that era) would solve the mystery or show himself to be an abject fool, relying on a gifted, and frequently eccentric, amateur to arrive at a conclusion. Clues were placed judiciously throughout the story as the author challenged the reader to solve the case before the protagonist did. The true colors of the least likely suspect were then revealed and he or she was taken into custody, returning the community to its formerly peaceful state.

Many current readers don't have the patience to follow the trail of clues in a detective story in which all suspects are interviewed (*interrogated* is a word for later mysteries), all having doubt cast on their alibis, their relationships with the victim, and their possible motives, until all the suspects are gathered for the explanation of how the crime was committed, who perpetrated it, and why they did it. It is not realistic and was never intended to be. It is entertainment, as all fiction is . . . or should be. Dorothy L. Sayers pointed out that people have amused themselves by creating riddles, conundrums, and puzzles of all kinds, apparently the sole purpose of which is the satisfaction they give themselves by deducing a solution. Struggling with a Rubik's Cube is a form of torment eliciting a tremendous sense of achievement and joy when it is solved. This is equally true of reading a good detective story, the apotheosis of which is the locked-room puzzle, with the added pleasure of becoming involved with fascinating, occasionally memorable characters, unusual backgrounds, and, when the sun is shining most brightly, told with captivating prose.

Don't read these stories on a subway train or in the backseat of a car. They want to be read when you are comfortably ensconced in an easy chair or a bed piled high with pillows, at your leisure, perhaps with a cup of tea or a glass of port. Oh, heaven!

FAMILLIAR AS THE ROSE IN SPRING

The most popular and frequently reprinted impossible-crime stories of all time.

THE MURDERS IN THE RUE MORGUE

EDGAR ALLAN POE

"THE MURDERS IN THE RUE MORGUE" is, without question, the single most important story in the history of mystery fiction. In these few pages, Edgar Allan Poe (1809–1849) invented most of the significant elements in a literary form that relied on this template for the next one hundred seventy years: the brilliant detective, his somewhat dimmer sidekick, the still dimmer official police, the apparently impossible crime, misleading clues, the observation of disparate bits of information and the inspired deduction that results, and the denouement in which all is made clear.

Born in Boston and orphaned at the age of two when both his parents died of tuberculosis, Poe was taken in by a wealthy merchant, John Allan, and his wife; although never legally adopted, Poe nonetheless took Allan for his name. He received a classical education in Scotland and England from 1815 to 1820. After returning to the United States, he published his first book, *Tamerlane and Other Poems* (1827). It, and his next two volumes of poetry, were financial disasters. He won a prize for his story "MS. Found in a Bottle" (1833) and began a series of jobs as editor and critic of several periodicals. While he dramatically increased their circulations, his alcoholism, strong views, and arrogance enraged his bosses, costing him one job after another. He married his thirteen-year-old cousin, Virginia, living in abject poverty for many years with her and her mother. Lack of money undoubtedly contributed to the death of his wife at twenty-four. The most brilliant literary critic of his time, the master of horror stories, the poet whose work remains familiar and beloved to the present day, and the inventor of the detective story, Poe died a pauper.

"The Murders in the Rue Morgue" was first published in the April 1841 issue of *Graham's Magazine*. It was first published in book form (if a forty-eight-page pamphlet may be counted as a book) in a very rare volume (a copy in collectors' condition would sell for at least two hundred fifty thousand dollars) titled *Prose Romances* (Philadelphia, Graham, 1843), which also contains "The Man That Was Used Up." It then was collected in *Tales* (New York, Wiley & Putnam, 1845).

THE MURDERS IN THE RUE MORGUE

EDGAR ALLAN POE

What song the Syrens sang, or what name Achilles assumed when he hid himself among women, although puzzling questions, are not beyond all conjecture.

—*Sir Thomas Browne*

THE MENTAL FEATURES discoursed of as the analytical, are, in themselves, but little susceptible of analysis. We appreciate them only in their effects. We know of them, among other things, that they are always to their possessor, when inordinately possessed, a source of the liveliest enjoyment. As the strong man exults in his physical ability, delighting in such exercises as call his muscles into action, so glories the analyst in that moral activity which *disentangles.* He derives pleasure from even the most trivial occupations bringing his talent into play. He is fond of enigmas, of conundrums, hieroglyphics; exhibiting in his solutions of each a degree of *acumen* which appears to the ordinary apprehension præternatural. His results, brought about by the very soul and essence of method, have, in truth, the whole air of intuition.

The faculty of re-solution is possibly much invigorated by mathematical study, and especially by that highest branch of it which, unjustly, and merely on account of its retrograde operations, has been called, as if *par excellence,* analysis. Yet to calculate is not in itself to analyze. A chess-player, for example, does the one, without effort at the other. It follows that the game of chess, in its effect upon mental character, is greatly misunderstood. I am not now writing a treatise, but simply prefacing a somewhat peculiar narrative by observations very much at random; I will, therefore, take occasion to assert that the higher powers of the reflective intellect are more decidedly and more usefully tasked by the unostentatious game of draughts than by all the elaborate frivolity of chess. In this latter, where the pieces have different and *bizarre* motions, with various and variable values, what is only complex, is mistaken (a not unusual error) for what is profound. The *attention* is here called powerfully into play. If it flag for an instant, an oversight is committed, resulting in injury or defeat. The possible moves being not only manifold, but involute, the chances of such oversights are multiplied; and in nine cases out of ten, it is the more concentrative rather than the more acute player who conquers. In draughts, on the contrary, where the moves are *unique* and have but little variation, the probabilities of inadvertence are diminished, and the mere attention being left comparatively unemployed, what advantages are obtained by either party are obtained by superior *acumen.* To be less abstract, let us suppose a game of draughts where the pieces are reduced to four kings, and where, of course, no oversight is to be expected. It is obvious that here the victory can be decided (the players being at all equal) only by some *recherché* movement, the result of some strong exertion of the intellect. Deprived of ordinary resources, the analyst throws himself into the spirit of his opponent, identifies himself therewith, and not unfrequently sees thus, at a glance, the sole methods (sometimes indeed absurdly simple ones) by which he may seduce into error or hurry into miscalculation.

Whist has long been known for its influence upon what is termed the calculating power; and men of the highest order of intellect have been known to take an apparently unaccountable delight in it, while eschewing chess as frivolous. Beyond doubt there is nothing of a similar nature so greatly tasking the faculty of analysis. The best chess-player in Christendom *may* be little more than the best player of chess; but proficiency in whist implies capacity for success in all these more important undertakings where mind struggles with mind. When I say proficiency, I mean that perfection in the game which includes a comprehension of *all* the sources whence legitimate advantage may be derived. These are not only manifold, but multiform, and lie frequently among recesses of thought altogether inaccessible to the ordinary understanding. To observe attentively is to remember distinctly; and, so far, the concentrative chess-player will do very well at whist; while the rules of Hoyle (themselves based upon the mere mechanism of the game) are sufficiently and generally comprehensible. Thus to have a retentive memory, and proceed by "the book" are points commonly regarded as the sum total of good playing. But it is in matters beyond the limits of mere rule that the skill of the analyst is evinced. He makes, in silence, a host of observations and inferences. So, perhaps, do his companions; and the difference in the extent of the information obtained, lies not so much in the validity of the inference as in the quality of the observation. The necessary knowledge is that of *what* to observe. Our player confines himself not at all; nor, because the game is the object, does he reject deductions from things external to the game. He examines the countenance of his partner, comparing it carefully with that of each of his opponents. He considers the mode of assorting the cards in each hand; often counting trump by trump, and honor by honor, through the glances bestowed by their holders upon each. He notes every variation of face as the play progresses, gathering a fund of thought from the differences in the expression of certainty, of surprise, of triumph, or chagrin. From the manner of gathering up a trick he judges whether the person taking it can make another in the suit. He recognizes what is played through feint, by the manner with which it is thrown upon the table. A casual or inadvertent word; the accidental dropping or turning of a card, with the accompanying anxiety or carelessness in regard to its concealment; the counting of the tricks, with the order of their arrangement; embarrassment, hesitation, eagerness, or trepidation—all afford, to his apparently intuitive perception, indications of the true state of affairs. The first two or three rounds having been played, he is in full possession of the contents of each hand, and thenceforward puts down his cards with as absolute a precision of purpose as if the rest of the party had turned outward the faces of their own.

The analytical power should not be confounded with simple ingenuity; for while the analyst is necessarily ingenious, the ingenious man is often remarkably incapable of analysis. The constructive or combining power, by which ingenuity is usually manifested, and to which the phrenologists (I believe erroneously) have assigned a separate organ, supposing it a primitive faculty, has been so frequently seen in those whose intellect bordered otherwise upon idiocy, as to have attracted general observation among writers on morals. Between ingenuity and the analytic ability there exists a difference far greater, indeed, than that between the fancy and the imagination, but of a character very strictly analogous. It will be found, in fact, that the ingenious are always fanciful, and the *truly* imaginative never otherwise than analytic.

The narrative which follows will appear to the reader somewhat in the light of a commentary upon the propositions just advanced.

Residing in Paris during the spring and part of the summer of 18——, I there became acquainted with a Monsieur C. Auguste Dupin. This young gentleman was of an excellent, indeed of an illustrious family, but, by a variety of untoward events, had been reduced to such poverty that the energy of his character succumbed beneath it, and he ceased to bestir himself in the world, or to care for the retrieval of his fortunes. By courtesy of his creditors, there still remained in his possession a small remnant of his patrimony; and, upon the income arising from this, he managed, by means of a rigorous economy, to procure the necessities of life, without troubling himself about its superfluities. Books, indeed, were his sole luxuries, and in Paris these are easily obtained.

Our first meeting was at an obscure library in the Rue Montmartre, where the accident of our both being in search of the same very rare and very remarkable volume brought us into closer communion. We saw each other again and again. I was deeply interested in the little family history which he detailed to me with all that candor which a Frenchman indulges whenever mere self is the theme. I was astonished, too, at the vast extent of his reading; and, above all, I felt my soul enkindled within me by the wild fervor, and the vivid freshness of his imagination. Seeking in Paris the objects I then sought, I felt that the society of such a man would be to me a treasure beyond price; and this feeling I frankly confided to him. It was at length arranged that we should live together during my stay in the city; and as my worldly circumstances were somewhat less embarrassed than his own, I was permitted to be at the expense of renting, and furnishing in a style which suited the rather fantastic gloom of our common temper, a time-eaten and grotesque mansion, long deserted through superstitions into which we did not inquire, and tottering to its fall in a retired and desolate portion of the Faubourg St. Germain.

Had the routine of our life at this place been known to the world, we should have been regarded as madmen—although, perhaps, as madmen of a harmless nature. Our seclusion was perfect. We admitted no visitors. Indeed the locality of our retirement had been carefully kept a secret from my own former associates; and it had been many years since Dupin had ceased to know or be known in Paris. We existed within ourselves alone.

It was a freak of fancy in my friend (for what else shall I call it?) to be enamored of the night for her own sake; and into this *bizarrerie,* as into all his others, I quietly fell; giving myself up to his wild whims with a perfect *abandon.* The sable divinity would not herself dwell with us always; but we could counterfeit her presence. At the first dawn of the morning we closed all the massy shutters of our old building; lighted a couple of tapers which, strongly perfumed, threw out only the ghastliest and feeblest of rays. By the aid of these we then busied our souls in dreams—reading, writing, or conversing, until warned by the clock of the advent of the true Darkness. Then we sallied forth into the streets, arm in arm, continuing the topics of the day, or roaming far and wide until a late hour, seeking, amid the wild lights and shadows of the populous city, that infinity of mental excitement which quiet observation can afford.

At such times I could not help remarking and admiring (although from his rich ideality I had been prepared to expect it) a peculiar analytic ability in Dupin. He seemed, too, to take an eager delight in its exercise—if not exactly in its display—and did not hesitate to confess the pleasure thus derived. He boasted to me, with a low chuckling laugh, that most men, in respect to himself, wore windows in their bosoms, and was wont to follow up such assertions by direct and very startling proofs of his intimate knowledge of my own. His manner at these moments was frigid and abstract; his eyes were vacant in expression; while his voice, usually a rich tenor, rose into a treble which would have sounded petulant but for the deliberateness and entire distinctness of the enunciation. Observing him in these moods, I often dwelt meditatively upon the old philosophy of the Bi-Part Soul, and amused myself with the fancy of a double Dupin—the creative and the resolvent.

Let it not be supposed, from what I have just said, that I am detailing any mystery, or penning any romance. What I have described in the Frenchman was merely the result of an excited, or perhaps of a diseased, intelligence. But of the character of his remarks at the periods in question an example will best convey the idea.

We were strolling one night down a long dirty street, in the vicinity of the Palais Royal. Being both, apparently, occupied with thought, neither of us had spoken a syllable for fifteen minutes at least. All at once Dupin broke forth with these words:

"He is a very little fellow, that's true, and would do better for the *Théâtre des Variétés.*"

"There can be no doubt of that," I replied, unwittingly, and not at first observing (so much had I been absorbed in reflection) the extraordinary manner in which the speaker had chimed in with my meditations. In an instant afterward I recollected myself, and my astonishment was profound.

"Dupin," said I, gravely, "this is beyond my comprehension. I do not hesitate to say that I am amazed, and can scarcely credit my senses. How was it possible you should know I was thinking of——?" Here I paused, to ascertain beyond a doubt whether he really knew of whom I thought.

"——of Chantilly," said he, "why do you pause? You were remarking to yourself that his diminutive figure unfitted him for tragedy."

This was precisely what had formed the subject of my reflections. Chantilly was a *quondam* cobbler of the Rue St. Denis, who, becoming stage-mad, had attempted the *rôle* of Xerxes, in Crébillon's tragedy so called, and been notoriously Pasquinaded for his pains.

"Tell me, for Heaven's sake," I exclaimed, "the method—if method there is—by which you have been enabled to fathom my soul in this matter." In fact, I was even more startled than I would have been willing to express.

"It was the fruiterer," replied my friend, "who brought you to the conclusion that the mender of soles was not of sufficient height for Xerxes *et id genus omne.*"

"The fruiterer!—you astonish me—I know no fruiterer whomsoever."

"The man who ran up against you as we entered the street—it may have been fifteen minutes ago."

I now remembered that, in fact, a fruiterer, carrying upon his head a large basket of apples, had nearly thrown me down, by accident, as we passed from the Rue C——into the thoroughfare where we stood; but what this had to do with Chantilly I could not possibly understand.

There was not a particle of *charlatanerie* about Dupin. "I will explain," he said, "and that you may comprehend all clearly, we will first retrace the course of your meditations, from the moment in which I spoke to you until that of the *rencontre* with the fruiterer in question. The larger links of the chain run thus—Chantilly, Orion, Dr. Nichols, Epicurus, Stereotomy, the street stones, the fruiterer."

There are few persons who have not, at some period of their lives, amused themselves in retracing the steps by which particular conclusions of their own minds have been attained. The occupation is often full of interest; and he who attempts it for the first time is astonished by the apparently illimitable distance and incoherence between the starting-point and the goal. What, then, must have been my amazement, when I heard the Frenchman speak what he had just spoken, and when I could not help acknowledging that he had spoken the truth. He continued:

"We had been talking of horses, if I remember aright, just before leaving the Rue C——. This was the last subject we discussed. As we crossed into this street, a fruiterer, with a large basket upon his head, brushing quickly past us, thrust you upon a pile of paving-stones collected at a spot where the causeway is undergoing repair. You stepped upon one of the loose fragments, slipped, slightly strained your ankle, appeared vexed or sulky, muttered a few words, turned to look at the pile, and then proceeded in silence. I was not particularly attentive to what you did; but observation has become with me, of late, a species of necessity.

"You kept your eyes upon the ground—glancing, with a petulant expression, at the holes and ruts in the pavement (so that I saw you were still thinking of the stones), until we reached the little alley called Lamartine, which has been paved, by way of experiment, with the overlapping and riveted blocks. Here your countenance brightened up, and, perceiving your lips move, I could not doubt that you murmured the word 'stereotomy,' a term very affectedly applied to this species of pavement. I knew that you could not say to yourself 'stereotomy' without being brought to think of atomies, and thus of the theories of Epicurus; and since, when we discussed this subject not very long ago, I mentioned to you how singularly, yet with how little notice, the vague guesses of that noble Greek had met with confirmation in the late nebular cosmogony, I felt that you could not avoid casting your eyes upward to the great *nebula* in Orion, and I certainly expected that you would do so. You did look up; and I was now assured that I had correctly followed your steps. But in that bitter *tirade* upon Chantilly, which appeared in yesterday's '*Musée*,' the satirist, making some disgraceful allusions to the cobbler's change of name upon assuming the buskin, quoted a Latin line about which we have often conversed. I mean the line

Perdidit antiquum litera prima sonum.

I had told you that this was in reference to Orion, formerly written Urion; and, from certain pungencies connected with this explanation, I was aware that you could not have forgotten it. It was clear, therefore, that you would not fail to combine the two ideas of Orion and Chantilly. That you did combine them I saw by the character of the smile which passed over your lips. You thought of the poor cobbler's immolation. So far, you had been stooping in your gait; but now I saw

you draw yourself up to your full height. I was then sure that you reflected upon the diminutive figure of Chantilly. At this point I interrupted your meditations to remark that as, in fact, he *was* a very little fellow—that Chantilly—he would do better at the *Théâtre des Variétés*."

Not long after this, we were looking over an evening edition of the *Gazette des Tribunaux*, when the following paragraphs arrested our attention.

"EXTRAORDINARY MURDERS.—This morning, about three o'clock, the inhabitants of the Quartier St. Roch were roused from sleep by a succession of terrific shrieks, issuing, apparently, from the fourth story of a house in the Rue Morgue, known to be in the sole occupancy of one Madame L'Espanaye, and her daughter, Mademoiselle Camille L'Espanaye. After some delay, occasioned by a fruitless attempt to procure admission in the usual manner, the gateway was broken in with a crowbar, and eight or ten of the neighbors entered, accompanied by two *gendarmes*. By this time the cries had ceased; but, as the party rushed up the first flight of stairs, two or more rough voices, in angry contention, were distinguished, and seemed to proceed from the upper part of the house. As the second landing was reached, these sounds, also, had ceased, and every thing remained perfectly quiet. The party spread themselves, and hurried from room to room. Upon arriving at a large back chamber in the fourth story (the door of which, being found locked, with the key inside, was forced open), a spectacle presented itself which struck every one present not less with horror than with astonishment.

"The apartment was in the wildest disorder—the furniture broken and thrown about in all directions. There was only one bedstead; and from this the bed had been removed, and thrown into the middle of the floor. On a chair lay a razor, besmeared with blood. On the hearth were two or three long and thick tresses of gray human hair, also dabbled with blood, and seeming to have been pulled out by the roots. Upon the floor were found four Napoleons, an ear-ring of topaz, three large silver spoons, three smaller of *métal d'Alger*, and two bags, containing nearly four thousand francs in gold. The drawers of a *bureau*, which stood in one corner, were open, and had been, apparently, rifled, although many articles still remained in them. A small iron safe was discovered under the *bed* (not under the bedstead). It was open, with the key still in the door. It had no contents beyond a few old letters, and other papers of little consequence.

"Of Madame L'Espanaye no traces were here seen; but an unusual quantity of soot being observed in the fire-place, a search was made in the chimney, and (horrible to relate!) the corpse of the daughter, head downward, was dragged therefrom; it having been thus forced up the narrow aperture for a considerable distance. The body was quite warm. Upon examining it, many excoriations were perceived, no doubt occasioned by the violence with which it had been thrust up and disengaged. Upon the face were many severe scratches, and, upon the throat, dark bruises, and deep indentations of finger nails, as if the deceased had been throttled to death.

"After a thorough investigation of every portion of the house without farther discovery, the party made its way into a small paved yard in the rear of the building, where lay the corpse of the old lady, with her throat so entirely cut that, upon an attempt to raise her, the head fell off. The body, as well as the head, was fearfully mutilated—the former so much so as scarcely to retain any semblance of humanity.

"To this horrible mystery there is not as yet, we believe, the slightest clew."

The next day's paper had these additional particulars:

"*The Tragedy in the Rue Morgue.*—Many individuals have been examined in relation to this most extraordinary and frightful affair," [the word '*affaire*' has not yet, in France, that levity of import which it conveys with us] "but nothing whatever has transpired to throw light upon it. We give below all the material testimony elicited.

"*Pauline Dubourg,* laundress, deposes that she has known both the deceased for three years, having washed for them during that period. The old lady and her daughter seemed on good terms—very affectionate toward each other. They were excellent pay. Could not speak in regard to their mode or means of living. Believe that Madame L. told fortunes for a living. Was reputed to have money put by. Never met any person in the house when she called for the clothes or took them home. Was sure that they had no servant in employ. There appeared to be no furniture in any part of the building except in the fourth story.

"*Pierre Moreau,* tobacconist, deposes that he has been in the habit of selling small quantities of tobacco and snuff to Madame L'Espanaye for nearly four years. Was born in the neighborhood, and has always resided there. The deceased and her daughter had occupied the house in which the corpses were found for more than six years. It was formerly occupied by a jeweller, who under-let the upper rooms to various persons. The house was the property of Madame L. She became dissatisfied with the abuse of the premises by her tenant, and moved into them herself, refusing to let any portion. The old lady was childish. Witness had seen the daughter some five or six times during the six years. The two lived an exceedingly retired life—were reputed to have money. Had heard it said among the neighbors that Madame L. told fortunes—did not believe it. Had never seen any person enter the door except the old lady and her daughter, a porter once or twice, and a physician some eight or ten times.

"Many other persons, neighbors, gave evidence to the same effect. No one was spoken of as frequenting the house. It was not known whether there were any living connections of Madame L. and her daughter. The shutters of the front windows were seldom opened. Those in the rear were always closed, with the exception of the large back room, fourth story. The house was a good house—not very old.

"*Isidore Musèt, gendarme,* deposes that he

was called to the house about three o'clock in the morning, and found some twenty or thirty persons at the gateway, endeavoring to gain admittance. Forced it open, at length, with a bayonet—not with a crowbar. Had but little difficulty in getting it open, on account of its being a double or folding gate, and bolted neither at bottom nor top. The shrieks were continued until the gate was forced—and then suddenly ceased. They seemed to be screams of some person (or persons) in great agony—were loud and drawn out, not short and quick. Witness led the way up stairs. Upon reaching the first landing, heard two voices in loud and angry contention—the one a gruff voice, the other much shriller—a very strange voice. Could distinguish some words of the former, which was that of a Frenchman. Was positive that it was not a woman's voice. Could distinguish the words '*sacré*' and '*diable*.' The shrill voice was that of a foreigner. Could not be sure whether it was the voice of a man or of a woman. Could not make out what was said, but believed the language to be Spanish. The state of the room and of the bodies was described by this witness as we described them yesterday.

"*Henri Duval*, a neighbor, and by trade a silver-smith, deposes that he was one of the party who first entered the house. Corroborates the testimony of Musèt in general. As soon as they forced an entrance, they reclosed the door, to keep out the crowd, which collected very fast, notwithstanding the lateness of the hour. The shrill voice, this witness thinks, was that of an Italian. Was certain it was not French. Could not be sure that it was a man's voice. It might have been a woman's. Was not acquainted with the Italian language. Could not distinguish the words, but was convinced by the intonations that the speaker was an Italian. Knew Madame L. and her daughter. Had conversed with both frequently. Was sure that the shrill voice was not that of either of the deceased.

"———*Odenheimer, restaurateur.*—This witness volunteered his testimony. Not speaking French, was examined through an interpreter. Is a native of Amsterdam. Was passing the house at the time of the shrieks. They lasted for several minutes—probably ten. They were long and loud—very awful and distressing. Was one of those who entered the building. Corroborated the previous evidence in every respect but one. Was sure that the shrill voice was that of a man—of a Frenchman. Could not distinguish the words uttered. They were loud and quick—unequal—spoken apparently in fear as well as in anger. The voice was harsh—not so much shrill as harsh. Could not call it a shrill voice. The gruff voice said repeatedly, '*sacré*,' '*diable*,' and once '*mon Dieu.*'

"*Jules Mignaud*, banker, of the firm of Mignaud et Fils, Rue Deloraine. Is the elder Mignaud. Madame L'Espanaye had some property. Had opened an account with his banking house in the spring of the year——(eight years previously). Made frequent deposits in small sums. Had checked for nothing until the third day before her death, when she took out in person the sum of 4000 francs. This sum was paid in gold, and a clerk sent home with the money.

"*Adolphe Le Bon*, clerk to Mignaud et Fils, deposes that on the day in question, about noon, he accompanied Madame L'Espanaye to her residence with the 4000 francs, put up in two bags. Upon the door being opened, Mademoiselle L. appeared and took from his hands one of the bags, while the old lady relieved him of the other. He then bowed and departed. Did not see any person in the street at the time. It is a bystreet—very lonely.

"*William Bird*, tailor, deposes that he was one of the party who entered the house. Is an Englishman. Has lived in Paris two years. Was one of the first to ascend the stairs. Heard the voices in contention. The gruff voice was that of a Frenchman. Could make out several words, but cannot now remember all. Heard distinctly '*sacré*' and '*mon Dieu.*' There was a sound at the moment as if of several persons struggling—a scraping and scuffling sound. The shrill voice was very loud—louder than the gruff one. Is sure that it was not the voice of an Englishman.

Appeared to be that of a German. Might have been a woman's voice. Does not understand German.

"Four of the above-named witnesses, being recalled, deposed that the door of the chamber in which was found the body of Mademoiselle L. was locked on the inside when the party reached it. Every thing was perfectly silent—no groans or noises of any kind. Upon forcing the door no person was seen. The windows, both of the back and front room, were down and firmly fastened from within. A door between the two rooms was closed but not locked. The door leading from the front room into the passage was locked, with the key on the inside. A small room in the front of the house, on the fourth story, at the head of the passage, was open, the door being ajar. This room was crowded with old beds, boxes, and so forth. These were carefully removed and searched. There was not an inch of any portion of the house which was not carefully searched. Sweeps were sent up and down the chimneys. The house was a four-story one, with garrets (*mansardes*). A trap-door on the roof was nailed down very securely—did not appear to have been opened for years. The time elapsing between the hearing of the voices in contention and the breaking open of the room door was variously stated by the witnesses. Some made it as short as three minutes—some as long as five. The door was opened with difficulty.

"*Alfonzo Garcio,* undertaker, deposes that he resides in the Rue Morgue. Is a native of Spain. Was one of the party who entered the house. Did not proceed up stairs. Is nervous, and was apprehensive of the consequences of agitation. Heard the voices in contention. The gruff voice was that of a Frenchman. Could not distinguish what was said. The shrill voice was that of an Englishman—is sure of this. Does not understand the English language, but judges by the intonation.

"*Alberto Montani,* confectioner, deposes that he was among the first to ascend the stairs. Heard the voices in question. The gruff voice was that of a Frenchman. Distinguished several words. The speaker appeared to be expostulat-

ing. Could not make out the words of the shrill voice. Spoke quick and unevenly. Thinks it the voice of a Russian. Corroborates the general testimony. Is an Italian. Never conversed with a native of Russia.

"Several witnesses, recalled, here testified that the chimneys of all the rooms on the fourth story were too narrow to admit the passage of a human being. By 'sweeps' were meant cylindrical sweeping-brushes, such as are employed by those who clean chimneys. These brushes were passed up and down every flue in the house. There is no back passage by which any one could have descended while the party proceeded up stairs. The body of Mademoiselle L'Espanaye was so firmly wedged in the chimney that it could not be got down until four or five of the party united their strength.

"*Paul Dumas,* physician, deposes that he was called to view the bodies about daybreak. They were both then lying on the sacking of the bedstead in the chamber where Mademoiselle L. was found. The corpse of the young lady was much bruised and excoriated. The fact that it had been thrust up the chimney would sufficiently account for these appearances. The throat was greatly chafed. There were several deep scratches just below the chin, together with a series of livid spots which were evidently the impression of fingers. The face was fearfully discolored, and the eyeballs protruded. The tongue had been partially bitten through. A large bruise was discovered upon the pit of the stomach, produced, apparently, by the pressure of a knee. In the opinion of M. Dumas, Mademoiselle L'Espanaye had been throttled to death by some person or persons unknown. The corpse of the mother was horribly mutilated. All the bones of the right leg and arm were more or less shattered. The left *tibia* much splintered, as well as all the ribs of the left side. Whole body dreadfully bruised and discolored. It was not possible to say how the injuries had been inflicted. A heavy club of wood, or a broad bar of iron—a chair—any large, heavy, and obtuse weapon would have produced such results, if wielded by the hands of a very powerful man. No woman could have inflicted the blows with any weapon. The head of the deceased, when seen by witness, was entirely separated from the body, and was also greatly shattered. The throat had evidently been cut with some very sharp instrument—probably with a razor.

"*Alexandre Etienne, surgeon, was called with M. Dumas to view the bodies. Corroborated the testimony, and the opinions of M. Dumas.

"Nothing further of importance was elicited, although several other persons were examined. A murder so mysterious, and so perplexing in all its particulars, was never before committed in Paris—if indeed a murder has been committed at all. The police are entirely at fault—an unusual occurrence in affairs of this nature. There is not, however, the shadow of a clew apparent."

The evening edition of the paper stated that the greatest excitement still continued in the Quartier St. Roch—that the premises in question had been carefully researched, and fresh examinations of witnesses instituted, but all to no purpose. A postscript, however, mentioned that Adolphe Le Bon had been arrested and imprisoned—although nothing appeared to criminate him beyond the facts already detailed.

Dupin seemed singularly interested in the progress of this affair—at least so I judged from his manner, for he made no comments. It was only after the announcement that Le Bon had been imprisoned that he asked me my opinion respecting the murders.

I could merely agree with all Paris in considering them an insoluble mystery. I saw no means by which it would be possible to trace the murderer.

"We must not judge of the means," said Dupin, "by this shell of an examination. The Parisian police, so much extolled for *acumen*, are cunning, but no more. There is no method in their proceedings, beyond the method of the moment. They make a vast parade of measures; but, not unfrequently, these are so ill-adapted to the objects proposed, as to put us in mind of Monsieur Jourdain's calling for his *robe-de-chambre—pour mieux entendre la musique.* The results attained by them are not unfrequently surprising, but, for the most part, are brought about by simple diligence and activity. When these qualities are unavailing, their schemes fail. Vidocq, for example, was a good guesser, and a persevering man. But, without educated thought, he erred continually by the very intensity of his investigations. He impaired his vision by holding the object too close. He might see, perhaps, one or two points with unusual clearness, but in so doing he, necessarily, lost sight of the matter as a whole. Thus there is such a thing as being too profound. Truth is not always in a well. In fact, as regards the more important knowledge, I do believe that she is invariably superficial. The depth lies in the valleys where we seek her, and not upon the mountain-tops where she is found. The modes and sources of this kind of error are well typified in the contemplation of the heavenly bodies. To look at a star by glances—to view it in a sidelong way, by turning toward it the exterior portions of the *retina* (more susceptible of feeble impressions of light than the interior), is to behold the star distinctly—is to have the best appreciation of its lustre—a lustre which grows dim just in proportion as we turn our vision *fully* upon it. A greater number of rays actually fall upon the eye in the latter case, but, in the former, there is the more refined capacity for comprehension. By undue profundity we perplex and enfeeble thought; and it is possible to make even Venus herself vanish from the firmament by a scrutiny too sustained, too concentrated, or too direct.

"As for these murders, let us enter into some examinations for ourselves, before we make up an opinion respecting them. An inquiry will afford us amusement," [I thought this an odd term, so applied, but said nothing] "and besides, Le Bon once rendered me a service for which I am not ungrateful. We will go and see the premises with our own eyes. I know G——, the Prefect of Police, and shall have no difficulty in obtaining the necessary permission."

The permission was obtained, and we proceeded at once to the Rue Morgue. This is one of those miserable thoroughfares which intervene between the Rue Richelieu and the Rue St. Roch. It was late in the afternoon when we reached it, as this quarter is at a great distance from that in which we resided. The house was readily found; for there were still many persons gazing up at the closed shutters, with an objectless curiosity, from the opposite side of the way. It was an ordinary Parisian house, with a gateway, on one side of which was a glazed watch-box, with a sliding panel in the window, indicating a *loge de concierge*. Before going in we walked up the street, turned down an alley, and then, again turning, passed in the rear of the building—Dupin, meanwhile, examining the whole neighborhood, as well as the house, with a minuteness of attention for which I could see no possible object.

Retracing our steps we came again to the front of the dwelling, rang, and, having shown our credentials, were admitted by the agents in charge. We went up stairs—into the chamber where the body of Mademoiselle L'Espanaye had been found, and where both the deceased still lay. The disorders of the room had, as usual, been suffered to exist. I saw nothing beyond what had been stated in the *Gazette des Tribunaux*. Dupin scrutinized every thing—not excepting the bodies of the victims. We then went into the other rooms, and into the yard; a *gendarme* accompanying us throughout. The examination occupied us until dark, when we took our departure. On our way home my companion stepped in for a moment at the office of one of the daily papers.

I have said that the whims of my friend were manifold, and that *Je les ménagais:*—for this phrase there is no English equivalent. It was his humor, now, to decline all conversation on the subject of the murder, until about noon the next day. He then asked me, suddenly, if I had observed any thing *peculiar* at the scene of the atrocity.

There was something in his manner of emphasizing the word *"peculiar,"* which caused me to shudder, without knowing why.

"No, nothing *peculiar,*" I said; "nothing more, at least, than we both saw stated in the paper."

"The *Gazette,*" he replied, "has not entered, I fear, into the unusual horror of the thing. But dismiss the idle opinions of this print. It appears to me that this mystery is considered insoluble, for the very reason which should cause it to be regarded as easy of solution—I mean for the *outré* character of its features. The police are confounded by the seeming absence of motive—not for the murder itself—but for the atrocity of the murder. They are puzzled, too, by the seeming impossibility of reconciling the voices heard in contention with the facts that no one was discovered upstairs but the assassinated Mademoiselle L'Espanaye, and that there were no means of egress without the notice of the party ascending. The wild disorder of the room; the corpse thrust, with the head downward, up the chimney; the frightful mutilation of the body of the old lady; these considerations, with those just mentioned, and others which I need not mention, have sufficed to paralyze the powers, by putting completely at fault the boasted *acumen,* of the government agents. They have fallen into the gross but common error of confounding the unusual with the abstruse. But it is by these deviations from the plane of the ordinary, that reason feels its way, if at all, in its search for the true. In investigations such as we are now pursuing, it should not be so much asked 'what has occurred,' as 'what has occurred that has never occurred before.' In fact, the facility with which I shall arrive, or have arrived, at the solution of this mystery, is in the direct ratio of its apparent insolubility in the eyes of the police."

I stared at the speaker in mute astonishment.

"I am now awaiting," continued he, looking toward the door of our apartment—"I am now awaiting a person who, although perhaps not the perpetrator of these butcheries, must have been in some measure implicated in their perpetration. Of the worst portion of the crimes committed, it is probable that he is innocent. I hope that I am right in this supposition; for upon it I build my expectation of reading the entire riddle. I look for the man here—in this room—every moment. It is true that he may not arrive; but the probability is that he will. Should he come, it will be necessary to detain him. Here are pistols; and we both know how to use them when occasion demands their use."

I took the pistols, scarcely knowing what I did, or believing what I heard, while Dupin went on, very much as if in a soliloquy. I have already spoken of his abstract manner at such times. His discourse was addressed to myself; but his voice, although by no means loud, had that intonation which is commonly employed in speaking to some one at a great distance. His eyes, vacant in expression, regarded only the wall.

"That the voices heard in contention," he said, "by the party upon the stairs, were not the voices of the women themselves, was fully proved by the evidence. This relieves us of all doubt upon the question whether the old lady could have first destroyed the daughter, and afterward have committed suicide. I speak of this point chiefly for the sake of method; for the strength of Madame L'Espanaye would have been utterly unequal to the task of thrusting her daughter's corpse up the chimney as it was found; and the nature of the wounds upon her own person entirely precludes the idea of self-destruction. Murder, then, has been committed by some third party; and the voices of this third party were those heard in contention. Let me now advert—not to the whole testimony respecting these voices—but to what was *peculiar* in that testimony. Did you observe any thing peculiar about it?"

I remarked that, while all the witnesses agreed in supposing the gruff voice to be that of a Frenchman, there was much disagreement in regard to the shrill, or, as one individual termed it, the harsh voice.

"That was the evidence itself," said Dupin, "but it was not the peculiarity of the evidence. You have observed nothing distinctive. Yet there *was* something to be observed. The witnesses, as you remark, agreed about the gruff voice; they were here unanimous. But in regard to the shrill voice, the peculiarity is—not that they disagreed—but that, while an Italian, an Englishman, a Spaniard, a Hollander, and a Frenchman attempted to describe it, each one spoke of it as that *of a foreigner*. Each is sure that it was not the voice of one of his own countrymen. Each likens it—not to the voice of an individual of any nation with whose language he is conversant—but the converse. The Frenchman supposes it the voice of a Spaniard, and 'might have distinguished some words *had he been acquainted with the Spanish*.' The Dutchman maintains it to have been that of a Frenchman; but we find it stated that '*not understanding French this witness was examined through an interpreter*.' The Englishman thinks it the voice of a German, and '*does not understand German*.' The Spaniard 'is sure' that it was that of an Englishman, but 'judges by the intonation' altogether, '*as he has no knowledge of the English*.' The Italian believes it the voice of a Russian, but '*has never conversed with a native of Russia*.' A second Frenchman differs, moreover, with the first, and is positive that the voice was that of an Italian; but, *not being cognizant of that tongue*, is, like the Spaniard, 'convinced by the intonation.' Now, how strangely unusual must that voice have really been, about which such testimony as this *could* have been elicited!—in whose *tones*, even, denizens of the five great divisions of Europe could recognize nothing familiar! You will say that it might have been the voice of an Asiatic—of an African. Neither Asiatics nor Africans abound in Paris; but, without denying the inference, I will now merely call your attention to three points. The voice is termed by one witness 'harsh rather than shrill.' It is represented by two others to have been 'quick and *unequal*.' No words—no sounds resembling words—were by any witness mentioned as distinguishable.

"I know not," continued Dupin, "what impression I may have made, so far, upon your own understanding; but I do not hesitate to say that legitimate deductions even from this portion of the testimony—the portion respecting the gruff and shrill voices—are in themselves sufficient to engender a suspicion which should give direction to all farther progress in the investigation of the mystery. I said 'legitimate deductions'; but my meaning is not thus fully expressed. I designed to imply that the deductions are the *sole* proper ones, and that the suspicion arises *inevitably* from them as the single result. What the suspicion is, however, I will not say just yet. I merely wish you to bear in mind that, with myself, it was sufficiently forcible to give a definite form—a certain tendency—to my inquiries in the chamber.

"Let us now transport ourselves, in fancy, to this chamber. What shall we first seek here? The means of egress employed by the murderers. It is not too much to say that neither of us believe in præternatural events. Madame and Mademoiselle L'Espanaye were not destroyed by spirits. The doers of the deed were material and escaped materially. Then how? Fortunately there is but one mode of reasoning upon the point, and that mode *must* lead us to a definite decision. Let us examine, each by each, the possible means of egress. It is clear that the assassins were in the room where Mademoiselle L'Espanaye was found, or at least in the room adjoining, when the party ascended the stairs. It is, then, only from these two apartments that we have to seek issues. The police have laid bare the floors, the ceiling, and the masonry of the walls, in every direction. No *secret* issues could have escaped their vigilance. But, not trusting to *their* eyes, I examined with my own. There were, then, *no* secret issues. Both doors leading from the rooms into the passage were securely locked, with the keys inside. Let us turn to the chimneys. These, although of ordinary width for some eight or ten feet above the hearths, will not admit, throughout their extent, the body of a large cat. The impossibility of egress, by means already stated, being thus absolute, we are reduced to the windows. Through those of the front room no one could have escaped without

notice from the crowd in the street. The murderers *must* have passed, then, through those of the back room. Now, brought to this conclusion in so unequivocal a manner as we are, it is not our part, as reasoners, to reject it on account of apparent impossibilities. It is only left for us to prove that these apparent 'impossibilities' are, in reality, not such.

"There are two windows in the chamber. One of them is unobstructed by furniture, and is wholly visible. The lower portion of the other is hidden from view by the head of the unwieldy bedstead which is thrust close up against it. The former was found securely fastened from within. It resisted the utmost force of those who endeavored to raise it. A large gimlet-hole had been pierced in its frame to the left, and a very stout nail was found fitted therein, nearly to the head. Upon examining the other window, a similar nail was seen similarly fitted in it; and a vigorous attempt to raise this sash failed also. The police were now entirely satisfied that egress had not been in these directions. And, *therefore*, it was thought a matter of supererogation to withdraw the nails and open the windows.

"My own examination was somewhat more particular, and was so for the reason I have just given—because here it was, I knew, that all apparent impossibilities *must* be proved to be not such in reality."

"I proceeded to think thus—*a posteriori.* The murderers *did* escape from one of these windows. This being so, they could not have re-fastened the sashes from the inside, as they were found fastened;—the consideration which put a stop, through its obviousness, to the scrutiny of the police in this quarter. Yet the sashes *were* fastened. They *must*, then, have the power of fastening themselves. There was no escape from this conclusion. I stepped to the unobstructed casement, withdrew the nail with some difficulty, and attempted to raise the sash. It resisted all my efforts, as I had anticipated. A concealed spring must, I now knew, exist; and this corroboration of my idea convinced me that my premises, at least, were correct, however mysterious still appeared the circumstances attending the nails. A careful search soon brought to light the hidden spring. I pressed it, and, satisfied with the discovery, forbore to upraise the sash.

"I now replaced the nail and regarded it attentively. A person passing out through this window might have reclosed it, and the spring would have caught—but the nail could not have been replaced. The conclusion was plain, and again narrowed in the field of my investigations. The assassins *must* have escaped through the other window. Supposing, then, the springs upon each sash to be the same, as was probable, there *must* be found a difference between the nails, or at least between the modes of their fixture. Getting upon the sacking of the bedstead, I looked over the head-board minutely at the second casement. Passing my hand down behind the board, I readily discovered and pressed the spring, which was, as I had supposed, identical in character with its neighbor. I now looked at the nail. It was as stout as the other, and apparently fitted in the same manner—driven in nearly up to the head.

"You will say that I was puzzled; but, if you think so, you must have misunderstood the nature of the inductions. To use a sporting phrase, I had not been once 'at fault.' The scent had never for an instant been lost. There was no flaw in any link of the chain. I had traced the secret to its ultimate result,—and that result was *the nail*. It had, I say, in every respect, the appearance of its fellow in the other window; but this fact was an absolute nullity (conclusive as it might seem to be) when compared with the consideration that here, at this point, terminated the clew. 'There *must* be something wrong,' I said, 'about the nail.' I touched it; and the head, with about a quarter of an inch of the shank, came off in my fingers. The rest of the shank was in the gimlet-hole, where it had been broken off. The fracture was an old one (for its edges were incrusted with rust), and had apparently been accomplished by the blow of a hammer, which had partially imbedded, in the top of the bottom sash, the head portion of the nail. I now carefully replaced this head portion in the indenta-

tion whence I had taken it, and the resemblance to a perfect nail was complete—the fissure was invisible. Pressing the spring, I gently raised the sash for a few inches; the head went up with it, remaining firm in its bed. I closed the window, and the semblance of the whole nail was again perfect.

"This riddle, so far, was now unriddled. The assassin had escaped through the window which looked upon the bed. Dropping of its own accord upon his exit (or perhaps purposely closed), it had become fastened by the spring; and it was the retention of this spring which had been mistaken by the police for that of the nail,—farther inquiry being thus considered unnecessary.

"The next question is that of the mode of descent. Upon this point I had been satisfied in my walk with you around the building. About five feet and a half from the casement in question there runs a lightning-rod. From this rod it would have been impossible for any one to reach the window itself, to say nothing of entering it. I observed, however, that the shutters of the fourth story were of the peculiar kind called by Parisian carpenters *ferrades*—a kind rarely employed at the present day, but frequently seen upon very old mansions at Lyons and Bordeaux. They are in the form of an ordinary door (a single, not a folding door), except that the lower half is latticed or worked in open trellis—thus affording an excellent hold for the hands. In the present instance these shutters are fully three feet and a half broad. When we saw them from the rear of the house, they were both about half open—that is to say they stood off at right angles from the wall. It is probable that the police, as well as myself, examined the back of the tenement; but, if so, in looking at these *ferrades* in the line of their breadth (as they must have done), they did not perceive this great breadth itself, or, at all events, failed to take it into due consideration. In fact, having once satisfied themselves that no egress could have been made in this quarter, they would naturally bestow here a very cursory examination. It was clear to me, however, that the shutter belonging to the window at the head of the bed, would, if swung fully back to the wall, reach to within two feet of the lightning-rod. It was also evident that, by exertion of a very unusual degree of activity and courage, an entrance into the window, from the rod, might have been thus effected. By reaching to the distance of two feet and a half (we now suppose the shutter open to its whole extent) a robber might have taken a firm grasp upon the trellis-work. Letting go, then, his hold upon the rod, placing his feet securely against the wall, and springing boldly from it, he might have swung the shutter so as to close it, and, if we imagine the window open at the time, might even have swung himself into the room.

"I wish you to bear especially in mind that I have spoken of a *very* unusual degree of activity as requisite to success in so hazardous and so difficult a feat. It is my design to show you first, that the thing might possibly have been accomplished:—but, secondly and *chiefly,* I wish to impress upon your understanding the *very extraordinary*—the almost præternatural character of that agility which could have accomplished it.

"You will say, no doubt, using the language of the law, that 'to make out my case,' I should rather undervalue than insist upon a full estimation of the activity required in this matter. This may be the practice in law, but it is not the usage of reason. My ultimate object is only the truth. My immediate purpose is to lead you to place in juxtaposition, that *very unusual* activity of which I have just spoken, with that *very peculiar* shrill (or harsh) and *unequal* voice, about whose nationality no two persons could be found to agree, and in whose utterance no syllabification could be detected."

At these words a vague and half-formed conception of the meaning of Dupin flitted over my mind. I seemed to be upon the verge of comprehension, without power to comprehend—as men, at times, find themselves upon the brink of remembrance, without being able, in the end, to remember. My friend went on with his discourse.

"You will see," he said, "that I have shifted the question from the mode of egress to that of ingress. It was my design to convey the idea that both were effected in the same manner, at the same point. Let us now revert to the interior of the room. Let us survey the appearances here. The drawers of the bureau, it is said, had been rifled, although many articles of apparel still remained within them. The conclusion here is absurd. It is a mere guess—a very silly one—and no more. How are we to know that the articles found in the drawers were not all these drawers had originally contained? Madame L'Espanaye and her daughter lived an exceedingly retired life—saw no company—seldom went out—had little use for numerous changes of habiliment. Those found were at least of as good quality as any likely to be possessed by these ladies. If a thief had taken any, why did he not take the best—why did he not take all? In a word, why did he abandon four thousand francs in gold to encumber himself with a bundle of linen? The gold *was* abandoned. Nearly the whole sum mentioned by Monsieur Mignaud, the banker, was discovered, in bags, upon the floor. I wish you, therefore, to discard from your thoughts the blundering idea of *motive,* engendered in the brains of the police by that portion of the evidence which speaks of money delivered at the door of the house. Coincidences ten times as remarkable as this (the delivery of the money, and murder committed within three days upon the party receiving it), happen to all of us every hour of our lives, without attracting even momentary notice. Coincidences, in general, are great stumbling-blocks in the way of that class of thinkers who have been educated to know nothing of the theory of probabilities—that theory to which the most glorious objects of human research are indebted for the most glorious of illustration. In the present instance, had the gold been gone, the fact of its delivery three days before would have formed something more than a coincidence. It would have been corroborative of this idea of motive. But, under the real circumstances of the case, if we are to suppose gold the motive of this outrage, we must also imagine the perpetrator so vacillating an idiot as to have abandoned his gold and his motive together.

"Keeping now steadily in mind the points to which I have drawn your attention—that peculiar voice, that unusual agility, and that startling absence of motive in a murder so singularly atrocious as this—let us glance at the butchery itself. Here is a woman strangled to death by manual strength, and thrust up a chimney head downward. Ordinary assassins employ no such mode of murder as this. Least of all, do they thus dispose of the murdered. In the manner of thrusting the corpse up the chimney, you will admit that there was something *excessively outré*—something altogether irreconcilable with our common notions of human action, even when we suppose the actors the most depraved of men. Think, too, how great must have been that strength which could have thrust the body *up* such an aperture so forcibly that the united vigor of several persons was found barely sufficient to drag it *down*!

"Turn, now, to other indications of the employment of a vigor most marvellous. On the hearth were thick tresses—very thick tresses—of gray human hair. These had been torn out by the roots. You are aware of the great force necessary in tearing thus from the head even twenty or thirty hairs together. You saw the locks in question as well as myself. Their roots (a hideous sight!) were clotted with fragments of the flesh of the scalp—sure token of the prodigious power which had been exerted in uprooting perhaps half a million hairs at a time. The throat of the old lady was not merely cut, but the head absolutely severed from the body: the instrument was a mere razor. I wish you also to look at the *brutal* ferocity of these deeds. Of the bruises upon the body of Madame L'Espanaye I do not speak. Monsieur Dumas, and his worthy coadjutor Monsieur Etienne, have pronounced that they were inflicted by some obtuse instrument; and so far these gentlemen are very correct. The obtuse instrument was clearly the stone pavement in the yard, upon which the victim had fallen from the window which looked in upon the bed. This idea, however simple it may now seem, escaped the police for the same reason that the breadth of the shutters escaped them—because, by the affair of the nails, their perceptions had been hermetically sealed against the possibility of the windows having ever been opened at all.

"If now, in addition to all these things, you have properly reflected upon the odd disorder of the chamber, we have gone so far as to combine the ideas of an agility astounding, a strength superhuman, a ferocity brutal, a butchery without motive, a *grotesquerie* in horror absolutely alien from humanity, and a voice foreign in tone to the ears of men of many nations, and devoid of all distinct or intelligible syllabification. What result, then, has ensued? What impression have I made upon your fancy?"

I felt a creeping of the flesh as Dupin asked me the question. "A madman," I said, "has done this deed—some raving maniac, escaped from a neighboring *Maison de Santé.*"

"In some respects," he replied, "your idea is not irrelevant. But the voices of madmen, even in their wildest paroxysms, are never found to tally with that peculiar voice heard upon the stairs. Madmen are of some nation, and their language, however incoherent in its words, has always the coherence of syllabification. Besides, the hair of a madman is not such as I now hold in my hand. I disentangled this little tuft from the rigidly clutched fingers of Madame L'Espanaye. Tell me what you can make of it."

"Dupin!" I said, completely unnerved; "this hair is most unusual—this is no *human* hair."

"I have not asserted that it is," said he; "but, before we decide this point, I wish you to glance at the little sketch I have here traced upon this paper. It is a *facsimile* drawing of what has been described in one portion of the testimony as 'dark bruises and deep indentations of finger nails' upon the throat of Mademoiselle L'Espanaye, and in another (by Messrs. Dumas and Etienne) as a 'series of livid spots, evidently the impression of fingers.'

"You will perceive," continued my friend, spreading out the paper upon the table before us, "that this drawing gives the idea of a firm and fixed hold. There is no *slipping* apparent. Each finger has retained—possibly until the death of the victim—the fearful grasp by which it originally imbedded itself. Attempt, now, to place all your fingers, at the same time, in the respective impressions as you see them."

I made the attempt in vain.

"We are possibly not giving this matter a fair trial," he said. "The paper is spread out upon a plane surface; but the human throat is cylindrical. Here is a billet of wood, the circumference of which is about that of the throat. Wrap the drawing around it, and try the experiment again."

I did so; but the difficulty was even more obvious than before. "This," I said, "is the mark of no human hand."

"Read now," replied Dupin, "this passage from Cuvier."

It was a minute anatomical and generally descriptive account of the large fulvous Ourang-Outang of the East Indian Islands. The gigantic stature, the prodigious strength and activity, the wild ferocity, and the imitative propensities of these mammalia are sufficiently well known to all. I understood the full horrors of the murder at once.

"The description of the digits," said I, as I made an end of the reading, "is in exact accordance with this drawing. I see that no animal but an Ourang-Outang, of the species here mentioned, could have impressed the indentations as you have traced them. This tuft of tawny hair, too, is identical in character with that of the beast of Cuvier. But I cannot possibly comprehend the particulars of this frightful mystery. Besides, there were *two* voices heard in contention, and one of them was unquestionably the voice of a Frenchman."

"True; and you will remember an expression attributed almost unanimously, by the evidence, to this voice,—the expression, '*mon Dieu!*' This, under the circumstances, has been justly characterized by one of the witnesses (Montani, the confectioner) as an expression of remonstrance or expostulation. Upon these two words, there-

fore, I have mainly built my hopes of a full solution of the riddle. A Frenchman was cognizant of the murder. It is possible—indeed it is far more than probable—that he was innocent of all participation in the bloody transactions which took place. The Ourang-Outang may have escaped from him. He may have traced it to the chamber; but, under the agitating circumstances which ensued, he could never have recaptured it. It is still at large. I will not pursue these guesses—for I have no right to call them more—since the shades of reflection upon which they are based are scarcely of sufficient depth to be appreciable by my own intellect, and since I could not pretend to make them intelligible to the understanding of another. We will call them guesses, then, and speak of them as such. If the Frenchman in question is indeed, as I suppose, innocent of this atrocity, this advertisement, which I left last night, upon our return home, at the office of *Le Monde* (a paper devoted to the shipping interest, and much sought by sailors), will bring him to our residence."

He handed me a paper, and I read thus:

"CAUGHT—*In the Bois de Boulogne, early in the morning of the——inst. (the morning of the murder), a very large, tawny Ourang-Outang of the Bornese species. The owner (who is ascertained to be a sailor, belonging to a Maltese vessel) may have the animal again, upon identifying it satisfactorily, and paying a few charges arising from its capture and keeping. Call at No.——Rue——, Faubourg St. Germain—au troisième.*"

"How was it possible," I asked, "that you should know the man to be a sailor, and belonging to a Maltese vessel?"

"I do *not* know it," said Dupin. "I am not *sure* of it. Here, however, is a small piece of ribbon, which from its form, and from its greasy appearance, has evidently been used in tying the hair in one of those long *queues* of which sailors are so fond. Moreover, this knot is one which few besides sailors can tie, and is peculiar to the

Maltese. I picked the ribbon up at the foot of the lightning-rod. It could not have belonged to either of the deceased. Now if, after all, I am wrong in my induction from this ribbon, that the Frenchman was a sailor belonging to a Maltese vessel, still I can have done no harm in saying what I did in the advertisement. If I am in error, he will merely suppose that I have been misled by some circumstance into which he will not take the trouble to inquire. But if I am right, a great point is gained. Cognizant although innocent of the murder, the Frenchman will naturally hesitate about replying to the advertisement—about demanding the Ourang-Outang. He will reason thus:—'I am innocent; I am poor; my Ourang-Outang is of great value—to one in my circumstances a fortune of itself—why should I lose it through idle apprehensions of danger? Here it is, within my grasp. It was found in the Bois de Boulogne—at a vast distance from the scene of that butchery. How can it ever be suspected that a brute beast should have done the deed? The police are at fault—they have failed to procure the slightest clew. Should they even trace the animal, it would be impossible to prove me cognizant of the murder or to implicate me in guilt on account of that cognizance. Above all, *I am known*. The advertiser designates me as the possessor of the beast. I am not sure to what limit his knowledge may extend. Should I avoid claiming a property of so great value, which it is known that I possess, I will render the animal, at least, liable to suspicion. It is not my policy to attract attention either to myself or to the beast. I will answer the advertisement, get the Ourang-Outang, and keep it close until this matter has blown over.'"

At this moment we heard a step upon the stairs.

"Be ready," said Dupin, "with your pistols, but neither use them nor show them until at a signal from myself."

The front door of the house had been left open, and the visitor had entered, without ringing, and advanced several steps upon the staircase. Now, however, he seemed to hesitate.

Presently we heard him descending. Dupin was moving quickly to the door, when we again heard him coming up. He did not turn back a second time, but stepped up with decision, and rapped at the door of our chamber.

"Come in," said Dupin, in a cheerful and hearty tone.

A man entered. He was a sailor, evidently—a tall, stout, and muscular-looking person, with a certain daredevil expression of countenance, not altogether unprepossessing. His face, greatly sunburnt, was more than half hidden by whisker and *mustachio*. He had with him a huge oaken cudgel, but appeared to be otherwise unarmed. He bowed awkwardly, and bade us "good evening," in French accents, which, although somewhat Neufchatelish, were still sufficiently indicative of a Parisian origin.

"Sit down, my friend," said Dupin. "I suppose you have called about the Ourang-Outang. Upon my word, I almost envy you the possession of him; a remarkably fine, and no doubt a very valuable animal. How old do you suppose him to be?"

The sailor drew a long breath, with the air of a man relieved of some intolerable burden, and then replied, in an assured tone:

"I have no way of telling—but he can't be more than four or five years old. Have you got him here?"

"Oh, no; we had no conveniences for keeping him here. He is at a livery stable in the Rue Dubourg, just by. You can get him in the morning. Of course you are prepared to identify the property?"

"To be sure I am, sir."

"I shall be sorry to part with him," said Dupin.

"I don't mean that you should be at all this trouble for nothing, sir," said the man. "Couldn't expect it. Am very willing to pay a reward for the finding of the animal—that is to say, any thing in reason."

"Well," replied my friend, "that is all very fair, to be sure. Let me think!—what should I have? Oh! I will tell you. My reward shall be this. You shall give me all the information in your power about these murders in the Rue Morgue."

Dupin said the last words in a very low tone, and very quietly. Just as quietly, too, he walked toward the door, locked it, and put the key in his pocket. He then drew a pistol from his bosom and placed it, without the least flurry, upon the table.

The sailor's face flushed up as if he were struggling with suffocation. He started to his feet and grasped his cudgel; but the next moment he fell back into his seat, trembling violently, and with the countenance of death itself. He spoke not a word. I pitied him from the bottom of my heart.

"My friend," said Dupin, in a kind tone, "you are alarming yourself unnecessarily—you are indeed. We mean you no harm whatever. I pledge you the honor of a gentleman, and of a Frenchman, that we intend you no injury. I perfectly well know that you are innocent of the atrocities in the Rue Morgue. It will not do, however, to deny that you are in some measure implicated in them. From what I have already said, you must know that I have had means of information about this matter—means of which you could never have dreamed. Now the thing stands thus. You have done nothing which you could have avoided—nothing, certainly, which renders you culpable. You were not even guilty of robbery, when you might have robbed with impunity. You have nothing to conceal. You have no reason for concealment. On the other hand, you are bound by every principle of honor to confess all you know. An innocent man is now imprisoned, charged with that crime of which you can point out the perpetrator."

The sailor had recovered his presence of mind, in a great measure, while Dupin uttered these words; but his original boldness of bearing was all gone.

"So help me God!" said he, after a brief pause, "I *will* tell you all I know about this affair;—but I do not expect you to believe one half I say—I would be a fool indeed if I did.

Still, I *am* innocent, and I will make a clean breast if I die for it."

What he stated was, in substance, this. He had lately made a voyage to the Indian Archipelago. A party, of which he formed one, landed at Borneo, and passed into the interior on an excursion of pleasure. Himself and a companion had captured the Ourang-Outang. This companion dying, the animal fell into his own exclusive possession. After great trouble, occasioned by the intractable ferocity of his captive during the home voyage, he at length succeeded in lodging it safely at his own residence in Paris, where, not to attract toward himself the unpleasant curiosity of his neighbors, he kept it carefully secluded, until such time as it should recover from a wound in the foot, received from a splinter on board ship. His ultimate design was to sell it.

Returning home from some sailors' frolic on the night, or rather in the morning, of the murder, he found the beast occupying his own bedroom, into which it had broken from a closet adjoining, where it had been, as was thought, securely confined. Razor in hand, and fully lathered, it was sitting before a looking-glass, attempting the operation of shaving, in which it had no doubt previously watched its master through the keyhole of the closet. Terrified at the sight of so dangerous a weapon in the possession of an animal so ferocious, and so well able to use it, the man, for some moments, was at a loss what to do. He had been accustomed, however, to quiet the creature, even in its fiercest moods, by the use of a whip, and to this he now resorted. Upon sight of it, the Ourang-Outang sprang at once through the door of the chamber, down the stairs, and thence, through a window, unfortunately open, into the street.

The Frenchman followed in despair; the ape, razor still in hand, occasionally stopping to look back and gesticulate at his pursuer, until the latter had nearly come up with it. It then again made off. In this manner the chase continued for a long time. The streets were profoundly quiet, as it was nearly three o'clock in the morning.

In passing down an alley in the rear of the Rue Morgue, the fugitive's attention was arrested by a light gleaming from the open window of Madame L'Espanaye's chamber, in the fourth story of her house. Rushing to the building, it perceived the lightning-rod, clambered up with inconceivable agility, grasped the shutter, which was thrown fully back against the wall, and, by its means, swung itself directly upon the head-board of the bed. The whole feat did not occupy a minute. The shutter was kicked open again by the Ourang-Outang as it entered the room.

The sailor, in the meantime, was both rejoiced and perplexed. He had strong hopes of now recapturing the brute, as it could scarcely escape from the trap into which it had ventured, except by the rod, where it might be intercepted as it came down. On the other hand, there was much cause for anxiety as to what it might do in the house. This latter reflection urged the man still to follow the fugitive. A lightning-rod is ascended without difficulty, especially by a sailor; but, when he had arrived as high as the window, which lay far to his left, his career was stopped; the most that he could accomplish was to reach over so as to obtain a glimpse of the interior of the room. At this glimpse he nearly fell from his hold through excess of horror. Now it was that those hideous shrieks arose upon the night, which had startled from slumber the inmates of the Rue Morgue. Madame L'Espanaye and her daughter, habited in their night clothes, had apparently been occupied in arranging some papers in the iron chest already mentioned, which had been wheeled into the middle of the room. It was open, and its contents lay beside it on the floor. The victims must have been sitting with their backs toward the window; and, from the time elapsing between the ingress of the beast and the screams, it seems probable that it was not immediately perceived. The flapping-to of the shutter would naturally have been attributed to the wind.

As the sailor looked in, the gigantic animal had seized Madame L'Espanaye by the hair (which was loose, as she had been combing it), and was flourishing the razor about her face, in imitation of the motions of a barber. The daughter lay prostrate and motionless; she had swooned. The screams and struggles of the old lady (during which the hair was torn from her head) had the effect of changing the probably pacific purposes of the Ourang-Outang into those of wrath. With one determined sweep of its muscular arm it nearly severed her head from her body. The sight of blood inflamed its anger into phrensy. Gnashing its teeth, and flashing fire from its eyes, it flew upon the body of the girl, and imbedded its fearful talons in her throat, retaining its grasp until she expired. Its wandering and wild glances fell at this moment upon the head of the bed, over which the face of its master, rigid with horror, was just discernible. The fury of the beast, who no doubt bore still in mind the dreaded whip, was instantly converted into fear. Conscious of having deserved punishment, it seemed desirous of concealing its bloody deeds, and skipped about the chamber in an agony of nervous agitation; throwing down and breaking the furniture as it moved, and dragging the bed from the bedstead. In conclusion, it seized first the corpse of the daughter, and thrust it up the chimney, as it was found; then that of the old lady, which it immediately hurled through the window headlong.

As the ape approached the casement with its mutilated burden, the sailor shrank aghast to the rod, and, rather gliding than clambering down it, hurried at once home—dreading the consequences of the butchery, and gladly abandoning, in his terror, all solicitude about the fate of the Ourang-Outang. The words heard by the party upon the staircase were the Frenchman's exclamations of horror and affright, commingled with the fiendish jabberings of the brute.

I have scarcely any thing to add. The Ourang-Outang must have escaped from the chamber, by the rod, just before the breaking of the door. It must have closed the window as it passed through it. It was subsequently caught by the owner himself, who obtained for it a very large sum at the *Jardin des Plantes*. Le Bon was instantly released, upon our narration of the circumstances (with some comments from Dupin) at the *bureau* of the Prefect of Police. This functionary, however well disposed to my friend, could not altogether conceal his chagrin at the turn which affairs had taken, and was fain to indulge in a sarcasm or two about the propriety of every person minding his own business.

"Let him talk," said Dupin, who had not thought it necessary to reply. "Let him discourse; it will ease his conscience. I am satisfied with having defeated him in his own castle. Nevertheless, that he failed in the solution of this mystery, is by no means that matter for wonder which he supposes it; for, in truth, our friend the Prefect is somewhat too cunning to be profound. In his wisdom is no *stamen*. It is all head and no body, like the pictures of the Goddess Laverna—or, at best, all head and shoulders, like a codfish. But he is a good creature after all. I like him especially for one master stroke of cant, by which he has attained his reputation for ingenuity. I mean the way he has '*de nier ce qui est, et d'expliquer ce qui n'est pas.*' "*

* Rousseau—Nouvelle Héloise.

THE PROBLEM OF CELL 13

JACQUES FUTRELLE

VERY FEW MYSTERY STORIES have been reprinted as often, or as deservedly, as "The Problem of Cell 13," the masterpiece by Jacques Futrelle (1875–1912) that introduced one of the great detectives of American literature, Professor Augustus S. F. X. Van Dusen, better known by the sobriquet given to him by admirers: The Thinking Machine.

Futrelle's reputation stands on this single story although he wrote forty-four other stories about the irascible little scientist, as well as many other stories and novels about different detectives. "The Problem of Cell 13" is the first story to be published about The Thinking Machine, but Futrelle's wife, May, also a writer, stated that he wrote *The Chase of the Golden Plate,* a short novel about the detective, a year earlier. It was published in 1906, whereas the short story made its first appearance in the pages of the *Boston American* on October 30, 1905. It was there that Van Dusen issued his challenge, declaring that he could escape from any prison merely by using his exceptional brain. This intriguing situation turned out to be a temporary frustration for readers because the story was published as a serial in six parts. It took the form of a contest with one hundred dollars in prize money offered to the reader who came up with the best solution to the apparently insoluble predicament. The contest began on a Monday and concluded on Sunday, presumably so judges could read and grade the submissions, though it is not entirely impossible that skipping an installment on Saturday was an encouragement to buy the more expensive Sunday edition. The fifty-dollar first prize was won by a gentleman named P. C. Hosmer, who was never again heard from in the world of mystery fiction.

"The Problem of Cell 13" was first collected in book form in *The Thinking Machine* (New York, Dodd, Mead, 1907).

THE PROBLEM OF CELL 13

JACQUES FUTRELLE

PRACTICALLY ALL THOSE letters remaining in the alphabet after Augustus S. F. X. Van Dusen was named were afterward acquired by that gentleman in the course of a brilliant scientific career, and, being honorably acquired, were tacked on to the other end. His name, therefore, taken with all that belonged to it, was a wonderfully imposing structure. He was a Ph.D., an LL.D., an F.R.S., an M.D., and an M.D.S. He was also some other things—just what he himself couldn't say—through recognition of his ability by various foreign educational and scientific institutions.

In appearance he was no less striking than in nomenclature. He was slender with the droop of the student in his thin shoulders and the pallor of a close, sedentary life on his clean-shaven face. His eyes wore a perpetual, forbidding squint—the squint of a man who studies little things—and, when they could be seen at all through his thick spectacles, were mere slits of watery blue. But above his eyes was his most striking feature. This was a tall, broad brow, almost abnormal in height and width, crowned by a heavy shock of bushy, yellow hair. All these things conspired to give him a peculiar, almost grotesque, personality.

Professor Van Dusen was remotely German. For generations his ancestors had been noted in the sciences; he was the logical result, the master mind. First and above all he was a logician. At least thirty-five years of the half century or so of his existence had been devoted exclusively to proving that two and two always equal four, except in unusual cases, where they equal three or five, as the case may be. He stood broadly on the general proposition that all things that start must go somewhere, and was able to bring the concentrated mental force of his forefathers to bear on a given problem. Incidentally it may be remarked that Professor Van Dusen wore a No. 8 hat.

The world at large had heard vaguely of Professor Van Dusen as The Thinking Machine. It was a newspaper catch-phrase applied to him at the time of a remarkable exhibition at chess; he had demonstrated then that a stranger to the game might, by the force of inevitable logic, defeat a champion who had devoted a lifetime to its study. The Thinking Machine! Perhaps that more nearly described him than all his honorary initials, for he spent week after week, month after month, in the seclusion of his small laboratory from which had gone forth thoughts that staggered scientific associates and deeply stirred the world at large.

It was only occasionally that The Thinking Machine had visitors, and these were usually men who, themselves high in the sciences, dropped in to argue a point and perhaps convince themselves. Two of these men, Dr. Charles Ransome and Alfred Fielding, called one evening to discuss some theory which is not of consequence here.

"Such a thing is impossible," declared Dr. Ransome emphatically, in the course of the conversation.

"Nothing is impossible," declared The Thinking Machine with equal emphasis. He always spoke petulantly. "The mind is master of all things. When science fully recognizes that fact a great advance will have been made."

"How about the airship?" asked Dr. Ransome.

"That's not impossible at all," asserted The Thinking Machine. "It will be invented some time. I'd do it myself, but I'm busy."

Dr. Ransome laughed tolerantly.

"I've heard you say such things before," he said. "But they mean nothing. Mind may be master of matter, but it hasn't yet found a way to apply itself. There are some things that can't be *thought* out of existence, or rather which would not yield to any amount of thinking."

"What, for instance?" demanded The Thinking Machine.

Dr. Ransome was thoughtful for a moment as he smoked.

"Well, say, prison walls," he replied. "No man can *think* himself out of a cell. If he could, there would be no prisoners."

"A man can so apply his brain and ingenuity that he can leave a cell, which is the same thing," snapped The Thinking Machine.

Dr. Ransome was slightly amused.

"Let's suppose a case," he said, after a moment. "Take a cell where prisoners under sentence of death are confined—men who are desperate and, maddened by fear, would take any chance to escape—suppose you were locked in such a cell. Could you escape?"

"Certainly," declared The Thinking Machine.

"Of course," said Mr. Fielding, who entered the conversation for the first time, "you might wreck the cell with an explosive—but inside, a prisoner, you couldn't have that."

"There would be nothing of that kind," said The Thinking Machine. "You might treat me precisely as you treated prisoners under sentence of death, and I would leave the cell."

"Not unless you entered it with tools prepared to get out," said Dr. Ransome.

The Thinking Machine was visibly annoyed and his blue eyes snapped.

"Lock me in any cell in any prison anywhere at any time, wearing only what is necessary, and I'll escape in a week," he declared, sharply.

Dr. Ransome sat up straight in the chair, interested. Mr. Fielding lighted a new cigar.

"You mean you could actually *think* yourself out?" asked Dr. Ransome.

"I would get out," was the response.

"Are you serious?"

"Certainly I am serious."

Dr. Ransome and Mr. Fielding were silent for a long time.

"Would you be willing to try it?" asked Mr. Fielding, finally.

"Certainly," said Professor Van Dusen, and there was a trace of irony in his voice. "I have done more asinine things than that to convince other men of less important truths."

The tone was offensive and there was an undercurrent strongly resembling anger on both sides. Of course it was an absurd thing, but Professor Van Dusen reiterated his willingness to undertake the escape and it was decided upon.

"To begin now," added Dr. Ransome.

"I'd prefer that it begin to-morrow," said The Thinking Machine, "because——"

"No, now," said Mr. Fielding, flatly. "You are arrested, figuratively, of course, without any warning locked in a cell with no chance to communicate with friends, and left there with identically the same care and attention that would be given to a man under sentence of death. Are you willing?"

"All right, now, then," said The Thinking Machine, and he arose.

"Say, the death cell in Chisholm Prison."

"The death cell in Chisholm Prison."

"And what will you wear?"

"As little as possible," said The Thinking Machine. "Shoes, stockings, trousers, and a shirt."

"You will permit yourself to be searched, of course?"

"I am to be treated precisely as all prisoners are treated," said The Thinking Machine. "No more attention and no less."

There were some preliminaries to be arranged in the matter of obtaining permission for the test, but all three were influential men and everything was done satisfactorily by telephone, albeit the prison commissioners, to whom the experiment was explained on purely scientific grounds, were sadly bewildered. Professor Van Dusen would be the most distinguished prisoner they had ever entertained.

When The Thinking Machine had donned those things which he was to wear during his incarceration he called the little old woman who was his housekeeper, cook, and maidservant all in one.

"Martha," he said, "it is now twenty-seven minutes past nine o'clock. I am going away. One week from to-night, at half past nine, these gentlemen and one, possibly two, others will take supper with me here. Remember Dr. Ransome is very fond of artichokes."

The three men were driven to Chisholm Prison, where the warden was awaiting them, having been informed of the matter by telephone. He understood merely that the eminent Professor Van Dusen was to be his prisoner, if he could keep him, for one week; that he had committed no crime, but that he was to be treated as all other prisoners were treated.

"Search him," instructed Dr. Ransome.

The Thinking Machine was searched. Nothing was found on him; the pockets of the trousers were empty; the white, stiff-bosomed shirt had no pocket. The shoes and stockings were removed, examined, then replaced. As he watched all these preliminaries, and noted the pitiful, childlike physical weakness of the man—the colorless face, and the thin, white hands—Dr. Ransome almost regretted his part in the affair.

"Are you sure you want to do this?" he asked.

"Would you be convinced if I did not?" inquired The Thinking Machine in turn.

"No."

"All right. I'll do it."

What sympathy Dr. Ransome had was dissipated by the tone. It nettled him, and he resolved to see the experiment to the end; it would be a stinging reproof to egotism.

"It will be impossible for him to communicate with anyone outside?" he asked.

"Absolutely impossible," replied the warden. "He will not be permitted writing materials of any sort."

"And your jailers, would they deliver a message from him?"

"Not one word, directly or indirectly," said the warden. "You may rest assured of that. They will report anything he might say or turn over to me, anything he might give them."

"That seems entirely satisfactory," said Mr. Fielding, who was frankly interested in the problem.

"Of course, in the event he fails," said Dr. Ransome, "and asks for his liberty, you understand you are to set him free?"

"I understand," replied the warden.

The Thinking Machine stood listening, but had nothing to say until this was all ended, then:

"I should like to make three small requests. You may grant them or not, as you wish."

"No special favors, now," warned Mr. Fielding.

"I am asking none," was the stiff response. "I should like to have some tooth powder—buy it yourself to see that it is tooth powder—and I should like to have one five-dollar and two ten-dollar bills."

Dr. Ransome, Mr. Fielding, and the warden exchanged astonished glances. They were not surprised at the request for tooth powder, but were at the request for money.

"Is there any man with whom our friend would come in contact that he could bribe with twenty-five dollars?"

"Not for twenty-five hundred dollars," was the positive reply.

"Well, let him have them," said Mr. Fielding. "I think they are harmless enough."

"And what is the third request?" asked Dr. Ransome.

"I should like to have my shoes polished."

Again the astonished glances were exchanged. This last request was the height of absurdity, so they agreed to it. These things all being attended to, The Thinking Machine was led back into the prison from which he had undertaken to escape.

"Here is Cell 13," said the warden, stopping three doors down the steel corridor. "This is where we keep condemned murderers. No one can leave it without my permission; and no one in it can communicate with the outside. I'll stake my reputation on that. It's only three doors back of my office and I can readily hear any unusual noise."

"Will this cell do, gentlemen?" asked The Thinking Machine. There was a touch of irony in his voice.

"Admirably," was the reply.

The heavy steel door was thrown open, there was a great scurrying and scampering of tiny feet, and The Thinking Machine passed into the gloom of the cell. Then the door was closed and double locked by the warden.

"What is that noise in there?" asked Dr. Ransome, through the bars.

"Rats—dozens of them," replied The Thinking Machine, tersely.

The three men, with final good nights, were turning away when The Thinking Machine called:

"What time is it exactly, Warden?"

"Eleven seventeen," replied the warden.

"Thanks. I will join you gentlemen in your office at half past eight o'clock one week from to-night," said The Thinking Machine.

"And if you do not?"

"There is no 'if' about it."

Chisholm Prison was a great, spreading structure of granite, four stories in all, which stood in the center of acres of open space. It was surrounded by a wall of solid masonry eighteen feet high, and so smoothly finished inside and out as to offer no foothold to a climber, no matter how expert. Atop of this fence, as a further precaution, was a five-foot fence of steel rods, each terminating in a keen point. This fence in itself marked an absolute deadline between freedom and imprisonment, for, even if a man escaped from his cell, it would seem impossible for him to pass the wall.

The yard, which on all sides of the prison building was twenty-five feet wide, that being the distance from the building to the wall, was by day an exercise ground for those prisoners to whom was granted the boon of occasional semi-liberty. But that was not for those in Cell 13. At all times of the day there were armed guards in the yard, four of them, one patrolling each side of the prison building.

By night the yard was almost as brilliantly lighted as by day. On each of the four sides was a great arc light which rose above the prison wall and gave to the guards a clear sight. The lights, too, brightly illuminated the spiked top of the wall. The wires which fed the arc lights ran up the side of the prison building on insulators and from the top story led out to the poles supporting the arc lights.

All these things were seen and comprehended by The Thinking Machine, who was only enabled to see out his closely barred cell window by standing on his bed. This was on the morning following his incarceration. He gathered, too, that the river lay over there beyond the wall somewhere, because he heard faintly the pulsation of a motor boat and high up in the air saw a river bird. From that same direction came the shouts of boys at play and the occasional crack of a batted ball. He knew then that between the prison wall and the river was an open space, a playground.

Chisholm Prison was regarded as absolutely safe. No man had ever escaped from it. The Thinking Machine, from his perch on the bed, seeing what he saw, could readily understand why. The walls of the cell, though built he judged twenty years before, were perfectly solid, and the window bars of new iron had not a shadow of rust on them. The window itself, even with the bars out, would be a difficult mode of egress because it was small.

Yet, seeing these things, The Thinking Machine was not discouraged. Instead, he thoughtfully squinted at the great arc light—there was bright sunlight now—and traced with his eyes the wire which led from it to the building. That electric wire, he reasoned, must come down the side of the building not a great distance from his cell. That might be worth knowing.

Cell 13 was on the same floor with the offices of the prison—that is, not in the basement, nor yet upstairs. There were only four steps up to the office floor, therefore the level of the floor must be only three or four feet above the ground. He couldn't see the ground directly beneath his window, but he could see it further out toward the wall. It would be an easy drop from the window. Well and good.

Then The Thinking Machine fell to remembering how he had come to the cell. First, there was the outside guard's booth, a part of the wall. There were two heavily barred gates there, both of steel. At this gate was one man always on guard. He admitted persons to the prison after much clanking of keys and locks, and let them out when ordered to do so. The warden's office was in the prison building, and in order to reach that official from the prison yard one had to pass a gate of solid steel with only a peephole in it. Then coming from that inner office to Cell 13, where he was now, one must pass a heavy wooden door and two steel doors into the corridors of the prison; and always there was the double-locked door of Cell 13 to reckon with.

There were then, The Thinking Machine recalled, seven doors to be overcome before one could pass from Cell 13 into the outer world, a free man. But against this was the fact that he was rarely interrupted. A jailer appeared at his cell door at six in the morning with a breakfast of prison fare; he would come again at noon, and again at six in the afternoon. At nine o'clock at night would come the inspection tour. That would be all.

"It's admirably arranged, this prison system," was the mental tribute paid by The Thinking Machine. "I'll have to study it a little when I get out. I had no idea there was such great care exercised in the prisons."

There was nothing, positively nothing, in his cell, except his iron bed, so firmly put together that no man could tear it to pieces save with sledges or a file. He had neither of these. There was not even a chair, or a small table, or a bit of tin or crockery. Nothing! The jailer stood by when he ate, then took away the wooden spoon and bowl which he had used.

One by one these things sank into the brain of The Thinking Machine. When the last possibility had been considered he began an examination of his cell. From the roof, down the walls on all sides, he examined the stones and the cement between them. He stamped over the floor carefully time after time, but it was cement, perfectly solid. After the examination he sat on the edge of the iron bed and was lost in thought for a long time. For Professor Augustus S. F. X. Van Dusen, The Thinking Machine, had something to think about.

He was disturbed by a rat, which ran across his foot, then scampered away into a dark corner of the cell, frightened at its own daring. After a while The Thinking Machine, squinting steadily into the darkness of the corner where the rat had gone, was able to make out in the gloom many little beady eyes staring at him. He counted six pair, and there were perhaps others; he didn't see very well.

Then The Thinking Machine, from his seat on the bed, noticed for the first time the bottom of his cell door. There was an opening there of two inches between the steel bar and the floor. Still looking steadily at this opening, The Thinking Machine backed suddenly into the corner where he had seen the beady eyes. There was a great scampering of tiny feet, several squeaks of frightened rodents, and then silence.

None of the rats had gone out the door, yet there were none in the cell. Therefore there must be another way out of the cell, however small. The Thinking Machine, on hands and knees, started a search for this spot, feeling in the darkness with his long, slender fingers.

At last his search was rewarded. He came upon a small opening in the floor, level with the cement. It was perfectly round and somewhat larger than a silver dollar. This was the way the rats had gone. He put his fingers deep into the opening; it seemed to be a disused drainage pipe and was dry and dusty.

Having satisfied himself on this point, he sat on the bed again for an hour, then made another inspection of his surroundings through the small cell window. One of the outside guards stood directly opposite, beside the wall, and happened to be looking at the window of Cell 13 when the head of The Thinking Machine appeared. But the scientist didn't notice the guard.

Noon came and the jailer appeared with the prison dinner of repulsively plain food. At home The Thinking Machine merely ate to live; here he took what was offered without comment. Occasionally he spoke to the jailer who stood outside the door watching him.

"Any improvements made here in the last few years?" he asked.

"Nothing particularly," replied the jailer. "New wall was built four years ago."

"Anything done to the prison proper?"

"Painted the woodwork outside, and I believe about seven years ago a new system of plumbing was put in."

"Ah!" said the prisoner. "How far is the river over there?"

"About three hundred feet. The boys have a baseball ground between the wall and the river."

The Thinking Machine had nothing further to say just then, but when the jailer was ready to go he asked for some water.

"I get very thirsty here," he explained. "Would it be possible for you to leave a little water in a bowl for me?"

"I'll ask the warden," replied the jailer, and he went away.

Half an hour later he returned with water in a small earthen bowl.

"The warden says you may keep this bowl," he informed the prisoner. "But you must show it to me when I ask for it. If it is broken, it will be the last."

"Thank you," said The Thinking Machine. "I shan't break it."

The jailer went on about his duties. For just the fraction of a second it seemed that The Thinking Machine wanted to ask a question, but he didn't.

Two hours later this same jailer, in passing the door of Cell No. 13, heard a noise inside and stopped. The Thinking Machine was down on his hands and knees in a corner of the cell, and from that same corner came several frightened squeaks. The jailer looked on interestedly.

"Ah, I've got you," he heard the prisoner say.

"Got what?" he asked, sharply.

"One of these rats," was the reply. "See?" And between the scientist's long fingers the jailer saw a small gray rat struggling. The prisoner brought it over to the light and looked at it closely.

"It's a water rat," he said.

"Ain't you got anything better to do than to catch rats?" asked the jailer.

"It's disgraceful that they should be here at all," was the irritated reply. "Take this one away and kill it. There are dozens more where it came from."

The jailer took the wriggling, squirmy rodent and flung it down on the floor violently. It gave one squeak and lay still. Later he reported the incident to the warden, who only smiled.

Still later that afternoon the outside armed guard on the Cell 13 side of the prison looked up again at the window and saw the prisoner looking out. He saw a hand raised to the barred window and then something white fluttered to the ground, directly under the window of Cell 13. It was a little roll of linen, evidently of white shirting material, and tied around it was a five-dollar bill. The guard looked up at the window again, but the face had disappeared.

With a grim smile he took the little linen roll and the five-dollar bill to the warden's office. There together they deciphered something which was written on it with a queer sort of ink, frequently blurred. On the outside was this:

"Finder of this please deliver to Dr. Charles Ransome."

"Ah," said the warden, with a chuckle. "Plan of escape number one has gone wrong." Then, as an afterthought: "But why did he address it to Dr. Ransome?"

"And where did he get the pen and ink to write with?" asked the guard.

The warden looked at the guard and the guard looked at the warden. There was no apparent solution of that mystery. The warden studied the writing carefully, then shook his head.

"Well, let's see what he was going to say to Dr. Ransome," he said at length, still puzzled, and he unrolled the inner piece of linen.

"Well, if that—what—what do you think of that?" he asked, dazed.

The guard took the bit of linen and read this:—

"Epa cseot d'net niiy awe htto n'si sih. T."

The warden spent an hour wondering what sort of a cipher it was, and half an hour wondering why his prisoner should attempt to communicate with Dr. Ransome, who was the cause of his being there. After this the warden devoted some thought to the question of where the prisoner got writing materials, and what sort of writing materials he had. With the idea of illuminating this point, he examined the linen again. It was a torn part of a white shirt and had ragged edges.

Now it was possible to account for the linen, but what the prisoner had used to write with was another matter. The warden knew it would have been impossible for him to have either pen or pencil, and, besides, neither pen nor pencil had been used in this writing. What, then? The warden decided to investigate personally. The Thinking Machine was his prisoner; he had orders to hold his prisoners; if this one sought to escape by sending cipher messages to persons outside, he would stop it, as he would have stopped it in the case of any other prisoner.

The warden went back to Cell 13 and found The Thinking Machine on his hands and knees on the floor, engaged in nothing more alarming than catching rats. The prisoner heard the warden's step and turned to him quickly.

"It's disgraceful," he snapped, "these rats. There are scores of them."

"Other men have been able to stand them," said the warden. "Here is another shirt for you—let me have the one you have on."

"Why?" demanded The Thinking Machine, quickly. His tone was hardly natural, his manner suggested actual perturbation.

"You have attempted to communicate with Dr. Ransome," said the warden severely. "As my prisoner, it is my duty to put a stop to it."

The Thinking Machine was silent for a moment.

"All right," he said, finally. "Do your duty."

The warden smiled grimly. The prisoner arose from the floor and removed the white shirt, putting on instead a striped convict shirt the warden had brought. The warden took the white shirt eagerly, and then and there compared the pieces of linen on which was written the cipher with certain torn places in the shirt. The Thinking Machine looked on curiously.

"The guard brought *you* those, then?" he asked.

"He certainly did," replied the warden triumphantly. "And that ends your first attempt to escape."

The Thinking Machine watched the warden as he, by comparison, established to his own satisfaction that only two pieces of linen had been torn from the white shirt.

"What did you write this with?" demanded the warden.

"I should think it a part of your duty to find out," said The Thinking Machine, irritably.

The warden started to say some harsh things, then restrained himself and made a minute search of the cell and of the prisoner instead. He found absolutely nothing; not even a match or toothpick which might have been used for a pen. The same mystery surrounded the fluid with which the cipher had been written. Although the warden left Cell 13 visibly annoyed, he took the torn shirt in triumph.

"Well, writing notes on a shirt won't get him

out, that's certain," he told himself with some complacency. He put the linen scraps into his desk to await developments. "If that man escapes from that cell I'll—hang it—I'll resign."

On the third day of his incarceration The Thinking Machine openly attempted to bribe his way out. The jailer had brought his dinner and was leaning against the barred door, waiting, when The Thinking Machine began the conversation.

"The drainage pipes of the prison lead to the river, don't they?" he asked.

"Yes," said the jailer.

"I suppose they are very small."

"Too small to crawl through, if that's what you're thinking about," was the grinning response.

There was silence until The Thinking Machine finished his meal. Then:

"You know I'm not a criminal, don't you?"

"Yes."

"And that I've a perfect right to be freed if I demand it?"

"Yes."

"Well, I came here believing that I could make my escape," said the prisoner, and his squint eyes studied the face of the jailer. "Would you consider a financial reward for aiding me to escape?"

The jailer, who happened to be an honest man, looked at the slender, weak figure of the prisoner, at the large head with its mass of yellow hair, and was almost sorry.

"I guess prisons like these were not built for the likes of you to get out of," he said, at last.

"But would you consider a proposition to help me get out?" the prisoner insisted, almost beseechingly.

"No," said the jailer, shortly.

"Five hundred dollars," urged The Thinking Machine. "I am not a criminal."

"No," said the jailer.

"A thousand?"

"No," again said the jailer, and he started away hurriedly to escape further temptation. Then he turned back. "If you should give me ten thousand dollars I couldn't get you out. You'd have to pass through seven doors, and I only have the keys to two."

Then he told the warden all about it.

"Plan number two fails," said the warden, smiling grimly. "First a cipher, then bribery."

When the jailer was on his way to Cell 13 at six o'clock, again bearing food to The Thinking Machine, he paused, startled by the unmistakable scrape, scrape of steel against steel. It stopped at the sound of his steps, then craftily the jailer, who was beyond the prisoner's range of vision, resumed his tramping, the sound being apparently that of a man going away from Cell 13. As a matter of fact he was in the same spot.

After a moment there came again the steady scrape, scrape, and the jailer crept cautiously on tiptoes to the door and peered between the bars. The Thinking Machine was standing on the iron bed working at the bars of the little window. He was using a file, judging from the backward and forward swing of his arms.

Cautiously the jailer crept back to the office, summoned the warden in person, and they returned to Cell 13 on tiptoes. The steady scrape was still audible. The warden listened to satisfy himself and then suddenly appeared at the door.

"Well?" he demanded, and there was a smile on his face.

The Thinking Machine glanced back from his perch on the bed and leaped suddenly to the floor, making frantic efforts to hide something. The warden went in, with hand extended.

"Give it up," he said.

"No," said the prisoner, sharply.

"Come, give it up," urged the warden. "I don't want to have to search you again."

"No," repeated the prisoner.

"What was it—a file?" asked the warden.

The Thinking Machine was silent and stood squinting at the warden with something very nearly approaching disappointment on his face—nearly, but not quite. The warden was almost sympathetic.

"Plan number three fails, eh?" he asked, good-naturedly. "Too bad, isn't it?"

The prisoner didn't say.

"Search him," instructed the warden.

The jailer searched the prisoner carefully. At last, artfully concealed in the waistband of the trousers, he found a piece of steel about two inches long, with one side curved like a half moon.

"Ah," said the warden, as he received it from the jailer. "From your shoe heel," and he smiled pleasantly.

The jailer continued his search and on the other side of the trousers waistband found another piece of steel identical with the first. The edges showed where they had been worn against the bars of the window.

"You couldn't saw a way through those bars with these," said the warden.

"I could have," said The Thinking Machine firmly.

"In six months, perhaps," said the warden, good-naturedly.

The warden shook his head slowly as he gazed into the slightly flushed face of his prisoner.

"Ready to give it up?" he asked.

"I haven't started yet," was the prompt reply.

Then came another exhaustive search of the cell. Carefully the two men went over it, finally turning out the bed and searching that. Nothing. The warden in person climbed upon the bed and examined the bars of the window where the prisoner had been sawing. When he looked he was amused.

"Just made it a little bright by hard rubbing," he said to the prisoner, who stood looking on with a somewhat crestfallen air. The warden grasped the iron bars in his strong hands and tried to shake them. They were immovable, set firmly in the solid granite. He examined each in turn and found them all satisfactory. Finally he climbed down from the bed.

"Give it up, Professor," he advised.

The Thinking Machine shook his head and the warden and jailer passed on again. As they disappeared down the corridor The Thinking Machine sat on the edge of the bed with his head in his hands.

"He's crazy to try to get out of that cell," commented the jailer.

"Of course he can't get out," said the warden. "But he's clever. I would like to know what he wrote that cipher with."

It was four o'clock next morning when an awful, heart-racking shriek of terror resounded through the great prison. It came from a cell, somewhere about the center, and its tone told a tale of horror, agony, terrible fear. The warden heard and with three of his men rushed into the long corridor leading to Cell 13.

As they ran there came again that awful cry. It died away in a sort of wail. The white faces of prisoners appeared at cell doors upstairs and down, staring out wonderingly, frightened.

"It's that fool in Cell 13," grumbled the warden.

He stopped and stared in as one of the jailers flashed a lantern. "That fool in Cell 13" lay comfortably on his cot, flat on his back with his mouth open, snoring. Even as they looked there came again the piercing cry, from somewhere above. The warden's face blanched a little as he started up the stairs. There on the top floor he found a man in Cell 43, directly above Cell 13, but two floors higher, cowering in a corner of his cell.

"What's the matter?" demanded the warden.

"Thank God you've come," exclaimed the prisoner, and he cast himself against the bars of his cell.

"What is it?" demanded the warden again.

He threw open the door and went in. The prisoner dropped on his knees and clasped the warden about the body. His face was white with terror, his eyes were widely distended, and he was shuddering. His hands, icy cold, clutched at the warden's.

"Take me out of this cell, please take me out," he pleaded.

"What's the matter with you, anyhow?" insisted the warden, impatiently.

"I heard something—something," said the prisoner, and his eyes roved nervously around the cell.

"What did you hear?"

"I—I can't tell you," stammered the prisoner. Then, in a sudden burst of terror: "Take me out of this cell—put me anywhere—but take me out of here."

The warden and the three jailers exchanged glances.

"Who is this fellow? What's he accused of?" asked the warden.

"Joseph Ballard," said one of the jailers. "He's accused of throwing acid in a woman's face. She died from it."

"But they can't prove it," gasped the prisoner. "They can't prove it. Please put me in some other cell."

He was still clinging to the warden, and that official threw his arms off roughly. Then for a time he stood looking at the cowering wretch, who seemed possessed of all the wild, unreasoning terror of a child.

"Look here, Ballard," said the warden, finally, "if you heard anything, I want to know what it was. Now tell me."

"I can't, I can't," was the reply. He was sobbing.

"Where did it come from?"

"I don't know. Everywhere—nowhere. I just heard it."

"What was it—a voice?"

"Please don't make me answer," pleaded the prisoner.

"You must answer," said the warden, sharply.

"It was a voice—but—but it wasn't human," was the sobbing reply.

"Voice, but not human?" repeated the warden, puzzled.

"It sounded muffled and—and far away—and ghostly," explained the man.

"Did it come from inside or outside the prison?"

"It didn't seem to come from anywhere—it was just here, here, everywhere. I heard it. I heard it."

For an hour the warden tried to get the story, but Ballard had become suddenly obstinate and would say nothing—only pleaded to be placed in another cell, or to have one of the jailers remain near him until daylight. These requests were gruffly refused.

"And see here," said the warden, in conclusion, "if there's any more of this screaming I'll put you in the padded cell."

Then the warden went his way, a sadly puzzled man. Ballard sat at his cell door until daylight, his face, drawn and white with terror, pressed against the bars, and looked out into the prison with wide, staring eyes.

That day, the fourth since the incarceration of The Thinking Machine, was enlivened considerably by the volunteer prisoner, who spent most of his time at the little window of his cell. He began proceedings by throwing another piece of linen down to the guard, who picked it up dutifully and took it to the warden. On it was written:

"Only three days more."

The warden was in no way surprised at what he read; he understood that The Thinking Machine meant only three days more of his imprisonment, and he regarded the note as a boast. But how was the thing written? Where had The Thinking Machine found this new piece of linen? Where? How? He carefully examined the linen. It was white, of fine texture, shirting material. He took the shirt which he had taken and carefully fitted the two original pieces of the linen to the torn places. This third piece was entirely superfluous; it didn't fit anywhere, and yet it was unmistakably the same goods.

"And where—where does he get anything to write with?" demanded the warden of the world at large.

Still later on the fourth day The Thinking Machine, through the window of his cell, spoke to the armed guard outside.

"What day of the month is it?" he asked.

"The fifteenth," was the answer.

The Thinking Machine made a mental astronomical calculation and satisfied himself that the moon would not rise until after nine o'clock that night. Then he asked another question:

"Who attends to those arc lights?"

"Man from the company."

"You have no electricians in the building?"

"No."

"I should think you could save money if you had your own man."

"None of my business," replied the guard.

The guard noticed The Thinking Machine at the cell window frequently during that day, but always the face seemed listless and there was a certain wistfulness in the squint eyes behind the glasses. After a while he accepted the presence of the leonine head as a matter of course. He had seen other prisoners do the same thing; it was the longing for the outside world.

That afternoon, just before the day guard was relieved, the head appeared at the window again, and The Thinking Machine's hand held something out between the bars. It fluttered to the ground and the guard picked it up. It was a five-dollar bill.

"That's for you," called the prisoner.

As usual, the guard took it to the warden. That gentleman looked at it suspiciously; he looked at everything that came from Cell 13 with suspicion.

"He said it was for me," explained the guard.

"It's a sort of a tip, I suppose," said the warden. "I see no particular reason why you shouldn't accept——"

Suddenly he stopped. He had remembered that The Thinking Machine had gone into Cell 13 with one five-dollar bill and two ten-dollar bills; twenty-five dollars in all. Now a five-dollar bill had been tied around the first pieces of linen that came from the cell. The warden still had it, and to convince himself he took it out and looked at it. It was five dollars; yet here was another five dollars, and The Thinking Machine had only had ten-dollar bills.

"Perhaps somebody changed one of the bills for him," he thought at last, with a sigh of relief.

But then and there he made up his mind. He would search Cell 13 as a cell was never before searched in this world. When a man could write at will, and change money, and do other wholly inexplicable things, there was something radically wrong with his prison. He planned to enter the cell at night—three o'clock would be an excellent time. The Thinking Machine must do all the weird things he did sometimes. Night seemed the most reasonable.

Thus it happened that the warden stealthily descended upon Cell 13 that night at three o'clock. He paused at the door and listened. There was no sound save the steady, regular breathing of the prisoner. The keys unfastened the double locks with scarcely a clank, and the warden entered, locking the door behind him. Suddenly he flashed his dark lantern in the face of the recumbent figure.

If the warden had planned to startle The Thinking Machine he was mistaken, for that individual merely opened his eyes quietly, reached for his glasses and inquired, in a most matter-of-fact tone:

"Who is it?"

It would be useless to describe the search that the warden made. It was minute. Not one inch of the cell or the bed was overlooked. He found the round hole in the floor, and with a flash of inspiration thrust his thick fingers into it. After a moment of fumbling there he drew up something and looked at it in the light of his lantern.

"Ugh!" he exclaimed.

The thing he had taken out was a rat—a dead rat. His inspiration fled as a mist before the sun. But he continued the search. The Thinking Machine, without a word, arose and kicked the rat out of the cell into the corridor.

The warden climbed on the bed and tried the steel bars in the tiny window. They were perfectly rigid; every bar of the door was the same.

Then the warden searched the prisoner's clothing, beginning at the shoes. Nothing hidden in them! Then the trousers waistband. Still nothing! Then the pockets of the trousers. From one side he drew out some paper money and examined it.

"Five one-dollar bills," he gasped.

"That's right," said the prisoner.

"But the—you had two tens and a five—what the—how do you do it?"

"That's my business," said The Thinking Machine.

"Did any of my men change this money for you—on your word of honor?"

The Thinking Machine paused just a fraction of a second.

"No," he said.

"Well, do you make it?" asked the warden. He was prepared to believe anything.

"That's my business," again said the prisoner.

The warden glared at the eminent scientist fiercely. He felt—he knew—that this man was making a fool of him, yet he didn't know how. If he were a real prisoner he would get the truth—but, then, perhaps, those inexplicable things which had happened would not have been brought before him so sharply. Neither of the men spoke for a long time, then suddenly the warden turned fiercely and left the cell, slamming the door behind him. He didn't dare to speak, then.

He glanced at the clock. It was ten minutes to four. He had hardly settled himself in bed when again came that heart-breaking shriek through the prison. With a few muttered words, which, while not elegant, were highly expressive, he relighted his lantern and rushed through the prison again to the cell on the upper floor.

Again Ballard was crushing himself against the steel door, shrieking, shrieking at the top of his voice. He stopped only when the warden flashed his lamp in the cell.

"Take me out, take me out," he screamed. "I did it, I did it, I killed her. Take it away."

"Take what away?" asked the warden.

"I threw the acid in her face—I did it—I confess. Take me out of here."

Ballard's condition was pitiable; it was only an act of mercy to let him out into the corridor. There he crouched in a corner, like an animal at bay, and clasped his hands to his ears. It took half an hour to calm him sufficiently for him to speak. Then he told incoherently what had happened. On the night before at four o'clock he had heard a voice—a sepulchral voice, muffled and wailing in tone.

"What did it say?" asked the warden, curiously.

"Acid—acid—acid!" gasped the prisoner. "It accused me. Acid! I threw the acid, and the woman died. Oh!" It was a long, shuddering, wail of terror.

"Acid?" echoed the warden, puzzled. The case was beyond him.

"Acid. That's all I heard—that one word, repeated several times. There were other things, too, but I didn't hear them."

"That was last night, eh?" asked the warden. "What happened to-night—what frightened you just now?"

"It was the same thing," gasped the prisoner. "Acid—acid—acid!" He covered his face with his hands and sat shivering. "It was acid I used on her, but I didn't mean to kill her. I just heard the words. It was something accusing me—accusing me." He mumbled, and was silent.

"Did you hear anything else?"

"Yes—but I couldn't understand—only a little bit—just a word or two."

"Well, what was it?"

"I heard 'acid' three times, then I heard a long, moaning sound, then—then—I heard 'No. 8 hat.' I heard that twice."

"No. 8 hat," repeated the warden. "What the devil—No. 8 hat? Accusing voices of conscience have never talked about No. 8 hats, so far as I ever heard."

"He's insane," said one of the jailers, with an air of finality.

"I believe you," said the warden. "He must be. He probably heard something and got frightened. He's trembling now. No. 8 hat! What the——"

When the fifth day of The Thinking Machine's imprisonment rolled around the warden was wearing a haunted look. He was anxious for the end of the thing. He could not help but feel that his distinguished prisoner had been amusing himself. And if this were so, The Thinking

Machine had lost none of his sense of humor. For on this fifth day he flung down another linen note to the outside guard, bearing the words: "Only two days more." Also he flung down half a dollar.

Now the warden knew—he *knew*—that the man in Cell 13 didn't have any half dollars—he *couldn't* have any half dollars, no more than he could have pen and ink and linen, and yet he did have them. It was a condition, not a theory; that is one reason why the warden was wearing a hunted look.

That ghastly, uncanny thing, too, about "Acid" and "No. 8 hat" clung to him tenaciously. They didn't mean anything, of course, merely the ravings of an insane murderer who had been driven by fear to confess his crime, still there were so many things that "didn't mean anything" happening in the prison now since The Thinking Machine was there.

On the sixth day the warden received a postal stating that Dr. Ransome and Mr. Fielding would be at Chisholm Prison on the following evening, Thursday, and in the event Professor Van Dusen had not yet escaped—and they presumed he had not because they had not heard from him—they would meet him there.

"In the event he had not yet escaped!" The warden smiled grimly. Escaped!

The Thinking Machine enlivened this day for the warden with three notes. They were on the usual linen and bore generally on the appointment at half past eight o'clock Thursday night, which appointment the scientist had made at the time of his imprisonment.

On the afternoon of the seventh day the warden passed Cell 13 and glanced in. The Thinking Machine was lying on the iron bed, apparently sleeping lightly. The cell appeared precisely as it always did from a casual glance. The warden would swear that no man was going to leave it between that hour—it was then four o'clock—and half past eight o'clock that evening.

On his way back past the cell the warden heard the steady breathing again, and coming close to the door looked in. He wouldn't have done so if The Thinking Machine had been looking, but now—well, it was different.

A ray of light came through the high window and fell on the face of the sleeping man. It occurred to the warden for the first time that his prisoner appeared haggard and weary. Just then The Thinking Machine stirred slightly and the warden hurried on up the corridor guiltily. That evening after six o'clock he saw the jailer.

"Everything all right in Cell 13?" he asked.

"Yes, sir," replied the jailer. "He didn't eat much, though."

It was with a feeling of having done his duty that the warden received Dr. Ransome and Mr. Fielding shortly after seven o'clock. He intended to show them the linen notes and lay before them the full story of his woes, which was a long one. But before this came to pass the guard from the river side of the prison yard entered the office.

"The arc light in my side of the yard won't light," he informed the warden.

"Confound it, that man's a hoodoo," thundered the official. "Everything has happened since he's been here."

The guard went back to his post in the darkness, and the warden phoned to the electric light company.

"This is Chisholm Prison," he said through the phone. "Send three or four men down here quick, to fix an arc light."

The reply was evidently satisfactory, for the warden hung up the receiver and passed out into the yard. While Dr. Ransome and Mr. Fielding sat waiting, the guard at the outer gate came in with a special delivery letter. Dr. Ransome happened to notice the address, and, when the guard went out, looked at the letter more closely.

"By George!" he exclaimed.

"What is it?" asked Mr. Fielding.

Silently the doctor offered the letter. Mr. Fielding examined it closely.

"Coincidence," he said. "It must be."

It was nearly eight o'clock when the warden returned to his office. The electricians had arrived in a wagon, and were now at work. The warden pressed the buzz-button communicating with the man at the outer gate in the wall.

"How many electricians came in?" he asked, over the short phone. "Four? Three workmen in jumpers and overalls and the manager? Frock coat and silk hat? All right. Be certain that only four go out. That's all."

He turned to Dr. Ransome and Mr. Fielding.

"We have to be careful here—particularly," and there was broad sarcasm in his tone, "since we have scientists locked up."

The warden picked up the special delivery letter carelessly, and then began to open it.

"When I read this I want to tell you gentlemen something about how——Great Cæsar!" he ended, suddenly, as he glanced at the letter. He sat with mouth open, motionless, from astonishment.

"What is it?" asked Mr. Fielding.

"A special delivery letter from Cell 13," gasped the warden. "An invitation to supper."

"What?" and the two others arose, unanimously.

The warden sat dazed, staring at the letter for a moment, then called sharply to a guard outside in the corridor.

"Run down to Cell 13 and see if that man's in there."

The guard went as directed, while Dr. Ransome and Mr. Fielding examined the letter.

"It's Van Dusen's handwriting; there's no question of that," said Dr. Ransome. "I've seen too much of it."

Just then the buzz on the telephone from the outer gate sounded, and the warden, in a semi-trance, picked up the receiver.

"Hello! Two reporters, eh? Let 'em come in." He turned suddenly to the doctor and Mr. Fielding. "Why, the man *can't* be out. He must be in his cell."

Just at that moment the guard returned.

"He's still in his cell, sir," he reported. "I saw him. He's lying down."

"There, I told you so," said the warden, and he breathed freely again. "But how did he mail that letter?"

There was a rap on the steel door which led from the jail yard into the warden's office.

"It's the reporters," said the warden. "Let them in," he instructed the guard; then to the two other gentlemen: "Don't say anything about this before them, because I'd never hear the last of it."

The door opened, and the two men from the front gate entered.

"Good-evening, gentlemen," said one. That was Hutchinson Hatch; the warden knew him well.

"Well?" demanded the other, irritably. "I'm here."

That was The Thinking Machine.

He squinted belligerently at the warden, who sat with mouth agape. For the moment that official had nothing to say. Dr. Ransome and Mr. Fielding were amazed, but they didn't know what the warden knew. They were only amazed; he was paralyzed. Hutchinson Hatch, the reporter, took in the scene with greedy eyes.

"How—how—how did you do it?" gasped the warden, finally.

"Come back to the cell," said The Thinking Machine, in the irritated voice which his scientific associates knew so well.

The warden, still in a condition bordering on trance, led the way.

"Flash your light in there," directed The Thinking Machine.

The warden did so. There was nothing unusual in the appearance of the cell, and there—there on the bed lay the figure of The Thinking Machine. Certainly! There was the yellow hair! Again the warden looked at the man beside him and wondered at the strangeness of his own dreams.

With trembling hands he unlocked the cell door and The Thinking Machine passed inside.

"See here," he said.

He kicked at the steel bars in the bottom of the cell door and three of them were pushed out of place. A fourth broke off and rolled away in the corridor.

"And here, too," directed the erstwhile prisoner as he stood on the bed to reach the small window. He swept his hand across the opening and every bar came out.

"What's this in bed?" demanded the warden, who was slowly recovering.

"A wig," was the reply. "Turn down the cover."

The warden did so. Beneath it lay a large coil of strong rope, thirty feet or more, a dagger, three files, ten feet of electric wire, a thin, powerful pair of steel pliers, a small tack hammer with its handle, and—and a derringer pistol.

"How did you do it?" demanded the warden.

"You gentlemen have an engagement to supper with me at half past nine o'clock," said The Thinking Machine. "Come on, or we shall be late."

"But how did you do it?" insisted the warden.

"Don't ever think you can hold any man who can use his brain," said The Thinking Machine. "Come on; we shall be late."

It was an impatient supper party in the rooms of Professor Van Dusen and a somewhat silent one. The guests were Dr. Ransome, Alfred Fielding, the warden, and Hutchinson Hatch, reporter. The meal was served to the minute, in accordance with Professor Van Dusen's instructions of one week before; Dr. Ransome found the artichokes delicious. At last the supper was finished and The Thinking Machine turned full on Dr. Ransome and squinted at him fiercely.

"Do you believe it now?" he demanded.

"I do," replied Dr. Ransome.

"Do you admit that it was a fair test?"

"I do."

With the others, particularly the warden, he was waiting anxiously for the explanation.

"Suppose you tell us how——" began Mr. Fielding.

"Yes, tell us how," said the warden.

The Thinking Machine readjusted his glasses, took a couple of preparatory squints at his audience, and began the story. He told it from the beginning logically; and no man ever talked to more interested listeners.

"My agreement was," he began, "to go into a cell, carrying nothing except what was necessary to wear, and to leave that cell within a week. I had never seen Chisholm Prison. When I went into the cell I asked for tooth powder, two ten- and one five-dollar bills, and also to have my shoes blacked. Even if these requests had been refused it would not have mattered seriously. But you agreed to them.

"I knew there would be nothing in the cell which you thought I might use to advantage. So when the warden locked the door on me I was apparently helpless, unless I could turn three seemingly innocent things to use. They were things which would have been permitted any prisoner under sentence of death, were they not, warden?"

"Tooth powder and polished shoes, yes, but not money," replied the warden.

"Anything is dangerous in the hands of a man who knows how to use it," went on The Thinking Machine. "I did nothing that first night but sleep and chase rats." He glared at the warden. "When the matter was broached I knew I could do nothing that night, so suggested next day. You gentlemen thought I wanted time to arrange an escape with outside assistance, but this was not true. I knew I could communicate with whom I pleased, when I pleased."

The warden stared at him a moment, then went on smoking solemnly.

"I was aroused next morning at six o'clock by the jailer with my breakfast," continued the scientist. "He told me dinner was at twelve and supper at six. Between these times, I gathered, I would be pretty much to myself. So immediately after breakfast I examined my outside surroundings from my cell window. One look told me it would be useless to try to scale the wall, even should I decide to leave my cell by the window, for my purpose was to leave not only the cell, but the prison. Of course, I could have gone over the wall, but it would have taken me longer to lay my plans that way. Therefore, for the moment, I dismissed all idea of that.

"From this first observation I knew the river

was on that side of the prison, and that there was also a playground there. Subsequently these surmises were verified by a keeper. I knew then one important thing—that anyone might approach the prison wall from that side if necessary without attracting any particular attention. That was well to remember. I remembered it.

"But the outside thing which most attracted my attention was the feed wire to the arc light which ran within a few feet—probably three or four—of my cell window. I knew that would be valuable in the event I found it necessary to cut off that arc light."

"Oh, you shut it off to-night, then?" asked the warden.

"Having learned all I could from that window," resumed The Thinking Machine, without heeding the interruption, "I considered the idea of escaping through the prison proper. I recalled just how I had come into the cell, which I knew would be the only way. Seven doors lay between me and the outside. So, also for the time being, I gave up the idea of escaping that way. And I couldn't go through the solid granite walls of the cell."

The Thinking Machine paused for a moment and Dr. Ransome lighted a new cigar. For several minutes there was silence, then the scientific jailbreaker went on:

"While I was thinking about these things a rat ran across my foot. It suggested a new line of thought. There were at least half a dozen rats in the cell—I could see their beady eyes. Yet I had noticed none come under the cell door. I frightened them purposely and watched the cell door to see if they went out that way. They did not, but they were gone. Obviously they went another way. Another way meant another opening.

"I searched for this opening and found it. It was an old drain pipe, long unused and partly choked with dirt and dust. But this was the way the rats had come. They came from somewhere. Where? Drain pipes usually lead outside prison grounds. This one probably led to the river, or near it. The rats must therefore come from that direction. If they came a part of the way, I reasoned that they came all the way, because it was

extremely unlikely that a solid iron or lead pipe would have any hole in it except at the exit.

"When the jailer came with my luncheon he told me two important things, although he didn't know it. One was that a new system of plumbing had been put in the prison seven years before; another that the river was only three hundred feet away. Then I knew positively that the pipe was a part of an old system; I knew, too, that it slanted generally toward the river. But did the pipe end in the water or on land?

"This was the next question to be decided. I decided it by catching several of the rats in the cell. My jailer was surprised to see me engaged in this work. I examined at least a dozen of them. They were perfectly dry; they had come through the pipe, and, most important of all, they were *not house rats, but field rats*. The other end of the pipe was on land, then, outside the prison walls. So far, so good.

"Then, I knew that if I worked freely from this point I must attract the warden's attention in another direction. You see, by telling the warden that I had come there to escape you made the test more severe, because I had to trick him by false scents."

The warden looked up with a sad expression in his eyes.

"The first thing was to make him think I was trying to communicate with you, Dr. Ransome. So I wrote a note on a piece of linen I tore from my shirt, addressed it to Dr. Ransome, tied a five-dollar bill around it and threw it out the window. I knew the guard would take it to the warden, but I rather hoped the warden would send it as addressed. Have you that first linen note, warden?"

The warden produced the cipher.

"What the deuce does it mean, anyhow?" he asked.

"Read it backward, beginning with the 'T' signature and disregard the division into words," instructed The Thinking Machine.

The warden did so.

"*T-h-i-s*, this," he spelled, studied it a moment, then read it off, grinning:

"This is not the way I intend to escape."

"Well, now what do you think o' that?" he demanded, still grinning.

"I knew that would attract your attention, just as it did," said The Thinking Machine, "and if you really found out what it was it would be a sort of gentle rebuke."

"What did you write it with?" asked Dr. Ransome, after he had examined the linen and passed it to Mr. Fielding.

"This," said the erstwhile prisoner, and he extended his foot. On it was the shoe he had worn in prison, though the polish was gone—scraped off clean. "The shoe blacking, moistened with water, was my ink; the metal tip of the shoe lace made a fairly good pen."

The warden looked up and suddenly burst into a laugh, half of relief, half of amusement.

"You're a wonder," he said, admiringly. "Go on."

"That precipitated a search of my cell by the warden, as I had intended," continued The Thinking Machine. "I was anxious to get the warden into the habit of searching my cell, so that finally, constantly finding nothing, he would get disgusted and quit. This at last happened, practically."

The warden blushed.

"He then took my white shirt away and gave me a prison shirt. He was satisfied that those two pieces of the shirt were all that was missing. But while he was searching my cell I had another piece of that same shirt, about nine inches square, rolled into a small ball in my mouth."

"Nine inches of that shirt?" demanded the warden. "Where did it come from?"

"The bosoms of all stiff white shirts are of triple thickness," was the explanation. "I tore out the inside thickness, leaving the bosom only two thicknesses. I knew you wouldn't see it. So much for that."

There was a little pause, and the warden looked from one to another of the men with a sheepish grin.

"Having disposed of the warden for the time being by giving him something else to think about, I took my first serious step toward freedom," said Professor Van Dusen. "I knew,

within reason, that the pipe led somewhere to the playground outside; I knew a great many boys played there; I knew that rats came into my cell from out there. Could I communicate with some one outside with these things at hand?

"First was necessary, I saw, a long and fairly reliable thread, so—but here," he pulled up his trousers legs and showed that the tops of both stockings, of fine, strong lisle, were gone. "I unraveled those—after I got them started it wasn't difficult—and I had easily a quarter of a mile of thread that I could depend on.

"Then on half of my remaining linen I wrote, laboriously enough I assure you, a letter explaining my situation to this gentleman here," and he indicated Hutchinson Hatch. "I knew he would assist me—for the value of the newspaper story. I tied firmly to this linen letter a ten-dollar bill—there is no surer way of attracting the eye of anyone—and wrote on the linen: 'Finder of this deliver to Hutchinson Hatch, *Daily American,* who will give another ten dollars for the information.'

"The next thing was to get this note outside on that playground where a boy might find it. There were two ways, but I chose the best. I took one of the rats—I became adept in catching them—tied the linen and money firmly to one leg, fastened my lisle thread to another, and turned him loose in the drain pipe. I reasoned that the natural fright of the rodent would make him run until he was outside the pipe and then out on earth he would probably stop to gnaw off the linen and money.

"From the moment the rat disappeared into that dusty pipe I became anxious. I was taking so many chances. The rat might gnaw the string, of which I held one end; other rats might gnaw it; the rat might run out of the pipe and leave the linen and money where they would never be found; a thousand other things might have happened. So began some nervous hours, but the fact that the rat ran on until only a few feet of the string remained in my cell made me think he was outside the pipe. I had carefully instructed Mr. Hatch what to do in case the note reached him. The question was: Would it reach him?

"This done, I could only wait and make other plans in case this one failed. I openly attempted to bribe my jailer, and learned from him that he held the keys to only two of seven doors between me and freedom. Then I did something else to make the warden nervous. I took the steel supports out of the heels of my shoes and made a pretense of sawing the bars of my cell window. The warden raised a pretty row about that. He developed, too, the habit of shaking the bars of my cell window to see if they were solid. They were—then."

Again the warden grinned. He had ceased being astonished.

"With this one plan I had done all I could and could only wait to see what happened," the scientist went on. "I couldn't know whether my note had been delivered or even found, or whether the rat had gnawed it up. And I didn't dare to draw back through the pipe that one slender thread which connected me with the outside.

"When I went to bed that night I didn't sleep, for fear there would come the slight signal twitch at the thread which was to tell me that Mr. Hatch had received the note. At half past three o'clock, I judge, I felt this twitch, and no prisoner actually under sentence of death ever welcomed a thing more heartily."

The Thinking Machine stopped and turned to the reporter.

"You'd better explain just what you did," he said.

"The linen note was brought to me by a small boy who had been playing baseball," said Mr. Hatch. "I immediately saw a big story in it, so I gave the boy another ten dollars, and got several spools of silk, some twine, and a roll of light, pliable wire. The professor's note suggested that I have the finder of the note show me just where it was picked up, and told me to make my search from there, beginning at two o'clock in the morning. If I found the other end of the thread I was to twitch it gently three times, then a fourth.

"I began the search with a small-bulb electric light. It was an hour and twenty minutes before I found the end of the drain pipe, half hidden in weeds. The pipe was very large there, say twelve inches across. Then I found the end of the lisle thread, twitched it as directed and immediately I got an answering twitch.

"Then I fastened the silk to this and Professor Van Dusen began to pull it into his cell. I nearly had heart disease for fear the string would break. To the end of the silk I fastened the twine, and when that had been pulled in I tied on the wire. Then that was drawn into the pipe and we had a substantial line, which rats couldn't gnaw, from the mouth of the drain into the cell."

The Thinking Machine raised his hand and Hatch stopped.

"All this was done in absolute silence," said the scientist. "But when the wire reached my hand I could have shouted. Then we tried another experiment, which Mr. Hatch was prepared for. I tested the pipe as a speaking tube. Neither of us could hear very clearly, but I dared not speak loud for fear of attracting attention in the prison. At last I made him understand what I wanted immediately. He seemed to have great difficulty in understanding when I asked for nitric acid, and I repeated the word 'acid' several times.

"Then I heard a shriek from a cell above me. I knew instantly that someone had overheard, and when I heard you coming, Mr. Warden, I feigned sleep. If you had entered my cell at that moment that whole plan of escape would have ended there. But you passed on. That was the nearest I ever came to being caught.

"Having established this improvised trolley it is easy to see how I got things in the cell and made them disappear at will. I merely dropped them back into the pipe. You, Mr. Warden, could not have reached the connecting wire with your fingers; they are too large. My fingers, you see, are longer and more slender. In addition I guarded the top of that pipe with a rat—you remember how."

"I remember," said the warden, with a grimace.

"I thought that if anyone were tempted to investigate that hole the rat would dampen his ardor. Mr. Hatch could not send me anything useful through the pipe until the next night, although he did send me change for ten dollars as a test, so I proceeded with other parts of my plan. Then I evolved the method of escape which I finally employed.

"In order to carry this out successfully it was necessary for the guard in the yard to get accustomed to seeing me at the cell window. I arranged this by dropping linen notes to him, boastful in tone, to make the warden believe, if possible, one of his assistants was communicating with the outside for me. I would stand at my window for hours gazing out, so the guard could see, and occasionally I spoke to him. In that way I learned that the prison had no electricians of its own, but was dependent upon the lighting company if anything should go wrong.

"That cleared the way to freedom perfectly. Early in the evening of the last day of my imprisonment, when it was dark, I planned to cut the feed wire which was only a few feet from my window, reaching it with an acid-tipped wire I had. That would make that side of the prison perfectly dark while the electricians were searching for the break. That would also bring Mr. Hatch into the prison yard.

"There was only one more thing to do before I actually began the work of setting myself free. This was to arrange final details with Mr. Hatch through our speaking tube. I did this within half an hour after the warden left my cell on the fourth night of my imprisonment. Mr. Hatch again had serious difficulty in understanding me, and I repeated the word 'acid' to him several times, and later on the words: 'No. 8 hat'—that's my size—and these were the things which made a prisoner upstairs confess to murder, so one of the jailers told me next day. This prisoner heard our voices, confused of course, through the pipe, which also went to his cell. The cell directly over me was not occupied, hence no one else heard.

"Of course the actual work of cutting the steel bars out of the window and door was comparatively easy with nitric acid, which I got through the pipe in tin bottles, but it took time. Hour after hour on the fifth and sixth and seventh days the guard below was looking at me as I worked on

the bars of the window with the acid on a piece of wire. I used the tooth powder to prevent the acid spreading. I looked away abstractedly as I worked and each minute the acid cut deeper into the metal. I noticed that the jailers always tried the door by shaking the upper part, never the lower bars, therefore I cut the lower bars, leaving them hanging in place by thin strips of metal. But that was a bit of dare-deviltry. I could not have gone that way so easily."

The Thinking Machine sat silent for several minutes.

"I think that makes everything clear," he went on. "Whatever points I have not explained were merely to confuse the warden and jailers. These things in my bed I brought in to please Mr. Hatch, who wanted to improve the story. Of course, the wig was necessary in my plan. The special delivery letter I wrote and directed in my cell with Mr. Hatch's fountain pen, then sent it out to him and he mailed it. That's all, I think."

"But your actually leaving the prison grounds and then coming in through the outer gate to my office?" asked the warden.

"Perfectly simple," said the scientist. "I cut the electric light wire with acid, as I said, when the current was off. Therefore when the current was turned on the arc didn't light. I knew it would take some time to find out what was the matter and make repairs. When the guard went to report to you the yard was dark. I crept out the window—it was a tight fit, too—replaced the bars by standing on a narrow ledge and remained in a shadow until the force of electricians arrived. Mr. Hatch was one of them.

"When I saw him I spoke and he handed me a cap, a jumper and overalls, which I put on within ten feet of you, Mr. Warden, while you were in the yard. Later Mr. Hatch called me, presumably as a workman, and together we went out the gate to get something out of the wagon. The gate guard let us pass out readily as two workmen who had just passed in. We changed our clothing and reappeared, asking to see you. We saw you. That's all."

There was silence for several minutes. Dr. Ransome was first to speak.

"Wonderful!" he exclaimed. "Perfectly amazing."

"How did Mr. Hatch happen to come with the electricians?" asked Mr. Fielding.

"His father is manager of the company," replied The Thinking Machine.

"But what if there had been no Mr. Hatch outside to help?"

"Every prisoner has one friend outside who would help him escape if he could."

"Suppose—just suppose—there had been no old plumbing system there?" asked the warden, curiously.

"There were two other ways out," said The Thinking Machine, enigmatically.

Ten minutes later the telephone bell rang. It was a request for the warden.

"Light all right, eh?" the warden asked, through the phone. "Good. Wire cut beside Cell 13? Yes, I know. One electrician too many? What's that? Two came out?"

The warden turned to the others with a puzzled expression.

"He only let in four electricians, he has let out two and says there are three left."

"I was the odd one," said The Thinking Machine.

"Oh," said the warden. "I see." Then through the phone: "Let the fifth man go. He's all right."

A TERRIBLY STRANGE BED

WILKIE COLLINS

WHILE IT IS TRUE that Edgar Allan Poe invented the detective story, and even wrote the first locked-room mystery, no one played a greater role in making this literary genre popular than (William) Wilkie Collins (1824–1889), a friend of and frequent collaborator with Charles Dickens and author of two of the greatest novels in the history of mystery fiction, *The Woman in White* (1860) and *The Moonstone* (1868). The inventor of what became known as the "sensation" novel and one of the most popular and highest paid of all Victorian novelists, he was born in London, the son of the very successful landscape painter William Collins, a member of the Royal Academy. Collins received a law degree but never practiced, deciding to become a full-time writer instead. Over the course of his life, he published twenty-five novels, fifteen plays, more than fifty short stories, and more than one hundred nonfiction articles. He met Dickens in 1851 and soon co-wrote a play with him, *The Frozen Deep*, then collaborated with him on short stories, articles, and numerous other projects. When Dickens founded a magazine, *All the Year Round*, in 1859, Collins assured its success by serializing *The Woman in White* in its pages. He later wrote Christmas stories for the periodical, serialized the long novel *No Name* (1862) and, in 1867, the classic *The Moonstone*, which T. S. Eliot described as "the first, the longest, and the best" detective novel of all time. Collins adapted *The Woman in White* for the stage in 1871; it has been filmed frequently, beginning with a Pathe silent in 1917 but most memorably in 1948 with Alexis Smith, Eleanor Parker, Gig Young, and Sydney Greenstreet as the evil Count Fosco. *The Moonstone* was also dramatized by Collins, opening in 1877; it has been filmed at least five times, first as a 1909 silent, followed by a 1915 silent, then as a lackluster 1934 low-budget film, as a garrulous five-part BBC production in 1972, and again as a BBC production in 1997.

"A Terribly Strange Bed" was first published in the April 24, 1852, issue of *Household Words*; it was first collected in *After Dark* (London, Smith, 1856).

A TERRIBLY STRANGE BED

WILKIE COLLINS

SHORTLY AFTER my education at college was finished, I happened to be staying at Paris with an English friend. We were both young men then, and lived, I am afraid, rather a wild life, in the delightful city of our sojourn. One night we were idling about the neighborhood of the Palais Royal, doubtful to what amusement we should next betake ourselves. My friend proposed a visit to Frascati's; but his suggestion was not to my taste. I knew Frascati's, as the French saying is, by heart; had lost and won plenty of five-franc pieces there, merely for amusement's sake, until it was amusement no longer, and was thoroughly tired, in fact, of all the ghastly respectabilities of such a social anomaly as a respectable gambling-house. "For Heaven's sake," said I to my friend, "let us go somewhere where we can see a little genuine, blackguard, poverty-stricken gaming, with no false gingerbread glitter thrown over it at all. Let us get away from fashionable Frascati's, to a house where they don't mind letting in a man with a ragged coat, or a man with no coat, ragged or otherwise." "Very well," said my friend, "we needn't go out of the Palais Royal to find the sort of company you want. Here's the place just before us; as blackguard a place, by all report, as you could possibly wish to see." In another minute we arrived at the door, and entered the house.

When we got upstairs, and had left our hats and sticks with the doorkeeper, we were admitted into the chief gambling-room. We did not find many people assembled there. But, few as the men were who looked up at us on our entrance, they were all types—lamentably true types—of their respective classes.

We have come to see blackguards; but these men were something worse. There is a comic side, more or less appreciable, in all blackguardism—here there was nothing but tragedy—mute, weird tragedy. The quiet in the room was horrible. The thin, haggard, long-haired young man, whose sunken eyes fiercely watched the turning up of the cards, never spoke; the flabby, fat-faced, pimply player, who pricked his piece of pasteboard perseveringly, to register how often black won, and how often red—never spoke; the dirty, wrinkled old man, with the vulture eyes and the darned great-coat, who had lost his last *sou*, and still looked on desperately, after he could play no longer—never spoke. Even the voice of the croupier sounded as if it were strangely dulled and thickened in the atmosphere of the room. I had entered the place to laugh, but the spectacle before me was something to weep over. I soon found it necessary to take refuge in excitement from the depression of spirits which was fast stealing on me. Unfortunately I sought the nearest excitement, by going to the table and beginning to play. Still more unfortunately, as the event will show, I won—won prodigiously; won incredibly; won at such a rate that the regular players at the table crowded round me; and staring at my stakes with hungry, superstitious eyes, whispered to one another that the English stranger was going to break the bank.

The game was *Rouge et Noir*. I had played at it in every city in Europe, without, however, the care or the wish to study the Theory of Chances—that philosopher's stone of all gamblers! And a gambler, in the strict sense of the word, I had never been. I was heart-whole from the corroding passion for play. My gaming was a mere idle amusement. I never resorted to it by necessity, because I never knew what it was to want money. I never practiced it so incessantly as to lose more than I could afford, or to gain more than I could coolly pocket without being thrown off my balance by my good luck. In short, I had hitherto frequented gambling-tables—just as I frequented ballrooms and opera-houses—because they amused me, and because I had nothing to do with my leisure hours.

But on this occasion it was very different—now, for the first time in my life, I felt what the passion for play really was. My success first bewildered, and then, in the most literal meaning of the word, intoxicated me. Incredible as it may appear, it is nevertheless true, that I only lost when I attempted to estimate chances, and played according to previous calculation. If I left everything to luck, and staked without any care or consideration, I was sure to win—to win in the face of every recognized probability in favor of the bank. At first some of the men present ventured their money safely enough on my color; but I speedily increased my stakes to sums which they dared not risk. One after another they left off playing, and breathlessly looked on at my game.

Still, time after time, I staked higher and higher, and still won. The excitement in the room rose to fever pitch. The silence was interrupted by a deep-muttered chorus of oaths and exclamations in different languages, every time the gold was shoveled across to my side of the table—even the imperturbable croupier dashed his rake on the floor in a (French) fury of astonishment at my success. But one man present preserved his self-possession, and that man was my friend. He came to my side, and whispering in English, begged me to leave the place, satisfied with what I had already gained. I must do him the justice to say that he repeated his warnings and entreaties several times, and only left me and went away after I had rejected his advice (I was to all intents and purposes gambling drunk) in terms which rendered it impossible for him to address me again that night.

Shortly after he had gone, a hoarse voice behind me cried: "Permit me, my dear sir—permit me to restore to their proper place two napoleons which you have dropped. Wonderful luck, sir! I pledge you my word of honor, as an old soldier, in the course of my long experience in this sort of thing, I never saw such luck as yours—never! Go on, sir—*Sacré mille bombes!* Go on boldly, and break the bank!"

I turned round and saw, nodding and smiling at me with inveterate civility, a tall man, dressed in a frogged and braided surtout.

If I had been in my senses, I should have considered him, personally, as being rather a suspicious specimen of an old soldier. He had goggling, blood-shot eyes, mangy mustaches, and a broken nose. His voice betrayed a barrack-room intonation of the worst order, and he had the dirtiest pair of hands I ever saw—even in France. These little personal peculiarities exercised, however, no repelling influence on me. In the mad excitement, the reckless triumph of that moment, I was ready to "fraternize" with anybody who encouraged me in my game. I accepted the old soldier's offered pinch of snuff; clapped him on the back, and swore he was the honestest fellow in the world—the most glorious relic of the Grand Army that I had ever met with. "Go on!" cried my military friend, snapping his fingers in ecstacy—"Go on, and win! Break the bank—*Mille tonnerres!* my gallant English comrade, break the bank!"

And I *did* go on—went on at such a rate, that in another quarter of an hour the croupier called out, "Gentlemen, the bank has discontinued for to-night." All the notes, and all the gold in that "bank," now lay in a heap under my hands; the whole floating capital of the gambling-house was waiting to pour into my pockets!

"Tie up the money in your pocket-handkerchief, my worthy sir," said the old soldier, as I wildly plunged my hands into my heap of gold. "Tie it up, as we used to tie up a bit of dinner in the Grand Army; your winnings are too heavy for any breeches-pockets that ever were sewed. There! that's it—shovel them in, notes and all! *Credié!* what luck! Stop! another napoleon on the floor! *Ah! sacré petit polisson de Napoleon!* have I found thee at last? Now then, sir—two tight double knots each way with your honorable permission, and the money's safe. Feel it! feel it, fortunate sir! hard and round as a cannon-ball—*Ah, bah!* if they had only fired such cannon-balls at us at Austerlitz—*nom d'une pipe!* if they only had! And now, as an ancient grenadier, as an ex-brave of the French Army, what remains for me to do? I ask what? Simply this, to entreat my valued English friend to drink a bottle of Champagne with me, and toast the goddess Fortune in foaming goblets before we part!"

"Excellent ex-brave! Convivial ancient grenadier! Champagne by all means! An English cheer for an old soldier! Hurra! hurra! Another English cheer for the goddess Fortune! Hurra! hurra! hurra!"

"Bravo! the Englishman; the amiable, gracious Englishman, in whose veins circulates the vivacious blood of France! Another glass? *Ah, bah!*—the bottle is empty! Never mind! *Vive le vin!* I, the old soldier, order another bottle, and half a pound of *bonbons* with it!"

"No, no, ex-brave; never—ancient grenadier! *Your* bottle last time; *my* bottle this! Behold it! Toast away! The French Army! the great Napoleon! the present company! the croupier! the honest croupier's wife and daughters—if he has any! the Ladies generally! everybody in the world!"

By the time the second bottle of Champagne was emptied, I felt as if I had been drinking liquid fire—my brain seemed all aflame. No excess in wine had ever had this effect on me before in my life. Was it the result of a stimulant acting upon my system when I was in a highly excited state? Was my stomach in a particularly disordered condition? Or was the Champagne amazingly strong?

"Ex-brave of the French Army!" cried I, in a mad state of exhilaration, "*I* am on fire! how are *you*? You have set me on fire! Do you hear, my hero of Austerlitz? Let us have a third bottle of Champagne to put the flame out!"

The old soldier wagged his head, rolled his goggle-eyes, until I expected to see them slip out of their sockets; placed his dirty forefinger by the side of his broken nose; solemnly ejaculated "Coffee!" and immediately ran off into an inner room.

The word pronounced by the eccentric veteran seemed to have a magical effect on the rest of the company present. With one accord they all rose to depart. Probably they had expected to profit by my intoxication; but finding that my new friend was benevolently bent on preventing me from getting dead drunk, had now abandoned all hope of thriving pleasantly on my winnings. Whatever their motive might be, at any rate they went away in a body. When the old soldier returned, and sat down again opposite to me at the table, we had the room to ourselves. I could see the croupier, in a sort of vestibule which opened out of it, eating his supper in solitude. The silence was now deeper than ever.

A sudden change, too, had come over the "ex-brave." He assumed a portentously solemn look; and when he spoke to me again, his speech was ornamented by no oaths, enforced by no finger-snapping, enlivened by no apostrophes or exclamations.

"Listen, my dear sir," said he, in mysteriously confidential tones—"listen to an old soldier's advice. I have been to the mistress of the house (a very charming woman, with a genius for cookery!) to impress on her the necessity of making us some particularly strong and good coffee. You must drink this coffee in order to get rid of your little amiable exaltation of spirits before you think of going home—you *must*, my good and gracious friend! With all that money to take home to-night, it is a sacred duty to yourself to have your wits about you. You are known to be a winner to an enormous extent by several gentlemen present to-night, who, in a certain point of view, are very worthy and excellent fellows; but they are mortal men, my dear sir, and they have their amiable weaknesses! Need I say more? Ah, no, no! you understand me! Now, this is what you must do—send for a cabriolet when you feel quite well again—draw up all the windows when you get into it—and tell the driver to take you home only through the large and well-lighted thoroughfares. Do this; and you and your money will be safe. Do this; and to-morrow you will thank an old soldier for giving you a word of honest advice."

Just as the ex-brave ended his oration in very lachrymose tones, the coffee came in, ready poured out in two cups. My attentive friend handed me one of the cups with a bow. I was parched with thirst, and drank it off at a draught. Almost instantly afterward, I was seized with a fit of giddiness, and felt more completely intoxicated than ever. The room whirled round and round furiously; the old soldier seemed to be regularly bobbing up and down before me like the piston of a steam-engine. I was half deafened by a violent singing in my ears; a feeling of utter bewilderment, helplessness, idiocy, overcame me. I rose from my chair, holding on by the table to keep my balance; and stammered out that I felt dreadfully unwell—so unwell that I did not know how I was to get home.

"My dear friend," answered the old soldier—and even his voice seemed to be bobbing up and down as he spoke—"my dear friend, it would be madness to go home in *your* state; you would be sure to lose your money; you might be robbed and murdered with the greatest ease. *I* am going to sleep here; do *you* sleep here, too—they make up capital beds in this house—take one; sleep off the effects of the wine, and go home safely with your winnings to-morrow—to-morrow, in broad daylight."

I had but two ideas left; one, that I must never let go hold of my handkerchief full of money; the other, that I must lie down somewhere immediately, and fall off into a comfortable sleep. So I agreed to the proposal about the bed, and took the offered arm of the old soldier, carrying my money with my disengaged hand. Preceded by the croupier, we passed along some passages and up a flight of stairs into the bedroom which I was to occupy. The ex-brave shook me warmly by the hand, proposed that we should breakfast together, and then, followed by the croupier, left me for the night.

I ran to the wash-hand stand; drank some of the water in my jug; poured the rest out, and plunged my face into it; then sat down in a chair and tried to compose myself. I soon felt better. The change for my lungs, from the fetid atmosphere of the gambling-room to the cool air of the apartment I now occupied, the almost equally refreshing change for my eyes, from the glaring gaslights of the "salon" to the dim, quiet flicker of one bedroom-candle, aided wonderfully the restorative effects of cold water. The giddiness left me, and I began to feel a little like a reasonable being again. My first thought was of the risk of sleeping all night in a gambling-house; my second, of the still greater risk of trying to get out after the house was closed, and of going home alone at night through the streets of Paris with a large sum of money about me. I had slept in worse places than this on my travels; so I determined to lock, bolt, and barricade my door, and take my chance till the next morning.

Accordingly, I secured myself against all intrusion; looked under the bed, and into the cupboard; tried the fastening of the window; and then, satisfied that I had taken every proper precaution, pulled off my upper clothing, put my light, which was a dim one, on the hearth among a feathery litter of wood-ashes, and got into bed, with the handkerchief full of money under my pillow.

I soon felt not only that I could not go to sleep, but that I could not even close my eyes. I was wide awake, and in a high fever. Every nerve in my body trembled—every one of my senses seemed to be preternaturally sharpened. I tossed and rolled, and tried every kind of position, and perseveringly sought out the cold corners of the bed, and all to no purpose. Now I thrust my arms over the clothes; now I poked them under the clothes; now I violently shot my legs straight out down to the bottom of the bed; now I convulsively coiled them up as near my chin as they would go; now I shook out my crumpled pillow, changed it to the cool side, patted it flat, and lay down quietly on my back; now I fiercely doubled it in two, set it up on end, thrust it against the board of the bed, and tried a sitting posture. Every effort was in vain; I groaned with vexation as I felt that I was in for a sleepless night.

What could I do? I had no book to read. And yet, unless I found out some method of diverting my mind, I felt certain that I was in the condition to imagine all sorts of horrors; to rack my brain with forebodings of every possible and impossible danger; in short, to pass the night in suffering all conceivable varieties of nervous terror.

I raised myself on my elbow, and looked about the room—which was brightened by a lovely moonlight pouring straight through the window—to see if it contained any pictures or ornaments that I could at all clearly distinguish. While my eyes wandered from wall to wall, a remembrance of Le Maistre's delightful little book, *Voyage autour de ma Chambre*, occurred to me. I resolved to imitate the French-author, and find occupation and amusement enough to relieve the tedium of my wakefulness, by making a mental inventory of every article of furniture I could see, and by following up to their sources the multitude of associations which even a chair, a table, or a wash-hand stand may be made to call forth.

In the nervous unsettled state of my mind at that moment, I found it much easier to make my inventory than to make my reflections, and thereupon soon gave up all hope of thinking in Le Maistre's fanciful track—or, indeed, of thinking at all. I looked about the room at the different articles of furniture, and did nothing more.

There was, first, the bed I was lying in; a four-post bed, of all things in the world to meet with in Paris—yes, a thorough clumsy British four-poster, with a regular top lined with chintz—the regular fringed valance all round—the regular stifling, unwholesome curtains, which I remembered having mechanically drawn back against the posts without particularly noticing the bed when I first got into the room. Then there was the marble-topped wash-hand stand, from which the water I had spilled, in my hurry to pour it out, was still dripping, slowly and more slowly, on to the brick floor. Then two small chairs, with my coat, waist-coat, and trousers flung on them. Then a large elbow-chair covered with dirty-white dimity, with my cravat and shirt collar thrown over the back. Then a chest of drawers with two of the brass handles off, and a tawdry, broken china inkstand placed on it by way of ornament for the top. Then the dressing-table, adorned by a very small looking-glass, and a very large pincushion. Then the window—an unusually large window. Then a dark old picture, which the feeble candle dimly showed me. It was the picture of a fellow in a high Spanish hat, crowned with a plume of towering feathers. A swarthy, sinister ruffian, looking upward, shading his eyes with his hand, and looking intently upward—it might be at some tall gallows at which he was going to be hanged. At any rate, he had the appearance of thoroughly deserving it.

This picture put a kind of constraint upon me to look upward too—at the top of the bed. It was a gloomy and not an interesting object, and I looked back at the picture. I counted the feathers in the man's hat—they stood out in relief—three white, two green. I observed the crown of his hat, which was of a conical shape, according to the fashion supposed to have been favored by Guido Fawkes. I wondered what he was looking up at. It couldn't be at the stars; such a desperado was neither astrologer nor astronomer. It must be at the high gallows, and he was going to be hanged presently. Would the executioner come into possession of his conical crowned hat and plume of feathers? I counted the feathers again—three white, two green.

While I still lingered over this very improving and intellectual employment, my thoughts insensibly began to wander. The moonlight shining into the room reminded me of a certain moonlight night in England—the night after a picnic party in a Welsh valley. Every incident of the drive homeward, through lovely scenery, which the moonlight made lovelier than ever, came back to my remembrance, though I had never given the picnic a thought for years; though, if I had *tried* to recollect it, I could certainly have recalled little or nothing of that scene long past. Of all the wonderful faculties that help to tell us we are immortal, which speaks the sublime truth more eloquently than memory? Here was I, in a strange house of the most suspicious character, in a situation of uncertainty, and even of peril, which might seem to make the cool exercise of my recollection almost out of the question; nevertheless, remembering, quite involuntarily, places, people, conversations, minute circumstances of every kind, which I had thought forgotten forever; which I could not possibly have recalled at will, even under the most favorable auspices. And what cause had produced in a moment the whole of this strange, complicated, mysterious effect? Nothing but some rays of moonlight shining in at my bedroom window.

I was still thinking of the picnic—of our merriment on the drive home—of the sentimental young lady who *would* quote "Childe Harold" because it was moonlight. I was absorbed by these past scenes and past amusements, when, in an instant, the thread on which my memories hung snapped asunder; my attention immediately came back to present things more vividly than ever, and I found myself, I neither knew why nor wherefore, looking hard at the picture again.

Looking for what?

Good God! the man had pulled his hat down on his brows! No! the hat itself was gone! Where

was the conical crown? Where the feathers—three white, two green? Not there! In place of the hat and feathers, what dusky object was it that now hid his forehead, his eyes, his shading hand?

Was the bed moving?

I turned on my back and looked up. Was I mad? drunk? dreaming? giddy again? or was the top of the bed really moving down—sinking slowly, regularly, silently, horribly, right down throughout the whole of its length and breadth—right down upon me, as I lay underneath?

My blood seemed to stand still. A deadly paralyzing coldness stole all over me as I turned my head round on the pillow and determined to test whether the bed-top was really moving or not, by keeping my eye on the man in the picture.

The next look in that direction was enough. The dull, black, frowzy outline of the valance above me was within an inch of being parallel with his waist. I still looked breathlessly. And steadily and slowly—very slowly—I saw the figure, and the line of frame below the figure, vanish, as the valance moved down before it.

I am, constitutionally, anything but timid. I have been on more than one occasion in peril of my life, and have not lost my self-possession for an instant; but when the conviction first settled on my mind that the bed-top was really moving, was steadily and continuously sinking down upon me, I looked up shuddering, helpless, panic-stricken, beneath the hideous machinery for murder, which was advancing closer and closer to suffocate me where I lay.

I looked up, motionless, speechless, breathless. The candle, fully spent, went out; but the moonlight still brightened the room. Down and down, without pausing and without sounding, came the bed-top, and still my panic terror seemed to bind me faster and faster to the mattress on which I lay—down and down it sank, till the dusty odor from the lining of the canopy came stealing into my nostrils.

At that final moment the instinct of self-preservation startled me out of my trance, and

I moved at last. There was just room for me to roll myself sidewise off the bed. As I dropped noiselessly to the floor, the edge of the murderous canopy touched me on the shoulder.

Without stopping to draw my breath, without wiping the cold sweat from my face, I rose instantly on my knees to watch the bed-top. I was literally spell-bound by it. If I had heard footsteps behind me, I could not have turned round; if a means of escape had been miraculously provided for me, I could not have moved to take advantage of it. The whole life in me was, at that moment, concentrated in my eyes.

It descended—the whole canopy, with the fringe round it, came down—down—close down; so close that there was not room now to squeeze my finger between the bed-top and the bed. I felt at the sides, and discovered that what had appeared to me from beneath to be the ordinary light canopy of a four-post bed was in reality a thick, broad mattress, the substance of which was concealed by the valance and its fringe. I looked up and saw the four posts rising hideously bare. In the middle of the bed-top was a huge wooden screw that had evidently worked it down through a hole in the ceiling, just as ordinary presses are worked down on the substance selected for compression. The frightful apparatus moved without making the faintest noise. There had been no creaking as it came down; there was now not the faintest sound from the room above. Amid a dead and awful silence I beheld before me—in the nineteenth century, and in the civilized capital of France—such a machine for secret murder by suffocation as might have existed in the worst days of the Inquisition, in the lonely inns among the Hartz Mountains, in the mysterious tribunals of Westphalia! Still, as I looked on it, I could not move, I could hardly breathe, but I began to recover the power of thinking, and in a moment I discovered the murderous conspiracy framed against me in all its horror.

My cup of coffee had been drugged, and drugged too strongly. I had been saved from being smothered by having taken an overdose of some narcotic. How I had chafed and fretted at the fever fit which had preserved my life by keeping me awake! How recklessly I had confided myself to the two wretches who had led me into this room, determined, for the sake of my winnings, to kill me in my sleep by the surest and most horrible contrivance for secretly accomplishing my destruction! How many men, winners like me, had slept, as I had proposed to sleep, in that bed, and had never been seen or heard of more! I shuddered at the bare idea of it.

But ere long all thought was again suspended by the sight of the murderous canopy moving once more. After it had remained on the bed—as nearly as I could guess—about ten minutes, it began to move up again. The villains who worked it from above evidently believed that their purpose was now accomplished. Slowly and silently, as it had descended, that horrible bed-top rose toward its former place. When it reached the upper extremities of the four posts, it reached the ceiling, too. Neither hole nor screw could be seen; the bed became in appearance an ordinary bed again—the canopy an ordinary canopy—even to the most suspicious eyes.

Now, for the first time, I was able to move—to rise from my knees—to dress myself in my upper clothing—and to consider of how I should escape. If I betrayed by the smallest noise that the attempt to suffocate me had failed, I was certain to be murdered. Had I made any noise already? I listened intently, looking toward the door.

No! no footsteps in the passage outside—no sound of a tread, light or heavy, in the room above—absolute silence everywhere. Besides locking and bolting my door, I had moved an only wooden chest against it, which I had found under the bed. To remove this chest (my blood ran cold as I thought of what its contents *might* be!) without making some disturbance was impossible; and, moreover, to think of escaping through the house, now barred up for the night, was sheer insanity. Only one chance was left me—the window. I stole to it on tiptoe.

My bedroom was on the first floor, above an

entresol, and looked into the back street. I raised my hand to open the window, knowing that on that action hung, by the merest hair-breadth, my chance of safety. They keep vigilant watch in a House of Murder. If any part of the frame cracked, if the hinge creaked, I was a lost man! It must have occupied me at least five minutes, reckoning by time—five *hours,* reckoning by suspense—to open that window. I succeeded in doing it silently—in doing it with all the dexterity of a house-breaker—and then looked down into the street. To leap the distance beneath me would be almost certain destruction! Next, I looked round at the sides of the house. Down the left side ran a thick water-pipe—it passed close by the outer edge of the window. The moment I saw the pipe I knew I was saved. My breath came and went freely for the first time since I had seen the canopy of the bed moving down upon me!

To some men the means of escape which I had discovered might have seemed difficult and dangerous enough—to *me* the prospect of slipping down the pipe into the street did not suggest even a thought of peril. I had always been accustomed, by the practice of gymnastics, to keep up my school-boy powers as a daring and expert climber; and knew that my head, hands, and feet would serve me faithfully in any hazards of ascent or descent. I had already got one leg over the window-sill, when I remembered the handkerchief filled with money under my pillow. I could well have afforded to leave it behind me, but I was revengefully determined that the miscreants of the gambling-house should miss their plunder as well as their victim. So I went back to the bed and tied the heavy handkerchief at my back by my cravat.

Just as I had made it tight and fixed it in a comfortable place, I thought I heard a sound of breathing outside the door. The chill feeling of horror ran through me again as I listened. No! dead silence still in the passage—I had only heard the night air blowing softly into the room. The next moment I was on the window-sill— and the next I had a firm grip on the water-pipe with my hands and knees.

I slid down into the street easily and quietly, as I thought I should, and immediately set off at the top of my speed to a branch "Prefecture" of Police, which I knew was situated in the immediate neighborhood. A "Sub-prefect," and several picked men among his subordinates, happened to be up, maturing, I believe, some scheme for discovering the perpetrator of a mysterious murder which all Paris was talking of just then. When I began my story, in a breathless hurry and in very bad French, I could see that the Sub-prefect suspected me of being a drunken Englishman who had robbed somebody; but he soon altered his opinion as I went on, and before I had anything like concluded, he shoved all the papers before him into a drawer, put on his hat, supplied me with another (for I was bareheaded), ordered a file of soldiers, desired his expert followers to get ready all sorts of tools for breaking open doors and ripping up brick flooring, and took my arm, in the most friendly and familiar manner possible, to lead me with him out of the house. I will venture to say that when the Sub-prefect was a little boy, and was taken for the first time to the play, he was not half as much pleased as he was now at the job in prospect for him at the gambling-house!

Away we went through the streets, the Subprefect cross-examining and congratulating me in the same breath as we marched at the head of our formidable *posse comitatus.* Sentinels were placed at the back and front of the house the moment we got to it; a tremendous battery of knocks was directed against the door; a light appeared at a window; I was told to conceal myself behind the police—then came more knocks and a cry of "Open in the name of the law!" At that terrible summons bolts and locks gave way before an invisible hand, and the moment after the Sub-prefect was in the passage, confronting a waiter half-dressed and ghastly pale. This was the short dialogue which immediately took place:

"We want to see the Englishman who is sleeping in this house."

"He went away hours ago."

"He did no such thing. His friend went away; *he* remained. Show us to his bedroom!"

"I swear to you, Monsieur le Sous-prefect, he is not here! he—"

"I swear to you, Monsieur le Garçon, he is. He slept here—he didn't find your bed comfortable—he came to us to complain of it—here he is among my men—and here am I ready to look for a flea or two in his bedstead. Renaudin! (calling to one of the subordinates, and pointing to the waiter) collar that man and tie his hands behind him. Now, then, gentlemen, let us walk upstairs!"

Every man and woman in the house was secured—the "Old Soldier" the first. Then I identified the bed in which I had slept, and then we went into the room above.

No object that was all extraordinary appeared in any part of it. The Sub-prefect looked round the place, commanded everybody to be silent, stamped twice on the floor, called for a candle, looked attentively at the spot he had stamped on, and ordered the flooring there to be carefully taken up. This was done in no time. Lights were produced, and we saw a deep raftered cavity between the floor of this room and the ceiling of the room beneath. Through this cavity there ran perpendicularly a sort of case of iron thickly greased; and inside the case appeared the screw, which communicated with the bed-top below. Extra lengths of screw, freshly oiled; levers covered with felt; all the complete upper works of a heavy press—constructed with infernal ingenuity so as to join the fixtures below, and when taken to pieces again to go into the smallest possible compass—were next discovered and pulled out on the floor. After some little difficulty the Sub-prefect succeeded in putting the machinery together, and, leaving his men to work it, descended with me to the bedroom. The smothering canopy was then lowered, but not so noiselessly as I had seen it lowered. When I mentioned this to the Sub-prefect, his answer, simple as it was, had a terrible significance. "My men," said he, "are working down the bed-top for the first time—the men whose money you won were in better practice."

We left the house in the sole possession of two police agents—every one of the inmates being removed to prison on the spot. The Sub-prefect, after taking down my *"procés verbal"* in his office, returned with me to my hotel to get my passport. "Do you think," I asked, as I gave it to him, "that any men have really been smothered in that bed, as they tried to smother *me?*"

"I have seen dozens of drowned men laid out at the Morgue," answered the Sub-prefect, "in whose pocketbooks were found letters stating that they had committed suicide in the Seine, because they had lost everything at the gaming-table. Do I know how many of those men entered the same gambling-house that *you* entered? won as *you* won? took that bed as *you* took it? slept in it? were smothered in it? and were privately thrown into the river, with a letter of explanation written by the murderers and placed in their pocketbooks? No man can say how many or how few have suffered the fate from which you have escaped. The people of the gambling-house kept their bedstead machinery a secret from *us*—even from the police! The dead kept the rest of the secret for them. Good-night, or rather good-morning, Monsieur Faulkner! Be at my office again at nine o'clock—in the meantime, *au revoir!*"

The rest of my story is soon told. I was examined and re-examined; the gambling-house was strictly searched all through from top to bottom; the prisoners were separately interrogated; and two of the less guilty among them made a confession. I discovered that the Old Soldier was the master of the gambling-house—*justice* discovered that he had been drummed out of the army as a vagabond years ago; that he had been guilty of all sorts of villainies since; that he was in possession of stolen property, which the owners identified; and that he, the croupier, another accomplice, and the woman who had made my cup of coffee, were all in the secret of the bedstead. There appeared some reason to doubt whether the inferior persons attached to the house knew anything of the suffocating machinery; and they received the benefit of that doubt, by being treated simply as thieves and vagabonds. As for the Old Soldier and his two head myrmidons, they went to the galleys; the woman who had drugged my coffee was imprisoned for I forget how many years; the regular attendants at the gambling-house were considered "suspicious" and placed under "surveillance"; and I became, for one whole week (which is a long time) the head "lion" in Parisian society. My adventure was dramatized by three illustrious play-makers, but never saw theatrical daylight; for the censorship forbade the introduction on the stage of a correct copy of the gambling-house bedstead.

One good result was produced by my adventure, which any censorship must have approved: it cured me of ever again trying *"Rouge et Noir"* as an amusement. The sight of a greencloth, with packs of cards and heaps of money on it, will henceforth be forever associated in my mind with the sight of a bed canopy descending to suffocate me in the silence and darkness of the night.

THE TWO BOTTLES OF RELISH
LORD DUNSANY

IN HIS EPONYMOUS MAGAZINE, Ellery Queen once ran a survey to determine the ten greatest mystery stories ever written and, to the surprise of no one who has ever read it, "The Two Bottles of Relish" made the list. Eighty years after it was written, it remains amazingly puzzling and, ultimately, shocking, resulting in its being one of the most anthologized stories of the twentieth century. Lord Dunsany, the byline used by Edward John Moreton Drax Plunkett, 18th Baron of Dunsany (1878–1957), is best known as one of the giants of fantasy and horror fiction, both for his own work and for his influence on such subsequent masters of the genre as H. P. Lovecraft, Fritz Leiber, and J. R. R. Tolkien. He was the scion of one of Ireland's oldest families, the Plunketts, tracing back to the eleventh century. Lord Dunsany lived in and cared for Dunsany Castle (construction of which began in 1180), Ireland's oldest residential castle. A polymath, he was a brilliant chess player, being the Irish National Champion who once played the great Capablanca to a draw. He also was an artist, poet, playwright, hunter, and unsuccessful politician.

"The Two Bottles of Relish" was adapted for the stage in 1961 by Edward Darby in *Two Bottles of Relish: A Play in One Act*. The story was first published in the November 12, 1932, issue of *Time & Tide*; it was first published in book form in the anonymously edited *Powers of Darkness: A Collection of Uneasy Tales* (London, Philip Allan, 1934) and first collected in *The Little Tales of Smethers* (London, Jarrolds, 1952).

THE TWO BOTTLES OF RELISH

LORD DUNSANY

SMITHERS IS MY NAME. I'm what you might call a small man and in a small way of business. I travel for Num-numo, a relish for meats and savouries—the world-famous relish I ought to say. It's really quite good, no deleterious acids in it, and does not affect the heart; so it is quite easy to push. I wouldn't have got the job if it weren't. But I hope some day to get something that's harder to push, as of course the harder they are to push, the better the pay. At present I can just make my way, with nothing at all over; but then I live in a very expensive flat. It happened like this, and that brings me to my story. And it isn't the story you'd expect from a small man like me, yet there's nobody else to tell it. Those that know anything of it besides me are all for hushing it up. Well, I was looking for a room to live in in London when first I got my job. It had to be in London, to be central; and I went to a block of buildings, very gloomy they looked, and saw the man that ran them and asked him for what I wanted. Flats they called them; just a bedroom and a sort of a cupboard. Well, he was showing a man round at the time who was a gent, in fact more than that, so he didn't take much notice of me—the man that ran all those flats didn't, I mean. So I just ran behind for a bit, seeing all sorts of rooms and waiting till I could be shown my class of thing. We came to a very nice flat, a sitting room, bedroom and bathroom, and a sort of little place that they called a hall. And that's how I came to know Linley. He was the bloke that was being shown round.

"Bit expensive," he said.

And the man that ran the flats turned away to the window and picked his teeth. It's funny how much you can show by a simple thing like. What he meant to say was that he'd hundreds of flats like that, and thousands of people looking for them, and he didn't care who had them or whether they all went on looking. There was no mistaking him, somehow. And yet he never said a word, only looked away out of the window and picked his teeth. And I ventured to speak to Mr. Linley then; and I said, "How about it, sir, if I paid half, and shared it? I wouldn't be in the way, and I'm out all day, and whatever you said would go, and really I wouldn't be no more in your way than a cat."

You may be surprised at my doing it; and you'll be much more surprised at him accepting it—at least, you would if you knew me, just a small man in a small way of business. And yet I could see at once that he was taking to me more than he was taking to the man at the window.

"But there's only one bedroom," he said.

"I could make up my bed easy in that little room there," I said.

"The Hall," said the man, looking round from the window, without taking his toothpick out.

"And I'd have the bed out of the way and hid in the cupboard by any hour you like," I said.

He looked thoughtful, and the other man looked out over London; and in the end, do you know, he accepted.

"Friend of yours?" said the flat man.

"Yes," answered Mr. Linley.

It was really very nice of him.

I'll tell you why I did it. Able to afford it? Of course not. But I heard him tell the flat man that he had just come down from Oxford and wanted to live for a few months in London. It turned out he wanted just to be comfortable and do nothing for a bit while he looked things over and chose a job, or probably just as long as he could afford it. Well, I said to myself, what's the Oxford manner worth in business, especially a business like mine? Why, simply everything you've got. If I picked up only a quarter of it from this Mr. Linley I'd be able to double my sales, and that would soon mean I'd be given something a lot harder to push, with perhaps treble the pay. Worth it every time. And you can make a quarter of an education go twice as far again, if you're careful with it. I mean you don't have to quote the whole of the *Inferno* to show that you've read Milton; half a line may do it.

Well, about that story I have to tell. And you mightn't think that a little man like me could make you shudder. Well, I soon forgot about the Oxford manner when we settled down in our flat. I forgot it in the sheer wonder of the man himself. He had a mind like an acrobat's body, like a bird's body. It didn't want education. You didn't notice whether he was educated or not. Ideas were always leaping up in him, things you'd never have thought of. And not only that, but if any ideas were about, he'd sort of catch them. Time and again I've found him knowing just what I was going to say. Not thought reading, but what they call intuition. I used to try to learn a bit about chess, just to take my thoughts off Num-numo in the evening, when I'd done with it. But problems I never could do. Yet he'd come along and glance at my problem and say, "You probably move that piece first," and I'd say, "But where?" and he'd say, "Oh, one of those three squares." And I'd say, "But it will be taken on all of them." And the piece a queen all the time, mind you. And he'd say, "Yes, it's doing no good there: you're probably meant to lose it."

And, do you know, he'd be right.

You see, he'd been following out what the other man had been thinking. That's what he'd been doing.

Well, one day there was that ghastly murder at Unge. I don't know if you remember it. But Steeger had gone down to live with a girl in a bungalow on the North Downs, and that was the first we had heard of him.

The girl had £200, and he got every penny of it, and she utterly disappeared. And Scotland Yard couldn't find her.

Well, I'd happened to read that Steeger had bought two bottles of Num-numo; for the Otherthorpe police had found out everything about him, except what he did with the girl; and that of course attracted my attention, or I should have never thought again about the case or said a word of it to Linley. Num-numo was always on my mind, as I always spent every day pushing it, and that kept me from forgetting the other thing. And so one day I said to Linley, "I wonder with all that knack you have for seeing through a chess problem, and thinking of one thing and another, that you don't have a go at that Otherthorpe mystery. It's a problem as much as chess," I said.

"There's not the mystery in ten murders that there is in one game of chess," he answered.

"It's beaten Scotland Yard," I said.

"Has it?" he asked.

"Knocked them endwise," I said.

"It shouldn't have done that," he said. And almost immediately after he said, "What are the facts?"

We were both sitting at supper, and I told him the facts, as I had them straight from the papers. She was a pretty blonde, she was small, she was called Nancy Elth, she had £200, they lived at the bungalow for five days. After that he stayed there for another fortnight, but nobody ever saw her alive again. Steeger said she had gone to South America, but later said he had never said South America, but South Africa. None of her money remained in the bank where she had kept it, and Steeger was shown to have come by at least £150 just at that time. Then Steeger turned out to be a vegetarian, getting all his food from the greengrocer, and that made the constable in the village of Unge suspicious of him, for a vegetarian was something new to the constable. He watched Steeger after that, and it's well he did, for there was nothing that Scotland Yard asked him that he couldn't tell them about him, except of course the one thing. And he told the police at Otherthorpe five or six miles away, and they came and took a hand at it too. They were able to say for one thing that he never went outside the bungalow and its tidy garden ever since she disappeared. You see, the more they watched him the more suspicious they got, as you naturally do if you're watching a man; so that very soon they were watching every move he made, but if it hadn't been for his being a vegetarian they'd never have started to suspect him, and there wouldn't have been enough evidence even for Linley. Not that they found out anything much against him, except that £150 dropping in from nowhere, and it was Scotland Yard that found that, not the police of Otherthorpe. No, what the constable of Unge found out was about the larch trees, and that beat Scotland Yard utterly, and beat Linley up to the very last, and of course it beat me. There were ten larch trees in the bit of a garden, and he'd made some sort of an arrangement with the landlord, Steeger had, before he took the bungalow, by which he could do what he liked with the larch trees. And then from about the time that little Nancy Elth must have died he cut every one of them down. Three times a day he went at it for nearly a week, and when they were all down he cut them all up into logs no more than two foot long and laid them all in neat heaps. You never saw such work. And what for? To give an excuse for the axe was one theory. But the excuse was bigger than the axe; it took him a fortnight, hard work every day. And he could have killed a little thing like Nancy Elth without an axe, and cut her up too. Another theory was that he wanted firewood, to make away with the body. But he never used it. He left it all standing there in those neat stacks. It fairly beat everybody.

Well, those are the facts I told Linley. Oh yes, and he bought a big butcher's knife. Funny thing, they all do. And yet it isn't so funny after all; if you've got to cut a woman up, you've got to cut her up; and you can't do that without a knife. Then, there were some negative facts. He hadn't burned her. Only had a fire in the small stove now and then, and only used it for cooking. They got on to that pretty smartly, the Unge constable did, and the men that were lending him a hand from Otherthorpe. There were some little woody places lying round, shaws they call them in that part of the country, the country people do, and they could climb a tree handy and unobserved and get a sniff at the smoke in almost any direction it might be blowing. They did that now and then, and there was no smell of flesh burning, just ordinary cooking. Pretty smart of the Otherthorpe police that was, though of course it didn't help to hang Steeger. Then later on the Scotland Yard men went down and got another fact—negative, but narrowing things down all the while. And that was that the chalk under the bungalow and under the little garden had none of it been disturbed. And he'd never been outside it since Nancy disappeared. Oh yes, and he had a big file besides the knife. But there was no sign of any ground bones found on the file, or any blood on the knife. He'd washed them of course. I told all that to Linley.

Now I ought to warn you before I go any further. I am a small man myself and you probably don't expect anything horrible from me. But I ought to warn you this man was a murderer, or at any rate somebody was; the woman had been made away with, a nice pretty little girl too, and the man that had done that wasn't necessarily going to stop at things you might think he'd stop at. With the mind to do a thing like that, and with the long thin shadow of the rope to drive him further, you can't say what he'll stop at. Murder tales seem nice things sometimes for a lady to sit and read all by herself by the fire. But murder isn't a nice thing, and when a murderer's desperate and trying to hide his tracks he isn't even as nice as he was before. I'll ask you to bear that in mind. Well, I've warned you.

So I says to Linley, "And what do you make of it?"

"Drains?" said Linley.

"No," I says, "you're wrong there. Scotland Yard has been into that. And the Otherthorpe people before them. They've had a look in the drains, such as they are, a little thing running into a cesspool beyond the garden; and nothing has gone down it—nothing that oughtn't to have, I mean."

He made one or two other suggestions, but Scotland Yard had been before him in every case. That's really the crab of my story, if you'll excuse the expression. You want a man who sets out to be a detective to take his magnifying glass and go down to the spot; to go to the spot before everything; and then to measure the footmarks and pick up the clues and find the knife that the police have overlooked. But Linley never even went near the place, and he hadn't got a magnifying glass, not as I ever saw, and Scotland Yard were before him every time.

In fact they had more clues than anybody could make head or tail of. Every kind of clue to show that he'd murdered the poor little girl; every kind of clue to show that he hadn't disposed of the body; and yet the body wasn't there. It wasn't in South America either, and not much more likely in South Africa. And all the time, mind you, that enormous bunch of chopped larchwood, a clue that was staring everyone in the face and leading nowhere. No, we didn't seem to want any more clues, and Linley never went near the place. The trouble was to deal with the clues we'd got. I was completely mystified; so was Scotland Yard; and Linley seemed to be getting no forwarder; and all the while the mystery was hanging on me. I mean if it were not for the trifle I'd chanced to remember, and if it were not for one chance word I said to Linley, that mystery would have gone the way of all the other mysteries that men have made nothing of, a darkness, a little patch of night in history.

Well, the fact was Linley didn't take much interest in it at first, but I was so absolutely sure that he could do it that I kept him to the idea. "You can do chess problems," I said.

"That's ten times harder," he said, sticking to his point.

"Then why don't you do this?" I said.

"Then go and take a look at the board for me," said Linley.

That was his way of talking. We'd been a fortnight together, and I knew it by now. He meant to go down to the bungalow at Unge. I know you'll say why didn't he go himself; but the plain truth of it is that if he'd been tearing about the countryside he'd never have been thinking, whereas sitting there in his chair by the fire in our flat there was no limit to the ground he could cover, if you follow my meaning. So down I went by train next day, and got out at Unge station. And there were the North Downs rising up before me, somehow like music.

"It's up there, isn't it?" I said to the porter.

"That's right," he said. "Up there by the lane; and mind to turn to your right when you get to the old yew tree, a very big tree, you can't mistake it, and then . . ." and he told me the way so that I couldn't go wrong. I found them all like that, very nice and helpful. You see, it was Unge's day at last. Everyone had heard of Unge now; you could have got a letter there any time just then without putting the county or post town; and this was what Unge had to show. I dare say if you tried to find Unge now . . . well, anyway, they were making hay while the sun shone.

Well, there the hill was, going up into sunlight, going up like a song. You don't want to hear about the spring, and all the may rioting, and the colour that came down over everything later on in the day, and all those birds; but I thought, "What a nice place to bring a girl to." And then when I thought that he'd killed her there, well I'm only a small man, as I said, but when I thought of her on that hill with all the birds singing, I said to myself, "Wouldn't it be odd if it turned out to be me after all that got that man killed, if he did murder her." So I soon found my way up to the bungalow and began prying about, looking over the hedge into the garden. And I didn't find much, and I found nothing at all that the police hadn't found already, but there were those heaps of larch logs staring me in the face and looking very queer.

I did a lot of thinking, leaning against the hedge, breathing the smell of the may, and looking over the top of it at the larch logs, and the neat little bungalow the other side of the garden. Lots of theories I thought of, till I came to the best thought of all; and that was that if I left the thinking to Linley, with his Oxford-and-Cambridge education, and only brought him the facts, as he had told me, I should be doing more good in my way than if I tried to do any big thinking. I forgot to tell you that I had gone to Scotland Yard in the morning. Well, there wasn't really much to tell. What they asked me was what I wanted. And, not having an answer exactly ready, I didn't find out very much from them. But it was quite different at Unge; everyone was most obliging; it was their day there, as I said. The constable let me go indoors, so long as I didn't touch anything, and he gave me a look at the garden from the inside. And I saw the stumps of the ten larch trees, and I noticed one thing that Linley said was very observant of me, not that it turned out to be any use, but anyway I was doing my best: I noticed that the stumps had been all chopped anyhow. And from that I thought that the man that did it didn't know much about chopping. The constable said that was a deduction. So then I said that the axe was blunt when he used it; and that certainly made the constable think, though he didn't actually say I was right this time. Did I tell you that Steeger never went outdoors, except to the little garden to chop wood, ever since Nancy disappeared? I think I did. Well, it was perfectly true. They'd watched him night and day, one or another of them, and the Unge constable told me that himself. That limited things a good deal. The only thing I didn't like about it was that I felt Linley ought to have found all that out instead of ordinary policemen, and I felt that he could have too. There'd have been romance in a story like that. And they'd never have done it if the news hadn't gone round that the man was a vegetarian and only dealt at the greengrocer's. Likely as not

even that was only started out of pique by the butcher. It's queer what little things may trip a man up. Best to keep straight is my motto. But perhaps I'm straying a bit away from my story. I should like to do that forever—forget that it ever was; but I can't.

Well, I picked up all sorts of information; clues I suppose I should call it in a story like this, though they none of them seemed to lead anywhere. For instance, I found out everything he ever bought at the village, I could even tell you the kind of salt he bought, quite plain with no phosphates in it, that they sometimes put in to make it tidy. And then he got ice from the fishmonger's, and plenty of vegetables, as I said, from the greengrocer, Mergin & Sons. And I had a bit of a talk over it all with the constable. Slugger he said his name was. I wondered why he hadn't come in and searched the place as soon as the girl was missing. "Well, you can't do that," he said. "And besides, we didn't suspect at once, not about the girl, that is. We only suspected there was something wrong about him on account of him being a vegetarian. He stayed a good fortnight after the last that was seen of her. And then we slipped in like a knife. But, you see, no one had been enquiring about her, there was no warrant out."

"And what did you find?" I asked Slugger, "when you went in?"

"Just a big file," he said, "and the knife and the axe that he must have got to chop her up with."

"But he got the axe to chop trees with," I said.

"Well, yes," he said, but rather grudgingly.

"And what did he chop them for?" I asked.

"Well, of course, my superiors has theories about that," he said, "that they mightn't tell to everybody."

You see, it was those logs that were beating them.

"But did he cut her up at all?" I asked.

"Well, he said that she was going to South America," he answered. Which was really very fair-minded of him.

I don't remember now much else that he told me. Steeger left the plates and dishes all washed up and very neat, he said.

Well, I brought all this back to Linley, going up by the train that started just about sunset. I'd like to tell you about the late spring evening, so calm over that grim bungalow, closing in with a glory all round it as though it were blessing it; but you'll want to hear of the murder. Well, I told Linley everything, though much of it didn't seem to me to be worth the telling. The trouble was that the moment I began to leave anything out, he'd know it, and make me drag it in. "You can't tell what may be vital," he'd say. "A tin tack swept away by a housemaid might hang a man."

All very well, but be consistent, even if you are educated at Eton and Harrow, and whenever I mentioned Num-numo, which after all was the beginning of the whole story, because he wouldn't have heard of it if it hadn't been for me, and my noticing that Steeger had bought two bottles of it, why then he said that things like that were trivial and we should keep to the main issues. I naturally talked a bit about Num-numo, because only that day I had pushed close on fifty bottles of it in Unge. A murder certainly stimulates people's minds, and Steeger's two bottles gave me an opportunity that only a fool could have failed to make something of. But of course all that was nothing at all to Linley.

You can't see a man's thoughts, and you can't look into his mind, so that all the most exciting things in the world can never be told of. But what I think happened all that evening with Linley, while I talked to him before supper, and all through supper, and sitting smoking afterwards in front of our fire, was that his thoughts were stuck at a barrier there was no getting over. And the barrier wasn't the difficulty of finding ways and means by which Steeger might have made away with the body, but the impossibility of finding why he chopped those masses of wood every day for a fortnight, and paid, as I'd just found out, £25 to his landlord to be allowed to do it. That's what was beating Linley. As for the ways by which Steeger might have hidden the body,

it seemed to me that every way was blocked by the police. If you said he buried it, they said the chalk was undisturbed; if you said he carried it away, they said he never left the place; if you said he burned it, they said no smell of burning was ever noticed when the smoke blew low, and when it didn't they climbed trees after it. I'd taken to Linley wonderfully, and I didn't have to be educated to see there was something big in a mind like his, and I thought that he could have done it. When I saw the police getting in before him like that, and no way that I could see of getting past them, I felt real sorry.

Did anyone come to the house, he asked me once or twice. Did anyone take anything away from it? But we couldn't account for it that way. Then perhaps I made some suggestion that was no good, or perhaps I started talking of Num-numo again, and he interrupted me rather sharply.

"But what would you do, Smithers?" he said. "What would you do yourself?"

"If I'd murdered poor Nancy Elth?" I asked.

"Yes," he said.

"I can't ever imagine doing such a thing," I told him.

He sighed at that, as though it were something against me.

"I suppose I should never be a detective," I said. And he just shook his head.

Then he looked broodingly into the fire for what seemed an hour. And then he shook his head again. We both went to bed after that.

I shall remember the next day all my life. I was till evening, as usual, pushing Num-numo. And we sat down to supper about nine. You couldn't get things cooked at those flats, so of course we had it cold. And Linley began with a salad. I can see it now, every bit of it. Well, I was still a bit full of what I'd done in Unge, pushing Num-numo. Only a fool, I know, would have been unable to push it there; but still, I *had* pushed it; and about fifty bottles, forty-eight to be exact, are something in a small village, whatever the circumstances. So I was talking about it a bit; and then all of a sudden I realized that Num-numo was nothing to Linley, and I pulled myself up with a jerk. It was really very kind of him; do you know what he did? He must have known at once why I stopped talking, and he just stretched out a hand and said, "Would you give me a little of your Num-numo for my salad?"

I was so touched I nearly gave it him. But of course you don't take Num-numo with salad. Only for meats and savouries. That's on the bottle.

So I just said to him, "Only for meats and savouries." Though I don't know what savouries are. Never had any.

I never saw a man's face go like that before.

He seemed still for a whole minute. And nothing speaking about him but that expression. Like a man that's seen a ghost, one is tempted to write. But it wasn't really at all. I'll tell you what he looked like. Like a man that's seen something that no one has ever looked at before, something he thought couldn't be.

And then he said in a voice that was all quite changed, more low and gentle and quiet it seemed, "No good for vegetables, eh?"

"Not a bit," I said.

And at that he gave a kind of sob in his throat. I hadn't thought he could feel things like that. Of course I didn't know what it was all about; but, whatever it was, I thought all that sort of thing would have been knocked out of him at Eton and Harrow, an educated man like that. There were no tears in his eyes, but he was feeling something horribly.

And then he began to speak with big spaces between his words, saying, "A man might make a mistake perhaps, and use Num-numo with vegetables."

"Not twice," I said. What else could I say?

And he repeated that after me as though I had told of the end of the world, and adding an awful emphasis to my words, till they seemed all clammy with some frightful significance, and shaking his head as he said it.

Then he was quite silent.

"What is it?" I asked.

"Smithers," he said.

"Yes," I said.

"Smithers," said he.

And I said, "Well?"

"Look here, Smithers," he said, "you must phone down to the grocer at Unge and find out from him this."

"Yes?" I said.

"Whether Steeger bought those two bottles, as I expect he did, on the same day, and not a few days apart. He couldn't have done that."

I waited to see if any more was coming, and then I ran out and did what I was told. It took me some time, being after nine o'clock, and only then with the help of the police. About six days apart they said; and so I came back and told Linley. He looked up at me so hopefully when I came in, but I saw that it was the wrong answer by his eyes.

You can't take things to heart like that without being ill, and when he didn't speak I said, "What you want is a good brandy, and go to bed early."

And he said, "No. I must see someone from Scotland Yard. Phone round to them. Say here at once."

But I said, "I can't get an inspector from Scotland Yard to call on us at this hour."

His eyes were all lit up. He was all there all right.

"Then tell them," he said, "they'll never find Nancy Elth. Tell one of them to come here, and I'll tell him why." And he added, I think only for me, "They must watch Steeger, till one day they get him over something else."

And, do you know, he came. Inspector Ulton; he came himself.

While we were waiting I tried to talk to Linley. Partly curiosity, I admit. But I didn't want to leave him to those thoughts of his, brooding away by the fire. I tried to ask him what it was all about. But he wouldn't tell me. "Murder is horrible," is all he would say. "And as a man covers his tracks up it only gets worse."

He wouldn't tell me. "There are tales," he said, "that one never wants to hear."

That's true enough. I wish I'd never heard this one. I never did actually. But I guessed it from Linley's last words to Inspector Ulton, the only ones that I overheard. And perhaps this is the point at which to stop reading my story, so that you don't guess it too; even if you think you want murder stories. For don't you rather want a murder story with a bit of a romantic twist, and not a story about real foul murder? Well, just as you like.

In came Inspector Ulton, and Linley shook hands in silence, and pointed the way to his bedroom; and they went in there and talked in low voices, and I never heard a word.

A fairly hearty-looking man was the inspector when they went into that room.

They walked through our sitting room in silence when they came out, and together they went into the hall, and there I heard the only words they said to each other. It was the inspector that first broke that silence.

"But why," he said, "did he cut down the trees?"

"Solely," said Linley, "in order to get an appetite."

THE INVISIBLE MAN

G. K. CHESTERTON

IT HAS BEEN widely and perhaps accurately stated that Father Brown is the second greatest English detective in all of literature, surpassed only, it is superfluous to say, by Sherlock Holmes. What separates him from most of his crime-fighting colleagues is his view that wrongdoers are souls in need of redemption rather than criminals to be brought to justice. The rather ordinary-seeming Roman Catholic priest possesses a sharp, subtle, sensitive mind, with which he demonstrates a deep understanding of human nature to solve mysteries.

Father Brown is a logical creation of Gilbert Keith Chesterton (1874–1936), a converted and extremely devout Catholic who believed that religion was the world's only refuge. There were five collections of stories about the gentle little priest: *The Innocence of Father Brown* (1911), *The Wisdom of Father Brown* (1914), *The Incredulity of Father Brown* (1926), *The Secret of Father Brown* (1927), and *The Scandal of Father Brown* (1935); *The Father Brown Omnibus*, assembled in 1951, added a stray story, "The Vampire of the Village." There were two films about the sleuth—*Father Brown, Detective* (1934, starring Walter Connolly) and *Father Brown*, released in the United States as *The Detective* (1954, with Alec Guinness in the titular role)—oddly both based on the same tale, "The Blue Cross," the first Father Brown story. Chesterton wrote many other stories and novels about various types of crime, notably the allegorical *The Man Who Was Thursday* (1908), and several volumes of stories that displayed his love of paradox and whimsicality.

"The Invisible Man" was first published in the February 1911 issue of *Cassell's Magazine*; it was first collected in *The Innocence of Father Brown* (London, Cassell, 1911).

THE INVISIBLE MAN

G. K. CHESTERTON

IN THE COOL blue twilight of two steep streets in Camden Town, the shop at the corner, a confectioner's, glowed like the butt of a cigar. One should rather say, perhaps, like the butt of a firework, for the light was of many colours and some complexity, broken up by many mirrors and dancing on many gilt and gaily-coloured cakes and sweetmeats. Against this one fiery glass were glued the noses of many gutter-snipes, for the chocolates were all wrapped in those red and gold and green metallic colours which are almost better than chocolate itself; and the huge white wedding-cake in the window was somehow at once remote and satisfying, just as if the whole North Pole were good to eat. Such rainbow provocations could naturally collect the youth of the neighbourhood up to the ages of ten or twelve. But this corner was also attractive to youth at a later stage; and a young man, not less than twenty-four, was staring into the same shop window. To him, also, the shop was of fiery charm, but this attraction was not wholly to be explained by chocolates; which, however, he was far from despising.

He was a tall, burly, red-haired young man, with a resolute face but a listless manner. He carried under his arm a flat, grey portfolio of black-and-white sketches, which he had sold with more or less success to publishers ever since his uncle (who was an admiral) had disinherited him for Socialism, because of a lecture which he had delivered against that economic theory. His name was John Turnbull Angus.

Entering at last, he walked through the confectioner's shop to the back room, which was a sort of pastry-cook restaurant, merely raising his hat to the young lady who was serving there. She was a dark, elegant, alert girl in black, with a high colour and very quick, dark eyes; and after the ordinary interval she followed him into the inner room to take his order.

His order was evidently a usual one. "I want, please," he said with precision, "one halfpenny bun and a small cup of black coffee." An instant before the girl could turn away he added, "Also, I want you to marry me."

The young lady of the shop stiffened suddenly and said, "Those are jokes I don't allow."

The red-haired young man lifted grey eyes of an unexpected gravity.

"Really and truly," he said, "it's as serious—as serious as the half-penny bun. It is expensive, like the bun; one pays for it. It is indigestible, like the bun. It hurts."

The dark young lady had never taken her dark eyes off him, but seemed to be studying him with almost tragic exactitude. At the end of her scrutiny she had something like the shadow of a smile, and she sat down in a chair.

"Don't you think," observed Angus, absently, "that it's rather cruel to eat these halfpenny buns? They might grow up into penny buns. I shall give up these brutal sports when we are married."

The dark young lady rose from her chair and walked to the window, evidently in a state of strong but not unsympathetic cogitation.

When at last she swung round again with an air of resolution she was bewildered to observe that the young man was carefully laying out on the table various objects from the shop-window. They included a pyramid of highly coloured sweets, several plates of sandwiches, and the two decanters containing that mysterious port and sherry which are peculiar to pastry-cooks. In the middle of this neat arrangement he had carefully let down the enormous load of white sugared cake which had been the huge ornament of the window.

"What on earth are you doing?" she asked.

"Duty, my dear Laura," he began.

"Oh, for the Lord's sake, stop a minute," she cried, "and don't talk to me in that way. I mean, what is all that?"

"A ceremonial meal, Miss Hope."

"And what is *that*?" she asked impatiently, pointing to the mountain of sugar.

"The wedding-cake, Mrs. Angus," he said.

The girl marched to that article, removed it with some clatter, and put it back in the shop window; she then returned, and, putting her elegant elbows on the table, regarded the young man not unfavourably but with considerable exasperation.

"You don't give me any time to think," she said.

"I'm not such a fool," he answered; "that's my Christian humility."

She was still looking at him; but she had grown considerably graver behind the smile.

"Mr. Angus," she said steadily, "before there is a minute more of this nonsense I must tell you something about myself as shortly as I can."

"Delighted," replied Angus gravely. "You might tell me something about myself, too, while you are about it."

"Oh, do hold your tongue and listen," she said. "It's nothing that I'm ashamed of, and it isn't even anything that I'm specially sorry about. But what would you say if there were something that is no business of mine and yet is my nightmare?"

"In that case," said the man seriously, "I should suggest that you bring back the cake."

"Well, you must listen to the story first," said Laura, persistently. "To begin with, I must tell you that my father owned the inn called the 'Red Fish' at Ludbury, and I used to serve people in the bar."

"I have often wondered," he said, "why there was a kind of a Christian air about this one confectioner's shop."

"Ludbury is a sleepy, grassy little hole in the Eastern Counties, and the only kind of people who ever came to the 'Red Fish' were occasional commercial travellers, and for the rest, the most awful people you can see, only you've never seen them. I mean little, loungy men, who had just enough to live on and had nothing to do but lean about in bar-rooms and bet on horses, in bad clothes that were just too good for them. Even these wretched young rotters were not very common at our house; but there were two of them that were a lot too common— common in every sort of way. They both lived on money of their own, and were wearisomely idle and over-dressed. But yet I was a bit sorry for them, because I half believe they slunk into our little empty bar because each of them had a slight deformity; the sort of thing that some yokels laugh at. It wasn't exactly a deformity either; it was more an oddity. One of them was a surprisingly small man, something like a dwarf, or at least like a jockey. He was not at all jockey-ish to look at, though; he had a round black head and a well-trimmed black beard, bright eyes like a bird's; he jingled money in his pockets; he jangled a great gold watch chain; and he never turned up except dressed just too much like a gentleman to be one. He was no fool though, though a futile idler; he was curiously clever at all kinds of things that couldn't be the slightest use; a sort of impromptu conjuring; making fifteen matches set fire to each other like a regular firework; or cutting a banana or some such thing into a dancing doll. His name was Isidore Smythe; and I can see him still, with his little dark face, just coming up to the counter, making a jumping kangaroo out of five cigars.

"The other fellow was more silent and more ordinary; but somehow he alarmed me much more than poor little Smythe. He was very tall and slight, and light-haired; his nose had a high bridge, and he might almost have been handsome in a spectral sort of way; but he had one of the most appalling squints I have ever seen or heard of. When he looked straight at you, you didn't know where you were yourself, let alone what he was looking at. I fancy this sort of disfigurement embittered the poor chap a little; for while Smythe was ready to show off his monkey tricks anywhere, James Welkin (that was the squinting man's name) never did anything except soak in our bar parlour, and go for great walks by himself in the flat, grey country all round. All the same, I think Smythe, too, was a little sensitive about being so small, though he carried it off more smartly. And so it was that I was really puzzled, as well as startled, and very sorry, when they both offered to marry me in the same week.

"Well, I did what I've since thought was perhaps a silly thing. But, after all, these freaks were my friends in a way; and I had a horror of their thinking I refused them for the real reason, which was that they were so impossibly ugly. So I made up some gas of another sort, about never meaning to marry anyone who hadn't carved his way in the world. I said it was a point of principle with me not to live on money that was just inherited like theirs. Two days after I had talked in this well-meaning sort of way, the whole trouble began. The first thing I heard was that both of them had gone off to seek their fortunes, as if they were in some silly fairy tale.

"Well, I've never seen either of them from that day to this. But I've had two letters from the little man called Smythe, and really they were rather exciting."

"Ever heard of the other man?" asked Angus.

"No, he never wrote," said the girl, after an instant's hesitation. "Smythe's first letter was simply to say that he had started out walking with Welkin to London; but Welkin was such a good walker that the little man dropped out of it, and took a rest by the roadside. He happened to be picked up by some travelling show, and,

partly because he was nearly a dwarf, and partly because he was really a clever little wretch, he got on quite well in the show business, and was soon sent up to the Aquarium, to do some tricks that I forget. That was his first letter. His second was much more of a startler, and I only got it last week."

The man called Angus emptied his coffee-cup and regarded her with mild and patient eyes. Her own mouth took a slight twist of laughter as she resumed, "I suppose you've seen on the hoardings all about this 'Smythe's Silent Service'? Or you must be the only person that hasn't. Oh, I don't know much about it, it's some clockwork invention for doing all the housework by machinery. You know the sort of thing: 'Press a Button—A Butler who Never Drinks.' 'Turn a Handle—Ten Housemaids who Never Flirt.' You must have seen the advertisements. Well, whatever these machines are, they are making pots of money; and they are making it all for that little imp whom I knew down in Ludbury. I can't help feeling pleased the poor little chap has fallen on his feet; but the plain fact is, I'm in terror of his turning up any minute and telling me he's carved his way in the world—as he certainly has."

"And the other man?" repeated Angus with a sort of obstinate quietude.

Laura Hope got to her feet suddenly. "My friend," she said, "I think you are a witch. Yes, you are quite right. I have not seen a line of the other man's writing; and I have no more notion than the dead of what or where he is. But it is of him that I am frightened. It is he who is all about my path. It is he who has half driven me mad. Indeed, I think he has driven me mad; for I have felt him where he could not have been, and I have heard his voice when he could not have spoken."

"Well, my dear," said the young man, cheerfully, "if he were Satan himself, he is done for now you have told somebody. One goes mad all alone, old girl. But when was it you fancied you felt and heard our squinting friend?"

"I heard James Welkin laugh as plainly as I

hear you speak," said the girl, steadily. "There was nobody there, for I stood just outside the shop at the corner, and could see down both streets at once. I had forgotten how he laughed, though his laugh was as odd as his squint. I had not thought of him for nearly a year. But it's a solemn truth that a few seconds later the first letter came from his rival."

"Did you ever make the spectre speak or squeak, or anything?" asked Angus, with some interest.

Laura suddenly shuddered, and then said, with an unshaken voice, "Yes. Just when I had finished reading the second letter from Isidore Smythe announcing his success, just then, I heard Welkin say, 'He shan't have you, though.' It was quite plain, as if he were in the room. It is awful; I think I must be mad."

"If you really were mad," said the young man, "you would think you must be sane. But certainly there seems to me to be something a little rum about this unseen gentleman. Two heads are better than one—I spare you allusions to any other organs—and really, if you would allow me, as a sturdy, practical man, to bring back the wedding-cake out of the window——"

Even as he spoke, there was a sort of steely shriek in the street outside, and a small motor, driven at devilish speed, shot up to the door of the shop and stuck there. In the same flash of time a small man in a shiny top hat stood stamping in the outer room.

Angus, who had hitherto maintained hilarious ease from motives of mental hygiene, revealed the strain of his soul by striding abruptly out of the inner room and confronting the new-comer. A glance at him was quite sufficient to confirm the savage guesswork of a man in love. This very dapper but dwarfish figure, with the spike of black beard carried insolently forward, the clever, unrestful eyes, the neat but very nervous fingers, could be none other than the man just described to him: Isidore Smythe, who made dolls out of banana skins and matchboxes; Isidore Smythe, who made millions out of undrinking butlers and unflirting housemaids of metal. For a moment the two men, instinctively understanding each other's air of possession, looked at each other with that curious cold generosity which is the soul of rivalry.

Mr. Smythe, however, made no allusion to the ultimate ground of their antagonism, but said simply and explosively. "Has Miss Hope seen that thing on the window?"

"On the window?" repeated the staring Angus.

"There's no time to explain other things," said the small millionaire shortly. "There's some tom-foolery going on here that has to be investigated."

He pointed his polished walking-stick at the window, recently depleted by the bridal preparations of Mr. Angus; and that gentleman was astonished to see along the front of the glass a long strip of paper pasted, which had certainly not been on the window when he had looked through it some time before. Following the energetic Smythe outside into the street, he found that some yard and a half of stamp paper had been carefully gummed along the glass outside, and on this was written in straggly characters, "If you marry Smythe, he will die."

"Laura," said Angus, putting his big red head into the shop, "you're not mad."

"It's the writing of that fellow Welkin," said Smythe gruffly. "I haven't seen him for years, but he's always bothering me. Five times in the last fortnight he's had threatening letters left at my flat, and I can't even find out who leaves them, let alone if it is Welkin himself. The porter of the flats swears that no suspicious characters have been seen, and here he has pasted up a sort of dado on a public shop window, while the people in the shop——"

"Quite so," said Angus modestly, "while the people in the shop were having tea. Well, sir, I can assure you I appreciate your common sense in dealing so directly with the matter. We can talk about other things afterwards. The fellow cannot be very far off yet, for I swear there was no paper there when I went last to the window, ten or fifteen minutes ago. On the other hand, he's too far off to be chased, as we don't even know the direction. If you'll take my advice, Mr. Smythe, you'll put this at once in the hands of some energetic inquiry man, private rather than public. I know an extremely clever fellow, who has set up in business five minutes from here in your car. His name's Flambeau, and though his youth was a bit stormy, he's a strictly honest man now, and his brains are worth money. He lives in Lucknow Mansions, Hampstead."

"That is odd," said the little man, arching his black eyebrows. "I live, myself, in Himylaya Mansions, round the corner. Perhaps you might care to come with me; I can go to my rooms and sort out these queer Welkin documents, while you run round and get your friend the detective."

"You are very good," said Angus politely. "Well, the sooner we act the better."

Both men, with a queer kind of impromptu fairness, took the same sort of formal farewell of the lady, and both jumped into the brisk little car. As Smythe took the handles and they turned the great corner of the street, Angus was amused to see a gigantesque poster of "Smythe's Silent Service," with a picture of a huge headless iron doll, carrying a saucepan with the legend, "A Cook Who is Never Cross."

"I use them in my own flat," said the little black-bearded man, laughing, "partly for advertisements, and partly for real convenience. Honestly, and all above board, those big clockwork dolls of mine do bring you coals or claret or a timetable quicker than any live servants I've ever known, if you know which knob to press. But I'll never deny, between ourselves, that such servants have their disadvantages, too."

"Indeed?" said Angus; "is there something they can't do?"

"Yes," replied Smythe coolly; "they can't tell me who left those threatening letters at my flat."

The man's motor was small and swift like himself; in fact, like his domestic service, it was of his own invention. If he was an advertising quack, he was one who believed in his own wares. The sense of something tiny and flying

was accentuated as they swept up long white curves of road in the dead but open daylight of evening. Soon the white curves came sharper and dizzier; they were upon ascending spirals, as they say in the modern religions. For, indeed, they were cresting a corner of London which is almost as precipitous as Edinburgh, if not quite so picturesque. Terrace rose above terrace, and the special tower of flats they sought, rose above them all to almost Egyptian height, gilt by the level sunset. The change, as they turned the corner and entered the crescent known as Himylaya Mansions, was as abrupt as the opening of a window; for they found that pile of flats sitting above London as above a green sea of slate. Opposite to the mansions, on the other side of the gravel crescent, was a bushy enclosure more like a steep hedge or dyke than a garden, and some way below that ran a strip of artificial water, a sort of canal, like the moat of that embowered fortress. As the car swept round the crescent it passed, at one corner, the stray stall of a man selling chestnuts; and right away at the other end of the curve, Angus could see a dim blue policeman walking slowly. These were the only human shapes in that high suburban solitude; but he had an irrational sense that they expressed the speechless poetry of London. He felt as if they were figures in a story.

The little car shot up to the right house like a bullet, and shot out its owner like a bomb shell. He was immediately inquiring of a tall commissionaire in shining braid, and a short porter in shirt sleeves, whether anybody or anything had been seeking his apartments. He was assured that nobody and nothing had passed these officials since his last inquiries; whereupon he and the slightly bewildered Angus were shot up in the lift like a rocket, till they reached the top floor.

"Just come in for a minute," said the breathless Smythe. "I want to show you those Welkin letters. Then you might run round the corner and fetch your friend." He pressed a button concealed in the wall, and the door opened of itself.

It opened on a long, commodious ante-room, of which the only arresting features, ordinarily speaking, were the rows of tall half-human mechanical figures that stood up on both sides like tailors' dummies. Like tailors' dummies they were headless; and like tailors' dummies they had a handsome unnecessary humpiness in the shoulders, and a pigeon-breasted protuberance of chest; but barring this, they were not much more like a human figure than any automatic machine at a station that is about the human height. They had two great hooks like arms, for carrying trays; and they were painted pea-green, or vermillion, or black for convenience of distinction; in every other way they were only automatic machines and nobody would have looked twice at them. On this occasion, at least, nobody did. For between the two rows of these domestic dummies lay something more interesting than most of the mechanics of the world. It was a white, tattered scrap of paper scrawled with red ink; and the agile inventor had snatched it up almost as soon as the door flew open. He handed it to Angus without a word. The red ink on it actually was not dry, and the message ran, "If you have been to see her to-day, I shall kill you."

There was a short silence, and then Isidore Smythe said quietly, "Would you like a little whisky? I rather feel as if I should."

"Thank you; I should like a little Flambeau," said Angus, gloomily. "This business seems to me to be getting rather grave. I'm going round at once to fetch him."

"Right you are," said the other, with admirable cheerfulness. "Bring him round here as quick as you can."

But as Angus closed the front door behind him he saw Smythe push back a button, and one of the clockwork images glided from its place and slid along a groove in the floor carrying a tray with syphon and decanter. There did seem something a trifle weird about leaving the little man alone among those dead servants, who were coming to life as the door closed.

Six steps down from Smythe's landing the man in shirt sleeves was doing something with a pail. Angus stopped to extract a promise, fortified with a prospective bribe, that he would remain in that place until the return with the detective, and would keep count of any kind of stranger coming up those stairs. Dashing down to the front hall he then laid similar charges of vigilance on the commissionaire at the front door, from whom he learned the simplifying circumstances that there was no back door. Not content with this, he captured the floating policeman and induced him to stand opposite the entrance and watch it; and finally paused an instant for a pennyworth of chestnuts, and an inquiry as to the probable length of the merchant's stay in the neighbourhood.

The chestnut seller, turning up the collar of his coat, told him he should probably be moving shortly, as he thought it was going to snow. Indeed, the evening was growing grey and bitter, but Angus, with all his eloquence, proceeded to nail the chestnut man to his post.

"Keep yourself warm on your own chestnuts," he said earnestly. "Eat up your whole stock; I'll make it worth your while. I'll give you a sovereign if you'll wait here till I come back, and then tell me whether any man, woman, or child has gone into that house where the commissionaire is standing."

He then walked away smartly, with a last look at the besieged tower.

"I've made a ring round that room, anyhow," he said. "They can't all four of them be Mr. Welkin's accomplices."

Lucknow Mansions were, so to speak, on a lower platform of that hill of houses, of which Himylaya Mansions might be called the peak. Mr. Flambeau's semi-official flat was on the ground floor, and presented in every way a marked contrast to the American machinery and cold hotel-like luxury of the flat of the Silent Service. Flambeau, who was a friend of Angus, received him in a rococo artistic den behind his office, of which the ornaments were sabres, harquebuses, Eastern curiosities, flasks of Italian wine, savage cooking-pots, a plumy Persian cat, and a small dusty-looking Roman Catholic priest, who looked particularly out of place.

"This is my friend Father Brown," said Flambeau. "I've often wanted you to meet him. Splendid weather, this; a little cold for Southerners like me."

"Yes, I think it will keep clear," said Angus, sitting down on a violet-striped Eastern ottoman.

"No," said the priest quietly, "it has begun to snow."

And, indeed, as he spoke, the first few flakes, foreseen by the man of chestnuts, began to drift across the darkening window-pane.

"Well," said Angus heavily. "I'm afraid I've come on business, and rather jumpy business at that. The fact is, Flambeau, within a stone's throw of your house is a fellow who badly wants your help; he's perpetually being haunted and threatened by an invisible enemy—a scoundrel whom nobody has even seen." As Angus proceeded to tell the whole tale of Smythe and Welkin, beginning with Laura's story, and going on with his own, the supernatural laugh at the corner of two empty streets, the strange distinct words spoken in an empty room, Flambeau grew more and more vividly concerned, and the little priest seemed to be left out of it, like a piece of furniture. When it came to the scribbled stamp-paper pasted on the window, Flambeau rose, seeming to fill the room with his huge shoulders.

"If you don't mind," he said, "I think you had better tell me the rest on the nearest road to this man's house. It strikes me, somehow, that there is no time to be lost."

"Delighted," said Angus, rising also, "though he's safe enough for the present, for I've set four men to watch the only hole to his burrow."

They turned out into the street, the small priest trundling after them with the docility of a small dog. He merely said, in a cheerful way, like one making conversation, "How quick the snow gets thick on the ground."

As they threaded the steep side streets already powdered with silver, Angus finished his story; and by the time they reached the crescent with the towering flats, he had leisure to turn his attention to the four sentinels. The chestnut seller, both before and after receiving a sovereign, swore stubbornly that he had watched the door and seen no visitor enter. The policeman was even more emphatic. He said he had had experience of crooks of all kinds, in top hats and in rags; he wasn't so green as to expect suspicious characters to look suspicious; he looked out for anybody, and, so help him, there had been nobody. And when all three men gathered round the gilded commissionaire, who still stood smiling astride of the porch, the verdict was more final still.

"I've got a right to ask any man, duke or dustman, what he wants in these flats," said the genial and gold-laced giant, "and I'll swear there's been nobody to ask since this gentleman went away."

The unimportant Father Brown, who stood back, looking modestly at the pavement, here ventured to say meekly, "Has nobody been up and down stairs, then, since the snow began to fall? It began while we were all round at Flambeau's."

"Nobody's been in here, sir, you can take it from me," said the official, with beaming authority.

"Then I wonder what that is?" said the priest, and stared at the ground blankly like a fish.

The others all looked down also; and Flambeau used a fierce exclamation and a French gesture. For it was unquestionably true that down the middle of the entrance guarded by the man in gold lace, actually between the arrogant, stretched legs of that colossus, ran a stringy pattern of grey footprints stamped upon the white snow.

"God!" cried Angus involuntarily, "the Invisible Man!"

Without another word he turned and dashed up the stairs, with Flambeau following; but Father Brown still stood looking about him in the snow-clad street as if he had lost interest in his query.

Flambeau was plainly in a mood to break down the door with his big shoulders; but the

Scotchman, with more reason, if less intuition, fumbled about on the frame of the door till he found the invisible button; and the door swung slowly open.

It showed substantially the same serried interior; the hall had grown darker, though it was still struck here and there with the last crimson shafts of sunset, and one or two of the headless machines had been moved from their places for this or that purpose, and stood here and there about the twilit place. The green and red of their coats were all darkened in the dusk; and their likeness to human shapes slightly increased by their very shapelessness. But in the middle of them all, exactly where the paper with the red ink had lain, there lay something that looked like red ink spilt out of its bottle. But it was not red ink.

With a French combination of reason and violence Flambeau simply said "Murder!" and, plunging into the flat, had explored every corner and cupboard of it in five minutes. But if he expected to find a corpse he found none. Isidore Smythe was not in the place, either dead or alive. After the most tearing search the two men met each other in the outer hall, with streaming faces and staring eyes. "My friend," said Flambeau, talking French in his excitement, "not only is your murderer invisible, but he makes invisible also the murdered man."

Angus looked round at the dim room full of dummies, and in some Celtic corner of his Scotch soul a shudder started. One of the life-size dolls stood, immediately overshadowing the blood stain, summoned, perhaps, by the slain man an instant before he fell. One of the high-shouldered hooks that served the thing for arms was a little lifted, and Angus had suddenly the horrid fancy that poor Smythe's own iron child had struck him down. Matter had rebelled, and these machines had killed their master. But even so, what had they done with him?

"Eaten him?" said the nightmare at his ear; and he sickened for an instant at the idea of rent, human remains absorbed and crushed into all that acephalous clockwork.

He recovered his mental health by an emphatic effort, and said to Flambeau, "Well, there it is. The poor fellow has evaporated like a cloud and left a red streak on the floor. The tale does not belong to this world."

"There is only one thing to be done," said Flambeau, "whether it belongs to this world or the other, I must go down and talk to my friend."

They descended, passing the man with the pail, who again asseverated that he had let no intruder pass, down to the commissionaire and the hovering chestnut man, who rigidly reasserted their own watchfulness. But when Angus looked round for his fourth confirmation he could not see it, and called out with some nervousness, "Where is the policeman?"

"I beg your pardon," said Father Brown; "that is my fault. I just sent him down the road to investigate something—that I just thought worth investigating."

"Well, we want him back pretty soon," said Angus abruptly, "for the wretched man upstairs has not only been murdered, but wiped out."

"How?" asked the priest.

"Father," said Flambeau, after a pause, "upon my soul I believe it is more in your department than mine. No friend or foe has entered the house, but Smythe is gone, as if stolen by the fairies. If that is not supernatural, I——"

As he spoke they were all checked by an unusual sight; the big blue policeman came round the corner of the crescent, running. He came straight up to Brown.

"You're right, sir," he panted, "they've just found poor Mr. Smythe's body in the canal down below."

Angus put his hand wildly to his head. "Did he run down and drown himself?" he asked.

"He never came down, I'll swear," said the constable, "and he wasn't drowned either, for he died of a great stab over the heart."

"And yet you saw no one enter?" said Flambeau in a grave voice.

"Let us walk down the road a little," said the priest.

As they reached the other end of the crescent

he observed abruptly, "Stupid of me! I forgot to ask the policeman something. I wonder if they found a light brown sack."

"Why a light brown sack?" asked Angus, astonished.

"Because if it was any other coloured sack, the case must begin over again," said Father Brown; "but if it was a light brown sack, why, the case is finished."

"I am pleased to hear it," said Angus with hearty irony. "It hasn't begun, so far as I am concerned."

"You must tell us all about it," said Flambeau with a strange heavy simplicity, like a child.

Unconsciously they were walking with quickening steps down the long sweep of road on the other side of the high crescent, Father Brown leading briskly, though in silence. At last he said with an almost touching vagueness, "Well, I'm afraid you'll think it so prosy. We always begin at the abstract end of things, and you can't begin this story anywhere else.

"Have you ever noticed this—that people never answer what you say? They answer what you mean—or what they think you mean. Suppose one lady says to another in a country house, 'Is anybody staying with you?' the lady doesn't answer 'Yes; the butler, the three footmen, the parlourmaid, and so on,' though the parlourmaid may be in the room, or the butler behind her chair. She says 'There is *nobody* staying with us,' meaning nobody of the sort you mean. But suppose a doctor inquiring into an epidemic asks, 'Who is staying in the house?' then the lady will remember the butler, parlourmaid, and the rest. All language is used like that; you never get a question answered literally, even when you get it answered truly. When those four quite honest men said that no man had gone into the Mansions, they did not really mean that *no man* had gone into them. They meant no man whom they could suspect of being your man. A man did go into the house, and did come out of it, but they never noticed him."

"An invisible man?" inquired Angus, raising his red eyebrows.

"A mentally invisible man," said Father Brown.

A minute or two after he resumed in the same unassuming voice, like a man thinking his way. "Of course you can't think of such a man, until you do think of him. That's where his cleverness comes in. But I came to think of him through two or three little things in the tale Mr. Angus told us. First, there was the fact that this Welkin went for long walks. And then there was the vast lot of stamp paper on the window. And then, most of all, there were the two things the young lady said— things that couldn't be true. Don't get annoyed," he added hastily, noting a sudden movement of the Scotchman's head; "she thought they were true. A person *can't* be quite alone in a street a second before she receives a letter. She can't be quite alone in a street when she starts reading a letter just received. There must be somebody pretty near her; he must be mentally invisible."

"Why must there be somebody near her?" asked Angus.

"Because," said Father Brown, "barring carrier-pigeons, somebody must have brought her the letter."

"Do you really mean to say," asked Flambeau, with energy, "that Welkin carried his rival's letters to his lady?"

"Yes," said the priest. "Welkin carried his rival's letters to his lady. You see, he had to."

"Oh, I can't stand much more of this," exploded Flambeau. "Who is this fellow? What does he look like? What is the usual get-up of a mentally invisible man?"

"He is dressed rather handsomely in red, blue, and gold," replied the priest promptly with precision, "and in this striking, and even showy, costume he entered Himylaya Mansions under eight human eyes; he killed Smythe in cold blood, and came down into the street again carrying the dead body in his arms——"

"Reverend sir," cried Angus, standing still, "are you raving mad, or am I?"

"You are not mad," said Brown, "only a little unobservant. You have not noticed such a man as this, for example."

He took three quick strides forward, and put his hand on the shoulder of an ordinary passing postman who had bustled by them unnoticed under the shade of the trees.

"Nobody ever notices postmen somehow," he said thoughtfully; "yet they have passions like other men, and even carry large bags where a small corpse can be stowed quite easily."

The postman, instead of turning naturally, had ducked and tumbled against the garden fence. He was a lean fair-bearded man of very ordinary appearance, but as he turned an alarmed face over his shoulder, all three men were fixed with an almost fiendish squint.

Flambeau went back to his sabres, purple rugs, and Persian cat, having many things to attend to. John Turnbull Angus went back to the lady at the shop, with whom that imprudent young man contrives to be extremely comfortable. But Father Brown walked those snow-covered hills under the stars for many hours with a murderer, and what they said to each other will never be known.

MELVILLE DAVISSON POST

REGARDED BY some critics as the best American short-story writer in the mystery genre since Edgar Allan Poe, Melville Davisson Post (1869–1930) was the most commercially successful magazine writer of his time, his popularity largely being due to his ability to create unusual situations with surprising twists at the conclusion. His technical skill in plotting stories is conceded even by those who do not consider his work of significant literary value. Post believed that the primary purpose of fiction was to entertain, and his fast-paced tales are reminiscent of O. Henry. While not a household name nowadays, Post did create two characters who are mainstays of mystery anthologies and whose adventures remain readable and fresh a century after they were written: Randolph Mason, an amoral lawyer, and Uncle Abner, the most famous detective in literature to be known only by his first name.

Abner lives in the America of Millard Fillmore's presidency in a rural area of Virginia. Not at all a cheerful individual, he is nonetheless likable in a rugged, pioneer-like way. He does not rely on exhaustive examination of scientific minutae or on brilliant flights of imagination, but instead embraces his knowledge of people and his judgment of their souls to help in his investigations. He has no official status in his community, nor has he sought the job of solving crimes, but his strong moral convictions (strengthened by a deep knowledge of the Bible) compel him to act as the righter of wrongs and protector of the innocent.

"The Doomdorf Mystery" was first published in the July 18, 1914, issue of *The Saturday Evening Post*; it was first collected in book form in *Uncle Abner: Master of Mysteries* (New York, Appleton, 1918).

THE DOOMDORF MYSTERY

MELVILLE DAVISSON POST

THE PIONEER was not the only man in the great mountains behind Virginia. Strange aliens drifted in after the Colonial wars. All foreign armies are sprinkled with a cockle of adventurers that take root and remain. They were with Braddock and La Salle, and they rode north out of Mexico after her many empires went to pieces.

I think Doomdorf crossed the seas with Iturbide when that ill-starred adventurer returned to be shot against a wall; but there was no Southern blood in him. He came from some European race remote and barbaric. The evidences were all about him. He was a huge figure of a man, with a black spade beard, broad, thick hands, and square, flat fingers.

He had found a wedge of land between the Crown's grant to Daniel Davisson and a Washington survey. It was an uncovered triangle not worth the running of the lines; and so, no doubt, was left out, a sheer rock standing up out of the river for a base, and a peak of the mountain rising northward behind it for an apex.

Doomdorf squatted on the rock. He must have brought a belt of gold pieces when he took to his horse, for he hired old Robert Steuart's slaves and built a stone house on the rock, and he brought the furnishings overland from a frigate in the Chesapeake; and then in the handfuls of earth, wherever a root would hold, he planted the mountain behind his house with peach trees. The gold gave out; but the devil is fertile in

resources. Doomdorf built a log still and turned the first fruits of the garden into a hell-brew. The idle and the vicious came with their stone jugs, and violence and riot flowed out.

The government of Virginia was remote and its arm short and feeble; but the men who held the lands west of the mountains against the savages under grants from George, and after that held them against George himself, were efficient and expeditious. They had long patience, but when that failed they went up from their fields and drove the thing before them out of the land, like a scourge of God.

There came a day, then, when my Uncle Abner and Squire Randolph rode through the gap of the mountains to have the thing out with Doomdorf. The work of this brew, which had the odors of Eden and the impulses of the devil in it, could be borne no longer. The drunken Negroes had shot old Duncan's cattle and burned his haystacks, and the land was on its feet.

They rode alone, but they were worth an army of little men. Randolph was vain and pompous and given over to extravagance of words, but he was a gentleman beneath it, and fear was an alien and a stranger to him. And Abner was the right hand of the land.

It was a day in early summer and the sun lay hot. They crossed through the broken spine of the mountains and trailed along the river in the shade of the great chestnut trees. The road was only a path and the horses went one before the other. It left the river when the rock began to rise and, making a detour through the grove of peach trees, reached the house on the mountain side. Randolph and Abner got down, unsaddled their horses and turned them out to graze, for their business with Doomdorf would not be over in an hour. Then they took a steep path that brought them out on the mountain side of the house.

A man sat on a big red-roan horse in the paved court before the door. He was a gaunt old man. He sat bare-headed, the palms of his hands resting on the pommel of his saddle, his chin sunk in his black stock, his face in retrospection, the wind moving gently his great shock of voluminous white hair. Under him the huge red horse stood with his legs spread out like a horse of stone.

There was no sound. The door to the house was closed; insects moved in the sun; a shadow crept out from the motionless figure, and swarms of yellow butterflies maneuvered like an army.

Abner and Randolph stopped. They knew the tragic figure—a circuit rider of the hills who preached the invective of Isaiah as though he were the mouthpiece of a militant and avenging overlord; as though the government of Virginia were the awful theocracy of the Book of Kings. The horse was dripping with sweat and the man bore the dust and the evidences of a journey on him.

"Bronson," said Abner, "where is Doomdorf?"

The old man lifted his head and looked down at Abner over the pommel of the saddle. "'Surely,'" he said, "'he covereth his feet in his summer chamber.'"

Abner went over and knocked on the closed door, and presently the white, frightened face of a woman looked out at him. She was a little, faded woman, with fair hair, a broad foreign face, but with the delicate evidences of gentle blood.

Abner repeated his question. "Where is Doomdorf?"

"Oh, sir," she answered with a queer lisping accent, "he went to lie down in his south room after his midday meal, as his custom is; and

I went to the orchard to gather any fruit that might be ripened." She hesitated and her voice lisped into a whisper: "He is not come out and I cannot wake him."

The two men followed her through the hall and up the stairway to the door.

"It is always bolted," she said, "when he goes to lie down." And she knocked feebly with the tips of her fingers.

There was no answer and Randolph rattled the doorknob. "Come out, Doomdorf!" he called in his big, bellowing voice.

There was only silence and the echoes of the words among the rafters. Then Randolph set his shoulder to the door and burst it open.

They went in. The room was flooded with sun from the tall south windows. Doomdorf lay on a couch in a little offset of the room, a great scarlet patch on his bosom and a pool of scarlet on the floor.

The woman stood for a moment staring; then she cried out: "At last I have killed him!" And she ran like a frightened hare.

The two men closed the door and went over to the couch. Doomdorf had been shot to death. There was a great ragged hole in his waistcoat. They began to look about for the weapon with which the deed had been accomplished, and in a moment found it—a fowling piece lying in two dogwood forks against the wall. The gun had just been fired; there was a freshly exploded paper cap under the hammer.

There was little else in the room—a loom-woven rag carpet on the floor; wooden shutters flung back from the windows; a great oak table, and on it a big, round glass water bottle, filled to its glass stopper with raw liquor from the still. The stuff was limpid and clear as spring water; and, but for its pungent odor, one would have taken it for God's brew instead of Doomdorf's. The sun lay on it and against the wall where hung the weapon that had ejected the dead man out of life.

"Abner," said Randolph, "this is murder! The woman took that gun down from the wall and shot Doomdorf while he slept."

Abner was standing by the table, his fingers round his chin. "Randolph," he replied, "what brought Bronson here?"

"The same outrages that brought us," said Randolph. "The mad old circuit rider has been preaching a crusade against Doomdorf far and wide in the hills."

Abner answered, without taking his fingers from about his chin: "You think this woman killed Doomdorf? Well, let us go and ask Bronson who killed him."

They closed the door, leaving the dead man on his couch, and went down into the court.

The old circuit rider had put away his horse and got an ax. He had taken off his coat and pushed his shirtsleeves up over his long elbows. He was on his way to the still to destroy the barrels of liquor. He stopped when the two men came out, and Abner called to him. "Bronson," he said, "who killed Doomdorf?"

"I killed him," replied the old man, and went on toward the still.

Randolph swore under his breath. "By the Almighty," he said, "everybody couldn't kill him!"

"Who can tell how many had a hand in it?" replied Abner.

"Two have confessed!" cried Randolph. "Was there perhaps a third? Did you kill him, Abner? And I too? Man, the thing is impossible!"

"The impossible," replied Abner, "looks here like the truth. Come with me, Randolph, and I will show you a thing more impossible than this."

They returned through the house and up the stairs to the room. Abner closed the door behind them. "Look at this bolt," he said; "it is on the inside and not connected with the lock. How did the one who killed Doomdorf get into this room, since the door was bolted?"

"Through the windows," replied Randolph.

There were but two windows, facing the south, through which the sun entered. Abner led Randolph to them. "Look!" he said. "The wall of the house is plumb with the sheer face of the rock. It is a hundred feet to the river and

the rock is as smooth as a sheet of glass. But that is not all. Look at these window frames; they are cemented into their casement with dust and they are bound along their edges with cobwebs. These windows have not been opened. How did the assassin enter?"

"The answer is evident," said Randolph: "The one who killed Doomdorf hid in the room until he was asleep; then he shot him and went out."

"The explanation is excellent but for one thing," replied Abner: "How did the assassin bolt the door behind him on the inside of this room after he had gone out?"

Randolph flung out his arms with a hopeless gesture. "Who knows?" he cried. "Maybe Doomdorf killed himself."

Abner laughed. "And after firing a handful of shot into his heart he got up and put the gun back carefully into the forks against the wall!"

"Well," cried Randolph, "there is one open road out of this mystery. Bronson and this woman say they killed Doomdorf, and if they killed him they surely know how they did it. Let us go down and ask them."

"In the law court," replied Abner, "that procedure would be considered sound sense; but we are in God's court and things are managed there in a somewhat stranger way. Before we go let us find out, if we can, at what hour it was that Doomdorf died."

He went over and took a big silver watch out of the dead man's pocket. It was broken by a shot and the hands lay at one hour after noon. He stood for a moment fingering his chin.

"At one o'clock," he said. "Bronson, I think, was on the road to this place, and the woman was on the mountain among the peach trees." Randolph threw back his shoulders. "Why waste time in a speculation about it, Abner?" he said. "We know who did this thing. Let us go and get the story of it out of their own mouths. Doomdorf died by the hands of either Bronson or this woman."

"I could better believe it," replied Abner, "but for the running of a certain awful law."

"What law?" said Randolph. "Is it a statute of Virginia?"

"It is a statute," replied Abner, "of an authority somewhat higher. Mark the language of it: 'He that killeth with the sword must be killed with the sword.'"

He came over and took Randolph by the arm. "Must! Randolph, did you mark particularly the word 'must'? It is a mandatory law. There is no room in it for the vicissitudes of chance or fortune. There is no way round that word. Thus, we reap what we sow and nothing else; thus, we receive what we give and nothing else. It is the weapon in our own hands that finally destroys us. You are looking at it now." And he turned him about so that the table and the weapon and the dead man were before him. "'He that killeth with the sword must be killed with the sword.' And now," he said, "let us go and try the method of the law courts. Your faith is in the wisdom of their ways."

They found the old circuit rider at work in the still, staving in Doomdorf's liquor casks, splitting the oak heads with his ax.

"Bronson," said Randolph, "how did you kill Doomdorf?"

The old man stopped and stood leaning on his ax. "I killed him, as Elijah killed the captains of Ahaziah and their fifties. But not by the hand of any man did I pray the Lord God to destroy Doomdorf, but with fire from heaven to destroy him." He stood up and extended his arms. "His hands were full of blood," he said. "With his abomination from these groves of Baal he stirred up the people to contention, to strife and murder. The widow and the orphan cried to heaven against him. 'I will surely hear their cry,' is the promise written in the Book. The land was weary of him; and I prayed the Lord God to destroy him with fire from heaven, as he destroyed the Princes of Gomorrah in their palaces!"

Randolph made a gesture as of one who dismisses the impossible, but Abner's face took on a deep, strange look.

"With fire from heaven!" he repeated slowly to himself. Then he asked a question. "A little while ago," he said, "when we came, I asked you where Doomdorf was, and you answered me in the language of the third chapter of the Book of Judges. Why did you answer me like that, Bronson?—'Surely he covereth his feet in his summer chamber.'"

"The woman told me that he had not come down from the room where he had gone up to sleep," replied the old man, "and that the door was locked. And then I knew that he was dead in his summer chamber like Eglon, King of Moab." He extended his arm toward the south. "I came here from the Great Valley," he said, "to cut down these groves of Baal and to empty out this abomination; but I did not know that the Lord had heard my prayer and visited His wrath on Doomdorf until I was come up into these mountains to his door. When the woman spoke I knew it." And he went away to his horse, leaving the ax among the ruined barrels.

Randolph interrupted. "Come, Abner," he said; "this is wasted time. Bronson did not kill Doomdorf."

Abner answered slowly in his deep, level voice: "Do you realize, Randolph, how Doomdorf died?"

"Not by fire from heaven, at any rate," said Randolph.

"Randolph," replied Abner, "are you sure?"

"Abner," cried Randolph, "you are pleased to jest, but I am in deadly earnest. A crime has been done here against the state. I am an officer of justice and I propose to discover the assassin if I can."

He walked away toward the house and Abner followed, his hands behind him and his great shoulders thrown loosely forward, with a grim smile about his mouth.

"It is no use to talk with the mad old preacher," Randolph went on. "Let him empty out the liquor and ride away. I won't issue a warrant against him. Prayer may be a handy implement to do a murder with, Abner, but it is not a deadly weapon under the statutes of Virginia. Doomdorf was dead when old Bronson got here with his Scriptural jargon. This woman killed Doomdorf. I shall put her to an inquisition."

"As you like," replied Abner. "Your faith remains in the methods of the law courts."

"Do you know of any better methods?" said Randolph.

"Perhaps," replied Abner, "when you have finished."

Night had entered the valley. The two men went into the house and set about preparing the corpse for burial. They got candles, and made a coffin, and put Doomdorf in it, and straightened out his limbs, and folded his arms across his shot-out heart. Then they set the coffin on benches in the hall.

They kindled a fire in the dining room and sat down before it, with the door open and the red firelight shining through on the dead man's narrow, everlasting house. The woman had put some cold meat, a golden cheese and a loaf on the table. They did not see her, but they heard her moving about the house; and finally, on the gravel court outside, her step and the whinny of a horse. Then she came in, dressed as for a journey.

Randolph sprang up. "Where are you going?" he said.

"To the sea and a ship," replied the woman. Then she indicated the hall with a gesture. "He is dead and I am free."

There was a sudden illumination in her face. Randolph took a step toward her. His voice was big and harsh. "Who killed Doomdorf?" he cried.

"I killed him," replied the woman. "It was fair!"

"Fair!" echoed the justice. "What do you mean by that?"

The woman shrugged her shoulders and put out her hands with a foreign gesture. "I remember an old, old man sitting against a sunny wall, and a little girl, and one who came and talked a long time with the old man, while the little girl plucked yellow flowers out of the grass and put them into her hair. Then finally the stranger gave the old man a gold chain and took the little girl away." She flung out her hands. "Oh, it

was fair to kill him!" She looked up with a queer, pathetic smile.

"The old man will be gone by now," she said; "but I shall perhaps find the wall there, with sun on it, and the yellow flowers in the grass. And now, may I go?"

It is the law of the story-teller's art that he does not tell a story. It is the listener who tells it. The story-teller does but provide him with the stimuli.

Randolph got up and walked about the floor. He was a justice of the peace in a day when that office was filled only by the landed gentry, after the English fashion; and the obligations of the law were strong on him. If he should take liberties with the letter of it, how could the weak and the evil be made to hold it in respect? Here was this woman before him a confessed assassin. Could he let her go?

Abner sat unmoving by the hearth, his elbow on the arm of his chair, his palm propping up his jaw, his face clouded in deep lines. Randolph was consumed with vanity and the weakness of ostentation, but he shouldered his duties for himself. Presently he stopped and looked at the woman, wan, faded like some prisoner of legend escaped out of fabled dungeons into the sun.

The firelight flickered past her to the box on the benches in the hall, and the vast, inscrutable justice of heaven entered and overcame him.

"Yes," he said. "Go! There is no jury in Virginia that would hold a woman for shooting a beast like that." And he thrust out his arm, with the fingers extended toward the dead man.

The woman made a little awkward curtsy. "I thank you, sir." Then she hesitated and lisped, "But I have not shoot him."

"Not shoot him!" cried Randolph. "Why, the man's heart is riddled!"

"Yes, sir," she said simply, like a child. "I kill him, but have not shoot him."

Randolph took two long strides toward the woman. "Not shoot him!" he repeated. "How then, in the name of heaven, did you kill Doomdorf?" And his big voice filled the empty places of the room.

"I will show you, sir," she said.

She turned and went away into the house. Presently she returned with something folded up in a linen towel. She put it on the table between the loaf of bread and the yellow cheese.

Randolph stood over the table, and the woman's deft fingers undid the towel from round its deadly contents; and presently the thing lay there uncovered.

It was a little crude model of a human figure done in wax with a needle thrust through the bosom.

Randolph stood up with a great intake of the breath. "Magic! By the eternal!"

"Yes, sir," the woman explained, in her voice and manner of a child. "I have try to kill him many times—oh, very many times!—with witch words which I have remembered; but always they fail. Then, at last, I make him in wax, and I put a needle through his heart; and I kill him very quickly."

It was clear as daylight, even to Randolph, that the woman was innocent. Her little harmless magic was the pathetic effort of a child to kill a dragon. He hesitated a moment before he spoke, and then he decided like the gentleman he was. If it helped the child to believe that her enchanted straw had slain the monster—well, he would let her believe it.

"And now, sir, may I go?"

Randolph looked at the woman in a sort of wonder. "Are you not afraid," he said, "of the night and the mountains, and the long road?"

"Oh no, sir," she replied simply. "The good God will be everywhere now."

It was an awful commentary on the dead man—that this strange half-child believed that all the evil in the world had gone out with him; that now he was dead, the sunlight of heaven would fill every nook and corner.

It was not a faith that either of the two men wished to shatter, and they let her go. It would be daylight presently and the road through the mountains to the Chesapeake was open.

Randolph came back to the fireside after he had helped her into the saddle, and sat down. He tapped on the hearth for some time idly with the iron poker; and then finally he spoke.

"This is the strangest thing that ever happened," he said. "Here's a mad old preacher who thinks that he killed Doomdorf with fire from heaven, like Elijah the Tishbite; and here is a simple child of a woman who thinks she killed him with a piece of magic of the Middle Ages— each as innocent of his death as I am. And, yet, by the eternal, the beast is dead!"

He drummed on the hearth with the poker, lifting it up and letting it drop through the hollow of his fingers.

"Somebody shot Doomdorf. But who? And how did he get into and out of that shut-up room? The assassin that killed Doomdorf must have gotten into the room to kill him. Now, how did he get in?"

He spoke as to himself; but my uncle sitting across the hearth replied: "Through the window."

"Through the window!" echoed Randolph. "Why, man, you yourself showed me that the window had not been opened, and the precipice below it a fly could hardly climb. Do you tell me now that the window was opened?"

"No," said Abner, "it was never opened."

Randolph got on his feet. "Abner," he cried, "are you saying that the one who killed Doomdorf climbed the sheer wall and got in through a closed window, without disturbing the dust or the cobwebs on the window frame?"

My uncle looked Randolph in the face. "The murderer of Doomdorf did even more," he said. "That assassin not only climbed the face of that precipice and got in through the closed window, but he shot Doomdorf to death and got out again through the closed window, without leaving a single track or trace behind, and without disturbing a grain of dust or a thread of a cobweb."

Randolph swore a great oath. "The thing is impossible!" he cried. "Men are not killed today in Virginia by black art or a curse of God."

"By black art, no," replied Abner; "but by the curse of God, yes. I think they are."

Randolph drove his clenched right hand into the palm of his left. "By the eternal!" he cried. "I would like to see the assassin who could do a murder like this, whether he be an imp from the pit or an angel out of heaven."

"Very well," replied Abner, undisturbed. "When he comes back tomorrow I will show you the assassin who killed Doomdorf."

When day broke they dug a grave and buried the dead man against the mountain among his peach trees. It was noon when that work was ended. Abner threw down his spade and looked up at the sun. "Randolph," he said, "let us go and lay an ambush for this assassin. He is on his way here."

And it was a strange ambush that he laid. When they were come again into the chamber where Doomdorf died he bolted the door; then he loaded the fowling piece and put it carefully back on its rack against the wall. After that he did another curious thing: He took the blood-stained coat, which they had stripped off the dead man when they had prepared his body for the earth, put a pillow in it and laid it on the couch precisely where Doomdorf had slept. And while he did these things Randolph stood in wonder and Abner talked:

"Look you, Randolph . . . We will trick the murderer . . . We will catch him in the act."

Then he went over and took the puzzled justice by the arm. "Watch!" he said. "The assassin is coming along the wall!"

But Randolph heard nothing, saw nothing. Only the sun entered. Abner's hand tightened on his arm. "It is here! Look!" And he pointed to the wall.

Randolph, following the extended finger, saw a tiny brilliant disk of light moving slowly up the wall toward the lock of the fowling piece. Abner's hand became a vise and his voice rang as over metal. "'He that killeth with the sword must be killed with the sword.' It is the water bottle, full of Doomdorf's liquid, focusing the sun. . . . And look, Randolph, how Bronson's prayer was answered!"

The tiny disk of light traveled on the plate of the lock.

"It is fire from heaven!"

The words rang above the roar of the fowling piece, and Randolph saw the dead man's coat leap up on the couch, riddled by the shot. The gun, in its natural position on the rack, pointed to the couch standing at the end of the chamber, beyond the offset of the wall, and the focused sun had exploded the percussion cap.

Randolph made a great gesture, with his arm extended. "It is a world," he said, "filled with the mysterious joinder of accident!"

"It is a world," replied Abner, "filled with the mysterious justice of God!"

THE ADVENTURE OF THE SPECKLED BAND
ARTHUR CONAN DOYLE

ONE OF THE MOST astonishing elements of the Sherlock Holmes stories by Arthur Conan Doyle (1859–1930) is that, although written in the Victorian era, they lack the overwrought verbosity so prevalent in the prose of that time and remain as readable and fresh as anything produced in recent times. Equally astonishing is that Doyle believed that his most important fiction was such historical novels and short-story collections as *Micah Clarke* (1889), *The White Company* (1891), *The Exploits of Brigadier Gerard* (1896), and *Sir Nigel* (1906). He believed his most significant nonfiction work was in the spiritualism field, to which he devoted the last twenty years of his life, a considerable portion of his fortune, and prodigious energy, producing many major and not-so-major works on the subject.

He was deluded, of course, as Holmes was his supreme achievement, arguably the most famous fictional character ever created. The great detective's first appearance was in the novel *A Study in Scarlet* (1887), followed by *The Sign of Four* (1890), neither of which changed the course of the detective story. This occurred when the first Holmes short story, "A Scandal in Bohemia," was published in *The Strand Magazine* (July 1891), bringing the world's first private detective to a huge readership. Monthly publication of new Holmes stories became so widely anticipated that eager readers queued up at news stalls awaiting each new issue.

One of the most famous Holmes axioms was that when the impossible was eliminated, whatever remained must be the truth. This theory is in great evidence in the present story.

"The Adventure of the Speckled Band" was first published in the February 1892 issue of *The Strand Magazine*; it was first collected in book form in *The Adventures of Sherlock Holmes* (London, Newnes, 1892).

THE ADVENTURE OF THE SPECKLED BAND

ARTHUR CONAN DOYLE

IN GLANCING over my notes of the seventy-odd cases in which I have during the last eight years studied the methods of my friend Sherlock Holmes, I find many tragic, some comic, a large number merely strange, but none commonplace; for, working as he did rather for the love of his art than for the acquirement of wealth, he refused to associate himself with any investigation which did not tend towards the unusual, and even the fantastic. Of all these varied cases, however, I cannot recall any which presented more singular features than that which was associated with the well-known Surrey family of the Roylotts of Stoke Moran. The events in question occurred in the early days of my association with Holmes, when we were sharing rooms as bachelors, in Baker-street. It is possible that I might have placed them upon record before, but a promise of secrecy was made at the time, from which I have only been freed during the last month by the untimely death of the lady to whom the pledge was given. It is perhaps as well that the facts should now come to light, for I have reasons to know that there are widespread rumours as to the death of Dr. Grimesby Roylott which tend to make the matter even more terrible than the truth.

It was early in April in the year '83 that I woke one morning to find Sherlock Holmes standing, fully dressed, by the side of my bed. He was a late riser as a rule, and, as the clock on the mantelpiece showed me that it was only a quarter past seven, I blinked up at him in some surprise, and perhaps just a little resentment, for I was myself regular in my habits.

"Very sorry to knock you up, Watson," said he, "but it's the common lot this morning. Mrs. Hudson has been knocked up, she retorted upon me, and I on you."

"What is it, then? A fire?"

"No, a client. It seems that a young lady has arrived in a considerable state of excitement, who insists upon seeing me. She is waiting now in the sitting-room. Now, when young ladies wander about the Metropolis at this hour of the morning, and knock sleepy people up out of their beds, I presume that it is something very pressing which they have to communicate. Should it prove to be an interesting case, you would, I am sure, wish to follow it from the outset. I thought at any rate that I should call you, and give you the chance."

"My dear fellow, I would not miss it for anything."

I had no keener pleasure than in following Holmes in his professional investigations, and in admiring the rapid deductions, as swift as intuitions, and yet always founded on a logical basis, with which he unravelled the problems which were submitted to him. I rapidly threw on my clothes, and was ready in a few minutes to accompany my friend down to the sitting-room. A lady dressed in black and heavily veiled, who had been sitting in the window, rose as we entered.

"Good morning, madam," said Holmes, cheerily. "My name is Sherlock Holmes. This is my intimate friend and associate, Dr. Watson, before whom you can speak as freely as before myself. Ha, I am glad to see that Mrs. Hudson has had the good sense to light the fire. Pray draw up to it, and I shall order you a cup of hot coffee, for I observe that you are shivering."

"It is not cold which makes me shiver," said the woman in a low voice, changing her seat as requested.

"What then?"

"It is fear, Mr. Holmes. It is terror." She raised her veil as she spoke, and we could see that she was indeed in a pitiable state of agitation, her face all drawn and grey, with restless, frightened eyes, like those of some hunted animal. Her features and figure were those of a woman of thirty, but her hair was shot with premature grey, and her expression was weary and haggard. Sherlock Holmes ran her over with one of his quick, all-comprehensive glances.

"You must not fear," said he, soothingly, bending forward and patting her forearm. "We shall soon set matters right, I have no doubt. You have come in by train this morning, I see."

"You know me, then?"

"No, but I observe the second half of a return ticket in the palm of your left glove. You must have started early, and yet you had a good drive in a dog-cart, along heavy roads, before you reached the station."

The lady gave a violent start, and stared in bewilderment at my companion.

"There is no mystery, my dear madam," said he, smiling. "The left arm of your jacket is spattered with mud in no less than seven places. The marks are perfectly fresh. There is no vehicle save a dog-cart which throws up mud in that way, and then only when you sit on the left hand side of the driver."

"Whatever your reasons may be, you are perfectly correct," said she. "I started from home before six, reached Leatherhead at twenty past, and came in by the first train to Waterloo. Sir, I can stand this strain no longer, I shall go mad if it continues. I have no one to turn to—none,

save only one, who cares for me, and he, poor fellow, can be of little aid. I have heard of you, Mr. Holmes; I have heard of you from Mrs. Farintosh, whom you helped in the hour of her sore need. It was from her that I had your address. Oh, sir, do you not think that you could help me too, and at least throw a little light through the dense darkness which surrounds me? At present it is out of my power to reward you for your services, but in a month or six weeks I shall be married, with the control of my own income, and then at least you shall not find me ungrateful."

Holmes turned to his desk, and unlocking it, drew out a small case-book which he consulted.

"Farintosh," said he. "Ah, yes, I recall the case; it was concerned with an opal tiara. I think it was before your time, Watson. I can only say, madam, that I shall be happy to devote the same care to your case as I did to that of your friend. As to reward, my profession is its own reward; but you are at liberty to defray whatever expenses I may be put to, at the time which suits you best. And now I beg that you will lay before us everything that may help us in forming an opinion upon the matter."

"Alas!" replied our visitor. "The very horror of my situation lies in the fact that my fears are so vague, and my suspicions depend so entirely upon small points, which might seem trivial to another, that even he to whom of all others I have a right to look for help and advice looks upon all that I tell him about it as the fancies of a nervous woman. He does not say so, but I can read it from his soothing answers and averted eyes. But I have heard, Mr. Holmes, that you can see deeply into the manifold wickedness of the human heart. You may advise me how to walk amid the dangers which encompass me."

"I am all attention, madam."

"My name is Helen Stoner, and I am living with my stepfather, who is the last survivor of one of the oldest Saxon families in England, the Roylotts of Stoke Moran, on the western border of Surrey."

Holmes nodded his head. "The name is familiar to me," said he.

"The family was at one time among the richest in England, and the estates extended over the borders into Berkshire in the north, and Hampshire in the west. In the last century, however, four successive heirs were of a dissolute and wasteful disposition, and the family ruin was eventually completed by a gambler in the days of the Regency. Nothing was left save a few acres of ground, and the two-hundred-year-old house, which is itself crushed under a heavy mortgage. The last squire dragged out his existence there, living the horrible life of an aristocratic pauper; but his only son, my stepfather, seeing that he must adapt himself to the new conditions, obtained an advance from a relative, which enabled him to take a medical degree, and went out to Calcutta, where, by his professional skill and his force of character, he established a large practice. In a fit of anger, however, caused by some robberies which had been perpetrated in the house, he beat his native butler to death, and narrowly escaped a capital sentence. As it was, he suffered a long term of imprisonment, and afterwards returned to England a morose and disappointed man.

"When Dr. Roylott was in India he married my mother, Mrs. Stoner, the young widow of Major-General Stoner, of the Bengal Artillery. My sister Julia and I were twins, and we were only two years old at the time of my mother's remarriage. She had a considerable sum of money, not less than a thousand a year, and this she bequeathed to Dr. Roylott entirely whilst we resided with him, with a provision that a certain annual sum should be allowed to each of us in the event of our marriage. Shortly after our return to England my mother died—she was killed eight years ago in a railway accident near Crewe. Dr. Roylott then abandoned his attempts to establish himself in practice in London, and took us to live with him in the old ancestral house at Stoke Moran. The money which my mother had left was enough for all our wants, and there seemed to be no obstacle to our happiness.

"But a terrible change came over our stepfather about this time. Instead of making friends and exchanging visits with our neighbours, who had at first been overjoyed to see a Roylott of Stoke Moran back in the old family seat, he shut himself up in his house, and seldom came out save to indulge in ferocious quarrels with whoever might cross his path. Violence of temper approaching to mania has been hereditary in the men of the family, and in my stepfather's case it had, I believe, been intensified by his long residence in the tropics. A series of disgraceful brawls took place, two of which ended in the police-court, until at last he became the terror of the village, and the folks would fly at his approach, for he is a man of immense strength, and absolutely uncontrollable in his anger.

"Last week he hurled the local blacksmith over a parapet into a stream, and it was only by paying over all the money which I could gather together that I was able to avert another public exposure. He had no friends at all save the wandering gipsies, and he would give these vagabonds leave to encamp upon the few acres of bramble-covered land which represent the family estate, and would accept in return the hospitality of their tents, wandering away with them sometimes for weeks on end. He has a passion also for Indian animals, which are sent over to him by a correspondent, and he has at this moment a cheetah and a baboon, which wander freely over his grounds, and are feared by the villagers almost as much as their master.

"You can imagine from what I say that my poor sister Julia and I had no great pleasure in our lives. No servant would stay with us, and for a long time we did all the work of the house. She was but thirty at the time of her death, and yet her hair had already begun to whiten, even as mine has."

"Your sister is dead, then?"

"She died just two years ago, and it is of her death that I wish to speak to you. You can understand that, living the life which I have described, we were little likely to see anyone of our own age and position. We had, however, an aunt, my mother's maiden sister, Miss Honoria Westphail, who lives near Harrow, and we were occasionally allowed to pay short visits at this lady's house.

Julia went there at Christmas two years ago, and met there a half-pay Major of Marines, to whom she became engaged. My stepfather learned of the engagement when my sister returned, and offered no objection to the marriage; but within a fortnight of the day which had been fixed for the wedding, the terrible event occurred which has deprived me of my only companion."

Sherlock Holmes had been leaning back in his chair with his eyes closed, and his head sunk in a cushion, but he half opened his lids now, and glanced across at his visitor.

"Pray be precise as to details," said he.

"It is easy for me to be so, for every event of that dreadful time is seared into my memory. The manor house is, as I have already said, very old, and only one wing is now inhabited. The bedrooms in this wing are on the ground floor, the sitting-rooms being in the central block of the buildings. Of these bedrooms the first is Dr. Roylott's, the second my sister's, and the third my own. There is no communication between them, but they all open out into the same corridor. Do I make myself plain?"

"Perfectly so."

"The windows of the three rooms open out upon the lawn. That fatal night Dr. Roylott had gone to his room early, though we knew that he had not retired to rest, for my sister was troubled by the smell of the strong Indian cigars which it was his custom to smoke. She left her room, therefore, and came into mine, where she sat for some time, chatting about her approaching wedding. At eleven o'clock she rose to leave me, but she paused at the door and looked back.

"'Tell me, Helen,' said she, 'have you ever heard anyone whistle in the dead of the night?'

"'Never,' said I.

"'I suppose that you could not possibly whistle yourself in your sleep?'

"'Certainly not. But why?'

"'Because during the last few nights I have always, about three in the morning, heard a low clear whistle. I am a light sleeper, and it has awakened me. I cannot tell where it came from— perhaps from the next room, perhaps from the lawn. I thought that I would just ask you whether you had heard it.'

"'No, I have not. It must be those wretched gipsies in the plantation.'

"'Very likely. And yet if it were on the lawn I wonder that you did not hear it also.'

"'Ah, but I sleep more heavily than you.'

"'Well, it is of no great consequence at any rate,' she smiled back at me, closed my door, and a few moments later I heard her key turn in the lock."

"Indeed," said Holmes. "Was it your custom always to lock yourselves in at night?"

"Always."

"And why?"

"I think that I mentioned to you that the Doctor kept a cheetah and a baboon. We had no feeling of security unless our doors were locked."

"Quite so. Pray proceed with your statement."

"I could not sleep that night. A vague feeling of impending misfortune impressed me. My sister and I, you will recollect, were twins, and you know how subtle are the links which bind two souls which are so closely allied. It was a wild night. The wind was howling outside, and the rain was beating and splashing against the windows. Suddenly, amidst all the hubbub of the gale, there burst forth the wild scream of a terrified woman. I knew that it was my sister's voice. I sprang from my bed, wrapped a shawl round me, and rushed into the corridor. As I opened my door I seemed to hear a low whistle, such as my sister described, and a few moments later a clanging sound, as if a mass of metal had fallen. As I ran down the passage my sister's door was unlocked, and revolved slowly upon its hinges. I stared at it horror-stricken, not knowing what was to issue from it. By the light of the corridor lamp I saw my sister appear at the opening, her face blanched with terror, her hands groping for help, her whole figure swaying to and fro like that of a drunkard. I ran to her and threw my arms round her, but at that moment her knees seemed to give way and she fell to the ground. She writhed as one who is in terrible pain, and her limbs were dreadfully convulsed. At first I thought that she had not recognised me, but as I bent over her she suddenly shrieked out in a voice which I shall never forget, 'Oh, my God! Helen! It was the band! The speckled band!' There was something else which she would fain have said, and she stabbed with her finger into the air in the direction of the Doctor's room, but a fresh convulsion seized her and choked her words. I rushed out, calling loudly for my stepfather, and I met him hastening from his room in his dressing-gown. When he reached my sister's side she was unconscious, and though he poured brandy down her throat, and sent for medical aid from the village, all efforts were in vain, for she slowly sank and died without having recovered her consciousness. Such was the dreadful end of my beloved sister."

"One moment," said Holmes; "are you sure about this whistle and metallic sound? Could you swear to it?"

"That was what the county coroner asked me at the inquiry. It is my strong impression that I heard it, and yet among the crash of the gale, and the creaking of an old house, I may possibly have been deceived."

"Was your sister dressed?"

"No, she was in her nightdress. In her right hand was found the charred stump of a match, and in her left a matchbox."

"Showing that she had struck a light and looked about her when the alarm took place. That is important. And what conclusions did the coroner come to?"

"He investigated the case with great care, for Dr. Roylott's conduct had long been notorious in the county, but he was unable to find any satisfactory cause of death. My evidence showed that the door had been fastened upon the inner side, and the windows were blocked by old-fashioned shutters with broad iron bars, which were secured every night. The walls were carefully sounded, and were shown to be quite solid all round, and the flooring was also thoroughly examined, with the same result. The chimney is wide, but is barred up by four large staples. It is

certain, therefore, that my sister was quite alone when she met her end. Besides, there were no marks of any violence upon her."

"How about poison?"

"The doctors examined her for it, but without success."

"What do you think that this unfortunate lady died of, then?"

"It is my belief that she died of pure fear and nervous shock, though what it was which frightened her I cannot imagine."

"Were there gipsies in the plantation at the time?"

"Yes, there are nearly always some there."

"Ah, and what did you gather from this allusion to a band—a speckled band?"

"Sometimes I have thought that it was merely the wild talk of delirium, sometimes that it may have referred to some band of people, perhaps to these very gipsies in the plantation. I do not know whether the spotted handkerchiefs which so many of them wear over their heads might have suggested the strange adjective which she used."

Holmes shook his head like a man who is far from being satisfied.

"These are very deep waters," said he; "pray go on with your narrative."

"Two years have passed since then, and my life has been until lately lonelier than ever. A month ago, however, a dear friend, whom I have known for many years, has done me the honour to ask my hand in marriage. His name is Armitage—Percy Armitage—the second son of Mr. Armitage, of Crane Water, near Reading. My stepfather has offered no opposition to the match, and we are to be married in the course of the spring. Two days ago some repairs were started in the west wing of the building, and my bedroom wall has been pierced, so that I have had to move into the chamber in which my sister died, and to sleep in the very bed in which she slept. Imagine, then, my thrill of terror when last night, as I lay awake, thinking over her terrible fate, I suddenly heard in the silence of the night the low whistle which had been the herald of her own death. I sprang up and lit the lamp, but nothing was to be seen in the room. I was too shaken to go to bed again, however, so I dressed, and as soon as it was daylight I slipped down, got a dog-cart at the 'Crown' inn, which is opposite, and drove to Leatherhead, from whence I have come on this morning with the one object of seeing you and asking your advice."

"You have done wisely," said my friend. "But have you told me all?"

"Yes, all."

"Miss Roylott, you have not. You are screening your stepfather."

"Why, what do you mean?"

For answer Holmes pushed back the frill of black lace which fringed the hand that lay upon our visitor's knee. Five little livid spots, the marks of four fingers and a thumb, were printed upon the white wrist.

"You have been cruelly used," said Holmes.

The lady coloured deeply, and covered over her injured wrist. "He is a hard man," she said, "and perhaps he hardly knows his own strength."

There was a long silence, during which Holmes leaned his chin upon his hands and stared into the crackling fire.

"This is a very deep business," he said at last. "There are a thousand details which I should desire to know before I decide upon our course of action. Yet we have not a moment to lose. If we were to come to Stoke Moran to-day, would it be possible for us to see over these rooms without the knowledge of your stepfather?"

"As it happens, he spoke of coming into town to-day upon some most important business. It is probable that he will be away all day, and that there would be nothing to disturb you. We have a housekeeper now, but she is old and foolish, and I could easily get her out of the way."

"Excellent. You are not averse to this trip, Watson?"

"By no means."

"Then we shall both come. What are you going to do yourself?"

"I have one or two things which I would wish to do now that I am in town. But I shall return by the twelve o'clock train, so as to be there in time for your coming."

"And you may expect us early in the afternoon. I have myself some small business matters to attend to. Will you not wait and breakfast?"

"No, I must go. My heart is lightened already since I have confided my trouble to you. I shall look forward to seeing you again this afternoon." She dropped her thick black veil over her face, and glided from the room.

"And what do you think of it all, Watson?" asked Sherlock Holmes, leaning back in his chair.

"It seems to me to be a most dark and sinister business."

"Dark enough, and sinister enough."

"Yet if the lady is correct in saying that the flooring and walls are sound, and that the door, window, and chimney are impassable, then her sister must have been undoubtedly alone when she met her mysterious end."

"What becomes, then, of these nocturnal whistles, and what of the very peculiar words of the dying woman?"

"I cannot think."

"When you combine the ideas of whistles at night, the presence of a band of gipsies who are on intimate terms with this old Doctor, the fact that we have every reason to believe that the Doctor has an interest in preventing his stepdaughter's marriage, the dying allusion to a band, and finally, the fact that Miss Helen Stoner heard a metallic clang, which might have been caused by one of those metal bars which secured the shutters falling back into their place, I think that there is good ground to think that the mystery may be cleared along those lines."

"But what, then, did the gipsies do?"

"I cannot imagine."

"I see many objections to any such theory."

"And so do I. It is precisely for that reason that we are going to Stoke Moran this day. I want to see whether the objections are fatal, or if they may be explained away. But what, in the name of the devil!"

The ejaculation had been drawn from my

companion by the fact that our door had been suddenly dashed open, and that a huge man had framed himself in the aperture. His costume was a peculiar mixture of the professional and of the agricultural, having a black top hat, a long frock coat, and a pair of high gaiters, with a hunting crop swinging in his hand. So tall was he that his hat actually brushed the cross bar of the doorway, and his breadth seemed to span it across from side to side. A large face, seared with a thousand wrinkles, burned yellow with the sun, and marked with every evil passion, was turned from one to the other of us, while his deep-set, bile-shot eyes, and his high thin fleshless nose, gave him somewhat the resemblance to a fierce old bird of prey.

"Which of you is Holmes?" asked this apparition.

"My name, sir, but you have the advantage of me," said my companion, quietly.

"I am Dr. Grimesby Roylott, of Stoke Moran."

"Indeed, Doctor," said Holmes, blandly. "Pray take a seat."

"I will do nothing of the kind. My stepdaughter has been here. I have traced her. What has she been saying to you?"

"It is a little cold for the time of the year," said Holmes.

"What has she been saying to you?" screamed the old man furiously.

"But I have heard that the crocuses promise well," continued my companion imperturbably.

"Ha! You put me off, do you?" said our new visitor, taking a step forward, and shaking his hunting crop. "I know you, you scoundrel! I have heard of you before. You are Holmes the meddler."

My friend smiled.

"Holmes the busybody!"

His smile broadened.

"Holmes the Scotland-yard Jack-in-office!"

Holmes chuckled heartily. "Your conversation is most entertaining," said he. "When you go out close the door, for there is a decided draught."

"I will go when I have said my say. Don't you dare to meddle with my affairs. I know that Miss Stoner has been here—I traced her! I am a dangerous man to fall foul of! See here." He stepped swiftly forward, seized the poker, and bent it into a curve with his huge brown hands.

"See that you keep yourself out of my grip," he snarled, and hurling the twisted poker into the fireplace, he strode out of the room.

"He seems a very amiable person," said Holmes, laughing. "I am not quite so bulky, but if he had remained I might have shown him that my grip was not much more feeble than his own." As he spoke he picked up the steel poker, and with a sudden effort straightened it out again.

"Fancy his having the insolence to confound me with the official detective force! This incident gives zest to our investigation, however, and I only trust that our little friend will not suffer from her imprudence in allowing this brute to trace her. And now, Watson, we shall order breakfast, and afterwards I shall walk down to Doctors' Commons, where I hope to get some data which may help us in this matter."

It was nearly one o'clock when Sherlock Holmes returned from his excursion. He held in his hand a sheet of blue paper, scrawled over with notes and figures.

"I have seen the will of the deceased wife," said he. "To determine its exact meaning I have been obliged to work out the present prices of the investments with which it is concerned. The total income, which at the time of the wife's death was little short of £1,100, is now through the fall in agricultural prices not more than £750. Each daughter can claim an income of £250, in case of marriage. It is evident, therefore, that if both girls had married this beauty would have had a mere pittance, while even one of them would cripple him to a very serious extent. My morning's work has not been wasted, since it has proved that he has the very strongest motives for standing in the way of anything of the sort. And now, Watson, this is too serious for dawdling, especially as the old man is aware that we are interesting ourselves in his affairs, so if you are ready we shall call a cab and drive to Waterloo. I should be very much obliged if you would slip your revolver into your pocket. An Eley's No. 2 is an excellent argument with gentlemen who can twist steel pokers into knots. That and a tooth-brush are, I think, all that we need."

At Waterloo we were fortunate in catching a train for Leatherhead, where we hired a trap at the station inn, and drove for four or five miles through the lovely Surrey lanes. It was a perfect day, with a bright sun and a few fleecy clouds in the heavens. The trees and wayside hedges were just throwing out their first green shoots, and the air was full of the pleasant smell of the moist earth. To me at least there was a strange contrast between the sweet promise of the spring and this sinister quest upon which we were engaged. My companion sat in the front of the trap, his arms folded, his hat pulled down over his eyes, and his chin sunk upon his breast, buried in the deepest thought. Suddenly, however, he started, tapped me on the shoulder, and pointed over the meadows.

"Look there!" said he.

A heavily-timbered park stretched up in a gentle slope, thickening into a grove at the highest point. From amidst the branches there jutted out the grey gables and high roof-tree of a very old mansion.

"Stoke Moran?" said he.

"Yes, sir, that be the house of Dr. Grimesby Roylott," remarked the driver.

"There is some building going on there," said Holmes; "that is where we are going."

"There's the village," said the driver, pointing to a cluster of roofs some distance to the left; "but if you want to get to the house, you'll find it shorter to get over this stile, and so by the footpath over the fields. There it is, where the lady is walking."

"And the lady, I fancy, is Miss Stoner," observed Holmes, shading his eyes. "Yes, I think we had better do as you suggest."

We got off, paid our fare, and the trap rattled back on its way to Leatherhead.

"I thought it as well," said Holmes, as we climbed the stile, "that this fellow should think we had come here as architects, or on some definite business. It may stop his gossip. Good afternoon, Miss Stoner. You see that we have been as good as our word."

Our client of the morning had hurried forward to meet us with a face which spoke her joy. "I have been waiting so eagerly for you," she cried, shaking hands with us warmly. "All has turned out splendidly. Dr. Roylott has gone to town, and it is unlikely that he will be back before evening."

"We have had the pleasure of making the Doctor's acquaintance," said Holmes, and in a few words he sketched out what had occurred. Miss Stoner turned white to the lips as she listened.

"Good heavens!" she cried, "he has followed me, then."

"So it appears."

"He is so cunning that I never know when I am safe from him. What will he say when he returns?"

"He must guard himself, for he may find that there is someone more cunning than himself upon his track. You must lock yourself up from him to-night. If he is violent, we shall take you away to your aunt's at Harrow. Now, we must make the best use of our time, so kindly take us at once to the rooms which we are to examine."

The building was of grey, lichen-blotched stone, with a high central portion, and two curving wings, like the claws of a crab, thrown out on each side. In one of these wings the windows were broken, and blocked with wooden boards, while the roof was partly caved in, a picture of ruin. The central portion was in little better repair, but the right-hand block was comparatively modern, and the blinds in the windows, with the blue smoke curling up from the chimneys, showed that this was where the family resided. Some scaffolding had been erected against the end wall, and the stonework had been broken into, but there were no signs of any workmen at the moment of our visit. Holmes walked slowly up and down the ill-trimmed lawn, and examined with deep attention the outsides of the windows.

"This, I take it, belongs to the room in which you used to sleep, the centre one to your sister's, and the one next to the main building to Dr. Roylott's chamber?"

"Exactly so. But I am now sleeping in the middle one."

"Pending the alterations, as I understand. By the way, there does not seem to be any very pressing need for repairs at that end wall."

"There were none. I believe that it was an excuse to move me from my room."

"Ah! that is suggestive. Now, on the other side of this narrow wing runs the corridor from which these three rooms open. There are windows in it, of course?"

"Yes, but very small ones. Too narrow for anyone to pass through."

"As you both locked your doors at night your rooms were unapproachable from that side. Now, would you have the kindness to go into your room, and to bar your shutters."

Miss Stoner did so, and Holmes, after a careful examination through the open window, endeavoured in every way to force the shutter open, but without success. There was no slit through which a knife could be passed to raise the bar. Then with his lens he tested the hinges, but they were of solid iron, built firmly into the massive masonry. "Hum!" said he, scratching his chin in some perplexity, "my theory certainly presents some difficulties. No one could pass these shutters if they were bolted. Well, we shall see if the inside throws any light upon the matter."

A small side door led into the white-washed corridor from which the three bedrooms opened. Holmes refused to examine the third chamber, so we passed at once to the second, that in which Miss Stoner was now sleeping, and in which her sister had met with her fate. It was a homely little room, with a low ceiling and a gaping fireplace, after the fashion of old country houses. A brown chest of drawers stood in one corner, a narrow white-counterpaned bed in another, and a dressing-table on the left-hand side of the window. These articles, with two small wickerwork chairs, made up all the furniture in the room, save for a square of Wilton carpet in the centre. The boards round and the panelling of the walls were of brown, worm-eaten oak, so old and discoloured that it may have dated from the original building of the house. Holmes drew one of the chairs into a corner and sat silent, while his eyes travelled round and round and up and down, taking in every detail of the apartment.

"Where does that bell communicate with?" he asked at last, pointing to a thick bell-rope which hung down beside the bed, the tassel actually lying upon the pillow.

"It goes to the housekeeper's room."

"It looks newer than the other things?"

"Yes, it was only put there a couple of years ago."

"Your sister asked for it, I suppose?"

"No, I never heard of her using it. We used always to get what we wanted for ourselves."

"Indeed, it seemed unnecessary to put so nice a bell-pull there. You will excuse me for a few minutes while I satisfy myself as to this floor." He threw himself down upon his face with his lens in his hand, and crawled swiftly backwards and forwards, examining minutely the cracks between the boards. Then he did the same with the woodwork with which the chamber was panelled. Finally he walked over to the bed and spent some time in staring at it, and in running his eye up and down the wall. Finally he took the bell-rope in his hand and gave it a brisk tug.

"Why, it's a dummy," said he.

"Won't it ring?"

"No, it is not even attached to a wire. This is very interesting. You can see now that it is fastened to a hook just above where the little opening for the ventilator is."

"How very absurd! I never noticed that before."

"Very strange!" muttered Holmes, pulling

at the rope. "There are one or two very singular points about this room. For example, what a fool a builder must be to open a ventilator into another room, when, with the same trouble, he might have communicated with the outside air!"

"That is also quite modern," said the lady.

"Done about the same time as the bell-rope?" remarked Holmes.

"Yes, there were several little changes carried out about that time."

"They seem to have been of a most interesting character—dummy bell-ropes, and ventilators which do not ventilate. With your permission, Miss Stoner, we shall now carry our researches into the inner apartment."

Dr. Grimesby Roylott's chamber was larger than that of his stepdaughter, but was as plainly furnished. A camp bed, a small wooden shelf full of books, mostly of a technical character, an armchair beside the bed, a plain wooden chair against the wall, a round table, and a large iron safe were the principal things which met the eye. Holmes walked slowly round and examined each and all of them with the keenest interest.

"What's in here?" he asked, tapping the safe.

"My stepfather's business papers."

"Oh! you have seen inside, then?"

"Only once, some years ago. I remember that it was full of papers."

"There isn't a cat in it, for example?"

"No. What a strange idea!"

"Well, look at this!" He took up a small saucer of milk which stood on the top of it.

"No; we don't keep a cat. But there is a cheetah and a baboon."

"Ah, yes, of course! Well, a cheetah is just a big cat, and yet a saucer of milk does not go very far in satisfying its wants, I daresay. There is one point which I should wish to determine." He squatted down in front of the wooden chair, and examined the seat of it with the greatest attention.

"Thank you. That is quite settled," said he, rising and putting his lens in his pocket. "Hullo! here is something interesting!"

The object which had caught his eye was a small dog lash hung on one corner of the bed. The lash, however, was curled upon itself, and tied so as to make a loop of whipcord.

"What do you make of that, Watson?"

"It's a common enough lash. But I don't know why it should be tied."

"That is not quite so common, is it? Ah, me! it's a wicked world, and when a clever man turns his brains to crime it is the worst of all. I think that I have seen enough now, Miss Stoner, and, with your permission, we shall walk out upon the lawn."

I had never seen my friend's face so grim, or his brow so dark, as it was when we turned from the scene of this investigation. We had walked several times up and down the lawn, neither Miss Stoner nor myself liking to break in upon his thoughts, before he roused himself from his reverie.

"It is very essential, Miss Stoner," said he, "that you should absolutely follow my advice in every respect."

"I shall most certainly do so."

"The matter is too serious for any hesitation. Your life may depend upon your compliance."

"I assure that I am in your hands."

"In the first place, both my friend and I must spend the night in your room."

Both Miss Stoner and I gazed at him in astonishment.

"Yes, it must be so. Let me explain. I believe that that is the village inn over there?"

"Yes, that is the 'Crown.'"

"Very good. Your windows would be visible from there?"

"Certainly."

"You must confine yourself to your room, on pretence of a headache, when your stepfather comes back. Then when you hear him retire for the night, you must open the shutters of your window, undo the hasp, put your lamp there as a signal to us, and then withdraw quietly with everything which you are likely to want into the room which you used to occupy. I have no doubt that, in spite of the repairs, you could manage there for one night."

"Oh, yes, easily."

"The rest you will leave in our hands."

"But what will you do?"

"We shall spend the night in your room, and we shall investigate the cause of this noise which has disturbed you."

"I believe, Mr. Holmes, that you have already made up your mind," said Miss Stoner, laying her hand upon my companion's sleeve.

"Perhaps I have."

"Then for pity's sake tell me what was the cause of my sister's death."

"I should prefer to have clearer proofs before I speak."

"You can at least tell me whether my own thought is correct, and if she died from some sudden fright."

"No, I do not think so. I think that there was probably some more tangible cause. And now, Miss Stoner, we must leave you, for if Dr. Roylott returned and saw us, our journey would be in vain. Good-bye, and be brave, for if you will do what I have told you, you may rest assured that we shall soon drive away the dangers that threaten you."

Sherlock Holmes and I had no difficulty in engaging a bedroom and sitting-room at the "Crown" Inn. They were on the upper floor, and from our window we could command a view of the avenue gate, and of the inhabited wing of Stoke Moran Manor House. At dusk we saw Dr. Grimesby Roylott drive past, his huge form looming up beside the little figure of the lad who drove him. The boy had some slight difficulty in undoing the heavy iron gates, and we heard the hoarse roar of the doctor's voice, and saw the fury with which he shook his clenched fists at him. The trap drove on, and a few minutes later we saw a sudden light spring up among the trees as the lamp was lit in one of the sitting-rooms.

"Do you know, Watson," said Holmes, as we sat together in the gathering darkness, "I have really some scruples as to taking you to-night. There is a distinct element of danger."

"Can I be of assistance?"

"Your presence might be invaluable."

"Then I shall certainly come."

"It is very kind of you."

"You speak of danger. You have evidently seen more in these rooms than was visible to me."

"No, but I fancy that I may have deduced a little more. I imagine that you saw all that I did."

"I saw nothing remarkable save the bell rope, and what purpose that could answer I confess is more than I can imagine."

"You saw the ventilator, too?"

"Yes, but I do not think that it is such a very unusual thing to have a small opening between two rooms. It was so small that a rat could hardly pass through."

"I knew that we should find a ventilator before ever we came to Stoke Moran."

"My dear Holmes!"

"Oh, yes, I did. You remember in her statement she said that her sister could smell Dr. Roylott's cigar. Now, of course that suggested at once that there must be a communication between the two rooms. It could only be a small one, or it would have been remarked upon at the Coroner's inquiry. I deduced a ventilator."

"But what harm can there be in that?"

"Well, there is at least a curious coincidence of dates. A ventilator is made, a cord is hung, and a lady who sleeps in the bed dies. Does not that strike you?"

"I cannot as yet see any connection."

"Did you observe anything very peculiar about that bed?"

"No."

"It was clamped to the floor. Did you ever see a bed fastened like that before?"

"I cannot say that I have."

"The lady could not move her bed. It must always be in the same relative position to the ventilator and to the rope—for so we may call it, since it was clearly never meant for a bell-pull."

"Holmes," I cried, "I seem to see dimly what you are hinting at. We are only just in time to prevent some subtle and horrible crime."

"Subtle enough, and horrible enough. When a doctor does go wrong, he is the first of criminals. He has nerve and he has knowledge. Palmer and Pritchard were among the heads of their profession. This man strikes even deeper, but I think, Watson, that we shall be able to strike deeper still. But we shall have horrors enough before the night is over; for goodness' sake let us have a quiet pipe, and turn our minds for a few hours to something more cheerful."

About nine o'clock the light among the trees was extinguished, and all was dark in the direction of the Manor House. Two hours passed slowly away, and then, suddenly, just at the stroke of eleven, a single bright light shone out right in front of us.

"That is our signal," said Holmes, springing to his feet; "it comes from the middle window."

As we passed out he exchanged a few words with the landlord, explaining that we were going on a late visit to an acquaintance, and that it was possible that we might spend the night there. A moment later we were out on the dark road, a chill wind blowing in our faces, and one yellow light twinkling in front of us through the gloom to guide us on our sombre errand.

There was little difficulty in entering the grounds, for unrepaired breaches gaped in the old park wall. Making our way among the trees, we reached the lawn, crossed it, and were about to enter through the window, when out from a clump of laurel bushes there darted what seemed to be a hideous and distorted child, who threw itself upon the grass with writhing limbs, and then ran swiftly across the lawn into the darkness.

"My God!" I whispered; "did you see it?"

Holmes was for the moment as startled as I. His hand closed like a vice upon my wrist in his agitation. Then he broke into a low laugh, and put his lips to my ear.

"It is a nice household," he murmured. "That is the baboon."

I had forgotten the strange pets which the Doctor affected. There was a cheetah, too; perhaps we might find it upon our shoulders at any moment. I confess that I felt easier in my mind

when, after following Holmes's example and slipping off my shoes, I found myself inside the bedroom. My companion noiselessly closed the shutters, moved the lamp on to the table, and cast his eyes round the room. All was as we had seen it in the day-time. Then creeping up to me and making a trumpet of his hand, he whispered into my ear again so gently that it was all that I could do to distinguish the words.

"The least sound would be fatal to our plans."

I nodded to show that I had heard.

"We must sit without light. He would see it through the ventilator."

I nodded again.

"Do not go asleep; your very life may depend upon it. Have your pistol ready in case we should need it. I will sit on the side of the bed, and you in that chair."

I took out my revolver and laid it on the corner of the table.

Holmes had brought up a long thin cane, and this he placed upon the bed beside him. By it he laid the box of matches and the stump of a candle. Then he turned down the lamp, and we were left in darkness.

How shall I ever forget that dreadful vigil? I could not hear a sound, not even the drawing of a breath, and yet I knew that my companion sat open-eyed, within a few feet of me, in the same state of nervous tension in which I was myself. The shutters cut off the least ray of light, and we waited in absolute darkness. From outside came the occasional cry of a night bird, and once at our very window a long-drawn, cat-like whine, which told us that the cheetah was indeed at liberty. Far away we could hear the deep tones of the parish clock, which boomed out every quarter of an hour. How long they seemed, those quarters! Twelve struck, and one, and two, and three, and still we sat waiting silently for what-ever might befall.

Suddenly there was the momentary gleam of a light up in the direction of the ventilator, which vanished immediately, but was succeeded by a strong smell of burning oil and heated metal. Someone in the next room had lit a dark lantern. I heard a gentle sound of movement, and then all was silent once more, though the smell grew stronger. For half an hour I sat with straining ears. Then suddenly another sound became audible—a very gentle, soothing sound, like that of a small jet of steam escaping continually from a kettle. The instant that we heard it, Holmes sprang from the bed, struck a match, and lashed furiously with his cane at the bell-pull.

"You see it, Watson?" he yelled. "You see it?"

But I saw nothing. At the moment when Holmes struck the light I heard a low, clear whistle, but the sudden glare flashing into my weary eyes made it impossible for me to tell what it was at which my friend lashed so savagely. I could, however, see that his face was deadly pale, and filled with horror and loathing.

He had ceased to strike, and was gazing up at the ventilator, when suddenly there broke from the silence of the night the most horrible cry to which I have ever listened. It swelled up louder and louder, a hoarse yell of pain and fear and anger all mingled in the one dreadful shriek. They say that away down in the village, and even in the distant parsonage, that cry raised the sleepers from their beds. It struck cold to our hearts, and I stood gazing at Holmes, and he at me, until the last echoes of it had died away into the silence from which it rose.

"What can it mean?" I gasped.

"It means that it is all over," Holmes answered. "And perhaps, after all, it is for the best. Take your pistol, and we shall enter Dr. Roylott's room."

With a grave face he lit the lamp, and led the way down the corridor. Twice he struck at the chamber door without any reply from within. Then he turned the handle and entered, I at his heels, with the cocked pistol in my hand.

It was a singular sight which met our eyes. On the table stood a dark lantern with the shutter half open, throwing a brilliant beam of light upon the iron safe, the door of which was ajar. Beside this table, on the wooden chair, sat Dr. Grimesby Roylott, clad in a long grey dressing-gown, his bare ankles protruding beneath, and his feet thrust into red heelless Turkish slippers. Across his lap lay the short stock with the long lash which we had noticed during the day. His chin was cocked upwards, and his eyes were fixed in a dreadful rigid stare at the corner of the ceiling. Round his brow he had a peculiar yellow band, with brownish speckles, which seemed to be bound tightly round his head. As we entered he made neither sound nor motion.

"The band! the speckled band!" whispered Holmes.

I took a step forward. In an instant his strange headgear began to move, and there reared itself from among his hair the squat diamond-shaped head and puffed neck of a loathsome serpent.

"It is a swamp adder!" cried Holmes—"the deadliest snake in India. He has died within ten seconds of being bitten. Violence does, in truth, recoil upon the violent, and the schemer falls into the pit which he digs for another. Let us thrust this creature back into its den, and we can then remove Miss Stoner to some place of shelter, and let the county police know what has happened."

As he spoke he drew the dog whip swiftly from the dead man's lap, and throwing the noose round the reptile's neck, he drew it from its horrid perch, and, carrying it at arm's length, threw it into the iron safe, which he closed upon it.

Such are the true facts of the death of Dr. Grimesby Roylott, of Stoke Moran. It is not necessary that I should prolong a narrative which has already run to too great a length, by telling how we broke the sad news to the terrified girl, how we conveyed her by the morning train to the care of her good aunt at Harrow, of how the slow process of official inquiry came to the conclusion that the Doctor met his fate while indiscreetly playing with a dangerous pet. The little which I had yet to learn of the case was told me by Sherlock Holmes as we travelled back next day.

"I had," said he, "come to an entirely erroneous conclusion, which shows, my dear Watson, how dangerous it always is to reason from insufficient data. The presence of the gipsies, and the use of the word 'band,' which was used by the poor girl, no doubt, to explain the appearance which she had caught a hurried glimpse of by the light of her match, were sufficient to put me upon an entirely wrong scent. I can only claim the merit that I instantly reconsidered my position when, however, it became clear to me that whatever danger threatened an occupant of the room could not come either from the window or the door. My attention was speedily drawn, as I have already remarked to you, to this ventilator, and to the bell rope which hung down to the bed. The discovery that this was a dummy, and that the bed was clamped to the floor, instantly gave rise to the suspicion that the rope was there as a bridge for something passing through the hole, and coming to the bed. The idea of a snake instantly occurred to me, and when I coupled it with my knowledge that the Doctor was furnished with a supply of creatures from India, I felt that I was probably on the right track. The idea of using a form of poison which could not possibly be discovered by any chemical test was just such a one as would occur to a clever and ruthless man who had had an Eastern training. The rapidity with which such a poison would take effect would also, from his point of view, be an advantage. It would be a sharp-eyed coroner indeed who could distinguish the two little dark punctures which would show where the poison fangs had done their work. Then I thought of the whistle. Of course, he must recall the snake before the morning light revealed it to the victim. He had trained it, probably by the use of the milk which we saw, to return to him when summoned. He would put it through this ventilator at the hour that he thought best, with the certainty that it would crawl down the rope, and land on the bed. It might or might not bite the occupant, perhaps she might escape every night for a week, but sooner or later she must fall a victim.

"I had come to these conclusions before ever I had entered his room. An inspection of his chair showed me that he had been in the habit of standing on it, which, of course, would be necessary in order that he should reach the ventilator. The sight of the safe, the saucer of milk, and the loop of whipcord were enough to finally dispel any doubts which may have remained. The metallic clang heard by Miss Stoner was obviously caused by her father hastily closing the door of his safe upon its terrible occupant. Having once made up my mind, you know the steps which I took in order to put the matter to the proof. I heard the creature hiss, as I have no doubt that you did also, and I instantly lit the light and attacked it."

"With the result of driving it through the ventilator."

"And also with the result of causing it to turn upon its master at the other side. Some of the blows of my cane came home, and roused its snakish temper, so that it flew upon the first person it saw. In this way I am no doubt indirectly responsible for Dr. Grimesby Roylott's death, and I cannot say that it is likely to weigh very heavily upon my conscience."

THIS WAS THE UNKINDEST CUT OF ALL

Stabbing in a completely sealed environment
appears to be the most common murder method.

THE WRONG PROBLEM

JOHN DICKSON CARR

THERE HAS NEVER BEEN, nor can there be, any argument that the greatest practitioner of the locked-room mystery is John Dickson Carr (1906–1977), the American (born and raised in Pennsylvania) who was described as more English than any English author of his time. On a trip abroad, he fell in love with an English girl and moved there because he thought it the ideal place in which to write detective fiction. He wrote so prolifically that he created the pseudonym Carter Dickson (originally Carr Dickson until Harper, his American publisher, objected) for the overflow. Soon after World War II broke out, he produced propaganda programs for the BBC. When a left-wing government was voted into power, Carr returned to the United States to "escape socialism," as he wrote. After the Labour Party was defeated in 1951, he moved back to England until 1958, when it again took office; he then returned to America permanently.

His most famous detective creation as Carr was Dr. Gideon Fell, who appeared in two dozen novels and numerous short stories. Based on one of Carr's literary heroes, G. K. Chesterton, Fell is a long-time policeman who has seen so much that the only crimes that interest him are those that have the appearance of being impossible. Carr's work was so quickly recognized as being superior that he was elected to England's prestigious Detection Club in 1936 after only a few years in England. He was honored as a Grand Master for lifetime achievement by the Mystery Writers of America in 1963.

"The Wrong Problem" was first published in the August 14, 1936, issue of the *London Evening Standard*. It was first published in the United States in slightly altered form in the July 1942 issue of *Ellery Queen's Mystery Magazine*. It was first collected in *Dr. Fell, Detective* (New York, Mercury, 1947). Note: All printings of this story except the first follow the text of the *EQMM* appearance.

THE WRONG PROBLEM

JOHN DICKSON CARR

AT THE DETECTIVES' CLUB it is still told how Dr. Fell went down into the valley in Somerset that evening and of the man with whom he talked in the twilight by the lake, and of murder that came up as though from the lake itself. The truth about the crime has long been known, but one question must always be asked at the end of it.

The village of Grayling Dene lay a mile away towards the sunset. And the rear windows of the house looked out towards it. This was a long gabled house of red brick, lying in a hollow of the shaggy hills, and its bricks had darkened like an old painting. No lights showed inside, although the lawns were in good order and the hedges trimmed.

Behind the house there was a long gleam of water in the sunset, for the ornamental lake— some yards across—stretched almost to the windows. In the middle of the lake, on an artificial island, stood a summerhouse. A faint breeze had begun to stir, despite the heat, and the valley was alive with a conference of leaves.

The last light showed that all the windows of the house, except one, had little lozenge-shaped panes. The one exception was a window high up in a gable, the highest in the house, looking out over the road to Grayling Dene. It was barred.

Dusk had almost become darkness when two men came down over the crest of the hill. One was large and lean. The other, who wore a shovel-hat, was large and immensely stout, and

he loomed even more vast against the skyline by reason of the great dark cloak billowing out behind him. Even at that distance you might hear the chuckles that animated his several chins and ran down the ridges of his waistcoat. The two travelers were engaged (as usual) in a violent argument. At intervals the larger one would stop and hold forth oratorically for some minutes, flourishing his cane. But, as they came down past the lake and the blind house, both of them stopped.

"There's an example," said Superintendent Hadley. "Say what you like, it's a bit too lonely for me. Give me the town—"

"We are not alone," said Dr. Fell.

The whole place had seemed so deserted that Hadley felt a slight start when he saw a man standing at the edge of the lake. Against the reddish glow on the water they could make out that it was a small man in neat dark clothes and a white linen hat. He seemed to be stooping forward, peering out across the water. The wind went rustling again, and the man turned around.

"I don't see any swans," he said. "Can you see any swans?" The quiet water was empty.

"No," said Dr. Fell, with the same gravity. "Should there be any?"

"There should be one," answered the little man, nodding. "Dead. With blood on its neck. Floating there."

"Killed?" asked Dr. Fell, after a pause. He has said afterwards that it seemed a foolish thing to say; but that it seemed appropriate to that time between the lights of the day and the brain.

"Oh, yes," replied the little man, nodding again. "Killed, like others—human beings. Eye, ear, and throat. Or perhaps I should say ear, eye, and throat, to get them in order."

Hadley spoke with some sharpness.

"I hope we're not trespassing. We knew the land was enclosed, of course, but they told us that the owners were away and wouldn't mind if we took a short cut. Fell, don't you think we'd better—?"

"I beg your pardon," said the little man, in a voice of such cool sanity that Hadley turned round again. From what they could see in the gloom, he had a good face, a quiet face, a somewhat ascetic face; and he was smiling. "I beg your pardon," he repeated in a curiously apologetic tone. "I should not have said that. You see, I have been far too long with it. I have been trying to find the real answer of thirty years. As for the trespassing, myself, I do not own this land, although I lived here once. There is, or used to be, a bench here somewhere. Can I detain you for a little while?"

Hadley never quite realized afterwards how it came about. But such was the spell of the hour, or of the place, or the sincere, serious little man in the white linen hat, that it seemed no time at all before the little man was sitting on a rusty iron chair beside the darkening lake, speaking as though to his fingers.

"I am Joseph Lessing," he said, in the same apologetic tone. "If you have not heard of me, I don't suppose you will have heard of my stepfather. But at one time he was rather famous as an eye, ear, and throat specialist. Dr. Harvey Lessing, his name was.

"In those days we—I mean the family—always came down here to spend our summer holidays. It is rather difficult to make biographical details clear. Perhaps I had better do it with dates, as though the matter were really important, like a history book. There were four children. Three of them were Dr. Lessing's children by his first wife, who died in 1899. I was

the stepson. He married my mother when I was seventeen, in 1901. I regret to say that *she* died three years later. Dr. Lessing was a kindly man, but he was very unfortunate in the choice of his wives."

The little man appeared to be smiling sadly.

"We were an ordinary, contented, and happy group, in spite of Brownrigg's cynicism. Brownrigg was the eldest. Eye, ear, and throat pursued us: he was a dentist. I think he is dead now. He was a stout man, smiling a good deal, and his face had a shine like pale butter. He was an athlete run to seed; he used to claim that he could draw teeth with his fingers. By the way, he was very fond of walnuts. I always seem to remember him sitting between two silver candlesticks at the table, smiling, with a heap of shells in front of him, and a little sharp nut-pick in his hand.

"Harvey Junior was the next. They were right to call him Junior; he was of the striding sort, brisk and high-colored and likable. He never sat down in a chair without first turning it the wrong way round. He always said 'Ho, my lads!' when he came into a room, and he never went out of it without leaving the door open so that he could come back in again. Above everything, he was nearly always on the water. We had a skiff and a punt for our little lake—would you believe that it is ten feet deep? Junior always dressed for the part as solemnly as though he had been on the Thames, wearing a red-and-white striped blazer and a straw hat of the sort that used to be called a boater. I say he was nearly always on the water: but not, of course, after tea. That was when Dr. Lessing went to take his afternoon nap in the summerhouse."

The summerhouse, in its sheath of vines, was almost invisible now. But they all looked at it, very suggestive in the middle of the lake.

"The third child was the girl, Martha. She was almost my own age, and I was very fond of her."

Joseph Lessing pressed his hands together.

"I am not going to introduce an unnecessary love story, gentlemen," he said. "As a matter of fact, Martha was engaged to a young man who had a commission in a line regiment, and she was expecting him down here any day when— the things happened. Arthur Somers, his name was. I knew him well; I was his confidant in the family.

"I want to emphasize what a hot, pleasant summer it was. The place looked then much as it does now, except that I think it was greener then. I was glad to get away from the city. In accordance with Dr. Lessing's passion for 'useful employment,' I had been put to work in the optical department of a jeweler's. I was always skillful with my hands. I dare say I was a spindly, snappish, suspicious lad, but they were all very good to me after my mother died, except butter-faced Brownrigg, perhaps. But for me that summer centers around Martha, with her brown hair piled up on the top of her head, in a white dress with puffed shoulders, playing croquet on a green lawn, and laughing. I told you it was a long while ago.

"On the afternoon of the fifteenth of August we had all intended to be out. Even Brownrigg had intended to go out after a sort of lunch-tea that we had at two o'clock in the afternoon. Look to your right, gentlemen. You see that bow window in the middle of the house, overhanging the lake? There was where the table was set.

"Dr. Lessing was the first to leave the table. He was going out early for his nap in the summerhouse. It was a very hot afternoon, as drowsy as the sound of a lawn mower. The sun baked the old bricks and made a flat blaze on the water. Junior had knocked together a sort of miniature landing-stage at the side of the lake—it was just about where we are sitting now—and the punt and the rowing-boat were lying there.

"From the open windows we could all see Dr. Lessing going down to the landing-stage with the sun on his bald spot. He had a pillow in one hand and a book in the other. He took the rowing-boat; he could never manage the punt properly, and it irritated a man of his dignity to try.

"Martha was the next to leave. She laughed and ran away, as she always did. Then Junior said, 'Cheerio, chaps'—or whatever the expression was then—and strode out leaving the door open. I went shortly afterwards. Junior had asked Brownrigg whether he intended to go out, and Brownrigg had said yes. But he remained, being lazy, with a pile of walnut shells in front of him. Though he moved back from the table to get out of the glare, he lounged there all afternoon in view of the lake.

"Of course, what Brownrigg said or thought might not have been important. But it happened that a gardener named Robinson had taken it into his head to trim some hedges on this side of the house. He had a full view of the lake. And all that afternoon nothing stirred. The summerhouse, as you can see, has two doors, one facing toward the house, the other in the opposite direction. These openings were closed by sunblinds, striped red and white like Junior's blazer, so that you could not see inside. But all the afternoon the summerhouse remained dead, showing up against the fiery water and that clump of trees at the far side of the lake. No boat put out. No one went in to swim. There was not so much as a ripple, any more than might have been caused by the swans (we had two of them), or by the spring that fed the lake.

"By six o'clock we were all back in the house. When there began to be a few shadows, I think something in the *emptiness* of the afternoon alarmed us. Dr. Lessing should have been there, demanding something. He was not there. We halloo'd for him, but he did not answer. The rowing-boat remained tied up by the summerhouse. Then Brownrigg, in his cool fetch-and-run fashion, told me to go out and wake up the old party. I pointed out that there was only the punt, and that I was a rotten hand at punting, and that whenever I tried it I only went 'round in circles or upset the boat. But Junior said, 'Come-along-old-chap-you-shall-improve-your-punting-I'll-give-you-a-hand.'

"I have never forgotten how long it took us to get out there while I staggered at the punt-pole, and Junior lent a hand.

"Dr. Lessing lay easily on his left side, almost

on his stomach, on a long wicker settee. His face was very nearly into the pillow, so that you could not see much except a wisp of sandy side-whisker. His right hand hung down to the floor, the fingers trailing into the pages of *Three Men in a Boat*.

"We first noticed that there seemed to be some—that is, something that had come out of his ear. More we did not know, except that he was dead, and in fact the weapon has never been found. He died in his sleep. The doctor later told us that the wound had been made by some round sharp-pointed instrument, thicker than a hat-pin but not so thick as a lead-pencil, which had been driven through the right ear into the brain."

Joseph Lessing paused. A mighty swish of wind uprose in the trees beyond the lake, and their tops ruffled under clear starlight. The little man sat nodding to himself in the iron chair. They could see his white hat move.

"Yes?" prompted Dr. Fell in an almost casual tone. Dr. Fell was sitting back, a great bandit-shape in cloak and shovel-hat. He seemed to be blinking curiously at Lessing over his eyeglasses. "And whom did they suspect?"

"They suspected me," said the little man.

"You see," he went on, in the same apologetic tone, "I was the only one in the group who could swim. It was my one accomplishment. It is too dark to show you now but I won a little medal by it, and I have kept it on my watch-chain ever since I received it as a boy."

"But you said," cried Hadley, "that nobody—"

"I will explain," said the other, "if you do not interrupt me. Of course, the police believed that the motive must have been money. Dr. Lessing was a wealthy man, and his money was divided almost equally among us. I told you he was always very good to me.

"First they tried to find out where everyone had been in the afternoon. Brownrigg had been sitting, or said he had been sitting, in the dining room. But there was the gardener to prove that not he or anyone else had gone out on the lake.

Martha (it was foolish, of course, but they investigated even Martha) had been with a friend of hers—I forget her name now—who came for her in the phaeton and took her away to play croquet. Junior had no alibi, since he had been for a country walk. But," said Lessing, quite simply, "everybody knew *he* would never do a thing like that. I was the changeling, or perhaps I mean ugly duckling, and I admit I was an unpleasant, sarcastic lad.

"This is how Inspector Deering thought I had committed the murder. First, he thought, I had made sure everybody would be away from the house that afternoon. Thus, later, when the crime was discovered, it would be assumed by everyone that the murderer had simply gone out in the punt and come back again. Everybody knew that I could not possibly manage a punt alone. You see?

"Next, the inspector thought, I had come down to the clump of trees across the lake, in line with the summerhouse and the dining room windows. It is shallow there, and there are reeds. He thought that I had taken off my clothes over a bathing suit. He thought that I had crept into the water under cover of the reeds, and that I had simply swum out to the summerhouse under water.

"Twenty-odd yards under water, I admit, are not much to a good swimmer. They thought that Brownrigg could not see me come up out of the water, because the thickness of the summerhouse was between. Robinson had a full view of the lake, but he could not see that one part at the back of the summerhouse. Nor, on the other hand, could I see them. They thought that I had crawled under the sun-blind with the weapon in the breast of my bathing suit. Any wetness I might have left would soon be dried by the intense heat. That, I think, was how they believed I had killed the old man who befriended me."

The little man's voice grew petulant and dazed.

"I told them I did not do it," he said with a hopeful air. "Over and over again I told them I did not do it. But I do not think they believed me. That is why for all these years I have wondered . . .

"It was Brownrigg's idea. They had me before a sort of family council in the library, as though I had stolen jam. Martha was weeping, but I think she was weeping with plain fear. She never stood up well in a crisis, Martha didn't; she turned pettish and even looked softer. All the same, it is not pleasant to think of a murderer coming up to you as you doze in the afternoon heat. Junior, the good fellow, attempted to take my side and call for fair play; but I could see the idea in his face. Brownrigg presided, silkily, and smiled down his nose.

"'We have either got to believe you killed him,' Brownrigg said, 'or believe in the supernatural. Is the lake haunted? No; I think we may safely discard that.' He pointed his finger at me. 'You damned young snake, you are lazy and wanted that money.'

"But, you see, I had one very strong hold over them—and I used it. I admit it was unscrupulous, but I was trying to demonstrate my innocence and we are told that the devil must be fought with fire. At mention of this hold, even Brownrigg's jowls shook. Brownrigg was a dentist, Harvey was studying medicine. What hold? That is the whole point. Nevertheless, it was not what the family thought I had to fear, it was what Inspector Deering thought.

"They did not arrest me yet, because there was not enough evidence, but every night I feared it would come the next day. Those days after the funeral were too warm; and suspicion acted like woolen underwear under the heat. Martha's tantrums got on even Junior's nerves. Once I thought Brownrigg was going to hit her. She very badly needed her fiancé Arthur Somers; but, though he wrote that he might be there any day, he still could not get leave of absence from his colonel.

"And then the lake got more food.

"Look at the house, gentlemen. I wonder if the light is strong enough for you to see it from here? Look at the house—the highest window there—under the gable. You see?"

There was a pause, filled with the tumult of the leaves.

"It's got bars," said Hadley.

"Yes," assented the little man. "I must describe the room. It is a little square room. It has one door and one window. At the time I speak of, there was no furniture at all in it. The furniture had been taken out some years before, because it was rather a special kind of furniture. Since then it had been locked up. The key was kept in a box in Dr. Lessing's room; but, of course, nobody ever went up there. One of Dr. Lessing's wives had died there in a certain condition. I told you he had bad luck with his wives. They had not even dared to have a glass window."

Sharply, the little man struck a match. The brief flame seemed to bring his face up towards them out of the dark. They saw that he had a pipe in his left hand. But the flame showed little except the gentle upward turn of his eyes, and the fact that his whitish hair (of such coarse texture that it seemed whitewashed) was worn rather long.

"On the afternoon of the twenty-second of August, we had an unexpected visit from the family solicitor. There was no one to receive him except myself. Brownrigg had locked himself up in his room at the front with a bottle of whiskey; he was drunk or said he was drunk. Junior was out. We had been trying to occupy our minds for the past week, but Junior could not have his boating or I my workshop; this was thought not decent. I believe it was thought that the most decent thing was to get drunk. For some days Martha had been ailing. She was not ill enough to go to bed, but she was lying on a long chair in her bedroom.

"I looked into the room just before I went downstairs to see the solicitor. The room was muffled up with shutters and velvet curtains, as all the rooms decently were. You may imagine that it was very hot in there. Martha was lying back in the chair with a smelling-bottle, and there was a white-globed lamp burning on a little round table beside her. I remember that her white dress looked starchy; her hair was piled up on top of her head and she wore a little gold watch on her breast. Also, her eyelids were so puffed that they seemed almost Oriental. When I asked her how she was, she began to cry and concluded by throwing a book at me.

"So I went on downstairs. I was talking to the solicitor when it took place. We were in the library, which is at the front of the house, and in consequence we could not hear distinctly. But we heard something. That was why we went upstairs—and even the solicitor ran. Martha was not in her own bedroom. We found out where she was from the fact that the door to the garret-stairs was open.

"It was even more intolerably hot up under the roof. The door to the barred room stood halfway open. Just outside stood a housemaid (her name, I think, was Jane Dawson) leaning against the jamb and shaking like the ribbons on her cap. All sound had dried up in her throat, but she pointed inside.

"I told you it was a little, bare, dirty brown room. The low sun made a blaze through the window, and made shadows of the bars across Martha's white dress. Martha lay nearly in the middle of the room, with her heel twisted under her as though she had turned 'round before she fell. I lifted her up and tried to talk to her; but a rounded sharp-pointed thing, somewhat thicker than a hat-pin, had been driven through the right eye into the brain.

"Yet there was nobody else in the room.

"The maid told a straight story. She had seen Martha come out of Dr. Lessing's bedroom downstairs. Martha was running, running as well as she could in those skirts; once she stumbled, and the maid thought that she was sobbing. Jane Dawson said that Martha made for the garret door as though the devil were after her. Jane Dawson, wishing anything rather than to be alone in the dark hall, followed her. She saw Martha come up here and unlock the door of the little brown room. When Martha ran inside, the maid thought that she did not attempt to close the door; but that it appeared to swing shut after her. You see?

"Whatever had frightened Martha, Jane Dawson did not dare follow her in—for a few seconds, at least, and afterwards it was too late. The maid could never afterwards describe exactly the sort of sound Martha made. It was something that startled the birds out of the vines and set the swans flapping on the lake. But the maid presently saw straight enough to push the door with one finger and peep round the edge.

"Except for Martha, the room was empty.

"Hence the three of us now looked at each other. The maid's story was not to be shaken in any way, and we all knew she was a truthful witness. Even the police did not doubt her. She said she had seen Martha go into that room, but that she had seen nobody come out of it. She never took her eyes off the door—it was not likely that she would. But when she peeped in to see what had happened, there was nobody except Martha in the room. That was easily established, because there was no place where anyone could have been. Could she have been blinded by the light? No. Could anyone have slipped past her? No. She almost shook her hair loose by her vehemence on this point.

"The window, I need scarcely tell you, was inaccessible. Its bars were firmly set, no farther apart than the breadth of your hand, and in any case the window could not have been reached. There was no way out of the room except the door or the window; and no—what is the word I want?—no mechanical device in it. Our friend Inspector Deering made certain of that. One thing I suppose I should mention. Despite the condition of the walls and ceiling, the floor of the room was swept clean. Martha's white dress with the puffed shoulders had scarcely any dirt when she lay there; it was as white as her face.

"This murder was incredible. I do not mean merely that it was incredible with regard to its physical circumstances, but also that there was Martha dead—on a holiday. Possibly she seemed all the more dead because we had never known her well when she was alive. She was (to me, at least) a laugh, a few coquetries, a pair of brown eyes. You felt her absence more than you would have felt that of a more vital person. And—on a holiday with that warm sun, and the tennis-net ready to be put up.

"That evening I walked with Junior here in the dusk by the lake. He was trying to express some of this. He appeared dazed. He did not know why Martha had gone up to that little brown room, and he kept endlessly asking why. He could not even seem to accustom himself to the idea that our holidays were interrupted, much less interrupted by the murders of his father and his sister.

"There was a reddish light on the lake; the trees stood up against it like black lace, and we were walking near that clump by the reeds. The thing I remember most vividly is Junior's face. He had his hat on the back of his head, as he usually did. He was staring down past the reeds, where the water lapped faintly, as though the lake itself were the evil genius and kept its secret. When he spoke I hardly recognized his voice.

"'God,' he said, 'but it's in the air!'

"There was something white floating by the reeds, very slowly turning 'round with a snaky discolored talon coming out from it along the water, the talon was the head of a swan, and the swan was dead of a gash across the neck that had very nearly severed it.

"We fished it out with a boathook," explained the little man as though with an afterthought. And then he was silent.

On the long iron bench Dr. Fell's cape shifted a little; Hadley could hear him wheezing with quiet anger, like a boiling kettle.

"I thought so," rumbled Dr. Fell. He added more sharply: "Look here, this tomfoolery has got to stop."

"I beg your pardon?" said Joseph Lessing, evidently startled.

"With your kind permission," said Dr. Fell, and Hadley has later said that he was never more glad to see that cane flourished or hear that common-sense voice grow fiery with controversy, "with your kind permission, I should like to ask you a question. Will you swear to me by anything you hold sacred (if you have anything, which I rather doubt) that you do not know the real answer?"

"Yes," replied the other seriously, and nodded.

For a little space, Dr. Fell was silent. Then he spoke argumentatively. "I will ask you another question, then. Did you ever shoot an arrow into the air?"

Hadley turned 'round. "I hear the call of mumbo-jumbo," said Hadley with grim feeling. "Hold on, now! You don't think that girl was killed by somebody shooting an arrow into the air, do you?"

"Oh, no," said Dr. Fell in a more meditative tone. He looked at Lessing. "I mean it figuratively—like the boy in the verse. Did you ever throw a stone when you were a boy? Did you ever throw a stone, not to hit anything, but for the sheer joy of firing it? Did you ever climb trees? Did you ever like to play pirate and dress up and wave a sword? I don't think so. That's why you live in a dreary, rarefied light; that's why you dislike romance and sentiment and good whiskey and all the noblest things of this world; and it is also why you do not see the unreasonableness of several things in this case.

"To begin with, birds do not commonly rise up in a great cloud from the vines because someone cries out. With the hopping and always-whooping Junior about the premises, I should imagine the birds were used to it. Still less do swans leap up out of the water and flap their wings because of a cry from far away; swans are not so sensitive. But did you ever see a boy throw a stone at a wall? Did you ever see a boy throw a stone at the water? Birds and swans would have been outraged only if something had *struck* both the wall and the water: something, in short, which fell from that barred window.

"Now, frightened women do not in their terror rush up to a garret, especially a garret with such associations. They go downstairs, where there is protection. Martha Lessing was not frightened. She went up to that room for some purpose. What purpose? She could not have been going to get anything, for there was nothing in the room to be got. What could have been on her mind? The only thing we know to have been on her mind was a frantic wish for her fiancé to get there. She had been expecting him for weeks. It is a singular thing about that room—but its window is the highest in the house, and commands the only good clear view of the road to the village.

"Now suppose someone had told her that he thought, he rather *thought,* he had glimpsed Arthur Somers coming up the road from the village. It was a long way off, of course, and the someone admitted he might have been mistaken in thinking so . . .

"H'm, yes. The trap was all set, you see. Martha Lessing waited only long enough to get the key out of the box in her father's room, and she sobbed with relief. But, when she got to the room, there was a strong sun pouring through the bars straight into her face—and the road to the village is a long way off. That, I believe, was the trap. For on the window-ledge of that room (which nobody ever used, and which someone had swept so that there should be no footprints) this someone conveniently placed a pair of—eh, Hadley?"

"Field-glasses," said Hadley, and got up in the gloom.

"Still," argued Dr. Fell, wheezing argumentatively, "there would be one nuisance. Take a pair of field-glasses, and try to use them in a window where the bars are set more closely than the breadth of your hand. The bars get in the way—wherever you turn you bump into them; they confuse sight and irritate you; and, in addition, there is a strong sun to complicate matters. In your impatience, I think you would turn the glasses sideways and pass them out through the bars. Then, holding them firmly against one bar with your hands through the bars on either side, you would look through the eyepieces.

"But," said Dr. Fell, with a ferocious geniality, "those were no ordinary glasses. Martha Lessing had noticed before that the lenses were blurred. Now that they were in position, she tried to adjust the focus by turning the little wheel in the middle. And as she turned the wheel, like a trigger of a pistol it released the spring mechanism and a sharp steel point shot out from the right-hand lens into her eye. She

dropped the glasses, which were outside the window. The weight of them tore the point from her eye; and it was this object, falling, which gashed and broke the neck of the swan just before it disappeared into the water below."

He paused. He had taken out a cigar, but he did not light it.

"Busy solicitors do not usually come to a house 'unexpectedly.' They are summoned. Brownrigg was drunk and Junior absent; there was no one at the back of the house to see the glasses fall. For this time the murderer had to have a respectable alibi. Young Martha, the only one who could have been gulled into such a trap, had to be sacrificed—to avert the arrest which had been threatening someone ever since the police found out how Dr. Lessing really had been murdered.

"There was only one man who admittedly did speak with Martha Lessing only a few minutes before she was murdered. There was only one man who was employed as optician at a jeweler's, and admits he had his 'workshop' here. There was only one man skillful enough with his hands—" Dr. Fell paused, wheezing, and turned to Lessing. "I wonder they didn't arrest you."

"They did," said the little man, nodding. "You see, I was released from Broadmoor only a month ago."

There was a sudden rasp and crackle as he struck another match.

"You—" bellowed Hadley, and stopped. "So it was your mother who died in that room? Then what the hell do you mean by keeping us here with this pack of nightmares?"

"No," said the other peevishly. "You do not understand. I never wanted to know who killed Dr. Lessing or poor Martha. You have got hold of the wrong problem. And yet I tried to tell you what the problem was.

"You see, it was not *my* mother who died mad. It was theirs—Brownrigg's and Harvey's and Martha's. That was why they were so desperately anxious to think I was guilty, for they could not face the alternative. Didn't I tell you I had a hold over them, a hold that made even

Brownrigg shake, and that I used it? Do you think they wouldn't have had me clapped into jail straightaway if it had been *my* mother who was mad? Eh?

"Of course," he explained apologetically, "at the trial they had to swear it was my mother who was mad; for I threatened to tell the truth in open court if they didn't. Otherwise I should have been hanged, you see. Only Brownrigg and Junior were left. Brownrigg was a dentist, Junior was to be a doctor, and if it had been known—But that is not the point. That is not the problem. Their mother was mad, but they

were harmless. I killed Dr. Lessing. I killed Martha. Yes, I am quite sane. Why did I do it, all those years ago? Why? Is there no rational pattern in the scheme of things, and no answer to the bedeviled of the earth?"

The match curled to a red ember, winked and went out. Clearest of all they remembered the coarse hair that was like whitewash on the black, the eyes, and the curiously suggestive hands. Then Joseph Lessing got up from the chair. The last they saw of him was his white hat bobbing and flickering across the lawn under the blowing trees.

THE THING INVISIBLE

WILLIAM HOPE HODGSON

IT HAS ALWAYS been a tricky business to combine supernatural elements and logical deductions in mystery fiction, but William Hope Hodgson (1875–1918) managed it wonderfully in his stories about Thomas Carnacki, a psychic detective.

Born in Essex, Hodgson left home at an early age to spend eight years at sea, traveling around the world three times. Living in the south of France with his wife when World War I erupted, he returned to England, received a commission, and was killed in action. Most of his fiction dealt with weird and occult subjects, the best of them being eerie tales of the sea and a series of stories about a shady smuggler, *Captain Gault: Being the Exceedingly Private Log of a Sea-Captain* (1917).

Carnacki is a ghost-finder brought into cases to discover or explain certain phenomena that have every indication of being connected to the supernatural, although many times that appearance is deceptive. He is a skeptic regarding the truth—or untruth—of ghost stories. He does not let "cheap laughter" deter him from ascertaining the possible truth of a fantastic legend. When he is on a case and alone (or possibly with some "Thing from the Other World") in the dark, he admits he is scared half to death. After a case is concluded and he is ready to talk about it, he sends a note to three friends who come to his house to listen. He settles into his easy chair, lights a pipe, and recounts the adventure without preamble. When the story is finished, he genially says "out you go" and the evening is concluded.

"The Thing Invisible" was first published in *The New Magazine* in 1912; it was first collected in book form in *Carnacki, the Ghost-Finder* (London, Nash, 1913); it was first published in the United States in 1947 by Mycroft and Moran with three additional stories.

THE THING INVISIBLE

WILLIAM HOPE HODGSON

CARNACKI HAD just returned to Cheyne Walk, Chelsea. I was aware of this interesting fact by reason of the curt and quaintly worded postcard which I was re-reading, and by which I was requested to present myself at his house not later than seven o'clock on that evening.

Mr. Carnacki had, as I and the others of his strictly limited circle of friends knew, been away in Kent for the past three weeks; but beyond that, we had no knowledge. Carnacki was genially secretive and curt, and spoke only when he was ready to speak. When this stage arrived, I and his three other friends, Jessop, Arkright, and Taylor, would receive a card or a wire, asking us to call. Not one of us ever willingly missed, for after a thoroughly sensible little dinner, Carnacki would snuggle down into his big armchair, light his pipe, and wait whilst we arranged ourselves comfortably in our accustomed seats and nooks. Then he would begin to talk.

Upon this particular night I was the first to arrive and found Carnacki sitting, quietly smoking over a paper. He stood up, shook me firmly by the hand, pointed to a chair and sat down again, never having uttered a word.

For my part, I said nothing either. I knew the man too well to bother him with questions or the weather, and so took a seat and a cigarette. Presently the three others turned up and after that we spent a comfortable and busy hour at dinner.

Dinner over, Carnacki snuggled himself down into his great chair, as I have said was his habit, filled his pipe and puffed for awhile, his gaze directed thoughtfully at the fire. The rest of us, if I may so express it, made ourselves cosy, each after his own particular manner. A minute or so later Carnacki began to speak, ignoring any preliminary remarks, and going straight to the subject of the story we knew he had to tell:

"I have just come back from Sir Alfred Jarnock's place at Burtontree, in South Kent," he began, without removing his gaze from the fire. "Most extraordinary things have been happening down there lately and Mr. George Jarnock, the eldest son, wired to ask me to run over and see whether I could help to clear matters up a bit. I went.

"When I got there, I found that they have an old Chapel attached to the castle which has had quite a distinguished reputation for being what is popularly termed 'haunted.' They have been rather proud of this, as I managed to discover, until quite lately when something very disagreeable occurred, which served to remind them that family ghosts are not always content, as I might say, to remain purely ornamental.

"It sounds almost laughable, I know, to hear of a long-respected supernatural phenomenon growing unexpectedly dangerous; and in this case, the tale of the haunting was considered as little more than an old myth, except after nightfall, when possibly it became more plausible seeming.

"But however this may be, there is no doubt

at all but that what I might term the Haunting Essence which lived in the place, had become suddenly dangerous—deadly dangerous too, the old butler being nearly stabbed to death one night in the Chapel, with a peculiar old dagger.

"It is, in fact, this dagger which is popularly supposed to 'haunt' the Chapel. At least, there has been always a story handed down in the family that this dagger would attack any enemy who should dare to venture into the Chapel after night-fall. But, of course, this had been taken with just about the same amount of seriousness that people take most ghost-tales, and that is not usually of a worryingly *real* nature. I mean that most people never quite know how much or how little they believe of matters ab-human or ab-normal, and generally they never have an opportunity to learn. And, indeed, as you are all aware, I am as big a sceptic concerning the truth of ghost-tales as any man you are likely to meet; only I am what I might term an unprejudiced sceptic. I am not given to either believing or disbelieving things 'on principle,' as I have found many idiots prone to be, and what is more, some of them not ashamed to boast of the insane fact. I view all reported 'hauntings' as un-proven until I have examined into them, and I am bound to admit that ninety-nine cases in a hundred turn out to be sheer bosh and fancy. But the hundredth! Well, if it were not for the hundredth, I should have few stories to tell you—eh?

"Of course, after the attack on the butler, it became evident that there was at least 'something' in the old story concerning the dagger, and I found everyone in a half belief that the queer old weapon did really strike the butler, either by the aid of some inherent force, which I found them peculiarly unable to explain, or else in the hand of some invisible thing or monster of the Outer World!

"From considerable experience, I knew that it was much more likely that the butler had been 'knifed' by some vicious and quite material human!

"Naturally, the first thing to do was to test this probability of human agency, and I set to work to make a pretty drastic examination of the people who knew most about the tragedy.

"The result of this examination both pleased and surprised me, for it left me with very good reasons for belief that I had come upon one of those extraordinarily rare 'true manifestations' of the extrusion of a Force from the Outside. In more popular phraseology—a genuine case of haunting.

"These are the facts: On the previous Sunday evening but one, Sir Alfred Jarnock's household had attended family service, as usual, in the Chapel. You see, the Rector goes over to officiate twice each Sunday, after concluding his duties at the public Church about three miles away.

"At the end of the service in the Chapel, Sir Alfred Jarnock, his son Mr. George Jarnock, and the Rector had stood for a couple of minutes, talking, whilst old Bellett the butler went round, putting out the candles.

"Suddenly, the Rector remembered that he had left his small prayer-book on the Communion table in the morning; he turned, and asked the butler to get it for him before he blew out the chancel candles.

"Now, I have particularly called your attention to this because it is important in that it provided witnesses in a most fortunate manner at an extraordinary moment. You see, the Rector's turning to speak to Bellett had naturally caused both Sir Alfred Jarnock and his son to glance in the direction of the butler, and it was at this identical instant and whilst all three were looking at him that the old butler was stabbed—there, full in the candle-light, before their eyes.

"I took the opportunity to call early upon the Rector, after I had questioned Mr. George Jarnock, who replied to my queries in place of Sir Alfred Jarnock, for the older man was in a nervous and shaken condition, as a result of the happening, and his son wished him to avoid dwelling upon the scene as much as possible.

"The Rector's version was clear and vivid, and he had evidently received the astonishment of his life. He pictured to me the whole affair—Bellett, up at the chancel gate, going for the prayer-book, and absolutely alone; and then the BLOW, out of the Void, he described it, and the *force* prodigious—the old man being driven headlong into the body of the Chapel. Like the kick of a great horse, the Rector said, his benevolent old eyes bright and intense with the effort he had actually witnessed, in defiance of all that he had hitherto believed.

"When I left him, he went back to the writing which he had put aside, when I appeared. I feel sure that he was developing the first unorthodox sermon that he had ever evolved. He was a dear old chap, and I should certainly like to have heard it.

"The last man I visited was the butler. He was, of course, in a frightfully weak and shaken condition, but he could tell me nothing that did not point to there being a Power abroad in the Chapel. He told the same tale, in every minute particle, that I had learned from the others. He had been just going up to put out the altar candles and fetch the Rector's book, when something struck him an enormous blow high up on the left breast and he was driven headlong into the aisle.

"Examination had shown that he had been stabbed by the dagger—of which I will tell you more in a moment—that hung always above the altar. The weapon had entered, fortunately some inches above the heart, just under the collarbone, which had been broken by the stupendous force of the blow, the dagger itself being driven clean through the body, and out through the scapula behind.

"The poor old fellow could not talk much, and I soon left him; but what he had told me was sufficient to make it unmistakable that no living person had been within yards of him when he was attacked; and, as I knew, this fact was verified by three capable and responsible witnesses, independent of Bellett himself.

"The thing now was to search the Chapel, which is small and extremely old. It is very massively built, and entered through only one door, which leads out of the castle itself, and the key of

which is kept by Sir Alfred Jarnock, the butler having no duplicate.

"The shape of the Chapel is oblong, and the altar is railed off after the usual fashion. There are two tombs in the body of the place; but none in the chancel, which is bare, except for the tall candlesticks, and the chancel rail, beyond which is the undraped altar of solid marble, upon which stand four small candlesticks, two at each end.

"Above the altar hangs the 'waeful dagger,' as I had learned it was named. I fancy the term has been taken from an old vellum, which describes the dagger and its supposed ab-normal properties. I took the dagger down, and examined it minutely and with method. The blade is ten inches long, two inches broad at the base, and tapering to a rounded but sharp point, rather peculiar. It is double-edged.

"The metal sheath is curious for having a cross-piece, which, taken with the fact that the sheath itself is continued three parts up the hilt of the dagger (in a most inconvenient fashion), gives it the appearance of a cross. That this is not unintentional is shown by an engraving of the Christ crucified upon one side, whilst upon the other, in Latin, is the inscription: 'Vengeance is Mine, I will Repay.' A quaint and rather terrible conjunction of ideas. Upon the blade of the dagger is graven in old English capitals: 'I Watch. I Strike.' On the butt of the hilt there is carved deeply a Pentacle.

"This is a pretty accurate description of the peculiar old weapon that has had the curious and uncomfortable reputation of being able (either of its own accord or in the hand of something invisible) to strike murderously any enemy of the Jarnock family who may chance to enter the Chapel after night-fall. I may tell you here and now, that before I left, I had very good reason to put certain doubts behind me; for I tested the deadliness of the thing myself.

"As you know, however, at this point of my investigation, I was still at that stage where I considered the existence of a supernatural Force unproven. In the meanwhile, I treated the Chapel drastically, sounding and scrutinising the walls and floor, dealing with them almost foot by foot, and particularly examining the two tombs.

"At the end of this search, I had in a ladder, and made a close survey of the groined roof. I passed three days in this fashion, and by the evening of the third day I had proved to my entire satisfaction that there is no place in the whole of that Chapel where any living being could have hidden, and also that the only way of ingress and egress to and from the Chapel is through the doorway which leads into the castle, the door of which was always kept locked, and the key kept by Sir Alfred Jarnock himself, as I have told you. I mean, of course, that this doorway is the only entrance practicable to *material* people.

"Yes, as you will see, even had I discovered some other opening, secret or otherwise, it would not have helped at all to explain the mystery of the incredible attack, in a normal fashion. For the butler, as you know, was struck in full sight of the Rector, Sir Jarnock, and his son. And old Bellett himself knew that no living person had touched him. . . . 'OUT OF THE VOID,' the Rector had described the inhumanly brutal attack. 'Out of the Void!' A strange feeling it gives one—eh?

"And this is the thing that I had been called in to bottom!

"After considerable thought, I decided on a plan of action. I proposed to Sir Alfred Jarnock that I should spend a night in the Chapel, and keep a constant watch upon the dagger. But to this, the old knight—a little, weasened, nervous man—would not listen for a moment. He, at least, I felt assured had no doubt of the *reality* of some dangerous supernatural Force a-roam at night in the Chapel. He informed me that it had been his habit every evening to lock the Chapel door; so that no one might foolishly or heedlessly run the risk of any peril that it might hold at night, and that he could not allow me to attempt such a thing, after what had happened to the butler.

"I could see that Sir Alfred Jarnock was very

much in earnest, and would evidently have held himself to blame, had he allowed me to make the experiment, and any harm come to me; so I said nothing in argument; and presently, pleading the fatigue of his years and health, he said goodnight, and left me; having given me the impression of being a polite, but rather superstitious, old gentleman.

"That night, however, whilst I was undressing, I saw how I might achieve the thing I wished, and be able to enter the Chapel after dark, without making Sir Alfred Jarnock nervous. On the morrow, when I borrowed the key, I would take an impression, and have a duplicate made. Then, with my private key, I could do just what I liked.

"In the morning I carried out my idea. I borrowed the key, as I wanted to take a photograph of the chancel by daylight. When I had done this I locked up the Chapel and handed the key to Sir Alfred Jarnock, having first taken an impression in soap. I had brought out the exposed plate—in its slide—with me; but the camera I had left exactly as it was, as I wanted to take a second photograph of the chancel that night, from the same position.

"I took the dark-slide into Burtontree, also the cake of soap with the impress. The soap I left with the local ironmonger, who was something of a locksmith and promised to let me have my duplicate, finished, if I would call in two hours. This I did, having in the meanwhile found out a photographer where I developed the plate, and left it to dry, telling him I would call next day. At the end of the two hours I went for my key and found it ready, much to my satisfaction. Then I returned to the castle.

"After dinner that evening, I played billiards with young Jarnock for a couple of hours. Then I had a cup of coffee and went off to my room, telling him I was feeling awfully tired. He nodded and told me he felt the same way. I was glad, for I wanted the house to settle as soon as possible.

"I locked the door of my room, then from under the bed—where I had hidden them earlier in the evening—I drew out several fine pieces of plate-armour, which I had removed from the armoury. There was also a shirt of chain-mail, with a sort of quilted hood of mail to go over the head.

"I buckled on the plate-armour, and found it extraordinarily uncomfortable, and over all I drew on the chain-mail. I know nothing about armour, but from what I have learned since, I must have put on parts of two suits. Anyway, I felt beastly, clamped, and clumsy and unable to move my arms and legs naturally. But I knew that the thing I was thinking of doing called for some sort of protection for my body. Over the armour I pulled on my dressing gown and shoved my revolver into one of the side-pockets—and my repeating flashlight into the other. My dark lantern I carried in my hand.

"As soon as I was ready I went out into the passage and listened. I had been some considerable time making my preparations and I found that now the big hall and staircase were in darkness and all the house seemed quiet. I stepped back and closed and locked my door. Then, very slowly and silently I went downstairs to the hall and turned into the passage that led to the Chapel.

"I reached the door and tried my key. It fitted perfectly and a moment later I was in the Chapel, with the door locked behind me, and all about me the utter dree silence of the place, with just the faint showings of the outlines of the stained, leaded windows, making the darkness and lonesomeness almost the more apparent.

"Now it would be silly to say I did not feel queer. I felt very queer indeed. You just try, any of you, to imagine yourself standing there in the dark silence and remembering not only the legend that was attached to the place, but what had really happened to the old butler only a little while gone. I can tell you, as I stood there, I could believe that something invisible was coming towards me in the air of the Chapel. Yet, I had got to go through with the business, and I just took hold of my little bit of courage and set to work.

"First of all I switched on my light, then I began a careful tour of the place, examining every corner and nook. I found nothing unusual. At the chancel gate I held up my lamp and flashed the light at the dagger. It hung there, right enough, above the altar, but I remember thinking of the word 'demure,' as I looked at it. However, I pushed the thought away, for what I was doing needed no addition of uncomfortable thoughts.

"I completed the tour of the place, with a constantly growing awareness of its utter chill and unkind desolation—an atmosphere of cold dismalness seemed to be everywhere, and the quiet was abominable.

"At the conclusion of my search I walked across to where I had left my camera focussed upon the chancel. From the satchel that I had put beneath the tripod I took out a dark-slide and inserted it in the camera, drawing the shutter. After that I uncapped the lens, pulled out my flashlight apparatus, and pressed the trigger. There was an intense, brilliant flash, that made the whole of the interior of the Chapel jump into sight, and disappear as quickly. Then, in the light from my lantern, I inserted the shutter into the slide, and reversed the slide, so as to have a fresh plate ready to expose at any time.

"After I had done this I shut off my lantern and sat down in one of the pews near to my camera. I cannot say what I expected to happen, but I had an extraordinary feeling, almost a conviction, that something peculiar or horrible would soon occur. It was, you know, as if I *knew*.

"An hour passed, of absolute silence. The time I knew by the far-off, faint chime of a clock that had been erected over the stables. I was beastly cold, for the whole place is without any kind of heating pipes or furnace, as I had noticed during my search, so that the temperature was sufficiently uncomfortable to suit my frame of mind. I felt like a kind of human periwinkle encased in boilerplate and frozen with cold and funk. And, you know, somehow the dark about me seemed to press coldly against my face. I cannot say whether any of you have ever had the feeling, but if you have, you will know just how disgustingly un-nerving it is. And then, all at once, I had a horrible sense that something was moving in the place. It was not that I could hear anything, but I had a kind of intuitive knowledge that something had stirred in the darkness. Can you imagine how I felt?

"Suddenly my courage went. I put up my mailed arms over my face. I wanted to protect it. I had got a sudden sickening feeling that something was hovering over me in the dark. Talk about fright! I could have shouted, if I had not been afraid of the noise. . . . And then, abruptly, I heard something. Away up the aisle, there sounded a dull clang of metal, as it might be the tread of a mailed heel upon the stone of the aisle. I sat immovable. I was fighting with all my strength to get back my courage. I could not take my arms down from over my face, but I knew that I was getting hold of the gritty part of me again. And suddenly I made a mighty effort and lowered my arms. I held my face up in the darkness. And, I tell you, I respect myself for the act, because I thought truly at that moment that I was going to die. But I think, just then, by the slow revulsion of feeling which had assisted my effort, I was less sick, in that instant, at the thought of having to die, than at the knowledge of the utter weak cowardice that had so unexpectedly shaken me all to bits, for a time.

"Do I make myself clear? You understand, I feel sure, that the sense of respect, which I spoke of, is not really unhealthy egotism; because, you see, I am not blind to the state of mind which helped me. I mean that if I had uncovered my face by a sheer effort of will, unhelped by any revulsion of feeling, I should have done a thing much more worthy of mention. But, even as it was, there were elements in the act worthy of respect. You follow me, don't you?

"And, you know, nothing touched me, after all! So that, in a little while, I had got back a bit to my normal, and felt steady enough to go through with the business without any more funking.

"I daresay a couple of minutes passed, and

then, away up near the chancel, there came again that clang, as though an armoured foot stepped cautiously. By Jove! but it made me stiffen. And suddenly the thought came that the sound I heard might be the rattle of the dagger above the altar. It was not a particularly sensible notion, for the sound was far too heavy and resonant for such a cause. Yet, as can be easily understood, my reason was bound to submit somewhat to my fancy at such a time. I remember now, that the idea of that insensate thing becoming animate, and attacking me, did not occur to me with any sense of possibility or reality. I thought rather, in a vague way, of some invisible monster of outer space fumbling at the dagger. I remembered the old Rector's description of the attack on the butler . . . OUT OF THE VOID. And he had described the stupendous force of the blow as being 'like the kick of a great horse.' You can see how uncomfortably my thoughts were running.

"I felt round swiftly and cautiously for my lantern. I found it close to me, on the pew seat, and with a sudden, jerky movement, I switched on the light. I flashed it up the aisle, to and fro across the chancel, but I could see nothing to frighten me. I turned quickly, and sent the jet of light darting across and across the rear end of the Chapel; then on each side of me, before and behind, up at the roof and down at the marble floor, but nowhere was there any visible thing to put me in fear, not a thing that need have set my flesh thrilling; just the quiet Chapel, cold, and eternally silent. You know the feeling.

"I had been standing, whilst I sent the light about the Chapel, but now I pulled out my revolver, and then, with a tremendous effort of will, switched off the light, and sat down again in the darkness, to continue my constant watch.

"It seemed to me that quite half an hour, or even more, must have passed, after this, during which no sound had broken the intense stillness. I had grown less nervously tense, for the flashing of the light round the place had made me feel less out of all bounds of the normal—it had given me something of that unreasoned sense of safety that a nervous child obtains at night, by covering its head up with the bedclothes. This just about illustrates the completely human illogicalness of the workings of my feelings; for, as you know, whatever Creature, Thing, or Being it was that had made that extraordinary and horrible attack on the old butler, it had certainly not been *visible*.

"And so you must picture me sitting there in the dark; clumsy with armour, and with my revolver in one hand, and nursing my lantern, ready, with the other. And then it was, after this little time of partial relief from intense nervousness, that there came a fresh strain on me; for somewhere in the utter quiet of the Chapel, I thought I heard something. I listened, tense and rigid, my heart booming just a little in my ears for a moment; then I thought I heard it again. I felt sure that something had moved at the top of the aisle. I strained in the darkness, to hark; and my eyes showed me blackness within blackness, wherever I glanced, so that I took no heed of what they told me; for even if I looked at the dim loom of the stained window at the top of the chancel, my sight gave me the shapes of vague shadows passing noiseless and ghostly across, constantly. There was a time of almost peculiar silence, horrible to me, as I felt just then. And suddenly I seemed to hear a sound again, nearer to me, and repeated, infinitely stealthy. It was as if a vast, soft tread were coming slowly down the aisle.

"Can you imagine how I felt? I do not think you can. I did not move, any more than the stone effigies on the two tombs; but sat there, *stiffened*. I fancied now that I heard the tread all about the Chapel. And then, you know, I was just as sure in a moment that I could not hear it—that I had never heard it.

"Some particularly long minutes passed, about this time; but I think my nerves must have quieted a bit; for I remember being sufficiently aware of my feelings, to realize that the muscles of my shoulders *ached*, with the way that they must have been contracted, as I sat there, hunching myself, rigid. Mind you, I was still in a disgusting funk; but what I might call

the 'imminent sense of danger' seemed to have eased from around me; at any rate, I felt, in some curious fashion that there was a respite—a temporary cessation of malignity from about me. It is impossible to word my feelings more clearly to you, for I cannot see them more clearly than this, myself.

"Yet, you must not picture me as sitting there, free from strain; for the nerve tension was so great that my heart action was a little out of normal control, the blood-beat making a dull booming at times in my ears, with the result that I had the sensation that I could not hear acutely. This is a simply beastly feeling, especially under such circumstances.

"I was sitting like this, listening, as I might say with body and soul, when suddenly I got that hideous conviction again that something was moving in the air of the place. The feeling seemed to stiffen me, as I sat, and my head appeared to tighten, as if all the scalp had grown *tense*. This was so real, that I suffered an actual pain, most peculiar and at the same time intense; the whole head pained. I had a fierce desire to cover my face again with my mailed arms, but I fought it off. If I had given way then to that, I should simply have bunked straight out of the place. I sat and sweated coldly (that's the bald truth), with the 'creep' busy at my spine. . . .

"And then, abruptly, once more I thought I heard the sound of that huge, soft tread on the aisle, and this time closer to me. There was an awful little silence, during which I had the feeling that something enormous was bending over towards me, from the aisle. . . . And then, through the booming of the blood in my ears, there came a slight sound from the place where my camera stood—a disagreeable sort of slithering sound, and then a sharp tap. I had the lantern ready in my left hand, and now I snapped it on, desperately, and shone it straight above me, for I had a conviction that there was something there. But I *saw* nothing. Immediately I flashed the light at the camera, and along the aisle, but again there was nothing visible. I wheeled round, shooting the beam of light in a great circle about the place; to and fro I shone it, jerking it here and there, but it showed me nothing.

"I had stood up the instant that I had seen that there was nothing in sight over me, and now I determined to visit the chancel, and see whether the dagger had been touched. I stepped out of the pew into the aisle, and here I came to an abrupt pause, for an almost invincible, sick repugnance was fighting me back from the upper part of the Chapel. A constant, queer prickling went up and down my spine, and a dull ache took me in the small of the back, as I fought with myself to conquer this sudden new feeling of terror and horror. I tell you, that no one who has not been through these kinds of experiences, has any idea of the sheer, *actual physical pain* attendant upon, and resulting from, the intense nerve-strain that ghostly-fright sets up in the human system. I stood there, feeling positively ill. But I got myself in hand, as it were, in about half a minute, and then I went, walking, I expect, as jerky as a mechanical tin man, and switching the light from side to side, before and behind, and over my head continually. And the hand that held my revolver sweated so much, that the thing fairly slipped in my fist. Does not sound very heroic, does it?

"I passed through the short chancel, and reached the step that led up to the small gate in the chancel-rail. I threw the beam from my lantern upon the dagger. Yes, I thought, it's all right. Abruptly, it seemed to me that there was something wanting, and I leaned forward over the chancel-gate to peer, holding the light high. My suspicion was hideously correct. *The dagger had gone.* Only the cross-shaped sheath hung there above the altar.

"In a sudden, frightened flash of imagination, I pictured the thing adrift in the Chapel, moving here and there, as though of its own volition; for whatever Force wielded it, was certainly beyond visibility. I turned my head stiffly over to the left, glancing frightenedly behind me, and flashing the light to help my eyes. In the same instant I was struck a tremendous blow over the left breast, and hurled backward from the chancel-rail, into the aisle, my armour clanging loudly in the horrible silence. I landed on my back, and slithered along on the polished marble. My shoulder struck the corner of a pew front, and brought me up, half stunned. I scrambled to my feet, horribly sick and shaken; but the fear that was on me, making little of that at the moment. I was minus both revolver and lantern, and utterly bewildered as to just where I was standing. I bowed my head, and made a scrambling run in the complete darkness and dashed into a pew. I jumped back, staggering, got my bearings a little, and raced down the centre of the aisle, putting my mailed arms over my face. I plunged into my camera, hurling it among the pews. I crashed into the font, and reeled back. Then I was at the exit. I fumbled madly in my dressing-gown pocket for the key. I found it and scraped at the door, feverishly, for the keyhole. I found the keyhole, turned the key, burst the door open, and was into the passage. I slammed the door and leant hard against it, gasping, whilst I felt crazily again for the keyhole, this time to lock the door upon what was in the Chapel. I succeeded, and began to feel my way stupidly along the wall of the corridor. Presently I had come to the big hall, and so in a little to my room.

"In my room, I sat for a while, until I had steadied down something to the normal. After a time I commenced to strip off the armour. I saw then that both the chain-mail and the plate-armour had been pierced over the breast. And, suddenly, it came home to me that the Thing had struck for my heart.

"Stripping rapidly, I found that the skin of the breast over the heart had just been cut sufficiently to allow a little blood to stain my shirt, nothing more. Only, the whole breast was badly bruised and intensely painful. You can imagine what would have happened if I had not worn the armour. In any case, it is a marvel that I was not knocked senseless.

"I did not go to bed at all that night, but sat upon the edge, thinking, and waiting for the dawn; for I had to remove my litter before Sir Alfred Jarnock should enter, if I were to hide from him the fact that I had managed a duplicate key.

"So soon as the pale light of the morning had strengthened sufficiently to show me the various details of my room, I made my way quietly down to the Chapel. Very silently, and with tense nerves, I opened the door. The chill light of the dawn made distinct the whole place—everything seeming instinct with a ghostly, unearthly quiet. Can you get the feeling? I waited several minutes at the door, allowing the morning to grow, and likewise my courage, I suppose. Presently the rising sun threw an odd beam right in through the big, East window, making coloured sunshine all the length of the Chapel. And then, with a tremendous effort, I forced myself to enter.

"I went up the aisle to where I had overthrown my camera in the darkness. The legs of the tripod were sticking up from the interior of a pew, and I expected to find the machine smashed to pieces; yet, beyond that the ground glass was broken, there was no real damage done.

"I replaced the camera in the position from which I had taken the previous photography; but the slide containing the plate I had exposed by flashlight I removed and put into one of my side pockets, regretting that I had not taken a second flash-picture at the instant when I heard those strange sounds up in the chancel.

"Having tidied my photographic apparatus, I went to the chancel to recover my lantern and revolver, which had both—as you know—been knocked from my hands when I was stabbed. I found the lantern lying, hopelessly bent, with smashed lens, just under the pulpit. My revolver I must have held until my shoulder struck the pew, for it was lying there in the aisle, just about where I believe I cannoned into the pew-corner. It was quite undamaged.

"Having secured these two articles, I walked up to the chancel-rail to see whether the dagger had returned, or been returned, to its sheath above the altar. Before, however, I reached the chancel-rail, I had a slight shock; for there on the floor of the chancel, about a yard away from where I had been struck, lay the dagger, quiet and demure upon the polished marble pavement. I wonder whether you will, any of you, understand the nervousness that took me at the sight of the thing. With a sudden, unreasoned action, I jumped forward and put my foot on it, to hold it there. Can you understand? Do you? And, you know, I could not stoop down and pick it up with my hands for quite a minute, I should think. Afterwards, when I had done so, however, and handled it a little, this feeling passed away and my Reason (and also, I expect, the daylight) made me feel that I had been a little bit of an ass. Quite natural, though, I assure you! Yet it was a new kind of fear to me. I'm taking no notice of the cheap joke about the ass! I am talking about the curiousness of learning in that moment a new shade or quality of fear that had hitherto been outside of my knowledge or imagination. Does it interest you?

"I examined the dagger, minutely, turning it over and over in my hands and never—as I suddenly discovered—holding it loosely. It was as if I were subconsciously surprised that it lay quiet in my hands. Yet even this feeling passed, largely, after a short while. The curious weapon showed no signs of the blow, except that the dull colour of the blade was slightly brighter on the rounded point that had cut through the armour.

"Presently, when I had made an end of staring at the dagger, I went up the chancel step and in through the little gate. Then, kneeling upon the altar, I replaced the dagger in its sheath, and came outside of the rail again, closing the gate after me and feeling awarely uncomfortable because the horrible old weapon was back again in its accustomed place. I suppose, without analysing my feelings very deeply, I had an unreasoned and only half conscious belief that there was a greater probability of danger when the dagger hung in its five-century resting place than when it was out of it! Yet, somehow I don't think this is a very good explanation, when I remember the *demure* look the thing seemed to have when I saw it lying on the floor of the chancel. Only I know this, that when I had replaced the dagger I had quite a touch of nerves and I stopped only to pick up my lantern from where I had placed it whilst I examined the weapon, after which I went down the quiet aisle at a pretty quick walk, and so got out of the place.

"That the nerve tension had been considerable, I realised, when I had locked the door behind me. I felt no inclination now to think of old Sir Alfred as a hypochondriac because he had taken such hyper-seeming precautions regarding the Chapel. I had a sudden wonder as to whether he might not have some knowledge of a long prior tragedy in which the dagger had been concerned.

"I returned to my room, washed, shaved and dressed, after which I read awhile. Then I went downstairs and got the acting butler to give me some sandwiches and a cup of coffee.

"Half an hour later I was heading for Burton-tree, as hard as I could walk; for a sudden idea had come to me, which I was anxious to test. I reached the town a little before eight-thirty, and found the local photographer with his shutters still up. I did not wait, but knocked until he appeared with his coat off, evidently in the act of dealing with his breakfast. In a few words I made clear that I wanted the use of his dark room immediately, and this he at once placed at my disposal.

"I had brought with me the slide which contained the plate that I had used with the flash-light, and as soon as I was ready I set to work to develop. Yet, it was not the plate which I had exposed, that I first put into the solution, but the second plate, which had been ready in the camera during all the time of my waiting in the darkness. You see, the lens had been uncapped all that while, so that the whole chancel had been, as it were, under observation.

"You all know something of my experiments in 'Lightless Photography,' that is, appreciating light. It was X-ray work that started me in that direction. Yet, you must understand, though I was attempting to develop this 'unexposed' plate, I had no definite idea of results—nothing more than a vague hope that it might show me something.

"Yet, because of the possibilities, it was with the most intense and absorbing interest that I watched the plate under the action of the developer. Presently I saw a faint smudge of black appear in the upper part, and after that others, indistinct and wavering of outline. I held the negative up to the light. The marks were rather small, and were almost entirely confined to one end of the plate, but as I have said, lacked definiteness. Yet, such as they were, they were sufficient to make me very excited and I shoved the thing quickly back into the solution.

"For some minutes further I watched it, lifting it out once or twice to make a more exact scrutiny, but could not imagine what the markings might represent, until suddenly it occurred to me that in one of two places they certainly had shapes suggestive of a cross-hilted dagger. Yet, the shapes were sufficiently indefinite to make me careful not to let myself be over-impressed by the uncomfortable resemblance, though I must confess, the very thought was sufficient to set some odd thrills adrift in me.

"I carried development a little further, then put the negative into the hypo, and commenced work upon the other plate. This came up nicely, and very soon I had a really decent negative that appeared similar in every respect (except for the difference of lighting) to the negative I had taken during the previous day. I fixed the plate, then having washed both it and the 'unexposed' one for a few minutes under the tap, I put them into methylated spirits for fifteen minutes, after which I carried them into the photographer's kitchen and dried them in the oven.

"Whilst the two plates were drying the photographer and I made an enlargement from the negative I had taken by daylight. Then we did the same with the two that I had just developed, washing them as quickly as possible, for I was not troubling about the permanency of the prints, and drying them with spirits.

"When this was done I took them to the window and made a thorough examination, commencing with the one that appeared to show shadowy daggers in several places. Yet, though it was now enlarged, I was still unable to feel convinced that the marks truly represented anything abnormal; and because of this, I put it on one side, determined not to let my imagination play too large a part in constructing weapons out of the indefinite outlines.

"I took up the two other enlargements, both of the chancel, as you will remember, and commenced to compare them. For some minutes I examined them without being able to distinguish any difference in the scene they portrayed, and then abruptly, I saw something in which they varied. In the second enlargement—the one made from the flashlight negative—the dagger was not in its sheath. Yet, I had felt sure it was there but a few minutes before I took the photograph.

"After this discovery I began to compare the two enlargements in a very different manner from my previous scrutiny. I borrowed a pair of calipers from the photographer and with these I carried out a most methodical and exact comparison of the details shown in the two photographs.

"Suddenly I came upon something that set me all tingling with excitement. I threw the calipers down, paid the photographer, and walked out through the shop into the street. The three enlargements I took with me, making them into a roll as I went. At the corner of the street I had the luck to get a cab and was soon back at the castle.

"I hurried up to my room and put the photographs away; then I went down to see whether I could find Sir Alfred Jarnock; but Mr. George Jarnock, who met me, told me that his father was too unwell to rise and would prefer that no one entered the Chapel unless he were about.

"Young Jarnock made a half apologetic excuse for his father; remarking that Sir Alfred Jarnock was perhaps inclined to be a little over careful; but that, considering what had happened, we must agree that the need for his carefulness had been justified. He added, also, that even before the horrible attack on the butler his father had been just as particular, always keep-ing the key and never allowing the door to be unlocked except when the place was in use for Divine Service, and for an hour each forenoon when the cleaners were in.

"To all this I nodded understandingly; but when, presently, the young man left me I took my duplicate key and made for the door of the Chapel. I went in and locked it behind me, after which I carried out some intensely interesting and rather weird experiments. These proved successful to such an extent that I came out of the place in a perfect fever of excitement. I inquired for Mr. George Jarnock and was told that he was in the morning room.

"'Come along,' I said, when I had found him. 'Please give me a lift. I've something exceedingly strange to show you.'

"He was palpably very much puzzled, but came quickly. As we strode along he asked me a score of questions, to all of which I just shook my head, asking him to wait a little.

"I led the way to the Armoury. Here I suggested that he should take one side of a dummy, dressed in half-plate armour, whilst I took the other. He nodded, though obviously vastly bewildered, and together we carried the thing to the Chapel door. When he saw me take out my key and open the way for us he appeared even more astonished, but held himself in, evidently waiting for me to explain. We entered the Chapel and I locked the door behind us, after which we carted the armoured dummy up the aisle to the gate of the chancel-rail where we put it down upon its round, wooden stand.

"'Stand back!' I shouted suddenly as young Jarnock made a movement to open the gate. "My God, man! you mustn't do that!'

"'Do what?' he asked, half startled and half irritated by my words and manner.

"'One minute,' I said. 'Just stand to the side a moment, and watch.'

"He stepped to the left whilst I took the dummy in my arms and turned it to face the altar, so that it stood close to the gate. Then, standing well away on the right side, I pressed the back of the thing so that it leant forward a little upon the gate, which flew open. In the same instant, the dummy was struck a tremendous blow that hurled it into the aisle, the armour rattling and clanging upon the polished marble floor.

"'Good God!' shouted young Jarnock, and ran back from the chancel-rail, his face very white.

"'Come and look at the thing,' I said, and led the way to where the dummy lay, its armoured upper limbs all splayed adrift in queer contortions. I stooped over it and pointed. There, driven right through the thick steel breastplate, was the 'waeful dagger.'

"'Good God!' said young Jarnock again. 'Good God! It's the dagger! The thing's been stabbed, same as Bellett!'

"'Yes,' I replied, and saw him glance swiftly towards the entrance of the Chapel. But I will do him the justice to say that he never budged an inch.

"'Come and see how it was done,' I said, and led the way back to the chancel-rail. From the wall to the left of the altar I took down a long, curiously ornamented, iron instrument, not unlike a short spear. The sharp end of this I inserted in a hole in the left-hand gate-post of the chancel gateway. I lifted hard, and a section of the post, from the floor upwards, bent inwards towards the altar, as though hinged at the bottom. Down it went, leaving the remaining part of the post standing. As I bent the movable portion lower there came a quick click and a section of the floor slid to one side, showing a long, shallow cavity, sufficient to enclose the post. I put my weight to the lever and hove the post down into the niche. Immediately there was a sharp clang, as some catch snicked in, and held it against the powerful operating spring.

"I went over now to the dummy, and after a few minutes' work managed to wrench the dagger loose out of the armour. I brought the old weapon and placed its hilt in a hole near the top of the post where it fitted loosely, the point upwards. After that I went again to the lever and gave another strong heave, and the post descended about a foot, to the bottom of the

cavity, catching there with another clang. I withdrew the lever and the narrow strip of floor slid back, covering post and dagger, and looking no different from the surrounding surface.

"Then I shut the chancel-gate, and we both stood well to one side. I took the spear-like lever, and gave the gate a little push, so that it opened. Instantly there was a loud thud, and something sang through the air, striking the bottom wall of the Chapel. It was the dagger. I showed Jarnock then that the other half of the post had sprung back into place, making the whole post as thick as the one upon the right-hand side of the gate.

"'There!' I said, turning to the young man and tapping the divided post. 'There's the "invisible" thing that used the dagger, but who the deuce is the person who sets the trap?' I looked at him keenly as I spoke.

"'My father is the only one who has a key,' he said. 'So it's practically impossible for anyone to get in and meddle.'

"I looked at him again, but it was obvious that he had not yet reached out to any conclusion.

"'See here, Mr. Jarnock,' I said, perhaps rather curter than I should have done, considering what I had to say. 'Are you quite sure that Sir Alfred is quite balanced—mentally?'

"He looked at me, half frightenedly and flushing a little. I realised then how badly I put it.

"'I—I don't know,' he replied, after a slight pause and was then silent, except for one or two incoherent half-remarks.

"'Tell the truth,' I said. 'Haven't you suspected something, now and again? You needn't be afraid to tell me.'

"'Well,' he answered slowly, 'I'll admit I've thought father a little—a little strange, perhaps, at times. But I've always tried to think I was mistaken. I've always hoped no one else would see it. You see, I'm very fond of the old guv-nor.'

"I nodded.

"'Quite right, too,' I said. 'There's not the least need to make any kind of scandal about this. We must do something, though, but in a quiet way. No fuss, you know. I should go and have a chat with your father, and tell him we've found out about this thing.' I touched the divided post.

"Young Jarnock seemed very grateful for my advice and after shaking my hand pretty hard, took my key, and let himself out of the Chapel. He came back in about an hour, looking rather upset. He told me that my conclusions were perfectly correct. It was Sir Alfred Jarnock who had set the trap, both on the night that the butler was nearly killed, and on the past night. Indeed, it seemed that the old gentleman had set it every night for many years. He had learnt of its existence from an old M.S.-book in the Castle library. It had been planned and used in an earlier age as a protection for the gold vessels of the Ritual, which were, it seemed, kept in a hidden recess at the back of the altar.

"This recess Sir Alfred Jarnock had utilised, secretly, to store his wife's jewellery. She had died some twelve years back, and the young man told me that his father had never seemed quite himself since.

"I mentioned to young Jarnock how puzzled I was that the trap had been set *before* the service, on the night that the butler was struck; for, if I understood him aright, his father had been in the habit of setting the trap late every night and unsetting it each morning before anyone entered the Chapel. He replied that his father, in a fit of temporary forgetfulness (natural enough in his neurotic condition), must have set it too early and hence what had so nearly proved a tragedy.

"That is about all there is to tell. The old man is not (so far as I could learn), really insane in the popularly accepted sense of the word. He is extremely neurotic and has developed into a hypochondriac, the whole condition probably brought about by the shock and sorrow resultant on the death of his wife, leading to years of sad broodings and to overmuch of his own company and thoughts. Indeed, young Jarnock told me that his father would sometimes pray for hours together, alone in the Chapel." Carnacki made an end of speaking and leant forward for a spill.

"But you've never told us just *how* you discovered the secret of the divided post and all that," I said, speaking for the four of us.

"Oh, that!" replied Carnacki, puffing vigorously at his pipe. "I found—on comparing the—photos, that the one—taken in the—daytime, showed a thicker left-hand gate-post, than the one taken at night by the flashlight. That put me on to the track. I saw at once that there might be some mechanical dodge at the back of the whole queer business and nothing at all of an abnormal nature. I examined the post and the rest was simple enough, you know.

"By the way," he continued, rising and going to the mantelpiece, "you may be interested to have a look at the so-called 'waeful dagger.' Young Jarnock was kind enough to present it to me, as a little memento of my adventure."

He handed it round to us and whilst we examined it, stood silent before the fire, puffing meditatively at his pipe.

"Jarnock and I made the trap so that it won't work," he remarked after a few moments. "I've got the dagger, as you see, and old Bellett's getting about again, so that the whole business can be hushed up, decently. All the same I fancy the Chapel will never lose its reputation as a dangerous place. Should be pretty safe now to keep valuables in."

"There's two things you haven't explained yet," I said. "What do you think caused the two clangey sounds when you were in the Chapel in the dark? And do you believe the soft tready sounds were real, or only a fancy, with your being so worked up and tense?"

"Don't know for certain about the clangs," replied Carnacki. "I've puzzled quite a bit about them. I can only think that the spring which worked the post must have 'given' a trifle, slipped you know, in the catch. If it did, under such a tension, it would make a bit of a ringing noise. And a little sound goes a long way in the middle of the night when you're thinking of 'ghostesses.' You can understand that—eh?"

"Yes," I agreed. "And the other sounds?"

"Well, the same thing—I mean the extraordinary quietness—may help to explain these a bit. They may have been some usual enough sound that would never have been noticed under ordinary conditions, or they may have been only fancy. It is just impossible to say. They were disgustingly real to me. As for the slithery noise, I am pretty sure that one of the tripod legs of my camera must have slipped a few inches; if it did so, it may easily have jolted the lens-cap off the base-board, which would account for that queer little tap which I heard directly after."

"How do you account for the dagger being in its place above the altar when you first examined it that night?" I asked. "How could it be there, when at that very moment it was set in the trap?"

"That was my mistake," replied Carnacki. "The dagger could not possibly have been in its sheath at the time, though I thought it was. You see, the curious cross-hilted sheath gave the appearance of the complete weapon, as you can understand. The hilt of the dagger protrudes very little above the continued portion of the sheath—a most inconvenient arrangement for drawing quickly!" He nodded sagely at the lot of us and yawned, then glanced at the clock.

"Out you go!" he said, in friendly fashion, using the recognised formula. "I want a sleep."

We rose, shook him by the hand, and went out presently into the night and the quiet of the Embankment, and so to our homes.

DEPARTMENT OF IMPOSSIBLE CRIMES

JAMES YAFFE

ALTHOUGH NOT A PROLIFIC AUTHOR, the stories and novels of James Yaffe (1927–) have acquired a following deeply devoted to his exceptional narratives of fair-play detective fiction. Born in Chicago, he moved to New York City at an early age and wrote his first story while still in high school. That effort, "Department of Impossible Crimes," was published in *Ellery Queen's Mystery Magazine,* launching a series of stories about Paul Dawn and the fictional division of the NYPD that he heads. Yaffe then created his most popular detective character, Mom, a Jewish widow who lives in the Bronx. A true armchair detective, Mom solves cases for her son, a detective, merely by listening to his accounts of the evidence during their traditional Friday-night dinners. These stories were frequent winners in the annual *EQMM* contests and spawned five novels, beginning with *A Nice Murder for Mom* (1988).

After Yaffe graduated from Yale, he served in the navy and spent a full year in Paris before launching his writing career. A book of non-mystery stories, *Poor Cousin Evelyn* (1951), received good reviews, followed by *Nothing but the Night* (1957), a fictionalized version of the famous Leopold-Loeb murder trial. He has written several plays, the best known being *The Deadly Game* (1960), an adaptation of Friedrich Dürrenmatt's *Traps*; it was the basis for a 1982 television movie with George Segal, Trevor Howard, and Robert Morley. With Jerome Weidman, Yaffe wrote the drama *Ivory Tower* (1969), in which an American poet in 1943 calls for soldiers to lay down their arms in the face of the Nazi onslaught and is accused of treason. Yaffe wrote for numerous TV series, including *Studio One, The U.S. Steel Hour, Suspicion,* and *The Alfred Hitchcock Hour.*

"Department of Impossible Crimes" was first published in the July 1943 issue of *Ellery Queen's Mystery Magazine.*

DEPARTMENT OF IMPOSSIBLE CRIMES

JAMES YAFFE

BLANK BLANK Blank Blank t. If he could only find those first four letters everything would be all right. He was sure of it.

"What's a five letter word meaning 'to fall prostrate'? The last letter is 't.'"

"I'm sure I couldn't tell you," said Inspector Stanley Fledge, of the New York Homicide Squad. "Now suppose you listen to me for a minute. We've got a case on our hands. A murder. It's running the force ragged. And you're just the man to solve it."

Paul Dawn was flattered. He liked it very much indeed when they came to him for advice, though he would have cut off his right arm rather than admit it. He took a cigarette from the box on his desk and lit it. He shook out the match and tossed it neatly into the waste paper basket. "Neat shot, eh?" Paul was a rather nice-looking young man. There was a faraway expression on his face most of the time. Paul could have the most rousing adventures in the barren ice stretches of the North Pole, while his body was firmly implanted in his office chair.

"Look here, Paul," Inspector Fledge insisted, "this isn't funny business, you know. We don't bother you very often, do we? Only in cases of emergency. So put away your crossword puzzles and whatchamacallits and listen to me."

Stanley Fledge was a grizzled old veteran of the Homicide Squad. Paul Dawn didn't mind Fledge, it was just that he couldn't understand him. Fledge was a Man of Action, and this jarred Paul's scheme of things. Paul's idea of action was to sit in an easy chair, fondling a bottle, and do nothing more than let his mind wander.

He saw Fledge's peering little rabbit-eyes focussed anxiously upon him, so he deposited himself back in this world.

"Is this crime in my department?"

"You bet. It's one of the most impossible crimes we've ever come across."

"Go ahead then." Paul leaned back in his chair, and as he listened he tapped the point of his pencil absently against the desk. It was because of his passion for impossible crimes—crimes which couldn't have happened—that he had persuaded the Commissioner to let him take charge of an obscure little office connected to the Homicide Squad, known as the D.I.C.—The Department of Impossible Crimes.

"Here's the problem," Fledge said. "A rich old stockbroker named George Seabrook was killed last night. He'd been spending the evening with some of his poor relations—his nephew Philip, and Philip's wife, Agnes.

"Around nine o'clock Seabrook got up to go. He wanted to be back at his home by ten. They said their good-byes and walked their uncle to the elevator."

Paul's attention was caught by Stanley Fledge's large and protruding Adam's apple. It bobbed up and down in a little bouncing motion as the Inspector spoke. And on the word "elevator" Paul received a special treat. The Adam's apple, caught up by the flow of syllables, not only bounded back and forth but wobbled slightly to the side.

If only Fledge would say "elevator" a few more times.

"The Seabrooks," continued the Inspector, "live in a small apartment house called the Lexington Arms. They have a couple of rooms on the fifth floor. The Lexington Arms has only one elevator"—*Hurray!*—"and it's one of those automatic, push-button affairs. You know. You push the button for the third floor and the elevator goes to the third floor.

"Anyway, George Seabrook got into the elevator"—*Again!*—"and pushed the button for the first floor. Philip Seabrook and Agnes Seabrook both saw him push the button for the first floor. So did Mrs. Battleman, a woman who lives in one of the other apartments on the fifth floor. Mrs. Battleman had just opened the door of her apartment in order to take in the evening paper which was lying on the mat. She saw Seabrook getting into the elevator. She saw him push the button. And Mrs. Battleman, Philip Seabrook, and Agnes Seabrook can testify that when that elevator started to go down George Seabrook was in perfectly good condition."

Something Fledge said made Paul switch his attention to the matter on hand. He would return to the elusive little Adam's apple later. "What do you mean by 'perfectly good condition'?"

"I mean alive." The Inspector cleared his throat and went on. "At the same time, Paul, two tenants of the Lexington Arms were waiting for the elevator on the first floor. One of them was a Dr. Herbert Martin, who was coming back from a call, and the other one was a stenographer, Miss Flora Kingsley. Incidentally, this Kingsley woman used to work for Seabrook years ago.

"These two waited at the first floor. Around nine o'clock this was. They saw the indicator above the elevator door stop at the fifth floor. Then they saw the indicator move from the fifth floor to the first floor. They were both watching that indicator all the time, and they swear that it didn't stop once on its way down to their floor.

In other words, from the time George Seabrook got into that elevator on the fifth floor to the time that elevator reached the first floor, it made no other stops.

"Now just a little about the construction of the elevator. It's made of good, thick wood. The walls, floor and ceiling are absolutely solid. There are no secret doorways or hidden entrances in it. The only way of getting into that elevator or out is by the door. And the mechanism is such that the door won't open if the elevator is in motion. Since the elevator *was* in motion from Floor 5 to Floor 1, the door couldn't have been opened. And since that door was the only entrance to the elevator, nobody could have possibly entered it or left it while George Seabrook took his trip down. Get the picture?"

Paul nodded. "But I don't see what you're leading up to, Fledge."

"Just this." The Inspector leaned forward and spoke intently. "George Seabrook was alive when he entered the elevator. No one else was in the elevator. It traveled straight down without any stops. And yet, when that elevator reached the first floor, Dr. Martin and Miss Kingsley pulled open the door, and found George Seabrook lying dead on the elevator floor, *with a knife in his back*."

Fledge slammed the palm of his hand down on the surface of the desk to emphasize his point. "And if that isn't an impossible crime," he said, "I don't know what is!"

A loud silence filled the room.

Paul Dawn was thinking. In a slow, lazy fashion of course—but for him any form of concentrated thought was an effort. He usually got better results by giving his mind a free hand and letting it spread out in whichever direction it liked. But now he was thinking about the Impossible Crime in the Elevator. Paul always tabbed his cases with titles. The labels helped him keep everything straight.

He kept on tapping his pencil lightly against a blotter that lay on his desk. Stanley Fledge's Adam's apple was entirely forgotten.

"Well, Paul," Fledge asked eagerly. "What do you think of it?"

"Think of what?"

"The case. The impossible murder."

"I try not to," said Paul. "It's interesting, though."

"It'll interest me when we clear it up."

Paul blew a nearly perfect smoke ring, a feat which gave him a great deal of satisfaction. "I have visions," he said suddenly, and Fledge looked at him queerly. Paul closed his eyes. "I see our victim, George Seabrook. He stands in the elevator probably with the idea that he is completely alone. And then without warning something happens. The machinery begins to turn. The automatic thingamajig, whatever it might be, starts to whirr, and a knife is plunged into George Seabrook's back. Then our murderer vanishes. Very melodramatic. Especially melodramatic since, from what you've told me, it couldn't have happened that way."

"And yet," said the Inspector, scratching his chin contemplatively, "it looks like it couldn't have happened any other way."

"I wonder how it did happen," Paul said. "Pigs don't fly. Automobiles can't change into kangaroos. And murderers don't disappear up elevator shafts whenever they please. This case is riddled with complexities."

"It's riddled with something, all right." Fledge shook his head gloomily. "How about it? Does it appeal to you?"

"Oh, vaguely." Of course it appeals, Paul thought. He hadn't had a case for weeks that appealed half as much. But it wouldn't do to show he was too anxious. Bored and superior. That was the proper effect. "By the way, Fledge, have you thought of a five letter word meaning 'to fall prostrate' yet? Remember, the last letter is 't.'"

"No, I haven't given it a thought," the Inspector said irritably. "Will you take the case?"

"I'll take the case."

He blew another smoke ring which, he was glad to note, was up to his usual high standard.

"This," said Paul Dawn out loud though he meant it to himself, "is going to be good."

The remark was prompted by his first glance at the automatic elevator in the Lexington Arms. A second glance was unnecessary. The elevator was solid all right. Impenetrable even. No suspicious cracks in the wall. No out-of-place bumps in the ceiling. No concealed crevices in the floor. With the door closed, Paul reflected, a bug would have trouble sneaking into that elevator. He thought of all the trouble it would have saved him if only the builder had obligingly placed a few trap doors in the floor, or several sliding panels in the wall. But this was the kind of difficult problem he liked, something like that troublesome five letter word meaning 'to fall prostrate.' He wondered whether, if he tried falling prostrate once or twice, it might not give him the answer.

With effort he pulled his mind back to more immediate things.

"Tight as a drum, isn't it?" Stanley Fledge said. "It doesn't look as if there's any way at all to get into it. But someone did. It's frightening, Paul. Can't say I'm particularly comforted by the idea of an invisible murderer running around loose. Come on, now. Let's get busy."

The Fledge philosophy in a few short words, Paul thought. Inspector Stanley Let's-Get-Busy Fledge. These get-up-and-go men upset Paul's nervous system.

"Let's get busy at what?" he asked.

"Questioning suspects! Hunting for clues! Solving the case! That's what. Come on."

Paul puffed tranquilly at his cigarette, and seated himself on the one chair in the cramped lobby of the Lexington Arms. "I'll get busy right here," he said. "I have a few questions to ask of *you.*"

"I didn't commit the murder."

Paul let that one pass. "First, what about fingerprints? Have you found any?"

Fledge snorted indelicately. "Too many. Just about everybody in the building rode up in that elevator yesterday. But the clearest sets are made by George Seabrook."

"Did you find his thumbprint on the first-floor button?"

"Sure we did. That's the first place we looked."

"Did you find Seabrook's print on *any of the other* push buttons?"

Fledge looked at him with a puzzled expression. "Why do you ask that?"

"Did you?"

"Yes, as a matter of fact we did."

If Paul felt any great interest or eagerness his face didn't show it. His expression was placid and mild. His eyes looked rather sleepy. He completely skipped over the obvious question. "What does the Medical Examiner say?" he asked instead.

"Death due to stabbing. Died instantly. Say! Hold on a minute." Fledge's face was a study in bewilderment. "Aren't you going to ask me on what button we found those other fingerprints of Seabrook's?"

"The fifth-floor button," said Paul absently. "What did the Medical Examiner say about Seabrook's general physical condition?"

Fledge's neck was reddening. "How did you know Seabrook's thumbprint was on the fifth-floor button?"

"Use your logic," Paul explained patiently. "When he came down from the fifth floor he pushed the first floor button. Therefore, earlier in the evening, when he went up from the first floor he must have pushed the *fifth*-floor button. Does it penetrate?"

Fledge nodded his head doubtfully. Paul blew another smoke ring. "I'll repeat my other question. What did the Medical Examiner say about Seabrook's general physical condition?"

"He said it was rotten. Seabrook was a sick man."

"What does his doctor say?"

"Seabrook's doctor? That's this Dr. Herbert Martin, who found the body. I haven't asked him yet."

"Why haven't you asked him?"

"I didn't think it was important."

"You didn't think it was important!" Paul gave him one of those very annoying and-you're-supposed-to-have-brains looks, and Fledge's face turned a livid shade of scarlet. Good tactics, thought Paul. Get him embarrassed. Impress him with his mediocrity and your own superiority. Mentally he patted himself on the back.

"When do you start questioning the suspects?" Fledge asked timidly.

"As soon as I find out what kind of a knife Seabrook was stabbed with."

"An ordinary pocket penknife. The murderer jabbed it in a few times."

"Fingerprints?"

"Not a single one. Only a few smudges, as if the man who handled the knife had been wearing gloves."

With a great deal of painful effort Paul pulled himself out of the chair. Inspector Fledge greeted the news that they would now question suspects with a great deal of pleasure. Paul knew why. The Inspector was known on the force as a suspect-pounder. He liked to squeeze information out of hostile witnesses. Sometimes he liked it even better than having the witness offer him the information in a perfectly friendly, cooperative manner.

"I've given instructions that no one in the building is to use the elevator," Fledge said. "But we can go up in it ourselves." They stepped into it, and Fledge pulled the door shut and then the steel elevator gate. His thumb stabbed the button marked five. "First, Mr. and Mrs. Philip Seabrook."

On the way up, Fledge pointed to a large X mark drawn in the very corner of the elevator in white chalk.

"That marks the spot where the body was found."

X marks the spot.

"Seabrook's body," the Inspector went on, "was kinda slumped up in the corner when Dr. Martin and Miss Kingsley first saw him. His back was against the wall, and the knife was sticking out his back."

The elevator had come to a stop. They walked out into the fifth-floor hallway.

"5-E," said the Inspector, pushing a doorbell. "Now, we can get busy solving this thing."

Paul winced.

———

Paul Dawn had a way with suspects. He managed to extract more information from witnesses in his own quiet, unintentional way than the bulldozing, browbeating Stanley Fledge. Paul explained it by saying that he "caught them off guard," which is probably just as good an explanation as any.

Agnes Seabrook was a cute little blonde with a nice smile and a vacant head. Her husband was more the studious type. He was a short young man, slightly pudgy in spots, with big eyes peering out from behind dark-rimmed glasses. With the appearance of two representatives of the Law, he appeared to be rather flustered.

"And I'll say right now," he said hotly, "that this is getting to be downright annoying. Police dropping in every minute of the day to ask me stupid questions. I couldn't even get down to the office today."

"I'm really very sorry, Mr. Seabrook," Fledge said soothingly, "but routine is routine. I think I can promise you that this will be the last time we question you."

"It better be. Enough is enough. I'll say right now that—"

Fledge cleared his throat. "Now, Mr. Seabrook, will you tell me again what happened last night?"

"For the five thousandth time. We had dinner with Uncle George. At nine o'clock he had to leave, so we walked him to the elevator. The elevator came. He said goodbye. He pushed the button for the first floor. He said goodbye again. The elevator door closed. And that was that."

"Your neighbor, Mrs. Battleman, saw all this too?"

"Yeah. Old leather-puss came out to take in her evening paper. Only I think she really wanted to catch a look at Uncle George. Big financier and all that. She's an old sneak, anyway."

"She is not an old sneak, Phil!" Mrs. Seabrook spoke up for the first time, indignantly. "She's a charming and cultured woman. And she's one of the nicest girls I know."

"Girls," Philip sneered. "If that 'girl' is a day under seventy-five I'll eat her bustle."

"You're absolutely certain that Mr. George Seabrook was alive when that elevator door closed?" Fledge asked.

"He didn't *look* dead," Agnes Seabrook said tentatively.

Philip drew himself up in what he meant to be a haughty manner. "I can still tell a live man from a corpse, Inspector," he said.

"Now," said Fledge, veering off on another tack, "what about motive? Mr. Seabrook, can you think of any possible reason why anyone should want to kill your uncle?"

"I'm sure I can't tell you." Philip glared at Fledge defiantly. "Seems to me that's your job, Inspector."

"So it is." Fledge turned to Agnes. "Can you think of any reason?"

"Of course," she said. "There are a lot of people who'd want to kill Uncle George."

"Ah! Who?"

"Well, Philip and myself, for instance."

Philip's face grew red. "You're a fool, Agnes," he exploded.

"No, I'm not." She faced the Inspector. "You were bound to find out sooner or later. We didn't like George Seabrook. Not many people did. He was horribly conceited, pompous, self-righteous, possessive—that's about all the words I can think of. Anyway, that's the kind of awful old man he was. He didn't like Philip getting married to me, and when he did he decided he was going to give me a sort of six months period of inspection. For the last six months, since we were married, George Seabrook has been inviting himself up to the apartment for dinner almost every week. And you know why? Just so he could look me over and see if he 'approved' of me. Well, we didn't like that. We don't like being pawed over, and dissected by a rich relative. There were times when I felt like killing him myself."

Here was a phenomenon, Paul thought. A dumb woman with brains. For lack of anything better to do, he decided to ask a question. "You'll pardon me, Mrs. Seabrook—" His voice was quiet enough but they all started at the sound of it. "I was just wondering—if you really detested your uncle so much, why did you tolerate him all this time?"

"Just what I was about to ask," Fledge said.

"Money!" Philip Seabrook burst out suddenly. "What did you think? Uncle George was a rich man, and I'm not. But I was his only living relative. And if you can't follow it from there—"

"You stood to gain everything?" Fledge asked.

"I stood! I do get everything. Uncle's lawyer phoned me this morning. And I'm not particularly sorry or humble about it either. As a matter of fact, it's a relief that he's dead. I never did get Rockefeller's salary."

There was a strained pause.

Well, now, this is nice, thought Paul Dawn. It isn't often that he had a perfect motive, wrapped in a neat little bundle, deposited in his lap. But Inspector Fledge was hesitating. Under ordinary circumstances, a police officer would arrest a suspect on an admission like that. But not in this case. Fledge could do nothing. Paul smiled as he wondered how the Inspector was going to charge anybody with a murder that nobody could have committed.

With a sudden pang of worry, Paul wondered how he himself was going to figure this thing out. The fact remained. Somebody must have got into that elevator—except that nobody *could* have got into it.

"Have any questions before we leave, Paul?" said Fledge rising.

"Uh—yes. Just one." He looked at the Seabrooks with that same sleepy expression. "Mr. or Mrs. Seabrook—perhaps you can tell me one thing. Can you think of a five letter word meaning 'to fall prostrate' and the last letter is 't'?"

The very puzzled Seabrooks stared blankly and the two detectives left.

Out in the hallway, Fledge was completely bewildered. "Listen, Paul, are you sure you know what you're doing?"

"Maybe it was suicide," Paul muttered.

"Suicide!" Fledge spoke in a murderously calm voice. "And how, tell me, did our suicidal corpse STAB HIMSELF IN THE BACK?"

"Perhaps," said Paul maliciously, "he was a contortionist."

Dr. Herbert Martin was one of those big, hearty, robust physicians who are never without their bedside manner. Paul and Fledge found him in his downtown office, and were treated to an effusive greeting.

"Sit down, gentlemen! Glad to see you. Anything I can do to help? Horrible affair, isn't it? Well, well, well. What is it you want to know?"

The doctor had a trick of rubbing his big ham-like hands together in a businesslike manner while speaking.

"We'd just like to know once more what happened, Doctor." Fledge was polite but still official.

"What happened? Now let me see." The doctor paused thoughtfully. "I'd just come back to the apartment from a call I'd been making. Patient was an old woman I've been treating for years. She's a hypochondriac and pays me a lot of money to tell her there's something the matter with her. She's as healthy as a horse, really. Healthier. But I've got to make a living. At any rate, I arrived at the house just as the elevator door was closing. I pushed the button and waited. The indicator started at the first floor and went up to the fifth. Then it started down again. Around that time, another tenant—a woman—arrived and we waited together."

"Miss Flora Kingsley?"

"So I discovered later. I'm new to the building and I don't usually get very friendly with neighbors anyway. Trouble with all us New Yorkers. Stick to ourselves too much. But that's beside the point. Miss Kingsley and I waited till the elevator reached our floor. It stopped and I pulled open the door. Then—then I saw him." It seemed to Paul that Dr. Martin was trembling just slightly. "He was bunched up in the corner of the elevator, his back to the wall. I rushed toward him, but I told Miss Kingsley to stay back. She waited in the doorway and watched. I bent down by the body and saw the knife. She screamed. 'He's dead,' I said. 'Go phone the police!' At first she was frozen to the spot. I didn't want her to get hysterical, so I ordered her to phone the police. In a few minutes she returned and we waited together. Then you arrived, Inspector."

Convincing enough, Paul thought. "Doctor," he drawled, "you were George Seabrook's physician?"

"Yes. I was." Martin's gaze was level and unflinching.

"Wasn't in good health, was he?"

"No, he wasn't. He had heart trouble. Bad kidneys. Fainting spells. Bad headaches. A great deal of pain, I imagine."

"Enough pain, do you think, to make him commit suicide?"

The doctor hesitated a moment. Then finally he said, "Perhaps."

"That's not very definite."

"That's as definite as I care to be."

"Thank you, Dr. Martin."

"Oh, by the way," Martin said. "That's a puzzler, isn't it—how the murder was committed?"

"Certainly is," said Paul. "Talking of puzzlers, do you know a five letter word meaning 'to fall prostrate'? The last letter is 't.'"

"Crossword puzzles?" Martin said jovially. "Used to work them. Got out of the habit these days."

"Do you know the word?" Paul inquired.

"No."

Paul could understand why Miss Flora Kingsley had remained a spinster all sixty years of her life. She had tight lips, a drawn white face, and two piercing, highly menacing eyes. She looked to Paul as if she had escaped from a Boris Karloff movie. And the fact that she wore her hair in a very modern fashion only served to increase the ghoulish effect.

"What do you want to ask me?" Miss Kingsley asked in a flat, metallic voice.

"Miss Kingsley, we'd just like your story of what happened last evening."

She told them in short, precise sentences as if she knew it by heart. It corroborated what Dr.

Martin had told them almost exactly. Paul especially noticed how she described her reactions to the murder.

"I was quite broken up," she said. "Dr. Martin said that the man was dead, and after that I must have screamed. An exceedingly undignified thing to do."

"You used to work for Mr. Seabrook, Miss Kingsley?"

"Yes. I did." Her lips tightened. "Many years ago."

"Why did you leave him?"

"He retired from business."

"Do you know why?"

"No."

Paul spoke suddenly in a lazy voice. "Miss Kingsley, is it possible that Mr. Seabrook retired because his business failed?"

Her fingers gripped the side of her chair.

"Yes. That's possible."

"And wasn't there a rumor at the time that the reason his business failed was because Mr. Seabrook had been drawing illegally from the funds of his stockholders?"

"It was never proved!" she cried, jumping to her feet. It was her first sign of emotion. She subsided wearily into the chair. "I'm sorry," she said. "Yes. I'd heard that."

"You believed it?"

She nodded her head.

"Thank you. Uh—do you ever do crossword puzzles, Miss Kingsley?"

She looked at him with a very suspicious expression for a moment. Then her face hardened. She rose to her feet and faced both of them squarely.

"Would you gentlemen leave now?"

"You didn't answer my question," Paul said gently.

"No. I didn't, did I? Good afternoon."

They were in police headquarters that evening.

"Blind alleys," Stanley Fledge shouted. "Dead ends," Stanley Fledge yelled. "Stone walls," Stanley Fledge screamed. "And elevators. Damn it all, that's what gets me. I could take each one of them and sweat it out of them—if I only had some sort of a clue about the elevator. How did the murderer get into that elevator? What happened? Am I going nuts? Am I dreaming all this? *How did the murderer get into that elevator?*"

"The murderer didn't get into that elevator," said Paul very calmly.

Fledge's mouth fell open; his eyes bulged.

"What?"

"I said—the murderer didn't get into that elevator."

"Do you know how it was done?"

Paul Dawn lit a cigarette with a steady hand. He puffed once and let the smoke pour out of his nostrils. "I knew how it was done some time ago. The question was," he said, "to prove it."

"And did you—" Fledge gulped helplessly, "did you—prove it?"

"I did. Come up to my office tomorrow morning and find out all about it." He rose from his chair. "You'd better come early. At ten-thirty the morning paper arrives, and I'll be very busy—doing the crossword puzzle."

Paul Dawn kept a bottle of scotch in his desk drawer—for medicinal purposes. After he learned what the real solution was, Inspector Fledge was astounded enough to dispose of half the bottle in three large gulps.

"It's so simple," Paul said. "So easy. I really saw it all the time."

And it *was* simple. Very simple. But ingenious, Paul hastened to add. It was especially ingenious the way he explained it.

"All you've got to do is look at it with imagination. That's why these impossible crimes are right up my alley. I might not have a lot of things. Initiative or energy. But I certainly have imagination."

Inspector Fledge would be the last to deny it.

"Here's the way it really happened," Paul said. "In solving these impossible murders we've got to take a hard, unsentimental view. You've got to discount ghosts, or invisible men, or complicated contraptions operated by radio control. You've got to get it into your head that *there is no such thing as an impossible murder.*

"That's what I got into my head right from the start. George Seabrook was killed. Someone entered that elevator and shoved a knife into his back. In order to enter the elevator, the murderer had to come in, obviously, by an entrance. There is, however, only one entrance to the elevator. You searched it through and through yourself. You found only one entrance. I searched it through and through. I found only one entrance. That entrance is the elevator door. Therefore the murderer must have entered when the elevator door was open.

"But it's impossible for the elevator door to be open while the elevator is in motion, and in the course of this affair the elevator door was open only twice. It was open while the elevator was on the fifth floor, and while the elevator was on the first floor.

"Therefore George Seabrook was killed while the elevator was either on the fifth floor or on the first floor.

"Well, let's see about these two times. When Seabrook got into the elevator he was alive. When he pushed the elevator button he was alive. When the door closed he was alive. Three different people confirmed that, including a woman who can be considered an outsider. From this we conclude that Seabrook couldn't have been killed while the elevator was on the fifth floor.

"So he must have been killed while the elevator was on the first floor!"

"But as soon as the elevator door opened at the first floor," objected Fledge, "two different witnesses *saw* Seabrook lying on the floor with a knife in his back!"

"Did they? That is where we've been making our mistake all along. What do we know, and what are we only surmising? The witnesses say that Seabrook was lying on the floor with a knife in his back. But the witnesses only saw Seabrook from the elevator doorway. Seabrook's back was toward the wall. Actually all that *both* of these witnesses saw was Seabrook lying on the floor. Miss Kingsley was standing in the doorway all the time. Contrary to what she says, she couldn't possibly have seen that knife in Seabrook's back."

Fledge waved his hand at Paul like a child asking to be called on in class. "Hold on!" the Inspector said. "The action is moving too fast for me. So what if Miss Kingsley didn't see the knife—Dr. Martin did!"

"Did he?" Paul paused and smiled with satisfaction. "That's exactly my point, Fledge. Did Dr. Martin see the knife in Seabrook's back, or did Dr. Martin *merely say that he saw a knife in Seabrook's back?*

"Let's piece together the facts. Martin says that Miss Kingsley screamed and then he said, 'He's dead!' Miss Kingsley says that Martin said 'He's dead!' first, and *then* she screamed. Why should one of them lie? It's my guess that Martin lied because he made that exclamation 'He's dead!' for a purpose. He cried out 'He's dead!' in order psychologically to plant in Miss Kingsley's mind the false idea that she had seen Seabrook dead, when all she had really seen was *Seabrook lying on the floor.*

"Well, knowing that Seabrook wasn't dead, what *was* wrong with him? And there comes one of the greatest twists of Fate that I have ever encountered in my life. Remember my five-letter word meaning 'to fall prostrate.' The last letter is a 't.' Well, that's exactly what Seabrook did. He gave me my definition. He 'fell prostrated.' He *fainted*!

"Don't you see? Seabrook had one of his fainting spells while going down in the elevator. Dr. Martin said he was subject to them. When the elevator reached the first floor, Martin saw Seabrook lying there. He realized instantly what had happened. An idea sprang to his mind. He saw how he could take advantage of the fact that Seabrook had fainted in an elevator.

"Immediately he began to play up the idea that Seabrook was dead, all for Miss Kingsley's benefit. He rushed over to the body. He shouted

'He's dead!' He pointed to an imaginary knife in Seabrook's back that Miss Kingsley couldn't possibly see because of the body's position. All the time he kept her at a safe distance from Seabrook. He made it all seem very cold-blooded and realistic. By the time Dr. Martin had finished his little scene he had poor Miss Kingsley actually believing she had seen a corpse.

"Then he got rid of her—he ordered her to phone the police.

"This is another point against Dr. Martin. He was the only one in the whole bunch who was *alone with Seabrook* from the moment the old man got into that elevator!

"While Miss Kingsley was phoning, Martin bent down beside Seabrook and put on his doctor's rubber gloves. He had them in his medical bag. And we know he had his medical bag with him because he had just come back from a call. He put on the gloves, stabbed Seabrook in the back, and put the gloves back in the bag.

"Martin probably felt absolutely safe. As long as Miss Kingsley held up—and he was sure she would—he had nothing to worry about. Because she could always alibi him by testifying that Seabrook was dead at a time when Martin couldn't possibly have killed him. Get it?"

Inspector Fledge was breathing deeply, and he started to mop the sweat off his brow. "Now only one more point. Tell me the motive and I'll put the handcuffs on Dr. Martin."

"The motive," Paul Dawn said, "was staring us in the face all the time. Miss Kingsley confirmed the fact that Seabrook's business had once gone bankrupt owing to Seabrook's shady dealings. A lot of stockholders lost money in that collapse, and it's conceivable that one of them would hold a grudge for a long, long time. Look up Martin's past, why don't you?"

"I'd better hurry off now," said Inspector Fledge heartily, "and do my duty. Oh, by the way, this has been somewhat of a strain. You don't happen to have a bit of liquid refreshment, do you?"

Paul did. And that was when the Inspector emptied half the bottle.

THE ALUMINIUM DAGGER

R. AUSTIN FREEMAN

THE CREATOR of Dr. John Thorndyke, the greatest of all scientific detectives, Richard Austin Freeman (1862–1943), denied that his character was a detective at all, claiming that he "is an investigator of crime but he is not a detective. . . . The technique of Scotland Yard would be neither suitable nor possible to [Thorndyke]." It is exactly this type of hair-splitting for which the character is known, too. The stories about him are precise, filled with descriptions of slow, painstaking technique, which is largely responsible for Freeman being less read today than he was in the first half of the twentieth century, when readers were more patient with his somewhat prolix prose style.

Born in London's Soho district, Freeman studied medicine and worked in Accra on Africa's Gold Coast as assistant colonial surgeon, returning to England in 1891 after seven years—in poor health, impoverished, and too ill to practice medicine. He took to writing fiction and became both prolific and successful with more than two dozen novels and stories about Dr. Thorndyke and nearly as many featuring other detectives and rogues. Thorndyke was introduced in *The Red Thumb Mark* (1907), followed by *John Thorndyke's Cases* (1909) and *The Singing Bone* (1912), where Freeman perfected the inverted detective story in which the culprit is known from the outset, the suspense arising from following the train of deductive reasoning that will catch him—the difficult subgenre executed so brilliantly on the television series *Columbo*.

"The Aluminium Dagger" was first published in the March 1909 issue of *Pearson's Magazine*; it was first collected in *John Thorndyke's Cases* (London, Chatto & Windus, 1909), which was first published in the United States as *Dr. Thorndyke's Cases* (New York, Dodd, Mead, 1931).

THE ALUMINIUM DAGGER

R. AUSTIN FREEMAN

THE "URGENT CALL"—the instant, peremptory summons to professional duty—is an experience that appertains to the medical rather than the legal practitioner, and I had supposed, when I abandoned the clinical side of my profession in favour of the forensic, that henceforth I should know it no more; that the interrupted meal, the broken leisure, and the jangle of the nightbell, were things of the past; but in practice it was otherwise. The medical jurist is, so to speak, on the borderland of the two professions, and exposed to the vicissitudes of each calling, and so it happened from time to time that the professional services of my colleague or myself were demanded at a moment's notice. And thus it was in the case that I am about to relate.

The sacred rite of the "tub" had been duly performed, and the freshly-dried person of the present narrator was about to be insinuated into the first instalment of clothing, when a hurried step was heard upon the stair, and the voice of our laboratory assistant, Polton, arose at my colleague's door.

"There's a gentleman downstairs, sir, who says he must see you instantly on most urgent business. He seems to be in a rare twitter, sir——"

Polton was proceeding to descriptive particulars, when a second and more hurried step became audible, and a strange voice addressed Thorndyke.

"I have come to beg your immediate assistance, sir; a most dreadful thing has happened. A horrible murder has been committed. Can you come with me now?"

"I will be with you almost immediately," said Thorndyke. "Is the victim quite dead?"

"Quite. Cold and stiff. The police think——"

"Do the police know that you have come for me?" interrupted Thorndyke.

"Yes. Nothing is to be done until you arrive."

"Very well. I will be ready in a few minutes."

"And if you would wait downstairs, sir," Polton added persuasively, "I could help the doctor to get ready."

With this crafty appeal, he lured the intruder back to the sitting-room, and shortly after stole softly up the stairs with a small breakfast-tray, the contents of which he deposited firmly in our respective rooms, with a few timely words on the folly of "undertaking murders on an empty stomach." Thorndyke and I had meanwhile clothed ourselves with a celerity known only to medical practitioners and quick-change artists, and in a few minutes descended the stairs together, calling in at the laboratory for a few appliances that Thorndyke usually took with him on a visit of investigation.

As we entered the sitting-room, our visitor, who was feverishly pacing up and down, seized his hat with a gasp of relief. "You are ready to come?" he asked. "My carriage is at the door," and without waiting for an answer, he hurried out, and rapidly preceded us down the stairs.

The carriage was a roomy brougham, which fortunately accommodated the three of us, and as soon as we had entered and shut the door, the coachman whipped up his horse and drove off at a smart trot.

"I had better give you some account of the circumstances, as we go," said our agitated friend. "In the first place, my name is Curtis, Henry Curtis; here is my card. Ah! and here is another card, which I should have given you before. My solicitor, Mr. Marchmont, was with me when I made this dreadful discovery, and he sent me to you. He remained in the rooms to see that nothing is disturbed until you arrive."

"That was wise of him," said Thorndyke. "But now tell us exactly what has occurred."

"I will," said Mr. Curtis. "The murdered man was my brother-in-law, Alfred Hartridge, and I am sorry to say he was—well, he was a bad man. It grieves me to speak of him thus—*de mortuis*, you know—but, still, we must deal with the facts, even though they be painful."

"Undoubtedly," agreed Thorndyke.

"I have had a great deal of very unpleasant correspondence with him—Marchmont will tell you about that—and yesterday I left a note for him, asking for an interview, to settle the business, naming eight o'clock this morning as the hour, because I had to leave town before noon. He replied, in a very singular letter, that he would see me at that hour, and Mr. Marchmont very kindly consented to accompany me. Accordingly, we went to his chambers together this morning, arriving punctually at eight o'clock. We rang the bell several times, and knocked loudly at the door, but as there was no response, we went down and spoke to the hall-porter. This man, it seems, had already noticed, from the courtyard, that the electric lights were full on in Mr. Hartridge's sitting-room, as they had been all night, according to the statement of the night-porter; so now, suspecting that something was wrong, he came up with us, and rang the bell and battered at the door. Then, as there was still no sign of life within, he inserted his duplicate key and tried to open the door—unsuccessfully, however, as

it proved to be bolted on the inside. Thereupon the porter fetched a constable, and, after a consultation, we decided that we were justified in breaking open the door; the porter produced a crowbar, and by our united efforts the door was eventually burst open. We entered, and—my God! Dr. Thorndyke, what a terrible sight it was that met our eyes! My brother-in-law was lying dead on the floor of the sitting-room. He had been stabbed—stabbed to death; and the dagger had not even been withdrawn. It was still sticking out of his back."

He mopped his face with his handkerchief, and was about to continue his account of the catastrophe when the carriage entered a quiet side-street between Westminster and Victoria, and drew up before a block of tall, new, red-brick buildings. A flurried hall-porter ran out to open the door, and we alighted opposite the main entrance.

"My brother-in-law's chambers are on the second-floor," said Mr. Curtis. "We can go up in the lift."

The porter had hurried before us, and already stood with his hand upon the rope. We entered the lift, and in a few seconds were discharged on to the second-floor, the porter, with furtive curiosity, following us down the corridor. At the end of the passage was a half-open door, considerably battered and bruised. Above the door, painted in white lettering, was the inscription, "Mr. Hartridge"; and through the doorway protruded the rather foxy countenance of Inspector Badger.

"I am glad you have come, sir," said he, as he recognized my colleague. "Mr. Marchmont is sitting inside like a watch-dog, and he growls if any of us even walks across the room."

The words formed a complaint, but there was a certain geniality in the speaker's manner which made me suspect that Inspector Badger was already navigating his craft on a lee shore.

We entered a small lobby or hall, and from thence passed into the sitting-room, where we found Mr. Marchmont keeping his vigil, in company with a constable and a uniformed inspector.

The three rose softly as we entered, and greeted us in a whisper; and then, with one accord, we all looked towards the other end of the room, and so remained for a time without speaking.

There was, in the entire aspect of the room, something very grim and dreadful. An atmosphere of tragic mystery enveloped the most commonplace objects; and sinister suggestions lurked in the most familiar appearances. Especially impressive was the air of suspense—of ordinary, every-day life suddenly arrested—cut short in the twinkling of an eye. The electric lamps, still burning dim and red, though the summer sunshine streamed in through the windows; the half-emptied tumbler and open book by the empty chair had each its whispered message of swift and sudden disaster, as had the hushed voices and stealthy movements of the waiting men, and, above all, an awesome shape that was but a few hours since a living man, and that now sprawled, prone and motionless, on the floor.

"This is a mysterious affair," observed Inspector Badger, breaking the silence at length, "though it is clear enough up to a certain point. The body tells its own story."

We stepped across and looked down at the corpse. It was that of a somewhat elderly man, and lay, on an open space of floor before the fireplace, face downwards, with the arms extended. The slender hilt of a dagger projected from the back below the left shoulder, and, with the exception of a trace of blood upon the lips, this was the only indication of the mode of death. A little way from the body a clock-key lay on the carpet, and, glancing up at the clock on the mantelpiece, I perceived that the glass front was open.

"You see," pursued the inspector, noting my glance, "he was standing in front of the fireplace, winding the clock. Then the murderer stole up behind him—the noise of the turning key must have covered his movements—and stabbed him. And you see, from the position of the dagger on the left side of the back, that the murderer must have been left-handed. That is all clear enough.

What is not clear is how he got in, and how he got out again."

"The body has not been moved, I suppose," said Thorndyke.

"No. We sent for Dr. Egerton, the police-surgeon, and he certified that the man was dead. He will be back presently to see you and arrange about the post-mortem."

"Then," said Thorndyke, "we will not disturb the body till he comes, except to take the temperature and dust the dagger-hilt."

He took from his bag a long, registering chemical thermometer and an insufflator or powder-blower. The former he introduced under the dead man's clothing against the abdomen, and with the latter blew a stream of fine yellow powder on to the black leather handle of the dagger. Inspector Badger stooped eagerly to examine the handle, as Thorndyke blew away the powder that had settled evenly on the surface.

"No finger-prints," said he, in a disappointed tone. "He must have worn gloves. But that inscription gives a pretty broad hint."

He pointed, as he spoke, to the metal guard of the dagger, on which was engraved, in clumsy lettering, the single word, "TRADITORE."

"That's the Italian for 'traitor,'" continued the inspector, "and I got some information from the porter that fits in with that suggestion. We'll have him in presently, and you shall hear."

"Meanwhile," said Thorndyke, "as the position of the body may be of importance in the inquiry, I will take one or two photographs and make a rough plan to scale. Nothing has been moved, you say? Who opened the windows?"

"They were open when we came in," said Mr. Marchmont. "Last night was very hot, you remember. Nothing whatever has been moved."

Thorndyke produced from his bag a small folding camera, a telescopic tripod, a surveyor's measuring-tape, a boxwood scale, and a sketch-block. He set up the camera in a corner, and exposed a plate, taking a general view of the room, and including the corpse. Then he moved to the door and made a second exposure.

"Will you stand in front of the clock, Jervis,"

he said, "and raise your hand as if winding it? Thanks; keep like that while I expose a plate."

I remained thus, in the position that the dead man was assumed to have occupied at the moment of the murder, while the plate was exposed, and then, before I moved, Thorndyke marked the position of my feet with a blackboard chalk. He next set up the tripod over the chalk marks, and took two photographs from that position, and finally photographed the body itself.

The photographic operations being concluded, he next proceeded, with remarkable skill and rapidity, to lay out on the sketch-block a ground-plan of the room, showing the exact position of the various objects, on a scale of a quarter of an inch to the foot—a process that the inspector was inclined to view with some impatience.

"You don't spare trouble, Doctor," he remarked; "nor time either," he added, with a significant glance at his watch.

"No," answered Thorndyke, as he detached the finished sketch from the block; "I try to collect all the facts that may bear on a case. They may prove worthless, or they may turn out of vital importance; one never knows beforehand, so I collect them all. But here, I think, is Dr. Egerton."

The police-surgeon greeted Thorndyke with respectful cordiality, and we proceeded at once to the examination of the body. Drawing out the thermometer, my colleague noted the reading, and passed the instrument to Dr. Egerton.

"Dead about ten hours," remarked the latter, after a glance at it. "This was a very determined and mysterious murder."

"Very," said Thorndyke. "Feel that dagger, Jervis."

I touched the hilt, and felt the characteristic grating of bone.

"It is through the edge of a rib!" I exclaimed.

"Yes; it must have been used with extraordinary force. And you notice that the clothing is screwed up slightly, as if the blade had been rotated as it was driven in. That is a very peculiar feature, especially when taken together with the violence of the blow."

"It is singular, certainly," said Dr. Egerton, "though I don't know that it helps us much. Shall we withdraw the dagger before moving the body?"

"Certainly," replied Thorndyke, "or the movement may produce fresh injuries. But wait." He took a piece of string from his pocket, and, having drawn the dagger out a couple of inches, stretched the string in a line parallel to the flat of the blade. Then, giving me the ends to hold, he drew the weapon out completely. As the blade emerged, the twist in the clothing disappeared. "Observe," said he, "that the string gives the direction of the wound, and that the cut in the clothing no longer coincides with it. There is quite a considerable angle, which is the measure of the rotation of the blade."

"Yes, it is odd," said Dr. Egerton, "though, as I said, I doubt that it helps us."

"At present," Thorndyke rejoined dryly, "we are noting the facts."

"Quite so," agreed the other, reddening slightly; "and perhaps we had better move the body to the bedroom, and make a preliminary inspection of the wound."

We carried the corpse into the bedroom, and, having examined the wound without eliciting anything new, covered the remains with a sheet, and returned to the sitting-room.

"Well, gentlemen," said the inspector, "you have examined the body and the wound, and you have measured the floor and the furniture, and taken photographs, and made a plan, but we don't seem much more forward. Here's a man murdered in his rooms. There is only one entrance to the flat, and that was bolted on the inside at the time of the murder. The windows are some forty feet from the ground; there is no rain-pipe near any of them; they are set flush in the wall, and there isn't a foothold for a fly on any part of that wall. The grates are modern, and there isn't room for a good-sized cat to crawl up any of the chimneys. Now, the question is, How did the murderer get in, and how did he get out again?"

"Still," said Mr. Marchmont, "the fact is that he did get in, and that he is not here now; and therefore he must have got out; and therefore it must have been possible for him to get out. And, further, it must be possible to discover how he got out."

The inspector smiled sourly, but made no reply.

"The circumstances," said Thorndyke, "appear to have been these: The deceased seems to have been alone; there is no trace of a second occupant of the room, and only one half-emptied tumbler on the table. He was sitting reading when apparently he noticed that the clock had stopped—at ten minutes to twelve; he laid his book, face downwards, on the table, and rose to wind the clock, and as he was winding it he met his death."

"By a stab dealt by a left-handed man, who crept up behind him on tiptoe," added the inspector.

Thorndyke nodded. "That would seem to be so," he said. "But now let us call in the porter, and hear what he has to tell us."

The custodian was not difficult to find, being, in fact, engaged at that moment in a survey of the premises through the slit of the letter-box.

"Do you know what persons visited these rooms last night?" Thorndyke asked him, when he entered, looking somewhat sheepish.

"A good many were in and out of the building," was the answer, "but I can't say if any of them came to this flat. I saw Miss Curtis pass in about nine."

"My daughter!" exclaimed Mr. Curtis, with a start. "I didn't know that."

"She left about nine-thirty," the porter added.

"Do you know what she came about?" asked the inspector.

"I can guess," replied Mr. Curtis.

"Then don't say," interrupted Mr. Marchmont. "Answer no questions."

"You're very close, Mr. Marchmont," said the inspector; "we are not suspecting the young lady. We don't ask, for instance, if she is left-handed."

He glanced craftily at Mr. Curtis as he made this remark, and I noticed that our client suddenly turned deathly pale, whereupon the inspector looked away again quickly, as though he had not observed the change.

"Tell us about those Italians again," he said, addressing the porter. "When did the first of them come here?"

"About a week ago," was the reply. "He was a common-looking man—looked like an organ-grinder—and he brought a note to my lodge. It was in a dirty envelope, and was addressed 'Mr. Hartridge, Esq., Brackenhurst Mansions,' in a very bad handwriting. The man gave me the note and asked me to give it to Mr. Hartridge; then he went away, and I took the note up and dropped it into the letter-box."

"What happened next?"

"Why, the very next day an old hag of an Italian woman—one of them fortune-telling swines with a cage of birds on a stand—came and set up just by the main doorway. I soon sent her packing, but, bless you! she was back again in ten minutes, birds and all. I sent her off again—I kept on sending her off, and she kept on coming back, until I was reg'lar wore to a thread."

"You seem to have picked up a bit since then," remarked the inspector with a grin and a glance at the sufferer's very pronounced bow-window.

"Perhaps I have," the custodian replied haughtily. "Well, the next day there was an ice-cream man—a reg'lar waster, *he* was. Stuck outside as if he was froze to the pavement. Kept giving the errand-boys tasters, and when I tried to move him on, he told me not to obstruct his business. Business, indeed! Well, there them boys stuck, one after the other, wiping their tongues round the bottoms of them glasses, until I was fit to bust with aggravation. And *he* kept me going all day.

"Then, the day after that there was a barrel-organ, with a mangy-looking monkey on it. He was the worst of all. Profane, too, *he* was. Kept mixing up sacred tunes and comic songs: 'Rock of Ages,' 'Bill Bailey,' 'Cujus Animal,' and 'Over the Garden Wall.' And when I tried to move him on, that little blighter of a monkey made a run at my leg; and then the man grinned and started playing, 'Wait Till the Clouds Roll By.' I tell you, it was fair sickening."

He wiped his brow at the recollection, and the inspector smiled appreciatively.

"And that was the last of them?" said the latter; and as the porter nodded sulkily, he asked: "Should you recognize the note that the Italian gave you?"

"I should," answered the porter with frosty dignity.

The inspector bustled out of the room, and returned a minute later with a letter-case in his hand.

"This was in his breast-pocket," said he, laying the bulging case on the table, and drawing up a chair. "Now, here are three letters tied together. Ah! this will be the one." He untied the tape, and held out a dirty envelope addressed in a sprawling, illiterate hand to "Mr. Hartridge, Esq." "Is that the note the Italian gave you?"

The porter examined it critically. "Yes," said he; "that is the one."

The inspector drew the letter out of the envelope, and, as he opened it, his eyebrows went up.

"What do you make of that, Doctor?" he said, handing the sheet to Thorndyke.

Thorndyke regarded it for a while in silence, with deep attention. Then he carried it to the window, and, taking his lens from his pocket, examined the paper closely, first with the low power, and then with the highly magnifying Coddington attachment.

"I should have thought you could see that with the naked eye," said the inspector, with a sly grin at me. "It's a pretty bold design."

"Yes," replied Thorndyke; "a very interesting production. What do you say, Mr. Marchmont?"

The solicitor took the note, and I looked over his shoulder. It was certainly a curious production. Written in red ink, on the commonest notepaper, and in the same sprawling hand as the address, was the following message: "You are given six days to do what is just. By the sign above, know what to expect if you fail." The sign referred to was a skull and crossbones, very

neatly, but rather unskilfully, drawn at the top of the paper.

"This," said Mr. Marchmont, handing the document to Mr. Curtis, "explains the singular letter that he wrote yesterday. You have it with you, I think?"

"Yes," replied Mr. Curtis; "here it is."

He produced a letter from his pocket, and read aloud:

" 'Yes: come if you like, though it is an ungodly hour. Your threatening letters have caused me great amusement. They are worthy of Sadler's Wells in its prime.

" 'Alfred Hartridge.' "

"Was Mr. Hartridge ever in Italy?" asked Inspector Badger.

"Oh yes," replied Mr. Curtis. "He stayed at Capri nearly the whole of last year."

"Why, then, that gives us our clue. Look here. Here are these two other letters; E.C. postmark—Saffron Hill is E.C. And just look at that!"

He spread out the last of the mysterious letters, and we saw that, besides the *memento mori*, it contained only three words: "Beware! Remember Capri!"

"If you have finished, Doctor, I'll be off and have a look round Little Italy. Those four Italians oughtn't to be difficult to find, and we've got the porter here to identify them."

"Before you go," said Thorndyke, "there are two little matters that I should like to settle. One is the dagger: it is in your pocket, I think. May I have a look at it?"

The inspector rather reluctantly produced the dagger and handed it to my colleague.

"A very singular weapon, this," said Thorndyke, regarding the dagger thoughtfully, and turning it about to view its different parts. "Singular both in shape and material. I have never seen an aluminium hilt before, and bookbinder's morocco is a little unusual."

"The aluminium was for lightness," explained the inspector, "and it was made narrow to carry up the sleeve, I expect."

"Perhaps so," said Thorndyke.

He continued his examination, and presently, to the inspector's delight, brought forth his pocket lens.

"I never saw such a man!" exclaimed the jocose detective. "His motto ought to be, 'We magnify thee.' I suppose he'll measure it next."

The inspector was not mistaken. Having made a rough sketch of the weapon on his block, Thorndyke produced from his bag a folding rule and a delicate calliper-gauge. With these instruments he proceeded, with extraordinary care and precision, to take the dimensions of the various parts of the dagger, entering each measurement in its place on the sketch, with a few brief, descriptive details.

"The other matter," said he at length, handing the dagger back to the inspector, "refers to the houses opposite."

He walked to the window, and looked out at the backs of a row of tall buildings similar to the one we were in. They were about thirty yards distant, and were separated from us by a piece of ground, planted with shrubs and intersected by gravel paths.

"If any of those rooms were occupied last night," continued Thorndyke, "we might obtain an actual eyewitness of the crime. This room was brilliantly lighted, and all the blinds were up, so that an observer at any of those windows could see right into the room, and very distinctly, too. It might be worth inquiring into."

"Yes, that's true," said the inspector; "though I expect, if any of them have seen anything, they will come forward quick enough when they read the report in the papers. But I must be off now, and I shall have to lock you out of the rooms."

As we went down the stairs, Mr. Marchmont announced his intention of calling on us in the evening, "unless," he added, "you want any information from me now."

"I do," said Thorndyke. "I want to know who is interested in this man's death."

"That," replied Marchmont, "is rather a queer story. Let us take a turn in that garden that we saw from the window. We shall be quite private there."

He beckoned to Mr. Curtis, and, when the inspector had departed with the police-surgeon, we induced the porter to let us into the garden.

"The question that you asked," Mr. Marchmont began, looking up curiously at the tall houses opposite, "is very simply answered. The only person immediately interested in the death of Alfred Hartridge is his executor and sole legatee, a man named Leonard Wolfe. He is no relation of the deceased, merely a friend, but he inherits the entire estate—about twenty thousand pounds. The circumstances are these: Alfred Hartridge was the elder of two brothers, of whom the younger, Charles, died before his father, leaving a widow and three children. Fifteen years ago the father died, leaving the whole of his property to Alfred, with the understanding that he should support his brother's family and make the children his heirs."

"Was there no will?" asked Thorndyke.

"Under great pressure from the friends of his son's widow, the old man made a will shortly before he died; but he was then very old and rather childish, so the will was contested by Alfred, on the grounds of undue influence, and was ultimately set aside. Since then Alfred Hartridge has not paid a penny towards the support of his brother's family. If it had not been for my client, Mr. Curtis, they might have starved; the whole burden of the support of the widow and the education of the children has fallen upon him.

"Well, just lately the matter has assumed an acute form, for two reasons. The first is that Charles's eldest son, Edmund, has come of age. Mr. Curtis had him articled to a solicitor, and, as he is now fully qualified, and a most advantageous proposal for a partnership has been made, we have been putting pressure on Alfred to supply the necessary capital in accordance with his father's wishes. This he had refused to do, and it was with reference to this matter that we were calling on him this morning. The second reason involves a curious and disgraceful story. There is a certain Leonard Wolfe, who has been an intimate friend of the deceased. He is, I may say, a man of bad character, and their association has been of a kind creditable to neither. There is also a certain woman named Hester Greene, who had certain claims upon the deceased, which we need not go into at present. Now, Leonard Wolfe and the deceased, Alfred Hartridge, entered into an agreement, the terms of which were these: (1) Wolfe was to marry Hester Greene, and in consideration of this service (2) Alfred Hartridge was to assign to Wolfe the whole of his property, absolutely, the actual transfer to take place on the death of Hartridge."

"And has this transaction been completed?" asked Thorndyke.

"Yes, it has, unfortunately. But we wished to see if anything could be done for the widow and the children during Hartridge's lifetime. No doubt, my client's daughter, Miss Curtis, called last night on a similar mission—very indiscreetly, since the matter was in our hands; but, you know, she is engaged to Edmund Hartridge—and I expect the interview was a pretty stormy one."

Thorndyke remained silent for a while, pacing slowly along the gravel path, with his eyes bent on the ground: not abstractedly, however, but with a searching, attentive glance that roved amongst the shrubs and bushes, as though he were looking for something.

"What sort of man," he asked presently, "is this Leonard Wolfe? Obviously, he is a low scoundrel, but what is he like in other respects? Is he a fool, for instance?"

"Not at all, I should say," said Mr. Curtis. "He was formerly an engineer, and, I believe, a very capable mechanician. Latterly he has lived on some property that came to him, and has spent both his time and his money in gambling and dissipation. Consequently, I expect he is pretty short of funds at present."

"And in appearance?"

"I only saw him once," replied Mr. Curtis, "and all I can remember of him is that he is rather short, fair, thin, and clean-shaven, and that he has lost the middle finger of his left hand."

"And he lives at——?"

"Eltham, in Kent. Morton Grange, Eltham," said Mr. Marchmont. "And now, if you have all the information that you require, I must really be off, and so must Mr. Curtis."

The two men shook our hands and hurried away, leaving Thorndyke gazing meditatively at the dingy flower-beds.

"A strange and interesting case, this, Jervis," said he, stooping to peer under a laurel-bush. "The inspector is on a hot scent—a most palpable red herring on a most obvious string; but that is his business. Ah, here comes the porter, intent, no doubt, on pumping us, whereas——" He smiled genially at the approaching custodian, and asked: "Where did you say those houses fronted?"

"Cotman Street, sir," answered the porter. "They are nearly all offices."

"And the numbers? That open second-floor window, for instance?"

"That is number six; but the house opposite Mr. Hartridge's rooms is number eight."

"Thank you."

Thorndyke was moving away, but suddenly turned again to the porter.

"By the way," said he, "I dropped something out of the window just now—a small flat piece of metal, like this." He made on the back of his visiting card a neat sketch of a circular disc, with a hexagonal hole through it, and handed the card to the porter. "I can't say where it fell," he continued; "these flat things scale about so; but you might ask the gardener to look for it. I will give him a sovereign if he brings it to my chambers, for, although it is of no value to anyone else, it is of considerable value to me."

The porter touched his hat briskly, and as we turned out at the gate, I looked back and saw him already wading among the shrubs.

The object of the porter's quest gave me considerable mental occupation. I had not seen Thorndyke drop anything, and it was not his way to finger carelessly any object of value. I was about to question him on the subject, when, turning sharply round into Cotman Street, he drew up at the doorway of number six, and began attentively to read the names of the occupants.

" 'Third-floor,' " he read out, " 'Mr. Thomas Barlow, Commission Agent.' Hum! I think we will look in on Mr. Barlow."

He stepped quickly up the stone stairs, and I followed, until we arrived, somewhat out of breath, on the third-floor. Outside the Commission Agent's door he paused for a moment, and we both listened curiously to an irregular sound of shuffling feet from within. Then he softly opened the door and looked into the room. After remaining thus for nearly a minute, he looked round at me with a broad smile, and noiselessly set the door wide open. Inside, a lanky youth of fourteen was practising, with no mean skill, the manipulation of an appliance known by the appropriate name of diabolo; and so absorbed was he in his occupation that we entered and shut the door without being observed. At length the shuttle missed the string and flew into a large waste-paper basket; the boy turned and confronted us, and was instantly covered with confusion.

"Allow me," said Thorndyke, rooting rather unnecessarily in the waste-paper basket, and handing the toy to its owner. "I need not ask if Mr. Barlow is in," he added, "nor if he is likely to return shortly."

"He won't be back to-day," said the boy, perspiring with embarrassment; "he left before I came. I was rather late."

"I see," said Thorndyke. "The early bird catches the worm, but the late bird catches the diabolo. How did you know he would not be back?"

"He left a note. Here it is."

He exhibited the document, which was neatly written in red ink. Thorndyke examined it attentively, and then asked:

"Did you break the inkstand yesterday?"

The boy stared at him in amazement. "Yes, I did," he answered. "How did you know?"

"I didn't, or I should not have asked. But I see that he has used his stylo to write this note."

The boy regarded Thorndyke distrustfully, as he continued:

"I really called to see if your Mr. Barlow was a gentleman whom I used to know; but I expect you can tell me. My friend was tall and thin, dark, and clean-shaved."

"This ain't him, then," said the boy. "He's thin, but he ain't tall or dark. He's got a sandy beard, and he wears spectacles and a wig. I know a wig when I see one," he added cunningly, " 'cause my father wears one. He puts it on a peg to comb it, and he swears at me when I larf."

"My friend had injured his left hand," pursued Thorndyke.

"I dunno about that," said the youth. "Mr. Barlow nearly always wears gloves; he always wears one on his left hand, anyhow."

"Ah well! I'll just write him a note on the chance, if you will give me a piece of notepaper. Have you any ink?"

"There's some in the bottle. I'll dip the pen in for you."

He produced, from the cupboard, an opened packet of cheap notepaper and a packet of similar envelopes, and, having dipped the pen to the bottom of the ink-bottle, handed it to Thorndyke, who sat down and hastily scribbled a short note. He had folded the paper, and was about to address the envelope, when he appeared suddenly to alter his mind.

"I don't think I will leave it, after all," he said, slipping the folded paper into his pocket. "No. Tell him I called—Mr. Horace Budge—and say I will look in again in a day or two."

The youth watched our exit with an air of perplexity, and he even came out on to the landing, the better to observe us over the balusters; until, unexpectedly catching Thorndyke's eye, he withdrew his head with remarkable suddenness, and retired in disorder.

To tell the truth, I was now little less perplexed than the office-boy by Thorndyke's proceedings, in which I could discover no relevancy to the investigation that I presumed he was engaged upon; and the last straw was laid upon the burden of my curiosity when he stopped at a staircase window, drew the note out of his pocket, examined it with his lens, held it up to the light, and chuckled aloud.

"Luck," he observed, "though no substitute for care and intelligence, is a very pleasant addition. Really, my learned brother, we are doing uncommonly well."

When we reached the hall, Thorndyke stopped at the housekeeper's box, and looked in with a genial nod.

"I have just been up to see Mr. Barlow," said he. "He seems to have left quite early."

"Yes, sir," the man replied. "He went away about half-past eight."

"That was very early; and presumably he came earlier still?"

"I suppose so," the man assented, with a grin; "but I had only just come on when he left."

"Had he any luggage with him?"

"Yes, sir. There was two cases, a square one and a long, narrow one, about five foot long. I helped him to carry them down to the cab."

"Which was a four-wheeler, I suppose?"

"Yes, sir."

"Mr. Barlow hasn't been here very long, has he?" Thorndyke inquired.

"No. He only came in last quarter-day—about six weeks ago."

"Ah well! I must call another day. Good-morning," and Thorndyke strode out of the building, and made directly for the cab-rank in the adjoining street. Here he stopped for a minute or two to parley with the driver of a four-wheeled cab, whom he finally commissioned to convey us to a shop in New Oxford Street. Having dismissed the cabman with his blessing and a half-sovereign, he vanished into the shop, leaving me to gaze at the lathes, drills, and bars of metal displayed in the window. Presently he emerged with a small parcel, and explained, in answer to my inquiring look: "A strip of tool steel and a block of metal for Polton."

His next purchase was rather more eccentric. We were proceeding along Holborn when his attention was suddenly arrested by the window of a furniture shop, in which was displayed a collection of obsolete French small-arms—relics of the tragedy of 1870—which were being sold for decorative purposes. After a brief inspection, he entered the shop, and shortly reappeared carrying a long sword-bayonet and an old Chassepôt rifle.

"What may be the meaning of this martial display?" I asked, as we turned down Fetter Lane.

"House protection," he replied promptly. "You will agree that a discharge of musketry, followed by a bayonet charge, would disconcert the boldest of burglars."

I laughed at the absurd picture thus drawn of the strenuous house-protector, but nevertheless continued to speculate on the meaning of my friend's eccentric proceedings, which I felt sure were in some way related to the murder in Brackenhurst Chambers, though I could not trace the connection.

After a late lunch, I hurried out to transact such of my business as had been interrupted by the stirring events of the morning, leaving Thorndyke busy with a drawing-board, squares, scale, and compasses, making accurate, scaled drawings from his rough sketches; while Polton, with the brown-paper parcel in his hand, looked on at him with an air of anxious expectation.

As I was returning homeward in the evening by way of Mitre Court, I overtook Mr. Marchmont, who was also bound for our chambers, and we walked on together.

"I had a note from Thorndyke," he explained, "asking for a specimen of handwriting, so I thought I would bring it along myself, and hear if he has any news."

When we entered the chambers, we found Thorndyke in earnest consultation with Polton, and on the table before them I observed, to my great surprise, the dagger with which the murder had been committed.

"I have got you the specimen that you asked for," said Marchmont. "I didn't think I should be able to, but, by a lucky chance, Curtis kept the only letter he ever received from the party in question."

He drew the letter from his wallet, and handed it to Thorndyke, who looked at it attentively and with evident satisfaction.

"By the way," said Marchmont, taking up the dagger, "I thought the inspector took this away with him."

"He took the original," replied Thorndyke. "This is a duplicate, which Polton has made, for experimental purposes, from my drawings."

"Really!" exclaimed Marchmont, with a glance of respectful admiration at Polton; "it is a perfect replica—and you have made it so quickly, too."

"It was quite easy to make," said Polton, "to a man accustomed to work in metal."

"Which," added Thorndyke, "is a fact of some evidential value."

At this moment a hansom drew up outside. A moment later flying footsteps were heard on the stairs. There was a furious battering at the door, and, as Polton threw it open, Mr. Curtis burst wildly into the room.

"Here is a frightful thing, Marchmont!" he gasped. "Edith—my daughter—arrested for the murder. Inspector Badger came to our house and took her. My God! I shall go mad!"

Thorndyke laid his hand on the excited man's shoulder. "Don't distress yourself, Mr. Curtis," said he. "There is no occasion, I assure you. I suppose," he added, "your daughter is left-handed?"

"Yes, she is, by a most disastrous coincidence. But what are we to do? Good God! Dr. Thorndyke, they have taken her to prison—to prison—think of it! My poor Edith!"

"We'll soon have her out," said Thorndyke. "But listen; there is someone at the door."

A brisk rat-tat confirmed his statement, and when I rose to open the door, I found myself confronted by Inspector Badger. There was a moment of extreme awkwardness, and then both the detective and Mr. Curtis proposed to retire in favour of the other.

"Don't go, inspector," said Thorndyke; "I want to have a word with you. Perhaps Mr. Curtis would look in again, say, in an hour. Will you? We shall have news for you by then, I hope."

Mr. Curtis agreed hastily, and dashed out of the room with his characteristic impetuosity. When he had gone, Thorndyke turned to the detective, and remarked dryly:

"You seem to have been busy, inspector?"

"Yes," replied Badger; "I haven't let the grass grow under my feet; and I've got a pretty strong case against Miss Curtis already. You see, she was the last person seen in the company of the deceased; she had a grievance against him; she is left-handed, and you remember that the murder was committed by a left-handed person."

"Anything else?"

"Yes. I have seen those Italians, and the whole thing was a put-up job. A woman, in a widow's dress and veil, paid them to go and play the fool outside the building, and she gave them the letter that was left with the porter. They haven't identified her yet, but she seems to agree in size with Miss Curtis."

"And how did she get out of the chambers, with the door bolted on the inside?"

"Ah, there you are! That's a mystery at present—unless you can give us an explanation." The inspector made this qualification with a faint grin, and added: "As there was no one in the place when we broke into it, the murderer must have got out somehow. You can't deny that."

"I do deny it, nevertheless," said Thorndyke. "You look surprised," he continued (which was undoubtedly true), "but yet the whole thing is exceedingly obvious. The explanation struck me directly I looked at the body. There was evidently no practicable exit from the flat, and there was certainly no one in it when you entered. Clearly, then, *the murderer had never been in the place at all.*"

"I don't follow you in the least," said the inspector.

"Well," said Thorndyke, "as I have finished with the case, and am handing it over to you, I will put the evidence before you *seriatim*. Now,

I think we are agreed that, at the moment when the blow was struck, the deceased was standing before the fireplace, winding the clock. The dagger entered obliquely from the left, and, if you recall its position, you will remember that its hilt pointed directly towards an open window."

"Which was forty feet from the ground."

"Yes. And now we will consider the very peculiar character of the weapon with which the crime was committed."

He had placed his hand upon the knob of a drawer, when we were interrupted by a knock at the door. I sprang up, and, opening it, admitted no less a person than the porter of Brackenhurst Chambers. The man looked somewhat surprised on recognizing our visitors, but advanced to Thorndyke, drawing a folded paper from his pocket.

"I've found the article you were looking for, sir," said he, "and a rare hunt I had for it. It had stuck in the leaves of one of them shrubs."

Thorndyke opened the packet, and, having glanced inside, laid it on the table.

"Thank you," said he, pushing a sovereign across to the gratified official. "The inspector has your name, I think?"

"He have, sir," replied the porter; and, pocketing his fee, he departed, beaming.

"To return to the dagger," said Thorndyke, opening the drawer. "It was a very peculiar one, as I have said, and as you will see from this model, which is an exact duplicate." Here he exhibited Polton's production to the astonished detective. "You see that it is extraordinarily slender, and free from projections, and of unusual materials. You also see that it was obviously not made by an ordinary dagger-maker; that, in spite of the Italian word scrawled on it, there is plainly written all over it 'British mechanic.' The blade is made from a strip of common three-quarter-inch tool steel; the hilt is turned from an aluminium rod; and there is not a line of engraving on it that could not be produced in a lathe by any engineer's apprentice. Even the boss at the top is mechanical, for it is just like an ordinary hexagon nut. Then, notice the dimensions, as shown

on my drawing. The parts A and B, which just project beyond the blade, are exactly similar in diameter—and such exactness could hardly be accidental. They are each parts of a circle having a diameter of 10.9 millimetres—a dimension which happens, by a singular coincidence, to be exactly the calibre of the old Chassepôt rifle, specimens of which are now on sale at several shops in London. Here is one, for instance."

He fetched the rifle that he had bought, from the corner in which it was standing, and, lifting the dagger by its point, slipped the hilt into the muzzle. When he let go, the dagger slid quietly down the barrel, until its hilt appeared in the open breech.

"Good God!" exclaimed Marchmont. "You don't suggest that the dagger was shot from a gun?"

"I do, indeed; and you now see the reason for the aluminium hilt—to diminish the weight of the already heavy projectile—and also for this hexagonal boss on the end?"

"No, I do not," said the inspector; "but I say that you are suggesting an impossibility."

"Then," replied Thorndyke, "I must explain and demonstrate. To begin with, this projectile had to travel point foremost; therefore it had to be made to spin—and it certainly was spinning when it entered the body, as the clothing and the wound showed us. Now, to make it spin, it had to be fired from a rifled barrel; but as the hilt would not engage in the rifling, it had to be fitted with something that would. That something was evidently a soft metal washer, which fitted on to this hexagon, and which would be pressed into the grooves of the rifling, and so spin the dagger, but would drop off as soon as the weapon left the barrel. Here is such a washer, which Polton has made for us."

He laid on the table a metal disc, with a hexagonal hole through it.

"This is all very ingenious," said the inspector, "but I say it is impossible and fantastic."

"It certainly sounds rather improbable," Marchmont agreed.

"We will see," said Thorndyke. "Here is a

makeshift cartridge of Polton's manufacture, containing an eighth charge of smokeless powder for a 20-bore gun."

He fitted the washer on to the boss of the dagger in the open breech of the rifle, pushed it into the barrel, inserted the cartridge, and closed the breech. Then, opening the office-door, he displayed a target of padded strawboard against the wall.

"The length of the two rooms," said he, "gives us a distance of thirty-two feet. Will you shut the windows, Jervis?"

I complied, and he then pointed the rifle at the target. There was a dull report—much less loud than I had expected—and when we looked at the target, we saw the dagger driven in up to its hilt at the margin of the bull's-eye.

"You see," said Thorndyke, laying down the rifle, "that the thing is practicable. Now for the evidence as to the actual occurrence. First, on the original dagger there are linear scratches which exactly correspond with the grooves of the rifling. Then there is the fact that the dagger was certainly spinning from left to right—in the direction of the rifling, that is—when it entered the body. And then there is this which, as you heard, the porter found in the garden."

He opened the paper packet. In it lay a metal disc, perforated by a hexagonal hole. Stepping into the office, he picked up from the floor the washer that he had put on the dagger, and laid it on the paper beside the other. The two discs were identical in size, and the margin of each was indented with identical markings, corresponding to the rifling of the barrel.

The inspector gazed at the two discs in silence for a while; then, looking up at Thorndyke, he said:

"I give in, Doctor. You're right, beyond all doubt; but how you came to think of it beats me into fits. The only question now is, Who fired the gun, and why wasn't the report heard?"

"As to the latter," said Thorndyke, "it is probable that he used a compressed-air attachment, not only to diminish the noise, but also to prevent any traces of the explosive from being left on the dagger. As to the former, I think I can give you the murderer's name; but we had better take the evidence in order. You may remember," he continued, "that when Dr. Jervis stood as if winding the clock, I chalked a mark on the floor where he stood. Now, standing on that marked spot, and looking out of the open window, I could see two of the windows of a house nearly opposite. They were the second- and third-floor windows of No. 6, Cotman Street. The second-floor is occupied by a firm of architects; the third-floor by a commission agent named Thomas Barlow. I called on Mr. Barlow, but before describing my visit, I will refer to another matter. You haven't those threatening letters about you, I suppose?"

"Yes, I have," said the inspector; and he drew forth a wallet from his breast-pocket.

"Let us take the first one, then," said Thorndyke. "You see that the paper and envelope are of the very commonest, and the writing illiterate. But the ink does not agree with this. Illiterate people usually buy their ink in penny bottles. Now, this envelope is addressed with Draper's dichroic ink—a superior office ink, sold only in large bottles—and the red ink in which the note is written is an unfixed, scarlet ink, such as is used by draughtsmen, and has been used, as you can see, in a stylographic pen. But the most interesting thing about this letter is the design drawn at the top. In an artistic sense, the man could not draw, and the anatomical details of the skull are ridiculous. Yet the drawing is very neat. It has the clean, wiry line of a machine drawing, and is done with a steady, practised hand. It is also perfectly symmetrical; the skull, for instance, is exactly in the centre, and, when we examine it through a lens, we see why it is so, for we discover traces of a pencilled centre-line and ruled cross-lines. Moreover, the lens reveals a tiny particle of draughtsman's soft, red, rubber, with which the pencil lines were taken out; and all these facts, taken together, suggest that the drawing was made by someone accustomed to making accurate mechanical drawings. And now we will return to Mr. Barlow. He was out when I called, but I took the liberty of glancing round the office, and this is what I saw. On the mantelshelf was a twelve-inch flat boxwood rule, such as engineers use, a piece of soft, red rubber, and a stone bottle of Draper's dichroic ink. I obtained, by a simple ruse, a specimen of the office notepaper and the ink. We will examine it presently. I found that Mr. Barlow is a new tenant, that he is rather short, wears a wig and spectacles, and always wears a glove on his left hand. He left the office at 8:30 this morning, and no one saw him arrive. He had with him a square case, and a narrow, oblong one about five feet in length; and he took a cab to Victoria, and apparently caught the 8:51 train to Chatham."

"Ah!" exclaimed the inspector.

"But," continued Thorndyke, "now examine those three letters, and compare them with this note that I wrote in Mr. Barlow's office. You see that the paper is of the same make, with the same water-mark, but that is of no great significance. What is of crucial importance is this: You see, in each of these letters, two tiny indentations near the bottom corner. Somebody has used compasses or drawing-pins over the packet of notepaper, and the points have made little indentations, which have marked several of the sheets. Now, notepaper is cut to its size after it is folded, and if you stick a pin into the top sheet of a section, the indentations on all the underlying sheets will be at exactly similar distances from the edges and corners of the sheet. But you see that these little dents are all at the same distance from the edges and the corner." He demonstrated the fact with a pair of compasses. "And now look at this sheet, which I obtained at Mr. Barlow's office. There are two little indentations—rather faint, but quite visible—near the bottom corner, and when we measure them with the compasses, we find that they are exactly the same distance apart as the others, and the same distance from the edges and the bottom corner. The irresistible conclusion is that these four sheets came from the same packet."

The inspector started up from his chair, and faced Thorndyke. "Who is this Mr. Barlow?" he asked.

"That," replied Thorndyke, "is for you to determine; but I can give you a useful hint. There is only one person who benefits by the death of Alfred Hartridge, but he benefits to the extent of twenty thousand pounds. His name is Leonard Wolfe, and I learn from Mr. Marchmont that he is a man of indifferent character—a gambler and a spendthrift. By profession he is an engineer, and he is a capable mechanician. In appearance he is thin, short, fair, and clean-shaven, and he has lost the middle finger of his left hand. Mr. Barlow is also short, thin, and fair, but wears a wig, a beard, and spectacles, and always wears a glove on his left hand. I have seen the handwriting of both these gentlemen, and should say that it would be difficult to distinguish one from the other."

"That's good enough for me," said the inspector. "Give me his address, and I'll have Miss Curtis released at once."

The same night Leonard Wolfe was arrested at Eltham, in the very act of burying in his garden a large and powerful compressed-air rifle. He was never brought to trial, however, for he had in his pocket a more portable weapon—a large-bore Derringer pistol—with which he managed to terminate an exceedingly ill-spent life.

"And, after all," was Thorndyke's comment, when he heard of the event, "he had his uses. He has relieved society of two very bad men, and he has given us a most instructive case. He has shown us how a clever and ingenious criminal may take endless pains to mislead and delude the police, and yet, by inattention to trivial details, may scatter clues broadcast. We can only say to the criminal class generally, in both respects, 'Go thou and do likewise.'"

THE CREWEL NEEDLE

GERALD KERSH

IT IS IMPOSSIBLE to slot Gerald Kersh (1911–1968) into any category of fiction, as his strange and powerful stories and novels run the gamut from crime to fantasy to literary fiction, with many of the works straddling more than one genre. A somewhat bizarre young life—he was pronounced dead at four, only to sit up in his coffin at the funeral—in which he described himself as being "a morose and tearful child," continued through the early years of adulthood, in which he worked as a baker, nightclub bouncer, salesman, and professional wrestler. He served in the Coldstream Guards in World War II until an injury forced him out; he became a war correspondent and was buried alive during bombing raids on three separate occasions. Although a successful writer, he moved to the United States after the war to escape what he regarded as confiscatory taxation and became a naturalized citizen.

His most famous novel is *Night and the City* (1938), set in the London underworld of professional wrestling, which was the basis for the classic 1950 film noir directed by Jules Dassin and starring Richard Widmark; it was remade in 1992 with Robert De Niro and Jessica Lange. Most critics regard the 1957 novel *Fowler's End* to be Kersh's masterpiece and one of the great novels of the twentieth century, but it remains largely unknown. He wrote more than a thousand magazine pieces and more than a thousand short stories, the best known in the crime field being those about Karmesin, a rogue who narrates his own adventures and was described by Ellery Queen as "either the greatest criminal or the greatest liar of all time." Typical of these stories is "Karmesin and the Crown Jewels," in which the thief may have stolen the jewels from the Tower of London.

"The Crewel Needle" was first published in *Lilliput* in 1953; it was first collected in *Guttersnipe* (London, Heinemann, 1954). It was reprinted in the October 1959 issue of *Ellery Queen's Mystery Magazine* as "Open Verdict."

THE CREWEL NEEDLE

GERALD KERSH

CERTAIN OTHERS I know, in my position, sir, have had "severe nervous breakdowns"— gone out of their minds—took to parading the streets with banners, and whatnot, shouting *Unfair!* Well, thank God, I was always steady-minded. I could always see the other side of things. So, although I was unjustly dismissed from the Force, I could still keep my balance. I could see the reason for the injustice behind my dismissal, and could get around to blaming myself for not keeping my silly mouth shut.

Actually, you know, I wasn't really sacked. I was told that if I wanted to keep what there was of my pension, I had better resign on grounds of ill health. So I did, and serves me right. I should never have made my statement without, first, having my evidence corroborated. However, no bitterness. Justifiable or unjustifiable, bitterness leads to prejudice which, carried far enough, is the same thing as madness . . . I started life in the Army, d'you see, where you learn to digest a bit of injustice here and there; because, if you do not, it gets you down and you go doolally.

Many is the good man I've known who has ruined himself by expecting too much justice. Now, I ask you, what sane man in this world really expects to get what he properly deserves?

If I had been thirty years wiser thirty years ago, I might have been retired, now, on an Inspector's pension. Only, in the matter of an open verdict, I didn't have the sense to say nothing. I was young and foolish, d'you see, and, therefore, overeager. There was a girl I was very keen on, and I was anxious to better myself—she was used to something a cut above what I could offer her. D'you see?

I was supposed to be an intelligent officer, as far as that goes in the Police Force. But that isn't quite good enough. In those days, all the so-called intelligence in the world wouldn't get a policeman very far—seniority aside—unless he had a kind of spectacular way of showing it.

I'm not embittered, mind you. Nothing against the Force. Only I ought to have known when to stop talking . . .

At first, like everybody else, I thought nothing of it. The Police were called in after the doctor, merely as a matter of routine, d'you see. I was on a beat, then, in Hammersmith. Towards about eight o'clock one Sunday morning, neighbors on either side of a little house on Spindleberry Road were disturbed by the hysterical crying of a child at No. 9.

At first there was some talk of the N.S.P.C.C., but there was no question of that, because the people at No. 9 were simply a little orphan girl, aged eight, and her aunt, Miss Pantile, who thought the world of her niece and, far from ill-treating the child, had a tendency to spoil her; because the little girl whose name was Titania was delicate, having had rheumatic fever.

As is not uncommon, the houses in Spindleberry Road are numbered odd coming up, and even going down. The neighbors in question, therefore, were Nos. 7 and 11. Spindleberry Road, like so many of them put up around Brook Green before the turn of the century, is simply a parallel of brick barracks, sort of sectionalized and numbered. Under each number, a porch. In front of each porch, iron railings and an iron gate. At the back of each and every house, a bit of garden. I mention this, d'you see, because these houses, from a policeman's point of view, present only an elementary problem: they are accessible from front or back only.

Beg pardon—I've never quite lost the habit of making everything I say a kind of Report.

. . . Well, hearing child crying, neighbors knock at door. No answer. No. 7 shouts through letter box: "Open the door and let us in, Titania!" Child keeps on crying. Various neighbors try windows, but every window is locked from the inside. At last, No. 11, a retired captain of the Mercantile Marine, in the presence of witnesses, bursts in the back door. Meanwhile, one of the lady neighbors has come to get a policeman, and has found me at the corner of Rowan Road. I appear on the scene.

Not to bother you, sir, with the formalities; being within my rights, as I see them in this case, I go in, having whistled for another policeman who happens to be my sergeant. The house is in no way disturbed, but all the time, upstairs, this child is screaming as if she is being murdered, over and over again: "Auntie Lily's dead! Auntie Lily's dead!"

The bedroom is locked on the inside. Sergeant and I force the lock, and there comes out at us a terrified little golden-headed girl, frightened out of her wits. The woman from No. 11 soothes her as best she can, but the sergeant and I concentrate our attention upon Miss Lily Pantile, who is lying on a bed with her eyes and mouth wide open, stone-dead.

The local doctor was called, of course, and he said that, as far as he could tell, this poor old maiden lady had died of something like a cerebral hemorrhage at about three o'clock in the

morning. On a superficial examination, this was as far as he cared to commit himself. He suggested that this was a matter for the coroner.

And that, as far as everybody was concerned, was that, d'you see? Only it was not. At the inquest it appeared that poor Miss Pantile had met her death through a most unusual injury. A gold-eyed crewel needle had been driven through her skull, and into her brain, about three inches above the left ear!

Now here, if you like, was a mystery with a capital M.

Miss Pantile lived alone with her eight-year-old niece. She had enough money of her own to support them both, but sometimes made a little extra by crewelwork—you know, embroidering with silks on a canvas background. She was especially good at creweling roses for cushion covers. The needle she favored—she had packets and packets of them—was the Cumberland Crewel Gold Eye, one of which had found its way, nobody knew how, through her skull and into her brain. But how could it possibly have found its way there?—that was the question.

There was no lack of conjecture, you may be sure. Doctors cited dozens of instances of women—tailoresses and dressmakers, particularly—who had suddenly fallen dead through having needles embedded in various vital organs. Involuntary muscular contractions, it was demonstrated, could easily send an accidentally stuck-in needle, or portion of a needle, working its way between the muscles for extraordinary distances, until it reached, for example, the heart . . .

The coroner was inclined to accept this as a solution, and declare a verdict of Death by Misadventure. Only the doctor wouldn't have that. Such cases, he said, had come to his attention, especially in the East End of London; and in every case the needle extracted had been in a certain way corroded, or calcified, as the case might be. In the case of Miss Lily Pantile, the crewel needle—upon the evidence of a noted pathologist—had been driven into the skull *from the outside*, with superhuman force. Part of the gold eye of the needle had been found protruding from the deceased's scalp . . . What did the coroner make of that?—the doctor asked.

The coroner was not anxious to make anything of it.

In the opinion of the doctor, could an able-bodied man have driven a needle through a human skull with his fingers?

Definitely, no.

Might this needle, then, have been driven into Miss Pantile's skull with some instrument, such as a hammer?

Possibly; but only by someone of "preternatural skill" in the use of fine steel instruments of exceptional delicacy . . .

The doctor reminded the coroner that even experienced needlewomen frequently broke far heavier needles than this gold-headed crewel needle, working with cloth of close texture. The human skull, the doctor said—calling the coroner, with his forensic experience, to witness—was a most remarkably difficult thing to penetrate, even with a specially designed instrument like a trephine.

The coroner said that one had, however, to admit the *possibility* of a crewel needle being driven through a middle-aged woman's skull with a hammer, in the hands of a highly skilled man.

. . . So it went on, d'you see. The doctor lost his temper and invited anyone to produce an engraver, say, or cabinetmaker, to drive a crewel needle through a human skull with a hammer "with such consummate dexterity"—they were his words, sir—as to leave the needle unbroken and the surrounding skin unmarked, as was the case with Miss Pantile.

There, d'you see, the coroner had him. He said, in substance: "You have proved that this needle could not have found its way into the late Miss Pantile's brain from inside. You have also proved that this needle could not have found its way into Miss Pantile's brain from outside."

Reprimanding somebody for laughing, he then declared an Open Verdict.

So the case was closed. A verdict is a verdict, but coroners are only coroners, even though they may be backed by the Home Office pathologist. And somehow or other, for me, this verdict was not good enough. If I had been that coroner, I would have made it: Willful Murder by a Person or Persons Unknown.

All fine and large. But what person or persons, known or unknown, with specialized skill enough to get into a sealed house, and into a locked room, hammer a fine needle into a lady's skull, and get out again, locking all the doors behind him, or them, from the inside—all without waking up an eight-year-old girl sleeping by the side of the victim?

And there was the question of Motive. Robbery? Nothing had been touched. The old lady had nothing worth stealing. Revenge? Most unlikely: she had no friends and no enemies, living secluded with her little niece, doing no harm to anyone . . . There was a certain amount of sense in the coroner's verdict . . . still . . .

Only let me solve this mystery, and I'm made, I thought.

I solved it, and I broke myself.

Now, as you must know, when you are in doubt you had better first examine yourself.

People get into a sloppy habit of mind. I once read a detective story called *The Invisible Man,* in which everybody swore he had seen nobody; yet there were footprints in the snow. "Nobody," of course, was the postman, in this story; "invisible" simply because nobody ever bothers to consider a postman as a person.

I was quite sure that in the mystery of Miss Pantile there *must* have been something somebody overlooked. I don't mean Sherlock Holmes stuff, like a cigarette ash, and whatnot. Not a clue, in the generally accepted sense of the term, but *something.*

And I was convinced that somehow, out of the corner of my mind's eye, I had seen in Miss Pantile's bedroom a certain something-or-other that was familiar to me, yet very much out of place. Nothing bad in itself—an object, in itself, perfectly innocent; but, in the circumstances, definitely queer. Now what was it?

I racked my brains trying to visualize in detail the scene of that bedroom. I was pretty observant as a youngster—I tell you, I might have got to be Detective-Inspector if I'd had the sense to keep my mouth shut at the right time—and the scene came back into my mind.

There was the room, about sixteen feet by fourteen. Main articles of furniture: a pair of little bedsteads with frames of stained oak; crewelworked quilts. Everything neat as a pin. A little dressing table, blue crockery with a pattern of pink roses. Wallpaper, white with a pattern of red roses. A little fire screen, black, crewel-worked again with yellow roses and green leaves. Over the fireplace, on the mantel shelf, several ornaments—one kewpie doll with a ribbon round its waist, one china cat with a ribbon round its neck, a cheap gift vase with a paper rose stuck in it, and a pink velvet pincushion. At the end of the mantel shelf nearest the little girl's side of the room, several books—

Ah-ah! Hold hard there! my memory said to me. *You're getting hot!* . . . You remember the old game of Hot and Cold in which you have to go out of the room, and then come back and find some hidden object? When you're close to it, you're hot; when you're not, you're cold. When my memory said *hot,* I stopped at the mental image of those books, and all of a sudden the solution to the Spindleberry Road mystery struck me like a blow between the eyes.

And here, in my excitement, I made my big mistake. I wanted, d'you see, to get the credit, and the promotion that would certainly come with it.

Being due for a weekend's leave, I put on my civilian suit and went down to Luton, where the orphan girl Titania was staying in the care of some distant cousin, and by making myself pleasant and tactful, I got to talking with the kid alone, in a tea shop.

She got through six meringues before we were done talking . . .

She was a pale-faced little girl, sort of pathetic in the reach-me-down black full mourning they'd dressed her in. One of those surprised-looking little girls with round eyes and mouth always part open. Bewildered, never quite sure whether to come or go, to laugh or cry. Devil of a nuisance to an officer on duty: He always thinks they've lost their way, or want to be taken across a street. It's difficult for a busy man to get any sense out of them, because they start crying at a sharp word.

Her only truly distinguishing mark was her hair, which was abundant and very pretty. Picture one of those great big yellow chrysanthemums combed back and tied with a bit of black ribbon.

I asked her, was she happy in her new home? She said, "Oh, yes. Auntie Edith says as soon as it's decent I can go to the pictures twice a week."

"Why," I asked, "didn't your Auntie Lily let you go to the pictures, then?"

Titania said, "Oh, no. Auntie Lily wouldn't go because picture houses are dangerous. They get burnt down."

"Ah, she was a nervous lady, your Auntie Lily, wasn't she," I said, "keeping the house all locked up like that at night?"

"She was afraid of boys," Titania said, in an old-fashioned way. "Those boys! What with throwing stones and letting off fireworks, they can burn you alive in your bed. A girl isn't safe with these boys around."

"That's what your poor Auntie said, isn't it, Titania? Now you're not afraid of boys, are you?"

"Oh, no," she said. "Brian was a boy. He was my brother."

"What, did Brian die, my little dear?" I asked.

"Oh, yes," she said. "He died of the flu, when Mummy did. I had the flu, too. But *I* didn't die; only I was delicate afterwards. I had the rheumatic fever, too."

"Your brother Brian must have been a fine big boy," I said. "Now about how old would he have been when he—passed away? Twelve?"

"Thirteen and a quarter," said Titania.

"And so he passed away, and I'm very sorry to

hear it," I said. "And your Auntie Lily wouldn't let you go to the pictures, wouldn't she? Well, you must always obey your elders, as you are told in the Catechism. Who did you like best in the pictures?"

Her face sort of lit up, then. She told me, "Best of all I liked Pearl White in a serial, *Peg o' the Ring*. Oh, it was good! And John Bunny and Flora Finch—" She giggled at the memory. "But we had only got to Part Three of *The Clutching Hand* when Mummy and Brian died, and I went to live with Auntie Lily . . . Apart from the danger of fire, picture palaces are unhealthy because they are full of microbes. Microbes carry germs . . . Auntie Lily used to wear an influenza mask on her face when she went out—you know, you can't be too careful these days," said this serious little girl.

"And kept all her windows locked up, too, I daresay," I said. "Well, your elders and betters know best, no doubt . . . But I mean to say, what did you do with yourself? Play with dolls?"

"Sometimes. Or sometimes I did sewing, or read books."

"Ah, you're a great one for reading, Titania," I said, "like your poor mother used to be. Why, Titania is a name out of a fairy story, isn't it? A clever girl like you could read anything she could get her hands on, if she were locked up with nobody to talk to. I bet you read your poor brother's old books, too. I remember noticing on the mantelpiece a bound volume of the *Boy's Own Paper*. And also . . . now let me see . . . a book with a black and red cover entitled *Ten Thousand Things a Young Boy Can Do*—is that it?"

She said, "Not *things*! *Tricks*."

"And right you are! And I'll bet you mastered every one of those tricks, didn't you?"

She said, "Not all of them. I didn't have the right things to do most of them with—"

"There's one trick in that book, which I have read myself," I said, "which you did master, though, and which you did have the right apparatus for, Titania, my dear. Tell me what it is. You get a medium needle and stick it down the center of a soft cork. Then you get a penny and place this penny between two little blocks of wood. Put your cork with the needle in it on top of the penny, and strike the cork a sharp blow with a hammer. The cork will hold the needle straight, so that it goes right through that penny. That's the way you killed your poor Auntie Lily, isn't it, Titania?"

Finishing the last of her meringue, she nodded. Having swallowed, she said, "Yes," and to my horror, she giggled.

"Why, then," I said, "you must come back to London with me, and tell my Inspector about it."

"Yes," she said, nodding. "Only you mustn't say anything to Auntie Edith."

I told her, "Nobody will do anything dreadful to you; only you must confess and get it off your poor little mind."

Titania's second cousin Edith, by courtesy called "Auntie," came with the child and me to London—and there, in the police station, she flatly denied every word of everything, and cried to be sent back home.

Put yourself in my position, stigmatized as a madman and a brute! I lost my temper, one word led to another, and I "tendered my resignation."

I shall never forget the sly expression on the girl Titania's face when she went back with her Auntie Edith to Luton.

I have no idea what has happened to her since. She will be about thirty-eight or thirty-nine by now, and I should not be at all surprised if she had turned out to be quite a handful.

THE DOCTOR'S CASE

STEPHEN KING

REMARKABLY MAINTAINING his position for nearly four decades as the most famous and beloved writer in America, Stephen Edwin King (1947–) was born in Portland, Maine, and graduated from the University of Maine with a BA in English. Unable to find a position as a high school teacher, he sold some stories to various publications, including *Playboy*. Heavily influenced by H. P. Lovecraft and the macabre stories published by EC Comics, he directed his energy toward horror and supernatural fiction, although he has dabbled in other genres, including mystery, western, and science fiction. The manuscript of his first book, *Carrie* (1973), about a girl with psychic powers, was thrown into a wastebasket and famously rescued by his wife, Tabitha, who encouraged him to polish and submit it. It received a very modest advance but was published as a hardcover and then had great success as a paperback, launching a career of such spectacular magnitude that King is a celebrity as recognizable as a movie star or athlete—not commonplace for authors.

In addition to writing numerous novels and short stories, King has written screenplays and nonfiction, proving himself an expert in macabre fiction and film. More than one hundred films and television programs have been made from his work, most notably *Carrie* (1976), *The Shining* (1980), *Stand By Me* (1986, based on the novella "The Body"), *The Shawshank Redemption* (1994, based on the short story "Rita Hayworth and Shawshank Redemption"), and *The Green Mile* (1999).

"The Doctor's Case" was originally published in *The New Adventures of Sherlock Holmes*, edited by Martin H. Greenberg, Carol-Lynn Rössel Waugh, and Jon L. Lellenberg (New York, Carroll & Graf, 1987).

THE DOCTOR'S CASE

STEPHEN KING

I BELIEVE THERE WAS only one occasion upon which I actually solved a crime before my slightly fabulous friend, Mr. Sherlock Holmes. I say *believe* because my memory began to grow hazy about the edges round the time I attained my ninth decade; now, as I approach my centennial, the whole has become downright misty. There *may* have been another occasion, but I do not remember it, if so.

I doubt if I should ever forget this particular case no matter how murky my thoughts and memories might become, but I suspect I haven't much longer to write, and so I thought I would set it down. It cannot humiliate Holmes now, God knows; he is forty years in his grave. That, I think, is long enough to leave the tale untold. Even Lestrade, who used Holmes upon occasion but never had any great liking for him, never broke his silence in the matter of Lord Hull—he hardly could have done so, considering the circumstances. Even if the circumstances had been different, I somehow doubt if he would have. He and Holmes might bait each other, but Lestrade had a queer respect for my friend.

Why do I remember so clearly? Because the case I solved—to the best of my belief the only one I *ever* solved during my long association with Holmes—was the very one Holmes wanted more than any other to solve himself.

It was a wet, dreary afternoon and the clock had just rung half past one. Holmes sat by the window, holding his violin but not playing it, looking silently out into the rain. There were times, especially after his cocaine days were behind him, when Holmes could grow moody to the point of surliness when the skies remained stubbornly gray for a week or more, and he had been doubly disappointed on this day, for the glass had been rising since late the night before and he had confidently predicted clearing skies by ten this morning at the latest. Instead, the mist which had been hanging in the air when I arose had thickened into a steady rain. And if there was anything which rendered Holmes moodier than long periods of rain, it was being wrong.

Suddenly he straightened up, tweaking a violin string with a fingernail, and smiled sardonically. "Watson! Here's a sight! The wettest bloodhound you ever saw!"

It was Lestrade, of course, seated in the back of an open waggon with water running into his close-set, fiercely inquisitive eyes. The waggon had no more than stopped before he was out, tossing the driver a coin, and striding toward 221B Baker Street. He moved so quickly that I thought he should run into our door.

I heard Mrs. Hudson remonstrating with him about his decidedly damp condition and the effect it might have on the rugs both downstairs and up, and then Holmes, who could make Lestrade look like a tortoise when the urge struck him, leaped across to the door and called down, "Let him up, Mrs. H.—I'll put a newspaper under his boots if he stays long, but I somehow think—"

Then Lestrade was bounding up the stairs, leaving Mrs. Hudson to expostulate below. His colour was high, his eyes burned, and his teeth—decidedly yellowed by tobacco—were bared in a wolfish grin.

"Inspector Lestrade!" Holmes cried jovially. "What brings you out on such a—"

No further did he get. Still panting from his climb, Lestrade said, "I've heard gypsies say the devil grants wishes. Now I believe it. Come at once if you'd have a try, Holmes; the corpse is still fresh and the suspects all in a row."

"What is it?"

"Why, what you in your pride have wished for a hundred times or more in my own hearing, my dear fellow. The perfect locked-room mystery!"

Now Holmes's eyes blazed. "You mean it? Are you serious?"

"Would I have risked wet lung riding here in an open waggon if I was not?" Lestrade countered.

Then, for the only time in my hearing (despite the countless times the phrase has been attributed to him), Holmes turned to me and cried: "Quick, Watson! The game's afoot!"

On our way to the home of Lord Hull, Lestrade commented sourly that Holmes also had the *luck* of the devil; although Lestrade had commanded the waggon-driver to wait, we had no more than emerged from our lodgings when that exquisite rarity clip-clopped down the street: an empty hansom cab in what had become a driving rain. We climbed in and were off in a trice. As always, Holmes sat on the left-hand side, his eyes darting restlessly about, cataloguing everything, although there was precious little to see on *that* day . . . or so it seemed, at least, to the likes of me. I've no doubt every empty street-corner and rain-washed shop window spoke volumes to Holmes.

Lestrade directed the driver to what sounded like an expensive address in Saville Row, and then asked Holmes if he knew Lord Hull.

"I know *of* him," Holmes said, "but have never had the good fortune of meeting him. Now it seems I never shall. Shipping, wasn't it?"

"Shipping it was," Lestrade returned, "but the good fortune was all yours. Lord Hull was, by all accounts (including those of his nearest and—ahem!—dearest), a thoroughly nasty fellow, and as dotty as a puzzle-picture in a child's novelty book. He's finished practicing both nastiness and dottiness for good, however; around eleven o'clock this morning, just—" he pulled his turnip of a pocket-watch and looked at it "—two hours and forty minutes ago, someone put a knife in his back as he sat in his study with his will on the blotter before him."

"So," Holmes said thoughtfully, lighting his pipe, "you believe the study of this unpleasant Lord Hull is the perfect locked room I've been looking for all my life, do you?" His eyes gleamed skeptically through a rising rafter of blue smoke.

"I believe," Lestrade said quietly, "that it is."

"Watson and I have dug such holes before and never struck water yet," Holmes said, and he glanced at me before returning to his ceaseless catalogue of the streets through which we passed. "Do you recall the 'Speckled Band,' Watson?"

I hardly needed to answer him. There had been a locked room in that business, true enough, but there had also been a ventilator, a snake full of poison, and a killer evil enough to allow the one into the other. It had been devilish, but Holmes had seen to the bottom of the matter in almost no time at all.

"What are the facts, Inspector?" Holmes asked.

Lestrade began to lay them before us in the clipped tones of a trained policeman. Lord Albert Hull had been a tyrant in business and a despot at home. His wife was a mousy, terrified thing. The fact that she had borne him three sons seemed to have in no way sweetened his feelings toward her. She had been reluctant to speak of their social relations, but her sons had no such reservations; their papa, they said, had missed no opportunity to dig at her, to criticize her, or to jest at her expense . . . all of this when they were in company. When they were alone, he virtually ignored her. And, Lestrade added, he sometimes beat her.

"William, the eldest, told me she always gave out the same story when she came to the breakfast table with a swollen eye or a mark on her cheek, that she had forgotten to put on her glasses and had run into a door. 'She ran into doors once and twice a week,' William said. 'I didn't know we had that many doors in the house.'"

"Hmmm!" Holmes said. "A cheery fellow! The sons never put a stop to it?"

"She wouldn't allow it," Lestrade said.

"Insanity," I returned. A man who would beat his wife is an abomination; a woman who would allow it an abomination and a perplexity.

"There was method in her madness, though," Lestrade said. "Although you'd not know it to look at her, she was twenty years younger than Hull. He had always been a heavy drinker and a champion diner. At age sixty, five years ago, he developed gout and angina."

"Wait for the storm to end and then enjoy the sunshine," Holmes remarked.

"Yes," Lestrade said. "He made sure they knew both his worth and the provisions of his will. They were little better than slaves—"

"—and the will was the document of indenture," Holmes murmured.

"Exactly so. At the time of his death, his worth was three hundred thousand pounds. He never asked them to take his word for this; he had his chief accountant to the house quarterly to detail the balance sheets of Hull Shipping . . . although he kept the purse-strings firmly in his own hands and tightly closed."

"Devilish!" I exclaimed, thinking of the cruel boys one sometimes sees in Eastcheap or Piccadilly, boys who will hold out a sweet to a starving dog to see it dance . . . and then gobble it themselves. Within moments I discovered this comparison was even more apt than I thought.

"On his death, Lady Rebecca Hull was to receive one hundred and fifty thousand pounds. William, the eldest, was to receive fifty thousand; Jory, the middler, forty; and Stephen, the youngest, thirty."

"And the other thirty thousand?" I asked.

"Seven thousand, five hundred each to his brother in Wales and an aunt in Brittany (not a cent for *her* relatives), five thousand in assorted bequests to the servants at the town-house and the place in the country, and—you'll like this, Holmes—ten thousand pounds to Mrs. Hemphill's Home for Abandoned Pussies."

"You're *joking*!" I cried, although if Lestrade expected a similar reaction from Holmes, he was disappointed. Holmes merely re-lighted his pipe and nodded as if he had expected this, or something like it. "With babies dying of starvation in the East End and homeless orphans still losing all the teeth out of their jaws by the age of ten in the sulphur factories, this fellow left ten thousand pounds to a . . . a boarding-hotel for *cats*?"

"I mean exactly that," Lestrade said pleasantly. "Furthermore, he should have left *twenty-seven times* that amount to Mrs. Hemphill's Abandoned Pussies if not for whatever happened this morning—and whoever who did the business."

I could only gape at this, and try to multiply in my head. While I was coming to the conclusion that Lord Hull had intended to disinherit both wife and children in favor of an orphanage for felines, Holmes was looking sourly at Lestrade and saying something which sounded to me like a total *non sequitur*. "I am going to sneeze, am I not?"

Lestrade smiled. It was a smile of transcendent sweetness. "Oh yes, my dear Holmes. I fear you will sneeze often and profoundly."

Holmes removed his pipe, which he had just gotten drawing to his satisfaction (I could tell by the way he settled back slightly in his seat), looked at it for a moment, and then held it out into the rain. I watched him knock out the damp and smouldering tobacco, more dumbfounded than ever. If you had told me then that I was to be the one to solve this case, I believe I should have been impolite enough to laugh in your face. At that point I didn't even know what the case was *about,* other than that someone (who more and more sounded the sort of person who deserved to stand in the courtyard of Buckingham Palace for a medal rather than in the Old Bailey for sentencing) had killed this wretched Lord Hull before he could leave his family's rightful due to a gaggle of street cats.

"How many?" Holmes asked.

"Ten," Lestrade said.

"I suspected it was more than this famous locked room of yours that brought you out in the back of an open waggon on such a wet day," Holmes said sourly.

"Suspect as you like," Lestrade said gaily. "I'm afraid I must go on, but if you'd like, I could let you and the good doctor out here."

"Never mind," Holmes said. "When did he become sure that he was going to die?"

"Die?" I said. "How can you know he—"

"It's obvious, Watson," Holmes said. "It amused him to keep them in bondage by the means of his will." He looked at Lestrade. "No trust arrangements, I take it?"

Lestrade shook his head.

"Nor entailments of any sort?"

"None."

"Extraordinary!" I said.

"He wanted them to understand all would be theirs when he did them the courtesy of dying, Watson," Holmes said, "but he never actually intended for them to have it. He realized he was dying. He waited . . . and then he called them together this morning . . . this morning, Inspector, yes?"

Lestrade nodded.

"Yes. He called them together this morning and told them that he had made a new will which disinherited them one and all . . . except for the servants and the distant relatives, I suppose."

I opened my mouth to speak, only to discover I was too outraged to say anything. The image which kept returning to my mind was that of those cruel boys, making the starving East End curs jump with a bit of pork or a crumb of crust

from a meat pie. I must add it never occurred to me to ask if such a will could not be disputed before the bar. Today a man would have a deuce of a time slighting his closest relatives in favor of a hotel for pussies, but in 1899, a man's will was a man's will, and unless many examples of insanity—not eccentricity but outright *insanity*—could be proved, a man's will, like God's, was done.

"This new will was properly witnessed?" Holmes asked, immediately putting his finger on the one possible loophole in such a wretched scheme.

"Indeed it was," Lestrade replied. "Yesterday Lord Hull's solicitor and one of his assistants appeared at the house and were shown into his study. There they remained for about fifteen minutes. Stephen Hull says the solicitor once raised his voice in protest about something—he could not tell what—and was silenced by Hull. Jory, the third son, was upstairs, painting, and Lady Hull was calling on a friend. But both Stephen and William saw them enter and leave. William said that when the solicitor and his assistant left, they did so with their heads down, and although William spoke, asking Mr. Barnes—the solicitor—if he was well, and making some social remark about the persistence of the rain, Barnes did not reply and the assistant seemed to actually cringe. It was as if they were ashamed, William said."

Well, there it was: witnesses. So much for *that* loophole, I thought.

"Since we are on the subject, tell me about the boys," Holmes said, putting his slender fingers together.

"As you like. It goes pretty much without saying that their hatred for the pater was exceeded only by the pater's boundless contempt for them . . . although how he could hold Stephen in contempt is . . . well, never mind, I'll keep things in their proper order."

"How good of you, Inspector Lestrade," Holmes said dryly.

"William is thirty-six. If his father had given him any sort of allowance, I suppose he would be a bounder. As he had little or none, he took long walks during the days, went out to the coffee-houses at night, or, if he happened to have a bit more money in his pockets, to a card-house, where he would lose it quickly enough. Not a pleasant man, Holmes. A man who has no purpose, no skill, no hobby, and no ambition (save to outlive his father), could hardly be a pleasant man. I had the queerest idea while I was talking to him—that I was interrogating an empty vase on which the face of the Lord Hull had been lightly stamped."

"A vase waiting for the pater's money to fill him up," Holmes commented.

"Jory is another matter. Hull saved most of his contempt for Jory, calling him from his earliest childhood by such endearing pet-names as 'fish-face' and 'keg-legs' and 'stoat-belly.' It's not hard to understand such names, unfortunately; Jory Hull stands no more than five feet tall, if that, is bow-legged, slump-shouldered, and of a remarkably ugly countenance. He looks a bit like that poet fellow, the pouf."

"Oscar Wilde?" asked I.

Holmes turned a brief, amused glance upon me. "I believe Lestrade means Algernon Swinburne," he said. "Who, I believe, is no more a pouf than you are, Watson."

"Jory Hull was born dead," Lestrade said. "After he remained blue and still for an entire minute, the doctor pronounced him so and put a napkin over his misshapen body. Lady Hull, in her one moment of heroism, sat up, removed the napkin, and dipped the baby's legs into the hot water which had been brought to attend the birth. The baby began to squirm and squall."

Lestrade grinned and lit a cigarillo with a match undoubtedly dipped by one of the urchins of whom I had just been thinking. "Hull himself, always munificent, blamed this immersion for his bow legs."

Holmes's only comment on this extraordinary (and to my physician's mind rather suspect) story was to suggest that Lestrade had gotten a large body of information from his suspects in a short period of time.

"One of the aspects of the case which I thought would appeal to you, my dear Holmes," Lestrade said as we swept into Rotten Row in a splash and a swirl. "They need no coercion to speak; coercion's what it would take to shut 'em up. They've had to remain silent all too long. And then there's the fact that the new will is gone. Relief loosens tongues beyond measure, I find."

"Gone!" I exclaimed, but Holmes took no notice. He asked Lestrade about this misshapen middle child.

"Ugly as he is, I believe his father continually heaped vituperation on his head because—"

"Because Jory was the only son who had no need to depend upon his father's money to make his way in the world," Holmes said complacently.

Lestrade started. "The devil! How did you know that?"

"Rating a man with faults which all can see is the act of a man who is afraid as well as vindictive," Holmes said. "What was his key to the cell door?"

"As I told you, he paints," Lestrade said.

"Ah!"

Jory Hull was, as the canvases in the lower halls of Hull House later proved, a very good painter indeed. Not great; I do not mean to suggest he was. But his renderings of his mother and brothers were faithful enough so that, years later, when I saw color photographs for the first time, my mind flashed back to that rainy November afternoon in 1899. And the one of his father, which he showed us later . . . perhaps it *was* Algernon Swinburne that Jory resembled, but his father's likeness—at least as seen through Jory's hand and eye—reminded me of an Oscar Wilde character: that nearly immortal *roué*, Dorian Gray.

His canvases were long, slow processes, but he was able to quick-sketch with such nimble rapidity that he might come home from Hyde Park on a Saturday afternoon with as much as twenty pounds in his pockets.

"I wager his father enjoyed *that*," Holmes

said. He reached automatically for his pipe and then put it back. "The son a Peer of the Realm quick-sketching well-off American tourists and their sweethearts like a French Bohemian."

"He raged over it," Lestrade said, "but Jory wouldn't give over his selling stall in Hyde Park . . . not, at least, until his father agreed to an allowance of thirty-five pounds a week. He called it low blackmail."

"My heart bleeds," I said.

"As does mine, Watson," Holmes said. "The third son, Lestrade—we've almost reached the house, I believe."

As Lestrade had said, surely Stephen Hull had the greatest cause to hate his father. As his gout grew worse and his head more befuddled, Lord Hull surrendered more and more of the company affairs to Stephen, who was only twenty-eight at the time of his father's death. The responsibilities devolved upon Stephen, and the blame devolved upon him if his least decision proved amiss . . . and yet no financial gain devolved upon him should he decide well.

As the only of his three children with an interest in the business he had founded, Lord Hull should have looked upon his son with approval. As a son who not only kept his father's shipping business prosperous when it might have foundered due to Lord Hull's own increasing physical and mental problems (and all of this as a young man) he should have been looked upon with love and gratitude as well. Instead, Stephen had been rewarded with suspicion, jealousy and his father's belief—spoken more and more often—that his son "would steal the pennies from a dead man's eyes."

"The b——d!" I cried, unable to contain myself.

"He saved the business and the fortune," Holmes said, steepling his fingers again, "and yet his reward was still to be the youngest son's share of the spoil. What, by the way, was to be the disposition of the company by the new will?"

"It was to be handed over to the Board of Directors, Hull Shipping, Ltd., with no provision for the son," Lestrade said, and pitched his cigarillo as the hackney swept up the curving drive of a house which looked extraordinarily ugly to me just then, as it stood amid its dead lawns in the rain. "Yet with the father dead and the new will nowhere to be found, Stephen Hull comes into thirty thousand. The lad will have no trouble. He has what the Americans call 'leverage.' The company will have him as managing director. They should have done anyway, but now it will be on Stephen Hull's terms."

"Yes," Holmes said. "Leverage. A good word." He leaned out into the rain. "Stop short, driver!" he cried. "We've not quite done!"

"As you say, guv'nor," the driver returned, "but it's devilish wet out here."

"And you'll go with enough in your pocket to make your innards as wet and devilish as your out'ards," Holmes said, which seemed to satisfy the driver, who stopped thirty yards from the door. I listened to the rain tip-tapping on the roof while Holmes cogitated and then said: "The old will—the one he teased them with—*that* document isn't missing, is it?"

"Absolutely not. It was on his desk, near his body."

"Four excellent suspects! Servants need not be considered . . . or so it seems now. Finish quickly, Lestrade—the final circumstances, and the locked room."

Lestrade complied in less than ten minutes, consulting his notes from time to time. A month previous, Lord Hull had observed a small black spot on his right leg, directly behind the knee. The family doctor was called. His diagnosis was gangrene, an unusual but far from rare result of gout and poor circulation. The doctor told him the leg would have to come off, and well above the site of the infection.

Lord Hull laughed at this until tears streamed down his cheeks. The doctor, who had expected any other reaction than this, was struck speechless. "When they stick me in my coffin, sawbones," Hull said, "it will be with both legs still attached, thank you."

The doctor told him that he sympathized with Lord Hull's wish to keep his leg, but that without amputation he would be dead in six months . . . and he would spend the last two in exquisite pain. Lord Hull asked the doctor what his chances of survival should be if he were to undergo the operation. He was still laughing, Lestrade said, as though it were the best joke he had ever heard. After some hemming and hawing, the doctor said the odds were even.

"Bunk," said I.

"Exactly what Lord Hull said," Lestrade replied. "Except he used a term a bit more vulgar."

Hull told the doctor that he himself reckoned his chances at no better than one in five. "As to the pain, I don't think it will come to that," he went on, "as long as there's laudanum and a spoon to stir it within stumping distance."

The next day, Hull finally sprang his nasty surprise—that he was thinking of changing his will. Just how he did not say.

"Oh?" Holmes said, looking at Lestrade from those cool gray eyes that saw so much. "And who, pray, was surprised?"

"None of them, I should think. But you know human nature, Holmes; how people hope against hope."

"And how some plan against disaster," Holmes said dreamily.

This very morning Lord Hull had called his family into the parlor, and when all were settled, he performed an act few testators are granted, one which is usually performed by the wagging tongues of their solicitors after their own have been silenced forever. In short, he read them his new will, leaving the balance of his estate to Mrs. Hemphill's wayward pussies. In the silence which followed he rose, not without difficulty, and favored them all with a death's-head grin. And leaning over his cane, he made the following declaration, which I find as astoundingly vile now as I did when Lestrade recounted it to us in that hackney cab: "So! All is fine, is it not? Yes, very fine! You have served me quite faithfully, woman and boys, for some forty years. Now I intend, with the clearest and most serene conscience imaginable, to cast you hence. But

take heart! Things could be worse! If there was time, the pharaohs had their favorite pets—cats, for the most part—killed before they died, so the pets might be there to welcome them into the after-life, to be kicked or petted there, at their masters' whims, forever . . . and forever . . . and forever." Then he began to laugh at them. He leaned over his cane and laughed from his doughy livid dying face, the new will—signed and witnessed, as all of them had seen—clutched in one claw of a hand.

William rose and said, "Sir, you may be my father and the author of my existence, but you are also the lowest creature to crawl upon the face of the earth since the serpent tempted Eve in the Garden."

"Not at all!" the old monster returned, still laughing. "I know four lower. Now, if you will pardon me, I have some important papers to put away in my safe . . . and some worthless ones to burn in the stove."

"He still had the old will when he confronted them?" Holmes asked. He seemed more interested than startled.

"Yes."

"He could have burned it as soon as the new one was signed and witnessed," Holmes mused. "He had all the previous afternoon and evening to do so. But that wasn't enough, was it? What do you suppose, Lestrade?"

"That he was teasing them. Teasing them with a chance he believed all would refuse."

"There is another possibility," Holmes said. "He spoke of suicide. Isn't it possible that such a man might hold out such a temptation, knowing that if one of them—Stephen seems most likely from what you say—would do it for him, be caught . . . and swing for it?"

I stared at Holmes in silent horror.

"Never mind," Holmes said. "Go on."

The four of them had sat in paralyzed silence as the old man made his long slow way up the corridor to his study. There were no sounds but the thud of his cane, the laboured rattle of his breathing, the plaintive *miaow* of a cat in the kitchen, and the steady beat of the pendulum in the parlour clock. Then they heard the squeal of hinges as Hull opened his study door and stepped inside.

"Wait!" Holmes said sharply, sitting forward. "No one actually saw him go in, did they?"

"I'm afraid that's not so, old chap," Lestrade returned. "Mr. Oliver Stanley, Lord Hull's valet, had heard Lord Hull's progress down the hall. He came from Hull's dressing chamber, went to the gallery railing, and called down to ask if Hull was all right. Hull looked up—Stanley saw him as plainly as I see you right now, old fellow—and said he was feeling absolutely tip-top. Then he rubbed the back of his head, went in, and locked the study door behind him. By the time he reached the door (the corridor is quite long and it may have taken him as long as two minutes to make his way up it without help) Stephen had shaken off his stupor and had gone to the parlour door. He saw the exchange between his father and his father's man. Of course his father was back-to, but he heard his father's voice and described the same gesture: Hull rubbing the back of his head."

"Could Stephen Hull and this Stanley fellow have spoken before the police arrived?" I asked—shrewdly, I thought.

"Of course they could, and probably did," Lestrade said wearily. "But there was no collusion."

"You feel sure of that?" Holmes asked, but he sounded uninterested.

"Yes. Stephen Hull would lie very well, I think, but Stanley would do so badly. Accept my professional opinion or not just as you like, Holmes."

"I accept it."

So Lord Hull passed into his study, the famous locked room, and all heard the click of the lock as he turned the key—the only key there was to that *sanctum sanctorum*. This was followed by a more unusual sound: the bolt being drawn across.

Then, silence.

The four of them—Lady Hull and her sons, so shortly to be blue-blooded paupers—looked at each other in silence. The cat *miaowed* again from the kitchen and Lady Hull said in a distracted voice that if the housekeeper wouldn't give that cat a bowl of milk, she supposed she must. She said the sound of it would drive her mad if she had to listen to it much longer. She left the parlour. Moments later, without a word among them, the three sons also left. William went to his room upstairs, Stephen wandered into the music room. And Jory went to sit upon a bench beneath the stairs where, he had told Lestrade, he had gone since earliest child when he was sad or had matters of deep difficulty to think over.

Less than five minutes later a terrible shriek arose from the study. Stephen bolted out of the music room, where he had been plinking out isolated notes on the piano. Jory met him at the door. William was already halfway downstairs and saw them breaking in when Stanley, the valet, came out of Lord Hull's dressing room and went to the gallery railing for the second time. He saw Stephen Hull burst the study door in; he saw William reach the foot of the stairs and almost fall on the marble; he saw Lady Hull come from the dining room doorway with a pitcher of milk still in one hand. Moments later the rest of the servants had gathered. Lord Hull was slumped over his writing desk with the three brothers standing by. His eyes were open. There was a snarl on his lips, a look of ineffable surprise in his eyes. Clutched in his hand was his will . . . the old one. Of the new one there was no sign. And there was a dagger in his back."

With this Lestrade rapped for the driver to go on.

We entered between two constables as stone-faced as Buckingham Palace sentinels. Here was a very long hall, floored in black and white marble tiles like a chessboard. They led to an open door at the end, where two more constables were posted. The infamous study. To the left were the stairs, to the right two doors: the parlour and the music room, I guessed.

"The family is gathered in the parlour," Lestrade said.

"Good," Holmes said pleasantly. "But perhaps Watson and I might first have a look at this locked room."

"Shall I accompany you?"

"Perhaps not," Holmes said. "Has the body been removed?"

"It had not been when I left for your lodgings, but by now it should be gone."

"Very good."

Holmes started away. I followed. Lestrade called, "Holmes!"

Holmes turned, eyebrows upraised.

"No secret panels, no secret doors. Take my word or not, as you like."

"I believe I'll wait until . . ." Holmes began, and then his breath began to hitch. He scrambled in his pocket, found a napkin probably carried absently away from the eating-house where we had dined the previous evening, and sneezed mightily into it. I looked down and saw a large scarred tomcat, as out of place here in this grand hall as would have been one of those sulphur-factory urchins, twining about Holmes's legs, One of its ears was laid back against its scarred skull. The other was gone, lost in some long-ago alley battle, I supposed.

Holmes sneezed repeatedly and kicked out at the cat. It went with a reproachful backward look rather than with the angry hiss one would have expected from such an old campaigner. Holmes looked at Lestrade over the napkin with reproachful, watery eyes. Lestrade, not in the least put out of countenence, grinned. "Ten, Holmes," he said. "*Ten*. House is full of felines. Hull loved 'em." With that Lestrade walked off.

"How long, old fellow?" I asked.

"Since forever," he said, and sneezed again. I still believe, I am bound to add, that the solution to the locked room problem would have been as readily apparent to Holmes as it was to me if not for this unfortunate affliction. The word *allergy* was hardly known all those years ago, but that, of course, was his problem.

"Do you want to leave?" I was a bit alarmed. I had once seen a case of near asphyxiation as the result of such an aversion to sheep.

"He'd like that," Holmes said. I did not

need him to tell me who he meant. Holmes sneezed once more (a large red welt was appearing on his normally pale forehead) and then we passed between the constables at the study door. Holmes closed it behind him.

The room was long and relatively narrow. It was at the end of something like a wing, the main house spreading to either side from an area roughly three-quarters of the way down the hall. Thus there were windows on both sides and the room was well-lit in spite of the gray, rainy day. There were framed shipping charts on most of the walls, but on one was a really handsome set of weather instruments in a brass-bound case: an anemometer (Hull had the little whirling cups mounted on one of the roof-peaks, I supposed), two thermometers (one registering the outdoor temperature and the other that of the study), and a barometer much like the one that had fooled Holmes into believing the bad weather would finally break. I noticed the glass was still rising, then looked outside. The rain was falling harder than ever, rising glass or no rising glass. We believe we know a great lot, with our instruments and things, but we don't know half as much as we think we do.

Holmes and I both turned to look at the door. The bolt was torn free, but leaning inward, as it should have been. The key was still in the lock, and still turned.

Holmes's eyes, watering as they were, were everywhere at once, noting, cataloging, storing.

"You are a little better," I said.

"Yes," he said, lowering the napkin and stuffing it indifferently back into his coat pocket. "He may have loved 'em, but he apparently didn't allow 'em in here. Not on a regular basis, anyway. What do you make of it, Watson?"

Although my eyes were slower than his, I was also looking around. The double windows were all locked with thumb-turns and small brass side-bolts. None of the panes had been broken. The framed charts and weather instruments were between these windows. The other two walls, before and behind the desk which dominated the room, were filled with books. There was a small coal-stove at the south end of the room but no fireplace . . . the murderer hadn't come down the chimney like St. Nicholas, not unless he was narrow enough to fit through a stove-pipe and clad in an asbestos suit, for the stove was still very warm. The north end of this room was a little library, with two high-backed upholstered chairs and a coffee-table between them. On this table was a random stack of books. The ceiling was plastered. The floor was covered with a large Turkish rug. If the murderer had come up through a trap-door, I hadn't the slightest idea how he could have gotten back under that rug without disarranging it, and it was not disarranged in the slightest: it was smooth, and the shadows of the coffee-table legs lay across it without a ripple.

"Did you believe it, Watson?" Holmes asked, snapping me out of something like a hypnotic trance. Something . . . something about that coffee-table . . .

"Believe what, Holmes?"

"That all four of them simply walked out of that parlour, in four different directions, four minutes before the murder?"

"I don't know," I said faintly.

"*I* don't believe it; not for a mo—" He broke off. "Watson! Are you all right?"

"No," I said in a voice I could hardly hear myself. I collapsed into one of the library chairs. My heart was beating too fast. I couldn't seem to catch my breath. My head was pounding; my eyes seemed to have suddenly grown too large for their sockets. I could not take them from the shadows of the coffee-table legs upon the rug. "I am most . . . most definitely not . . . not all right."

At that moment Lestrade appeared in the study doorway. "If you've looked your fill, H—" He broke off. "What the devil's the matter with Watson?"

"I believe," said Holmes in a calm, measured voice, "that Watson has solved the case. Have you, Watson?"

I nodded my head. Not all of it, perhaps, but most. I knew who; I knew how.

"Is it this way with you, Holmes?" I asked. "When you . . . see?"

"Yes," he said.

"*Watson's* solved the case?" Lestrade said impatiently. "Bah! Watson's offered a thousand solutions to a hundred cases before this, Holmes, as you very well know—all of them wrong. Why, I remember just this late summer—"

"I know more about Watson than you shall ever know," Holmes said, "and this time he has hit upon it. I know the look." He began to sneeze again; the cat with the missing ear had wandered into the room through the door, which Lestrade had left open. It headed directly for Holmes with an expression of what seemed to be affection on its ugly face.

"If this is how it is for you," I said, "I'll never envy you again, Holmes. My heart should burst."

"One becomes enured even to insight," Holmes said, with not the slightest trace of conceit in his voice. "Out with it, then . . . or shall we bring in the suspects, as in the last chapter of a detective novel?"

"No!" I cried in horror. I had seen none of them; I had no urge to. "Only I think I must *show* you how it was done. If you and Inspector Lestrade will only step out into the hall for a moment—"

The cat reached Holmes and jumped into his lap, purring like the most satisfied creature on earth.

Holmes exploded into a perfect fusillade of sneezes. The red patches on his face, which had begun to fade, burst out afresh. He pushed the cat away and stood up.

"Be quick, Watson, so we can be away from this damned place," he said in a muffled voice, and left his perfect locked room with his shoulders in an uncharacteristic hunch, his head down, and with not a single look back. Believe me when I say that a little of my heart went with him.

Lestrade stood leaning against the door, his wet coat steaming slightly, his lips parted in a detestable grin. "Shall I take Holmes's new admirer, Watson?"

"Leave it," I said, "but close the door."

"I'd lay a fiver you're wasting our time, old

man," Lestrade said, but I saw something different in his eyes: if I'd offered to take him up on the wager, he would have found a way out of it.

"Close the door," I repeated. "I shan't be long."

He closed the door. I was alone in Hull's study . . . except for the cat, of course, which was now sitting in the middle of the rug, tail curled neatly about its paws, green eyes watching me.

I felt in my pockets and found my own souvenir from last night's dinner—bachelors are rather untidy people, I fear, but there was a reason for the bread other than general slovenliness. I almost always kept a crust in one pocket or the other, for it amused me to feed the pigeons that landed outside the very window where Holmes had been sitting when Lestrade drove up.

"Pussy," said I, and put the bread beneath the coffee-table—the coffee-table to which Lord Hull would have presented his back when he sat down with his two wills—the wretched old one and the even more wretched new one. "Pussy-pussy-pussy."

The cat rose and walked languidly beneath the table to investigate.

I went to the door and opened it. "Holmes! Lestrade! Quickly!"

They came in.

"Step over here." I walked to the coffee-table. Lestrade looked about and began to frown, seeing nothing; Holmes, of course, began to sneeze again. "Can't we have that wretched thing out of here?" he managed from behind the table-napkin, which was now quite soggy.

"Of course," said I. *"But where is it, Holmes."*

A startled expression filled his eyes above the napkin. Lestrade whirled, walked toward Hull's writing desk, and behind it. Holmes knew his reaction should not have been so violent if the cat had been on the far side of the room. He bent and looked beneath the coffee-table, saw nothing but empty space and the bottom row of the two book-cases on the north wall of the room, and straightened up again. If his eyes had not been spouting like fountains, he should have seen the illusion then; he was right on top of it. But

all the same, it was devilishly good. The empty space under that coffee-table had been Jory Hull's masterpiece.

"I don't—" Holmes began, and then the cat, who found Holmes much more to its liking than the bread, strolled out from beneath the table and began once more to twine ecstatically about his ankles. Lestrade had returned, and his eyes grew so wide I thought they might actually fall out. Even having seen through it, I myself was amazed. The scarred tomcat seemed to be materializing out of thin air; head, body, white-tipped tail last.

It rubbed against Holmes leg, purring as Holmes sneezed.

"That's enough," I said. "You've done your job and may leave."

I picked it up, took it to the door (getting a good scratch for my pains), and tossed it unceremoniously into the hall. I shut the door behind it.

Holmes was sitting down. "My God," he said in a nasal, clogged voice. Lestrade was incapable of any speech at all. His eyes never left the table and the faded red Turkish rug beneath its legs: and empty space that had somehow given birth to a cat.

"I should have seen," Holmes was muttering. "Yes . . . but you . . . how did you understand so *quickly?*" I detected the faintest hurt and pique in that voice . . . and forgave it.

"It was *those*," I said, and pointed at the shadows thrown by the table-legs.

"Of course!" Holmes nearly groaned. He slapped his welted forehead. "Idiot! I'm a perfect *idiot!*"

"Nonsense," I said tartly. "With ten cats in the house and one who has apparently picked you out for a special friend, I suspect you were seeing ten of everything."

Lestrade finally found his voice. "What about the shadows?"

"Show him, Watson," Holmes said wearily, lowering the napkin into his lap.

So I bent and picked one of the shadows off the floor.

Lestrade sat down in the other chair, hard, like a man who has been unexpectedly punched.

"I kept looking at them, you see," I said, speaking in a tone which could not help being apologetic. This seemed all wrong. It was Holmes's job to explain the whos and hows. Yet while I saw that he now understood everything, I knew he would refuse to speak in this case. And I suppose a part of me—the part that knew I would probably never have another chance to do something like this—*wanted* to be the one to explain. And the cat was rather a nice touch, I must say. A magician could have done no better with a rabbit and a top-hat.

"I knew something was wrong, but it took a moment for it to sink in. This room is extremely well lighted, but today it's pouring down rain. Look around and you'll see that not a single object in this room casts a shadow . . . *except for these table-legs.*"

Lestrade uttered an oath.

"It's rained for nearly a week," I said, "but both Holmes's barometer and the late Lord Hull's"—I pointed to it—"said that we could expect sun today. In fact, it seemed a sure thing. So he added the shadows as a final touch."

"Who did?"

"Jory Hull," Holmes said in that same weary tone. "Who else?"

I bent down and reached my hand beneath the right end of the coffee-table. It disappeared into thin air, just as the cat had appeared. Lestrade uttered another startled oath. I tapped the back of the canvas stretched tightly between the forward legs of the coffee-table. The books and the rug bulged and rippled, and the illusion, nearly perfect as it had been, was dispelled.

Jory Hull had painted the nothing under his father's coffee-table; had crouched behind the nothing as his father entered the room, locked the door, and sat at his desk with his two wills, the new and the old. And when he began to rise again from his seat, he rushed out from behind the nothing, dagger in hand.

"He was the only one who could execute such a piece of realism," I said, this time running my hand down the face of the canvas. We could all hear the low rasping sound it made, like the purr of a very old cat. "The only one who could execute it, and the only one who could hide behind it: Jory Hull, who was no more than five feet tall, bow-legged, slump-shouldered.

"As Holmes said, the surprise of the new will was no surprise. Even if the old man had been secretive about the possibility of cutting the relatives out of the will, which he wasn't, only simpletons could have mistaken the import of the visit from the solicitor and, more important, the assistant. It takes two witnesses to make a will a valid document at Chancery. What Holmes said about some people preparing for disaster was very true. A canvas as perfect as this was not made overnight, or in a month. You may find he had it ready—should it need to be used—for as long as a year—"

"Or five," Holmes interpolated.

"I suppose. At any rate, when Hull announced that he wanted to see his family in the parlour this morning, I suppose Jory knew the time had come. After his father had gone to bed last night, he would have come down here and mounted his canvas. I suppose he may have put down the false shadows at the same time, but if I had been him I should have tip-toed in here for another peek at the glass this morning, before the parlour gathering, just to make sure it was still rising. If the door was locked, I suppose he filched the key from his father's pocket and returned it later."

"Wasn't locked," Lestrade said shortly. "As a rule he kept it closed to keep the cats out, but rarely locked it."

"As for the shadows, they are just strips of felt, as you now see. His eye was good; they are about where they would have been at eleven this morning . . . if the glass had been right."

"If he expected the sun to be shining, why did he put down shadows at all?" Lestrade grumped. "Sun puts 'em down as a matter of course, just in case you've never noticed your own, Watson."

Here I was at a loss. I looked at Holmes, who seemed grateful to have *any* part in the answer.

"Don't you see? That is the greatest irony of all! If the sun had shone as the glass suggested it would, the canvas would have *blocked* the shadows. Painted shadow-legs don't cast them, you know. He was caught by shadows on a day when there were none because he was afraid he would be caught by none on a day when his father's barometer said they would almost certainly be everywhere else in the room."

"I still don't understand how Jory got in here without Hull seeing him," Lestrade said.

"That puzzled me as well," Holmes said— dear old Holmes! I doubt if it puzzled him a bit, but that was what he said. "Watson?"

"The parlor where the four of them sat has a door which communicates with the music room, does it not?"

"Yes," Lestrade said, "and the music room has a door which communicates with Lady Hull's morning-room, which is next in line as one goes toward the back of the house. But from the morning-room one can only go back into the hall, Doctor Watson. If there had been *two* doors into Hull's study, I should hardly have come after Holmes on the run as I did."

He said this last in tones of faint self-justification.

"Oh, he went back into the hall, all right," I said, "but his father didn't see him."

"Rot!"

"I'll demonstrate," I said, and went to the writing-desk, where the dead man's cane still leaned. I picked it up and turned toward them. "The very instant Lord Hull left the parlour, Jory was up and on the run."

Lestrade shot a startled glance at Holmes; Holmes gave the Inspector a cool, ironic look in return. And I must say I did not understand the wider implications of the picture I was drawing for yet awhile. I was too wrapped up in my own recreation, I suppose.

"He nipped through the first connecting door, ran across the music room, and entered Lady Hull's morning-room. He went to the hall door then and peeked out. If Lord Hull's gout had gotten so bad as to have brought on gangrene, he would have progressed no more than a quarter of the way down the hall, and that is optimistic. Now mark me, Inspector Lestrade, and I will show you how a man has spent a lifetime eating rich foods and imbibing the heavy waters ends up paying for it. If you doubt it, I shall bring you a dozen gout sufferers who will show you exactly what I'm going to show you now."

With that I began to stump slowly across the room toward them, both hands clamped tightly on the ball of the cane. I would raise one foot quite high, bring it down, pause, and then draw the other leg along. Never did my eyes look up. Instead, they alternated between the cane and that forward foot.

"Yes," Holmes said quietly. "The good Doctor is exactly right, Inspector Lestrade. The gout comes first; then (if the sufferer lives long enough, that is) there comes the characteristic stoop brought on by always looking down."

"He knew it, too," I said. "Lord Hull was afflicted with worsening gout for five years. Jory would have marked the way he had come to walk, always looking down at the cane and his own feet. Jory peeped out of the morning room, saw he was safe, and simply nipped into the study. Three seconds and no more, if he was nimble." I paused. "That hall floor is marble, isn't it? He must have kicked off his shoes."

"He was wearing slippers," Lestrade said curtly.

"Ah. I see. Jory gained the study and slipped behind his stage-flat. Then he withdrew the dagger and waited. His father reached the end of the hall. He heard Stanley call down to his father. That must have been a bad moment for him. Then his father called back that he was fine, came into the room and closed the door."

They were both looking at me intently, and I understood some of the Godlike power Holmes must have felt at moments like that, telling others what only you could know. And yet, I must repeat that it is a feeling I shouldn't have wanted to have too often. I believe the urge for such a feeling would have corrupted most men—men with less iron in their souls than was possessed by my friend Sherlock Holmes is what I mean.

"Jory—old Keg-Legs, old Stoat-Belly—would have made himself as small as possible before the locking-up went on, knowing that his father would have one good look round before turning the key and shooting the bolt. He may have been gouty and going a bit soft about the edges, but that doesn't mean he was going blind."

"His valet says his eyes were quite good," Lestrade said. "One of the first things I asked."

"Bravo, Inspector," Holmes said softly, and Inspector Lestrade favored him with a jaundiced glance.

"So he looked round," I said, and suddenly I could *see* it, and I supposed this was also the way with Holmes; this reconstruction which, while based only upon facts and deduction, seemed to be half a vision, "and he saw nothing but the study as it always was, empty save for himself. It is a remarkably open room, I see no closet door, and with the windows on both sides, there are no dark nooks even on such a day as this.

"Satisfied, he closed the door, turned his key, and shot the bolt. Jory would have heard him stump his way across to the desk. He would have heard the heavy thump and wheeze of the chair-cushion as his father sat down—a man in whom gout is well-advanced does not sit so much as position himself over a soft spot and then drop into it, seat-first—And then Jory would at last have risked a look out."

I glanced at Holmes. "Go on, old man," he said warmly. "You are doing splendidly. Absolutely first rate." I saw he meant it. Thousands would have called him cold, and they would not have been wrong, precisely, but he also had a large heart. Holmes simply protected it better than some men do.

"Thank you. Jory would have seen his father put his cane aside, and place the papers—the two packets of papers—on the blotter. He did

not kill his father immediately, although he could have done; that's what's so gruesomely pathetic about this business, and that's why I wouldn't go into that parlour where they are for a thousand pounds. I wouldn't go in unless you and your men dragged me."

"How do you know he didn't do it immediately?" Lestrade asked.

"The scream came at least two minutes after the key was turned and the bolt drawn; I assume you have enough testimony on that to believe it. Yet it can only be seven paces from door to desk. Even for a gouty man like Lord Hull, it would have taken half a minute, forty seconds at the outside, to cross to the chair and sit down. Add fifteen seconds for him to prop his cane where you found it, and put his wills on the blotter.

"What happened then? What happened during that last minute or two, which must have seemed—to Jory Hull, at least—all but endless? I believe Lord Hull simply sat there, looking from one will to the other. Jory would have been able to tell the difference between the two easily enough; the parchment of the older would have been darker.

"He knew his father intended to throw one of them into the stove.

"I believe he waited to see which one it would be.

"There was, after all, a chance that his father was only having a cruel practical joke at his family's expense. Perhaps he would burn the new will, and put the old one back in the safe. Then he could have left the room and told his family the new will was safely put away. Do you know where it is, Lestrade? The safe?"

"Five of the books in that case swing out," Lestrade said briefly, pointing to a shelf in the library area.

"Both family and old man would have been satisfied then; the family would have known their earned inheritances were safe, and the old man would have gone to his grave believing he had perpetrated one of the cruellest practical jokes of all time . . . but he would have gone as God's victim or his own, and not Jory Hull's."

Again, that look I did not understand passed between Holmes and Lestrade.

"Myself, I rather think the old man was only savoring the moment, as a man may savor the prospect of an after-dinner drink in the middle of the afternoon or a sweet after a long period of abstinence. At any rate, the minute passed, and Lord Hull began to rise . . . but with the darker parchment in his hand, and facing the stove rather than the safe. Whatever his hopes may have been, there was no hesitation on Jory's part when the moment came. He burst from hiding, crossed the distance between the coffee-table and the desk in an instant, and plunged the knife into his father's back before he was fully up.

"I suspect the autopsy will show the thrust clipped through the heart's upper ventricle and into the lung—that would explain the quantity of blood expelled from the mouth. It also explains why Lord Hull was able to scream before he died, and that's what did for Mr. Jory Hull."

"Explain," Lestrade said.

"A locked-room mystery is a bad business unless you intend to pass murder off as a case of suicide," I said, looking at Holmes. He smiled and nodded at this maxim of his. "The last thing Jory would have wanted was for things to look as they did . . . the locked room, the locked windows, the man with a knife in him where the man himself never could have put it. I think he had never forseen his father dying with such a squall. His plan was to stab him, burn the new will, rifle the desk, unlock one of the windows, and escape that way. He would have entered the house by another door, resumed his seat under the stairs, and then, when the body was finally discovered, it would have looked like robbery."

"Not to Hull's solicitor," Lestrade said.

"He might well have kept his silence," Holmes said, and then added brightly "I'll bet Jory intended to open one of the windows and add as few tracks, too. I think we all agree it would have seemed a suspiciously convenient murder, under the circumstances, but even if the solicitor spoke up, nothing could have been *proved*."

"By screaming, Lord Hull spoiled everything," I said, "as he had been spoiling things all his life. The house was roused. Jory, probably in a panic, probably only stood there like a nit.

"It was Stephen Hull who saved the day, of course—or at least Jory's alibi, the one which had him sitting on the bench under the stairs when his father was murdered. He rushed down the hall from the music room, smashed the door open, and must have hissed for Jory to get over to the desk with him, at once, so it would look as if they had broken in toget—"

I broke off, thunderstruck. At last I understood the glances between Holmes and Lestrade. I understood what they must have seen from the moment I showed them the trick hiding place: it could not have been done alone. The killing, yes, but the rest . . .

"Stephen testified that he and Jory met at the study door," I said slowly. "That he, Stephen, burst it in and they entered together, discovered the body together. He lied. He might have done it to protect his brother, but to lie so well when one doesn't know what has happened seems . . . seems . . ."

"Impossible," Holmes said, "is the word for which you are searching, Watson."

"Then Jory and Stephen were in on it together," I said. "They planned it together . . . and in the eyes of the law, both are guilty of their father's murder! My God!"

"Not both of them, my dear Watson," Holmes said in a tone of curious gentleness. "*All* of them."

I could only gape.

He nodded. "You have shown remarkable insight this morning, Watson. For once in your life you have burned with a deductive heat I'll wager you'll never generate again. My cap is off to you, dear fellow, as it is to any man who is able to transcend his normal nature, no matter how briefly. But in one way you have remained the same dear chap as you've always been: while you understand how good people can be, you have no understanding of how black they *may* be."

I looked at him silently, almost humbly.

"Not that there was much blackness here, if half of what we've heard of Lord Hull was true," Holmes said. He rose and began to pace irritably about the study. "Who testifies that Jory was with Stephen when the door was smashed in? Jory, naturally. Stephen, naturally. But there were two others. One was William—the third brother. Am I right, Lestrade?"

"Yes. He said he was halfway down the stairs when he saw the two of them go in together, Jory a little ahead."

"How interesting!" Holmes said, eyes gleaming. "Stephen breaks in the door—as the younger and stronger of course he must—and so one would expect simple forward motion would have carried him into the room first. Yet William, halfway down the stairs, saw *Jory* enter first. Why was that, Watson?"

I could only shake my head numbly.

"Ask yourself whose testimony, *and whose testimony alone,* we can trust here. The answer is the fourth witness, Lord Hull's man, Oliver Stanley. He approached the gallery railing in time to see Stephen enter the room, and that is perfectly correct, since *Stephen* was alone when he broke it in. It was *William,* with a better angle from his place on the stairs, who said he saw Jory precede Stephen into the study. William said so because he had seen Stanley and knew what he must say. It boils down to this, Watson: we know Jory was inside this room. Since both of his brothers testify he was *outside,* there was, at the very least, collusion. But as you say, the lack of confusion, the way they all pulled together so neatly, suggests something more."

"Conspiracy," I said dully.

"Yes. But, unfortunately for the Hulls, that's not all. Do you recall me asking you, Watson, if you believe that all four of them simply walked wordlessly out of that parlour in four different directions at the very moment they heard the study door locked?"

"Yes. Now I do."

"The *four* of them." He looked at Lestrade. "All four testified they were four, yes?"

"Yes."

"That includes Lady Hull. And yet we know Jory had to have been up and off the moment his father left the room; we know he was in the study when the door was locked, *yet all four—including Lady Hull—*claimed all four of them were still in the parlour when they heard the door locked. There might as well have been four hands on that dagger, Watson. The murder of Lord Hull was very much a family affair."

I was too staggered to say anything. I looked at Lestrade and saw a look on his face I had never seen before or ever did again; a kind of tired sickened gravity.

"What may they expect?" Holmes said, almost genially.

"Jory will certainly swing," Lestrade said. "Stephen will go to gaol for life. William Hull may get life, but will more likely get twenty years in Broadmoor, and there such a weakling as he will almost certainly be tortured to death by his fellows. The only difference between what awaits Jory and what awaits William is that Jory's end will be quicker and more merciful."

Holmes bent and stroked the canvas stretched between the legs of the coffee-table. It made that odd hoarse purring noise.

"Lady Hull," Lestrade went on, "would go to Beechwood Manor—more commonly know to the female inmates as Cut-Purse Palace—for five years . . . but, having met the lady, I rather suspect she will find another way out. Her husband's laudanum would be my guess."

"All because Jory Hull missed a clean strike," Holmes remarked, and sighed. "If the old man had had the common decency to die silently, all would have been well. He would, as Watson says, have left by the window. Taking his canvas with him, of course . . . not to mention his trumpery shadows. Instead, he raised the house. All the servents were in, exclaiming over the dead master. The family was in confusion. How shabby their luck was, Lestrade! How close was the constable when Stanley summoned him? Less than fifty yards, I should guess."

"He was actually on the walk," Lestrade said.

"Their luck *was* shabby. He was passing, heard the scream, and turned in."

"Holmes," I said, feeling much more comfortable in my old role, "how did you know a constable was so nearby?"

"Simplicity itself, Watson. If not, the family would have shooed the servants out long enough to hide the canvas and 'shadows.'"

"Also to unlatch at least one window, I should think," Lestrade added in a voice uncustomarily quiet.

"They *could* have taken the canvas and the shadows," I said suddenly.

Holmes turned toward me. "Yes."

Lestrade raised his eyebrows.

"It came down to a choice," I said to him. "There was time enough to burn the new will or get rid of the hugger-mugger . . . this would have been just Stephen and Jory, of course, in the moments after Stephen burst in the door. They—or, if you've got the temperature of the characters right, and I suppose you do, *Stephen*—decided to burn the will and hope for the best. I suppose there was just time enough to chuck it into the stove."

Lestrade turned, looked at it, then looked back. "Only a man as black as Hull would have found strength enough to scream at the end," he said.

"Only a man as black as Hull would have required a son to kill him," Holmes returned.

He and Lestrade looked at each other, and again something passed between them, something perfectly communicated which I myself did not understand.

"Have you ever done it?" Holmes asked, as if picking up on an old conversation.

Lestrade shook his head. "Once came damned close," he said. "There was a girl involved, not her fault, not really. I came close. Yet . . . that was one."

"And these are four," Holmes returned. "Four people ill used by a foul man who should have died within six months anyway."

Now I understood.

Holmes turned his gray eyes on me. "What

say you, Lestrade? Watson has solved this one, although he did not see all the ramifications. Shall we let Watson decide?"

"All right," Lestrade said gruffly. "Just be quick. I want to get out of this damned room."

Instead of answering, I bent down, picked up the felt shadows, rolled them into a ball, and put them in my coat pocket. I felt quite odd doing it: much as I had felt when in the grip of the fever which almost took my life in India.

"Capital fellow, Watson!" Holmes said. "You've solved your first case and became an accessory to murder all in the same day, and before tea-time! And here's a souvenir for myself—an original Jory Hull. I doubt it's signed, but one must be grateful for whatever the gods send us on rainy days." He used his pen-knife to loosen the glue holding the canvas to the legs of the coffee-table. He made quick work of it; less than a minute later he was slipping a narrow canvas tube into the inner pocket of his voluminous greatcoat.

"This is a dirty piece of work," Lestrade said, but he crossed to one of the windows and, after a moment's hesitation, released the locks which held it and raised it half an inch or so.

"Some is dirtier done than undone," Holmes observed. "Shall we?"

We crossed to the door. Lestrade opened it. One of the constables asked Lestrade if there was any progress.

On another occasion Lestrade might show the man the rough side of his tongue. This time he said shortly, "Looks like attempted robbery gone to something worse. I saw it at once, of course; Holmes a moment later."

"Too bad!" the other constable ventured.

"Yes, too bad," Lestrade said. "But the old man's scream sent the thief packing before he could steal anything. Carry on."

We left. The parlour door was open, but I kept my head as we passed it. Holmes looked, of course; there was no way he could not have done. It was just the way he was made. As for me, I never saw any of the family. I never wanted to.

Holmes was sneezing again. His friend was

twining around his legs and miaowing blissfully. "Let me out of here," he said, and bolted.

An hour later we were back at 221B Baker Street, in much the same positions we occupied when Lestrade came driving up: Holmes in the window-seat, myself on the sofa.

"Well, Watson," Holmes said presently, "how do you think you'll sleep tonight?"

"Like a top," I said. "And you?"

"Likewise," he said. "I'm glad to be away from those damned cats, I can tell you that."

"How will Lestrade sleep, d'you think?"

Holmes looked at me and smiled. "Poorly tonight. Poorly for a week, perhaps. But then he'll be all right. Among his other talents, Lestrade has a great one for creative forgetting."

That made me laugh, and laugh hard.

"Look, Watson!" Holmes said. "Here's a sight!" I got up and went to the window, sure I would see Lestrade riding up in the waggon once more. Instead I saw the sun breaking through the clouds, bathing London in a glorius late afternoon light.

"It came out after all," Holmes said. "Top-hole!" He picked up his violin and began to play, the sun strong on his face. I looked at his barometer and saw it was falling. That made me laugh so hard I had to sit down. When Holmes looked at me and asked what it was, I could only shake my head. Strange man, Holmes: I doubt if he would have understood, anyway.

MANLY WADE WELLMAN

THE VERSATILE AND PROLIFIC Manly Wade Wellman (1903–1986) began writing, mainly in the horror field, in the 1920s and by the 1930s was selling stories to the leading pulps in the genre: *Weird Tales*, *Wonder Stories*, and *Astounding Stories*. He had three series running simultaneously in *Weird Tales*. They featured Silver John, also known as John the Balladeer, the backwoods minstrel with a silver-stringed guitar; John Thunstone, the New York playboy and adventurer who was also a psychic detective; and Judge Keith Hilary Pursuivant, an elderly occult detective (Wellman wrote this last series under the pseudonym Gans T. Fields).

His short story "A Star for a Warrior" won the Best Story of the Year award from *Ellery Queen's Mystery Magazine* in 1946, beating out a story by William Faulkner, who wrote an angry letter of protest. Other major honors include Lifetime Achievement Awards from the World Fantasy Writers (1980) and the British Fantasy Writers (1985), and the World Fantasy Award for Best Collection for *Worse Things Waiting* (1975).

Several of his stories have been adapted for television, including "The Valley Was Still" for *The Twilight Zone* (1961), "The Devil Is Not Mocked" for *Night Gallery* (1971), and "Larroes Catch Meddlers" (1951) and "School for the Unspeakable" (1952) for two episodes of *Lights Out*.

Wellman also wrote for comic books, producing the first Captain Marvel issue for Fawcett Publishers. When DC Comics sued Fawcett for plagiarizing their Superman character, Wellman testified against Fawcett, and DC won the case after three years of litigation.

"A Knife Between Brothers" was originally published in the February 1947 issue of *Ellery Queen's Mystery Magazine*.

A KNIFE BETWEEN BROTHERS

MANLY WADE WELLMAN

STRIPPED TO TROUSERS and mocca-
sins, young David Return needed only a feather
jutting from his black hair to reincarnate the
most picturesque of his warrior-chief ancestors
of the Tsichah. Sweat and sunlight conferred to
his brown back and shoulders a sheen like that of
a well-used, well-kept saddle. His hands were as
knowledgeable with spanner and screwdriver as
they might have been, two generations ago, with
warclub or scalping knife. Rather incongruously for one who so well fitted the ideal picture
of a savage, he was tinkering successfully with
the ignition system of an old Plymouth sedan
behind the whitewashed police shack of the Tsichah Agency.

Tightening a last connection, David Return
slipped into the driver's seat, stepped on the
starter, and listened intently to the response of
the engine. Satisfied, he snapped off the ignition, wiped his hands and face on a morsel of
ancient towelling, then caught up and put on his
flannel shirt with its silver-plated star badge of
the agency police. Tucking in his shirt tails, he
entered the shack.

"*Ahi*, that car will run now," he announced
to the Indian, much older and more picturesque
than himself, who sat behind the desk with his
hands full of papers. "The whole automotive
industry ought to come and watch the things I
did to it. And I'm dried out like jerked beef."
From a hook by the window he lifted a canvas
water bag and drank gratefully from it. "Are we
running a police detail or a garage?"

Tough Feather, David's grandsire and senior
agency policeman, reached for a pen and signed
his name to a report. His profile was almost
exactly similar to that of the noble old chief on
the buffalo nickel. Had he not been so good a
police officer, he might have been notable as
an artists' model or a character actor. Tough
Feather grinned, his teeth startlingly white in
the seamed duskiness of his face.

"We run both those things, and ten or twenty
more, David. Here," and he held up the paper,
"is our monthly report to the agent. Here," and
he turned his chin to indicate a high piled wire
basket, "is unanswered correspondence—on
almost every subject but law enforcement. By
day after tomorrow, for instance, we must have
something definite on the survey of how many
dogs are kept on this reservation—"

"How many dogs!" David almost whooped.
"Who's going to count all the dogs of all the Tsichah?"

"Two policemen are going to count them,"
Tough Feather informed him. "They're at it
now. And there's a request for a police escort
to accompany the school children visiting the
historical exhibit over at Smith City," continued Tough Feather, "and an advance man's
coming to look this reservation over for a travel
newsreel company. He needs a guide and interpreter."

"Don't give me either of those assignments,"
begged David. "Police college taught me to
gather evidence and disarm violent lawbreakers,

but not to be a governess or a public relations expert."

"Your education is incomplete," Tough Feather told him. "Indian police have to be everything—almost. You've started well, son of my son, but you still think the job begins and ends in trailing criminals and locking them up. If that's all you do, what will the Tsichah call you? A white man's Indian."

David winced at that.

"I'm an Indian's Indian," he said harshly, "and they'd better realize it. I believe in being a good citizen and a good policeman, but I was born a chief of the Tsichah, and that's a priority. I don't want to do anything but help my tribe, which is what police are for."

"Because police must do other things than make arrests," amplified Tough Feather gravely. "We have to explain the law as well as enforce it. We must uphold the government with the Indians, and uphold the Indians with the government." He filled his ancient stone pipe and lighted it. "We Indians might still be masters of this hemisphere if we'd been able to stop fighting each other."

David's broad young brow creased, as if troubled by thoughts evoked by his grandfather's words. "I'm still a rookie policeman," he said. "What I need is experience. How about assigning me to gather some?"

"I was waiting for you to finish fixing the car," said Tough Feather, and held out a scribbled card. "Drive out the Squaw Hill trail to the cabin of Yellow Bird and Stone Wolf. They have a dispute. Judge between them."

David's brow-crease became a frown. He was young, and well-reared young Indians are shy about giving advice to old ones. "I've not been trained as a judge," he demurred.

"You were born a chief," his grandfather reminded him. "Now you're a grown warrior, and a qualified police officer of this agency. Yellow Bird and Stone Wolf sent me a message last night, asking for my help, but this paperwork will keep me busy today and tomorrow." He thrust the card into David's hesitating hand. "Go and

act in my place. Because of your blood, they'll accept your word as though it were mine."

David felt better for that assurance. He studied the names on the card. "Yellow Bird and Stone Wolf—I haven't seen those old brothers since I was a boy. They never come here to the agency. Aren't they old, old Tsichah, remembering nothing but wars and hunts? How do they stay alive?"

"They have lands on the reservation," replied Tough Feather. "Between their two head rights there are about eighty acres worth cultivating; but they never learned to farm, and they live among the hills and speak only to each other. Not even that now, since they quarreled. They rent their land to a step-kinsman."

"Step-kinsman?" echoed David.

"It was he who brought me their message last night. Both of them were married when they were young warriors, before their last fight with the white men." Tough Feather's face grew momentarily harder, for the bloody finish of that conflict was the most vivid and least pleasant memory of his own boyhood. "There was cannon-fire at the Tsichah camp, and it killed both their families, except for Stone Wolf's little daughter."

"She went to Chicago," David remembered.

"And married a white man. Now she's dead, too, without children of her own; but her husband had a son by a first marriage, and that son farms for Stone Wolf and Yellow Bird. He began while you were away at the police college. His name's Avery Packer—a good farmer."

"He brought the message, you say. Can he help me?"

"He's a good farmer," repeated Tough Feather, "but no white man can decide the private quarrels of old Tsichah. They must have a chief's word."

Tough Feather's sinewy old hand shook the ashes from the stone pipe. "Any more questions?"

David brought his moccasined heels together and whipped his brown hand to his brown temple in salute.

"No questions. I'll get a bite of lunch at the trader's and go. My report will be on your desk before evening."

The afternoon was hotter than the morning had been. David drove up the trail with the car windows open, but the breeze he stirred was dry and heavy. Flat red-brown dryness stretched away to right and left, with occasional dimples where buffaloes had wallowed long ago, and more distant clumps and stragglings of brushy willow or cottonwood scrub to mark scanty watercourses. Now and then the hot air danced and blurred, as though a ghost had dared come out in broad daylight and shake his robe.

It was weary country, conquered country, mused David. His people, the Tsichah, had been almost the last Indian tribe to admit the mastery of the white men. This, their reservation, was the worst and driest portion of their vast ancient roaming-grounds. If Avery Packer, Stone Wolf's step-grandson, actually paid rent on eighty acres of it, he must be a spendthrift fool. But as David decided that, his car topped a knoll and he saw the land of the disputing brothers.

It was all welcome, restful green, a smooth expanse of it to the very trailside and reaching ahead and beyond to a confining curve of knolls and bluffs. The only break in the pleasant expanse was a patch in the center, a patch as silver-bright in the sun as David's new star. It was quiet water, a whole pondful, as rare on Tsichah acres as the rich, sturdy grass itself. David's moccasin pushed down the brake and he leaned back in the driver's seat to gaze in admiration.

Toward him walked a figure, a burly white man in rough clothes, carefully parting the grass to avoid trampling too much of it.

"Looking for me?"

"If you're Avery Packer, I am," said David, his eyes still in the field. "Nice hay crop you've got here. Must have worked hard on it."

Packer nodded. "I did. That pond of mine's the secret." He glanced back toward the still surface of water, and his profile showed a short, straight nose and a jutting brow. "It catches rain and soaks it out through the loose earth. Otherwise whatever I planted would die out in the first hot spell."

"Lucky break having it," David congratulated him, and Packer grinned.

"Lucky back-break, you ought to say. When I first rented, it was just a mud-puddle. I dredged and scooped out for days to make it worthwhile. This year I'll make a dollar or two on this hay, and next year I may go in for corn." Packer's eye caught the glint of the star on David's flannel shirt. "Agency policeman, aren't you?"

"Right. That's why I stopped. You rent from Yellow Bird and Stone Wolf, don't you? I'm going out to settle their squabble."

"They were kind of expecting old Tough Feather."

"He can't come. I'm his grandson, handling the case for him. What can you tell me about it?"

Packer's grin came back. "Just that it's over money. A little bit of money I paid 'em a week ago."

He paused, as though awaiting a question, but David sat relaxed, watching him and listening. Packer went on:

"I pay in silver. Paper they don't savvy. Rent's two dollars an acre a year, about fifteen bucks each month. They make out on that, buying a little flour and bacon and canned stuff, and sometimes a few cartridges to hunt rabbits and ducks. They keep it, as I hear, under a loose floor board in their cabin. Well, old Stone Wolf was clawing for some of it yesterday, to buy supplies at the agency. There wasn't none."

"They told you this?" prompted David.

"In about eleven words between the both of 'em. I'm sort of kinfolk—my dad married Stone Wolf's daughter—but they don't jaw a lot, not even to me. Anyhow, they wound up accusing each other of stealing. That's all I know, except I went to the agency for 'em, to ask Tough Feather would he come out and hear their argument."

"Thanks," said David, "that's a help. Where do they live?"

"Right yonder, past the bluff." Packer's big hand gestured ahead. "Mind if I come along?"

"Glad to have you." David opened the door for him.

Beyond the bluff they came in sight of the cabin, a sagging little structure on a rise above the trail. The open front door was full of darkness.

"Wait here," David told Parker, and trotted up the footpath to the flat rock that served as a front stoop.

"*Ahi*," grunted someone inside, and David stepped across the threshold.

In the hot still darkness inside the front room, squatting on the floor, was a spare old man as brown as leather. Despite the bitter heat, he was wrapped from skinny chin to skinny toes in a blanket that seemed as old and worn as himself. Two braids of gray-salted hair framed his wrinkled face. His licorice eyes looked sunken and sad.

David glanced quickly around the room. Its two windows were curtained with tattered blankets. In one corner lay a few poor possessions—rolled bedding, a battered coffee pot, a clay water-jar that surely dated back to the days of savage freedom, some other small odds and ends. The only furniture was a rickety old chair with but three legs that leaned against the inner wall beside a closed door.

"*Ahi*, uncle," David greeted the oldster politely. "I am Tough Feather's grandson."

"I am Stone Wolf," replied the other.

"You asked for a chief to judge your quarrel," David reminded him. "Where is your brother Yellow Bird?"

The gray-black head perked toward the closed inner door. "In the kitchen. We have not spoken or sat together since—"

"I know something about it, but will speak to both at one time," announced David with chiefly dignity.

"Speak to Yellow Bird if you want to," said Stone Wolf. "He will not hear you. He is out in the kitchen. Dead."

Yellow Bird, prone on the floor of the oven-hot kitchen, was a replica of Stone Wolf in all things—gray braids, wrinkled face, meager limbs, seedy old blanket—save the slack immobility of his body and the knife-handle that jutted from between his shoulders.

David stood over him, and pondered sagely that a policeman must do many right things at once, and must likewise refrain from doing many wrong things. In case of a homicide, first study the surroundings, he remembered from a lecture at police college. Carefully he looked to either side of him, up, down. At his left as he stood just inside the doorway was a single window, both its broken panes mended with flour sacking nailed on. To his right slouched a rusty stove. Straight ahead was the cabin's back door, with a broken lock and a heavy home-made bar of wood.

Stone Wolf rose and came to David's elbow, gazing at his quiet brother. "Who killed him?" asked David.

Out of the folded blanket crept Stone Wolf's skinny hand. A thumb like a stub of twig jabbed at Stone Wolf's chest.

"I," rumbled the old man. "I killed him."

David turned quickly to meet the gaze of the sunken eyes. "But you wanted your quarrel judged," he protested.

"I killed him," repeated Stone Wolf. "Who else could have struck my brother?"

Decrepitly he shuffled into the kitchen. The gaunt hand crept further into view, lifting to indicate with its spread palm, Indian-fashion, the back door.

"The bar is in place—inside. And the window"—Stone Wolf paused, turned and lifted his palm toward it—"could not open far enough to let an enemy in. See for yourself, young chief."

David stepped to the window and prodded both sashes. Warped by many hot seasons and by many soaking rains, they were stubbornly wedged in position—the upper closed, the lower raised perhaps two inches. Not even a crowbar could dislodge them, judged David; they would splinter before they would budge. Nor had the sacking over the glass been disturbed; the nails that held it were rusted into their holes. David felt shame. Stone Wolf, in his self-accusation, weighed the evidence far better than he, David.

"Is it your knife in Yellow Bird's back?" he demanded.

"*Yuh.* It is my knife." Stone Wolf bent creakily, his hand extending.

"Don't touch it!" commanded David sharply, and the old Indian stepped back obediently. David returned to the body—it lay two long strides from the window—and knelt.

"White men's police wisdom," he lectured importantly, "can show what hand held a knife, by things called fingerprints."

But not this time, he decided even as he spoke. The weapon, an old butcher knife such as traders have sold Indians for a century, had been driven to the very hilt, and blood had gushed from the wound over the worn brass-studded grip.

Stone Wolf was speaking again: "Such wisdom is not needed. I said that I killed him. Does a Tsichah lie?"

Rising, David faced the old man. "Was it self-defense, Stone Wolf?"

The exposed hand quivered its spread fingers, the universal plains sign for a question, a mystification, a lack of understanding. "I do not know. Maybe I slept squatting, and in my sleep crept upon my brother. Or a *djiba,* an enemy ghost, put a spell on me to make me do the thing. Or, because I am grown old, I forget at one time what I did another."

Stone Wolf's face was mournful, but calm and stubborn, even a bit disdainful.

"A man cannot kill and not know," David half-scolded him.

"You are the chief," Stone Wolf replied gravely, turning away. "Use your wisdom to find out."

He shuffled back into the front room and sat down on the floor again. Left alone in the stuffy kitchen, David again gazed thoughtfully at the body, at the stove, at the barred door, at the immovable window, and back at the body.

Yellow Bird had fallen on his left side, head toward the back door, feet drawn up, knees together. Plainly he had been squatting. Awake, then, or at most dozing lightly; and his right side, not his back, had been nearest to the communicating door. In any case the old floor boards creaked loudly, even under David's careful moccasins. How could Stone Wolf, asleep or in a trance or even awake and stealthy, have crept upon him?

Perhaps Stone Wolf had thrown his knife. Many Tsichah could do that—David himself was a fair knife-thrower. But another study of the dead man ruled that out. The knife had struck his back—it had come, not from the direction of the front room, but from the direction of the window.

David turned his attention to that jammed, sack-cloaked window with its crack of opening. Yellow Bird had been sitting some six feet away, no difficult target. Crossing the creaky floor to the back door, David lifted the wooden bar and walked out and around the cabin. Avery Packer was watching him curiously from the car's running board, below on the trail. David approached the window from outside.

Stacked against the wall below the sill was the cabin's supply of firewood—old broken boxes and planks, branches and roots, a few shingles blown from the ruinous roof, three broken pieces of an old bamboo fishing pole. David smiled thinly. The two old brothers must have ranged far to gather this fuel in an almost timberless country, but meditations on such chores were not part of an investigator's job. The stacked wood was enough to prevent a knife-thrower from pushing close to the window and inserting his hand. Even if a hand were inserted, it would be too cramped to whip strength behind the cast. David stepped several paces backward. Only the most skillful of thrown blades could sail through that narrow slit, and the dimness beyond would cloak any target.

A flutter of motion from the car registered in his eye-corner. Packer was beckoning. David hurried down to him.

"What's all this about?" demanded the white man. "You having trouble?"

David told him, briefly. Packer frowned. "You think Stone Wolf did it? After all, he's my step-granddad."

"I believe him when he says he doesn't know how it happened," replied David, "and it's plain that nobody else could have got to Yellow Bird. The set-up's like those sealed-room killings in the mystery stories. The police college instructors used to joke about them."

"It's no joke when the story's true," said Packer weightily. "Well, what next? If Stone Wolf goes to jail—" He stopped, with his mouth half open, and his face lighted up. "Look," he said, more animatedly, "if his memory lapsed, he can't be tried for murder. He's mentally incompetent."

"At Stone Wolf's age he'd probably beat a conviction on those grounds," agreed David.

"I certainly hope so," said Packer earnestly. "I'd do anything for that old duck. I'm the closest to a family he's got left. Maybe—"

"Tell me later." Again David was scrambling up the slope. He rounded the cabin again, entered the back door, and dropped the bar in place. Once more he paced around Yellow Bird's motionless body, thoughtful and silent.

He could see now that a knife-throw from outside was impossible. The position of the hilt showed that the blade had gone in, not flat down but edge down. Not even a circus star could have counted on sailing it through the narrow space beneath the window in that fashion. David produced his bandana, knelt, and with his cloth-wrapped hand tugged at the bloody hilt. It was wedged hard, in spine or rib.

He got up quickly and went back into the front room. Stone Wolf sat motionless on the floor. David felt elation mingling with the gravity of his mood. He was being a policeman after all, finding out many small things that fitted together into a picture of growing clarity. He asked:

"Stone Wolf, when did you last see Yellow Bird alive?"

"This morning."

"Tell me how."

"Since our quarrel I kept to this room, he to the kitchen. Men who call each other thief and liar do not speak until the question is properly settled."

"*Yuh,*" agreed David. "That is good Tsichah custom. And then?"

"We cooked at different times. I came this morning to fry bacon on the kitchen stove. When Yellow Bird saw me he unbarred the back door and went out. He looked at me without speaking." Stone Wolf's eyes fluttered briefly in their bracketing of pouchy wrinkles. "I think he was like me, anxious for a settlement. I cooked but I ate only a little, for my stomach was sad in me. When I came back in here, Yellow Bird came into the kitchen. He barred the door again and closed the door to this room. I heard him sit down and wait."

"When did you leave this room again?"

"When the sun was high. I felt hungry, for I had eaten so little in the morning. I opened the door to the kitchen and I saw that I had killed my brother."

Stone Wolf's hand, again emerging, rubbed its fingertips together as if casting away a pinch of sand—the sign of loss. David looked at him with eyes that brightened.

"You can kill with a knife? Show me."

Slowly Stone Wolf got to his feet and took the knife that David held out, hilt foremost. David picked up the ruined old chair. "Stab here," he directed. "I am a chief. Do not ask questions about what I want. Obey me."

Stone Wolf gripped the knife, his hand knowledgeable upon it. He struck with considerable suddenness for an old man. David lifted the chair by its shaky legs, catching the driving point on the wooden seat.

"That was a weak stab, uncle," he taunted. "Again."

Stone Wolf stepped closer and struck, with all his force. David caught the point as before, then tilted the chair to see. He curled his lip scornfully as he studied the splintery little nick.

"I have not your young arm," reminded Stone Wolf. "Once my blow would have split that chair, or even a heavier thing."

"Take the knife in both your hands," bade David. He set the chair upright and steadied it by the back. "With all your strength this time. Strike down."

Stone Wolf's left hand cupped around and over his right, gripping the knife daggerwise. He poised himself, summoning and tensing every fiber of his stringy muscles, then drove downward from shoulder height, and stepped back. The blade stood upright and vibrating, its point lodged in the seat of the chair.

Stooping, David dislodged the knife with a little shake. He slid it back into the sheath at his hip. His white teeth flashed through the gloom of the curtained cabin in a happy smile.

"You did not kill your brother, Stone Wolf."

The gray head shook, its two braids quivered on Stone Wolf's shoulders. "But I have shown that I did."

"I say you did not," insisted David. "A stronger hand than yours struck Yellow Bird. The blow drove your knife through bone and flesh. You could never have done it."

Again Stone Wolf's hand made the quivering mystery-sign. "I see the truth of that. Your wisdom is big."

"You must help me." David seized the scrawny old shoulder in his earnestness. "Someone else killed Yellow Bird. Who?"

"A *djiba*? A devil?"

"No squaw's tales here! A man did it, somebody strong and bad. We will find him, you and I. First," and he used an English word, "we must search for a—motive."

Stone Wolf was as baffled as David. "I am a child in these things. I do not know your meaning."

"A motive means, why did the man kill him?"

"Why does any man kill another?" rejoined Stone Wolf. "He hates the other. He wants the other man's horse or wife or weapons. He is afraid the other means to kill him, and strikes first."

"But who hated Yellow Bird? Not even you, though you had quarrelled. Yellow Bird had no wife or horse or other things. Even the little money itself was already stolen. And who would fear him?"

"Those things are for a chief to find out." Stone Wolf doddered over to the corner where odds and ends were piled. He fumbled in a worn buckskin pouch, cradled something in his palm, and from the water jug carefully sluiced a few drops upon it.

"Nobody but you could have stabbed Yellow Bird inside this cabin," David amplified, as much for himself as for Stone Wolf. "It was someone else—at the window. But he did not throw. He struck." Breaking off, David watched his companion. "What are you doing there?"

"This is red paint for mourning." The old fellow dipped from the wet mass in his palm and smeared broad patches on his wrinkled cheeks, his parchment brow. Even in the dim room, the color was vivid.

Almost leaping at Stone Wolf, David thrust his own thumb into the palmful of watered powder. "Vermilion," said David at once. "Where did you get this?"

Stone Wolf jerked his chin doorward. "Out there, near where the grass is growing. My father and my father's father got red paint-powder in that place, long before white men ever came here."

"Red paint-powder," echoed David. He studied his stained thumb as if it were writing he had just learned to read.

"I mourn," continued Stone Wolf, "for my brother. He did not die by my hand. I may honestly show sorrow."

"And I," said David Return, "may honestly show the man who killed him."

He hastened outside.

For a moment only he paused, under the kitchen window, to snatch at the woodpile. As he headed downslope to the car, Avery Packer rose from the running board.

"Ready to bring Stone Wolf along?" asked the white man.

"I'm ready to bring you along," said David Return.

He held out the three broken lengths of the bamboo.

"When these were all in one piece," he said, "they made a pole. Here, in the hollow butt end, you put that knife you'd stolen from Stone Wolf. Through the crack of the window you jabbed at Yellow Bird's back—hard. The knife stuck in his bones, and you pulled the pole free and broke it up to lose in the kindling pile."

Packer stared. He fumbled out tobacco-bag and papers. "I don't get you," he said, and for the first time he sounded foolish.

"But I get you," David assured him. "Stone Wolf's innocent. That leaves you. You were the only one in contact with the brothers. You knew where they kept their money, how the cabin was arranged, you were able to steal Stone Wolf's knife. You took the money to make them suspicious of each other and start quarrelling—you even carried a message for them to my grandfather. Then you hurried back and killed Yellow Bird. For this."

Tucking the pieces of bamboo under one arm, David thrust his other hand under Packer's nose, waggling the red-smeared thumb.

"That's only Indian paint," said Packer, his eyes goggling.

"You recognize it. We both know what it is. Cinnabar—vermilion. For centuries the Tsichah and other Indians made their brightest red from it. But white men make something else— mercury. A deposit's worth a fortune to the right developer."

Packer had started to roll a cigarette. He threw the paper and the pinch of tobacco grains on the ground. Again he opened his mouth, but this time no words came out.

"You discovered the cinnabar deposit when you were dredging your pond," went on David. "Your rent for the farming rights was low; but mineral rights would come high. It would be cheaper, you decided, to get them by killing."

"You're crazy!" Packer exploded. "Yellow Bird was killed. I can't claim anything of *his*. It's Stone Wolf who's my kin."

"And he's alive," David wound up for him. "You had that figured out, too. He'd stand trial, be called a crazy old man, and be put away in comfort—with a guardian named to handle his affairs. You'd be the logical one. You were all ready to offer yourself. You even started to explain all that to me, a moment ago when I was out here looking at the window and the wood-pile. You sounded very kind and dutiful. Yellow Bird dead, Stone Wolf in a hospital or asylum— and you with a free hand to coin all that cinnabar into money."

David turned to the car, tossing in one piece of bamboo, then another. His right hip was within the white man's reach.

Packer shot out his own hand, whipping the knife from David's belt.

With the thickest piece of bamboo still in his hand, David struck Packer calculatingly across the knuckles. Packer swore in pain, and the knife dropped among the crumbs of spilled tobacco.

"I gave you that chance on purpose, and you practically confessed," announced David in tones sweet with triumph. "You knew I had you, so you were going to knife me as you knifed Yellow Bird."

Stooping swiftly, he caught up the knife. It gleamed authoritatively, point toward Packer.

"Come to the agency with me," commanded David Return.

THE GLASS GRAVESTONE

JOSEPH COMMINGS

IT SHOULD BE NO SURPRISE that as one of the masters of the locked-room mystery, Joseph Commings (1913–1992) enjoyed the friendship of Edward D. Hoch, one of the greatest and most prolific writers in that challenging sub-genre, and Robert Adey, one of the foremost experts of detective fiction generally and impossible crimes specifically. Born in New York City, Commings lived there most of his life and met Hoch when the latter was stationed there for his army service in 1952 and 1953. They began a weekly correspondence that lasted until Commings had a stroke in 1971 and then continued sporadically until his death.

Senator Brooks U. Banner, the giant (6'3", 270-pound) accomplished magician and adventurer, was his series character, born from when Commings made up stories to entertain his fellow soldiers in Sardinia during World War II. With some rewriting after the war, he found a ready market for them in the pulps *10-Story Detective* and *Ten Detective Aces* (whose editor changed the character's name to Mayor Tom Landin; when later reprinted, the name was changed back to Banner). Although the pulps were dying in the late 1940s, new digest-sized magazines came to life and Commings sold stories to *Mystery Digest*, *The Saint Mystery Magazine*, and *Mike Shayne Mystery Magazine*. Although he wrote several full-length mystery novels, none was published, in spite of the encouragement of his friend John Dickson Carr. The only Commings novels to see print were paperback original soft-core porn novels. The only book edition of his stories was published posthumously: *Banner Deadlines: The Impossible Files of Senator Brooks U. Banner* (Norfolk, Virginia, Crippen & Landru, 2004).

"The Glass Gravestone" was first published in the October 1966 issue of *The Saint Mystery Magazine*. This is its first appearance in book form.

THE GLASS GRAVESTONE

JOSEPH COMMINGS

THE MAN STANDING at the foot of the escalator, wearing the purple turban and the silver-tipped black beard, was Surendranath Das. He was a United Nations delegate from India. I walked toward him, the lobby floor under my feet all black and white marble, like a giant checkerboard.

Das seemed to be hesitating. This was the *down* escalator from the mezzanine in the Secretariat. So he wasn't thinking of taking it up. I hadn't expected to see him. I hadn't expected to see anybody except Sir Quiller Selwyn and Senator Banner. Like any other office building, The United Nations Secretariat closed up shop at six. It was now a dark nine p.m.

At the rap of my heels, Das turned. He was a fat-bodied man with a handshake that was moist and flabby. Squinting across the deserted lobby through his glasses with the tortoise-shell rims, he placed me. His brindled beard parted in a grinning grimace. "How do you do?" He spoke in cultured English in a high piping voice. "You're—ah—the newspaper reporter."

"Bob Farragut," I said with a return grimace. "Associated Press." There was a fine distinction and I wanted to keep it. I glanced upward toward the mezzanine with its subdued lights. "Mr. Das, have you seen Sir Quiller?"

"Not yet. I was waiting for him. He sent for me."

"You?" I wanted to ask more, but there was no time.

Sir Quiller Selwyn appeared at the top of the descending escalator. He was a squat bald-headed man with bushy eyebrows and a taciturn way. Even at this distance I could see a look on his face that I had never seen there before. It was a look of naked alarm.

He didn't seem to see me at all.

"Das!" he cried. "Have you taken leave of your senses? They're the most deadly—!" He put his feet on the moving steps. "Wait till I get down there!"

Das and I were standing together. I glanced sideways at him to see how he was taking this severe admonition. Oddly, his coffee-colored face had turned toward me. His brown eyes looked sensitive and full of hurt.

Yet his tone was calm. "I should like to ask you, Mr. Farragut, what *you* are doing here."

"I—"

There was a sharp sound above us like a pistol shot.

We both looked up at the escalator.

Sir Quiller was now about halfway down, still over twenty feet away from us. I was shocked to see him beginning to crumple over. His hands were half lifted involuntarily toward his head. The most horrifying thing about the man was that his throat, above his stiff white collar, was all a red gash. And blood was already coming from it in bright red spurts.

His throat had been cut!

His body pitched forward on the glittering metal steps, being brought automatically down to where we stood dumbfounded. At that moment I tried to remember my newspaper training to see *everything*. But there was nothing else—not near him, above him, or around him.

He came rolling off the endless treadmill at our feet, immaculately dressed and thoroughly dead.

Even the blood was beginning to stop pumping out of the slash that had opened his throat from ear to ear.

Das breathed something in his own language.

I bent over Sir Quiller.

"Look!" said Das. He was pointing.

Pushed up against the body from behind was an open old-fashioned razor. Its keen blade lay polished and gleaming under the lights.

I straightened up. I didn't touch anything except the emergency button that stopped the escalator.

"Get the guard at the door," I said to Rass.

I didn't wait to see if he obeyed me or not. I was already running up the stalled steps to the mezzanine.

I encountered nothing on my way up. At the top, I was in a wide corridor flanked by office doors. Straight ahead of me, about two dozen feet away, was an open door with a light showing through. I ran toward it and looked in.

Seated at a desk under the glow of neon tubing was Bernice Harper. She was opating a trilingual typewriter. Papers were scattered about her as she worked industriously. But you never bothered to look at papers when you saw Bernice Harper.

Her hair was blonde, light and beautiful, fanning down below her wide clean shoulders. She glanced questioningly up at me with large blue eyes. There was strength in her face, in the large red mouth and in the dimpled chin. But most men looked at her face last. Her body was stronger even than her face. Earthy but never dirty was the way I liked to put it. Yet she disdained plunging necklines. Tonight everything was modestly covered up in a blue taffeta dress that was closed to the frilly throat with platter buttons.

She was Sir Quiller Selwyn's personal secretary.

"Bernice," I said, slowing down and walking in, "Promise me. No hysterics."

"What is it?" She stood up. I couldn't imagine her having hysterics.

"It's Sir Quiller. Gentle, girl. He's dead."

"Dead!" Her face streamed white under the makeup. "He left this office only a minute ago!"

"Yes. It happened on the escalator."

"You mean his heart? But he never complained—"

"I can't say for sure just what did happen. I've got to find out. Are you the only one up here?"

"I think—" She paused.

From the dim corridor outside came a mechanical sound. *Spok-spok. Spok-spok.*

We both stared at the door.

A tall, well-built, youngish fellow walked in with a limp. Every time he moved his left leg you heard the artificial knee-socket. Jack Croydon was one Anzac who had left a leg in Viet Nam while his volunteer company was fighting Cong guerrillas.

"Hullo!" he said, staring quizzically back at us. "Am I as frightening as all that?"

Croydon was from Queensland, Australia. He spoke with a burr that was cousin to a Tipperary brogue. And how the women ate it up when he told them about his rugged days on a stock farm before he took himself off to war. He was now a member of the Secretariat.

"Croydon," I said, "I'm only one step ahead of the police. They'll be here in a few minutes. Sir Quiller's napoo. Dead. His throat's cut."

"Good God!" said Croydon, limping briskly to Bernice's side. "Did he do it himself?"

I thought about the highly polished razor that had come down the escalator with the body. "I don't think so," I said. "Bernice, I'll have to use your phone. I want to get this story in to a rewrite man. This is one scoop I don't relish."

"Of course," murmured Bernice.

I dialed and began to talk. Sir Quiller was this month's President of the Security Council. He had been handling delicate diplomatic secrets and he would be sorely missed.

As I rattled off what few facts I knew into the phone, I saw Croydon rest his tanned hand over Bernice's in a comforting fashion. I could have kicked myself for being such a slowpoke about doing that myself. Now he had the edge on me. In spite of her generous body, the hand under his was small and fragile. The kind of hand you want to hold. A little girl's hand. Her feet and ankles were small too.

The look she gave him in return was pure catnip.

I put down the phone. "Croydon, have you seen anybody around the escalator?"

"There's nobody on this floor but us," said Croydon with finality.

"Why was Sir Quiller meeting Senator Banner?"

"He never told me," said Bernice. "He merely asked me to stay and work late. Shouldn't we—shouldn't we go down?"

"You'd better stay put, Bernice," said Croydon. "A cut throat is a bit nasty. Watch the office. I'll face it out with Farragut. Come along."

I followed Croydon and his mechanical leg outside. He closed the door after us.

He caught my arm. "This sounds ugly. We must try to spare Bernice all we can."

"I'll go along with that," I said.

"Lord, she's a handsome girl. Some people in my country would call her a bonzer peach."

"They'd call her a peach anywhere," I said grudgingly.

"Do you think I stand half a chance?" he asked.

He wasn't really asking me. He was asking himself.

Downstairs again. The first of the police had arrived. I stayed long enough with them to corroborate Surendranath Das's story. Then I heard him say: "If you want me further, I'll be at India House."

I walked out of the Secretariat lobby with him.

Outside it was a cold, raw April night, thick with fog. Ceiling zero. It could explain why Senator Banner had not shown up if he was taking a plane in from Washington.

Das melted away toward his parked car.

Mournful foghorns croaked on the East River. I buttoned up my putty-colored Aquascutum against the mist and walked north on First to catch the bus at 49th Street that would take me crosstown to Park Avenue and the Waldorf.

The Waldorf lobby was all old rose carpet and tall alabaster marble columns and dignified hush. I could have used some of this kind of luxury. Thick rugs and thick wallets and thick bodies. I walked to the elevator bank. I didn't have to ask where the Selwyns were staying. They had a permanent suite in the Tower.

I rode up to the 33rd floor, went to a door, and bumped a brass knocker.

Moira Selwyn opened the door as if on cue and for a long moment we looked at each other. Her shoulders were set stiffly.

After that tense moment there was a slight thaw. Her smile was as dangerous as thin ice. "Come in," she said in clipped British. "I was expecting you."

I almost dropped my hat. "Me?"

"You—or someone like you."

I was in and she shut the door softly.

"It's about—" I began.

"Something dreadful's happened to my husband. You wouldn't have any other reason to come to me." There was practically no change in her placid expression. "How did I know? Call it intuition. Or premonition. Anything you like. I'm strongly psychic."

"I never believed in it."

"You don't know enough about women. But that's to be expected. You're an American. Metaxa?"

"Who?" I said with a start.

While she was speaking she had lit a cigaret. One of those foreign brands. The brittle smile continued, as if she were mocking me. "Greek grape brandy."

I watched her walk across the room to a cut-glass decanter. She was wearing an ashes-of-roses cocktail suit over a foundation that was a corsetiere's sonnet. Moira was lithe anyway. Her face had those sharp, taut lines that must have made her look boyish in her teens. Her hair was blue-black and cut crisply short like a poodle's and in one pink earlobe was only one blue chip of an earring. I watched her long legs move provocatively underneath the sheath skirt. And I was incensed at her remark that I didn't know enough about women.

In her lurked potentialities neither banal nor restrained. Yet, while sexually she had whet many a man's appetite, I had never heard of any having an affair with her.

She was in her proper setting. On the floor was an all-over carpet of midnight blue and there were chairs with seats of lustrous black satin.

She returned with the decanter and two glasses. The cigaret glowed in her plum-red mouth. Her black and brilliant eyes were half closed in the drifting smoke. At a low, lacquer-black cocktail table she bent over and poured two drinks—sweet, heavy, and dark.

Her moist lips moved slightly around the cigaret as she handed me the Greek brandy. "As a race, you're all so very practical, though when it comes to us—and I mean women—you just don't know beans. An American, my dear, gives more attention to his motorcar than he does to his wife. Reading a newspaper, he'll stop to ogle a man in a baseball suit before he'll turn to a picture of a girl showing her legs."

Sipping her brandy, she walked to a settee in dusky violet, with orange-tan pillows, and sat down with the fluid grace of a mannequin. Every movement she made was deliberately for effect. She attended to the gratification of her senses as carefully as somebody else would cultivate a rose garden.

"What is it you see in *baseball*?" She crossed her legs. They were long and slim, a golden honey color in seamless nylons. A thin silver love chain winked roguishly on one slender ankle. Her perfect teeth showed and her ripe-red tongue darted. "Nine young morons running around a pasture on a bloody hot afternoon."

I wanted to make a sneering reply that some of them weren't so young—but she had two strikes on her already. I took brandy to cover my silence. It had a slight resin flavor.

She carefully tapped ash from her cigaret into a bronze tray. "In most European countries a boy is under the bridge with a girl when he's fifteen. In this country he's still playing baseball at twenty-one." She looked me over from my Heidelburg haircut to the toes of my oxfords as if trying to commit me to memory. "I haven't anything personal against you. What do you think of all this? . . . Stop standing there mum, dear boy, and *say* something."

I said: "I think you're an extraordinary woman."

"Now you're beginning to show some perception."

"But if this baseball talk got out, you'd be rated as the most unsympathetic woman in America . . . I'm sorry."

The smoke of her cigaret was clinging wraithlike to her attractive angular face and to her dark poodle hair. "Why?"

"Your husband is dead."

Poised, she sniffed brandy. "I told you I was expecting dire news."

"The details are a little grim," I warned.

"Then don't go into them. It'll be gruesome enough when the police come tramping in. Is this why you came to me so quickly—to prepare me?"

"I wanted to see you first. Sir Quiller knew many diplomatic secrets. He may have shared some with you."

She tilted her glass. "You mean my own life may be in danger? You *are* a dear boy . . . As his wife, I *did* share confidences with him. He always thought I was very astute."

"I'd say so too." I put down my glass. "I hate to run. But this'll be a hectic night."

"Yes," she said. She didn't stir. "Shall I see you again?"

"I'm sure of it."

"Good night."

I nodded at her and walked toward the suite door, feeling her eyes like ice cubes sliding down my back all the way out.

In a booth I phoned long distance to my pipeline in Washington.

"He hopped off in a copter about three hours ago," was the reply.

I went out to Lexington Avenue and stopped a taxi and told the cabbie to take me to LaGuardia Airport. Hang the expense. It'd all go on my well-padded swindle sheet.

The cab crawled over Queensboro Bridge.

At the airfield everything was grounded. "Bird-walking weather," said one of the loafing pilots.

I meandered out into the soup, the airport lights fuzzy around me. Finally I heard a whirring sound making erratic movements somewhere up above. An invisible aircraft landed out on a strip. Loud voices swirled in on the fog. Heavy footfalls approached on the concrete.

Senator Brooks U. Banner loomed out of the thick brew, coming in on the beam of his own Pittsburgh stogie. He was big and fat, with a rain-barrel figure. His white campaign hat was crammed down on his square head. An old tarp was thrown over his beefy shoulders like a poncho. I stepped out of the weak glow of the landing lights.

I said: "Let me introduce myself, Senator. I'm Bob Farragut, the AP district man at the UN."

Banner stopped dead, peering around like a buffalo making up his mind to charge. And Banner was just as shaggy. "Lemme get my bearings, sonny boy. That gyrene that brought me here in a flying windmill flew by the seat of his pants all the way . . . How in hell'd you know I was coming?"

"Right from the Washington grapevine."

"Goddammit! I'm supposed to be on a secret mission! Ain't your stoolies got anything else to do besides tapping my telephones!"

"I've got news for you, Senator. Bad news. You're too late to meet Sir Quiller. He was killed in the Secretariat at nine o'clock."

"Killed!" He turned so that the murky light fell across his grim jowls for an instant.

"We don't know how or why."

"I'll tell you *why* in one word." He peered around at the fog-shapes suspiciously. *"Spies!"*

Then he didn't say another word as we plowed in through the rotunda and out to the ramp to a taxi.

"The UN," said Banner to the driver as he stumbled in. "C'mon, bloodhound!" I followed. We settled back as the cab lurched forward. Banner growled. "So they got old Quill! I thought mebbe he'd make news some day by moving into 10 Downing Street as prime minister. Now it's just an obit. Haaak. He phoned me only this morning. Hush-hush secrets have been leaking out to the Commies. Secrets from *his* files. Rotten business. I was gonna meet him tonight, cuz he said he'd hand over the bugger that was doing it . . . Tell me how he got killed."

By the time we reached the Secretariat, Banner knew as much about it as I did.

There was a corps of police brass on the scene now. The Secretary General was there, pale but trying not to show his anxiety.

The tarp rustling on his shoulders, Banner lumbered over to the Secretary General, sweeping off his hat to reveal a mop of grizzled hair. They talked quietly for a few minutes. Banner's ruddy face was even grimmer as he turned back to me.

"No score," he said. He prowled around the foot of the escalator, went up to the mezzanine, and came down again. "Shenanigans at the UN! You were one of the eyewitnesses, Farragut— prob'ly the only reliable one. Where's a quiet place we can talk? Hah? The delegates' lounge!"

I could tell that he was quite familiar with the buildings the way he found the right doors. The Conference Building is a low-lying structure catercorner behind the tall glass headstone of the Secretariat. We went in that direction.

Banner was saying, "The diplomatic game is

the toughest in the world. It's the iron claw in the velvet mitt, all right. You gamble millions of lives at every throw of the dice. And if you ever crap-out, like old Quill did, you're a dead man."

By the time we reached the delegates' lounge we were all by ourselves.

We were in a block-long room with slanted glass paneling at the north end of the Conference Building. The lounge was thickly carpeted and stuffed with fan-backed Danish chairs, as well as tables and leather sofas. The chief feature of the room was the Honduras mahogany bar. Overhanging it was a huge relief map of the world, made of Cuban mahogany overlaid on Canadian ash. The only discouraging aspect was that there was no bartender.

"We call this the chicken yard," I said, thinking of ruffled feathers.

"Waal," rumbled Banner, "tonight we're the only two roosters on the manure pile." He looked thirstily at the bar, then made up his mind. He wore a shabby frockcoat bulging at the pockets. Grubbing into one of the pockets, he dug out a key. "See if that'll open the likker cabinet." He tossed it at me.

Miraculously the key fitted.

I placed my arms akimbo on the bar. "What'll it be, Senator? There's Dutch gin, Polish slivovitz, Mexican tequila, Russian vodka."

He glided a five-dollar-bill across the bar. "Stick that in the till and hand out that dimple bottle of Haig & Haig and we'll shoot the breeze."

I did. He took his straight. I had soda with mine.

"Now," said Banner in the hush of the deserted lounge, "how was it done?"

I'd been doing a lot of thinking about that. "Werewolves," I said.

Banner smacked his lips. He liked the sound of that word. But he didn't say anything. He waited for me to continue.

I said: "That hard core of Nazis that were left in Germany after the Second World War. They called themselves Werewolves. They fought dirty. They'd stretch a thin wire across a country

road and when one of our jeeps would whiz by, the wire'd lop the GI's head off."

"Ho!" said Banner. "You've been thinking that old Quill was killed on the escalator by the same gimmick. A thin wire stretched across would ketch him just under the chin as he traveled down." He frowned. "Waal, sir, I hate to throw cold water on you at the start, but there're too many counts against it. An escalator moves slow—not fast like one of those jeeps in Germany. A wire might've given Quill a bad nick and knocked him over backwards. But you told me he fell forward. What's more, you scooted up that escalator half a minute later and you didn't encounter any wires. Wires! Judas priest! You saw the condition of his throat. A deep vicious razorlike slash!"

"But it wasn't the razor!"

"No. Not *that* razor. Not the one that was found with him. The coppers told me that there wasn't a trace of blood or a fingerprint found on it. Why was it there? The killer knew we'd look for a weapon, so as a mocking gesture we were given one."

"What else do you think, Senator?"

"I think that the killer was actually holding the weapon at the instant of the murder. Yaas. That could be."

"How so? There was nobody within twenty-five feet of him when he was struck down."

Banner scowled. "Waal mebbe *you* got some explanations. Let's hear 'em!"

I said carefully: "There's a balcony effect around the escalator on the mezzanine. If somebody were standing on that balcony, we couldn't see him from below. Croydon and Bernice were both on the mezzanine. Croydon comes from the wilds of Australia. He'd know more than any of us how to handle a boomerang. Suppose he threw some sort of boomerang at Sir Quiller. It'd return—"

"Wrong!" said Banner with a thump on the leather chair-arm. "A boomerang'd return to the thrower only if it *missed* its target!"

After a painful pause I said: "I've wondered about Surendranath Das."

"I've been wondering about him too," muttered Banner.

"That turban he wears. Do you know that when you unwind one of those turbans they reach six or eight feet?"

Banner howled with glee. "Now *you're* reaching!"

I felt angry. He was simply playing with me. "Of course I'm reaching! I'm turning over every possibility to guess what the murder weapon was!"

"Yass?" He was hardly paying attention. "I know what the weapon is. What I wanna know is—where's it hidden?" His eyes were speculating on the walls.

"You know!"

"It's still in the building," he went on, yammering to himself. "Everybody that's gone out has had a police shakedown. That gal Bernice and Croydon are still here. So it ain't been spirited out."

"What's it look like, Senator?"

"You'll see—when we find it."

Sometimes, in spite of his fame as a murder expert, I wondered if he weren't an old fraud. It could be that he knew no more what it looked like than I did. Yet he was so acute that he'd recognize it for what it was the instant somebody else dug it up.

"Not even a hint?" I coaxed. "Is it some strange instrument?"

"Strange? No sir. It's a pretty common thing. Though they ain't as common as they once were."

"That explains a *lot*," I said sarcastically.

He chuckled. "Yass, it does, doesn't it? It explains, frinstance, that Moira Selwyn, though a logical suspect, could not have done it. She's the only one of our li'l group who wasn't here tonight. The guards know who came and went . . . D'you know," he said suddenly, "where Bernice Harper comes from?"

I nodded wearily. "She was born and brought up in Brooklyn. Lives on Columbia Heights. Why?"

"This's one place," he said tormentingly,

"where people come naturally from all parts of the world."

"Really?" I said acidly.

Banner swallowed the last of his whisky. "I wanna have a chat with Das. Where's he at?"

"I heard him tell the police he'd be at India House."

Banner struggled up out of his soft leather chair. I put away the bottle, soda, and glasses.

We went back through the quiet, darkened corridors to the lobby of the Secretariat.

It was crawling like a beehive.

Banner took one sour look around. Then he said: "They ain't found it. Why wait? Let's scram up to 64th Street."

64th Street, just off Fifth Avenue, was a canyon of cold fog. We got out of the cab at India House, stumbled up the front steps and entered the pink marble foyer.

We took the spinsterish self-service elevator up to the fourth floor, where Surendranath Das had a temporary office. Under a green-shaded desk lamp we found a lotus-eyed girl in a sari reading a thick book. She smiled at me and said hello, then looked a little frightened at Banner. He had that effect on some people.

I said: "Hello, Happy." I'd got to know her around the UN. She had told me that the red dot she had on her forehead just over her eyebrows was not a sign of caste. It was a dab of kumkum denoting happiness. So I called her Happy. "This is Senator Banner."

Banner, his tarp in fat folds, pushed forward. "Lemme see Das."

"Yes, sair," said Happy obediently. "This way, if you please."

She rapped discreetly on a closed door before opening it. I could see Das's purple turban and coffee-colored face and speckled black beard hovering over another desk. He was having a midnight snack of chicken curry, pickled onions in a bottle, fritters, and saki. He half rose at Banner's blundering entrance

"Senator Banner!"

"Whaddya know, Das! No innerductions needed! Good! If I had more time I'd chin with you about the Crims."

"Crims?"

"Those hereditary criminals in your country, saheeb. They operate by paralyzing geese 'n' sheep before stealing 'em. Interesting rascals. Only there's the more pressing problem of a man getting his throat slashed on an escalator without a soul being near him."

"Ah yes. Sir Quiller." Das subsided again to absently spear a pickled onion out of the bottle. "Will you sit down, gentlemen?" he went on in his high piping English.

"Yass." Banner headed for the most comfortable chair. Out of the corner of my eye I saw Happy slip out again. Banner was saying: "This here now AP feller, Bob Farragut, says both you and he were witnesses to the killing. He says he saw nothing but old Quill. Did you see anything else?"

"Nothing else," answered Das.

"You *heard* something!"

I stirred uneasily. Yes, we heard something. Something that didn't fit in at all.

"Ah yes, Senator," said Das. "I heard a loud report like a pistol shot. I'm sure Mr. Farragut did too."

"Wait a minute, saheeb! What businesses have you been in? How qualified are you to judge the sound of a pistol shot?"

"I come from a family of rich clothing merchants," said Das placidly. "My father and brothers have shops in New Delhi and on the Chowringee in Calcutta. But I know firearms, Senator. I've been on many a shoot with the Maharajah of Jubbulpore. I've used everything from the big bore for tigers to a small automatic. Yet *that* sounded like no caliber I'd ever heard."

"Yass," muttered Banner, "I didn't think it would . . . Now, sir! This's more personal. Old Quill was gonna meet me at the Secretariat tonight. It was gonna be a meeting that'd spell curtains for somebody. What were you doing there?"

Das screwed closed the lid on the pickled onions bottle. "Sir Quiller had sent a message to come and see him. He sounded urgent."

"Did he say why?"

"No, Senator."

"Hey? He musta given some indication."

"I really—"

I butted in finally. "There *was* something. He looked alarmed. As soon as he saw Mr. Das he shouted."

Banner swarmed around in his chair. "Shouted what?"

"How *was* that again?" I tried to recollect. "As well as I can remember—*Das! Have you taken leave of your senses! They're the most deadly—!* Then he cut himself off and started down. Correct, Mr. Das?"

Das was leaning forward at his desk, absorbed in my recitation, grimacing through his thick beard. "I'm afraid you are correct, Mr. Farragut. But I assure you, Sir Quiller was unduly alarmed. Everything was quite safe. They—"

Banner thumped the desktop and the china dishes rattled. "Lemme be judge of that, Das! What in blue blazes are you talking about?"

Das leaned back and sighed. "I'm sure Sir Quiller was referring to what I have in a big satchel in my office at the Secretariat. It's a pair of king cobras that I brought from India as a good-will gesture. I was going to present them to the Bronx Zoo."

I wasn't as bland as he was. "King cobras! The most deadly of all poisonous snakes!"

"As Sir Quiller feared," nodded Das. "But, gentlemen, the satchel is securely closed with safety catches. They can't possibly get—"

I turned to look at Banner to see how he was taking all this. There was a silence from his side of the room that was overwhelming. He was sitting there thunderstruck, his jaw unhinged, the stogie having fallen out of his mouth into his vast lap.

Then—

"Snakes!" he hollered. "Great Caesar's ghost! We gotta get back there!"

And he went out through the door like a hurricane.

On the wild ride back to the UN I got a grim briefing on king cobras.

Their fangs inject a poison so venomous that it can kill a man inside of a few minutes. They have great lashlike bodies, loops of pale olive, that grow to a length of fifteen feet.

What this had to do with the murder of Sir Quiller I couldn't even grasp. Sir Quiller hadn't been poisoned. Banner wasn't explaining. After the king cobra lecture, he spent the rest of the ride chomping the dead stogie and scowling at the back of the cabbie's neck.

We beat our way out of the fog, came into the court around the great basin of the pool, and, leaving the cab, spun in through the revolving glass doors of the Secretariat.

A big husky Irish cop was standing there with a UN guard.

Banner halted and snapped: "Has any staff member left?"

The Irish cop gave Banner a half salute. "Yes, sir. The young fella with the limp and the girl. Only not together. He left a bit before she did."

"And one of 'em," said Banner slowly, "was carrying a satchel!"

He had a knowing look, as if he meant to amaze everybody with his remarkable powers of second sight.

But he was the one to get surprised.

"Yes, sir," said the cop. "The girl was."

"The girl!" Banner, his tarp flapping like the membranous wings of a bat, rocked back on his heels. He'd had a set-back, that was for sure. He braced himself again. "You looked inside it, I hope!"

"I did. I was ordered to search everything. There was two of the foulest divils you ever clapped your eyes on, their bodies all twined up in one another. As soon as they saw me they began to raise up their orange-colored heads. They had ruddy yella eyes that glowed. Wide-awake, they was. I took one good look and I saw all I wanted to see. There was nothing in there but those snakes' bodies. And I slammed it shut on them again."

Banner worried his double chins with his fat fingers. "Where'd she say she was taking 'em?"

"To the Bronx Zoo. Where else could you take them? And that's the same direction I heard her give to the cab driver. There was something else she had him do. She told him to tie that satchel to the outside of the cab before they drove away. Not that I blame her any. I wouldn't want them divils inside the cab with me neither."

The UN guard nodded solemn agreement.

Banner was gone. He was flouncing out into the murky night again with me sticking as close behind him as a splinter in the seat of his pants. I wouldn't have lost him now—or the story—no matter how hard he tried. He ran down a cab on First Avenue. I reached it in time to hear him bellow: "Bronx Zoo! And there's a sawbuck for you if you break all traffic rules!"

I leaped in behind him. The cab started so fast I almost dislocated my neck.

Banner was howling: "For crissakes, never mind that red light! We gotta ketch 'em before they turn those snakes loose!"

The cabbie drove as if he had two maniacs in back—and we weren't far from it.

The memory of that journey northward remains a blur. I hardly knew where we were. Banner kept peering through the fog-curtained windows and finally announced: "Southern Boulevard. We're tearing past the Zoo now. Turn right, cabbie, at Fordham. We'll try the Pelham Parkway entrance."

The cab skidded greasily on wet pavement, and I thought I heard a faint scream as we missed a pedestrian by a hair, then we came to a squealing stop at some mist-enshrouded ornate gates.

Banner flopped out and flung money at the cabbie. "You earned it!" He ran full tilt at the driveway's iron gates and crashed into them. "Locked! . . . They're outside somewhere. Foller the railing along, Farragut. Lissen for voices!"

I listened.

The sparse traffic on the Parkway was a muffled whir. We blundered among some bare trees and budding shrubbery. Banner, beside me, hissed and raised his hand.

"Look! Over on the left! See those shadders!"

Muzzy silhouettes stood close together in the bushes. A man and a woman. There were murmuring sounds as they spoke. The man had taken the satchel.

"He's opening it," hissed Banner.

I could barely see.

Banner gulped. "Suffering sunfish! He's dumped 'em out on the ground!"

"The snakes?"

"What else, you nitwit? We're almost too late now. We gotta charge in and ketch 'em red-handed. I'll scare 'em stiff with a Comanche war whoop. And you—wait!"

He let out a howl like a dervish sitting on a hot cookstove. I felt my skin shrivel.

Then he wallowed forward, shouting: "The game's up!" or something just as corny.

There was a stir of real agitation from the man and woman.

Banner whirled, pointing. "And you, Farragut, dive into that bush! Quick!"

By now I was beginning to have an unreasoning regard for his screwball orders. Tonight we'd all gone mad. I flung myself in a foolhardy dive into the crackling brush.

When I landed I knew how foolhardy.

Smack under me was a thick coil. I supported myself against it with my outstretched hands. It was scaly and long and as thick as my wrist. And as I instinctively grasped it, it began to glide from under my faltering fingers.

Sweat soaked me like a cold shower.

I heard Banner's holler: "Hold on to it, Farragut! One end's dangerous!"

Both ends were dangerous as far as I was concerned!

I heard the girl scream. There was a thrashing of bodies. Night birds screeched in their vaulted cages. In the distance a restless lion roared.

The coil under my fingers was yanking violently to get free. I fastened myself onto it.

I heard Banner's warning. "Don't let go, Farragut! Your life depends on it!"

I'd heard of riding a tiger—but never a king cobra.

"Grab holt and *pull*!"

When you face a life span of only a few minutes, you get mighty reckless.

I got my knees braced on the ground underneath me, tightened my grip on the sliding thing, and tugged backwards. It held staunchly, as if the front end of the cobra were snubbed around a post. It was all very unusual. It gave me the courage to yank back again.

It yanked in return—so roughly that I was dragged a few feet through the shrubs.

I dug my heels in hard and hauled away with all my strength.

Something came loose.

I toppled over backwards, falling flat on my spine. The coils came hissing through the air, landing in a heap on my chest.

For a moment I didn't breathe, as sweat drenched me.

It lay over me and around me. Gingerly I touched the end. Then I knew I was safe.

It was an incredibly long rawhide whip!

The most fitting place for the last act was the delegates' lounge. Led by the Secretary General and the police inspector, our headliners trooped in—Surendranath Das, Bernice Harper, Jack Croydon, and Moira Selwyn.

Banner told them all to be seated, then he scowled around at their faces. "I got all of you here so that if I say something wrong you can stick in your two cents. But," he added ominously, "I don't expect any interruptions."

Stretched out full length on the immaculate carpeting was the whip. It had a shortish handle, a long trunk about two inches thick, which gradually tapered to a mere ribbon at the end. A good twenty-five feet in all.

"That," said Banner, pointing, "is called, among other things, a Spanish bull whip." He paused. "There was a wunnerful old movie. Old Doug Fairbanks in *Don Q, Son of Zorro*." For a moment his frosty blue eyes had a faraway look of nostalgia. Overcome by memory, he bleated: "Why ain't they making pitchers like *that* anymore? . . . Haaak! Waal, in that whizbang movie Fairbanks used a whip like this 'un.

With it he could snuff out burning candles without disturbing the wick, or flick seegars outta a stooge's mouth. In the Old West, bullwhackers could cut a notch in a maverick's ear at twenty paces, or snap a bandana outta a man's hip pocket and still leave the seat of the pants. What I'm driving at is that there's no dispute about how skillful a man can become in using one of these bullwhacks."

He stopped and stared at the faces.

"They're not used in this country much anymore, 'cept at Wild West shows. But there's another place as woolly as our West ever was. Right now! I kinda forgot to tell you, accidentally on purpose, that this's also called an Australian stock whip. And a stock farm is just another way of saying a cattle ranch!"

Everybody involuntarily glanced at Jack Croydon. It was then that I saw that two cops had come in to stand behind his chair. Yet he was sitting there, his mechanical leg stretched out comfortably in front of him, taking it all in as if it were being put on for his amusement. As cool a cuss as I've ever seen.

Banner's buzzsaw voice droned into the silence. "Only one of us, y'see, has had the background to be able to use this thing. Now you say, as vicious as a whip of this sort is, it couldn't've sliced a man's throat as if with a razor. True. But lookit the thin end! A piece of steel, about three inches long, honed razor-sharp on both sides, has been fastened to the end of the whip. With the deadly accuracy of long practice, you could slash a man's throat while standing twenty-five feet away from him. It could be all over in an instant. And the only clue as to how it was done would be the pistol-like crack of the whip!"

I wondered now why it hadn't occurred to me in the very beginning.

"Sure," said Banner, with pure disgust, "it was you, Croydon. You were peddling old Quill's secrets to the Commies. You found out that he was gonna expose your filthy hide. You killed him to prevent exposure. It's as simple as that!"

Croydon finally spoke. His voice was strong, though he had to clear his throat with a slight cough before he could begin. "How would I know what Sir Quiller's secrets were? How did I know he was going to expose me?" He looked like a man with an ace up his sleeve.

"Quit being coy!" snapped Banner. "You're Moira Selwyn's lover! Is that blunt enough for you? Hah! That scourges like the whip, don't it? . . . Yass, Farragut, are *you* surprised, after the front you saw him putting up with Bernice Harper? Nice diversion. Actually he was smooching after hours with Moira. Moira admitted to you that her hubby confided in her. Poor old Quill didn't suspect her hand in it at all. What she learned from Quill she passed on to Croydon. *She* knew the secrets—and *she* knew that Quill was gonna jerk the rug from under Croydon tonight. She warned her lover in ample time. No wonder she was expecting bad news about her husband when you showed up at the Waldorf suite!

"So, knowing the game was up, Croydon had plenty of time to prepare the whip. Carrying it into the building was no trouble. Nobody'd search him. He then stalked Quill, waiting for the opportune moment. It came when Quill was going down the escalator. Croydon was in a perfect position on that balcony facing the escalator, hidden from the sight of anybody below. He trailed out the long whip—then let it fly at Quill's throat."

There was a sob. It came from Bernice. I could have knocked out all of Croydon's teeth then and there for causing Bernice one moment of unhappiness.

Banner considered. "Croydon's pretense with Bernice served its purpose. He hadda get the whip outta the building again, before we found it. This time it wouldn't be easy. Everybody was being shaken down. Then he remembered Das' snakes and the fuss Quill'd been kicking up about 'em. I gotta give you credit for that cunning bit, Croydon. You simply put the snakelike whip in with the whiplike snakes. A quick gander into that crawling satchel would only reveal a twisted mass of greenish folds. The cops'd let it pass out the door. Still, *you* didn't wanna chance carrying it. You sweet-talked li'l Bernice!"

"I did it for him," she murmured, clutching a handkerchief. "But I thought it was only the snakes. He said I ought to bring them up to the Bronx Zoo right away."

"What excuse did he give for not bringing 'em by himself?"

"He said he had to see the curator first about opening the Zoo at that time of night. Naturally he left first and I followed—with the satchel. We met there."

"Uh-huh," said Banner. "He also instructed you to have the satchel carted *outside* the cab you took. Y'know why? So the snakes wouldn't get nice 'n' warm in the heated cab. Outside it was cold. The cold'd make the snakes sluggish. They'd be pretty near harmless when he dumped both outta the satchel to get the whip."

That was right, of course. I'd mentioned how chilly the night was several times.

Banner's face was grim. "The real danger, then, was the whip in Croydon's hand. That was what was lying along the ground, Farragut. That was what I wanted you to pounce on and hold useless. Cuz if he'd been able to use that on us, we'd've been slashed to ribbons. There was a minute there when I thought it was a narrer squeak."

"*You* thought it was!"

"What utter rot!" said Moira's clipped voice. Her black brilliant eyes glittered at Banner.

Croydon's face glowed with anger. "It is rot! I left a leg in a rice paddy while fighting those bastards. Do you think I'd turn traitor for them now?"

Banner snapped back: "Benedict Arnold almost lost a leg too when he was on our side. That didn't stop him from ratting out later."

The Secretary General cut in: "The Senator's logic is irrefutable. Nothing else could have happened."

"Take 'em out," ordered Banner. "Her too. She's an accessory before the fact. When you get him into court he won't have *one* leg to stand on!"

After they had gone, the Secretary General shook Banner's hand strongly, not saying anything. He was too sincere for a speech.

Banner said: "I'll leave the legal headache of imprisoning them to you."

Surendranath Das, picking his way out, was murmuring a gem of wisdom from the Code of Manu, the old Hindu law: "The house which is cursed by a woman perishes utterly."

This time I wasn't such a slowpoke with Bernice. I rested my hand on hers while at the same time trying to look like a sheep dog finding a shorn lamb that had been lost in a snowdrift.

Perhaps, as Moira said, I didn't know much about women. But I was learning.

THE TEA LEAF

EDGAR JEPSON
& ROBERT EUSTACE

THE AUTHOR OF mainly rather dull, lightweight detective novels produced soon after the turn of the nineteenth century, as well as the creator of pedestrian adventure novels with which he began his career as a novelist, Edgar Alfred Jepson (1863–1938) is read today primarily as the translator of novels and stories from the French of Maurice Leblanc, for whom he brought to the English reading public many of the famous Arsene Lupin adventures. He also translated the once-popular novel *The Man with the Black Feather* (1912) by Gaston Leroux.

Born in London, he graduated from Baliol College, Oxford, then spent five years in Barbados before returning to take a job as editor at *Vanity Fair*. He became involved, albeit tangentially, with such members of the Decadent Movement as Ernest Dawson, John Gawsworth (with whom he collaborated on several short stories), and Arthur Machen. The first novel he wrote under his own name, *Sibyl Falcon* (1895), features a female adventurer, and he followed this with such fantasy novels as *The Horned Shepherd* (1904), about the worship of Pan. His son, Selwyn Jepson, was a prolific mystery writer, and his granddaughter is the noted British novelist Fay Weldon.

The only book Dr. Eustace Robert Barton (1854–1943) wrote by himself, under the pseudonymn Robert Eustace, was *The Human Bacillus* (1907), a crime novel, but he collaborated on mystery fiction with such popular authors as L. T. Meade, Gertrude Warden, and Dorothy L. Sayers, as well as Jepson.

"The Tea Leaf" was originally published in the October 1925 issue of *The Strand Magazine*.

THE TEA LEAF

EDGAR JEPSON & ROBERT EUSTACE

ARTHUR KELSTERN and Hugh Willoughton met in the Turkish bath in Duke Street, St. James's, and rather more than a year later in that Turkish bath they parted. Both of them were bad-tempered men, Kelstern cantankerous and Willoughton violent. It was indeed difficult to decide which was the worse-tempered; and when I found that they had suddenly become friends, I gave that friendship three months. It lasted nearly a year.

When they did quarrel they quarrelled about Kelstern's daughter Ruth. Willoughton fell in love with her and she with him and they became engaged to be married. Six months later, in spite of the fact that they were plainly very much in love with one another, the engagement was broken off. Neither of them gave any reason for breaking it off. My belief was that Willoughton had given Ruth a taste of his infernal temper and got as good as he gave.

Not that Ruth was at all a Kelstern to look at. Like the members of most of the old Lincolnshire families, descendants of the Vikings and the followers of Canute, one Kelstern is very like another Kelstern, fair-haired, clear-skinned, with light-blue eyes and a good bridge to the nose. But Ruth had taken after her mother: she was dark with a straight nose, dark-brown eyes of the kind often described as liquid, dark-brown hair, and as kissable lips as ever I saw. She was a proud, rather self-sufficing, high-spirited girl, with a temper of her own. She needed it to

live with that cantankerous old brute Kelstern. Oddly enough in spite of the fact that he always would try to bully her, she was fond of him; and I will say for him that he was very fond of her. Probably she was the only creature in the world of whom he was really fond. He was an expert in the application of scientific discoveries to industry; and she worked with him in his laboratory. He paid her five hundred a year, so that she must have been uncommonly good.

He took the breaking off of the engagement very hard indeed. He would have it that Willoughton had jilted her. Ruth took it hard too: her warm colouring lost some of its warmth; her lips grew less kissable and set in a thinner line. Willoughton's temper grew worse than ever; he was like a bear with a perpetually sore head. I tried to feel my way with both him and Ruth with a view to help to bring about a reconciliation. To put it mildly, I was rebuffed. Willoughton swore at me; Ruth flared up and told me not to meddle in matters that didn't concern me. Nevertheless my strong impression was that they were missing one another badly and would have been glad enough to come together again if their stupid vanity could have let them.

Kelstern did his best to keep Ruth furious with Willoughton. One night I told him—it was no business of mine; but I never did give a tinker's curse for his temper—that he was a fool to meddle and had much better leave them alone. It made him furious, of course; he would have

199

it that Willoughton was a dirty hound and a low blackguard—at least those were about the mildest things he said of him. It struck me of a sudden that there must be something much more serious in the breaking off of the engagement than I had guessed.

That suspicion was strengthened by the immense trouble Kelstern took to injure Willoughton. At his clubs, the Athenæum, the Devonshire, and the Savile, he would display an astonishing ingenuity in bringing the conversation round to Willoughton; then he would declare that he was a scoundrel and a blackguard of the meanest type. Of course it did Willoughton harm, though not nearly as much harm as Kelstern desired, for Willoughton knew his job as few engineers knew it; and it is very hard indeed to do much harm to a man who really knows his job. People have to have him. But of course it did him some harm; and Willoughton knew that Kelstern was doing it. I came across two men who told me that they had given him a friendly hint. That did not improve Willoughton's temper.

An expert in the construction of those ferro-concrete buildings which are rising up all over London, he was as distinguished in his sphere as Kelstern in his. They were alike not only in the matters of brains and bad temper but I think that their minds worked in very much the same way. At any rate both of them seemed determined not to change their ordinary course of life because of the breaking off of that engagement.

It had been the habit of both of them to have a Turkish bath, at the baths in Duke Street, at four in the afternoon on the second and last Tuesday in every month. To that habit they stuck. The fact that they must meet on those Tuesdays did not cause either of them to change his hour of taking his Turkish bath by the twenty minutes which would have given them no more than a passing glimpse of one another. They continued to take them, as they always had, simultaneously. Thick-skinned? They were thick-skinned. Neither of them pretended that he did not see the other; he scowled at him; and he scowled at him

most of the time. I know this, for sometimes I had a Turkish bath myself at that hour.

It was about three months after the breaking off of the engagement that they met for the last time at that Turkish bath, and there parted for good.

Kelstern had been looking ill for about six weeks: there was a grayness and a drawn look to his face; and he was losing weight. On the second Tuesday in October he arrived at the bath punctually at four, bringing with him, as was his habit, a thermos flask full of a very delicate China tea. If he thought that he was not perspiring freely enough he would drink it in the hottest room; if he did perspire freely enough, he would drink it after his bath. Willoughton arrived about two minutes later. Kelstern finished undressing and went into the bath a couple of minutes before Willoughton. They stayed in the hot room about the same time; Kelstern went into the hottest room about a minute after Willoughton. Before he went into it he sent for his thermos flask which he had left in the dressing room and took it into the hottest room with him.

As it happened, they were the only two people in the hottest room; and they had not been in it two minutes before the four men in the hot room heard them quarrelling. They heard Kelstern call Willoughton a dirty hound and a low blackguard, among other things, and declare he would do him in yet. Willoughton told him to go to the devil twice. Kelstern went on abusing him and presently Willoughton fairly shouted: "Oh, shut up, you old fool! Or I'll make you!"

Kelstern did not shut up. About two minutes later Willoughton came out of the hottest room, scowling, walked through the hot room into the shampooing room and put himself into the hands of one of the shampooers. Two or three minutes after that a man of the name of Helston went into the hottest room and fairly yelled. Kelstern was lying back on a blood-drenched couch, with the blood still flowing from a wound over his heart.

There was a devil of a hullabaloo. The police

were called in; Willoughton was arrested. Of course he lost his temper and, protesting furiously that he had had nothing whatever to do with the crime, abused the police. That did not incline them to believe him.

After examining the room and the dead body the detective-inspector in charge of the case came to the conclusion that Kelstern had been stabbed as he was drinking his tea. The thermos flask lay on the floor in front of him and some of the tea had evidently been spilt, for some tea leaves—the tea in the flask must have been carelessly strained off the leaves by the maid who filled it—lay on the floor about the mouth of the empty flask. It looked as if the murderer had taken advantage of Kelstern's drinking his tea to stab him while the flask rather blocked his vision and prevented him from seeing what he would be at.

The case would have been quite plain sailing but for the fact that they could not find the weapon. It had been easy enough for Willoughton to take it into the bath in the towel in which he was draped. But how had he got rid of it? Where had he hidden it? A Turkish bath is no place to hide anything in. It is as bare as an empty barn—if anything, barer; and Willoughton had been in the barest part of it. The police searched every part of it—not that there was much point in doing that, for Willoughton had come out of the hottest room, and gone through the hot room into the shampooers' room. When Helston started shouting murder, Willoughton had rushed back with the shampooers to the hottest room and there he had stayed. Since it was obvious that he had committed the murder the shampooers and the bathers had kept their eyes on him. They were all of them certain that he had not left them to go to the dressing rooms; they would not have allowed him to do so.

It was obvious that he must have carried the weapon into the bath, hidden in the folds of the towel in which he was draped, and brought it away in the folds of that towel. He had laid the towel down beside the couch on which he was being shampooed; and there it still lay when they came to look for it, untouched, with no weapon in it, with no traces of blood on it. There was not much in the fact that it was not stained with blood, since Willoughton could have wiped the knife, or dagger, or whatever weapon he used, on the couch on which Kelstern lay. There were no marks of any such wiping on the couch; but the blood, flowing from the wound, might have covered them up.

There was no finding the weapon; and its disappearance puzzled the police and later puzzled the public.

Then the doctors who made the autopsy came to the conclusion that the wound had been inflicted by a circular, pointed weapon nearly three-quarters of an inch in diameter. It had penetrated rather more than three inches and supposing that its handle was only four inches long it must have been a sizeable weapon, quite impossible to overlook. The doctors also discovered a further proof of the theory that Kelstern had been drinking his tea when he was stabbed. Half-way down the wound they found two halves of a tea leaf which had evidently fallen on to Kelstern's body, been driven into the wound and cut in half by the weapon. Also they discovered that Kelstern was suffering from cancer. This fact was not published in the papers; I heard it at the Devonshire.

Willoughton was brought before the magistrates and to most people's surprise did not reserve his defense. He went into the witness box and swore that he had never touched Kelstern, that he had never had anything to touch him with, that he had never taken any weapon into the Turkish bath and so had had no weapon to hide, that he had never even seen any such weapon as the doctors described. He was committed for trial.

The papers were full of the crime; every one was discussing it; and the question which occupied every one's mind was: where had Willoughton hidden the weapon? People wrote to the papers to suggest that he had ingeniously put it in some place under everybody's eyes and that it had been overlooked because it was so obvious.

Others suggested that, circular and pointed, it must be very like a thick lead pencil, that it was a thick lead pencil; and that was why the police had overlooked it in their search. The police had not overlooked any thick lead pencil; there had been no thick lead pencil to overlook. They hunted England through—Willoughton did a lot of motoring—to discover the man who had sold him this curious and uncommon weapon. They did not find the man who had sold it to him; they did not find a man who sold such weapons at all. They came to the conclusion that Kelstern had been murdered with a piece of a steel, or iron, rod filed to a point like a pencil.

In spite of the fact that only Willoughton *could* have murdered Kelstern, I could not believe that he had done it. The fact that Kelstern was doing his best to injure him professionally and socially was by no means a strong enough motive. Willoughton was far too intelligent a man not to be very well aware that people do not take much notice of statements to the discredit of a man whom they need to do a job for them; and for the social injury he would care very little. Besides, he might very well injure, or even kill, a man in one of his tantrums; but his was not the kind of bad temper that plans a cold-blooded murder; and if ever a murder had been deliberately planned, Kelstern's had.

I was as close a friend as Willoughton had, and I went to visit him in prison. He seemed rather touched by my doing so, and grateful. I learnt that I was the only person who had done so. He was subdued and seemed much gentler. It might last. He discussed the murder readily enough and naturally with an harassed air. He said quite frankly that he did not expect me, in the circumstances, to believe that he had not committed it; but he had not, and he could not for the life of him conceive who had. I did believe that he had not committed it; there was something in his way of discussing it that wholly convinced me. I told him that I was quite sure that he had not killed Kelstern; and he looked at me as if he did not believe the assurance. But again he looked grateful.

Ruth was grieving for her father; but Willoughton's very dangerous plight to some degree distracted her mind from her loss. A woman can quarrel with a man bitterly without desiring to see him hanged; and Willoughton's chance of escaping hanging was not at all a good one. But she would not believe for a moment that he had murdered her father.

"No; there's nothing in it—nothing whatever," she said firmly. "If Dad had murdered Hugh I could have understood it. He had reasons—or at any rate he had persuaded himself that he had. But whatever reason had Hugh for murdering Dad? It's all nonsense to suppose that he'd mind Dad's trying all he knew to injure him, as much as that. All kinds of people are going about trying to injure other people in that way, but they don't really injure them very much; and Hugh knows that quite well."

"Of course they don't; and Hugh wouldn't really believe that your father was injuring him much," I said. "But you're forgetting his infernal temper."

"No: I'm not," she protested. "He might kill a man in one of his rages on the spur of the moment. But this wasn't the spur of the moment. Whoever did it had worked the whole thing out and came along with the weapon ready."

I had to admit that that was reasonable enough. But who had done it? I pointed out to her that the police had made careful enquiries about every one in the bath at the time, the shampooers and the people taking their baths, but they had found no evidence whatever that any one of them had at any time had any relations, except that of shampooer, with her father.

"Either it was one of them, or somebody else who just did it and got right away, or there's a catch somewhere," she said, frowning thoughtfully.

"I can't see how there can possibly have been anyone in the bath except the people who are known to have been there," said I. "In fact, there can't have been."

Then the Crown subpœnaed her as a witness for the prosecution. It seemed rather unnecessary and even a bit queer, for it could have found plenty of evidence of bad blood between the two men without dragging her into it. Plainly it was bent on doing all it knew to prove motive enough. Ruth seemed more upset by the prospect of going into the witness box than I should have expected her to be. But then she had been having a very trying time.

On the morning of the trial I called for her after breakfast to drive her down to the New Bailey. She was pale and looked as if she had had a poor night's rest, and, naturally enough, she seemed to be suffering from an excitement she had to control. It was not like her to show any excitement she might be feeling.

We had of course been in close touch with Willoughton's solicitor, Hamley; and he had kept seats for us just behind him. He wished to have Ruth at hand to consult should some point turn up on which she could throw light, since she knew more than anyone about the relations between Willoughton and her father. I had timed our arrival very well; the jury had just been sworn in. Of course the Court was full of women, the wives of Peers and bookmakers and politicians, most of them overdressed and overscented.

Then the judge came in; and with his coming the atmosphere of the Court became charged with that sense of anxious strain peculiar to trials for murder. It was rather like the atmosphere of a sick room in a case of fatal illness, but worse.

It was unfortunate for Willoughton that the judge was Garbould. A hard-faced, common-looking fellow, and coarse in the grain, he has a well-founded reputation as a hanging judge and the habit of acting as an extra counsel for the prosecution.

Willoughton came into the box, looking under the weather and very much subdued. But he certainly looked dignified and he said that he was not guilty in a steady enough voice.

Greatorex, the leading Counsel for the Crown, opened the case for the prosecution. There was no suggestion in his speech that the police had discovered any new fact.

Then Helston gave evidence of finding the body of the dead man and he and the other three men who had been with him in the hot room gave evidence of the quarrel they had overheard between Willoughton and the dead man, and that Willoughton came out of the hottest room, scowling and obviously furious. One of them, a fussy old gentleman of the name of Underwood, declared that it was the bitterest quarrel he had ever heard. None of the four of them could throw any light on the matter of whether Willoughton was carrying the missing weapon in the folds of the towel in which he was draped; all of them were sure that he had nothing in his hands.

The medical evidence came next. In cross-examining the doctors who had made the autopsy, Hazeldean, Willoughton's counsel, established the fact quite definitely that the missing weapon was of a fair size; that its rounded blade must have been over half an inch in diameter and between three and four inches long. They were of the opinion that to drive a blade of that thickness into the heart, a handle of at least four inches in length would be necessary to give a firm enough grip. It might have been a piece of a steel, or iron, rod sharpened like a pencil. At any rate it was certainly a sizeable weapon, not one to be hidden quickly, or to disappear wholly in a Turkish bath. Hazeldean could not shake their evidence about the tea leaf; they were confident that it had been driven into the wound and cut in half by the blade of the missing weapon, and that that went to show that the wound had been inflicted while Kelstern was drinking his tea.

Detective-Inspector Brackett, who was in charge of the case, was cross-examined at great length about his search for the missing weapon. He made it quite clear that it was nowhere in that Turkish bath, neither in the hot rooms, nor the shampooing room, nor the dressing rooms, nor the vestibule, nor the office. He had had the plunge bath emptied; he had searched the roofs, though it was practically certain that the skylight above the hot room, not the hottest, had been shut at the time of the crime. In re-examination he scouted the idea of Willoughton's having had an accomplice who had carried away the weapon for him. He had gone into that matter most carefully.

The shampooer stated that Willoughton came to him scowling so savagely that he wondered what had put him into such a bad temper. In cross-examining him Arbuthnot, Hazeldean's junior, made it clearer than ever that, unless Willoughton had already hidden the weapon in the bare hottest room, it was hidden in the towel. Then he drew from the shampooer the definite statement that Willoughton had set down the towel beside the couch on which he was shampooed, that he had hurried back to the hot rooms in front of the shampooer; that the shampooer had come back from the hot rooms, leaving Willoughton still in them discussing the crime, to find the towel lying just as Willoughton had set it down, with no weapon in it and no trace of blood on it.

Since the Inspector had disposed of the possibility that an accomplice had slipped in, taken the weapon from the towel, and slipped out of the bath with it, this evidence really made it clear that the weapon had never left the hottest room.

Then the prosecution called evidence of the bad terms on which Kelstern and Willoughton had been. Three well-known and influential men told the jury about Kelstern's efforts to prejudice Willoughton in their eyes and the damaging statements he had made about him. One of them had felt it to be his duty to tell Willoughton about this; and Willoughton had been very angry. Arbuthnot, in cross-examining, elicited the fact that any damaging statement that Kelstern made about anyone was considerably discounted by the fact that everyone knew him to be in the highest degree cantankerous.

I noticed that during the end of the cross-examination of the shampooer, and during this evidence, Ruth had been fidgeting and turning to look impatiently at the entrance to the Court, as if she were expecting someone. Then, just as she was summoned to the witness box, there came in a tall, stooping, grey-headed, grey-bearded man of about sixty, carrying a brown-paper parcel. His face was familiar to me; but I could not place him. He caught her eye and nodded to her. She breathed a sharp sigh of relief and bent over and handed a letter she had in her hand to Willoughton's solicitor and pointed out the grey-bearded man to him. Then she went quietly to the witness box.

Hamley read the letter and at once bent over and handed it to Hazeldean and spoke to him. I caught a note of excitement in his hushed voice. Hazeldean read the letter and appeared to grow excited too. Hamley slipped out of his seat and went to the grey-bearded man who was still standing just inside the door of the Court and began to talk to him earnestly.

Greatorex began to examine Ruth; and naturally I turned my attention to her. His examination was directed also to show on what bad terms Kelstern and Willoughton had been. Ruth was called on to tell the jury some of Kelstern's actual threats. Then—it is astonishing how few things the police fail to ferret out in a really important case—the examination took a curious turn. Greatorex began to question Ruth about her own relations with Willoughton and the plain trend of his questions was to bring out the fact that they had not merely been engaged to be married but had also been lovers.

I saw at once what the prosecution was aiming at. It was trying to make use of the tendency of a British jury and a British judge, in a natural effort to champion morality, to hang a man or a woman, who is on trial for murder, for behaving immorally in relations with the other sex. There was no better way of prejudicing Willoughton than by proving that he had seduced Ruth under the promise of marriage.

Of course Hazeldean was on his feet at once protesting that this evidence was irrelevant and inadmissible; and of course Garbould was against him—he does not enjoy the nickname by which he is known to the junior bar for nothing. Hazeldean was magnificent. He had one of the worst rows with Garbould he had ever had; and he has had many. Garbould is a fool to let him have these rows. Hazeldean always gets the better of him, or seems to; and it does him good with the jury. But then Garbould was raised to the bench not for intelligence but for political merit. He ruled that the questions were admissible and put one or two to Ruth himself.

Then Willoughton lost his temper and protested that this had nothing to do with the case and that it was an outrage. Willoughton has a ringing voice of considerable volume. He is not at all an easy man to hush when he does not wish to hush; and they were some time hushing him. By the time they succeeded Garbould was purplish-red with fury. Anything that he could do to hang Willoughton would certainly be done. But, observing the jury, my impression was that Willoughton's outburst had done him good with it and that Hazeldean's protests had shaken its confidence in Garbould. When I looked at the faces, just a trifle sickly, of the counsel for the prosecution, I felt sure that the Crown had bungled this business rather badly.

Greatorex, assisted by Garbould, went on with his questions; and Ruth defiant rather than abashed, and looking in her flushed animation a more charming creature than ever, admitted that she and Willoughton had been lovers; that more than once when he had brought her home from a dance or a theatre he had not left her till the early morning. One of the maids had spied on them; and the Crown had the facts.

I was afraid, in spite of Hazeldean's protests, that the fact that Willoughton had seduced her under the promise of marriage, as Greatorex put it, would do him great harm with the jury—very likely it would hang him.

Then Ruth, still flushed, but not greatly discomposed, said: "That would be a reason for my father's murdering Mr. Willoughton, not for Mr. Willoughton's murdering my father."

That brought Garbould down upon her like a ton of bricks. She was there to answer questions, not to make idle remarks and so forth and so on.

Then Greatorex came to the breaking off of the engagement and put it to her that Willoughton had broken it off, had in fact jilted her after compromising her. That she would not have for a moment. She declared that they had had a quarrel and she had broken it off. To that she stuck and there was no shaking her, though Garbould himself took a hearty hand in trying to shake her.

In the middle of it Willoughton, who was looking quite himself again, now that the atmosphere of the Court might be said to be charged almost with violence, said in a very unpleasant, jeering voice: "What she says is perfectly true— what's the good of bothering her?"

Again Garbould was to the fore, and angrily reprimanded him for speaking, bade him keep silent, and said that he would not have his Court turned into a beargarden.

"With the bear on the bench," said Hazeldean to Arbuthnot in a whisper that carried well.

Two or three people laughed. One of them was a juryman. By the time Garbould had finished with him I did not think that that juryman would have convicted Willoughton, if he had actually seen him stab Kelstern.

Willoughton was writing a note which was passed to Hazeldean.

Hazeldean rose to cross-examine Ruth with a wholly confident air. He drew from her the facts that her father had been on excellent terms with Willoughton until the breaking off of the engagement; that in that matter he had taken her part warmly; and that when the maid who had spied upon them had informed him of her relations with Willoughton he had been very little more enraged than he was already.

Then Hazeldean asked: "Is it a fact that since the breaking off of your engagement the prisoner has more than once begged you to forgive him and renew it?"

"Four times," said Ruth.

"And you refused?"

"Yes," said Ruth. She looked at Willoughton queerly and added: "He wanted a lesson."

"Did he then beg you at least to go through

the form of marriage with him, and promise to leave you at the church door?"

"Yes."

"And you refused?"

"Yes," said Ruth.

Garbould bent forward and said in his most unpleasant tone: "And why did you reject the opportunity of repairing your shameful behaviour?"

"It wasn't shameful," Ruth almost snapped; and she scowled at him frankly. Then she added naïvely: "I refused because there was no hurry. He would always marry me if I changed my mind and wanted to."

There was a pause. To me it seemed clearer than ever that the Crown had bungled badly in raising the question of the relations between her and Willoughton since he had evidently been more than ready to save her from any harm that might come of their indiscretion. But then, with a jury, you can never tell. Then Hazeldean started on a fresh line.

In sympathetic accents he asked: "Is it a fact that your father was suffering from cancer in a painful form?"

"It was beginning to grow very painful," said Ruth sadly.

"Did he make a will and put all his affairs in order a few days before he died?"

"Three days," said Ruth.

"Did he ever express an intention of committing suicide?"

"He said that he would stick it out for a little while and then end it all," said Ruth. She paused and added: *"And that is what he did do."*

One might almost say that the Court started. I think that everyone in it moved a little, so that there was a kind of rustling murmur. Garbould threw himself back in his seat with a snort of incredulity and glowered at Ruth.

"Will you tell the Court your reasons for that statement?" said Hazeldean.

Ruth seemed to pull herself together; the flush had faded from her face and she was looking very tired; then she began in a quiet, even voice: "I never believed for a moment that Mr.

Willoughton murdered my father. If my father had murdered Mr. Willoughton it would have been a different matter."

Garbould leaned forward and snarled that it was not her beliefs or fancies that were wanted, but facts.

I did not think that she heard him; she was concentrating on giving her reasons exactly; she went on in the same quiet tone: "Of course, like everybody else I puzzled over the weapon: what it was and where it had got to. I did not believe that it was a pointed piece of a half-inch steel rod. If anybody had come to the Turkish bath meaning to murder my father and hide the weapon, they wouldn't have used one so big and so difficult to hide, when a hatpin would have done just as well and could be hidden much more easily. But what puzzled me most was the tea leaf in the wound. All the other tea leaves that came out of the flask were lying on the floor. Inspector Brackett told me they were. And I couldn't believe that one tea leaf had fallen onto my father at the very place above his heart at which the point of the weapon had penetrated the skin and got driven in by it. It was too much of a coincidence for me to swallow. But I got no nearer understanding it than anyone else."

Garbould broke in in a tone of some exasperation and told her to come to the facts. Hazeldean rose and protested that the witness should not be interrupted; that she had solved a mystery which had puzzled some of the best brains in England, and she should be allowed to tell her story in her own way.

Again Ruth did not appear to listen to them, and when they stopped she went on in the same quiet voice: "Of course I remembered that Dad had talked of putting an end to it; but no one with a wound like that could get up and hide the weapon. Then, the night before last I dreamt that I went into the laboratory and saw a piece of steel rod, pointed, lying on the table at which my father used to work."

"Dreams now!" murmured Garbould contemptuously; and he leaned back and folded his hands over his stomach.

"I didn't think much of the dream, of course," Ruth went on. "I had been puzzling about it all so hard for so long that it was only natural to dream about it. But after breakfast I had a sudden feeling that the secret was in the laboratory if I could only find it. I did not attach any importance to the feeling; but it went on growing stronger; and after lunch I went to the laboratory and began to hunt.

"I looked through all the drawers and could find nothing. Then I went round the room looking at everything and into everything, instruments and retorts and tubes and so on. Then I went into the middle of the floor and looked slowly round the room pretty hard. Against the wall, near the door, lying ready to be taken away, was a gas cylinder. I rolled it over to see what gas had been in it and found no label on it."

She paused to look round the Court as if claiming its best attention; then she went on: "Now that was very queer because every gas cylinder must have a label on it—so many gases are dangerous. I turned on the cylinder and nothing came out of it. It was quite empty. Then I went to the book in which all the things which come in are entered, and found that ten days before Dad died he had had in a cylinder of CO_2 and seven pounds of ice. Also he had had seven pounds of ice every day till the day of his death. It was the ice and the CO_2 together that gave me the idea. CO_2, carbon dioxide, has a very low freezing point—eighty degrees centigrade—and as it comes out of the cylinder and mixes with the air it turns into very fine snow; and that snow, if you compress it, makes the hardest and toughest ice possible. It flashed on me that Dad could have collected this snow and forced it into a mould and made a weapon that would not only inflict that wound but would *disappear instantly*!"

She paused again to look round the Court at about as rapt a lot of faces as any narrator could desire. Then she went on: "I knew that that was what he had done. I knew it for certain. Carbon dioxide ice would make a hard, tough dagger, and it would melt quickly in the hottest room of a Turkish bath and leave no smell because it is scentless. So there wouldn't be any weapon. And it explained the tea leaf too. Dad had made a carbon dioxide dagger perhaps a week before he used it, perhaps only a day. And he had put it into the thermos flask as soon as he had made it. The thermos flask keeps out the heat as well as the cold, you know. But to make sure that it couldn't melt at all he kept the flask in ice till he was ready to use the dagger. It's the only way you can explain that tea leaf. It came out of the flask sticking to the point of the dagger and was driven into the wound!"

She paused again and one might almost say that the Court heaved a deep sigh of relief.

Then Garbould asked in an unpleasant and incredulous voice: "Why didn't you take this fantastic theory straight to the police?"

"But that wouldn't have been any good," she protested quickly. "It was no use my knowing it myself; I had to make other people believe it; I had to find evidence. I began to hunt for it. I felt in my bones that there was some. What I wanted was the mould. I found it!"

She uttered the words in a tone of triumph and smiled at Willoughton; then she went on: "At least I found bits of it. In the box into which we used to throw odds and ends, scraps of material, damaged instruments, and broken test tubes, I found some pieces of vulcanite; and I saw at once that they were bits of a vulcanite container. I took some wax and rolled it into a rod about the right size and then I pieced the container together on the outside of it—at least most of it—there are some small pieces missing. It took me nearly all night. But I found the most important bit—*the pointed end*!"

She dipped her hand into her handbag and drew out a black object about nine inches long and three quarters of an inch thick and held it up for everyone to see.

Someone, without thinking, began to clap; and there came a storm of applause that drowned the voice of the Clerk calling for order and the bellowing of Garbould.

When the applause died down, Hazeldean, who never misses the right moment, said: "I have no more questions to ask the witness, my lord," and sat down.

That action seemed to clinch it in my eyes and, I have no doubt, it clinched it in the eyes of the jury.

The purple Garbould leant forward and almost bellowed at Ruth: "Do you expect the jury to believe that a well-known man like your father died in the act of deliberately setting a dastardly trap to hang the prisoner?"

Ruth looked at him, shrugged her shoulders, and said with a calm acceptance of the facts of human nature one would expect to find only in a much older woman: "Oh, well, Daddy was like that. And he certainly believed he had very good reasons for killing Mr. Willoughton."

There was that in her tone and manner which made it absolutely certain that Kelstern was not only like that but that he had acted according to his nature.

Greatorex did not re-examine Ruth; he conferred with Hazeldean. Then Hazeldean rose to open the case for the defence. He said that he would not waste the time of the Court, and that in view of the fact that Miss Kelstern had solved the problem of her father's death, he would only call one witness, Professor Mozley.

The grey-headed, grey-bearded, stooping man, who had come to the Court so late, went into the witness box. Of course his face had been familiar to me; I had seen his portrait in the newspapers a dozen times. He still carried the brown-paper parcel.

In answer to Hazeldean's questions he stated that it was possible, not even difficult, to make a weapon of carbon dioxide hard enough and tough enough and sharp enough to inflict such a wound as that which had caused Kelstern's death. The method of making it was to fold a piece of chamois leather into a bag, hold that bag with the left hand, protected by a glove, over the nozzle of a cylinder containing liquid carbon dioxide, and open the valve with the right hand. Carbon dioxide evaporates so quickly that its freezing point, 80° centigrade, is soon reached; and it solidifies in the chamois leather

bag as a deposit of carbon dioxide snow. Then turn off the gas, spoon that snow into a vulcanite container of the required thickness, and ram it down with a vulcanite plunger into a rod of the required hardness. He added that it was advisable to pack the container in ice while filling it and ramming down the snow, then put the rod into a thermos flask; and keep it till it is needed.

"And you have made such a rod?" said Hazeldean.

"Yes," said the Professor, cutting the string of the brown-paper parcel. "When Miss Kelstern hauled me out of bed at half past seven this morning to tell me her discoveries, I perceived at once that she had found the solution of the problem of her father's death, which had puzzled me considerably. I had breakfast quickly and got to work to make such a weapon myself for the satisfaction of the Court. Here it is."

He drew a thermos flask from the brown paper, unscrewed the top of it, and inverted it. There dropped into his gloved hand a white rod about eight inches long. He held it out for the jury to see.

"This carbon dioxide ice is the hardest and toughest ice we know of; and I have no doubt that Mr. Kelstern killed himself with a similar rod. The difference between the rod he used and this is that his rod was pointed. I had no pointed vulcanite container; but the container that Miss Kelstern pieced together is pointed. Doubtless Mr. Kelstern had it specially made, probably by Messrs. Hawkins and Spender."

He dropped the rod back into the thermos flask and screwed on the top.

Hazeldean sat down. The juryman who had been reprimanded by Garbould leaned forward and spoke earnestly to the foreman. Greatorex rose.

"With regard to the point of the rod, Professor Mozley: would it remain sharp long enough to pierce the skin in that heat?" he asked.

"In my opinion it would," said the Professor. "I have been considering that point and bearing in mind the facts that Mr. Kelstern would from his avocation be very deft with his hands, and being a scientific man, would know exactly what to do, he would have the rod out of the flask and the point in position in very little more than a second—perhaps less. He would, I think, hold it in his left hand and drive it home by striking the butt of it hard with his right. The whole thing would not take him two seconds. Besides, if the point of the weapon had melted the tea leaf would have fallen off it."

"Thank you," said Greatorex, and turned and conferred with the Crown solicitors.

Then he said: "We do not propose to proceed with the case, my lord."

The foreman of the jury rose quickly and said: "And the jury doesn't want to hear anything more, my lord. We're quite satisfied that the prisoner isn't guilty."

Garbould hesitated. For two pins he would have directed the case to proceed. Then his eye fell on Hazeldean, who was watching him; I fancied that he decided not to give him a chance of saying more disagreeable things.

Looking black enough, he put the question formally to the jury, who returned a verdict of "Not guilty," and then he discharged Willoughton.

I came out of the Court with Ruth, and we waited for Willoughton.

Presently he came out of the door and stopped and shook himself. Then he saw Ruth and came to her. They did not greet one another. She just slipped her hand through his arm; and they walked out of the New Bailey together.

We made a good deal of noise, cheering them.

THE FLUNG-BACK LID

PETER GODFREY

DESCRIBED AS "The Simenon of South Africa," Peter Godfrey (1917–1992) was a playwright, broadcaster, and journalist who was exiled to London from his native country for his outspoken opposition to apartheid. He wrote hundreds of short stories, mainly in the 1940s and 1950s, which were translated into eight languages. However, until Crippen & Landru published *The Newtonian Egg* (2002), he had had only one book published, *Death Under the Table* (1954), a very rare collection of detective stories issued by the obscure South African publishing house S. A. Scientific Publishing Co., the address of which was a post office box in Cape Town.

Godfrey's series character, lawyer and psychologist Rolf le Roux, with his assistants Inspector Joubert, Sergeant Johnson, and Doc McGregor, works in Cape Town and provides a look into every corner of that great international city. The homicide squad and le Roux confront the most elusive type of mystery, the seemingly impossible crime, and display extraordinary intelligence in their solutions. One case challenges them to understand how a quantity of cyanide got inside an unbroken hard-boiled egg. Another, published in *Death Under the Table*, "The Wanton Murders," served as the basis for the 1957 motion picture *The Girl in Black Stockings*, which starred Anne Bancroft.

"The Flung-Back Lid" was first published in *John Creasey's Crime Collection* (London, Gollancz, 1979). It is a rewritten and improved version of "Out of This World," first collected in *Death Under the Table* (Cape Town, South Africa, S. A. Scientific Publishing Co., 1954).

THE FLUNG-BACK LID

PETER GODFREY

ALL THAT DAY, the last day of March, the cableway to the top of Table Mountain had operated normally. Every half hour the car on the summit descended, and the car below ascended, both operating on the same endless cable. The entire journey took seven minutes.

Passengers going up or coming down gawked at the magnificent panorama over the head of the blase conductor in each car. In his upper-station cabin the driver of the week, Clobber, hunched conscientiously over his controls during each run, and was usually able to relax for the rest of the half hour.

In the restaurant on the summit, Mrs. Orvin worked and chatted and sold curios and postcards and buttered scones, and showed customers how to post their cards in the little box which would ensure their stamps would be canceled with a special Table Mountain franking.

In the box-office at the lower station, the station master, Brander, sold tickets for the journey, and chatted with the conductor who happened to be down at the time, and drank tea.

Then, at 5:30 p.m., the siren moaned its warning that the last trip of the day was about to commence. Into the upper car came the last straggling sightseers, the engineer on duty, Mrs. Orvin, and the conductor, Skager. Alone in the lower car was the other conductor, Heston, who would sleep overnight on the summit.

Then two bells rang, and the cars were on their way. For the space of seven minutes Clob-

ber and the Native labourer, Ben, were the only two on top of the mountain. Then the cars docked, and Heston stepped jauntily onto the landing platform.

He joined Clobber, but neither spoke. Their dislike was mutual and obvious. They ate their evening meal in silence.

Clobber picked up a book. Heston took a short walk, and then went to bed.

Some hours later, he woke up. Somewhere in the blackness of the room he could hear Clobber snoring softly.

Heston bared his teeth. Snore now, he thought, snore now. But tomorrow . . .

The night began to grow less black. The stars faded first, then the lights far below in the city also winked out. The east changed colour. The sun rose.

It was tomorrow.

Brander came into the room which housed the lower landing platform, and peered myopically up along the giant stretch of steel rope.

The old Cape Coloured, Piet, was sweeping out the car which had remained overnight at the lower station—the right-hand car. He said: "Dag,* Baas Brander."

"Dag, Piet," said Brander.

Two thousand feet above, the upper station

---

* *Afrikaans: "Good day."*

looked like a doll's house, perched on the edge of the cliff. The outlines of Table Mountain stood deep-etched by the morning sun. On the flat top of the elevation there was no sign of cloud—the tablecloth, as people in Cape Town call it—and there was no stirring of the air.

Brander thought: Good weather. We will be operating all day.

Piet was sweeping carefully, poking the broom edgeways into the corners of the car. He noticed Brander looking at him, and his old parchment flat-nosed face creased suddenly into a myriad of grins. "Baas Dimple is the engineer today," he said. "The car must be very clean."

"That's right, Piet," said Brander. "Make a good job for Baas Dimble. You still have twenty minutes."

In the upper station, Clobber settled himself in his chair in the driver's cabin, and opened the latest issue of *Armchair Scientist*. He had just about enough time, he reckoned, to finish the latest article on the new rocket fuels before the test run at nine-thirty.

Line by line his eyes swallowed words, phrases and sentences. Then, interrupting the even flow of his thoughts, he felt the uneasy consciousness of eyes staring at the back of his neck. He had an annoying mental image of Heston's thin lips contorting in a sardonic smile.

He turned. It was Heston, but this time his face was unusually serious. "Did I interrupt you?" he asked.

"Oh, go to hell," said Clobber. He marked the place in his magazine, and put it down. He asked: "Well?"

"I wanted a few words with you," said Heston.

"If it's chit-chat you're after, find someone else."

Heston looked hurt. "It's . . . well, it's rather a personal problem. Do you mind?"

"All right. Go ahead."

"I'm a bit worried about the trip down."

"Why? You know as well as I do that nothing can go wrong with the cable."

"No, it's not that. It's just . . . Look, Clobber, I don't want you to think I'm pulling your leg, because I'm really very serious. I don't think I'm going to get down alive. You see, yesterday was my birthday—I turned thirty-one and it was 31 March—and I had to spend last night up here. Now, I'm not being superstitious or anything, but I've been warned that the day after my birthday I'd not be alive if my first trip was from the top to the bottom of the mountain. If I hadn't forgotten, I'd have changed shifts with someone, but as it is . . ."

"Look here, Heston, if you're not bluffing, you're the biggest damned fool—"

"I'm not bluffing, Clobber. I mean it. You see, I haven't got a relation in the world. If anything does happen, I'd like to see that each of the men gets something of mine as a sort of keepsake. You can have my watch. Dimble gets my binoculars—"

"Sure, sure. And your million-rand bank account goes to Little Orphan Annie. Don't be a damned fool. Who gave you this idiotic warning, anyway?"

"I had a dream—"

"Get to hell out of here, you little rat! Coming here and—"

"But I mean it, Clobber—"

"Get out! It would be a damned good thing for all of us if you didn't reach the bottom alive!"

Dimble, neat and officious but friendly, arrived at the lower station wagon, and with him were Skager and Mrs. Orvin.

Brander shuffled forward to meet them.

"Nice day," said Dimble. "What's your time, Brander? Nine-twenty-five? Good, our watches agree. Everything ship-shape here? Fine."

Skager scratched a pimple on his neck.

Mrs. Orvin said: "How's your hand, Mr. Brander?"

The station-master peered below his glasses at his left hand, which was neatly bound with fresh white bandages. "Getting better slowly, thanks. It's still a little painful. I can't use it much, yet."

"Don't like that Heston," said Dimble. "Nasty trick he played on you, Brander."

"Perhaps it wasn't a trick, Mr. Dimble. Perhaps he didn't know the other end of the iron was hot."

"Nonsense," said Mrs. Orvin. "He probably heated it up, specially. I can believe anything of him. Impertinent, that's what he is."

"Even if he did do it," said Brander, "I can't bear any hard feelings."

Dimble said: "You're a religious man, eh, Brander? All right in its way, but too impractical. No good turning the other cheek to a chap like Heston. Probably give you another clout for good measure. No, I'm different. If he'd done it to me, I'd have my knife into him."

"He'll get a knife into him one of these days," said Skager, darkly. He hesitated. "He'll be coming down in the first car, won't he?"

"Yes," said Brander.

"And it's just about time," said Dimble. "We'd better get in our car. After you, Mrs. Orvin. So long, Brander."

"Goodbye, Mr. Dimble—Mrs. Orvin—Skager."

Heston came through the door leading to the landing platform at the upper station. In the car, the Native Ben was still sweeping.

"Hurry up, you lazy black swine," said Heston. "What in hell have you been doing with yourself this morning? It's almost time to go, and you're still messing about. Get out of my way."

The Native looked at him with a snarl. "You mustn't talk to me like that. I'm not your dog. I've been twenty years with this company, and in all that time nobody's ever spoken to me like that—"

"Then it's time someone started. Go on—get out!"

Ben muttered: "I'd like to—"

"You'd like to what? Come up behind me when I'm not looking, I suppose? Well, you won't get much chance for that. And don't hang around—voetsak!"*

From the driver's cabin they heard the two sharp bells that indicated that the cars were ready to move. Ben stepped aside. As the upper car began to slide down and away Heston went through the door, up the short flight of stairs and into the driver's cabin. He looked over Clobber's shoulder at the plate-glass window.

The upper car was then twenty or thirty yards from the station. Both men saw Heston lean over the side of the car, and salute them with an exaggerated sweep of his right arm. Both men muttered under their breath.

As the seconds ticked by, the two cars approached each other in mid-air.

In the ascending car Dimble looked at the one that was descending with a critical eye. Suddenly, he became annoyed. "That fool," he said. "Look how he's leaning out over the door. Dangerous . . ."

His voice tailed off. As the cars passed each other, he saw something protruding from Heston's back—something that gleamed silver for an inch or two, and was surmounted by a handle of bright scarlet. Dimble said: "God!" He reached and jerked the emergency brake. Both cars stopped suddenly, swaying drunkenly over the abyss.

Skager moaned: "He's not leaning . . ."

Mrs. Orvin gulped audibly. "That's my knife," she said, "the one he said . . ."

The telephone bell in the car rang shrilly. Dimble answered it.

"What's the trouble?" came Clobber's voice.

"It's Heston. He's slumped over the door of the car. There seems to be a knife in his back."

"A knife? Hell! He was alive when he left here. He waved to me . . . What should we do?"

"Hang on a second. Brander, are you on the other end? Have you heard this conversation?"

* *Afrikaans: "Scram!"*

"Yes, Mr. Dimble."

"Okay, Clobber. I'm releasing the brake now. Speed it up a little."

"Sure."

The cars moved again.

At the top, Dimble led the rush up the stairs to the driver's cabin, where Clobber's white face greeted them. They waited.

The telephone rang.

Clobber stretched out a tentative hand, but Dimble was ahead of him.

"I've seen him," said Brander, queerly. "He's dead."

"Are you sure?"

"Yes. He's dead."

"Now look, Brander, we must make sure nothing is touched. Get on the outside phone to the police right away. And let Piet stand guard over the body until they get here, OK?"

"It might be difficult, Mr. Dimble. There are people here already for tickets, so I can't leave here, and Piet is scared. He's said so. I've locked the door leading to the landing stage—won't that be enough?"

"No. If anyone there is curious, they can climb round the side of the station to the car, and possibly spoil evidence. Let me speak to Piet."

"Here he is, Mr. Dimble."

"Hullo, Piet. Now listen—I want you to stand guard on the landing stage and see nobody touches the car until the police arrive."

"No, Baas. Not me, Baas. Not with a dead body, Baas."

"Oh, dammit. OK, Let me speak to Mr. Brander. Brander? Listen—this is the best plan. Don't sell any tickets—we won't be operating today, anyway. We'll start the cars and stop them halfway so nobody will be able to get near them. In the meantime you telephone the police. Do you get that?"

"Yes, I will telephone the police."

"And give me a ring the moment they are here."

"Yes, Mr. Dimble."

The police came. Caledon Square had sent its top murder team. Lieutenant Dirk Joubert was in charge of the party, and with him was his uncle, Rolf le Roux, the "expert on people" as he jocularly styled himself, the inevitable krom-steel* protruding through the forest of his beard. Happy Detective-Sergeant Johnson was there, Lugubrious Sergeant Botha, Doc McGregor and several uniformed men. They mounted the steps to the lower station building and found Brander waiting for them.

"Where is the body?" asked Joubert.

Brander pointed out the two tiny cars on their thin threads a thousand feet above. "Will you please speak on the internal phone to Mr. Dimble, the engineer in charge, who's at the upper station?" he asked.

"Get him for me," said Joubert.

Brander made the connection, and then handed over the phone.

"Mr. Dimble? I am Inspector Joubert of the Cape Town C.I.D. I want the cable car with the body to be allowed to come down here. What? No, it'd be better if you people stayed on top of the mountain while we do our preliminary work here. I'll ring you when we're ready. Hullo! Just one moment, just bring me up to date on the discovery of the crime—briefly, please. I see. You were going up in the right-hand car, and when you passed the other one at half-way, you saw a knife sticking out of the conductor's back. His name? Heston . . . yes, I have that. And then? I see. Yes. Yes. And why did you move the car with the body half-way back up the mountain? Mm. No, that's all right—it was a good idea. Right, better get the body back here now."

Almost as soon as he put the receiver down, the cable began to whine.

From the landing-stage they watched the approaching car. Even at some distance they could see the slumped figure quite clearly, with

* *Curved Boer pipe.*

the scarlet splash of the knife handle protruding from its back.

"I can tell you one thing right now," said McGregor. "It's not a suicide."

As the car came closer to the landing-stage, Johnson began checking his photographic and fingerprint equipment.

Brander mumbled: "It is the will of the Lord . . ."

He looked almost grateful when Joubert said: "There's nothing we can do here, Brander. Let's go into the ticket office. There are one or two questions . . ."

Rolf went with them.

Joubert said: "I've had the rough details of the story from Mr. Dimble. You were here when the body first came down. Did you examine it?"

"No."

"Why not?"

"He was dead. I could see that."

"And did anyone else come near the body? This Coloured, Piet?"

"No, not Piet. He was afraid. He wouldn't go near the car. He stood at the door until the motors started, though, in case anyone else wanted to go through."

"Anyone else? Who else was here?"

"Well, there was a man and two women— passengers—but they left when I wouldn't sell them tickets."

Joubert tried a new tack. "This Heston, now. Tell me, Brander, what sort of a man was he? Was there anyone working here who hated him?"

Brander hesitated. "I do not like to talk about him. He is dead now. What does it matter what he was like in life?"

Joubert said: "Answer my question. Is there anyone here who hated him?"

"He was not liked," said Brander, "but nobody here hated him enough to kill him."

"No? Someone stuck a knife in his back, all the same. Who could have done it?"

"What does it matter?" said Brander. "He's dead now. Let him rest in peace."

The experts had finished. Two constables carried a long basket clumsily down the steps to a waiting ambulance.

"Well, Doc?" asked Joubert.

"One blow," said McGregor. "A very clean swift blow. No mess. The murderer struck him from behind and above. Either the killer stood on something, or he was a very tall man."

"Or woman?"

"Maybe. I canna say one way or another."

Johnson made his report. "No fingerprints on the knife, Dirk. Couple of blurred smears, that's all. Probably wore gloves."

Joubert said: "All right. Doc, you go back with the body, and do the P.M. If you come up with anything new, telephone me here . . . Now let's talk to this Coloured, Piet."

But Piet knew nothing. He was old and superstition-ridden. He had not even looked at the body. The nearest he had come to it was to stand on guard on the other side of a closed door.

Joubert phoned Dimble. "We're coming up. What is the signal for starting the car? Two bells—right. I'm not interested in rules about conductors on every trip. We're coming up without one, and the car at the top must come down completely empty. All right—so it's irregular. So is murder. I'll take the responsibility . . . We'll want to interview you one at a time. Is there a room there we can use? The restaurant? Right. You'll hear the signal in a couple of minutes."

Joubert, Rolf le Roux and Johnson. Four uniformed policemen. Going up in the car in which death had come down.

"I don't think we'll be long," said Joubert. "The solution's on top, obviously."

Rolf said: "How do you make that out?"

"When the cars reached the middle of the run, Heston already had the knife in his back. He was alone in the cable-car. Therefore he must have been killed before he left the summit. One of the men stationed up there is the chap we're looking for."

Rolf looked worried. He said: "I hope you are right."

"Of course I'm right. It's the only possible explanation."

"So you'll start off by concentrating on the men who were on the mountain when the cars started this morning?"

"No, let them stew in their own juice for a while. This Dimble seems a proper fuss-pot—better get him over first."

Dimble

". . . And so I told Brander to see the body was guarded, and when I found Piet was afraid I told him . . ."

"Right, Dimble. We've got all that. Now, let me get one thing clear. Apart from Heston, there were two men who stayed overnight at the summit—Clobber, and the Native, Ben?"

"Yes."

"Did either of these two have anything against Heston?"

"Probably. Heston wasn't very likable, you know. But I don't think anyone would murder him."

Joubert said again: "Someone did. Now look, Dimble—to your knowledge did either Clobber or Ben have anything against Heston?"

"Not to my knowledge, no. They may have. For that matter, we all disliked him. He was always doing something . . . objectionable. Like practical jokes—only there was malice behind them, and he never acted as though he was joking. Never could be sure. Nasty type."

Rolf asked: "Exactly what sort of objectionable actions do you mean, Mr. Dimble?"

"Well, like putting an emetic in my sandwiches when I wasn't looking. Couldn't prove it was him, though. And burning Brander's hand."

Joubert said: "I noticed his left hand was bandaged. What happened?"

"Heston handed him a length of iron to hold, and his end was all but red-hot."

"I see. So it would appear that both you and Brander had cause to hate the man?"

"'Cause, yes, and I must admit I didn't like him. But Brander's different. We were talking about it this morning, and he didn't seem to bear any grudge. He's a religious type, you know."

"So I gathered," said Joubert, drily.

Dimble went on: "And that reminds me—Skager had it in for Heston too. When I mentioned that if it had been my hand he burnt, I'd have my knife in for him, Skager said that one day someone would . . . Hey! That's ironic, isn't it?"

"Yes," said Joubert. "All right, Dimble. Let's have Skager."

Skager

A pasty, pimply young man, with a chip on his shoulder.

"I didn't mean anything by it, Inspector. It's just an expression. I didn't like him."

"So you didn't like him, and you just used an expression? Doesn't it strike you as strange that a few minutes later Heston did have a knife in his back?"

"I didn't think about it."

"Well, think now, Skager. Why did you hate him?"

"Look, Inspector, I had nothing to do with the murder. How could I have killed him?"

"How do you know how he was killed? I tell you, Skager, I am prepared to arrest any man who attempts to hide his motives . . . Now answer my question?"

A slight pause of defiance, then—

"Well, I don't suppose it makes any difference. I've got a girlfriend. Some time ago, someone rang her up and warned her not to go out with me because I had an incurable disease. It took me weeks before I could convince her it was a lie."

"And you thought Heston made the phone call?"

"Yes."

"Why?"

"Maybe because he was always making snide

remarks about my pimples. Besides, it's just the kind of sneaky trick he would get up to."

"So you hated him, eh, Skager—hated him enough to kill him?"

"Why do you pick on me, Inspector? I know nothing about any murder. Why don't you speak to Mrs. Orvin? At least she recognised the knife . . ."

Mrs. Orvin

Mrs. Orvin said: "Yes, the knife is mine. My brother-in-law sent it to me from the Congo."

"What did you use it for?"

"Mainly as an ornament. Occasionally for cutting. It was kept on this shelf under the glass of the counter."

"So anyone could have taken it while you were in the kitchen?"

"Yes, that's what must have happened."

"When did you find it was missing?"

"Yesterday afternoon."

"And before that, when did you last notice it?"

"Only a few minutes earlier. I'd been using it to cut some string, and I put it down to attend to something in the kitchen—"

"Was there anyone else in the restaurant at the time?"

"Yes, quite a few people. Four or five tourists and Heston and Clobber."

"Clobber was here?"

"Yes, having his tea. He sat at the far corner table."

"And Heston?"

"At first he was on the balcony, but when I came back from the kitchen he was sitting at this table."

"So when you missed the knife, what did you do?"

"I spoke to Heston . . ."

Heston looked up innocently at her. "Yes, Mrs. Orvin?"

"Mr. Heston, have you by any chance seen my knife?"

"You mean the big one with the red handle? The voodoo knife? Of course I have. You were using it a minute ago."

"Well, it's gone now. Did you see anyone take it?"

"No, I didn't see anyone take it, Mrs. Orvin, but I know what happened to it all the same."

"What?"

"It suddenly rose in the air, and sort of fluttered out through the door. All by itself . . ."

"Mr. Heston, you're being stupid and impertinent—"

"But it's true, Mrs. Orvin, it's true. Some of the other people here must have seen it, too. Why don't you ask Clobber?"

Joubert said: "And did you ask Clobber, Mrs. Orvin?"

"Yes."

"And what did he say?"

"He knew nothing about the knife. He was very angry when I told him about Heston."

"Well, thanks, Mrs. Orvin—I think that'll be all for now."

Mrs. Orvin left.

Rolf allowed a puff of smoke to billow through his beard. He said to Johnson: "So now we have a flying voodoo dagger."

"Utter nonsense," said Joubert. "This is murder, not fantasy. Someone wearing gloves killed Heston, and the murder was done on top of the mountain. It can only be one of two—the Native or Clobber. I fancy Clobber."

"You're quite sure, eh?" said Rolf. "What will you say if we find Heston was alive when he left the summit?"

"It just couldn't happen. There is no possible way of stabbing a man alone in a cable-car in mid-journey."

Rolf said: "I still have a feeling about this case . . ."

"There are too many feelings altogether. What we need are a few facts. Let's send for Clobber."

Clobber

Clobber was pale. He was still wearing the soiled dustcoat he used while driving. Joubert looked at something protruding from the pocket and glanced significantly at Johnson and Rolf.

"Do you always wear cotton gloves?" he asked.

"Yes. They keep my hands clean."

"They also have another very useful purpose. They don't leave fingerprints."

Clobber's face went even whiter. "What are you getting at? I didn't kill Heston. He was alive when he left the summit."

"And dead when he passed the other car half-way down? Come off it, Clobber. He must have been killed up here. Either you or Ben are guilty."

Clobber said, stubbornly: "Neither of us did it. I tell you he was alive when he left."

"That's what you say. The point is, can you prove it?"

"Yes, I think so. After the car had started, when he was about twenty yards out, he leant over the side of the car and waved to me. Ben had just come into my cabin. He saw him too."

"Where was Ben before that?"

"He was with Heston at the car."

"A new gleam came into Joubert's eye. "Look, Clobber," he said, "couldn't Ben have stabbed Heston just as the car pulled away?"

"I suppose he could, but don't forget, Ben was with me when Heston waved."

"Are you sure it was a wave? Couldn't it have been a body wedged upright, and then slumping over the door?"

"No, definitely not. The arm moved up and down two or three times. He was alive. I'm sure of that."

Joubert flung up his hands in a gesture of impatience. "All right, then. Say he was alive. Then how did the knife get in his back half-way down?" Clobber looked harassed. "I don't know. He had an idea . . . but that's nonsense—"

"Idea? What idea?"

"He told me this morning he didn't expect to get to the bottom of the mountain alive."

Rolf echoed: "Didn't expect?"

"Yes. He said he'd been warned. His thirty-first birthday was yesterday—the 31st of the month—and he'd been told that if he spent last night on top of the mountain, he'd never reach the bottom alive. I thought he was pulling my leg."

"Who was supposed to have told him that?"

"He said it was a dream."

Joubert said: "Oh, my God!" but Rolf's face was serious.

"Tell me, Mr. Clobber," he said, "did Heston ever mention prophetic dreams to you before?"

"Just once. About a month ago."

"And the circumstances?"

"I'd just come off duty, and I was at the lower station with Heston and Brander. Somehow or the other the conversation led to the subject of death . . ."

Clobber said: "When a man dies, he's dead. Finished. A lot of chemical compounds grouped round a skeleton. No reason to hold a body in awe. The rituals of funerals and cremations are a lot of useless hooey. There should be a law compelling the use of bodies for practical purposes—for transplants, medical research, making fertiliser—anything except burning them up or hiding them in holes in the ground under fancy headstones."

Brander was uneasy. "I don't think I can agree with you . . ."

"The trouble with you, Brander, is that you're a religious man, which also means you are a superstitious one. Try looking at hard facts. What we do with our dead is not only irrational, it's also economically wasteful.

"Last night I went to a municipal-election meeting. The speaker made what the crowd thought was a joke, but he was really being sensible. He said the wall round Woltemade cemetery was an example of useless spending—the people outside didn't want to get in, and the people inside couldn't get out . . . What's the matter with you, Brander?"

Heston suddenly interrupted. "You've upset him with all your callous talk. Can't you realise that Brander's a decent religious man who has a proper respect for the dead?"

Brander dabbed his forehead and his lips in an obvious effort to pull himself together. "No . . . no . . . it's not just that. This business about the wall and the people inside reminds me of something that's always horrified me. The idea of the dead coming to life. Even the Bible story of Lazarus . . . you see, ever since I can remember, every now and again I have a terrible nightmare. I'm with a coffin at a funeral, and suddenly from inside the box there's a loud knock . . . I feel my insides twisting in fear . . ."

Clobber said, hastily: "Sorry, Brander. Didn't mean to upset you. But if you think about it for a moment, you'll realise the whole thing's a lot of nonsense—the dead coming to life, and things like that. Absolute rubbish."

"Really?" said Heston. "What about Zombies?"

Brander gasped: "What?"

"Zombies. Dead men brought to life by voodoo in the West Indies to work in the fields. And dreams, too. I know all about prophetic dreams."

Clobber was almost spitting with rage. "What do you mean, you know? What are you getting at?"

"I'll tell you some other time," said Heston. "Here's the station wagon, and I'm in a hurry."

Joubert said: "And the next time he mentioned a dream to you was to tell you he wouldn't reach the lower station alive?"

"Yes."

"And now do you believe in prophetic dreams?"

"It's got so I don't know what to believe."

Joubert rose. "Well, I do. There are no prophesies and nothing here except a cleverly planned murder, and God help you if you did it, Clobber—because I'm going to smash your alibi."

"You can't smash the truth," said Clobber. "In any case, why should I be the one under suspicion?"

"One of the reasons," said Joubert, "is that you wear gloves."

Clobber grinned for the first time. "Then you'll have to widen your suspect list. We all wear them up here. Dimble has a pair. Ben, too. And, yes, Mrs. Orvin generally carries kid gloves."

"All right," said Joubert savagely. "That's enough for now. Tell Ben we want to see him."

Ben came, gave his evidence, and went.

"If I could prove that he and Clobber were collaborating," Joubert started, but Rolf stopped him with a shake of his head.

"No, Dirk. There is nothing between them. I could see that. You could see it, too."

"We're stymied," said Johnson. "Apparently nobody could have done it. I examined the cable-car myself, and I'm prepared to swear there's no sign of any sort of apparatus which could explain the stabbing of a man in mid-air. He was alive when he left the top, and dead at the half-way mark. It's just . . . plain impossible."

"Not quite," said Joubert. "We do know some facts. First, this is a carefully premeditated crime. Secondly, it was done before the car left the summit—"

Rolf said: "No, Dirk. The most important facts in this case lie in what Heston told Clobber—his dream of death—his thirty-first birthday—"

"What are you getting at, Oom?"

"I think I know how and why Heston was killed, Dirk. It's only a theory now, and I do not like to talk until I have proof. But you can help me get that proof . . ."

The word went round. A reconstruction of the crime. Everyone must do exactly as he did when Heston was killed.

Whispers.

"Who's going to take Heston's place?"

"The elderly chap with a beard: le Roux I think his name is. The one they call Oom Rolf."

"Do you think they'll find out anything? Do you think—?"

"We'll know soon enough, anyway."

On the lower station Joubert rang the signal for the reconstruction to start. Dimble, Mrs. Orvin, and Skager went towards the bottom car. Sergeant Botha went, too.

Rolf le Roux came through the door of the upper landing platform, and looked at Ben sweeping out the empty car.

He said: "Baas Heston spoke to you, and you stopped sweeping?"

"Yes. And then I came out of the car, like this."

"And then?"

"Then we talked."

"Where did Baas Heston stand?"

He got into the car, and stood near the door. "Yes, just about there." He paused. "Do you think you will find out who killed him?"

"It is possible."

"I hope not, Baas. This Heston was a bad man."

"All the same, it is not right that he should be killed. The murderer must be punished."

Two sharp bells rang in the driver's cabin. The car began to move. Ben went through the door up the stairs and stood in the cabin with Clobber and Johnson. They saw Rolf lean over and wave with an exaggerated gesture.

Clobber reached to lift a pair of binoculars, but Johnson gripped his arm. "Wait. Did you pick them up at this stage the first time?"

"No. I only used them after the emergency brake was applied."

"Then leave them alone now."

They watched the two cars crawling slowly across space towards each other.

In the ascending car Dimble peered approvingly at the one which was descending. "That's right," he said to Botha. "He's leaning over the door exactly as Heston . . . Good God!"

He pulled the emergency brake. Mrs. Orvin sobbed and then screamed.

The telephone rang. Botha clapped the instrument to his ear.

"Everything OK?" asked Johnson.

"No!" said Botha, "no! Something's happened to Rolf. There's a knife sticking out of his back. It looks like the same knife . . ."

From the lower station Joubert cut in excitedly. "What are you saying, Botha? It's impossible . . ."

"It's true, Inspector. I can see it quite clearly from here. And he's not moving . . ."

"Get him down here," said Joubert. "Quick!"

The cars moved again.

In the driver's cabin Johnson, through powerful binoculars, watched the car with the sagging figure go down, down, losing sight of it only as it entered the lower station.

Joubert, with Brander, stood on the landing-stage watching the approaching car. He felt suddenly lost and bewildered and angry.

"Oom Rolf," he muttered.

Brander's eyes were sombre with awe. "The Lord has given," he said, "and the Lord has taken away. Blessed be the name of the Lord."

He and Joubert stepped forward as the car bumped to a stop.

The head of the corpse with the knife in its back suddenly twisted, grinned, said gloatingly: "April fool!"

Brander shivered into shocked action. His arms waved in an ecstasy of panic. His bandaged left hand gripped the hilt of the knife held between Rolf's left arm and his body, and raised it high in a convulsive gesture. Rolf twisted away, but his movement was unnecessary. Joubert had acted, too.

Brander struggled, but only for a second. Then he stood meekly, peering in myopic surprise at the handcuffs clicking round his wrists.

"And that is how Heston was killed," said Rolf. "He died because he remembered today was April the first—All Fools Day—and because he had that type of mind, he thought of a joke, and he played it to the bitter end. A joke on Clobber, on the people in the ascending car, on Brander.

"But to Brander it was not a joke—it was horror incarnate. A dead man come to life. This was infinitely more terrible than the dream he feared of a knock from a coffin. This was like the very lid being suddenly flung open in his face. And his reaction was the typical response to panic when there is no escape—a wild uncontrollable aggression, striking out in every direction—as he struck out at me when the unthinkable happened again.

"The first time he plunged the knife into Heston. The joke became reality. The dead stopped walking."

"And now you see why there were no fingerprints on the knife. Brander is left-handed—he reached for the hot iron with that hand, remember. So it was burnt and bandaged. Bandages—no fingerprints. The way Heston was crouched, too, explains the angle of the wound."

Joubert said: "So it was not premeditated after all." Then, to Brander: "Why did you not tell the truth?"

Brander said, meekly: "Who would believe the truth?" Then, louder, with undertones of a new hysteria: "The dead are dead. They must rest in peace. Always rest. They are from hell if they walk . . ."

Then he mumbled, and his voice trailed off as he raised his eyes, and his gaze saw far beyond the mountain and the blue of the sky.

THE CROOKED PICTURE
JOHN LUTZ

HAD HE BEEN BORN a few decades earlier, John Thomas Lutz (1939–)
would have been a star in the pulp world. With more than forty novels and two
hundred short stories to his credit, he has demonstrated both the ingenuity and
work ethic of those early writers who turned out readable, entertaining prose
year after year. Born in Dallas, Texas, Lutz moved to St. Louis when young and
has lived there ever since. Before becoming a full-time writer in 1975, he had
jobs as a construction worker, theater usher, warehouse worker, truck driver,
and switchboard operator for the St. Louis Metropolitan Police Department.
His writing career is as varied as his background, producing private eye stories, political suspense, humor, occult stories, psychological suspense, tales of
espionage, historical works, futuristic writings, police procedurals, and urban
suspense fiction. His first series character, Alo Nudger, who made his debut in
Buyer Beware (1976), may be the least likely private eye in the mystery genre. He
is so compassionate that he is downright meek, a borderline coward who is an
out-and-out loser paralyzed by overdue bills, clients who refuse to pay him, and
a blood-sucking former wife. A more traditional character is the Florida-based
P.I. Fred Carver, a former cop forced off the job after a Latino street punk kneecaps him; his first appearance was in *Tropical Heat* (1986). Lutz's most commercially successful book is probably *SWF Seeks Same* (1990), a suspense thriller
that served as the basis for the 1992 movie *Single White Female* starring Bridget
Fonda and Jennifer Jason Leigh. Lutz has served as the president of the Mystery
Writers of America and has been nominated for four Edgar Awards, winning in
1986 for best short story for "Ride the Lightning."

   "The Crooked Picture" was first published in the November 1967 issue of
The Man from U.N.C.L.E. Magazine.

THE CROOKED PICTURE

JOHN LUTZ

THE ROOM was a mess. The three of them, Paul Eastmont, his wife, Laura, and his brother, Cuthbert, were sitting rigidly and morosely. They were waiting for Louis Bratten.

"But just who is this Bratten?" Laura Eastmont asked in a shaking voice. She was a very beautiful woman, on the edge of middle age.

Cuthbert, recently of several large eastern universities, said, "A drunken, insolent sot."

"And he's a genius," Paul Eastmont added, "in his own peculiar way. More importantly, he's my friend." He placed a hand on his wife's wrist. "Bratten is the most discreet man I know."

Laura shivered. "I hope so, Paul."

Cuthbert rolled his king-size cigarette between thumb and forefinger, an annoyed look on his young, aquiline face. "I don't see why you put such stock in the man, Paul. He's run the gamut of alcoholic degeneration. From chief of homicide to—what? If I remember correctly, you told me some time ago that they'd taken away his private investigator's license."

He saw that he was upsetting his sister-in-law even more and shrugged his thin shoulders. "My point is that he's hardly the sort of man to be confided in concerning *this*." He looked thoughtful. "On the other hand, half of what he says is known to be untrue anyway."

The butler knocked lightly, pushed one of the den's double doors open, and Louie Bratten entered. He was a blocky, paunchy little man of about forty, with a perpetual squint in one eye.

His coarse, dark hair was mussed, his suit was rumpled, and his unclasped tie hung crookedly outside one lapel. He looked as if he'd just stepped out of a hurricane.

"Bratten!" Paul Eastmont said in warm greeting. "You don't know how glad I am to have you in on this!"

Cuthbert nodded coldly. "Mr. Bratten."

Laura stared intently at her hands, which were folded in her lap.

"Give me a drink," Bratten said.

Paul crossed to the portable bar and poured him a straight scotch, no ice.

Bratten sipped the scotch, smacked his lips in satisfaction, and then slouched in the most comfortable leather armchair in the den.

"Now, what's bugging you, Paul?" he asked.

Cuthbert stood and leaned on the mantel. "It's hardly a matter to be taken lightly," he said coldly.

"How in the hell can I take it lightly," Bratten asked, "when I don't even know what the matter is?"

Paul raised a hand for silence. "Let me explain briefly. Several years ago, before Laura and I had met, a picture was taken of her in a very—compromising pose. This photo fell into the hands of a blackmailer named Hays, who has been milking us for two hundred dollars a month for the past four years. Recently Hays needed some cash badly. He offered to give me the photo for five thousand dollars."

Paul Eastmont glanced protectively at his embarrassed wife. "Naturally I agreed, and the deal was made. The negative, incidentally, was destroyed long ago, and I happen to know that the photo wasn't reproduced at any time since by taking a picture of it. That was part of the original blackmail arrangement. It's the only picture in existence, an eight-by-ten glossy."

"Interesting," Bratten said.

"But Hays turned out to be a stubborn sort," Paul went on. "He gave me the photograph yesterday, and like a fool I didn't destroy it. He saw me put it in my wall safe. Last night he broke in here and tried to steal it back."

"And did he?"

"We don't know. Clark, the butler, sleeps in that part of the house, and he heard Hays tinkering about. He surprised him as he ran in here."

"Terrific scotch," Bratten said. "Did he have the photo?"

"Yes. It wasn't in the wall safe. As you can see, he hurriedly rummaged about in this room, lifting cushions, knocking over the lamp, we think looking for a place to hide the photo. Then he leaped out the window."

"Caught?"

"Hurt himself when he landed and couldn't run fast enough. Shot dead by the police just outside the gate. And he didn't have the photo on his body, nor was it on the grounds."

"Hays was a smart blackmailer," Bratten said. He squinted at Paul. "You left the room as it was?"

Paul nodded. "I know your peculiar way of working. But the photo must be in this room. We looked everywhere, but we didn't disturb anything, put everything back exactly the way we found it."

"Ah, that's good," Bratten said, either of the scotch or of the Eastmonts' actions. "Another drink, if you please." He handed the empty glass up to Cuthbert, who was the only one standing.

"Really," Cuthbert said, grabbing the glass. "If I had my way we wouldn't have confided this to you."

"We never did hit it off, did we?" Bratten laughed. "That's probably because you have too much education. Ruins a man sometimes. Restricts his thinking."

Cuthbert reluctantly gave Bratten his fresh drink. "You should be an expert on ruination."

"Touch. That means touché in English." Bratten leaned back and ran his tongue over his lips. "This puts me in mind of another case. One about ten years ago. There was this locked-room-type murder—"

"What on earth does a locked-room murder have to do with this case?" Cuthbert interrupted in agitation.

"Everything, you idiot."

Paul motioned for Cuthbert to be silent, and Bratten continued.

"Like they say," Bratten said, "there's a parallel here." He took a sip of scotch and nonchalantly hung one leg over an arm of his chair. "There were these four brothers, rich, well bred—like Cuthbert here, only with savvy. They'd made their pile on some cheap real estate development out West. The point is, the business was set up so one of the brothers controlled most of the money, and they didn't get along too well to start off with."

He raised his glass and made a mock bow to Cuthbert. "In language you'd understand, it was a classic sibling rivalry intensified by economic inequality. What it all meant was that if this one brother was dead, the other three would profit a hell of a lot. And lo and behold, this one brother did somehow get dead. That's when I was called into the case by a friend of mine, a local sheriff in Illinois.

"Seems one of the brothers had bought a big old house up in a remote wooded area, and six months later the four of them met up there for a business conference or something. The three surviving brothers' story was simply that their brother had gone into this room, locked the door, and never came out. Naturally not, lying in the middle of the floor with a knife in his chest."

"I fail to see any parallel whatever so far," Cuthbert said.

"The thing of it was, this room was locked from the inside with a sliding bolt and a key still in the keyhole. The one window that opened was locked and there wasn't a mark on the sill. It was summer, and the ground was hard, but I don't think we would have found anything outside anyway."

"Secret panel, no doubt," Cuthbert said.

"Nope. It did happen to be a paneled room, though. We went over that room from wall to wall, ceiling to floor. There was no way out but the door or the window. And to make the thing really confusing, the knife was wiped clean of prints, and there was nothing nearby the dying man could have used to do that, even if he'd been crazy enough to want to for some reason. There was no sign of a struggle, or of any blood other than what had soaked into the rug around the body.

"Without question the corpse was lying where it fell. On the seat of a chair was an open book, and on an end table was a half-empty cup of coffee with the dead man's prints on it. But there was one other thing in the room that caught my attention."

"Well, get it over with and get to the business at hand," Cuthbert said, trying to conceal his interest. "Who was it and how was it done?"

"Another drink," Bratten said, handing up his glass. "Now here was the situation: dead man in a locked room, three suspects with good motives who were in the same house at the time of the murder, and a knife without prints. The coroner's inquest could come to no conclusion but suicide unless the way the murderer left the room was explained. Without that explanation, no jury could convict."

Bratten paused to take a long pull of scotch. "The authorities thought they were licked, and my sheriff friend and I were walking around the outside of the house, talking about how hopeless things were, when I found it."

"The solution?" Cuthbert asked.

"No. A nail. And a shiny one."

"Good Lord," Cuthbert said.

"Doesn't that suggest something to you?"

"It suggests somebody dropped a nail," Cuthbert said furiously.

"Well, I tied that in with what had caught my attention inside the room," Bratten said, "and like they say, everything fell into place. We contacted the former owners of the house, who were in Europe, snooped around a bit, and that was that. We got a confession right away."

Cuthbert was incredulous. "Because of a nail?"

"Not entirely," Bratten said. "How about another drink, while you're up?"

Cuthbert turned to Paul. "How do you expect this sot to help us if he's dead drunk?"

"Give him another," Paul said, "and let him finish."

His face livid, Cuthbert poured Bratten another glass of scotch. "What was it you saw in the room that you connected with the nail you found?"

"A picture," Bratten said. "It was hanging crooked, though everything else in the room was in order. It's things like that that bring first daylight to a case." He looked at Cuthbert as if he were observing some kind of odd animal life. "You still don't get it?"

"No," Cuthbert said, controlling himself. "And as I first suspected, there is no parallel whatsoever with our problem."

Bratten shrugged. "What the brothers did was this: through their business, they gathered the materials secretly over a period of time and got things ready. When the time was right, they got their victim to go out there with them and stabbed him on the spot, then wiped the knife handle clean. They had the concrete block foundation, the floor, the roof, and all but one of the walls up. They built in an L of the big house so there were only two walls to bother with. They even had the rug and furniture down and ready."

"After the victim was dead, they quickly put up the last wall, already paneled like the rest on the inside and shingled with matching shingles on the outside, and called the police. In short, the locked room was prefabricated and built around the body."

Cuthbert's mouth was open. "Unbelievable!"

"Not really," Bratten said. "No one would think to check and see how many rooms the house had, and they did a real good job on the one they built. Of course on close examination you could tell. The heating duct was a dummy, and the half of the molding that fitted against the last wall had dummy nail heads in it."

"But from the outside the room was perfect. The shingles matched and the metal corner flashing was a worn piece taken from another part of the house. The trouble was they didn't think to use old nails, and they didn't want to leave the inside of that last wall bare when they fit it in place."

"An amusing story, I admit," Cuthbert said.

"True or not. Now if you'll be so kind as to point out this damned parallel you keep talking about . . ."

Bratten looked surprised. "Why, the picture, you imbecile! The crooked picture on the last wall!" He pointed to a cheap oil painting that hung on the Eastmonts' wall.

"But that picture is straight!" Cuthbert yelled in frustration. "It is immaculately straight!"

"Exactly, you learned jackass. It's the only thing in this fouled-up room besides my drink that is immaculately straight. And I suspect if you look between the painting and the cardboard backing, you'll find your photograph."

They did.

CARTER DICKSON

BY THE TIME John Dickson Carr (1906–1977) turned twenty-four, he had seen more than fifty of his stories and poems published in high school and Haverford College magazines and his first novel, *It Walks by Night* (1930), released by Harper & Brothers. He went on to write nearly ninety books, three dozen short stories, seven plays, and more than ninety radio dramas. Most of his output was written under his own name, but he produced a historical adventure novel, *Devil Kinsmere* (1934), as Roger Fairbairn; a mystery novel, *The Bowstring Murders* (1933), as Carr Dickson; and twenty-six books as Carter Dickson, mostly in the series about Sir Henry Merrivale. The series of twenty-two novels begins with *The Plague Court Murders* (1934), one of the greatest locked-room mysteries of all time. Carr also enjoyed collaborating with other writers, producing *Fatal Descent* (1939; British title: *Drop to His Death*) with Major C. J. C. Street (using the pseudonym John Rhode), on whom he based one of his detectives, Colonel March of Scotland Yard, and *The Exploits of Sherlock Holmes* (1954) with Adrian Conan Doyle.

Merrivale, who liked to refer to himself as "The Old Man," was Carr's personal favorite among his protagonists. Although it has often been suggested that the barrel-shaped, cigar-chomping detective was based on Sir Winston Churchill, Carr denied it, though it may be easily perceived that Merrivale becomes more and more like the distinguished prime minister as the series progresses.

"Blind Man's Hood" was first published in the April 1938 issue of *The Strand Magazine*; it was first collected in *The Department of Queer Complaints* (London, William Heinemann, 1940).

BLIND MAN'S HOOD

CARTER DICKSON

ALTHOUGH ONE snowflake had already sifted past the lights, the great doors of the house stood open. It seemed less a snowflake than a shadow; for a bitter wind whipped after it, and the doors creaked. Inside, Rodney and Muriel Hunter could see a dingy, narrow hall paved in dull red tiles, with a Jacobean staircase at the rear. (At that time, of course, there was no dead woman lying inside.)

To find such a place in the loneliest part of the Weald of Kent—a seventeenth-century country house whose floors had grown humped and its beams scrubbed by the years—was what they had expected. Even to find electricity was not surprising. But Rodney Hunter thought he had seldom seen so many lights in one house, and Muriel had been wondering about it ever since their car turned the bend in the road. "Clearlawns" lived up to its name. It stood in the midst of a slope of flat grass, now wiry white with frost, and there was no tree or shrub within twenty yards of it. Those lights contrasted with a certain inhospitable and damp air about the house, as though the owner were compelled to keep them burning.

"But why is the front door *open*?" insisted Muriel.

In the drive-way, the engine of their car coughed and died. The house was now a secret blackness of gables, emitting light at every chink, and silhouetting the stalks of the wisteria vines which climbed it. On either side of the front door were little-paned windows whose curtains had not been drawn. Towards their left they could see into a low dining-room, with table and sideboard set for a cold supper; towards their right was a darkish library moving with the reflections of a bright fire.

The sight of the fire warmed Rodney Hunter, but it made him feel guilty. They were very late. At five o'clock, without fail, he had promised Jack Bannister, they would be at "Clearlawns" to inaugurate the Christmas party.

Engine-trouble in leaving London was one thing; idling at a country pub along the way, drinking hot ale and listening to the wireless sing carols until a sort of Dickensian jollity stole into you, was something else. But both he and Muriel were young; they were very fond of each other and of things in general; and they had worked themselves into a glow of Christmas, which—as they stood before the creaking doors of "Clearlawns"—grew oddly cool.

There was no real reason, Rodney thought, to feel disquiet. He hoisted their luggage, including a big box of presents for Jack and Molly's children, out of the rear of the car. That his footsteps should sound loud on the gravel was only natural. He put his head into the doorway and whistled. Then he began to bang the knocker. Its sound seemed to seek out every corner of the house and then come back like a questing dog; but there was no response.

"I'll tell you something else," he said. "There's nobody in the house."

Muriel ran up the three steps to stand beside

him. She had drawn her fur coat close around her, and her face was bright with cold.

"But that's impossible!" she said. "I mean, even if they're out, the servants——! Molly told me she keeps a cook and two maids. Are you sure we've got the right place?"

"Yes. The name's on the gate, and there's no other house within a mile."

With the same impulse they craned their necks to look through the windows of the dining-room on the left. Cold fowl on the sideboard, a great bowl of chestnuts; and, now they could see it, another good fire, before which stood a chair with a piece of knitting put aside on it. Rodney tried the knocker again, vigorously, but the sound was all wrong. It was as though they were even more lonely in that core of light, with the east wind rushing across the Weald, and the door creaking again.

"I suppose we'd better go in," said Rodney. He added, with a lack of Christmas spirit: "Here, this is a devil of a trick! What do you think has happened? I'll swear that fire has been made up in the last fifteen minutes."

He stepped into the hall and set down the bags. As he was turning to close the door, Muriel put her hand on his arm.

"I say, Rod. Do you think you'd better close it?"

"Why not?"

"I—I don't know."

"The place is getting chilly enough as it is," he pointed out, unwilling to admit that the same thought had occurred to him. He closed both doors and shot their bar into place; and, at the same moment, a girl came out of the door to the library on the right.

She was such a pleasant-faced girl that they both felt a sense of relief. Why she had not answered the knocking had ceased to be a question; she filled a void. She was pretty, not more than twenty-one or -two, and had an air of primness which made Rodney Hunter vaguely associate her with a governess or a secretary, though Jack Bannister had never mentioned any such person. She was plump, but with a curiously narrow waist; and she wore brown. Her brown

hair was neatly parted, and her brown eyes— long eyes, which might have given a hint of secrecy or curious smiles if they had not been so placid—looked concerned. In one hand she carried what looked like a small white bag of linen or cotton. And she spoke with a dignity which did not match her years.

"I am most terribly sorry," she told them. "I *thought* I heard someone, but I was so busy that I could not be sure. Will you forgive me?"

She smiled. Hunter's private view was that his knocking had been loud enough to wake the dead; but he murmured conventional things. As though conscious of some faint incongruity about the white bag in her hand, she held it up.

"For Blind Man's Bluff," she explained. "They do cheat so, I'm afraid, and not only the children. If one uses an ordinary handkerchief tied round the eyes, they always manage to get a corner loose. But if you take this, and you put it fully over a person's head, and you tie it round the neck"—a sudden gruesome image occurred to Rodney Hunter—"then it works so much better, don't you think?" Her eyes seemed to turn inward, and to grow absent. "But I must not keep you talking here. You are——?"

"My name is Hunter. This is my wife. I'm afraid we've arrived late, but I understood Mr. Bannister was expecting——"

"He did not tell you?" asked the girl in brown.

"Tell me what?"

"Everyone here, including the servants, is always out of the house at this hour on this particular date. It is the custom; I believe it has been the custom for more than sixty years. There is some sort of special church service."

Rodney Hunter's imagination had been devising all sorts of fantastic explanations: the first of them being that this demure lady had murdered the members of the household, and was engaged in disposing of the bodies. What put this nonsensical notion into his head he could not tell, unless it was his own profession of detective-story writing. But he felt relieved to hear a commonplace explanation. Then the woman spoke again.

"Of course, it is a pretext, really. The rector,

that dear man, invented it all those years ago to save embarrassment. What happened here had nothing to do with the murder, since the dates were so different; and I suppose most people have forgotten now why the tenants *do* prefer to stay away during seven and eight o'clock on Christmas Eve. I doubt if Mrs. Bannister even knows the real reason, though I should imagine Mr. Bannister must know it. But what happens here cannot be very pleasant, and it wouldn't do to have the children see it—would it?"

Muriel spoke with such sudden directness that her husband knew she was afraid. "Who are you?" Muriel said. "And what on earth are you talking about?"

"I am quite sane, really," their hostess assured them, with a smile that was half-cheery and half-coy. "I dare say it must be all very confusing to you, poor dear. But I am forgetting my duties. Please come in and sit down before the fire, and let me offer you something to drink."

She took them into the library on the right, going ahead with a walk that was like a bounce, and looking over her shoulder out of those long eyes. The library was a long, low room with beams. The windows towards the road were uncurtained; but those in the side-wall, where a faded red-brick fireplace stood, were bay windows with draperies closed across them. As their hostess put them before the fire, Hunter could have sworn he saw one of the draperies move.

"You need not worry about it," she assured him, following his glance towards the bay. "Even if you looked in there, you might not see anything now. I believe some gentleman did try it once, a long time ago. He stayed in the house for a wager. But when he pulled the curtain back, he did not see anything in the bay—at least, anything quite. He felt some hair, and it moved. That is why they have so many lights nowadays."

Muriel had sat down on a sofa, and was lighting a cigarette: to the rather prim disapproval of their hostess, Hunter thought.

"May we have a hot drink?" Muriel asked crisply. "And then, if you don't mind, we might walk over and meet the Bannisters coming from church."

"Oh, please don't do that!" cried the other. She had been standing by the fireplace, her hands folded and turned outwards. Now she ran across to sit down beside Muriel; and the swiftness of her movement, no less than the touch of her hand on Muriel's arm, made the latter draw back.

Hunter was now completely convinced that their hostess was out of her head. Why she held such fascination for him, though, he could not understand. In her eagerness to keep them there, the girl had come upon a new idea. On a table behind the sofa, book-ends held a row of modern novels. Conspicuously displayed—probably due to Molly Bannister's tact—were two of Rodney Hunter's detective stories. The girl put a finger on them.

"May I ask if you wrote these?"

He admitted it.

"Then," she said with sudden composure, "it would probably interest you to hear about the murder. It was a most perplexing business, you know; the police could make nothing of it, and no one ever has been able to solve it." An arresting eye fixed on his. "It happened out in the hall there. A poor woman was killed where there was no one to kill her, and no one could have done it. But she was murdered."

Hunter started to get up from his chair; then he changed his mind, and sat down again. "Go on," he said.

"You must forgive me if I am a little uncertain about dates," she urged. "I think it was in the early eighteen-seventies, and I am sure it was in early February—because of the snow. It was a bad winter then; the farmers' livestock all died. My people have been bred up in the district for years, and I know that. The house here was much as it is now, except that there was none of this lighting (only paraffin lamps, poor girl!); and you were obliged to pump up what water you wanted; and people read the newspaper quite through, and discussed it for days.

"The people were a little different to look at, too. I am sure I do not understand why we think beards are so strange nowadays; they seem to think that men who had beards never had any emotions. But even young men wore them then, and looked handsome enough. There was a newly married couple living in this house at the time: at least, they had been married only the summer before. They were named Edward and Jane Waycross, and it was considered a good match everywhere.

"Edward Waycross did not have a beard, but he had bushy side-whiskers which he kept curled. He was not a handsome man, either, being somewhat dry and hard-favoured; but he was a religious man, and a good man, and an excellent man of business, they say: a manufacturer of agricultural implements at Hawkhurst. He had determined that Jane Anders (as she was) would make him a good wife, and I dare say she did. The girl had several suitors. Although Mr. Waycross was the best match, I know it surprised people a little when she accepted him, because she was thought to have been fond of another man—a more striking man, whom many of the young girls were after. This was Jeremy Wilkes: who came of a very good family, but was considered wicked. He was no younger than Mr. Waycross, but he had a great black beard, and wore white waistcoats with gold chains, and drove a gig. Of course, there had been gossip, but that was because Jane Anders was considered pretty."

Their hostess had been sitting back against the sofa, quietly folding the little white bag with one hand, and speaking in a prim voice. Now she did something which turned her hearers cold.

You have probably seen the same thing done many times. She had been touching her cheek lightly with the fingers of the other hand. In doing so, she touched the flesh at the corner under her lower eyelid, and accidentally drew down the corner of that eyelid—which should have exposed the red part of the inner lid at the corner of the eye. It was not red. It was of a sickly pale colour.

"In the course of his business dealings," she went on, "Mr. Waycross had often to go to London, and usually he was obliged to remain overnight. But Jane Waycross was not afraid to remain alone in the house. She had a good servant, a staunch old woman, and a good dog. Even so, Mr. Waycross commended her for her courage."

The girl smiled. "On the night I wish to tell you of, in February, Mr. Waycross was absent. Unfortunately, too, the old servant was absent; she had been called away as a midwife to attend her cousin, and Jane Waycross had allowed her to go. This was known in the village, since all such affairs are well known, and some uneasiness was felt—this house being isolated, as you know. But she was not afraid.

"It was a very cold night, with a heavy fall of snow which had stopped about nine o'clock. You must know, beyond doubt, that poor Jane Waycross was alive after it had stopped snowing. It must have been nearly half-past nine when a Mr. Moody—a very good and sober man who lived in Hawkhurst—was driving home along the road past this house. As you know, it stands in the middle of a great bare stretch of lawn; and you can see the house clearly from the road. Mr. Moody saw poor Jane at the window of one of the upstairs bedrooms, with a candle in her hand, closing the shutters. But he was not the only witness who saw her alive.

"On that same evening, Mr. Wilkes (the handsome gentleman I spoke to you of a moment ago) had been at a tavern in the village of Five Ashes with Dr. Sutton, the local doctor, and a racing gentleman named Pawley. At about half-past eleven they started to drive home in Mr. Wilkes's gig to Cross-in-Hand. I am afraid they had been drinking, but they were all in their sober senses. The landlord of the tavern remembered the time because he had stood in the doorway to watch the gig, which had fine yellow wheels, go spanking away as though there were no snow; and Mr. Wilkes in one of the new round hats with a curly brim.

"There was a bright moon. 'And no danger,' Dr. Sutton always said afterwards; 'shadows of trees and fences as clear as though a silhouette-cutter had made 'em for sixpence.' But when they were passing this house Mr. Wilkes pulled up sharp. There was a bright light in the window of one of the downstairs rooms—this room, in fact. They sat out there looking round the hood of the gig, and wondering.

"Mr. Wilkes spoke: 'I don't like this,' he said. 'You know, gentlemen, that Waycross is still in London; and the lady in question is in the habit of retiring early. I am going up there to find out if anything is wrong.'

"With that he jumped out of the gig, his black beard jutting out and his breath smoking. He said: 'And if it is a burglar, then, by Something, gentlemen'—I will not repeat the word he used—'by Something, gentlemen, I'll settle him.' He walked through the gate and up to the house—they could follow every step he made—and looked into the windows of this room here. Presently he returned looking relieved (they could see him by the light of the gig lamps), but wiping the moisture off his forehead.

"'It is all right,' he said to them; 'Waycross has come home. But, by Something, gentlemen, he is growing thinner these days, or it is shadows.'

"Then he told them what he had seen. If you look through the front windows—there—you can look sideways and see out through the doorway into the main hall. He said he had seen Mrs. Waycross standing in the hall with her back to the staircase, wearing a blue dressing-wrap over her nightgown, and her hair down round her shoulders. Standing in front of her, with his back to Mr. Wilkes, was a tallish, thin man like Mr. Waycross, with a long greatcoat and a tall hat like Mr. Waycross's. *She* was carrying either a candle or a lamp; and he remembered how the tall hat seemed to wag back and forth, as though the man were talking to her or putting out his hands towards her. For he said he could not see the woman's face.

"Of course, it was not Mr. Waycross; but how were they to know that?

"At about seven o'clock next morning, Mrs. Randall, the old servant, returned. (A fine boy had been born to her cousin the night before.) Mrs. Randall came home through the white

dawn and the white snow, and found the house all locked up. She could get no answer to her knocking. Being a woman of great resolution, she eventually broke a window and got in. But, when she saw what was in the front hall, she went out screaming for help.

"Poor Jane was past help. I know I should not speak of these things; but I must. She was lying on her face in the hall. From the waist down her body was much charred and—unclothed, you know, because fire had burnt away most of the nightgown and the dressing-wrap. The tiles of the hall were soaked with blood and paraffin oil, the oil having come from a broken lamp with a thick blue-silk shade which was lying a little distance away. Near it was a china candlestick with a candle. This fire had also charred a part of the panelling of the wall, and a part of the staircase. Fortunately, the floor is of brick tiles, and there had not been much paraffin left in the lamp, or the house would have been set afire.

"But she had not died from burns alone. Her throat had been cut with a deep slash from some very sharp blade. But she had been alive for a while to feel both things, for she had crawled forward on her hands while she was burning. It was a cruel death, a horrible death for a soft person like that."

There was a pause. The expression on the face of the narrator, the plump girl in the brown dress, altered slightly. So did the expression of her eyes. She was sitting beside Muriel; and moved a little closer.

"Of course, the police came. I do not understand such things, I am afraid, but they found that the house had not been robbed. They also noticed the odd thing I have mentioned, that there was both a lamp *and* a candle in a candlestick near her. The lamp came from Mr. and Mrs. Waycross's bedroom upstairs, and so did the candlestick: there were no other lamps or candles downstairs except the lamps waiting to be filled next morning in the back kitchen. But the police thought she would not have come downstairs carrying both the lamp *and* the candle as well.

"She must have brought the lamp, because that was broken. When the murderer took hold of her, they thought, she had dropped the lamp, and it went out; the paraffin spilled, but did not catch fire. Then this man in the tall hat, to finish his work after he had cut her throat, went upstairs, and got a candle, and set fire to the spilled oil. I am stupid at these things; but even I should have guessed that this must mean someone familiar with the house. Also, if she came downstairs, it must have been to let someone in at the front door; and that could not have been a burglar.

"You may be sure all the gossips were like police from the start, even when the police hemm'd and haw'd, because they knew Mrs. Waycross must have opened the door to a man who was not her husband. And immediately they found an indication of this, in the mess that the fire and blood had made in the hall. Some distance away from poor Jane's body there was a medicine-bottle, such as chemists use. I think it had been broken in two pieces; and on one intact piece they found sticking some fragments of a letter that had not been quite burned. It was in a man's handwriting, not her husband's, and they made out enough of it to understand. It was full of—expressions of love, you know, and it made an appointment to meet her there on that night."

Rodney Hunter, as the girl paused, felt impelled to ask a question.

"Did they know whose handwriting it was?"

"It was Jeremy Wilkes's," replied the other simply. "Though they never proved that, never more than slightly suspected it, and the circumstances did not bear it out. In fact, a knife stained with blood was actually found in Mr. Wilkes's possession. But the police never brought it to anything, poor souls. For, you see, not Mr. Wilkes—or anyone else in the world—could possibly have done the murder."

"I don't understand that," said Hunter, rather sharply.

"Forgive me if I am stupid about telling things," urged their hostess in a tone of apology. She seemed to be listening to the chimney growl under a cold sky, and listening with hard, placid eyes. "But even the village gossips could tell that. When Mrs. Randall came here to the house on that morning, both the front and the back doors were locked and securely bolted on the inside. All the windows were locked on the inside. If you will look at the fastenings in this dear place, you will know what that means.

"But, bless you, that was the least of it! I told you about the snow. The snowfall had stopped at nine o'clock in the evening, hours and hours before Mrs. Waycross was murdered. When the police came, there were only two separate sets of footprints in the great unmarked half-acre of snow round the house. One set belonged to Mr. Wilkes, who had come up and looked in through the window the night before. The other belonged to Mrs. Randall. The police could follow and explain both sets of tracks; but there were no other tracks at all, and no one was hiding in the house.

"Of course, it was absurd to suspect Mr. Wilkes. It was not only that he told a perfectly straight story about the man in the tall hat; but both Dr. Sutton and Mr. Pawley, who drove back with him from Five Ashes, were there to swear he could not have done it. You understand, he came no closer to the house than the windows of this room. They could watch every step he made in the moonlight, and they did. Afterwards he drove home with Dr. Sutton, and slept there, or, I should say, they continued their terrible drinking until daylight. It is true that they found in his possession a knife with blood on it, but he explained that he had used the knife to gut a rabbit.

"It was the same with poor Mrs. Randall, who had been up all night about her midwife's duties, though naturally it was even more absurd to think of *her*. But there were no other footprints at all, either coming to or going from the house, in all that stretch of snow; and all the ways in or out were locked on the inside."

It was Muriel who spoke then, in a voice that

tried to be crisp, but wavered in spite of her. "Are you telling us that all this is true?" she demanded.

"I am teasing you a little, my dear," said the other. "But, really and truly, it all did happen. Perhaps I will show you in a moment."

"I suppose it was really the husband who did it?" asked Muriel in a bored tone.

"Poor Mr. Waycross!" said their hostess tenderly. "He spent that night in a temperance hotel near Charing Cross Station, as he always did, and, of course, he never left it. When he learned about his wife's duplicity"—again Hunter thought she was going to pull down a corner of her eyelid—"it nearly drove him out of his mind, poor fellow. I think he gave up agricultural machinery and took to preaching, but I am not sure. I know he left the district soon afterwards, and before he left he insisted on burning the mattress of their bed. It was a dreadful scandal."

"But in that case," insisted Hunter, "who did kill her? And, if there were no footprints and all the doors were locked, how did the murderer come or go? Finally, if all this happened in February, what does it have to do with people being out of the house on Christmas Eve?"

"Ah, that is the real story. That is what I meant to tell you."

She grew very subdued.

"It must have been very interesting to watch the people alter and grow older, or find queer paths, in the years afterwards. For, of course, nothing did happen as yet. The police presently gave it all up; for decency's sake it was allowed to rest. There was a new pump built in the market square; and the news of the Prince of Wales's going to India in '75 to talk about; and presently a new family came to live at 'Clearlawns,' and began to raise their children. The trees and the rains in summer were just the same, you know. It must have been seven or eight years before anything happened, for Jane Waycross was very patient.

"Several of the people had died in the meantime. Mrs. Randall had, in a fit of quinsy; and

so had Dr. Sutton, but that was a great mercy, because he fell by the way when he was going out to perform an amputation with too much of the drink in him. But Mr. Pawley had prospered—and, above all, so had Mr. Wilkes. He had become an even finer figure of a man, they tell me, as he drew near middle age. When he married he gave up all his loose habits. Yes, he married; it was the Tinsley heiress, Miss Linshaw, whom he had been courting at the time of the murder; and I have heard that poor Jane Waycross, even after *she* was married to Mr. Waycross, used to bite her pillow at night because she was so horribly jealous of Miss Linshaw.

"Mr. Wilkes had always been tall, and now he was finely stout. He always wore frock-coats. Though he had lost most of his hair, his beard was full and curly; he had twinkling black eyes, and twinkling ruddy cheeks, and a bluff voice. All the children ran to him. They say he broke as many feminine hearts as before. At any wholesome entertainment he was always the first to lead the cotillion or applaud the fiddler, and I do not know what hostesses would have done without him.

"On Christmas Eve, then—remember, I am not sure of the date—the Fentons gave a Christmas party. The Fentons were the very nice family who had taken this house afterwards, you know. There was to be no dancing, but all the old games. Naturally, Mr. Wilkes was the first of all to be invited, and the first to accept; for everything was all smoothed away by time, like the wrinkles in last year's counterpane; and what's past *is* past, or so they say. They had decorated the house with holly and mistletoe, and guests began to arrive as early as two in the afternoon.

"I had all this from Mrs. Fenton's aunt (one of the Warwickshire Abbotts), who was actually staying here at the time. In spite of such a festal season, the preparations had not been going at all well that day, though such preparations usually did. Miss Abbott complained that there was a nasty earthy smell in the house. It was a dark and raw day, and the chimneys did not seem to draw as well as they should. What is more, Mrs. Fenton cut her finger when she was carving the cold fowl, because she said one of the children had been hiding behind the window-curtains in here, and peeping out at her; she was very angry. But Mr. Fenton, who was going about the house in his carpet slippers before the arrival of the guests, called her 'Mother' and said that it was Christmas.

"It is certainly true that they forgot all about this when the fun of the games began. Such squealings you never heard!—or so I am told. Foremost of all at Bobbing for Apples or Nuts in May was Mr. Jeremy Wilkes. He stood, gravely paternal, in the midst of everything, with his ugly wife beside him, and stroked his beard. He saluted each of the ladies on the cheek under the mistletoe; there was also some scampering to salute him; and, though he *did* remain for longer than was necessary behind the window-curtains with the younger Miss Twigelow, his wife only smiled. There was only one unpleasant incident, soon forgotten. Towards dusk a great gusty wind began to come up, with the chimneys smoking worse than usual. It being nearly dark, Mr. Fenton said it was time to fetch in the Snapdragon Bowl, and watch it flame. You know the game? It is a great bowl of lighted spirit, and you must thrust in your hand and pluck out a raisin from the bottom without scorching your fingers. Mr. Fenton carried it in on a tray in the half-darkness; it was flickering with that bluish flame you have seen on Christmas puddings. Miss Abbott said that once, in carrying it, he started and turned round. She said that for a second she thought there was a face looking over his shoulder, and it wasn't a nice face.

"Later in the evening, when the children were sleepy and there was tissue-paper scattered all over the house, the grown-ups began their games in earnest. Someone suggested Blind Man's Bluff. They were mostly using the hall and this room here, as having more space than the dining-room. Various members of the party were blindfolded with the men's handkerchiefs; but there was a dreadful amount of cheating. Mr.

Fenton grew quite annoyed about it, because the ladies almost always caught Mr. Wilkes when they could; Mr. Wilkes was laughing and perspiring heartily, and his great cravat with the silver pin had almost come loose.

"To make it certain nobody could cheat, Mr. Fenton got a little white linen bag—like this one. It was the pillow-cover off the baby's cot, really; and he said nobody could look through that if it were tied over the head.

"I should explain that they had been having some trouble with the lamp in this room. Mr. Fenton said: 'Confound it, Mother, what is wrong with that lamp? Turn up the wick, will you?' It was really quite a good lamp from Spence and Minstead's, and should not have burned so dull as it did. In the confusion, while Mrs. Fenton was trying to make the light better, and he was looking over his shoulder at her, Mr. Fenton had been rather absently fastening the bag on the head of the last person caught. He has said since that he did not notice who it was. No one else noticed, either, the light being so dim and there being such a large number of people. It seemed to be a girl in a broad bluish kind of dress, standing over near the door.

"Perhaps you know how people act when they have just been blindfolded in this game. First they usually stand very still, as though they were smelling or sensing in which direction to go. Sometimes they make a sudden jump, or sometimes they begin to shuffle gently forward. Everyone noticed what an air of *purpose* there seemed to be about this person whose face was covered; she went forward very slowly, and seemed to crouch down a bit.

"It began to move towards Mr. Wilkes in very short but quick little jerks, the white bag bobbing on its face. At this time Mr. Wilkes was sitting at the end of the table, laughing, with his face pink above the beard, and a glass of our Kentish cider in his hand. I want you to imagine this room as being very dim, and much more cluttered, what with all the tassels they had on the furniture then; and the high-piled hair of the ladies, too. The hooded person got to the edge of the table. It began to edge along towards Mr. Wilkes's chair; and then it jumped.

"Mr. Wilkes got up and skipped (yes, skipped) out of its way, laughing. It waited quietly, after which it went, in the same slow way, towards him again. It nearly got him again, by the edge of the potted plant. All this time it did not say anything, you understand, although everyone was applauding it and crying encouraging advice. It kept its head down. Miss Abbott says she began to notice an unpleasant faint smell of burnt cloth or something worse, which turned her half-ill. By the time the hooded person came stooping clear across the room, as certainly as though it could see him, Mr. Wilkes was not laughing any longer.

"In the corner by one bookcase, he said out loud: 'I'm tired of this silly, rotten game; go away, do you hear?' Nobody there had ever heard him speak like that, in such a loud, wild way, but they laughed and thought it must be the Kentish cider. 'Go away!' cried Mr. Wilkes again, and began to strike at it with his fist. All this time, Miss Abbott says, she had observed his face gradually changing. He dodged again, very pleasant and nimble for such a big man, but with the perspiration running down his face. Back across the room he went again, with it following him; and he cried out something that most naturally shocked them all inexpressibly.

"He screamed out: 'For God's sake, Fenton, take it off me!'

"And for the last time the thing jumped.

"They were over near the curtains of that bay window, which were drawn as they are now. Miss Twigelow, who was nearest, says that Mr. Wilkes could not have seen anything, because the white bag was still drawn over the woman's head. The only thing she noticed was that at the lower part of the bag, where the face must have been, there was a curious kind of discoloration, a stain of some sort which had not been there before: something seemed to be seeping through. Mr. Wilkes fell back between the curtains, with the hooded person after him, and screamed again. There was a kind of thrashing noise in or behind

the curtains; then they fell straight again, and everything grew quiet.

"Now, our Kentish cider is very strong, and for a moment Mr. Fenton did not know what to think. He tried to laugh at it, but the laugh did not sound well. Then he went over to the curtains, calling out gruffly to them to come out of there and not play the fool. But, after he had looked inside the curtains, he turned round very sharply and asked the rector to get the ladies out of the room. This was done, but Miss Abbott often said that she had one quick peep inside. Though the bay windows were locked on the inside, Mr. Wilkes was now alone on the window seat. She could see his beard sticking up, and the blood. He was dead, of course. But, since he had murdered Jane Waycross, I sincerely think that he deserved to die."

For several seconds the two listeners did not move. She had all too successfully conjured up this room in the late 'seventies, whose stuffiness still seemed to pervade it now.

"But look here!" protested Hunter, when he could fight down an inclination to get out of the room quickly. "You say he killed her after all? And yet you told us he had an absolute alibi. You said he never went closer to the house than the windows. . . ."

"No more he did, my dear," said the other.

"He was courting the Linshaw heiress at the time," she resumed; "and Miss Linshaw was a very proper young lady who would have been horrified if she had heard about him and Jane Waycross. She would have broken off the match, naturally. But poor Jane Waycross meant her to hear. She was much in love with Mr. Wilkes, and she was going to tell the whole matter publicly: Mr. Wilkes had been trying to persuade her not to do so."

"But——"

"Oh, don't you see what happened?" cried the other in a pettish tone. "It is so dreadfully simple. I am not clever at these things, but I should have seen it in a moment: even if I did not already know. I told you everything so that you should be able to guess.

"When Mr. Wilkes and Dr. Sutton and Mr. Pawley drove past here in the gig that night, they saw a bright light burning in the windows of this room. I told you that. But the police never wondered, as anyone should, what caused that light. Jane Waycross never came into this room, as you know; she was out in the hall, carrying either a lamp or a candle. But that lamp in the thick blue-silk shade, held out there in the hall, would not have caused a bright light to shine through this room and illuminate it. Neither would a tiny candle; it is absurd. And I told you there were no other lamps in the house except some empty ones waiting to be filled in the back kitchen. There is only one thing they could have seen. They saw the great blaze of the paraffin oil round Jane Waycross's body.

"Didn't I tell you it was dreadfully simple? Poor Jane was upstairs waiting for her lover. From the upstairs window she saw Mr. Wilkes's gig drive along the road in the moonlight, and she did not know there were other men in it; she thought he was alone. She came downstairs——

"It is an awful thing that the police did not think more about that broken medicine-bottle lying in the hall, the large bottle that was broken in just two long pieces. She must have had a use for it; and, of course, she had. You knew that the oil in the lamp was almost exhausted, although there was a great blaze round the body. When poor Jane came downstairs, she was carrying the unlighted lamp in one hand; in the other hand she was carrying a lighted candle, and an old medicine-bottle containing paraffin oil. When she got downstairs, she meant to fill the lamp from the medicine-bottle, and then light it with the candle.

"But she was too eager to get downstairs, I am afraid. When she was more than half-way down, hurrying, that long nightgown tripped her. She pitched forward down the stairs on her face. The medicine-bottle broke on the tiles under her, and poured a lake of paraffin round her body. Of course, the lighted candle set the paraffin blaz-

ing when it fell; but that was not all. One intact side of that broken bottle, long and sharp and cleaner than any blade, cut into her throat when she fell on the smashed bottle. She was not quite stunned by the fall. When she felt herself burning, and the blood almost as hot, she tried to save herself. She tried to crawl forward on her hands, forward into the hall, away from the blood and oil and fire.

"That was what Mr. Wilkes really saw when he looked in through the window.

"You see, he had been unable to get rid of the two fuddled friends, who insisted on clinging to him and drinking with him. He had been obliged to drive them home. If he could not go to 'Clearlawns' now, he wondered how at least he could leave a message; and the light in the window gave him an excuse.

"He saw pretty Jane propped up on her hands in the hall, looking out at him beseechingly while the blue flame ran up and turned yellow. You might have thought he would have pitied, for she loved him very much. Her wound was not really a deep wound. If he had broken into the house at that moment, he might have saved her life. But he preferred to let her die: because now she would make no public scandal and spoil his chances with the rich Miss Linshaw. That was why he returned to his friends and told a lie about a murderer in a tall hat. It is why, in heaven's truth, he murdered her himself. But when he returned to his friends, I do not wonder that they saw him mopping his forehead. You know now how Jane Waycross came back for him, presently."

There was another heavy silence.

The girl got to her feet, with a sort of bouncing motion which was as suggestive as it was vaguely familiar. It was as though she were about to run. She stood there, a trifle crouched, in her prim brown dress, so oddly narrow at the waist after an old-fashioned pattern; and in the play of light on her face Rodney Hunter fancied that its prettiness was only a shell.

"The same thing happened afterwards, on some Christmas Eves," she explained. "They played Blind Man's Bluff over again. That is why people who live here do not care to risk it nowadays. It happens at a quarter-past seven——"

Hunter stared at the curtains. "But it was a quarter-past seven when we got here!" he said. "It must now be——"

"Oh, yes," said the girl, and her eyes brimmed over. "You see, I told you you had nothing to fear; it was all over then. But that is not why I thank you. I begged you to stay, and you did. You have listened to me, as no one else would. And now I have told it at last, and now I think both of us can sleep."

Not a fold stirred or altered in the dark curtains that closed the window bay; yet, as though a blurred lens had come into focus, they now seemed innocent and devoid of harm. You could have put a Christmas-tree there. Rodney Hunter, with Muriel following his gaze, walked across and threw back the curtains. He saw a quiet window-seat covered with chintz, and the rising moon beyond the window. When he turned round, the girl in the old-fashioned dress was not there. But the front doors were open again, for he could feel a current of air blowing through the house.

With his arm round Muriel, who was white-faced, he went out into the hall. They did not look long at the scorched and beaded stains at the foot of the panelling, for even the scars of fire seemed gentle now. Instead, they stood in the doorway looking out, while the house threw its great blaze of light across the frosty Weald. It was a welcoming light. Over the rise of a hill, black dots trudging in the frost showed that Jack Bannister's party was returning; and they could hear the sound of voices carrying far. They heard one of the party carelessly singing a Christmas carol for glory and joy, and the laughter of children coming home.

FOOTPRINTS IN THE SANDS OF TIME

Is there a more baffling scenario than to find a body in smooth sand or snow with no footprints leading to or from the victim?

THE MAN FROM NOWHERE
EDWARD D. HOCH

OVER THE COURSE of the last half century or more, it has been virtually impossible for an author to earn a living as a short-story writer, but Edward Dentinger Hoch (1930–2008) was that rare exception. He produced about nine hundred stories in his career, approximately half of them published in *Ellery Queen's Mystery Magazine*, beginning in 1962. In May of 1973, Hoch started a remarkable run of publishing at least one story in every issue of *EQMM* until his death—and beyond, as he had already delivered additional stories.

Readers have never been able to decide which is their favorite of Hoch's series characters, but there can be little argument that his most unusual is Simon Ark, who was the protagonist of his first published story, "Village of the Dead," which ran in the December 1955 issue of *Famous Detective Stories*, one of the last pulp magazines. Ark looks to be an ordinary man in his sixties but claims to be a two-thousand-year-old Coptic priest who has spent the past two millennia touring the globe in search of Satan in order to do battle with him. Is he really what he claims to be? The author has never answered the question, preferring to leave the decision to readers. The stories always present a fantastic situation (the disappearance of all the people in a village, the murder of one member of a cult in a dark cellar while all the other members are hanging from crucifixes) but are resolved in the classic detective manner of observation and deduction, without any supernatural elements playing a role. Ark stories have been collected in several volumes: *The Judges of Hades and Other Simon Ark Stories* (1971), *City of Brass and Other Simon Ark Stories* (1971), and *The Quests of Simon Ark* (1984).

"The Man from Nowhere" was first published in the June 1956 issue of *Famous Detective Stories*; it was first collected in *The Quests of Simon Ark* (New York, Mysterious Press, 1984).

THE MAN FROM NOWHERE

EDWARD D. HOCH

THE INTERESTED READER may find the tale of Kaspar Hauser's strange life and stranger death related at some length in volume eleven of the Encyclopedia Britannica. And perhaps the story of Douglas Zadig's life and death will be there some day, too.

For Douglas Zadig was also a man from nowhere, a man who came out of the mists and died in the snow—just as Kaspar Hauser had over one hundred years ago.

This is the story of Douglas Zadig's last day on earth, and of the people who were with him when he died. . . .

It was a cold, bleak Friday afternoon in early November when Simon Ark called me at my office. I was in the midst of checking some final galley proofs for our January books, but I tossed them aside when I recognized his voice on the line. "Simon! How've you been?"

"Busy," he replied. "How would you like to go up to Maine for the weekend?"

"Maine? In November? Nobody goes up there except hunters this time of year."

"Hunters and publishers," Simon Ark corrected; "I want to see a man, and since he's a writer of sorts, I thought it might be good to take you along. That is, if you're free. . . ."

I'd learned long ago that an invitation from Simon Ark was never as casual as it sounded. If he was going up to Maine for the weekend, there was a reason for it, and I wanted to be with him. "I'm free," I said. "When should I meet you?"

"Can you be at Grand Central at six? We'll take the New Haven part of the way."

"I'll be there. At the information booth. . . ."

I called my wife after that, explaining the reason for my sudden trip. She knew Simon Ark almost as well as I did, and she was one of the few people in this world who understood. She said goodbye to me with that little catch in her breath that told me she'd be waiting for whatever adventures I had to relate upon my return.

And then I was off, on a weekend I was never to forget. . . .

I'd first met Simon Ark years before, when I was still a newspaper reporter; and though I'd lost track of him for several years, he'd turned up again recently to renew our friendship. He was an odd man by any standards, a tall, heavy-set figure with an expression that was at times saintly.

My experiences with him in the past, together with the tales he'd related to me over a beer or a glass of wine, told me that he was someone not really of our world at all. He belonged to the world of the past—to the world of the supernatural, perhaps, but certainly not to the world of twentieth century America.

He was a man who was searching, searching for what he called the Ultimate Evil, the devil himself. I'd laughed at first, or thought possibly that he was a little crazy; but I didn't laugh any more, and I knew that if anything he was the sanest man in the world. He found evil everywhere, because there was evil everywhere, and I knew that someday he would have his wish; someday he would confront Satan himself.

That was why I always went with him when he asked. He'd been searching for a long time, and the meeting might never take place in my lifetime; but if it did I wanted to be there, too.

So that was why I was with him as the train rumbled north toward New England that night. "What's it all about this time, Simon?" I asked finally, when no information was forthcoming.

He gazed out the train window, almost as if he could see something in the darkness besides the irregular patterns of light from buildings and roads.

Presently he asked, "Did you ever hear of a man called Douglas Zadig?"

The name seemed somehow familiar, but I had to shake my head. "Who is he?"

"He is a man from nowhere, a man without family or country, a man without a past. You may have read about him some ten years ago, when he walked out of an English mist one night to become an overnight sensation."

"I remember now," I said. "He was a youth of about twenty at the time, and he claimed to have no memory of his past life. He spoke English very poorly, and his clothes were almost rags. The only thing he remembered was that his first name was Douglas. When they found him, he was carrying a worn French copy of Voltaire's novel, *Zadig,* so the newspapers named him Douglas Zadig."

"You have a good memory for details," Simon Ark said. "As you probably remember, this Douglas Zadig has remained a complete mystery. His fingerprints were not on file anywhere in the world; his picture has never been identified by anyone. He is simply a man without a past."

"I lost track of him a few years back, though," I told Simon. "What's he been doing recently?"

"I ran into him a few years ago in London," Simon Ark continued. "I was in England to investigate an odd happening in Devonshire, and I happened to hear him speaking at a sort of rally. He's become quite a writer and speaker in some circles—a sort of prophet, I suppose you'd call him."

"Is this the man we're going up to Maine to see?"

"Quite correct. He came to this country with an American doctor two years ago. The doctor—a man named Adam Hager—has actually adopted him as a son, and the two of them are living in Maine."

"Odd, but hardly in your field of investigation, is it, Simon?"

The train rumbled on through the small New England towns, along the dark waiting waters of Long Island Sound. Around us, people were drifting into sleep, and the seat lights were being dimmed.

Simon Ark took a slim volume from his pocket and held it out for my examination. I glanced at the cover and saw that the unlikely title was *On the Eternal War Between the Forces of Good and the Forces of Evil.* The author was Douglas Zadig.

"So?" I questioned.

Simon Ark returned the book to his pocket. "The odd thing about this book—as with all of Douglas Zadig's writings and speeches—is that his apparently new philosophy is actually lifted almost word for word from the teachings of a religious leader named Zoroaster, who lived seven centuries before Christ. . . ."

It took us until Saturday noon to reach our destination, a small town called Katahdin in the northern part of the state. It was cold up here, and a fresh layer of snow already covered the ground. All around us were mountains and lakes and forests, and it seemed impossible that such a place could be only a single night's journey from New York.

There was a small hotel of sorts, where we

left what few belongings we'd brought along. It was all but empty now, but in another week I imagined it would be full of sportsmen up from Bangor and Boston.

"You fellows hunters?" the room clerk asked us. "Little early in the season for good hunting."

"We're hunters of a very special type of game," Simon Ark replied. "Can you direct us to the house of Doctor Hager?"

"Sure; it's right at the edge of town, where the road turns. Big white place. You can't miss it."

"Thank you."

The house of Doctor Hager was indeed easy to find; and from the look of the barren white fields that surrounded it, I guessed that someone had once tried farming the land.

Doctor Hager himself was average in almost every respect. He might have been a typical country doctor, but he might just as well have been a big-city businessman. There was a look of shrewdness about his eyes that contrasted with the weak smile that seemed always on his lips.

Simon Ark explained that we were from a New York publishing company, and had come up to speak with Douglas Zadig about the possibility of doing one of his books.

"Come in, by all means," Doctor Hager urged us. "I'm sure Douglas will be happy to speak with you. There are so many people interested in his work. . . ."

The house was even larger than it had seemed from outside, and we saw at once that we were not the only visitors. A handsome young woman of perhaps thirty, and an older man with thin, drawn features were sitting in the living room.

Doctor Hager took charge of the introductions, and I learned that the woman was a Mrs. Eve Brent, from Chicago. The older man was Charles Kingsley, and I recognized him as a retired manufacturer, whose name was prominent in financial circles.

"These are some New York publishers," Doctor Hager announced proudly, "who have come all the way up here to talk with Douglas." Then, turning to us, he explained, "Our house here is always open to visitors. Mrs. Brent and

Mr. Kingsley are staying with us for a few weeks to try and find themselves spiritually."

I had taken the chair next to Mrs. Brent, and I asked her where Douglas Zadig was, just to get the conversation started.

"He's upstairs in his room; I think he'll be down shortly."

"You're a long way from Chicago, aren't you?" I asked.

"My . . . my husband died a few years back. Since then, I've just been at loose ends, traveling to Europe and South America; it wasn't until I read one of Douglas Zadig's books that I found myself again."

I saw that Simon was busy talking with Hager and Mr. Kingsley. But all conversation stopped with the sudden entrance of a thin young man whom I knew to be Douglas Zadig.

He was taller than I'd supposed, with gaunt, pointed features of the type that stayed in your memory. There was a slight limp to his walk, and I remembered reading now that he'd had the limp when he first appeared, more than ten years ago in England.

"I'm sorry to be late," he apologized, in a rich full voice, with barely a trace of English accent. "But it happened again."

Whatever it was that had "happened" was enough to bring gasps from the Doctor and the two guests. Hager rushed to Douglas Zadig's side and quickly examined his head.

"The same side as before, Adam," the young man said. "I was shaving, when suddenly I felt this blow on the temple; there's not much blood this time, though."

"The skin is broken, though," Doctor Hager said. "Just like the other time."

Simon Ark arose from his chair and went forward to examine the young man. "Just what is the trouble here?" he asked, addressing the question to the four of them.

It was Mrs. Brent at my side who answered. "Douglas has been the victim of two mysterious attacks, both while he was alone in his room. We . . . we think it might be the . . . the devil. . . ."

I saw Simon Ark's quiet eyes come alive at the word, and I knew that in some mysterious way he'd come into conflict again with the Evil he eternally sought. From outside, a slight wind stirred the barren trees; and through the window I could see a brief gust of snow eddy up into the air.

Charles Kingsley snorted and took out a cigar. "This whole business is nonsense. We're not living in the Middle Ages anymore; the devil doesn't come around attacking people."

"I fear you're quite wrong." Simon Ark spoke quietly. "Satan is just as real today as he was a thousand years ago; and there's no reason to suppose that his tactics have changed any in that time. If I were more certain he was among us, in fact, I'd suggest a rite of exorcism."

"We'd need a priest for that," Mrs. Brent said; "there isn't one within miles of here."

Simon Ark shook his head. "In the early days of Christianity, it was quite common for lay persons to exorcise the devil. But I would not want to attempt it under the present circumstances."

Douglas Zadig spoke from the doorway, where he'd remained during Simon Ark's brief examination. "Just what do you mean by that, sir? You talk oddly for a book publisher."

"I have other professions. I refer to the peculiar doctrine you preach as to the eternal war between the two great forces of good and evil. It reminds one somewhat of the teachings of Zoroaster."

The young man seemed to pale slightly at the name "I . . . I have read about his doctrines, of course. But if you'd completed your study of my teachings and published works, I think you'd find that my theory of evil holds that, as a force, it is a part of God, and is willed by Him—not that it is a separate and distinct power."

"Oh, come now, Mr. Zadig," Simon Ark said with almost a chuckle, "Thomas Aquinas disproved that idea seven hundred years ago. In case you're not familiar with it, I refer you to chapters thirty-nine and ninety-five in Book One of his *Summa Contra Gentiles*. For a preacher of a new religion, you seem to be quite confused as to your own doctrine."

Douglas Zadig turned on him with blazing eyes. "I need not listen to these insults in my own house," he said, and turned from the room. Doctor Hager ran after him and followed him onto the front porch.

Kingsley and Mrs. Brent seemed shocked at Simon Ark's tactics; I walked over close enough to speak to him without their hearing us. "Perhaps you were a little hard on the fellow, Simon; I'm sure he means no harm."

"Whether he *means* harm or not, the fact remains that false teachings like that can always cause harm."

Doctor Hager returned to us then, and through the window we could see Douglas Zadig walking off across a snow-covered field, his open jacket flapping in the breeze. "He's gone for a walk," the doctor informed us; "he wants to be alone with his thoughts."

Simon Ark walked to the window and watched him until he was out of sight over a hill of snow.

"Really," Mrs. Brent said, "I think you owe him an apology when he returns. In his own way, he's a great man."

Simon Ark turned from the window and faced the four of us. "Have any of you ever heard the story of Kaspar Hauser?" he asked quietly. And when he saw our blank expressions, he went on, "Kaspar Hauser was a German youth of about sixteen, who appeared suddenly in Nuremberg in May of 1828. He was dressed as a peasant, and seemed to remember nothing of his past life. In his possession were found two letters, supposedly written by the boy's mother and his guardian. A professor in Nuremberg undertook his education, and he remained there and in Ansbach until his death in 1833. Twice before his death, while he was living with the professor, he suffered mysterious wounds; and his death from a stab wound while he was walking in a park during the winter has never been explained."

Doctor Hager spoke from between tightened lips. "Just what are you driving at?"

"I am suggesting that Douglas Zadig's life, his appearance out of nowhere in England ten years ago, his friendship with you, Doctor, and even the two odd wounds he has recently suffered, follow very closely the life of Kaspar Hauser."

Mrs. Brent was still beside me, and her fingers dug unconsciously into my arm. "Perhaps you're right. What does that prove?"

"Don't any of you see it?" Simon Ark asked. "This man we all know as Douglas Zadig has no life of his own. Everything he has done and said has been done and said before in this world. He bears the name of a fictional character from French literature; he teaches a doctrine of a man dead nearly three thousand years, and he lives the life of a man from the nineteenth century. I don't propose to explain it—I am only stating the facts. . . ."

There was silence when he finished speaking, and the four of us who were with him in the room looked at each other with questioning glances. There was something here which was beyond our understanding. Something . . .

Doctor Hager broke the silence. "How . . . how did this man . . . this Kaspar Hauser die?"

"He was stabbed to death while walking alone in a park. There were no other footprints in the snow, and yet the wound could not have been self-inflicted. The mystery has never been solved."

As if with one body our eyes went toward the window where last we'd seen Douglas Zadig walking. And I knew there was but a single thought in our minds.

Doctor Hager pulled a coat from the closet and threw it over his shoulders. "No, not that way," he said, giving voice to the fear that was in all our minds. "He'll come back the other way, at the rear of the house."

We ran out, Hager and Simon Ark in the lead, closely followed by Kingsley, Mrs. Brent, and

myself. We gave only a passing glance to the single set of footprints leading off over the hill, and then we ran around the back of the big white house.

It was cold, but somehow we didn't notice the cold. We saw only the snow—clear and white and unmarked ahead of us—and far away in the distance across the field, the lone figure of Douglas Zadig walking back toward us.

He walked quickly, with the steady gait of a young, vigorous man. The thin layer of snow did not impede his feet, and his short jacket flapped in the breeze as if it were a summer's day. When he saw us he waved a greeting, and seemed to walk a little faster toward us.

He was perhaps a hundred yards away when it happened. He stopped short, as if struck by a blow, and his hands flew to his left side. And even at this distance we could see the look of shock and surprise on his face.

He staggered, almost fell, and then continued staggering toward us, his hands clutching at his side. "I've been stabbed," he shouted, "I've been stabbed." And already we could see the bloody trail he was leaving in the snow. . . .

Doctor Hager was the first to break the spell, and he dashed forward to meet the wounded man, with the rest of us in close pursuit. When Hager was still some twenty yards from him, Douglas Zadig fell to his knees in the snow; and now the blood was reddening his shirt and gushing out between his fingers. He looked at us once more, with that same surprised expression on his face, and then he toppled over in the snow.

Hager was the first to reach him, and he bent over and quickly turned the body back to examine the wound. Then he let it fall again and looked up at us.

"He's dead . . ." he said simply. . . .

We knew it was impossible, and we stood there and looked down at the impossible and perhaps we prayed.

"He must have been shot," Eve Brent said; but then Doctor Hager showed us the wound, and it was clearly that of a knife.

"He stabbed himself," Charles Kingsley said, but I knew that Kingsley didn't even believe it himself. There was no knife in the wound, no knife back there in the snow; and Hager settled it by pointing out that such a wound would be difficult to self-inflict, and impossible while the five of us watched him.

We went back to where the bloodstains started, and searched in the snow for something, anything—even the footprints of an invisible man. But there was nothing. The snow was unmarked, except for the bloodstains and the single line of footprints.

And then we stood there and looked at the body and looked at each other and waited for somebody else to say something.

"I suggest we call the local police, or the state troopers," Simon Ark said finally.

And so we left the body of Douglas Zadig where it lay in the snow and went back into the house. And waited for the police.

And when they came—a bent old man, who was the local barber and also at times the constable, and a wiser one, who was the town doctor and also its coroner, we knew no more.

Could the wound have been inflicted by someone on the other side of the hill, before he came into view? That was my question, but the half-formed theory in my mind died even before it was born. The blood had only started at the point where we'd seen him grip his side; and besides that both doctors agreed that such a wound would cause almost instantaneous death. It was a wonder he'd even managed to walk as far as he did.

And presently the barber, who was the constable, and the doctor who was the coroner, left, taking the body of Douglas Zadig with them.

Simon Ark continued to gaze out the window at the occasional snowflakes that were drifting down from above. Mrs. Brent and I managed somehow to make coffee for the others, but for a long time no one spoke.

Presently I heard Simon Ark mumble, "The man from nowhere. . . . Nowhere. . . ." And seeing me watching him, he continued, "Dear, beauteous death, the jewel of the just! Shining

nowhere but in the dark; what mysteries do lie beyond thy dust, could man outlook that mark!"

When he saw my puzzled expression, he explained, "The lines are not original with me. They were written back in the seventeenth century by Henry Vaughan."

"Does that tell you what killed Douglas Zadig out there in the snow?"

He smiled at me, something he rarely did. "The answer to our mystery might better be found in Shakespeare than in Vaughan."

"Then you do know!"

"Perhaps. . . ."

"I read a story once, about a fellow who was murdered with a dagger made of ice."

"That melted and left no trace? Well, you'd hardly expect a dagger of ice to melt when the outside temperature is below freezing, would you?"

"I guess not," I admitted. "But if it wasn't done in any of the ways we've mentioned, then it must have been supernatural. Do you really mean that Douglas Zadig was possessed of the devil?"

But Simon Ark only repeated his favorite word. "Perhaps. . . ."

"I don't care," Charles Kingsley was saying, in the loud voice I'd come to expect from him. "I'm not a suspect, and I don't intend to stay here any longer. I came because I believed in the teachings and writings of Douglas Zadig; now that he's dead there's no reason for me to remain any longer."

Doctor Hager shrugged and gave up the argument. "You're certainly free to leave any time you want to, Mister Kingsley. Believe me, this awful tragedy strikes me a much greater blow than anyone else."

Mrs. Brent had taken out a checkbook and her pen. "Well, I'll still give you the money as I promised, Dr. Hager. If nothing else perhaps you can erect a memorial of some sort."

I could see that she was serious. I had known Douglas Zadig for only a short time on the final day of his life, but I could see that he'd had a profound effect on the lives of these people and others like them. To me he had been only a name half-remembered from the news stories of ten years ago, but to some he had become apparently the preacher of a new belief.

And then Simon Ark spoke again. "I would like you people to remain for another hour if you would. I think I will be able to show you the manner in which Douglas Zadig died."

"If you can do that," Kingsley said, "it's worth waiting for. But if there really is some sort of devil around here, I sure don't want to stay."

"I promise you that I'll protect you all from the force that struck down Douglas Zadig," Simon Ark said. "I have one question, though: Dr. Hager, do you keep any chickens here?"

"Chickens?" Hager repeated with a puzzled frown. "Why, no; there's a place down the road that raises them, though. Why?"

"I wondered," he replied, and then he would say no more. After that, he disappeared into a remote section of the house and the four of us were left alone. We knew that the state police would be arriving before long, to continue the investigation; and I could understand why Kingsley and Mrs. Brent were anxious to get away.

They were beginning to grow restless again when Simon Ark reappeared, this time holding in his hands the small ansated cross he always carried. "If you people will accompany me outside, I believe I will be able to show you how Douglas Zadig met his death."

"You mean you know who killed him."

"In a way I suppose I was responsible for his death," Simon Ark answered. "The least I can do is to avenge it. . . ."

We followed him outside, to the snow-covered field very near the spot where Douglas Zadig had died just an hour earlier. The four of us paused at the edge of the snow, but Simon Ark walked on, until he was some fifty feet away from us.

Then he stood there, looking up at the bleak November sky and at the distant trees and mountains. And he seemed to be very much alone. . . .

He held the strange ansated cross above his head, and chanted a few words in the Coptic language I'd come to know so well.

From somewhere a large bird swooped in a giant circle overhead. It might have been an eagle, or a vulture, lured north into the cold weather by some unknown quirk of nature. We watched it until it disappeared into a low brooding cloud bank, and then our eyes returned to Simon Ark.

He stood there, chanting in the strange tongue, as if calling upon some demons from the dark past. He stood there for what seemed an eternity, and what must have been the longest five minutes of my life.

And then it happened.

Again.

He dropped his hands suddenly to his side, and when they came away we could see the blood. He took a single step forward and then collapsed on his face in the snow, one outstretched hand still clutching the ansated cross.

We rushed forward behind Adam Hager, and I could feel my knees growing weak at the sight before us. Simon Ark, whom I'd come to think of as almost an invincible man, had been struck down by the same force that had killed Douglas Zadig. . . .

Dr. Hager reached him first, and felt for his heart. And then . . .

. . . In a moment I'll never forget, Simon Ark suddenly came alive, and rolled over in the snow, pinning Hager beneath him.

And we all saw, in Hager's outstretched helpless hand, the gleaming blade of a thin steel dagger. . . .

"They were just a couple of small-time swindlers who came close to hitting the big money," Simon Ark said later, when the state police had taken away the cursing, struggling, figure of Dr. Hager.

We were back inside—Kingsley, Mrs. Brent, several police officers, and myself—and listening to Simon Ark's explanation. Somehow the tension of the past few hours was gone, and we were a friendly group of people who might have been discussing the results of the day's football games.

"It's always difficult to imagine yourself as the victim of a swindler," he was saying, "but I saw at once that Zadig and Hager had invited you two here for the purpose of getting money from you. We might never know how many dozens were here before you, people who'd read Zadig's book and written to him. If you'll check further, I think you'll find that the book's publication was paid for by Zadig and Hager, and that most of his speaking engagements were phony, too—like his occasional limping."

"He did ask us for money to carry out various projects," Kingsley admitted.

"As I've already told you," Simon Ark continued, "the very fact that his name, his life, and his so-called doctrine were copied from the past made me suspect a swindle of some sort. There was just nothing original about the man; his was a life copied out of an encyclopedia. I suppose after he met Hager in London, the two of them thought up the scheme. I imagine you'll find that Hager has tried this sort of thing before under various names."

"But what about the murder?" Mrs. Brent wanted to know. "Why should Hager kill his partner in crime?"

"I fear it was because of my arrival. My detailed questions about Zadig's teachings caught them both off guard; and Hager, especially, knew that I might uncover their whole phony plot. When I mentioned the parallels between the attacks on Zadig and Kaspar Hauser, as well as those between the doctrines of Zadig and Zoroaster, Hager knew I was getting too close. When he and Zadig went out on the porch together before, I imagine they set up the final act of the Hauser drama, in which Zadig was to be wounded by a devil that had taken possession of him. I suppose this was the final try for the money, and perhaps they'd done the whole performance before."

"Only this time it was real," I said; "this time Hager really killed him. . . ."

"Correct. You'll remember it was Hager who asked how Hauser had been killed—and Hager who got us out of the house, so we could have front row seats for the final act. The actual mechanics of the murder are simple, once you know they were both swindlers. There's an old trick among confidence men—I believe it's called a 'cackle-bladder'—a small membranous bag filled with chicken blood or the like, which the swindler crushes to his body in order to appear wounded, after his confederate has fired a blank pistol at him. Douglas Zadig, walking toward us across the field, simply burst the bladder on his side and did a good job of acting. Hager, who naturally was expecting it all, easily managed to move fastest and reach the 'body' first. At this point, to make it look as realistic as possible, Hager was to wound Zadig slightly with a spring-knife hidden up his sleeve. . . ."

He paused, and we remembered the scene in the snow; and the horror of what was coming dawned on us all.

"And then, while Douglas Zadig braced himself so as to remain motionless when the knife cut into him, his partner released the spring knife up his sleeve, and sent the steel blade deep into Zadig's side, straight for the heart. . . ."

Charles Kingsley stirred slightly, and Mrs. Brent was beginning to look sick. But there wasn't much more, and Simon Ark continued. "Both doctors told us such a wound would have caused almost instantaneous death, and that made me wonder about the wounded man walking as far as he did. Anything's possible, of course, but it seemed far more likely that Hager had killed him as he bent over the body."

"But," I objected, "why did he have the nerve to try to kill you in the same way? When you pulled the trick with the chicken blood he must have realized you knew."

"It wasn't chicken blood," Simon Ark corrected with a slight smile. "I was forced to use ordinary ketchup, but I knew Hager would try to kill me, even though he realized I was only waiting to grab the knife from his sleeve. He had no choice, really. Once I was on to his trick, I had only to explain it; and an analysis of the various blood stains on Zadig's shirt would have proved me correct. His only chance was to be faster with his spring-knife that I was with my hands. Luckily, he wasn't, or you might have had a second impossible death on your hands."

He said it as if he meant it; but somehow I had the feeling that his life had never really been in danger. I had the feeling that it would be awfully difficult to kill Simon Ark. . . .

And so we departed from the little town in Maine, and journeyed back toward the slightly warmer wilds of Manhattan. A search of the house had turned up nearly a hundred thousand dollars in contributions from Zadig's swindled followers, and we began to think that Hager had possibly been thinking of that, too, when he plunged the knife into his partner's side.

"One thing, though, Simon," I said as the train thundered through the New England night. "Just where did Douglas Zadig ever come from? What happened in that London mist ten years ago?"

"There are things that are never explained," he answered simply. "But several explanations present themselves. The copy of the novel in French suggests—now that we know the man's true character—that even at this early age he was trying to fool the public into thinking him French instead of English. I don't know the real answer, and probably never will; but if a young man had avoided military service during England's darkest hours, he might well have had to think up a scheme to protect himself in a postwar world full of returning veterans."

"Of course!" I agreed. "He was a draft-dodger; that would explain why his fingerprints weren't on file with the army, or elsewhere!"

But Simon Ark was gazing out the window, into the night, and he replied in a quiet voice. "There are other possible explanations, of course, but I prefer not to dwell on them. Douglas Zadig is dead, like Kasper Hauser before him, and there are some things better left unexplained, at least in this world."

And after that he said no more about it. . . .

FREDRIC BROWN

CLAIMING THAT HE WROTE mysteries for the money but science fiction for fun, Fredric William Brown (1906–1972) is equally revered in both genres. He was born in Cincinnati, Ohio, and attended the University of Cincinnati at night and then spent a year at Hanover College, Indiana. He was an office worker for a dozen years before becoming a proofreader for the *Milwaukee Journal* for a decade. He was not able to devote his full time to writing fiction until 1949. He had for several years, however, already been a prolific writer of short stories and in the form that he mastered and for which he is much loved today, the difficult-to-write short-short story (generally one to three pages).

Brown was never financially secure, which forced him to write at a prodigious pace, yet he seemed to be enjoying himself in spite of the work load. Many of his stories and novels are imbued with humor, including a devotion to puns and word play. A "writer's writer," he was highly regarded by his colleagues, including Mickey Spillane, who called him his favorite writer of all time; Robert Heinlein, who made him a dedicatee of *Stranger in a Strange Land*; and Ayn Rand, who in *The Romantic Manifesto* regarded him as ingenious. After more than three hundred short stories, he wrote his first novel, *The Fabulous Clipjoint* (1947), for which he won an Edgar. His best-known work is *The Screaming Mimi* (1949), which served as the basis for the 1957 Columbia Pictures film of the same title that starred Anita Ekberg, Philip Carey, and Gypsy Rose Lee.

"The Laughing Butcher" was first published in the Fall 1948 issue of *Mystery Book*; it was first collected in *Mostly Murder* (New York, Dutton, 1953).

THE LAUGHING BUTCHER

FREDRIC BROWN

YESTERDAY MUST have been a dull day for news, because the Chicago *Sun* gave three inches to the funeral of a dwarf downstate, in Corbyville.

"Listen to this, Bill," Kathy said, and Wally—(that's my only in-law, Kathy's brother)—and I looked up from our game of cribbage.

"Yeah?" I said. Kathy read it to us.

Then she said, "Bill, wasn't that—" She let it trail off.

I looked at her warningly, because of her brother being there with us, and I said, "The dwarf that beat you at a game of chess five years ago? Yeah, that was the one."

Wally put down his last card, said, "Thirty-one for two," and pegged it. I scored my hand and he scored his and the crib, and it put him out and ended the game.

"Five years ago," he said. "And yesterday was your anniversary. That's put it on your honeymoon, if it was exactly five years ago, I mean. She play chess with dwarfs on your honeymoon?"

"One dwarf," I told him. "One game. In Corbyville. And she got beaten."

"Served her right," Wally said. "Look, Bill—wasn't it about that time, five years ago, they lynched a guy in Corbyville? The case they called the 'The Corbyville Horror'?"

"A few weeks after that," I said.

"The guy was a butcher, and a black magician, or something. Or they thought he was. Killed somebody by magic, or . . . What was it about, anyway?"

I was looking at the window, and the window was a black, blank square of night, and I wanted to shiver, but with Wally watching me that way, I couldn't. I got up and walked over to the window instead, so I could look down on the lights and traffic of Division Street instead of at the black night above it.

"It was the butcher they lynched," I said. I turned around from the window. "We saw him, too."

Wally picked up his glass of beer and took a sip of it.

"Some of it's coming back to me," he said. "Corbyville's that circus town, isn't it? Town where a lot of ex-circus people live?"

I nodded.

"And this Corbyville Horror business. Wasn't a guy found out in the middle of a field of snow, dead, with two sets of footprints leading up to his body and none leading away from it?"

"That's right," I said.

"And one set of footprints was his own and the other set just led to the body and vanished as though the guy had flown?"

"Yes," I said.

"I remember now. And the town lynched this butcher-magician because he had a down on the guy who was killed, and—"

"Something like that."

"They never did find out what really happened?" Wally asked.

"No."

He took another sip of beer and shook his head.

"I remember now that it puzzled me. How could a set of tracks go halfway across a field of snow and then stop, and not either come back or go on?"

"One set's easy to explain," I said. "I mean those of the guy they found dead out there in the field."

"Sure, him. But what about the one who chased him? He did chase him, didn't he? I mean, if I remember rightly, his footprints were on top of the dead man's in the snow."

"That's right," I said. "I saw those footprints myself. Of course by the time I saw them there were a lot of other prints around and they'd taken the body away, but I talked to the men who found the body, and they were sure of their description of those prints, and of the fact that there weren't any other ones around, within a hundred yards."

"Didn't somebody suggest ropes?"

"No trees or telephone poles anywhere near. Nope."

Kathy went and got us some more beer. I asked Wally if he wanted another game of cribbage. "No," he said. "The story."

I poured his glass full and then mine.

"What do you want to know, Wally?" I asked.

"What killed him?"

"Heart failure," I said.

"But—what was chasing him?"

"Nothing was chasing him," I said slowly. "Nothing at all. He wasn't running away from anybody or anything. It was more horrible than that."

I went over and sat down in the big armchair. Kathy came over and curled up on my lap like a contented kitten. Over her shoulder I could see that black square of night that was the open window.

"It was much more horrible than that, Wally," I repeated slowly. "He wasn't running away from something. He was running toward something. Something out in the middle of that field."

Wally laughed uneasily. "Bill," he said, "you don't talk like a Chicago copper. You talk like a fey Irishman. What was out in that field?"

"Death," I told him.

That held him for a minute. Then he asked, "What about the one-way tracks, the ones that led to the body and not away from it?"

It was warm and pleasant up there on top of the hill, I remember. I stopped the car at the side of the muddy road, put my arm around Kathy and kissed her, with the soundness that a second-day-of-honeymoon kiss deserves. We had been married the morning before, in Chicago, and were driving south. I had arranged a month off and we figured to get to New Orleans and back, driving leisurely, and stopping off wherever we wished. We had spent the first night of our honeymoon in Decatur, a town I'll never forget.

I won't forget Corbyville, either, although not for the same reason. But of course I didn't know that then. I pointed to the view through the windshield and down the hill into the valley, bright green and muddy brown from the recent rains. And with a little village at the bottom of it—three score or so of houses huddled together like frightened sheep.

"Ain't it purty?" I said.

"Beautiful," Kathy said. "The valley, I mean. Is that Corbyville? Where are the elephants? Didn't I read they used elephants for the plowing outside Corbyville?"

I laughed at her. "One elephant, and it died years ago. I guess there are a lot of the circus people left there, though. Maybe we'll see some of them when we drive through."

"I forget the story, Bill," Kathy said. "Why is it so many circus people live there? Some circus owner—"

"Old John Corby," I said. "He owned about the third biggest circus in the country and made a fortune from it. That was the town he came from—it had some other name then—and he put all his profits into the land there, got to own nearly the whole town and valley.

"And when he died, his will left houses and

stores and farms to people in his circus, on the condition that they live there. A lot of 'em wouldn't, of course; weren't ready to settle down, and went with some other circus instead. But a lot of 'em did take what was left them and live there. Out of a population of a thousand or so, over a hundred, I think, are ex-circus people. . . . Did I ever tell you I love you, Kathy?"

"I seem to remem . . . Bill, not here! You—"

So after a minute I slid the car in gear and started down the slippery, winding road into the valley. We were off the main highway, coming in on a side road that wasn't used much, and it was pretty bad. The mud was inches deep in the ruts. It wasn't too bad until we were just a half-mile outside the village, and then suddenly the wheels were sliding and the back end of the car, despite my efforts with the wheel, slewed around and went off the road. I tried to start, and the back wheels spun in mud that was like soup.

I said appropriate words, suitably modified to fit Kathy's presence, and got out of the car, then looked around.

There was a little three-room frame farmhouse only a few dozen paces away, and a stocky, blond man of about thirty was already walking from the house toward the car.

He grinned at me.

"Nice roads we got here," he said. "You in very deep?"

"Not too bad," I told him. "If you can give me a hand, maybe two of us—"

"Wish I could," he said. "But anything heavy's against the rules. I've got a bum ticker. The doc won't let me pick up anything heavier than a potato, and I got to do that slow." He looked up and down the road. "We might get you out with some gunny sacks or boards, but it'd hardly be worth the trouble. Pete Hobbs is about due by here. He's the mailman."

"Drive a truck?"

The blond man laughed. "Sure, but he won't need it. Pete used to be a strongman with Corby. He's getting old, but he can still pick up the back end of your car with one hand. You and the missus want to drop in the house till Pete gets here?"

Kathy had been listening, and she must have liked the man because she said sure, we'd be glad to.

So we went in, and it was half an hour before the mailman came along and we got to know the Wilsons fairly well, for half an hour. That was the blond man's name, Len Wilson. His wife, Dorothy, was a stunner. Almost as pretty as Kathy.

No, Len Wilson told us, he hadn't been with any circus. He had been born right here on this small farm, and Dorothy had been born in Corbyville. They had been married four years, and you could see they were still in love. I noticed how considerate they were of each other; how, when he started up to get an ash tray for me, Dorothy spoke almost sharply to him to make him sit down again. The sort of sharpness one might use on a child.

I remember wondering how, since Len couldn't exert himself physically, he managed to run a farm, even a small one. Maybe he knew I'd be wondering that. Anyway, he told me the answer.

"I can work all right," he told me, "as long as it isn't heavy, and I keep at a steady, dogged pace. I can lift a thousand pounds—about ten pounds at a time. I can walk a hundred miles, if I walk slowly and rest once in a while. And I can run a farm, a little one like this, the same way. Not that I get rich doing it." He grinned a little.

A honking out front brought us to our feet, and Dorothy Wilson said:

"That's Pete. I'll run ahead and be sure to catch him."

The rest of us followed more slowly, Kathy and I matching our pace to Len's. The ex-strongman got out of his mail truck and he and I easily lifted the car's back end around to where the wheels would find traction.

As I got under the wheel, Len waved.

"Might see you in town, if you're stopping there," he said. "I'm riding in with Pete."

Anyway, that was how we met Len Wilson. We saw him only once more, in Corbyville, a little later.

I was going to drive on through, I remember,

but Kathy wanted to stop and eat. I parked the car in front of a clean-looking hamburger joint and we went in. That was where we met the dwarf.

I remember thinking, when we first went in and sat down at the counter, that there was something strange and out of proportion about the five-foot-tall little man who nodded to us from behind the counter and took our orders. But I didn't realize what it was until he walked back to the grill to put on the hamburgers we ordered. He wasn't five feet tall at all; he was about three feet. The area back of the counter was built up, about two feet higher than the floor in the rest of the room.

He saw me lean over the counter and look down, and grinned at me.

"My chin'd just about come to the level of the counter without that arrangement," he said.

"You ought to get a patent on it," Kathy said. "Say, isn't that a chess board down there at the end of the counter?"

He nodded. "I was working out a problem. You play?"

That was better than the smell of the hamburgers to Kathy. Few women like chess, but she's one of the few, even if she doesn't look like it. To look at Kathy you'd think gin rummy would be her top intellectual entertainment, but you'd be fooled. She's got more brains and more education than I. Got a master's degree and would probably be teaching if she hadn't decided to marry me instead. Which, I'll admit, was a big waste of brains.

Kathy told him she played and how about a quick game? And she wasn't kidding on the quick part; she really does move fairly fast, and the dwarf—I noticed with relief—kept up with the pace she set. I know enough about chess, due to Kathy, to follow the moves, and when a game goes fairly quick, I can stay interested watching it.

Kathy had the men set up by the time he brought our hamburgers and coffee, and I watched until midgame while I ate. Then I strolled front to the doorway and stood leaning against the jamb, looking out across the street.

Directly across from me, in the doorway of the butcher shop, a butcher in a white apron was doing the same thing. My gaze passed him over lightly the first time, then went back to him and got stuck there. At first, I didn't even know why.

Then a child—a girl of about six or seven—came skipping along the street, noticed him when she was a dozen paces away, and stopped skipping. She circled widely, almost to the outer curb, to keep as much distance as possible between herself and the butcher. He didn't seem to notice her at all, and once she was safely behind his back, she started skipping again.

Definitely, I realized, she had been afraid of him.

It could have been nothing, of course; a child who'd been scolded for filching a wiener from the butcher shop, but—well, it didn't seem like that.

It didn't seem like that because what happened made me look at the butcher's face. It was calm, impassive. If he had noticed the child, he had neither frowned nor smiled at the wide circle she had made. And the face itself was handsome, but . . . I shivered a little.

A Chicago cop gets used to seeing faces that aren't nice to look at. He sees faces daily that might be Greek masks of hate or lust or avarice. He gets used to hopped-up torpedoes and crazy killers. He takes faces like that in his stride; they're his business.

But this wasn't that sort of face. It was an evil face, but subtly evil. The man's features were straight and regular and his eyes were clear. The evil was behind the face, behind the eyes. I couldn't even put my finger on how I knew it was there. It wasn't something I could see; it was something I felt.

The part of my brain that's trained to observe and remember was cataloguing the rest of him as well—I don't know why. Height, five eleven; weight, one eighty; age, about forty; black hair, brown eyes, olive complexion; distinguishing features—an aura of evil.

I wondered what the looie in charge of my precinct would say if I turned in a report like that.

I strolled back into the restaurant and looked at the chess game, mildly wishing Kathy would be through so she could leave with me while the butcher was still standing there. I wondered what her reaction to him would be.

There were still a lot of pieces on the board, though. Kathy looked up at me.

"Having trouble," she admitted. "This gentleman really knows how to play chess. Why aren't you smart like that, Bill?"

The dwarf grinned without looking up, and moved a pawn.

"She's played this game before, too," he said. "It's even so far."

"But not now," Kathy said.

I looked at the pieces and saw what she meant. The dwarf had left one of his knights unprotected. Kathy's hand hovered over the board a moment, then her bishop swooped to conquer.

"Attababy," I said to Kathy and patted her shoulder. "Take your time," I told her. "It's only our honeymoon."

I strolled back to the doorway. The white-aproned butcher was still there.

Out of the doorway of the store next door to the butcher shop came Len Wilson. He walked, as before, slowly. He walked toward the butcher shop. I started to hail him, to ask him to come over and have a cup of coffee with me while Kathy and the dwarf finished their game. I had my mouth open to call to him, but I didn't.

Len Wilson caught the butcher's eye, and stopped. There was something so peculiar about his way of stopping, as though he had run into a brick wall, that I didn't call. I watched, instead.

The butcher was smiling, but it wasn't a nice smile. He said something, but I couldn't hear it across the street, nor could I hear what Len answered. It was like watching a movie whose sound track had stopped working.

I saw the butcher reach into his pocket and take something out, hold it casually in his hand. It looked like a tiny doll, about two inches long. It could have been made of wax. He did something, I couldn't see what, with the doll between his hands.

Then he said something again—several sentences—and laughed again. I could hear that laugh across the street, even though I hadn't heard the words. It wasn't loud, but it carried. And Len Wilson's fists clenched, and he started forward—not slowly at all—for the butcher.

I started, too, at the same time. There wasn't any mistaking the expression on Len's face. His intention wasn't any intention that a man with a bad ticker should have. He was going to take a poke at that butcher, a man bigger than he was and husky looking besides, and for a man in Len's shape it was going to be just too bad unless that one poke did the work.

But Len had been only a few steps away, and I'd been across the street. I saw him swing wildly and miss, and then an auto horn and squealing brakes made me step back just in time to keep from getting killed in the middle of the street. When I looked again, the tableau had changed. The big butcher was standing behind Len, with Len's arm doubled in a hammerlock. Len's face was red with either pain or futile anger, or both.

I took a quick look for traffic both ways this time before I started across toward them. I don't mind telling you that I was afraid. Not physically afraid of that butcher, but—well, there was something about him that had made me want to hit him, even before Len had come along, but that made me afraid to do it, too.

Suddenly I noticed that Kathy and the dwarf were with me, Kathy abreast of me on one side, and the dwarf scuttling by me on the other side, his short legs going like piston rods as he passed me.

"Let go of him, Kramer, damn you!" he was yelling.

The butcher let go of Len, and Len almost collapsed, leaning back against the building. The dwarf got to Len first, and reached into Len's vest pocket. He came out with a little box of pills. He handed them to me.

"Give him one, quick," he said. "I can't reach."

I got the box open—they were nitro pills, I noticed—and got Len to take one.

"Take him across to my place," the dwarf was saying. "Make him sit down and rest."

And Kathy was on Len's other side and we were helping him across the street.

The dwarf wasn't with us. I saw that Len seemed to be breathing normally and making it all right, then I glanced back over my shoulder.

Again it was a conversation I couldn't hear, but could see. The dwarf's face, on a level with the butcher's belt, was dark with fierce anger. There was smiling amusement on the butcher's face, and again I felt that impact of evil.

The butcher said something. The dwarf took a step forward and kicked viciously at the butcher's shin. He connected, too.

I almost stopped, thinking I'd have to let Kathy support Len while I ran back to rescue the foolhardy dwarf.

But the butcher didn't make a move. Instead, he leaned back against the door post of his shop and laughed. Great peals of loud laughter that must have been audible a full block away. He didn't even lean down to rub his kicked shin. He laughed.

He was still laughing when Kathy and I had taken Len through the open doorway of the restaurant. I turned around and the dwarf, his face almost purple with thwarted anger, was crossing the street after us, and the butcher still stood there laughing. It wasn't a nice laugh at all. It made me want to kill him, and I've got a pretty even disposition myself.

We let Len down into one of the seats at a booth, and the dwarf was beside us, his face calm again. I glanced out through the window and saw that the butcher was gone, probably back into his shop. And the silence, after that laughter, seemed blessed.

"Shall I get Doc?" the dwarf asked Len.

Len Wilson shook his head. "I'm all right. That nitro pill fixed me up. Just let me sit and rest a minute or two."

"Cup of coffee while you're resting?"

"Sure," Len said. "And make me a hamburger, will you, Joe? Haven't eaten much."

Kathy sat down across from Len in the booth

and I went back with the dwarf named Joe. He went up the ramp that led to the raised area back of the counter and he again wasn't a dwarf anymore. He was five feet tall and his eyes were higher than mine as I sat at one of the counter stools opposite the hamburger grill. He took a hamburger patty from the refrigerator and slapped it on the grill, and then I caught his eye.

"What," I asked, jerking my thumb in the direction of the butcher shop, "was that?"

"That," he said, "was Gerhard Kramer." He made it sound like profanity.

"And who is Gerhard Kramer?"

"A nice guy," he said, "if you listen to some people who think so. Most of us don't. Some of us are pretty close to thinking he's the devil himself."

"Outside of a butcher," I asked, "who is he? What was he?"

"Used to be with Corby's circus. Sideshow magician and mentalist. He makes a better butcher. But he still keeps on with magic—only the black kind, the serious kind."

"He really believes in it? Wax dolls and that sort of stuff?"

"You saw that doll, then? Well, he makes people believe he believes in it. Got half the town scared stiff of him."

"Yet they buy in his store?"

He flipped over the hamburger frying on the grill. "They're afraid not to, I guess, if it comes to that. Oh, and some of the women aren't afraid of him. He's attractive to women. He does all right. He owns a good share of the town. Probably likes cutting up dead animals or he wouldn't have to run that shop. Yeah, he does all right."

Something in his tone of voice made me ask, "Except what?"

He slit a bun and put the hamburger in it, drew a cup of coffee, and started around the counter with them. I stayed still. I knew he'd answer my question when he got back.

He came back and said, "Len's wife, mister. That's the one thing he wants and can't have."

"Dorothy?" I asked, surprised. I don't know why I was surprised.

He looked so puzzled that I realized he hadn't known that we had stopped at the Wilsons' place on our way into Corbyville. He had thought that our first sight of Len had been across the street. I told him about it.

"Yes, Dorothy," he said. "She was a town girl before she married Len. Kramer wanted her and Len took her out from under his nose. Kramer's hated Len ever since. And, damn him, he'll probably get her if Len isn't more careful of himself. He'll keel over and leave a clear field."

"But won't Dorothy Wilson have something to say about that?" I asked. "Would she marry a—a guy like Kramer?"

He looked gloomy. "I told you women like him. She likes him—can't see anything wrong with him. Oh, I don't mean she'd cheat on Len, or anything like that. But if Len would die, why, after a year or so—"

"And that doll," I said. "That wax doll. Does that mean Kramer doesn't want to wait till Len dies naturally, if he does? Does Kramer really believe in that kind of magic?"

The dwarf looked at me cynically. "Sometimes that kind of magic can work, mister," he said. "You saw it blame near work just now, when he showed it to Len."

I saw what he meant. I got up and went back to the front of the store. Len looked better, and Kathy was talking to him animatedly.

"I've just learned Len plays chess, Bill," she said. "He's a friend of Joe Laska—that's the man who runs the restaurant here—and says they play a lot. We could have played a game out at Len's house while we were there."

"Sure," I said, "only you didn't. How'd you come out on the game with Joe? You were a knight ahead, I remember, and I see he put the board back, so I guess you finished the game."

"Yes, we finished. We were coming out to join you just when—when the trouble started across the street."

With Len sitting there I didn't want to go into that; I'd tell Kathy later what it was all about. "Who won?" I asked quickly.

"Joe, darn him. That business of giving me

the knight was a gambit. He checkmated me four moves later."

Len grinned, a little weakly. "Joe's a great guy for those gambits, lady. If you play with him again, watch out any time he offers you a piece for free."

The dwarf came back then and said that he was going to get a car to take Len home. But I wouldn't hear of that, of course. I made Len get into my car—he could walk all right by now—and Kathy and I drove him home.

Dorothy Wilson took a look at Len as he came through the door and took him off upstairs to put him to bed for the rest of the day. She had called back, asking us to wait, and we did.

But when she came down it turned out she had wanted us to wait so she could offer us something to eat, and we explained that we had just eaten in town. So Dorothy walked out to the car with us.

"Joe Laska phoned me," she said. "He said—well, I gathered that Len tried again to start a fight with Gerry Kramer. Oh, I wish Len wouldn't be so foolish. To hear Len—and Joe, too—talk, you'd think Gerry was a devil or something."

Something made me ask, "And isn't he?"

She laughed a little. "He's one of the nicest men in town. The men around here don't like him because he's handsome and polished and—well, you know how small-town people are."

"Oh," I said.

"But he's nice, really. Why, he holds a mortgage on this place of ours, overdue. He could put Len and me off any time he wanted, but he doesn't, in spite of the way Len acts about him."

I didn't want to hear any more of it. I wanted to say, "Sure, he'd rather let Len stay on a farm and work himself to death than maybe go to a city somewhere and get a softer job where he could last a longer time."

But I didn't say it. I had no business to, just because I hadn't liked a man's face and his laugh.

We said good-by to Mrs. Wilson and drove off.

After a while, I said, "Women—" disgustedly, and then asked Kathy what she had thought of the butcher.

"I don't really know," she said. "He is good-looking all right, and maybe Mrs. Wilson is right, but—well, I wouldn't trust him. There seemed to be something wrong about him, Bill. Something—uh—wicked, evil."

And since she was smart enough to have seen that for herself, I told her, as we drove along, everything that I had seen and what Joe, the dwarf, had told me.

We talked about it quite a while. There had been something about that scene in front of the butcher shop, and about the situation back of it, that wasn't going to be easy to forget. We wouldn't have forgotten it, I'm sure, even if it had ended there.

But after a while it slid into the back of our minds. We were, after all, on our honeymoon.

We drove to New Orleans and spent a wonderful two weeks in the marvelous fall weather they have there, and I remember the warmth was all the more wonderful when we read in the papers that Illinois and Indiana had been having freezing weather and early snows.

We started driving back then, leisurely. We didn't plan our route from day to day, and I don't know whether we would have driven through Corbyville at all, if we hadn't happened to buy a Centralia newspaper in Metropolis, just after we'd crossed the Ohio River from Paducah.

There was a headline:

BUTCHER LYNCHED IN CORBYVILLE

And in that first story there wasn't any play-up at all of the "Corbyville Horror" angle that made Sunday supplements all over the country. The lynching—it was the first in a long time in the State of Illinois—was the angle of the Centralia paper.

Apparently the reporters hadn't actually been on the scene as yet, because there weren't many details. I read the story out loud to Kathy, then she took the paper away from me and read it again to herself, while I sat and thought, and finished my coffee.

It seemed, according to the Centralia paper, that one Len Wilson, a farmer living just outside Corbyville, had died under rather mysterious circumstances, and that the people of the town blamed the local butcher, Gerhard Kramer, for Wilson's death. The sheriff, summoned from Centralia, had refused, for lack of evidence, to arrest Kramer.

And while the sheriff was out at the farm a group of townsmen, who had already been out at the farm, yanked Gerhard Kramer out of his butcher shop and strung him up on the light pole right in front of the store. Sheriff's deputies had been unable to find out who—outside, I suppose, of Kramer himself—had been involved in the lynching.

I paid our check in the restaurant and we went out and got in the car.

"Are you going through Corbyville?" Kathy asked.

"Yes," I said. "I want to know what happened. Don't you?"

"I guess so, Bill," she said.

We got to Corbyville about two o'clock. It was a quiet town when we drove down the main street. It was unnaturally quiet.

I drove slowly. The butcher shop, I noticed, was closed, although there wasn't any wreath on the door. The hamburger stand across from it, the dwarf's place, was closed too. There, there was a sign on the door that read:

CLOSED TILL MONDAY

I drove on out to the Wilson farm.

There was still an inch of snow on the ground, and it was cold, unseasonably cold for early October. There were cars parked in front— four of them.

We got out and walked back where there was a little knot of men standing beside a fence, and beyond the fence was an open field. I could see the footprints—the two sets of footprints that the Sunday supplements and all the newspapers made so much of. Alongside of them were other prints now, of course, ones that would not have been there when the first ones were made.

I took a good look at those tracks, without climbing over the fence. You've read about them, and they were just what the papers said. Two sets of tracks led out across that snow-covered field; neither set came back. It put a little chill down your spine to look at them, to visualize how they had looked to the first men there, those who had discovered the body, when the rest of the field was virgin white.

Len Wilson's footprints were a little the smaller of the two sets. You could tell which they were easily enough. He had been running, fast. The other set had been made after Len's. In places one of the bigger prints came on top of one of Len's.

Kathy stood staring at them, studying them.

I talked a few minutes to the men who were standing around. One was a deputy sheriff stationed there. He wanted to know who I was, and I showed him my Chicago credentials, and explained that I'd known Len slightly, and was interested for that reason. The other three men were reporters. One all the way from Chicago.

"Where is Mrs. Wilson?" I asked.

I didn't particularly want to talk to Dorothy Wilson, but I felt that if she was in the house, Kathy and I should go there, at least for a minute.

"With her folks in Corbyville," the Chicago reporter told me. "Say, those tracks. It's the damnedest thing." He turned and stared at them. Then he said, "I guess I can see why they lynched that butcher. If he hated Len Wilson, and if he went in for black magic—well, if this isn't what the hell is?"

The deputy sheriff spat over the fence. He started to say something, noticed Kathy, and changed his mind. He cleared his throat and said, "Black magic, phooey! But I'd still like to know how he did it. He was a circus sideshow magician, but even so—"

"Are those other footprints his?" I asked.

"His size. We haven't found the particu-

lar pair of shoes that made them. He probably ditched 'em."

"I—I guess I'm a little scared," Kathy said.

"I'm a lot scared," I told her.

We got in the car and drove away, north toward Chicago and home.

"It—it's horrible, Bill," Kathy said, after a while.

"What was he running from?"

"Nothing, Kathy," I told her. "He was running toward."

I told her how I figured it and why, and her eyes got wider and scareder. When I finished, she grabbed my arm. "Bill," she said, "You're a—a policeman. Does that mean you'll have to—to tell?"

I shook my head. "If I had any evidence, yes. But an opinion is my own, even if we know it's right."

Kathy relaxed, but we didn't talk much the rest of the way to Chicago.

Wally said, "All right, my beloved brother-in-law, I'm dumb and you're a big, smart copper. I don't get it." He downed the last of his beer and put the empty glass down quietly. "What was he running toward?"

"Death," I said. "I told you that. Death, out in the middle of the field, standing there waiting for him. He was pretty sick, Wally. I'm guessing he knew he didn't have long to live anyway. Otherwise, it wouldn't have made too much sense. But he loved Dorothy, and he hated that laughing butcher, Kramer. He knew that he was going to die, anyway, and if he died in such a manner that the town would figure Kramer did it, either by black magic or by some trick of sleight of hand—"

"Sleight of foot," said Wally.

"All right, sleight of foot," I amended. "He'd have his revenge on Kramer. And the town knowing Kramer, knowing how Kramer hated Len and wanted him to die, would blame the butcher if there was any supernatural-looking angle to Len's death, anything unexplainable.

Even if he wasn't arrested or lynched, the town would believe he had something to do with it. He'd have to leave. So by dying that way, a little sooner, Len got his revenge on a man he must have hated almost as much as he loved Dorothy—and he saved Dorothy from her blindness. If Len had waited to die naturally, she probably would have married Kramer after a while, because for some reason she was blind to the evil in him. Don't you see?"

Kathy stirred in my lap.

"Like in chess, Wally," she said. "A gambit—where you make a sacrifice to win. Like Joe, the dwarf, gave me a knight, and then checkmated me. That's how Joe and Len, playing chess on the same side of the board for once, checkmated the butcher."

"Huh?" Wally said. "The dwarf was in on it?"

"He had to be," I said. "Who else could have made the footprints that led only one way from the body to the fence? Who besides the dwarf could have ridden on Len's back while he ran like mad out into the field until his heart gave way, and who but a dwarf could have fastened a pair of Kramer's shoes on, backward?"

THE SANDS OF THYME

MICHAEL INNES

JOHN INNES MACKINTOSH STEWART (1906–1994), the Scottish-born author, established a great reputation as a literary critic and producer of contemporary novels and short stories. Many of those who were intimately familiar with his work, which included biographies of Rudyard Kipling and Joseph Conrad, had no idea that as Michael Innes he also was a prolific writer of detective fiction, most notably featuring the Scotland Yard inspector, later commissioner, John Appleby. Born in Edinburgh, Stewart attended Oxford University, winning the Matthew Arnold Memorial Prize and honors in English. Upon graduating, he taught at the University of Leeds (1930–1935), was a professor at the University of Adelaide for the next decade, briefly taught at Queen's University Belfast, and, from 1949 to 1973, was on the faculty of Christ Church, Oxford. His first book was written on the long sea journey to Australia; subsequent books were produced between semesters or, during the academic year, by two hours of daily writing before breakfast. His detective novels are generally rich with literary allusions, quotations, and satire, endearing him to readers and critics alike, though these elements begin to wear in later books and have sometimes been described as showing off. Innes's hero, Appleby, is as erudite as his creator, frequently to the bafflement of his superiors at the Yard.

"The Sands of Thyme" was first published in *Appleby Talking* (London, Gollancz, 1954); it was published in the United States under the title *Dead Man's Shoes* (New York, Dodd, Mead, 1954).

THE SANDS OF THYME

MICHAEL INNES

THE SEA SPARKLED and small waves splashed drowsily on the beach. Donkeys trotted to and fro bearing the children of holiday-makers who themselves slumbered under handkerchiefs and newspapers. On the horizon lay the smoke of a Channel steamer, on a day trip to Boulogne. And at all this the vicar glanced down with contentment from the promenade. "Fastidious persons," he said, "would call it vulgar."

"I like a deserted beach myself," said the Doctor.

Appleby looked up from his novel. "Do you know Thyme Bay?" he asked. "No? It's as lonely as you could wish, Doctor."

The Vicar removed his pipe from his mouth. "You have a story to tell us," he said.

Appleby smiled. "Quite frankly, Vicar, I have!"

I was there (said Appleby) on special duty with the Security people at the experimental air station. It was summer, and when the tide allowed it I used to walk across the bay before breakfast.

Thyme is a tremendous stretch of sand; you may remember that in the old days they held motor races there.

But the great thing is the shells. Thyme is the one place I know of to which you can go and feel that sea-shells are still all that they were in your childhood. Both on the beach itself and among the rocks, you find them in inexhaustible variety.

On the morning of which I'm speaking, I was amusing myself so much with the shells that it was some time before I noticed the footprints.

It was a single line of prints, emerging from the sandhills, and taking rather an uncertain course towards a group of rocks, islanded in sand, near the centre of the bay. They were the prints of a fairly long-limbed man, by no means a light-weight, and more concerned to cover the ground than to admire the view. But I noticed more than that. The tracks were of a man who limped. I tried to work out what sort of limp it would be.

This had the effect, of course, of making me follow the prints. Since the man had not retraced his steps, he had presumably gone on to the rocks, and then found his way back to the coastal road somewhere farther on. So I continued to follow in his tracks.

Presently I was feeling that something was wrong, and instead of going straight up to those rocks I took a circle round them. No footprints led away from them. So I searched. And there the chap was—tall, heavy, and lying on his tummy. . . . He was dead.

I turned him over—half-expecting what, in fact, I found. There was a bullet-hole plumb center of his forehead. And a revolver was lying beside him.

But that wasn't all. Suicides, you know, are fond of contriving a little décor of pathos.

On a flat ledge of the rock a score or so of

shells—the long, whorled kind—had been ranged in straight lines, like toy soldiers drawn up for battle. Beside them lay an open fountain-pen, and a scrap of paper that looked as if it had been torn from the top edge of a notebook. There was just a sentence: *"As a child, I played with these for hours."*

Of course I did the routine things at once. The dead man was a stranger to me.

He carried loose change, a few keys on a ring, a handkerchief, a gold cigarette-case, and a box of matches—absolutely nothing else. But his clothes were good, and I found his name sewn inside a pocket of the jacket. A. G. Thorman, Esqre. It seemed familiar.

I made one other discovery. The right ankle was badly swollen. I had been right about that limp.

Thorman was in late middle-age, and it turned out that I was remembering his name from the great days of aviation—the era of the first long-distance flights. He had made some of the most famous of these with Sir Charles Tumbril, and he had been staying with Tumbril at the time of his death.

But he had belonged to the district, too, having been born and brought up in a rectory just beyond Thyme Point. So it seemed likely enough that he had chosen to cut short his life in some haunt holding poignant memories of his childhood.

I took Tumbril the news of his guest's death myself. It was still quite early, and he came out from his wife's breakfast-table to hear it. I had a glimpse of both the Tumbrils from the hall, and there was Thorman's place, empty, between them.

Tumbril showed me into his study and closed the door with a jerk of his shoulder. He was a powerful, lumbering, clumsy man.

He stood in front of an empty fireplace, with his hands deep in his trouser pockets. I told him my news, and he didn't say a word. "It comes completely as a surprise to you, Sir Charles?"

He looked at me as if this was an impertinence. "It's not for us to conjecture," he said. "What has prompted Thorman to suicide can be neither your business nor mine."

"That doesn't quite cover the matter, Sir Charles. Our circumstances are rather exceptional here. You are in control of this experimental station, and I am responsible to the Ministry on the security side. You have three planes here on the secret list, including the P.2204 itself. Any untoward incident simply must be sifted to the bottom."

Tumbril took it very well, and said something about liking a man who kept his teeth in his job. I repeated my first question.

"A surprise?" Tumbril considered. "I can't see why it shouldn't be a surprise."

"But yet it isn't?"

"No, Appleby—it is not. Since Thorman came down to us a few days ago there has been something in the air. We were very old friends, and I couldn't help feeling something wrong."

"Thorman didn't give any hint of what it might be?"

"None at all. He was always a reticent fellow."

"He might have had some sort of secret life?"

"I hope he had nothing as shoddy as that sounds, Appleby. And I don't think you'd find any of the very obvious things: money gone wrong, a jam between two women, or anything of that sort. But serious disease is a possibility. He looked healthy enough, but you never know."

"Were there any relations?"

"A brother. I suppose I ought to contact him now." Tumbril crossed the room to the old upright telephone he kept on his desk. Then he said: "I'll do that later."

I thought this might be a hint for me to clear out. But I asked one more question. "You had confidence, Sir Charles, in Thorman's probity?"

He looked at me with a startled face. "Probity?" he repeated. "Are you suggesting, Appleby, that Thorman may have been a spy—something of that sort?"

THE SANDS OF THYME

"Yes, Sir Charles. That is what I have in mind."

He looked at me in silence for almost half a minute, and his voice when he spoke was uncomfortably cold. "I must repeat that Arthur Thorman was one of my oldest friends. Your suggestion is ridiculous. It is also personally offensive to me. Good morning."

So that was that, and I left the room well and truly snubbed.

All the same, I didn't precisely banish the puzzle of Arthur Thorman from my mind.

And there *was* a puzzle; it was a perfectly plain puzzle, which appears clearly in the facts as I've already given them.

Tumbril must have felt he'd been a bit stiff with me, and that I'd shown the correct reactions. At least that, I suppose, is why I received a telephone call from Lady Tumbril later in the morning, inviting me in to tea. I went along at the time named.

Thorman's brother had arrived. He must have been much older than the dead man; his only interest in life was the Great Pyramid of Cheops; and he gave no indication of finding a suicide in the family anything very out of the way.

Lady Tumbril coped with the situation very well, but it wasn't a cheerful tea. Tumbril himself didn't appear—his wife explained that he was working—and we ate our crumpets in some abstraction, while the elder Thorman explained that something in the proportions of his pyramid made it certain that London would be destroyed by an earthquake in 1958.

It was only at the end of the meal that this tedious old person appeared to make any contact with the lesser catastrophe of that morning. And what he was mainly prompted to, it seemed, was a concern over his brother's clothes and baggage, as these must still repose in a bedroom upstairs.

The tea-party ended with the old man's going up to inspect and pack his brother's things, and with myself accompanying him to lend a hand.

I suppose I should be ashamed of the next incident in the story. Waste-paper baskets and fireplaces have a strong professional fascination for me. I searched those in Arthur Thorman's room. It was not quite at random. I had come to have a good idea of what I might find there. Ten minutes later I was once more in Sir Charles Tumbril's study.

"Will you please look at this, sir?"

He was again standing before the fireplace with his hands in his pockets, and he gave that sombre glance at what I was holding out to him. "Put it on the desk," he said.

"Sir Charles—is there any point in this concealment? I saw how it was with your arm when you stopped yourself from telephoning this morning."

"I've certainly had an accident. But I'm not aware that I need exhibit it to you, Appleby."

"Nor to your doctor?"

He looked at me in silence. "What do you want?" he asked.

"I should like to know, sir, whether Thorman was writing a book—a book of memoirs, or anything of that sort?"

Tumbril glanced towards the piece of charred paper I had laid on his desk. "Yes," he said, "I believe he was."

"You must know what I've got here, sir. I had to find it." I was looking at him steadily. "You see, the thing didn't make sense as it stood. That last message of Thorman's could be the product only of complete spontaneity—a final spur-of-the-moment touch to his suicide.

"But, although it had the appearance of having been written on the spot, there wasn't another scrap of paper on him. That it should just happen that he had that one fragment from a notebook——"

"I see. And what, in fact, have you got there?"

"The bottom of another leaf of the same paper, Sir Charles. And on it, also in Thorman's writing, just two words: *paper gliders*."

———

"I must tell you the truth." Tumbril had sat down. "I must tell you the truth, Appleby.

"It so happens that I am a very light sleeper. That fact brought me down here at two o'clock this morning, to find Thorman with the safe open, and the P.2204 file in front of him on this desk. He brought out a revolver and fired at me.

"The bullet went through my arm. I don't doubt now that he meant to kill. And then he grabbed the file and bolted out through the french window. He must have opened it in case of just such a need to cut and run.

"He jumped from the terrace and I heard a yelp of pain. He tried to run on, but could only limp, and I knew that he had sprained an ankle. The result, of course, was that I caught up with him in no time.

"He still had the revolver; we struggled for it; it went off again—and there was Thorman, dead. I carried the body back to the house.

"I went up to his room with the idea of searching it for anything else he might have stolen, and there I saw the manuscript of this book he had begun. My eye fell on the last words he had written. I saw them as pathetic. And suddenly I saw how that pathos might be exploited to shield poor Arthur's name.

"My wife and I between us had the whole plan worked out within half an hour. Shortly before dawn we got out her helicopter from the private hangar—we fly in and out here, you know, at all sorts of hours—and hoisted in the body.

"Thorman and I were of the same weight and build; I put on his shoes, which I found fitted well enough; and then I set out for the shore.

The tide was just right, and I walked out to those rocks—limping, of course, for I remembered Thorman's ankle. My wife followed in the machine, and lowered the body to me on the winch.

"I restored the shoes and made the various dispositions which you found—and which you were meant to find, Appleby, for I had noticed your regular morning walk.

"Then I went up the rope and we flew home. We thought that we had achieved our aim: to make it appear irrefutable that poor Arthur Thorman had committed suicide—and in circumstances which, although mysterious, were wholly unconnected with any suspicion of treason."

When Appleby had concluded his narrative, neither of his hearers spoke.

"My dear Appleby," the Vicar said presently, "you were in a very difficult position. I shall be most interested to hear what your decision was."

"I haven't the slightest idea." And Appleby smiled at the astonishment of his friends. "Did you ever hear of Arthur Thorman?"

The Doctor considered. "I can't say that I ever did."

"Or, for that matter, of the important Sir Charles Tumbril?"

The Vicar shook his head. "No. When you come to mention it——"

And Appleby picked up his novel again. "Didn't I say," he murmured, "that I was going to tell you a story? And there it is—a simple story about footprints on the sands of Thyme."

THE FLYING DEATH

SAMUEL HOPKINS ADAMS

A PROLIFIC WRITER of fiction and once one of America's most popular authors, Samuel Hopkins Adams (1871–1958) was also a noted muckraking journalist whose investigations into patent medicines and medical quackery were instrumental in bringing about the passage of the first Pure Food and Drug Act.

Born in Dunkirk, New York, he received BA and LHD degrees from Hamilton College but was not ambitious, preferring to fish and search for antiques. When he turned to journalism, his ability to popularize research in science and medicine brought him great success. He used the background of phony medical practices for many of the stories in his highly regarded detective story collection, *Average Jones* (1911), a series he abandoned when he was unable to come up with additional plots. His only other mystery-related books were *The Secret of Lonesome Cove* (1912) and a chapter of *The President's Mystery Plot* (1935), a round-robin mystery by seven authors based on a plot idea by Franklin D. Roosevelt. Among his many non-mystery stories, the most notable is "Night Bus," which was made into the motion picture classic *It Happened One Night* (1934), starring Clark Gable and Claudette Colbert. Other films based on Adams's work were *The Gorgeous Hussy* (1936), starring Joan Crawford, Robert Taylor, and Lionel Barrymore, and *The Harvey Girls* (1946), starring Judy Garland.

"The Flying Death" was first published in the January and February 1903 issues of *McClure's*; it was later expanded into a full-length novel of the same title (New York, McClure, 1908).

THE FLYING DEATH

SAMUEL HOPKINS ADAMS

Document No. 1.—A letter of explanation from Harris Haynes, Reporter for the *New Era*, New York, off on Vacation to his Managing Editor.

Montauk Point, L. I., Sept. 20th, 1902. Mr. John Clare, Managing Editor, the *New Era*, New York City.

MY DEAR Mr. Clare,—here is a case for your personal consideration. At present it is—or, at least, it would appear on paper—a bit of pure insanity. Lest you should think it that, and myself the victim, I have two witnesses of character and reputation who will corroborate every fact in the case, and who go further with the incredible inferences than I can bring myself to do. They are Professor Willis Ravenden, expert in entomology and an enthusiast in every other branch of science, and Stanford Colton, son of old Colton, of the Button Trust, and himself a medical student about to obtain his diploma. Colton, like myself, is recuperating. Professor Ravenden is studying the metamorphosis of a small, sky-blue butterfly species of insect with a disjointed name which inhabits these parts.

We three constitute the total late-season patronage of Third House, and probably five per cent of the population of this forty square miles of grassland, the remainder being the men of the Life Saving Service, the farmer families of First, Second, and Third Houses, and a little settlement of fishermen on the Sound side.

This afternoon—yesterday, to be accurate, as it is now past midnight—we three went out for a tramp. On our return we ran into a fine, driving rain that blotted out the landscape. It's no trick at all to get lost in this country, where the hillocks were all hatched out of the same egg and the scrub-oak patches out of the same acorn. For an hour or so we circled around. Then we caught the booming of the surf plainly, and came presently to the crest of the sand-cliff, eighty feet above the beach. As the mist blew away we saw, a few yards out from the cliff's foot and a short distance to the east, the body of a man lying on the hard sand.

There was something in the huddled posture that struck the eye with a shock as of violence. With every reason for assuming at first sight the body to have been washed up, I somehow knew that the man had not met death by the waves. Where we stood the cliff fell too precipitously to admit of descent, but opposite the body it was lower, and here a ravine cut sharply through a dip between the hills at right angles to the beach. We half fell, half slipped down the cliff, made our way to the gully's opening, and came upon a soft and pebbly beach only a few feet wide, beyond which the hard, clean level of sand stretched to the receding waves. As we reached the open a man appeared around a point to the eastward, saw the body, and broke into a run. Colton had started toward the body, but I called him back. I didn't want the sand marked just then. Keeping close to the cliff's edge, we went forward to meet the man. As soon as he could make himself heard above the surf he hailed us.

"How long has that been there?"

"We've just found it," said Colton, as we turned out toward the sea. "It must have been washed up at high tide."

"I'm the coastguardsman from the Bow Hill Station," said the man.

"We are guests at Third House," said I. "We'll go through with this together."

"Come along, then," said he.

We were now on a line with the body, which lay with the head toward the waves. The coastguardsman suddenly checked his steps and exclaimed, "It's Paul Serdholm." Then he rushed forward with a great cry, "He's been murdered!"

"Oh, surely not murdered," expostulated the Professor, nervously. "He's been drowned, and——"

"Drowned!" cried the other. "And how about that gash in the back of his neck? He's the guard from Sand Spit, two miles below. Three hours ago I saw him on the cliff yonder. Since then he's come and gone between here and his station. And"—he gulped suddenly and turned upon us so sharply that the Professor jumped—"what's he met with?"

"The wound might have been made by the surf dashing him on a sharp rock," I suggested.

"No, sir," said the coastguardsman, with emphasis. "The tide ain't this high once in a month. It's murder, that's what it is—foul murder," and he bent over the dead man with twitching shoulders.

"He's right," said Colton, who had been hastily examining the corpse. "This is no drowning case. The man was stabbed and died instantly. Was he a friend of yours?" he asked of the guard.

"No; nor of nobody's, was Paul Serdholm," replied the man. "No later than last week we quarrelled." He paused, looking blankly at us.

"How long would you say he had been dead?" I asked Colton.

"A very few minutes."

"Then get to the top of the cliff and scatter," I said; "the murderer must have escaped that way. From the hilltop you can see the whole country. Keep off that sand, can't you? Make a detour to the gully."

"And what will you do?" inquired Colton, looking at me curiously.

"Stay here and study this out," I replied, in a low tone. "You and the Professor meet me at Sand Spit in half an hour. Guard, if you don't see anything, come back here in fifteen minutes." He hesitated. "I've had ten years' experience in murder cases," I added. "If you will do as you're told for the next few minutes we should clear this thing up."

No sooner had they disappeared on the high ground than I set myself to the solution of the problem. Inland from the body stretched the hard beach. Not one of us had stepped between the body and the soft sand into which the cliff sloped. In this soft, pebbly mass of rubble footprints would be indeterminable. Anywhere else they should stand out like the stamp on a coin. As we approached I had noticed that there were no prints to the east. On the side of the sea there was nothing except numerous faint bird tracks extending almost to the water. Taking off my shoes I followed the spoor of the dead man. It stood out plain as a poster, to the westward. For a hundred yards I followed it. There was no parallel track. To make certain that his slayer had not crept upon him from that direction, I examined the prints for the marks of superimposed steps. None was there. Three sides, then, were eliminated. My first hasty glance at the sand between the body and the cliff had shown me nothing. Here, however, must be the evidence. Striking off from the dead man's line, I walked out upon the hard surface.

The sand was deeply indented beyond the body, where the three men had hurried across to begin the hunt. But no other footmark broke its evenness. Not until I was almost on a line between the corpse and the mouth of the gully did I find a clue. Clearly imprinted on the clean level was the outline of a huge claw. There were the five talons and the nub of the foot. A little forward and to one side was a similar mark, except that it was slanted differently. Step by step, with starting eyes and shuddering mind, I followed the trail. Then I became aware of a second, confusing the first, the track of the same creature. At first the second track was distinct, then it merged with the first, only to diverge again. In this second series the points of the talons were toward the cliff. From the body to the soft sand stretched the unbroken lines. *Nowhere else within a radius of many yards was there any other indication.* The sand lay blank as a white sheet of paper; as blank as my mind, which struggled with one stupefying thought—that between the dead life-saver and the refuge of the cliff no creature had passed except one that stalked on monstrous clawed feet!

My first thought was to preserve the evidence for a more careful examination. I hastily collected some flat rocks and had covered those marks nearest the soft sand when I heard a hail. For the present I didn't want the others to know what I had found. I wanted to think it out, undisturbed by conflicting theories. So I hastily returned, and was putting on my shoes when the Bow Hill coastguardsman—his name was Schenck—came out of the gully.

"See anything?" I called.

"Nothing to the northward. Have you found anything?"

"Nothing definite," I replied. "Don't cross the sand there. Keep along down. We'll go to the Sand Spit Station and report this."

But the man was staring out beyond my little column of rock shelters.

"What's that thing?" he said, pointing to the nearest unsheltered print. "Heavens! It looks like a bird track. And it leads straight to the body," he cried, in a voice that jangled on my nerves. But when he began to look fearfully overhead into the gathering darkness, drawing in his shoulders like one shrinking from a blow, that was too much. I jumped to my feet, grabbed him by the arm, and started him along.

"Don't be a fool," I said. "Keep this to yourself. I won't have a lot of idiots prowling around those tracks. Understand? You're to report this murder and say nothing about what you don't know. Later we'll take it up again."

The man seemed stunned. He walked along quietly, close to me, and it was no comfort to feel him now and again shaken by a violent shudder. We had nearly reached the station when Professor Ravenden and Colton came down to the beach in front of us. But they had nothing to tell.

Before we reached the station I cleared another point to my satisfaction.

"The man wasn't stabbed; he was shot," I said.

"I'll stake my life that's no bullet wound," cried Colton, quickly. "I've seen plenty of shooting cases. The bullet never was cast that made such a gap in a man's head as that. It was a sharp instrument, with power behind it."

"To Mr. Colton's opinion I must add my own for what it is worth," said Professor Ravenden.

"Can you qualify as an expert?" I demanded, with the rudeness of rasped nerves and in some surprise at the tone of certainty in the old boy's voice.

"When in search of a sub-species of the Papilionidae in the Orinoco region," said he, mildly, "my party was attacked by the Indians that infest the river. After we had beaten them off it fell to my lot to attend the wounded. I thus had opportunity to observe the wounds made by their slender spears. The incision under consideration bears a rather striking resemblance to the spear-gashes which I then saw. I may add that I brought away my specimens of Papilionidae intact, although we lost most of our provisions."

"No man has been near enough the spot where Serdholm was struck down to stab him," I said. "Our footprints are plain; so are his. There are no others. The man was shot by someone lying in the gully or on the cliff."

"I'll bet you five hundred to five dollars that the post-mortem doesn't result in the finding of a bullet," cried Colton.

I accepted, and it was agreed that he should stay and report from the post-mortem. At the station I talked with several of the men, and, assuming for the time that the case presented no unusual features of murder, tried to get at some helpful clue. Motive was my first aim. Results were scant. It is true that there was a general dislike of Serdholm, who was a moody and somewhat mysterious character, having come from nobody knew whence. On the other hand, no one had anything serious against him. The four clues that I struck, such as they were, can tabulate briefly:—

(I) A week ago Serdholm returned from Amagansett with a bruised face. He had been in a street fight with a local loafer who had attacked him when drunk. Report brought back by one of the farmers that the life-saver beat the other fellow soundly, who went away threatening vengeance. Found out by telephone that the loafer was in Amagansett as late as five o'clock this afternoon.

(II) Two months ago Serdholm accused a local fisherman of stealing some tobacco. Nothing further since heard of the matter.

(III) Three weeks ago a stranded juggler and mountebank found his way here and asked aid of Serdholm; claimed to be his cousin. Serdholm sent him away next day. Played some tricks and collected a little money from the men. Serdholm, angry at the jeers of the men about his relative, threw a heavy stick at him, knocking him down. As soon as he was able to walk juggler went away crying. Not since seen.

(IV) This is the most direct clue for motive and opportunity. Coastguard Schenck (the man who met us at the scene of the murder) quarrelled with the dead man over the daughter of a farmer, who prefers Schenck. They fought, but were separated. Schenck blacked Serdholm's eye. Serdholm threatened to get square. Schenck cannot prove absolute alibi. His bearing and behaviour, however, are those of an innocent man. Moreover, the knife he carried was too small to have made the wound that killed Serdholm. And how could Schenck—or any other

man—have stabbed the victim and left no track on the sand? That is the blank wall against which I come at every turn of conjecture.

Professor Ravenden, Schenck, and I started back, we two to Third House, Schenck to his station. Colton remained to wait for the coroner, who had sent word that he would be over as soon as a horse could bring him. As we were parting Schenck said:

"Gentlemen, I'm afraid there's likely to be trouble for me over this."

"It's quite possible," I said, "that they may arrest you."

"Heaven knows I never thought of killing Serdholm or any other man. But I had a grudge against him, and I wasn't far away when he was killed. The only evidence to clear me is those queer tracks."

"I shall follow those until they lead me somewhere," said I, "and I do not myself believe, Schenck, that you had any part in the thing."

"Thank you," said the guard. "Good-night."

Professor Ravenden turned to me as we entered the house.

"Pardon a natural curiosity. Did I understand that there were prints on the sand which might be potentially indicative?"

"Professor Ravenden," said I, "there is an inexplicable feature to this case. If you'll come up to my room I should very much like to draw on your fund of natural history."

When we were comfortably settled I began.

"Would it be possible for a wandering ostrich or other huge bird, escaped from some zoo, to have made its home here?"

"Scientifically quite possible. May I inquire the purpose of this? Can it be that the tracks referred to by the guard were the cloven hoof-prints of——"

"Cloven hoofs!" I cried, in sharp disappointment. "Is there no member of the ostrich family that has claws?"

"None now extant. In the processes of evolution the claws of the ostrich, like its wings, have gradually——"

"Is there any huge-clawed bird large enough

and powerful enough to kill a man with a blow of its beak?"

"No, sir," said the Professor. "I know of no bird which would venture to attack man except the ostrich, emu, or cassowary, and the fighting weapon of this family is the hoof, not the beak. But you will again pardon me if I ask——"

"Professor Ravenden, the only thing that approached Serdholm within striking distance walked on a foot armed with five great claws." I rapidly sketched on a sheet of paper a rough, but careful, drawing. "And there's its sign-manual," I added, pushing it towards him.

Imagination could hardly picture a more precise, unemotional, and conventionally scientific man than Professor Ravenden. Yet at sight of the paper his eyes sparkled, he half started from his chair, a flush rose in his cheeks, he looked briskly and keenly from the sketch to me, and spoke in a voice that rang with a deep under-thrill of excitement.

"Are you sure, Mr. Haynes—are you quite sure that this is substantially correct?"

"Minor details may be inexact. In all essentials that will correspond to the marks made by a thing that walked from the mouth of the gully to the spot where we found the body, and back again."

Before I had fairly finished the Professor was out of the room. He returned almost immediately with a flat slab of considerable weight. This he laid on the table, and taking my drawing sedulously compared it with an impression, deep-sunken into the slab. For me a single glance was enough. That impression, stamped as it was on my brain, I would have identified as far as the eye could see it.

"That's it," I cried, with the eagerness of triumphant discovery. "The bird from whose foot that cast was made is the thing that killed Serdholm."

"Mr. Haynes," said the entomologist, drily, "this is not a cast."

"Not a cast?" I said, in bewilderment. "What is it, then?"

"It is a rock of the Cretaceous period."

"A rock?" I repeated, dully. "Of what period?"

"The Cretaceous. The creature whose footprint you see there trod that rock when it was soft ooze. That may have been one hundred million years ago. It was at least ten million."

I looked again at the rock, and strange emotions stirred among the roots of my hair.

"Where did you find it?" I asked.

"It formed a part of Mr. Stratton's stone fence. Probably he picked it up in his pasture yonder. The maker of the mark inhabited the island where we now are—this land was then distinct from Long Island—in the incalculably ancient ages."

"What did this bird thing call itself?" I demanded.

"It was not a bird. It was a reptile. Science knows it as the Pteranodon."

"Could it kill a man with its beak?"

"The first man came millions of years later—or so science thinks," said the Professor. "However, primeval man, unarmed, would have fallen an easy prey to so formidable a brute as this. The Pteranodon was a creature of prey," he continued, with an attempt at pedantry which was obviously a ruse to conquer his own excitement. "From what we can reconstruct, a reptile stands forth spreading more than twenty feet of bat-like wings, and bearing a four-foot beak as terrible as a bayonet. This monster was the undisputed lord of the air; as dreadful as his cousins of the earth, the Dinosaurs, whose very name carries the significance of terror."

"And you mean to tell me that this billion-years-dead flying sword-fish has flitted out of the darkness of eternity to kill a miserable coast-guard within a hundred miles of New York in the year 1902?" I cried. He had told me nothing of the sort. I didn't want to be told anything of the sort. I wanted reassuring. But I was long past weighing words.

"I have not said so," replied the entomologist, quickly. "But if your diagram is correct, Mr. Haynes—if it is reasonably accurate—I can tell you that no living bird ever made the print which it reproduces, that science knows no five-toed bird and no bird whatsoever of sufficiently formidable beak to kill a man. Furthermore, that the one creature known to science which could make that print, and could slay man or a creature far more powerful than man, is the tiger of the air, the Pteranodon. Probably, however, your natural excitement, due to the distressing circumstances, has led you into error, and your diagram is inaccurate."

"Will you come with me and see?" I demanded.

"Willingly. I shall have to ask your help, however, with the rock."

We got a light, for it was now very dark, and, taking turns with the lantern and the Cretaceous slab (which hadn't lost any weight with age, by the way), we went direct to the shore and turned westward. Presently a light appeared around the face of the cliff and Colton hailed us. He was on his way back to Third House, but, of course, joined us in our excursion.

I hastily explained to him the matter of the footprints, the diagram, and the fossil marks. "Professor Ravenden would have us believe that Serdholm was killed by a beaked ghoul that lived a hundred million years ago."

"I'll tell you one thing," said Colton, gravely. "He wasn't killed by a bullet. It was a stab wound—a broad-bladed knife or something of that sort, but driven with terrific power. The post-mortem settled that. You lose your bet, Haynes. Why," he cried, suddenly, "if you come to that it wasn't unlike what a heavy, sharp beak would make. But—but—this Pteranodon—is that it? Oh, the deuce! I thought all those Pterano-things were dead and buried before Adam's great-grandfather was a protoplasm."

"Science has assumed that they were extinct," said the Professor. "But a scientific assumption is a mere makeshift, useful only until it is overthrown by new facts. We have prehistoric survivals—the gar of our rivers is unchanged from his ancestors of fifteen million years ago. The creature of the water has endured; why not the creature of the air?"

"Oh, come off," said Colton, seriously. "Where could it live and not have been discovered?"

"Perhaps at the North or South Pole," said the Professor. "Perhaps in the depths of unexplored islands. Or possibly inside the globe. Geographers are accustomed to say loosely that the earth is an open book. Setting aside the exceptions which I have noted, there still remains the interior, as unknown and mysterious as the planets. In its possible vast caverns there may well be reproduced the conditions in which the Pteranodon and its terrific contemporaries found their suitable environment on the earth's surface ages ago."

"Then how would it get out?"

"The violent volcanic disturbances of this summer might have opened an exit. However, I am merely defending the Pteranodon's survival as an interesting possibility. My own belief is that your diagram, Mr. Haynes, is faulty."

"Hold the light here, then," I said, laying down the slab, for we were now at the spot. "I will convince you as to that."

While the Professor held the light I uncovered one of the tracks. A quick exclamation escaped him. He fell on his knees beside the print, and as he compared the today's mark on the sand with the rock print of millions of years ago his breath came hard. When he lifted his head his face was twitching nervously, but his voice was steady.

"I have to ask your pardon, Mr. Haynes," he said. "Your drawing was faithful. The marks are the same."

"But what in Heaven's name does it mean?" cried Colton.

"It means that we are on the verge of the most important discovery of modern times," said the Professor. "Savants have hitherto scouted the suggestions to be deduced from the persistent legend of the roc, and from certain almost universal North American Indian lore, notwithstanding that the theory of some monstrous winged creature widely different from any recognised existing forms is supported by more convincing proofs. In the North of England, in 1844, reputable witnesses found the tracks, after a night's fall of snow, of a creature with a pendent tail, which made flights over houses and other obstructions, leaving a trail much like this before us. There are other corroborative instances of a similar nature. In view of the present evidence I would say that this was unquestionably a Pteranodon, or a descendant little altered, and a very large specimen, as the tracks are distinctly larger than the fossil prints. Gentlemen, I congratulate you both on your part in so epoch-making a discovery."

"Do you expect a sane man to believe this thing?" I demanded.

"That's what I feel," said Colton. "But, on your own showing of the evidence, what else is there to believe?"

"But see here," I expostulated, all the time feeling as if I were arguing in and against a dream. "If this is a *flying* creature, how explain the footprints leading up to Serdholm's body as well as away from it?"

"Owing to its structure," said the Professor, "the Pteranodon could not rapidly rise from the ground in flight. It either sought an acclivity from which to launch itself or ran swiftly along the ground, gathering impetus for a leap into the air with outspread wings. Similarly, in alighting, it probably ran along on its hind feet before coming to a halt. Now, suppose the Pteranodon to be on the cliff's edge, about to start upon its evening flight. Below it appears a man. Its ferocious nature is aroused. Down it swoops, skims swiftly with pattering feet toward him, impales him on its dreadful beak, then returns to climb the cliff and again launch itself for flight."

"If the shore was covered with these footprints," I said vehemently, "I wouldn't believe it. It's too——"

I never finished that sentence. From out of the darkness there came a hoarse cry. Heavy wings beat the air with swift strokes. In that instant panic seized me. I ran for the shelter of the cliff, and after me came Colton. Only the Professor stood his ground, but it was with a tremulous voice that he called to us:

"That was a common marsh or short-eared owl that arose; the Asio accipitrinus is not rare hereabouts. There is nothing further to do tonight, and I believe that we are in some peril in remaining here, as the Pteranodon appears to be nocturnal."

We returned to him ashamed. But all the way home, despite my better sense, I walked under an obsession of terror hovering in the blackness above.

So here is the case as clearly as I can put it. I shall have time to work it out unhampered, as the remoteness of the place is a safeguard so far as news is concerned, and only we three know of the Pteranodon prints.

It seems like a nightmare—formless, meaningless. What you will think of it I can only conjecture. But you must not think that I have lost my senses. I am sane enough; so is Colton; so, to all appearances, is Professor Ravenden. The facts are exactly as I have written them down. I have left no clue untouched thus far. I will stake my life on the absence of footprints. And it all comes down to this, Mr. Clare: Pteranodon or no Pteranodon, as sure as my name is Haynes, the thing that killed Paul Serdholm never walked on human feet.

Very sincerely yours,
HARRIS D. HAYNES.

Document No. 2—Extract from letter written by Stanford Colton to his father, John Colton, Esq., of New York City. Date, September 21st, 4 p.m.

So there, my dear dad, is the case against the Pteranodon. To your hard business sense it will seem a thing for laughter. You wouldn't put a cent in Pteranodon stock on the word of an idealistic, scientific theorist like old Ravenden, backed by a few queer marks on a beach. Very well, neither would I. All the same, I ducked and ran when the owl flapped out from the cliff. And I wonder if you wouldn't have been dragging us to shelter yourself if you had been there.

At six o'clock this morning Haynes woke me out of a troubled dream by walking along the hall.

"Is that you, Haynes?" I called.

"Yes," he said. "I'm off for the beach."

"Wait fifteen minutes and I'll go with you," I suggested.

"If you don't mind, Colton, I'd rather you wouldn't. I want to go over the ground alone first. A good night's rest has scared the Professor's Cretaceous jub-jub bird out of my mental premises."

I was now up and at the door.

"Well, good luck!" I said and for some reason I reached out and shook hands with him.

He looked rather surprised—perhaps just a bit startled—but he only said, "See you in a couple of hours."

Sleep was not for me after that. I tried it, but it was no go. The Stratton family almost expired of amazement when I showed up for seven o'clock breakfast. Half an hour later I was on the way to find Haynes. I went direct down the beach. Haynes had gone this way before me, as I saw by his tracks. It was a dead-and-alive sort of morning—grey, with a mist that seemed to smother sound as well as sight. I went forward with damped spirits and little heart in the enterprise. As I came to the turn of the cliff that opens up the view down the shore I halloaed for Haynes. No reply came. Again I shouted, and this time, as my call drew no answer, I confess that a clammy feeling of loneliness hastened my steps. I rounded the cliff at a good pace and saw ahead what checked me like a blow.

Almost at the spot where we had found Serdholm a man lay sprawled grotesquely. Though the face was hidden and the posture distorted, I knew him instantly for Haynes, and as instantly knew that he was dead. I went forward to the body, sickening at every step.

Haynes had been struck opposite the gully. The weapon that killed him had been driven with fearful impetus between his ribs, from the back. A dozen staggering prints showed where he had plunged forward before he fell. The heart was touched, and he must have been dead almost on the stroke. His flight was involuntary—the blind, mechanical instinct of escape from death. To one who had seen its like before there was no mistaking that great gash in his back. Haynes had been killed as Serdholm was. But for what cause? What possible motive of murder could embrace those two who had never known or so much as spoken to each other? No; it was motiveless: the act of a thing without mind, inspired by no motive but the blood-thirst, the passion of slaughter. At that the picture of the Pteranodon, as the Professor had drawn it, took hold of my mind. I ran to the point whence Haynes had staggered. Beginning there, in double line over the clean sand, stretched the grisly track of the talons. *Except for them the sand was untouched.*

Of the formalities that succeeded there is no need to speak; but following what I thought Haynes's method would have been, I investigated the movements of Schenck, the coast-guard, that morning. From six o'clock till eight he was at the station. His alibi is perfect. In the killing of poor Haynes he had no part. That being proved sufficiently establishes his innocence of the Serdholm crime. Both were done by the same murderer.

Professor Ravenden is now fixed in his belief that the Pteranodon, or some little-altered descendant, did the murders. I am struggling not to believe it, yet it lies at the back of all my surmises as a hideous probability. One thing I know, that nothing would tempt me alone upon that beach tonight. Tomorrow morning I shall load my Colt and go down there with the Professor, who is a game old theorist, and can be counted on to see this through. He is sketching out, this afternoon, a monograph on the survival of the Pteranodon. It will make a stir in the scientific world. Don't be worried about my part in this. I'll be cautious tomorrow. No other news to tell; nothing but this counts.

Your affectionate son,
STANFORD.

Document No. 3—Statement by Stanford Colton regarding his part in the events of the morning of September 22nd, 1902.

On the morning of the day after the killing of Harris Haynes I went to the beach opposite Stony Gully. It was seven o'clock when I reached the point where the bodies were found. Professor Ravenden was to have accompanied me. He had started out while I was at breakfast, however, through a misunderstanding as to time. His route was a roundabout one, bringing him to the spot after my arrival, as will appear in his report. I went directly down the shore. In my belt was a forty-five-calibre revolver.

As I came opposite Stony Gully I carefully examined the sand. The five-taloned tracks were in several places almost as distinct as on the previous day. Fortunately, owing to the scanty population and the slow transmission of news, there had been very few visitors to the scene, and those few had been careful in their movements, so the evidence was not trodden out.

For a closer examination I got down on my hands and knees above one of the tracks. There was the secret, if I could but read it. The mark was in all respects the counterpart of the sketch made by Haynes, and of the impress on the Cretaceous rock of Professor Ravenden. I might have been in that posture two or three minutes, my mind immersed in conjecture. Then I rose, and as I stood and looked down there suddenly flashed into my brain the solution. I started forward to the next mark, and as I advanced something sang in the air behind me. I knew it was some swiftly flying thing; knew in the same agonizing moment that I was doomed; tried to face my death; and then there was a dreadful, grinding shock, a flame tore through my brain, and I fell forward into darkness.

Document No. 4—The explanation by Professor Willis Ravenden, F.R.S., etc., of the events of September 20th, 21st, and 22nd, 1902, surrounding the deaths of Paul Serdholm and Harris Haynes and the striking down of Stanford Colton.

Upon the death of my esteemed young friend, Mr. Haynes, I made minute examination of the vestigia near the body. These were obviously the footprints of the same creature that killed Serdholm, the coastguard. Not only the measurements and depth of indentation, but the intervals corresponded exactly to those observed in the first investigation. The non-existence of any known five-toed birds drove me to consideration of other winged creatures, and certainly none may say that, with the evidence on hand, my hypothesis of the survival and reappearance of the Pteranodon was not justified.

Having concluded my examination into the circumstances of Mr. Haynes's death, I returned to Third House and set about embodying the remarkable events in a monograph. In this work I employed the entire afternoon and evening, with the exception of an inconsiderable space devoted to a letter which it seemed proper to write to the afflicted family of Mr. Haynes, and in which I suggested for their comfort the fact that he met his death in the noble cause of scientific investigation. In pursuance of an understanding with Mr. Colton, he and I were to have visited, early on the following morning, the scene of the tragedies. By a misconception of the plan I set out before he left, thinking that he had already gone. My purpose was to proceed to the spot along the cliffs instead of by the beach, this route affording a more favourable view, though an intermittent one, as it presents a succession of smoothly rolling hillocks. Hardly had I left the house when the disturbance of the grasses incidental to my passage put to flight a fine specimen of the Lycaena pseudoargiolus, whose variations I have been investigating. I had, of course, taken my net with me, partly, indeed, as a weapon of defence, as the butt is readily detachable and heavily loaded.

In the light of subsequent events I must confess my culpability in allowing even so absorbing an interest as this that suddenly beset my path to turn me from my engagement to meet Mr. Colton. Instinctively, however, I pursued the insect. Although this species, as is well known, exhibits a power of sustained flight possessed by none other of the lepidopterae of corresponding wing area, I hoped that, owing to the chill morning air, this specimen would be readily captured. Provokingly it alighted at short intervals, but on each occasion rose again as I was almost within reach. Thus lured on I described a half-circle and was, approximately, a third of a mile inland when finally I netted my prey on the leaves of a Quercus ilicifolia. Having deposited it in the poison jar which I carried on a shoulder-strap, I made haste, not without some quickenings of self-reproach, toward the cliff. Incentive to greater haste was furnished by a fog-bank that was approaching from the south. Heading directly for the nearest point of the cliff, I reached it before the fog arrived. The first object that caught my eyes, as it ranged for the readiest access to the beach, was the outstretched body of Colton lying upon the hard sand where Serdholm and Haynes had met their deaths.

For the moment I was stunned into inaction. Then came the sense of my own guilt and responsibility. Along the cliff I ran at full speed, dipped down into a hollow, where, for the time, the beach was shut off from view, and surmounted the hill beyond, which brought me almost above the body a little to the east of the gully. The fog, too, had been advancing swiftly, and now as I reached the cliff's edge it spread a grey mantle over the body lying there alone. Already I had reached the head of the gully, when there moved very slowly out upon the hard sand a thing so out of all conception, an apparition so monstrous to the sight, that my net fell from my hand and a loud cry burst from me. In the grey folds of mist it wavered, assuming shapes beyond comprehension. Suddenly it doubled on itself, contracted to a compact mass, underwent a strange inversion, and before my clearing vision there arose a man, dreadful of aspect indeed, but still a human being, and, as such, not beyond human powers to cope with. Coincident with this recognition I noted a knife, inordinately long of blade and bulky of handle, on the sand almost under Colton. Toward this the man had been moving when my cry arrested

him, and now he stood facing the height with strained eye and gnashing teeth.

There was no time for delay. The facile descent of the gully was out of the question. It was over the cliff or nothing; for if Colton was alive his only chance was that I should reach his assailant before the latter could come at the knife. Upon the flash of the thought I was in mid-air, a giddy terror dulling my brain as I plunged down through the fog. Fortunately for me—for the bones of sixty years are brittle—I landed upon a slope of soft sand. Forward I pitched, threw myself completely over, and, carried to my feet by the impetus, ran down the lesser slope upon the man. That he was obsessed by a mania of murder was written on his face and in his eyes. But now his expression, as he turned toward me, was that of a beast alarmed. To hold his attention I shouted. The one desideratum was to reach him before he turned again to the knife and Colton.

The maniac crouched as I ran in upon him, and I must confess to a certain savage exultation as I noted that he had little the advantage of me in size or weight. Although not a large man, I may say that I am of wiry frame, which my out-of-door life has kept in condition. So I felt no great misgivings as to the outcome. We closed. As my opponent's muscles tightened on mine I knew, with a sudden, daunting shock, that I had met the strength of fury. For a moment we strained, I striving for a hold which would enable me to lift him from his feet. Then with a rabid scream the creature dashed his face into my shoulder and bit through shirt and flesh until the teeth grated on my shoulder blade.

Not improbably this saved my life and Colton's. For, upon the outrage of that assault, a fury not less insane than that of my enemy fired me, and I, who have ever practised a certain scientific austerity of emotional life, became a raging beast. Power flashed through every vein; strength distended every muscle. Clutching at the throat of my assailant I tore that hideous face from my shoulder. My right hand, drawn back for a blow, twitched the cord of my heavy poison bottle. Shouting aloud I swung the formidable weapon up and brought it down upon his head with repeated blows. His grasp relaxed. I sprang back for a fuller swing and beat him to the ground. The jar was shattered, but such was my ecstasy of murderousness that I forgot the specimen of pseudo-argiolus, which fell with the fragments and was trodden into the sand.

In my hand I still held the base of the jar. My head was whirling. I staggered backward, and with just sense enough left to know that the deadly fumes of the cyanide were doing their work flung it far away. A mist fell like a curtain somewhere between my eyes and my brain, befogging the processes of thought.

The next thing I knew, I was lying on my back, looking into a white face—Colton's! I must have been saying something, for Colton replied, as if to a question:

"It's all right, Professor. There's no pseudo-argiolus or Pteranodon, or anything. Just lie quiet."

But it was borne in upon me that I had lost my prize. "Let me up!" I cried. "I've lost it—it fell when the poison jar broke."

"There, there," he said, soothingly, as one calms a delirious person. "Just wait——"

"I'm speaking of my specimen, the pseudo-argiolus." The mist was beginning to lift from my brain, and the mind now swung dizzily back to the great speculation. "The Pteranodon?" I gasped.

"There!" Colton laughed shakily as he pointed to the blood-besmeared form lying quiet on the sand.

"But the footprints! The fossil marks on the rock!"

"Footprints on the rock? Handprints here."

"Handprints!" I repeated. "Tell me slowly. I must confess to a degree of bewilderment to which I am not accustomed."

"No wonder, sir. Here it is. I saw it all just before I was hit. This man is Serdholm's cousin, the juggler. He's crazy, probably from Serdholm's blow. He's evidently been waiting for a chance to kill Serdholm. The gully's mouth is where he waited. You've seen circus-jugglers throw knives—well, that's the way he killed Serdholm. In his crazy cunning he saw that footprints would give him away, so he utilized another of his circus tricks and recovered the knife by walking on his hands. His handprints are what we mistook for the footprints of a giant, prehistoric bird!"

"But Mr. Haynes? And yourself?"

"I don't know why he wanted to kill us, unless he feared we would discover his secret. I escaped because I was going forward as he threw, and that must have disturbed his aim so that the knife turned in the air and the handle struck me, knocking me senseless."

Here the juggler groaned, and we busied ourselves with bringing him to.

My monograph on the Pteranodon, it is hardly needful to state, will not be published. At the same time I maintain that the survival of this formidable creature, while now lacking definite proof, is none the less strictly within the limits of scientific possibility. . . .

WILLIS RAVENDEN.

THE FLYING CORPSE

A. E. MARTIN

A MYSTERY AUTHOR who seemed at one time to have great potential to become a major figure on the literary scene, Archibald Edward Martin (1885–1955) never quite succeeded in going beyond being a much-loved cult writer. Born in South Australia, his obsession was travel (he went as far as Invercargill, the town closest to the South Pole) and meeting all kinds of people as he took on a wide variety of unconventional jobs, including managing prize fighters, freaks, and film stars, as well as touring with a vaudeville show. His novel *The Bridal Bed Murders* (1954; published in England as *The Chinese Bed Mysteries* in 1955) employed some of these colorful vocations, with a traveling freak show touring Australia as a background. While in Europe, he bought the rights to numerous documentary films and exhibited them in Australia. Martin was nearly sixty when he tried his hand at mystery writing, producing three books in 1944: *Sinners Never Die*, *The Misplaced Corpse*, and *The Common People* (retitled from its Australian publication as *The Outsiders* in the United States and England). The last title served as the basis for the 1955 Hammer film titled *The Glass Cage* (released in America as *The Glass Tomb*), which starred John Ireland and Honor Blackman and was directed by Montgomery Tully. These novels were followed by a short-story collection, *The Shudder Show* (1945), and two detective novels, *Death in the Limelight* (1946) and *The Curious Crime* (1952). His most famous short story, "The Power of the Leaf" (1948), is a story of a nineteenth-century aboriginal tribe living in the Bush in which the protagonist, Ooloo of the Narranyeri, uses observation and deduction in true Holmesian fashion to solve a mystery that has baffled the medicine man.

"The Flying Corpse" was first published in the September 1947 issue of *Ellery Queen's Mystery Magazine*.

THE FLYING CORPSE

A. E. MARTIN

"THERE MUST be some little thing wrong that's not quite right," my wife said.

I gave her a look, but she settled back in the front seat of the car and closed her eyes. "You go right ahead, dear, and fix it," she went on, snuggling deeper into the cushions. "After all, it's broken down in a nice spot."

I thought, if she were going to sleep and I, in my shirt sleeves, was to dig and delve into the disgusting entrails of the wretched bus, it didn't matter what sort of place the thing had chosen to break down in. Nevertheless, as I looked about me, I confessed that Mona was right.

So far as the motor road knew them we were on the crest of the Hummocks, a line of low, bare hills that provided the tail to the range that stretched Northward to God knows where. We had climbed no noble height, but at least we commanded a view, even if it was only one of flat land stretching in an immense green carpet to the shores of the distant gulf. It was one of those clear, crisp mornings when we should have been able to see ships a-sailing. But there were no ships. As far as I could see, between us and the gulf, there was nothing but grass and stunted bush, with no sign of habitation. Watching closely you could discern the lazy movement of inaudible waves as they curled in to make patterns in foam along the flat, deserted beach. Except for that there was no movement. For miles around the country appeared to be holding its breath, sluggish in the welcome warmth of a perfect winter's day. The sunshine was no more than a caress and twenty feet below the built-up highway, dew still glistened.

Lighting my pipe I scowled at the car.

Mona's voice came drowsily: "Unless you're going to make it work, Rodney, I think we should telephone Nell."

"Mona, my true love," I retorted, "there is no chance of telephoning your adorable sister." I added, malevolently, "Let the sausages wither."

"Oh, Nell wouldn't have sausages," Mona said.

I didn't pursue the subject but peered into the innards of the ailing Retallick. I am not mechanically minded. I am a physician, not a surgeon. I felt that whatever I did to the inside of the automobile would be wrong, and I prayed fervently for the approach of a car driven by one of those cool, efficient fellows who talk off-handedly of carburetors and sparkplugs as if they were mere thromboses or polypi.

"Have you got it going?" Mona asked, after I had, by rattling the spanner against this and that, awakened the echoes with some hearty industrial noises.

"No, I haven't," I said, shortly. "If only I had a hairpin . . ." I was well aware she never used them.

"I really think, Rodney, we should telephone," my wife said again.

"For the hundredth time, Mona," I cried,

exasperated into exaggeration, "how can we telephone from the midst of nowhere?"

"Well, it seems quite unfair to Nellie," she
retorted, as illogical as ever. "She's probably put
her best bib on. We're hours late."

I wanted to say, "And whose fault is that?" but
asked myself, "What's the use?" I'd wanted to
start at eight. We could have been at my sister-
in-law's country home comfortably by noon and
settled down to the holiday we'd planned. But
by the time Mona had been ready to start, it was
ten. And there had been the delay at the gipsy
camp. My wife had insisted on having her fortune told. It had been a little queer the way that
paunchy Romany had looked at her and said,
"So you've come back, eh? Looking for *more* bad
luck?" Of course she'd never been there before,
as he realized when she spoke. All the rigmarole
about prospective offspring and halcyon days
ahead had taken up the best part of an hour and
now the effete Retallick had played up.

Opening her eyes, Mona said, "For goodness'
sake, Rodney, make an effort. Hit a bolt or something."

"Do you realize, my girl, that tinkering
with the unknown may have disastrous consequences?" I asked grimly. "Hit a bolt, indeed!
Suppose it was the *right* bolt. The car might leap
suddenly forward and hurtle into the depths
with you in it. How'd you like to be shot off the
highway? You'd be dead in a jiffy. Worse . . . your
new hat crushed beyond recognition."

She patted the crazy thing affectionately and
stepped out of the car, stretching her arms ador-
ably.

"I know," I said, feeling better for the nearness of her, "I'll climb through the railing and
hide below the level of the road. At the first sign
of a car you'll proceed to fix your stocking. I've
heard it's infallible. Every motorist stops dead in
his tracks."

"And when he stops?"

"I shall leap out—I mean up—and render
him unconscious with this spanner. We will then
leap lightly into his car, push our own over the
nearest precipice, and live happily ever after."

"It sounds enthralling," Mona said, "but
haven't I heard crime doesn't pay? Seriously,
Rod, we can't stay here and perish. I think we—I
mean *you* should walk back and enquire at the
hut we just passed."

"I saw no hut," I said.

"I suppose you had your eyes on the road and
your thoughts on some other woman," she said,
and led me round the bend and pointed. Sure
enough there was a mud excrescence on the side
of the drab hill and, emerging from it, a tall and
very thin man who waved furiously. I waved
back, glad of anyone who might perhaps deal
with the refractory car.

We stood leaning on the road railing, looking down on him as he approached. He was
not exactly prepossessing. Hatless, his hair fell
untidily over an abnormally high brow. His eyes
were too small for the swollen dome above, and
his face narrowed to a weak chin and simpering
mouth. As he climbed the steepish slope to the
highway, I noticed the scrawniness of the wrists
and saw that he was barefooted. Mentally I classified him as hydrocephalic.

"Anyhow," Mona said, sensing my thoughts,
"he's wearing his best suit—even it it wasn't
made for him."

He was on the highway at last, towering over
us, his beady eyes focused on my wife. Putting
his fingers beside his absurd mouth he shuffled
like a shy schoolboy.

"My!" he giggled.

Mona smiled at him brazenly, and I coughed
significantly.

"Oh, let the boy have his hour," she said,
and like a mannequin, pirouetted. The stranger
gazed spellbound; then said, mincingly:

"I'm going to see you tonight."

Mona stopped abruptly in the middle of a
pose.

"Yes," he went on eagerly. "You're in the
circus, aren't you? All night I been hearing the
trucks go by."

Mona was too surprised to speak.

"That's what comes of wearing that hat," I
grinned.

"It's a rare pretty hat," the stranger said and Mona wrinkled her nose at me.

The man was grubbing into the inside pocket of his ridiculously inadequate coat. "But most I like you without clothes," he said simply, and as Mona blinked, held out a printed paper. "Like that."

I glanced over my wife's shoulder. The paper had been torn from some cheap publication and the tall man pointed a crudely bandaged forefinger at a picture of a girl posing in tights. Before he carefully restored it to his pocket I had time to notice that there was certainly some resemblance to Mona. So far as the hut dweller was concerned there was no doubt at all. He said, like a child telling of promised pleasures, "*I'm going to the circus tonight.*" He looked pensively at the automobile.

It was a chance in a million. "If you can make it go," I said, "we'll take you." I added mischievously, "You shall ride in the back with the lady."

"You shouldn't," Mona whispered as he walked across to the car. "It's not fair promising Mr. Simon . . ."

"Simon?"

"Sh-h." She nodded warningly toward the gangling creature who was poking an experimental finger into the belly of the Retallick.

"But how do you know it's Simon?"

She whispered. "Pieman . . . going to the fair. No money. Remember?"

I said, "If that poor devil can get the car going, I'll eat my hat."

And, surprisingly, at that moment the Retallick sprang to life.

"Oh-oh," Mona said. "I hope you're hungry." She reached up, and removing my hat, handed it to me.

"Well," I said, "your Mr. Simon deserves to ride beside his princess."

He stood, wiping greasy fingers on his newly-pressed pants, gazing into the interior of the car. With one foot on the running board he suddenly looked round. There was the strangest expression in his eyes. Suspicion was there, certainly, but something of fear too.

"We better see *him* first," he said.

"Him?"

"He's down there," he told us, pointing to the paddock below the road.

"Who?" I asked, and as he didn't reply, shook his sleeve. "What's he doing there?"

"I didn't go near," he said defensively. "I see him lying but I didn't go near. I called, but he didn't answer."

"Better have a look-see," Mona counselled and began to scramble under the railing. I helped her down the slope. When we reached the bottom Simple Simon was standing motionless, pointing at a spot some thirty feet from the roadway above. We followed his gaze and Mona caught her breath.

In the thin grass was a naked man. Even at that distance, and it must have been a dozen yards at least, I knew he was dead.

The tall man suddenly began whimpering.

"When did you find him?" I asked.

He turned slowly, blinking. "Before I put on this new suit." He added eagerly, "But I haven't been near him. No closer'n this," and asked, "Who put him there?"

My eyes roamed the patches of grass and bare dampish earth surrounding the body. Then bidding them stay where they were, I walked forward gingerly. I knew the importance of footprints. The body was lying, face down, in a curiously humped position, almost as if it had been in the first stage of turning a somersault. The temple rested in an indentation in the soft earth but the head was twisted and part of the cheek and chin was visible.

I looked back to where Mona and the stranger were standing and could clearly distinguish the tracks I had made. Then my eyes carefully surveyed the area surrounding the corpse. There was not the slightest indentation. How then, I wondered, did the man come to be lying there, thirty feet from the road. Of course, I'd known at once the cause of death. There was a bullet hole behind his ear. I straightened, frowning, to find Mona beside me.

"Now, don't be fussy," she said. "Simon's

run away to be sick." She looked down at the nude figure, ludicrous even in death, and made a little grimace.

"He's been shot," I told her. "See, the bullet went in there." I pointed to the hole behind the ear. "He was shot at very close quarters."

"And in the early morning," Mona said. "That's why he's undressed." She snapped her fingers. "I know. He was shot in the bath and dumped here. He must have shaved, finished his bath, and then got himself shot. It's a lesson, isn't it, always to lock your bathroom door and risk having a fainting fit?"

"O.K., Mrs. Sherlock Holmes," I said. "Now tell me something else. How did he get thirty feet from the highway? Peek around. You can see my footprints, can't you?" I raised my eyebrows. "Where are yours?"

"Oh," she said, "I was very clever about that. I tiptoed in your marks."

"Good for you," I said. "Now, do you see any other prints? Any indentations? Any wheel tracks? There isn't a sign. Then how did he get here?"

"Oh, you'll never make a detective," she said, calmly. "He was dropped, of course. Out of an airplane. He was murdered thousands of miles away and flown here."

"But," I objected, "airplanes have to travel at a good bat to keep up. When he hit the ground wouldn't he roll or bounce or something? This man looks as if he'd just plopped!"

"I know," she said. "Balloon! They were coming down and when they threw him out the balloon hurtled up again."

"Balloons are extinct," I told her. "Anyway, it's not our worry. After all, my pet, you're not going to ride with Simple Simon. Whether he likes it or not he's got to stay here and watch the body."

As her sister embraced her, Mona said breathlessly, "Oh, Nell, we're so sorry we're late. We've seen a murder."

"Nothing of the sort," I said, cutting short further exaggerations. "We came across a dead man."

"A gipsy," Mona said. "He was disgustingly naked in the middle of nowhere."

"We know nothing about him," I said. "We don't know *who* he is or *what* he is. Now you two gossip about something else while I find the policeman."

"He'll be watching the circus," Nell advised. "Half the population has gone to see the tent go up." She added apologetically, "The circus is an event in this little town."

Sergeant Copestone was watching an elephant hauling on some gadget affixed to a pulley that lifted the soiled and sagging canvas and gave it the shape and substance and magic that is the circus. He was frankly irritated when his attention was distracted from the unusual scene.

"Dead in a paddock, eh? Well it *would* have to happen today."

I explained about Simple Simon. "Oh, Daffy!" he said lightly. "Did *he* find him? Well, he's harmless. A half-wit and that's an exaggeration."

"He's at least a mechanic," I said.

"Daffy?" he scoffed. "A mechanic!"

"My car stalled. He made it go."

"I didn't think he'd ever ridden in one," Copestone chortled. "He must have had a lucky break." He looked at me keenly. "Did you say this chap was naked?"

"He wore less than Adam. And your Daffy had on a new suit—one that didn't fit."

"Don't tell me Daffy shot him just to get his clothes," Copestone grinned.

"In any case," I said, "how would he get the corpse to where we found it without leaving any tracks? There's no sign of anything."

"*You're* saying it," Copestone said. "I know the spot. He could have been emptied off the highway."

"No," I said, definitely, "He was too far from the road. I guess he was dropped from a plane."

Copestone groaned. "That means all sorts of blinking experts. Of course the stripping's to avoid identification. That won't help if it's a local lad, but if he was thrown from a plane he might have come from anywhere."

Well, he wasn't a local lad, and Cincotta, the circus proprietor, at the Sergeant's request, had a look at the body and said it was no one from his show. When I had a close-up with the local doctor I knew the man had died late the previous night, probably not more than an hour or so before he'd been dumped. He'd a number of injuries all consistent with a fall from a height, and for a moment I wondered if he could have come down in a parachute that had landed him none too gently. But, then, where was the parachute? I told Copestone I'd be in the town for two weeks and left him with his headache.

I'd been warned that tea would be served promptly at three-thirty and although I arrived on the dot, the girls were already taking theirs. Opposite them a young woman sat bolt upright, a cup held stiffly in her right hand. She gave me quite a shock because, as far as features went, she was the counterpart of Mona. She made as if to rise but Mona said:

"Don't move. It's only my brute of a husband." She turned to me. "This is M'lle. Valda from the circus," and left me to wonder while Nell served tea as if it were quite usual to have itinerant show-folk dropping in.

After some desultory conversation Mona said abruptly, "Rodney, you've got to give M'lle. Valda a certificate or something to say she can't perform tonight. She's had a great shock."

The circus woman attempted to wipe her eye with her free hand. I said, "I'm sorry to hear that." And with that the cup fell from M'lle. Valda's fingers and she burst into tears.

"There, there," Nell said, putting her arms about her. "You come to my room and rest."

When she had led the sobbing girl away I said: "Now what *is* all this? What's she doing here?"

"I met her at the chemist's," Mona explained. "The chemist introduced us . . . sort of. He

said, 'Are you ladies sisters?' I remembered the picture poor silly Simon showed us and I knew who she was. I couldn't help being interested. When the chemist went away to mix something she'd ordered, she began to dab her eyes. I said, 'You're M'lle. Valda, aren't you? Can I help you?' I think she was just dying to talk to somebody. She broke down and on the spur of the moment, I invited her round for a cup of tea. I knew Nell wouldn't mind. And she told me all about it."

"And what was it all about?"

"Her boy friend has run away. He's not coming back."

"How does she know that?"

"He wrote her a letter. He wanted to be free."

"Nothing unusual in that," I said.

"Now you're being Dr. Smug," Mona said. "And, anyway, I'll bet my suspenders against your stethoscope that Valda's boy friend is the naked lad Simple Simon found in the paddock."

"Oh, that's just guessing," I said. "The circus boss saw the body. It's no one from the show."

"He might be lying."

"Mona," I protested, "that's unreasonable. However, if you wish to satisfy your romantic little mind, why not ask the girl to describe her friend. You can then check with the corpse. Heaven knows you saw enough of him."

"I'll get it out of her," she promised. "He must have been a detestable man sending a letter like that."

"Oh, so you've seen the note?"

"He didn't actually write it," Mona said. "He got someone to do it. He can't write."

"Well, we *are* moving in nice company," I said, smugly. "Naked men dropping from the sky! Crying circus girls! Illiterate Casanovas!"

"Maybe writing isn't so important in a circus," Mona said. "Valda's friend is a bareback rider. I don't see that knowing how to write would help him to stick on."

Nell returned just then, looking a mite serious. "If Rod would like to assume his bedside manner he could visit the patient." She added in another tone, "You've only my word, but I fancy our visitor is going to have a baby."

"There!" Mona exploded. "What a beast of a man!"

Nell asked: "What man?"

"The jockey . . . the bareback rider. Saying in his letter 'I'm sick of you. You won't ever see me again.' He *must* have known about the baby. I bet he's some monkey-faced, under-sized rat," she said, entirely forgetting that she'd previously identified him with the man in the paddock who had been slim and well-shaped and not bad-looking.

"He's nothing of the sort, Mona," Nell said, unexpectedly. "I've seen his picture. She asked me to get something from her bag and it was there. He's quite picturesque with the fiercest mustache and a tuft on his chin that might have come off Napoleon the Third."

"There!" I said. "That disposes of your idea about Valda's lover being the corpse in the copse."

"Anyway," Mona said, "he deserved to be murdered. Writing such a brutal letter!" She regarded me sternly. "If you were half a doctor," she said, "you wouldn't stand eating your head off while that poor child . . ."

"Oh, all right," I said, swallowing my cream cake. "I'll see the lady."

"And if it's what Nell thinks," my wife went on, "you've got to march over and tell the ring-master she can't possibly perform tonight. I'm not going to have that girl bounding about on a slack-wire."

"Oh, she's a wire-walker?"

"I don't know," Mona admitted. "In the circus they do everything. She might even go in with the lion."

"Oh, go on in with the patient," Nell said, laughing, pushing me through the door.

I found it was true enough about the baby, but there'd be quite an interval before its birth. M'lle. Valda wept as she told me, "I don't want you to think I'm bad," she said. "You've all been so kind. You're not snobs. We were going to be married and now he's run away."

"He knew about the baby?"

She nodded.

I sighed. "I'll walk across and tell your boss you can't perform tonight."

She regarded me curiously. There was something in her expression I couldn't fathom. "You're a doctor," she said at length. "You know men—men who are going to have babies they think will be a tie. Do you think Joe will come back?"

I patted her hand. "In time, yes," I lied. "I feel sure of it. Don't you?"

"No," she said, "I don't think he'll ever come back."

On my way to the circus I met Sergeant Copestone. "They're round the body like bees," he told me. "It's got 'em guessing. The absence of tracks, I mean. Cincotta lent us a blacktracker who does a boomerang act in the circus but he couldn't pick up a damn thing. I think you're right, doc. He was dropped from a plane." He sighed prodigiously. "That's where the tax-payers' money goes. He could have been flown from anywhere in Australia and Australia's a damn big place. I hear the newspapers are playing it up. 'The Flying Corpse' or something."

I found Cincotta suave and swarthy—all teeth and sideburns. I imagined, in make-up, under arc lights, he'd look well in a dress-suit. Just now he was a little grimy in oil-smeared slacks and dirty pullover. I began with some politeness about intruding upon him at a busy time and with an African lion in a cage roaring in my ears, broached the subject of my visit.

"I've called to see you regarding M'lle. Valda," I said. "I have advised her to rest tonight. She is suffering from shock."

He shrugged. "She will get over it. They all do. Her man has run away."

"Oh, you know that?"

He shrugged again. "The girl, she rides him too hard. Joe Varella, he is never serious." He looked at me slyly. "Maybe something has happened?"

I ignored the implication. I certainly wasn't going to tell him about Valda's condition.

He went on: "Mister, if you knew Joe, you would understand. Two days ago he hands me his notice. I am not surprised. I am sorry but I understand. Joe!—he can pick up dames like that . . ." he snapped his fingers. "Why should he stick to one woman? She wants he should marry her, he tells me. Joe Varella marry? *pouf!*"

"You mean he gave up his job because Valda was pressing him to marry her?"

"Why not?" he asked. "Joe can get plenty jobs. Valda can get plenty men. But me? I am the poor mug because Varella must have his fun and maybe carries the game too far. I lose a good rider the dames come twice to see in the two-night stands and now you want I should lose little Valda." He smiled, deprecatingly, showing all his teeth. "Well, mister, I still got that mangy lion and a good elephant. I should worry." He spat into the tanbark, then lit a cigarette without offering me one. "Where is she now?" he asked.

"Quite safe," I told him.

He grinned. "Wherever she is, she will not stay, my friend. She is circus. When she hears the band tonight she will come running. Tomorrow she forgets you. The day after she forgets Varella."

He bawled instructions to a man fixing some gear at the top of the tent, then turned to me apologetically.

"Excuse me," he said. "Plenty to do, you understand. Tell Valda she shall take it easy. I find her some simple act. Not too much jolt, eh?" He smirked, knowingly. "Later, maybe, she sells the tickets." He took my arm familiarly and steered me toward the entrance. "Don't worry too much, doc. Circus girls is tough."

"What exactly does Valda do?" I asked, but he was no longer interested. His eyes had gone to the tent top again and he directed such a spate of obscenity at the fellow perched there that I was glad to escape. I paused at the entrance, feeling for a cigarette, and heard a complaining circus hand: "Listen to him. I feel like turning the game in. There's no programs tonight. How does he think a man can live without side-lines?"

As I lit my cigarette a telegraph messenger thrust an envelope at me. "Mr. Cincotta?" I pointed to the ring. A moment later I heard Cincotta shout. "Doc!" He came hurrying, waving a telegram, then held it under my nose. "See! Joe, he is not such a bad fellow, eh?"

I read the message: "I admit nothing but give Valda ten pounds for me."

Cincotta said: "He has got a conscience, that fellow. I'll bet he's been worrying and this morning he sends the telegram." He tapped the paper. "See—from the city." He put the envelope in his pocket. "Poor Joe. He thinks maybe he'll have bad luck if he don't do the right thing. Very superstitious. D'you know, doc, that man is so superstitious he has a picture of some saint pasted in his watch-case so he can get protection any minute! Well," he clapped his hands, rubbing them together as if all were well with the world, "now I get Valda back tonight, sure. Ten pounds, eh? That makes everything okey-doke."

I was a little disgusted with Mr. Cincotta but had to admit he knew his people. At any rate M'lle. Valda refused Nell's invitation to remain for dinner. I impressed upon her the wisdom of resting and she promised to take it easy.

"And," Mona said, "you must on no account walk any wires or things."

Valda stood at the door looking back at us with that queer enigmatic expression. "She reminds me of someone," I said, when she had gone.

"It's me," Mona said, promptly.

I shook my head. "Not the face, the expression."

"Mona Lisa," Nell suggested and of course that was it.

We assured ourselves we didn't want to see the circus. Distantly we could hear the band and noisy ballyhoo and occasionally the poor lion roared. The footsteps and excited chatter of people on their way to the show came to us clearly.

"I wish I knew what that girl is doing," Mona said. "I bet that brute of a circus man will make her go in with the animals."

"He promised she would do some simple act," I protested.

"Simple!" she cried. "What's simple about circus acts? Do you call swinging by your toes from a trapeze ninety miles high simple?" She eyed me sternly. "You ought to be there to forbid it."

"Which adds up to—you'd like to see the circus?" I said.

"It's all very well to be complacent," Mona said, "but I keep thinking of that poor lamb."

"All right," Nell said, good-naturedly. "Just to satisfy ourselves Valda isn't being cruelly exploited, we'll go."

Cincotta was standing near the entrance, a picturesque figure in his evening clothes. He flashed me a smile and I asked after Valda. He shrugged, characteristically. "My friend, I have done my best." He went on hurriedly, "But it is only a little act. Just looking pretty."

As we were hustled along the gangway by those following, Mona whispered, "Who was that?"

"Cincotta. Valda's boss," I told her.

"He looks every inch a white-slaver," she commented, and just then a megaphone voice announced the grand parade and we had only just reached our seats when the cavalcade entered.

When, later, Valda tripped into the ring Mona gasped and clutched my arm. "It's her," she said.

"Looking exactly like you, only in pink tights," I whispered.

"Oh, shut up," she said, her eyes on the ring. "Now, listen, Rodney, if she starts performing catherine wheels you must stop the show."

"I'll do nothing of the kind," I said. "Besides, she isn't going to perform catherine wheels."

Valda had advanced to the centre of the ring followed by Cincotta. The latter cupped his hand and into it she placed a pink-slippered foot. Her hands grasped a hanging rope and she began to climb. At the tent top she rested a moment on a trapeze and then, while Mona protested so audibly that even Nell shushed her, she began posing on the rope. Cincotta, from the ring below, pulled upon the end so that Valda, clinging now by her feet, now by her hands, swayed gently while a spotlight picked up her rounded figure and the band played "Dreaming."

Mona said: "It's ghastly. She'll be dashed to pieces."

It would be a nasty drop, I thought, but there was nothing harmful in the exercises themselves even if, sooner or later, she *was* going to have a baby.

When it was over and Valda had bowed herself out of the ring, Mona said indignantly: "And that's what that white-slaver calls a simple little act? Butchering her to make a Roman holiday! Making her swing in mid-air with a breaking heart!"

In bed that night Mona tossed and turned and suddenly was wide-awake, sitting up so abruptly that, startled, I switched on the light.

"I've just remembered," she said. "That fat gipsy mistook me for someone. He thought I was Valda. They'd prophesied misfortune for her."

"What of it?" I asked. "They were right for once. Her man's run away."

"Listen, Rodney," my wife said, "You can turn over and go to sleep in cold blood if you like, but there was something foreboding about that gipsy. There was death in his eye."

"You've been dreaming," I said.

"Anyway," she said, settling down, "tomorrow you're driving us to the gipsies' camp. I'm going to see what I can find out. It's high time Nell had her fortune told."

"Maybe Nell doesn't want to know her fate."

"Nonsense," Mona said. "Everyone should know their fate. How else can they guard against it?" And with that piece of logic ringing in my ears I fell asleep.

The gipsy camp looked deserted but when I hallooed, the paunchy Romany we had met previously appeared. He was flashily dressed with an opal tie-pin and several rings on fingers more bronzed by dirt than nature.

"Remember me?" Mona said, using the smile Nell calls male-bait.

"Could I forget, lady?" he responded, and Mona looked pleased.

She pointed to Nell. "This lady wants to cross your palm, but first I want to ask you something. Yesterday you mistook me for someone."

I fancied the man's eyes narrowed.

"You said," Mona went on, "'Have you come back for more back luck?' Please, I want to know. Did you prophesy something bad for the lady like me? I will pay, just as if you were telling her fortune again."

The gipsy smiled. "If someone else asked me," he said, "I would never tell. For you, it is different. You are so lovely." Mona cast down her eyes. "To you I say the woman is like you only in face. Her ways are dark ways. Her fate is a dark fate. For you there is love and happiness and children—let me see! How many?"

"Really, I think that will do, thank you very much," Mona said in a rush. "My husband's a doctor, you see," she added with seeming irrelevance. "Now you can tell my sister all about some tall dark man." She smiled at him, bewitchingly.

As I walked discreetly away, I heard Nell giggle. "Goodness! I don't believe a word of this but I hope it will be good."

They were so long about the business that, becoming restless, I sauntered back. "I don't want to interfere with fate," I began, "but—"

"Pooh!" Mona interrupted. "It's quite early." She rested her hand on the Romany's sleeve as if she'd known him for years. "What time is it, Mr. er—?"

"Rialando," he volunteered, his eyes avid. Somehow she seemed to have hypnotized the fellow for, without a by-your-leave, she took hold of his massive gold chain and jerked his watch

from his pocket. She released the spring and the lid flew open. "Why, it's only three," she said, snapping it shut and thrusting it back. It was an outrageous familiarity and it angered me to see the gipsy pass his tongue over his thick lips; but Mona seemed oblivious and Nell was laughing.

"I can't believe it," she was saying, "*Five* children!" And then, suddenly, I remembered what I had seen. The highly-colored picture of some saint pasted inside the lid of the gipsy's watch!

"I knew it," Mona exclaimed when, later, I told her about the picture and Cincotta's reference to Varella's superstition. "The gipsies lured him to the camp, robbed and murdered him, and heaved his body into that paddock."

"My dear girl," I remonstrated, "why will you persist in associating Mr. Varella with the corpse? In the first place, Joe was a man with whiskers and rings in his ears. . . ."

"There!" Mona cried, excitedly. "I knew there was something. That body had *had* rings in its ears. Don't you remember how I told Nell we'd found a dead gipsy? I'd forgotten, but now I remember. Surely you noticed his ears had been pierced?"

"No, I didn't," I said, a little sulky. Then I shook my head. "It won't do. It's purely coincidence. Cincotta didn't recognize the body. And your gipsy friends are not so strong they could heave a corpse thirty feet. No, Mona my love, they'd have had to drag him and they'd have left traces. And don't forget, my precious, he wrote a valedictory message to Valda."

"I told you he can't write," she countered.

"Well, got someone to write for him. And while your naked friend was in the morgue the bareback rider was in the city sending a telegram to Mr. Cincotta instructing him to salve Valda's feelings with ten pounds."

"I don't care," Mona said, obstinately. "I think we should tell the policeman."

"I'll tell him about the watch," I said, "but I don't expect him to do anything about it. That is, unless there's been a complaint that it was stolen." I put my arms around her. "Don't let this thing get you down, my pet. The circus has gone. Cincotta has gone. Valda has gone. And Varella has gone. Stop being Mrs. Sherlock and be the doctor's wife."

"I suppose I should," she said, "but I can't help thinking of that poor girl hanging by her toes."

"Actually, you're being sorry for yourself," I said. "Because Valda resembles you, you put yourself in her place. If she'd been a frowsy little imitation blonde you'd have forgotten her long ago."

"You can be terribly wise, Rodney," she said, meekly, then kissed me excitingly. "If ever I run away, be sure to smack me when I come back."

When I awoke next morning she'd gone. An envelope stuck on the mirror bore the dramatic message, FAREWELL, in Mona's characteristic scrawl.

I was at the door in a bound, shouting for Nell. She appeared at once.

"Now, don't get excited," she said. "She's only eloped."

"What *is* this joke?"

"She's motored to the city with Tommy Stewart," she informed me in mock horror, then grinned impishly. "Tommy's wife went with them."

I suppose I looked a little sheepish for she patted my arm. "There," she said, consolingly. "It takes time getting used to Mona. You've only had her two years. I've known her a lifetime."

When Mona came back she looked radiant. "Darling," she cried, throwing her arms about me, "I hope you were frantic. But I was quite safe. Tommy drives beautifully and his wife kept her eye on him all the time."

"And that's all the explanation I get?"

"For the present, Dr. Fusspot." She was thoughtful a moment. "Could you find out where the circus is?"

"No, I can't," I said. "I'm sick of the circus."

"Then I shall ask that nice policeman, Mr. Cobblestone."

"Copestone," I corrected, and added, ungraciously, "What is it you want him to do?"

"Get a circus pass for you and me. You know—a free ticket. Admit Two."

"For heaven's sake, Mona, be sensible," I said. "The circus is probably a hundred miles away. We've seen it, and we don't want to see it again. Even if we did we could afford to pay. We don't want a free ticket."

"Ah, but we do, darling," she replied. "Just an admit-two from that white-slaver."

"Cincotta is *not* a white-slaver."

"Well, he looks like one," Mona said, unperturbed. "Another thing! I want that poor girl taken off the trapeze and brought here."

I sat down heavily and she caressed my hair. "Darling," she said, "you weren't really upset about my clearing out with Tommy, were you? I'll get you some aspirin."

"I don't want aspirin," I said. "All I want is some sense out of what you're saying. All this nonsense about bringing Valda back! *Why?*"

"Why?" she repeated in surprise. "To identify Mr. Varella's body. It's still here, isn't it?"

"No," I said, "they've taken it to the city. And it isn't Varella. Varella is alive and probably kicking. I'm not going to Copestone with any cock-and-bull story."

"You don't have to talk about cocks and bulls at all," Mona retorted with spirit. "All right," she added, "we'll forget about it. Every single thing."

From experience I knew that was just what she was not going to do.

We had barely finished dinner when a goggling maid informed us that the policeman wanted Mona on the phone. She rose hurriedly and we heard her honey-sweet voice. "Oh, that's splendid, Mr. Cob—Copestone. I think you're wonderful. We'll be right over."

Nell raised her eyebrows. "Here we go," she said. "Plunging into crime again."

Mona bustled in as if we were all dying for a good old romp with a corpse. "Mr. Copestone says we can go over at once," she said, her eyes shining. "It won't take a minute. Just fancy, Rodney, he remembered that the white-slaver gave him a pass for the sanitary inspector and the sanitary inspector's wife was having a ten-pound baby girl and couldn't go so he's still got it."

On our way I said: "Listen, Mona. I haven't a notion what this is all about."

"Oh, but you *have*, darling," she said in genuine surprise. "It's about the admit-two and the telegram the white-slaver got from Varella."

"Don't keep on calling Cincotta a white-slaver," I said sternly, as a passer-by, who had caught the word, turned and stared.

"All right," she agreed. "I'll just say W. S. and you'll know."

Copestone made quite a fuss over Mona, settling her in the best chair, then dived into a drawer. "There you are, ma'am," he said. Mona took the pasteboard he produced. It was characteristic of her that she gave him a dazzling smile before she looked at the card on which she had built high hopes. When at last she looked at it she said, "Yes, it's the same," and from her bag produced a folded paper, spreading it before us.

The paper was a telegraph form—one that had been handed in for transmission. It read: "I admit nothing but give Valda ten pounds for me."

"What is this?" Copestone asked.

"That," Mona said, with a little note of triumph, "is the telegram Mr. Varella sent to the W. S.—I mean to Cincotta—after he died."

"Died?" Copestone exclaimed. "How could he send it if he was dead?"

"He didn't," Mona explained. "Cincotta sent it himself to make it look as if Mr. Varella was alive."

I studied the form with new interest, recalling how Cincotta had thrust the message into my hand impressing upon me it had been sent that morning.

"Where did you get this?" I asked Mona.

Just for a moment she appeared confused.

"Well, dear," she said. "I suddenly remembered Leo White. He's something awfully important in the head post office. I knew he could get it for me." She hurried on. "You remember Leo, surely, dear? The tall dark boy who took me to the theatre on nights when you had to study."

"I don't understand," Copestone said. "Who is Varella?"

"He's the dead man in the paddock," Mona said, promptly.

"Nothing of the sort, Sergeant," I objected. "She's guessing."

"Varella was a circus man?" Copestone asked.

"With rings in his ears and whiskers. Cincotta shaved them off—the whiskers I mean—and put him in the paddock," my wife told him.

"Mona!" I exclaimed. "This is outrageous. We have nothing against Mr. Cincotta. All the experts say the body fell from an airplane."

"That's right, ma'am," the policeman said. "It's the only conclusion you could come to. There were absolutely no signs of anyone ever being near the body."

"Well," Mona said, "I don't know how it got there but I am sure Cincotta did it."

"He didn't recognize the body," Copestone said, heavily.

"Well, you wouldn't expect him to bound in and say, 'Oh, goody, here's the man I murdered,' now would you?" Mona smiled.

"But," I objected, "we don't even know he sent the wire."

"Oh, yes, we do," she replied. "But we wouldn't have found out if Mr. Copestone hadn't so cleverly remembered about the sanitary man's free pass." She took up the pasteboard. "See, it says, Admit Two. Look at the 'Admit.' Now look at the 'Admit' on the telegraph form."

There wasn't the slightest doubt that the words had been written by the same hand.

"Cincotta killed Varella," Mona announced, definitely. "And he wants you to think Joe is alive. I bet the note Valda got was written by Cincotta, too. When I think of that poor girl going to have a baby on the high trapeze—"

Copestone cleared his throat loudly. "Perhaps you had better tell it *all*," he said and spread an enormous sheaf of paper before him. Carefully he selected a nib. "Now then, nice and clear like, eh?"

It was over at last and the sergeant said: "There's some funny aspects but it all hinges on the identity of the corpse. Perhaps this M'lle. Valda should view the body."

"Yes," my wife said, quietly. "I think that, too. It's hateful, but she would have to know sometime."

"We'll be tactful," Copestone promised. "Now, ma'am, you're sure you have told us everything?"

"Why, yes," Mona said, picking up her bag. She suddenly put it down again. "Oh, I forgot all about the gipsy and the watch."

"Gipsy? Watch?" Copestone blinked.

"Yes," Mona went on, "yesterday I went to the camp again." She gave me an apologetic glance. "I persuaded Mrs. Stewart to have her fortune told. It was awfully good. She's going to have three husbands. And while the woman was telling it I got that fat gipsy on one side and I told him he was going to be arrested for murder."

"Mona! for heaven's sake!" I ejaculated.

"I told him he had the corpse's watch and I asked him if he didn't kill him, how did he get it? He was terribly flustered."

"I'll bet he was," Nell said, dryly.

"He told me all about it—in confidence, of course," Mona went on. "He pinched it off Varella the night he was murdered."

"*If* he was murdered," Copestone amended, painstakingly. "So this Varella was at the camp?"

"Yes," Mona said, blandly. "He was there with Mr. Cincotta."

I leaned across Copestone's desk. "Mona," I said, "don't make such definite statements unless you're sure."

"But I am sure, darling," she said. "Didn't the gipsy tell me?" She appealed to Nell. "You

know him. The fat one who told you you'd have five children. You said yourself that you thought he told the truth."

I hardly noticed Nell's blush. "And Valda was there, too?"

Mona nodded. "Varella and Valda had their fortunes told, then they all drove off in their truck." She thrust her hand into her bag. "There's the watch to prove it," she said and handed it to Copestone. "Mr. Rialando says he never wants to see the damn thing again."

"If it wasn't for the way the corpse was found," Copestone said as we left, "this would look very pretty, but even if Valda recognizes the body we still don't know how it got where Daffy found it."

"Did Daffy hear any plane that morning?" I enquired.

"Yes, he heard one," Copestone grinned, "but he also heard the Angel Gabriel."

"Perhaps," suggested Nell, "it was Mr. Cincotta who dropped the body from the plane."

Copestone dealt with the suggestion with official gravity. "No, miss, if he was at the camp as alleged, there wouldn't have been time. You can't pick up a plane like a taxi."

"Unless," I said, "he'd arranged for one. That's pretty flat country."

Copestone telephoned me late next afternoon. He'd caught up with the circus and rushed Valda to the city. No, Cincotta hadn't objected. "But it's no go," the sergeant told me. "The girl couldn't recognize the corpse."

When I told Mona she stared at me as if she couldn't believe it; then she burst into tears.

For the next two days golf had my serious and undivided attention. In the evenings my wife appeared quieter than usual but seemed to have forgotten the murder.

It was a shock, therefore, when meeting Copestone on my first morning free from golf, he said, "If I might say so, doctor, that wife of yours is a very remarkable woman."

"Indeed," I said with foreboding.

He watched me slyly. "Says I'll become Chief of Police."

I recognized Mona's brand of flattery and sighed. "Tell me the worst, Copestone. What is she up to now?"

"As a matter of fact, doc," he said. "I'm running her up to Parriwatta. Cincotta's circus is there tonight."

"Now, listen, sergeant," I said. "If my wife is still harking—"

He interrupted me. "I thought you'd come along, doc. I think it might be interesting."

I taxed Mona later. "But you were at Parriwatta yesterday," I said. "With that Stewart fellow and his mother."

She nodded. "We had a bush picnic on the way. The circus is there two nights. Darling, do please come. I promise I won't open my mouth about the old murder the whole way."

Which, just then, was exactly what I didn't want.

As we parked at Parriwatta it was dark. We could hear the circus music and see the shadows of people sitting on the back bleachers. Mona led the way, stepping carefully over guy ropes and moving in and out among the caravans surrounding the big top. In a few minutes she stopped, pointing. "There's her tent, Mr. Copestone."

Copestone said: "You two wait." I drew Mona into the shadows and watched him step up to Valda's tent. A shadow appeared on the canvas, grew enormously, and the girl came into view. She was wearing tights as in the picture Daffy had shown us, and started as she saw the uniformed figure. We heard Copestone mumble something.

She appeared to hesitate, then her voice came clearly: "Not here—I share this tent. Let's walk across the lot." She disappeared, returning instantly, a cloak draped about her, and with the policeman, moved out of the line of light.

Mona leaned against me suddenly, breathing hard. "It's hot," she said.

"It isn't hot at all," I said, alarmed. "You're fainting."

Despite her protests I carried her across the intervening gloom into Valda's tent, and sat her on a trunk, then looked about for water. Finding none, I stepped outside and moved toward the caravan alongside. The door was open and the interior lit. There was no one inside. I glanced back and saw Mona's profile silhouetted on the side of the tent; and then, suddenly, there was a man standing alongside the shadow with only the canvas dividing him and her.

I heard him whisper, *"Valda,"* and saw the shadowed head lift slightly. The voice continued: "Listen, the policeman is here. You must be careful. Behave naturally. You must do the act. Understand?"

The silhouetted head nodded and in a moment the man had gone. Without moving from where I stood, I reached out and pushed the caravan door slightly so that a beam of light streamed directly across his path. I had no more than a glimpse, but it was sufficient to show me it was Cincotta. I had barely time to rush over and ask Mona if she were all right when Copestone and Valda returned.

Valda stared at my wife, then that enigmatic smile altered her whole expression. "I might have known," she said.

Someone bawled in the darkness. "Valda, you've got five minutes!"

The smile never left her face. She turned to Copestone. "The show's got to go on. You don't mind?" She looked at Mona. "Excuse me," she said. "There's a letter I must send." She walked inside the tent and sat at a make-shift table, her back to us. Nobody spoke.

After what seemed an age, the voice bawled again: "Valda, you're on!"

She rose. "I must go," she said and handed Mona an envelope. "Would you post it?"

"Of course," Mona said.

The girl regarded Copestone quietly. "You ought to go in and watch," she said. "You get in for nothing, don't you?" Next moment the darkness had swallowed her and I heard the band start the music for her act.

Copestone was preoccupied as we walked to

the entrance of the big top, and Mona said, "I'll stand in the air. You go in."

"You're sure you're all right?"

"Please. Go in," she urged.

Standing in the entrance I could see Valda high in the tent posing on the rope, wrapping it about her tinselled waist, kissing her fingers to the crowd outside the orbit of the spotlight. Occasionally the beam picked up the gleaming white of Cincotta's shirt in the ring below.

The music ceased as Valda returned to the trapeze and gracefully acknowledged the applause. Suddenly, she stood and reaching up, detached a rope from some gear above her head. It had a buckled end and this she clipped to the seat of the trapeze. Then, sitting with lower limbs extended, and with every gesture and movement reeking of circus, she began to manipulate the other end of the rope.

I heard Cincotta's surprised ejaculation and heard him call *"Valda!"* There was consternation in his voice. Copestone sensed something unrehearsed was happening and made a step forward. The queer Mona Lisa smile played about the lips of the girl and as Cincotta cried again, *"Valda!"* I saw that she had contrived a loop in the free end of the rope. This she held up for the audience to see, smiling through it; then she looped the rope about her slender neck. She looked down and around her again, kissing her fingertips to each section of the audience in turn.

There was that deathly silence that showmanship insists must preface all death-defying acts and then the unbelievable happened. We heard Cincotta cry *"No!"* I am sure the crowd thought it was *"Go!"* Copestone cried, "Good God," and then Valda dropped from the trapeze like a stone. Down, down, down, until she stopped suddenly in mid-air with a hideous jerk and the silver sequins on her pink tights threw out myriad flashes as the shapely body spun, then twitched convulsively and hung in an attitude of shameful death.

"You shouldn't let it worry you," Copestone said later at Nell's house. "It saved a lot of trouble."

"I only wanted to help her," Mona said. "I thought Cincotta killed him, but when she said she didn't recognize the body, I knew she was hiding something. I believed Cincotta was frightening her into silence."

The policeman said: "I think they were both in it."

"It was Valda who killed him," Mona said, and handed Copestone a letter. "I didn't realize it was addressed to me. It's all there." While Copestone read, she told me.

Cincotta, Varella, and Valda left the gipsy camp, Varella driving the truck. He'd had a big win at the races and Valda said: "Now you can marry me." He laughed at her and produced a roll of notes waving them in her face. "Look!" he said. "There's a thousand pounds there and I wouldn't give you a single tenner for yourself *or* Cincotta's brat."

Mona said: "It was the first time Valda realized he knew who was the baby's father. Cincotta couldn't marry her even if he wanted to because he was married already. Varella kept boasting about the money he could make and the women he could have, and how he would eventually settle down and marry some *nice* girl."

All the while, it seemed, Valda sitting between the two men could feel the bulge in Cincotta's pocket that was his gun. In the end she couldn't stand Varella's taunts. She shot him while he was waving the notes in her face. Cincotta leaned over and took the money. He owed Varella five hundred on a gambling debt so he was fifteen hundred up if he could get away with it. But it was his gun, and his word against Valda's.

He said: "We'll split fifty-fifty. I know just what to do."

I glanced quickly through Valda's letter. "It doesn't say what he did," I said. "How did they get his body into the paddock?"

Copestone said: "Cincotta is a showman. He knows how easily the mind can be diverted. Conjurers always keep you watching something that really doesn't matter. He and Valda cooked up a plausible excuse for Varella leaving the circus, and their method of disposing of the body clinched the whole thing. Afterwards he whipped back to the city somehow and arranged for a wire to be sent while Valda drove the lorry on here. Everybody but your good wife forgot the circus."

"And my good wife discovered how Varella's body got into the paddock?"

"Yes, I did, darling," Mona admitted, "but you have to take the credit because you told me all the important things *like about the boy complaining there weren't any programs.* I thought to myself, there's something that W. S. is trying to hide. Then you told me he'd promised Valda would do *another* act. Somehow that made me remember there was something I'd forgotten about the picture Daffy showed us. So I went and had tea with him . . . out of a pannikin."

"But why, in heaven's name?"

"I asked him to show me Valda's picture—the one he thought was me without clothes."

Copestone coughed and I gritted my teeth. "And he did?"

"He was awfully sweet, darling. He gave it to me." She began fiddling in her bag. "We'll have to find some theatrical costumers when we go home and hire the tights."

"Tights?" Nell gasped. "Who for?"

"Why, for me," Mona said. "I had to promise Daffy I'd give him a lovely framed picture for the one I took away."

"Over my dead body," I said.

"Now, darling," she said, "don't be difficult.

After all, Daffy's picture of Valda put us on the track." She handed me the print the half-wit had shown us. "I remembered the wonderful clue you gave me the day we discovered the body."

"What clue?" I asked and read the caption under the picture.

M'LLE. VALDA, THE HUMAN CANNON BALL

"What clue?" she repeated. "Why, surely you remember? You asked me how I'd like to be *shot off the highway.* I began thinking and asked Mr. Copestone had he seen many circuses and then he said, "Well, I'm b——"

Copestone coughed. He said: "It struck me all of a heap, Doc."

"So," Mona went on, "he had a good look through the circus and there it was."

"There what was?" I asked.

"Why, the big, wooden cannon, darling. Don't be so dense."

"It was there all right, doc," Copestone said. "After they'd done him in, they stripped him, shaved him, pushed him into the muzzle of the cannon which is really a camouflaged catapult and which they were carrying on the truck as part of the circus props, drove to the crest of the Hummocks, and shot him over."

"Don't you see, darling?" Mona said. "The Human Cannon Ball. It was a copy of the act Valda did in the circus. They used to shoot her out of the gun into a net . . . only there was no net for Mr. Varella."

VINCENT CORNIER

NEVER HAVING WRITTEN a novel, Vincent Cornier (1898–1976) is a name recognized only by devoted aficionados of detective fiction, especially those who are drawn to locked rooms and impossible crimes, a form in which he excelled. Born in Redcar, Yorkshire, he began writing at a very young age, earning the not inconsiderable sum of a hundred guineas a year at fourteen, selling articles to newspapers and magazines for a half guinea each. After serving in the Royal Air Force as a pilot in World War I, he became a journalist and soon began writing fiction, placing stories in both English and American magazines such as *Pearson's*, *The Storyteller*, and *Argosy*. Cornier created a series character for some of his stories, Barnabas Hildreth, who is similar to R. Austin Freeman's famous Dr. Thorndyke. A scientist, Hildreth brings careful analysis to the mysteries with which he is confronted, meticulously examining the most minute details and bringing scientific knowledge to interpreting them. A member of British Intelligence, he is known as "The Black Monk" by those who work with him, a moniker perhaps a bit more colorful than the character himself.

"The Flying Hat" was first published in the May 1929 issue of *The Storyteller*; it was then published in book form in the British anthology *The Best Detective Stories of 1929*, edited anonymously by Ronald Knox and H. Harrington (London, Faber & Faber, 1930).

THE FLYING HAT

VINCENT CORNIER

I

The wearer of the hat was tall and wan and spare in frame—that bleak and shabby young man who kissed Mary Sugden good night at the top of the area steps of Number 24, Bellington Square, W.1. He kissed her in a resounding fashion that brought a laugh from a nearing policeman, unheard of approach on his rubber-soled boots.

The young man looked up, and Mary Sugden gasped: "Oh, lor'!"

"A nasty raw night," the constable remarked.

"Er—yes, it is that," mumbled the swain.

"Doesn't know whether to snow again or thaw."

"No, it doesn't," agreed the young man. "Pretty rotten, underfoot."

The constable glanced at the man's cracked shoes, nodded benignantly, smiled, and sauntered on. The man tried to grip at Mary's hand, but she giggled and scuttled three steps downward, to her kitchen.

"Then t'morrow night, same time," she hoarsely ordered.

"Maybe," grunted the young man.

"What d'y' mean—*mebbe?*"

"I'm sick of messing about. I'm going in to see him." The young man nodded at the golden windows of the dining-room above his head.

"I thought so—now I just thought so! Well, Harry Greenwood, y've precious little respec' for me—as you've asked to be y'r wife—if y' can't be guided by me; you have! I've warned y'—he doesn't bother his head about the likes of us. I've told you over an' over again; but y're that pig-headed, y' are . . . Shut up an' don't be so soft!"

"Well, my argument is, you never know—"

"All right then, have y'r own silly way. Go on in an' see him—an' get chucked out! *Do it* . . . an' it's the last you ever see of me, Harry! He knows you by sight; seen you callin' here . . . get me the blinkin' sack you would! . . . An' a fat lot you'd care—" And here, a gulping and a break to tears.

The constable had halted to pat his hands together in the cold night. Out of sidelong eyes he was watching. He had little else to do, for the relief was already five minutes late and he was at the defined end of his beat. Very soon now the sergeant from Harford Street Police Station would appear with a file of fifteen constables—cutting through Bellington Square, relieving duty-men all the way, eventually to post the last man out in Edgware Road. The sudden little quarrel he regarded whimsically, as men at their ease always regard the unease of others.

A second five-minutes' period passed. The constable lost his complacency. Hang the relief! He took three or four slow steps toward the still quarrelsome twain. He saw, quite distinctly, for all that a swift whirry of snow sailed into the square, that Mary Sugden's eyes were shining wide with tears. He heard her sobbing; but then he saw the tall man stoop quickly and kiss those tears away . . . fondle her with some fierce gentility of passion: heard him murmuring earnestly as he threw aside all his forces that had made for discord. And the constable, smiling again, retraced those three steps.

A second good-night call; a sweeter reply; a treading of feet and the closing of a heavy door. The constable turned to see the tall lover striding away across the narrow roadway to the high railings that bounded the private central gardens of the square. Mary Sugden had vanished. Save for the constable and the lover the great quadrangle was deserted . . . The time was twelve minutes past ten o'clock.

. . . The terrible scream and the crash as of a shot came within the ensuing twenty seconds.

P.C. Pentony was a man of decision and a good runner. He whistled double calls and sped to the fallen Harry Greenwood. He only had to traverse thirty-seven snowy yards . . . to reach the silent huddle beneath the lamp, beside the railings.

Doors were opening on all sides and windows glared as their hangings were drawn aside by alarmed residents. Bellington Square, W.I., wherein the only usual sounds were the far-away drone of traffic in Oxford Street and the solemn snoring of that in Edgware Road, became as the court-yard of Babel. The relief sergeant with his file of officers rushed up at the double, and a second constable, unrelieved, who had been on duty at the top end of the square—on the far side of the railed-in central gardens—ran around and joined the busy group.

Greenwood lay in the snow that covered the concrete pathway which was a bound outside the railings, with his knees bent under him as though he had slumped asleep at prayer. He was hatless and the shoulder of his jacket (he had no overcoat) was torn. His pitiful face was a livid mask, and frozen, so it seemed. One feeble and fluttering hand tried to claw the red slush in which he lay. But then this twitched and was awfully still. Constable Pentony turned him over and looked.

"Shot through the head, poor bloke!" he muttered.

A second policeman smoothed him out and covered him with a cape. "Stand back there—keep back, will you!" snapped a third to the ever clustering crowd, and out of the plenitude of men he had, the sergeant drew a cordon.

"Pentony, where's the fellow's hat; seen it?"

"No, Sergeant, I haven't."

"*Ugh!*—How far away were you when the shot was heard?"

"Not forty yards . . . just across the road, as a matter of fact."

"*What?*" The sergeant started and grew red in the face. "And—and you didn't see anyone?"

"Not a soul!"

The sergeant glanced around and took survey of all the close vicinity. Then he cocked one eye and regarded P.C. Pentony as one regards a puling child: tolerantly, yet pitying.

"And you never noticed—"

"Sergeant Arnott, I saw this chap fall; saw him fall, I tell you"—Pentony's voice was shrill—"but there wasn't anyone about."

"You—you poor fish!" Sergeant Arnott was icily violent. "Didn't it dawn on your mind—hadn't you the hoss-sense to realise—that the fellow was shot from *inside* these railings?" He snorted now. "Here, get a move on: you've got a key . . . half-a-dozen of you men . . . light up, and search these gardens. It's an eight-feet-high barrier; take some getting over—might be just possible that the fellow who did the job is still inside!"

Seven electric hand-lamps flashed white arcs on the snow, and P.C. Pentony, trembling now, clumsily opened a resident's gate in the tall railings. The searchers sidled through into the snowy waste, and very slowly began to scour the ground; methodically to scour. They were trained men. They missed little, as they moved about with those brilliant fans of light poured on the clear snow.

. . . The time was nineteen minutes past ten o'clock.

Sergeant Arnott had sent an officer back to

Harford Street Station to report and to summon an ambulance and a doctor. This man found that an inspector of the C.I.D. was in the charge-room. He had listened and had taken matters in hand; he covered the hundred-and-eighty yards between the station and the scene of the crime at a rush. Sergeant Arnott sighed in relief as the inspector pushed through the cordon and hurriedly he recounted all he had done, and had learned . . . Into the top of the square, from Edgware Road, a clanging ambulance-car, from St. Asaph's Hospital, Paddington, turned.

. . . The time was twenty-two minutes past ten o'clock.

"Good evening, Inspector Templeton—good evening, Sergeant Arnott"—this was a very steady voice—"What's the trouble?"

The two officers saluted. Each recognised the newcomer; each with differing emotions. To the sergeant, the advent of Sir Richard Thorreston Brantyngham, from his stately house—Number 24, Bellington Square, W.I.—was almost as the advent of doom to his career. P.C. Pentony had been on special detail . . . had been guarding the residence of this officer of State, as always it was guarded; by day and by night. And a man who had talked to a maid in that house had been murdered—almost on the doorstep and actually within sight of the warden.

On the contrary, the C.I.D. man welcomed Brantyngham. Inspector Templeton knew Sir Richard, not alone as a Third Service Chief, but as a clever doctor and one who had power to advance by his influence what years of careful service, otherwise, could not move. He felt that here, at last, was his chance to display himself, to the finest advantage. . . .

"Man, at present unknown, Sir Richard, shot through the head—dead, Sir Richard."

Sir Richard Brantyngham examined the man under the clustered coverings of many capes and the glowing of electric lamps.

"I'll have him taken into my house, Inspector," Sir Richard quietly remarked. "He is not dead, nor has he been shot. There's not the slightest chance for him if he's taken off in the ambulance; a single jolt will end him. . . . Tell

the ambulance orderlies to bring a stretcher. . . . *Ah*—good; here's a doctor. I shall need help."

"Very good, sir!" The Inspector spoke to Sergeant Arnott and this man gave his orders. The heavy mass of curiosity was pressed back, not gently, and the supine body of Harry Greenwood was delicately lifted and borne up the steps to the house. The hospital doctor, conferring with Sir Richard, whom he knew, followed.

The door of 24, Bellington Square was widely opened, and as the stretcher-bearers passed into the large hall, Sir Richard halted for a moment to scan the railed-in garden, in which the bobbing lines of light made by the police searchers still moved—away at the farthermost end, nearest, now, to Edgware Road.

Looking so . . . he saw the black thing . . . flying.

Fully a hundred feet above the ground, high above the tallest of the magnificent plane trees that dotted the enclosure—dim in the sailing snow—it sped along; it seemed a ball of blackness, madly sportive. The air in the square was very still, yet a movement of currents was indicated at that height usurped by the flying thing. For it bounced aloft in a mighty arc; lofting strangely, too—as though it had impetus from more cause than the little high-crying wind above the house-tops—cutting aerial angles and graceful curves and gyratory figures, all admirably . . . Until it swerved, lost power, and made a sudden swoop downward, until it fell below the level of the highest eaves, where no wind was. Then it shot away in an oblique line—to scrape across the upper twigs of a tree—to be deflected, and so to fall . . . into the roadway almost at the feet of Sergeant Arnott, as he stood at the tailboard of the ambulance.

It was a hat; a simple bowler hat—the one that Harry Greenwood had worn, and that which P.C. Pentony could not find—a bowler hat . . . yet it battered into the slushy snow with the sounding weight of a hammer blow. It crashed heavily, and its brim broke off . . . and a long rain of golden discs rolled from its ruin.

Sir Richard Brantyngham took the wrecked thing, and the golden discs, from the sergeant.

He beckoned, and Arnott followed him indoors. The door of Number 24, Bellington Square closed on a hundred gaping faces.

. . . The time was twenty-six minutes past ten o'clock.

‖

Sir Richard Brantyngham took up one of the three champagne goblets he had ordered to be brought him. He poured in it a few drops of pure alcohol which he obtained from Doctor Fletchley's case of drugs and instruments. He ignited the spirit and watched it flare within the thin glass hemisphere . . . and allowed the newly sterilised vessel to cool.

He next took a pair of sterile forceps and went over to the chair on which Greenwood's jacket lay. From the bloodstained left shoulder he carefully plucked five pieces of ice, none larger than a pea.

He let these fragments tinkle into the prepared vessel and instantly covered them.

Only now did he manifest interest in Doctor Fletchley's final work on Greenwood's moaning body. He watched the swift stitches that the surgeon was making in the left shoulder. His own turn had already been served: he had worried like a delicately determined dog to help Fletchley in his major operation of setting to rights the back of the poor skull and the alleviation of danger from the injured throat.

"Miraculous escape the artery had—what?"

Doctor Fletchley nodded without looking up.

"About the nearest thing I've ever seen," he agreed.

"D'you think he'll make it, Fletchley?"

"Don't see why he shouldn't; you gave him the only chance. Not a bad physique for a youngster. Yes, I think he'll get over this—it's that damned base I'm fearing."

"So am I." Brantyngham was very grave. "I'm far from satisfied . . . believe you'll find a smash, under X-rays."

"Aye—before that!" Greenwood began to stir. "Look at him; he's showing up . . . very like it!"

"Poor devil! He'd better be taken away as soon as you've tied that lot, don't you agree?"

"Certainly! I'll only be a minute or so longer. Then, if I can use your phone, I'll prepare 'em up at St. Asaph's for what's coming."

"The whole thing's absolutely beyond me," Fletchley continued. "Simply can't make head or tail of it. How the devil a man can suffer a cracked cranium from a stab, I'm at a loss to determine! *Jove!*—if he snuffs it, my evidence at the inquest'll put a new point into medical— 'ju' . . . I'm baffled!"

"Oh, I shouldn't let it worry, Fletchley," Sir Richard drawled. "I realise your quandry, but take advice from an old hand in such relation— never allow surprise at the phenomenal to fester into concern, else your peace of mind will suffer beyond all remedy. Admittedly the whole affair is a maddening riddle, but just let it rest at that; what sense is there in fraying nerves about it?" He mused; smiled obliquely at the eager-looking inspector and said, softly: "Look at Templeton here—he's all but springing at your neck, to throttle out of you what you mean by stating that Greenwood was stabbed, when he's already as sure as light that the fellow was shot."

"He—he *was* shot!" declared the Inspector. "Not much doubt about that, I should say."

Doctor Fletchley raised his shaggy, sandy head and glared over the curves of his pince-nez.

"*I* said that this man was stabbed! You C.I.D. fellows are just too confoundedly omnipotent, on occasion—for all that, I've yet to find one of you capable of teaching me my own business, sir! This man was stabbed—was seriously injured, if you like that better—by a blow from some sharp and triangular instrument that was driven downwards with tremendous force; a blow that cracked the left base of the skull first—that tore the neck and the left shoulder last. Nothing more certain than that, Inspector!" He rounded on Sir Richard. "You substantiate that?"

"Without qualification, Fletchley."

So buffeted, Inspector Templeton became dogged.

"With all respects to you, Sir Richard—"

"Here, Templeton—pull up! You're in charge

of this case; it's essentially a police affair . . . up to now. Don't you fret your soul about undue respects. Say what you like—don't mind me!"

"Thank you, Sir Richard. I mayn't be able to teach you your job, Doctor, but the same salt's on your bird: I know mine. And, knowing it, Doctor, I'll take a dickens of a lot of convincing that those wounds were caused by stabbing. What about the scream and the sound of the shot? How d'you get over those? So far as I can go, at present, what's more feasible than that the fellow was shot at from a distance—the bullet striking his shoulder first, glancing up to cut the side of his neck and then glancing again—to smash him on the lower bulge of his head, so fracturing the skull?"

"I—I tell you, once and for all, Inspector, this was a *downwards* driven blow!"

"Then the bullet could have been fired, say, from an upper window in this square; that would yield you the point and still fit in with known facts."

"Really? Then will you tell me something else that my poor talents cannot grapple with—where's the bullet? You saw that wound in the shoulder; it had no point of exit . . . And do you think I'm such a fool as to imperil my career by stitching up a cavity without being certain beyond all shadow of doubt that no foreign body lay embedded in it?" Doctor Fletchley snorted. "No, Inspector, you'll have to try again; that cat won't fight—this—is—not—a—bullet—wound . . . it's purely and simply a stab!"

"I'm very much afraid, Inspector Templeton," Sir Richard Brantyngham quietly said, "that you'll have to drop your bullet theory. Eliminate it altogether, now! You'll never get anywhere otherwise. Doctor Fletchley is absolutely sure, and so am I, that this ragged wound, despite the complication of the fractured base, *is* in every way compatible with a theorising about there being a downwards driven blow, akin to a stabbing, delivered on this man's upper body."

"You—you told me that you heard the scream and the sound of the shot, and—"

"Inspector Templeton—*please!* I told you nothing of the kind, sir! When you first questioned me, I most deliberately referred to: 'a shrill and scream-like sound, succeeded by a detonation, as that one might attribute to the discharge of a fire-arm' . . . Come, get your wits to work—were those, or were they not, my actual words?"

"They *were* your actual words, Sir Richard. But I cannot see, save that they are guarded, they are any different from the making of a definite statement to the effect that you heard this man scream out in fear and then you heard the shot that knocked him out."

Sir Richard Brantyngham sighed and turned to Sergeant Arnott. "Would you mind, Sergeant? . . . Ring up the Senior United Forces' Club—ask if Lord Passingford is present, and, if he is—tell him to come to this house as fast as he can."

The sergeant saluted and went off to the telephone. Sir Richard left the group in the hall and entered his study. A safe door clanged and he returned . . . to place in Inspector Templeton's hands a warrant, given under the twin seals of two of His Majesty's Principal Secretaries of State for Home and Foreign Affairs . . .

"As this man never uttered a scream and as a shot was not fired in this square to-night, Inspector Templeton, and, as you will not rid your mind of a prejudicial theory of 'shooting,' that annuls all your efforts from the outset . . . I shall take charge of this case from now. From now you act only under my orders!"

III

. . . The foregoing I have edited and accurately transcribed from Sir Richard Thorreston Brantyngham's minutely elaborate notes on the case of "The Flying Hat," entered in his journals. On my arrival at 24, Bellington Square I found that Greenwood had been removed to St. Asaph's Hospital, and that Sir Richard had received a report from P.C. Pentony, on the result of the search of the central gardens of the square. Essentially, now, does my task begin:

For all that every inch of the snow-covered surface had been scoured—time after time—not a trace of a footstep was to be found in those gardens. The police searchers left long black lines in the grass wherever they moved; lines that cut down through the lightly-lain snow, betraying all well. Naught save these remained . . . attention alone had been centred on three small holes, not far from the scene of the crime, which marked the snow as points of an isosceles triangle, four-feet long in the base and six-feet seven inches from basal points to apex. Since no other similar markings were seen, these the police were inclined to treat perfunctorily. Brantyngham smiled on hearing of them.

P.C. Pentony, eager no doubt to wipe off the black patch on his service, indicated in Sergeant Arnott's earlier attitude toward him—and, strangely enough, appointed control-officer of the squad of searchers by reason, also, of that attitude—made some very fine points. He had every vertical railing examined: none was loose in its socket; none was bent; not one had in any way been started. Now, beneath the rather savage-looking ornamental spikes, topping these eight-feet-high rails, is a flat horizontal rail. Pentony, brilliant fellow, had the snow that lay on top of this flat rail carefully inspected. In no place was its unbroken surface marred. Apparently then no one had got out of that inner plot by way of clambering over the railings . . . and of the residents' gates . . . all save the one that Pentony had opened with his private key, were not only locked, but chained and re-padlocked.

Further than all this, P.C. Pentony took it upon himself to carry out certain other tests. He ran from the scene of the crime to each of the boundary rails in turn; allowed two minutes—in mind—for that time necessary for an agile man to clamber over the railings and then assessed that, at the very lowest estimate, a running and athletic man could not hope to escape from the inner garden, via the railings, in a time under four minutes. And, so bonded by seconds and

moments is the chronology of this case, such a period would have certainly admitted the possibility of that man's capture. . . . Let it be recalled that the square was fully aroused within two minutes, and the police were already in the central gardens, searching, within five minutes of the detonation (I shall not call it "shot"). Surely anyone decamping from the scene would have been noticed. . . .

Eliminated, the possibility of a shot from some upper window of the square; admitted, a stabbing . . . necessitated therefore: some human agency that was in very close proximity to the victim. *Then*—how had that human being escaped? How had it consummated the crime? Trackless and invisible, that agent—entity—being, call it what you will; *how* had it struck and felled and gone from all men's knowing, within a few short minutes; out of a well-lighted quadrangle, alive with police officers and stirring people? Such was the riddle Brantyngham set himself to solve!

He began to work in earnest when he looked over the "property" found in Greenwood's pockets; when he carefully examined the man's clothing—his shoes, stocking-feet pulled over holed socks; his miserable rag of a dirty shirt; his greasy waistcoat; his blood-stained jacket . . . and his exquisitely woven silk underwear—that which was labelled by a Bond Street name, that only uncared price purchases . . .

"Funny kit for an out-of-work dental mechanic, worth two-and-threepence-'a-penny and fourteen pawn-tickets—*eh?*" grunted Brantyngham, looking at that labelled name.

"Damned funny," I agreed.

"Beg your pardon, Sir Richard," said the massive Inspector Templeton, "but I've been able to get a bit of news out of that hysterical kitchen-maid of yours—this fellow Greenwood was a waiter, not a dental mechanic!"

Sir Richard calmly looked up and smoothed his mane of iron-grey hair. A smile was twitching around his lean mouth that seemed a preface to a laugh, but one I knew—from long and sorry knowledge—to be a disguise.

"I shouldn't question the point, Inspector Templeton." I laughed. "Rather shall we ask him to prove it . . ."

"Proof—*proof*, you ask?" Brantyngham was started from his mood, like a terrier started at a sudden rat; I was wary enough *not* to smile! "What proof d'you want more than this?" And he pointed to the front of the waistcoat. "Apart from the physical peculiarities of the man— sorry you didn't get here in time to scan 'em, Passingford; rather interesting—this waistcoat tells me as much as is necessary to know."

"His waistcoat—?"

"Yes; d'you see these?" Brantyngham pointed to a clutter of waxen spottings about the middle button of the garment. Greasy, pink, brown and reddish were they . . . and long veinings of rusty-looking dust adhered to the wax and so deeply entered the very fabric of the thing as to obliterate its rough texture of warp and weft. "Those marks were made by dental wax, dropped on the serge in a molten state, and the rusty dust is that of finely pulverised—or, shall I say, milled— vulcanite. I don't know whether you are aware of the fact, Inspector, but a dental mechanic in making false dentures first of all arranges artificial teeth on waxen plates, these being formed upon plaster-of-Paris models of the human mouth into which the finished product has to go. . . . Very well then . . . Wax and plaster and vulcanite—this last being the material of which false denture-plates are usually fashioned.

"Here, on this waistcoat are distinct traces of two of these materials; especially about a horizontal patch which coincides with the wearer's level of body, when seated, at a work-bench. And a dental mechanic's bench is usually shaped like that of a working jeweller—a table-like structure with a bay in it, in which to press the round of the upper abdomen. Here are markings at that level, as I have said . . . they betray as much as they help to prove.

"Then again, had you taken perfect note of his physical peculiarities, you would have found a curious malformation of Greenwood's right index finger, and another of the inner curve of his right thumb. . . . Flat and shining surfaces, these . . . and the nails were bevelled cross-wise, deeper than the most exquisitely manicured Viennese beauty dare allow herself to go, in pursuit of V-contours. . . . Those nails had been ground away to their quicks on the inner rounds of each digit.

"When a dental mechanic shapes the tiny artificial porcelain bodies of teeth that are to fit against the gum-contours of a human mouth, he grinds those bodies on a small carborundum wheel; rotated at high speed. His fingers and their nails cannot help but suffer—they get ground as well. . . . Greenwood's nails and fingers had been malformed in such fashion. When I examined them, they showed signs of regaining their normal shape; a month or so of growth, I guessed. They were badly stunted; their recovery will be slow.

"Keep so much in mind—now for the tiny blobs of dirty grey stuff, like minute 'marbles,' that are, as you can see, dotted all over these trousers' legs. . . . Those are made of plaster-of-Paris. In mechanical dentistry that material is used in quantities, every hour. And these are old spottings: they have gone to the hardness of common pottery. None is new." Sir Richard picked up one of the man's broken shoes. "Then, look at this; see how it's also marked and marred? Absolutely ingrained with plaster; rotted by the stuff. And what else strikes you as noteworthy about these lines of rot?"

The gaping Inspector did not answer. I murmured that they seemed to have been repeatedly blackened and polished over.

"Exactly, Passingford . . . *exactly*!" Brantyngham was childishly exultant. "No fresh markings of plaster made on the shoe. Those that are, repeatedly concealed. I'm getting to my final point. . . . I told you that the man was out of work, didn't I?"

We agreed.

"No recent grindings of the nails; no recent sullying of clothes and footgear by plaster . . . no recent work, at his craft."

The Inspector graciously approved.

"Then, Sir Richard, I'll have inquiries made, at once, to ascertain the name of his old employer. The fact that his pawn-tickets are in his correct name seems to indicate that the fellow has not gone under an *alias*—and Theobalds Road district is the address on all of 'em."

"That's the way, Templeton; do that, and we'll get on like a house a-fire. . . . And by the way, just to narrow down your search, Greenwood worked for a very second-rate man; probably some recently registered, but actually semi-qualified, man. I saw the abnormal development of his right leg. The thigh and calf muscles were enormously bunched, but going flabby because not used for a while. Those muscles were developed by reason of his having been used to a foot-treadle; a grinding and polishing lathe . . . which he had worked himself. Most flourishing dentists can afford electric power for those jobs; moreover a dentist who does not have mains' supply, and has to use the old-time foot power, usually delegates such work to an apprentice. You can argue from such statements, Inspector, that Greenwood's employer is in quite a small way—could only afford one man to do everything. . . . Now you get the Yard at work; it will be interesting to discover how near I am getting at truths. . . ."

Before midnight it was found that Harry Greenwood was a dental mechanic who had worked for a Mr. Eric Pinnersby, registered dentist, of Theobalds Road—a man who had closed down because of lack of trade. He shut up shop exactly five weeks before that tragic night in Bellington Square!

Inspector Templeton became, at that news, Sir Richard Thorreston Brantyngham's most devoted ally.

IV

"Ever heard that yarn, Passingford,"—Sir Richard was studying a heap of gold; those heavy coins that had fallen out of Greenwood's hat when it fell at Arnott's feet—"about the doctor who stopped before the statue of the 'Dying Alexander' in the Uffizi Galleries of Florence, and, 'That chap died of cerebro-spinal meningitis,'" said he. . . . The medical eye and the artist's eye in the sculptor had each seen straightly across the centuries; each found accordance. "Rather neat—what?"

I told him that I had never heard the yarn before, although I had been in the Galleries.

"I—I thought you had!" Brantyngham glanced up and smiled, ever so gently; I grew cold. Here was some test. "I thought you had, Passingford . . . d'you remember the gold room?"

"*By Jove!*" I looked with a more avid interest at the coins. "I do! . . . Here, let me have another look at that largest piece." Brantyngham gave it to me. "Yes; I've seen that before—"

"—In the gold room; precisely!" He was still gently smiling. "The only existing medallion-of-homage known to modern history . . . struck by the Emperor Diocletian; portraying his full body, supported by rather abandoned goddesses, soaring above the cluster of ancient Rome. The only specimen . . . and that found in the hatband of one Harry Greenwood, out-of-work!" He coughed and laughed together; his peculiar betrayal of violent interest in a problem. "And here we also have, at least to my poor knowledge, another thousand-pounds' worth of coins. Rare as the devil's bath-nights—*eh?* Look at 'em—Rose Nobles and Ducats; an Armada token in soft gold and a Henry piece that has a double 'Lady' . . . Roman, Assyrian, Babylonian, and mediæval. . . . How, in the name of wonder, do they connect up with that poverty-stricken beggar—?"

"—Who wore ten-guinea silken underwear," I reminded him.

"Oh, I'm not letting that fact escape me, Passingford! Not for a moment!" He stopped his noisy laughing and lit a cigar. . . . The clock chimed out that the hour was three of the morning. "As you know, that maid, Mary Sugden, has stated that she met Greenwood first of all when he came down to her kitchen making guarded inquiries: he had heard I was in the way of being some weird kind of a private detective—he sought my aid, as he had some mysterious trouble that could not be dealt with at police hands. I submit, in theory, that this trouble also was connected with these coins. Well, Mary Sugden assured him that I wouldn't touch his affairs . . . but asked him to call again. The result was a wooing; that pair are engaged to be married.

"Now, here's something that you do not know"—he passed a heavy gold ring across to me—"that ring signified the betrothal; Sugden never wore it in the house, but gave it to me when she told me her private relations with the fellow. And that ring, my puzzled Passingford, drops us further into the mire! Undoubtedly it is ancient Egyptian . . . a salt-ring: a circlet denoting that its one-time owner was a vendor of salt, at that time rare and precious stuff in Egypt, to people with money enough to buy. And that ring, Passingford, I dare wager, has come from some other great numismatic and olden goldworks' collection.

"Assuming that all these mysterious pieces of gold formed the subject of Greenwood's trouble, why the dickens did he carry them about with him so negligently? Assuming that he was worn down by poverty—why didn't he melt the lot down and sell the result, bit by bit, as scrap gold? Being a dental mechanic he could have got away with it, easily—such men always consider scrap-metal as perquisites, and sell quite openly. For all that the buyer could tell, the melted result might have once formed gold plates of artificial teeth, and—"

He stopped; gasped, went quite grey . . . Then, musing:

"By the Lord Harry—I see it! A—a track at last! Passingford—a track I tell you—*a track* . . . Now we might be able to correlate the apparently irreconcilable parts of this astounding whole! Thanks for reminding me about that silken underwear. . . . A man who has such tastes usually goes the whole hog; but there may be men who have such tastes and have to conceal them."

"Force of circumstances, you mean?"

"Oh, there are various kinds of force." Brantyngham was airily vague; an attitude that told me he had truly struck a light in mental darkness. "Let's ring up the hospital and find out how Greenwood's progressing."

. . . Doctor Fletchley said: "As well as can be expected. He's unconscious. It *is* a fractured base. He keeps on muttering two words—'lorry' and 'queer'; 'lorry-queer,' in succession, like that."

"Interesting," muttered Brantyngham, "but not enlightening. . . . Who's that?" He put down the receiver and looked up at his sleepy butler who had entered. "*Who?*—Oh, Inspector Templeton; very good, I'll see him."

Templeton's face was one vast smile. He carried himself stiffly and with pride. Sir Richard gave him a drink and we listened to what he had to tell.

It appeared that he had acquitted himself with remarkable skill. It had already been ascertained that Harry Greenwood had lodged near to his old employer's place and had not moved, although out of work. For all his apparent poverty he had not claimed the "dole," and for all that he went about almost in rags the sum of eight-hundred and forty pounds, in pound and ten-shilling notes, had been found concealed under a loose board in his bedroom. Further, a search of his rooms had shown the police that he was possessed of a valuable set of gold and ivory toilet requisites, although the brush and comb and shaving-brush he habitually used had not cost five shillings all told. The expensive set was also hidden beneath the floor. Behind a door hung an overcoat that had cost every penny of fifteen guineas, and between mattress and springings of his bed two suits of perfect cut and finish were discovered.

Brantyngham smiled as he listened to all this. He smiled as gently and as happily as when he tested me on the point concerning the Uffizi Galleries. "I am beginning to admire this fellow Greenwood," he murmured. "Behold the struggle indicated in and by all this; must have a backbone! I wish to heavens that little Mary Sugden had not prevented him from seeing me! I'd have helped . . ."

Greenwood's landlady stated that she had another boarder until recently, a man with whom Greenwood had been friendly, yet one whom he seemed to fear. A fortnight ago the landlady heard high words passing between her two tenants, and the sound of a blow. That night Zweiterbach, the Jewish boarder, left her house. He went away in a violent rage and had a black eye. Another friend of Greenwood's was a tall Frenchman—a man whose name she said was Lorrequier—who was a student and was always travelling abroad. She knew this because the fellow had rather fascinated her eldest daughter . . . he was forever sending her post-cards from foreign parts—Paris, Berlin, Vienna and Rome and Florence.

Brantyngham whistled a little stave; a bird-note that was full of glee. "Behold the unholy trinity." He chuckled. "Lorrequier—'lorry-queer' . . . the force that was not of circumstances and the victim of something that may have been because Greenwood was above circumstances—for the force, read 'the Jew' . . . Go on, Inspector, you've done remarkably well!"

The Jew, Zweiterbach, was a small and ill-favoured fellow. He was described as having a black beard and stubby hands, loose teeth—mis-shapen and prominent; a shuffle in his gait and reddish-rimmed eyes; the pupils a brilliant brown, the landlady said. Lorrequier was a fair-haired fellow with merry blue eyes—and "as open as the day." His hands were lean and long fingered and his mien, usually one of laughing insouciance.

One more fact elicited: both the Jew and Greenwood were often in receipt of buff envelopes stamped "O.H.M.S.," and, according to their printed superscription, emanating from the Patents Office.

Sir Richard Brantyngham got to his feet and stretched himself.

"Inspector, I congratulate you. You haven't let much slip past you!"

Templeton also got up, awkwardly. "There's one last point, Sir Richard," he said. "I set afoot inquiries among all the taxi-drivers round about here, describing the Jew. You see, I remembered the quarrel and the black eye and thought of possible motive and revenge. And sure enough, one Jerry Butterworth, a driver, tells me that he took up a fare from the corner of Edgware Road, at eleven o'clock, who answered to our descriptions. He drove him into Hyde Park, and there the man rapped at the window and stopped the cab. He got out and disappeared along a side-path."

"Butterworth seems to have taken a lot of notice of his fare, Inspector!"

"Yes, I thought of that point—but it appears that the Jew was trembling and cursing like some madman; not only that, he paid over a ten-bob note for that drive and didn't stop for change. . . . More than this, he was carrying a small brass fire-extinguisher and a heavy metal tripod; a collapsible affair such as wandering photographers use, only much stouter—"

"Yes, I thought he would have something like that," was Brantyngham's superbly indifferent statement. "And of course the cabby would also notice that his beard and clothing was all ice—not snow—*ice*!"

The Inspector goggled and stepped back a pace. He looked at Sir Richard, as a man looks at menacing death.

"*B'gad*—beg pardon, sir—but—but that's exactly right! He was coated with ice, about the head and shoulders and the right arm: 'Looked as 'ow 'e'd bin in a hice-'ouse, 'e did,' said Butterworth."

"As a matter of fact he had, in a way—only it wasn't ice, you see, Inspector; no more than there was a scream and a shot!" He twitted, but his eyes were kindly. "No human scream and no sound of a fire-arm's discharge; yet a simulation of each. A man coated with ice—yet not. Remember, Inspector, that this Jew didn't get into the taxi until eleven o'clock, long after the wounding. . . . Had that been ice, for all the snow was falling in a cold night, it would have melted; alternately, he could have cracked it off his clothing . . . ice, yet not ice . . . damned funny business altogether—*eh?*" He laughed. "Here, have another drink, Templeton, you'll have apoplexy if you don't! This is rather a pretty little mystery and—"

Again the telephone-bell began to ring.

"Hello! . . . Yes, speaking . . . You've analysed it all? . . . Yes—now let's get that right: the contents of glasses *B* and *C* are simply neutral . . . London grime and simple H-two-O . . . Yes? . . . And that in glass *A*, rich in mineral salts and evidently taken from over magnesium limestone . . . Yes . . . Deposits showing that galena-ore excretions also present . . . *Yes* . . . A fragmentary, almost microscopical, frond of moss . . . Identified as sphagnum . . . Yes . . . That all? . . . Very well, thank you very much; sorry I had to dig you out of bed, but it was vitally urgent . . . Oh, if you don't mind—I don't. . . . Good-night . . ."

Brantyngham gave that little coughing laugh again.

"That's the result of the analysis of ice-water taken from Greenwood's shoulder and two separate specimens of snowwater taken from the square. Rather neat—what? Taught me a lot. . . . No wonder people get goitre, is it? 'Derbyshire neck,' as it's commonly called. . . ." With which cryptic observation he stopped.

He glanced at the clock and yawned.

"But look here, we'll have to be getting off to bed; it's late—or rather, early! What about staying the night here, Passingford? I'd like you to . . . I'm off for a little trip to the Peak district, in the morning; nothing like a change of air."

I said, eagerly, that I'd stay. He turned, then, to Inspector Templeton. "As for you, Inspector, try to dream over a gentle little drama of a stabbing done without a blow being struck; by a man who wasn't there; by a trackless and invisible something that became a Jew coated with ice that wasn't ice . . . who carried a fire-extinguisher that wasn't one and a tripod that also was not; that Jew who missed his mark—the one who flung that bowler hat in the air—because he'd

got, or hadn't got, what he wanted out of it . . . that Jew who was in Bellington Square all the time your fellows were searching—yet, actually, was nowhere near. And also try by the morning to tell me how water frozen in Derbyshire should come to be on the shoulder of a man injured in the middle of London." He laughed and laughed again. "Oh, yes—all that lot—told you it was a pretty little problem, didn't I?"

V

Gustav Lorrequier entered the gates of Danton Lodge and locked them after him. He re-pocketed the wallet that held that key and sauntered along the snow-covered drive toward the great secret house that lay like a squat beast behind the tall guardian walls that bounded the little park.

Now it was that he died.

Only fifty yards on his way between the gates and the lodge, a happy and care-free man . . . now he was a twitching thing of death; killed by some unknown force that had taken him between the eyes and crumpled him up like a burst balloon. And as he died so suddenly he could never have heard that swift scream and that stunning sound as of a shot, heralding the end. Then something also laughed—high in the air; and laughing and laughing, it went away.

Sir Richard Brantyngham and myself were on the scene of the killing within three hours. We came over from Buxton, where we had been staying for four days. The local superintendent of police welcomed us at the gates of the lodge.

"Hope I've done right, Sir Richard, but it's a general order from the Yard that instant information has to be sent to you if anyone is discovered in the possession of ancient foreign or British coins. The dead man's trousers' pockets were full of 'em!"

"You certainly did right, Superintendent. The Yard phoned me and I got here as quickly as possible. Hope the snow's not been roughed and trampled about."

"No, sir, we've been very careful, but of course my men have had to do a bit of moving. The body's been taken to the mortuary, sir—shot in the centre of the forehead."

"Instantly killed?"

"So the doctors say, sir. But a very funny thing arises, they also tell—although the bullet did not leave the skull—it not having force enough, they say—it's nowhere to be found! The body has not been tampered with, and certain it is that the shot went in . . . but, where is it now? Queer, ain't it?"

"Very, Superintendent. Now, what about tracks in all this snow? Couldn't find any—eh? Not a mark, I expect."

"Not a mark," the officer repeated, looking curiously from one to the other of us, "not the hide or hair of one, anywhere!"

"No, there wouldn't be feet impresses. But, tell me, did you not by any chance discover three hollows in the snow anywhere? Three holes set in the form of an isosceles triangle?"

"Now—now that's funny and all, sir! We did come across such a lot of marks, but we didn't think anything on 'em like. I—I believe they're not touched, any. If I can find 'em again, should you like to see 'em?"

"Most decidedly!"

The awe-stricken Superintendent muttered in his throat (I verily believe he thought Brantyngham an intimate of the Devil!) and led us across the snow to a point some twelve yards distanced from the roughened and blood-stained patch that betrayed where the body had fallen and lain. Under the light of his lamp we saw . . . points as those of a triangle: exactly similar to those found in the inner garden of Bellington Square.

"Ah—here's where the hell-hound lurked—eh? Cover those marks over very carefully," Brantyngham ordered; "I want them to hang a man—or a beast—I really cannot tell which."

. . . The Superintendent now began to tell us that the police theory was that the unfortunate Lorrequier had been shot at from behind the gates—from the road.

"What? Shot at from the road, in the dark? A hell of an expert marksman would be required. And how is a man facing that house to be shot in the forehead by another, hidden fifty yards away behind his back? Use your commonsense, please!"

Then I saw Brantyngham put his head in the air and sniff, as a hound does. His mood changed; his voice softened and his eyes opened wider. Quite quietly and gently he asked:

"You have rather extensive moors hereabouts, have you not? There's a smell of peat and ling in the air."

"Can't say that I notice it much," growled the officer; "got something else to do but sniff at wind."

Brantyngham chuckled. "But you see, Superintendent, I am also doing things. For instance, I'm helping to hang that man I was telling you about—partly by that smelling of air! Tell me, there are moors near at hand, and mines and quarries, are there not?"

He was told that he judged rightly.

"And I gather that your water supply comes off those moors?"

"It does—worse luck; gives people 'Derbyshire neck,' they do say."

My heart leapt; here was a connection indeed! Here was that place for which Sir Richard had sought. Here was the reason for our mysterious advent into the Peak district.

"Sphagnum moss . . . plenty of that; can smell iodine in the air."

"Aye—that's t'main cause, they say—that and water that runs from the galena-ore in the limestone."

"And now you can give me details of all found on Lorrequier's person . . . and tell me all that you know of the tenant of that house."

The Superintendent did as he was bade . . . told us about the wallet of keys and the coins; then, referring to the tenant:

"He calls himself Charles Dixon now. Once we had him registered as an alien: a Hungarian, and he was named Zickel—Pether Zickel. He's naturalised and as wealthy as needs be. Retired broker, I'm told, with a turn for inventing things. Anyway he has a laboratory, as he calls it, into which he never allows anyone to set foot—all his servants are local folk; they talk, y'know. Makes a lot of trips to London, he does. Up to some six weeks ago he stayed in Town for weeks."

"And he's a shuffling fellow with red-rimmed eyes and prominent teeth—broken and yellow teeth; dark eyes; Jewish looking?"

"Aye—that's right," the officer agreed. "B'gow, but y've got him to a 'T' . . . and he is a Jew—a Hungarian Jew, now you mention it!"

"Thank you—we'll go up to the house and have a talk with him."

VI

We entered the warm wide hall of Danton Lodge. "Dixon" invited us from it to a room, but Brantyngham curtly refused. He would stay in the hall, he said; and stay he did—his careful eyes taking note of all therein.

"The dead man, Lorrequier—he was a friend of yours?"

"Vell, not vat you would call ein vriend."

"Surely not an enemy?"

"Dixon" twitched and drew back.

"*Ach nein!* . . . Vell, then, ein vriend."

"Did you expect his visit to you to-night?"

"No, he was callin' all on his owns."

"A regular habit with him—eh?"

"*Ach*, no! No 'abit at all—*nein*."

"Not a great friend of yours, nor yet an enemy?"

"So!"

"An acquaintance, unexpected?"

"Right; an ackvaintance—*ja!*"

"Do you usually allow your acquaintances to carry on their persons a private key to your well-locked and walled demesne, Mr. Dixon?"

The man shrank a little, but laughed, easily.

"If this Lorrequier 'ad ein key 'e gotten it vrom som'vher I not know."

"Um—but that lock on your gate is very subtle in its wards, Mr. Dixon. I really think you

must be forgetting—yes, forgetting. Hardly anyone could make a duplicate for such a piece of work, or get hold of one without the knowledge of the man who brought that lock." He yawned. "However, let that pass, Mr. Dixon . . . not your right name, by the way?"

"My right nom—Yes! Why not it? I am ein natralised Englishman, sir!"

"A Jewish Hungarian, I believe—from Central Hungary?"

"*Vas*—why you damn' vell ask?"

"Oh, I was just taking an interest in these beautiful rams' horns and these fleeces—wonderful things—you use as ornaments and rugs in this hall." He negligently waved around. "Rather out-of-the-way specimens—what? D'you know the Hungarian sheep is by way of being almost a noble animal! Semi-wild, too."

"*Ach so;* verry 'ard to control. . . . But, *hell*, ya not gome to me to talk about sheeps—*hein?*"

"And of course the wolves, that are always nosing about the flocks on the Hungarian plains, take pretty hefty toll of their numbers—*eh?*"

"*Ja*, d' volves do—*ja!*"

"And that fact necessitates the shepherds taking strange precautions"—I saw a sudden film come over the man's brilliant eyes, like the veiling of the orbs of a fowl, and there was a change in his face, as though slowly-pouring mud was silting down behind his yellowish skin—"to guard their flocks. I suppose they have eyes like eagles, yet even so they must find it very difficult to penetrate the rising clouds of dust that the sheep set up. . . . Again, for all the flatness of the plains, and the keenness of their keepers' vision—it would be almost impossible to tell over an enormous flock without the shepherds used—*Ah*, grab him there—*Get the devil*—!"

They shackled Pether Zickel, *alias* Dixon, *alias* Zweiterbach, and formally charged him on the dual points of murder and attempted murder: of Lorrequier and of Greenwood.

Then: "By the way, Zickel"—Brantyngham slurred the cruel words—"you didn't let me finish my little chat about telling over the flocks of Hungarian sheep; impossible, without overlooking them, above the dust-clouds they raise—impossible, without the shepherds use . . . *stilts!*"

VII

Two days after Pether Zickel was hanged I went around to Bellington Square to see Brantyngham. Harry Greenwood was making slow progress and his account of the affair was all in the Third Service Chief's possession. From it I can knit together the remainder to be told.

It appears that Greenwood met Zickel at the Patents Office when the first-named was registering the designs of a gold-casting machine for dental work, and the Hungarian was protecting a new kind of refrigerating plant. Dentists, Greenwood told Zickel, have always needed a machine to cast molten gold into the form of plates to cover the human palate—so perfectly cast as to reproduce every tiniest line and contour of the palate . . . from wax impressions. Several casting machines were already on the market; but Greenwood swore that his would oust them. It would cast a hair in gold—a butterfly's wing; a flower petal. And he proved it by exhibiting specimens of such casting.

The evil brain of Zickel saw certain possibilities. He mentioned them, and Greenwood unfortunately fell in with the scheme. Now enters Lorrequier, a marvellous artist and an expert numismatist. He had a "students' permit" allowing him, in certain foreign museums and so on, to handle, examine and take detailed notes and drawings of the world's richest treasures in ancient gold-work. From the time of Zickel's employment of him he no longer took drawn copies and notes—he took waxen impressions. These Greenwood cast in his machine . . . and when next Lorrequier visited a museum to examine pieces, he substituted the miraculously exact fraud for the real treasure.

But after a while, when half the European centres had been so denuded of their priceless pieces, Greenwood's conscience began to prick.

Zickel would not allow him to indulge his expensive tastes lest suspicion should be aroused, and here again was cause for disorder. And as Zickel took the lion's share of all monies accruing from the secret sale of the stolen pieces, in the United States, there arose more cause.

By some means Greenwood heard of Sir Richard Brantyngham, and evidently got it into his head that here was some kind of a private detective—instead of knowing he was wishing to deal with the head of a Department of State Intelligence. He determined on consulting Sir Richard, and fell in love with the little Sugden girl. But Zickel, getting wind of his plan, was forever on the watch. Each night he was there in the gardens of Bellington Square watching from his collapsible stilts, high among the branches of the plane trees. And those stilts functioned for him as do the stilts of the Hungarian sheepwatchers—they not only supported his legs, but also had a third stilt that could be used as a shooting stick is used. High in the air, comfortably seated, as a shepherd sits all day out on the Hungarian plains, he watched and waited . . . not wanting to kill Greenwood unless there was grim cause. Greenwood's telling Mary Sugden that he was no longer going to take her advice and intended to see Sir Richard—overheard by the sinister Zickel, lurking just across the narrow road—meant death to him.

Zickel grabbed Greenwood's hat, in which the plans of the casting machine were always concealed, struck his death-dealing blow . . . pulled his stilts up after him into the tree, and sat there, grinning, no doubt, at the futility of the police searchers. But overhearing and overseeing all that went on, he realised that Greenwood would have a chance to recover; hence his cursing and his shivering as he made off in the taxi, long after all had quieted down . . . after he had flung away the hat.

And now Lorrequier, returning to England with more waxen models, would surely hear of the crime—put two and two together and condemn. Lorrequier had also to die . . . and he did. The second time, Zickel made no mistake.

He straddled there above the dark and snow-covered road and just shot down on the walker's head. . . .

Sir Richard had argued stilts, from the beginning, after thinking about that isosceles triangle in the garden. The ice nodules directed him to look for a place where mining and moors ran together; recognised in the analysis the composition of minerals and salts that give rise to "Derbyshire neck," and acted accordingly. Then the ice on Zickel's clothing, that night . . . as it had not melted, he assumed that it was not frozen water—*but frozen air*, an intensely colder matter.

Zickel had intended his patent refrigerating plant to make use of this principle. He killed with it instead. All was done simply: he contrived a brazen cylinder, like a fire-extinguisher or a miniature pneumatic drill, such as they employ to break up concrete, and instead of a charge of air—compressed and hot—he charged up with compressed liquid air—compressed and intensely cold. He had a barrel in this thing: as the true barrel in a machine-gun's outer coil. In that barrel was a spicule of frozen water, an icicle like a barb.

Discharging the novel weapon, he flashed down that frozen bolt on his victims. The contact of the liquid air with ordinary air produced the simulation of a human scream; the "shot" sound was the mark of its sudden release—as of fulminated gun-powder bursting to gas. And the mist of frozen air plated the very cloth he wore, and his beard, with ice that would not melt for hours, so cold was it . . . frozen air.

All things considered, my old chief did not make to Inspector Templeton any statement that over-rode subsequent fact; and all things told, I do not think he enjoyed a problem more.

AND WE MISSED IT, LOST FOREVER

It is a fantasy for many people to disappear from their present lives. Some people disappear because they want to; others disappear because someone else wants them to. And objects—large objects—sometimes disappear in the same manner.

THE DAY THE CHILDREN VANISHED

HUGH PENTECOST

THE BEST-KNOWN pseudonym of the prolific mystery novelist and short-story writer Judson Philips (1903–1989) is Hugh Pentecost, taken from a great-uncle who was a noted criminal lawyer in New York at the turn of the last century. The author's other pseudonym, Philip Owen, was also borrowed from a relative. Although Philips wrote thirty novels and more than a hundred stories under his own name, the Pentecost pseudonym became better known and many of his earlier stories were reprinted under that more familiar name.

Born in Massachusetts, the author's family traveled extensively when he was young and he was educated in England before returning to get his AB degree from Columbia University in 1925. Selling his first story while still in school, he became a full-time writer for the rest of his life, even when suffering from emphysema and near blindness in later years. He was one of the founders of the Mystery Writers of America, became its third president, and was honored with the Grand Master Award for lifetime achievement in 1973.

"The Day the Children Vanished" became part of newspaper headlines when a California school bus was hijacked in July 1976 and the FBI was alerted to the Pentecost short story. It became abundantly clear that the kidnappers had no knowledge of the story, but the publicity garnered with the appearance of life following art resulted in Pentecost expanding the plot into a full-length novel of the same title, rushed into print later in the same year of the crime.

"The Day the Children Vanished" was first published in *This Week* magazine in 1958.

THE DAY THE CHILDREN VANISHED

HUGH PENTECOST

ON A BRIGHT, clear winter's afternoon the nine children in the town of Clayton who traveled each day to the Regional School in Lakeview disappeared from the face of the earth, along with the bus in which they traveled and its driver, as completely as if they had been sucked up into outer space by some monstrous interplanetary vacuum cleaner.

Actually, in the time of hysteria which followed the disappearance, this theory was put forward by some distraught citizen of Clayton, and not a few people, completely stumped for an explanation, gave consideration to it.

There was, of course, nothing interplanetary or supernatural about the disappearance of nine children, one adult, and a special-bodied station wagon which was used as a school bus. It was the result of callous human villainy. But, because there was no possible explanation for it, it assumed all the aspects of black magic in the minds of tortured parents and a bewildered citizenry.

Clayton is seven miles from Lakeview. Clayton is a rapidly growing quarry town. Lakeview, considerably larger and with a long history of planning for growth, recently built a new school. It was agreed between the boards of education of the two towns that nine children living at the east end of Clayton should be sent to the Lakeview School where there was adequate space and teaching staff. It was to be just a temporary expedient.

Since there were only nine children, they did not send one of the big, forty-eight passenger school buses to get them. A nine-passenger station wagon was acquired, properly painted and marked as a school bus, and Jerry Mahoney, a mechanic in the East Clayton Garage, was hired to make the two trips each day with the children.

Jerry Mahoney was well liked and respected. He had been a mechanic in the Air Force during his tour of duty in the armed services. He was a wizard with engines. He was engaged to be married to Elizabeth Deering, who worked in the Clayton Bank and was one of Clayton's choice picks. They were both nice people, responsible people.

The disappearance of the station wagon, the nine children, and Jerry Mahoney took place on a two-mile stretch of road where disappearance was impossible. It was called the "dugway," and it wound along the side of the lake. Heavy wire guard rails protected the road from the lake for the full two miles. There was not a gap in it anywhere.

The ground on the other side of the road rose abruptly upward into thousands of acres of mountain woodlands, so thickly grown that not even a tractor could have made its way up any part of it except for a few yards of deserted road that led to an abandoned quarry. Even over this old road nothing could have passed without leaving a trail of torn brush and broken saplings.

At the Lakeview end of the dugway was a filling station owned by old Jake Nugent. On the afternoon of the disappearance the bus, with Jerry Mahoney at the wheel and his carload of kids laughing and shouting at each other, stopped at old man Nugent's. Jerry Mahoney had brought the old man a special delivery letter from the post office, thus saving the RFD driver from making a special trip. Jerry and old Jake exchanged greetings, the old man signed the receipt for his letter—which was from his son in Chicago asking for a loan of fifty dollars—and Jerry drove off into the dugway with his cargo of kids.

At the Clayton end of the dugway was Joe Gorman's Diner, and one of the children in Jerry's bus was Peter Gorman, Joe's son. The diner was Jerry's first stop coming out of the dugway with his cargo of kids.

It was four-thirty in the afternoon when Joe Gorman realized that the bus was nearly three-quarters of an hour late. Worried, he called the school in Lakeview and was told by Miss Bromfield, the principal, that the bus had left on schedule.

"He may have had a flat or something," Miss Bromfield suggested.

This was one of seven calls Miss Bromfield was to get in the next half hour, all inquiring about the bus. Nine children; seven families.

Joe Gorman was the first to do anything about it seriously. He called Jake Nugent's filling station to ask about the bus, and Old Jake told him it had gone through from his place on schedule. So something had happened to Jerry and his busload of kids in the dugway. Joe got out his jeep and headed through the dugway toward Lakeview. He got all the way to Jake Nugent's without seeing the bus or passing anyone coming the other way.

Jake Nugent was a shrewd old gent, in complete possession of all his faculties. He didn't drink. When he said he had seen the bus—that it had stopped to deliver him his letter—and that he had watched it drive off into the dugway, you had to believe it. Cold sweat broke out on Joe Gorman's face as he listened. The dugway had a tendency to be icy. He had noticed coming over that it hadn't been sanded. Joe hadn't been looking for a major tragedy. But if the bus had skidded, gone through the guard rail . . .

He used Jake's phone to call the Dicklers in Clayton. The Dicklers' two children, Dorothy and Donald, were part of Jerry's load and they were the next stop after Joe's Diner. The Dicklers were already alarmed because their children hadn't appeared.

Joe didn't offer any theories. He was scared, though. He called the trooper barracks in Lakeview and told them about the missing bus. They didn't take it too seriously, but said they'd send a man out.

Joe headed back for Clayton. This time his heart was a lump in his throat. He drove slowly, staring at every inch of the wire guard rails. There was not a break anywhere, not a broken or bent post. The bus simply couldn't have skidded over the embankment into the lake without smashing through the wire guard rail.

Joe Gorman felt better when he came out at his diner at the Clayton end. He felt better, but he felt dizzy. Five minutes later Trooper Teliski came whizzing through from Lakeview and stopped his car.

"What's the gag?" he asked Joe.

Joe tried to light a cigarette and his hands were shaking so badly he couldn't make it. Teliski snapped on his lighter and held it out. Joe dragged smoke deep into his lungs.

"Look," he said. "The bus started through the dugway at the regular time." He told about Jerry's stop at Nugent's. "It never came out this end."

A nerve twitched in Teliski's cheek. "The lake," he said.

Joe shook his head. "I—I thought of that, right off. I just came through ahead of you—looking. Not a break in the guard rail anywhere. Not a scratch. Not a bent post. The bus didn't go into the lake. I'll stake my life on that."

"Then what else?" Teliski asked. "It couldn't go up the mountain."

"I know," Joe said, and the two men stared at each other.

"It's some kind of a joke," Teliski said.

"What kind of a joke? It's no joke to me—or the Dicklers. I talked to them."

"Maybe they had permission to go to a special movie or something," Teliski said.

"Without notifying the parents? Miss Bromfield would have told me, anyway. I talked to her. Listen, Teliski. The bus went into the dugway and it didn't come out. It's not in the dugway now, and it didn't go into the lake."

Teliski was silent for a moment, and then he spoke with a solid attempt at common sense. "It didn't come out this end," he said, "We'll check back on that guard rail, but let's say you're right. It didn't skid into the lake. It couldn't go up the mountain. So where does that leave us?"

"Going nuts!" Joe said.

"It leaves us with only one answer. The station wagon never went into the dugway."

Joe Gorman nodded. "That's logic," he said. "But why would Jake Nugent lie? Jerry's an hour and three-quarters late now. If he didn't go in the dugway, where is he? Where *could* he go? Why hasn't he telephoned if everything is okay?"

A car drove up and stopped. A man got out and came running toward them. It was Karl Dickler, father of two of the missing children. "Thank God you're here, Teliski. What's happened?"

"Some kind of a gag," Teliski said. "We can't figure it out. The bus never came through the dugway."

"But it did!" Karl Dickler said.

"It never came out this end," Joe Gorman said. "I was watching for Pete, naturally."

"But it did come through!" Dickler said. "I passed them myself on the way to Lakeview. They were about half a mile this way from Jake Nugent's. I saw them! I waved at my own kids!"

The three men stared at each other.

"It never came out this end," Joe Gorman said, in a choked voice.

Dickler swayed and reached out to the trooper to steady himself. "The lake!" he whispered.

But they were not in the lake. Joe Gorman's survey proved accurate; no broken wire, no bent post, not even a scratch . . .

It was nearly dark when the real search began. Troopers, the families of the children, the selectmen, the sheriff and twenty-five or thirty volunteer deputies, a hundred or more school friends of the missing children.

The lake was definitely out. Not only was the guard rail intact, but the lake was frozen over with about an inch of ice. There wasn't a break in the smooth surface of the ice anywhere along the two miles of shore bordering the dugway.

Men and women and children swarmed through the woods on the other side of the road, knowing all the time it was useless. The road was called the "dugway" because it had been dug out of the side of the mountain. There was a gravel bank about seven feet high running almost unbrokenly along that side of the road. There was the one old abandoned trail leading to the quarry. It was clear, after walking the first ten yards of it, that no car had come that way. It couldn't.

A hundred phone calls were made to surrounding towns and villages. No one had seen the station wagon, the children or Jerry Mahoney. The impossible had to be faced.

The bus had gone into the dugway and it hadn't come out. It hadn't skidded into the lake and it hadn't climbed the impenetrable brush of the mountain. It was just gone! Vanished into thin air! . . .

Everyone was deeply concerned for and sympathetic with the Dicklers, and Joe Gorman, and the Williams, the Trents, the Ishams, the Nortons, and the Jennings, parents of the missing children. Nobody thought much about Jerry Mahoney's family, or his girl.

It wasn't reasonable, but as the evening wore on and not one speck of evidence was found or one reasonable theory advanced, people began to talk about Jerry Mahoney. He was the driver. The bus had to have been driven somewhere. It couldn't navigate without Jerry Mahoney at the wheel. Jerry was the only adult involved. However it had been worked—this disappearance—Jerry must have had a hand in it.

It didn't matter that, until an hour ago, Jerry had been respected, trusted, liked. Their children were gone and Jerry had taken them somewhere. Why? Ransom. They would all get ransom letters in the morning, they said. A mass kidnapping. Jerry had the kids somewhere. There weren't any rich kids in Clayton, so he was going to demand ransom from all seven families.

So Jerry Mahoney became a villain because there was no one else to suspect. Nobody stopped to think that Jerry's father and Jerry's girl might be as anxious about his absence as the others were about the missing children.

At nine-thirty Sergeant Mason and Trooper Teliski of the State Police, George Peabody, the sheriff, and a dozen men of the community including Joe Gorman and Karl Dickler stormed into the living room of Jerry Mahoney's house where an old man with silvery white hair sat in an overstuffed armchair with Elizabeth Deering, Jerry's fiancée, huddled on the floor beside him, her face buried on his knees, weeping.

The old man wore a rather sharply cut gray flannel suit, a bright scarlet vest with brass buttons and a green necktie that must have been designed for a Saint Patrick's Day parade. As he stroked the girl's blond hair, the light from the lamp reflected glittering shafts from a square-cut diamond in a heavy gold setting he wore on his little finger. He looked up at Sergeant Mason and his small army of followers, and his blue eyes stopped twinkling as he saw the stern look on the Sergeant's face.

"All right, Pat," Sergeant Mason said. "What's Jerry done with those kids?" Pat Mahoney's pale blue eyes met the Sergeant's stare steadily. Then crinkles of mirth appeared at the corners of his eyes and mouth.

"I'd like to ask you something before I try to answer that," Pat Mahoney said.

"Well?"

"Have you stopped beating your wife, Sergeant?" Pat Mahoney asked. His cackle of laughter was the only sound in the room . . .

There are those who are old enough to remember the days when Mahoney and Faye were listed about fourth on a bill of eight star acts all around the Keith-Orpheum vaudeville circuit. Pat Mahoney was an Irish comic with dancing feet, and Nora Faye—Mrs. Mahoney to you—could match him at dancing and had the soprano voice of an angel.

Like so many people in show business, Pat was a blusterer, a boaster, a name dropper, but with it all a solid professional who would practice for hours a day to perfect a new routine, never missed an entrance in forty years, and up to the day young Jerry was born in a cheap hotel in Grand Rapids, Michigan, had given away half what he earned to deadbeats and hopeless failures.

The diamond ring he wore today had been in and out of a hundred hock shops. It had been the basis of his and Nora's security for more years than he liked to remember.

If you were left alone with Pat for more than five minutes, he went back to the old days—to the people he had idolized, like Sophie Tucker, and Smith and Dale, and Williams and Wolfus, and Joe Jackson. He'd known them all, played on the same bills with them all. "But," he would tell you, and a strange radiance would come into the pale blue eyes, "the greatest of them all was Nora Faye—Mrs. Mahoney to you."

Once he was started on his Nora, there was no way of stopping Pat Mahoney. He told of her talents as a singer and dancer, but in the end it was a saga of endless patience, of kindness and understanding, of love for a fat-headed, vain little Irish comic, of tenderness as a mother, and finally of clear-eyed courage in the face of stark tragedy.

Mahoney and Faye had never played the Palace, the Broadway goal of all vaudevillians. Pat had worked on a dozen acts that would crack the ice and finally he'd made it.

"We'd come out in cowboy suits, all covered with jewels, and jeweled guns, and jeweled boots, and we'd do a little soft shoe routine, and then suddenly all the lights would go out and only the jewels would show—they were made special for that—and we'd go into a fast routine, pulling the guns, and twirling and juggling them, and the roof would fall in! Oh, we tried it out of town, and our agent finally got us the booking at the Palace we'd always dreamed of."

There'd be a long silence then, and Pat would take a gaudy handkerchief from his hip pocket and blow his nose with a kind of angry violence. "I can show you the costumes still. They're packed away in a trunk in the attic. Just the way we wore them—me and Nora—the last time we ever played. Atlantic City it was. And she came off after the act with the cheers still ringing in our ears, and down she went on the floor of the dressing room, writhing in pain.

"Then she told me. It had been getting worse for months. She didn't want me to know. The doctor had told her straight out. She'd only a few months she could count on. She'd never said a word to me—working toward the Palace— knowing I'd dreamed of it. And only three weeks after that—she left us. Me and Jerry—she left us. We were standing by her bed when she left— and the last words she spoke were to Jerry. 'Take care of Pat,' she says to him. 'He'll be helpless without someone to take care of him.' And then she smiled at me, and all the years were in that smile."

And then, wherever he happened to be when he told the story, Pat Mahoney would wipe the back of his hand across his eyes and say: "If you'll excuse me, I think I'll be going home. . . ."

Nobody laughed when Pat pulled the old courtroom wheeze about "have you stopped beating your wife" on Sergeant Mason. Pat looked past the Sergeant at Trooper Teliski, and Joe Gorman, and Karl Dickler, and Mr. and Mrs. Jennings, whose two daughters were in the missing bus, and George Peabody, the fat, wheezing sheriff.

"The question I asked you, Sergeant," he said, "makes just as much sense as the one you asked me. You asked me what Nora's boy had done with those kids. There's no answer to that question. Do I hear you saying, 'I know what you must be feeling, Pat Mahoney, and you, Elizabeth Deering? And is there anything we can do for you in this hour of your terrible anxiety?' I don't hear you saying that, Sergeant."

"I'm sorry, Pat," Mason said. "Those kids are missing. Jerry had to take them somewhere."

"No!" Liz Deering cried. "You all know Jerry better than that!"

They didn't, it seemed, but they could be forgiven. You can't confront people with the inexplicable without frightening them and throwing them off balance. You can't endanger their children and expect a sane reaction. They muttered angrily, and old Pat saw the tortured faces of Joe Gorman and Karl Dickler and the swollen red eyes of Mrs. Jennings.

"Has he talked in any way queerly to you, Pat?" Mason asked. "Has he acted normal of late?"

"Nora's boy is the most normal boy you ever met," Pat Mahoney said, "You know that, Sergeant. Why, you've known him since he was a child."

Mrs. Jennings screamed out: "He'd protect his son. Naturally he'd protect his son. But he's stolen our children!"

"The Pied Piper rides again," Pat Mahoney said.

"Make him talk!" Mrs. Jennings cried, and the crowd around her muttered louder.

"When did you last see Jerry, Pat?"

"Breakfast," Pat said. "He has his lunch at Joe Gorman's Diner." The corner of his mouth twitched. "He should have been home for dinner long ago."

"Did he have a need for money?" Mason asked.

"Money? He was a man respected—until now—wasn't he? He was a man with a fine girl in love with him, wasn't he? What need would he have for money?"

"Make him answer sensibly!" Mrs. Jennings pleaded in a despairing voice.

Joe Gorman stepped forward. "Pat, maybe

Jerry got sick all of a sudden. It's happened to men who saw action overseas. Maybe you saw signs of something and wouldn't want to tell of it. But my Pete was on that bus, and Karl's two, and Mrs. Jennings's two. We're nowhere. Pat—so if you can tell us anything! Our kids were on that bus!"

Pat Mahoney's eyes, as he listened to Joe Gorman, filled with pain. "My kid is on that bus, too, Joe," he said.

They all stared at him, some with hatred. And then, in the distance, they heard the wail of a siren. The troopers' car was coming from Lakeview, hell-bent.

"Maybe it's news!" someone shouted.

"News!"

And they all went stumbling out of the house to meet the approaching car—all but Elizabeth Deering, who stayed behind, clinging to the old man.

"I don't understand it," she said, her voice shaken. "They think he's harmed their children, Pat! Why? Why would they think he'd do such a thing? Why?"

Old Pat's eyes had a faraway look in them. "Did I ever tell you about The Great Thurston?" he asked. "Greatest magic act I ever saw."

"Pat!" Elizabeth said, her eyes widening in horror.

"First time I ever caught his act was in Sioux City," Pat said. "He came out in a flowing cape, and a silk hat, and he . . ."

Dear God, he's losing his reason, Elizabeth Deering told herself. Let the news be good! Let them be found safe!

Outside the siren drew close.

The police car with its wailing siren carried news, but it was not the sort the people of Clayton were hoping to hear.

It was reassuring to know that within a few hours of the tragedy the entire area was alerted, that the moment daylight came a fleet of army helicopters would cover the area for hundreds of miles around, that a five-state alarm was out for the missing station wagon and its passengers, and that the Attorney General had sent the best

man on his staff to direct and coordinate the search.

Top officials, viewing the case coldly and untouched by the hysteria of personal involvement, had a theory. Of course there had to be a rational explanation of the disappearance of the bus, and Clyde Haviland, tall, stoop-shouldered, scholarly looking investigator from the Attorney General's office, was ordered to produce that explanation as soon as possible upon his arrival in Clayton. But beyond that, officials had no doubt as to the reason for the disappearance: this was a mass kidnapping; something novel in the annals of crime.

Since none of the families involved had means, Haviland and his superiors were convinced the next move in this strange charade would be a demand on the whole community to pay ransom for the children. The FBI was alerted to be ready to act the moment there was any indication of involvement across state lines.

While mothers wept and the menfolk grumbled angrily that Jerry Mahoney, the driver, was at the bottom of this, officialdom worked calmly and efficiently. The Air Force turned over its complete data on Technical Sergeant Jerry Mahoney to the FBI. Men who had known Jerry in the service were waked from their sleep or pulled out of restaurants or theaters to be questioned. Had he ever said anything that would indicate he might move into a world of violence? Did his medical history contain any record of mental illness?

Sitting at a desk in town hall, Clyde Haviland reported on some of this to George Peabody, the Sheriff, the town's three selectmen, Sergeant Mason and a couple of other troopers. Haviland, carefully polishing his shell-rimmed glasses, was a quiet, reassuring sort of man. He had a fine reputation in the state. He was not an unfamiliar figure to people in Clayton because he had solved a particularly brutal murder in the neighboring town of Johnsville, and his investigation had brought him in and out of Clayton for several weeks.

"So far," he said, with a faint smile, "the

report on Jerry Mahoney is quite extraordinary."

"In what way?" Sergeant Mason asked, eager for the scent of blood.

"Model citizen," Haviland said. "No one has a bad word for him. No bad temper. Never held grudges. Never chiseled. Saves his money. His savings account in the Clayton bank would surprise some of you. On the face of it, this is the last person in the world to suspect."

"There has to be a first time for everything," Karl Dickler said. He was a selectman as well as one of the bereaved parents.

"It's going down toward zero tonight," George Peabody, the sheriff, said glumly. "If those kids are out anywhere—"

"They're one hell of a long way from here by now, if you ask me," Sergeant Mason said.

Haviland looked at him, his eyes unblinking behind the lenses of his glasses. "Except that they never came out of the dugway."

"Nobody saw them," Mason said. "But they're not there so they did come out."

"They didn't come out," Joe Gorman said. "I was watching for them from the window of my diner at this end."

"That was the three seconds you were getting something out of the icebox in your pantry," Mason said.

"And I suppose everyone else along Main Street had his head in a closet at just that time!" Joe Gorman said.

"Or someone reached down out of the heavens and snatched that station wagon up into space," Haviland said. He was looking at Peabody's pudgy face as he spoke, and something he saw there made him add quickly: "I'm kidding, of course."

Peabody laughed nervously. "It's the only good explanation we've had so far."

Karl Dickler put his hand up to his cheek. There was a nerve there that had started to twitch, regularly as the tick of a clock. "I like Jerry. I'd give the same kind of report on him you've been getting, Mr. Haviland. But you can't pass up the facts. I'd have said he'd defend those kids with his life. But did he? And the old man—his father. He won't answer questions directly. There's something queer about him. Damn it, Mr. Haviland, my kids are—out there, somewhere!" He waved toward the frost-coated window panes.

"Every highway within two hundred miles of here is being patrolled, Mr. Dickler," Haviland said. "If they'd driven straight away from here in daylight—granting Mason is right and everybody was in a closet when the station wagon went through town—they'd have been seen a hundred times after they left Clayton. There isn't one report of anyone having seen the station wagon with the school-bus markings." Haviland paused to light a cigarette. His tapering fingers were nicotine stained.

"If you'd ever investigated a crime, Mr. Dickler, you'd know we usually are swamped with calls from people who think they've seen the wanted man. A bus—a busload of kids. Somebody *had* to see it! But there isn't even a crackpot report. If there was some place he could have stayed undercover—and don't tell me, I know there isn't—and started moving after dark, he might get some distance. But alarms are out everywhere. He couldn't travel five miles now without being trapped."

"We've told ourselves all these things for hours!" Dickler said, pinching savagely at his twitching cheek. "What are you going to *do*, Haviland?"

"Unless we're all wrong," Haviland said, "we're going to hear from the kidnappers soon. Tonight—or maybe in the morning—by mail, or phone or in some unexpected way. But we'll hear. They'll demand money. What other purpose can there be? Once we hear, we'll have to start to play it by ear. That's the way those cases are."

"Meanwhile you just sit here and wait!" Dickler said, a kind of despair rising in his voice. "What am I going to say to my wife?"

"I think all the parents of the children should go home. You may be the one the kidnappers contact. It may be your child they put on the phone to convince you the kids are safe," Haviland said. "As soon as it's daylight—"

"You think the kids *are* safe?" Dickler cried out.

Haviland stared at the distraught father for a minute. Then he spoke, gently. "What kind of assurance could I give you, Mr. Dickler? Even if I tried, you wouldn't believe me. People who play this kind of game are without feelings, not rational. When you fight them, you have to walk quietly. If you scare them, God knows what to expect. That's why I urge you all to go home and wait." He dropped his cigarette on the floor and heeled it out. "And pray," he said. . . .

Elizabeth Deering, Jerry Mahoney's girl, was sick with anxiety. Jerry was foremost in her mind; Jerry, missing with the children; Jerry, worse than that, suspected by his friends. But on top of that was old Pat Mahoney.

He hadn't made the slightest sense since the angry crowd had left his house. He had talked on endlessly about the old days in vaudeville. He seemed obsessed with the memory of the first time he had seen The Great Thurston in Sioux City. He remembered card tricks, and sawing the lady in half, and his wife Nora's childish delight in being completely bewildered. He seemed to remember everything he had seen the great man do.

Elizabeth tried, but she could not bring Pat back to the present. The tragedy seemed to have tipped him right out of the world of reason. She was partly relieved when she heard firm steps on the front porch. The other part of her, when she saw Sergeant Mason and the tall stranger, was the fear that they had news—bad news about Jerry.

Mason was less aggressive than he had been on his first visit. He introduced Haviland and said they wanted to talk to Pat. Elizabeth took them back into the living room where old Pat still sat in the overstuffed armchair.

Mason introduced Haviland. "Mr. Haviland is a special investigator from the Attorney General's office, Pat."

Pat's eyes brightened. "Say, you're the fellow that solved that murder over in Johnsville, aren't you?" he said. "Smart piece of work."

"Thanks," Haviland said. He looked at Pat, astonished at his gaudy vest and tie and the glittering diamond on his finger. He had been prepared for Pat, but not adequately.

"Sit down," Pat said. "Maybe Liz would make us some coffee if we asked her pretty."

Mason nodded to Liz, who went out into the kitchen. He followed her to tell her there was no news. Haviland sat down on the couch next to Pat, stretched out his long legs and offered Pat a cigarette.

"Don't smoke," Pat said. "Never really liked anything but cigars. Nora hated the smell of 'em. So what was I to do? You go to vaudeville in the old days, Mr. Haviland?"

"When I was a kid," Haviland said, lighting a cigarette. "I never had the pleasure of seeing you, though, Mr. Mahoney."

"Call me Pat," Pat said. "Everyone does. I was nothing, Mr. Haviland. Just a third-rate song-and-dance man. But Nora—well, if you ever saw my Nora . . ."

Haviland waited for him to go on, but Pat seemed lost in his precious memories.

"You must be very worried about your son, Pat," he said.

For a fractional moment the mask of pleasant incompetence seemed to be stripped from Pat's face. "Wouldn't you be?" he asked harshly. Then, almost instantly, the mask was fitted back into place, and old Pat gave his cackling laugh. "You got theories, Mr. Haviland? How're you going to handle this case?"

"I think," Haviland said, conversationally, "the children and your son have been kidnapped. I think we'll hear from the kidnappers soon. I think, in all probability, the whole town will be asked to get up a large ransom."

Pat nodded. "I'll chip in this diamond ring," he said. "It's got Jerry out of trouble more than once."

Haviland's eyes narrowed. "He's been in trouble before?"

"His main trouble was his Pop," Pat said.

"Sometimes there wasn't enough to eat. But we could always raise eating money on this ring." He turned his bright, laughing eyes directly on Haviland. "You figured out how the bus disappeared?"

"No," Haviland said.

"Of course it doesn't really matter, does it?" Pat said.

"Well, if we knew—" Haviland said.

"It wouldn't really matter," Pat said. "It's what's going to happen now that matters."

"You mean the demand for money?"

"If that's what's going to happen," Pat said. The cackling laugh suddenly grated on Haviland's nerves. The old joker did know something!

"You have a different theory, Pat?" Haviland asked, keeping his exasperation out of his voice.

"You ever see The Great Thurston on the Keith-Orpheum circuit?" Pat asked.

"I'm afraid not," Haviland said.

"Greatest magic act I ever saw," Pat said. "Better than Houdini. Better than anyone. I first saw him in Sioux City—"

"About the case here, Pat," Haviland interrupted. "You have a theory?"

"I got no theory," Pat said. "But I know what's going to happen."

Haviland leaned forward. "What's going to happen?"

"One of two things," Pat said. "Everybody in this town is going to be looking for that station wagon in the lake, where they know it isn't, and they're going to be looking for it in the woods, where they know it isn't. That's one thing that may happen. The other thing is, they buy this theory of yours, Mr. Haviland—and it's a good theory, mind you—and they all stay home and wait to hear something. There's one same result from both things, isn't there?"

"Same result?"

"Sure. Nobody in Clayton goes to work. The quarries don't operate. The small businesses will shut down. People will be looking and people will be waiting . . ."

"So?"

"So what good will that do anyone?" Pat asked.

Haviland ground out his cigarette in an ashtray. "It won't do anyone any good. The quarry owners will lose some money. The small businesses will lose some money."

"Not much point in it, is there?" Pat said, grinning.

Haviland rose. He'd had about enough. Mason and Elizabeth were coming back from the kitchen with coffee. "There isn't much point to anything you're saying, Mr. Mahoney."

Pat's eyes twinkled. "You said you never saw The Great Thurston, didn't you?"

"I never saw him," Haviland said.

"Well, we'll see. If they're supposed to stay home and wait, they'll stay home and wait. If they're supposed to be out searching, they'll be out searching. Ah, coffee! Smells real good. Pull up a chair, Sergeant. By the way, Mr. Haviland, I'll make you a bet," Pat said.

"I'm not a betting man," Haviland said.

"Oh, just a manner-of-speaking bet," Pat said. "I'll make you a bet that tomorrow morning they'll be out searching. I'll make you a bet that even if you order them to stay home and wait, they'll be out searching."

"Look here, Pat, if you know something . . ."

A dreamy look came into Pat's eyes. "Nora was so taken with The Great Thurston that time in Sioux City I went around to see him afterwards. I thought maybe he'd show me how to do a few simple tricks. I pretended it was for Nora, but really I thought we might use 'em in our act. He wouldn't tell me anything—that is, not about any of his tricks. But he told me the whole principle of his business."

"Sugar?" Elizabeth asked Haviland. Poor old man, she thought.

"The principle is," Pat said, "to make your audience think only what you want them to think, and see only what you want them to see." Pat's eyes brightened. "Which reminds me, there's something I'd like to have you see, Mr. Haviland."

Haviland gulped his coffee. Somehow he felt

mesmerized by the old man. Pat was at the foot of the stairs, beckoning. Haviland followed.

Elizabeth looked at Mason and there were tears in her eyes. "It's thrown him completely off base," she said. "You know what he's going to show Mr. Haviland?" Sergeant Mason shook his head.

"A cowboy suit!" Elizabeth said, and dropped down on the couch, crying softly. "He's going to show him a cowboy suit."

And she was right. Haviland found himself in the attic, his head bowed to keep from bumping into the sloping beams. Old Pat had opened a wardrobe trunk and, with the gesture of a waiter taking the silver lid off a tomato surprise, revealed two cowboy suits, one hanging neatly on each side of the trunk—Nora's and his. Chaps, shirt, vest, boots, Stetsons, and gun belts—all studded with stage jewelry.

". . . and when the lights went out," Pat was saying, "all you could see was these jew jaws, sparkling. And we'd take out the guns . . ." And suddenly Pat had the two jeweled six-shooters in his hands, twirling and spinning them. "In the old days I could draw these guns and twirl 'em into position faster than Jesse James!"

The spell was broken for Haviland. The old guy was cuckoo. "I enjoyed seeing them, Mr. Mahoney," he said. "But now, I'm afraid I've got to get back. . . ."

As soon as dawn broke, Haviland had Sergeant Mason and Sheriff George Peabody take him out to the scene of the disappearance. Everyone else was at home, waiting to hear from the kidnappers. It had been a terrible night for the whole town, a night filled with forebodings and dark imaginings. Haviland covered every inch of the two-mile stretch of the dugway. You couldn't get away from the facts. There was no way for it to have happened—but it had happened.

About eight-thirty he was back in Clayton in Joe's Diner, stamping his feet to warm them and waiting eagerly for eggs and toast to go with his steaming cup of black coffee. All the parents had been checked. There'd been no phone calls, no notes slipped under doors, nothing in the early-morning mail.

Haviland never got his breakfast. Trooper Teliski came charging into the diner just as Joe Gorman was taking the eggs off the grill. Teliski, a healthy young man, was white as parchment and the words came out of him in a kind of choking sob. "We've found 'em," he said. "Or at least we know where they are. Helicopters spotted 'em. I just finished passing the word in town."

Joe Gorman dropped the plate of eggs on the floor behind the counter. Haviland spun around on his counter stool. Just looking at Teliski made the hair rise on the back of his neck.

"The old quarry off the dugway," Teliski said, and gulped for air. "No sign of the bus. It didn't drive up there. But the kids." Teliski steadied himself on the counter. "Schoolbooks," he said. "A couple of coats—lying on the edge of the quarry. And in the quarry—more of the same. A red beret belonging to one of the kids—"

"Peter!" Joe Gorman cried out.

Haviland headed for the door. The main street of Clayton was frightening to see. People ran out of houses, screaming at each other, heading crazily toward the dugway. Those who went for their cars scattered the people in front of them. There was no order—only blind panic.

Haviland stood on the curb outside the diner, ice in his veins. He looked down the street to where old Pat Mahoney lived, just in time to see a wildly weeping woman pick up a stone and throw it through the front window of Pat's home.

"Come on—what's the matter with you?" Teliski shouted from behind the wheel of the State Police car.

Haviland stood where he was, frozen, staring at the broken window of Pat Mahoney's house. The abandoned quarry, he knew, was sixty feet deep, full to within six feet of the top with icy water fed in by constantly bubbling springs.

A fire engine roared past. They were going to try to pump out the quarry. It would be like bailing out the Atlantic Ocean with a tea cup.

"Haviland!" Teliski called desperately.

Haviland still stared at Pat Mahoney's house. A cackling old voice rang in his ears. "I'll make you a bet, Mr. Haviland. I'll make you a bet that even if you order them to stay at home and wait, they'll be out searching."

Rage such as he had never known flooded the ice out of Haviland's veins. So Pat had known! The old codger had known *last night*!

Haviland had never witnessed anything like the scene at the quarry.

The old road, long since overgrown, which ran about two hundred yards in from the dugway to the quarry, had been trampled down as if by a herd of buffalo.

Within three-quarters of an hour of the news reaching town, it seemed as if everyone from Clayton and half the population of Lakeview had arrived at the quarry's edge.

One of the very first army helicopters which had taken to the air at dawn had spotted the clothes and books at the edge of the abandoned stone pit.

The pilot had dropped down close enough to identify the strange objects and radioed immediately to State Police. The stampede had followed.

Haviland was trained to be objective in the face of tragedy, but he found himself torn to pieces by what he saw. Women crowded forward, screaming, trying to examine the articles of clothing and the books. Maybe not all the children were in this icy grave. It was only the hope of desperation. No one really believed it. It seemed, as Trooper Teliski had said, to be the work of a maniac.

Haviland collected as many facts about the quarry as he could from a shaken Sheriff Peabody.

"Marble's always been Clayton's business," Peabody said. "Half the big buildings in New York have got their marble out of Clayton quarries. This was one of the first quarries opened up by Clayton Marble Company nearly six years

ago. When they started up new ones, this one was abandoned."

In spite of the cold, Peabody was sweating. He wiped the sleeve of his plaid hunting shirt across his face. "Sixty feet down, and sheer walls," he said. "They took the blocks out at ten-foot levels, so there is a little ledge about every ten feet going down. A kid couldn't climb out of it if it was empty."

Haviland glanced over at the fire engine which had started to pump water from the quarry. "Not much use in that," he said.

"The springs are feeding it faster than they can pump it out," Peabody said. "There's no use telling them. They got to feel they're doing something." The fat sheriff's mouth set in a grim slit. "Why would Jerry Mahoney do a thing like this? *Why?* I guess you can only say the old man is a little crazy, and the son has gone off his rocker too."

"There are some things that don't fit," Haviland said. He noticed his own hands weren't steady as he lit a cigarette. The hysterical shrieking of one of the women near the edge of the quarry grated on his nerves. "Where is the station wagon?"

"He must have driven up here and—and done what he did to the kids," Peabody said. "Then waited till after dark to make a getaway."

"But you searched this part of the woods before dark last night," Haviland said.

"We missed it somehow, that's all," Peabody said, stubbornly.

"A nine-passenger station wagon is pretty hard to miss," Haviland said.

"So we missed it," Peabody said. "God knows how, but we missed it." He shook his head. "I suppose the only thing that'll work here is grappling hooks. They're sending a crane over from one of the active quarries. Take an hour or more to get it here. Nobody'll leave here till the hooks have scraped the bottom of that place and they've brought up the kids."

Unless, Haviland thought to himself, the lynching spirit gets into them. He was thinking of an old man in a red vest and a green necktie and a diamond twinkling on his little finger. He was thinking of a broken window pane—and of the way he'd seen mobs act before in his time.

Someone gripped the sleeve of Haviland's coat and he looked down into the horror-struck face of Elizabeth Deering, Jerry Mahoney's girl.

"It's true then," she whispered. She swayed on her feet, holding tight to Haviland for support.

"It's true they found some things belonging to the kids," he said. "That's all that's true at the moment, Miss Deering." He was a little astonished by his own words. He realized that, instinctively, he was not believing everything that he saw in front of him. "This whole area was searched last night before dark," he said. "No one found any schoolbooks or coats or berets then. No one saw the station wagon."

"What's the use of talking that way?" Peabody said. His eyes were narrowed, staring at Liz Deering. "I don't want to believe what I see either, Mr. Haviland. But I got to." The next words came out of the fat man with a bitterness that stung like a whiplash. "Maybe you're the only one in Clayton that's lucky, Liz. You found out he was a homicidal maniac in time—before you got married to him."

"Please, George!" the girl cried. "How can you believe—"

"What can anyone believe but that?" Peabody said, and turned away.

Liz Deering clung to Haviland, sobbing. The tall man stared over her head at the hundreds of people grouped around the quarry's edge. He was reminded of a mine disaster he had seen once in Pennsylvania; a whole town waiting at the head of the mine shaft for the dead to be brought to the surface.

"Let's get out of here," he said to Liz Deering, with sudden energy. . . .

Clayton was a dead town. Stores were closed. Joe's Diner was closed. The railroad station agent was on the job, handling dozens of telegrams that were coming in from friends and relatives of the parents of the missing children. The two girls in the telephone office, across the street from the bank, were at their posts.

Old Mr. Granger, a teller in the bank, and one of the stenographers were all of the bank staff that had stayed on the job. Old Mr. Granger was preparing the payroll for the Clayton Marble Company. He didn't know whether the truck from the company's offices with the two guards would show up for the money or not.

Nothing else was working on schedule today. Even the hotel down the street had shut up shop. One or two salesmen had driven into town, heard the news, and gone off down the dugway toward the scene of the tragedy. A few very old people tottered in and out the front doors of houses, looking anxiously down Main Street toward the dugway. Even the clinic was closed. The town's doctors and nurses had all gone to the scene of the disaster.

Down the street a piece of newspaper had been taped over the hole in Pat Mahoney's front window. Pat Mahoney sat in the big overstuffed armchair in his living room. He rocked slowly back and forth, staring at an open scrapbook spread across his knees. A big black headline from a show-business paper was pasted across the top.

MAHONEY AND FAYE
BOFFO BUFFALO

Under it were pictures of Pat and Nora in their jeweled cowboy suits, their six-shooters drawn, pointing straight at the camera. There was a description of the act, the dance in the dark with only the jewels showing and the six-shooters spouting flame. "Most original number of its kind seen in years," a Buffalo critic had written. "The ever popular Mahoney and Faye have added something to their familiar routines that should please theater audiences from coast to coast. We are not surprised to hear that they have been booked into the Palace."

Pat closed the scrapbook and put it down on the floor beside him. From the inside pocket of his jacket he took a wallet. It bulged with papers and cards. He was an honorary Elk, honorary police chief of Wichita in 1927, a Friar, a Lamb.

Carefully protected by an isinglass guard were some snapshots. They were faded now, but anyone could see they were pictures of Nora with little Jerry at various stages of his growth. There was Jerry at six months, Jerry at a year, Jerry at four years. And Nora, smiling gently at her son. The love seemed to shine right out of the pictures, Pat thought.

Pat replaced the pictures and put the wallet back in his pocket. He got up from his chair and moved toward the stairway. People who knew him would have been surprised. No one had ever seen Pat when movements weren't brisk and youthful. He could still go into a tap routine at the drop of a hat, and he always gave the impression that he was on the verge of doing so. Now he moved slowly, almost painfully—a tired old man, with no need to hide it from anyone. There was no one to hide it from; Jerry was missing, Liz was gone.

He climbed to the second floor and turned to the attic door. He opened it, switched on the lights, and climbed up to the area under the eaves. There he opened the wardrobe trunk he'd shown to Haviland. From the left side he took out the cowboy outfit—the chaps, the boots, the vest and shirt and Stetson hat, and the gun belt with the two jeweled six-shooters. Slowly he carried them down to his bedroom on the second floor. There Pat Mahoney proceeded to get into costume.

He stood, at last, in front of the full-length mirror on the back of the bathroom door. The high-heeled boots made him a couple of inches taller than usual. The Stetson was set on his head at a rakish angle. The jeweled chaps and vest glittered in the sunlight from the window. Suddenly old Pat jumped into a flat-footed stance, and the guns were out of the holsters, spinning dizzily and then pointed straight at the mirror.

"Get 'em up, you lily-livered rats!" old Pat shouted. A bejeweled gunman stared back at him fiercely from the mirror.

Then, slowly, he turned away to a silver picture frame on his bureau. Nora, a very young girl, looked at him with her gentle smile.

"It'll be all right, honey," Pat said. "You'll see. It'll be another boffo, honey. Don't you worry about your boy. Don't you ever worry about him while I'm around. You'll see. . . ."

It was a terrible day for Clayton, but Gertrude Naylor, the chief operator in the telephone office, said afterward that perhaps the worst moment for her was when she spotted old Pat Mahoney walking down the main street—right in the middle of the street—dressed in that crazy cowboy outfit. He walked slowly, looking from right to left, staying right on the white line that divided the street.

"I'd seen it a hundred times before in the movies," Gertrude Naylor said, afterward. "A cowboy, walking down the street of a deserted town, waiting for his enemy to appear—waiting for the moment to draw his guns. Old Pat's hands floated just above the crazy guns in his holster, and he kept rubbing the tips of his fingers against his thumb. I showed him to Millie, and we started to laugh, and then, somehow, it seemed about the most awful thing of all. Jerry Mahoney had murdered those kids and here was his old man, gone nutty as a fruitcake."

Old Mr. Granger, in the bank, had much the same reaction when the aged, bejeweled gun toter walked up to the teller's window.

"Good morning, Mr. Granger," Pat said, cheerfully.

Mr. Granger moistened his pale lips. "Good morning, Pat."

"You're not too busy this morning, I see," Pat said.

"N-no," Mr. Granger said. The killer's father—dressed up like a kid for the circus. He's ready for a padded cell, Mr. Granger thought.

"Since you're not so busy," Pat said, "I'd like to have a look at the detailed statement of my account for the last three months." As he spoke, he turned and leaned against the counter, staring out through the plate-glass bank window at the street. His hands stayed near the guns, and he kept rubbing his fingertips against the ball of his thumb.

"You get a statement each month, Pat," Mr. Granger said.

"Just the same, I'd like to see the detailed statement for the last three months," Pat said.

"I had to humor him, I thought," Mr. Granger said later, "So I went back to the vault to get his records out of the files. Well, I was just inside the vault door when he spoke again, in the most natural way. "If I were you, Mr. Granger," he said, "I'd close that vault door, and I'd stay inside, and I'd set off all the alarms I could lay my hands on. You're about to be stuck up, Mr. Granger."

"Well, I thought it was part of his craziness," Mr. Granger said, later. "I thought he meant *he* was going to stick up the bank. I thought that was why he'd got all dressed up in that cowboy outfit. Gone back to his childhood, I thought. I was scared, because I figured he was crazy. So I *did* close the vault door. And I *did* set off the alarm, only it didn't work. I didn't know then all the electric wires into the bank had been cut."

Gertrude and Millie, the telephone operators, had a box seat for the rest of it. They saw the black sedan draw up in front of the bank and they saw the four men in dark suits and hats get out of it and start up the steps of the bank. Two of them were carrying small suitcases and two of them were carrying guns.

Then suddenly the bank doors burst open and an ancient cowboy appeared, hands poised over his guns. He did a curious little jig step that brought him out in a solid square stance. The four men were so astonished at the sight of him they seemed to freeze.

"Stick 'em up, you lily-livered rats!" old Pat shouted. The guns were out of the holsters, twirling. Suddenly they belched flame, straight at the bandits.

The four men dived for safety, like men plunging off the deck of a sinking ship. One of them made the corner of the bank building.

Two of them got to the safe side of the car. The fourth, trying to scramble back into the car, was caught in the line of fire.

"I shot over your heads that first time!" Pat shouted. "Move another inch and I'll blow you all to hell!" The guns twirled again and then suddenly aimed steadily at the exposed bandit. "All right, come forward and throw your guns down," Pat ordered.

The man in the direct line of fire obeyed at once. His gun bounced on the pavement a few feet from Pat and he raised his arms slowly. Pat inched his way toward the discarded gun.

The other men didn't move. And then Gertrude and Millie saw the one who had gotten around the corner of the bank slowly raise his gun and take deliberate aim at Pat. She and Millie both screamed, and it made old Pat jerk his head around. In that instant there was a roar of gunfire.

Old Pat went down, clutching at his shoulder. But so did the bandit who'd shot him and so did one of the men behind the car. Then Gertrude and Millie saw the tall figure of Mr. Haviland come around the corner of the hotel next door, a smoking gun in his hand. He must have spoken very quietly because Gertrude and Millie couldn't hear him, but whatever he said made the other bandits give up. Then they saw Liz Deering running across the street to where old Pat lay, blood dripping through the fingers that clutched at his shoulder. . . .

Trooper Teliski's car went racing through the dugway at breakneck speed, siren shrieking. As he came to the turn-in to the old quarry, his tires screamed and he skidded in and up the rugged path, car bounding over stones, ripping through brush. Suddenly just ahead of him on the path loomed the crane from the new quarry, inching up the road on a caterpillar tractor. Trooper Teliski sprang out of his car and ran past the crane, shouting at the tractor driver as he ran.

"To hell with that!" Teliski shouted. Stumbling and gasping for breath, he raced out into the clearing where hundreds of people waited in a grief-stricken silence for the grappling for bodies to begin.

"Everybody!" Teliski shouted. "Everybody! Listen!" He was half laughing, half strangling for breath. "Your kids aren't there! They're safe. They're all safe—the kids, Jerry Mahoney, everyone! They aren't there. They'll be home before you will! Your kids—" And then he fell forward on his face, sucking in the damp, loam-scented air.

Twenty minutes later Clayton was a madhouse. People running, people driving, people hanging on to the running boards of cars and clinging to bumpers. And in the middle of the town, right opposite the bank, was a station wagon with a yellow school bus sign on its roof, and children were spilling out of it, waving and shouting at their parents, who laughed and wept. And a handsome young Irishman with bright blue eyes was locked in a tight embrace with Elizabeth Deering. . . .

Haviland's fingers shook slightly as he lit a cigarette. Not yet noon and he was on his third pack.

"You can't see him yet," he said to Jerry Mahoney. "The doctor's with him. In a few minutes."

"I still don't get it," Jerry said. "People thought I had harmed those kids?"

"You don't know what it's been like here," Liz Deering said, clinging tightly to his arm.

Jerry Mahoney turned and saw the newspaper taped over the broken front window, and his face hardened. "Try and tell me, plain and simple, about Pop," he said.

Haviland shook his head, smiling like a man still dazed. "Your Pop is an amazing man, Mr. Mahoney," he said. "His mind works in its own peculiar ways . . . The disappearance of the bus affected him differently from some others. He saw it as a magic trick, and he thought of it as a magic trick—or, rather, as *part* of a magic trick. He said it to me and I wouldn't listen. He said it is a magician's job to get you to think what he wants you to think and see what he wants you

to see. The disappearance of the children, the ghastly faking of their death in the quarry—it meant one thing to your Pop, Mr. Mahoney. Someone wanted all the people in Clayton to be out of town. Why?

"There was only one good reason that remarkable Pop of yours could think of. The quarry payroll. Nearly a hundred thousand dollars in cash, and not a soul in town to protect it. Everyone would be looking for the children, and all the bandits had to do was walk in the bank and take the money. No cops, no nothing to interfere with them."

"But why didn't Pop tell you his idea?" Jerry asked.

"You still don't know what it was like here, Mr. Mahoney," Haviland said. "People thought you had done something to those kids; they imagined your Pop knew something about it. If he'd told his story, even to me, I think I'd have thought he was either touched in the head or covering up. So he kept still—although he did throw me a couple of hints. And suddenly, he was, to all intents and purposes, alone in the town. So he went upstairs, got dressed in those cowboy clothes and went, calm as you please, to the bank to meet the bandits he knew must be coming. And they came."

"But why the cowboy suit?" Liz Deering asked.

"A strange and wonderful mind," Haviland said. "He thought the sight of him would be screwy enough to throw the bandits a little off balance. He thought if he started blasting away with his guns they might panic. They almost did."

"What I don't understand," Liz said, "is how, when he fired straight at them, he never hit anybody!"

"Those were stage guns—prop guns," Jerry said. "They only fire blanks."

Haviland nodded. "He thought he could get them to drop their own guns and then he'd have a real weapon and have the drop on them. It almost worked. But the one man who'd ducked around the corner of the building got in a clean shot at him. Fortunately, I arrived at exactly the same minute, and I had them all from behind."

"But how did you happen to turn up?" Jerry asked.

"I couldn't get your father out of my mind," Haviland said. "He seemed to know what was going to happen. He said they'd be searching for the kids, whether I told them to wait at home or not. Suddenly I had to know why he'd said that."

"Thank God," Jerry said. "I gather you got them to tell you where we were?"

Haviland nodded. "I'm still not dead clear how it worked, Jerry."

"It was as simple as pie a la mode," Jerry said. "I was about a half mile into the dugway on the home trip with the kids. We'd just passed Karl Dickler headed the other way when a big trailer truck loomed up ahead of me on the road. It was stopped, and a couple of guys were standing around the tail end of it.

"Broken down, I thought. I pulled up. All of a sudden guns were pointed at me and the kids. They didn't talk much. They just said to do as I was told. They opened the back of the big truck and rolled out a ramp. Then I was ordered to drive the station wagon right up into the body of the truck. I might have tried to make a break for it except for the kids. I drove up into the truck, they closed up the rear end, and that was that. They drove off with us—right through the main street of town here!"

Haviland shook his head. "An old trick used hundreds of times back in the bootleg days. And I never thought of it!"

"Not ten minutes later," Jerry went on, "they pulled into that big deserted barn on the Has-

kell place. We've been shut up there ever since. They were real decent to the kids—hot dogs, ice cream cones, soda.

"So we just waited there, not knowing why, but nobody hurt, and the kids not as scared as you might think," Jerry laughed. "Oh, we came out of the dugway all right—and right by everybody in town. But nobody saw us."

The doctor appeared in the doorway. "You can see him for a minute now, Jerry," he said. "I had to give him a pretty strong sedative. Dug the bullet out of his shoulder and it hurt a bit. He's pretty sleepy—but he'll do better if he sees you, I think. Don't stay too long, though."

Jerry bounded up the stairs and into the bedroom where Pat Mahoney lay, his face very pale, his eyes half closed. Jerry knelt by the bed.

"Pop," he whispered, "You crazy old galoot!"

Pat opened his eyes. "You okay, Jerry?"

"Okay, Pop."

"And the kids?"

"Fine. Not a hair on their heads touched." Jerry reached out and covered Pat's hand with his. "Now look here. Two-Gun Mahoney . . ."

Pat grinned at him. "It was a boffo, Jerry. A real boffo."

"It sure was," Jerry said. He started to speak, but he saw that Pat was looking past him at the silver picture frame on the dresser.

"I told you it'd be all right, honey," Pat whispered. "I told you not to worry about your boy while I was around to take care of him." Then he grinned at Jerry, and his eyes closed and he was asleep.

Jerry tiptoed out of the room to find his own girl.

THE TWELFTH STATUE

STANLEY ELLIN

ONE OF AMERICA'S greatest but most underappreciated mystery writers was the Brooklyn-born Stanley Bernard Ellin (1916–1986), a three-time Edgar Award winner and the Mystery Writers of America's Grand Master honoree in 1981. Upon his return to civilian life after serving in the army during World War II, his wife agreed to support him for a year (they had a small chicken farm) while he tried to make a career as a writer. Just before the deadline, *Ellery Queen's Mystery Magazine* accepted his short story "The Specialty of the House" (1948), which went on to become a relentlessly anthologized classic of crime fiction and was adapted for an episode of the television series *Alfred Hitchcock Presents.* Many more of his stories were adapted for TV by Hitchcock and other series. Six of his stories were nominated for Edgars, two of which, "The House Party" (1954) and "The Blessington Method" (1956), won; his superb novel *The Eighth Circle* (1958) also won an Edgar. In addition to a number of his works having been adapted for television, many have been produced as feature films. *Dreadful Summit* (1948), his first novel, was filmed by Joseph Losey as *The Big Night* (1951), starring John Drew Barrymore, Preston Foster, and Joan Lorring. *Leda* (1959), a French film directed by Claude Chabrol and starring Madeline Robinson and Jean-Paul Belmondo, was based on his second novel, *The Key to Nicholas Street* (1952). A short story, "The Best of Everything" (1952), became *Nothing But the Best* (1964), directed by Clive Donner and starring Alan Bates, Denholm Elliott, and Harry Andrews. *House of Cards* (1967) was filmed with the same title in 1968, directed by John Guillermin and starring George Peppard, Inger Stevens, and Orson Welles. The abysmal *Sunburn* (1979), starring Farrah Fawcett, Charles Grodin, and Art Carney, was based so loosely on *The Bind* (1970) that Ellin asked that his name be removed from the credits.

"The Twelfth Statue" was first published in the February 1967 issue of *Ellery Queen's Mystery Magazine*; it was first collected in *Kindly Dig Your Grave and Other Wicked Stories* (New York, Davis, 1975).

THE TWELFTH STATUE

STANLEY ELLIN

ONE FINE MIDSUMMER evening, in the
environs of the ancient city of Rome, an American motion picture producer named Alexander
File walked out of the door of his office and vanished from the face of the earth as utterly and
completely as if the devil had snatched him
down to hell by the heels.

However, when it comes to the mysterious
disappearance of American citizens, the Italian
police are inclined to shrug off the devil and his
works and look elsewhere for clues. There had
been four people remaining in the office after
File had slammed its door behind him and
apparently stepped off into limbo. One of the
people had been Mel Gordon. So Mel was not
surprised to find the note in his letter box at the
hotel politely requesting him to meet with *Com-
missario* Odoardo Ucci at Police Headquarters to
discuss *l'affaire* File.

He handed the note to his wife at the breakfast table.

"A Commissioner, no less," Betty said gloomily after she had skimmed through it. "What are
you going to tell him?"

"I guess the best policy is to answer everything with a simple yes or no and keep my private thoughts private." The mere sight of the
coffee and roll before him made Mel's stomach
churn. "You'd better drive me over there. I don't
think I'm up to handling the car in this swinging
Roman traffic, the way I feel right now."

His first look at Commissioner Ucci's office

didn't make him feel any better. It was as bleak
and uninviting as the operating room of a rundown hospital, its walls faced with grimy white
tile from floor to ceiling, and, in a corner, among
a tangle of steam and water pipes, there was a
faucet which dripped with a slow, hesitant tinkle
into the wash basin below it.

The Commissioner seemed to fit these surroundings. Bald, fat, sleepy-eyed, his clothing
rumpled, his tie askew, he asked his questions in
precise, almost uninflected English, and painstakingly recorded the answers with a pencil
scarred by toothmarks. Sublimation, thought
Mel. He can't chew up witnesses, so he chews
up pencils. But don't let those sleepy-looking
eyes fool you, son. There might be a shrewd
brain behind them. So stay close to the facts and
try to keep the little white lies to a minimum.

*"Signor File was a cinema producer exclusively?
He had no other business interests?"*

"That's right, Commissioner."

And so it was. File might have manufactured
only the cheapest quickies of them all, the slea-
ziest kind of gladiator-and-slave-girl junk, but
he was nonetheless a movie producer. And his
other interests had nothing to do with business,
but with dewy and nubile maidens, unripe love-
lies all the more enticing to him because they
were unripe. He loved them, did File, with a
mouth-watering, hard-breathing, popeyed love.
Loved them, in fact, almost as much as he loved
his money.

"There were two other people besides yourself and your wife who were the last to see the missing man, Signor Gordon. One of them, Cyrus Goldsmith, was the director of the picture you were making?"

"Yes, he was."

And a sad case, too, was Cy Goldsmith. Started as a stunt man in horse operas, got to be a Second Unit Director for DeMille—one of those guys who handled chariot races and cavalry charges for the Maestro—and by the time he became a full director of his own, of low-budget quickies, he had absorbed too much DeMille into his system for his own good.

The trouble was that, whatever else De-Mille's pictures might be, as spectacles they are the best. They are demonstrations of tender loving care for technical perfection, of craftsmanship exercised on every detail, and hang the expense. Quickies, on the other hand, have to be belted out fast and cheap. So Cy made them fast and cheap, but each time he did it he was putting an overdeveloped conscience on the rack, he was betraying all those standards of careful movie-making that had become ingrained in him. And, as the psychology experts would have it, a compulsive perfectionist forced to do sloppy work is like someone with claustrophobia trapped in an elevator between floors. And to be trapped the rest of your lifetime this way—!

That's what happened to Cy, that's why he hit the bottle harder and harder until he was marked unreliable, on the skids, all washed up, so that finally the only producer who would give him work was good old Alexander File, who paid him as little as possible to turn out those awful five-and-dime spectaculars of his. This is no reflection on others who might have been as charitable to Cy. The sad truth is that Signor File was the only producer on record who, as time went on, could keep Cy sober enough for a few weeks at a stretch to get a picture out of him, although, unless you like watching a sadistic animal trainer put a weary old lion through its paces, it wasn't nice to watch the way he did it. A razor-edged tongue can be a cruel instrument when wielded by a character like File.

And, of course, since he was as small and skinny as Cy was big and brawny it must have given him a rich satisfaction to abuse a defenseless victim who towered over him. It might have been as much the reason for his taking a chance on Cy, picture after picture, as the fact that Cy always delivered the best that could be made of the picture, and at the lowest possible price.

"Regarding this Cyrus Goldsmith, Signor Gordon—"

"Yes?"

"Was he on bad terms with the missing man?"

"Well—no."

Commissioner Ucci rubbed a stubby forefinger up and down his nose. A drop of water tinkled into the wash basin approximately every five seconds. Very significant, that nose rubbing. Or was it simply that the Commissioner's nose itched?

"And this other man who was with you that evening, this Henry MacAaron. What was his function?"

"He was director of photography for the picture, in charge of all the cameramen. Is, I should say. We still intend to finish the picture."

"Even without Signor File?"

"Yes."

"Ah. And this MacAaron and Goldsmith are longtime associates of each other, are they not?"

"Yes."

Very longtime, Commissioner. From as far back as the DeMille days, in fact, when Cy gave MacAaron his first chance behind a camera. Since then, like Mary and her lamb, where Cy is, there is MacAaron, although he's a pretty morose and hardbitten lamb. And, incidentally, one hell of a good cameraman. He could have done just fine for himself if he hadn't made it his life's work to worshipfully tag after Cy and nurse him through his binges.

"And you yourself, Signor Gordon, are the author who wrote this cinema work for Signor File?"

"Yes."

Yes, because it's not worth explaining to this dough-faced cop the difference between an author and a rewrite man. When it comes to that, who's to say which is the real creator of any script—the author of the inept original or the long-suffering expert who has to make a mountain out of its molehill of inspiration?

Commissioner Ucci rubbed his nose again, slowly and thoughtfully.

"When all of you were with Signor File in the office that evening, was there a quarrel? A violent disagreement?"

"No."

"No. Then is it possible that immediately after he left he had a quarrel with someone else working on the picture?"

"Well, as to that, Commissioner—"

An hour later, Mel escaped at last to the blessed sunlight of the courtyard where Betty was waiting in the rented Fiat.

"Head for the hills," he said as he climbed in beside her. "They're after us."

"Very funny. How did it go?"

"All right, I guess." He was dripping with sweat, and when he lit a cigarette he found that his hands were trembling uncontrollably. "He wasn't very friendly though."

Betty maneuvered the car through the traffic jamming the entrance to the bridge across the Tiber. When they were on the other side of the river she said, "You know, I can understand how the police feel about it because it's driving me crazy, too. A man just can't disappear the way Alex did. He just can't, Mel. It's impossible."

"Sure it is. All the same he *has* disappeared."

"But where? Where is he? What happened to him?"

"I don't know. That's the truth, baby. You can believe every word of it."

"I do," Betty sighed. "But, my God, if Alex had only not mailed you that script—"

That was when it had all started, of course, when File airmailed that script the long distance from Rome to Los Angeles. It had been a surprise, getting the script, because a few years before, Mel had thought he was done with File forever and had told him so right there on the job. And File had shrugged it off to indicate he couldn't care less.

The decision that day to kiss off File and the deals he sometimes offered hadn't been an act of bravado. A TV series Mel had been doctoring was, according to the latest ratings, showing a vast improvement in health, and with a successful series to his credit he envisioned a nice secure future for a long time to come. It worked out that way, too. The series had a good run, and when it folded, the reruns started paying off, which meant there was no reason for ever working for File again or even of thinking of working for him.

Now File suddenly wanted him again, although it was hard to tell why since it was obvious that a Mel Gordon with those residuals rolling in would be higher-priced than the old Mel Gordon who took what he could get. In the end they compromised, with File, as usual, getting the better of the deal. The trouble was that he knew Mel's weakness for tinkering with defective scripts, knew that once Mel had gone through the unbelievably defective script of *Emperor of Lust* he might be hooked by the problems it presented, and if hooked he could be reeled in without too much trouble.

That was how it worked out. File's Hollywood lawyer—a Big Name who openly despised File and so, inevitably, was the one man in the world File trusted—saw to the signing of the contract, and before the ink was dry on it, Mel, his wife at his side, and the script of *Emperor of Lust* under his arm, was on his way to a reunion with File.

They held the reunion at a sidewalk café on the Via Veneto, the tables around crowded by characters out of Fellini gracefully displaying their ennui in the June sunlight and by tourists ungracefully gaping at the Fellini characters.

There were four at their table besides Mel and Betty. File, of course, as small and pale and hard-featured as ever, his hair, iron-gray when Mel had last seen it, now completely white; and Cy Goldsmith, gaunt and craggy and bleary-eyed with hangover; and the dour MacAaron with that perpetual squint as if he were always sizing up camera angles; and a newcomer on the scene, a big, breasty, road-company version of Loren named Wanda Pericola who, it turned out, was going to get a leading role in the picture and who really had the tourists all agape.

Six of them at the table altogether. Four Camparis, a double Scotch for Cy, a cup of tea for File. File, although living most of each year abroad, distrusted all foreign food and drink.

The reunion was short and to the point. File impatiently allowed the necessary time to renew old acquaintance and for an introduction to Wanda who spoke just enough English to say hello, and then he said abruptly to Mel, "How much have you done on the script?"

"On the script? Alex, we just got in this morning."

"What's that got to do with it? You used to take one look at a script and start popping with ideas like a real old-fashioned corn popper. You mean making out big on the idiot box has gone and ruined that gorgeous talent?"

Once, when payments on house, car, and grocer's bills depended on the inflections of File's voice, Mel had been meek as a lamb. Now, braced by the thought of those residuals pouring out of the TV cornucopia, he found he could be brave as a lion.

"You want to know something, Alex?" he said. "If my gorgeous talent is ruined you're in real bad trouble, because the script is a disaster."

"So you say. All it needs is a couple of touches here and there."

"It needs a whole new script, that's what it needs, before we make sense out of all that crummy wordage. After I read it I looked up the life of the emperor Tiberius in the history books—"

"Well, thanks for that much anyhow."

"—and I can tell you everything has to build up the way he's corrupted by power and suspicion and lust until he goes mad, holed up in that palace on Capri where they have the daily orgies. And the key scene is where he goes off his rocker."

"So what? That's in the script right now, isn't it?"

"It's all wrong right now, with this Jekyll into Hyde treatment. All that raving and rug chewing makes the whole thing low comedy. But suppose no one around him can see that Tiberius has gone mad—if only the audience realizes it—"

"Yeah?" File was warily interested now. "And how do you show that?"

"This way. In that corridor outside Tiberius' bedroom in the palace we want a row of life-sized marble statues. Let's say six of them, a round half dozen. Statues of some great Romans, all calmly looking down at this man who's supposed to be carrying on their traditions. We establish in advance his respect for those marble images, the way he squares his shoulders with dignity when he passes them. Then the big moment arrives when he cracks wide open.

"How do we punch it across? We leave the bedroom with him, truck with him past those statues, see them as *he* sees them—and what we see is all his madness engraved on *their* faces! Get it, Alex? The faces of those statues Tiberius is staring at are now distorted, terrifying reflections of the madman he himself has finally become. That's it. A few feet of film and we're home free."

"Home free," echoed Cy Goldsmith. He gingerly pivoted his head toward MacAaron. "What do you think, Mac?" and MacAaron grunted, "It'll do"—which from him was a great deal of conversation, as well as the stamp of high approval.

"Do?" Wanda said anxiously. "*Che succede?*"—because, as Mel knew sympathetically, what she wanted to hear was her name being bandied about by these people in charge of her destiny; so it was only natural when Betty explained to her in her San Francisco Italian what had been said that Wanda should look disappointed.

But it was File's reaction that mattered, and Mel was braced for it.

"Statues," File finally said with open distaste.

"Twelve of them, Alex," Mel said flatly. "Six sanes and six mads. Six befores and six afters.

This is the key scene, the big scene. Don't short-change it."

"You know what artwork like that costs, sonny boy? You look at our budget—"

"Ah, the hell with the budget on this shot," Cy protested. "This scene can make all the difference, Alex. The way I see it—"

"You?" File turned to him open-mouthed, as if thunderstruck by this interruption. And File's voice was penetrating enough to be heard over all the racket of the traffic behind him. "Why, you're so loaded right now you can't see your hand in front of your face, you miserable lush. And with the picture almost ready to shoot, too. Now go on and try to sober up before next week. You heard me. Get going."

The others at the table—and this, Mel saw, included even Wanda who must have got the music if not the words—sat rigid with embarrassment while Cy clenched his empty glass in his fist as if to crush it into splinters, then lurched to his feet and set off down the street full-tilt, ricocheting into bypassers as he went. When MacAaron promptly rose to follow him File said, "Where are you going? I didn't say I was done with you yet, did I?"

"Didn't you?" said MacAaron, and then was gone, too.

File shrugged off this act of mutiny.

"A great team," he observed. "A rummy has-been and his nurse-maid. A fine thing to be stuck with." He picked up his cup of tea and sipped it, studying Mel through drooping eyelids. "Anyhow, the statues are out."

"They're in, Alex. All twelve of them. Otherwise, it might take me a long, long time to get going on the script."

This was the point where, in the past, File would slap his hand down on the table to end all argument. But now, Mel saw as File digested his tea, there was no slapping of the table.

"If I say okay," said File, "you should be able to give me a synopsis of the whole story tomorrow, shouldn't you?"

You give me my synopsis and I'll give you your statues. It was File's way of bargaining,

because File never gave something for nothing. And even though it meant a long night's work ahead, Mel said, with a sharp sense of triumph, "I'll have it for you tomorrow." For once—for the first time in all his dealings with File—he hadn't knuckled under at the mention of that sacred word Budget.

When he and Betty departed, not even the thought of the ugly scene with Cy could dim his pleasure in knowing he had brow-beaten File into allotting the picture a few thousand dollars more than his precious budget provided. After all, Mel told himself, Cy hardly needed others to comfort him in his sad plight when he had MacAaron to do that for him on a full-time basis.

Back in the hotel room, Mel stretched out on the bed with the script of *Emperor of Lust*—a title, he was sure, that had to be File's inspiration—while Betty readied herself at her portable typewriter, waiting for her husband to uncork the creative flow. Fifteen years before, she had been the secretary assigned him on his first movie job; they were married the second week on the job, and ever since then she had admirably combined the dual careers of amanuensis and wife. Married this long and completely, it was hard for them to surprise each other with anything said or done, but still Mel was surprised when Betty, who had been sitting in abstracted silence, said out of a clear sky, "She isn't the one."

"What?"

"Wanda. I mean, she's not Alex's playmate-of-the-month. She's not the one he's going to bed with."

"I'd say that's their problem. Anyhow, what makes you so sure about it?"

"For one thing, she's too old."

"She must be a fast twenty or twenty-one."

"That's still past the schoolgirl age. And she's just too much woman for him, no matter how you look at it. I think Alex is afraid of real women, the way he always goes for the Alice in Wonderland type."

"So?"

"So you know what I'm getting at. We've been through it before with him. Sooner or later he'll turn up with some wide-eyed little Alice, and it makes me sick if it does sound terribly quaint, but I think a man of sixty parading down the Via Veneto with a kid in her first high heels is really obscene. And sitting at the table with us, playing footsie with her. And showing her what a big man he is by putting down someone like Cy—"

"Oh?" said Mel. "And which one is really on your mind? The Alice type or Cy?"

"I pity both of them. Mel, you said last time you'd never work for Alex again. Why did you take this job anyhow?"

"So that I could put him down, the way I did about those statues. I needed that for the good of my soul, sweetheart; it was long overdue. Also because *The New York Times* said that the last one I did for Alex was surprisingly literate, and maybe I can get them to say it again."

"Still and all—"

"Still and all, it'll be a hectic enough summer without worrying about Cy and Alice in Movieland and all the rest of it. Right now we've got to put together some kind of story synopsis, so tomorrow we'll run over to Cinecitta to see what sets we'll have to work with, and after that we'll be so busy manufacturing stirring dialogue that there won't be time to think of other people's troubles."

"Unless they're shoved down your throat," said Betty. "Poor Cy. The day he kills Alex, I want to be there to see it."

Cinecitta is the Italian-style Hollywood outside Rome where most of File's pictures were shot. But when Mel phoned him about meeting him there, he was told to forget it; this one would be made in a lot a few miles south of the city right past Forte Appia on the Via Appia Antica, the Old Appian Way.

This arrangement, as File described it, was typical of his manipulations. Pan-Italia Productions had built its sets on that lot for an elaborate picture about Saint Paul, and when the picture was completed File had rented the lot, sets and all, dirt-cheap, on condition that he clear away everything when he left. The fact that the sets might be useless in terms of the script File had bought—also dirt-cheap—didn't bother him any. They were out of Roman history and that was good enough for him.

In a way, it was this kind of thing which often made working for File as intriguing to Mel as it was infuriating. The script he was handed and the sets and properties File provided usually had as much relationship to each other as the traditional square peg and round hole, and there was a fascination in trying to fit them together. When it came to an Alexander File Production, Mel sometimes reflected, necessity was without doubt the mother of improvisation.

The next day he and Betty rented a car and drove out to the lot to see what Pan-Italia had left him to improvise with. They went by way of the Porta San Sebastiano, past the catacombs, and along the narrow ancient Roman road through green countryside until they arrived at what looked like a restoration of Caesar's forum rising out of a meadow half a mile off the road. Beyond it was the production's working quarters, a huddle of buildings surrounding a structure the size of a small airplane hangar which was undoubtedly the sound stage.

There was a ten-foot-high wire fence running around the entire lot, and the guard at its gate, a tough-looking character with a pistol strapped to his hip, made a big project out of checking them through. Once inside, it wasn't hard to find File's headquarters, which was the building nearest the gate and had a few cars parked before it, among them File's big Cadillac convertible. The only sign of activity in the area was a hollow sound of hammering from inside the sound stage nearby.

File was waiting in his office along with Cy, MacAaron, and a couple of Italian technicians whom Mel remembered from the last picture, a Second Unit Director and a lighting man. Neither of them was much good at his job, Cy had once told him—DeMille wouldn't have let them sweep up for him—but they came cheap and understood English, which was all File wanted of them.

Mel found that the procedure of starting work for File hadn't varied over the years.

"All right, all right, let's see it," File said to him without preliminary, and when the story synopsis was handed across the desk to him he read it through laboriously, then said, "I guess it'll have to do. When can you have some stuff to start shooting?"

"In about a week."

"That's what you think. This is Friday. Monday morning, Wanda and the other leads are showing up bright and early along with a flock of extras for mob scenes. So eight o'clock Monday morning you'll be here with enough for Goldsmith to work on for a couple of days. And you'll have some interior scenes ready, too, in case it rains. Then everybody won't be sitting around on the payroll doing nothing."

"Look, Alex, let's get one thing straight right now—"

"Let's, sonny boy. And what we'll get straight is that it don't matter how big you made it on TV, when you work for me you produce like you always did. You are not Ernie Hemingway, understand? You are a hack, a shoemaker, and all you want to do is get some nails into the shoes before the customer gets sore. And no use looking daggers about it, because if you got any ideas of making trouble or walking out on this contract, I'll tie you up so tight in court you'll never write another script for anybody for the next fifty years. What do you think of that?"

Mel felt his collar grow chokingly tight, knew his face must be scarlet with helpless, apoplectic rage. The worst of it, as far as he was concerned, was that everyone else in the room was embarrassedly trying to avoid his eye the way those at the table the day before had tried to avoid Cy's when File had put him in his place. Only Betty aimed an outraged forefinger at File and said, "Listen, Alex—!"

"Stay out of this," File said evenly. "You're married to him, so maybe you like it when he makes like a genius. I don't."

Before Betty could fire back, Mel shook his head warningly at her. After all, the contract had been signed, sealed, and delivered. There was no way out of it now.

"All right, Alex," he said, hating to say it, "Monday, I'll have some nails in your shoes."

"I figured you would. Now let's go take a look at the layout."

They all trooped out into the blazing sunshine, File leading the way, Mel lagging behind with Betty's hand clutching his in consolation. As insurance against mud and dust, Pan-Italia had laid down a tarmac, a hard-surfaced shell, on this section of the lot, and although it was hardly noon Mel could feel it already softening underfoot in the heat. Most of Rome closed up shop and took a siesta during the worst of the midday heat in summer, but there were no siestas on an Alexander File Production.

Cy Goldsmith fell in step beside Mel. The heat seemed to weigh heavily on Cy; yesterday's ruddiness was gone from his face, leaving it jaundiced and mottled, and his lips with an unhealthy blueish tinge. But his eyes were bright and sharp, the bleariness cleared from them, which meant that he was, temporarily at least, off the bottle.

"What the hell," he said. "It figured Alex would want to slip the knife into you because of those statues, didn't it?"

"Did it? Well, if it wasn't for the contract I'm stuck with he could shove his whole picture. And if he thinks I'm going to really put out for him—"

"Don't talk like that, Mel. Look, for once we've got everything going for us—a good story, first-class sets, even some actors who know what it's all about. I signed them on myself."

"Like Wanda, our great big beautiful leading lady? Who are you kidding, Cy? What kind of performance can you get out of someone whose lines have to be written in phonetic English?"

"I'll get a good performance out of her. Just don't let Alex sour you on this job, Mel. You never dogged it on the job yet. This is no time to start doing it."

The pleading note in his voice sickened Mel. Bad enough this big hulk should have taken what File dished out over the years. Now, God help him, he seemed to be gratefully licking File's hand for it.

The tarmac came to an end beyond the huge structure housing the sound stage, and another high wire fence here bisected the property and barred the way to the backlot and the replica of the forum on it. The guard at the backlot gate, like his counterpart at the front gate, wore a pistol on his hip.

When they had passed through the fence and caught up to File he jerked a thumb in the direction of the guard.

"That's how the money goes," he said. "You need a guy like that on duty twenty-four hours a day around here. Otherwise, these ginzos would pick the place clean."

"Well, thanks," said Betty, whose maiden name happened to be Capoletta. *"Mille grazie, padrone."*

"Don't be so touchy," File said. "I'm not talking about any Italians from Fisherman's Wharf, I'm talking strictly about the local talent"; and Mel observed that the pair of technicians who must have understood every word of this looked as politely expressionless as if they didn't. After all, a job was a job.

The tour of the sets on the backlot indicated that File had got himself a real bargain. Pan-Italia had built not only the replica of the forum for its Saint Paul picture, but also a beautifully detailed full-scale model of an ancient Roman street complete with shops and houses, and a magnificent porticoed villa which stood on a height overlooking the rest.

This last, said File, would serve as Tiberius' palace in Capri, although its interiors would be done on the sound stage. MacAaron and a couple of the camera crew had already been to Capri the week before and taken some footage of the scenery there to make establishing shots look authentic. A Cy Goldsmith brainstorm, that Capri

footage, he added irritably, because what difference could it make to the slobs in the audience—

To get away from File, Mel climbed alone to the portico of the villa. Standing there, looking out over the forum and the umbrella pines and cypresses lining the Appian Way, he could see the time-worn curves of the Alban Hills on the horizon and had the feeling that all this might well be ancient Rome come to life again. Only a dazzle of sunlight reflected from a passing car in the distance intruded on that feeling, but even that flash of light might have been from the burnished armor of some Roman warrior heading south to Ostia in his chariot.

Then Cy was there beside him, looking at him quizzically.

"How do you like it?" he asked.

"I like it."

"And everything fits in with the Tiberius period. Now do you get what I meant about making an honest-to-God picture this time out? I mean, with everything done right. It's all here waiting to be made."

"Not by us. Why don't you quit pushing so hard, Cy? It takes rewrites and retakes and rehearsals to make the kind of picture you're talking about. The three R's. And you know how Alex feels about them."

"I know. But we can fight it out with Alex right down the line."

"Sure we can."

"Mel, I'm on the level. Would you believe me if I told you this was the last picture I'll ever work on?"

"You're kidding."

Cy smiled crookedly. "Not from what the doctors had to say. This is strictly between you and me and Mac—Betty, too, if you want to let her know—but I'm all gone inside." He patted his sagging belly. "It'll be a big deal if the machinery in here holds out for this picture, let alone another next year."

So that was it, Mel thought wonderingly, and just how corny can a man wind up being after a long hard lifetime? That explained everything. Cy Goldsmith was a dying man close to the end of his string, and this picture was to be his swan song. A good one, the best he was capable of, no matter how Alexander File felt about it.

"Look, Cy, doctors can make mistakes. If you went back to the States right now and saw a specialist there—maybe tried the Mayo Clinic—"

"That's where they gave me the word, Mel, at Mayo. Straight from the shoulder. You want to know how straight? Well, the first thing I did before flying out here on this job was to hop back to L.A. and make all the arrangements to be put away in Elysian Park when the time came. A big mausoleum, a nice box, everything. The funny part was that I felt a hell of a lot better when I signed those papers. It gave me a good idea why those old Romans and Egyptians wanted to make sure everything was all set for the big day. It makes you look the facts in the face. After that, you can live with them."

At least, Mel thought, until this picture was made the way you wanted it made. And, in the light of that, Cy had paid him the handsomest tribute he could. Everything depended on the script, and it was Mel Gordon who had been called a long way to work on it.

"Tell me one thing, Cy," he said. "It was your idea to get me out here on this script, wasn't it? Not Alex's."

"That's right. Doesn't that prove I can win a battle with Alex when I have to?"

"I guess it does," said Mel. "Now all we have to do is win the war."

And it was war, even without shot and shell being fired. Once File had the first draft of the complete script in his hands and had drawn up a shooting schedule from it, he quickly caught on to the fact that something strange was going on. After that, life became merry hell for everyone involved in the making of *Emperor of Lust*.

Including, as Mel pointed out to Betty with satisfaction, File himself. For the first time in File's career one of his pictures lagged steadily behind its schedule as Cy grimly ordered retake after retake until he got what he wanted of a scene, doubled in brass as his own Second Unit Director, drilling Roman legions and barbarian hordes in the fields outside the lot until they threatened open rebellion, bullied Mel into endlessly rewriting one scene after another until the dialogue suited the limited capabilities of the cast without losing any of its color or sense.

For that matter, all the conspirators doubled in brass. Mel found himself directing two-shots between his writing chores. MacAaron took over lighting and sound mixing despite roars of protest from outraged union delegates. Even Betty, toiling without pay, spent hours drilling Wanda Pericola in the pronunciation of her lines until the two of them hated the sight of each other.

Long days, long nights for all of them, culminated usually in the projection room where they wearily gathered to see the latest rushes while File sat apart from them in a cold fury delivering scathing comment on what he viewed on the screen and what it was costing him. The most grotesque part of it, Mel saw, was that File never understood what they were trying to do and flatly refused to believe the explanation of it that Betty gave him in a loud and frustrating private conference. As far as File was concerned, they were deliberately and maliciously goldbricking on the job, sabotaging him, driving him to ruin, and he let them know it at every turn.

In the long run it was his own cheapness that kept him from doing more than that. As Cy noted, he could have fired them all, but contracts cut ice both ways. Firing them would mean paying them off in full for having done only part of the picture, and replacing them would mean paying others in full for doing the other part, and this for File was unthinkable.

"I know," Mel said. "All the same, I wish there was some way of keeping him off our backs for five minutes at a time. Now if he'd only find himself some nice little distraction—"

It wasn't the wish that made it so, of course. But for better or worse, early the next morning along came the distraction.

_____

She arrived riding pillion on a noisy motorbike—a small slender girl with one arm around the waist of the bearded young man who drove the motorbike and the other arm clutching to her a bulky parcel done up in wrapping paper. A northerner, Mel surmised, taking in the fair skin, the honey-colored hair, the neatly chiseled, slightly upturned Tuscan nose. A skinny, underfed kid, really, but pretty as they come.

They were standing in front of File's headquarters when the bike pulled up—Mel and Betty, Cy, MacAaron, and File—having the usual morning squabble about the day's shooting schedule. As the girl dismounted, now gingerly holding the parcel in both hands as if it were made of fine glass, her skirt rode up over her thighs, and Mel saw File do almost a comic double-take, the man's eyes fixing on the whiteness of exposed thigh, then narrowing with interest as they moved up to take in the whole girl.

What made it worse, Mel thought, was the quality of flagrant innocence about her, of country freshness. He glanced at Betty. From her expression he knew the same word must have flashed through her mind as his at that instant. *Alice.*

The bearded driver of the motorbike came up to them, the girl following in his shadow as if trying to keep out of sight. Close up, Mel saw that the driver's straggling reddish beard was a hopeless attempt to add years and dignity to a guileless and youthful face.

"Signor File, I am here as you requested."

"Yeah," File grunted. He turned sourly to Mel. "You wanted statues? He's the guy who'll take care of them for you."

"Paolo Varese," said the youth. "And this is my sister, Claudia." He reached a hand behind him to draw her forward. "What are you afraid of, you stupid girl?" he asked her teasingly. "You must forgive her," he said to the others. "She is only a month from Campofriddo, and all this is new to her. It impresses her very much."

"Where's Campofriddo?" asked Betty.

"Near Lucca, in the hills there." Paolo laughed deprecatingly. "You know. Twenty people, forty goats. That kind of place. So Papa and Mama let Claudia come to live with me in Rome where she could get good schooling, because she did well in school at home."

He put an arm around the girl's narrow shoulders and gave her a brotherly hug which made her blush right red. "But you know how girls are about the cinema. When she heard I was to work here where you are photographing one—"

"Sure," Cy said impatiently, "but about those statues—"

"Yes, yes, of course." Paolo took the parcel from his sister, tore open its wrappings, and held up before them a statuette of a robed figure. It was beautifully carved out of what looked like polished white marble, and, Mel saw with foreboding, it was not quite two feet tall.

"The statues were supposed to be lifesized," he said, bracing himself for another bout with File. "This one—"

"But this is only the—the—" Paolo struck his knuckles to his forehead, groping for the word "—the sample. They will be lifesized. Twelve of them, all lifesized." He held out the sample at arm's length and regarded it with admiration. "This is Augustus. The others will be Sulla, Marius, Pompey, Caesar, and Tiberius himself, all copies of the pieces in the Museo Capitoline, all lifesized."

Mel took the figurine and found it surprisingly light. "It's not marble?"

"How could it be?" Paolo said. "Marble would take months to work, perhaps more. No, no, this is a trick. A device of my own. If you will show me where I am to work, I can demonstrate it for you."

His sister anxiously tugged at his arm. *"Che cosa devo fare, Paolo?"* she asked, then whispered to him in more rapid Italian.

"Oh, yes." Paolo nodded apologetically at File. "Claudia has a little time before she must go along to school, and she would like to look around here and see how a cinema is made. She would be very careful."

"Look around, hey?" File considered this frowningly, his eyes on the girl. "Well, why not? I'll even show her around myself," and from the way Claudia's face lit up, Mel saw she knew at least enough English to understand this. "And I have to go back to town in a little while," said File, "so I can drop her off at her school on the way."

Paolo seemed simultaneously alarmed and delighted by this kindness. "But, Signor File, to take such trouble—"

"It's all right, it's all right." File curtly waved aside the stammered gratitude. "You just get on the job and do what you're being paid for. Goldsmith here'll show you the shop."

Watching File motion the girl to follow him and then briskly stride off with her in his wake, Mel felt an angry admiration for the way the man handled these little situations. You had to know him to know the score. Otherwise, what you were seeing was a small white-haired grandfatherly type, concealing a heart of gold beneath a crusty exterior.

A sculptor's studio had been partitioned off in the carpenters' shop near the entrance to the sound stage, and it was already crowded with the materials and equipment for the making of the statues. The sculpturing process itself, as Paolo described it in rapt detail, was intriguing. A pipework armature, the size of the subject, was set up, its crosspiece at shoulder height. From the crosspiece, wire screening was then unspooled around and around down to the base where it was firmly attached, the whole thing making a cylinder of screening in roughly human proportions. To this was applied a thin layer of clay which was etched into the flowing lines of a Roman toga. As for the head—

Paolo took the statuette, and, despite Betty's wail of protest, ruthlessly chipped away its features with a knifeblade.

"It would take a long time to model the head in clay," he said, "but this way it can be done very quickly."

He brushed away marble-colored flakes, revealing beneath them what appeared to be a skull, although its eyes and nose sockets were filled in. He tapped it with a fingernail. "Hollow, you see. *Papier maché,* such as masks are made of. One merely soaks it in this stuff—*colla*—you know?"

"Glue," said Betty.

"Yes, yes. Then it can be quickly shaped into a whole head. It dries almost at once. Then clay goes over it for the fine work, and here is our Roman."

"How do you get it to look like marble?" Cy asked.

"Enamel paint is sprayed on, white and ivory mixed. That, too, dries while you wait."

"But the clay under it is still wet, isn't it?"

"Oh, no. Before the paint goes on, one uses the torch—the blowtorch, that is—up and down and back and forth for a few hours. But with all this it takes only one day. So there will be twelve statues in twelve days, as I have promised Signor File."

"Do you have the designs for the other statues with you?" Cy asked, and when they were produced, much crumpled and stained, from Paolo's pocket, it was clear that File had once again made himself an excellent deal.

Standing at the open door of the shop ready to take their departure, they saw File heave into sight with Claudia, direct her into the Cadillac, and climb behind the wheel.

"Beautiful," breathed Paolo, his eyes on the car rather than his sister. Then as the car headed for the gate, he reminded himself of something. *"La bicicletta! La bicicletta!"* he shouted after the girl, waving toward the motorbike propped on the ground before File's office, but she only made a small gesture of helplessness, and then the car was out of range.

Paolo shrugged in resignation.

"The autobus out here is very irregular, so she is supposed to bring me here on the bicycle each morning and then use it herself to go to school. That means I must take the autobus home at night, but today it looks as if I will be able to drive myself home without any trouble."

"There's a piece of luck," Betty said drily. "You know, Paolo, Claudia is a very pretty girl."

"But how well I know." Paolo raised his eyes to heaven in despair. "That was one reason I had so much trouble with Mama and Papa about permitting her to live with me here, where she could improve herself, become educated, perhaps become a teacher at school, not the wife of some stupid peasant. They are good people, Mama and Papa, but they hear stories, you know? So they think all the men in Rome want to do is eat the pretty little girls. They forget Claudia is with me, and that I—"

"Paolo," Betty cut in, "sometimes she is not with you. And while I don't know about all the other men in Rome, I know about Signor File. Signor File likes to eat pretty little girls."

The boy looked taken aback.

"He? Really, *signora,* he does not seem like someone who—"

"Faccia attenzione, signore," said Betty in a hard voice. *"Il padrone è un libertino. Capisce?"*

Paolo nodded gravely.

"Capisco, signora. Thank you. I will tell Claudia. She is already sixteen, not a child. She will understand."

But, Mel observed, there were days after that when File, contrary to his custom, left the lot in midafternoon and returned only late in the evening, if at all.

Betty observed this as well.

"And you know where he goes, don't you?" she said to her husband.

"I don't know. I suspect. That's different from knowing."

"Look, dear, let's not split hairs. He's with that child, and you darn well know it."

"So what? For one thing, Mother of the Gracchi, sixteen, going on seventeen, is not a child in these parts, as her brother himself remarked. For another thing, you've done all you could about it—angels could do no more. As far as I'm concerned—"

"Oh, sure. As far as you're concerned—and Cy and Mac, too—you're just glad Alex isn't around all the time, no matter what."

There was no denying that. It was a godsend not having File always underfoot, and they weren't going to question whatever reason he had for staying away from them. Their nerves were ragged with overwork and tension, but the picture was near completion, and all they needed was enough stamina to finish it in style. Considering the drain that File was on their stamina—complaining, threatening, countermanding orders—the sight of that Cadillac convertible pulling out of the gate in the afternoon was like a shot in the arm.

For that matter, Mel wasn't sure that even if Paolo suspected what might be going on he would be so anxious to rock the boat himself. The commission to do the statues, he had confided to Mel, meant enough money to see him through a difficult time. It was lucky Signor File had asked the Art Institute to recommend someone who would handle the commission at the lowest possible rate, because as one of their prize graduates the year before, he, Paolo, had got the recommendation. Very lucky. Money was hard to come by for a young sculptor without a patron; the family at home had no money to spare, so it was a case of always scratching for a few lire, taking odd jobs, doing anything to get up enough for the next rent day. But now—!

So from early morning to late at night, stripped to the waist and pouring sweat, Paolo toiled happily at the statues, and one by one they were carted away to the sound stage and mounted in place on the set there. The first six, faces in stern repose, looked good in the establishing shots; the ones that followed, faces distorted with madness, looked even better. The last to be done, and, Mel thought, the most effective of all according to the sketches of those agonized features, would be Tiberius in his madness.

When this was in its place along with the other five in the corridor of the palace, and MacAaron had made his trucking shots and closeups, the picture was all but finished. Finished, that is, except for Cy's editing—the delicate job of cutting, rearranging, finding the proper rhythm for each scene, and finally resplicing the whole thing into what would be shown on the screen. In the last analysis, everything depended on the editing, but this would be Cy's baby alone.

With the end in sight none of them wanted to rock the boat. And then, one stormy night, it came close to capsizing.

The storm had begun in the late afternoon, one of those drought-breaking Roman downpours that went on hour after hour, turning the meadows around them into a quagmire and covering even the tarmac with an inch of water. At midnight, when Mel and Betty splashed their way to the car, they saw Paolo standing hopelessly in the doorway of the carpenter's shop looking out into the deluge, and so they stopped to pick him up.

He was profusely grateful as he scrambled past Betty into the backseat. He lived in Trastevere, but if they dropped him anywhere in the city he could easily find his way home from there.

"No, it won't be any trouble taking you right to the door," Mel lied. "You just show me the way."

The way, as Paolo pointed it out, lay across the Ponte Sublicio and to the Piazza Matrai, in the heart of a shabby, working-class district. The apartment he and his sister occupied was in a tenement that looked centuries old and stood in an alleyway leading off from the piazza. And parked in solitary grandeur at the head of the alley was a big Cadillac convertible.

Mel's foot came down involuntarily on the brake when he saw it, and the little Fiat lurched to a stop halfway across the piazza. At the same moment he heard Paolo make a hissing sound between his teeth, felt the pressure of the boy's body against the back of the driver's seat as he leaned forward and stared through the rain-spattered windshield.

And then, as if timing his approach to settle all doubts, File came into view down the alley, heading for the Cadillac at a fast trot, head down and shoulders hunched against the rain. He had

almost reached it before Paolo suddenly roused himself from his paralysis of horror.

He pushed frantically at the back of Betty's seat. "*Signora,* let me out!"

Betty stubbornly remained unmoving. "Why? So you can commit murder and wind up in jail for the rest of your life? What good will that do Claudia now?"

"That is my affair. Let me out. I insist!"

From his tone Mel had the feeling there would be murder committed if Betty yielded. Then File was out of reach. The Cadillac's taillights blinked on, started to move away, then disappeared down the Via della Luce. Paolo hammered his fist on his knee.

"You had no right!" he gasped. "Why should you protect him?"

Mel thought of the next morning when this half-hysterical boy would have a chance to catch up to File on the lot.

"Now look," he said reasonably, although it struck him that under the circumstances reason was the height of futility. "Nobody knows exactly what happened up in that apartment, so if you keep your head and talk to Claudia—"

"Yes," Paolo said savagely, "and when I do—!"

"But I'll talk to her first," Betty announced. "I know," she said as Paolo started to blurt out an angry protest. "It's not my affair, I have no right to interfere, but I'm going to do it just the same. And you'll wait here with Signor Gordon until I'm back."

It was a tedious, nerve-racking wait, and the ceaseless drumming of the rain on the roof of the car made it that much more nerve-racking. The trouble was, Mel glumly reflected, that not having children of her own, Betty was always ready to adopt any waif or stray in sight and recklessly try to solve his problems for him. Only in this case, nothing she could say or do would mean anything. The boy sitting in deadly silence behind him had too much of a score to settle. The one practical way of forestalling serious trouble was to warn File about it and hope he had sense enough to take the warning to heart. If he didn't—

At last Betty emerged from the building and ducked into the car.

"Well," said Paolo coldly, "you have talked to her?"

"Yes."

"And she told you how much she was paid to—to—?"

"Yes."

Paolo had not expected this. "She would never tell you that," he said incredulously. "She would lie, try to deceive you the way she did with me. She—"

"First let me tell you what she said. She said your agreement with Signor File was that you would get a small payment for the statues in advance and the rest of the money when the work was done. Is that the truth?"

"Yes. But what does that have to do with it?"

"A great deal. Everything, in fact. Because Signor File told her that if she wasn't nice to him, you would never get the rest of the money. He would say your work was no good, and, more than that, he would let everyone know this so that you'd never get a chance at such commissions again. So what your sister thought she was sacrificing herself for, *signore*, was the money and the reputation she was sure you would otherwise be cheated out of."

Paolo clapped a hand to his forehead.

"But how could she think this?" he said wildly. "She knows there was a paper signed before the lawyers. How could she believe such lies?"

"Because she is only a child, no matter what your opinion is of that, and she had no one to tell her better. Now when you go upstairs, you must let her know you understand that. Will you?"

"*Signora*—"

"Will you?"

"Yes, yes, I will. But as for that man—?"

"Paolo, listen to me. I know how you feel about it, but anything you do to him can only mean a scandal that will hurt Claudia. Whatever happens will be in all the newspapers. After that, can the girl go back to school? Can she ever go back home to Campofriddo without everyone staring at her and whispering about her? Even if you take him to court—"

"Even that," Paolo said bitterly. He placed a hand on the latch of the door. "But I must not keep you any longer with my affairs." And when Betty reluctantly leaned forward so that he could climb past her out of the car, he added, "You do not understand these things, *signora*, but I will think over what you have said. *Ciao*."

Mel watched him disappear into the tenement, and then started the car.

"It doesn't sound very promising," he said. "I guess I'll have to slip Alex a word of warning tomorrow, much as I'd like to see him get what's coming to him."

"I know." Betty shook her head despairingly. "My God, you ought to see the way those kids are living. A room like a rathole with a curtain across the middle so they can each have a little privacy. And rain seeping right through the walls. And the furniture all orange crates. And a stinking, leaky toilet out in the hall. You wouldn't believe that in this day and age—"

"Oh, sure, but *la vie Boheme* is hardly ever as fancy as *la dolce vita*. Anyhow, whatever Alex is paying for this commission means some improvement in those living standards when he settles up."

"Does it? Mel, how much do you think Alex is paying?"

"How would I know? Why? Did Claudia tell you how much?"

"She did. Now take a guess. Please."

Mel did some swift mental arithmetic.

"Well," he said, "since the statues are all Paolo's work from the original designs up to the finished product, they ought to be worth between five and ten thousand bucks. But I'll bet the kid never got more than two thousand from Alex."

"Mel, he got five hundred. One hundred down, and the rest on completion. Five hundred dollars altogether!"

You couldn't beat File, Mel thought almost with awe as they recrossed the bridge over the swollen and murky Tiber. A lousy $500 for all twelve statues. And with Claudia Varese thrown in for good measure.

Mel had it out with File the next morning, glad that Cy and MacAaron were there in the office with them to get an earful about what had been going on.

Physically, File was not the bravest man in the world. He was plainly alarmed by the outlook.

"What the hell," he blustered, "you know these girls around here. If it wasn't me yesterday, it would be somebody else today. But if this brother of hers got any ideas about sticking a shiv in my back, maybe I can—"

"I didn't say that," Mel pointed out. "All I said was you'd be smart to steer clear of him. He'll be done with his job tomorrow. You might find something to do in town until he's gone."

"You mean, let this ginzo kid run me off my own property?"

"You started the whole thing, didn't you? Your bad luck you just happened to pick the wrong kind of girl this time."

"All right, all right! But I'll be back in the evening to see that last set of rushes, and we've got an important meeting in the office here right afterward. All of us, you understand? So you all be here."

That had an ominous sound, they agreed after File left, but it didn't bother them. There were only a couple of scenes left to be shot, about a week's work editing the picture, and that was it. File had done his worst, but it hadn't stopped them from doing their best. Whatever card he now had up his sleeve—and File could always produce some kind of nasty surprise at those meetings—it was too late for him to play it. That was all that mattered.

They were wrong. File returned late in the evening to view the rushes with them, and when they gathered in his office afterward, he pulled from his sleeve, not a card, but a bombshell.

"I want to clear up one little point," he said, "and then the meeting's over. One little point

is all. Goldsmith, I got an idea you're finally supposed to be done with the photography this week. Is that a fact?"

"By Friday," Cy said.

"Then it's settled. So Friday night when you all walk out of here it'll be for the last time. Get the point? Once you're on the other side of that gate you're staying there. And don't try to con the guard into anything, because he'll have special instructions about keeping you there."

"Sure," said Cy, "except that you overlooked one little detail, Alex. The picture has to be edited. You'll have to wait another week before you tell the guard to pull his gun on me."

"Oh?" said File with elaborate interest. "Another week?" His face hardened. "No, thanks, Goldsmith. We're already carrying a guy on the payroll as film editor, so you just wave goodbye Friday and forget you ever knew me."

"Alex, you're not serious about Gariglia doing the editing. But he's completely useless. If I'm not there to tell him what to do—"

"So from now on I'll tell him what to do."

"You?"

"That's right. Me." File angrily jabbed a forefinger into his chest. "Me. Alex File who was making pictures when you were still jumping ponies over a cliff for Monogram at ten bucks a jump."

"You never made a picture like this in your life."

"You bet I didn't." File's voice started to rise. "A month over schedule. Twenty per cent over budget. Twenty per cent, you hear?"

Cy's face was bloodless now, his breath coming hard.

"Alex, I won't let you or anybody else butcher this picture. If you try to bar me from the lot before the editing is done—"

"If I try to?" File smashed his fist down on the desk. "I'm not trying to, Goldsmith, I'm doing it! And this meeting is finished, do you hear? It's all over. And there won't be any more meetings, because I'm staying away from here until Saturday. All I got from this picture so far is ulcers, but Saturday the cure begins!"

This was no feigned fury, Mel saw. The man was blind with rage, literally shaking with it. The gods he worshipped were Budget and Schedule, and he had seen them spat on and overthrown. Now, like a high priest fleeing a place of sacrilege, he strode to the door bristling with outrage.

Cy's pleading voice stopped him there, hand on the knob.

"Look, Alex, we've known each other too long for this kind of nonsense. If we—"

"If we what?" File wheeled around, hand still on the knob. "If we sit and talk about it all night, maybe I'll change my mind? After what's been going on here all summer? Well, get this straight, you lousy double-crosser, I wouldn't!"

The door was flung open. It slammed shut. File was gone.

The four of them stood there staring at each other. It was so silent in the room that Mel heard every sound from outside as if it were being amplified—the highpitched piping of a train whistle in the distance, the creaking of the light globe outside the building swinging back and forth on its chain in the warm nighttime breeze, the sharp rapping of File's footsteps as he walked toward his car.

It was Betty who broke the silence in the room.

"Dear God," she whispered, and it sounded as if she didn't know whether to laugh or cry, "he meant it. He'll ruin the picture and not even know he's ruining it."

"Wait a second," Mel said. "If Cy's contract provides him with the right to edit the picture—"

"Only it don't," said MacAaron. He was watching Cy closely. "How do you feel?" he asked.

Cy grimaced.

"Great. It only hurts when I laugh."

"You look lousy. If I thought you'd settle for one little drink—"

"I'll settle for it. Let's just get the hell out of here, that's all."

They went outside. The moon, low on the horizon, was only a wafer-thin crescent, but the stars were so thickly clustered overhead that they seemed to light the way to the parked cars with a pale phosphorescence.

Then Mel noticed that File's Cadillac was still standing there, headlights not on, but door to the driver's seat swung open. And File was not in the car.

Mel looked around at the dark expanse of the lot. Strange, he thought. File was a creature of rigid habit who got into his car when the day's work was done and headed right out of the gate. He had never before been known to go wandering around the deserted lot after working hours, and what reason he might have for doing it now—

Cy and MacAaron had been walking ahead, and Mel saw Cy suddenly pull up short. He walked back to Mel with MacAaron at his heels.

"I could have sworn I heard that little punk going this way when we were inside," he said. "He doesn't have another car stashed around here, does he?"

Mel shook his head. "Just the Caddie. The door is open, too, so it looks as if he was getting in when he changed his mind about it. Where do you figure he went?"

"I don't know," said Cy. "All I know is that it's not like him to make any tour of inspection this time of night."

They all stood and looked vaguely around the emptiness of the lot. There was a dim light suspended over the office door, another light over the gate, half revealing the gatekeeper's house which was the size of a telephone booth, and that was all there was to be seen by way of illumination. The rest was the uncertain shadowy forms of buildings against pitch blackness, the outline of the sound stage towering over all the others.

"Well, what are we waiting for?" MacAaron said at last. "If something happened to him, we can always send poison ivy to the funeral. Come on, let's get going."

It would have been better if he hadn't said it, Mel thought resentfully. Then they could have shrugged off the mystery and left. Now the spoken suggestion that something might be wrong seemed to impose on them the burden of doing something about it, no matter how they felt about File.

It appeared that Cy shared this thought.

"You know," he said to Mel, "Mac is right. There's no need for you and Betty to hang around."

"What about you?"

"I'll wait it out a while. He'll probably show up in a few minutes."

"Then we can wait with you," Mel said, closing his ears to Betty's muttered comment on File.

The minutes dragged by. Then, at the sound of approaching footsteps, they all came to attention. But it wasn't File who showed up out of the darkness, it was the projectionist who had screened the rushes for them. He had been rewinding the film, he explained in answer to Cy's questions, and no, he had not seen Signor File since the screening. *Buona sera, signora, signori*—and off he went on his scooter amid a noisome belching of gasoline fumes.

They watched the guard emerge from his booth to open the gate for him, the scooter disappear through the gate, and then all was silence again.

"Hell," Cy said abruptly, "we should have thought of it right off. That guard might have seen Alex." And he shambled off to engage the guard in brisk conversation.

When he returned, shaking his head, he said, "No dice. The guard heard the office door slam, but he was reading his paper in the booth so he didn't see anything. And he says the only ones he hasn't signed out yet are Alex and us—and Paolo Varese."

That was it, Mel thought. If they all felt about it the way he did, that was the ominous possibility they had all been trying to close their eyes to. It was the real reason for this sense of disaster in the air. File and Paolo Varese. The boy hidden out of sight in back of the car, File opening the door, seating himself behind the wheel, the knife or gun suddenly menacing him, the two figures, one prodding the other out of the car, moving

off into the darkness so that the job could be finished in some safe corner.

Or was there a skull-crushing blow delivered right there on the spot with one of those iron bars used in assembling the armatures for the statues, then the body hoisted to a muscular shoulder and borne away into that all-enveloping darkness? But the evidence would remain. Spatters of blood. Worse, perhaps.

The temptation to look into the car, see what there was to be seen on its leather upholstery, rose in Mel along with a violent nausea. He weakly gestured toward the car.

"Maybe we ought to—"

"It's all right," Cy said, clearly taking pity on him, "I'll do it."

Mel gratefully watched him walk to the car and lean inside it. Then the small glow of the light on the instrument panel could be seen behind the windshield.

"The keys are in the lock," Cy called in a muffled voice, "but there's no sign of any trouble here."

The dashboard light went off, and he withdrew from the car. Keys in hand, he went around behind it, opened the trunk lid, and peered inside. He closed the lid and returned to them.

"Nothing," he said. "All we know is that Alex got into the car and then got out again."

"So?" Betty said.

"So I'm going to look in at the carpenters' shop and see if Varese is there in that studio of his. Meanwhile, Mac can take a look through the sound stage. But there's no need for you and Mel—"

"Don't worry about that," Betty said. "It's still the shank of the evening."

"All right, then you two take your car and run over to the backlot gate and check with the guard there. On the way back here cruise around and look over as much of the grounds as you can. Take your time and keep the headlights on full."

They followed instructions to the letter, and when they rejoined Cy and MacAaron in front of the office twenty minutes later, Mel was relieved to see that both still reflected only puzzlement.

"Mac tells me the sound stage is all clear," Cy said. "As for the kid, he's in the shop working on that last statue, and he swears on his mother's life he hasn't been out of there since dinner. I believe him, too, not that he made any secret about how happy he'd be if Alex broke his neck. The fact is, if he really intended to jump Alex, he'd never do it out here in the open with that guard only fifty feet away and with us likely to walk out of the office any minute. So unless you can picture a chickenheart like Alex walking into that studio all by himself and looking for trouble—"

"Not a chance," said Mel.

"That's how I feel about it. What did the guard at the backlot have to say?"

"Nothing, except that he locked up the gate at quitting time and hasn't seen a soul around here since then. We covered the lot, too, and all we turned up was a couple of stray cats. Now where does that leave us?"

Cy shook his head. "With a ten-foot fence all around and no way out for Alex unless he learned how to fly with his hands and feet. He's sure as hell around here somewhere, but I can't think where. The only thing left to do is comb through every building and see what turns up. Mac will help me with that. You get Betty back to the hotel. She looks dead on her feet."

She did, Mel saw. And he could well imagine what she was thinking. As long as Paolo was in the clear—

"Well, if you can get along without us," he said.

"We'll manage. Oh, yeah, on your way out, find some excuse to have the guard look into your car trunk. Make sure he gets a good look. And don't worry about what he'll find there, because I already checked it. You don't mind, do you?"

"No," said Mel, "not as long as Alex wasn't in it."

He was wakened early the next morning by a phone call from Cy at the lot reporting that he and MacAaron—and Paolo Varese, too, when he had finished the twelfth statue—had searched every inch of the lot and turned up no trace of File.

"He's gone, all right," Cy said tiredly. "I even called his hotel just now on the wild chance he somehow got out of here, but they told me he didn't show up all night and isn't there now. So I figured the best thing to do was call in the police. They'll be here in a little while."

"I'll get out there right away. But wasn't this calling in the police pretty fast, Cy? It's only been a few hours altogether."

"I know, but later on someone might ask why we didn't get the cops in as soon as we smelled something wrong. Anyhow, it's done now, and the only question is what we tell them about that little fracas in the office just before Alex walked out. I'll be honest with you, Mel. I think it would be a mistake to say anything about the film editing or about being barred from the lot after Friday. Betty was there, too, so if they want to start pinning things on us—"

Mel glanced at Betty who was sitting up in bed and regarding him with alarm. "What is it?" she whispered. "What's wrong?"

"Nothing. No," he said in answer to Cy's query, "I was talking to Betty. I'll explain everything to her. She'll understand. I suppose you already talked it over with Mac?"

"Yes. He sees it the way we do."

"And how much do we tell about Paolo?"

"Anything we're asked to tell. Why not?"

"Don't play dumb, Cy. If the cops find out what happened when I drove the kid home in the rain the other night—"

"Let them. As long as he had nothing to do with Alex disappearing, there's nothing they can pin on him. And maybe you didn't notice, but Wanda Pericola was standing right outside that office window when you were giving Alex hell about him and Varese's sister. What'll you bet Wanda spills the beans first chance she gets?"

It was not a fair bet, Mel knew. It was too much of a sure thing.

The police, two men in plainclothes, were

already at the lot when he and Betty arrived there, and, as the day passed, Mel saw that in terms of the official attitude it was divided into three distinct periods.

First, there was the cynical period when the two plainclothesmen smilingly indicated that this whole affair was obviously a publicity stunt arranged by File Productions.

Then, persuaded otherwise, they became the sober investigators, ordering everyone to report to the sound stage for a brisk questioning and a show of identification papers.

And finally, now thoroughly baffled and angry, they called headquarters for help and led a squad of uniformed men through a painstaking search of the entire lot.

Close behind the squad of police came reporters and a gang of *paparazzi*—free-lance photographers, most of them mounted on battered scooters—and the sight of them gathered before the front gate, aiming their cameras through the wiring, shouting questions at anyone who passed within hailing distance, seemed to annoy Inspector Conti, the senior of the two plainclothesmen, almost as much as his failure to locate the missing Alexander File.

"Nuisances," he said when Cy asked about holding some sort of press conference in the office. "They will stay on the other side of that fence where they belong. There can be no doubt that Signor File, alive or dead, is here inside the perimeter of that fence, and until we find him no one is permitted to enter or leave. It will not take long. Assuming the worst, that a crime has been committed, it is impossible to dispose of the victim beneath the pavement which covers the entire area. And thanks to your foresight, *signore*—" he nodded at Cy who wearily shrugged off the compliment "—this place has been hermetically sealed since immediately after the disappearance. There can be no question about it. Signor File is here. It is only a matter of hours at the most before we find him."

The Inspector was a stubborn man. Not until sunset, after his squad had, to no avail, moved across the lot like a swarm of locusts, not until

File's records and correspondence had futilely been examined page by page, did he acknowledge temporary defeat.

"You may leave now," he announced to the company assembled in the sound stage, "but you will make yourselves available for further questioning when called on. Until permission is granted by the authorities, no one will enter here."

By now Cy was groggy with exhaustion, but this brought him angrily to his feet. "Look, we've got a movie to finish, and if you—"

"All in good time, *signore*." The Inspector's voice was flat with finality. "Those of you who are not citizens will now surrender their passports to me, please. They will be held for you at headquarters."

Outside in the parking space, Mel saw that the door of File's Cadillac had been closed but was discolored by a grayish powder. It took him a moment to realize that this must have been the work of a fingerprint expert, and that realization, more than anything else that had happened during the day, made File's disappearance real and menacing. The questions asked by the police had only scratched the surface so far—there had been no need to mention either Claudia Varese or the editing of the picture; but there was further questioning to come, and next time it was likely to do much more than scratch the surface.

Cy was pursuing a different line of thought.

"First thing," he said, "is to make sure everybody we need for those last scenes stays on call."

"For what?" Mel said. "Without Alex, who takes care of the payroll, the release, the promotion? We can't sign anything for him."

"We won't have to. Look," Cy said urgently, "that big Hollywood lawyer of Alex's is empowered to act for him in his absence. He also happens to have a lot of dough tied up in this picture, and he's damn near as tight as Alex about money. When I get in touch with him and tell him what's going on here he'll see to it we finish the job. I guarantee that."

"Only if Alex is absent," Mel said. "But what if he's dead?"

"Then we're licked. The footage we shot so far is part of his estate, and by the time the Surrogates Court settles the estate we'll all be dead and gone ourselves. But we don't know Alex is dead, do we? Nobody knows if he is or not. So what we do is get his lawyer's okay to finish the picture in return for an agreement to deliver it to him for release."

"Without being allowed back on the lot?" said Betty. "And who knows how long it'll be before we are allowed back? Further questioning, the detective said. It might take weeks before they get around to it. Or months."

"It might," said Cy, "but I have a hunch it won't."

He was right. The very next morning Mel was called to his interview with Commissioner Odoardo Ucci at Police Headquarters and had as unpleasant a time of it as he had anticipated.

The worst of it was when the Commissioner, after much deliberation nose scratching, suddenly introduced the subject of Paolo Varese's hostility toward his employer, and when Mel hedged in his answers, Ucci revealed an astonishing familiarity with the scene played that rainy night on the Piazza Matrai. Which meant, Mel thought hopelessly, that Wanda had indeed spilled the beans at the first opportunity.

Under such conditions, Mel knew, there was no use being evasive about it. So he described the scene in detail and took what consolation he could from the memory of Cy's reminder that since Paolo had nothing to do with File's disappearance, there was nothing that could be pinned on him.

Ucci's reaction jolted him.

"If you had given this vital information to Inspector Conti at once—" he said.

"Vital?" Mel said. "Listen, Commissioner, we walked out of that office a minute or two after Mr. File. If Varese had tried to do anything to him out there—"

"But the possibility did enter your mind, *signore*, that he might have tried?"

"Yes, and I found out very quickly that I was wrong about it."

"I think I will soon prove otherwise, *signore*. Before the day is over, in fact. So you and Signora Gordon will please remain *incommunicado* in your hotel until then. As a favor to yourself, no telephone calls and no visitors, please."

It was Ucci himself who picked them up in a chauffeured car late in the afternoon.

"Where are we going?" Betty asked him as the car swung away from the curb.

"To the location of your cinema company, *signora*, to demonstrate that the mystery of Signor File's disappearance was never a mystery at all."

"Then you found him? But where? What happened to him?"

"Patience, *signora*, patience." The Commissioner's manner was almost playful. "You will shortly see the answer for yourself. If," he added grimly, "you have the stomach for it."

A *carabiniere* bearing a Tommy gun admitted them through the gate of the lot; another came to attention at the door of the carpenters' shop as they entered it. In the sculptor's studio behind the partition at the rear of the shop was a small gathering waiting for them.

Cy and MacAaron stood at one side of the room and Paolo Varese, tight-lipped and smoldering, stood at the other side between Inspector Conti and the subordinate plainclothesman. And in the center of the room, towering over them all on its pedestal, was a life-sized statue.

Tiberius mad, Mel thought, and then recoiled as understanding exploded in him. There was a distinct resemblance between this statue and the one of Tiberius sane which had already been photographed and stored away in the prop room; but there was an even greater resemblance between these distorted features and the face of Alexander File in a paroxysm of rage.

"Oh, no," Betty whispered in anguish, "it looks like—"

"Yes?" prompted Ucci, and when Betty mutely shook her head he said, "I am sorry, *signora*, but I wanted you to observe for yourself why the mystery never was a mystery. Once

I had compared this statue with photographs of Signor File, the solution was clear. Wet *papier maché* molded to the face seems to reproduce it so that even a layer of clay over the mask, skillfully worked as it may be, does not conceal the true image underneath.

"However"—he nodded toward Inspector Conti—"it was my assistant who unearthed the most important clue. A series of these statues had been made before the disappearance. Only one—this one—was completed *after* the disappearance, and the use it was put to is obvious. Also, *signora*, highly unpleasant. So if you wish to leave the room now while we produce the evidence of the crime—"

When she left, moving as if she were sleepwalking through a nightmare, Mel knew guiltily that he should have gone with her; but he found himself helplessly rooted to the spot, transfixed by the sight of the Commissioner picking up a mallet and chisel and approaching the statue.

The sight stirred Paolo Varese to violent action. He suddenly flung himself at Ucci, almost overthrowing him in the effort to wrest the tools from his hands. When the two plainclothesmen locked their arms through his and dragged him back he struggled furiously to free himself from their grasp, then subsided, gasping.

"You can't!" he shouted at Ucci. "That is a work of art!"

"And a clever one," said Ucci coldly. "Almost brilliant, in fact. A work of art that can be removed from here at your leisure and sent anywhere in the world without a single person knowing its contents. A fine business, young man, to use such a talent as yours for the purpose of concealing a murder. Do you at least confess to that murder now?"

"No! Whatever you find in my statue, I will never confess to any murder!"

"Ah? Then perhaps this will change your mind?"

The Commissioner placed the edge of the chisel into a fold of the toga draping the figure and struck it a careful blow. Then another and another.

As shards of white-enameled clay fell to the floor Mel closed his eyes, but that couldn't keep him from hearing the sound of those remorseless blows, the thudding on the floor of chunks of clay.

Then there was a different sound—the striking of metal against metal.

And finally a wrathful exclamation by Ucci.

Mel opened his eyes. What he saw at first glance was Ucci's broad face, almost ludicrous in its open-mouthed incredulity. Cy, MacAaron, the two plainclothesmen, all wore the same expression; all stared unbelievingly at the exposed interior of the statue which revealed the rods of an armature, a cylinder of wire screening—and nothing more.

"Impossible," Ucci muttered. "But this is impossible."

As if venting his frustration on the statue, he swung the mallet flush against its head. The head bounded to the floor and lay there, an empty mask of *papier maché*, patches of whitened clay still adhering to it.

Paolo pulled himself free of the plainclothesmen's grasp. He picked up the mask and tenderly ran his fingers over the damage in it made by the mallet.

"Barbarian," he said to Ucci. "Vandal. Did you really think I was a murderer? Did you have to destroy my work to learn better?"

Ucci shook his head dazedly.

"Young man, I tell you that everything, all the evidence—"

"What evidence? Do I look like some peasant from the south who lives by the vendetta?" The boy thrust out the mask toward Ucci who recoiled as if afraid it would bite him. "This was my revenge—to shape this so that the whole world would know what an animal that man was. And it was all the revenge I asked, because I am an artist, you understand, not a butcher. Now you can try to put the pieces of my statue together, because I am finished here." He looked at Cy. "As soon as I have packed my tools, *signore*, I will go."

"But we'll be back tomorrow," Cy pleaded.

He turned to Ucci. "You can't have any objections to that now, can you?"

"Objections?" The Commissioner still seemed lost in a daze. "No, no, *signore*. The premises have been fully investigated, so you are free to use them. But it is impossible—I cannot understand—"

"You see?" Cy said to Paolo. "And all I ask is one more day's work. Just one more day."

"No, *signore*. I have done the work I agreed to do. I am finished here."

As Mel started out of the studio, Cy followed him with lagging steps.

"Damn," he said. "I hate to do that scene one statue short."

"You can shoot around it. Hell, I'm glad it turned out like this, statue or not. For a minute, that cop had me convinced—"

"You? He had us all convinced. When Betty walked out of here she looked like she was ready to cave in. You want my advice, Mel, you'll book the first flight home tomorrow and get her away from here as quick as you can. The picture's just about done anyhow, and Betty's the one you have to worry about, not Alex."

The *carabiniere* on guard at the door motioned around the building, and they found Betty waiting for them there, her eyes red and swollen, the traces of tears shiny of her cheeks.

"What happened?" she asked, as if dreading to ask it. "Did they—?"

"No," said Mel, "they didn't. Paolo is out of it." And then as she stood there, helplessly shaking her head from side to side—looking, in fact, as if she were ready to cave in—Mel put his arms tight around her.

"It's all right, baby," he said, "it's all right. We're going home tomorrow."

Cy Goldsmith died the first day of winter that year, a few weeks after the picture was released; so at least, as Betty put it, he knew before he went that the critics thought the picture was good. Not an Oscar winner, of course, but plausible, dramatic, beautifully directed. It wasn't a bad send-off for a man on his deathbed.

The mystery of File's disappearance didn't hurt at the box office either. The press had a field day when the story first broke, and even when interest had died down somewhat it didn't take much to revive it. Every week or so Alexander File would be reported seen in some other corner of the world, a victim of amnesia, of drug addiction, of a Red plot, and the tabloids would once more heat up the embers of public interest. Then there was the release of the picture and Cy's death soon afterward to keep the embers burning.

Mel and Betty were in San Francisco getting ready to spend the Christmas week with her family when they saw the news in the paper—Cyrus Goldsmith died in Cedars of Lebanon Hospital after a long illness and would be buried at Elysian Park Cemetery—and it was the unpleasant thought of the reporters and photographers flocking around again that made Mel decide not to attend the funeral, but to settle instead for an extravagant wreath.

Reading that mention of Elysian Park reminded him also of the time when he and Cy had stood on the portico of the make-believe palace in the backlot, looking down on the Appian Way, and Cy had confided to him how comforting it had been to arrange for the mausoleum he would soon be occupying. He had been like a relic of antiquity, had Cyrus Goldsmith. A devout believer in the idea that a chamber of granite with one's name on it somehow meant a happier afterlife than a six-foot hole in the ground.

Mel shook his head at the thought. Cy had no family to mourn him, the only person in the world close to him had been MacAaron so MacAaron must have been in charge of the funeral arrangements. Too bad Mac wasn't the kind of man to do things up in real imaginative style. Seen to it, perhaps, that, just as the pharaohs had been buried with the full equipage for a happy existence in heaven, Cy should have been provided with his idea of the necessities for a pleasant eternity—a supply of Scotch, a print of *Emperor of Lust*, even a handsomely mounted picture of a futilely snarling Alexander File on the mausoleum wall to keep fresh that taste of the final victory.

A few days later—the day after Christmas when the household was still trying to recover from the festivities—Mel and Betty slipped away and drove downtown to see the picture for the first time. Mel had long ago given up attending public showings of anything he had worked on because watching the audience around him fail to appreciate his lines was too much like sitting in a dentist's chair and having a tooth needlessly drilled; but this time Betty insisted.

"After all, we didn't go to the funeral," she argued with a woman's logic, "so this is the least we can do for Cy."

"Darling, no disrespect intended, but where Cy is now, he couldn't care less what we do for him."

"Then I'll go see it by myself. Don't be like that, Mel. You know this one is different."

And so it was, he saw. Different and shocking in a way that no one else in the audience would appreciate. At his suggestion, and to Betty's pleased bewilderment, they sat through it a second time. Then, while Betty was in the theater lounge, he raced to a phone in the lobby and put through a call to MacAaron's home in North Hollywood.

"Mac, this is Mel Gordon."

"Sure. Say, I'm sorry you couldn't make it to the funeral, but those flowers you sent—"

"Never mind that. Mac, I just saw the picture, and there's one shot in it—well, I have to get together with you about it as soon as possible."

There was a long silence at the other end of the line.

"Then you know," MacAaron said at last.

"That's right. I see you do, too."

"For a long time. And Betty?"

"I'm sure she doesn't."

"Good," said MacAaron with obvious relief. "Look, where are you right now?"

"With my in-laws, in San Francisco. But I can be at your place first thing tomorrow."

"Well, first thing tomorrow I have to go over to Elysian Park and settle Cy's account for him. He put me in charge of it. You ever see the way he's fixed up there?"

"No."

"Then this'll give you a chance to. You can meet me there at ten. The man at the gate will show you where Cy is."

Punctuality was a fetish with MacAaron. When Mel arrived for the meeting a few minutes after ten, Mac was already there, seated on a bench close by a mausoleum with the name GOLDSMITH inscribed over its massive bronze door. The structure was made of roughhewn granite blocks without ornamentation or windows, and it stood on a grassy mount overlooking a somewhat unkempt greensward thickly strewn with grave markers. Unlike the fashionable new cemeteries around Los Angeles, Elysian Park looked distinctly like a burial ground.

MacAaron moved to make room for Mel on the bench.

"How many times did you see the picture?" he asked without preliminary.

"Twice around."

"That all? You caught on quick."

"It was simple arithmetic," Mel said, wondering why he felt impelled to make it almost an apology. "Six statues already used and locked up in the prop room, six more in that long shot of the corridor—and the one in the studio that the police smashed up. Thirteen statues. Not twelve. Thirteen."

"I know, I caught wise the day we shot the last scenes with those statues, and I counted six of them standing there, not five. That's when I backed Cy into a corner and made him tell me everything, much as he didn't want to. After he did, I had sense enough to cut away from that sixth statue before the camera could get it; but I never did notice that one long shot of the whole corridor showing all six of those damn things until the night of the big premiere, and then it was too late to do anything about it. So there they were, just waiting for you to turn up and start counting them." He shook his head dolefully.

"As long as the police didn't start counting them," Mel said. "Anyhow, all it proves is that Paolo Varese was a lot smarter than we gave him credit for. The statue in his studio was just a dummy, a red herring. All that time we were watching the Commissioner chop it apart, Alex was sealed up in the sixth one in the corridor. Right there on that set in the sound stage, with everyone walking back and forth past him."

"He was. But do you really think it was Varese who had the brains to handle the deal? He was as green as he looked, that kid. Him and his little sister both. A real pair of babes in the woods."

"You mean it was Cy who killed Alex?"

"Hell, no. The last thing Cy wanted was Alex dead, because then the picture would be tied up in Surrogates Court. No, the kid did it, all right, but it was Cy—look, maybe the best way to tell it is right from the beginning."

"Maybe it is," said Mel.

"Then first of all, you remember what Cy had us do after we saw the Caddie standing there that night with the door open and Alex nowhere around?"

"Yes. He had you go through the sound stage hunting for Alex, and Betty and me look around the grounds."

"Because he wanted all three of us out of the way for the time being. He had an idea Alex had gone to see the kid and that something might have happened. So he—"

"Hold on," Mel said. "We all agreed right there that Alex would never have the guts to face the kid."

"That's the track Cy put us on, but in the back of his mind he figured Alex might have one good reason for getting together with Varese. Just one. Alex was yellow right down to the bottom of the backbone, right? But he also had to do business in Rome every year, and that's where the kid lived. Who knew when they'd bump into each other, or when the kid would get all steamed up after a few drinks and come looking for him?

"So what does a guy like Alex do about it? He goes to the kid waving a white flag and tries to buy him off. Cheap, of course, but the way things are with Varese and the sister he feels a few hundred bucks should settle the case very nicely. About three hundred bucks, in fact. Twenty thousand lire. Cy knew how much it was because when he walked into the studio there was the money all over the floor, and Alex lying there dead with his face all black, and the kid standing there not knowing what had happened. Cy says it took him five minutes just to bring him out of shock.

"Anyhow, he finally got the kid to making sense, and it turned out that Alex had walked into the studio, waving the money in his hand, a big smile on that mean little face of his, and he let the kid know that, what the hell, the girl wasn't really hurt in any way, but if it would make her feel better to buy something nice for herself—"

"But how stupid could he be? To misjudge anyone that way!"

"Yeah, that's about the size of it." MacAaron nodded somberly. "Anyhow, it sure lit the kid's fuse. He didn't even know what happened next. All he knew was that he got his hands around that skinny throat, and when he let go it was too late."

"Even so," Mel said unhappily, "it was still murder."

"It was," agreed MacAaron. "And a long stretch in jail, and the papers full of how the little sister had gone wrong. It sure looked hopeless, all right. And you know the weirdest part of it?"

"What?"

"That the only thing on Varese's mind was the way he'd let his folks down, his Mama and his Papa. Going to jail didn't seem to bother him one bit as much as that he had argued his people into letting the girl go to Rome and then he had let her become a pigeon for Alex. It never struck him anything could be done about Alex being dead. As far as he was concerned, it was just a case of calling in the cops now and getting it over with.

"But, naturally, the last thing Cy wanted was

for anyone to know Alex was dead, because then the picture was really washed up. And looking at that Tiberius statue which was almost finished, he got the idea that maybe something *could* be done. The hitch was that you and me and Betty were right there on the spot, but once he got you two off the lot and then had me hunting for Alex like a fool through all those buildings and shops, he had room to move in.

"First off, he had the kid rush through a whole new Tiberius statue. That was the thirteenth statue, the one they stuck Alex inside of, and Cy said it was all he and the kid could do to keep their dinner down while they were at it. It took almost all night, too, and when it was done they trucked it over to the sound stage and set it up there and brought the other one back to the studio."

"But he told me he had Paolo helping you and him look for Alex most of the night. If I had asked you about it—"

"Oh, that." The ghost of a smile showed on MacAaron's hardbitten face. "He wasn't taking any chance with that story, because he had the kid go by me a couple of times looking around the lot with a flashlight in his hand. If I had any doubts about him up to then, that settled them. When Inspector Conti questioned me next day I didn't even mention the kid, I was so sure he was in the clear about Alex."

"You didn't have to mention him. Wanda was only waiting to."

"Wanda?" MacAaron said with genuine surprise. "What would she know? Hell, it was Cy who told the Inspector about what happened when you took the kid home that night. But the right way, you understand, sort of letting it be dragged out of him. And sort of steered him around to the studio so he could get a good look at that statue after seeing some photos of Alex.

"It was Cy all the way. Once he made sure the Inspector and the Commissioner knew those other statues in the prop room and on the sound stage had absolutely been there before Alex disappeared, Cy wanted that showdown in the studio. He wanted everything pinned on the kid

and then cleared up once and for all. The only question was whether the kid could hold up under pressure in the big scene, and you saw for yourself how he did.

"Now do you get the whole setup? Make the lot look like it was sealed up airtight, make it look like the kid was the only possible suspect, and then clear him completely. If I could swear on the Bible that the kid was helping us hunt for Alex that night, and if Alex isn't in that statue— what's left?"

"A statue with a body in it," Mel said. "A murder."

"Yeah, I understand," MacAaron said sympathetically. "Now you're sorry you know the whole thing. But I'm not, Mel. And I don't mean because it's been so hard keeping it to myself. What's been eating me is that up to now nobody else in the world knew how Cy proved the kind of man he was."

"Proved what?" Mel said harshly. "It wasn't hard for him to be that kind of man, feeling the way he did about the picture and knowing he had only a little while to live. How much was he really risking under those conditions? If things went wrong, he'd be dead before they could bring him to trial, and the kid would take the whole rap."

"You still don't get it. You don't get it at all. How could you if you weren't even there at the finish? Well, I was."

To Mel's horror, MacAaron, the imperturbable, the stoic, looked as if he were fighting back tears, his face wrinkling monkeylike in his effort to restrain them. "Mel, it went on forever in that hospital. Week after week, and every day of it the pain got worse. It was like knives being run into him. But all that time he would never let them give him a needle to kill the pain. They wanted to, but he wouldn't let them. He told them it was all right, he wouldn't make any fuss about how it hurt, and he didn't. Just lay there twisting around in that bed, chewing on a handkerchief he kept stuffed in his mouth, and sweat, the size of marbles, dripping down his face. But no needles. Not until right near the end after he didn't know what was going on anymore."

"So what? If he was afraid of a lousy needle—"

"But don't you see why?" MacAaron said despairingly. "Don't you get it? He was scared that if he had any dope in him he might talk about Alex and the kid without even knowing it. He might give the whole thing away and send the kid to jail after all. That was the one big thing on his mind. That was the kind of man he was. So however you want to fault him—"

He stared at Mel, searching for a response, and was evidently satisfied with what he saw.

"It'll be tough keeping this to ourselves," he said. "I know that, Mel. But we have to. If we didn't, it would mean wasting everything Cy went through."

"And how long do you think we'll get away with it? There's still the statue with Alex rotting away inside of it, wherever it is. Sooner or later—"

"Not sooner," MacAaron said. "Maybe a long time later. A couple of lifetimes later." He got up stiffly, walked over to the mausoleum and inserted a key into the lock of the bronze door. "Take a look," he said. "This is the only key, so now's your chance."

An unseen force lifted Mel to his feet and propelled him toward that open door. He knew he didn't want to go, didn't want to see what was to be seen, but there was no resisting that force.

Sunlight through the doorway flooded the chill depths of the granite chamber and spilled over an immense casket on a shelf against its far wall. And standing at its foot, facing it with features twisted into an eternal, impotent fury, was the statue of Tiberius mad.

ALL AT ONCE, NO ALICE

WILLIAM IRISH

A SAD AND LONELY MAN who desperately dedicated books to his typewriter and to his hotel room, Cornell George Hopley-Woolrich (1903–1968) was born in New York City, grew up in Latin America and New York, and was educated at Columbia University, to which he left his literary estate. Almost certainly a closeted homosexual (his marriage was terminated almost immediately) and an alcoholic, Woolrich was so antisocial and reclusive that he refused to leave his hotel room when his leg became infected, ultimately resulting in its amputation. Perhaps not surprisingly, then, the majority of his work has an overwhelming darkness, and few of his characters, whether good or evil, have much hope for happiness—or even justice. Whether writing as Cornell Woolrich, William Irish, or George Hopley, no twentieth-century author equaled his ability to create suspense, and Hollywood producers recognized it early on; few writers have had as many films based on their work as Woolrich, beginning with *Convicted* (1938), starring Rita Hayworth, and based on "Face Work." *Street of Chance* (1942) was based on *The Black Curtain*, and starred Burgess Meredith and Claire Trevor; *The Leopard Man* (1943), based on *Black Alibi*, featured Dennis O'Keefe and Jean Brooks; and *Phantom Lady* (1944), based on the novel of the same title, starred Ella Raines and Alan Curtis. "Chance" led to *Mark of the Whistler* (1944), with Richard Dix and Janis Carter; *Deadline at Dawn* became a movie with the same name in 1946, starring Susan Hayward; and "It Had to Be Murder" was made into *Rear Window* (1954), with Grace Kelly and James Stewart. There were at least fifteen other film adaptations, not including scores for television programs. Arguably the worst film ever made from any work by Woolrich is *The Return of the Whistler*, a 1948 Columbia Pictures movie so loosely based on "All at Once, No Alice" that it is barely recognizable and so leaden-paced that it is barely watchable.

"All at Once, No Alice" was first published in the March 2, 1940, issue of *Argosy*; it was first collected in *Eyes That Watch You* (New York, Rinehart, 1952).

ALL AT ONCE, NO ALICE

WILLIAM IRISH

IT WAS OVER so quickly I almost thought something had been left out, but I guess he'd been doing it long enough to know his business. The only way I could tell for sure it was over was when I heard him say: "You may kiss the bride." But then, I'd never gone through it before.

We turned and pecked at each other, a little bashful because they were watching us.

He and the motherly-looking woman who had been a witness—I guess she was his house-keeper—stood there smiling benevolently, and also a little tiredly. The clock said one fifteen. Then he shook hands with the two of us and said, "Good luck to both of you," and she shook with us too and said, "I wish you a lot of happiness."

We shifted from the living room, where it had taken place, out into the front hall, a little awkwardly. Then he held the screen door open and we moved from there out onto the porch.

On the porch step Alice nudged me and whispered, "You forgot something."

I didn't even know how much I was supposed to give him. I took out two singles and held them in one hand, then I took out a five and held that in the other. Then I went back toward him all flustered and said, "I—I guess you thought I was going to leave without remembering this."

I reached my hand down to his and brought it back empty. He kept right on smiling, as if this happened nearly every time too, the bridegroom forgetting like that. It was only after I turned

away and rejoined her that I glanced down at my other hand and saw which it was I'd given him. It was the five. That was all right; five thousand of them couldn't have paid him for what he'd done for me, the way I felt about it.

We went down their front walk and got into the car. The lighted doorway outlined them both for a minute. They raised their arms and said, "Good night."

"Good night, and much obliged," I called back. "Wait'll they go in," I said in an undertone to Alice, without starting the engine right away.

As soon as the doorway had blacked out, we turned and melted together on the front seat, and this time we made it a real kiss. "Any regrets?" I whispered to her very softly.

"It must have been awful before I was married to you," she whispered back. "How did I ever stand it so long?"

I don't think we said a word all the way in to Michianopolis. We were both too happy. Just the wind and the stars and us. And a couple of cigarettes.

We got to the outskirts around two thirty, and by three were all the way in downtown. We shopped around for a block or two. "This looks like a nice hotel," I said finally. I parked outside and we went in.

I think the first hotel was called the Commander. I noticed that the bellhops let us strictly alone; didn't bustle out to bring in our bags or anything.

I said to the desk man, "We'd like one of your best rooms and bath."

He gave me a sort of rueful smile, as if to say, "You should know better than that." . . . "I only wish I had something to give you," was the way he put it.

"All filled up?" I turned to her and murmured, "Well, we'll have to try someplace else."

He overheard me. "Excuse me, but did you come in without making reservations ahead?"

"Yes, we just drove in now. Why?"

He shook his head compassionately at my ignorance. "I'm afraid you're going to have a hard time finding a room in any of the hotels tonight."

"Why? They can't all be filled up."

"There's a three-day convention of the Knights of Balboa being held here. All the others started sending their overflow to us as far back as Monday evening, and our own last vacancy went yesterday noon."

The second one was called the Stuyvesant, I think. "There must be something in a city this size," I said when we came out of there. "We'll keep looking until we find it."

I didn't bother noticing the names of the third and fourth. We couldn't turn around and go all the way back to our original point of departure—it would have been midmorning before we reached it—and there was nothing that offered suitable accommodations between; just filling stations, roadside lunch-rooms, and detached farmsteads.

Besides, she was beginning to tire. She refused to admit it, but it was easy to tell. It worried me.

The fifth place was called the Royal. It was already slightly less first-class than the previous ones had been; we were running out of them now. Nothing wrong with it, but just a little seedier and older.

I got the same answer at the desk, but this time I wouldn't take it. The way her face drooped when she heard it was enough to make me persist. I took the night clerk aside out of her hearing.

"Listen, you've got to do something for me,

I don't care what it is," I whispered fiercely. "We've just driven all the way from Lake City and my wife's all in. I'm not going to drag her around to another place tonight."

Then as his face continued impassive, "If you can't accommodate both of us, find some way of putting her up at least. I'm willing to take my own chances, go out and sleep in the car or walk around the streets for the night."

"Wait a minute," he said, hooking his chin, "I think I could work out something like that for you. I just thought of something. There's a little bit of a dinky room on the top floor. Ordinarily it's not used as a guest room at all, just as a sort of storeroom. You couldn't possibly both use it, because there's only a single cot in it; but if you don't think your wife would object, I'd be glad to let her have it, and I think you might still be able to find a room for yourself at the Y. They don't admit women, and most of these Knights have brought their wives with them."

I took a look at her pretty, drawn face. "Anything, anything," I said gratefully.

He still had his doubts. "You'd better take her up and let her see it first."

A colored boy came with us, with a passkey. On the way up I explained it to her. She gave me a rueful look, but I could see she was too tired even to object as much as she felt she should have. "Ah, that's mean," she murmured. "Our first night by ourselves."

"It's just for tonight. We'll drive on right after breakfast. It's important that you get some rest, hon. You can't fool me, you can hardly keep your eyes open anymore."

She tucked her hand consolingly under my arm. "I don't mind if you don't. It'll give me something to look forward to, seeing you in the morning."

The bellboy led us along a quiet, green-carpeted hall, and around a turn, scanning numbers on the doors. He stopped three down from the turn, on the right-hand side, put his key in. "This is it here, sir." The number was 1006.

The man at the desk hadn't exaggerated. The room itself was little better than an alcove, long and narrow. I suppose two could have gotten into it; but it would have been a physical impossibility for two to sleep in it the way it was fitted up. It had a cot that was little wider than a shelf.

To give you an idea how narrow the room was, the window was narrower than average, and yet not more than a foot of wall-strip showed on either side of its frame. In other words it took up nearly the width of one entire side of the room.

I suppose I could have sat up in the single armchair all night and slept, or tried to, that way; but as long as there was a chance of getting a horizontal bed at the Y, why not be sensible about it? She agreed with me in this.

"Think you can go this, just until the morning?" I asked her, and the longing way she was eying that miserable cot gave me the answer. She was so tired, anything would have looked good to her right then.

We went down again and I told him I'd take it. I had the bellboy take her bag out of the car and bring it in, and the desk clerk turned the register around for her to sign.

She poised the inked pen and flashed me a tender look just as she was about to sign. "First time I've used it," she breathed. I looked over her shoulder and watched her trace *Mrs. James Cannon* along the lined space. The last entry above hers was *A. Krumbake, and wife.* I noticed it because it was such a funny name.

The desk clerk had evidently decided by now that we were fairly desirable people. "I'm terribly sorry I couldn't do more for you," he said. "It's just for this one night. By tomorrow morning a lot of them'll be leaving."

I went up with her a second time, to see that she was made as comfortable as she could be under the circumstances. But then there was nothing definitely wrong with the room except its tininess, and the only real hardship was our temporary separation.

I tipped the boy for bringing up her bag, and then I tipped him a second time for going and digging up a nice, fluffy quilt for her at my request—not to spread over her but to spread on top of the mattress and soften it up a little.

Those cots aren't as comfortable as regular beds by a darned sight. But she was so tired I was hoping she wouldn't notice the difference.

Then after he'd thanked me for the double-header he'd gotten out of it, and left the room, I helped her off with her coat and hung it up for her, and even got down on my heels and undid the straps of her little sandals, so she wouldn't have to bend over and go after them herself. Then we kissed a couple of times and told each other all about it, and I backed out the door.

The last I saw of her that night she was sitting on the edge of that cot in there, her shoeless feet partly tucked under her. She looked just like a little girl. She raised one hand, wriggled the fingers at me in good night as I reluctantly eased the door closed.

"Until tomorrow, sweetheart," she called gently, when there was a crack of opening left.

"Until tomorrow."

The night was as still around us as if it were holding its breath. The latch went *cluck,* and there we were on opposite sides of it.

The bellboy had taken the car down with him just now after he'd checked her in, and I had to wait out there a minute or two for him to bring it back up again at my ring. I stepped back to the turn in the hall while waiting, to look at the frosted glass transom over her door; and short as the time was, her light was already out. She must have just shrugged off her dress, fallen back flat, and pulled the coverings up over her.

Poor kid, I thought, with a commiserating shake of my head. The glass elevator panel flooded with light and I got in the car. The one bellhop doubled for liftman after twelve.

"I guess she'll be comfortable," he said.

"She was asleep before I left the floor," I told him.

The desk man told me where the nearest branch of the Y was, and I took the car with me as the quickest way of getting over there at that hour. I had no trouble at all getting a room, and not a bad one at that for six bits.

I didn't phone her before going up, to tell her I'd gotten something for myself, because I knew by the way I'd seen that light go out she was fast asleep already, and it would have been unnecessarily cruel to wake her again.

I woke up at eight and again I didn't phone her, to find out how she was, because in the first place I was going right over there myself in a few more minutes, and in the second place I wanted her to get all the sleep she could before I got there.

I even took my time, showered and shaved, and drove over slowly, to make sure of not getting there any earlier than nine.

It was a beautiful day, with the sun as brand-new-looking as if it had never shone before; and I even stopped off and bought a gardenia for her to wear on the shoulder of her dress. I thought: I'll check her out of that depressing dump. We'll drive to the swellest restaurant in town, and she'll sit having orange juice and toast while I sit looking at her face.

I braked in front of the Royal, got out, and went in, lighting up the whole lobby the way I was beaming.

A different man was at the desk now, on the day shift, but I knew the number of her room so I rode right up without stopping. I got out at the tenth, went down the hall the way we'd been led last night—still green-carpeted but a little less quiet now—and around the turn.

When I came to the third door down, on the right-hand side—the door that had 1006 on it—I stopped and listened a minute to see if I could tell whether she was up yet or not. If she wasn't up yet, I was going back downstairs again, hang around in the lobby, and give her another half-hour of badly needed sleep.

But she was up already. I could hear a sound in there as if she were brushing out her dress or coat with a stiff-bristled brush—*skish, skish, skish*—so I knocked, easy and loving, on the door with just three knuckles.

The *skish-skish-skish* broke off a minute, but then went right on again. But the door hadn't been tightly closed into the frame at all, and my knocking sent it drifting inward an inch or two. A whiff of turpentine or something like that nearly threw me over, but without stopping to distinguish what it was, I pushed the door the rest of the way in and walked in.

Then I pulled up short. I saw I had the wrong room.

There wasn't anything in it—no furniture, that is. Just bare floorboards, walls and ceiling. Even the light fixture had been taken down, and two black wires stuck out of a hole, like insect feelers, where it had been.

A man in spotted white overalls and peaked cap was standing on a stepladder slapping a paint brush up and down the walls. *Skish-skish-splop!*

I grunted, "Guess I've got the wrong number," and backed out.

"Guess you must have, bud," he agreed, equally laconic, without even turning his head to see who I was.

I looked up at the door from the outside. Number 1006. But that was the number they'd given her, sure it was. I looked in a second time. Long and narrow, like an alcove. Not more than a foot of wall space on either side of the window frame.

Sure, this was the room, all right. They must have found out they had something better available after all, and changed her after I left last night. I said, "Where'd they put the lady that was in here, you got any idea?"

Skish-skish-skish. "I dunno, bud, you'll have to find out at the desk. It was empty when I come here to work at seven." *Skish-skish-splop!*

I went downstairs to the desk again, and I said, "Excuse me. What room have you got Mrs. Cannon in now?"

He looked up some chart or other they use, behind the scenes, then he came back and said, "We have no Mrs. Cannon here."

I pulled my face back. Then I thrust it forward again. "What's the matter with you?" I said curtly. "I came here with her myself last night. Better take another look."

He did. A longer one. Then he came back and said, "I'm sorry, there's no Mrs. Cannon registered here."

I knew there was nothing to get excited about; it would probably be straightened out in a minute or two; but it was a pain in the neck. I was very patient. After all, this was the first morning of my honeymoon. "Your night man was on duty at the time. It was about three this morning. He gave her 1006."

He looked that up too. "That's not in use," he said. "That's down for redecorating. It's been empty for—"

"I don't care what it is. I tell you they checked my wife in there at three this morning, I went up with her myself! Will you quit arguing and find out what room she's in, for me? I don't want to stand here talking to you all day; I want to be with her."

"But I'm telling you, mister, the chart shows no one by that name."

"Then look in the register if you don't believe me. I watched her sign it myself."

People were standing around the lobby looking at me now, but I didn't care.

"It would be on the chart," he insisted. "It would have been transferred—" He ran the pad of his finger up the register page from bottom to top. Too fast, I couldn't help noticing: without a hitch, as if there were nothing to impede it. Then he went back a page and ran it up that, in the same streamlined way.

"Give it to me," I said impatiently. "I'll find it for you in a minute." I flung it around my way.

A. Krumbake, and wife stared at me. And then under that just a blank space all the way down to the bottom of the page. No more check-ins.

I could feel the pores of my face sort of closing up. That was what it felt like, anyway. Maybe it was just the process of getting pale. "She signed right under that name. It's been rubbed out."

"Oh, no, it hasn't," he told me firmly. "No one tampers with the register like that. People may leave, but their names stay on it."

Dazedly, I traced the ball of my finger back and forth across the white paper under that name, *Krumbake.* Smooth and unrubbed, its semi-glossy finish unimpaired by erasure. I held the page up toward the light and tried to squint through it, to see whether it showed thinner there, either from rubbing or some other means of eradication. It was all of the same even opacity.

I spoke in a lower voice now; I wasn't being impatient anymore. "There's something wrong. Something wrong about this. I can't understand it. I saw her write it. I saw her sign it with my own eyes. I've known it was the right hotel all along, but even if I wasn't sure, this other name, this name above, would prove it to me. Krumbake. I remember it from last night. Maybe they changed her without notifying you down here."

"That wouldn't be possible; it's through me, down here, that all changes are made. It isn't that I don't know what room she's in; it's that there's absolutely no record of any such person ever having been at the hotel, so you see you must be mis—"

"Call the manager for me," I said hoarsely.

I stood there waiting by the onyx-topped desk until he came. I stood there very straight, very impassive, not touching the edge of the counter with my hands in any way, about an inch clear of it.

People were bustling back and forth, casually, normally, cheerily, behind me; plinking their keys down on the onyx; saying, "Any mail for me?"; saying, "I'll be in the coffee shop if I'm called." And something was already trying to make me feel a little cut off from them, a little set apart. As if a shadowy finger had drawn a ring around me where I stood, and mystic vapors were already beginning to rise from it, walling me off from my fellow men.

I wouldn't let the feeling take hold of me—yet—but it was already there, trying to. I'd give an imperceptible shake of my head every once in a while and say to myself, "Things like this don't happen in broad daylight. It's just some kind of misunderstanding; it'll be cleared up presently."

The entrance, the lobby, had seemed so bright when I first came in, but I'd been mistaken. There were shadows lengthening in the far corners that only I could see. The gardenia I had for her was wilting.

The manager was no help at all. He tried to be, listened attentively, but then the most he could do was have the clerk repeat what he'd already done for me, look on the chart and look in the register. After all, details like that were in the hands of the staff. I simply got the same thing as before, only relayed through him now instead of direct from the desk man. "No, there hasn't been any Mrs. Cannon here at any time."

"Your night man will tell you," I finally said in despair, "he'll tell you I brought her here. Get hold of him, ask him. He'll remember us."

"I'll call him down; he rooms right here in the house," he said. But then with his hand on the phone he stopped to ask again, "Are you quite sure it was this hotel, Mr. Cannon? He was on duty until six this morning, and I hate to wake him up unless you—"

"Bring him down," I said. "This is more important to me than his sleep. It's got to be cleared up." I wasn't frightened yet, out-and-out scared; just baffled, highly worried, and with a peculiar lost feeling.

He came down inside of five minutes. I knew him right away, the minute he stepped out of the car, in spite of the fact that other passengers had come down with him. I was so sure he'd be able to straighten it out that I took a step toward him without waiting for him to join us. If they noticed that, which was a point in favor of my credibility—my knowing him at sight like that—they gave no sign.

I said, "You remember me, don't you? You remember checking my wife into 1006 at three this morning, and telling me I'd have to go elsewhere?"

"No," he said with polite regret. "I'm afraid I don't."

I could feel my face go white as if a soundless bombshell of flour or talcum had just burst all over it. I put one foot behind me and set the heel down and stayed that way.

The manager asked him, "Well, did the gentleman stop at the desk perhaps, just to inquire, and then go elsewhere? Do you remember him at all, Stevens?"

"No, I never saw him until now. It must have been some other hotel."

"But look at me; look at my face," I tried to say. But I guess I didn't put any voice into it, it was just lip motion, because he didn't seem to hear.

The manager shrugged amiably, as if to say, "Well, that's all there is to it, as far as we're concerned."

I was breathing hard, fighting for self-control. "No. No, you can't close this matter. I dem—I ask you to give me one more chance to prove that I—that I—Call the night porter, the night bellboy that carried up her bag for her."

They were giving one another looks by now, as if I were some sort of crank.

"Listen, I'm in the full possession of my faculties, I'm not drunk, I wouldn't come in here like this if I weren't positive—"

The manager was going to try to pacify me and ease me out. "But don't you see you must be mistaken, old man? There's absolutely no record of it. We're very strict about those things. If any of my men checked a guest in without entering it on the chart of available rooms, and in the register, I'd fire him on the spot. Was it the Palace? Was it the Commander, maybe? Try to think now, you'll get it."

And with each soothing syllable, he led me a step nearer the entrance.

I looked up suddenly, saw that the desk had already receded a considerable distance behind us, and balked. "No, don't do this. This is no way to— Will you get that night-to-morning bellhop? Will you do that one more thing for me?"

He sighed, as if I were trying his patience sorely. "He's probably home sleeping. Just a minute; I'll find out."

It turned out he wasn't. They were so overcrowded and undermanned at the moment that instead of being at home he was sleeping right down in the basement, to save time coming and going. He came up in a couple of minutes, still buttoning the collar of his uniform. I knew him right away. He didn't look straight at me at first, but at the manager.

"Do you remember seeing this gentleman come here with a lady, at three this morning? Do you remember carrying her bag up to 1006 for her?"

Then he did look straight at me—and didn't seem to know me. "No, sir, Mr. DeGrasse."

The shock wasn't as great as the first time; it couldn't have been, twice in succession.

"Don't you remember that quilt you got for her, to spread over the mattress, and I gave you a second quarter for bringing it? You must remember that—dark blue, with little white flowers all over it—"

"No, sir, boss."

"But I know your face! I remember that scar just over your eyebrow. And—part your lips a little—that gold cap in front that shows every time you grin."

"No, sir, not me."

My voice was curling up and dying inside my throat. "Then when you took me down alone with you, the last time, you even said, 'I guess she'll be comfortable'—" I squeezed his upper arm pleadingly. "Don't you remember? Don't you remember?"

"No, sir." This time he said it so low you could hardly hear it, as if his training wouldn't let him contradict me too emphatically, but on the other hand he felt obliged to stick to the facts.

I grabbed at the hem of my coat, bunched it up to emphasize the pattern and the color of the material. "Don't you know me by this?" Then I let my fingers trail helplessly down the line of my jaw. "Don't you know my face?"

He didn't answer anymore, just shook his head each time.

"What're you doing this for? What're you trying to do to me? All of you?" The invisible fumes from that necromancer's ring, that seemed to cut me off from all the world, came swirling up thicker and thicker about me. My voice was strident with a strange new kind of fear, a fear I hadn't known since I was ten.

"You've got me rocky now! You've got me down! Cut it out, I say!"

They were starting to draw back little by little away from me, prudently widen the tight knot they had formed around me. I turned from one to the other, from bellhop to night clerk, night clerk to day clerk, day clerk to manager, and each one as I turned to him retreated slightly.

There was a pause, while I fought against this other, lesser kind of death that was creeping over me—this death called *strangeness*, this snapping of all the customary little threads of cause and effect that are our moorings at other times. Slowly they all drew back from me step by step, until I was left there alone, cut off.

Then the tension exploded. My voice blasted the quiet of the lobby. "I want my wife!" I yelled shatteringly. "Tell me what's become of her. What've you done with her? I came in here with her last night; you can't tell me I didn't. . . ."

They circled, maneuvered around me. I heard the manager say in a hurried undertone, "I knew this was going to happen. I could have told you he was going to end up like this. George! Archer! Get him out of here fast!"

My arms were suddenly seized from behind and held. I threshed against the constriction, so violently both my legs flung up clear of the floor at one time, dropped back again, but I couldn't break it. There must have been two of them behind me.

The manager had come in close again, now that I was safely pinioned, no doubt hoping that his nearness would succeed in soft-pedaling the disturbance. "Now will you leave here quietly, or do you want us to call the police and turn you over to them?"

"You'd better call them anyway, Mr. DeGrasse," the day clerk put in. "I've run into this mental type before. He'll only come back in again the very minute your back's turned."

"No, I'd rather not, unless he forces me to. It's bad for the hotel. Look at the crowd collecting down here on the main floor already. Tchk! Tchk!"

He tried to reason with me. "Now listen, give me a break, will you? You don't look like the kind of a man who—Won't you please go quietly? If I have you turned loose outside, will you go away and promise not to come in here again?"

"Ali-i-i-i-ice!" I sent it baying harrowingly down the long vista of lobby, lounges, foyers. I'd been gathering it in me the last few seconds while he was speaking to me. I put my heart and soul into it. It should have shaken down the big old-fashioned chandeliers by the vibration it caused alone. My voice broke under the strain. A woman onlooker somewhere in the background bleated at the very intensity of it.

The manager hit himself between the eyes in consternation. "Oh, this is fierce! Hurry up, call an officer quick, get him out of here."

"See, what did I tell you?" the clerk said knowingly.

I got another chestful of air in, tore loose with it. "Somebody help me! You people standing around looking, isn't there one of you will help me? I brought my wife here last night; now she's gone and they're trying to tell me I never—"

A brown hand suddenly sealed my mouth, was as quickly withdrawn again at the manager's panic-stricken admonition. "George! Archer! Don't lay a hand on him. No rough stuff. Make us liable for damages afterwards, y'know."

Then I heard him and the desk man both give a deep breath of relief. "At last!" And I knew a cop must have come in behind me.

The grip on my arms behind my back changed, became single instead of double, one arm instead of two. But I didn't fight against it.

Suddenly I was very passive, unresistant. Because suddenly I had a dread of arrest, confinement. I wanted to preserve my freedom of movement more than all else, to try to find her again. If they threw me in a cell, or put me in a straitjacket, how could I look for her, how could I ever hope to get at the bottom of this mystery?

The police would never believe me. If the very people who had seen her denied her existence, how could I expect those who hadn't to believe in it?

Docile, I let him lead me out to the sidewalk in front of the hotel. The manager came out after us, mopping his forehead, and the desk clerk, and a few of the bolder among the guests who had been watching.

They held a three-cornered consultation in which I took no part. I even let the manager's version of what the trouble was pass unchallenged. Not that he distorted what had actually happened just now, but he made it seem as if I were mistaken about having brought her there last night.

Finally the harness cop asked, "Well, do you want to press charges against him for creating a disturbance in your lobby?"

The manager held his hands palms out, horrified. "I should say not. We're having our biggest rush of the year right now; I can't take time off to run down there and go through all that tommyrot. Just see that he doesn't come in again and create any more scenes."

"I'll see to that, all right," the cop promised truculently.

They went inside again, the manager and the clerk and the gallery that had watched us from the front steps. Inside to the hotel that had swallowed her alive.

The cop read me a lecture, to which I listened in stony silence. Then he gave me a shove that sent me floundering, said, "Keep moving now, hear me?"

I pointed, and said, "That's my car standing there. May I get in it?" He checked first to make sure it was, then he opened the door, said, "Yeah, get in it and get out of here."

He'd made no slightest attempt to find out what was behind the whole thing, whether there was some truth to my story or not, or whether it was drink, drugs, or mental aberration. But then he was only a harness cop. That's why I hadn't wanted to tangle with him.

This strangeness that had risen up around me was nothing to be fought by an ordinary patrolman. I was going to them—the police—

but I was going of my own free will and in my own way, not to be dragged in by the scruff of the neck and then put under observation for the next twenty-four hours.

Ten minutes or so later I got out in front of the first precinct house I came upon, and went in, and said to the desk sergeant, "I want to talk to the lieutenant in charge."

He stared at me coldly.

"What about?"

"About my wife."

I didn't talk to him alone. Three of his men were present. They were just shapes in the background as far as I was concerned, sitting there very quietly, listening.

I told it simply, hoping against hope I could get them to believe me, feeling somehow I couldn't even before I had started.

"I'm Jimmy Cannon, I'm twenty-five years old, and I'm from Lake City. Last evening after dark my girl and I—her name was Alice Brown—we left there in my car, and at 1:15 this morning we were married by a justice of the peace.

"I think his name was Hulskamp—anyway it's a white house with morning glories all over the porch, about fifty miles this side of Lake City.

"We got in here at three, and they gave her a little room at the Royal Hotel. They couldn't put me up, but they put her up alone. The number was 1006. I know that as well as I know I'm sitting here. This morning when I went over there, they were painting the room and I haven't been able to find a trace of her since.

"I saw her sign the register, but her name isn't on it anymore. The night clerk says he never saw her. The bellboy says he never saw her. Now they've got me so I'm scared and shaky, like a little kid is of the dark. I want you men to help me. Won't you men help me?"

"We'll help you"—said the lieutenant in charge. Slowly, awfully slowly; I didn't like that slowness—"if we're able to." And I knew what

he meant; if we find any evidence that your story is true.

He turned his head toward one of the three shadowy listeners in the background, at random. The one nearest him. Then he changed his mind, shifted his gaze further along, to the one in the middle. "Ainslie, suppose you take a whack at this. Go over to this hotel and see what you can find out. Take him with you."

So, as he stood up, I separated him from the blurred background for the first time. I was disappointed. He was just another man like me, maybe five years older, maybe an inch or two shorter. He could feel cold and hungry and tired, just as I could. He could believe a lie, just as I could. He couldn't see around corners or through walls, or into hearts any more than I could. What good was he going to be?

He looked as if he'd seen every rotten thing there was in the world. He looked as if he'd once expected to see other things beside that, but didn't anymore. He said, "Yes, sir," and you couldn't tell whether he was bored or interested, or liked the detail or resented it, or gave a rap.

On the way over I said, "You've got to find out what became of her. You've got to make them—"

"I'll do what I can." He couldn't seem to get any emotion into his voice. After all, from his point of view, why should he?

"You'll do what you can!" I gasped. "Didn't you ever have a wife?"

He gave me a look, but you couldn't tell what was in it.

We went straight back to the Royal. He was very businesslike, did a streamlined, competent job. Didn't waste a question or a motion, but didn't leave out a single relevant thing either.

I took back what I'd been worried about at first; he was good.

But he wasn't good enough for this, whatever it was.

It went like this: "Let me see your register." He took out a glass, went over the place I pointed out to him where she had signed. Evidently couldn't find any marks of erasure any more than I had with my naked eye.

Then we went up to the room, 1006. The painter was working on the wood trim by now, had all four walls and the ceiling done. It was such a small cubbyhole it wasn't even a half-day's work. He said, "Where was the furniture when you came in here to work this morning? Still in the room, or had the room been cleared?"

"Still in the room; I cleared it myself. There wasn't much; a chair, a scatter rug, a cot."

"Was the cot made or unmade?"

"Made up."

"Was the window opened or closed when you came in?"

"Closed tight."

"Was the air in the room noticeably stale, as if it had been closed up that way all night, or not noticeably so, as if it had only been closed up shortly before?"

"Turrible, like it hadn't been aired for a week. And believe me, when I notice a place is stuffy, you can bet it's stuffy all right."

"Were there any marks on the walls or floor or anywhere around the room that didn't belong there?"

I knew he meant blood, and gnawed the lining of my cheek fearfully.

"Nothing except plain grime, that needed painting bad."

We visited the housekeeper next. She took us to the linen room and showed us. "If there're any dark blue quilts in use in this house, it's the first I know about it. The bellboy *could* have come in here at that hour—but all he would have gotten are maroon ones. And here's my supply list, every quilt accounted for. So it didn't come from here."

We visited the baggage room next. "Look around and see if there's anything in here that resembles that bag of your wife's." I did, and there wasn't. Wherever she had gone, whatever had become of her, her bag had gone with her.

About fifty minutes after we'd first gone in, we were back in my car outside the hotel again. He'd done a good, thorough job; and if I was willing to admit that, it must have been.

We sat there without moving a couple of minutes, me under the wheel. He kept looking at me steadily, sizing me up. I couldn't tell what he was thinking. I threw my head back and started to look up the face of the building, story by story. I counted as my eyes rose, and when they'd come to the tenth floor I stopped them there, swung them around the corner of the building to the third window from the end, stopped them there for good. It was a skinnier window than the others. So small, so high up, to hold so much mystery. "Alice," I whispered up to it, and it didn't answer, didn't hear.

His voice brought my gaze down from there again. "The burden of the proof has now fallen on you. It's up to you to give me some evidence that she actually went in there. That she actually was with you. That she actually *was.* I wasn't able to find a single person in that building who actually saw her."

I just looked at him, the kind of a look you get from someone right after you stick a knife in his heart. Finally I said with quiet bitterness, "So now I have to prove I had a wife."

The instant, remorseless way he answered that was brutal in itself. "Yes, you do. Can you?"

I pushed my hat off, raked my fingers through my hair, with one and the same gesture. "Could you, if someone asked you in the middle of the street? Could you?"

He peeled out a wallet, flipped it open. A tiny snapshot of a woman's head and shoulders danced in front of my eyes for a split second. He folded it and put it away again. He briefly touched a gold band on his finger, token of that old custom that is starting to revive again, of husbands wearing marriage rings as well as wives.

"And a dozen other ways. You could call Tremont 4102. Or you could call the marriage clerk at the City Hall—"

"But we were just beginning," I said bleakly. "I have no pictures. She was wearing the only ring we had. The certificate was to be mailed to us at Lake City in a few days. You could call this justice of the peace, Hulskamp, out near U.S. 9; he'll tell you—"

"Okay, Cannon, I'll do that. We'll go back to headquarters, I'll tell the lieutenant what I've gotten so far, and I'll do it from there."

Now at last it would be over, now at last it would be straightened out. He left me sitting in the room outside the lieutenant's office, while he was in there reporting to him. He seemed to take a long time, so I knew he must be doing more than just reporting; they must be talking it over.

Finally Ainslie looked out at me, but only to say, "What was the name of that justice you say married you, again?"

"Hulskamp."

He closed the door again. I had another long wait. Finally it opened a second time, he hitched his head at me to come in. The atmosphere, when I got in there, was one of hard, brittle curiosity, without any feeling to it. As when you look at somebody afflicted in a way you never heard of before, and wonder how he got that way.

I got that distinctly. Even from Ainslie, and it was fairly oozing from his lieutenant and the other men in the room. They looked and looked and looked at me.

The lieutenant did the talking. "You say a Justice Hulskamp married you. You still say that?"

"A white house sitting off the road, this side of Lake City, just before you get to U.S. 9—"

"Well, there is a Justice Hulskamp, and he does live out there. We just had him on the phone. He says he never married anyone named James Cannon to anyone named Alice Brown, last night or any other night. He hasn't married anyone who looks like you, recently, to anyone who looks as you say she did. He didn't marry anyone at all at any time last night—"

He was going off someplace while he talked to me, and his voice was going away after him. Ainslie filled a paper cup with water at the cooler in the corner, strewed it deftly across my face, once each way, as if I were some kind of a potted plant, and one of the other guys picked me up from the floor and put me back on the chair again.

The lieutenant's voice came back again stron-ger, as if he hadn't gone away after all. "Who were her people in Lake City?"

"She was an orphan."

"Well, where did she work there?"

"At the house of a family named Beresford, at 20 New Hampshire Avenue. She was in service there, a maid; she lived with them—"

"Give me long distance. Give me Lake City. This is Michianopolis police headquarters. I want to talk to a party named Beresford, 20 New Hampshire Avenue."

The ring came back fast. "We're holding a man here who claims he married a maid working for you. A girl by the name of Alice Brown."

He'd hung up before I even knew it was over. "There's no maid employed there. They don't know anything about any Alice Brown, never heard of her."

I stayed on the chair this time. I just didn't hear so clearly for a while, everything sort of fuzzy.

". . . Hallucinations . . . And he's in a semi-hysterical condition right now. Notice how jerky his reflexes are?" Someone was chopping the edge of his hand at my kneecaps. "Seems harmless. Let him go. It'll probably wear off. I'll give him a sedative." Someone snapped a bag shut, left the room.

The lieutenant's voice was as flat as it was deadly, and it brooked no argument. "You never had a wife, Cannon!"

I could see only Ainslie's face in the welter before me. "You have, though, haven't you?" I said, so low none of the others could catch it.

The lieutenant was still talking to me. "Now get out of here before we change our minds and call an ambulance to take you away. And don't go back into any more hotels raising a row."

I hung around outside; I wouldn't go away. Where was there to go? One of the others came out, looked at me fleetingly in passing, said with humorous tolerance, "You better get out of here before the lieutenant catches you," and went on about his business.

I waited until I saw Ainslie come out. Then I

went up to him. "I've got to talk to you; you've got to listen to me—"

"Why? The matter's closed. You heard the lieutenant."

He went back to some sort of a locker room. I went after him.

"You're not supposed to come back here. Now look, Cannon, I'm telling you for your own good, you're looking for trouble if you keep this up."

"Don't turn me down," I said hoarsely, tugging away at the seam of his sleeve. "Can't you see the state I'm in? I'm like someone in a dark room, crying for a match. I'm like someone drowning, crying for a helping hand. I can't make it alone anymore."

There wasn't anyone in the place but just the two of us. My pawing grip slipped down his sleeve to the hem of his coat, and I was looking up at him from my knees. What did I care? There was no such thing as pride or dignity anymore. I would have crawled flat along the floor on my belly, just to get a word of relief out of anyone.

"Forget you're a detective, and I'm a case. I'm appealing to you as one human being to another. I'm appealing to you as one husband to another. Don't turn your back on me like that, don't pull my hands away from your coat. I don't ask you to do anything for me anymore; you don't have to lift a finger. Just say, 'Yes, you had a wife, Cannon.' Just give me that one glimmer of light in the dark. Say it even if you don't mean it, even if you don't believe it, say it anyway. Oh, say it, will you—"

He drew the back of his hand slowly across his mouth, either in disgust at my abasement or in a sudden access of pity. Maybe a little of both. His voice was hoarse, as if he were sore at the spot I was putting him on.

"Give me anything," he said, shaking me a little and jogging me to my feet, "the slightest thing, to show that she ever existed, to show that there ever was such a person outside of your own mind, and I'll be with you to the bitter end. Give me a pin that she used to fasten her dress with. Give me a grain of powder, a stray hair; but

prove that it was hers. But I can't do it unless you do."

"And I have nothing to show you. Not a pin, not a grain of powder."

I took a few dragging steps toward the locker room door. "You're doing something to me that I wouldn't do to a dog," I mumbled. "What you're doing to me is worse than if you were to kill me. You're locking me up in shadows for the rest of my life. You're taking my mind away from me. You're condemning me slowly but surely to madness, to being without a mind. It won't happen right away, but sooner or later, in six months or in a year—Well, I guess that's that."

I fumbled my way out of the locker room and down the passageway outside, guiding myself with one arm along the wall, and past the sergeant's desk and down the steps, and then I was out in the street.

I left my car there where it was. What did I want with it? I started to walk, without knowing where I was going. I walked a long time, and a good long distance.

Then all of a sudden I noticed a lighted drugstore—it was dark by now—across the way. I must have passed others before now, but this was the first one I noticed.

I crossed over and looked in the open doorway. It had telephone booths; I could see them at the back, to one side. I moved on a few steps, stopped, and felt in my pockets. I found a quill toothpick, and I dug the point of it good and hard down the back of my finger, ripped the skin open. Then I threw it away. I wrapped a handkerchief around the finger, and I turned around and went inside.

I said to the clerk, "Give me some iodine. My cat just scratched me and I don't want to take any chances."

He said, "Want me to put it on for you?"

I said, "No, gimme the whole bottle. I'll take it home; we're out of it."

I paid him for it and moved over to one side and started to thumb through one of the directories in the rack. Just as he went back inside the prescription room, I found my number. I went into the end booth and pulled the slide closed. I took off my hat and hung it over the phone mouthpiece, sort of making myself at home.

Then I sat down and started to undo the paper he'd just wrapped around the bottle. When I had it off, I pulled the knot of my tie out a little further to give myself lots of room. Then I took the stopper out of the bottle and tilted my head back and braced myself.

Something that felt like a baseball bat came chopping down on the arm I was bringing up, and nearly broke it in two, and the iodine sprayed all over the side of the booth. Ainslie was standing there in the half-opened slide.

He said, "Come on outta there!" and gave me a pull by the collar of my coat that did it for me. He didn't say anything more until we were out on the sidewalk in front of the place. Then he stopped and looked me over from head to foot as if I were some kind of a microbe. He said, "Well, it was worth coming all this way after you, at that!"

My car was standing there; I must have left the keys in it and he must have tailed me in that. He thumbed it, and I went over and climbed in and sat there limply. He stayed outside.

I said, "I can't live with shadows, Ainslie. I'm frightened, too frightened to go on. You don't know what the nights'll be like from now on. And the days won't be much better. I'd rather go now, fast. Show her to me on a slab at the morgue and I won't whimper. Show her to me all cut up in small pieces and I won't bat an eyelash. But don't say she never was."

"I guessed what was coming from the minute I saw you jab yourself with that toothpick." He watched sardonically while I slowly unwound the handkerchief, that had stayed around my finger all this time. The scratch had hardly bled at all. Just a single hairline of red was on the handkerchief.

We both looked at that.

Then more of the handkerchief came open. We both looked at the initials in the corner. *A.B.* We both, most likely, smelled the faint sweetness that still came from it at the same time. Very faint, for it was such a small handkerchief.

We both looked at each other, and both our minds made the same discovery at the same time. I was the one who spoke it aloud. "It's hers," I said grimly; "the wife that didn't exist."

"This is a fine time to come out with it," he said quietly. "Move over, I'll drive." That was his way of saying, "I'm in."

I said, "I remember now. I got a cinder in my eye, during the drive in, and she lent me her handkerchief to take it out with; I didn't have one of my own on me. I guess I forgot to give it back to her. And this—is it." I looked at him rebukingly. "What a difference a few square inches of linen can make. Without it, I was a madman. With it, I'm a rational being who enlists your co-operation."

"No. You didn't turn it up when it would have done you the most good, back at the station house. You only turned it up several minutes after you were already supposed to have gulped a bottle of iodine. I could tell by your face you'd forgotten about it until then yourself. I think that does make a difference. To me it does, anyway." He meshed gears.

"And what're you going to do about it?"

"Since we don't believe in the supernatural, our only possible premise is that there's been some human agency at work."

I noticed the direction he was taking. "Aren't you going back to the Royal?"

"There's no use bothering with the hotel. D'you see what I mean?"

"No, I don't," I said bluntly. "That was where she disappeared."

"The focus for this wholesale case of astigmatism is elsewhere, outside the hotel. It's true we could try to break them down, there at the hotel. But what about the justice, what about the Beresford house in Lake City? I think it'll be simpler to try to find out the reason rather than the mechanics of the disappearance.

"And the reason lies elsewhere. Because you brought her to the hotel from the justice's. And to the justice's from Lake City. The hotel was the last stage. Find out why the justice denies he married you, and we don't have to find out why the hotel staff denies having seen her. Find out why the Beresford house denies she was a maid there, and we don't have to find out why the justice denies he married you.

"Find out, maybe, something else, and we don't have to find out why the Beresford house denies she was a maid there. The time element keeps moving backward through the whole thing. Now talk to me. How long did you know her? How well? How much did you know about her?"

"Not long. Not well. Practically nothing. It was one of those story-book things. I met her a week ago last night. She was sitting on a bench in the park, as if she were lonely, didn't have a friend in the world. I don't make a habit of accosting girls on park benches, but she looked so dejected it got to me.

"Well, that's how we met. I walked her home afterwards to where she said she lived. But when we got there—holy smoke, it was a mansion! I got nervous, said: 'Gee, this is a pretty swell place for a guy like me to be bringing anyone home to, just a clerk in a store.'

"She laughed and said, 'I'm only the maid. Disappointed?' I said, 'No, I would have been disappointed if you'd been anybody else, because then you wouldn't be in my class.' She seemed relieved after I said that. She said, 'Gee, I've waited so long to find someone who'd like me for myself.'

"Well, to make a long story short, we made an appointment to meet at that same bench the next night. I waited there for two hours and she never showed up. Luckily I went back there the next night again—and there she was. She explained she hadn't been able to get out the night before; the people where she worked were having company or something.

"When I took her home that night I asked her name, which I didn't know yet, and that seemed to scare her. She got sort of flustered, and I saw her look at her handbag. It had the initials *A.B.* on it; I'd already noticed that the first night I met her. She said, 'Alice Brown.'

"By the third time we met we were already nuts about each other. I asked her whether she'd take a chance and marry me. She said, 'Is it possible someone wants to marry little Alice Brown, who hasn't a friend in the world?' I said yes, and that was all there was to it.

"Only, when I left her that night, she seemed kind of scared. First I thought she was scared I'd change my mind, back out, but it wasn't that. She said, 'Jimmy, let's hurry up and do it, don't let's put it off. Let's do it while—while we have the chance'; and she hung on to my sleeve tight with both hands.

"So the next day I asked for a week off, which I had coming to me from last summer anyway, and I waited for her with the car on the corner three blocks away from the house where she was in service. She came running as if the devil were behind her, but I thought that was because she didn't want to keep me waiting. She just had that one little overnight bag with her.

"She jumped in, and her face looked kind of white, and she said, 'Hurry, Jimmy, hurry!' And away we went. And until we were outside of Lake City, she kept looking back every once in a while, as if she were afraid someone was coming after us."

Ainslie didn't say much after all that rigmarole I'd given him. Just five words, after we'd driven on for about ten minutes or so. "She was afraid of something." And then in another ten minutes, "And whatever it was, it's what's caught up with her now."

We stopped at the filling station where Alice and I had stopped for gas the night before. I looked over the attendants, said: "There's the one serviced us." Ainslie called him over, played a pocket light on my face.

"Do you remember servicing this man last night? This man, and a girl with him?"

"Nope, not me. Maybe one of the oth—"

Neither of us could see his hands at the moment; they were out of range below the car door. I said, "He's got a white scar across the back of his right hand. I saw it last night."

Ainslie said, "Hold it up."

He did, and there was a white cicatrix across it, where stitches had been taken or something. Ainslie said, "Now whaddye say?"

It didn't shake him in the least. "I still say no.

Maybe he saw me at one time or another, but I've never seen him, to my knowledge, with or without a girl." He waited a minute, then added: "Why should I deny it, if it was so?"

"We'll be back, in a day or in a week or in a month," Ainslie let him know grimly, "but we'll be back—to find that out."

We drove on. "Those few square inches of linen handkerchief will be wearing pretty thin, if this keeps up," I muttered dejectedly after a while.

"Don't let that worry you," he said, looking straight ahead. "Once I'm sold, I don't unsell easily."

We crossed U.S. 9 a half-hour later. A little white house came skimming along out of the darkness. "This is where I was married to a ghost," I said.

He braked, twisted the grip of the door latch. My hand shot down, stopped his arm.

"Wait; before you go in, listen to this. It may help out that handkerchief. There'll be a round mirror in the hall, to the left of the door, with antlers over it for a hatrack. In their parlor, where he read the service, there'll be an upright piano, with brass candle holders sticking out of the front of it, above the keyboard. It's got a scarf on it that ends in a lot of little plush balls. And on the music rack, the top selection is a copy of *Kiss Me Again*. And on the wall there's a painting of a lot of fruit rolling out of a basket. And this housekeeper, he calls her Dora."

"That's enough," he said in that toneless voice of his. "I told you I was with you anyway, didn't I?" He got out and went over and rang the bell. I went with him, of course.

They must have been asleep; they didn't answer right away. Then the housekeeper opened the door and looked out at us. Before we could say anything, we heard the justice call down the stairs, "Who is it, Dora?"

Ainslie asked if we could come in and talk to him, and straightened his necktie in the round mirror to the left of the door, with antlers over it.

Hulskamp came down in a bathrobe, and

Ainslie said: "You married this man to a girl named Alice Brown last night." It wasn't a question.

The justice said, "No. I've already been asked that once, over the phone, and I said I hadn't. I've never seen this young man before." He even put on his glasses to look at me better.

Ainslie didn't argue the matter, almost seemed to take him at his word. "I won't ask you to let me see your records," he said drily, "because they'll undoubtedly—bear out your word."

He strolled as far as the parlor entrance, glanced in idly. I peered over his shoulder. There was an upright piano with brass candle sconces. A copy of *Kiss Me Again* was topmost on its rack. A painting of fruit rolling out of a basket daubed the wall.

"They certainly will!" snapped the justice resentfully.

The housekeeper put her oar in. "I'm a witness at all the marriages the justice performs, and I'm sure the young man's mistaken. I don't ever recall—"

Ainslie steadied me with one hand clasping my arm, and led me out without another word. We got in the car again. Their door closed, somewhat forcefully.

I pounded the rim of the wheel helplessly with my fist. I said, "What is it? Some sort of wholesale conspiracy? But *why*? She's not important; I'm not important."

He threw in the clutch, the little white house ebbed away in the night darkness behind us.

"It's some sort of a conspiracy, all right," he said. "We've got to get the reason for it. That's the quickest, shortest way to clear it up. To take any of the weaker links, the bellboy at the hotel or that filling station attendant, and break them down, would not only take days, but in the end would only get us some anonymous individual who'd either threatened them or paid them to forget having seen your wife, and we wouldn't be much further than before. If we can get the reason behind it all, the source, we don't have to bother with any of these small fry. That's why we're heading back to Lake City instead of just concentrating on that hotel in Michianopolis."

We made Lake City by one a.m. and I showed him the way to New Hampshire Avenue. Number 20 was a massive corner house, and we glided up to it from the back, along the side street; braked across the way from the service entrance I'd always brought her back to. Not a light was showing.

"Don't get out yet," he said. "When you brought her home nights, you brought her to this back door, right?"

"Yes."

"Tell me, did you ever actually see her open it and go in, or did you just leave her here by it and walk off without waiting to see where she went?"

I felt myself get a little frightened again. This was something that hadn't occurred to me until now. "I didn't once actually see the door open and her go inside, now that I come to think of it. She seemed to—to want me to walk off without waiting. She didn't say so, but I could tell. I thought maybe it was because she didn't want her employers to catch on she was going around with anyone. I'd walk off, down that way—"

I pointed to the corner behind us, on the next avenue over. "Then when I got there, I'd look back from there each time. As anyone would. Each time I did, she wasn't there anymore. I thought she'd gone in, but—it's funny, I never saw her go in."

He nodded gloomily. "Just about what I thought. For all you know, she didn't even belong in that house, never went in there at all. A quick little dash, while your back was turned, would have taken her around the corner of the house and out of sight. And the city would have swallowed her up."

"But why?" I said helplessly.

He didn't answer that. We hadn't had a good look at the front of the house yet. As I have said, we had approached from the rear, along the side street. He got out of the car now, and I followed suit. We walked down the few remaining yards to the corner, and turned and looked all up and down the front of it.

It was an expensive limestone building; it spelt real dough, even looking at it in the dark as we were. There was a light showing from the front, through one of the tall ground-floor windows—but a very dim one, almost like a night light. It didn't send any shine outside; just peered wanly around the sides of the blind that had been drawn on the inside.

Something moved close up against the door-facing, stirred a little. If it hadn't been white limestone, it wouldn't have even been noticeable at all. We both saw it at once; I caught instinctively at Ainslie's arm, and a cold knife of dull fear went through me—though why I couldn't tell.

"Crepe on the front door," he whispered. "Somebody's dead in there. Whether she did go in here or didn't, just the same I think we'd better have a look at the inside of this place."

I took a step in the direction of the front door. He recalled me with a curt gesture. "And by that I don't mean march up the front steps, ring the doorbell, and flash my badge."

"Then how?"

Brakes ground somewhere along the side street behind us. We turned our heads and a lacquered sedan-truck had drawn up directly before the service door of 20 New Hampshire Avenue. "Just in time," Ainslie said. "This is how."

We started back toward it. The driver and a helper had gotten down, were unloading batches of camp chairs and stacking them up against the side of the truck, preparatory to taking them in.

"For the services tomorrow, I suppose," Ainslie grunted. He said to the driver: "Who is it that died, bud?"

"Mean to say you ain't heard? It's in alla papers."

"We're from out of town."

"Alma Beresford, the heiress. Richest gal in twenty-four states. She was an orphum, too. Pretty soft for her guardian; not another soul to get the cash but him."

"What was it?" For the first time since I'd known him, you couldn't have called Ainslie's voice toneless; it was sort of springy like a rubber band that's pulled too tight.

"Heart attack, I think." The truckman snapped his fingers. "Like that. Shows you that rich or poor, when you gotta go, you gotta go."

Ainslie asked only one more question. "Why you bringing these setups at an hour like this? They're not going to hold the services in the middle of the night, are they?"

"Nah, but first thing in the morning; so early there wouldn't be a chance to get 'em over here unless we delivered 'em ahead of time." He was suddenly staring fascinatedly at the silvery lining of Ainslie's hand.

Ainslie's voice was toneless again. "Tell you what you fellows are going to do. You're going to save yourselves the trouble of hauling all those camp chairs inside, and you're going to get paid for it in the bargain. Lend us those work aprons y'got on."

He slipped them something apiece; I couldn't see whether it was two dollars or five. "Gimme your delivery ticket; I'll get it receipted for you. You two get back in the truck and lie low."

We both doffed our hats and coats, put them in our own car, rolled our shirt sleeves, put on the work aprons, and rang the service bell. There was a short wait and then a wire-sheathed bulb over the entry glimmered pallidly as an indication someone was coming. The door opened and a gaunt-faced sandy-haired man looked out at us. It was hard to tell just how old he was. He looked like a butler, but he was dressed in a business suit.

"Camp chairs from the Thebes Funerary Chapel," Ainslie said, reading from the delivery ticket.

"Follow me and I'll show you where they're to go," he said in a hushed voice. "Be as quiet as you can. We've only just succeeded in getting Mr. Hastings to lie down and try to rest a little." The guardian, I supposed. In which case this anemic-looking customer would be the guardian's Man Friday.

We each grabbed up a double armful of the camp chairs and went in after him. They were corded together in batches of half a dozen. We could have cleared up the whole consignment at once—they were lightweight—but Ainslie gave me the eye not to; I guess he wanted to have an excuse to prolong our presence as much as possible.

You went down a short delivery passageway, then up a few steps into a brightly lighted kitchen.

A hatchet-faced woman in maid's livery was sitting by a table crying away under one eye-shading hand, a teacup and a tumbler of gin before her. Judging by the redness of her nose, she'd been at it for hours. "My baby," she'd mew every once in a while.

We followed him out at the other side, through a pantry, a gloomy-looking dining room, and finally into a huge cavernous front room, eerily suffused with flickering candlelight that did no more than heighten the shadows in its far corners. It was this wavering pallor that we must have seen from outside of the house.

An open coffin rested on a flower-massed bier at the upper end of the place, a lighted taper glimmering at each corner of it. A violet velvet pall had been spread over the top of it, concealing what lay within.

But a tiny peaked outline, that could have been made by an uptilted nose, was visible in the plush at one extremity of its length. That knife of dread gave an excruciating little twist in me, and again I didn't know why—or refused to admit I did. It was as if I instinctively sensed the nearness of something familiar.

The rest of the room, before this monument to mortality, had been left clear, its original furniture moved aside or taken out. The man who had admitted us gave us our instructions.

"Arrange them in four rows, here in front of the bier. Leave an aisle through them. And be sure and leave enough space up ahead for the divine who will deliver the oration." Then he retreated to the door and stood watching us for a moment.

Ainslie produced a knife from the pocket of his borrowed apron, began severing the cord-ing that bound the frames of the camp chairs together. I opened them one at a time as he freed them and began setting them up in quadruple rows, being as slow about it as I could.

There was a slight sound and the factotum had tiptoed back toward the kitchen for a moment, perhaps for a sip of the comforting gin. Ainslie raised his head, caught my eye, speared his thumb at the bier imperatively. I was the nearer of us to it at the moment. I knew what he meant: look and see who it was.

I went cold all over, but I put down the camp chair I was fiddling with and edged over toward it on arched feet. The taper flames bent down flat as I approached them, and sort of hissed. Sweat needled out under the roots of my hair. I went around by the head, where that tiny little peak was, reached out, and gingerly took hold of the corners of the velvet pall, which fell loosely over the two sides of the coffin without quite meeting the headboard.

Just as my wrists flexed to tip it back, Ainslie coughed warningly. There was a whispered returning tread from beyond the doorway. I let go, took a quick side-jump back toward where I'd been.

I glanced around and the secretary fellow had come back again, was standing there with his eyes fixed on me. I pretended to be measuring off the distance for the pulpit with my foot.

"You men are rather slow about it," he said, thin-lipped.

"You want 'em just so, don't you?" Ainslie answered. He went out to get the second batch. I pretended one of the stools had jammed and I was having trouble getting it open, as an excuse to linger behind. The secretary was on his guard. He lingered too.

The dick took care of that. He waited until he was halfway back with his load of camp chairs, then dropped them all over the pantry floor with a clatter, to draw the watchdog off.

It worked. He gave a huff of annoyance, turned, and went in to bawl Ainslie out for the noise he had made. The minute the doorway cleared, I gave a catlike spring back toward the velvet mound. This time I made it. I flung the pall back—

Then I let go of it, and the lighted candles started spinning around my head, faster and faster, until they made a comet-like track of fire. The still face staring up at me from the coffin was Alice's.

I felt my knees hit something, and I was swaying back and forth on them there beside the bier. I could hear somebody coming back toward the room, but whether it was Ainslie or the other guy I didn't know and didn't care. Then an arm went around me and steadied me to my feet once more, so I knew it was Ainslie.

"It's her," I said brokenly. "Alice. I can't understand it; she must—have—been this rich girl, Alma Beresford, all the time—"

He let go of me, took a quick step over to the coffin, flung the pall even further back than I had. He dipped his head, as if he were staring nearsightedly. Then he turned and I never felt my shoulder grabbed so hard before, or since. His fingers felt like steel claws that went in, and met in the middle. For a minute I didn't know whether he was attacking me or not; and I was too dazed to care.

He was pointing at the coffin. "Look at that!" he demanded. I didn't know what he meant. He shook me brutally, either to get me to understand or because he was so excited himself. "*She's not dead.* Watch her chest cavern."

I fixed my eyes on it. You could tell only by watching the line where the white satin of her burial gown met the violet quilting of the coffin lining. The white was faintly, but unmistakably and rhythmically, rising and falling.

"They've got her either drugged or in a coma—"

He broke off short, let go of me as if my shoulder were red-hot and burned his fingers. His hand flashed down and up again, and he'd drawn and sighted over my shoulder. "Put it down or I'll let you have it right where you are!" he said.

Something thudded to the carpet. I turned and the secretary was standing there in the doorway, palms out, a fallen revolver lying at his feet.

"Go over and get that, Cannon," Ainslie ordered. "This looks like the finale now. Let's see what we've got."

There was an arched opening behind him, leading out to the front entrance hall, I suppose, and the stairway to the upper floors. We'd come in from the rear, remember. Velvet drapes had been drawn closed over that arch, sealing it up, the whole time we'd been in there.

He must have come in through there. I bent down before the motionless secretary, and, with my fingers an inch away from the fallen gun at his feet, I heard the impact of a head blow and Ainslie gave the peculiar guttural groan of someone going down into unconsciousness.

The secretary's foot snaked out and sped the gun skidding far across to the other side of the room. Then he dropped on my curved back like a dead weight and I went down flat under him, pushing my face into the parquet flooring.

He kept aiming blows at the side of my head from above, but he had only his fists to work with at the moment, and even the ones that landed weren't as effective as whatever it was that had been used on Ainslie. I reached upward and over, caught the secretary by the shoulders of his coat, tugged and at the same time jerked my body out from under him in the opposite direction; and he came flying up in a backward somersault and landed sprawling a few feet away.

I got up and looked. Ainslie lay inert, face down on the floor to one side of the coffin, something gleaming wet down the part of his hair. There was a handsome but vicious-looking gray-haired man in a brocaded dressing gown standing behind him holding a gun on me, trying to cow me with it.

"Get him, Mr. Hastings," panted the one I'd just flung off.

It would have taken more than a gun to hold me, after what I'd been through. I charged at him, around Ainslie's form. He evidently didn't want to fire, didn't want the noise of a shot to be heard there in the house. Instead, he reversed his gun, swung the butt high up over his shoulder; and my own headfirst charge undid me. I couldn't swerve or brake in time, plunged right in under it. A hissing, spark-shedding skyrocket seemed to tear through the top of my head, and I went down into nothingness as Ainslie had.

For an hour after I recovered consciousness I was in complete darkness. Such utter darkness that I couldn't be sure the blow hadn't affected my optic nerve.

I was in a sitting position, on something cold—stone flooring probably—with my hands lashed behind me, around something equally cold and sweating moisture, most likely a water pipe. My feet were tied too, and there was a gag over my mouth. My head blazed with pain.

After what seemed like an age, a smoky gray light began to dilute the blackness; so at least my eyesight wasn't impaired. As the light strengthened it showed me first a barred grate high up on the wall through which the dawn was peering in. Next, a dingy basement around me, presumably that of the same New Hampshire Avenue house we had entered several hours ago.

And finally, if that was any consolation to me, Ainslie sitting facing me from across the way, in about the same fix I was. Hands and feet secured, sitting before another pipe, mouth also gagged. A dark stain down one side of his forehead, long since dried, marked the effect of the blow he had received.

We just stared at each other, unable to communicate. We could turn our heads. He shook his from side to side deprecatingly. I knew what he meant: "Fine spot we ended up in, didn't we?" I nodded, meaning, "You said it."

But we were enjoying perfect comfort and peace of mind, compared to what was to follow. It came within about half an hour at the most. Sounds of activity began to penetrate to where we were. First a desultory moving about sounded over our heads, as if someone were looking things over to make sure everything was in order. Then something heavy was set down: it might have been a table, a desk—or a pulpit.

This cellar compartment we were in seemed to be directly under that large front room where the coffin was and where the obsequies were to be held.

A dawning horror began to percolate through me. I looked at Ainslie and tried to make him understand what I was thinking. I didn't need to, he was thinking the same thing.

She'd been alive when we'd last seen her, last night. Early this same morning, rather. What were they going to do—go ahead with it anyway?

A car door clashed faintly, somewhere off in the distance outside. It must have been at the main entrance of this very house we were in, for within a moment or two new footsteps sounded overhead, picking their way along, as down an aisle under guidance. Then something scraped slightly, like the leg rests of a camp chair straining under the weight of a body.

It repeated itself eight or ten times after that. The impact of a car door outside in the open, then the sedate footsteps over us—some the flat dull ones of men, some the sharp brittle ones of women—then the slight shift and click of the camp chairs. I didn't have to be told its meaning; probably Ainslie didn't either. The mourners were arriving for the services.

It was probably unintentional, our having been placed directly below like this; but it was the most diabolic torture that could ever have been devised. Was she dead yet, or wasn't she? But she had to be before—

They couldn't be that low. Maybe the drug she'd been under last night was timed to take fatal effect between then and now. But suppose it hadn't?

The two of us were writhing there like maimed snakes. Ainslie kept trying to bring his knees up and meet them with his chin, and at first I couldn't understand what his idea was. It was to snag the gag in the cleft between his two tightly pressed knees and pull it down, or at least dislodge it sufficiently to get some sound out. I immediately began trying the same thing myself.

Meanwhile an ominous silence had descended above us. No more car-door thuds, no more footsteps mincing down the aisle to their seats. The services were being held.

The lower half of my face was all numb by now from hitting my bony up-ended knees so many times. And still I couldn't work it. Neither could he. The rounded structure of the kneecaps kept them from getting close enough to our lips to act as pincers. If only one of us could have made it. If we could hear them that clearly down here, they would have been able to hear us yell up there. And they couldn't all be in on the plot, all those mourners, friends of the family or whoever they were.

Bad as the preliminaries had been, they were as nothing compared to the concluding stages that we now had to endure listening to. There was a sudden concerted mass shifting and scraping above, as if everyone had risen to his feet at one time.

Then a slow, single-file shuffling started in, going in one direction, returning in another. The mourners were filing around the coffin one by one for a last look at the departed. The departed who was still living.

After the last of them had gone out, and while the incessant cracking of car doors was still under way outside, marking the forming of the funeral cortege, there was a quick, businesslike converging of not more than two pairs of feet on one certain place—where the coffin was. A hurried shifting about for a moment or two, then a sharp hammering on wood penetrated to where we were, and nearly drove me crazy; they were fastening down the lid.

After a slight pause that might have been employed in reopening the closed room doors, more feet came in, all male, and moving toward that one certain place where the first two had preceded them. These must be the pallbearers, four or six of them. There was a brief scraping and jockeying about while they lifted the casket to their shoulders, and then the slow, measured tread with which they carried it outside to the waiting hearse.

I let my head fall inertly downward as far over as I could bend it, so Ainslie wouldn't see the tears running out of my eyes.

Motion attracted me and I looked blurredly up again. He was shaking his head steadily back and forth. "Don't give up, keep trying," he meant to say. "It's not too late yet."

About five or ten minutes after the hearse had left, a door opened surreptitiously somewhere close at hand; and a stealthy, frightened tread began to descend toward us, evidently along some steps that were back of me.

Ainslie could see who it was—he was facing that way—but I couldn't until the hatchet-faced maid we had seen crying in the kitchen the night before suddenly sidled out between us. She kept looking back in the direction from which she'd just come, as if scared of her life. She had an ordinary kitchen bread knife in her hand. She wasn't in livery now, but black-hatted, coated and gloved, as if she had started out for the cemetery with the rest and then slipped back unnoticed.

She went for Ainslie's bonds first, cackling terrifiedly the whole time she was sawing away at them. "Oh, if they ever find out I did this, I don't know what they'll do to me! I didn't even know you were down here until I happened to overhear Mr. Hastings whisper to his secretary just now before they left, 'Leave the other two where they are, we can attend to them when we come back.' Which one of you is her Jimmy? She confided in me; I knew about it; I helped her slip in and out of the house that whole week. I took her place under the bedcovers, so that when he'd look in he'd think she was asleep in her room.

"They had no right to do this to you and your friend, Jimmy, even though you were the cause of her death. The excitement was too much for her, she'd been so carefully brought up. She got this heart attack and died. She was already unconscious when they brought her back—from wherever it was you ran off with her to.

"I don't know why I'm helping you. You're a reckless, bad, fortune-hunting scoundrel; Mr. Hastings says so. The marriage wouldn't have been legal anyway; she didn't use her right name. It cost him all kinds of money to hush everyone up about it and destroy the documents, so it wouldn't be found out and you wouldn't have a chance to blackmail her later.

"You killed my baby! But still he should have turned you over to the police, not kept you tied up all ni—"

At this point she finally got through, and Ainslie's gag flew out of his mouth like one of those feathered darts kids shoot through a blowtube. "I *am* the police!" he panted. "And your 'baby' has been murdered, or will be within the next few minutes, by Hastings himself, not this boy here! She was still alive in that coffin at two o'clock this morning."

She gave a scream like the noon whistle of a factory. He kept her from fainting, or at any rate falling in a heap, by pinning her to the wall, took the knife away from her. He freed me in one-tenth of the time it had taken her to rid him of his own bonds. "No," she was groaning hollowly through her hands, "her own family doctor, a lifelong friend of her father and mother, examined her after she was gone, made out the death certificate. He's an honest man, he wouldn't do that—"

"He's old, I take it. Did he see her face?" Ainslie interrupted.

A look of almost stupid consternation froze on her own face. "No. I was at the bedside with him; it was covered. But only a moment before she'd been lying there in full view. The doctor and I both saw her from the door. Then Mr. Hastings had a fainting spell in the other room, and we ran to help him. When the doctor came in again to proceed with his examination, Mr. Chivers had covered her face—to spare Mr. Hastings' feelings.

"Dr. Meade just examined her body. Mr. Hastings pleaded with him not to remove the covering, said he couldn't bear it. And my pet was still wearing the little wrist watch her mother gave her before she died—"

"They substituted another body for hers,

that's all; I don't care how many wrist watches it had on it," Ainslie told her brutally. "Stole that of a young girl approximately her own age who had just died from heart failure or some other natural cause, most likely from one of the hospital morgues, and put it over on the doddering family doctor and you both.

"If you look, you'll probably find something in the papers about a vanished corpse. The main thing is to stop that burial; I'm not positive enough on it to take a chance. It may be she in the coffin after all, and not the substitute. Where was the interment to be?"

"In the family plot, at Cypress Hill."

"Come on, Cannon; got your circulation back yet?" He was at the top of the stairs already. "Get the local police and tell them to meet us out there."

Ainslie's badge was all that got us into the cemetery, which was private. The casket had already been lowered out of sight. They were throwing the first shovelful of earth over it as we burst through the little ring of sedate, bowing mourners.

The last thing I saw was Ainslie snatching an implement from one of the cemetery workers and jumping down bodily into the opening, feet first.

The face of that silver-haired devil, her guardian Hastings, had focused in on my inflamed eyes.

A squad of Lake City police, arriving only minutes after us, were all that saved his life. It took three of them to pull me off him.

Ainslie's voice was what brought me to, more than anything else. "It's all right, Cannon," he was yelling over and over from somewhere behind me. "It's the substitute."

I stumbled over to the lip of the grave between two of the cops and took a look down. It was the face of a stranger that was peering up at me through the shattered coffin lid. I turned away, and they made the mistake of letting go of me.

I went at the secretary this time; Hastings was still stretched out more dead than alive. "What've you done with her? Where've you got her?"

"That ain't the way to make him answer," Ainslie said, and for the second and last time throughout the whole affair his voice wasn't toneless. "*This* is!"

Wham! We had to take about six steps forward to catch up with the secretary where he was now.

Ainslie's method was all right at that. The secretary talked—fast.

Alice was safe; but she wouldn't have been, much longer. After the mourners had had a last look at her in the coffin, Hastings and the secretary had locked her up for safekeeping—stupefied, of course—and substituted the other body for burial.

And Alice's turn was to come later, when, under cover of night, she was to be spirited away to a hunting lodge in the hills—the lodge that had belonged to her father. There she could have been murdered at leisure.

When we'd flashed back to the New Hampshire Avenue house in a police car, and unlocked the door of the little den where she'd been secreted; and when the police physician who accompanied us brought her out of the opiate they'd kept her under—whose arms were the first to go around her?

"Jimmy"—She sighed a little, after we took time off from the clinches—"he showed up late that night with Chivers, in that dinky little room you left me in.

"They must have been right behind us all the way, paying all those people to say they'd never seen me.

"But he fooled me, pretended he wasn't angry, said he didn't mind if I married and left him. And I was so sleepy and off guard I believed him. Then he handed me a glass of salty-tasting water to drink, and said, 'Come on down to the car. Jimmy's down there waiting for you; we've got him with us.' I staggered down there between them, that's all I remember."

Then she remembered something else and looked at me with fright in her eyes. "Jimmy, you didn't mind marrying little Alice Brown, but I don't suppose Alma Beresford would stand a show with you—?"

"You don't-suppose right," I told her gruffly, "because I'm marrying Alice Brown all over again—even if we've gotta change her name first.

"And this ugly-looking bloke standing up here, name of Ainslie, is going to be best man at our second wedding. Know why? Because he was the only one in the whole world believed there really was a you."

EDMUND CRISPIN

ROBERT BRUCE MONTGOMERY (1921–1978) had a long, successful career as a pianist, organist, conductor, and composer, creating operas, requiem masses, and even the background music for many British motion pictures, including six of the famous *Carry On . . .* comic film series, such as *Carry on Nurse* (1959). Using the pseudonym Edmund Crispin, he enjoyed a career as the author of detective novels and stories featuring Gervase Fen, a literary critic and professor at Oxford University, which he attended as well. Although he published only nine novels (all with Fen) and two short-story collections, Crispin quickly became a favorite of readers who like intelligent, witty, fair-play detective fiction. Two of his novels, *The Moving Toyshop* (1946) and *Love Lies Bleeding* (1948), were selected for the Haycraft-Queen Cornerstone Library. In the former, a poet stumbles upon a corpse in a room above a toy shop and is immediately knocked unconscious. When he comes to, the corpse is missing—and so is the entire toy shop. The latter focuses on the search for a long-lost, priceless Shakespearean manuscript. Eight of Crispin's novels and a short-story collection were written during a ten-year stretch (1944–1953), and it appeared that he would take his place with the greatest of the greats when he abruptly stopped writing detective fiction to devote his career to music, reviewing crime fiction, and editing science fiction anthologies. He wrote only one more novel, *Glimpses of the Moon* (1977), before his death; *Fen Country* (1979), his second collection, was published posthumously.

"Beware of the Trains" was first published as "Nine Minus Nine Equals One" in the March 1951 issue of *Ellery Queen's Mystery Magazine*; it was first collected in *Beware of the Trains* (London, Gollancz, 1953).

BEWARE OF THE TRAINS

EDMUND CRISPIN

A WHISTLE BLEW; jolting slightly, the big posters on the hoardings took themselves off rearwards—and with sudden acceleration, like a thrust in the back, the electric train moved out of Borleston Junction, past the blurred radiance of the tall lamps in the marshalling-yard, past the diminishing constellations of the town's domestic lighting, and so out across the eight-mile isthmus of darkness at whose further extremity lay Clough. Borleston had seen the usual substantial exodus, and the few remaining passengers—whom chance had left oddly, and, as it turned out, significantly distributed—were able at long last to stretch their legs, to transfer hats, newspapers and other impedimenta from their laps to the vacated seats beside them, and for the first time since leaving Victoria to relax and be completely comfortable. Mostly they were somnolent at the approach of midnight, but between Borleston and Clough none of them actually slept. Fate had a conjuring trick in preparation, and they were needed as witnesses to it.

The station at Clough was not large, nor prepossessing, nor, it appeared, much frequented; but in spite of this, the train, once having stopped there, evinced an unexpected reluctance to move on. The whistle's first confident blast having failed to shift it, there ensued a moment's offended silence; then more whistling, and when that also failed, a peremptory, unintelligible shouting. The train remained inanimate, however, without even the usual rapid ticking to enliven it. And presently Gervase Fen, Professor of English Language and Literature in the University of Oxford, lowered the window of his compartment and put his head out, curious to know what was amiss.

Rain was falling indecisively. It tattooed in weak, petulant spasms against the station roof, and the wind on which it rode had a cutting edge. Wan bulbs shone impartially on slot-machines, timetables, a shuttered newspaper-kiosk; on governmental threat and commercial entreaty; on peeling green paint and rust-stained iron. Near the clock, a small group of men stood engrossed in peevish altercation. Fen eyed them with disapproval for a moment and then spoke.

"Broken down?" he enquired unpleasantly. They swivelled round to stare at him. "Lost the driver?" he asked.

This second query was instantly effective. They hastened up to him in a bunch, and one of them—a massive, wall-eyed man who appeared to be the Station-master—said: "For God's sake, sir, *you* 'aven't seen 'im, 'ave you?"

"Seen whom?" Fen demanded mistrustfully.

"The motorman, sir. The driver."

"No, of course I haven't," said Fen. "What's happened to him?"

"'E's gorn, sir. 'Ooked it, some'ow or other. 'E's not in 'is cabin, nor we can't find 'im any-where on the station, neither."

"Then he has absconded," said Fen, "with

valuables of some description, or with some other motorman's wife."

The Station-master shook his head—less, it appeared, by way of contesting this hypothesis than as an indication of his general perplexity—and stared helplessly up and down the deserted platform. "It's a rum go, sir," he said, "and that's a fact."

"Well, there's one good thing about it, Mr. Maycock," said the younger of the two porters who were with him. "'E can't 'ave got clear of the station, not without being seen."

The Station-master took some time to assimilate this, and even when he had succeeded in doing so, did not seem much enlightened by it. "'Ow d'you make that out, Wally?" he enquired.

"Well, after all, Mr. Maycock, the place is surrounded, isn't it?"

"Surrounded, Wally?" Mr. Maycock reiterated feebly. "What d'you mean, surrounded?"

Wally gaped at him. "Lord, Mr. Maycock, didn't you know? I thought you'd 'a' met the Inspector when you came back from your supper."

"Inspector?" Mr. Maycock could scarcely have been more bewildered if his underling had announced the presence of a Snab or a Greevey. "What Inspector?"

"Scotland Yard chap," said Wally importantly. "And 'alf a dozen men with 'im. They're after a burglar they thought'd be on this train."

Mr. Maycock, clearly dazed by this melodramatic intelligence, took refuge from his confusion behind a hastily contrived breastwork of outraged dignity. "And why," he demanded in awful tones, "was I not *hin*formed of this 'ere?"

"You 'ave bin informed," snapped the second porter, who was very old indeed, and who appeared to be temperamentally subject to that vehement, unfocused rage which one associates with men who are trying to give up smoking. "You 'ave bin informed. We've just informed yer."

Mr. Maycock ignored this. "*If* you would be so kind," he said in a lofty manner, "it would be 'elpful for me to know at what time these per-

sons of 'oom you are speaking put in an appearance 'ere."

"About twenty to twelve, it'd be," said Wally sulkily. "Ten minutes before this lot was due in."

"And it wouldn't 'ave occurred to you, would it"—here Mr. Maycock bent slightly at the knees, as though the weight of his sarcasm was altogether too much for his large frame to support comfortably—"to 'ave a dekko in my room and see if I was 'ere? *Ho* no. I'm only the Station-master, that's all I am."

"Well, I'm very sorry, Mr. Maycock," said Wally, in a tone of voice which effectively cancelled the apology out, "but I wasn't to know you was back, was I? I told the Inspector you was still at your supper in the village."

At this explanation, Mr. Maycock, choosing to overlook the decided resentment with which it had been delivered, became magnanimous. "Ah well, there's no great 'arm done, I dare say," he pronounced; and the dignity of his office having by now been adequately paraded, he relapsed to the level of common humanity again. "Burglar, eh? Was 'e on the train? Did they get 'im?"

Wally shook his head. "Not them. False alarm, most likely. They're still 'angin' about, though." He jerked a grimy thumb towards the exit barrier. "That's the Inspector, there."

Hitherto, no one had been visible in the direction indicated. But now there appeared, beyond the barrier, a round, benign, clean-shaven face surmounted by a grey Homburg hat, at which Fen bawled, "Humbleby!" in immediate recognition. And the person thus addressed, having delivered the injunction "Don't *move* from here, Millican" to someone in the gloom of the ticket-hall behind him, came on to the platform and in another moment had joined them.

He was perhaps fifty-five: small, as policemen go, and of a compact build which the neatness of his clothes accentuated. The close-cropped greying hair, the pink affable face, the soldierly bearing, the bulge of the cigar-case in the breast pocket and the shining brown shoes—these things suggested the more malleable sort of German *petit bourgeois;* to see him close at hand, however, was to see the grey eyes—bland, intelligent, sceptical—which effectively belied your first, superficial impression, showing the iron under the velvet. "Well, well," he said. "Well, well, well. Chance is a great thing."

"What," said Fen severely, his head still projecting from the compartment window like a gargoyle from a cathedral tower, "is all this about a burglar?"

"And you will be the Station-master." Humbleby had turned to Mr. Maycock. "You were away when I arrived here, so I took the liberty——"

"*That* I wasn't, sir," Mr. Maycock interrupted, anxious to vindicate himself. "I was in me office all the time, only these lads didn't think to look there. . . . 'Ullo, Mr. Foster." This last greeting was directed to the harassed Guard, who had clearly been searching for the missing motorman. "Any luck?"

"Not a sign of 'im," said the Guard sombrely. "Nothing like this 'as ever 'appened on one of *my* trains before."

"It is 'inkson, isn't it?"

The Guard shook his head. "No. Phil Bailey."

"Bailey?"

"Ah. Bailey sometimes took over from 'inkson on this run." Here the Guard glanced uneasily at Fen and Humbleby. "It's irregular, o' course, but it don't do no 'arm as I can see. Bailey's 'ome's at Bramborough, at the end o' this line, and 'e'd 'ave to catch this train any'ow to get to it, so 'e took over sometimes when 'Inkson wanted to stop in Town. . . . And now this 'as to 'appen. There'll be trouble, you mark my words." Evidently the unfortunate Guard expected to be visited with a substantial share of it.

"Well, I can't 'old out no longer," said Mr. Maycock. "I'll 'ave to ring 'eadquarters straight away." He departed in order to do this, and Humbleby, who still had no clear idea of what was going on, required the others to enlighten him. When they had done this: "Well," he said, "one thing's certain, and that is that your motorman hasn't left the station. My men are all

round it, and they had orders to detain anyone who tried to get past them."

At this stage, an elderly business man, who was sharing the same compartment with Fen and with an excessively genteel young woman of the sort occasionally found behind the counters of Post Offices, irritably enquired if Fen proposed keeping the compartment window open all night. And Fen, acting on this hint, closed the window and got out on to the platform.

"None the less," he said to Humbleby, "it'll be as well to interview your people and confirm that Bailey *hasn't* left. I'll go the rounds with you, and you can tell me about your burglar."

They left the Guard and the two porters exchanging theories about Bailey's defection, and walked along the platform towards the head of the train. "Goggett is my burglar's name," said Humbleby. "Alfred Goggett. He's wanted for quite a series of jobs, but for the last few months he's been lying low, and we haven't been able to put our hands on him. Earlier this evening, however, he was spotted in Soho by a plain-clothes man named, incongruously enough, Diggett . . ."

"Really, Humbleby . . ."

". . . And Diggett chased him to Victoria. Well, you know what Victoria's like. It's rather a rambling terminus, and apt to be full of people. Anyway, Diggett lost his man there. Now, about mid-day today one of our more reliable narks brought us the news that Goggett had a hideout here in Clough, so this afternoon Millican and I drove down here to look the place over. Of course the Yard rang up the police here when they heard Goggett had vanished at Victoria; and the police here got hold of me; and here we all are. There was obviously a very good chance that Goggett would catch this train. Only unluckily he didn't."

"No one got off here?"

"No one got off or on. And I understand that this is the last train of the day, so for the time being there's nothing more we can do. But sooner or later, of course, he'll turn up at his cottage here, and then we'll have him."

"And in the meantime," said Fen thoughtfully, "there's the problem of Bailey."

"In the meantime there's that. Now let's see. . . ."

It proved that the six damp but determined men whom Humbleby had culled from the local constabulary had been so placed about the station precincts as to make it impossible for even a mouse to have left without their observing it; and not even a mouse, they stoutly asserted, had done so. Humbleby told them to stay where they were until further orders, and returned with Fen to the down platform.

"No loophole there," he pronounced. "And it's an easy station to—um—invest. If it had been a great sprawling place like Borleston, now, I could have put a hundred men round it, and Goggett might still have got clear. . . . Of course, it's quite possible that Borleston's where he did leave the train."

"One thing at a time," said Fen rather peevishly. "It's Bailey we're worrying about now—not Goggett."

"Well, Bailey's obviously still on the station. Or else somewhere on the train. I wonder what the devil he thinks he's up to?"

"In spite of you and your men, he must have been able to leave his cabin without being observed." They were passing the cabin as Fen spoke, and he stopped to peer at its vacant interior. "As you see, there's no way through from it into the remainder of the train."

Humbleby considered the disposition of his forces, and having done so: "Yes," he admitted, "he could have left the cabin without being seen; and for that matter, got to shelter somewhere in the station buildings."

"Weren't the porters on the platform when the train came in?"

"No. They got so overwrought when I told them what I was here for—the younger one especially—that I made them keep out of the way. I didn't want them gaping when Goggett got off the train and making him suspicious—he's the sort of man who's quite capable of using a gun when he finds himself cornered."

"Maycock?"

"He was in his office—asleep, I suspect. As to the Guard, I could see his van from where I was standing, and he didn't even get out of it till he was ready to start the train off again. . . ." Humbleby sighed. "So there really wasn't anyone to keep an eye on the motorman's doings. However, we're bound to find him: he can't have left the precincts. I'll get a search-party together, and we'll have another look—a systematic one, this time."

Systematic or not, it turned out to be singularly barren of results. It established one thing only, and that was that beyond any shadow of doubt the missing motorman was not anywhere in, on, or under the station, nor anywhere in, on, or under his abandoned train.

And unfortunately, it was also established that he could not, in the nature of things, be anywhere else.

Fen took no part in this investigation, having already foreseen its inevitable issue. He retired, instead, to the Station-master's office, by whose fire he was dozing when Humbleby sought him out half an hour later.

"One obvious answer," said Humbleby when he had reported his failure, "is of course that Bailey's masquerading as someone else—as one of the twelve people (that's not counting police) who definitely *are* cooped up in this infernal little station."

"And is he doing that?"

"No. At least, not unless the Guard and the two porters and the Station-master are in a conspiracy together—which I don't for a second believe. They all know Bailey by sight, at least, and they're all certain that no one here can possibly be him."

Fen yawned. "So what's the next step?" he asked.

"What I ought to have done long ago: the next step is to find out if there's any evidence Bailey was driving the train when it left Borleston. . . . Where's the telephone?"

"Behind you."

"Oh, yes. . . . I don't understand these

inter-station phones, so I'll use the ordinary one. . . . God help us, hasn't that dolt Maycock made a note of the number anywhere?"

"In front of you."

"Oh, yes . . . 51709." Humbleby lifted the receiver, dialled, and waited. "Hello, is that Borleston Junction?" he said presently. "I want to speak to the Station-master. Police business. . . . Yes, all right, but be *quick*." And after a pause: "Station-master? This is Detective-Inspector Humbleby of the Metropolitan C.I.D. I want to know about a train which left Borleston for Clough and Bramborough at—at——"

"A quarter to midnight," Fen supplied.

"At a quarter to midnight. . . . Good heavens, yes, this last midnight that we've just had. . . . Yes, I know it's held up at Clough; so am I. . . . No, no, what I want is information about who was driving it when it left Borleston: eyewitness information. . . . *You did?* . . . You actually saw Bailey yourself? Was that immediately before the train left? . . . It was; well then, there's no chance of Bailey's having hopped out, and someone else taken over, after you saw him? . . . I see: the train was actually moving out when you saw him at the controls. Sure you're not mistaken? This is important. . . . Oh, there's a porter who can corroborate it, is there? . . . No, I don't want to talk to him now. . . . All right. . . . Yes. . . . Goodbye."

Humbleby rang off and turned back to Fen. "So that," he observed, "is that."

"So I gathered."

"And the next thing is, could Bailey have left the train between Borleston and here?"

"The train," said Fen, "didn't drive itself in, you know."

"Never mind that for the moment," said Humbleby irritably. "*Could* he?"

"No. He couldn't. Not without breaking his neck. We did a steady thirty-five to forty all the way, and we didn't stop or slow down once."

There was a silence. "Well, I give up," said Humbleby. "Unless this wretched man has vanished like a sort of soap-bubble——"

"It's occurred to you that he may be dead?"

"It's occurred to me that he may be dead and cut up into little pieces. But I still can't find any of the pieces. . . . Good Lord, Fen, it's like—it's like one of those Locked-Room Mysteries you get in books: an Impossible Situation."

Fen yawned again. "Not impossible, no," he said. "Rather a simple device, really. . . ." Then more soberly: "But I'm afraid that what we have to deal with is something much more serious than a mere vanishing. In fact——"

The telephone rang, and after a moment's hesitation Humbleby answered it. The call was for him; and when, several minutes later, he put the receiver back on its hook, his face was grave.

"They've found a dead man," he said, "three miles along the line towards Borleston. He's got a knife in his back and has obviously been thrown out of a train. From their description of the face and clothes, it's quite certainly Goggett. And equally certainly, *that*"—he nodded towards the platform—"is the train he fell out of. . . . Well, my first and most important job is to interview the passengers. And anyone who was alone in a compartment will have a lot of explaining to do."

Most of the passengers had by now disembarked, and were standing about in various stages of bewilderment, annoyance, and futile enquiry. At Humbleby's command, and along with the Guard, the porters, and Mr. Maycock, they shuffled, feebly protesting, into the waiting-room. And there, with Fen as an interested onlooker, a Grand Inquisition was set in motion.

Its results were both baffling and remarkable. Apart from the motorman, there had been nine people on the train when it left Borleston and when it arrived at Clough; and each of them had two others to attest the fact that during the whole crucial period he (or she) had behaved as innocently as a newborn infant. With Fen there had been the elderly business man and the genteel girl; in another compartment there had likewise been three people, no one of them connected with either of the others by blood, acquaintance, or vocation; and even the Guard had witnesses to his harmlessness, since from Victoria onwards he had been accompanied in the van by two melancholy men in cloth caps, whose mode of travel was explained by their being in unremitting personal charge of several doped-looking whippets. None of these nine, until the first search for Bailey was set on foot, had seen or heard anything amiss. None of them (since the train was not a corridor train) had had any opportunity of moving out of sight of his or her two companions. None of them had slept. And unless some unknown, travelling in one of the many empty compartments, had disappeared in the same fashion as Bailey—a supposition which Humbleby was by no means prepared to entertain—it seemed evident that Goggett must have launched himself into eternity unaided.

It was at about this point in the proceedings that Humbleby's self-possession began to wear thin, and his questions to become merely repetitive; and Fen, perceiving this, slipped out alone on to the platform. When he returned, ten minutes later, he was carrying a battered suitcase; and regardless of Humbleby, who seemed to be making some sort of speech, he carried this impressively to the centre table and put it down there.

"In this suitcase," he announced pleasantly, as Humbleby's flow of words petered out, "we shall find, I think, the motorman's uniform belonging to the luckless Bailey." He undid the catches. "And in addition, no doubt . . . *Stop him, Humbleby!*"

The scuffle that followed was brief and inglorious. Its protagonist, tackled round the knees by Humbleby, fell, struck his head against the fender, and lay still, the blood welling from a cut above his left eye.

"Yes, that's the culprit," said Fen. "And it will take a better lawyer than there is alive to save *him* from a rope's end."

Later, as Humbleby drove him to his destination through the December night, he said: "Yes, it had to be Maycock. And Goggett and Bailey had, of course, to be one and the same person. But what about motive?"

Humbleby shrugged. "Obviously, the money in that case of Goggett's. There's a lot of it, you know. It's a pretty clear case of thieves falling out. We've known for a long time that Goggett had an accomplice, and it's now certain that that accomplice was Maycock. Whereabouts in his office did you find the suitcase?"

"Stuffed behind some lockers—not a very good hiding-place, I'm afraid. Well, well, it can't be said to have been a specially difficult problem. Since Bailey wasn't on the station, and hadn't left it, it was clear he'd never entered it. But *someone* had driven the train in—and who could it have been *but* Maycock? The two porters were accounted for—by you; so were the Guard and the passengers—by one another; and there just wasn't anyone else.

"And then, of course, the finding of Goggett's body clinched it. He hadn't been thrown out of either of the occupied compartments, or the Guard's van; he hadn't been thrown out of any of the *un*occupied compartments, for the simple reason that there was nobody to throw him. *Therefore* he was thrown out of the motorman's cabin. And since, as I've demonstrated, Maycock was unquestionably *in* the motorman's cabin, it was scarcely conceivable that Maycock had not done the throwing.

"Plainly, Maycock rode or drove into Borleston while he was supposed to be having his supper, and boarded the train—that is, the motorman's cabin—there. He kept hidden till the train was under way, and then took over from Goggett-Bailey while Goggett-Bailey changed into the civilian clothes he had with him. By the way, I take it that Maycock, to account for his presence, spun some fictional (as far as he knew) tale about the police being on Goggett-Bailey's track, and that the change was Goggett-Bailey's idea; I mean, that he had some notion of its assisting his escape at the end of the line."

Humbleby nodded. "That's it, approximately. I'll send you a copy of Maycock's confession as soon as I can get one made. It seems he wedged the safety handle which operates these trains, knifed Goggett-Bailey and chucked him out, and then drove the train into Clough and there simply disappeared, with the case, into his office. It must have given him a nasty turn to hear the station was surrounded."

"It did," said Fen. "If your people hadn't been there, it would have looked, of course, as if Bailey had just walked off into the night. But chance was against him all along. Your siege, and the grouping of the passengers, and the cloth-capped men in the van—they were all part of an accidental conspiracy—if you can talk of such a thing—to defeat him; all part of a sort of fortu-itous conjuring trick." He yawned prodigiously, and gazed out of the car window. "Do you know, I believe it's the dawn. . . . Next time I want to arrive anywhere, I shall travel by bus."

THE LOCKED BATHROOM

H. R. F. KEATING

STARTING HIS WRITING CAREER as a journalist, Henry Reymond Fitzwalter Keating (1926–2011), known to all as "Harry," worked for several newspapers until 1960, when he became a full-time author, producing several general novels and mysteries, achieving success with *The Perfect Murder* (1964). Introducing his most famous character, Inspector Ganesh Ghote of the Bombay CID, it won the (British) Crime Writers' Association (CWA) Gold Dagger for the best novel of the year; it also was nominated for an Edgar Award by the Mystery Writers of America. Ghote (pronounced GO-tay), one of the most revered characters in British crime fiction for more than four decades, is the homicide expert in Bombay but is nonetheless a man beset by doubts. He is dominated by his wife and gives the impression while on the job of being bullied or victimized by his superiors, tough criminals, and powerful witnesses or suspects. Nevertheless, in spite of his simple naïveté, he is often shrewd and seems always to come through with the correct solution to any mystery with which he is confronted. Although praised for his accurate and sensitive portrayal of life in India in the Ghote novels, Keating did not visit India until he had written nine books set there.

Keating was born in Sussex and, after joining the BBC Engineering Department as a youth-in-training, served in the army from 1945 to 1948. He attended Trinity College in Dublin, then returned to England to work at various newspapers. As a freelance writer, he reviewed for the *Times* (London) for fifteen years, beginning in 1967. Regarded as one of the great writers of fair-play detective fiction, Keating served as president of the prestigious Detection Club (1985–2000) and was awarded a Cartier Diamond Dagger for lifetime achievement by the CWA in 1996.

"The Locked Bathroom" was first published in the June 2, 1980, issue of *Ellery Queen's Mystery Magazine*.

THE LOCKED BATHROOM

H. R. F. KEATING

MRS. CRAGGS HAD very often nearly left the cleaning job she had with Mrs. Marchpane, of Fitzjames Avenue. But somehow, for some reason or no reason, she stayed on week after week. And so she was there, a witness, when in that luxury flat—as later the newspaper headline writers were to insist on calling it—there occured one of the great mysteries of our time. Or, anyhow, a mystery. And one that made the papers for nearly two weeks.

Certainly Mrs. Craggs had no regard at all for her employer, silly, gabbling Mrs. Marchpane, wife of Squadron Leader John (Jumping Jack) Marchpane, retired. Every other week at least, when it came to the Friday, the second of the two days on which she "did" for Mrs. Marchpane, she had been on the point of saying, "Sorry, madam, but I shan't be able to oblige after next Friday," and then she had said nothing. It might, to some extent, have been because of the Squadron Leader. There he was, a hero, called "Jumping Jack" in the war because he had had to bail out on twenty-three different occasions and had gone back to pilot another Spitfire next day every single time. But now he was retired with only a bit of a job to keep himself occupied and spending all the rest of his time being given orders by Mrs. Marchpane. And ridiculous orders, too, often as not.

So, although the Squadron Leader was always very nice to her, never failing to ask about her rheumatism—and listening to her reply—producing a little bunch of flowers when he discovered it was her birthday and sending her a card at Christmas, she could not help mingling her liking for him with a little half-contemptuous pity.

The trouble was that Mrs. Marchpane was such a fusspot. Everything had to be just right for her. If the frail figurines on the sitting-room mantelpiece were not each one at its exactly accustomed angle when Mrs. Craggs had finished dusting, it was as if the whole fabric of society had been made to totter. If each one of Mrs. Marchpane's delicately scented toilet articles was not in its exact place on the shelf in front of the bathroom mirror, to a hair's-breadth, it was as if the very foundations of the ever-spinning world had been lifted up and moved. If after Mrs. Craggs had taken the vacuum cleaner over the hall carpet the Squadron Leader was forgetful enough to walk across it and leave footmarks in the immaculate pile, it was as if someone had impiously challenged the Thirty-nine Articles of the Church of England and had to be rushed to the stake forthwith.

Yet Mrs. Craggs stayed on. Which did at least mean she was there on the day of the Great Locked Bathroom Mystery.

It happened just after she had finished the hall carpet, a task Mrs. Marchpane liked done first of all. Both the Squadron Leader and his wife were in the bathroom. They did not get up early, and it was very much a regular thing that the Squadron Leader should be taking his shower at this time. Mrs. Marchpane insisted—of course—that any husband of hers should shower each morning and she even timed her own twenty minutes spent at the bathroom basin to coincide with his. She insisted too that he should have a complete change of clothes each day, in summer even putting his lightweight trousers into the Ali Baba dirty-linen basket in the corner of the bathroom.

And hair. What a fuss she made about hair caught in the bath wastepipe.

You'd think, Mrs. Craggs used to murmur to herself whenever she heard from the other side of the locked bathroom door that unending sing-song voice, poor old Jumping Jack's hairs were great poisonous tropical wrigglies, the palaver she's making. "Really, John, if I've asked you once I've asked you a thousand times." Mrs. Marchpane never called her hero husband by any other less dignified name than John. "Really, John, I can't have the charwoman finding hair in the plug-hole." Though Mrs. Craggs's own feelings were that life made its share of muck, and muck had got to be cleared up.

But on this memorable day, just as she had switched off the vacuum cleaner, she heard from behind the bathroom door, not a comparatively restrained rebuke, but a sudden ear-shattering scream.

"Gone. Gone. He's gone. He's gone."

Then there came the sound of the bolt on the door being banged back with desperate force and the next second Mrs. Marchpane came rushing out full pelt into the hall.

At first Mrs. Craggs thought the Squadron Leader must have had a heart attack as he stood there in the shower. But Mrs. Marchpane's next shrill words dissipated the notion in an instant.

"He's disappeared. John. My John. He's gone. He's vanished."

"What you mean 'gone'?" Mrs. Craggs was eventually forced to shout sharply into Mrs. Marchpane's ear.

"Mrs. Craggs, my husband. He was there in the shower. I was looking at him in the mirror.

I was massaging my face. Then—then I looked again and he wasn't—he wasn't there, Mrs. Craggs."

And the good lady burst into such a howl of tears that Mrs. Craggs could do nothing else but guide her into the kitchen, ease her down onto a chair at the table, and hastily put a light under the kettle for that universal remedy, a good strong cup of tea.

"There, there," she said. "You'll be all right, dear. He can't've gone. Not *gone*. You just didn't see him, that's all."

But she knew at that moment that these were no more than mere words of comfort. Because the plain fact of the matter was that standing in front of the bathroom mirror, you could see plainly and fully right to the back of the sort of sentry box made by the shower curtain at the far end of the bath. She had often noticed this herself when she had cleaned the glass shelf over the wash basin and was making sure that each one of Mrs. Marchpane's toilet articles was back in its exact place.

At last she saw with relief that the kettle had boiled. She tumbled hot water into the teapot, poured a quick cup—it wouldn't be very strong, but at least it would be hot—and put it in front of Mrs. Marchpane.

But already that lady was beginning to recover.

"Tea?" she exclaimed. "In the kitchen? What can you be thinking of? I'll be in the sitting room. In the sitting room, Mrs. Craggs."

She rose to her feet, somewhat unsteadily.

"Oh, no, you won't," Mrs. Craggs said, her voice exactly mingling sternness and kindliness. "You'll sit just there where you are and swaller that cup right down. A nasty shock you've 'ad, an' tea you need."

And she even planted her sturdy legs squarely in front of the kitchen door to stop her employer from getting up and opening it.

Mrs. Marchpane, to Mrs. Craggs's relief, seemed to lack enough of her customary hammering willpower to resist. She fell back onto the kitchen chair and began to sip the hot liquid.

"Now," said Mrs. Craggs, "I'll just go along to that old bathroom an' see what all this is about."

She marched off, not without urgency, neglecting indeed in this emergency to take care to walk round and not across the hall carpet.

But, true enough, in the bathroom there was no sign of the Squadron Leader. And when, joined by Mrs. Marchpane, she looked through all the rest of the flat, there was still not the faintest trace of him to be found.

It had been some time before Mrs. Craggs allowed her employer to go to the length of telephoning the police. But in the end she had had to agree to that portentous step. And that had been the start of a process that had gone on for at least the two weeks during which the mysterious disappearance had made the national press. A series of ever more important police officers had one by one confessed themselves baffled. Fingerprint experts, photographers, Geiger counters, stethoscopes—all had been used, but none had helped.

At last the mystery entered the history books, and Mrs. Craggs brought herself to utter the words she had wanted to say ever since her first week of employment at the flat in Fitzjames Avenue, "Sorry, madam, but I shan't be able to oblige after next Friday."

Even her friend Mrs. Milhorne, who had pestered her night and morning for new details of the affair—and had had to be content with meagre pickings indeed—at last transferred her riotous imagination to the latest Hollywood scandal.

Until just a week before Christmas, nearly six months later.

That was when Mrs. Craggs received a particularly splendid Christmas card. Even if it was one not particularly in the spirit of Yuletide, consisting as it did of a reproduced painting of that hallowed air-war machine of old, the Spitfire.

Mrs. Milhorne, dropping in for a chat and a cup of tea, took it from the mantelpiece, without asking, and looked inside.

"From Jack Mayglass—and Jill," she read aloud. "Who's he then? I didn't know you knew any Jack Mayglass."

Mrs. Craggs pondered for a moment.

"Well," she said at last, "I don't suppose it matters if I tell you now, in confidence like. I don't know no Jack May-glass. But I used ter know a John March-pane."

"John March—the Great Locked Bathroom Mystery?"

"Locked bathroom. That bathroom weren't locked fer very long," Mrs. Craggs said. "It weren't locked from the moment that silly cow unbolted it when she thought her poor long-suffering hubby had disappeared."

"But he *had* disappeared. It said so in the papers."

"Oh, yes. He disappeared all right. Then. Disappeared from a dog's life, to start up somewhere new. Walked right out o' that bathroom 'e did, soon as I 'appened to take his missus into the kitchen an' shut the door behind me. Stuck on 'is shirt an' trousers what 'e took out o' that Ali Baba basket where he'd just put 'em, an' walked right out o' the house. An' jolly good luck to 'im."

"Yes," said Mrs. Milhorne slowly. "Yes, I can see that. I can see he might of been driven to that, driven by a force greater than what he was. But what I can't see is, how he wasn't there when she looked for him in that mirror."

"Easy," said Mrs. Craggs. "Hair."

"Hair? What you mean 'hair'?"

"He must of been cleaning 'is hair out o' the plug-'ole," Mrs. Craggs answered. "Like what she was always on an' on at him to do. Crouched down 'e must of been ter hoick the stuff out. An' just then the silly cow would've looked back in the mirror again an' not seen 'im. 'Course she wouldn't, not with 'im tucked away beneath 'er sight the way 'e was an' with that curtain there an' all. But what's she do? Blows 'er top straight away, goes rushing to the door, yanks open that bolt, comes yelling up ter me an' clasps me in 'er arms like what we was Rudy Valentino an' Mary Pickford. An' then it must of come to 'im.

This was his chance. His sudden chance. An' 'e took it."

Mrs. Milhorne looked at the card with the picture of the sunlit Spitfire on it.

"But you knew," she said suddenly. "You must of known all along."

"Well, not quite all along. But I did 'ear some little noises in the 'all while we was in the kitchen, an' I knew then I'd better keep that dratted woman in there. An' it was a good thing I did. Footsteps all across the 'all carpet there was. 'Ad to tread on 'em meself to blot 'em out. Couldn't 'ave the Great Locked Bathroom Mystery come to an end before it'd really begun, could I?"

MIKE, ALEC, AND RUFUS

DASHIELL HAMMETT

AS WRITERS TURNED from the orotund style of Henry James and his Victorian predecessors to lean and swift prose, scholars have pointed to the undeniably profound force of Ernest Hemingway, but the argument could be made that the most influential writer of the twentieth century was Dashiell Hammett (1894–1961), whose crisp and realistic (one might say Hemingwayesque) dialogue appears to have influenced the great Papa.

Publishing dates are hard facts, not esoteric theories. Hammett's first Continental Op story appeared in *Black Mask* on October 1, 1923. The quintessential hard-boiled private eye appeared frequently in the ensuing years. Hemingway's first book, *In Our Time,* was published in Paris in a limited edition in 1924, and published in a tiny edition of 1,335 copies in the United States in October 1925, by which time Hammett was already well established and a highly popular regular contributor to the most important pulp magazine of its time.

In addition to the nameless operative of the Continental Detective Agency, Hammett created Sam Spade, the hero of the most famous American detective novel ever written or filmed, *The Maltese Falcon* (1930), which had been serialized in *Black Mask,* as were all of his novels except the last, *The Thin Man* (1934).

"Mike, Alec, or Rufus" was published in the January 1925 issue of *Black Mask*; it was first published in book form under the title "Tom, Dick, or Harry" (as it had been retitled for its publication in *Ellery Queen's Mystery Magazine*) in *Twentieth Century Detective Stories* (Cleveland, World, 1948). It was first collected in the Hammett short-story collection *The Creeping Siamese* (New York, Jonathan Press, 1950).

MIKE, ALEC, AND RUFUS

DASHIELL HAMMETT

I DON'T KNOW whether Frank Toplin was tall or short. All of him I ever got a look at was his round head—naked scalp and wrinkled face, both of them the color and texture of Manila paper—propped up on white pillows in a big four-poster bed. The rest of him was buried under a thick pile of bedding.

Also in the room that first time were his wife, a roly-poly woman with lines in a plump white face like scratches in ivory; his daughter Phyllis, a smart popular-member-of-the-younger-set type; and the maid who had opened the door for me, a big-boned blond girl in apron and cap.

I had introduced myself as a representative of the North American Casualty Company's San Francisco office, which I was in a way. There was no immediate profit in admitting I was a Continental Detective Agency sleuth, just now in the casualty company's hire, so I held back that part.

"I want a list of the stuff you lost," I told Toplin, "but first—"

"Stuff?" Toplin's yellow sphere of a skull bobbed off the pillows, and he wailed to the ceiling, "A hundred thousand dollars if a nickel, and he calls it stuff!"

Mrs. Toplin pushed her husband's head down on the pillows again with a short-fingered fat hand.

"Now, Frank, don't get excited," she soothed him.

Phyllis Toplin's dark eyes twinkled, and she winked at me.

The man in bed turned his face to me again, smiled a bit shame-facedly, and chuckled.

"Well, if you people want to call your seventy-five-thousand-dollar-loss stuff, I guess I can stand it for twenty-five thousand."

"So it adds up to a hundred thousand?" I asked.

"Yes. None of them were insured to their full value, and some weren't insured at all."

That was very usual. I don't remember ever having anybody admit that anything stolen from them was insured to the hilt—always it was half, or at most, three-quarters covered by the policy.

"Suppose you tell me exactly what happened," I suggested, and added, to head off another speech that usually comes, "I know you've already told the police the whole thing, but I'll have to have it from you."

"Well, we were getting dressed to go to the Bauers' last night. I brought my wife's and daughter's jewelry—the valuable pieces—home with me from the safe-deposit box. I had just got my coat on and had called to them to hurry up when the doorbell rang."

"What time was this?"

"Just about half-past eight. I went out of this room into the sitting-room across the passageway and was putting some cigars in my case when Hilda"—nodding at the blond maid—"came walking into the room, backward. I started to ask her if she had gone crazy, walking around backward, when I saw the robber. He—"

"Just a moment." I turned to the maid. "What happened when you answered the bell?"

"Why, I opened the door, of course, and this man was standing there, and he had a revolver in his hand, and he stuck it against my—my stomach, and pushed me back into the room where Mr. Toplin was, and he shot Mr. Toplin, and—"

"When I saw him and the revolver in his hand"—Toplin took the story away from his servant—"it gave me a fright, sort of, and I let my cigar case slip out of my hand. Trying to catch it again—no sense in ruining good cigars even if you are being robbed—he must have thought I was trying to get a gun or something. Anyway, he shot me in the leg. My wife and Phyllis came running in when they heard the shot and he pointed the revolver at them, took all their jewels, and had them empty my pockets. Then he made them drag me back into Phyllis's room, into the closet, and he locked us all in there. And mind you, he didn't say a word all the time, not a word—just made motions with his gun and his left hand."

"How bad did he bang your leg?"

"Depends on whether you want to believe me or the doctor. He says it's nothing much. Just a scratch, he says, but it's my leg that's shot, not his!"

"Did he say anything when you opened the door?" I asked the maid.

"No, sir."

"Did any of you hear him say anything while he was here?"

None of them had.

"What happened after he locked you in the closet?"

"Nothing that we knew about," Toplin said, "until McBirney and a policeman came and let us out."

"Who's McBirney?"

"The janitor."

"How'd he happen along with a policeman?"

"He heard the shot and came upstairs just as the robber was starting down after leaving here. The robber turned around and ran upstairs, then into an apartment on the seventh floor, and stayed there—keeping the woman who lives there, a Miss Eveleth, quiet with his revolver—until he got a chance to sneak out and get away. He knocked her unconscious before he left, and—and that's all. McBirney called the police right after he saw the robber, but they got here too late to be any good."

"How long were you in the closet?"

"Ten minutes—maybe fifteen."

"What sort of looking man was the robber?"

"Short and thin and—"

"How short?"

"About your height, or maybe shorter."

"About five feet five or six, say? What would he weigh?"

"Oh, I don't know—maybe a hundred and fifteen or twenty. He was kind of puny."

"How old?"

"Not more than twenty-two or -three."

"Oh, Papa," Phyllis objected, "he was thirty, or near it!"

"What do you think?" I asked Mrs. Toplin.

"Twenty-five, I'd say."

"And you?" to the maid.

"I don't know exactly, sir, but he wasn't very old."

"Light or dark?"

"He was light," Toplin said. "He needed a shave and his beard was yellowish."

"More of a light brown," Phyllis amended.

"Maybe, but it was light."

"What color eyes?"

"I don't know. He had a cap pulled down over them. They looked dark, but that might have been because they were in the shadow."

"How would you describe the part of his face you could see?"

"Pale, and kind of weak-looking—small chin. But you couldn't see much of his face; he had his coat collar up and his cap pulled down."

"How was he dressed?"

"A blue cap pulled down over his eyes, a blue suit, black shoes, and black gloves—silk ones."

"Shabby or neat?"

"Kind of cheap-looking clothes, awfully wrinkled."

"What sort of gun?"

Phyllis Toplin put in her word ahead of her father.

"Papa and Hilda keep calling it a revolver, but it was an automatic—a thirty-eight."

"Would you folks know him if you saw him again?"

"Yes," they agreed.

I cleared a space on the bedside table and got out a pencil and paper.

"I want a list of what he got, with as thorough a description of each piece as possible, and the price you paid for it, where you bought it, and when." I got the list half an hour later.

"Do you know the number of Miss Eveleth's apartment?" I asked.

"702, two floors above.

"I went up there and rang the bell. The door was opened by a girl of twenty-something, whose nose was hidden under adhesive tape. She had nice clear hazel eyes, dark hair, and athletics written all over her.

"Miss Eveleth?"

"Yes."

"I'm from the insurance company that insured the Toplin jewelry, and I'm looking for information about the robbery."

She touched her bandaged nose and smiled ruefully.

"This is some of my information."

"How did it happen?"

"A penalty of femininity. I forgot to mind my own business. But what you want, I suppose, is what I know about the scoundrel. The doorbell rang a few minutes before nine last night and when I opened the door he was there. As soon as I got the door opened he jabbed a pistol at me and said, 'Inside, kid!'

"I let him in with no hesitancy at all; I was quite instantaneous about it and he kicked the door to behind him.

"'Where's the fire escape?' he asked.

"The fire escape doesn't come to any of my windows, and I told him so, but he wouldn't take my word for it. He drove me ahead of him to each of the windows; but of course he didn't find his fire escape, and he got peevish about it, as if it were my fault. I didn't like some of the things he called me, and he was such a little half-portion of a man so I tried to take him in hand. But—well, man is still the dominant animal so far as I'm concerned. In plain American, he busted me in the nose and left me where I fell. I was dazed, though not quite all the way out, and when I got up he had gone. I ran out into the corridor then, and found some policemen on the stairs. I sobbed out my pathetic little tale to them and they told me of the Toplin robbery. Two of them came back here with me and searched the apartment. I hadn't seen him actually leave, and they thought he might be foxy enough or desperate enough to jump into a closet and stay there until the coast was clear. But they didn't find him here."

"How long do you think it was after he knocked you down that you ran out into the corridor?"

"Oh, it couldn't have been five minutes. Perhaps only half that time."

"What did Mr. Robber look like?"

"Small, not quite so large as I; with a couple of days' growth of light hair on his face; dressed in shabby blue clothes, with black cloth gloves."

"How old?"

"Not very. His beard was thin, patchy, and he had a boyish face."

"Notice his eyes?"

"Blue; his hair, where it showed under the edge of his cap, was very light yellow, almost white."

"What sort of voice?"

"Very deep bass, though he may have been putting that on."

"Know him if you'd see him again?"

"Yes, indeed!" She put a gentle finger on her bandaged nose. "My nose would know, as the ads say, anyway!"

From Miss Eveleth's apartment I went down to the office on the first floor, where I found McBirney, the janitor, and his wife, who managed the apartment building. She was a scrawny little woman with the angular mouth and nose of a nagger; he was big, broad-shouldered, with sandy hair and mustache, good-humored, shiftless red face, and genial eyes of a pale and watery blue.

He drawled out what he knew of the looting.

"I was fixin' a spigot on the fourth floor when I heard the shot. I went up to see what was the matter, an' just as I got far enough up the front stairs to see the Toplins' door, the fella came out. We seen each other at the same time, an' he aims his gun at me. There's a lot o' things I might of done, but what I did do was to duck down an' get my head out o' range. I heard him run upstairs, an' I got up just in time to see him make the turn between the fifth and sixth floors.

"I didn't go after him. I didn't have a gun or nothin', an' I figured we had him cooped. A man could get out o' this buildin' to the roof of the next from the fourth floor, an' maybe from the fifth, but not from any above that; an' the Toplins' apartment is on the fifth. I figured we had this fella. I could stand in front of the elevator an' watch both the front an' back stairs; an' I rang for the elevator, an' told Ambrose, the elevator boy, to give the alarm an' run outside an' keep his eye on the fire escape until the police came.

"The missus came up with my gun in a minute or two, an' told me that Martinez—Ambrose's brother, who takes care of the switchboard an' the front door—was callin' the police. I could see both stairs plain, an' the fella didn't come down them; an' it wasn't more'n a few minutes before the police—a whole pack of 'em—came from the Richmond Station. Then we let the Toplins out of the closet where they were, an' started to search the buildin'. An' then Miss Eveleth came runnin' down the stairs, her face an' dress all bloody, an' told about him bein' in her apartment; so we were pretty sure we'd land him. But we didn't. We searched every apartment in the buildin', but didn't find hide nor hair of him."

"Of course you didn't!" Mrs. McBirney said unpleasantly. "But if you had—"

"I know," the janitor said with the indulgent air of one who has learned to take his pannings

as an ordinary part of married life, "if I'd been a hero an' grabbed him, an' got myself all mussed up. Well, I ain't foolish like old man Toplin, gettin' himself plugged in the foot, or Blanche Eveleth, gettin' her nose busted. I'm a sensible man that knows when he's licked—an' I ain't jumpin' at no guns!"

"No! You're not doing anything that—"

This Mr. and Mrs. stuff wasn't getting me anywhere, so I cut in with a question to the woman. "Who is the newest tenant you have?"

"Mr. and Mrs. Jerald—they came the day before yesterday."

"What apartment?"

"704—next door to Miss Eveleth."

"Who are these Jeralds?"

"They come from Boston. He told me he came out here to open a branch of a manufacturing company. He's a man of at least fifty, thin and dyspeptic-looking."

"Just him and his wife?"

"Yes. She's poorly too—been in a sanatorium for a year or two."

"Who's the next newest tenant?"

"Mr. Heaton, in 535. He's been here a couple of weeks, but he's down in Los Angeles right now. He went away three days ago and said he would be gone for ten or twelve days."

"What does he look like and what does he do?"

"He's with a theatrical agency and he's kind of fat and red-faced."

"Who's the next newest?"

"Miss Eveleth. She's been here about a month."

"And the next?"

"The Wageners in 923. They've been here going on two months."

"What are they?"

"He's a retired real-estate agent. The others are his wife and son Jack—a boy of maybe nineteen. I seen him with Phyllis Toplin a lot."

"How long have the Toplins been here?"

"It'll be two years next month."

I turned from Mrs. McBirney to her husband.

"Did the police search all these people's apartments?"

"Yeah," he said. "We went into every room, every alcove, an' every closet from cellar to roof."

"Did you get a good look at the robber?"

"Yeah. There's a light in the hall outside of the Toplins' door, an' it was shinin' full on his face when I saw him."

"Could he have been one of your tenants?"

"No, he couldn't."

"Know him if you saw him again?"

"You bet."

"What did he look like?"

"A little runt, a light-complected youngster of twenty-three or -four in an old blue suit."

"Can I get hold of Ambrose and Martinez—the elevator and door boys who were on duty last night—now?"

The janitor looked at his watch.

"Yeah. They ought to be on the job now. They come on at two."

I went out into the lobby and found them together, matching nickels. They were brothers, slim, bright-eyed Filipino boys. They didn't add much to my dope.

Ambrose had come down to the lobby and told his brother to call the police as soon as McBirney had given him his orders, and then he had to beat it out the back door to take a plant on the fire escapes. The fire escapes ran down the back and one side wall. By standing a little off from the corner of those walls, the Filipino had been able to keep his eyes on both of them, as well as on the back door.

There was plenty of illumination, he said, and he could see both fire escapes all the way to the roof, and he had seen nobody on them.

Martinez had given the police a rap on the phone and had then watched the front door and the foot of the front stairs. He had seen nothing.

I had just finished questioning the Filipinos when the street door opened and two men came in. I knew one of them: Bill Garren, a police detective on the Pawnshop Detail. The other was a small blond youth all flossy in pleated pants, short, square-shouldered coat, and patent-leather shoes with fawn spats to match his hat and gloves. His face wore a sullen pout. He didn't seem to like being with Garren.

"What are you up to around here?" the detective hailed me.

"The Toplin doings for the insurance company," I explained.

"Getting anywhere?" he wanted to know.

"About ready to make a pinch," I said, not altogether in earnest and not altogether joking.

"The more the merrier," he grinned. "I've already made mine," nodding at the dressy youth. "Come on upstairs with us."

The three of us got into the elevator and Ambrose carried us to the fifth floor. Before pressing the Toplin bell, Garren gave me what he had.

"This lad tried to soak a ring in a Third Street shop a little while ago—an emerald and diamond ring that looks like one of the Toplin lot. He's doing the clam now; he hasn't said a word—yet. I'm going to show him to these people; then I'm going to take him down to the Hall of Justice and get words out of him—words that fit together in nice sentences and everything!"

The prisoner looked sullenly at the floor and paid no attention to this threat. Garren rang the bell and the maid Hilda opened the door. Her eyes widened when she saw the dressy boy, but she didn't say anything as she led us into the sitting-room, where Mrs. Toplin and her daughter were. They looked up at us.

"Hello, Jack!" Phyllis greeted the prisoner.

"'Lo, Phyl," he mumbled, not looking at her.

"Among friends, huh? Well, what's the answer?" Garren demanded of the girl.

She put her chin in the air and although her face turned red, she looked haughtily at the police detective.

"Would you mind removing your hat?" she asked.

Bill isn't a bad bimbo, but he hasn't any meekness. He answered her by tilting his hat over one eye and turning to her mother.

"Ever seen this lad before?"

"Why, certainly!" Mrs. Toplin exclaimed. "That's Mr. Wagener who lives upstairs."

"Well," said Bill, "Mr. Wagener was picked up in a hock shop trying to get rid of this ring." He fished a gaudy green and white ring from his pocket. "Know it?"

"Certainly!" Mrs. Toplin said, looking at the ring. "It belongs to Phyllis, and the robber—" Her mouth dropped open as she began to understand. "How could Mr. Wagener—?"

"Yes, how?" Bill repeated.

The girl stepped between Garren and me, turning her back on him to face me. "I can explain everything," she announced.

That sounded too much like a movie subtitle to be very promising, but—

"Go ahead," I encouraged her.

"I found that ring in the passageway near the front door after the excitement was over. The robber must have dropped it. I didn't say anything to Papa and Mamma about it, because I thought nobody would ever know the difference, and it was insured, so I thought I might as well sell it and be in that much money. I asked Jack last night if he could sell it for me and he said he knew just how to go about it. He didn't have anything to do with it outside of that, but I did think he'd have sense enough not to try to pawn it right away!"

She looked scornfully at her accomplice.

"See what you've done!" she accused him.

He fidgeted and pouted at his feet.

"Ha! Ha! Ha!" Bill Garren said sourly. "That's a nifty! Did you ever hear the one about the two Irishmen that got in the Y.W.C.A. by mistake?"

She didn't say whether she had heard it or not.

"Mrs. Toplin," I asked, "making allowances for the different clothes and the unshaven face, could this lad have been the robber?"

She shook her head with emphasis. "No! He could not!"

"Set your prize down, Bill," I suggested, "and let's go over in a corner and whisper things at each other."

"Right."

He dragged a heavy chair to the center of the floor, sat Wagener on it, anchored him there with handcuffs—not exactly necessary, but Bill was grouchy at not getting his prisoner identified as the robber—and then he and I stepped out into the passageway. We could keep an eye on the sitting-room from there without having our low-voiced conversation overheard.

"This is simple," I whispered into his big red ear. "There are only five ways to figure the lay. First: Wagener stole the stuff for the Toplins. Second: the Toplins framed the robbery themselves and got Wagener to peddle it. Third: Wagener and the girl engineered the deal without the old folks being in on it. Fourth: Wagener pulled it on his own hook and the girl is covering him up. Fifth: she told us the truth. None of them explains why your little playmate should have been dumb enough to flash the ring downtown this morning, but that can't be explained by any system. Which of the five do you favor?"

"I like 'em all," he grumbled. "But what I like most is that I've got this baby right—got him trying to pass a hot ring. That suits me fine. You do the guessing. I don't ask for anymore than I've got."

"It doesn't irritate me any either," I agreed. "The way it stands the insurance company can welsh on the policies—but I'd like to smoke it out a little further, far enough to put away anybody who has been trying to run a hooligan on the North American. We'll clean up all we can on this kid, stow him in the can, and then see what further damage we can do."

"All right," Garren said. "Suppose you get hold of the janitor and that Eveleth woman while I'm showing the boy to old man Toplin and getting the maid's opinion."

I nodded and went out into the corridor, leaving the door unlocked behind me. I took the elevator to the seventh floor and told Ambrose to get hold of McBirney and send him to the Toplins' apartment. Then I rang Blanche Eveleth's bell.

"Can you come downstairs for a minute or

two?" I asked her. "We've a prize who might be your friend of last night."

"Will I?" She started toward the stairs with me. "And if he's the right one, can I pay him back for my battered beauty?"

"You can," I promised. "Go as far as you like, so you don't maul him too badly to stand trial."

I took her into the Toplins' apartment without ringing the bell, and found everybody in Frank Toplin's bedroom. A look at Garren's glum face told me that neither the old man nor the maid had given him a nod on the prisoner.

I put the finger on Jack Wagener. Disappointment came into Blanche Eveleth's eyes. "You're wrong," she said. "That's not he."

Garren scowled at her. It was a pipe that if the Toplins were tied up with young Wagener, they wouldn't identify him as the robber. Bill had been counting on that identification coming from the two outsiders—Blanche Eveleth and the janitor—and now one of them had flopped.

The other one rang the bell just then and the maid brought him in.

I pointed at Jack Wagener, who stood beside Garren staring sullenly at the floor.

"Know him, McBirney?"

"Yeah, Mr. Wagener's son, Jack."

"Is he the man who shooed you away with a gun last night?"

McBirney's watery eyes popped in surprise.

"No," he said with decision, and began to look doubtful.

"In an old suit, cap pulled down, needing a shave—could it have been him?"

"No-o-o-o," the janitor drawled, "I don't think so, though it— You know, now that I come to think about it, there was something familiar about that fella, an' maybe— By cracky, I think maybe you're right—though I couldn't exactly say for sure."

"That'll do!" Garren grunted in disgust.

An identification of the sort the janitor was giving isn't worth a damn one way or the other. Even positive and immediate identifications aren't always the goods. A lot of people who don't know any better—and some who do, or

should—have given circumstantial evidence a bad name. It is misleading sometimes. But for genuine, undiluted, pre-war untrustworthiness, it can't come within gunshot of human testimony. Take any man you like—unless he is the one in a hundred thousand with a mind trained to keep things straight, and not always even then—get him excited, show him something, give him a few hours to think it over and talk it over, and then ask him about it. It's dollars to doughnuts that you'll have a hard time finding any connection between what he saw and what he says he saw. Like this McBirney—another hour and he'd be ready to gamble his life on Jack Wagener's being the robber.

Garren wrapped his fingers around the boy's arm and started for the door.

"Where to, Bill?" I asked.

"Up to talk to his people. Coming along?"

"Stick around a while," I invited. "I'm going to put on a party. But first, tell me, did the coppers who came here when the alarm was turned in do a good job?"

"I didn't see it," the police detective said. "I didn't get here until the fireworks were pretty well over, but I understand the boys did all that could be expected of them."

I turned to Frank Toplin. I did my talking to him chiefly because we—his wife and daughter, the maid, the janitor, Blanche Eveleth, Garren, and his prisoner, and I—were grouped around the old man's bed and by looking at him I could get a one-eyed view of everybody else.

"Somebody has been kidding me somewhere," I began my speech. "If all the things I've been told about this job are right, then so is Prohibition. Your stories don't fit together, not even almost. Take the bird who stuck you up. He seems to have been pretty well acquainted with your affairs. It might be luck that he hit your apartment at a time when all of your jewelry was on hand, instead of another apartment, or your apartment at another time. But I don't like luck. I'd rather figure that he knew what he was doing. He nicked you for your pretties, and then he galloped up to Miss Eveleth's apartment. He may have been about to go downstairs when he ran into McBirney, or he may not. Anyway, he went upstairs, into Miss Eveleth's apartment, looking for a fire escape. Funny, huh? He knew enough about the place to make a push-over out of the stick-up, but he didn't know there were no fire escapes on Miss Eveleth's side of the building.

"He didn't speak to you or to McBirney, but he talked to Miss Eveleth, in a bass voice. A very, very deep voice. Funny, huh? From Miss Eveleth's apartment he vanished with every exit watched. The police must have been here before he left her apartment and they would have blocked the outlets first thing, whether McBirney and Ambrose had already done that or not. But he got away. Funny, huh? He wore a wrinkled suit, which might have been taken from a bundle just before he went to work, and he was a small man. Miss Eveleth isn't a small woman, but she would be a small man. A guy with a suspicious disposition would almost think Blanche Eveleth was the robber."

Frank Toplin, his wife, young Wagener, the janitor, and the maid were gaping at me. Garren was sizing up the Eveleth girl with narrowed eyes, while she glared white-hot at me. Phyllis Toplin was looking at me with a contemptuous sort of pity for my feeble-mindedness.

Bill Garren finished his inspection of the girl and nodded slowly.

"She could get away with it," he gave his opinion, "indoors and if she kept her mouth shut."

"Exactly," I said.

"Exactly, my eye!" Phyllis Toplin exploded. "Do you two correspondence-school detectives think we wouldn't know the difference between a man and a woman dressed in man's clothes? He had a day or two's growth of hair on his face—real hair, if you know what I mean. Do you think he could have fooled us with false whiskers? This happened, you know, it's not in a play!"

The others stopped gaping, and heads bobbed up and down.

"Phyllis is right." Frank Toplin backed up his offspring. "He was a man—no woman dressed like one."

His wife, the maid, and the janitor nodded vigorous endorsements.

But I'm a bull-headed sort of bird when it comes to going where the evidence leads. I spun to face Blanche Eveleth.

"Can you add anything to the occasion?" I asked her.

She smiled very sweetly at me and shook her head.

"All right, bum," I said. "You're pinched. Let's go."

Then it seemed she could add something to the occasion. She had something to say, quite a few things to say, and they were all about me. They weren't nice things. In anger her voice was shrill, and just now she was madder than you'd think anybody could get on short notice. I was sorry for that. This job had run along peacefully and gently so far, hadn't been marred by any rough stuff, had been almost ladylike in every particular; and I had hoped it would go that way to the end. But the more she screamed at me the nastier she got. She didn't have any words I hadn't heard before, but she fitted them together in combinations that were new to me. I stood as much of it as I could.

Then I knocked her over with a punch in the mouth.

"Here! Here!" Bill Garren yelled, grabbing my arm.

"Save your strength, Bill," I advised him, shaking his hand off and going over to yank the Eveleth person up from the floor. "Your gallantry does you credit, but I think you'll find Blanche's real name is Tom, Dick, or Harry."

I hauled her (or him, whichever you like) to his or her feet and asked it: "Feel like telling us about it?"

For answer I got a snarl.

"All right," I said to the others, "in the absence of authoritative information I'll give you my dope. If Blanche Eveleth could have been the robber except for the beard and the difficulty of a woman passing for a man, why couldn't the robber have been Blanche Eveleth before and after the robbery by using a—what do you call it?—strong depilatory on his face, and a wig? It's hard for a woman to masquerade as a man, but there are lots of men who can get away with the feminine role. Couldn't this bird, after renting his apartment as Blanche Eveleth and getting everything lined up, have stayed in his apartment for a couple of days letting his beard grow? Come down and knock the job over? Beat it upstairs, get the hair off his face, and get into his female rig in, say, fifteen minutes? My guess is that he could. And he had fifteen minutes. I don't know about the smashed nose. Maybe he stumbled going up the stairs and had to twist his plans to account for it—or maybe he smacked himself intentionally."

My guesses weren't far off, though his name was Fred—Frederick Agnew Rudd. He was known in Toronto, having done a stretch in the Ontario Reformatory as a boy of nineteen, caught shoplifting in his she-make-up. He wouldn't come though, and we never turned up his gun or the blue suit, cap, and black gloves, although we found a cavity in his mattress where he had stuffed them out of the police's sight until later that night, when he could get rid of them. But the Toplin sparklers came to light piece by piece when we had plumbers take apart the drains and radiators in apartment 702.

THE EPISODE OF THE *TORMENT IV*

C. DALY KING

OF THE MERE SEVEN volumes of detective fiction that Charles Daly King (1895–1963) produced in his lifetime, his undoubted masterpiece is the short-story collection *The Curious Mr. Tarrant*. Although King was an American, the book was first published in England in 1935 and was among the rarest mystery books of the twentieth century until Dover issued the first American edition as a paperback in 1977.

Because of their uneven nature and occasional long, boring passages, King's novels are not often read today, despite the ingenuity of their plotting. In *Obelists at Sea* (1932), four psychologists, each a specialist in a different area of study, investigate a murder from their perspective and knowledge; all are proved wrong. In *Arrogant Alibi* (1938), the nine suspects for two murders all have impeccable, unshakable alibis. Trevis Tarrant, the amateur detective in the eponymous story collection, is a wealthy, cultured gentleman of leisure who believes in cause and effect; they "rule the world," he says. He takes it on himself to explain locked-room mysteries and impossible crimes that involve such improbabilities as mysterious footsteps by an invisible entity heard even in broad daylight, horrible images of a hanged man haunting a modern house, headless corpses found on a heavily traveled highway, as well as dealing with apparent ghosts and other supernormal happenings. It entertains him to bring his gift of being able to see things clearly and solve mysteries by the use of inarguable logic. He is accompanied at all times by his valet, Katoh, a Japanese doctor and spy.

"The Episode of the *Torment IV*" was first published in *The Curious Mr. Tarrant* (London, Collins, 1935).

THE EPISODE OF THE TORMENT IV

C. DALY KING

Characters of the Episode

JERRY PHELAN, the narrator
VALERIE PHELAN, his wife
MORGAN WHITE, their host
LESTER BLACK, a neighbour
AMELIE BLACK, his wife
JULIE BLACK, their daughter
TOM CONSTABLE, Black's cousin
TOM CONSTABLE, JUN., his son
MARGARET CONSTABLE, his widow
JIM DUFF, hired man
TREVIS TARRANT, interested in puzzles

W E   W E R E driving straight towards horror. Though we didn't know it yet.

Valerie said, "Dar*ling,* I do hope Trevis's friend has a decent place. I want a big room, with blinds to make it dim, and none of those awful New Hampshire spiders. And I want a nice, long bath."

"Oh, I guess his place is all right. Nothing much any one can do about New Hampshire spiders, though; they're big and nasty. But there won't be any in our room. The fellow probably has a good enough shack. Why shouldn't he?"

"Ugh! . . . Spiders." Valerie grimaced. "Yes, I suppose it'll be a good house. Trevis is rather tasteful about places himself."

We were motoring down from Canada and had arranged to pick up Tarrant at Winnespequam Lake where he had been staying with a friend named Morgan White, whom neither Valerie nor I had met. Tarrant planned to come along with us to New York a couple of days later, for White had been good enough to write, asking us to break our trip at his place for a day or so. We had gotten well along now, had passed Lancaster and were scooting through the Crawford Notch as fast as we could. It was as hot as blazes.

I said, "Another hour and a half will get us there. Then a swim, before anything else. I feel like a strip of wilted cardboard."

"I want a nice, long bath," Valerie repeated.

Ahead of us a small truck and a touring car loaded with about eighteen sweating travellers in their shirt sleeves were creeping along the hot asphalt through the centre of the valley. I gave the horn some lusty digs and we swerved past them.

And that, though we didn't know it, either, was our introduction to the episode of *Torment IV.*

"The most intriguing problem I have ever heard of," said Tarrant, "is the mystery of the *Mary Celeste.* It is practically perfect."

As he spoke, he leaned back in the hammock chair an the moonlight glinted through dusk against the sharp lines of his lean, strong face. Across the water came the twinkle of little twin lights, red and green, where a motor-boat, a mere shadow on the darkening lake, put out from the opposite shore.

Valerie and I had arrived, hot and tired, about five in the afternoon. And I had had a most refreshing swim. Winnespequam, as a good many people know, is a New Hampshire lake. It is typical. Surrounded by hills, it has gathered around itself an almost unbroken line of the estates of prosperous merchants and professional men whose winter homes are in New York and Philadelphia. Some of the natives, too, boast modest bungalows nestling near the water, to which they repair during the summer months from their more permanent quarters in the little town that runs down to the northern tip of the lake. Even the motor highway that circles the shore travels chiefly between forested slopes and does little to disfigure the scene. It is a pleasant and carefree resort.

White, a big man and a good host, grunted, "Don't know it. I'm sure you do. What's the *Mary Celeste*?"

"You don't know the *Mary Celeste*?" Tarrant was plainly surprised. "Why, it's the perfect problem of all time. Dozens of people have had a whack at it, including some fairly clever ones, but it remains to-day as unsolved and apparently insoluble as it was sixty years ago."

He paused; then, as we were all quiet, obviously waiting for further information, he went on again. "The *Mary Celeste*, sometimes wrongly called the *Marie Celeste*, was a two-hundred-ton brig owned by an American called Winchester. She was picked up by the barque *Dei Gratia* one pleasant afternoon early in December, 1872, about three hundred miles west of Gibraltar. This was what was wrong about her: there was not a soul on board and she was sailing derelict on the starboard tack against a north wind that was driving her off her course. Her chronometer, her manifest, bills of lading and register were missing. A further examination showed that a cutlass hanging in her cabin bore stains as if blood had been wiped from it; but a medical officer in Gibraltar, who subsequently analysed these stains, declared that they

were not of blood. There was a deep cut in her rail, as if made by an axe; but no axe has been mentioned as having been found aboard. On both sides of the bows a small strip, a little more than an inch wide and six or seven feet long had recently been cut from her outer planking a few feet above the water line; this strip was only about three-eighths of an inch deep and had no effect upon her seaworthiness. Her log had been written up to the evening of the twelfth day previous and the slate log carried to eight a.m. of the eleventh day before. In other words the log was not up-to-date.

"But what was right about her was more astonishing. In the galley were the remains of a burnt-out fire above which stood the victuals for the crew's breakfast. Some of their clothes were hanging upon a line to dry and their effects were in good order and undisturbed. In the master's cabin breakfast had been partly eaten; some porridge was left in a bowl and an egg had been cut open and left standing in its holder. A bottle of cough mixture had been left on the table, its cork beside it. An harmonium stood in one corner and in a sewing machine was a child's garment, partly sewed. None of these articles were in any way disturbed. In the first mate's quarters, moreover, was found a piece of paper with an unfinished sum upon it, just as he had put it aside when interrupted. For the eleven days during which the log had not been kept, the weather over the course from which the point last noted in the log to the position where the *Mary Celeste* was found, had been mild. The cargo, some casks of alcohol for Genoa, was intact and securely stowed. The boat itself was staunch in all respects, hull, masts, and rigging. There was no sign whatsoever of fire or other hazard. And last of all, the single small boat with which the brig was equipped, was upon its davits, untouched, and properly secured.

"Those are the essential facts, as evidenced by many and reliable witnesses. They make a very pretty problem. . . . Of course, a good many hypotheses have been advanced. But actually not one of them is even as easy to credit as the curious state of affairs that was discovered when the *Mary Celeste* was boarded that December afternoon. . . . What could possibly have happened to make a competent crew, not to mention the captain's wife and small daughter, abandon a perfectly sound ship in fine weather, without so much as attempting to launch her boat? . . . "

There was a little silence.

"Match your mystery," White grunted. "Right here."

Tarrant twisted round in his chair. "Yes? I think you would be put to it to find another enigma with such simple and such contradictory factors."

"Judge for yourself," said our host. . . . "The Blacks. That big place just across the lake is theirs. Closed up now. They had the *Torment IV* and they were——"

Struck by his unusual expression, I interrupted. "What in heaven's name is a torment four?" I asked. "How do you mean they had it?"

"Oh, no mystery there," he assured us. "That is the name of their motor-boat. Blacks have been coming up here for years, and a good many years ago now they got their first boat. Just when steam launches were going out and gas engines coming in. Wasn't much of a boat; jerky and spasmodic, and among other essentials it lacked a self-starter. A fairly thorough nuisance, and they named it, quite properly, *Torment*.

"Presently they got another; though the second one had a self-starter it was just one more thing to be spasmodic and *Torment II* was a good name for that one also. The third was much better, really a proper boat, but by that time the name had become traditional. *Torment III* was turned in only a year ago and the new one, *Torment IV*, is a beauty; long, fast, polished up like a new dime. I was out in her early this summer; I remember at the time that *Torment* seemed a foolish title for such a beautiful piece of machinery, but now—well, I don't know."

He paused, and, "Yes, but what happened?" asked Valerie.

"All killed. Lester Black and his wife, Amelie, and their small daughter. Just like your captain and his family."

"I didn't say the captain had been killed." Tarrant's reservation came softly across from the railing.

"Touch," said White. "Wrong myself. They're dead; at least two of 'em are. Said they were killed, but I don't even know that. No one knows what actually happened to them."

The voice from the railing was plainly interested now. "Come on, Morgan, what did happen?"

"I tell you I don't know. It was really extraordinary. . . . Well, here's the story. Blacks came up early this year and so did I. It occurred about the end of June; hot spell then, if you remember, and we got it here, too. It was a beautiful, bright day and very warm for that time of year. Middle of the afternoon, *Torment IV* ran ashore a little way up the lake from here; that was the first we knew anything was wrong.

"Let me take your method and tell you want was right about her first. To begin with, her keel was hardly scratched and that came from her grounding, which happened by good luck on a strip of sand. Later, when the affair turned into a tragedy, I went over her carefully with the sheriff and there wasn't another mark or dent of any kind on her. Engine, transmission, and so on, in perfect condition—ran her back to the Blacks' dock myself after we found her. Have to tell you the cushions and pillows on the after-deck are life preservers in themselves, filled with some kind of stuff that will keep you afloat if necessary. Not one of 'em had been disturbed in any way; all present and accounted for. Not a leak, not a single miss from the motor—nothing.

"In fact, only two items were wrong. First, one of the chairs on the afterdeck was overturned; might have happened when she ran ashore. Second, no one was in her. I know, for I saw the boat a hundred yards or so off land and watched her bump. . . . That's all."

Tarrant threw the remains of his cigar in a wide arc and, three seconds later, came a tiny *phizz* as it struck the water below. "You mean these three people simply vanished?" he demanded. "How do you know they even went out in the boat in the first place?"

"Found that out when I took the boat back. They had gone out after lunch, apparently for a joy ride. And they were drowned somewhere in the middle of the lake—two of the bodies were recovered later, Black's and his wife's, not the child's—but how or why is a complete mystery."

"But in the middle of a bright after-noon——" Tarrant began. "There were no witnesses at all? No one saw them?"

"Well, they went up to the town dock at the end of the lake and got some gas; that was established. Then they headed out again—Lester Black was running the boat—and that is the last any one saw of them. Of course, end of June, not many people around the lake, still a bit early for the summer people. Just the same it *is* strange. Inquiries were made all around the lake, of course, but no one was found to throw even a glimmer on the thing."

"H'm," remarked Tarrant. "There was no obvious cause, I suppose? No trouble, financial or otherwise? An estrangement between hus-band and wife, something serious?"

"Not a chance," White grunted. "I wasn't an intimate friend but I've known them for years. Man had plenty of money, lived a leisurely life, great family man, as a matter of fact. Very fond of his wife and daughter and they of him. Last thing in the world he would do, kill them and drown himself, if you've anything like that in your head."

Tarrant, meantime, had lit a cigarette and now smoked silently for some minutes. Finally he spoke. "Still, something like that is all you leave, if your other facts are right, isn't it? Peo-ple don't jump out of a perfectly good motor-boat in the middle of a lake for nothing. Could they swim?"

"They could all swim, though probably none of them would have been good for a mile or more. And I've told you about the life preserv-ers, every one of them in the boat. We made a careful check of that, naturally."

"Well, there you are. The more you say, the more it appears to have been a purpose-ful performance. . . . There are lots of things in people's lives that are kept pretty well hid-den. . . . What happened to the boat?"

"I don't believe there was a thing in Lester Black's life that would account for that kind of tragedy," our host insisted. "Prosaic man, pro-saic as hell. The boat was inherited by the Con-stables, cousins of the Blacks. Live next them up here, down the road a bit. They didn't use the boat for some time; didn't care to, I guess. Lately they've been taking her out once in a while. Boat's really too good to throw away."

Again there came a pause, but just as I was about to enter an opinion, Tarrant summed the matter up. "Let's see; here it is, then. Black took his wife and daughter out for a spin on a nice, clear day. First they went to the village dock and bought gas. Then they turned out into the lake once more. From the time when they left the village—— By the way, when was that?"

"Between two and two thirty."

"And when did the boat come ashore?"

"Just about four o'clock."

"Then some time during that hour and a half the man and his wife went overboard and doubt-less the child, too. There is no way, apparently, of fixing it closer than that?"

"No, none. Boat may have come ashore directly they were out of it or it may have cruised around for an hour or more. No one noticed it."

"The boat was entirely unharmed and, in any event, they would not have abandoned it ordinarily in the middle of the lake without the precaution of providing themselves with the life preservers so readily at hand. I'm sure there was no fire or you would have mentioned it."

"Absolutely not," White declared. "Not a trace of anything like fire. Anyhow, since it obviously didn't burn up, they would have had plenty of time to throw over *all* the preservers in that case."

I had a sudden thought. "How about some sort of fumes from the engine that might have affected all of them at once so that they were forced to jump without waiting for anything?"

White merely grunted and Tarrant's tone was quizzical. "Hardly, Jerry. In an open boat proceeding at a fair speed no fumes would get much of a chance to affect the passengers. And some mysterious poison fumes that would make them jump instantly are simply incredible. If the engine burned ordinary gas, as it did, carbon monoxide is all that could possibly come off. So that if we grant the impossible and assume that it came through the floor instead of going out the exhaust—and then stayed near the deck—the result would surely have been to asphyxiate the people, certainly not to throw them overboard. . . . No, that's out.

"There remain, of course, several alternatives," he continued. "The first is that Black threw his wife and daughter out and followed them as a suicide. That's the one you don't care for, Morgan."

"Can't see it at all. Silly."

"There are a number of reasons to account for such an action. A bitter quarrel is only one of them. There is temporary aberration, followed by remorse, for example."

"Nonsense. Still silly. You didn't know Black."

"All right, we'll reverse it. The wife hits the man over the head while he is running the boat, throws him out and then follows *him* with the child. The aberration theory fits a woman better than a man, anyhow; they are more highly strung. How about that?"

"Trevis, come off it." White seemed almost provoked by the last notion. "Aside from Amelie's being incapable of such a thing psychologically, I'll tell you why it's absurd. She was a little woman, much smaller than Black. She couldn't possibly have tossed him out *unless* she hit him first. And he hadn't been hit. The autopsies showed that neither of them had a single mark of violence on them."

Undoubtedly Tarrant was smiling in the darkness as he said, "Very well, we'll leave that theory entirely. I was only thinking abstractly, you know; no reflections intended. . . . Then we are left with one more hypothesis, the accident one."

"Ugh."

"Perhaps it's the most reasonable of all, anyhow. The child falls overboard, the mother jumps to save it, the father, who is running the boat, is the last to act. He jumps to save them both, and they are all drowned, while the boat, which in the excitement he has failed to close off, speeds away."

White answered at once. "Won't do, either. Naturally, we've been over that possibility up here. There is not merely one, but three or four points, against it. Altogether too many. As I said, they all knew how to swim and the daughter was about ten, not helpless in the water by any means, even with her clothes on. In the second place, the Blacks have been aquaplaning for years, and aquaplaning behind a fast boat is no joke. Matter of fact, not even aquaplaning; they did it on water skis, much harder. The point is, if any one had fallen over, they would naturally have followed what they have done so often when there was a spill off the skis; swung the boat about and come up to the swimmer. They were used to doing that; they could do it quickly; it was a habit. They were all used to the water, to being on it and in it; couldn't possibly have lost their heads completely over a mere tumble.

"But last and most impressive of all, I tell you that Black was a prosaic and methodical man, known for it. Supposing some real emergency— though what it could have been, God knows— supposing the wife did jump and he prepared to go after her. He would never have left his boat empty without shutting off the motor, it doesn't take an instant. Granting even that impossibility, however, it is simply beyond belief that he would have jumped to their rescue himself before throwing them at least a couple of preservers, which would reach them more quickly than he and be of as much use. You must remember that they weren't at all helpless in the water, either of them. He would surely have done that first. Then, I grant you, he *might* have gone in, just to make sure. But the theory you built won't do. . . . No, it won't. . . . Really."

"The objections are strong," Tarrant acknowledged. "Of course, I didn't know the people at all. . . . Well, that's the end of the list, so far as I can see now. You discard them all; the first as being impossible on grounds of character, the second on physical grounds, the third on grounds of habit and familiarity with the water and its hazards. I——"

For the first time during the discussion Valerie interrupted. She had been sitting quietly beyond Tarrant and smoking while the talk went on. Now she said, "May I suggest something? Perhaps it's pretty wild. . . . What about this? The parents had received some kind of threat, kidnapping or something. No, this is better. They were hailed from the shore while they were riding about and they landed. There the child actually *was* kidnapped. The parents were stricken with grief, they were quite out of their heads for a time. They went out on the lake again and presently made a suicide pact and both honoured it at once. That covers it all, doesn't it? The child's body, I understood, hasn't been found."

Tarrant's chair creaked as he turned towards her and a match, flaring in his hand, showed his surprised and interested expression. "Valerie," he said, "you have constructed the best theory yet. Really, that's very good. It covers all the facts of the case except one. So I'm afraid it won't work, but I can see that you and I are going to get on famously. It's too bad you have forgotten that one little point. Black was a well-to-do man. Kidnapping is done for ransom; and surely he would have paid a ransom as an alternative to his wife's and his own suicide. It is unreasonable to suppose that even a week's separation would cause him to choose so absurdly. The only possibility would be that the child was taken by some enemy for revenge and no return intended. That's too much like a bad shocker; I'm afraid it won't do. . . . It was a good try, though."

He rose and stretched. "I'm going to take a stroll for a bit and then turn in early. I imagine Valerie and Jerry would like to, too, after their ride." He turned and wandered slowly down the verandah.

"So you give it up?" White called after him. "No answer?"

"No. All the first answers are washed out. I'll grant you this, though, Morgan. You have a very good replica of the *Mary Celeste;* all the essential items are there. It's a problem all right; I'm not through thinking about it yet."

The matter remained in this state of suspense while we were sitting about the following morning after breakfast. The day was bright and clear but gave promise of becoming even hotter than the previous one; I was distinctly glad that Valerie and I were not to be touring the roads again.

A half-hour or so later Morgan White made the suggestion that we try his tennis court, since if we delayed much longer it might well become too uncomfortable for playing. Every one was agreeable and we trouped down to the court, which turned out to be of clay in excellent condition. "Jim Duff, the Constable's hired man, rolls it for me every other morning before he goes up to their place," White confided.

We proceeded to enjoy the fruits of Duff's labours. After several sets it was getting considerably hotter and Valerie voted for doubles. We won, though I am not at all sure it was due entirely to our play; during the second and last set I, for one, was beginning to feel a touch weary.

Every one agreed, at the conclusion of that set, that swimming was the form of exercise now indicated. All of us except Val were dripping. In fifteen minutes or less we had reassembled at White's boathouse in bathing suits and stood smoking a final cigarette along the little platform by the side of the boathouse proper that covers his *Grey Falcon.* I remarked upon the diving-board protruding over the water at the platform's end and White assured us all that the lake here was seven or eight feet deep, so that diving was feasible. The afternoon before I had simply jumped off the end of his dock.

"I think I'll be trying it," I informed the rest, just as White turned to Tarrant and pointed out over the water.

"There, see that boat?" he said. "About two-thirds across the lake, heading north. That's *Tor-*

ment IV, the one we were discussing last night. Wait till I get my glasses from the boathouse and you can have a good look at her, Trevis."

He unlocked the boathouse door and disappeared inside, returning at once with a pair of binoculars which he handed over. At the moment, however, I was more interested in getting wet than seeing a motor-boat. Valerie was already in the water, shouting that it was perfect and calling the rest of us sissies. "You look," I told Tarrant. "I'm for a dive." White apparently felt the same way, for upon turning the glasses over to his friend, he immediately took a header into the lake.

Thus it happened that the first intimation of excitement reached me in mid-air. I had struck the end of the board hard and it threw me high. At the top of the spring I was just touching my feet for a jack-knife when Tarrant's shout came to me. "Morgan! Morgan, come here! Hurry! We must get your——" Swish into the water went my head and his words were cut off; but on the way I got an upside-down view of Tarrant holding the binoculars steadily to his eyes, his mouth suddenly grim as he called out.

Under the water I twisted back towards the dock and, reaching an arm over the platform above me, pulled myself partway up. "What ho?" I demanded.

White was already clambering up and Tarrant disappearing through the door. "The boat," he called after him. "Hurry up! How fast can we get her out?"

Tarrant's calm is proverbial, but when he wants to, he can certainly work quickly. By the time I got inside he had the slide-door at the end almost up and White, dropping into the driving seat of the *Grey Falcon,* was pushing the starter-button. "All clear," called Tarrant; the rat-tat-tat of the motor fell to a grind as the clutch went into reverse. Just as the boat began to back out, Valerie jumped down into the rear deck.

We came around in a wide circle and headed out into the lake, the motor coughing a little as it was opened full without any preliminary warning. Tarrant said, "They jumped. You'll have another tragedy unless we can get there in time."

"*What is* this about?" cried Valerie. "Who jumped where? Have you boys all gone crazy?" Valerie has noticed, I think, that men of Tarrant's age rather like to have her call them boys.

His voice was unpleasantly serious as he answered. "The people in that boat I was watching, this *Torment* of yours, Morgan. There were two people in her, a big man and a little one, or maybe a man and a boy——"

"Tom Constable and junior, his son, undoubtedly," White put in, without turning his head.

"Suddenly the man who was driving scrambled out of his seat and into the rear deck, where the boy was riding. He grabbed the boy's arm and immediately jumped overboard, pulling the boy with him. . . . Here, Morgan, don't follow the boat! There's no one in it. The place where they went out is almost on a direct line between your boat and that big rock on the other shore."

All of us except White were on our feet looking helplessly across the water to where, a good two miles away now, *Torment IV* was still speeding up the lake with her bow waves curving high on both sides. It gave me a queer feeling, that boat which I could just see was empty (now that I had been told), driving along as if operated by an invisible pilot. The sun was burning down, making such a glare on the lake that it was impossible to discern any small object on the surface. Such as a man's head, for example. Tarrant had the binoculars (being Tarrant, of course, he had not failed to bring them) held to his eyes with one hand, attempting to shade their glasses with the other.

"Have you got her at top speed, Morgan?" he demanded. "Best part of a mile yet to go, as I judge it."

"Everything she's got," grunted White. "Full out. Check my direction if you see anything."

"Thought I saw them a minute ago. Right together. Lost them now."

"Not good swimmers. Nowhere nearly as good as the Blacks. Doubt if they can stay up long enough."

"Oh," said Valerie, and sat down abruptly, her rubber bathing trunks making a squdging sound on a cushion. "Hurry, Mr. White. Oh, hurry!"

White said, "Agh!"

"Lost 'em," Tarrant announced definitely. "Not a sign."

Nor was there a sign when, some minutes later, we came up to the spot where, as closely as Tarrant was able to guess, the thing had happened. For five or ten minutes we floated, with the motor cut off, peering over the sides and in all directions around the *Grey Falcon*. Nothing but the calm, bright water of Winnespequam, ruffled by the lightest of breezes, met our gaze. Valerie, too, searched with the rest of us, although I could see from her expression that she wasn't very anxious to discover anything. "Of course," Tarrant pointed out, "I can't be positive as to the spot. The line is right, but the exact distance from your boathouse, Morgan, is another thing."

We began to circle slowly, in wider and wider courses.

"Any use diving?" I asked, having some vague notion that these people could possibly be brought up and resuscitated.

"No good. Deep here; take a deep-sea diver to fetch bottom. Besides, we don't know where they went down. Even if the line is right, they may have swum some distance in any direction before they gave out. . . . Not to the shore, though. They never made that."

Our search went on. But though we circled over a large area for more than two hours, not a trace did we find either of the man or of the boy. Finally, "Nothing more we can do," said White gloomily. "They sink in this lake. Didn't recover the others for three days. . . . Might as well run up towards Winnespequam and see what happened to the boat." He turned the wheel and we headed north.

Scarcely had we gone a mile when on the shore off our starboard side we saw a knot of persons gathered at the edge of the lake; and a little distance from them, what was obviously the boat we sought. I wondered, as we approached, at the unmistakable signs of excitement evidenced by the small group, for surely *Torment IV* must have grounded here nearly two hours previously. We landed a hundred yards to the south at a disused and ramshackle dock, and made our way to the scene. An old man passed us as we drew near; he was hobbling along, shaking his head, and his mumbling reached us clearly enough—"'Tis bewitched, she be a devil's boat."

It took us some time to discover, from the excited replies of the people we came up with, that yet a further tragedy had occurred. They interrupted each other and told the story backwards rather than forwards, but at last we pieced together the following account.

Torment IV, after the affair that Tarrant had witnessed, had run ashore upon a small island so close to the town wharf that she had been seen by numerous loungers. Among these was Jim Duff, in the village on an errand, and he had at once procured another boat and been taken out to salvage that of the Constable's. The latter seemed, at any rate, to possess her own luck, for neither in running afoul of the island nor in her present landing had she suffered much harm. Duff had put himself aboard and, finding all in good order, had set off towards the Constable's dock alone, after expressing his fears to his companions that some ill must have befallen his employers.

The story then passed to four fishermen who, having been almost where we now stood, had witnessed the sequel. Duff, they asserted, had been passing not far from shore on his way south when, without any evident cause, he leapt from the seat he occupied and dived overboard. No doubt he twisted the wheel as he jumped away, for *Torment IV* turned and headed in. Two of the fishermen, however, seeing their friend struggling in the water, had immediately put out in their row-boat and gone to his rescue. Duff was a strong swimmer, accustomed to the lake since boyhood, but to their astonishment, no sooner did he note their approach than he turned and, in place of coming ashore, swam out into the lake with every appearance of panic. They were still some distance away from him when this happened and, though they made all possible efforts to overtake the man, he had sunk three times before they reached him, and he had drowned.

Nevertheless, after much exertion they had been able to recover his body.

For the first time we noticed a still form, covered by one of the fisherman's blankets, lying farther up the bank among the trees.

"Have you tried resuscitation?" asked Tarrant sharply.

"More'n an hour an' a half we tried," he was told. "He be dead, he be."

White and Tarrant walked over to the body and, after sending Valerie back to the *Grey Falcon*, I followed. When I arrived, they had drawn back the blanket and were looking at the corpse. It was not a pleasant sight. I have been led to believe that persons who have drowned wear a peaceful expression but this one assuredly did not. He was a man of about forty-eight or fifty, a native New Hampshireman, bony and obviously strong. But on his face there was stamped a hideous grimace, an expression so obviously of extreme horror that it would have been essentially identical on any cast of features.

With a grunt Morgan quietly replaced the blanket. "That's him, all right; that's Jim Duff."

When we returned to the shoreline, arrangements were being made to tow *Torment IV* back to the Constable's dock. No one seemed anxious to pilot her, and I noted a bit absently that our host did not volunteer his services this time, however willing he may have been on the first occasion he had told us about. Once more in the *Grey Falcon*, we backed out on the water and steered for home. A subdued party. It was Tarrant who broke the silence after it had continued to several minutes.

"No use trying to avoid the subject," he said. "We're all thinking about it. . . . If what I saw earlier, and what has just happened here, isn't due to some form of insanity arising with the utmost suddenness, God knows what it may be."

Silence again.

White spoke this time, gruffly. "How can a boat drive people insane? Certainly not a hard-boiled old-timer like Duff."

"Could it, could it be sunstroke?" Valerie asked in a small voice. "It's awfully hot."

Tarrant admitted, "There's no question it's hot. But I don't see a sunstroke theory. None of us feel any symptoms, do we? And we have been on the lake longer than any of them were."

"But what *can* have made them do it?"

"I don't know," said Tarrant in a low tone. "I confess I don't know. . . . At first I felt that some deep cause for suicide must be operating in the Black-Constable family. What I saw surely looked like nothing so much as a determined suicide combined with murder, or perhaps a double suicide. . . . But that's out now, definitely. This man Duff could hardly be involved in such a thing and, furthermore, I don't believe for a moment that he had the least idea of doing away with himself when he started that boat down the lake."

No one had even a conjecture to add. The rest of our return was only the purring of the engine and the slap-slither of the little waves against our boat. As for me, I was completely bewildered. Here were a succession of calamities; first three persons, then two, finally one, who for no reason at all had abruptly cast themselves into the lake to drown. The last two tragedies had been amply witnessed, one by Tarrant himself through the binoculars, the other by no less than four fishermen, friends of the unfortunate man, and this time at a reasonably short range.

One must suppose, at all events, that the first disaster had been similar to its successors, a finding that scarcely did much to account for any of them. The last victim's relations with the others had certainly not been of a nature so serious as to form a bond of death. What could possibly have caused such different types of people, in broad daylight, on this peaceful lake, and plainly menaced by no danger, to jump and die? Duff's reported actions, surely, appeared to indicate that, once out of the boat, he was determined to drown. Suicide seemed absurd; and yet his actions had comported with it. Both sight and sound—for his friends had shouted at him—had combined to assure him that help was close at hand. But he had renounced all aid. Involuntarily I shook my head. It just didn't make sense.

When we landed, Tarrant made an abrupt excuse and hurried off to the house in his bathing suit. Apparently he changed with some speed, for he was nowhere to be found when the rest of us climbed the path.

He was late for dinner. We were half-way through the main course when he came in and sat down at the table. "Glad you didn't wait for me," he said, a little absently. On his forehead there still lingered the trace of the frown that always accompanies his most strenuous thinking.

"Didn't know whether you'd show up or not," White remarked in explanation. "Where have you been?"

"Looking over that boat."

"Thought so. Find anything?"

"Not a thing," answered Tarrant frankly. "That is, if you mean, as I take it you do, anything that throws light on these strange deaths."

For a time he applied himself to his meal, but when he had caught up with us at its end, he pushed back his chair and addressed us. "I examined this *Torment IV* from stem to stern. She is a beautiful boat, Morgan, no doubt about it; and she has gotten out of these mishaps herself with no more than a few dents in the bows. And a long gash coming back from the bow on one side where she careened off a rock when grounding on the island. It's above the water-line and scarcely an eighth of an inch deep. No real harm; but just another item resembling the *Mary Celeste*. You remember *she* had strips in her, running back from the bows, too. It's a strange coincidence how these circumstances match, even down to the condition of the boat—so far as a motor-boat *can* exhibit the same conditions as a two hundred-ton brig. . . ."

In the short pause I queried, "Still, that doesn't get us anywhere, does it?"

He agreed. "As you say. Even if we had reason to believe that the same causes were operating—since several of the same symptoms have appeared—we have no further clue, since we don't know what could have brought about the situation on the *Mary Celeste*. And of course we have no right to assume even similar causes; a hundred to one this is merely a superficial resemblance."

Came one of White's grunts. "Nothing at all, eh? Nothing? What were you looking for?"

"To tell you the truth," Tarrant confessed with a smile, "I'm afraid I was looking for some sort of mechanical arrangement. I don't know exactly what. Something along the lines of Jerry's idea of a poison gas, possibly. Since it obviously couldn't come from the motor in the routine way, I considered the possibility of a small, hidden tank concealed somewhere on board. With a blower or insufflator arrangement, of course. Although I have some knowledge of gases and have never heard of one having the observed effects, it is still possible. That would at least indicate malice, murder, in fact; and we should have a reasonable background for these events. Pretty far-fetched, I admit. You see to what conjectures I have been reduced by the apparently inexplicable data. . . . I have never cared much for supernatural explanations."

"Hmph. Why 'apparently' inexplicable? Looks actually inexplicable to me."

"Nothing," said Tarrant shortly, "is actually inexplicable. That is, if you credit Causation. I do. What is loosely called the 'inexplicable' is only the unexplained, certainly not the unexplainable. The term is quite literally a mere catchword for ignorance. That's our present relation to the deaths; we are still ignorant of their cause."

"Guess we'll have to remain so this time."

"Oh, no. After our experience to-day, it's a challenge I accept."

Something in his tone interested Valerie. She said, "I'm glad you won't give it up. But what else can you do now, if you have already examined the boat?"

"I've examined the boat. Thoroughly. I even had the floorboards up; I couldn't take the engine out but I did everything else. Had a boy go under her in the dock and he reported everything shipshape and just as it ought to be along the keel."

"Well, then," Val repeated, "what is left that you can do?"

Tarrant smiled. "Now I'm disappointed in you, Valerie. Surely that is obvious. There is something pretty drastic that happens to people in that boat. There is only one alternative left now. With Jerry's help I propose to find out to-morrow what it is that happens. When we know that, it may be possible for us to deal with it."

"Oh. Oh, I see. Of course. You're going out in the boat yourself." Val paused; and added suddenly, "Not with Jerry, you're not! No, I won't listen to it. I won't let Jerry go anywhere near the horrible thing!"

I expostulated. If Tarrant was willing to risk his neck, it seemed only fair that someone else should go with him. Morgan White offered to go immediately, but it appeared that Trevis preferred me for some reason.

"He won't have to go very near it, Valerie," Tarrant assured her. "I wouldn't myself permit him to come with me in the boat. I only want him to follow me at a respectful distance in the *Grey Falcon*, so that, if I jump over, he can pick me up. . . . There must be a reason why people jump."

In the end we persuaded her, though Tarrant did most of it. There are times when Valerie seems hardly to listen to *me*. He persuaded her not only to permit me to follow him but not to come along herself. As usual, he had his way.

We all went down to the boathouse after breakfast. White explained to me how to run his boat, which was simple enough; and Tarrant and I started off for the Constable's dock, leaving Valerie and our host behind. He agreed to run *Torment IV* up and down the lake opposite the boathouse, so that they could observe what happened, if anything.

On the way over, Tarrant produced the implements with which he had equipped the *Grey Falcon* earlier in the day—so as not to worry Val-

erie unnecessarily, he said. They made a curious collection. There was a shotgun and, somewhat redundantly, a rifle; an axe and a long rope with a lasso at its end completed his equipment.

Naturally my attention was caught by the firearms. "But what can we use those for?" I inquired curiously. "Is there some one to shoot at? But no, there wasn't any one in the boat except the people who jumped out of it, each time. And this morning you are going alone, aren't you?"

"I don't know. I'm going alone, yes. On the other hand, there is certainly villainy of some kind here, and where there is villainy, it has been my experience that there is usually a villain. . . . I'm glad it turned out a good, hot day again."

More puzzled than ever, I said, "We threw out the sunstroke theory, didn't we? What in heaven's name has a hot day got to do with it?"

"I don't know, Jerry, honestly I don't," Tarrant grinned. "I have the haziest notion about this thing, but it is much too vague for me to tell you. So far as I know, there are only two conditions leading up to these deaths, a ride in *Torment IV* and a bright, warm day. Since I want to see duplicated whatever happens, I am glad that both conditions are fulfilled."

There was no time for more, as we had now reached the Constable's dock. Tarrant, who had taken the precaution of donning his bathing trunks, landed and was admitted to the boathouse by a man who evidently had been waiting for him. After a short delay—no doubt he was making another examination of *Torment IV*—I heard him start the motor and, a moment later, the ill-omened motor-boat slid slowly out of its shelter.

The events that succeeded constituted a series of complete surprises for me, culminating in sheer amazement. He turned and headed the boat out into the lake, opening her up fairly wide, and I brought the *Grey Falcon* along in his wake as closely as I dared, constantly alert for any change of direction or other sudden action on his part. *Torment IV* had a driving seat stretching entirely across the centre of the boat, and my first surprise was to observe Tarrant clamber up on this and crouch there in a most uncomfortable position, as he manipulated the controls. Nothing further happened, however, and while continuing to watch carefully, I could not avoid wondering again for what purpose he had provided the weapons in my own craft.

I realised that it was foolish and yet I could think of no other type of explanation of the tragedies than a supernatural one. A ghost or ghoul? In broad daylight, on a motor-boat? Even so, a shotgun isn't of much use against a ghost. But of course that was nonsense, anyhow. Even the strange coincidence of sudden, self-destructive madness on the part of these diverse people in similar circumstances was better. And again, you can't shoot madness. The rope and the axe I abandoned hopelessly.

By now we had reached the centre of the lake and Tarrant motioned to me, without turning around, that he proposed to slow down. As I did so, too, I saw that he had produced a length of stout cord and was lashing *Torment IV*'s wheel in such a way that the boat would continue forward in a large circle.

When he had done so, he scrambled out of the driver's seat altogether and, passing right by the rear well-deck with its comfortable chairs, gained the upper decking of the hull itself as far astern as he could get, immediately over the propeller, in fact. There he stood upright, balancing easily on both feet and intently observing the entire boat ahead of him, almost all of which was visible from his position.

And nothing happened. *Torment IV* continued to circle at a reduced speed and Tarrant continued to watch as tensely as ever. It went on for so long that I am afraid I was beginning to get a little careless. I must have been all of seventy-five yards away when suddenly I saw him stiffen, start to turn away, take one more glance forward—and dive!

I strained my eyes, but I could see no change whatsoever in his boat, which was keeping placidly on her circular course. It certainly looked as if he had seen something, but if so, it remained invisible to me. Abruptly I came to and swung

the *Grey Falcon* towards where he was swimming with more speed than I had thought him capable of. Even yet I was not much concerned. Tarrant was neither a Philadelphian merchant nor a backwoodsman. Furthermore, he was a good swimmer and in his bathing suit. Accordingly my astonishment all but took my breath away entirely when, as I came up towards him, he gave a horrified glance over his shoulder and twisting abruptly away from the *Grey Falcon*, dug his arms into the water in a panic-stricken Australian crawl!

In that moment I realised we were up against something serious. I threw in the clutch and went after him. Fortunately I could always overtake him with the motor-boat I had; and I prepared to jump in for him if he showed signs of sinking. I was sure that, no matter how good a swimmer he was, he would sink before he reached Winnespequam, some eight miles away, for he was heading up the lake directly towards the town, although the nearest shore was well within a mile.

I was drawing up to him again, but this time, instead of slowing down, I sent the boat past him as closely as I dared. And as I went past, I yelled at the top of my voice, "Tarrant! For God's sake, what the hell has gotten into you!"

Evidently one of his ears was out of the water, for he hesitated and raised his head. For a moment he regarded my boat and myself without recognition, then he trod water and looked anxiously all about. I was coming about now, having been carried beyond him, and I heard his hoarse shout, "All right. I'm coming aboard."

He was literally shaking when I helped pull him over the side and for a minute or so he merely stood in the *Grey Falcon* and gasped. Then he said suddenly, "Where is that devil's boat?" I was struck by the same expression the old man had used the day before.

"There she is," he went on. "She's getting too close in to shore. She mustn't land again!" In the chase after Tarrant I had almost forgotten *Torment IV*, but now I saw that she was, in fact, circling closer and closer to the edge of the lake.

"We shall have to get near enough, Jerry, so

that I can rope that little mast on her bow," he grated. "Don't get *any* closer than you have to, though." And he added under his breath, "God, I hate to do this." Well, I gave up; in view of these unbelievable happenings it didn't seem even worthwhile asking questions. No matter what occurred, I didn't think my friend had gone mad.

I settled down to the job and soon made a parallel course with *Torment IV.* "Not so close, for God's sake!" yelled Tarrant. I eased off a little; and he threw his coiled rope. The third time he succeeded; the noose settled accurately over the small mast and he jerked it tight. "Make for the centre of the lake now, Jerry. Give it all you've got; you'll have to pull the other boat out of her course. I didn't dare stop her completely for fear it wouldn't happen." As he spoke he was securing his end of the rope to a cleat, and immediately caught up the axe and took his stand above the taut line, looking anxiously along it. So that was why he had brought the axe! Apparently he foresaw the possibility of having to sever the rope even before it could be released. It was hard going, pulling against *Torment IV*'s powerful engine, but finally we were well out in the lake again. With an audible sigh of relief Tarrant brought down the axe, the rope snapped.

"Now," he said, "the rifle," retrieving it from the floor and slipping in a cartridge. It was a regulation Winchester, a heavy weapon. "Go parallel again but at least twice as far away from her," he admonished me.

When this course had been taken up to his satisfaction and we were a good hundred yards and more from *Torment IV,* he commenced firing at the empty boat. The shots crashed out over the lake, a round dozen of them, and I saw that he was quite literally attacking the motor-boat itself. A little series of spurts appeared just along its waterline as the bullets punched a neat row of holes through the hull.

"Enough, I guess," he observed, putting down the rifle and catching up the shotgun, hastily loading both chambers. We waited then, still accompanying *Torment IV* at the same dis-

tance; and shortly she began to list on the side towards us. This had the effect of straightening her course somewhat but only for a few hundred yards, for she was filling rapidly now and beginning to plough down into the water. Deliberately she settled on her starboard side until the lake poured over her rail; then with a final swirl her stern lifted a little and she went under.

But, just as she did so, something climbed up on her port side and hopped away. At the distance I couldn't see what it was, except that I should have judged it to be about two feet or more in diameter. It made a dark spot against the bright water, and it did not sink. On the contrary it scrambled over the surface and it was making directly for our boat. "Easy, Jerry," Tarrant grated, as I instinctively put on speed; "we've got to get it."

Reluctantly I swung to port in order not to catch the thing in our wake. It seemed to be coming towards us with the speed of lightning; I doubt if we could have distanced it, anyhow. Tarrant's face was white and strained, and a tremor ran over his body as he raised his gun. For a few seconds he waited, then fired. Just behind the creature the water splattered where the shot struck the lake. He had one more shot; the thing was closer now and still coming rapidly. It was so close I could begin to see it clearly—the most repulsive animal I have ever looked at. Spiders always make me creepy, but this monstrous creature with its flashing legs, its horribly hairy bulb of a body, was nauseating and worse than nauseating. There was something so horrifying about it that I very nearly jumped before it reached us. I could see, or imagined that I could, a beady, malignant eye fixed definitely upon me. If Tarrant had missed his last shot I don't know what would have happened. It's one of those things I don't let myself think about.

He didn't miss. Simultaneously with the roar of the gun, the water about it churned and the monster disappeared, blown to bits.

For the next ten minutes we drifted aimlessly. I was being sick over the side of the *Grey Falcon.*

"I think," said Tarrant that evening, "that it was some member of the *Lycosidæ* or wolf-spider species. Or else one of the larger species of *Aviculariidæ,* some of which grow to great size. Even so, I have never heard of anything as large as this having been reported. And judging from the experiences here I judge it unlikely that many observers will live to report it. Although the poisonous effects of most spider bites are exaggerated, I have a feeling that this one's bite was fatal.

"Of course I had some inkling as to what to expect. Oh, not such a spider, I couldn't guess that. Although I should have done. When I was examining the motor yesterday, I did see some heavy cob-webbing way up under the bow, but at that time I didn't think that any sort of spider could be so terrifying; I am not greatly upset by spiders myself. Just the same, reason told me that something appeared on that boat which drove people overboard in a panic. And since the motor was the only portion of it that I was unable to examine thoroughly, it was from that direction that I looked for it. That is why, as soon as I could, I lashed the wheel and got as far away from the driving seat as was possible. The heat, I believe, brought it out; not only the heat of the motor but also that of the sun pouring down on the forward deck. How it got into the driver's cockpit I don't know; the first I saw of it was when it sprang up on the back of the seat.

"I can't express the horror and loathing its appearance inspired. It was sufficient to make Jerry pretty ill—and it never got with twenty yards of him. Sheer panic, that's what one felt in its presence. When I struck the water, I had no thought of where I was going, only a hopeless conviction that I would surely be overtaken. I forgot everything, all my own preparations; and the mere swish of Jerry's boat when he first came toward me only increased my terror. That is why Duff turned away from his rescuers; in his panic-stricken condition he may even have imagined that the rowboat with its oars was the beast itself. . . . Well, thank God I recovered sufficiently to get into the *Grey Falcon* and finish the job."

"Suppose there'll be no trouble about the motor-boat?"

"Oh, no. I didn't see the widow, but she sent word that I could blow it up if I wished and good riddance. The loss of the boat was a small price, I think."

Valerie shuddered and reached for my hand. "Jerry," she said, "it's nice here, but take me home to-morrow, please?"

JULIAN HAWTHORNE

JULIAN HAWTHORNE (1846–1934), the only son of Nathaniel Hawthorne, followed in his father's footsteps and decided to become a writer—very much against his family's wishes, as he had been educated at Harvard to be a civil engineer and previously had expressed interest in philosophy and had shown great artistic skill with his ability to draw. What he lacked in genius he compensated for with perspicacity, producing a vast number of novels and short stories, many uncollected from their magazine appearances. Much of his writing was in the mystery, horror, and supernatural genres.

His first story, "Love & Counter Love; or, Masquerading," was immediately accepted by *Harper's Weekly*, which paid the then generous sum of fifty dollars for it, and he quickly sold more stories to *Scribner's*, *Lippincott's*, and other leading magazines. He was one of the first American mystery writers to use a series detective, Inspector Byrnes, who serves as the protagonist in several novels, including *A Tragic Mystery* (1887), *An American Penman* (1887), *Another's Crime* (1888), and *The Great Bank Robbery* (1888). Working as a journalist, he covered the Indian famine for *Cosmopolitan* magazine in 1897 and the Spanish-American War for the *New York Journal* in 1898. Having lost his money in a farming venture in Jamaica, he entered a contest, reputedly writing *A Fool of Nature* in eighteen days under a pseudonym (it was published under his own name in 1896), for which he won a ten-thousand-dollar prize. He was later caught in a silver-mine stock fraud and served a year in prison.

"Greaves' Disappearance" was first published in *Six Cent Sam's* (St. Paul, Minnesota, Price-McGill, 1893).

GREAVES' DISAPPEARANCE

JULIAN HAWTHORNE

WE WERE FOUR in the club smoking room that October afternoon. The weather was gusty and inclement, and we were out of sorts. Perhaps our having been up till two or three o'clock the night before may have had something to do with our gloomy sensations. Twelve hours had elapsed since we had left the card table, and permitted yawning Thomas to go to bed. We had dispersed to our various abiding places, slept till noon, and drifted back to the club and breakfast. Hardly anyone besides ourselves was in the house. It was intolerably dull. What is one to do in town at three o'clock of a rainy October afternoon, after being up all night?

Allardice, the man-about-town *par excellence,* lay languid and relaxed in his easy-chair, his legs outstretched, his chin on his breast, and a black Mexican cigar between his teeth. His prominent gray eyes were half closed, some cigar ashes lay unheeded on his vest, and the light from the window was reflected dimly on the bald summit of his cranium. Tinling, the poet and dramatic critic, reclined on the divan, his gray, abundant hair contrasting oddly with his smooth pink-and-white face; the hand with the big seal ring on it lay romantically and conspicuously on his heart. Gawtrey sat with his elbows on his knees, and his face between his hands, the small eyes in his big fat countenance blinking stupidly at the fire. He and Tinling had been wrangling about the merits or demerits of the new Persian dancer who had been attracting the town for some days past, and who was being advertised, free and otherwise, to a degree unexampled. Tinling had declared that she was "the peer—I do not say of Ellsler or Taglioni, but of Salome, the daughter of Herodias." Gawtrey had replied that he had never seen the Herodias girl, or the other two, either; but that he could find women in any ordinary music hall, here or in London, who could knock the stuffing out of Mlle. Saki. Thereupon fell a silence, finally broken by Allardice.

"If no one else will, I suppose I must," said he, leaning forward and touching the electric bell in the panel. "Think of what it's to be, gentlemen."

We sighed and changed the position of our legs.

"There should be a by-law specifying the correct drink for each hour of the day," said someone. "Up to eleven p.m., at any rate, it's too fatiguing to choose for one's self."

"You might always order the same drink, you know, like Greaves," suggested Gawtrey. "Grand Vin Sec is his tipple, and he never touches any other."

"Gawtrey has no discrimination," murmured Tinling. "Greaves has a hundred thousand a year, youth, health and happiness."

"No rose without the thorn," said Allardice. "He's going to get married."

"That's a pretty cheap article of cynicism, even before dinner," rejoined Tinling. "In the first place, the girl comes of one of our best families. Baddely was a name famous in the old country centuries ago, and always respected. Secondly, Miss Baddely is a mighty fine girl, both in looks and otherwise; and fifthly and sixthly, and to conclude, Greaves is dead in love with her."

"The Baddely, is it?" grunted Gawtrey. "Why, they don't amount to a row of pins! Met the old boy downtown. Ain't worth a hundred thousand."

"The greater her good sense, to look with favor on Greaves's suit," was contributed by Allardice.

Tinling closed his eyes. "You weary me," he said. "She's the most independent girl I know. If anything could make her jilt Greaves, it would be precisely his income. If Greaves were poor, she'd support him. She thinks women ought to support themselves, anyway."

"What can she do for a living?" someone inquired.

"What couldn't she? Anything—from keeping a dancing school to running an American railroad system. She's got genius."

"That's the reason Greaves didn't join us last night," remarked Gawtrey. "When a fellow gets gone on a girl, he may as well resign from his clubs. But I wish he'd given me my revenge first. Never saw anything like the hands that fellow held last time. Two flushes and a four-ace were some of 'em."

"What is yours, sir?" inquired the pale but ever respectful Thomas, appearing at this juncture. Whereupon we all wearily began to try to think of something.

In the midst of our deliberations, in came Fred Guise, looking quite pale and haggard. He nodded to us without speaking, and dropped into a chair.

"Just in time," said Allardice, "and you look as if you needed it. Ask Mr. Guise what he'll have, Thomas."

"Absinthe cocktail," said Guise, without faltering. "I'm knocked out. Haven't seen the color of a bed since night before last. None of

you chaps have heard anything new about him, of course?"

"Guess not. About whom?"

"Greaves, of course. Did you think I meant the Shah of Persia?" inquired Guise, with a fine irony.

"All we know about Greaves here is, that he promised to be here last night and didn't materialize," said Gawtrey, with a yawn. "He owes me my revenge—"

"Do you mean to say you chaps haven't heard?" interrupted Guise, sitting up and speaking slowly, as if astonishment weighted his utterance. "Why it's nearly a day old!"

"Is its father known?" asked Allardice, languidly.

"What's the matter, Fred?" demanded Tinling, struck by something peculiar in Guise's manner. "We've only just got up, you know, and you're the first man that's come in since—"

"Why, good God, the man's disappeared," exclaimed Guise, always in his characteristic low but distinct voice. "He vanished like the blowing out of a candle! He was with me one moment, and the next, he was—well, he was gone!"

"I say," grunted Gawtrey, "draw it mild. What are you giving us?"

"What are the circumstances? How disappeared? When? Where?" put in Tinling, erecting himself, and shaking back his long gray hair.

"Why, I supposed the report would have got here the first thing. It's the most inexplicable thing I ever came across. Let me see—to begin at the beginning, I'd breakfasted with him in the forenoon yesterday at his rooms. He was quite jolly—rather more so than usual, I thought. I took it for natural high spirits—going to be married soon, and all that sort of thing, you know. But I've thought since it may have been excitement from some other cause, you know. He talked a bit about his private affairs—we're pretty intimate, you know—but nothing was said in particular that I remember. We talked of the Ingledew's ball, and that escapade of Mrs. Revell's, you know, and that Mlle. Saki, the Persian dancer—whom he didn't seem to think much of, by the by—and of the gold-find in Alaska; he said he thought that looked promising, and that he might like to take some stock in that; and then—"

"For pity's sake, do tell us the story first, and we can join you in your comments afterward," someone exclaimed. "Get to the point, can't you?"

"I was only trying to recall anything that might possibly throw some light on the thing, you know," rejoined Fred, unhurriedly. "I can't make out any motive for it myself. Everything was all right about him—property, health, love affair—well, everything. And it's inconceivable to me that he could have planned anything beforehand—to make away with himself, or anything of that sort; but then it's even more inconceivable he should have vanished involuntarily, don't you know. I can't make it out," and here Fred accepted the absinthe cocktail that Thomas silently extended to him, and emptied it with deliberate circumspection.

Allardice elevated one eyebrow, and hunted in his pocket for a cigar. "Take your time, my dear boy," said he. "We've got the afternoon before us, and we're none of us curious. Won't you take another absinthe before you continue?"

Guise leaned back in his chair, seemed to consult his memory, and finally went on:

"Well, after breakfast, you know, we lay about for a while, looking over his books and pictures, and talking philosophy and art. Toward three or four o'clock—just about this time, you know—we agreed to go out for a little stroll. It looked as if it might rain, and Greaves put on a light gray Mackintosh overcoat, that he'd just had over from London—rather a peculiar looking thing it was, by the by—and a soft felt hat, and out we went. We turned into Broadway, and walked on the west side up past the hotels toward Thirty-Fourth Street. There were comparatively few people out. I remember we passed a long file of those sandwich men, you know, with Persian turbans on, and boards with Saki's portrait on them. She's at the Fifth Avenue, you know. Just as we reached the corner of

Twenty-Eighth Street, we came across a bit of an excitement. There was a man running down the middle of the street, with his hat in his hand, and making good time; and about a dozen yards behind him were a couple of bobbies. Greaves and I stopped on the corner, to see what would happen. Greaves said he was a fool to run in that direction, because he could never get across Broadway. The bobbies thought so, too, I fancy, and it threw them off their guard. Almost at the entrance of the street the chap turned like a flash, and dashed straight at them. Before they knew where they were he had tripped them both and sent them sprawling, and was flying up the street. Halfway along the block there's an empty house, going to be torn down. The basement door was open and he went through it, and that was the last ever seen of him, I fancy. I turned round to Greaves, who had spoken to me, you know, just the instant before, and saw him across the other side of Broadway, walking on toward Thirtieth. There he was, you know, in his gray Mackintosh and soft felt hat. I hurried to catch up with him, and took his arm. I said, 'He was no fool, after all, that chap. I fancy he must have played on a football team.'

"That's what I said, and then Greaves pulled away his arm and turned round on me, and you may imagine I was surprised when I found it wasn't Greaves at all, nor anyone a bit like him. It was a fellow of fifty, with a stubble of gray beard a week old, a red potato nose, and one eye gone. 'I beg your pardon, young fellow,' he said to me, 'I guess you've made a mistake.'

"Well, you know, at first I didn't think so much of it; I'd been misled by the similarity of dress, that was all. Greaves must be somewhere, of course, and close at hand, too; it was hardly thirty seconds since he'd spoken to me, and there were only three directions in which he could have gone—up Broadway, or down or up the side street toward Fifth Avenue. If he had gone down the street toward Sixth Avenue I should have seen him, for that was the direction I'd been looking. But the Broadway sidewalks in both directions were nearly empty, the crowd having run down Twenty-Eighth after the fellow and the bobbies. There was nobody going toward Fifth Avenue either, and he couldn't have got away more than a dozen rods, anyhow. I should have recognized him at any distance in that gray Mackintosh. It was true, he might have gone into some shop, so I looked into all of them up and down the blocks, but it was no use. Unless he'd dropped through a manhole in the pavement, there was nowhere he could have gone; but he was gone just the same. There never was a disappearance on the stage managed quicker or neater, or half so inexplicable. I began to feel mighty queer about it—something as if I'd seen a ghost. Here was an effect without a cause. I assure you it was as unpleasant a shock as ever I had in my life."

We all stared at one another. At last Gawtrey said:

"See here, Fred, make a clean breast of it; how many bottles of the Grand Vin Sec did you polish off at the breakfast?"

"I'm entirely serious, gentlemen," returned Fred, gravely; "and recollect, even if Greaves could have eluded me in any ordinary way, he would still have been heard from somewhere by this time. But he's given no sign. Whether he went voluntarily or not, he's vanished, and I'm afraid when news does come it will not be the sort of news we shall like to hear."

Gawtrey now poured his pony of brandy into a tumbler, added a dash of water, swallowed the mixture, looked in the bottom of the glass for inspiration, and said, "I don't believe, for my part, that Greaves has been kidnapped in broad daylight in the center of New York; and on the other hand, I don't believe in miracles—this year, anyway. What he did, depend upon it, was just to step quietly out of sight somewhere, when you weren't looking. Probably he saw Miss Baddely on a horse car, and boarded it to join her."

"There's something in that idea," said Allardice.

Guise shook his head. "There wasn't, as it happens, a single car passing, for there was a block across both tracks at Twenty-Fifth Street.

And as for Miss Baddely, I afterward ascertained that she was at home at the time. No, gentlemen; ordinary explanations won't work. Last evening, I went down and had a talk with Inspector Byrnes, and he has put two of his best men on the case. But they had found out nothing when I looked in at Headquarters just now."

"You called on Miss Baddely, did you? How does she take it?" inquired Tinling.

"I saw her father; she was not to be seen. Of course they are all upset. I told him all I've told you. He said one thing—the old man did—that struck me as a bit odd; he said that both his daughter and Greaves were persons of arbitrary will and extraordinary whims. They were capable of almost anything. If one of them did a crazy thing, the other would be apt to do something to cap it. He said he had no control over either of 'em, and never had had. But he said this last business did surprise him. I thought that was queer language to use on such an occasion. It might mean that he suspected something."

"A quarrel, for instance, and desperation on Greaves's part."

"A wager of some kind, maybe."

"I never did think much of that fellow Baddely. He's a poor sort of an old dude. Where does he get his pocket money from? He never made a cent in his life. Shouldn't wonder if his daughter supported him somehow. Takes in sewing on the quiet, or paints fans, or gives music lessons. Rum things go on in some of these old families." It was Gawtrey who made these observations.

"Upon the whole," said another of the party, "it looks to me as if Greaves's kidnapper must have been Greaves himself. But how he arranged it—the circumstances being what they were—I can't figure out. My impression is, Guise should have followed up that fellow in the gray Mackintosh."

"I agree with the last honorable member," said Tinling. "Such a coincidence as that similarity of costume is too remarkable not to be suspicious. Looks like a plot of some sort. But there's nothing to throw any light on his motive."

"Let's have another drink," said Gawtrey. "What are we going to do this evening?"

"I am going to the Fifth Avenue to see Saki," said Allardice. "Your talk about her has aroused my curiosity. I saw some oriental dancers at the Paris Exhibition a while ago, and I'd like to see how she compares with them."

The evening papers had just been brought in, and I had picked up one of them. A paragraph headed "Illness of the Persian Dancer" caught my eye.

"She won't appear this evening," said I. "It says: 'Mlle. Saki was so unfortunate as to sprain her ankle yesterday while alighting from her carriage. While the injury is not regarded as serious, it will prevent her from dancing this evening. Tickets purchased in advance will be accepted for later dates.'"

"Nothing in the paper about Greaves?" asked Tinling.

"Seems not."

Soon after we broke up, and drifted away in various directions, somewhat preoccupied with speculations about Greaves.

The next morning, however, the papers were full of the story, and though no light was thrown upon the manner of Greaves's disappearance, certain facts of interest were mentioned. On the very day before his disappearance, it appears, he had executed a deed conveying the bulk of his large property to Sophie Baddely. This deed was not a will, but a deed of gift simply. Its provisions went into effect immediately, and, in view of what had occurred, one could not help suspecting that Greaves had prepared it as part of a predetermined scheme of action, whether of suicide or something else. And here there was a coincidence that drew my attention. The "indisposition" of Mlle. Saki corresponded very nearly with the disappearance of Greaves. She had not returned to the theater since the evening of that occurrence, and it was now stated that her absence might be prolonged for a week. I knew from Guise, the most intimate friend that Greaves had, that the latter had been several times to see Saki dance, and that he had betrayed rather marked interest in her performance. Mr.

Baddely had said that his intending son-in-law was capable of strange escapades; was it possible, then, that he and the too-fascinating Persian had eloped together—he having first salved his conscience by bestowing his wealth upon the woman he was abandoning? Moreover, Tinling, having made inquiries at the theater, brought news that there was now no prospect of Saki's returning at all; on the contrary, her agent had paid a heavy forfeit, and she had departed none knew whither. The sprained ankle was obviously a fiction. Of course, the manner in which Greaves had effected his exit was no less than ever a mystery. A conceivable motive had been suggested, that was all.

The establishment known as Six Cent Sam's extends clear through the narrow block in which it stands, and has an entrance in the street on the other side, a fact not generally known. For the rear face of the eating house is a pawnshop, kept, as the sign board indicates, by one Samuel Jonathan, who is, in fact, no other than Six Cent Sam himself; and to the initiated there is a passageway leading out of the pawnshop into the eating house. I am of the initiated; and as I was passing down this passage on the day after the scene at the club, I met Sam—or Mr. Jonathan—and he said:

"Turn back, sir; I've something to say to you."

I followed him into the office of the pawnshop, where we sat down.

"One way or another," began Sam, "I hear a good deal of what's going on. Pawnshops and eating houses bring news. Now, there's young Greaves, for instance."

I became interested at once. Sam is always interesting.

"When last seen," continued the latter, "had on gray Mackintosh and soft hat. Could you identify them? Look at these," and from a shelf he drew out just such an English-made garment as Guise had described to us, with the hat to match.

"He's been here, then?" I asked.

Sam shook his head, and went on in his terse, deep-toned way. "A fellow came here yesterday with a carbuncle on his nose, and a game eye. Had these duds under his arm; wanted to sell 'em. How did he come by 'em? Gent had given 'em to him. How and why? Oh, quite a yarn. Gent met him on street doing sandwich act for Fifth Avenue Theatre. Pursuant to bargain then and there made, and instructions given, met him again next day, same place. Another gent along. Disturbance on street; other man's attention distracted; garments exchanged inside ten seconds. Gent, in sandwiches, marches down street after other sandwiches; no one ever thinks of looking at face of sandwich, only the announcement on board. Thus gent became invisible, and has so remained."

So this was the simple but ingenious solution of the puzzle.

"And where is Greaves now, and what did he do it for?" I asked.

Sam looked me straight in the face with his powerful eyes.

"Where's Saki?" he replied.

"So they're together after all?" said I, rather vain of my insight.

"Guess not; but they ought to be."

That was a queer thing to say, and I stared at Sam without answering.

"Newspapers say he gave a pot of money to Miss Baddely," resumed the latter. "Proud, independent girl, father poor. She will be beholden to nobody, not even Greaves. Wanted to support herself. Greaves objects; quarrel. Now, if Greaves were to make away with himself, after deeding property to her, she would naturally give up her scheme of earning her own living. Do you see how the cat is going to jump?"

"You think Greaves has committed suicide?"

Sam gave me a reproachful glance. "Wasn't I asking to bring him and Saki together? Do you know either of the ladies?"

"Either of them?"

"Well, do you know Saki?" said Sam, a trifle impatiently.

"No, I don't."

"Nor Miss Baddely?"

"I haven't that pleasure."

"I'll introduce you to both of them. We'll go now. Great friends; always together."

"Who? Miss Baddely and Saki?"

"The same."

"What are we to do there?"

"I want 'em to settle which of 'em's to marry Greaves."

"Is Greaves in love with both of them?"

"That's his fix, precisely."

"And they with him?"

"That's what I'm figuring on."

"And you expect them to agree which of them—"

"We have to hurry," remarked Sam, rising. "Let me get into a clean shirt, and we're off." He stepped into a side room as he spoke, and shut the door.

I did not know what to make of it, but I knew enough of Sam to know that he, who knew everything and everybody, from a pawnshop *habitué* to a wealthy club man, was not acting in the dark. In a few minutes he reappeared, in the garb of a well-to-do man-about-town. Silk hat, Prince Albert coat, striped trousers, white scarf, yellow gloves, and silver-headed umbrella. Not a finer gentleman in the city.

"We'll look up Mlle. Saki first," he said, as we sallied forth together. "Do you speak Persian fluently? Never mind, she speaks as good English as you or I do, and is a very intelligent woman."

To us, awaiting her in a tasteful but simple sitting room up-town, entered the famous Persian dancer. She was a handsome brunette, with superb black eyes and hair. Her figure and bearing were all grace and elegance. She was plainly dressed, and looked, as Sam had said, very intelligent.

"Now, Mademoiselle," said Sam, after the greetings were over, "I have called as your manager, to learn what you want to do. You may speak freely before this gentleman."

"Tell me first what has become of him?" she replied, in a slightly tremulous voice. "I can never forgive myself. Is he—"

"He is a pig-headed donkey, if you must have

my opinion," returned Sam. "And he's as well as such a monster deserves to be. Now, shall we temporize with him, or shall we keep on our course and let him go to—" Sam's finger at this juncture was pointing downward.

"Temporize with him? I'll go down on my knees to him if he will but give me the chance. He was right from the beginning, and I was wrong. I saw that almost from the first—long before this terrible thing happened. But for my miserable obstinacy, I'd have given it up then. I had no conception what the life was till I had tried it. It was an awful lesson. I shall never forget it. I feel as if I had actually done all the bad things every one seemed to suspect me of. And yet, when I was looking forward to it, it all appeared good and right. I thought I would elevate and ennoble my art. But the world is hard."

"Well, it is unless we take it the right way," said Sam. "The best way to find out is to make experiments. I helped you to do that, and you're the better for it, because you now know what you would never have believed if it had been told you. Some girls go through life believing all they are told, good or bad, but you're not that sort. You can do other things just as clever as dancing, and not so open to remarks. For one thing, you can make a man happy, and bring up his children."

Mlle. Saki blushed, and tears stood in her eyes.

"It's too late to think of that now," she said. "He must despise me and hate me; he couldn't help it."

"Pooh! Besides, there are other men in the world as good as he, and a great deal better."

"You know that is not so," exclaimed Mlle. Saki, with a naïve indignation that was enchanting. "I should like to see him again, though, just once," she added, "to tell him how sorry and ashamed I am, and to ask his forgiveness."

"I guess it would be more politic for you to forgive him," said Sam, with a smile. "However, we'll see what can be done," and thereupon we took our leave.

It was a mysterious affair altogether, and has never been cleared up to this day. As everybody knows, Greaves is married, but he married Miss Sophie Baddely. Mlle. Saki was never again heard of. It is the impression among the general public that she returned to Paris. Be that as it may, I saw Mrs. Greaves driving out in the park the other day with her husband, and remarked that the lady bore a striking resemblance to the Persian dancer. Guise and Tinling, however, have never spoken of any likeness. No doubt, she must have looked very different in her Persian costume from what she did in the plain American dress that she wore when I saw her.

THE HOUSE OF HAUNTS

ELLERY QUEEN

IN WHAT REMAINS one of the most brilliant marketing decisions of all time, the two Brooklyn cousins who collaborated under the pseudonym Ellery Queen, Frederic Dannay (born Daniel Nathan) (1905–1982) and Manfred Bennington Lee (born Manford Lepofsky) (1905–1971), also named their detective Ellery Queen. They reasoned that if readers forgot the name of the author, *or* the name of the character, they might remember the other. It worked, as Ellery Queen is counted among the handful of best-known names in the history of mystery fiction.

Lee was a full collaborator on the fiction created as Ellery Queen, but Dannay on his own was also one of the most important figures in the mystery world. He founded *Ellery Queen's Mystery Magazine* in 1941, and it remains, more than seventy years later, the most significant periodical in the genre. He also formed one of the first great collections of detective fiction first editions, the rare contents leading to reprinted stories in the magazines and anthologies he edited, which are among the best ever produced, most notably *101 Years' Entertainment* (1941), which gets my vote as the greatest mystery anthology ever published. He also produced such landmark reference books as *Queen's Quorum* (1951), a listing and appreciation of the 106 (later expanded to 125) most important short-story collections in the genre, and *The Detective Short Story* (1942), a bibliography of all the collections Dannay had identified up to the publication date. More than a dozen movies were based on Queen books. There were several radio and television shows as well as comics; it was not far-fetched to describe the ubiquitous Ellery Queen in the 1930s, 1940s, and 1950s as the personification of the American detective story.

"The House of Haunts" was first published in the November 1935 issue of *Detective Story*; it was retitled "The Lamp of God" when it was collected in *The New Adventures of Ellery Queen* (New York, Stokes, 1940). It was also published in 1951 as a single story by Dell in its short-lived ten-cent series.

THE HOUSE OF HAUNTS

ELLERY QUEEN

The Black House

IF A STORY BEGAN: "Once upon a time in a house cowering in wilderness there lived an old and hermetical creature named Mayhew, a crazy man who had buried two wives and lived a life of death; and this house was known as *The Black House*"—if a story began in this fashion, it would strike no one as especially remarkable. There are people like that who live in houses like that, and very often mysteries materialize like ectoplasm about their wild-eyed heads.

Now, however disorderly Mr. Ellery Queen may be by habit, mentally he is an orderly person. His neckties and shoes might be strewn about his bedroom helter-skelter, but inside his skull hums a perfectly oiled machine, functioning as neatly and inexorably as the planetary system. So if there was a mystery about one Sylvester Mayhew, deceased, and his buried wives and gloomy dwelling, you may be sure the Queen brain would seize upon it and worry it and pick it apart and get it all laid out in neat and shiny rows. Rationality, that was it. No esoteric mumbo-jumbo could fool *that fellow*. Lord, no! His two feet were planted solidly on God's good earth, and one and one made two—always—and that's all there was that.

Of course, Macbeth had said that stones have been known to move and trees to speak; but, pshaw! for these literary fancies. In this day and age, with its *Cominterns*, its wars of peace, its

fasces, and its rocketry experiments? Nonsense! The truth is, Mr. Queen would have said, there is something about the harsh, cruel world we live in that's very rough on miracles. Miracles just don't happen anymore, unless they are miracles of stupidity or miracles of national avarice. Everyone with a grain of intelligence knows that.

"Oh, yes," Mr. Queen would have said; "there are yogis, voodoos, fakirs, shamans, and other tricksters from the effete East and primitive Africa, but nobody pays any attention to such pitiful monkeyshines—I mean, nobody with sense. This is a reasonable world and everything that happens in it must have a reasonable explanation."

You couldn't expect a sane person to believe, for example, that a three-dimensional, flesh-and-blood, veritable human being could suddenly stoop, grab his shoelaces, and fly away. Or that a water-buffalo could change into a golden-haired little boy before your eyes. Or that a man dead one hundred and thirty-seven years could push aside his tombstone, step out of his grave, yawn, and then sing three verses of "Mademoiselle from Armentières." Or even, for that matter, that a stone could move or a tree speak—yea, though it were in the language of Atlantis or Mu.

Or . . . *could you?*

The tale of Sylvester Mayhew's house is a strange tale. When what happened happened, proper minds tottered on their foundations and porcelain beliefs threatened to shiver into shards. Before the whole fantastic and incomprehensible business was done, God Himself came into it. Yes, God came into the story of Sylvester Mayhew's house, and that is what makes it quite the most remarkable adventure in which Mr. Ellery Queen, that lean and indefatigable agnostic, has ever become involved. . . .

The early mysteries in the Mayhew case were trivial—mysteries merely because certain pertinent facts were lacking; pleasantly provocative mysteries, but scarcely savorous of the supernatural.

Ellery was sprawled on the hearthrug before the hissing fire that raw January morning, debating with himself whether it was more desirable to brave the slippery streets and biting wind on a trip to Centre Street in quest of amusement, or to remain where he was in idleness but comfort, when the telephone rang.

It was Thorne on the wire. Ellery, who never thought of Thorne without perforce visualizing a human monolith—a long-limbed, gray-thatched male figure with marbled cheeks and agate eyes, the whole man coated with a veneer of ebony, was rather startled. Thorne was excited; every crack and blur in his voice spoke eloquently of emotion. It was the first time, to Ellery's recollection, that Thorne had betrayed the least evidence of human feeling.

"What's the matter?" Ellery demanded. "Nothing's wrong with Ann, I hope?" Ann was Thorne's wife.

"No, no." Thorne spoke hoarsely and rapidly, as if he had been running.

"Where the deuce have you been? I saw Ann only yesterday and she said she hadn't heard from you for almost a week. Of course, your wife's used to your preoccupation with those interminable legal affairs, but an absence of six days—"

"Listen to me, Queen, and don't hold me up. I must have your help. Can you meet me at Pier 54 in half an hour? That's North River."

"Of course."

Thorne mumbled something that sounded absurdly like: "Thank God!" and hurried on: "Pack a bag. For a couple of days. And a revolver. Especially a revolver, Queen."

"I see," said Ellery, not seeing at all.

"I'm meeting the Cunarder *Coronia*. Docking this morning. I'm with a man by the name of Reinach, Dr. Reinach. You're my colleague; get that? Act stern and omnipotent. Don't be friendly. Don't ask him—or me—questions. And don't allow yourself to be pumped. Understood?"

"Understood," said Ellery, "but not exactly clear. Anything else?"

"Call Ann for me. Give her my love and tell her I shan't be home for days yet, but that you're with me and that I'm all right. And ask her to telephone my office and explain matters to Crawford."

"Do you mean to say that not even your partner knows what you've been doing?"

But Thorne had hung up.

Ellery replaced the receiver, frowning. It was stranger than strange. Thorne had always been a solid citizen, a successful attorney who led an impeccable private life and whose legal practice was dry and unexciting. To find old Thorne entangled in a web of mystery . . .

Ellery drew a happy breath, telephoned Mrs. Thorne, tried to sound reassuring, yelled for Djuna, hurled some clothes into a bag, loaded his .38 police revolver with a grimace, scribbled a note for Inspector Queen, dashed downstairs and jumped into the cab Djuna had summoned, and landed on Pier 54 with thirty seconds to spare.

There was something terribly wrong with Thorne, Ellery saw at once, even before he turned his attention to the vast fat man by the lawyer's side. Thorne was shrunken within his Scotch-plaid greatcoat like a pupa which has died prematurely in its cocoon. He had aged years in the few weeks since Ellery had last seen him. His ordinarily sleek cobalt cheeks were covered with a straggly stubble. Even his clothing looked tired and uncared-for. And there was a glitter of furtive relief in his bloodshot eyes as he pressed Ellery's hand that was, to one who knew Thorne's self-sufficiency, almost pathetic.

But he merely remarked, "Oh, hello, there, Queen. We've a longer wait than we anticipated, I'm afraid. Want you to shake hands with Dr. Herbert Reinach. Doctor, this is Ellery Queen."

"'D'you do," said Ellery curtly, touching the man's immense gloved hand. If he was to be omnipotent, he thought, he might as well be rude, too.

"Surprise, Mr. Thorne?" said Dr. Reinach in the deepest voice Ellery had ever heard; it rumbled up from the caverns of his chest like the echo of thunder. His little purplish eyes were very, very cold.

"A pleasant one, I hope," said Thorne.

Ellery snatched a glance at his friend's face as he cupped his hands about a cigarette, and he read approval there. If he had struck the right tone, he knew how to act thenceforth. He flipped the match away and turned abruptly to Thorne. Dr. Reinach was studying him in a half-puzzled, half-amused way.

"Where's the *Coronia*?"

"Held up in quarantine," said Thorne. "Somebody's seriously ill aboard with some disease or other and there's been difficulty in clearing her passengers. It will take hours, I understand. Suppose we settle down in the waiting-room for a bit."

They found places in the crowded room, and Ellery set his bag between his feet and disposed himself so that he was in a position to catch every expression on his companions' faces. There was something in Thorne's repressed excitement, an even more piquing aura enveloping the fat doctor, that violently whipped his curiosity.

"Alice," said Thorne in a casual tone, as if Ellery knew who Alice was, "is probably becoming impatient. But that's a family trait with the Mayhews, from the little I saw of old Sylvester. Eh, Doctor? It's trying, though, to come all the way from England only to be held up on the threshold."

So they were to meet an Alice Mayhew, thought Ellery, arriving from England on the *Coronia*. Good old Thorne! He almost chuckled

aloud. "Sylvester" was obviously a senior Mayhew, some relative of Alice's.

Dr. Reinach fixed his little eyes on Ellery's bag and rumbled politely, "Are you going away somewhere, Mr. Queen?"

Then Reinach did not know Ellery was to accompany them—wherever they were bound for.

Thorne stirred. "Queen's coming back with me, Dr. Reinach." There was something brittle and hostile in his voice.

The fat man blinked, his eyes buried beneath half-moons of damp flesh. "Really?" he said, and by contrast his bass voice was tender.

"Perhaps I should have explained," said Thorne abruptly. "Queen is a colleague of mine. This case has interested him."

"Case?" said the fat man.

"Legally speaking. I really hadn't the heart to deny him the pleasure of helping me—ah—protect Alice Mayhew's interests. I trust you won't mind?"

This was a deadly game, Ellery became certain. Something important was at stake, and Thorne in his stubborn way was determined to defend it by force or guile.

Reinach's puffy lids dropped over his eyes as he folded his paws on his stomach. "Naturally, naturally not," he said in a hearty tone. "Only too happy to have you, Mr. Queen. A little unexpected, perhaps, but delightful surprises are as essential to life as to poetry. Eh?" And he chuckled.

Samuel Johnson, thought Ellery, recognizing the source of the doctor's remark. The physical analogy struck him. There was iron beneath those layers of fat and a good brain under that dolichocephalic skull. The man sat there on the waiting-room bench like an octopus, lazy and inert and peculiarly indifferent to his surroundings. Indifference—that was it, thought Ellery! the man was a colossal remoteness, as vague and darkling as a storm cloud on an empty horizon.

Thorne said in a weary voice, "Suppose we have lunch. I'm famished. . . ."

By three in the afternoon Ellery felt old and worn. Several hours of nervous, cautious silence, threading his way smiling among treacherous shoals, had told him just enough to put him on guard. He often felt knotted-up and tight inside when a crisis loomed or danger threatened from an unknown quarter. Something extraordinary was going on.

As they stood on the pier watching the *Coronia*'s bulk being nudged alongside, he chewed on the scraps he had managed to glean during the long, heavy, pregnant hours. He knew definitely now that the man called Sylvester Mayhew was dead, that he had been pronounced paranoiac, that his house was buried in an almost inaccessible wilderness on Long Island. Alice Mayhew, somewhere on the decks of the *Coronia* doubtless straining her eyes pierward, was the dead man's daughter, parted from her father since childhood.

And he had placed the remarkable figure of Dr. Reinach in the puzzle. The fat man was Sylvester Mayhew's half brother. He had also acted as Mayhew's physician during the old man's last illness. This illness and death seemed to have been very recent, for there had been some talk of "the funeral" in terms of fresh if detached sorrow. There was also a Mrs. Reinach glimmering unsubstantially in the background, and a queer old lady who was the dead man's sister. But what the mystery was, or why Thorne was so perturbed, Ellery could not figure out.

The liner tied up to the pier at last. Officials scampered about, whistles blew, gang-planks appeared, passengers disembarked in droves. Interest crept into Dr. Reinach's little eyes, and Thorne was shaking.

"There she is!" croaked the lawyer. "I'd know her anywhere from her photographs. That slender girl in the brown turban!"

As Thorne hurried away Ellery studied the girl eagerly. She was anxiously scanning the crowd, a tall charming creature with an elasticity of movement more esthetic than athletic and a harmony of delicate feature that approached beauty. She was dressed so simply and inexpensively that he narrowed his eyes.

Thorne came back with her, patting her gloved hand and speaking quietly to her. Her face was alight and alive, and there was a natural gaiety in it which convinced Ellery that whatever mystery or tragedy lay before her, it was still unknown to her. At the same time there were certain signs about her eyes and mouth—fatigue, strain, worry, he could not put his finger on the exact cause—which puzzled him.

"I'm so glad," she murmured in a cultured voice, strongly British in accent. Then her face grew grave and she looked from Ellery to Dr. Reinach.

"This is your uncle, Miss Mayhew," said Thorne. "Dr. Reinach. This other gentleman is not, I regret to say, a relative. Mr. Ellery Queen, a colleague of mine."

"Oh," said the girl; and she turned to the fat man and said tremulously, "Uncle Herbert. How terribly odd. I mean—I've felt so all alone. You've been just a legend to me, Uncle Herbert, you and Aunt Sarah and the rest, and now—" She choked a little as she put her arms about the fat man and kissed his pendulous cheek.

"My dear," said Dr. Reinach solemnly; and Ellery could have struck him for the Judas quality of his solemnity.

"But you must tell me everything! Father—how is Father? It seems so strange to be—to be saying that."

"Don't you think, Miss Mayhew," said the lawyer quickly, "that we had better see you through the Customs? It's growing late and we have a long trip before us. Long Island, you know."

As they made their way toward the Customs, Ellery dropped a little behind and devoted himself to watching Dr. Reinach. But that vast lunar countenance was as inscrutable as a gargoyle. . . .

Dr. Reinach drove. It was not Thorne's car; Thorne had a regal new Lincoln limousine and this was a battered if serviceable old Buick sedan.

The girl's luggage was strapped to the back and sides; Ellery was puzzled by the scantness of it—three small suitcases and a tiny steamer-trunk. Did these four pitiful containers hold all of her worldly possessions?

Sitting beside the fat man, Ellery strained his

ears. He paid little attention to the road Reinach was taking.

The two behind were silent for a long time. Then Thorne cleared his throat with an oddly ominous finality. Ellery saw what was coming; he had often heard that throat-clearing sound emanate from the mouths of judges pronouncing sentence of doom.

"We have something sad to tell you, Miss Mayhew. You may as well learn it now."

"Sad?" murmured the girl after a moment. "Oh, it's not—"

"Your father," said Thorne inaudibly. "He's dead."

She cried, "Oh!" in a small voice; and then she grew quiet.

"I'm dreadfully sorry to have to greet you with such news," said Thorne in the silence. "We'd anticipated— And I realize how awkward it must be for you. After all, it's quite as if you had never known him at all. Love for a parent, I'm afraid, lies in direct ratio to the degree of childhood association. Without any association at all—"

"It's a shock, of course," Alice said in a muffled voice. "And yet, as you say, he was a stranger to me, a mere name. As I wrote you, I was only a toddler when Mother got her divorce and took me off to England. I don't remember Father at all. And I've not seen him since, or heard from him. I might have learned more about Father if Mother hadn't died when I was six; but she did, and my people—her people—in England— Uncle John died last fall. He was the last one. And then I was left all alone. When your letter came I was—I was so glad, Mr. Thorne. I didn't feel lonely anymore. I was really happy for the first time in years. And now—" She broke off.

Dr. Reinach swiveled his massive head and smiled benignly. "But you're not alone, my dear. There's my unworthy self, and your Aunt Sarah, and Milly—Milly's my wife, Alice; naturally you wouldn't know anything about her—and there's even a husky young fellow named Keith who works about the place—bright lad who's come down in the world." He chuckled. "So you see

there won't be a dearth of companionship for you."

"Thank you, Uncle Herbert," she murmured. "I'm sure you're all terribly kind. Mr. Thorne, how did Father— When you replied to my letter you wrote me he was ill, but—"

"He fell into a coma unexpectedly nine days ago. You hadn't left England yet and I cabled you at your antique-shop address. But somehow it missed you."

"I'd sold the shop by that time. When did he—die?"

"A week ago Thursday. The funeral— Well, we couldn't wait, you see. I might have caught you by cable or telephone on the *Coronia*, but I didn't have the heart to spoil your voyage."

"I don't know how to thank you for all the trouble you've taken." Without looking at her Ellery knew there were tears in her eyes. "It's good to know that someone—"

"It's been hard for all of us," rumbled Dr. Reinach.

"Of course, Uncle Herbert. I'm sorry." She fell silent. When she spoke again, it was as if there were a compulsion expelling the words. "When Uncle John died, I didn't know where to reach Father. The only American address I had was yours, Mr. Thorne, which some patron or other had given me. It was the only thing I could think of. I was sure a solicitor could find Father for me. That's why I wrote to you in such detail, with photographs and all."

"Naturally we did what we could." Thorne seemed to be having difficulty with his voice. "When I found your father and went out to see him the first time and showed him your letter and photographs, he—I'm sure this will please you, Miss Mayhew. He wanted you badly. He'd apparently been having a hard time of late years—ah, mentally, emotionally. And so I wrote you at his request. On my second visit, the last time I saw him alive, when the question of the estate came up—"

Ellery thought that Dr. Reinach's paws tightened on the wheel. But the man's face bore the same bland, remote smile.

"Please," said Alice wearily. "Do you greatly mind, Mr. Thorne? I—I don't feel up to discussing such matters now."

The car was fleeing along the deserted road as if it were trying to run away from the weather. The sky was gray lead; a frowning, gloomy sky under which the countryside lay cowering. It was growing colder, too, in the dark and drafty tonneau; the cold seeped in through the cracks and their overclothes.

Ellery stamped his feet a little and twisted about to glance at Alice Mayhew. Her oval face was a glimmer in the murk; she was sitting stiffly, her hands clenched into tight little fists in her lap. Thorne was slumped miserably by her side, staring out the window.

"By George, it's going to snow," announced Dr. Reinach with a cheerful puff of his cheeks. No one answered.

The drive was interminable. There was a dreary sameness about the landscape that matched the weather's mood. They had long since left the main highway to turn into a frightful byroad, along which they jolted in an unsteady eastward curve between ranks of leafless woods. The road was pitted and frozen hard; the woods were tangles of dead trees and underbrush densely packed but looking as if they had been repeatedly seared by fire. The whole effect was one of widespread and oppressive desolation.

"Looks like No Man's Land," said Ellery at last from his bouncing seat beside Dr. Reinach. "And feels like it, too."

Dr. Reinach's cetaceous back heaved in a silent mirth. "Matter of fact, that's exactly what it's called by the natives. Land-God-forgot, eh? But then Sylvester always swore by the Greek unities."

The man seemed to live in a dark and silent cavern, out of which he maliciously emerged at intervals to poison the atmosphere.

"It isn't very inviting-looking, is it?" remarked Alice in a low voice. It was clear she was brooding over the strange old man who had lived in this wasteland, and of her mother who had fled from it so many years before.

"It wasn't always this way," said Dr. Reinach, swelling his cheeks like a bullfrog. "Once it was pleasant enough; I remember it as a boy. Then it seemed as if it might become the nucleus of a populous community. But progress has passed it by, and a couple of uncontrollable forest fires did the rest."

"It's horrible," murmured Alice, "simply horrible."

"My dear Alice, it's your innocence that speaks there. All life is a frantic struggle to paint a rosy veneer over the ugly realties. Why not be honest with yourself? Everything in this world is stinking rotten; worse than that, a bore. Hardly worth living, in any impartial analysis. But if you have to live, you may as well live in surroundings consistent with the rottenness of everything."

The old attorney stirred beside Alice, where he was buried in his greatcoat. "You're quite a philosopher, Doctor," he snarled.

"I'm an honest man."

"Do you know, Doctor," murmured Ellery, despite himself, "you're beginning to annoy me."

The fat man glanced at him. Then he said, "And do you agree with this mysterious friend of yours, Thorne?"

"I believe," snapped Thorne, "that there is a platitude extant which says that actions speak with considerably more volume than words. I haven't shaved for six days, and today has been the first time I left Sylvester Mayhew's house since his funeral."

"Mr. Thorne!" cried Alice, turning to him. "Why?"

The lawyer muttered, "I'm sorry, Miss Mayhew. All in good time, in good time."

"You wrong us all," smiled Dr. Reinach, deftly skirting a deep rut in the road. "And I'm afraid you're giving my niece quite the most erroneous impression of her family. We're odd, no doubt, and our blood is presumably turning sour after so many generations of cold storage; but then don't the finest vintages come from the deepest cellars? You've only to glance at Alice to see my point. Such vital loveliness could only have been produced by an old family."

"My mother," said Alice, with a faint loathing in her glance, "had something to do with that, Uncle Herbert."

"Your mother, my dear," replied the fat man, "was merely a contributory factor. You have the typical Mayhew features."

Alice did not reply. Her uncle, whom until today she had not seen, was an obscene enigma; the others, waiting for them at their destination, she had never seen at all, and she had no great hope that they would prove better. A livid streak ran through her father's family; he had been a paranoiac with delusions of persecution. The Aunt Sarah in the dark distance, her father's surviving sister, was apparently something of a character. As for Aunt Milly, Dr. Reinach's wife, whatever she might have been in the past, one had only to glance at Dr. Reinach to see what she undoubtedly was in the present.

Ellery felt prickles at the nape of his neck. The farther they penetrated this wilderness the less he liked the whole adventure. It smacked vaguely of a fore-ordained theatricalism, as if some hand of monstrous power were setting the stage for the first act of a colossal tragedy. . . . He shrugged this sophomoric foolishness off, settling deeper into his coat. It was queer enough, though. Even the lifelines of the most indigent community were missing; there were no telephone poles and, so far as he could detect, no electric cables. That meant candles. He detested candles.

The sun was behind them, leaving them. It was a feeble sun, but feeble as it was, Ellery wished it would stay.

They crashed on and on, endlessly, shaken like dolls. The road kept lurching toward the east in a stubborn curve. The sky grew more and more leaden. The cold seeped deeper and deeper into their bones.

When Dr. Reinach finally rumbled, "Here we are," and steered the jolting car leftward off the road into a narrow, wretchedly graveled driveway, Ellery came to with a start of surprise

and relief. So their journey was really over, he thought.

He roused himself, stamping his icy feet, looking about. The same desolate tangle of woods to either side of the byroad. He recalled now that they had not once left the main road nor crossed another road since turning off the highway. No chance, he thought grimly, to stray off this path to perdition.

Dr. Reinach said, "Welcome home, Alice."

Alice murmured something incomprehensible; her face was buried to the eyes in the motheaten lap robe Reinach had flung over her. Ellery glanced sharply at the fat man; there had been a note of mockery, of derision, in that heavy rasping voice. But the face was smooth and damp and bland, as before.

Dr. Reinach ran the car up the driveway and brought it to rest a little before, and between, two houses. These structures flanked the drive, standing side by side, separated by only the width of the drive, which led straight ahead to a ramshackle garage. Ellery caught a glimpse of Thorne's glittering Lincoln within its crumbling walls. The three buildings huddled in a ragged clearing, surrounded by the tangle of woods, like three desert islands in an empty sea.

"That," said Dr. Reinach heartily, "is the ancestral mansion, Alice. To the left."

The house to the left was of stone; once gray, but now so tarnished by the elements and perhaps the ravages of fire that it was almost black. Its face was blotched and streaky, as if it had succumbed to an insensate leprosy. Rising three stories, elaborately ornamented with stone flora and gargoyles, it was unmistakably Victorian in its architecture. The façade had a neglected, granular look that only the art of great age could have etched. The whole structure appeared to have thrust its roots immovably into the forsaken landscape.

Ellery saw Alice Mayhew staring at it with a sort of speechless horror; it had nothing of the pleasant hoariness of old English mansions. It was simply old, old with the dreadful age of this seared and blasted countryside. He cursed

Thorne beneath his breath for subjecting the girl to such a shocking experience.

"Sylvester called it The Black House," said Dr. Reinach cheerfully as he turned off the ignition. "Not pretty, I admit, but as solid as the day it was built, seventy-five years ago."

"Black House," grunted Thorne. "Rubbish."

"Do you mean to say," whispered Alice, "that Father—Mother lived *here?*"

"Yes, my dear. Quaint name, eh, Thorne? Another illustration of Sylvester's preoccupation with the morbidly colorful. Built by your grandfather, Alice. The old gentleman built this one, too, later; I believe you'll find it considerably more habitable. Where the devil is everyone?"

He descended heavily and held the rear door open for his niece. Mr. Ellery Queen slipped down to the driveway on the other side and glanced about with the sharp, uneasy sniff of a wild animal. The old mansion's companion-house was a much smaller and less pretentious dwelling, two stories high and built of an originally white stone which had turned gray. The front door was shut and the curtains at the lower windows were drawn. But there was a fire burning somewhere inside; he caught the tremulous glimmers. In the next moment they were blotted out by the head of an old woman, who pressed her face to one of the panes for a single instant and then vanished. But the door remained shut.

"You'll stop with us, of course," he heard the doctor say genially; and Ellery circled the car. His three companions were standing in the driveway, Alice pressed close to old Thorne as if for protection. "You won't want to sleep in the Black House, Alice. No one's there, it's in rather a mess; and a house of death, y'know."

"Stop it," growled Thorne. "Can't you see the poor child is half-dead from fright as it is? Are you trying to scare her away?"

"Scare me away?" repeated Alice, dazedly.

"Tut, tut," smiled the fat man. "Melodrama doesn't become you at all, Thorne. I'm a blunt old codger, Alice, but I mean well. It will really be more comfortable in the White House." He chuckled suddenly again. "White House. That's

what *I* named it to preserve a sort of atmospheric balance."

"There's something frightfully wrong here," said Alice in a tight voice. "Mr. Thorne, what is it? There's been nothing but innuendo and concealed hostility since we met at the pier. And just why *did* you spend six days in father's house after the funeral? I think I've a right to know."

Thorne licked his lips. "I shouldn't—"

"Come, come, my dear," said the fat man. "Are we to freeze here all day?"

Alice drew her thin coat more closely about her. "You're all being beastly. Would you mind, Uncle Herbert? I should like to see the inside—where Father and Mother—"

"I don't think so, Miss Mayhew," said Thorne hastily.

"Why not?" said Dr. Reinach tenderly, and he glanced once over his shoulder at the building he had called the White House. "She may as well do it now and get it over with. There's still light enough to see by. Then we'll go over, wash up, have a hot dinner, and you'll feel worlds better." He seized the girl's arm and marched her toward the dark building, across the dead, twig-strewn ground. "I believe," he continued blandly, as they mounted the steps of the stone porch, "that Mr. Thorne has the keys."

The girl stood quietly waiting, her dark eyes studying the faces of the three men. The attorney was pale, but his lips were set in a stubborn line. He did not reply. Taking a bunch of large rusty keys out of a pocket, he fitted one into the lock of the front door. It turned over with a creak. Then Thorne pushed open the door and they stepped into the house.

It was a tomb. It smelled of must and damp. The furniture, ponderous pieces which once no doubt had been regal, was uniformly dilapidated and dusty. The walls were peeling, showing broken, discolored laths beneath. There was dirt and debris everywhere. It was inconceivable that a human being could once have inhabited this grubby den.

The girl stumbled about, her eyes a blank horror, Dr. Reinach steering her calmly. How long the tour of inspection lasted Ellery did not know; even to him, a stranger, the effect was so oppressive as to be almost unendurable. They wandered about, silent, stepping over trash from room to room, impelled by something stronger than themselves. Once Alice said in a strangled voice, "Uncle Herbert, didn't anyone—take care of Father? Didn't anyone ever clean up this horrible place?"

The fat man shrugged. "Your father had notions in his old age, my dear. There wasn't much anyone could do with him. Perhaps we had better not go into that."

The sour stench filled their nostrils. They blundered on, Thorne in the rear, watchful as an old cobra. His eyes never left Dr. Reinach's face.

On the middle floor they came upon a bedroom in which, according to the fat man, Sylvester Mayhew had died. The bed was unmade; indeed, the impress of the dead man's body on the mattress and tumbled sheets could still be discerned. It was a bare and mean room, not as filthy as the others, but infinitely more depressing. Alice began to cough.

She coughed and coughed, hopelessly, standing still in the center of the room and staring at the dirty bed in which she had been born. Then suddenly she stopped coughing and ran over to a lopsided bureau with one foot missing. A large, faded chromo was propped on its top against the yellowed wall. She looked at it for a long time. Then she took it down.

"It's mother," she said slowly. "It's really mother. I'm glad now I came. He did love her, after all. He's kept it all these years."

"Yes, Miss Mayhew," muttered Thorne. "I thought you'd like to have it."

"I've only one portrait of mother, and that's a poor one. This—why, she was beautiful, wasn't she?"

She held the chromo up proudly, almost laughing in her hysteria. The time-dulled colors revealed a stately young woman with hair worn high. The features were piquant and regular. There was little resemblance between Alice and the woman in the picture.

"Your father," said Dr. Reinach with a sigh, "often spoke of your mother toward the last, and of her beauty."

"If he had left me nothing but this, it would have been worth the trip from England." Alice trembled a little. Then she hurried back to them, the chromo pressed to her breast. "Let's get out of here," she said in a shriller voice. "I—I don't like it here. It's ghastly. I'm—afraid."

They left the house with half-running steps, as if someone were after them. The old lawyer turned the key in the lock of the front door with great care, glaring at Dr. Reinach's back as he did so. But the fat man had seized his niece's arm and was leading her across the driveway to the White House, whose windows were now flickeringly bright with light and whose front door stood wide open.

As they crunched along behind, Ellery said sharply to Thorne, "Thorne. Give me a clue. A hint. Anything. I'm completely in the dark."

Thorne's unshaven face was haggard in the setting sun. "Can't talk now," he muttered. "Suspect everything, everybody. I'll see you tonight, in your room. Or wherever they put you, if you're alone. Queen, for God's sake, be careful!"

"Careful?" Ellery frowned.

"As if your life depended on it." Thorne's lips made a thin, grim line. "For all I know, it does."

Then they were crossing the threshold of the White House. . . .

Ellery's impressions were curiously vague. Perhaps it was the effect of the sudden smothering heat after the hours of cramping cold outdoors; perhaps he thawed out too suddenly, and the heat went to his brain.

He stood about for a while in a state almost of semiconsciousness, basking in the waves of warmth that eddied from a roaring fire in a fireplace black with age. He was only dimly aware of the two people who greeted them, and of the interior of the house. The room was old, like everything else he had seen, and its furniture might have come from an antique shop. They were standing in a large living-room, comfortable enough; strange to his senses only because it was so old-fashioned in its appointments. There were actually antimacassars on the overstuffed chairs! A wide staircase with worn brass treads wound from one corner to the sleeping-quarters above.

One of the two persons awaiting them was Mrs. Reinach, the doctor's wife. The moment Ellery saw her, even as she embraced Alice, he knew that this was inevitably the sort of woman the fat man would choose for a mate. She was a pale and weazened midge, almost fragile in her delicacy of bone and skin; and she was plainly in a silent convulsion of fear. She wore a hunted look on her dry and bluish face; and over Alice's shoulder she glanced timidly, with the fascinated obedience of a whipped bitch, at her husband.

"So you're Aunt Milly," sighed Alice, pushing away. "You'll forgive me if I—It's all so very new to me."

"You must be exhausted, poor darling," said Mrs. Reinach in the chirping twitter of a bird; and Alice smiled wanly and looked grateful. "And I quite understand. After all we're no more than strangers to you. Oh!" she said, and stopped. Her faded eyes were fixed on the chromo in the girl's hands. "Oh," she said again. "You've been over to the other house *already*."

"Of course she has," said the fat man; and his wife grew even paler at the sound of his bass voice. "Now, Alice, why don't you let Milly take you upstairs and get you comfortable?"

"I am rather done in," confessed Alice; and then she looked at her mother's picture and smiled again. "I suppose you think I'm very silly, dashing in this way with just—" She did not finish; instead, she went to the fireplace. There was a broad flame-darkened mantel above it, crowded with gewgaws of a vanished era. She set the chromo of the handsome Victorian-garbed woman among them. "There! Now I feel much better."

"Gentlemen, gentlemen," said Dr. Reinach. "Please don't stand on ceremony. Nick!

Make yourself useful. Miss Mayhew's bags are strapped to the car."

A gigantic young man, who had been leaning against the wall, nodded in a surly way. He was studying Alice Mayhew's face with a dark absorption. He went out.

"Who," murmured Alice, flushing, "is that?"

"Nick Keith." The fat man slipped off his coat and went to the fire to warm his flabby hands. "My morose protégé. You'll find him pleasant company, my dear, if you can pierce that thick defensive armor he wears. Does odd jobs about the place, as I believe I mentioned, but don't let that hold you back. This is a democratic country."

"I'm sure he's very nice. Would you excuse me? Aunt Milly, if you'd be kind enough to—"

The young man reappeared under a load of baggage, clumped across the living-room, and plodded up the stairs. And suddenly, as if at a signal, Mrs. Reinach broke out into a noisy twittering and took Alice's arm and led her to the staircase. They disappeared after Keith.

"As a medical man," chuckled the fat man, taking their wraps and depositing them in a hall-closet, "I prescribe a large dose of—this, gentlemen." He went to a sideboard and brought out a decanter of brandy. "Very good for chilled bellies." He tossed off his own glass with an amazing facility, and in the light of the fire the finely etched capillaries in his bulbous nose stood out clearly. "Ah-h! One of life's major compensations. Warming, eh? And now I suppose you feel the need of a little sprucing up yourselves. Come, I'll show you to your rooms."

Ellery shook his head in a dogged way, trying to clear it. "There's something about your house, Doctor, that's unusually soporific. Thank you, I think both Thorne and I would appreciate a brisk wash."

"You'll find it brisk enough," said the fat man, shaking with silent laughter. "This is the forest primeval, you know. Not only haven't we any electric light or gas or telephone, but we've no running water, either. Well behind the house keeps us supplied. The simple life, eh? Better for you than the pampering influences of modern civilization. Our ancestors may have died more easily of bacterial infections, but I'll wager they had a greater body immunity to coryza! . . . Well, well, enough of this prattle. Up you go."

The chilly corridor upstairs made them shiver, but the very shiver revived them; Ellery felt better at once. Dr. Reinach, carrying candles and matches, showed Thorne into a room overlooking the front of the house, and Ellery into one on the side. A fire burned crisply in the large fireplace in one corner, and the basin on the old-fashioned washstand was filled with icy-looking water.

"Hope you find it comfortable," drawled the fat man, lounging in the doorway. "We were expecting only Thorne and my niece, but one more can always be accommodated. Ah—colleague of Thorne's, I believe he said?"

"Twice," replied Ellery. "If you don't mind—"

"Not at all." Reinach lingered, eyeing Ellery with a smile. Ellery shrugged, stripped off his coat, and made his ablutions. The water *was* cold; it nipped his fingers like the mouths of little fishes. He scrubbed his face vigorously.

"That's better," he said, drying himself. "Much. I wonder why I felt so peaked downstairs."

"Sudden contrast of heat after cold, no doubt." Dr. Reinach made no move to go.

Ellery shrugged again. He opened his bag with pointed nonchalance. There, plainly revealed on his haberdashery, lay the .38 police revolver. He tossed it aside.

"Do you always carry a gun?" murmured Dr. Reinach.

"Always." Ellery picked up the revolver and slipped it into his hip pocket.

"Charming!" The fat man stroked his triple chin. "Charming. Well, Mr. Queen, if you'll excuse me I'll see how Thorne is getting on. Stubborn fellow, Thorne. He could have taken pot luck with us this past week, but he insisted on isolating himself in that filthy den next door."

"I wonder," murmured Ellery, "why."

Dr. Reinach eyed him. Then he said, "Come downstairs when you're ready. Mrs. Reinach has an excellent dinner prepared and if you're as hungry as I am, you'll appreciate it." Still smiling, the fat man vanished.

Ellery stood still for a moment, listening. He heard the fat man pause at the end of the corridor; a moment later the heavy tread was audible again, this time descending the stairs. Ellery went swiftly to the door on tiptoe. He had noticed that the instant he had come into the room.

There was no lock. Where a lock had been there was a splintery hole, and the splinters had a newish look about them. Frowning, he placed a rickety chair against the doorknob and began to prowl.

He raised the mattress from the heavy wooden bedstead and poked beneath it, searching for he knew not what. He opened closets and drawers; he felt the worn carpet for wires. But after ten minutes, angry with himself, he gave up and went to the window. The prospect was so dismal that he scowled in sheer misery. Just brown stripped woods and the leaden sky; the old mansion picturesquely known as the Black House was on the other side, invisible from this window.

A veiled sun was setting; a bank of storm clouds slipped aside for an instant and the brilliant rim of the sun shone directly into his eyes, making him see colored, dancing balls. Then other clouds, fat with snow, moved up and the sun slipped below the horizon. The room darkened rapidly.

Lock taken out, eh? Someone had worked fast. They could not have known he was coming, of course. Then someone must have seen him through the window as the car stopped in the drive. The old woman who had peered out for a moment? Ellery wondered where she was. At any rate, a few minutes' work by a skilled hand at the door— He wondered, too, if Thorne's door had been similarly mutilated. And Alice Mayhew's. . . .

Thorne and Dr. Reinach were already seated before the fire when Ellery came down, and the fat man was rumbling, "Just as well. Give the poor girl a chance to return to normal. With the shock she's had today, it might be the finisher. I've told Mrs. Reinach to break it to Sarah gently. . . . Ah, Queen. Come and join us. We'll have dinner as soon as Alice comes down."

"Dr. Reinach was just apologizing," said Thorne casually, "for this Aunt Sarah of Miss Mayhew's—Mrs. Fell, Sylvester Mayhew's sister. The excitement of anticipating her niece's arrival seems to have been a bit too much for her."

"Indeed," said Ellery, sitting down and planting his feet on the nearest firedog.

"Fact is," said the fat man, "my poor half sister is cracked. The family paranoia. She's off-balance; not violent, you know, but it's wise to humor her. She isn't normal, and for Alice to see her—"

"Paranoia," said Ellery. "An unfortunate family, it seems. Your half brother Sylvester's weakness seems to have expressed itself in rubbish and solitude. What's Mrs. Fell's delusion?"

"Common enough—she thinks her daughter is still alive. As a matter of fact, poor Olivia was killed in an automobile accident three years ago. It shocked Sarah's maternal instinct out of plumb. Sarah's been looking forward to seeing Alice, her brother's daughter, and it may prove awkward. Never can tell how a diseased mind will react to an unusual situation."

"For that matter," drawled Ellery, "I should have said the same remark might be made about any mind, diseased or not."

Dr. Reinach laughed. Thorne said, "This Keith boy."

The fat man set his glass down slowly. "Drink, Queen."

"No, thank you."

"This Keith boy," said Thorne again.

"Eh? Oh, Nick. Yes, Thorne? What about him?"

The lawyer shrugged. Dr. Reinach picked up his glass again. "Am I imagining things, or is there the vaguest hint of hostility in the circumambient ether?"

"Reinach—" began Thorne harshly.

"Don't worry about Keith, Thorne. We let

him pretty much alone. He's sour on the world, which demonstrates his good sense; but I'm afraid he's unlike me in that he hasn't the emotional buoyancy to rise above his wisdom. You'll probably find him antisocial. . . . Ah, there you are, my dear! Lovely, lovely."

Alice was wearing a different gown, a simple unfrilled frock, and she had freshened up. There was color in her cheeks and her eyes were sparkling with a light and tinge they had not had before. Seeing her for the first time without her hat and coat, Ellery thought she looked different, as all women contrive to look different divested of their outer clothing and refurbished by the mysterious activities which go on behind the closed doors of feminine dressing-rooms. Apparently the ministrations of another woman, too, had cheered her; there were still rings under her eyes, but her smile was more cheerful.

"Thank you, Uncle Herbert." Her voice was slightly husky. "But I do think I've caught a nasty cold."

"Whisky and hot lemonade," said the fat man promptly. "Eat lightly and go to bed early."

"To tell the truth, I'm famished."

"Then eat as much as you like. I'm one hell of a physician, as no doubt you've already detected. Shall we go in to dinner?"

"Yes," said Mrs. Reinach in a frightened voice. "We shan't wait for Sarah, or Nicholas."

Alice's eyes dulled a little. Then she sighed and took the fat man's arm and they all trooped into the dining-room.

Dinner was a failure. Dr. Reinach divided his energies between gargantuan inroads on the viands and copious drinking. Mrs. Reinach donned an apron and served, scarcely touching her own food in her haste to prepare the next course and clear the plates; apparently the household employed no domestic. Alice gradually lost her color, the old strained look reappearing on her face; occasionally she cleared her throat. The oil lamp on the table flickered badly, and every mouthful Ellery swallowed was flavored with the taste of oil. Besides, the *pièce de résistance* was curried lamb: if there was one dish he detested, it was lamb; and if there was one culinary style that sickened him, it was curry. Thorne ate stolidly, not raising his eyes from his plate.

As they returned to the living-room the old lawyer managed to drop behind. He whispered to Alice, "Is everything all right? Are you?"

"I'm a little scarish, I think," she said quietly. "Mr. Thorne, please don't think me a child, but there's something so strange about—everything. I wish now I hadn't come."

"I know," muttered Thorne. "And yet it was necessary, quite necessary. If there was any way to spare you this, I should have taken it. But you obviously couldn't stay in that horrible hole next door—"

"Oh, no." She shuddered.

"And there isn't a hotel for miles and miles. Miss Mayhew, have any of these people—"

"No, no. It's just that they're so strange to me. I suppose it's my imagination and this cold. Would you greatly mind if I went to bed? Tomorrow will be time enough to talk."

Thorne patted her hand. She smiled gratefully, murmured an apology, kissed Dr. Reinach's cheek, and went upstairs with Mrs. Reinach again.

They had just settled themselves before the fire again and were lighting cigarettes when feet stamped somewhere at the rear of the house.

"Must be Nick," wheezed the doctor. "Now where's *he* been?"

The gigantic young man appeared in the living-room archway, glowering. His boots were soggy with wet. He growled, "Hello," in his surly manner and went to the fire to toast his big reddened hands. He paid no attention whatever to Thorne, although he glanced once, swiftly, at Ellery in passing.

"Where've you been, Nick? Go in and have your dinner."

"I ate before you came."

"What's been keeping you?"

"I've been hauling firewood. Something you didn't think of doing." Keith's tone was truculent, but Ellery noticed that his hands were shaking. Damnably odd! His manner was noticeably

not that of a servant, and yet he was apparently employed in a menial capacity. "It's snowing."

"Snowing?" They crowded to the front windows. The night was moonless; big fat snowflakes were sliding down the panes.

"Ah, snow," sighed Dr. Reinach; and for all the sigh there was something in his tone that made the nape of Ellery's neck prickle. "'The whited air hides hills and woods, the river, and the heaven, and veils the farmhouse at the garden's end.'"

"You're quite the countryman, Doctor," said Ellery.

"I like Nature in her more turbulent moods. Spring is for milksops. Winter brings out the fundamental iron." The doctor slipped his arm about Keith's broad shoulders. "Smile, Nick. Isn't God in His heaven?"

Keith flung the arm off without replying.

"Oh, you haven't met Mr. Queen. Queen, this is Nick Keith. You know Mr. Thorne already." Keith nodded shortly. "Come, come, my boy, buck up. You're too emotional, that's the trouble with you. Let's all have a drink. The disease of nervousness is infectious."

Nerves! thought Ellery grimly. His nostrils were pinched, sniffing the little mysteries in the air. They tantalized him. Thorne was tied up in knots, as if he had cramps; the veins at his temples were pale blue swollen cords and there was sweat on his forehead. Above their heads the house was soundless.

Dr. Reinach went to the sideboard and began hauling out bottles—gin, bitters, rye, vermouth. He busied himself mixing drinks, talking incessantly. There was a purr in his hoarse undertones, a vibration of pure excitement. What in Satan's name, thought Ellery in a sort of agony, was going on here?

Keith passed the cocktails around, and Ellery's eyes warned Thorne. Thorne nodded slightly; they had two drinks apiece and refused more. Keith drank doggedly, as if he were anxious to forget something.

"Now that's better," said Dr. Reinach, settling his bulk into an easy-chair. "With the women out of the way and a fire and liquor, life becomes almost endurable."

"I'm afraid," said Thorne, "that I shall prove an unpleasant influence, Doctor. I'm going to make it unendurable."

Dr. Reinach blinked. "Well, now," he said. "Well, now." He pushed the brandy decanter carefully out of the way of his elbow and folded his pudgy paws on his stomach. His purple little eyes shone.

Thorne went to the fire and stood looking down at the flames, his back to them. "I'm here in Miss Mayhew's interests, Dr. Reinach," he said, without turning. "In her interests alone. Sylvester Mayhew died last week very suddenly. Died while waiting to see the daughter whom he hadn't seen since his divorce from her mother almost twenty years ago."

"Factually exact," rumbled the doctor, without stirring.

Thorne spun about. "Dr. Reinach, you acted as Mayhew's physician for over a year before his death. What was the matter with him?"

"A variety of things. Nothing extraordinary. He died of cerebral hemorrhage."

"So your certificate claimed." The lawyer leaned forward. "I'm not entirely convinced," he said slowly, "that your certificate told the truth."

The doctor stared at him for an instant, then he slapped his bulging thigh. "Splendid!" he roared. "Splendid! A man after my own heart. Thorne, for all your desiccated exterior you have juicy potentialities." He turned on Ellery, beaming, "You heard that, Mr. Queen? Your friend openly accuses me of murder. This is becoming quite exhilarating. So! Old Reinach's a fratricide. What do you think of that, Nick? Your patron accused of cold-blooded murder. Dear, dear."

"That's ridiculous, Mr. Thorne," growled Nick Keith. "You don't believe it yourself."

The lawyer's gaunt cheeks sucked in. "Whether I believe it or not is immaterial. The possibility exists. But I'm more concerned with Alice Mayhew's interests at the moment than with a possible homicide. Sylvester Mayhew

is dead, no matter by what agency—divine or human; but Alice Mayhew is very much alive."

"And so?" asked Reinach softly.

"And so I say," muttered Thorne, "it's damnably queer her father should have died when he did. Damnably."

For a long moment there was silence. Keith put his elbows on his knees and stared into the flames, his shaggy boyish hair over his eyes. Dr. Reinach sipped brandy with enjoyment.

Then he set his glass down and said with a sigh, "Life is too short, gentlemen, to waste in cautious skirmishings. Let us proceed without feinting movements to the major engagement. Nick Keith is in my confidence and we may speak freely before him." The young man did not move. "Mr. Queen, you're very much in the dark, aren't you?" went on the fat man with a bland smile.

Ellery did not move, either. "And how did you know that?"

Reinach kept smiling. "Pshaw. Thorne hadn't left the Black House since Sylvester's funeral. Nor did he receive or send any mail during his self-imposed vigil last week. This morning he left me on the pier to telephone someone. You showed up shortly after. Since he was gone only a minute or two, it was obvious that he hadn't had time to tell you much, if anything. Allow me to felicitate you, Mr. Queen, upon your conduct today. It's been exemplary. An air of omniscience covering a profound and desperate ignorance."

Ellery removed his pince-nez and began to polish their lenses. "You're a psychologist as well as a physician, I see."

Thorne said abruptly, "This is all beside the point."

"No, no, it's all very much *to* the point," replied the fat man in a sad bass. "Now the canker annoying your friend, Mr. Queen—since it seems a shame to keep you on tenterhooks any longer—is roughly this: My half-brother Sylvester, God rest his troubled soul, was a miser. If he'd been able to take his gold with him to the grave—with any assurance that it would remain there—I'm sure he would have done so."

"Gold?" asked Ellery, raising his brows.

"You may well titter, Mr. Queen. There was something medieval about Sylvester; you almost expected him to go about in a long black velvet gown muttering incantations in Latin. At any rate, unable to take his gold with him to the grave, he did the next best thing. He hid it."

"Oh, Lord," said Ellery. "You'll be pulling clanking ghosts out of your hat next."

"Hid," beamed Dr. Reinach, "the filthy lucre in the Black House."

"And Miss Alice Mayhew?"

"Poor child, a victim of circumstances. Sylvester never thought of her until recently, when she wrote from London that her last maternal relative had died. Wrote to friend Thorne, he of the lean and hungry eye, who had been recommended by some friend as a trustworthy lawyer. As he is, as he is! You see, Alice didn't even know if her father was alive, let alone where he was. Thorne, good Samaritan, located us, gave Alice's exhaustive letters and photographs to Sylvester, and has acted as liaison officer ever since. And a downright circumspect one, too, by thunder!"

"This explanation is wholly unnecessary," said the lawyer stiffly. "Mr. Queen knows—"

"Nothing," smiled the fat man, "to judge by the attentiveness with which he's been following my little tale. Let's be intelligent about this, Thorne." He turned to Ellery again, nodding very amiably. "Now, Mr. Queen, Sylvester clutched at the thought of his new-found daughter with the pertinacity of a drowning man clutching a life-preserver. I betray no secret when I say that my half brother, in his paranoiac dotage, suspected his own family—imagine!—of having evil designs on his fortune."

"A monstrous slander, of course."

"Neatly put, neatly put! Well, Sylvester told Thorne in my presence that he had long since converted his fortune into specie, that he'd hidden this gold somewhere in the house next door, and that he wouldn't reveal the hiding-place to anyone but Alice, his daughter, who was to be his sole heir. You see?"

"I see," said Ellery.

"He died before Alice's arrival, unfortunately. Is it any wonder, Mr. Queen, that Thorne thinks dire things of us?"

"This is fantastic," snapped Thorne, coloring. "Naturally, in the interests of my client, I couldn't leave the premises unguarded with that mass of gold lying about loose somewhere—"

"Naturally not," nodded the doctor.

"If I may intrude my still, small voice," murmured Ellery, "isn't this a battle of giants over a mouse? The possession of gold is a clear violation of the law in this country, and has been for some years. Even if you found it, wouldn't the government confiscate it?"

"There's a complicated legal situation, Queen," said Thorne; "but one which cannot come into existence before the gold is found. Therefore my efforts to—"

"And successful efforts, too." Dr. Reinach grinned. "Do you know, Mr. Queen, your friend has slept behind locked, barred doors, with an old cutlass in his hand—one of Sylvester's prized mementos of a grandfather who was in the Navy? It's terribly amusing."

"I don't find it so," said Thorne shortly. "If you insist on playing the buffoon—"

"And yet—to go back to this matter of your little suspicions, Thorne—have you analyzed the facts? Whom do you suspect, my dear fellow? Your humble servant? I assure you that I am spiritually an ascetic—"

"An almighty fat one!" snarled Thorne.

"—and that money, per se, means nothing to me," went on the doctor imperturbably. "My half sister Sarah? An anile wreck living in a world of illusion, quite as antediluvian as Sylvester—they were twins, you know—who isn't very long for this world. Then that leaves my estimable Milly and our saturnine young friend Nick. Milly? Absurd; she hasn't had an idea, good or bad, for two decades. Nick? Ah, an outsider—we may have struck something there. Is it Nick you suspect, Thorne?" chuckled Dr. Reinach.

Keith got to his feet and glared down into the bland damp lunar countenance of the fat man.

He seemed quite drunk. "You damned porker," he said thickly.

Dr. Reinach kept smiling, but his little porcine eyes were wary. "Now, now, Nick," he said in a soothing rumble.

It all happened very quickly. Keith lurched forward, snatched the heavy cut-glass brandy decanter, and swung it at the doctor's head. Thorne cried out and took an instinctive forward step; but he might have spared himself the exertion. Dr. Reinach jerked his head back like a fat snake and the blow missed. The violent effort pivoted Keith's body completely about; the decanter slipped from his fingers and flew into the fireplace, crashing to pieces. The fragments splattered all over the fireplace, strewing the hearth, too; the little brandy that remained in the bottle hissed into the fire, blazing with a blue flame.

"That decanter," said Dr. Reinach angrily, "was almost a hundred and fifty years old!"

Keith stood still, his broad back to them. They could see his shoulders heaving.

Ellery sighed with the queerest feeling. The room was shimmering as in a dream, and the whole incident seemed unreal, like a scene in a play on a stage. Were they acting? Had the scene been carefully planned? But, if so, why? What earthly purpose could they have hoped to achieve by pretending to quarrel and come to blows? The sole result had been the wanton destruction of a lovely old decanter. It didn't make sense.

"I think," said Ellery, struggling to his feet, "that I shall go to bed before the Evil One comes down the chimney. Thank you for an altogether extraordinary evening, gentlemen. Coming, Thorne?"

He stumbled up the stairs, followed by the lawyer, who seemed as weary as he. They separated in the cold corridor without a word to stumble to their respective bedrooms. From below came a heavy silence.

It was only as he was throwing his trousers over the footrail of his bed that Ellery recalled hazily Thorne's whispered intention hours before to visit him that night and explain the whole fantastic business. He struggled into his dressing-gown and slippers and shuffled down the hall to Thorne's room. But the lawyer was already in bed, snoring stertorously. Ellery dragged himself back to his room and finished undressing. He knew he would have a head the next morning; he was a notoriously poor drinker. His brain spinning, he crawled between the blankets and fell asleep almost instantly. . . .

He opened his eyes after a tossing, tiring sleep with the uneasy conviction that something was wrong. For a moment he was aware only of the ache in his head and the fuzzy feel of his tongue; he did not remember where he was. Then, as his glance took in the faded wallpaper, the pallid patches of sunlight on the worn blue carpet, his trousers tumbled over the footrail where he had left them the night before, memory returned; and, shivering, he consulted his wrist watch, which he had forgotten to take off on going to bed. It was five minutes to seven. He raised his head from the pillow in the frosty air of the bedroom; his nose was half-frozen. But he could detect nothing wrong; the sun looked brave if weak in his eyes; the room was quiet and exactly as he had seen it on retiring; the door was closed. He snuggled between the blankets again.

Then he heard it. It was Thorne's voice. It was Thorne's voice raised in a thin faint cry, almost a wall, coming from somewhere outside the house.

He was out of bed and at the window in his bare feet in one leap. But Thorne was not visible at this side of the house, upon which the dead woods encroached directly; so he scrambled back to slip shoes on his feet and his gown over his pajamas, darted toward the footrail and snatched his revolver out of the hip pocket of his trousers, and ran out into the corridor, heading for the stairs, the revolver in his hand.

"What's the matter?" grumbled someone, and he turned to see Dr. Reinach's vast skull protruding nakedly from the room next to his.

"Don't know. I heard Thorne cry out," and

Ellery pounded down the stairs and flung open the front door.

He stopped within the doorway, gaping.

Thorne, fully dressed, was standing ten yards in front of the house, facing Ellery obliquely, staring at something outside the range of Ellery's vision with the most acute expression of terror on his gaunt face Ellery had ever seen on a human countenance. Beside him crouched Nicholas Keith, only half-dressed; the young man's jaws gaped foolishly and his eyes were enormous glaring disks.

Dr. Reinach shoved Ellery roughly aside and growled, "What's the matter? What's wrong?" The fat man's feet were encased in carpet slippers and he had pulled a raccoon coat over his nightshirt; he looked like a particularly obese bear.

Thorne's Adam's-apple bobbed nervously. The ground, the trees, the world were blanketed with snow of a peculiarly unreal texture; and the air was saturated with warm woolen flakes, falling softly. Deep drifts curved upward to clamp the boles of trees.

"Don't move," croaked Thorne as Ellery and the fat man stirred. "Don't move, for the love of God. Stay where you are." Ellery's grip tightened on the revolver and he tried perversely to get past the doctor; but he might have been trying to budge a stone wall. Thorne stumbled through the snow to the porch, paler than his background, leaving two deep ruts behind him. "Look at me," he shouted. "*Look at me.* Do I seem all right? Have I gone mad?"

"Pull yourself together, Thorne," said Ellery sharply. "What's the matter with you? I don't see anything wrong."

"Nick!" bellowed Dr. Reinach. "Have you gone crazy, too?"

The young man covered his sunburned face suddenly with his hands; then he dropped his hands and looked again.

He said in a strangled voice, "Maybe we all have. This is the most— Take a look yourself."

Reinach moved then, and Ellery squirmed by him to land in the soft snow beside Thorne, who was trembling violently. Dr. Reinach came

lurching after. They ploughed through the snow toward Keith, squinting, straining to see.

They need not have strained. What was to be seen was plain for any seeing eye to see. Ellery felt his scalp crawl as he looked; and at the same instant he was aware of the sharp conviction that this was inevitable, this was the only possible climax to the insane events of the previous day. The world had turned topsy-turvy. Nothing in it meant anything sane.

Dr. Reinach gasped once; and then he stood blinking like a huge owl. A window rattled on the second floor of the White House. None of them looked. It was Alice Mayhew in a wrapper, staring from the window of her bedroom, which was on the side of the house facing the driveway. She screamed once; and then she, too, fell silent.

There was the house from which they had just emerged, the house Dr. Reinach had dubbed the White House, with its front door quietly swinging open and Alice Mayhew at an upper side window. Substantial, solid, an edifice of stone and wood and plaster and glass and the patina of age. It was everything a house should be. That much was real, a thing to be grasped.

But beyond it, beyond the driveway and the garage, where the Black House had stood, the house of the filth and the stench, the house of the equally stone walls, wooden facings, glass windows, chimneys, gargoyles, porch; the house of the blackened look; the old Victorian house built during the Civil War where Sylvester Mayhew had died, where Thorne had barricaded himself with a cutlass for a week; the house which they had all seen, touched, smelled— there, *there stood nothing.*

No walls. No chimney. No roof. No ruins. No debris. No house. Nothing. Nothing but empty space covered smoothly and warmly with snow.

The house had vanished during the night.

Magic or Miracle?

There's even, thought Mr. Ellery Queen dully, *a character named Alice.*

He looked again. The only reason he did not

rub his eyes was that it would have made him feel ridiculous; besides, his sight, all his senses, had never been keener.

He simply stood there in the snow and looked and looked and looked at the empty space where a three-story stone house seventy-five years old had stood the night before.

"Why, it isn't there," said Alice feebly from the upper window. "It—isn't—there."

"Then I'm not insane." Thorne stumbled toward them. Ellery watched the old man's feet sloughing through the snow, leaving long tracks. A man's weight still counted for something in the universe, then. Yes, and there was his own shadow; so material objects still cast shadows. Absurdly, the discovery brought a certain faint relief.

"It *is* gone!" said Thorne in a cracked voice.

"Apparently." Ellery found his own voice thick and slow; he watched the words curl out on the air and become nothing. "Apparently, Thorne." It was all he could find to say.

Dr. Reinach arched his fat neck, his wattles quivering like a gobbler's. "Incredible. Incredible!"

"Incredible," said Thorne in a whisper.

"Unscientific. It can't be. I'm a man of sense. Of senses. My mind is clear. Things like this—damn it, they just don't happen!"

"As the man said who saw a giraffe for the first time," sighed Ellery. "And yet—there it was."

Thorne began wandering helplessly about in a circle. Alice stared, bewitched into stone, from the upper window. And Keith cursed and began to run across the snow-covered driveway toward the invisible house, his hands outstretched before him like a blind man's.

"Hold on," said Ellery. "Stop where you are."

The giant halted, scowling. "What d'ye want?"

Ellery slipped his revolver back into his pocket and sloshed through the snow to pause beside the young man in the driveway. "I don't know precisely. Something's wrong. Something's out of kilter either with us or with the world. It isn't the world as we know it. It's almost—almost a matter of transposed dimen-sions. Do you suppose the solar system has slipped out of its niche in the universe and gone stark crazy in the uncharted depths of space-time? I suppose I'm talking nonsense."

"You know best," shouted Keith. "I'm not going to let this screwy business stampede *me.* There was a solid house on that plot last night, by God, and nobody can convince me it still isn't there. Not even my own eyes. We've—we've been hypnotized! The hippo could do it here—he could do anything. Hypnotized. You hypnotized us, Reinach!"

The doctor mumbled, "What?" and kept glaring at the empty lot.

"I tell you it's there!" cried Keith angrily.

Ellery sighed and dropped to his knees in the snow; he began to brush aside the white, soft blanket with chilled palms. When he had laid the ground bare, he saw wet gravel and a rut. "This *is* the driveway, isn't it?" he asked, not looking up.

"The driveway," snarled Keith, "or the road to hell. You're as mixed up as we are. Sure it's the driveway! Can't you see the garage? Why shouldn't it be the driveway?"

"I don't know." Ellery got to his feet, frowning. "I don't know anything. I'm beginning to learn all over again. Maybe—maybe it's a matter of gravitation. Maybe we'll all fly into space any minute now."

Thorne groaned, "My God."

"All I can be sure of is that something very strange happened last night."

"I tell you," growled Keith, "it's an optical illusion!"

"Something strange." The fat man stirred. "Yes, decidedly. What an inadequate word! A house has disappeared. Something strange." He chuckled in a choking, mirthless way.

"Oh, that," said Ellery impatiently. "Certainly. Certainly, Doctor. That's a *fact.* As for you, Keith, you don't really believe this mass-hypnosis bilge. The house is gone, right enough. It's not the fact of its being gone that bothers me. It's the agency, the *means.* It smacks of—of—" He shook his head. "I've never believed in—this sort of thing, damn it all!"

Dr. Reinach threw back his vast shoulders and glared, red-eyed, at the empty snow-covered space. "It's a trick," he bellowed. "A rotten trick, that's what it is. That house is right there in front of our noses. Or—or— They can't fool *me!*"

Ellery looked at him. "Perhaps Keith has it in his pocket?"

Alice clattered out on the porch in high-heeled shoes over bare feet, her hair streaming, a cloth coat flung over her night-clothes. Behind her crept little Mrs. Reinach. The women's eyes were wild.

"Talk to them," muttered Ellery to Thorne. "Anything; but keep their minds occupied. We'll all go balmy if we don't preserve at least an air of sanity. Keith, get me a broom."

He shuffled up the driveway, skirting the invisible house very carefully and not once taking his eyes off the empty space. The fat man hesitated; then he lumbered along in Ellery's tracks. Thorne stumbled back to the porch and Keith strode off, disappearing behind the White House.

There was no sun now. A pale and eerie light filtered down through the clouds. The snow continued its soft, thick fall.

They looked like dots, small and helpless, on a sheet of blank paper.

Ellery pulled open the folding doors of the garage and peered. A healthy odor of raw gasoline and rubber assailed his nostrils. Thorne's car stood within, exactly as Ellery had seen it the afternoon before, a black monster with glittering chromework. Beside it, apparently parked by Keith after their arrival, stood the battered Buick in which Dr. Reinach had driven them from the city. Both cars were perfectly dry.

He shut the doors and turned back to the driveway. Aside from the catenated links of their footprints in the snow, made a moment before, the white covering on the driveway was virgin.

"Here's your broom," said the giant. "What are you going to do—ride it?"

"Hold your tongue, Nick," growled Dr. Reinach.

Ellery laughed. "Let him alone, Doctor. His angry sanity is infectious. Come along, you two.

This may be the Judgment Day, but we may as well go through the motions."

"What do you want with a broom, Queen?"

"It's hard to decide whether the snow was an accident or part of the plan," murmured Ellery. "Anything may be true today. Literally anything."

"Rubbish," snorted the fat man. "Abracadabra. *Om mani padme hum.* How could a man have planned a snowfall? You're talking gibberish."

"I didn't say a human plan, Doctor."

"Rubbish, rubbish, rubbish!"

"You may as well save your breath. You're a badly scared little boy whistling in the dark—for all your bulk, Doctor."

Ellery gripped the broom tightly and stamped out across the driveway. He felt his own foot shrinking as he tried to make it step upon the white rectangle. His muscles were gathered in, as if in truth he expected to encounter the adamantine bulk of a house which was still there but unaccountably impalpable. When he felt nothing but cold air, he laughed a little self-consciously and began to wield the broom on the snow in a peculiar manner. He used the most delicate of sweeping motions, barely brushing the surface crystals away, so that layer by layer he reduced the depth of the snow. He scanned each layer with anxiety as it was uncovered. And he continued to do this until the ground itself lay revealed; and at no depth did he come across the minutest trace of a human imprint.

"Elves. Nothing less than elves. I confess it's beyond me."

"Even the foundation—" began Dr. Reinach heavily.

Ellery poked the tip of the broom at the earth. It was hard as corundum.

The front door slammed as Thorne and the two women crept into the White House. The three men outside stood still.

"Well," said Ellery at last, "this is either a bad dream or the end of the world." He made off diagonally across the plot, dragging the broom behind him like a tired charwoman, until he reached the snow-covered drive; and then he trudged down the drive toward the invisible road, disappearing around a bend under the stripped white-dripping trees.

It was a short walk to the road. Ellery remembered it well. It had curved steadily in a long arc all the way from the turn-off at the main highway. There had been no crossroad in all the jolting journey.

He went out into the middle of the road, snow-covered now but plainly distinguishable between the powdered tangles of woods as a gleaming, empty strip. There was the long curve exactly as he remembered it. Mechanically he used the broom again, sweeping a small area clear. And there were the pits and ruts of the old Buick's journeys.

"What are you looking for," said Nick Keith quietly, "gold?"

Ellery straightened up by degrees, turning about slowly until he was face to face with the giant. "So you thought it was necessary to follow me? Or—no, I beg your pardon. Undoubtedly it was Dr. Reinach's idea."

The sun-charred features did not change expression. "You're crazy. Follow you? I've got all I can do to follow myself."

"Of course," said Ellery. "But did I understand you to ask me if I was looking for gold, my dear young Prometheus?"

"You're a queer one," said Keith as they made their way back toward the house.

"Gold," repeated Ellery. "Hmm. There was gold in that house, and now the house is gone. In the shock of the discovery that houses fly away like birds, I'd quite forgotten that little item. Thank you, Mr. Keith," said Ellery grimly, "for reminding me. . . ."

"Mr. Queen," said Alice. She was crouched in a chair by the fire, white to the lips. "What's happened to us? What are we to do? Have we— Was yesterday a dream? Didn't we walk into that house, go through it, touch things? . . . I'm frightened."

"If yesterday *was* a dream," smiled Ellery, "then we may expect that tomorrow will bring a vision; for that's what holy Sanskrit says, and we may as well believe in parables as in miracles."

He sat down, rubbing his hands briskly. "How about a fire, Keith? It's arctic in here."

"Sorry," said Keith with surprising amiability, and he went away.

"We could use a vision," shivered Thorne. "My brain is—sick. It just isn't possible. It's horrible." His hand slapped his side and something jangled in his pocket.

"Keys," said Ellery, "and no house. It *is* staggering."

Keith came back under a mountain of firewood. He grimaced at the litter in the fireplace, dropped the wood, and began sweeping together the fragments of glass, the remains of the brandy decanter he had smashed against the brick wall the night before. Alice glanced from his broad back to the chromo of her mother on the mantel. As for Mrs. Reinach, she was as silent as a scared bird; she stood in a corner like a weazened little gnome, her wrapper drawn about her, her stringy sparrow-colored hair hanging down her back, and her glassy eyes fixed on the face of her husband.

"Milly," said the fat man.

"Yes, Herbert, I'm going," said Mrs. Reinach instantly, and she crept up the stairs and out of sight.

"Well, Mr. Queen, what's the answer? Or is this riddle too esoteric for your taste?"

"No riddle is esoteric," muttered Ellery, "unless it's the riddle of God; and that's no riddle—it's a vast blackness. Doctor, is there any way of reaching assistance?"

"Not unless you can fly."

"No phone," said Keith, "and you saw the condition of the road. You'd never get a car through those drifts."

"If you had a car," chuckled Dr. Reinach. Then he seemed to remember the disappearing house, and his chuckle died.

"What do you mean?" demanded Ellery. "In the garage are—"

"Two useless products of the machine age. Both cars are out of fuel."

"And mine," said old Thorne suddenly, with a resurrection of grim personal interest, "mine has something wrong with it besides. I left my chauffeur in the city, you know, Queen, when I drove down last time. Now I can't get the engine running on the little gasoline that's left in the tank."

Ellery's fingers drummed on the arm of his chair. "Bother! Now we can't even call on other eyes to test whether we've been bewitched or not. By the way, Doctor, how far is the nearest community? I didn't pay attention on the drive down."

"Over fifteen miles by road. If you're thinking of footing it, Mr. Queen, you're welcome to the thought."

"You'd never get through the drifts," muttered Keith. The drifts appeared to trouble him.

"And so we find ourselves snowbound," said Ellery, "in the middle of the fourth dimension—or perhaps it's the fifth. A pretty kettle! Ah there, Keith, that feels considerably better."

"You don't seem bowled over by what's happened," said Dr. Reinach, eyeing him curiously. "I'll confess it's given even me a shock."

Ellery was silent for a moment. Then he said lightly, "There wouldn't be any point to losing our heads, would there?"

"I fully expect dragons to come flying over the house," groaned Thorne. He eyed Ellery a bit bashfully. "Queen—perhaps we had better—try to get out of here."

"You heard Keith, Thorne."

Thorne bit his lips. "I'm frozen," said Alice, drawing nearer the fire. "That was well done, Mr. Keith. It—it—a fire like this makes me think of home, somehow." The young man got to his feet and turned around. Their eyes met for an instant.

"It's nothing," he said shortly. "Nothing at all."

"You seem to be the only one who—Oh!"

An enormous old woman with a black shawl over her shoulders was coming downstairs. She might have been years dead, she was so yellow and emaciated and mummified. And yet she gave the impression of being very much alive, with a sort of ancient, ageless life; her black eyes were young and bright and cunning, and her face was extraordinarily mobile. She was sidling down stiffly, feeling her way with one foot and clutching the banister with two dried claws, while her lively eyes remained fixed on Alice's face. There was a curious hunger in her expression, the flaring of a long-dead hope suddenly, against all reason.

"Who—who—" began Alice, shrinking back.

"Don't be alarmed," said Dr. Reinach quickly. "It's unfortunate that she got away from Milly. . . . Sarah!" In a twinkling he was at the foot of the staircase, barring the old woman's way. "What are you doing up at this hour? You should take better care of yourself, Sarah."

She ignored him, continuing her snail's pace down the stairs until she reached his pachyderm bulk. "Olivia," she mumbled, with a vital eagerness. "It's Olivia come back to me. Oh, my sweet, sweet darling."

"No, Sarah," said the fat man, taking her hand gently. "Don't excite yourself. This isn't Olivia, Sarah. It's Alice—Alice Mayhew. Sylvester's girl, come from England. You remember Alice, little Alice? Not Olivia, Sarah."

"Not Olivia?" The old woman peered across the banister, her wrinkled lips moved. "Not Olivia?"

The girl jumped up. "I'm Alice, Aunt Sarah. Alice—"

Sarah Fell darted suddenly past the fat man and scurried across the room to seize the girl's hand and glare into her face. As she studied those shrinking features her expression changed to one of despair. "Not Olivia. Olivia's beautiful black hair. . . . Not Olivia's voice. Alice? Alice?" She dropped into Alice's vacated chair, her skinny broad shoulders sagging, and began to weep. They could see the yellow skin of her scalp through the sparse gray hair.

Dr. Reinach roared, "Milly!" in an enraged voice. Mrs. Reinach popped into sight like a Jack-in-the-box. "Why did you let her leave her room?"

"B–But I thought she was—" began Mrs. Reinach.

"Take her upstairs at once!"

"Yes, Herbert," whispered the sparrow, and Mrs. Reinach hurried downstairs in her wrapper and took the old woman's hand and, unopposed, led her away. Mrs. Fell kept repeating, between sobs, "Why doesn't Olivia come back? Why did they take her away from her mother?" until she was out of sight.

"Sorry," panted the fat man, mopping himself. "One of her spells. I knew it was coming on from the curiosity she exhibited the moment she heard you were coming, Alice. There *is* a resemblance; you can scarcely blame her."

"She's—she's horrible," said Alice faintly. "Mr. Queen—Mr. Thorne, must we stay here? I'd feel so much easier in the city. And then my cold, these frigid rooms—"

"By Heaven," burst out Thorne, "I feel like chancing it on foot!"

"And leave Sylvester's gold to our tender mercies?" smiled Dr. Reinach. Then he scowled.

"I don't want Father's legacy," said Alice desperately. "At this moment I don't want anything but to get away. I—I can manage to get along all right. I'll find work to do—I can do so many things. I want to go away. Mr. Keith, couldn't you—"

"*I'm* not a magician," said Keith rudely; and he buttoned his mackinaw and strode out of the house. They could see his tall figure stalking off behind a veil of snowflakes.

Alice flushed, turning back to the fire.

"Nor are any of us," said Ellery. "Miss Mayhew, you'll simply have to be a brave girl and stick it out until we can find a means of getting out of here."

"Yes," murmured Alice, shivering; and stared into the flames.

"Meanwhile, Thorne, tell me everything you know about this case, especially as it concerns Sylvester Mayhew's house. There may be a clue in your father's history, Miss Mayhew. If the house has vanished, so has the gold *in* the house; and whether you want it or not, it belongs to you. Consequently we must make an effort to find it."

"I suggest," muttered Dr. Reinach, "that you find the house first. House!" he exploded, waving his furred arms. And he made for the sideboard.

Alice nodded listlessly. Thorne mumbled, "Perhaps, Queen, you and I had better talk privately."

"We made a frank beginning last night; I see no reason why we shouldn't continue in the same candid vein. You needn't be reluctant to speak before Dr. Reinach. Our host is obviously a man of parts—unorthodox parts."

Dr. Reinach did not reply. His globular face was dark as he tossed off a water-goblet full of gin.

Through air metallic with defiance, Thorne talked in a hardening voice; not once did he take his eyes from Dr. Reinach.

His first suspicion that something was wrong had been germinated by Sylvester Mayhew himself.

Hearing by post from Alice, Thorne had investigated and located Mayhew. He had explained to the old invalid his daughter's desire to find her father, if he still lived. Old Mayhew, with a strange excitement, had acquiesced; he was eager to be reunited with his daughter; and he seemed to be living, explained Thorne defiantly, in mortal fear of his relatives in the neighboring house.

"Fear, Thorne?" The fat man sat down, raising his brows. "You know he was afraid, not of us, but of poverty. He was a miser."

Thorne ignored him. Mayhew had instructed Thorne to write Alice and bid her come to America at once; he meant to leave her his entire estate and wanted her to have it before he died. The repository of the gold he had cunningly refused to divulge, even to Thorne; it was "in the house," he had said, but he would not reveal its hiding-place to anyone but Alice herself. The "others," he had snarled, had been looking for it ever since their "arrival."

"By the way," drawled Ellery, "how long have you good people been living in this house, Dr. Reinach?"

"A year or so. You certainly don't put any credence in the paranoiac ravings of a dying man?

449

There's no mystery about our living here. I looked Sylvester up over a year ago after a long separation and found him still in the old homestead, and this house boarded up and empty. The White House, this house, incidentally, was built by my stepfather—Sylvester's father—on Sylvester's marriage to Alice's mother; Sylvester lived in it until my stepfather died, and then moved back to the Black House. I found Sylvester, a degenerated hulk of what he'd once been, living on crusts, absolutely alone and badly in need of medical attention."

"Alone—here, in this wilderness?" said Ellery incredulously.

"Yes. As a matter of fact, the only way I could get his permission to move back to this house, which belonged to him, was by dangling the bait of free medical treatment before his eyes. I'm sorry, Alice; he was quite unbalanced. . . . And so Milly and Sarah and I—Sarah had been living with us ever since Olivia's death—moved in here."

"Decent of you," remarked Ellery. "I suppose you had to give up your medical practice to do it, Doctor?"

Dr. Reinach grimaced. "I didn't have much of a practice to give up, Mr. Queen."

"But it was an almost pure brotherly impulse, eh?"

"Oh, I don't deny that the possibility of falling heir to some of Sylvester's fortune had crossed our minds. It was rightfully ours, we believed, not knowing anything about Alice. As it's turned out—" He shrugged. "I'm a philosopher."

"And don't deny, either," shouted Thorne, "that when I came back here at the time Mayhew sank into that fatal coma you people watched me like a—like a band of spies! I was in your way!"

"Mr. Thorne," whispered Alice, paling.

"I'm sorry, Miss Mayhew, but you may as well know the truth. Oh, you didn't fool me, Reinach! You wanted that gold, Alice or no Alice. I shut myself up in that house just to keep you from getting your hands on it!"

Dr. Reinach shrugged again; his rubbery lips compressed.

"You want candor; here it is!" rasped Thorne. "I was in that house, Queen, for six days after Mayhew's funeral and before Miss Mayhew's arrival, *looking for the gold*. I turned that house upside down. And I didn't find the slightest trace of it. I tell you it isn't there." He glared at the fat man. "I tell you it was stolen before Mayhew died!"

"Now, now," sighed Ellery. "That makes less sense than the other. Why then has somebody intoned an incantation over the house and caused it to disappear?"

"I don't know," said the old lawyer fiercely. "I know only that the most dastardly thing's happened here, that everything is unnatural, veiled in that—that false creature's smile! Miss Mayhew, I'm sorry I must speak this way about your own family. But I feel it my duty to warn you that you've fallen among human wolves. Wolves!"

"I'm afraid," said Reinach sourly, "that I shouldn't come to you, my dear Thorne, for a reference."

"I wish," said Alice very low, "I truly wish I were dead."

But the lawyer was past control. "That man Keith," he cried. "Who is he? What's he doing here? He looks like a gangster. I suspect him, Queen—"

"Apparently," smiled Ellery, "you suspect everybody."

"Mr. Keith?" murmured Alice. "Oh, I'm sure not. I—I don't think he's that sort at all, Mr. Thorne. He looks as if he's had a hard life. As if he's suffered terribly from something."

Thorne threw up his hands, turning to the fire.

"Let us," said Ellery amiably, "confine ourselves to the problem at hand. We were, I believe, considering the problem of a disappearing house. Do any architect's plans of the so-called Black House exist?"

"Lord, no," said Dr. Reinach.

"Who has lived in it since your stepfather's death besides Sylvester Mayhew and his wife?"

"Wives," corrected the doctor, pouring himself another glassful of gin. "Sylvester married

twice; I suppose you didn't know that, my dear."
Alice shivered by the fire. "I dislike raking over
old ashes, but since we're at confessional—
Sylvester treated Alice's mother abominably."

"I—guessed that," whispered Alice.

"She was a woman of spirit and she rebelled;
but when she'd got her final decree and returned
to England, the reaction set in and she died very
shortly afterward, I understand. Her death was
recorded in the New York papers."

"When I was a baby," whispered Alice.

"Sylvester, already unbalanced, although
not so anchoretic in those days as he became
later, then wooed and won a wealthy widow and
brought her out here to live. She had a son, a
child by her first husband, with her. Father'd
died by this time, and Sylvester and his second
wife lived in the Black House. It was soon evident that Sylvester had married the widow for
her money; he persuaded her to sign it over to
him—a considerable fortune for those days—
and promptly proceeded to devil the life out of
her. Result: the woman vanished one day, taking
her child with her."

"Perhaps," said Ellery, seeing Alice's face,
"we'd better abandon the subject, Doctor."

"We never did find out what actually
happened—whether Sylvester drove her out or
whether, unable to stand his brutal treatment
any longer, she left voluntarily. At any rate, I discovered by accident, a few years later, through
an obituary notice, that she died in the worst
sort of poverty."

Alice was staring at him with a wrinkle-nosed
nausea. "Father—did that?"

"Oh, stop it," growled Thorne. "You'll have
the poor child gibbering in another moment.
What has all this to do with the house?"

"Mr. Queen asked," said the fat man mildly.
Ellery was studying the flames as if they fascinated him.

"The real point," snapped the lawyer, "is
that you've watched me from the instant I set
foot here, Reinach. Afraid to leave me alone
for a moment. Why, you even had Keith meet
me in your car on both my visits—to 'escort'
me here! And I didn't have five minutes alone

with the old gentleman—you saw to that. And
then he lapsed into the coma and was unable to
speak again before he died. Why? Why all this
surveillance? God knows I'm a forbearing man;
but you've given me every ground for suspecting
your motives."

"Apparently," chuckled Dr. Reinach, "you
don't agree with Caesar."

"I beg your pardon?"

"'Would,'" quoted the fat man, "'he were
fatter.' Well, good people, the end of the world
may come, but that's no reason why we shouldn't
have breakfast. Milly!" he bellowed. . . .

Thorne awoke sluggishly, like a drowsing
old hound dimly aware of danger. His bedroom
was cold; a pale morning light was struggling in
through the window. He groped under his pillow.

"Stop where you are!" he said harshly.

"So you have a revolver, too?" murmured
Ellery. He was dressed and looked as if he had
slept badly. "It's only I, Thorne, stealing in for
a conference. It's not so hard to steal in here, by
the way."

"What do you mean?" grumbled Thorne, sitting up and putting his old-fashioned revolver
away.

"I see your lock has gone the way of mine,
Alice's, the Black House, and Sylvester Mayhew's elusive gold."

Thorne drew the patchwork comforter about
him, his old lips blue. "Well, Queen?"

Ellery lit a cigarette and for a moment stared
out Thorne's window at the streamers of crepy
snow still dropping from the sky. The snow had
fallen without a moment's let-up the entire previous day. "This is a curious business all round,
Thorne. The queerest medley of spirit and matter. I've just reconnoitered. You'll be interested
to learn that our young friend the Colossus is
gone."

"Keith gone?"

"His bed hasn't been slept in at all. I looked."

"And he was away most of yesterday, too!"

"Precisely. Our surly Crichton, who
seems afflicted by a particularly acute case of
Weltschmerz, periodically vanishes. Where does

451

he go? I'd give a good deal to know the answer to that question."

"He won't get far in those nasty drifts," mumbled the lawyer.

"It gives one, as the French say, to think. Comrade Reinach is gone, too." Thorne stiffened. "Oh, yes; his bed's been slept in, but briefly, I judge. Have they eloped together? Separately? Thorne," said Ellery thoughtfully, "this becomes an increasingly subtle devilment."

"It's beyond me," said Thorne with another shiver. "I'm just about ready to give up. I don't see that we're accomplishing a thing here. And then there's always that annoying, incredible fact—the house—vanished."

Ellery sighed and looked at his wrist watch. It was a minute past seven.

Thorne threw back the comforter and groped under the bed for his slippers. "Let's go downstairs," he snapped. . . .

"Excellent bacon, Mrs. Reinach," said Ellery. "I suppose it must be a trial carting supplies up here."

"We've the blood of pioneers," said Dr. Reinach cheerfully, before his wife could reply. He was engulfing mounds of scrambled eggs and bacon. "Luckily, we've enough in the larder to last out a considerable siege. The winters are severe out here—we learned that last year."

Keith was not at the breakfast table. Old Mrs. Fell was. She ate voraciously. Nevertheless, although she did not speak, she contrived as she ate to keep her eyes on Alice, who wore a haunted look.

"I didn't sleep very well," said Alice, toying with her coffee-cup. Her voice was huskier. "This abominable snow! Can't we manage somehow to get away today?"

"Not so long as the snow keeps up, I'm afraid," said Ellery gently. "And you, Doctor? Did you sleep badly, too? Or hasn't the whisking away of a whole house from under your nose affected your nerves at all?"

The fat man's eyes were rid-rimmed and his lids sagged. Nevertheless, he chuckled and said, "I? I always sleep well. Nothing on my conscience. Why?"

"Oh, no special reason. Where's friend Keith this morning? He's a seclusive sort of chap, isn't he?"

Mrs. Reinach swallowed a muffin whole. Her husband glanced at her and she rose and fled to the kitchen. "Lord knows," said the fat man. "He's as unpredictable as the ghost of Banquo. Don't bother yourself about the boy; he's harmless."

Ellery sighed and pushed back from the table. "The passage of twenty-four hours hasn't softened the wonder of the event. May I be excused? I'm going to have another peep at the house that isn't there anymore." Thorne started to rise. "No, no, Thorne; I'd rather go alone."

He put on his warmest clothes and went outdoors. The drifts reached the lower windows now; and the trees had almost disappeared under the snow. A crude path had been hacked by someone from the front door for a few feet; already it was half-refilled with snow.

Ellery stood still in the path, breathing deeply of the raw air and staring off to the right at the empty rectangle where the Black House had once stood. Leading across that expanse to the edge of the woods beyond were barely discernible tracks. He turned up his coat-collar against the cutting wind and plunged into the snow waist-deep.

It was difficult going, but not unpleasant. After a while he began to feel quite warm. The world was white and silent—a new, strange world.

When he had left the open area and struggled into the woods, it was with a sensation that he was leaving even that new world behind. Everything was so still and white and beautiful, with a pure beauty not of the earth; the snow draping the trees gave them a fresh look, making queer patterns out of old forms.

Here, where there was a roof between ground and sky, the snow had not filtered into the mysterious tracks so quickly. They were purposeful tracks, unwandering, striking straight as a dotted line for some distant goal. Ellery pushed on more rapidly, excited by a presentiment of discovery.

Then the world went black. It was a curious thing. The snow grew gray, and grayer, and finally very dark gray, becoming jet black at the last instant, as if flooded from underneath by ink. And with some surprise he felt the cold wet kiss of the drift on his cheek.

He opened his eyes to find himself flat on his back in the snow and Thorne in the great-coat stooped over him, nose jutting from blued face like a winter thorn.

"Queen!" cried the old man, shaking him. "Are you all right?"

Ellery sat up, licking his lips. "As well as might be expected," he groaned. "What hit me? It felt like one of God's angrier thunderbolts." He caressed the back of his head, and staggered to his feet. "Well, Thorne, we seem to have reached the border of the enchanted land."

"You're not delirious?" asked the lawyer anxiously.

Ellery looked about for the tracks which should have been there. But except for the double line at the head of which Thorne stood, there were none. Apparently he had lain unconscious in the snow for a long time.

"Farther than this," he said with a grimace, "we may not go. Hands off. Nose out. Mind your own business. Beyond this invisible boundary-line lie Sheol and Domdaniel and Abaddon. *Lasciate ogni speranza voi ch'entrate*. . . . Forgive me, Thorne. Did you save my life?"

Thorne jerked about, searching the silent woods. "I don't know. I think not. At least I found you lying here, alone. Gave me quite a start—thought you were dead."

"As well," said Ellery with a shiver, "I might have been."

"When you left the house Alice went upstairs, Reinach said something about a cat-nap, and I wandered out of the house. I waded through the drifts on the road for a spell, and then I thought of you and made my way back. Your tracks were almost obliterated; but they were visible enough to take me across the clearing to the edge of the woods, and I finally blundered upon you. By now the tracks are gone."

"I don't like this at all," said Ellery, "and yet in another sense I like it very much."

"What do you mean?"

"I can't imagine," said Ellery, "a divine agency stooping to such a mean assault."

"Yes, it's open war now," muttered Thorne. "Whoever it is—he'll stop at nothing."

"A benevolent war, at any rate. I was quite at his mercy, and he might have killed me as easily as—"

He stopped. A sharp report, like a pine-knot snapping in a fire or an ice-stiffened twig breaking in two, but greatly magnified, had come to his ears. Then the echo came to them, softer but unmistakable.

It was the report of a gun.

"From the house!" yelled Ellery. "Come on!"

Thorne was pale as they scrambled through the drifts. "Gun—I forgot. I left my revolver under the pillow in my bedroom. Do you think—?"

Ellery scrabbled at his own pocket. "Mine's still here. . . . No, by George, I've been scotched!" His cold fingers fumbled with the cylinder. "Bullets taken out. And I've no spare ammunition." He fell silent, his mouth hardening.

They found the women and Reinach running about like startled animals, searching for they knew not what.

"Did you hear it, too?" cried the fat man as they burst into the house. He seemed extraordinarily excited. "Someone fired a shot!"

"Where?" asked Ellery, his eyes on the rove. "Keith?"

"Don't know where he is. Milly says it might have come from behind the house. I was napping and couldn't tell. Revolvers! At least he's come out in the open."

"Who has?" asked Ellery.

The fat man shrugged. Ellery went through to the kitchen and opened the back door. The snow outside was smooth, untrodden. When he returned to the living-room Alice was adjusting a scarf about her neck with fingers that shook.

"I don't know how long you people intend to stay in this ghastly place," she said in a passionate voice. "But I've had *quite* enough, thank you. Mr. Thorne, I insist you take me away at once. At once! I shan't stay another instant."

"Now, now, Miss Mayhew," said Thorne in a distressed way, taking her hands. "I should like nothing better. But can't you see—"

Ellery, on his way upstairs three steps at a time, heard no more. He made for Thorne's room and kicked the door open, sniffing. Then, with rather a grim smile, he went to the tumbled bed and pulled the pillow away. A long-barreled, old-fashioned revolver lay there. He examined the cylinder; it was empty. Then he put the muzzle to his nose.

"Well?" said Thorne from the doorway. The English girl was clinging to him.

"Well," said Ellery, tossing the gun aside, "we're facing fact now, not fancy. It's war, Thorne, as you said. The shot was fired from your revolver. Barrel's still warm, muzzle still reeks, and you can smell the burned gunpowder if you sniff this cold air hard enough. *And* the bullets are gone."

"But what does it mean?" moaned Alice.

"It means that somebody's being terribly cute. It was a harmless trick to get Thorne and me back to the house. Probably the shot was a warning as well as a decoy."

Alice sank into Thorne's bed. "You mean we—"

"Yes," said Ellery, "from now on we're prisoners, Miss Mayhew. Prisoners who may not stray beyond the confines of the jail. I wonder," he added with a frown, "precisely why. . . ."

The day passed in a timeless haze. The world of outdoors became more and more choked in the folds of the snow. The air was a solid white sheet. It seemed as if the very heavens had opened to admit all the snow that ever was, or ever would be.

Young Keith appeared suddenly at noon, taciturn and leaden-eyed, gulped down some hot food, and without explanation retired to his bedroom. Dr. Reinach shambled about quietly for some time; then he disappeared, only to show up, wet, grimy, and silent, before dinner. As the day wore on, less and less was said. Thorne in desperation took to a bottle of whisky. Keith came down at eight o'clock, made himself some coffee, drank three cups, and went upstairs again. Dr. Reinach appeared to have lost his good nature; he was morose, almost sullen, opening his mouth only to snarl at his wife.

They all retired early, without conversation.

At midnight the strain was more than even Ellery's iron nerves could bear. He had prowled about his bedroom for hours, poking at the brisk fire in the grate, his mind leaping from improbability to fantasy until his head throbbed with one great ache. Sleep was impossible.

Moved by an impulse which he did not attempt to analyze, he slipped into his coat and went out into the frosty corridor. Thorne's door was closed; Ellery heard the old man's bed creaking and groaning. It was pitch-dark in the hall as he groped his way about. Suddenly Ellery's toe caught in a rent in the carpet and he staggered to regain his balance, coming up against the wall with a thud, his heels clattering on the bare planking at the bottom of the baseboard.

He had no sooner straightened up than he heard the stifled exclamation of a woman. It came from across the corridor; if he guessed right, from Alice Mayhew's bedroom. It was such a weak, terrified exclamation that he sprang across the hall, fumbling in his pockets for a match as he did so. He found match and door in the same instant; he struck one and opened the door and stood still, the tiny light flaring up before him.

Alice was sitting up in bed, quilt drawn about her shoulders, her eyes gleaming in the quarter-light. Before an open drawer of a tallboy across the room, one hand arrested in the act of scattering its contents about, loomed Dr. Reinach, fully dressed. His shoes were wet; his expression was blank.

"Please stand still, Doctor," said Ellery softly as the match sputtered out. "My revolver is useless as a percussion weapon, but it still can inflict damage as a blunt instrument." He moved to a nearby table, where he had seen an oil-lamp before the match went out, struck another match, lighted the lamp, and stepped back again to stand against the door.

"Thank you," whispered Alice.

"What happened, Miss Mayhew?"

"I—don't know. I slept badly. I came awake a moment ago when I heard the floor creak. And then you dashed in." She cried suddenly, "Bless you!"

"You cried out."

"Did I?" She sighed like a tired child. "I—Uncle Herbert!" she said suddenly, fiercely. "What's the meaning of this? What are you doing in my room?"

The fat man's eyes came open, innocent and beaming; his hand withdrew from the drawer and closed it; and he shifted his elephantine bulk until he was standing erect. "Doing, my dear?" he rumbled. "Why, I came in to see if you were all right." His eyes were fixed on a patch of her white shoulders visible above the quilt. "You were so overwrought today. Purely an avuncular impulse, child. Forgive me if I startled you."

"I think," sighed Ellery, "that I've misjudged you, Doctor. That's not clever of you at all. Downright clumsy, in fact; I can only attribute it to a certain understandable confusion of the moment. Miss Mayhew isn't normally to be found in the top drawer of a tallboy, no matter how capacious it may be." He said sharply to Alice, "Did this fellow touch you?"

"Touch me?" Her shoulders twitched with repugnance. "No. If he had, in the dark, I—I think I should have died."

"What a charming compliment," said Dr. Reinach ruefully.

"Then what," demanded Ellery, "*were* you looking for, Dr. Reinach?"

The fat man turned until his right side was toward the door. "I'm notoriously hard of hearing," he chuckled, "in my right ear. Good night, Alice; pleasant dreams. May I pass, Sir Lancelot?"

Ellery kept his gaze on the fat man's bland face until the door closed. For some time after the last echo of Dr. Reinach's chuckle died away they were silent.

Then Alice slid down in the bed and clutched the edge of the quilt. "Mr. Queen, please! Take

me away tomorrow. I mean it. I truly do. I—can't tell you how frightened I am of—all this. Every time I think of that—that— How can such things be? We're not in a place of sanity, Mr. Queen. We'll all go mad if we remain here much longer. Won't you take me away?"

Ellery sat down on the edge of her bed. "Are you really so upset, Miss Mayhew?" he asked gently.

"I'm simply terrified," she whispered.

"Then Thorne and I will do what we can tomorrow." He patted her arm through the quilt. "I'll have a look at his car and see if something can't be done with it. He said there's some gas left in the tank. We'll go as far as it will take us and walk the rest of the way."

"But with so little petrol— Oh, I don't care!" She stared up at him wide-eyed. "Do you think—he'll let us?"

"He?"

"Whoever it is that—"

Ellery rose with a smile. "We'll cross that bridge when it gets to us. Meanwhile, get some sleep; you'll have a strenuous day tomorrow."

"Do you think I'm—he'll—"

"Leave the lamp burning and set a chair under the doorknob when I leave." He took a quick look about. "By the way, Miss Mayhew, is there anything in your possession which Dr. Reinach might want to appropriate?"

"That's puzzled me, too. I can't imagine what I've got he could possibly want. I'm so poor, Mr. Queen—quite the Cinderella. There's nothing; just my clothes, the things I came with."

"No old letters, records, mementos?"

"Just one very old photograph of Mother."

"Hmm, Dr. Reinach doesn't strike me as *that* sentimental. Well, good night. Don't forget the chair. You'll be quite safe, I assure you."

He waited in the frigid darkness of the corridor until he heard her creep out of bed and set a chair against the door. Then he went into his own room.

And there was Thorne in a shabby dressing-gown, looking like an ancient and disheveled specter of gloom.

"What ho! The ghost walks. Can't you sleep, either?"

"Sleep!" The old man shuddered. "How can an honest man sleep in this God-forsaken place? I notice you seem rather cheerful."

"Not cheerful. Alive." Ellery sat down and lit a cigarette. "I heard you tossing about your bed a few minutes ago. Anything happen to pull you out into this cold?"

"No. Just nerves." Thorne jumped up and began to pace the floor. "Where have you been?"

Ellery told him. "Remarkable chap, Reinach," he concluded. "But we mustn't allow our admiration to overpower us. We'll really have to give this thing up, Thorne, at least temporarily. I *had* been hoping—But there! I've promised the poor girl. We're leaving tomorrow as best we can."

"And be found frozen stiff next March by a rescue party," said Thorne miserably. "Pleasant prospect! And yet even death by freezing is preferable to this abominable place." He looked curiously at Ellery. "I must say I'm a trifle disappointed in you, Queen. From what I'd heard about your professional cunning—"

"I never claimed"—Ellery shrugged—"to be a magician. Or even a theologian. What's happened here is either the blackest magic or palpable proof that miracles can happen."

"It would seem so," muttered Thorne. "And yet, when you put your mind to it— It goes against reason, by thunder!"

"I see," said Ellery dryly, "the man of law is recovering from the initial shock. Well, it's a shame to have to leave here now, in a way. I detest the thought of giving up—especially at the present time."

"At the present time? What do you mean?"

"I dare say, Thorne, you haven't emerged far enough from your condition of shock to have properly analyzed this little problem. I gave it a lot of thought today. The goal eludes me—but I'm near it," he said softly, "very near it."

"You mean," gasped the lawyer, "you mean you actually—"

"Remarkable case," said Ellery. "Oh, extraordinary—there isn't a word in the English language or any other, for that matter, that properly describes it. If I were religiously inclined—" He puffed away thoughtfully. "It gets down to the very simple elements, as all truly great problems do. A fortune in gold exists. It is hidden in a house. The house disappears. To find the gold, then, you must first find the house. I believe—"

"Aside from that mumbo-jumbo with Keith's broom the other day," cried Thorne, "I can't recall that you've made a single effort in that direction. Find the house!—why, you've done nothing but sit around and wait."

"Exactly," murmured Ellery.

"What?"

"Wait. That's the prescription, my lean and angry friend. That's the sigil that will exorcise the spirit of the Black House."

"Sigil?" Thorne stared. "Spirit?"

"Wait. Precisely. Lord, how I'm waiting!"

Thorne looked puzzled and suspicious, as if he suspected Ellery of a contrary midnight humor. But Ellery sat soberly smoking. "Wait! For what, man? You're more exasperating than that fat monstrosity! What are you waiting for?"

Ellery looked at him. Then he rose and flung his butt into the dying fire and placed his hand on the old man's arm. "Go to bed, Thorne. You wouldn't believe me if I told you."

"Queen, you *must*. I'll go mad if I don't see daylight on this thing soon!"

Ellery looked shocked, for no reason that Thorne could see. And then, just as inexplicably, he slapped Thorne's shoulder and began to chuckle. "Go to bed," he said, still chuckling.

"But you must tell me!"

Ellery sighed, losing his smile. "I can't. You'd laugh."

"I'm not in a laughing mood!"

"Nor is it a laughing matter. Thorne, I began to say a moment ago that if I, poor sinner that I am, possessed religious susceptibilities, I should have become permanently devout in the past three days. I suppose I'm a hopeless case. But even I see a power not of earth in this."

"Play-actor," growled the old lawyer. "Professing to see the hand of God in—Don't be sacrilegious, man. We're not all heathen."

Ellery looked out his window at the moonless night and the glimmering grayness of the snow-swathed world.

"Hand of God?" he murmured. "No, not hand, Thorne. If this case is ever solved, it will be by—a lamp."

"Lamp?" said Thorne faintly. "Lamp?"

"In a manner of speaking. *The lamp of God.*"

A Question of Murder

The next day dawned sullenly, as ashen and hopeless a morning as ever was. Incredibly, it still snowed in the same thick fashion, as if the whole sky were crumbling bit by bit.

Ellery spent the better part of the day in the garage, tinkering at the big black car's vitals. He left the doors wide open, so that anyone who wished might see what he was about. He knew little enough of automotive mechanics, and he felt from the start that he was engaged in a futile business. But in the late afternoon, after hours of vain experimentation, he suddenly came upon a tiny wire which seemed to him to be out of joint with its environment. It simply hung, a useless thing. Logic demanded a connection. He experimented. He found one.

As he stepped on the starter and heard the cold motor sputter into life, a shape darkened the entrance of the garage. He turned off the ignition quickly and looked up.

It was Keith, a black mass against the background of snow, standing with widespread legs, a large can hanging from each big hand.

"Hello, there," murmured Ellery. "You've assumed human shape again, I see. Back on one of your infrequent jaunts to the world of men, Keith?"

Keith said quietly, "Going somewhere, Mr. Queen?"

"Certainly. Why—do you intend to stop me?"

"Depends on where you're going."

"Ah, a threat. Well, suppose I tell *you* where to go?"

"Tell all you want. You don't get off these grounds until I know where you're bound for."

Ellery grinned. "There's a naïve directness about you, Keith, that draws me in spite of myself. Well, I'll relieve your mind. Thorne and I are taking Miss Mayhew back to the city."

"In that case it's all right." Ellery studied his face; it was worn deep with ruts of fatigue and worry. Keith dropped the cans to the cement floor of the garage. "You can use these, then. Gas."

"Gas! Where on earth did you get it?"

"Let's say," said Keith grimly, "I dug it up out of an old Indian tomb."

"Very well."

"You've fixed Thorne's car, I see. Needn't have. I could have done it."

"Then why didn't you?"

"Because nobody asked me to." The giant swung on his heel and vanished.

Ellery sat still, frowning. Then he got out of the car, picked up the cans, and poured their contents into the tank. He reached into the car again, got the engine running, and leaving it to purr away like a great cat he went back to the house. He found Alice in her room, a coat over her shoulders, staring out her window. She sprang up at his knocks.

"Mr. Queen, you've got Mr. Thorne's car going!"

"Success at last." Ellery smiled. "Are you ready?"

"Oh, yes! I feel so much better, now that we're actually to leave. Do you think we'll have a hard time? I saw Mr. Keith bring those cans in. Petrol, weren't they? Nice of him. I never did believe such a nice young man—" She flushed. There were hectic spots in her cheeks and her eyes were brighter than they had been for days. Her voice seemed less husky, too.

"It may be hard going through the drifts, but the car is equipped with chains. With luck we should make it. It's a powerful—" Ellery stopped very suddenly indeed, his eyes fixed on the worn carpet at his feet, stony yet startled.

"What is the matter, Mr. Queen?"

"Matter?" Ellery raised his eyes and drew a deep, deep breath. "Nothing at all. God's in His heaven and all's right with the world."

She looked down at the carpet. "Oh—the sun!" With a little squeal of delight she turned to the window. "Why, Mr. Queen, it's stopped snowing. There's the sun setting—at last!"

"And high time, too," said Ellery briskly. "Will you please get your things on? We leave at once." He picked up her bags and left her, walking with a springy vigor that shook the old boards. He crossed the corridor to his room opposite hers and began, whistling, to pack his bag. . . .

The living-room was noisy with a babble of adieus. One would have said that this was a normal household, with normal people in a normal human situation. Alice was positively gay, quite as if she were not leaving a fortune in gold for what might turn out to be all time.

She set her purse down on the mantel next to her mother's chromo, fixed her hat, flung her arms about Mrs. Reinach, pecked gingerly at Mrs. Fell's withered cheek, and even smiled forgivingly at Dr. Reinach. Then she dashed back to the mantel, snatched up her purse, threw one long enigmatic glance at Keith's drawn face, and hurried outdoors as if the devil himself were after her.

Thorne was already in the car, his old face alight with incredible happiness, as if he had been reprieved at the very moment he was to set his foot beyond the little green door. He beamed at the dying sun.

Ellery followed Alice more slowly. The bags were in Thorne's car; there was nothing more to do. He climbed in, raced the motor, and then released the brake.

The fat man filled the doorway, shouting, "You know the road, now, don't you? Turn to the right at the end of this drive. Then keep going in a straight line. You can't miss. You'll hit the main highway in about . . .."

His last words were drowned in the roar of the engine. Ellery waved his hand. Alice, in the tonneau beside Thorne, twisted about and laughed a little hysterically. Thorne sat beaming at the back of Ellery's head.

The car, under Ellery's guidance, trundled unsteadily out of the drive and made a right turn into the road.

It grew dark rapidly. They made slow progress. The big machine inched its way through the drifts, slipping and lurching despite its chains. As night fell, Ellery turned the powerful headlights on. He drove with unswerving concentration. None of them spoke.

It seemed hours before they reached the main highway. But when they did the car leaped to life on the road, which had been partly cleared by snowplows, and it was not long before they were entering the nearby town.

At the sight of the friendly electric lights, the paved streets, the solid blocks of houses, Alice gave a cry of sheer delight. Ellery stopped at a gasoline station and had the tank filled.

"It's not far from here, Miss Mayhew," said Thorne reassuringly. "We'll be in the city in no time. The Triborough Bridge—"

"Oh, it's wonderful to be alive!"

"Of course you'll stay at my house. My wife will be delighted to have you. After that—"

"You're so kind, Mr. Thorne. I don't know how I shall ever be able to thank you enough." She paused, startled. "Why, what's the matter, Mr. Queen?"

For Ellery had done a strange thing. He had stopped the car at a traffic intersection and asked the officer on duty something in a low tone. The officer stared at him and replied with gestures. Ellery swung the car off into another street. He drove slowly.

"What's the matter?" asked Alice again, leaning forward.

Thorne said, frowning, "You can't have lost your way. There's a sign which distinctly says—"

"No, it's not that. I've just thought of something."

The girl and the old man looked at each other, puzzled. Ellery stopped the car at a large stone building with green lights outside and went in, remaining there for fifteen minutes. He came out whistling.

"Queen!" said Thorne abruptly, eyes on the green lights. "What's up?"

"Something that must be brought down." Ellery swung the car about and headed it for the traffic intersection. When he reached it he turned left.

"Why, you've taken the wrong turn," said Alice nervously. "This is the direction from which we've just come. I'm sure of that."

"And you're quite right, Miss Mayhew. It is." She sank back, pale, as if the very thought of returning terrified her. "We're going back, you see," said Ellery.

"Back!" exploded Thorne, sitting up straight.

"Oh, can't we just forget all those horrible people!" moaned Alice.

"I've a viciously stubborn memory. Besides, we have reinforcements. If you'll look back you'll see a car following us. It's a police car, and in it are the local Chief of Police and a squad of picked men."

"But why, Mr. Queen?" cried Alice.

"Because," said Ellery grimly, "I have my own professional pride. Because I've been on the receiving end of a damnably cute magician's trick."

"Trick?" she repeated dazedly.

"Now I shall turn magician myself. You saw a house disappear." He laughed softly. "I shall make it appear again!"

They could only stare at him, too bewildered to speak.

"And then," said Ellery, his voice hardening, "even if we chose to overlook such trivia as dematerialized houses, in all conscience we can't overlook—*murder*."

The White House

And there was the Black House again. Not a wraith. A solid house, a strong, dirty, time-encrusted house, looking as if it would never dream of taking wings and flying off into space. It stood on the other side of the driveway, where it had always stood.

They saw it even as they turned into the drive from the drift-covered road, its bulk looming black against the brilliant moon, as substantial a house as could be found in the world of sane things.

Thorne and the girl were incapable of speech; they could only gape, dumb witnesses of a miracle even greater than the disappearance of the house in the first place.

As for Ellery, he stopped the car, sprang to the ground, signaled to the car snuffling up behind, and darted across the snowy clearing to the White House, whose windows were bright with lamp- and fire-light. Out of the police car swarmed men, and they ran after Ellery like hounds. Thorne and Alice followed in a daze.

Ellery kicked open the White House door. There was a revolver in his hand and there was no doubt, from the way he gripped it, that its cylinder had been replenished.

"Hello again," he said, stalking into the living-room. "Not a ghost; Inspector Queen's little boy in the too, too solid flesh. Nemesis, perhaps. I bid you good evening. What—no welcoming smile, Dr. Reinach?"

The fat man had paused in the act of lifting a glass of Scotch to his lips. It was wonderful how the color seeped out of his pouchy cheeks, leaving them gray. Mrs. Reinach whimpered in a corner, and Mrs. Fell stared stupidly. Only Nick Keith showed no great astonishment. He was standing by a window, muffled to the ears; and on his face there was bitterness and admiration and, strangely, a sort of relief.

"Shut the door." The detectives behind Ellery spread out silently. Alice stumbled to a chair, her eyes wild, studying Dr. Reinach with a fierce intensity. . . . There was a sighing little sound and one of the detectives lunged toward the window at which Keith had been standing. But Keith was no longer there. He was bounding toward the woods like a huge deer.

"Don't let him get away!" cried Ellery. Three men dived through the window after the giant, their guns out. Shots began to sputter. The night was streaked with orange lightning.

Ellery went to the fire and warmed his hands. Dr. Reinach slowly, very slowly, sat down in the armchair. Thorne sank into a chair, too, putting his hands to his head.

Ellery turned around and said, "I've told you, Captain, enough of what's happened since our arrival to allow you an intelligent understanding of what I'm about to say." A stocky man in uniform nodded curtly.

"Thorne, last night for the first time in my career," continued Ellery whimsically, "I acknowledged the assistance of— Well, I tell you, who are implicated in this extraordinary crime, that had it not been for the good God above you would have succeeded in your plot against Alice Mayhew's inheritance."

"I'm disappointed in you," said the fat man.

"A loss I keenly feel." Ellery looked at him, smiling. "Let me show you, skeptic. When Mr. Thorne, Miss Mayhew, and I arrived the other day, it was late afternoon. Upstairs, in the room you so thoughtfully provided, I looked out the window and saw the sun setting. This was nothing and meant nothing, surely: sunset. Mere sunset. A trivial thing, interesting only to poets, meteorologists, and astronomers. But this was one time when the sun was vital to a man seeking truth—a veritable lamp of God shining in the darkness.

"For, see. Miss Mayhew's bedroom that first day was on the opposite side of the house from mine. If the sun *set* in my window, then I faced west and she faced east. So far, so good. We talked, we retired. The next morning I awoke at seven—shortly after sunrise in this winter month—and what did I see? *I saw the sun streaming into my window.*"

A knot hissed in the fire behind him. The stocky man in the blue uniform stirred uneasily.

"Don't you understand?" cried Ellery. "The sun had *set* in my window, and now it was *rising* in my window!"

Dr. Reinach was regarding him with a mild ruefulness. The color had come back to his fat cheeks. He raised the glass he was holding in a gesture curiously like a salute. Then he drank, deeply.

And Ellery said, "The significance of this unearthly reminder did not strike me at once. But much later it came back to me; and I dimly saw that chance, cosmos, God, whatever you may choose to call it, had given me the instrument for understanding the colossal, the mind-staggering phenomenon of a house which vanished overnight from the face of the earth."

"Good Lord," muttered Thorne.

"But I was not sure; I did not trust my memory. I needed another demonstration from heaven, a bulwark to bolster my own suspicions. And so, as it snowed and snowed and snowed, the snow drawing a blanket across the face of the sun through which it could not shine, I waited. I waited for the snow to stop, and for the sun to shine again."

He sighed. "When it shone again, there could no longer be any doubt. It appeared first to me in Miss Mayhew's room, which had faced the east the afternoon of our arrival. But what as it I saw in Miss Mayhew's room late this afternoon? I saw the sun *set.*"

"Good Lord," said Thorne again; he seemed incapable of saying anything else.

"Then her room faced west today. How could her room face west today when it had faced east the day of our arrival? How could my room face west the day of our arrival and face east today? Had the sun stood still? Had the world gone mad? Or was there another explanation—one so extraordinary simple that it staggered the imagination?"

Thorne muttered, "Queen, this is the most—"

"Please," said Ellery, "let me finish. The only logical conclusion, the only conclusion that did not fly in the face of natural law, of science itself, was that while the house we were in today, the rooms we occupied, *seemed* to be identical with the house and the rooms we had occupied on the day of our arrival, *they were not.* Unless this solid structure had been turned about on its foundation like a toy on a stick, which was palpably absurd, then *it was not the same house.* It looked the same inside and out, it had identical furniture, identical carpeting, identical decorations— but it was not the same house. It was another house. It was another house exactly like the first in every detail except one: and that was its terrestrial position in relation to the sun."

A detective outside shouted a message of failure, a shout carried away by the wind under the bright cold moon.

"See," said Ellery softly, "how everything fell into place. If this White House we were in was not the same White House in which we had slept that first night, but was a twin house in a different position in relation to the sun, then the Black House, which apparently had vanished, had not vanished at all. It was where it had always been. It was not the Black House which had vanished, but we who had vanished. It was not the Black House which had moved away, but we who had moved away. We had been transferred during that first night to a new location, where the surrounding woods looked similar, where there was a similar driveway with a similar garage at its terminus, where the road outside was similarly old and pitted, where everything was similar except that there was no Black House, only an empty clearing.

"So we must have been moved, body and baggage, to this twin White House during the time we retired the first night and the time we awoke the next morning. We, Miss Mayhew's chromo on the mantel, the holes in our doors where locks had been, even the fragments of a brandy decanter which had been shattered the night before in a cleverly staged scene against the brick wall of the fireplace at the original house—all, all transferred to the twin house to further the illusion that we were still in the original house the next morning."

"Drivel," said Dr. Reinach, smiling. "Such pure drivel that it smacks of fantasmagoria."

"It was beautiful," said Ellery. "A beautiful plan. It had symmetry, the polish of great art. And it made a beautiful chain of reasoning, too, once I was set properly at the right link. For what followed? Since we had been transferred without our knowledge during the night, it must have been while we were unconscious. I recalled the two drinks Thorne and I had had, and the fuzzy tongue and head that resulted the next morning. Mildly drugged, then; and the drinks had been mixed the night before by Dr. Reinach's own hand. Doctor—drugs; very simple." The fat man shrugged with amusement, glancing sidewise at the stocky man in blue. But the stocky man in blue wore a hard, unchanging mask.

"But Dr. Reinach alone?" murmured Ellery. "Oh, no, impossible. One man could never have accomplished all that was necessary in the scant few hours available—fix Thorne's car, carry us and our clothes and bags from the one White House to its duplicate—by machine—put Thorne's car out of commission again, put us to bed again, arrange our clothing identically, transfer the chromo, the fragments of the cut-glass decanter in the fireplace, perhaps even a few knickknacks and ornaments not duplicated in the second White House, and so on. A prodigious job, even if most of the preparatory work had been done before our arrival. Obviously the work of a whole group. Of accomplices. Who but everyone in the house? With the possible exception of Mrs. Fell, who in her condition could be swayed easily enough, with no clear perception of what was occurring."

Ellery's eyes gleamed. "And so I accuse you all—including young Mr. Keith who has wisely taken himself off—of having aided in the plot whereby you would prevent the rightful heiress of Sylvester Mayhew's fortune from taking possession of the house in which it was hidden."

Dr. Reinach coughed politely, flapping his paws together like a great seal. "Terribly interesting, Queen, terribly. I don't know when I've been more captivated by sheer fiction. On the other hand, there are certain personal allusions in your story which, much as I admire their ingenuity, cannot fail to provoke me." He turned to the stock man in blue. "Certainly, Captain," he chuckled, "you don't credit this incredible story? I believe Mr. Queen has gone a little mad from sheer shock."

"Unworthy of you, Doctor," sighed Ellery. "The proof of what I say lies in the fact that we are here, at this moment."

"You'll have to explain that," said the police chief, who seemed out of his depth.

"I mean that we are now in the original White House. I led you back here, didn't I? And I can lead you back to the twin White House, for now I know the basis of the illusion. After our departure this evening, incidentally, all these people returned to this house. The other White House had served its purpose and they no longer needed it

"As for the geographical trick involved, it struck me that this side-road we're on makes a steady curve for miles. Both driveways lead off this same road, one some six miles farther up the road; although, because of the curve, which is like a number nine, the road makes a wide sweep and virtually doubles back on itself, so that as the crow flies the two settlements are only a mile or so apart, although by the curving road they are six miles apart.

"When Dr. Reinach drove Thorne and Miss Mayhew and me out here the day the *Coronia* docked, he deliberately passed the almost imperceptible drive leading to the substitute house and went on until he reached this one, the original. We didn't notice the first driveway.

"Thorne's car was put out of commission deliberately to prevent his driving. The driver of a car will observe landmarks when his passengers notice little or nothing. Keith even met Thorne on both Thorne's previous visits to Mayhew— ostensibly 'to lead the way,' actually to prevent Thorne from familiarizing himself with the road. And it was Dr. Reinach who drove the three of us here that first day. They permitted me to drive away tonight for what they hoped was a one-way trip because we started from the substitute house—of the two, the one on the road nearer to town. We couldn't possibly, then, pass the telltale second drive and become suspicious. They knew the relatively shorter drive would not impress our consciousness."

"But even granting all that, Mr. Queen," said the policeman, "I don't see what these people expected to accomplish. They couldn't hope to keep you folks fooled forever."

"True," cried Ellery, "but don't forget that by the time we caught on to the various tricks involved they hoped to have laid hands on Mayhew's fortune and disappeared with it. Don't you see that the whole illusion was planned *to give them time*? Time to dismantle the Black House without interference, raze it to the ground if necessary, to find that hidden hoard of gold? I don't doubt that if you examine the house next door you'll find it a shambles and a hollow shell. That's why Reinach and Keith kept disappearing. They were taking turns at the Black House, picking it apart, stone by stone, in a frantic search for the cache, while we were occupied in the duplicate White House with an apparently supernatural phenomenon. That's why someone—probably the worthy doctor here—slipped out of the house behind your back, Thorne, and struck me over the head when I rashly attempted to follow Keith's tracks in the snow. I could not be permitted to reach the original settlement, for if I did the whole preposterous illusion would be revealed."

"How about that gold?" growled Thorne.

"For all I know," said Ellery with a shrug, "they've found it and salted it away again."

"Oh, but we didn't," whimpered Mrs. Reinach, squirming in her chair. "Herbert, I *told* you not to—"

"Idiot," said the fat man. "Stupid swine." She jerked as if he had struck her.

"If you hadn't found the loot," said the police chief to Dr. Reinach brusquely, "why did you let these people go tonight?"

Dr. Reinach compressed his blubbery lips; he raised his glass and drank quickly.

"I think I can answer that," said Ellery in a gloomy tone. "In many ways it's the most remarkable element of the whole puzzle. Certainly it's the grimmest and least excusable. The other illusion was child's play compared to it. For it involves two apparently irreconcilable elements—Alice Mayhew and a murder."

"A murder!" exclaimed the policeman, stiffening.

"Me?" said Alice in bewilderment.

Ellery lit a cigarette and flourished it at the policeman. "When Alice Mayhew came here that first afternoon, she went into the Black House with us. In her father's bedroom she ran across an old chromo—I see it's not here, so it's still in the other White House—portraying her long-dead mother as a girl. Alice Mayhew fell on the chromo like a Chinese refugee on a bowl of rice. She had only one picture of her mother, she explained, and that a poor one. She treasured this unexpected discovery so much that she took it with her, then and there, to the White House—this house. And she placed it on the mantel over the fireplace here in a prominent position."

The stocky man frowned; Alice sat very still; Thorne looked puzzled. And Ellery put the cigarette back to his lips and said, "Yet when Alice Mayhew fled from the White House in our company tonight for what seemed to be the last time, *she completely ignored her mother's chromo,* that treasured memento over which she had gone into such raptures the first day! She could not have failed to overlook it in, let us say, the excitement of the moment. She had placed her purse on the mantel, a moment before, next to the chromo. She returned to the mantel for her purse. And yet she passed the chromo up without a glance. Since its sentimental value to her was overwhelming, by her own admission, it's the one thing in all this property she would not have left. *If she had taken it in the beginning, she would have taken it on leaving.*"

Thorne cried, "What in the name of Heaven are you saying, Queen?" His eyes glared at the girl, who sat glued to her chair, scarcely breathing.

"I am saying," said Ellery curtly, "that we were blind. I am saying that not only was a house impersonated, but a woman as well. *I am saying that this woman is not Alice Mayhew.*"

The girl raised her eyes after an infinite interval in which no one so much as stirred a foot.

"I thought of everything," she said with the queerest sigh, "but that. And it was going off so beautifully."

"Oh, you fooled me very neatly," drawled Ellery. "That pretty little bedroom scene last night. I know now what happened. This precious Dr. Reinach of yours had stolen into your room at midnight to report to you on the progress of the search at the Black House, perhaps to urge you to persuade Thorne and me to leave today—at any cost. I happened to pass along the hall outside your room, stumbled, and fell against the wall with a clatter; not knowing who it might be or what the intruder's purpose, you both fell instantly into that cunning deception. Actors! Both of you missed a career on the stage."

The fat man closed his eyes; he seemed asleep. And the girl murmured, with a sort of tired defiance, "Not missed, Mr. Queen. I spent several years in the theater."

"You were devils, you two. Psychologically this plot has been the conception of evil genius. You knew that Alice Mayhew was unknown to anyone in this country except by her photographs. Moreover, there was a startling resemblance between the two of you, as Miss Mayhew's photographs showed. And you knew Miss Mayhew would be in the company of Thorne and me for only a few hours, and then chiefly in the murky light of a sedan."

"Good Lord," groaned Thorne, staring at the girl in horror.

"Alice Mayhew," said Ellery grimly, "walked into this house and was whisked upstairs by Mrs. Reinach. *And Alice Mayhew, the English girl, never appeared before us again.* It was you who came downstairs; you, who had been secreted from Thorne's eyes during the past six days deliberately, so that he would not even suspect your existence; you who probably conceived the entire plot when Thorne brought the photographs of Alice Mayhew here, and her gossipy, informative letters; you, who looked enough like the real Alice Mayhew to get by with an impersonation in the eyes of two men to whom Alice Mayhew was a total stranger. I did think you looked different, somehow, when you appeared for dinner that first night; but I put it down to the fact that I was seeing you for the first time refreshed, brushed up, and without your hat and coat. Naturally, after that, the more I saw of you the less I remembered the details of the real Alice Mayhew's appearance and so became more and more convinced, unconsciously, that you were Alice Mayhew. As for the husky voice and the excuse of having caught cold on the long automobile ride from the pier, that was a clever ruse to disguise the inevitable difference between your voices. The only danger that existed lay in Mrs. Fell, who gave us the answer to the whole riddle the first time we met her. She thought you were her own daughter Olivia. Of course. *Because that's who you are!*"

Dr. Reinach was sipping brandy now with a steady indifference to his surroundings. His little eyes were fixed on a point miles away. Old Mrs. Fell sat gaping stupidly at the girl.

"You even covered that danger by getting Dr. Reinach to tell us beforehand that trumped-up story of Mrs. Fell's 'delusion' and Olivia Fell's 'death' in an automobile accident several years ago. Oh, admirable! Yet even this poor creature, in the frailty of her anile faculties, was fooled by a difference in voice and hair—two of the most easily distinguishable features. I suppose you fixed up your hair at the time Mrs. Reinach brought the real Alice Mayhew upstairs and you had a living model to go by. . . . I could find myself moved to admiration if it were not for one thing."

"You're so clever," said Olivia Fell coolly. "Really a fascinating monster. What do you mean?"

Ellery went to her and put his hand on her shoulder. "Alice Mayhew vanished and you took her place. Why did you take her place? For two possible reasons. One—to get Thorne and me away from the danger zone as quickly as possible, and to keep us away by 'abandoning' the fortune or dismissing us, which as Alice Mayhew would be your privilege: in proof, your vociferous insistence that we take you away. Two—of infinitely greater importance to the scheme: if your confederates did not find the

gold at once, you were still Alice Mayhew in our eyes. You could then dispose of the house when and as you saw fit. Whenever the gold was found, it would be yours and your accomplices'. But the real Alice Mayhew vanished. For you, her impersonator, to be in a position to go through the long process of taking over Alice Mayhew's inheritance, it was necessary that Alice Mayhew remain *permanently invisible*. For you to get possession of her rightful inheritance and live to enjoy its fruits, it was necessary that Alice Mayhew die. And that, Thorne," snapped Ellery, gripping the girl's shoulder hard, "is why I said that there was something besides a disappearing house to cope with tonight. Alice Mayhew was murdered."

There were three shouts from outside which rang with tones of great excitement. And then they ceased, abruptly.

"Murdered," went on Ellery, "by the only occupant of the house who was not *in* the house when this impostor came downstairs that first evening—Nicholas Keith. A hired killer. Although these people are all accessories to that murder."

A voice said from the window, "Not a hired *killer*."

They wheeled sharply, and fell silent. The three detectives who had sprung out of the window were there in the background, quietly watchful. Before them were two people.

"Not a killer," said one of them, a woman. "That's what he was supposed to be. Instead, and without their knowledge, he saved my life— dear Nick."

And now the pall of grayness settled over the faces of Mrs. Fell, and of Olivia Fell, and of Mrs. Reinach, and of the burly doctor. For by Keith's side stood Alice Mayhew. She was the same woman who sat near the fire only in general similitude of feature. Now that both women could be compared in proximity, there were obvious points of difference. She looked worn and grim, but happy withal; and she was holding to the arm of bitter-mouthed Nick Keith with a grip that was quite possessive.

Addendum

Afterward, when it was possible to look back on the whole amazing fabric of plot and event, Mr. Ellery Queen said, "The scheme would have been utterly impossible except for two things: the character of Olivia Fell and the—in itself—fantastic existence of that duplicate house in the woods."

He might have added that both of these would in turn have been impossible except for the aberrant strain in the Mayhew blood. The father of Sylvester Mayhew—Dr. Reinach's stepfather—had always been erratic, and he had communicated his unbalance to his children. Sylvester and Sarah, who became Mrs. Fell, were twins, and they had always been insanely jealous of each other's prerogatives. When they married in the same month, their father avoided trouble by presenting each of them with a specially-built house, the houses being identical in every detail. One he had erected next to his own house and presented to Mrs. Fell as a wedding gift; the other he built on a piece of property he owned some miles away and gave to Sylvester.

Mrs. Fell's husband died early in her married life; and she moved away to live with her half brother Herbert. When old Mayhew died, Sylvester boarded up his own house and moved into the ancestral mansion. And there the twin houses stood for many years, separated by only a few miles by road, completely and identically furnished inside—fantastic monuments to the Mayhew eccentricity.

The duplicate White House lay boarded up, waiting, idle, requiring only the evil genius of an Olivia Fell to be put to use. Olivia was beautiful, intelligent, accomplished, and as unscrupulous as Lady Macbeth. It was she who had influenced the others to move back to the abandoned house next to the Black House for the sole purpose of coercing or robbing Sylvester Mayhew. When Thorne appeared with the news of Sylvester's long-lost daughter, she recognized the peril to their scheme and, grasping her own resemblance to her English cousin from the photographs Thorne brought, conceived the whole extraordinary plot.

Then obviously the first step was to put Sylvester out of the way. With perfect logic, she bent Dr. Reinach to her will and caused him to murder his patient before the arrival of Sylvester's daughter. (A later exhumation and autopsy revealed traces of poison in the corpse.) Meanwhile, Olivia perfected the plans of the impersonation and illusion.

The house illusion was planned for the benefit of Thorne, to keep him sequestered and bewildered while the Black House was being torn down in the search for the gold. The illusion would perhaps not have been necessary had Olivia felt certain that her impersonation would succeed perfectly.

The illusion was simpler, of course, then appeared on the surface. The house was there, completely furnished, ready for use. All that was necessary was to take the boards down, air the place out, clean up, put fresh linen in. There was plenty of time before Alice's arrival for this preparatory work.

The one weakness of Olivia Fell's plot was objective, not personal. That woman would have succeeded in anything. But she made the mistake of selecting Nick Keith for the job of murdering Alice Mayhew. Keith had originally insinuated himself into the circle of plotters, posing as a desperado prepared to do anything for sufficient pay. Actually, he was the son of Sylvester Mayhew's second wife, who had been so brutally treated by Mayhew and driven off to die in poverty.

Before his mother expired she instilled in Keith's mind a hatred for Mayhew that waxed, rather than waned, with the ensuing years. Keith's sole motive in joining the conspirators was to find his stepfather's fortune and take that part of it which Mayhew had stolen from his mother. He had never intended to murder Alice—his ostensible role. When he carried her from the house that first evening under the noses of Ellery and Thorne, it was not strangle and bury her, as Olivia had directed, but to secrete her in an ancient shack in the nearby woods known only to himself.

He had managed to smuggle provisions to her while he was ransacking the Black House. At first he had held her frankly prisoner, intending to keep her so until he found the money, took his share, and escaped. But as he came to know her he came to love her, and he soon confessed the whole story to her in the privacy of the shack. Her sympathy gave him new courage; concerned now with her safety above everything else, he prevailed upon her to remain in hiding until he could find the money and outwit his fellow-conspirators. Then they both intended to unmask Olivia. . . .

The ironical part of the whole affair, as Mr. Ellery Queen was to point out, was that the goal of all this plotting and counterplotting—Sylvester Mayhew's gold—remained as invisible as the Black House apparently had been. Despite the most thorough search of the building and grounds no trace of it had been found.

"I've asked you to visit my poor diggings," Ellery said, smiling, a few weeks later, "because something occurred to me that simply cried out for investigation."

Keith and Alice glanced at each other blankly; and Thorne, looking clean, rested, and complacent for the first time in weeks, sat up straighter in Ellery's most comfortable chair.

"I'm glad something occurred to somebody," said Nick Keith with a grin. "I'm a pauper; and Alice is only one jump ahead of me."

"You haven't the philosophic attitude toward wealth," said Ellery dryly, "that's so charming a part of Dr. Reinach's personality. Poor Colossus! I wonder how he likes our jails." He poked a log into the fire. "By this time, Miss Mayhew, our common friend Thorne has had your father's house virtually annihilated. No gold. Eh, Thorne?"

"Nothing but dirt," said the lawyer sadly.

"Why, we've taken that house apart stone by stone."

"Exactly. Now there are two possibilities, since I am incorrigibly categorical: either your father's fortune exists, Miss Mayhew, or it does not. If it does not and he was lying, there's an end to the business, of course, and you and your precious Keith will have to put your heads together and agree to live either in noble, rugged individualistic poverty or by the grace of the Relief Administration. But suppose there was a fortune, as your father claimed, and suppose he did secret it somewhere in that house. What then?"

"Then," sighed Alice, "it's flown away."

Ellery laughed. "Not quite; I've had enough of vanishments for the present, anyway. Let's tackle the problem differently. Is there anything which was in Sylvester's Mayhew's house before he died which is not there now?"

Thorne stared. "If you mean the—er—the body—"

"Don't be gruesome, Literal Lyman. Besides, there's been an exhumation. No, guess again."

Alice looked slowly down at the package in her lap. "So that's why you asked me to fetch this with me today!"

"You mean," cried Keith, "the old fellow was deliberately putting everyone off the track when he said his fortune was gold?"

Ellery chuckled and took the package from the girl. He unwrapped it and for a moment gazed appreciatively at the large old chromo of Alice's mother.

And then, with the self-assurance of the complete logician, he stripped away the back of the frame.

Gold-and-green documents cascaded into his lap.

"Converted into bonds." Ellery grinned. "Who said your father was cracked, Miss Mayhew? A very clever gentleman! Come, come, Thorne, stop rubbernecking and let's leave these children of fortune alone!"

THE MONKEY TRICK

J. E. GURDON

THE HERO OF "The Monkey Trick" appears in only one collection of short stories by John Everard Gurdon (1898–1973) and both he and his creator are utterly unknown today. Although this short story presents a situation that is one of the most baffling in the realm of impossible crimes, and its solution one of the neatest, it does not appear to ever have been reprinted after its initial publication.

Gurdon was born in London and educated at Sandhurst Royal Military College. He served as an officer in the British army during World War I and suffered severe injuries, being invalided out in 1919. While he was recovering in the hospital, he began to write fiction, primarily on aviation subjects, both for adults and younger readers, mostly under the byline Capt. J. E. Gurdon, D.F.C. Among his adult thrillers are his first book, *Over and Above* (1919); *Feeling the Wind* (1924), about Kekulen, a superanarchist outsmarted by a British Secret Service Agent and a former R.F.C. pilot; and a story collection, *The Sky Trackers* (1931).

In addition to writing aviation stories for anthologies and such magazines as *Modern Boys' Annual* and *Air Stories*, Gurdon wrote several popular young adult novels that were often reprinted, including *Wings of Death* (1929), *The Kings' Pipe* (1934), *The Secret of the Lab* (1936), *The Secret of the South* (1950), and *The Riddle of the Forest* (1952). He also translated the nonfiction book *The German Air Force in the Great War* by Georg Paul Neumann. "The Monkey Trick" was first published in *The Monkey Trick* (London, Newnes, 1936).

THE MONKEY TRICK

J. E. GURDON

THE NOTE which His Excellency had just handed in was lying on the table, eyed in silence by three tired men upon whose shoulders rested all the weight of a nation's decision.

"War!" murmured one.

The tall man facing him nodded.

"They've never intended the dispute to go to arbitration," he complained bitterly.

From the depths of the chair which was almost engulfing him the fat little man spoke pipingly, a reflective smile creasing that famous chubbiness which a disgruntled colleague had once described as a "cartoonist's dream come true."

"Would any nation force war upon her neighbour," he demanded, "if aware that that neighbour possessed a type of aircraft which could be controlled by wireless when empty, and was capable of a speed of eight hundred miles an hour through the upper atmosphere?"

Neither of his two companions answered, but sat very still, yet alert.

"The possession of such a weapon," pursued the high-pitched voice in prim enunciation, "is a factor which must inevitably exercise the most far-reaching influence upon the development of this situation."

"So far as I am aware, no such machine exists," observed the tall man slowly. "What is your meaning?"

The smile vanished and suddenly the jovial mobile features set.

"I mean that although at the moment no such machine exists, I propose to call one into existence, and to demonstrate its powers in a manner which cannot fail to carry conviction. Moreover, I intend that this demonstration shall be made in the presence of Lobley, the Chief of their Secret Service, who is prowling about this country in blissful ignorance of the fact that our own men have had him under observation since the moment he landed."

"'Call one into existence,' eh?" echoed the tall man thoughtfully.

A slow, understanding grin lit up his haggard face; then, for the first time in many anxious weeks, he laughed long and joyously.

Of regular habits, Police-Sergeant Dunsterman played bowls every Wednesday evening, returning along the Snetch road as the light began to fade. On Wednesday, the 27th, having defeated the vicar of Ingoldsburgh in a warmly-contested match, he strolled home to become a figure of international importance.

Peace brooded over the flats that stretched eastward from the roadside to the sea a mile away, a peace whose smoothness was scarcely scoured by the screams of wheeling swallows. Sergeant Dunsterman, humming a marching song, watched the swallows and the samphire and the distant dunes, cast a weatherwise glance at the June sunset, and himself sank into that peace peculiar to an East Anglian man on East Anglian soil.

Half a mile ahead, where the road spanned the meandering River Wych, he glimpsed a white-clad figure that moved erratically. A chuckle rumbled in his deep chest as he recognized both figure and occupation. Mr. Kinley, the amiable young visitor from London, had already excited the amused comments of the neighbourhood by his habit of fishing in flannels at all hours of daylight.

As he reached the bridge the fisherman looked up with a friendly smile.

"Evening, Sergeant. How wags the world?"

"Mustn't grumble, sir. Have you had any luck?"

The young man grimaced and jerked his head at an empty creel which lay by his gaudy yellow blazer on the grass behind him.

"Never a nibble! I'll swear there's nothing but water in this darned stream. Ever try yourself?"

Dunsterman did not immediately reply, for he was staring with considerable surprise and interest at a pair of binoculars which also lay beside the blazer. For years he had been practising observation and accumulating a very wide fund of useful knowledge; even from where he stood he could see that those binoculars were in all probability a Zeiss instrument of exceptional power—at any rate a most unusual item of equipment for a young man fishing in flannels.

"Ever try yourself?"

The policeman pulled himself together at the repeated question and smiled.

"Not in my line. Haven't the patience." He hesitated, then went on casually: "Looks like a fine pair of glasses you've got there, sir."

Somewhat to his disappointment the response was remarkable for undoubted gratification. Promptly the young man picked up the glasses and offered them by swinging the strap at the low parapet.

"Catch," he invited. "You'll find 'em as good as any you've looked through. My brother won 'em from a German officer . . . Hello! . . . Hear

an aeroplane? . . . Sounds as though she's coming from that direction."

He pointed seaward.

Although he was justly proud of his hearing and listened intently, the sergeant could detect no sound remotely resembling an engine. He trained his glasses on the sea horizon and swept it from north to south. Through the splendid prisms and lenses he saw seabirds innumerable, but never a speck that might be an aeroplane.

"She's getting nearer!" exclaimed Kinley.

"Then, sir," laughed the policeman, "I must be getting deaf!"

"Can't you spot any machine?"

Dunsterman put down the binoculars and stared at the fisherman with sudden interest, for there had been a queer, tense ring of anxiety in his voice. Beneath his scrutiny Kinley flushed and became very busy packing up his tackle.

"Must have been mistaken," he mumbled. "Motor-bike, perhaps."

"No," answered the sergeant slowly, a few seconds later. "You were not mistaken. There *is* a machine coming in from the sea—though how you managed to hear her before beats me hollow!"

To this Kinley made no comment, nor did either utter a word during the crowded minutes that followed.

It all happened so swiftly that Dunsterman afterwards told his superintendent that it reminded him of going over the top. Out of the east droned a winged shape that grew with frightening rapidity, became suddenly silent, dipped, sank, and vanished behind a row of stunted willows.

"Gosh! Crashed!" breathed the policeman, and vaulted the parapet. Still without a word Kinley kept by his side as he forced his way through the clumps of reeds that fringed the stream. Together they reached the row of willows and together halted as at a word of command.

Between the willows and the nearest dunes was a strip of level turf, roughly triangular in shape and scarcely more than two hundred yards in length from apex to base. Quite undamaged, but with motionless propeller, a tiny aeroplane faced them from the tip of the triangle.

"Some landing," remarked Kinley.

"You're right. This is about the only possible patch for a mile around."

"Queer sort of bus!"

Dunsterman agreed. A low-wing monoplane, showing only a pair of planes protruding on either side of an immense tapering engine cowling, the intruder ridiculously reminded him of a bullet wearing a bow tie. The moment that they reached the machine and rounded one of the wing-tips he made a discovery, however, which drove all fanciful analogies from his mind, for nowhere on planes, sides, fins, or rudder was there a vestige of either international marking or registration number.

"Totally enclosed cabin," remarked Kinley, chattily, indicating the deep, glass-panelled fuselage. "Never seen such a fat body on such thin wings, have you?"

"Never. Don't go too close yet, sir. I don't want that turf messed up with footprints—not that there seems to be any except our own." His quick glances covered every tuft of the soft marshy grass before he nodded satisfaction. "Can't have got out yet," he concluded. "Not unless he's got wings himself!"

In France, Sergeant Dunsterman had behaved in a manner which earned him two very significant strips of ribbons. Regarding his courage, therefore, neither his fellowmen nor he himself had ever had cause for doubt, yet eyeing that inert mass of machinery, his heart misgave him as though he had been asked to lead some desperate venture. It was not that he feared the unknown pilot, although his conduct in remaining concealed was at least suspicious; what made the sergeant's scalp tingle were the altogether unaccountable sounds that came from within the sealed cockpit—sounds clearly made by something alive fighting to escape.

Squaring his shoulders he rapped authoritatively upon the panelled cabin, and assumed official tones—"Now then. What's up in there?"

To this came no articulate reply, although the sounds of struggling became frenzied.

"What is it?" whispered Kinley.

Examining the catch of the cockpit door the sergeant snorted with pardonable irritation. A fool question, he thought. For some seconds he fumbled at the unfamiliar device, then the door clicked and slid silently sideways.

A small monkey jumped out, bounced on to his shoulder, chattered agitatedly, and scampered away towards the dunes. The sergeant said nothing, for his jaw had dropped and he was staring incredulously into an empty cockpit where the joystick lolled to one side as though just released from the pilot's hand.

"Humph!" he grunted at length, sliding the door back. "Whoever flew this machine is just about the swiftest mover I've ever run across! I could have sworn it was impossible for any man to get out and disappear in the time it took us to come here from the bridge."

"But his footprints!" exclaimed Kinley. "There aren't any."

"Must be. Stands to reason. In failing light it's easy to overlook a footprint, even on squashy turf like this."

"I suppose," put in the young man, hesitantly, "I suppose the monkey—I mean to say they're awfully intelligent little beasts and one can train 'em to do almost anything. Supposing it was a pet monkey who'd been taught to fly, and managed to bolt with its owner's machine?"

Dunsterman laughed harshly, because he himself had just been guilty of equally fantastic speculations.

"The monkey's about the size of a cat," he retorted, "and it would take quite a reasonably tall man to sit on that seat and reach the rudder gadget with his feet. Besides the whole idea's too damn silly!"

It was not at all correct, he fully realized, to speak to a member of the public in this fashion, but for the moment he was too rattled to care. Not only was the affair from beginning to end so incredible as to be exasperating, but its developments seemed full of unpleasant possibilities for himself.

There were a great many points for him to consider, and the most important of them all was the immediate tracing of the vanished pilot. That, however, meant getting assistance, and while he was attending to this the pilot might return and fly off. Of course, he mused, he could leave Kinley on guard, but in the peculiar circumstances that was a risky thing to do; anything might happen; he might come back to find the machine gone and the unfortunate young man with his head knocked in. On the other hand, if he stayed himself and sent Kinley back to the station with a written report and instructions, it would inevitably be some hours before an effective search could be organized—and Sergeant Dunsterman was most uncomfortably sure that his superiors would be vengeful if, through any dilatoriness on his part, the pilot of this unregistered machine managed to get away.

"I quite see your difficulties," said Kinley suddenly, as though his companion had indeed been thinking aloud, "but if you like to leave me on guard while you get things moving I shall be quite O.K. My idea is to get into the cabin and shut the door. Then, if the blighter does return he's done in the eye. Moreover, he can't very well give me a swipe without first of all busting up his own 'plane."

"That, sir," returned the sergeant promptly, "is a good idea. Very good indeed. I am obliged to you. At the very most I shall not be away more than an hour."

"Right-o, old man." Kinley slid open the door and squeezed into the seat. "Don't you worry about me. It's jolly snug in here."

The door closed as Dunsterman nodded his thanks and strode rapidly off. Scarcely had he reached the row of willows when the monoplane's engine snarled. Feeling slightly sick, the policeman instinctively dodged behind the nearest tree as the little machine, like an unleashed beast, raged straight at him across the turf, bumped, rose, missed the topmost twigs by a bare foot, and sped with a dwindling scream into the gathering dusk.

That for the moment he should be deprived of all power either to think or act was inevitable, but with surprising swiftness training and disci-

pline resumed command. In a flashing sequence of tableaux his mind visualized what must have happened during those few seconds—the sudden reappearance of the pilot; some ruse that induced Kinley to open the cabin; then a savage blow, the body dragged out, and flight.

Shouting the young man's name, he sped back to where the machine had rested. Nothing lay sprawling on the turf, as he had feared; no signs of a struggle; no tracks, even, other than those which he and Kinley had made.

Swearing with all the fervour of a badly-frightened man, Dunsterman peered around into the bewildering shadows, then was struck to cold, sweating silence by a hand that clutched his leg. Hissing, the breath escaped between his teeth as he looked down and saw the monkey.

The tiny creature was holding his trouser leg, staring up, and making forlorn, twittering noises. Very gently Dunsterman stooped.

"Clarence," he said, tucking the animal under his jacket. "You're coming along with me!"

During all the breathless rush back to the police station at Snetch, Sergeant Dunsterman was thanking his lucky stars for the monkey. Without the reassuring warmth of the living body under his arm he would almost have doubted his own sanity and, even with the monkey to show as evidence, he dreaded the coming explanations to a notoriously caustic and sceptical superintendent.

On this point his misgivings were destined to be speedily removed, for as he panted up the station path, the Superintendent appeared in the doorway.

"What's all this about an aeroplane down on Wych marshes?" he demanded abruptly. "And why the devil are you running about with a monkey?"

"It j-j-jumped out of the aeroplane!"

The Superintendent grunted and led the way into the parlour, which also served the sergeant at his office.

"Now then," he commanded, "fire ahead, keep cool, and miss nothing."

Even the critical attention of his superior could find no fault with Dunsterman's crisp and circumstantial account of the incident or with his handling of it.

"This man Kinley," snapped the Superintendent when the tale was ended. "Know anything about him?"

"Nothing, sir, except that he turned up a few days ago and has been staying at the Sanger Arms. Just an ordinary visitor, I've understood, and I heard that he came from London."

"Humph! Go down to the pub at once. Go through his effects. Never mind formalities!" The Superintendent hesitated. He was a man of exceptional reserve and caution, even with trusted subordinates, but he was also an exceptionally worried man, with all a worried man's hankering after confidence. "Serious business this, Dunsterman," he growled at last. "London's been burning the wires blue. Now cut and——"

"See here, sir," broke in the sergeant excitedly. "This monkey! There's a collar on it with a brass plate—a name and address—'Sammy—Warnford Durrant—Hylton.'"

"So that's it!" he breathed. "Warnford Durrant, the Government aircraft designer, and the biggest man at his job in the country! Hylton in Essex is his experimental station—all passwords, barb wire, and sentries. I know 'cause I took leave down that way this spring. See now what's happened? That machine's one of Durrant's secret models—and it's been stolen!"

The faces of the two men as they exchanged a long, understanding look were grave, yet aglow with the curious pleasure of patriotic citizens drawn into deep and secret waters. Dunsterman was the first to break the silence.

"Will you take charge of the animal, sir," he inquired, "or shall I leave it with my wife? She is in the kitchen, and it will be perfectly safe if I chain it to the table-leg."

"Do that. I must report to the Chief Constable. Go down to the Sanger Arms and let me know immediately what you find."

Forty minutes later, Dunsterman and the Superintendent were closeted together in a small annexe to the hall of the Chief Constable's house.

"Everything's been cleared clean out," announced the harassed sergeant. "Just after nine o'clock this evening a young man drove up in a small open two-seater car and gave the landlord a note purporting to come from Kinley. The note said that he, Kinley, had been recalled to London and that the bearer of the note would settle his bill and collect his kit. The landlord says that he compared the signature on the note with Kinley's own signature in the visitors' book, and concluded that the note was genuine. I've compared 'em myself, and to me also the note seems genuine enough. So the landlord let the kit go. There was only one old suit-case, he says, and a haversack and some fishing-tackle."

"Search the room?"

"Yes, sir. But someone might just have gone over it with a vacuum-cleaner for all there was to find!"

"Landlord take the car number?"

"No. Says he had a rush of customers at the time."

"He would. Nine o'clock was well chosen. Does he know any facts about Kinley? Did he get any letters?"

"He knows nothing, sir, and swears there were no letters."

The Superintendent rubbed his chin reflectively.

"You met Kinley fishing at a quarter to ten," he murmured. "He was then in flannels, yet all his luggage had been collected from the pub three-quarters of an hour earlier. It doesn't make sense!"

The door opened and two men entered. One, the Chief Constable, was well enough known to Dunsterman, but at first he took his companion for a stranger; then his mind stirred to the memories of a thousand cartoons, and his heart beat quicker with anticipation of great events, good or evil. There was a quality about the tubby little figure and rounded, jovial features that had often struck terror into the hearts of harder-bitten men than Sergeant Dunsterman.

"I want you to describe for me this man Kinley," said the high, reedy voice. "There is no occasion for you to feel nervous, Sergeant, but I would impress upon you the necessity for absolute accuracy."

Unwinkingly, the great little man stared into his eyes while the sergeant provided him with a descriptive report which would have done credit to an expert in mnemonics.

"Excellent!" he wheezed at length. "I see that you are an exceptionally efficient officer. You are, then, perfectly clear in your mind that shortly after ten o'clock a young man named Kinley, wearing flannels, carrying a brightly-coloured yellow blazer and a pair of powerful binoculars, vanished from a meadow near the Wych river in very singular circumstances, and in an aeroplane bearing neither identification marks nor a registration number?"

"That is right, sir."

"No, Sergeant, it is not right. In all innocence, and with the best of intentions, you are reporting an event which has not occurred. I repeat—has—not—occurred. That this is so you will at once perceive when I tell you that at ten-thirty-five, only half an hour after the time you thought you saw Kinley, an aeroplane of the type you describe crashed in some fields on the outskirts of Edinburgh. The police could find no trace of an occupant, but in the pilot's cockpit they discovered a yellow blazer marked 'A. Kinley' and a pair of powerful binoculars of foreign make. Also the parachute and harness, which had been encased in a pack under the cushion of the seat, were missing, while to the instrument-board was pinned a note, signed A. Kinley, explaining to whoever found the wreckage that the writer had no control over the machine and was about to jump in a desperate attempt to save his life. Now all this evidence, Sergeant, is concrete, indisputable, and already in the hands of the police. Also, inevitably, it has already attracted a great deal of attention from press-men—as you will observe when you look at your paper in the morning. You follow me, I hope?"

"Yes, sir," croaked Sergeant Dunsterman, seriously wondering if it were he or the Minister who had gone mad.

"I am glad of that because, you see, if you were correct in your previous impression that Kinley and the aeroplane were in Norfolk at ten o'clock they could only have crashed in Edinburgh at ten-thirty if the machine had travelled at something like eight hundred miles an hour; and if some such ridiculous rumour began to spread it might, in the present temperamental conditions of the world, have unforeseen repercussions. You are, I am fully persuaded, far too intelligent an officer not to appreciate this point. Do you not see?"

Not immediately did the sergeant reply, for suddenly and stunningly he certainly did see—saw the jealously-guarded secret 'plane, saw the foreign agent—Kinley—keeping a rendezvous with an accomplice, flying away, losing control of the monster, wrenching open the cockpit door and being whirled away with his parachute like a spider slung from a blown leaf.

With an effort he jerked his thoughts back to realities as the Minister's voice continued.

"Kinley, I should inform you, was a young ex–flying officer, recently retired, who had just joined the staff of a great national journal. How he came to hear of the existence of this—er—experimental aircraft we shall probably never know. The fact remains that he did, that he proceeded to—er—investigate—no doubt with the object of securing for his paper what I believe is popularly known as a 'scoop'—and that he has, without the slightest doubt, paid for his temerity with his life. These points are of importance because, of course, the fact of his being a journalist will intensify the interest of the Press in the discovery at Edinburgh. You follow me?"

"Absolutely, sir, but"—Sergeant Dunsterman hesitated, greatly perturbed lest he should be about to commit an impertinence—"but I was not able to locate the man who was first flying the machine. The man, I mean, in charge when it landed on Wych marshes."

"Sergeant, you disappoint me! I have already demonstrated to you that no such landing could have taken place." The thin voice broke into an astonishingly bass chuckle. "You must not forget, Sergeant, that some persons might conclude, were they to learn of your curious and erroneous impressions, that the machine actually had been empty and under the control of—shall we say wireless, or some similar agency?"

Sergeant Dunsterman nodded dumbly. The implied revelation came to him as a shock, not of surprise but of confirmation, for his own astute brain had already read this interpretation of the empty cockpit.

"You do not answer, Sergeant. I wish to know if it is perfectly clear to you that this evening you have seen no unregistered aeroplane, no yellow blazer and no Zeiss binoculars, and that the young man named Kinley, who has been staying at the local inn, left for London, bag and baggage, at nine o'clock."

"I quite understand, sir," returned Sergeant Dunsterman earnestly. "There is no connexion whatever between the wreckage found in Scotland at half-past ten and a machine which some people hereabouts may have heard flying half an hour earlier."

"Exactly. Admirably put. No connexion. That is the whole point. And that is what you will all bear in mind, I beg, when making out official reports or dealing with local gossip."

The great man had already turned to go when the Superintendent cleared his throat.

"About the monkey, sir?" he began diffidently.

"*What?*" The word was a squeak.

"The monkey, sir, which jumped out of the machine which the sergeant—which the sergeant didn't see. It appears to belong to Professor Warnford Durrant. We left it at the station."

For the first time the fat face lost its air of benign complacency.

"Ring up at once. You, Sergeant. There's the telephone. Ring up."

White to the lips, Sergeant Dunsterman turned away from the instrument when the call went through.

"It's—it's been taken, sir," he whispered brokenly. "My wife says a man came with a message from the Superintendent ordering her to hand it over—and she did!"

Not a word of anger or reproach did the Minister utter, but silently nodded dismissal, then took the Chief Constable's arm and, still in silence, led him from the room, down the long hall, and out along the drive to his waiting car.

"Two first-rate men, those officers," he said, one neat and podgy foot on the running-board. "I will see that a friendly eye is kept on them."

The Chief Constable nodded absently.

"Do you know, sir," he remarked suddenly, "even now I can hardly believe you are right about that new footman of mine. He seemed such a—such a——"

"Nice, quiet, respectful and efficient servant," completed the Minister with a chuckle. "I have no doubt that he possesses all those qualities and that his references were unimpeachable. Nevertheless, my dear Colonel, I do assure you that his name is not Lovat but Lobley, that he is the Chief of the Secret Service of a Power which has been causing us a lot of anxiety recently, that he entered your service for the specific purpose of spying, that he had installed a dictaphone in that room which we have just left, and that at this very moment he is on his way to his Government with a record of every word that was spoken."

Again came the surprising bass chuckle.

"All the same," ended the great man inconsequently, "it's just as well we added the monkey."

Flight-Lieutenant Alastair Kinley, enjoying a few days' leave after his exceedingly fateful spell of "special service," lounged at ease in a favourite club arm-chair and beamed at his old friend Tony Carew.

"It is pleasant," he observed amiably, "to see your ugly features blotting the landscape once again. Pleasant but surprising. From your last letter, which I only got a month ago, I gathered that you fully expected to remain in China for at least another year."

"So I did. Then that war scare flared up and I made a bolt for home. Just in case, you know."

Kinley laughed.

"And instead of finding the recruiting offices doing a brisk trade," he murmured, "you discover the good old British Public happily wrangling about the Test matches, and all our international bothers referred to Geneva for polite arbitration."

"A dashed good job, too," responded Tony soberly. "You can bet I'm not disappointed. Even now, though, I can hardly believe the danger's over. D'you know I was told by one chap, who's usually pretty well informed, that a week ago to-day we were within one hour of general mobilization! Is that true, d'you think?"

"I happen to know that it's perfectly true."

Tony looked up with sudden quick interest.

"Aha!" he exclaimed softly. "So you've been up to your hush-hush tricks again! Excellent! I will lend you my ears, both of 'em, for half an hour. Tell the tale. Say your piece. Spill the beans."

"It's all so dashed confidential," demurred Kinley.

Very red in the face, Tony became busy with cigarette and lighter.

"Sorry," he muttered. "Shouldn't have asked, I suppose. Still, I'm not a blamed reporter, you know, and——"

"Don't be an ass, old man," Kinley put in hastily. "Of course I know you're as safe as houses, but in this game one gets so into the habit of swearing chaps to secrecy, and all that sort of thing, that—well—that it becomes second nature."

"Consider me sworn," grunted Tony.

"Good enough. Here goes, then. . . . You saw all that gaff in the papers last week about a marvellous and mysterious aeroplane which crashed near Edinburgh?"

"I did. Some of the papers hinted that it was controlled by wireless, and flew at eight hundred miles per hour, and heaven knows what! Silly season stuff, I thought it was. You don't mean to say it was genuine?"

"Genuine enough to frighten a Great Power into preferring arbitration to war."

"Great Scot!"

"You see, luckily the Chief of their Secret Service, an awfully nice chap whom we all know and love by the name of 'Little Lobley,'

happened to be in England on business, and although, of course, he was travelling strictly incognito, our fellows were unobtrusively by his side night and day.

"Now a certain fat and fanciful statesman, sometimes irreverently spoken of as the Cherubic Cham, conceived the really bright idea of persuading Little Lobley that we possessed an aeroplane of such fearsome potentialities that his country was absolutely bound to get it in the neck if it came to a scrap. Little Lobley was therefore allowed to hear strange and wonderful rumours. He was told, for example, that the famous Professor Warnford Durrant had himself designed the secret 'plane. Then he was instructed where to go to witness a trial flight, and was given a job as footman in the household of a Chief Constable in East Anglia. Every facility was allowed him to install his little dictaphones and other gadgets, and as soon as he was all set and comfortable, on Wednesday, the twenty-seventh instant, the curtain went up on the first and only performance of 'The Monkey Trick,' a fine and fruity melodrama with a highly original plot which I will now proceed to divulge."

With a wealth of picturesque and flippant detail Kinley related the events of the memorable Wednesday evening.

"And really," he concluded, "one can hardly blame Little Lobley for jumping to conclusions. The sergeant, stout fellow, was the most transparently honest and reliable witness that ever said 'swelp me'—in fact, he was chosen for that very quality, plus the commendable habit of being at a certain spot at a certain time every Wednesday evening. Then consider the monkey—an artistic touch, that! which Little Lobley was permitted to scrounge from the local police station. That inestimable animal proved quite indisputably to belong to Warnford Durrant. And remember the stuff the Cherubic Cham spouted, for the benefit of the dictaphone. Surely that was nicely calculated to prove that a sinister aircraft *must* have travelled from Norfolk to Edinburgh in some thirty minutes?"

"Quite neat," allowed Tony. "I must confess I don't see the catch myself. Expound."

"Two of everything, dear old idiot. Two machines, two yellow blazers, two conspicuous Zeisses. Aircraft carrier Number One, lounging about the North Sea, sends up machine A, which lands and collects me after I've duly impressed my personality upon the honest sergeant. We return to our ocean home and our own little turn is over. Aircraft carrier Number Two, idling away the hours in the Firth, sends up exactly similar machine B, complete with trimmings in the shape of blazer, binoculars, and perfectly genuine note, written by myself, at a moment nicely chosen to pile up on the outskirts of Edinburgh. Whereupon the inquisitive and intelligent observer will not unnaturally assume that machine A and machine B are one and the same,

and that a journey of some three hundred miles has been accomplished with remarkable celerity."

Tony laughed.

"A pretty idea! I didn't know, though, that they actually could control 'planes by wireless."

"Ass! Alan Arkwright was in mine, nicely tucked away in the front cockpit. You couldn't see him unless you climbed up on the wing, and I took jolly good care the excellent sergeant didn't do that. Grimshaw flew the Edinburgh bus, got it heading for the appointed mark, and floated gracefully away into the darkness with his parachute. With which, my good Tony, I bring my enthralling narrative to a close. Now what about a cocktail? Shall it be a 'Little Lobley' or a 'Monkey Trick'? They know how to mix 'em both here."

"So it seems," said Tony.

E. C. BENTLEY

IN THE HISTORIC CORNERSTONE of detective fiction, *Trent's Last Case* (1913; titled *The Woman in Black* in the United States), Philip Trent makes his debut and breaks several of the unwritten, if widely accepted, rules of the genre: he falls in love with the chief suspect and, after delivering a brilliant solution to the mystery, discovers that he is completely wrong.

Edmund Clerihew Bentley (1875–1956) is often credited with being the father of the modern detective story (even though his first novel was written a century ago) in that he insisted that his protagonist be human, which is to say fallible, unlike such contemporary characters as Sherlock Holmes, Craig Kennedy, and Martin Hewitt. Born in a suburb of London, Bentley attended Oxford University, then left to study law; he was admitted to the bar in 1902. He also turned to journalism at this time, making it his lifelong career.

In 1905, he published *Biography for Beginners* under the name E. Clerihew, a collection of nonsense poems in a four-line form that he invented and that still bears the name Clerihew, which for years rivaled the limerick in popularity. It was illustrated by Bentley's closest friend, G. K. Chesterton, who influenced his colleague's literary style in its clarity and humor.

Trent's Last Case was filmed three times: as a 1920 silent with Gregory Scott as Trent, as a Howard Hawks–directed version in 1929 with Raymond Griffith in the titular role, and in 1952 with Michael Wilding as Trent, Margaret Lockwood as the prime suspect, and Orson Welles as the murdered millionaire. Bentley wrote only two other books featuring the amateur detective Trent: the novel *Trent's Own Case* (1936) and *Trent Intervenes* (1938), a short-story collection.

"The Ordinary Hairpins" was first published in the October 1916 issue of *The Strand Magazine*; it was first collected in *Trent Intervenes* (London, Nelson, 1938).

THE ORDINARY HAIRPINS

E. C. BENTLEY

A SMALL COMMITTEE of friends had persuaded Lord Aviemore to sit for a presentation portrait, and the painter to whom they gave the commission was Philip Trent. It was a task that fascinated him, for he had often seen and admired, in public places, the high, half-bald skull, vulture nose, and grim mouth of the peer who was said to be deeper in theology than any other layman, and all but a few of the clergy; whose devotion to charitable work had made him nationally honoured. It was not until the third sitting that Lord Aviemore's sombre taciturnity was laid aside.

"I believe, Mr. Trent," he said abruptly, "you used to have a portrait of my late sister-in-law here. I was told that it hung in the studio."

Trent continued his work quietly. "It was just a rough drawing I made after seeing her in *Carmen*—before her marriage. It has been hung in here ever since. Before your first visit I removed it."

The sitter nodded slowly. "Very thoughtful of you. Nevertheless, I should like very much to see it, if I may."

"Of course." Trent drew the framed sketch from behind a curtain. Lord Aviemore gazed long in silence at Trent's very spirited likeness of the famous singer, while the artist worked busily to capture the first expression of feeling that he had so far seen on that impassive face. Lighted and softened by melancholy, it looked for the first time noble.

At last the sitter turned to him. "I would give a good deal," he said simply, "to possess this drawing."

Trent shook his head. "I don't want to part with it." He laid a few strokes carefully on the canvas. "If you care to know why, I'll tell you. It is my personal memory of a woman whom I found more admirable than any other I ever saw. Lillemor Wergeland's beauty and physical perfection were unforgettable. Her voice was a marvel; her spirit matched them; her fearlessness, her kindness, her vigour of mind and character, her feeling for beauty, were what I heard talked about even by people not given to enthusiasm. She had weaknesses, I dare say—I never spoke to her. I heard her sing very many times, but I knew no more about her than many other strangers. A number of my friends knew her, though, and all I ever gathered about her made me inclined to place her on a pedestal. I was ten years younger then; it did me good."

Lord Aviemore said nothing for a few minutes. Then he spoke slowly. "I am not of your temperament or your circle, Mr. Trent. I do not worship anything of this world. But I do not think you were far wrong about Lady Aviemore. Once I thought differently. When I heard that my eldest brother was about to marry a prima donna, a woman whose portrait was sold all over the world, who was famous for extravagance in dress and what seemed to me self-advertising conduct—I was appalled when I heard from him of this engagement. I will not deny that I was shocked, too, at the idea of a marriage with the daughter of Norwegian peasants."

"She was country-bred, then," Trent observed. "One never heard much about her childhood."

"Yes. She was an orphan of ten years old when Colonel Stamer and his wife went to lodge at her brother's farm for the fishing. They fell in love with the child, and having none of their own, they adopted her. All this my brother told me. He knew, he said, just what I would think; he only asked me to meet her, and then to judge if he had done well or ill. Of course I asked him to introduce me at the first opportunity."

Lord Aviemore paused and stared thoughtfully at the portrait. "She charmed every one who came near her," he went on presently. "I resisted the spell; but before they had been long married she had conquered all my prejudice. It was like a child, I saw, that she delighted in the popularity and the great income her gifts had brought her. But she was not really childish. It was not that she was what is called intellectual; but she had a singular spaciousness of mind in which nothing little or mean could live—it had, I used to fancy, some kinship with her Norwegian landscapes of mountain and sea. She was, as you say, extremely beautiful, with the vigorous purity of the fair-haired northern race. Her marriage with my brother was the happiest I have ever known."

He paused again, while Trent worked on in silence; and soon the low, meditative voice resumed. "It was about this time six years ago— the middle of March—that I had the terrible news from Taormina, the day after my return from Canada. I went out to her at once. When I saw her I was aghast. She showed no emotion; but there was in her calmness the most unearthly sense of desolation that I have ever received. From time to time she would say, as if she spoke to herself, 'It was all my fault.'"

At Trent's exclamation of surprise Lord Aviemore looked up. "Few people," he said, "know the whole of the tragedy. You have heard that a slight shock of earthquake caused the collapse of the villa, and that my brother and his child were found dead in the ruins; you have heard, I suppose, that Lady Aviemore was not in the house at the time. You have heard that she drowned herself afterwards. But you have evidently not heard that my brother had a presentiment that this visit to Sicily would end in death, and wished to abandon it at the last moment; that his wife laughed away his forebodings with her strong common-sense. But we belong to the Highlands, Mr. Trent; we are of that blood and tradition, and such interior warnings as my brother had are no trifles to us. However, she charmed his fears away; he had, she told me, entirely lost all sense of uneasiness. On the tenth day of their stay her husband and only child were killed. She did not think, as you may think, that there was coincidence here. The shock had changed her whole mental being; she believed then, as I believed, that my brother inwardly foreknew that death awaited him if he went to that place." He relapsed into silence.

"I know slightly," Trent remarked, "a man called Selby, a solicitor, who was with Lady Aviemore just after her husband's death."

Lord Aviemore said that he remembered Mr. Selby. He said it with such a total absence of expression of any kind that the subject of Selby was killed instantly; and he did not resume that of the tragedy of the woman whom the world remembered still as Lillemor Wergeland.

It was a few months later, when the portrait of Lord Aviemore was to be seen at the show of the N.S.P.P., that Trent received a friendly letter from Arthur Selby. After praising the picture, Selby went on to ask if Trent would do him the favour of calling at his office by appointment for a private talk. "I should like," he wrote, "to put a certain story before you, a story with a problem in it. I gave it up as a bad job long ago, myself, but seeing your portrait of A. reminded me of your reputation as an unraveller."

Thus it happened that, a few days later, Trent

found himself alone with Selby in the offices of the firm in which that very capable, somewhat dandified lawyer was a partner. They spoke of the portrait, and Trent told of the strange exaltation with which his sitter had spoken of the dead lady. Selby listened rather grimly.

"The story I referred to," he said, "is the Aviemore story. I acted for the Countess when she was alive. I was with her at the time of her suicide. I am an executor of her will. In the strictest confidence, I should like to tell you that story as I know it, and hear what you think about it."

Trent was all attention; he was deeply interested, and said so. Selby, with gloomy eyes, folded his arms on the broad writing-table between them, and began.

"You know all about the accident," he said. "I will start with the fifteenth of March, when Lord Aviemore and his son were buried in the cemetery at Taormina. That was before I came on the scene. Lady Aviemore had already discharged all the servants except her own maid, with whom she was living at the Hotel Cavour. There, as I gathered afterwards, she seldom left her rooms. She was undoubtedly overwhelmed by what had happened, though she seems never to have lost her grip on herself. Her brother-in-law, the present Lord Aviemore, had come out to join her. He had only just returned from Canada"—Selby raised a finger and repeated slowly—"from Canada, you will remember. He had gone out to get ideas about the emigration prospect, I understand. He remained at the hotel, meaning to accompany Lady Aviemore home when she should feel equal to the journey.

"It was not until the eighteenth that we received a long telegram from her, asking us to send some one representing the firm to her at Taormina. She stated that she wished to discuss business matters without delay, but did not yet feel able to travel. At the cost of some inconvenience, I went out myself, as I happen to speak Italian pretty well. You understand that Lady Aviemore, who already possessed considerable means of her own, came into a large income under her husband's will."

"She was a client who could afford to indulge her whims," Trent observed. "If you were already her adviser, she probably expected you to come."

"Just so. Well, I went out to Taormina, as I say. On my arrival Lady Aviemore saw me, and told me quite calmly that she was acquainted with the provisions of her late husband's will, and that she now wished to make her own. I took her instructions, and prepared the will at once. The next day, the British Consul and I witnessed her signature. You may remember, Trent, that when the contents of her will became public after her death, they attracted a good deal of attention."

"I don't think I heard of it," Trent said. "If I was giving myself a holiday at the time, I wouldn't know much about what was going on."

"Well, there were some bequests of jewellery and things to intimate friends. She left £2,000 to her brother, Knut Wergeland, of Myklebostad in Norway, and £100 to her maid, Maria Krogh, also a Norwegian, who had been with her a long time. The whole of the rest of her property she left to her brother, the new Lord Aviemore, unconditionally. That surprised me, because I had been told that he had disapproved bitterly of the marriage, and hadn't concealed his opinion from her or any one else. But she never bore malice, I knew; and what she said to me at Taormina was that she could think of nobody who would do so much good with the money as her brother-in-law. From that point of view she was justified. He is said to spend nine-tenths of his income on charities of all sorts, and I shouldn't wonder if it was true. Anyhow, she made him her heir."

"And what did he say to it?"

Selby coughed. "There is no evidence that he knew anything about it before her death. No evidence," he repeated slowly. "And when told of it afterwards he showed precious little feeling of any kind. Of course, that's his way. But now let me get on with the story. Lady Aviemore asked me to remain to transact business for her until she should leave Taormina. She did so on the twenty-seventh of March, accompanied by Lord Aviemore, myself, and her maid. To shorten the railway journey, as she told us, she had planned to go by boat first to Brindisi, then to Venice, and so home by rail. The boats from Brindisi to Venice all go in the daytime, except once a week, when a boat from Corfu arrives in the evening and goes on about eleven. She decided to get to Brindisi in time to catch that boat. So that was what we did; had a few hours in Brindisi, dined there, and went on board about ten o'clock. Lady Aviemore complained of a bad headache. She went at once to her cabin, which was a deck-cabin, asking me to send some one to collect her ticket at once, as she wanted to sleep as soon as possible and not be awakened again. That was soon done. Shortly before the boat left, the maid came to me on her way to her own quarters and told me her mistress had retired. Soon after we were out of the harbour, I turned in myself. At that time Lord Aviemore was leaning over the rail on the deck onto which Lady Aviemore's cabin opened, and some distance from the cabin. There was nobody else about that I could see. It was just beginning to blow, but it didn't trouble me, and I slept very well.

"It was a quarter to eight next morning when Lord Aviemore came into my cabin. He was fearfully pale and agitated. He told me that the Countess could not be found; that the maid had gone to her cabin to call her at seven-thirty and found it empty.

"I got up in a hurry, and went with him to the cabin. The dressing-case she had taken with her was there, and her fur coat and her hat and her jewellery-case and her hand-bag lay on the berth, which had not been slept in. The only other thing was a note, unaddressed, lying open on the table. Lord Aviemore and I read it together. After the inquiry at Venice, I kept the note. Here it is."

Selby unfolded and handed over a sheet of thin ruled paper, torn from a block. Trent read the following words, written in a large, firm, rounded hand:

"Such an ending to such a marriage is far worse than death. It was all my fault. This is not sorrow, it is complete destruction. I

have been kept up till now only by the reso-lution I took on the day when I lost them, by the thought of what I am going to do now. I take my leave of a world I cannot bear any more."

There followed the initials "L.A." Trent read and reread the pitiful message, so full of the awful egotism of grief, then he looked up in silence at Selby.

"The Italian authorities found that she had met her death by drowning. They could not sup-pose anything else—nor could I. But now listen, Trent. Soon after her death I got an idea into my head, and I have puzzled over the affair a lot without much result. I did find out a fact or two, though; and it struck me the other day that if I could discover something, you could probably do much better."

Trent, still studying the paper, ignored this tribute. "Well," he said, "what is your idea, Selby?"

Selby, evading the direct question, said, "I'll tell you the facts I referred to. That sheet, you see, is torn from an ordinary ruled writing-pad. Now I have shown it to a friend of mine who is in the paper business. He has told me that it is a make of paper never sold in Europe, but sold very largely in Canada. Next, Lady Aviemore never was in Canada. And there was no paper-pad in her dressing-case or anywhere in the cabin. Neither was there any pen or ink, or any fountain pen. The ink, you see, is a pale sort of grey ink."

Trent nodded. "Continental hotel ink, in fact. This was written in a hotel, then—probably the one where you had dinner in Brindisi. You could identify her writing, of course."

"Except that it seems to have been written with a bad pen—a hotel pen, no doubt—it is her usual handwriting."

"Any other exhibits?" Trent asked after a brief silence.

"Only this." Selby took from a drawer a woman's hand-bag of elaborate bead-work. "Later on, when I saw Lord Aviemore about the disposal of her valuables and personal effects,

I mentioned that there was this bag, with a few trifles in it. 'Give it away,' he said. 'Do what you like with it.' Well," Selby went on, smoothing the back of his head with an air of slight embarrassment, "I kept it. As a sort of memento— what? The things in it don't mean anything to me, but you have a look at them." He turned the bag out upon the writing-table. "Here you are— handkerchief, notes and change, nail-file, keys, powder-thing, lipstick, comb, hairpins—"

"Four hairpins." Trent took them in his hand. "Quite new ones, I should say. Have they anything to tell us, Selby?"

"I don't see how. They're just ordinary black hairpins—as you say, they look too fresh and bright to have been used."

Trent looked at the small heap of objects on the table. "And what's that last thing—the little box?"

"That's a box of Ixtil, the anti-sea-sick stuff. Two doses are gone. It's quite good, I believe."

Trent opened the box and stared at the pink capsules. "So you can buy it abroad?"

"I was with her when she bought it in Brindisi, just before we went on board."

Again Trent was silent a few moments. "Then all you discovered that was odd was this about the Canadian paper, and the note having obviously been prepared in advance. Queer enough, certainly. But going back before that last day or two—all through the time you were with Lady Aviemore, did nothing come under your notice that seemed strange?"

Selby fingered his chin. "If you put it like that, I do remember a thing that I thought curious at the time, though I never dreamed of its having anything to do—"

"Yes, I know, but you asked me here to go over the thing properly, didn't you? That question of mine is one of the routine inquiries."

"Well, it was simply this. A day or two before we left Sicily I was standing in the hotel lobby when the mail arrived. As I was waiting to see if there was anything for me, the porter put down on the counter a rather smart-looking package that had just come—done up the way they do

it at a really first-class shop, if you know what I mean. It looked like a biggish book, or box of chocolates, or something; and it had French stamps on it, but the postmark I didn't notice. And this was addressed to Mlle. Maria Krogh— you remember, the Countess's maid. Well, she was there waiting, and presently the man handed it to her. Maria went off with it, and just then her mistress came down the big stairs. She saw the parcel, and just held out her hand for it, and Maria passed it over as if it was a matter of course, and Lady Aviemore went upstairs with it. I thought it was quaint if she was ordering goods in her maid's name; but I thought no more of it, because Lady Aviemore decided that evening about leaving the place, and I had plenty to attend to. And if you want to know," Selby went on, as Trent opened his lips to speak, "where Maria Krogh is, all I can tell you is that I took her ticket in London for Christiansand, where she lives, and where I sent her legacy to her, which she acknowledged. Now then!"

Trent laughed at the solicitor's tone, and Selby laughed too. His friend walked to the fireplace, and pensively adjusted his tie. "Well, I must be off," he announced. "How about dining with me on Friday at the Cactus? If by that time I've anything to suggest about all this, I'll tell you. You will? All right, make it eight o'clock." And he hastened away.

But on the Friday he seemed to have nothing to suggest. He was so reluctant to approach the subject that Selby supposed him to be chagrined at his failure to achieve anything, and did not press the matter.

It was six months later, on a sunny afternoon in September, that Trent walked up the valley road at Myklebostad, looking farewell at the mountain far ahead, the white-capped mother of the torrent that roared down a twenty-foot fall beside him. He had been a week in this remote backwater of Europe, seven hours by motor-boat from the nearest place that ranked as a town. The savage beauty of that watery landscape, where sun and rain worked together daily to achieve an unearthly purity in the scene, had justified far better than he had hoped his story that he had come there in search of matter for his brush. He had worked and he had explored, and had learnt as much as he could of his neighbours. It was little enough, for the postmaster, in whose house he had a room, spoke only a trifle of German, and no one else, as far as he could discover, had anything but Norwegian, of which Trent knew no more than what could be got from a traveller's phrase-book. But he had seen every dweller in the valley, and he had paid close attention to the household of Knut Wergeland, the rich man of the valley, who had the largest farm. He and his wife, elderly and grim-faced peasants, lived with one servant in an old turf-roofed steading not far from the post office. Not another person, Trent was sure, inhabited the house.

He had decided at last that his voyage of curiosity to Myklebostad had been ill-inspired. Knut and his wife were no more than a thrifty peasant pair. They had given him a meal one day when he was sketching near the place, and they had refused with gentle firmness to take any payment. Both had made on him an impression of complete trustworthiness and competency in the life they led so utterly out of the world.

That day, as Trent gazed up to the mountain, his eye was caught by a flash of sunlight against the dense growth of birches running from top to bottom of the steep cliff that walled the valley to his left. It was a bright blink, about half-a-mile from where he stood; it remained steady, and at several points above and below he saw the same bright appearance. He perceived that there must be a wire, and a well-used wire, led up the precipitous hill-face among the trees. Trent went on towards the spot on the road whence the wire seemed to be taken upwards. He had never been so far in this direction until now. In a few minutes he came to the opening among the trees of a rough track leading upwards among rocks and roots, at such an angle that only a vigorous climber could attempt it. Close by, in the edge of the thicket, stood a tall post, from the top of which a wire stretched upwards through the branches in the same direction as the path.

Trent slapped the post with a resounding blow. "Heavens and earth!" he exclaimed. "I had forgotten the *saeter*!"

And at once he began to climb.

A thick carpet of rich pasture began where the deep birch-belt ended at the top of the height. It stretched away for miles over a gently-sloping upland. As Trent came into the open, panting after a strenuous forty-minute climb, the heads of a score of browsing cattle were sleepily turned towards him. Beyond them wandered many more; and two hundred yards away stood a tiny hut, turf-roofed.

This plateau was the *saeter*; the high grass-land, attached to some valley farm. Trent had heard long ago, and never thought since, of this feature of Norway's rural life. At the appointed time, the cattle would be driven up by an easier detour to the mountain pastures for their summer holiday, to be attended there by some peasant—usually a young girl—who lived solitary with the herd. Such wires as that he had seen were kept bright by the daily descent of milk-churns, let down by a line from above, received by a farm-hand at the road below.

And there, at the side of the hut, a woman stood. Trent, as he approached, noted her short, rough skirt and coarse, sack-like upper garment, her thick grey stockings and clumsy clogs. About her bare head her pale-gold hair was fastened in tight plaits. As she looked up on hearing Trent's footfall, two heavy silver earrings dangled about the tanned and careworn face of this very type of the middle-aged peasant women of the region.

She ceased her task of scraping a large cake of chocolate into a bowl, and straightened her tall body. Smiling, with lean hands on her hips, she spoke in Norwegian, greeting him.

Trent made the proper reply. "And that," he added in his own tongue, "is a large part of all the Norwegian I know. Perhaps, madam, you speak English." Her light blue eyes looked puzzlement, and she spoke again, pointing down to the valley. He nodded; and she began to talk pleasantly in her unknown speech. From within the hut she brought two thick mugs; she pointed rapidly to the chocolate in the bowl, to himself and herself.

"I should like it of all things," he said. "You are most kind and hospitable, like all your people. What a pity it is we have no language in common!" She brought him a stool and gave him the chocolate-cake and a knife, making signs that he should continue the scraping; then within the hut she kindled a fire of twigs and began to boil water in a black pot. Plainly this was her dwelling, the roughest Trent had ever seen. He could discern that on two small shelves were ranged a few pieces of chipped earthenware. A wooden bed-place, with straw and two neatly-folded blankets, filled a third of the space in the hut. All the carpentering was of the rudest. From a small chest in a corner she drew a biscuit-tin, half full of flat cakes of stale rye bread. There seemed to be nothing else in the tiny place but a heap of twigs for fuel.

She made chocolate in the two mugs, and then, at Trent's insistence in dumb show, she sat on the only stool at a rude table outside the hut, while her guest made a seat of an upturned milking-pail. She continued to talk amiably and unintelligibly, while he finished with difficulty the half of a bread-cake.

"I believe, madam," he said at last, setting down his empty mug, "you are talking simply to hear the sound of your own voice. In your case, that is excusable. You don't understand English, so I will tell you to your face that it is a most wonderful voice. I should say," he went on thoughtfully, "that you ought to have been one of the greatest sopranos that ever lived."

She heard him calmly, and shook her head as not understanding.

"Well, don't say I didn't break it gently," Trent protested. He rose to his feet. "Madam, I know that you are Lady Aviemore. I have broken in on your solitude, and I ask pardon for that; but I could not be sure unless I saw you. I give you my word that no one else knows or ever shall know from me, what I have discovered." He made as if to return by the way he had come.

But the woman held up a hand. A singular change had come over her brown face. A lively spirit now looked out of her desolate blue eyes; she smiled another and a much more intelligent smile. After a few moments she spoke in English, fluent but with a slight accent of her country.

"Sir," she said, "you have behaved very nicely up till now. It has been an amusement for me; there is not much comedy on the *saeter*. Now, will you have the goodness to explain?"

He told her in a few words that he had suspected she was still alive, that he had thought over such facts as had come to his knowledge, and had been led to think she was probably in that place. "I thought you might guess I had recognized you," he added, "so it seemed best to assure you that your secret was safe. Was it wrong to speak?"

She shook her head, gazing at him with her chin on a hand. Presently she said, "I think you are not against me. I can feel that, though I do not understand why you wanted to search out my secret, and why you kept it when you had dragged it into the light."

"I dragged it because I am curious," he answered. "I have kept it and will keep it because—oh well, because it is your own, and because to me Lillemor Wergeland is a sort of divinity."

She laughed suddenly. "Incense! And I in these rags, in this hovel, with what unpleasantness I can see in this little spotty piece of cheap mirror! . . . Ah well! You have come a long way, curious man, and it would be cruel not to gratify your curiosity a little more. Shall I tell you? After all, it was simple.

"It was very soon after the disaster that the resolve came to me. I never hesitated. It was my fault that we had gone to Sicily—you have heard that? Yes, I see it in your face. I felt I must leave the world I knew, and that knew me. I never really thought of suicide. As for a convent, unhappily there is none for people with minds like mine. I meant simply to disappear, and the only way to succeed was to get the reputation of being dead. I thought it out for some days and nights. Then I wrote, in the name of my maid, to an establishment in Paris where I used to buy things for the stage."

"Ha!" Trent exclaimed. "I heard of that, and I guessed."

"I sent money," she went on, "and I ordered a dark-brown transformation—that is a lady's word for wig—some stuff for darkening the skin, various pigments, pencils, *et tout le bazar.* My maid did not know what I had sent for; she only handed the parcel to me when it came. She would have thrown herself in the fire for me, I think, my maid Maria. When the things arrived, I announced that I would return to England by the route you have heard of, perhaps."

He nodded. "The route that gave you a night passage to Venice. And you disguised yourself in your cabin at Brindisi, and slipped off in the dark before the boat started."

"Indeed, I was not such a fool!" she returned. "What if my absence had been discovered somehow before the boat left Brindisi? That could easily happen, and then good-bye to the fiction of my suicide. No; when we reached Brindisi, we had, as I knew, some hours there. We left our things at a hotel, where we were to dine, and then I put on a thick veil and went out alone. At the office near the harbour I took a second-class passage to Venice for myself, in the name of Miss Julia Simmons, in the same boat I had planned to take. It would be at the quay, they told me, in an hour. Then I went into the poorer streets of the town, and bought some clothes, very ugly ones, some shoes, toilet things—"

"Some black hairpins," Trent murmured.

"Naturally, black," she assented. "My own gilt pins would have looked queer in a dark-brown wig, and I had to have pins to fasten it properly. I bought also a little cheap portmanteau-thing, and put my purchases in it. Then I took a cab to the quay, found the boat had arrived, and gave one of the stewards a tip to show me the berth named on my ticket, and

to carry my baggage there. After that I went shopping again on shore. I bought a long mackintosh coat and a funny little cap, the very things for Miss Simmons; took them to the hotel and pushed them under the things my maid had already packed in my big case.

"On the steamer, when Maria had left me and I had locked the cabin-door, I arranged a dark, rather catty sort of face for myself, and fitted on Miss Simmons's hair. I put on her mackintosh coat and cap. When the boat began to move away from the quay, I opened my door an inch and peeped out. As I expected, every one was looking over the rail, and so—the sooner the better—I just slipped out, shut the cabin door, and walked straight to Miss Simmons's berth at the other end of the ship. . . . There is not much more to say. At Venice, I did not look for the others, and never saw them. I went on to Paris, and wrote to my brother Knut that I was alive, telling him what I meant to do if he would help me. Such things do not seem so mad to a true child of Norway."

"What things?" Trent asked.

"Things of deep sorrow, malady of the soul, escape from the world. . . . He and his wife have been true and good to me. I am supposed to be her cousin, Hilda Bjoernstad. In my will I left them money, more than enough to pay for me, but they did not know that when they welcomed me here."

She ceased, and smiled vaguely at Trent, who was considering her story with eyes that gazed fixedly at the skyline.

"Yes, of course," he remarked presently in an abstracted manner. "That was it. As you say, so simple. And now let me tell you," he went on with a change of tone, "one or two little details you have forgotten.

"At Brindisi you bought, just before going on board with the others, a box of the stuff called Ixtil, because it looked as if there might be bad weather. You took a dose at once, and another a little later, as the directions told you. You might have needed more of it before reaching Venice, but as Mr. Selby was with you when you bought it, you thought it wiser to leave it behind when you vanished. Also, you left behind you four new black hairpins, which had somehow, I suppose, got loose inside your hand-bag, and were found there by Selby. You see, Lady Aviemore, it was Selby who brought me into this. He told me all the facts he knew, and he showed me your bag and its contents. But he didn't attach any importance to the two things I have just mentioned."

She raised her eyebrows just perceptibly. "I cannot see why he should. And I cannot see why he should bring in you or anybody."

"Because he had some vague notion of your brother-in-law having either caused your death, or at least having known of your intention to commit suicide. He never told me so outright, but it was plain that that was in his mind. Selby wanted me to clear that up, if I could. You see, your brother-in-law stood to benefit enormously by your death, and then there was the matter of the note announcing your suicide."

"It announced," she remarked, "the truth; that I was leaving a world I could not bear any longer. The words might mean one thing or another. But what about the note?"

"The perfectly truthful note was written with pen and ink, of which there was none in your cabin. It was written on paper which had been torn from a writing-pad, and no pad was found. Also that make of paper is sold in Canada, never in Europe. You had never been in Canada. Your brother-in-law had just come back from Canada. You see?"

"But did not Selby perceive that Charles is a saint?" inquired the lady with a touch of impatience. "Surely that was plain! More Dominic than Francis, no doubt; but an evident saint."

"In my slight knowledge of him," Trent admitted, "he did strike me in that way. But Selby is a lawyer, you see, and lawyers don't understand saints. Besides, your brother-in-law had taken a dislike to him, I think, and so perhaps he felt critical about your brother-in-law."

"It is true," she said, "he did not care about Mr. Selby, because he disliked all men who were foppish and worldly. But now I will tell you.

That evening in the hotel at Brindisi I wanted to write that note, and I asked Charles for a sheet from the block he had in his hand and was just going to write on. That is all. I wrote it in the hotel writing-room, and took it afterwards in my bag to the cabin."

"We supposed you had written it beforehand," Trent said, "and that was one of the things that led me to feel morally certain you were still alive. I'll explain. If, as we thought, you had written the note in the hotel, your suicide was a premeditated act. Yet it was afterwards that Selby saw you buying that Ixtil stuff, and it was plain that you had taken two doses. And it struck me, though it didn't seem to have struck Selby, that it was unlikely any one already resolved to drown herself at sea would begin treating herself against sea-sickness.

"Then there were those new black hairpins. The sight of them was a revelation to me. For I knew, of course, that with that hair of yours you had probably never used a black hairpin in your life."

The Countess felt at her pale-gold plaits, and gravely held out to him a black hairpin. "In the valley we use nothing else."

"It is very different in the valley, I know," he said gently. "I was speaking of my world— the world that you have left. I was led by those hairpins to think of your having changed your appearance, and I even guessed at what was in the parcel that came for your maid, which Selby had told me about."

She regarded her guest with something of respect. "It still remains," she said, "to explain how you knew it was in Norway, and here, as a poor farm servant, that I should hide myself. It seemed to me the last thing in the world—your world—that a woman who had lived my life would be expected to do."

"All the same, I thought it was a strong possibility," he answered. "Your problem, you see, was just what you say—to hide yourself. And you had another—you had to make a living somehow. Everything you possessed—except some small amount in cash, I suppose—you left behind when you disappeared. And a woman can't go on acting and disguising herself forever. A man can grow hair on his face, or shave it off; for a woman, disguise must be a perpetual anxiety. If she has to get employment, and especially if she has no references, it's something very like an impossibility."

She nodded gravely. "That was how I saw it."

"So," he pursued, "it came to this: that the world-famous Lillemor Wergeland had to come to the surface again somewhere, and in no long time—Lillemor Wergeland, whose type of beauty and general appearance were so marked and unmistakable, whose photographs were known everywhere. The fact is that for some time I couldn't see for the life of me how it could possibly have been done. There were only a few countries, I supposed, of which you knew enough of the language to attempt to live in any of them; and if you did, you would always be conspicuous by your physical type and your accent. If you attracted attention, discovery might follow at any moment. The more I thought of it, the more marvellous it seemed that you had not been recognized—assuming you were still alive—during the six years or so that had passed before I heard the full story and guessed at the truth.

"And then an idea came. There was one country in which your looks and speech would not betray you as a foreigner—your own country. And if there were any corners of the world where you could go with a fair certainty of being unrecognized, the remoter villages of Norway would be among them. And at Myklebostad, on the Langfjord, which the map told me was one of the remotest, you had a brother, who was two thousand pounds richer by your supposed death. You see how it was, then, that I came to this place on a sketching holiday."

Trent stood up and gazed across the valley to the sunlit white peaks beyond. "I have visited Norway before, but never had such an interesting time. And now, before I return to the haunts

of men, let me say again that I shall forget at once all that has happened to-day. Don't think it was merely a vulgar curiosity that brought me here. There was once a supreme artist, whose gifts made me her debtor and servant. Anything that happened to her touched me; I had a sort of right to go seeking what it really was that had happened."

She stood before him in her coarse and stained clothes, her hands clasped behind her, with a face and attitude of perfect dignity. "Very well—you stand on your right, and I on mine—to arrange my own life, since I am alone in it. I will spend it here, where it began. My soul was born here before it went out to have adventures, and it has crept home again for comfort. Believe me, it is not only that, as you say, I am safe from discovery here. That counts for very much; but also I felt I must go and live out my life in my own place, this far-away, lonely valley, where everything is humble and unspoilt, and the hills and the fjords are as God made them before there were any men. It is all my own, own land!

"And now," she ended suddenly, "we understand one another, and we can part friends." She extended her hand, saying, "I do not know your name."

"Why should you?" he asked. He bent over the hand, then went quickly from her. At the beginning of the descent he glanced back once; she waved to him.

Half-way down the rugged track he stopped. Far above a wonderful voice was singing to the glory of the Norse land.

"Ja, herligt er mit Fodeland
Der ewig trodser Tidens Tand"

sang the voice.

Trent looked out upon the wild landscape. "Her fatherland!" he soliloquised. "Well, well! They say the strictest parents have the most devoted children."

THE PHANTOM MOTOR

JACQUES FUTRELLE

WHILE VIRTUALLY EVERY READER of detective fiction is familiar with Jacques Futrelle's (1875–1912) brilliant debut, "The Problem of Cell 13," the central figure, Professor Augustus S. F. X. Van Dusen, better known as The Thinking Machine, appeared in forty-four other stories, some of which are first-rate, and "The Phantom Motor" is one of the best. Most of the early Van Dusen stories involve investigations of "impossible" (a word despised by the professor) crimes, while his later stories generally deal with bizarre, seemingly inexplicable, situations without falling into the former subgenre.

Born in Georgia of French Huguenot ancestry, Futrelle became a newspaperman, first in Richmond, Virginia, then in Boston, where he worked on the *Boston American*, which published much of his fiction as well as his reportage. He married L. May Peel in 1895. To celebrate his thirty-seventh birthday, the Futrelles left the children home and took a romantic cruise on the infamous maiden voyage of the R.M.S. *Titanic*. After the ship crashed into an iceberg and began its trip to the bottom of the icy sea, Futrelle forced his wife into one of the lifeboats and helped other women as well, refusing to board himself, dying in the tragedy.

Although his career as a fiction writer was relatively short, he wrote more than sixty stories and several novels popular in their time but forgotten today, including light romances and crime stories, the best of which are *The Diamond Master* (1909) and *My Lady's Garter* (1912), which features The Hawk, a gentleman thief.

"The Phantom Motor" was first published in the *Boston American* in 1905; it was first collected in book form in *The Thinking Machine* (New York, Dodd, Mead, 1907).

THE PHANTOM MOTOR

JACQUES FUTRELLE

TWO DAZZLING WHITE eyes bulged through the night as an automobile swept suddenly around a curve in the wide road and laid a smooth, glaring pathway ahead. Even at the distance the rhythmical crackling-chug informed Special Constable Baker that it was a gasoline car, and the headlong swoop of the unblinking lights toward him made him instantly aware of the fact that the speed ordinance of Yarborough County was being a little more than broken—it was being obliterated.

Now the County of Yarborough was a wide expanse of summer estates and superbly kept roads, level as a floor and offered distracting temptations to the dangerous pastime of speeding. But against this was the fact that the county was particular about its speed laws, so particular in fact that it had stationed half a hundred men upon its highways to abate the nuisance. Incidentally it had found that keeping record of the infractions of the law was an excellent source of income.

"Forty miles an hour if an inch," remarked Baker to himself.

He arose from a camp stool where he was wont to make himself comfortable from six o'clock until midnight on watch, picked up his lantern, turned up the light and stepped down to the edge of the road. He always remained on watch at the same place—at one end of a long stretch which autoists had unanimously dubbed The Trap. The Trap was singularly tempting—a perfectly macadamized road bed lying between two tall stone walls with only enough of a sinuous twist in it to make each end invisible from the other. Another man, Special Constable Bowman, was stationed at the other end of The Trap and there was telephonic communication between the points, enabling the men to check each other and incidentally, if one failed to stop a car or get its number, the other would. That at least was the theory.

So now, with the utmost confidence, Baker waited beside the road. The approaching lights were only a couple of hundred yards away. At the proper instant he would raise his lantern, the car would stop, its occupants would protest and then the county would add a mite to its general fund for making the roads even better and tempting autoists still more. Or sometimes the cars didn't stop. In that event it was part of the Special Constable's duties to get the number as it flew past, and reference to the monthly automobile register would give the name of the owner. An extra fine was always imposed in such cases.

Without the slightest diminution of speed the car came hurtling on toward him and swung wide so as to take the straight path of The Trap at full speed. At the psychological instant Baker stepped out into the road and waved his lantern.

"Stop!" he commanded.

The crackling-chug came on, heedless of the cry. The auto was almost upon him before

489

he leaped out of the road—a feat at which he was particularly expert—then it flashed by and plunged into The Trap. Baker was, at the instant, so busily engaged in getting out of the way that he couldn't read the number, but he was not disconcerted because he knew there was no escape from The Trap. On the one side a solid stone wall eight feet high marked the eastern boundary of the John Phelps Stocker country estate, and on the other side a stone fence nine feet high marked the western boundary of the Thomas Q. Rogers country estate. There was no turnout, no place, no possible way for an auto to get out of The Trap except at one of the two ends guarded by the special constables. So Baker, perfectly confident of results, seized the phone.

"Car coming through sixty miles an hour," he bawled. "It won't stop. I missed the number. Look out!"

"All right," answered Special Constable Bowman.

For ten, fifteen, twenty minutes Baker waited expecting a call from Bowman at the other end. It didn't come and finally he picked up the phone again. No answer. He rang several times, battered the box and did some tricks with the receiver. Still no answer. Finally he began to feel worried. He remembered that at that same post one Special Constable had been badly hurt by a reckless chauffeur who refused to stop or turn his car when the officer stepped out into the road. In his mind's eye he saw Bowman now lying helpless, perhaps badly injured. If the car held the pace at which it passed him it would be certain death to whoever might be unlucky enough to get in its path.

With these thoughts running through his head and with genuine solicitude for Bowman, Baker at last walked on along the road of The Trap toward the other end. The feeble rays of the lantern showed the unbroken line of the cold, stone walls on each side. There was no shrubbery of any sort, only a narrow strip of grass close to the wall. The more Baker considered the matter the more anxious he became and he increased his pace a little. As he turned a gen-

tle curve he saw a lantern in the distance coming slowly toward him. It was evidently being carried by some one who was looking carefully along each side of the road.

"Hello!" called Baker, when the lantern came within distance. "That you, Bowman?"

"Yes," came the hallooed response.

The lanterns moved on and met. Baker's solicitude for the other constable was quickly changed to curiosity.

"What're you looking for?" he asked.

"That auto," replied Bowman. "It didn't come through my end and I thought perhaps there had been an accident so I walked along looking for it. Haven't seen anything."

"Didn't come through your end?" repeated Baker in amazement. "Why it must have. It didn't come back my way and I haven't passed it so it must have gone through."

"Well, it didn't," declared Bowman conclusively. "I was on the lookout for it, too, standing beside the road. There hasn't been a car through my end in an hour."

Special Constable Baker raised his lantern until the rays fell full upon the face of Special Constable Bowman and for an instant they stared each at the other. Suspicion glowed from the keen, avaricious eyes of Baker.

"How much did they give you to let 'em by?" he asked.

"Give me?" exclaimed Bowman, in righteous indignation. "Give me nothing. I haven't seen a car."

A slight sneer curled the lips of Special Constable Baker.

"Of course that's all right to report at headquarters," he said, "but I happened to know that the auto came in here, that it didn't go back my way, that it couldn't get out except at the ends, therefore it went your way." He was silent for a moment. "And whatever you got, Jim, seems to me I ought to get half."

Then the worm—i.e., Bowman—turned. A polite curl appeared about his lips and was permitted to show through the grizzled mustache.

"I guess," he said deliberately, "you think

because you do that everybody else does. I haven't seen any autos."

"Don't I always give you half, Jim?" Baker demanded, almost pleadingly.

"Well I haven't seen any car and that's all there is to it. If it didn't go back your way there wasn't any car." There was a pause; Bowman was framing up something particularly unpleasant. "You're seeing things, that's what's the matter."

So was sown discord between two officers of the County of Yarborough. After awhile they separated with mutual sneers and open derision and went back to their respective posts. Each was thoughtful in his own way. At five minutes of midnight when they went off duty Baker called Bowman on the phone again.

"I've been thinking this thing over, Jim, and I guess it would be just as well if we didn't report it or say anything about it when we go in," said Baker slowly. "It seems foolish and if we did say anything about it it would give the boys the laugh on us."

"Just as you say," responded Bowman.

Relations between Special Constable Baker and Special Constable Bowman were strained on the morrow. But they walked along side by side to their respective posts. Baker stopped at his end of The Trap; Bowman didn't even look around.

"You'd better keep your eyes open tonight, Jim," Baker called as a last word.

"I had 'em open last night," was the disgusted retort.

Seven, eight, nine o'clock passed. Two or three cars had gone through The Trap at moderate speed and one had been warned by Baker. At a few minutes past nine he was staring down the road which led into The Trap when he saw something that brought him quickly to his feet. It was a pair of dazzling white eyes, far away. He recognized them—the mysterious car of the night before.

"I'll get it this time," he muttered grimly, between closed teeth.

Then when the onrushing car was a full two hundred yards away Baker planted himself in the middle of the road and began to swing the lantern. The auto seemed, if anything, to be traveling even faster than on the previous night. At a hundred yards Baker began to shout. Still the car didn't lessen speed, merely rushed on. Again at the psychological instant Baker jumped. The auto whisked by as the chauffeur gave it a dextrous twist to prevent running down the Special Constable.

Safely out of its way Baker turned and stared after it, trying to read the number. He could see there was a number because a white board swung from the tail axle, but he could not make out the figures. Dust and a swaying car conspired to defeat him. But he did see that there were four persons in the car dimly silhouetted against the light reflected from the road. It was useless, of course, to conjecture as to sex for even as he looked the fast-receding car swerved around the turn and was lost to sight.

Again he rushed to the telephone; Bowman responded promptly.

"That car's gone in again," Baker called. "Ninety miles an hour. Look out!"

"I'm looking," responded Bowman.

"Let me know what happens," Baker shouted.

With the receiver to his ear he stood for ten or fifteen minutes, then Bowman hallooed from the other end.

"Well?" Baker responded. "Get 'em?"

"No car passed through and there's none in sight," said Bowman.

"But it went in," insisted Baker.

"Well it didn't come out here," declared Bowman. "Walk along the road till I meet you and look out for it."

Then was repeated the search of the night before. When the two men met in the middle of The Trap their faces were blank—blank as the high stone walls which stared at them from each side.

"Nothing!" said Bowman.

"Nothing!" echoed Baker.

Special Constable Bowman perched his head on one side and scratched his grizzly chin.

"You're not trying to put up a job on me?" he inquired coldly. "You did see a car?"

"I certainly did," declared Baker, and a belligerent tone underlay his manner. "I certainly saw it, Jim, and if it didn't come out your end, why—why—"

He paused and glanced quickly behind him. The action inspired a sudden similar caution on Bowman's part.

"Maybe—maybe—" said Bowman after a minute, "maybe it's a—a spook auto?"

"Well it must be," mused Baker. "You know as well as I do that no car can get out of this trap except at the ends. That car came in here, it isn't here now and it didn't go out your end. Now where is it?"

Bowman stared at him a minute, picked up his lantern, shook his head solemnly and wandered along the road back to his post. On his way he glanced around quickly, apprehensively three times—Baker did the same thing four times.

On the third night the phantom car appeared and disappeared precisely as it had done previously. Again Baker and Bowman met half way between posts and talked it over.

"I'll tell you what, Baker," said Bowman in conclusion, "maybe you're just imagining that you see a car. Maybe if I was at your end I couldn't see it."

Special Constable Baker was distinctly hurt at the insinuation.

"All right, Jim," he said at last, "if you think that way about it we'll swap posts tomorrow night. We won't have to say anything about it when we report."

"Now that's the talk," exclaimed Bowman with an air approaching enthusiasm. "I'll bet I don't see it."

On the following night Special Constable Bowman made himself comfortable on Special Constable Baker's camp-stool. And *he* saw the phantom auto. It came upon him with a rush and a crackling-chug of engine and then sped on leaving him nerveless. He called Baker over the wire and Baker watched half an hour for the phantom. It didn't appear.

Ultimately all things reach the newspapers. So with the story of the phantom auto. Hutchinson Hatch, reporter, smiled incredulously when his City Editor laid aside an inevitable cigar and tersely stated the known facts. The known facts in this instance were meager almost to the disappearing point. They consisted merely of a corroborated statement that an automobile, solid and tangible enough to all appearances, rushed into The Trap each night and totally disappeared.

But there was enough of the bizarre about it to pique the curiosity, to make one wonder, so Hatch journeyed down to Yarborough County, an hour's ride from the city, met and talked to Baker and Bowman and then, in broad daylight strolled along The Trap twice. It was a leisurely, thorough investigation with the end in view of finding out how an automobile once inside might get out again without going out either end.

On the first trip through Hatch paid particular attention to the Thomas Q. Rogers side of the road. The wall, nine feet high, was an unbroken line of stone with not the slightest indication of a secret wagon-way through it anywhere. Secret wagon-way! Hatch smiled at the phrase. But when he reached the other end—Bowman's end—of The Trap he was perfectly convinced of one thing—that no automobile had left the hard, macadamized road to go over, under, or through the Thomas Q. Rogers wall. Returning, still leisurely, he paid strict attention to the John Phelps Stocker side, and when he reached the other end—Baker's end—he was convinced of another thing—that no automobile had left the road to go over, under or through the John Phelps Stocker wall. The only opening of any sort was a narrow footpath, not more than sixteen inches wide.

Hatch saw no shrubbery along the road, nothing but a strip of scrupulously cared for grass, therefore the phantom auto could not be hidden any time, night or day. Hatch failed, too, to find any holes in the road so the automobile didn't go down through the earth. At this point he involuntarily glanced up at the blue sky above. Perhaps, he thought, whimsically, the automobile was a strange sort of bird, or—or—and he stopped suddenly.

"By George!" he exclaimed. "I wonder if—"

And the remainder of the afternoon he spent systematically making inquiries. He went from house to house, the Stocker house, the Rogers house, both of which were at the time unoccupied, then to cottage, cabin, and hut in turn. But he didn't seem overladen with information when he joined Special Constable Baker at his end of The Trap that evening about seven o'clock.

Together they rehearsed the strange points of the mystery and as the shadows grew about them until finally the darkness was so dense that Baker's lantern was the only bright spot in sight. As the chill of evening closed in a certain awed tone crept into their voices. Occasionally an auto bowled along and each time as it hove in sight Hatch glanced at Baker questioningly. And each time Baker shook his head. And each time, too, he called Bowman, in this manner accounting for every car that went into The Trap.

"It'll come all right," said Baker after a long silence, "and I'll know it the minute it rounds the curve coming toward us. I'd know its two lights in a thousand."

They sat still and smoked. After awhile two dazzling white lights burst into view far down the road and Baker, in excitement, dropped his pipe.

"That's her," he declared. "Look at her coming!"

And Hatch did look at her coming. The speed of the mysterious car was such as to make one look. Like the eyes of a giant the two lights came on toward them, and Baker perfunctorily went through the motions of attempting to stop it. The car fairly whizzed past them and the rush of air which tugged at their coats was convincing enough proof of its solidity. Hatch strained his eyes to read the number as the auto flashed past. But it was hopeless. The tail of the car was lost in an eddying whirl of dust.

"She certainly does travel," commented Baker, softly.

"She does," Hatch assented.

Then, for the benefit of the newspaperman, Baker called Bowman on the wire.

"Car's coming again," he shouted. "Look out and let me know!"

Bowman, at his end, waited twenty minutes, then made the usual report—the car had not passed. Hutchinson Hatch was a calm, cold, dispassionate young man but now a queer, creepy sensation stole along his spinal column. He lighted a cigarette and pulled himself together with a jerk.

"There's one way to find out where it goes," he declared at last, emphatically, "and that's to place a man in the middle just beyond the bend of The Trap and let him wait and see. If the car goes up, down, or evaporates he'll see and can tell us."

Baker looked at him curiously.

"I'd hate to be the man in the middle," he declared. There was something of uneasiness in his manner.

"I rather think I would, too," responded Hatch.

On the following evening, consequent upon the appearance of the story of the phantom auto in Hatch's paper, there were twelve other reporters on hand. Most of them were openly, flagrantly sceptical; they even insinuated that no one had seen an auto. Hatch smiled wisely.

"Wait!" he advised with deep conviction.

So when the darkness fell that evening the newspapermen of a great city had entered into a conspiracy to capture the phantom auto. Thirteen of them, making a total of fifteen men with Baker and Bowman, were on hand and they agreed to a suggestion for all to take positions along the road of The Trap from Baker's post to Bowman's, watch for the auto, see what happened to it and compare notes afterwards. So they scattered themselves along a few hundred feet apart and waited. That night the phantom auto didn't appear at all and twelve reporters jeered at Hutchinson Hatch and told him to light his pipe with the story. And next night when Hatch and Baker and Bowman alone were watching the phantom auto reappeared.

Like a child with a troublesome problem, Hatch took the entire matter and laid it before Professor Augustus S. F. X. Van Dusen, the master brain. The Thinking Machine, with squint eyes turned steadily upward and long, slender fingers pressed tip to tip listened to the end.

"Now I know of course that automobiles don't fly," Hatch burst out savagely in conclusion, "and if this one doesn't fly, there is no earthly way for it to get out of The Trap, as they call it. I went over the thing carefully—I even went so far as to examine the ground and the tops of the walls to see if a runway had been let down to the auto to go over."

The Thinking Machine squinted at him inquiringly.

"Are you sure you saw an automobile?" he demanded irritably.

"Certainly I saw it," blurted the reporter. "I not only saw it—I smelled it. Just to convince myself that it was real I tossed my cane in front of the thing and it smashed it to tooth-picks."

"Perhaps, then, if everything is as you say the auto actually *does* fly," remarked the scientist.

The reporter stared into the calm, inscrutable face of The Thinking Machine, fearing first that he had not heard aright. Then he concluded that he had.

"You mean," he inquired eagerly, "that the phantom may be an auto-areoplane affair, and that it actually does fly?"

"It's not at all impossible," commented the scientist.

"I had an idea something like that myself," Hatch explained, "and questioned every soul within a mile or so but I didn't get anything."

"The perfect stretch of road there might be the very place for some daring experimenter to get up sufficient speed to soar a short distance in a light machine," continued the scientist.

"Light machine?" Hatch repeated. "Did I tell you that this car had four people in it?"

"Four people!" exclaimed the scientist. "Dear me! Dear me! That makes it very differ-ent. Of course four people would be too great a lift for an—"

For ten minutes he sat silent, and tiny, cob-webby lines appeared in his dome-like brow. Then he arose and passed into the adjoining room. After a moment Hatch heard the tele-phone bell jingle. Five minutes later The Think-ing Machine appeared, and scowled upon him unpleasantly.

"I suppose what you really want to learn is if the car is a—a material one, and to whom it belongs?" he queried.

"That's it," agreed the reporter, "and of course why it does what it does, and how it gets out of The Trap."

"Do you happen to know a fast, long-distance bicycle rider?" demanded the scientist abruptly.

"A dozen of them," replied the reporter promptly. "I think I see the idea, but—"

"You haven't the faintest inkling of the idea," declared The Thinking Machine posi-tively. "If you can arrange with a fast rider who can go a distance—it might be thirty, forty, fifty miles—we may end this little affair without dif-ficulty."

Under these circumstances Professor Augus-tus S. F. X. Van Dusen, Ph.D., LL.D., F.R.S., M.D., etc., etc., scientist and logician, met the famous Jimmie Thalhauer, the world's cham-pion long distance bicyclist. He held every record from five miles up to and including six hours, had twice won the six-day race and was, altogether, a master in his field. He came in chewing a tooth-pick. There were introductions.

"You ride the bicycle?" inquired the crusty little scientist.

"Well, *some*," confessed the champion mod-estly with a wink at Hatch.

"Can you keep up with an automobile for a distance of, say, thirty or forty miles?"

"I can keep up with anything that ain't got wings," was the response.

"Well, to tell you the truth," volunteered The Thinking Machine, "there is a growing belief that this particular automobile has wings. How-ever if you can keep up with it—"

"Ah, quit your kiddin'," said the champion, easily. "I can ride rings around anything on wheels. I'll start behind it and beat it where it's going."

The Thinking Machine examined the champion, Jimmie Thalhauer, as a curiosity. In the seclusion of his laboratory he had never had an opportunity of meeting just such another worldly young person.

"How fast *can* you ride, Mr. Thalhauer?" he asked at last.

"I'm ashamed to tell you," confided the champion in a hushed voice. "I can ride so fast that I scare myself." He paused a moment. "But it seems to me," he said, "if there's thirty or forty miles to do I ought to do it on a motor cycle."

"Now that's just the point," explained The Thinking Machine. "A motor-cycle makes noise and if it could have been used we would have hired a fast automobile. This proposition briefly is: I want you to ride without lights behind an automobile which may also run without lights and find out where it goes. No occupant of the car must suspect that it is followed."

"Without lights?" repeated the champion. "Gee! Rubber shoe, eh?"

The Thinking Machine looked his bewilderment.

"Yes, that's it," Hatch answered for him.

"I guess it's good for a four column head? Hunh?" inquired the champion. "Special pictures posed by the champion? Hunh?"

"Yes," Hatch replied.

"'Tracked on a Bicycle' sounds good to me. Hunh?"

Hatch nodded.

So arrangements were concluded and then and there The Thinking Machine gave definite and conclusive instructions to the champion. While these apparently bore broadly on the problem in hand they conveyed absolutely no inkling of his plan to the reporter. At the end the champion arose to go.

"You're a most extraordinary young man, Mr. Thalhauer," commented The Thinking Machine, not without admiration for the sturdy, powerful figure.

And as Hatch accompanied the champion out the door and down the steps Jimmie smiled with easy grace.

"Nutty old guy, ain't he? Hunh?"

Night! Utter blackness, relieved only by a white, ribbon-like road which winds away mistily under a starless sky. Shadowy hedges line either side and occasionally a tree thrusts itself upward out of the sombreness. The murmur of human voices in the shadows, then the crackling-chug of an engine and an automobile moves slowly, without lights, into the road. There is the sudden clatter of an engine at high speed and the car rushes away.

From the hedge comes the faint rustle of leaves as of wind stirring, then a figure moves impalpably. A moment and it becomes a separate entity; a quick movement and the creak of a leather bicycle saddle. Silently the single figure, bent low over the handle bars, moves after the car with ever increasing momentum.

Then a long, desperate race. For mile after mile, mile after mile the auto goes on. The silent cyclist has crept up almost to the rear axle and hangs there doggedly as a racer to his pace. On and on they rush together through the darkness, the chauffeur moving with a perfect knowledge of his road, the single rider behind clinging on grimly with set teeth. The powerful, piston-like legs move up and down to the beat of the engine.

At last, with dust-dry throat and stinging, aching eyes the cyclist feels the pace slacken and instantly he drops back out of sight. It is only by sound that he follows now. The car stops; the cyclist is lost in the shadows.

For two or three hours the auto stands deserted and silent. At last the voices are heard again, the car stirs, moves away and the cyclist drops in behind. Another race which leads off in another direction. Finally, from a knoll, the lights of a city are seen. Ten minutes elapse, the auto stops, the head lights flare up and more leisurely it proceeds on its way.

On the following evening The Thinking Machine and Hutchinson Hatch called upon Fielding Stanwood, President of the Fordyce National Bank. Mr. Stanwood looked at them with interrogative eyes.

"We called to inform you, Mr. Stanwood," explained The Thinking Machine, "that a box of securities, probably United States bonds, is missing from your bank."

"What?" exclaimed Mr. Stanwood, and his face paled. "Robbery?"

"I only know the bonds were taken out of the vault tonight by Joseph Marsh, your assistant cashier," said the scientist, "and that he, together with three other men, left the bank with the box and are now at—a place I can name."

Mr. Stanwood was staring at him in amazement.

"You know where they are?" he demanded.

"I said I did," replied the scientist, shortly.

"Then we must inform the police at once, and—"

"I don't know that there has been an actual crime," interrupted the scientist. "I do know that every night for a week these bonds have been taken out through the connivance of your watchman and in each instance have been returned, intact, before morning. They will be returned tonight. Therefore I would advise, if you act, not to do so until the four men return with the bonds."

It was a singular party which met in the private office of President Stanwood at the bank just after midnight. Marsh and three companions, formally under arrest, were present as were President Stanwood, The Thinking Machine and Hatch, besides detectives. Marsh had the bonds under his arms when he was taken. He talked freely when questioned.

"I will admit," he said without hesitating, "that I have acted beyond my rights in removing the bonds from the vault here, but there is no ground for prosecution. I am a responsible officer of this bank and have violated no trust. Nothing is missing, nothing is stolen. Every bond that went out of the bank is here."

"But why—why did you take the bonds?" demanded Mr. Stanwood.

Marsh shrugged his shoulders.

"It's what has been called a get-rich-quick scheme," said The Thinking Machine. "Mr. Hatch and I made some investigations today. Mr. Marsh and these other three are interested in a business venture which is ethically dishonest but which is within the law. They have sought backing for the scheme amounting to about a million dollars. Those four or five men of means with whom they have discussed the matter have called each night for a week at Marsh's country place. It was necessary to make them believe that there was already a million or so in the scheme, so these bonds were borrowed and represented to be owned by themselves. They were taken to and fro between the bank and his home in a kind of an automobile. This is really what happened, based on knowledge which Mr. Hatch has gathered and what I myself developed by the use of a little logic."

And his statement of the affair proved to be correct. Marsh and the others admitted the statement to be true. It was while The Thinking Machine was homeward bound that he explained the phantom auto affair to Hatch.

"The phantom auto as you call it," he said, "is the vehicle in which the bonds were moved about. The phantom idea came merely by chance. On the night the vehicle was first noticed it was rushing along—we'll say to reach Marsh's house in time for an appointment. A road map will show you that the most direct line from the bank to Marsh's was through The Trap. If an automobile should go half way through there, then out across the Stocker estate to the other road, the distance would be lessened by a good five miles. This saving at first was of course valuable, so the car in which they rushed into the trap was merely taken across the Stocker estate to the road in front."

"But how?" demanded Hatch. "There's no road there."

"I learned by phone from Mr. Stocker

that there is a narrow walk from a very narrow foot-gate in Stocker's wall on The Trap leading through the grounds to the other road. The phantom auto wasn't really an auto at all—it was merely two motor cycles arranged with seats and a steering apparatus. The French Army has been experimenting with them. The motor cycles are, of course, separate machines and as such it was easy to trundle them through a narrow gate and across to the other road. The seats are light; they can be carried under the arm."

"Oh!" exclaimed Hatch suddenly, then after a minute: "But what did Jimmie Thalhauer do for you?"

"He waited in the road at the other end of the footpath from The Trap," the scientist explained. "When the auto was brought through and put together he followed it to Marsh's home and from there to the bank. The rest of it you and I worked out today. It's merely logic, Mr. Hatch, logic."

There was a pause.

"That Mr. Thalhauer is really a marvelous young man, Mr. Hatch, don't you think?"

THE THEFT OF THE BERMUDA PENNY

EDWARD D. HOCH

WITH THE PASSING of Edward Dentinger Hoch (1930–2008), the pure detective story lost its most inventive and prolific practitioner of the past half century. While never hailed as a great stylist, Hoch's mystery fiction presented old-fashioned puzzles in clear, no-nonsense prose that rarely took a false step and consistently proved satisfying in most of his approximately nine hundred stories.

Born in Rochester, New York, Hoch (pronounced hoke) attended the University of Rochester before serving in the army (1950–1952). He then worked in advertising while writing on the side. When sales became sufficiently frequent, he became a full-time fiction writer in 1968, producing stories for all the major digest-sized magazines, including *Ellery Queen's Mystery Magazine*, *Alfred Hitchcock's Mystery Magazine*, *The Saint*, and *Mike Shayne Mystery Magazine*. Hoch wanted to create a series character specifically for *EQMM*, who turned out to be the professional thief Nick Velvet (whose original name was Nicholas Velvetta), the author's attempt to create an American counterpart to the hugely successful James Bond. The character quickly changed because Hoch didn't like the idea of his protagonist being a woman-chasing killer; Velvet remained faithful to his longtime girlfriend, Gloria Merchant, whom he met while he was burgling her apartment and who had no idea that he was a thief until 1979. The first Nick Velvet story, "The Theft of the Clouded Tiger," was published in the September 1966 issue of *EQMM*. Two major elements in the stories have made them among Hoch's most popular work: since he will not steal anything of intrinsic value, there is the mystery of why someone would pay Nick Velvet twenty thousand dollars (fifty thousand dollars in later stories) to steal it, and then the near impossibility of the theft itself (which included such items as a spider web, the water from a swimming pool, a day-old newspaper, a baseball team, and a sea serpent).

"The Theft of the Bermuda Penny" was first published in the June 1975 issue of *Ellery Queen's Mystery Magazine*; it was first collected in *The Thefts of Nick Velvet* (New York, Mysterious Press, 1978).

THE THEFT OF
THE BERMUDA PENNY

EDWARD D. HOCH

"NICKY?"

Nick Velvet had been far away in some private dream world when Gloria's voice summoned him back. He put down his beer and asked, "What is it?"

"Nicky, how can a person vanish from the back seat of a car that's traveling sixty miles an hour on an expressway?"

"He can't," Nick answered, picking up the beer again.

"But it's right here in the paper, Nicky! People along the New York State Thruway report picking up a young long-haired hitchhiker dressed all in white. He gets into the back seat, fastens his seat belt, and talks to the people about God. Then, suddenly they look around and he's gone! And the seat belt is still fastened!"

Nick grunted, only half hearing her. "If I was a detective I could solve it."

"Don't you get any cases like that in your government work, Nicky?"

"Not often." Gloria's mistaken impression of his government service helped cover his awkward absences, so he did nothing to correct it.

"What about—?" she began, but the telephone interrupted her.

It was for Nick, and he took it in the little den out of Gloria's hearing. The voice was that of a man for whom he'd worked on two prior occasions. "Velvet? I have someone with an urgent assignment. Can you handle it?"

"If it's in my line."

"It is. The client is a young woman. Her father was a dear friend of mine. Could you meet her at the marina, where you keep your boat?"

It was a good place for a meeting. On a summer's weekend one or two more people would attract no attention. "How soon?"

"One hour?"

"Make it two," Nick said.

As he'd expected, the Saturday sailors were lounging on the grass in their trunks and bikinis, sipping beer or gin-and-tonics. No one noticed him as he worked around his cabin cruiser. He'd been there less than half an hour when a young woman in white slacks and a blue shirt approached him. "Nice boat," she said.

"I like it."

"You're Nick Velvet?" She could have been past thirty, but her face and mane of blonde hair made her look younger.

"That's right."

"I'm Jeanne Kraft, I want to hire you."

He glanced around to make certain no one could hear. "You know I never steal money or anything of value."

She hesitated. "This *is* money, but—"

"Then I can't do it."

"—it's only a penny. A Bermuda penny, to be exact."

She took one from the pocket of her slacks and handed it to him. The penny had the identical size and copper color of an American cent, with the likeness of Queen Elizabeth on the obverse together with the words BERMUDA and ELIZABETH II. The reverse had some sort of pig with a curly tail, and the words ONE CENT with the date 1971. A deep gouge ran across the pig's back, as if the coin had been scratched with a knife.

"What's the pig for?" Neck asked.

"Early Bermuda coins—the first coins struck in North America—were called hog money because of the wild hog shown on them. I think it's been a tradition on Bermuda coins ever since."

"Is this some sort of rare coin that's worth a fortune?"

"Not at all. It's worth one cent in Bermuda and the same here, where it can be passed as an American penny."

"And you want me to steal one just like this?"

"That's right. The same date and the same sort of scratch on it."

"Who from?"

"A man named Alfred Cazar. He's in New York now, at the Waldorf. But he'll be leaving in a couple of days to drive upstate."

"Where upstate?"

"Saratoga Springs, for the August racing season." She reached out her hand and took back the penny. "A man named Blaze will be with him. He's a sort of hired traveling companion."

"You know my minimum fee is twenty thousand dollars?"

"Yes. I have a down payment here." She passed him an envelope. "You'll get the rest when you deliver the duplicate of this penny."

"Where can I contact you?"

"I'll be in Saratoga too, at the Grand Union Motel."

Nick smiled. "Then I'll see you there, Miss Kraft."

Making contact with Alfred Cazar proved to be the easiest part of it. Nick simply phoned his suite at the Waldorf and asked for an appoint-

ment, representing himself as a magazine writer doing an article on the Saratoga racing season. Because he might have to show his driver's license later, he used his real name.

When he reached the room, a spry little man in his sixties met him at the door. "I'm Cazar. You must be Velvet."

"That's right." Nick followed him inside, passing the remains of a room-service breakfast for two. He wondered if there was a girl in the next room, but then he remembered the male companion Jeanne had mentioned.

"Don't know how you happened to pick me," Cazar said as he finished knotting his necktie. "But it's true—I've been goin' up to Saratoga every August for the past twenty-four years. Used to be a lot different in the old days, of course. You'd get these big-money men and really high rollers from all over the country—bigwigs, Vegas stickmen, nomad hustlers—all comin' to Saratoga for August."

"But not anymore?" Nick said.

"Not anymore. The town's pretty much had it. Hell, in New York State you got off-track bettin' now. Who wants to go all the way to Saratoga for the action?"

Nick made a few notes. "Then why do you still go, Mr. Cazar?"

The little man grinned. "The springs are good for my arthritis. I bathe in them every mornin', then go to the track in the afternoon. At my age it helps the body and the wallet both."

From the beginning Nick's only problem in stealing the Bermuda penny was in locating it. He doubted if the little man carried it on him—not if it had value to someone—and searching this suite of rooms for an object that small could be a near-impossible task. He had to get the man away from here, where the possessions to be searched would be limited to the clothes on his back and a suitcase. "I'd like to go with you to Saratoga," he suggested now.

"Go with me? I'll be driving up, in a rented car."

"I could do part of the driving for you," Nick offered. "To properly research my article

I really should spend as much time with you as possible."

"I have someone to do the driving," Alfred Cazar said. He raised his voice and called, "Hugo, come in here for a moment!"

A bulky man who looked like an ex-prizefighter appeared in the doorway. Apparently he'd been listening from the next room and Nick didn't doubt for a moment that he carried a gun under the jacket of his summer suit. "You want me, boss?"

"Hugo Blaze—Nick Velvet, a magazine writer. He's doing a story on the season at Saratoga. Wants to drive up there with us."

The newcomer shook Nick's hand with a powerful grip. "Pleased to meet you."

Close up, Nick was forced to revise his first impression. Hugo Blaze's rough features were partly the result of pock-marks that made him look more sinister than he normally would. But his eyes were friendly, and Nick decided maybe he wasn't carrying a gun under his jacket after all.

"Are you a gambling man?" Cazar asked Nick.

"At times," Nick admitted. "But not so it interferes with my work."

"The drive to Saratoga Springs, along the Thruway and the Northway, can be a boring one. You can come along if you'll join me in a little wagering along the way."

"Fair enough," Nick agreed.

Cazar motioned to Blaze. "Hugo, bring along some of those sugar cubes from the breakfast table. We may want to picnic along the way."

The drive up to Albany, in the air-conditioned comfort of the closed car, was quickly enlivened by Cazar's betting games. "Now, Velvet," he said from the back seat, "call out any two-digit number."

"Sixty-three," Nick responded.

"Sixty-three. Fine! I'll bet you twenty dollars even money that none of the first fifty cars to pass us will have a sixty-three as the last two digits of its license plate."

It was difficult to see the plates on cars across the dividing mall, but they were going slowly enough so that fifty cars had passed them in the left lane during the first half hour. Cazar won his bet, and Nick passed a twenty-dollar bill to him in the back seat.

Hugo Blaze, sitting behind the wheel, smirked and said, "Never bet against the boss."

Cazar patted Nick on the shoulder. "Come on, let's stop at the next service area for lunch and I'll give you a chance to win it back."

The service area, about halfway to Albany, was nearly empty when they drove in. Blaze brought out a plastic cloth and spread it over one of the wooden picnic tables while Nick and Alfred Cazar went in to buy coffee and sandwiches. "You can drive the rest of the way to Albany if you want," Cazar suggested. "Then Hugo will take over from Albany to Saratoga."

"Fine."

The little man eyed him speculatively. "You know, Velvet, you don't seem like a writer. A guy I know told me once about a thief named Velvet. You wouldn't be him, would you?"

Nick merely grinned. "You seem to be doing the stealing, the way you got that twenty off me."

"I'll give you a chance to win it back." They'd reached the picnic table by the side of the parking lot where Hugo Blaze waited. "Hugo, have you got those sugar cubes?"

Blaze dug into his pocket and took out a handful of wrapped sugar cubes from the hotel. He unwrapped two of them and placed them on the tablecloth. "What's that for?" Nick asked.

Alfred Cazar smiled. "Picnics always attract flies. You choose one sugar cube and I'll take the other. I'll bet twenty, even money, that a fly lands on my cube first."

"You'll bet on anything, won't you?" Nick said, but he took a twenty-dollar bill from his wallet.

"Which cube?"

"The one on the right."

Cazar nodded. "Then I'll move mine over here and we'll see what happens."

While they ate their sandwiches they kept an eye on the twin cubes of sugar, resting about a foot apart. Presently a fly appeared, attracted by the food, and swooped low over the table. But it flew off without landing on the sugar. A second fly came by, hesitated a moment, and then settled on top of Cazar's cube.

"You win," Nick said, handing him the money.

"Let's try it again. I'll give you the other cube this time, just to prove it's honest. Another twenty?"

Nick showed his depleted wallet. "I can't afford it."

"Hell, I thought you were a gamblin' man!"

"How about we play for the change in our pockets?" Nick suggested. He emptied out his own pocket, placing a quarter, four dimes, a nickel, and eight pennies on the table.

"Seventy-eight cents? You want me to gamble for seventy-eight cents?"

"Sure. Give me a break—you've won forty bucks from me already!"

Cazar produced a little zippered purse which he emptied on the table. "Seventy-one cents. It's the best I can do. Hugo, you got seven cents?"

The bulky Blaze flipped a dime onto the pile. But Alfred Cazar had another thought. He reached into a pocket of his wallet and extracted another penny. "My lucky coin—I'll bet that, too."

Nick could hardly believe it would be this easy. There, before his eyes, was the Bermuda penny he'd been hired to steal. Even the scratch was the same as on Jeanne Kraft's coin. "That's just a penny," he said, hoping his voice was under control.

"A very special one, Velvet. But let's get on with this. Your cube is on the left this time, and I'll move mine down to the other end of the table just so the flies can make a clear choice."

Nick held his breath and waited. Maybe, just maybe—

A fly came close, almost landed on his cube, then darted away toward the far end of the table. After a moment's inspection it came to rest on Cazar's sugar.

"Another win!" the little gambler chortled. "You don't bet against Alfred Cazar!"

"It certainly wasn't my idea," Nick agreed.

"We'd better get back on the road," Blaze suggested. "We want to make Saratoga before evening."

While Cazar and Blaze went off to the Men's Room, Nick drove the car up to the gas pump and had the tank filled. They were an odd pair, and he wondered if Blaze might be more than an employee. At times the two men seemed more like partners—gentle grifters plying their trade on the road to Saratoga Springs.

Presently he saw them returning to the car. Blaze got in front next to him and explained the automatic shift. He heard Cazar buckle his seat belt in back, then shut the door. "Come on, you two, let's go!"

Nick pulled onto the Thruway, taking it easy until he got the feel of the unfamiliar vehicle. "It's straight ahead about seventy-five miles to Albany," Blaze advised him.

"Thanks." Nick stepped up the speed to the legal 55, then gradually worked it to 60.

"How about another license-plate bet?" Cazar's voice asked.

"I'm broke."

"I thought I saw a ten in that wallet."

"I need something for Saratoga. Hell, you'll win more off me than I'll get paid for this article."

Blaze lit a cigarette and smoked in silence, but his boss wasn't to be shut up. "Come on, Velvet, put up that ten!"

"No, thanks."

Nick lapsed into silence and Cazar did, too. After a few more miles he glanced in the rearview mirror but he couldn't see the little man. "Don't mind him," Blaze said softly. "If you won't bet with him he'll probably doze off for a bit."

"You been working for him long?" Nick asked, making conversation.

"A year or so. He's a good boss. It's easy work."

They passed two cars and had a clear highway ahead. Before Nick realized it, his speed had slipped past 65, on the way to 70. That was when he heard the siren and glanced in the mirror. "Damn! State Police."

Blaze cursed and put out his cigarette. "Take the ticket. Mr. Cazar will pay it."

As the trooper strolled up and asked for his license, Nick glanced into the back seat for Cazar. "Where is he?" he asked Blaze. "Is he on the floor?"

Blaze peered over the seat back. "He's not there. He's gone! His seat belt is still fastened, but he's gone!"

"What is all this?" the trooper asked.

"We lost a passenger," Nick said. He got out on his side and yanked open the rear door. It was true. Alfred Cazar had vanished.

"You mean you forgot him somewhere?"

"He was in the car," Blaze insisted, looking blank.

"I saw him get in," Nick agreed. "We were talking to him!"

Nick bit his lip. His mind had a vision of the Bermuda penny—and his twenty thousand dollar fee—flying away from him. "I know! He's a small man, and some cars have back seats that have access to the trunk compartment. There's where he's got to be!"

He unlocked the trunk, but it was empty except for a spare tire and a jack. Blaze was on his knees, peering beneath the car, and Nick joined him.

There was no trace of Alfred Cazar.

"Maybe he jumped out when we stopped," Blaze said. "But we didn't hear the door open."

The trooper shook his head. "Nobody jumped out when you stopped. Now let's quit the kidding around. I don't care how many people vanished from the back seat—you're still gettin' a ticket for speeding!"

As the trooper wrote the ticket, Nick was forced to admit Cazar had vanished into thin air, from the back seat of a closed car going nearly seventy miles an hour.

For eleven months of the year Saratoga Springs had a quiet village atmosphere befitting its population of less than twenty thousand people. Even the one-time fame of its waters and mud baths had declined in recent years, leaving it with the perpetual gloom of an off-season spa. Only in August, during the racing days, was there still a flash of the old glory. It wasn't quite like the early days, when the racing season brought the country's biggest mobsters to the spa for wide-open gambling. But enough remained on this fine August afternoon to give Nick a feeling of what once had been.

He dropped Hugo Blaze at the old Gideon Putnam Hotel and then drove on in search of a room for himself. It was difficult to find one without a reservation, but just then a room for the night was the least of his worries.

A few horse trailers were parked along Union Avenue, shaded by the stately elms, and he discovered to his surprise that the racetrack was quite near the center of town. He might want to visit the track later, but right now he was more interested in seeing Jeanne Kraft. He parked in the lot next to the Grand Union Motel and went inside to find her.

She wasn't in her room, but he located her in the hotel coffee shop, munching on a tuna-fish sandwich. "I'm glad you got here," she said as he slipped into the booth. "Any trouble?"

"Depends what you mean by trouble. Alfred Cazar has disappeared and taken the Bermuda penny with him."

"You mean he's run off?"

"I mean he's disappeared." He told her everything that had happened. "This guy Blaze is at the Gideon Putnam Hotel, hoping he'll get some word from Cazar. I'm supposed to see him there later."

"It was a trick of some sort," Jeanne Kraft said. "Cazar used to do some night-club magic, along with being a mimic and impressionist. He showed you the penny to watch your reaction. When you were interested, he must have guessed I hired you. He disappeared to keep you from stealing the penny."

"But how? And where do I find him now?"

"That's what I'm paying you twenty thousand dollars for."

"Yeah."

"Don't blame yourself entirely. He's a clever man."

"My only chance of finding him now is to learn what this is all about—what makes his Bermuda penny so valuable. Isn't it about time you told me?"

"I—" She hesitated, glancing around nervously. "All right, I suppose I have to tell you. It started some years back, in Bermuda. My father, Jesse Kraft, was one of the wealthiest men in Hamilton. My mother was dead and I was the only child, so I was naturally very close to him. His one weakness was poker. He'd meet once a week for a high-stakes game with a half-dozen other wealthy men and whoever happened to be visiting the island. Sometimes these Friday night games would go on till Sunday morning."

"Did he usually win or lose?"

"Mostly win. But one night there was a really big game with over a hundred thousand dollars on the table. My father was in it, and Alfred Cazar, and a Canadian named Brian Chetwind. They kept raising each other until everyone else was forced to drop out. Then, when my father and Cazar raised Chetwind more cash than he had on him, the Canadian said he'd have to use IOUs. Anyway, to make the story brief, by the end of the evening my father and Cazar were each in possession of a Bermuda penny on which the Canadian had scratched his mark with a knife. And each of these pennies was an IOU for sixty thousand dollars!"

"Why a penny? Why not a traditional IOU?"

"The pennies were still new in 1971. Bermuda had only adopted a dollar-decimal currency a year earlier. Then too, Chetwind was an important Canadian businessman who couldn't risk having his name signed to an ordinary IOU. Naturally the marked pennies had no legal standing as collectable debts, but then neither would regular IOUs."

"Why hasn't the money been collected from Chetwind before this?"

"My father and Cazar met him here at Saratoga in August of '71, but he persuaded them to let the gambling debt ride. He promised they could double their money through investments he'd made in Canadian mines. Since they had none of their own money to lose, they agreed. This August full payment is to be made. Each of the two shares is now worth something like $130,000."

"A goodly sum," Nick admitted. "But where's your father?"

"Some months back, when the full value of their shares became known, my father was struck and killed by a hit-and-run driver in Miami Beach. I'm convinced he was murdered by Alfred Cazar."

"For the penny?"

"For the penny. Chetwind knows both men were inveterate gamblers. If Cazar produced both pennies, with the story that he'd won my father's in a poker game, Chetwind would accept it without question."

"But you have the penny." Nick said. "You showed it to me."

"My father had it hidden where Cazar couldn't find it. But the very fact that both my father's body and his home were searched told me that Cazar was behind the crime. If I can't bring him to justice any other way, I'll at least turn the tables on him—by stealing his Bermuda penny."

"I don't kill people," Nick warned her.

"I didn't ask you to kill him. I asked you to steal the penny."

"He might not surrender it while he lives. He's already proven to be a very clever customer."

Jeanne Kraft eyed Nick with something close to disdain. "Those things he pulled on you were tricks and nothing more. If you fell for them, you deserved to lose your money."

"What do you mean 'tricks'?"

"The license-plate bet. It's not a 50-50 proposition at all. The odds were seven to five in Cazar's favor. You can find the mathematics of it in any good book on gambling. Try *Scarne's Complete Guide to Gambling* and it'll also tell you how he worked the sugar-cube stunt."

"You mean that was a trick, too?"

She nodded. "Sometime before the bet the two sugar cubes were doctored. A drop of insecticide was placed on one side of each cube. To start with, both of these sides were facing up. Then, after you chose your cube, he turned his over while positioning it. The flies were kept away from your cube, but landed on his."

"I'll be damned," Nick said.

"It's so simple when you know how."

"But what about his vanishing trick in the car? Any ideas about that?"

Jeanne Kraft shook her head. "I've never heard that one done before."

But Nick had. He'd heard about it quite recently, in fact. Gloria had read something in the newspaper about it.

"I have to find a phone," he said.

"What about the penny?"

"When are you meeting Chetwind?"

"Tomorrow morning at the racing museum. Ten o'clock."

"I'll be there."

Nick took a room for himself at the Holiday Inn and phoned home to Gloria. "Nicky, what's happened?" she asked, alarmed to be hearing from him. He wasn't in the habit of calling while away.

"Nothing. I'm okay. I just need some information. Remember that newspaper article you read about the hitchhiker vanishing from the back seat of a car?"

"Yes?"

"Get it and read it to me, will you?"

She left the phone and returned after a few minutes. The newspaper article was just as she'd first reported it—a bizarre account of a white-clad hippie hitchhiker who vanished from the back seats of autos after speaking of religion and judgment. The source for the story was given as a Professor Trout, folklorist at State University in Albany.

"Thanks, Gloria. That's what I wanted."

"Will you be home soon?"

"Maybe by tomorrow night, the way things are going."

"Be careful."

"I always am."

He hung up and put through a call to the State University. Professor Trout was not on campus during the summer, but he managed to obtain a home phone number. With one more call he had the man on the wire.

"I know," Trout said, speaking briskly. "It's the damned article. The phone's been ringing here all week. I suppose you have a disappearance to report too."

"In a way," Nick admitted. "But I have a couple of questions to ask you first. The paper says you're a folklorist."

"That's right."

"Meaning you don't really believe any of these happenings."

"Not exactly," Trout answered carefully. "Folklore is often based on distorted truths."

"I just want an answer, Professor. Are these reports about vanishing hitchhikers to be believed?"

"Oh, yes, as far as they go. You have to realize that the original reports came from young people—kids pretty well into the drug culture."

"Oh? Does that explain how he disappeared?"

"I think so. These kids often drive when they're high on something—just as adults do, unfortunately. Since many hallucinogens give one a distorted time-sense, it's quite likely a driver picked up a hitchhiker, talked with him, dropped him off somewhere without realizing or remembering it, and then really believed he simply vanished from the car. Once a story like that gets started, you always receive accounts of people with similar experiences."

"That's the only explanation you've come up with?" Nick asked, unable to conceal his disappointment. He knew he hadn't been high on anything when Alfred Cazar vanished.

"What other possibility is there?"

"None, I suppose," Nick answered with a sigh. "Thank you, Professor."

Though it was late afternoon, Nick walked a mile east on Lincoln Avenue to the Saratoga Race Course. The day's races were just finishing as he reached the gate, and he stood aside to watch the faces of the people as they exited.

Happy, sad, glowing, disgruntled—their faces told their day's fortunes. He watched one man empty his pockets of losing tickets and walk on, while another immediately pounced on them to search for an overlooked winner.

He'd come in hopes of catching a glimpse of a reincarnated Alfred Cazar, but the little man was nowhere visible in the crowd. Finally, as the departing throng thinned, he gave up and headed back to the red-brick Gideon Putnam Hotel to see Hugo Blaze.

The bulky man was in his room, and when he let Nick in he motioned him to a chair. "I'm on the phone," he explained. "Won't be a minute."

Nick heard him talking to New York, apparently reporting to someone on the disappearance of Alfred Cazar. When he hung up, Nick asked, "Any word of him back there?"

"Not a thing. He seems to have dropped off the face of the earth."

"Are you going to stay here?"

Blaze shrugged. "Why not? My salary is paid for another two weeks, and my job was to accompany him up here. I can only assume he'll turn up."

Nick nodded. "Let's get something to eat."

All the while they were dining in the elegant and spacious room downstairs, Nick's thoughts were somewhere else. Cazar had the Bermuda penny, and Cazar had disappeared. There was no way to steal it unless he could find the man, and that seemed impossible.

"Saratoga has changed a great deal these past years," Blaze was saying. "The gambling casino is now a museum, and most of the big old hotels are gone. They even issue health warnings about the mineral water."

"There must be someplace you can find a decent poker game," Nick suggested.

"Oh, sure. You interested?"

"I might be." Nick was remembering the Canadian, Brian Chetwind, and his liking for poker. If he planned to meet Jeanne in the morning at the racing museum, the odds were he was already in town. And he might well be found at a high-stakes game.

So after dinner they took the rented car and drove up North Broadway to a rambling white guest house on the edge of town. "This place was here at the turn of the century," Hugo Blaze explained. "And there was gambling here then."

He led Nick inside, through sitting rooms still lush with opulence of another era. Finally, in the rear, they passed through a double door into a large game room. Here seven men sat around a green-topped poker table moving their stacks of chips in and out of play like the money moguls they probably were. Nick noticed a craps table at one side of the room too, but for the moment all the action was on poker.

Nick studied the faces of the men at the table, trying to decide if one might be the Canadian. He listened to the names they called each other, but there seemed to be no Brian at the table. "This the only game around?" Nick asked Blaze.

"It's the best game around. There's usually one in the back room at the Orange Dollar, too."

"Let's try that."

The Orange Dollar was an old-fashioned roadhouse a bit farther along North Broadway. The back-room poker game was noisier and more crowded here, and Nick knew at once he'd found the right place. "Raise you, Chetwind," one of the players was saying as he entered, addressing a tall man who sat with his back to the door.

"You going to stay around here?" Blaze asked Nick.

"I think so, for a while."

"I'm going off to the track. Rather lose my money on a horse than a deck of cards, any day."

"Racing at night?"

"They've got a harness track that operates at night. I told you this was a swinging place."

After Hugo Blaze left, Nick remained watching the poker game. One busted player offered his chair, but Nick shook his head. He hadn't come to gamble, only to speak to Brian Chetwind.

After about an hour the Canadian cashed in his chips and rose from the chair with a wide stretch of his arms. "Enough for now. I'll see you birds tomorrow."

He sauntered over to a little bar at one end of the room and Nick joined him there. "You're Brian Chetwind, aren't you?"

The Canadian was tall and handsome, with gray hair fashionably styled across his forehead. He looked like money. "That's me. Do I know you?"

"Nick Velvet's the name. I'm doing some work for an acquaintance of yours—Jeanne Kraft."

The tall Canadian nodded. "Lovely young lady. Terrible thing about her father."

"I understand you're meeting her tomorrow."

"That's correct. We have a business deal to close."

"And Alfred Cazar?"

"Cazar? You know him, too?"

"Yes," Nick admitted. "I drove up here with him from New York."

"Glad he's here. I've been looking for him."

"I'll be frank, Mr. Chetwind. I know something of your dealings with Cazar and the late Jesse Kraft. I know about the Bermuda pennies."

"I see. And what is your interest?"

"I'm looking after Miss Kraft's interests. It's important that I know if Cazar has contacted you today."

"I told you I'd been looking for him, didn't I?" Chetwind was growing impatient. "If you're some sort of strongarm man hired by Miss Kraft, you can be assured that I intend to pay my debts."

"Nothing like that," Nick said. "She'll see you in the morning, Mr. Chetwind."

He left the Canadian and went outside. Hugo Blaze had taken the car, and it was necessary to hire a taxi to drive him to the Grand Union Motel where Jeanne was staying. During the ride he couldn't help considering a possibility which hadn't occurred to Jesse Kraft's daughter. There was someone besides Alfred Cazar with a motive for killing Kraft and stealing his Bermuda penny.

Brian Chetwind would have the strongest motive in the world—if he wasn't able to pay off his debts.

Nick hadn't really expected Jeanne Kraft to sit in her room all night, but it was frustrating nonetheless when she failed to answer his knock. There were too many places where she might be—the harness track, the concert, the summer theater, or even one of the mineral baths.

He was about to walk away when he heard a sound, very low, from the other side of her door. "Jeanne? Are you in there?" he called.

The low sound was repeated, and now he recognized it as a moan. He tried the door but it was locked. "Jeanne!"

". . . help me . . ." she said from the other side of the door, her voice little more than a whisper.

"Can you reach the knob to open the door?"

There was a few moments' pause, then the door opened. Jeanne Kraft was sagging against the wall, holding her head. "He was waiting for me, Nick. He hit me."

"Who hit you?"

"I didn't see him, but it must have been—" Her eyes caught sight of the purse on the floor, its contents scattered across the rug. She dropped to her knees and pawed through the purse, then gasped out, "Cazar! He stole my Bermuda penny!"

"You're sure it's gone?"

"Of course I'm sure! I had it hidden inside the lining here."

"Sorry I didn't get here sooner."

Her face was a picture of dejection. "So now he's got both pennies."

"Or neither."

"What?"

"Have you considered the possibility that Chetwind might have killed your father, made Cazar disappear from that car, and assaulted you—all to keep from paying his gambling debts?"

"But he's a wealthy man!"

"Is he? I was with him tonight. He left a poker game quite early, and it wasn't the biggest game in town."

"I still think it was Cazar. If only you could find him!"

"To know where he is I have to know how he pulled that vanishing act," Nick said. "Believe me, I've been thinking about it ever since it happened. Funny thing—it's almost as if the wrong man disappeared. If it had been Hugo Blaze who vanished instead of Cazar, I'd know how it was done."

But she wasn't listening. She sat looking at her purse and shaking her head. "What will I do now, Nick?"

"Meet Chetwind as planned tomorrow morning, just as if you still had the penny. In fact, I think we'll both go meet him."

The town awoke slowly, perhaps with a hangover from the night before, and Nick and Jeanne had the coffee shop almost to themselves for breakfast. "What happens at the museum?" he asked. "It would seem a pretty public place for a meeting."

"At ten each morning they show films of the previous day's races. I'm to meet Chetwind there, but we'll probably go elsewhere for the actual exchange." Then, remembering, she added, "Of course, I no longer have anything to exchange."

"Let me worry about that. If Cazar has both pennies, he'll show up for the meeting, too. If he doesn't have them, that puts the finger on Chetwind."

"And you'll get them back for me? Both of them?"

"Both of them," he assured her. "And it won't cost you anything extra. Two for the price of one."

By ten o'clock there was a fair crowd at the National Museum of Racing, across Union Avenue from the track itself. Nick let Jeanne walk ahead of him and enter the darkened area where films of the previous day's races would be shown. He stayed near a display case, looking over past racing trophies while he kept an eye on the main entrance.

He'd only been watching a few moments when Brian Chetwind hurried through the doors, heading straight for the film without a glance to his right or left. A minute later Hugo Blaze strode in.

Nick hesitated only an instant. The whole caper had been one big gamble from the beginning, with license plates, sugar cubes, horses, and cards. Now it was time for him to gamble. "Blaze!" he called out. "Over here!"

Hugo Blaze paused, hesitated, then walked over to the display case where Nick stood. "What's up?"

"In here," Nick said, motioning toward the Men's Room door. "It's important."

Hugo Blaze stepped inside, looking puzzled, and Nick followed him. A moment later Nick came out alone and headed across the lobby toward the film showing. Jeanne Kraft was just emerging with Chetwind.

"Nick, what can I do? He's ready to pay off, but he needs the coins!"

"Wait here a moment," Nick told the Canadian. Then he steered Jeanne back across the lobby to the Men's Room door.

"In there?"

Nick nodded. "I want you to meet Mr. Hugo Blaze."

He opened the door wide enough so she could see the unconscious man sprawled on the tile floor. "But—but, Nick, that's not Blaze! That's Alfred Cazar!"

Nick Velvet smiled. "I just won a bet with myself. And here, young lady, are your two Bermuda pennies."

Nick and Jeanne left Saratoga by car later that day. For them the season was over. "Look!" she exclaimed, holding up for Nick the thick packets of bonds that Brian Chetwind had given her. "They're worth more than a quarter of a million on today's market!"

"He's an honest man."

She nodded agreement. "That's more than I can say about Cazar. But how did you know he was Blaze? And how did they work that disappearance from the car?"

"When I first met the older man in his hotel room at the Waldorf, he simply said he was Cazar and I believed him. But right from the start I felt there was something funny. Blaze kept calling him 'boss,' overdoing the supposed relationship."

"The fake Cazar showed me the Bermuda penny for two reasons—to see if I was interested, and to fool me as to its location. When I revealed my interest, they knew I'd been hired by you, and they used a lever dodge like the old shell game. The fake Cazar simply slipped the penny to the real Cazar and then the fake Cazar disappeared. I couldn't steal it if I thought it had vanished along with him. The penny was only inches away from me all the time, yet it was safer than in a bank vault."

"But *how* did the fake Cazar disappear?"

"They'd just given me the job of driving a strange car. I saw them come back and heard the fake Cazar in the rear seat. Fastening his seat belt. Then he slammed the door. That should have told me something. It's far more natural to close the door *before* you fasten the belt. But back-seat belts aren't connected to any buzzer system, and I simply assumed he was still in the car.

"Meanwhile, the real Cazar—or Blaze—was distracting my attention by explaining the car's automatic shift. I started up, with Cazar's voice talking to me from the back seat, and drove away. In reality my back seat passenger was left behind, probably crouched behind a gas pump. His work was done, and he probably got a cab or hitched a ride back to New York."

"But the voice!"

"You told me yourself that Cazar had been a night-club entertainer—a mimic and impressionist. I suspect he knew a little ventriloquism, too. While he sat in the front seat calmly smoking a cigarette, he was imitating the absent man's voice in such a way that it appeared to come from the rear. I couldn't see him in my rearview mirror, but I certainly believed he was there.

"I suppose the article in the newspaper the other day about the vanishing hitchhiker gave them the idea for the stunt. Its main purpose was to send me off after a phantom Cazar while the Bermuda penny made a safe trip to Saratoga Springs."

"But what put you onto Blaze—or Cazar—this morning?"

"Remember, I told you last night the wrong man had disappeared. I was considering the possibility I'd been duped by a ventriloquist and mimic. Cazar fitted the bill, but he was the one who vanished. I couldn't believe both men in the car had that talent.

"But then I remembered how quickly Blaze left me last night when we stopped by a poker game where Chetwind was playing. He couldn't risk the Canadian seeing him and calling him by his real name. This morning Blaze showed up when I was expecting Cazar, and I took a gamble. I slugged him in the Men's Room and went through his pockets. He had both Bermuda pennies, ready to hand over to Chetwind."

"Will he come after me now?"

"I doubt it. He's a gambler and he knows when he's beaten. Besides, he won't want the police digging into your father's death. If he does give you trouble, have him arrested for assaulting you in your room last night."

"How can I ever thank you?"

Nick had an answer. "You can start by paying me the balance of my fee. Then we'll go on from there."

ROOM NUMBER 23
JUDSON PHILIPS

ONE CAN ONLY WONDER at how many books and stories an author can produce while also working as a sportswriter, writing movies, television, and radio scripts, and founding and running a theater. These are among the major accomplishments of Judson Pentecost Philips (1903–1989). During his prolific and highly professional career, Philips wrote more than ninety novels under his own name and as Hugh Pentecost and Philip Owen, and virtually countless short stories, of which more than a hundred appeared in *Ellery Queen's Mystery Magazine*, and scores of others in such major fiction magazines as *Colliers*, *The Saturday Evening Post*, *Liberty*, and *Cosmopolitan*. Writing for the pulps, he produced between forty and fifty thousand words a month for more than a decade, including his popular series about The Park Avenue Hunt Club in *Detective Fiction Weekly*. Philips was the coauthor of *General Crack*, John Barrymore's first talkie, and worked on many other motion pictures; he also wrote numerous episodes of *Suspense* and adapted the Father Brown mysteries for radio. He contributed to television scripts for such television drama series as *The Web*, *The Ray Milland Show*, *The Hallmark Hall of Fame*, and *Studio One*. He covered sports for *The New York Times* while still a teenager, was the co-owner and editor of the *Harlem Valley Times*, and founded the Sharon Playhouse, for which he produced plays for twenty-eight years (1950–1977).

"Room Number 23" was the first short story Philips wrote, and he sold it to a pulp magazine while still a student at Columbia University. The detective character in the story, James W. Bellamy, was based on his roommate, James Warner Bellah, who went on to become a successful writer. The story was first published in *Flynn's* magazine in 1925; it was reprinted in the June 1949 issue of *Ellery Queen's Mystery Magazine* under the author's frequently used pseudonym of Hugh Pentecost.

ROOM NUMBER 23

JUDSON PHILIPS

I FIRST MET James Bellamy during the war and was immediately conscious that he was a remarkable fellow. He was young, scarcely twenty-five, yet he had written two novels and was an Ace in the Royal Flying Corps.

I had not been as fortunate as some others in my war experience.

When the United States went in, I tried to enlist, but discovered that I had a "leaky valve," or some such tommyrot. I finally got into a Red Cross unit, and it was at a field hospital that I ran across James Bellamy. He had come in to have an infected hand dressed and he was much disgruntled at having to give up flying for a week because of so small an injury.

One afternoon while he was there I had to go to the other side of the town for something, and Bellamy offered to go with me. He was a striking figure as he walked down the shell-riddled street in his handsome uniform, twirling a little cane.

We said nothing, as we scarcely knew each other, and Bellamy was just a little too reserved to inspire loquacity. Before we had reached our destination, a heavy fire of enemy shells began dropping about us and we realized that at any minute we might be blown to bits. I was frightened silly, but Bellamy appeared entirely unmoved.

He sauntered along whistling a little tune and twiddling his stick. He looked at me and his eyes twinkled humorously. If I looked half as frightened as I was I must have been a sorry sight.

"I say, old bean," said Bellamy, "if we've got to die, let's die like gentlemen. Nothing like adopting the proper pose under such circumstances. Pose is all that counts in life." And he offered me a cigarette.

I took one and he held a match for me with steady hands.

"Do you ever read poetry?" he asked.

We continued to our destination discussing poets. Bellamy's utter indifference, at least externally, to the exploding shells was infectious, and I soon found that my pretense of bravery had actually made me forget my fear to a large extent.

The next day I had a few hours to myself, and Bellamy and I went to a little wine shop which had escaped destruction. He ordered Scotch whisky and soda, and I joined him. We continued our discussion of poetry. I found that he was intensely fascinated by all the romanticists in literature, and I confess it surprised me.

Bellamy's air of cynicism had led me to suspect entirely different tastes. I asked him about it. He sat puffing at his pipe for a few moments before he answered.

"It's because I like liars," he said at last. "Lying is dying out altogether too swiftly, and if I get through this fracas I shall devote my time to perfecting the Art of Lying."

"Explain," I said.

"Why, my dear fellow, we can see the hardships and horrors of life on every hand. Why, when we go to literature for entertainment must we read about obvious things? I hate these modern realists. They have no imaginations, so they must write about what they see. But the true artist doesn't care about what he sees, he only cares about what he'd *like* to see. Personally, aside from literature, I believe the truth is a bad habit.

"If you tell the truth you are sure to be found out sooner or later. If you don't tell the truth you amuse your friends a great deal more, and it is much more stimulating to yourself."

"Don't you ever tell the truth?" I asked.

"Only when it is so improbable that no one will believe it," he replied.

The next day Bellamy went back to his post and I didn't see him again. The armistice came and I found myself back in New York. I was fortunate in being able to get back my job on the *Republican*.

I had been reporting for them when war was declared. Donaldson, the managing editor, soon discovered that the war had developed in me a rather keen power of observation and he began sending me out on gruesome leads. I found myself covering all the important and unimportant crimes committed in and about the city.

One morning I was walking up the avenue when I saw the resplendent figure of a man coming toward me from the opposite direction. He was dressed in a smartly cut dark blue suit, with vest and spats of a lighter color. He wore a slouch hat pulled down at a rakish angle, and smoked a cigarette through a long amber holder. He was twirling a malacca walking-stick carelessly. Something about the way he carried that stick was familiar to me.

"Bellamy!" I cried, as he came abreast. "How the devil are you?"

He looked somewhat bewildered for a moment.

"I say, if it isn't old Renshaw," he drawled.

We shook hands heartily.

"What are you doing with yourself?" I asked.

"Idling, old bean, idling. It's the only profession left open for a gentleman. And you?"

"Unfortunately I have a bestial appetite," I said, "I must work to feed it. I'm reporting for the *Republican*. I'm a journalist."

"Journalist sounds better than reporter," he drawled. "Always put your best foot forward."

"Idling seems to agree with you," I said. "You look exceedingly prosperous."

"As a matter of fact, I have exactly thirty cents to my name," he said.

"Still lying?" I asked suspiciously.

"No. This is one of the times when it is unlikely that you'll believe the truth."

"You really mean you're that hard up?" I asked.

"Well, I've got some duds, furniture and the like, stored away. I'm looking for some simple soul who will supply an apartment and let me supply the furnishings. Some young fellow ought to jump at the chance to live with me. I would be a liberal education to him."

"Are you serious?" I demanded.

"Quite, old bean."

"Well, I'm your man," I said. "I've been looking for some one to share with me and I should be delighted to have you."

He tapped the curbing with his cane thoughtfully before answering.

"Can't tell when I'll have any money," he said shortly.

"That's all right. When you get it will be time enough to worry about that."

"I shall be devilish cross at times. When I'm writing I'm a bear."

"I understand," I said. "Besides, I shall scarcely be in except to sleep and for breakfast."

"I have a gilt angel in a frame and a set of Casanova that I should insist on having around," he said doubtfully.

"Suits me," I said.

He looked up at me with his rare but charming smile.

"I say, this is bully," he said. "You're sure you mean it?"

"Absolutely."

The next few days were hectic—I was at work all day for the *Republican* and in the evenings Bellamy and I fussed about trying to settle the little apartment on Gramercy Park. Bellamy's furnishings were really lovely, and at the end of the week we had a place that was perfect.

The apartment was in one of those old remodeled houses, and was blessed with a fireplace in the high ceilinged living-room. Two great windows looked out over the park and Bellamy had put a comfortable chair by each window. A heavy oak table stood in the center of the room and a couch was backed up against it, facing the fireplace.

Our first night at home we felt like kings. Bellamy, wrapped in a well worn dressing-gown, sat before a little blaze in the hearth and smoked his pipe thoughtfully. He had just filled it from a red can which bore the name of an English tobacconist.

"What kind of tobacco do you smoke?" he asked, seeing me take my pipe and pouch from the mantelpiece.

"Hampshire," I said.

"Try some of this," he suggested, handing me the red can.

I filled my pipe and lit it. He watched me speculatively.

"How do you like it?" he asked.

"It's very smooth," I said.

"How does it compare with Hampshire?"

"Well, it's much smoother," I said, puffing carefully. "It has a quality which a more expensive tobacco is bound to have."

Bellamy chuckled.

"That shows the unreliability of the senses," he said. "That's Hampshire you're smoking. I just keep it in this can because there's a little sponge in the top that keeps it moist."

The next morning, when I got to the office, the chief sent me out on a new case. Something had happened at the old Nathan Hotel, and I was to investigate. The Nathan is one of the landmarks of a society which once centered about Washington Square, but which has since migrated uptown.

Nothing of its ancient splendor remains, except the fine courtesy of employees and the clientele of old New Yorkers depressed in fortune. One could still get a delicious chicken and waffle supper there, the fame of which had lasted through a century. It was not the sort of place where one expected to find a crime of any sort.

But there had been a crime at the Nathan, at least the police thought there had been. It was a very odd thing. A Miss Wilson and her brother Robert had put up there for the night. The Wilsons' father had been one of the Nathan's old customers, and his children, who lived out of town, stayed there when in the city.

With the Wilsons on this occasion was a private detective named Herbert Horton. The reason for the detective's presence was this: Miss Wilson had been left a considerable fortune in jewels by an aunt, recently deceased. These jewels had been left with the family lawyer and Miss Wilson and her brother had come to get them.

It seems that they had insisted against the lawyer's advice, on taking the jewels with them to their home in Stamford. It was late in the afternoon when they left the lawyer's office, too late to deposit them in a safety vault, and too late to get home without being swallowed in the crush.

The Wilsons had decided to stay at the Nathan for the night and take an early train home in the morning. The lawyer, feeling that the whole procedure was a bit rash, had finally persuaded them to let Horton, the detective, accompany them and see that nothing happened to the jewels.

They had no trouble in getting three rooms at the Nathan. These rooms were on the sixth floor, which, by the way, was the top. The rooms were adjoining, though not connecting, and they looked out over the avenue. The numbers of these rooms were Twenty-One, Twenty-Three and Twenty-Five. Miss Wilson had the center room, with Horton in Twenty-One, and Robert Wilson in Twenty-Five.

When they had got settled in their rooms, Miss Wilson had decided she wanted some tea. Her brother had some letters to write and refused to go down. Miss Wilson left the jewels with him and went down to the old bar, which had been converted into a tea room. Horton remained in his room.

The clerk at the desk saw Miss Wilson go into the tea room, and about half an hour later he saw her go upstairs again. A chambermaid working in the hall saw her get off the elevator at the sixth floor and go to her room. Almost immediately there was a loud scream, apparently from Miss Wilson's room.

The maid stood terrified, staring at the door of Twenty-Three. Horton rushed out of his room and Wilson out of his. They hammered on the door of Twenty-three. They called Miss Wilson, but there was no answer. The door was locked. Horton turned and saw the chambermaid.

He asked her if she had seen Miss Wilson go into her room and she said she had. They redoubled their cries but to no avail. Wilson finally grabbed a fire ax from the wall and soon demolished the door. Horton rushed in, revolver in hand, and stopped on the threshold, amazed. Wilson stared over his shoulder.

The room was absolutely undisturbed. It was empty. Miss Wilson's coat and other articles hung in the closet. Everything was just as it must have been when she left the room. The window was locked on the inside.

Horton concluded that they had made a mistake, despite the chambermaid's evidence, and that the cry had come from someone else. Wilson went down to see if his sister was still in the tea room.

He came back shortly, white-faced, and told Horton what the clerk had seen. This clerk swore that he had just seen Miss Wilson go upstairs. The Wilsons had often stopped at the

hotel, he couldn't be mistaken. Then they questioned the chambermaid.

She had seen Miss Wilson go into her room. She described Miss Wilson perfectly. There could be no doubt about it.

Horton examined the room carefully. He unlocked and opened the window. There was no means of egress that way. It was a straight drop of six stories to the street. There was no cornice around the building on which any one could walk. Escape by the window was impossible.

There was absolutely no exit from that room except the door, and Miss Wilson hadn't come out of the door. There was no sign of a struggle, nothing to indicate that anything unusual had happened. Yet Miss Wilson had gone into that room, had screamed, hadn't come out, and yet wasn't there.

Horton hinted at foul play, but there was nothing to indicate that such a thing had happened. It seemed that it must have been some peculiar mistake. Miss Wilson couldn't have gone into that room or she'd be there now. They finally concluded that, despite all evidence to the contrary, Miss Wilson hadn't come up, that she had stepped out of the hotel for something.

They waited for her return. But she didn't come back. All night they waited, and during this time the clerk and the maid persisted that what they had said was true. About four in the morning Horton summoned the police.

The police examined the witnesses and the room with the same result. There could be no question of a murder. It was simply a mysterious disappearance. That the girl had gone against her will seemed apparent, inasmuch as she certainly wouldn't have gone off of her own volition without telling her brother.

Immediately a wide-spread search was organized. Every policeman in New York was supplied with a description of Miss Wilson. But nothing happened.

When I finally returned to the *Republican* office to write my story the only additional evidence of any sort was a corroboration of the evidence given by the clerk and the chambermaid. The elevator boy testified that he took Miss Wilson—describing her—up at the time the clerk said he saw her.

He remembered the time because he went off duty at six o'clock. In fact, Miss Wilson was the last passenger he had carried.

But the police obstinately refused to believe that Miss Wilson had ever returned to her room. With a certain sort of stolid logic, they argued that if she had returned she would be there now. No, Miss Wilson was somewhere about the city.

Perhaps some accident, a coincidence under the circumstances, had occurred and Miss Wilson was in a hospital. Every accident ward in the city was searched, but no trace of the missing girl was found.

My own personal opinion was that this was just another of those queer disappearances that always have a logical explanation when the lost person turns up. I could not believe, as the police did, that Miss Wilson's disappearance was involuntary. But then, unlike the police, I believed that the girl had returned to her room.

The evidence of those three people was, to my mind, conclusive. One person might make a mistake, but not three. Therefore, since there was no sign of any sort of a struggle, it seemed probable to me that for some inexplicable reason the girl had left the hotel of her own accord. The only thing I couldn't explain was the scream.

If Miss Wilson wanted to get away unnoticed, why did she scream? What was the cause of that scream? Horton, Wilson, and the chambermaid all described it as unquestionably a scream of terror. What was the meaning of it?

I finished my article and walked uptown toward Gramercy Park. Though I was very tired, I wanted some fresh air.

It was after midnight when I got to our apartment and I found that Bellamy had already turned in. I went quietly to bed, but it was not to be for long. I was awakened about three by the frantic ring of the phone. It was the editor of the *Republican*.

"Run over to the Nathan," he ordered. "They've found that girl—murdered," he added after a pause.

"Good God," I cried. "Where did they find her?"

"The body was hidden behind some ash barrels in the basement, said the editor. "The hotel porter discovered it accidentally. Shake a leg and get over there. I'm holding up the presses of the next edition for your story."

I began to dress hurriedly, without making any attempt to be quiet. Bellamy came out of his room, wrapped in his long bath robe.

"Devil of a thing to wake up a fellow at this hour," he grumbled. "Never can get to sleep again after I awaken. What's up?"

I told him briefly.

"What are the facts of the case?" he asked, stretching himself out on the couch.

I told him, finishing the narrative as I was putting on my hat to go out.

"Are all the police reporters such fools as you?" he asked.

It was his way of asking a question, like the old legal trick of inquiring of the defendant if he has "given up beating his wife." An answer either way is an indictment.

There was little to learn at the Nathan besides what the night editor had told me. William Graham, a porter at the Nathan, had made a cache of a bottle of Scotch behind some ash barrels in the cellar. When he reached behind the barrels for his forbidden treasure his hand touched the corpse.

He speedily notified the police and when I reached the Nathan I found that a special officer had been sent down to question Graham.

This officer was a rather intelligent fellow named Milliken. He got the porter's story from him and was about to dismiss him when Graham, with a puzzled frown, asked if he might add something to the evidence.

"There's something I'd like to tell, sir," he said, "but in telling you I have to confess to a crime myself. If you'll agree not to prosecute me I can tell you something valuable."

Milliken looked at him shrewdly.

"What sort of a crime have you committed?" he asked.

"You won't pull me in?"

"No. Spill it," demanded the officer shortly.

"Well, sir," began Graham, and he actually blushed, "I'm a bootlegger!" Milliken scowled blackly at some of us who laughed. Graham went on, somewhat hesitantly: "I was in the habit, sir, of keeping a case of liquor back of them barrels. The night that the young girl disappeared, last night, I had some customers.

"They came into the cellar for a case of gin I had for them. What I'm getting at is, that I had that case of gin back of them barrels, right where I found the young girl. She wasn't there, sir, yesterday at this time. What's more she wasn't there this afternoon, that is, yesterday afternoon, strictly speaking.

"I put a bottle of Scotch there about five o'clock when I came on duty. She wasn't there then, sir. That girl was put there, sir, some time between five last night and half-past two this morning."

Milliken smoked a cigarette thoughtfully.

"You'd swear to that, Graham? You'd swear she wasn't there last night at five o'clock? That means that the body was put there at least twenty-four hours *after* she disappeared."

"Yes, sir."

"Could anyone get into the basement without you seeing him?" asked the detective.

"Oh, yes, sir. The basement's a big place. I wasn't near them barrels after five o'clock until I found the young girl."

That was all the porter's evidence. But it made the case more difficult than ever. The police now switched their opinion about Miss Wilson's having gone to her room. There never had been any doubt in my mind. She had gone to her room, some one hiding in the room had struck her down, and had escaped himself, *with the body*!

Miss Wilson must have seen her assailant before he struck her, for she had screamed. But how, by all that's wonderful, had they got out of that room? There simply wasn't any way to get out except by the door, and there hadn't been any escape that way.

The chambermaid had been watching, and Horton and young Wilson had come out of their rooms almost immediately as they heard the scream. There had been less than three minutes before they broke in the door. Three minutes in which the murderer escaped with the body. Then, a day later, this murderer had come from wherever he had been hiding and put the body back of those ash barrels.

"The queer part of it is," said Milliken, "that he couldn't have been hiding in the hotel. Mr. Horton and I searched every square inch of it the day after the disappearance. He must have hidden outside somewhere and brought the body back to the hotel last night."

The whole problem was getting too deep for me, and I hurried back to the *Republican* to get an article into the breakfast-table edition. As I reassembled the facts I became more puzzled. A girl is waylaid, probably in an attempt to rob her of the jewels which she didn't have. She screams, and the robber strikes her down. The cause of her death had been a shattering blow on the head.

Then, in three minutes' time, the murderer escapes with his victim from a room from which escape is impossible. He drags the body somewhere outside the hotel, and then, a day later, brings it back and hides it in the basement.

After writing my article I returned once more to Gramercy Park to freshen up. I found Bellamy still stretched out on the couch. He had been smoking a great deal, for the carpet was littered with ashes.

He looked a little pale from his sleepless night. The coffee percolator was bubbling on the table, and the smell of it made me realize that I was ravishingly hungry.

"I was just about to throw together some bacon and eggs," said Bellamy. "You're just in time. What happened?"

I told him between gasps, as I drenched my face and head with cold water from the basin. He lay there, smoking, a queer smile on his face.

"Look here," I said when I had dried my face and hands, "I didn't have time to take up your parting jab this morning. What the devil do you mean by insinuating that I was a fool?"

"Did I insinuate that?" he drawled.

"Yes," I said. "You asked me if all police reporters were such fools as I."

"Did I? Well, perhaps they are. Crime is usually so elemental, the kindergarten of emotions, and you fellows make such a hullabaloo about it. It's ridiculous."

"If you have some brilliant solution to this Wilson business," I said dryly, "explode it. Every poet thinks he knows a devil of a lot about humanity. Suppose you explain this puzzle."

"It looks so simple to me," said Bellamy, "but of course I can't be sure. However, answer these questions if you can."

"Shoot," I said.

"First," said Bellamy, tapping down the ashes in his pipe, "Let us get the scene straight. Miss Wilson has a very valuable lot of jewels. They are obviously worth an attempted robbery. But did Miss Wilson publish the fact in the papers that she had them?"

"What are you driving at?" I asked.

"Just this, old bean. Either it was a coincidence, and some common burglar, a sneak thief hanging about the hotel corridors, chanced into Miss Wilson's room and, being surprised, killed her, or it was not a coincidence, and someone who knew about those jewels was the murderer.

"Now, the people who knew about those jewels were comparatively few. They were her brother and Horton, who were with her, the lawyer who gave them to her, and perhaps one or two of his office force. Now, my dear Renshaw, what do you say? Was it one of these, or was it just a chance burglar?"

"Most likely a chance burglar," I said.

"Very well. Question number two: the police and the reporters have been able to find no exit from that room but the door. Suppose, for the sake of argument, that there is another exit, which I hasten to assure you that I don't believe, do you think that, with Horton and Wilson banging on that door with a fire ax, he would stop to drag off the lifeless body of his victim?

"Remember, we are presuming that it was a chance burglar who knew nothing of the jewels. Someone who knew about the jewels might have thought Miss Wilson had them on her person and made the effort to get the body out with him for further search. But do you think even this is probable?"

I admitted that I didn't.

"Question number three," drawled Bellamy. "Presuming that we are wrong about this and that the murderer did drag the body out with him—out of the hotel, mind you, for the police searched every nook and cranny the day after the disappearance, and she wasn't in the hotel—presuming, I say, that he did drag the body out of the hotel, and concealed it in safety somewhere, which is presuming a great deal, can you by any stretch of imagination conceive of his returning the next day with the body and concealing it in the hotel?"

"No, I can't."

"The fourth question is very simple, but to my mind quite pertinent. Presuming that all this happened, can you imagine that in the struggle which took place in Room Twenty-Three, the falling body, the dragging of that body out of the room through the unknown exit—which doesn't exist—nothing would have been disturbed—no chair misplaced, no rumpled carpet—nothing?"

"Frankly, I can't," I admitted.

"Now one more point," he said. "We have been imagining that all this was done by a chance burglar. Is it any more likely that one who knew about the jewels would do these things?"

"No," I said, "it isn't."

Bellamy rose from the couch and pulled the plug out of the coffee percolater.

"Me for some breakfast," he said.

"But the solution?" I cried. "All you've done is to make it seem more difficult than ever."

Bellamy smiled. "You'll admit," he said,

"that none of these suppositions we have made are possible. Therefore an entirely different set of circumstances must have attended the crime. Use your head, old bean, use your head. I'm for a little bacon and eggs, and then I'm going to write a sonnet about the mayor."

"But you can't leave me in the air this way," I complained.

Bellamy wandered toward the kitchenette to cook his eggs.

"Look up the Wilsons' family history," he suggested. "Family histories are always interesting at a time like this."

And Bellamy would say no more, though I pestered him all through breakfast. I went back to the office then and wrote another article in which I embodied all of Bellamy's questions.

My chief was much pleased and wanted me to continue with a theory as to what actually happened. I couldn't do that, as I hadn't the vaguest notion about it.

I did follow Bellamy's advice, however, and found out what I could about the Wilsons. When I got home that night I told Bellamy what I had discovered.

"They are a family who once had means," I told him. "The father died about three years ago and left nothing but a mass of debts. The girl took a position as private secretary to some man, and Robert Wilson went on the stage. From what I could find out at his club, he is a man of good habits, though usually rather badly in debt."

Bellamy nodded. "Just as I thought," he said cryptically.

"And you have solved the riddle?"

"Been working on the mayor all day," he said. "I knew the solution this morning."

"Good Heavens," I cried, "if you really have any idea of what happened, you ought to tell me. The murderer may be making good his escape."

Bellamy thought for a moment.

"There is just one fact which might scatter my theory to the four winds," he said, "but I'm inclined to think that fact doesn't exist."

"What is that fact?" I asked.

"Were the rooms of Herbert Horton and Robert Wilson searched when the police were looking through the hotel for the body?"

"I see what you are driving at," I said excitedly. "You think the murderer might actually have concealed the body in one of those rooms while Wilson, Horton, and the police were searching the premises!

"Of course the police didn't bother to search those rooms because they knew that they had been occupied by the girl's brother and their own detective when the murder was committed. I think you've hit it," I concluded jubilantly.

"I didn't mean that at all," said Bellamy, "or at least not the way you think I did."

He sat smoking a minute, and then turned to me; and I saw his eyes were unusually bright.

"Renshaw," he said, "you know how absolutely worthless evidence of the visual sort is. I mean one can't count on the eye of a witness. It's been tried over and over again. A whole roomful of men will be asked to describe a pantomime which has been enacted before them, and no two of them will give the same answer.

"You know that a witness may swear to having seen something, swear honestly, that never happened at all."

"That's true."

"Bear in mind, then, old bean, that the chambermaid's testimony was absolutely false, although she thinks she has told the truth."

"What do you mean?" I cried.

"Wait—tell me, Renshaw, why do the police never believe their own conclusions? They say in this case that there is no possible means of escape from Room Twenty-Three except the door, yet they are trying to find out how Miss Wilson's murderer got out of that room. Renshaw, if there is no way out of that room but the door, *then the murderer never got out.*"

"What do you mean, he was hidden in there? That's impossible, they searched the room immediately when they got in."

"I mean," said Bellamy slowly, "*that he never was in that room.*"

"Look here," I said, laughing, "I thought you were being serious."

"That's the trouble with you duffers," said Bellamy with unwonted sharpness, "you haven't the brains to accept the truth. You sit by, in this instance, and solemnly assert that the murderer couldn't have escaped from Room Twenty-Three, and when I tell you he didn't, you scoff at it. Work out your own solution! You'll never find the truth, if you spend all your time contradicting yourself."

"Oh, come, Bellamy, don't be offended," I said. "I thought you were joking. You must admit it sounds ridiculous to say that the murderer didn't escape from the room in which the murder was committed and then that he never was in that room!"

Bellamy smiled.

"Sorry, old bean. I get awfully bored with pig-headedness at moments. But, see here, I said that the murderer wasn't in Room Twenty-Three. The reason he wasn't there was because *the murder wasn't committed in Room Twenty-Three.*"

"Bellamy!" I ejaculated.

Bellamy paused and filled his pipe.

"Thanks for not laughing at that one," he said dryly as he lit his pipe. "Let me get down to what actually happened," he continued, and I detected an unusual enthusiasm in his tone. His eyes were glowing and he twined and untwined his long fingers nervously.

"Look at the scene, Renshaw. Three rooms stand next to each other in the corridor. A chambermaid is cleaning up in the hall. A young girl gets off the elevator and goes to her room. The maid only casually notices this. But when a loud scream is heard the maid looks up, panic-stricken. For a moment she doubts which room the girl entered.

"There are a dozen similar doors in the corridor. However, she is soon made certain that it was Number Twenty-Three since the gentlemen who have the rooms on either side of Twenty-Three rush out and bang on that door. Then comes the excitement of breaking into the room. It was found empty. Horton turns to the maid and asks her if she saw Miss Wilson go into Room Twenty-Three.

"She swears that she did. But she didn't, Renshaw! She didn't! The thing that made her certain that Miss Wilson *had* entered Twenty-Three was that Horton and Wilson came out and banged on *that* door. Could anything be more natural?"

"It still isn't quite clear," I said.

Bellamy smiled tolerantly. "Listen, old bean, Miss Wilson never went into Twenty-Three. She went either into Horton's room or her brother's. One of those two men attacked her for some reason and killed her. Just before the attack Miss Wilson screamed.

"The murderer had great presence of mind, a presence of mind bordering on genius. Instead of trying to escape he rushes out into the hall—after pushing the body under the bed, say—and bangs on the door that Miss Wilson *ought to have entered.*

"The guiltless man, I won't say which he is for the moment, naturally supposed that the other fellow was acting on the same impulse as himself. He had heard the scream which he suspected came from Miss Wilson. The guiltless man was completely disarmed, never suspected for a moment.

"The chambermaid might have given the whole game away had she carefully noticed which room the girl entered, but she hadn't noticed carefully. When the two men came out and banged on the door of Twenty-Three she thought she was certain, only thought she was certain."

"But, Bellamy," I cried, "which one is it?"

Bellamy leaned forward. He seemed to be thrilled by his own reasoning. He was as excited as a schoolboy.

"What would have made that maid certain about the room?" he asked. "Remember, the evidence of the eyes is not certain, but there is another kind of evidence which is more reliable. The ear, Renshaw, the ear! What might she have heard that would have made her certain about the room?"

"I give up," I said.

"A knock," said Bellamy. "If Miss Wilson

had knocked on the door the maid would have looked up, waiting to see who let her in. It was because she *didn't knock* that the murderer has escaped so far and been able to make it seem that the murder took place in Room Twenty-Three.

"But it is because she didn't knock that we can pick the guilty man with absolute certainly. Come, Renshaw, surely you see it now? Which is it, Horton or Wilson?"

"I give up," I said. "My mind is whirling round like a pinwheel."

"So simple," chuckled Bellamy. "It was her brother, of course. If she had gone into Horton's room, she would have knocked! Don't you see? But she walked into her brother's room without a word. Have I convinced you, old bean?"

"But why—why would her brother kill her?"

"Ah, that's not in my province," said Bellamy, stretching contentedly.

"I have delivered the murderer to you, now you find out why he did it."

Bellamy was right. I took his theory to Milliken and explained the process of reasoning. He was thunderstruck that it had never occurred to him.

Wilson, when confronted with the crime, broke down and confessed everything. He had been heavily in debt.

When his sister had left the jewels with him he had decided to extract some of them from the box and pawn them. But the box was locked and his sister had the key. He had been in the act of prying it open when she walked into his room unannounced. She argued with him and in a fit of passion he struck her down with his walking-stick, a stout piece of Irish thorn.

She had screamed just before he struck her. He knew this scream would attract attention. His mind worked very fast. He pushed his sister's body under the bed and rushed out into the hall. He was startled when he saw the maid, and still more frightened when Horton questioned her, but his ruse had worked.

The only problem that remained was to get the body out of his room. The police searched the hotel from garret to cellar the first day, all except his room and Horton's. There was no thread of suspicion against them. After this rigorous search and failure to find any trace of the girl, the police activities were largely outside the hotel.

He took a chance on the second night and carried his sister's body to the freight elevator, which he manipulated himself. He hid the body back of the ash barrels. He was undetected and apparently free from danger.

The police force very generously gave me the credit for the solution which I, in turn, tried to shift to Bellamy. He refused to take any credit, saying his reputation as a poet would be seriously damaged if it became known that he was an amateur detective.

I have written this story now, several years later, since Bellamy's fame in the field of crime has spread far and wide, and I think it only right that he should receive his due in the famous mystery of Room Number Twenty-Three.

HOW EASILY IS MURDER DISCOVERED

There are so many ways for the creative killer to accomplish the act.

LYNNE WOOD BLOCK AND LAWRENCE BLOCK

AMONG THE MOST VERSATILE, prolific, accomplished, and popular writers in the mystery genre (and in others as well), Lawrence Block (1938–) has created numerous series characters that range from the light humor of Bernie Rhodenbarr (star of the "Burglar" series), Chip Harrison (an homage to the Nero Wolfe character, written as Chip Harrison), and Evan Tanner (a reluctant spy with a sleep disorder that keeps him constantly awake), to the very dark Matthew Scudder series about an alcoholic former cop who functions as an unpaid private detective drawn into mysteries by a desire to aid friends or just those who need help. While it is generally acknowledged that the Scudder novels are his greatest work, ranking among the best private eye fiction ever written, it is possible that his most brilliant stories feature a shady lawyer, Ehrengraf, who has no problem subverting the law to free his clients. His short stories featuring Keller, a hit man, have won him two of his four Edgar Awards (he also won for best short story with "By Dawn's Early Light" in 1985 and best novel with *A Dance at the Slaughterhouse* in 1992). For lifetime achievement, the Mystery Writers of America honored him with the Grand Master Award in 1994.

Lynne Wood Block (1943–), Lawrence Block's wife since 1983, was born in New Orleans and moved to New York in 1964 for her career as a fashion model (both print and runway). She also worked as an antiques dealer before establishing The Lynne Wood Company, a bookkeeping and accounting practice with the motto "You Make It, We Count It."

"The Burglar Who Smelled Smoke" was first published in the Summer/Fall 1997 issue of *Mary Higgins Clark's Mystery Magazine*; it was first collected in *The Collected Mystery Stories* (London, Orion, 1999).

THE BURGLAR WHO SMELLED SMOKE

LYNNE WOOD BLOCK AND LAWRENCE BLOCK

I WAS GEARING UP to poke the bell a second time when the door opened. I'd been expecting Karl Bellermann, and instead I found myself facing a woman with soft blond hair framing an otherwise severe, high-cheekboned face. She looked as if she'd been repeatedly disappointed in life but was damned if she would let it get to her.

I gave my name and she nodded in recognition. "Yes, Mr. Rhodenbarr," she said. "Karl is expecting you. I can't disturb him now as he's in the library with his books. If you'll come into the sitting room I'll bring you some coffee, and Karl will be with you in—" she consulted her watch "—in just twelve minutes."

In twelve minutes it would be noon, which was when Karl had told me to arrive. I'd taken a train from New York and a cab from the train station, and good connections had got me there twelve minutes early, and evidently I could damn well cool my heels for all twelve of those minutes.

I was faintly miffed, but I wasn't much surprised. Karl Bellermann, arguably the country's leading collector of crime fiction, had taken a cue from one of the genre's greatest creations, Rex Stout's incomparable Nero Wolfe. Wolfe, an orchid fancier, spent an inviolate two hours in the morning and two hours in the afternoon with his plants, and would brook no disturbance at such times. Bellermann, no more flexible in real life than Wolfe was in fiction, scheduled even longer sessions with his books, and would neither greet visitors nor take phone calls while communing with them.

The sitting room where the blond woman led me was nicely appointed, and the chair where she planted me was comfortable enough. The coffee she poured was superb, rich and dark and winey. I picked up the latest issue of *Ellery Queen* and was halfway through a new Peter Lovesey story and just finishing my second cup of coffee when the door opened and Karl Bellermann strode in.

"Bernie," he said. "Bernie Rhodenbarr."

"Karl."

"So good of you to come. You had no trouble finding us?"

"I took a taxi from the train station. The driver knew the house."

He laughed. "I'll bet he did. And I'll bet I know what he called it. 'Bellermann's Folly,' yes?"

"Well," I said.

"Please, don't spare my feelings. That's what all the local rustics call it. They hold in contempt that which they fail to understand. To their eyes, the architecture is overly ornate, and too much a mixture of styles, at once a Rhenish castle and an alpine chalet. And the library dwarfs the rest of the house, like the tail that wags the dog. Your driver is very likely a man who owns a single book, the Bible given to him for Confirmation and unopened ever since. That a man might choose to devote to his books the greater portion of his house—and, indeed, the greater portion of his life—could not fail to strike him as an instance of remarkable eccentricity." His eyes twinkled. "Although he might phrase it differently."

Indeed he had. "The guy's a nut case," the driver had reported confidently. "One look at his house and you'll see for yourself. He's only eating with one chopstick."

A few minutes later I sat down to lunch with Karl Bellermann, and there were no chopsticks in evidence. He ate with a fork, and he was every bit as agile with it as the fictional orchid fancier. Our meal consisted of a crown loin of pork with roasted potatoes and braised cauliflower, and Bellermann put away a second helping of everything.

I don't know where he put it. He was a long lean gentleman in his mid-fifties, with a full head of iron-grey hair and a moustache a little darker than the hair on his head. He'd dressed rather elaborately for a day at home with his books—a tie, a vest, a Donegal tweed jacket—and I didn't flatter myself that it was on my account. I had a feeling he chose a similar get-up seven days a week, and I wouldn't have been surprised to learn he put on a black tie every night for dinner.

He carried most of the lunchtime conversation, talking about books he'd read, arguing the relative merits of Hammett and Chandler, musing on the likelihood that female private eyes in fiction had come to out-number their real-life counterparts. I didn't feel called upon to contribute much, and Mrs. Bellermann never uttered a word except to offer dessert (*apfelküchen*, lighter than air and sweeter than revenge) and coffee (the mixture as before but a fresh pot of it, and seemingly richer and darker and stronger and winier this time around). Karl and I both turned down a second piece of the cake and said yes to a second cup of coffee, and then Karl turned significantly to his wife and gave her a formal nod.

"Thank you, Eva," he said. And she rose, all but curtseyed, and left the room.

"She leaves us to our brandy and cigars," he said, "but it's too early in the day for spirits, and no one smokes in Schloss Bellermann."

"Schloss Bellermann?"

"A joke of mine. If the world calls it Bellermann's Folly, why shouldn't Bellermann call it his castle? Eh?"

"Why not?"

He looked at his watch. "But let me show you my library," he said, "and then you can show me what you've brought me."

Diagonal mullions divided the library door into a few dozen diamond-shaped sections, each set with a mirrored pane of glass. The effect was unusual, and I asked if they were one-way mirrors.

"Like the ones in police stations?" He raised an eyebrow. "Your past is showing, eh, Bernie? But no, it is even more of a trick than the police play on criminals. On the other side of the mirror—" he clicked a fingernail against a pane "—is solid steel an inch and a half thick. The library walls themselves are reinforced with steel sheeting. The exterior walls are concrete, reinforced with steel rods. And look at this lock."

It was a Poulard, its mechanism intricate beyond description, its key one that not a locksmith in ten thousand could duplicate.

"Pickproof," he said. "They guarantee it."

"So I understand."

He slipped the irreproducible key into the impregnable lock and opened the unbreachable door. Inside was a room two full stories tall, with a system of ladders leading to the upper levels. The library, as tall as the house itself, had an eighteen-foot ceiling panelled in light and dark wood in a sunburst pattern. Wall-to-wall carpet covered the floor, and oriental rugs in turn covered most of the broadloom. The walls, predictably enough, were given over to floor-to-ceiling bookshelves, with the shelves themselves devoted entirely to books. There were no paintings, no Chinese ginger jars, no bronze animals, no sets of armour, no cigar humidors, no framed photographs of family members, no hand-coloured engravings of Victoria Falls, no hunting trophies, no Lalique figurines, no Limoges boxes. Nothing but books, sometimes embraced by bronze bookends, but mostly extending without interruption from one end of a section of shelving to the other.

"Books," he said reverently—and, I thought, unnecessarily. I own a bookstore, I can recognize books when I see them.

"Books," I affirmed.

"I believe they are happy."

"Happy?"

"You are surprised? Why should objects lack feelings, especially objects of such a sensitive nature as books? And, if a book can have feelings, these books ought to be happy. They are owned and tended by a man who cares deeply for them. And they are housed in a room perfectly designed for their safety and comfort."

"It certainly looks that way."

He nodded. "Two windows only, on the north wall, of course, so that no direct sunlight ever enters the room. Sunlight fades book spines, bleaches the ink of a dust jacket. It is a book's enemy, and it cannot gain entry here."

"That's good," I said. "My store faces south, and the building across the street blocks some of the sunlight, but a little gets through. I have to make sure I don't keep any of the better volumes where the light can get at them."

"You should paint the windows black," he said, "or hang thick curtains. Or both."

"Well, I like to keep an eye on the street," I said. "And my cat likes to sleep in the sunlit window."

He made a face. "A cat? In a room full of books?"

"He'd be safe," I said, "even in a room full of rocking chairs. He's a Manx. And he's an honest working cat. I used to have mice damaging the books, and that stopped the day he moved in."

"No mice can get in here," Bellermann said, "and neither can cats, with their hair and their odour. Mould cannot attack my books, or mildew. You feel the air?"

"The air?"

"A constant sixty-four degrees Fahrenheit," he said. "On the cool side, but perfect for my books. I put on a jacket and I am perfectly comfortable. And, as you can see, most of them are already wearing their jackets. Dust jackets! Ha ha!"

"Ha ha," I agreed.

"The humidity is sixty per cent," he went on. "It never varies. Too dry and the glue dries out. Too damp and the pages rot. Neither can happen here."

"That's reassuring."

"I would say so. The air is filtered regularly, with not only air conditioning but special filters to remove pollutants that are truly microscopic. No book could ask for a safer or more comfortable environment."

I sniffed the air. It was cool, and neither too moist nor too dry, and as immaculate as modern science could make it. My nose wrinkled, and I picked up a whiff of something.

"What about fire?" I wondered.

"Steel walls, steel doors, triple-glazed windows with heat-resistant bulletproof glass. Special insulation in the walls and ceiling and floor. The whole house could burn to the ground, Bernie, and this room and its contents would remain unaffected. It is one enormous fire-safe."

"But if the fire broke out in here . . ."

"How? I don't smoke, or play with matches. There are no cupboards holding piles of oily rags, no bales of mouldering hay to burst into spontaneous combustion."

"No, but——"

"And even if there were a fire," he said, "it would be extinguished almost before it had begun." He gestured and I looked up and saw round metal gadgets spotted here and there in the walls and ceiling.

I said, "A sprinkler system? Somebody tried to sell me one at the store once and I threw him out on his ear. Fire's rough on books, but water's sheer disaster. And those things are like smoke alarms, they can go off for no good reason, and then where are you? Karl, I can't believe——"

"Please," he said, holding up a hand. "Do you take me for an idiot?"

"No, but——"

"Do you honestly think I would use water to forestall fire? Credit me with a little sense, my friend."

"I do, but——"

"There will be no fire here, and no flood, either. A book in my library will be, ah, what is the expression? Snug as a slug in a rug."

"A bug," I said.

"I beg your pardon?"

"A bug in a rug," I said. "I think that's the expression."

His response was a shrug, the sort you'd get, I suppose, from a slug in a rug. "But we have no time for language lessons," he said. "From two to six I must be in the library with my books, and it is already one-fifty."

"You're already in the library."

"Alone," he said. "With only my books for company. So. What have you brought me?"

I opened my briefcase, withdrew the padded mailer, reached into that like Little Jack Horner and brought forth a plum indeed. I looked up in time to catch an unguarded glimpse of Beller-mann's face, and it was a study. How often do you get to see a man salivate less than an hour after a big lunch?

He extended his hands and I placed the book in them. *"Fer-de-Lance,"* he said reverently. "Nero Wolfe's debut, the rarest and most desirable book in the entire canon. Hardly the best of the novels, I wouldn't say. It took Stout several books fully to refine the character of Wolfe and to hone the narrative edge of Archie Goodwin. But the brilliance was present from the beginning, and the book is a prize."

He turned the volume over in his hands, inspected the dust jacket fore and aft. "Of course I own a copy," he said. "A first edition in dust wrapper. This dust wrapper is nicer than the one I have."

"It's pretty cherry," I said.

"Pristine," he allowed, "or very nearly so. Mine has a couple of chips and an unfortunate

tear mended quite expertly with tape. This does look virtually perfect."

"Yes."

"But the jacket's the least of it, is it not? This is a special copy."

"It is."

He opened it, and his large hands could not have been gentler had he been repotting orchids. He found the title page and read, " 'For Frank-lin Roosevelt, with the earnest hope of a brighter tomorrow. Best regards from Rex Todhunter Stout.' " He ran his forefinger over the inscrip-tion. "It's Stout's writing," he announced. "He didn't inscribe many books, but I have enough signed copies to know his hand. And this is the ultimate association copy, isn't it?"

"You could say that."

"I just did. Stout was a liberal Democrat, ultimately a World Federalist. FDR, like the present incumbent, was a great fan of detective stories. It always seems to be the Democratic presidents who relish a good mystery. Eisen-hower preferred Westerns, Nixon liked history and biography, and I don't know that Reagan read at all."

He sighed and closed the book. "Mr. Gul-benkian must regret the loss of this copy," he said.

"I suppose he must."

"A year ago," he said, "when I learned he'd been burglarized and some of his best volumes stolen, I wondered what sort of burglar could possibly know what books to take. And of course I thought of you."

I didn't say anything.

"Tell me your price again, Bernie. Refresh my memory."

I named a figure.

"It's high," he said.

"The book's unique," I pointed out.

"I know that. I know, too, that I can never show it off. I cannot tell anyone I have it. You and I alone will know that it is in my possession."

"It'll be our little secret, Karl."

"Our little secret. I can't even insure it. At least Gulbenkian was insured, eh? But he can never replace the book. Why didn't you sell it back to him?"

"I might," I said, "if you decide you don't want it."

"But of course I want it!" He might have said more but a glance at his watch reminded him of the time. "Two o'clock," he said, motioning me toward the door. "Eva will have my afternoon coffee ready. And you will excuse me, I am sure, while I spend the afternoon with my books, including this latest specimen."

"Be careful with it," I said.

"Bernie! I'm not going to *read* it. I have plenty of reading copies, should I care to renew my acquaintance with *Fer-de-Lance.* I want to hold it, to be with it. And then at six o'clock we will conclude our business, and I will give you a dinner every bit as good as the lunch you just had. And then you can return to the city."

He ushered me out, and moments later he disappeared into the library again, carrying a tray with coffee in one of those silver pots they used to give you on trains. There was a cup on the tray as well, and a sugar bowl and creamer, along with a plate of shortbread cookies. I stood in the hall and watched the library door swing shut, heard the lock turn and the bolt slide home. Then I turned, and there was Karl's wife, Eva.

"I guess he's really going to spend the next four hours in there," I said.

"He always does."

"I'd go for a drive," I said, "but I don't have a car. I suppose I could go for a walk. It's a beautiful day, bright and sunny. Of course your husband doesn't allow sunlight into the library, but I suppose he lets it go where it wants in the rest of the neighbourhood."

That drew a smile from her.

"If I'd thought ahead," I said, "I'd have brought something to read. Not that there aren't a few thousand books in the house, but they're all locked away with Karl."

"Not all of them," she said. "My husband's collection is limited to books published before

1975, along with the more recent work of a few of his very favourite authors. But he buys other contemporary crime novels as well, and keeps them here and there around the house. The bookcase in the guest room is well stocked."

"That's good news. As far as that goes, I was in the middle of a magazine story."

"In *Ellery Queen,* wasn't it? Come with me, Mr. Rhodenbarr, and I'll——"

"Bernie."

"Bernie," she said, and coloured slightly, those dangerous cheekbones turning from ivory to the ink you find inside a seashell. "I'll show you where the guest room is, Bernie, and then I'll bring you your magazine."

The guest room was on the second floor, and its glassed-in bookcase was indeed jam-packed with recent crime fiction. I was just getting drawn into the opening of one of Jeremiah Healy's Cuddy novels when Eva Bellermann knocked on the half-open door and came in with a tray quite like the one she'd brought her husband. Coffee in a silver pot, a gold-rimmed bone china cup and saucer, a matching plate holding shortbread cookies. And, keeping them company, the issue of *EQMM* I'd been reading earlier.

"This is awfully nice of you," I said. "But you should have brought a second cup so you could join me."

"I've had too much coffee already," she said. "But I could keep you company for a few minutes if you don't mind."

"I'd like that."

"So would I," she said, skirting my chair and sitting on the edge of the narrow captain's bed. "I don't get much company. The people in the village keep their distance. And Karl has his books."

"And he's locked away with them . . ."

"Three hours in the morning and four in the afternoon. Then in the evening he deals with correspondence and returns phone calls. He's retired, as you know, but he has investment decisions to make and business matters to deal with. And books, of course. He's always buying more of them." She sighed. "I'm afraid he doesn't have much time left for me."

"It must be difficult for you."

"It's lonely," she said.

"I can imagine."

"We have so little in common," she said. "I sometimes wonder why he married me. The books are his whole life."

"And they don't interest you at all?"

She shook her head. "I haven't the brain for it," she said. "Clues and timetables and elaborate murder methods. It is like working a crossword puzzle without a pencil. Or worse—like assembling a jigsaw puzzle in the dark."

"With gloves on," I suggested.

"Oh, that's funny!" She laughed more than the line warranted and laid a hand on my arm. "But I should not make jokes about the books. You are a bookseller yourself. Perhaps books are your whole life, too."

"Not my whole life," I said.

"Oh? What else interests you?"

"Beautiful women," I said recklessly.

"Beautiful women?"

"Like you," I said.

Believe me, I hadn't planned on any of this. I'd figured on finishing the Lovesey story, then curling up with the Healy book until Karl Bellermann emerged from his lair, saw his shadow, and paid me a lot of money for the book he thought I had stolen.

In point of fact, the *Fer-de-Lance* I'd brought him was legitimately mine to sell—or very nearly so. I would never have entertained the notion of breaking into Nizar Gulbenkian's fieldstone house in Riverdale. Gulbenkian was a friend as well as a valued customer, and I'd rushed to call him when I learned of his loss. I would keep an ear cocked and an eye open, I assured him, and I would let him know if any of his treasures turned up on the grey or black market.

"That's kind of you, Bernie," he'd said. "We will have to talk of this one day."

And, months later, we talked—and I learned

there had been no burglary. Gulbenkian had gouged his own front door with a chisel, looted his own well-insured library of its greatest treasures, and tucked them out of sight (if not out of mind) before reporting the offence—and pocketing the payoff from the insurance company.

He'd needed money, of course, and this had seemed a good way to get it without parting with his precious volumes. But now he needed more money, as one so often does, and he had a carton full of books he no longer legally owned and could not even show off to his friends, let alone display to the public. He couldn't offer them for sale, either, but someone else could. Someone who might be presumed to have stolen them. Someone rather like me.

"It will be the simplest thing in the world for you, Bernie," old Nizar said. "You won't have to do any breaking or entering. You won't even have to come to Riverdale. All you'll do is sell the books, and I will gladly pay you ten per cent of the proceeds."

"Half," I said.

We settled on a third, after protracted negotiations, and later over drinks he allowed that he'd have gone as high as forty per cent, while I admitted I'd have taken twenty. He brought me the books, and I knew which one to offer first, and to whom.

The FDR *Fer-de-Lance* was the prize of the lot, and the most readily identifiable. Karl Bellermann was likely to pay the highest price for it, and to be most sanguine about its unorthodox provenance.

You hear it said of a man now and then that he'd rather steal a dollar than earn ten. (It's been said, not entirely without justification, of me.) Karl Bellermann was a man who'd rather buy a stolen book for a thousand dollars than pay half that through legitimate channels. I'd sold him things in the past, some stolen, some not, and it was the volume with a dubious history that really got him going.

So, as far as he was concerned, I'd lifted *Fer-de-Lance* from its rightful owner, who would turn purple if he knew where it was. But I knew better—Gulbenkian would cheerfully pocket two-thirds of whatever I pried out of Bellermann, and would know exactly where the book had wound up and just how it got there.

In a sense, then, I was putting one over on Karl Bellermann, but that didn't constitute a breach of my admittedly elastic moral code. It was something else entirely, though, to abuse the man's hospitality by putting the moves on his gorgeous young wife.

Well, what can I say? Nobody's perfect.

Afterward I lay back with my head on a pillow and tried to figure out what would make a man choose a leather chair and room full of books over a comfortable bed with a hot blonde in it. I marvelled at the vagaries of human nature, and Eva stroked my chest and urged a cup of coffee on me.

It was great coffee, and no less welcome after our little interlude. The cookies were good, too. Eva took one, but passed on the coffee. If she drank it after lunchtime, she said, she had trouble sleeping nights.

"It never keeps me awake," I said. "In fact, this stuff seems to be having just the opposite effect. The more I drink, the sleepier I get."

"Maybe it is I who have made you sleepy."

"Could be."

She snuggled close, letting interesting parts of her body press against mine. "Perhaps we should close our eyes for a few minutes," she said.

The next thing I knew she had a hand on my shoulder and was shaking me awake. "Bernie," she said. "We fell asleep!"

"We did?"

"And look at the time! It is almost six o'clock. Karl will be coming out of the library any minute."

"Uh-oh."

She was out of bed, diving into her clothes. "I'll go downstairs," she said. "You can take your time dressing, as long as we are not together." And, before I could say anything, she swept out of the room.

I had the urge to close my eyes and drift right off again. Instead I forced myself out of bed, took a quick shower to clear the cobwebs, then got dressed. I stood for a moment at the head of the stairs, listening for conversation and hoping I wouldn't hear any voices raised in anger. I didn't hear any voices, angry or otherwise, or anything else.

It's quiet out there, I thought, like so many supporting characters in so many Westerns. And the thought came back, as it had from so many heroes in those same Westerns: *Yeah . . . too quiet.*

I descended the flight of stairs, turned a corner and bumped into Eva. "He hasn't come out," she said. "Bernie, I'm worried."

"Maybe he lost track of the time."

"Never. He's like a Swiss watch, and he *has* a Swiss watch and checks it constantly. He comes out every day at six on the dot. It is ten minutes past the hour and where is he?"

"Maybe he came out and——"

"Yes?"

"I don't know. Drove into town to buy a paper."

"He never does that. And the car is in the garage."

"He could have gone for a walk."

"He hates to walk. Bernie, he is still in there."

"Well, I suppose he's got the right. They're his rooms and his books. If he wants to hang around——"

"I'm afraid something has happened to him. Bernie, I knocked on the door. I knocked loud. Perhaps you heard the sound upstairs?"

"No, but I probably wouldn't. I was all the way upstairs, and I had the shower on for a while there. I take it he didn't answer."

"No."

"Well, I gather it's pretty well soundproofed in there. Maybe he didn't hear you."

"I have knocked before. And he has heard me before."

"Maybe he heard you this time and decided to ignore you." Why was I raising so many objections? Perhaps because I didn't want to let myself think there was any great cause for alarm.

"Bernie," she said, "what if he is ill? What if he has had a heart attack?"

"I suppose it's possible, but——"

"I think I should call the police."

I suppose it's my special perspective, but I almost never think that's a great idea. I wasn't mad about it now, either, being in the possession of stolen property and a criminal record, not to mention the guilty conscience that I'd earned a couple of hours ago in the upstairs guest room.

"Not the police," I said. "Not yet. First let's make sure he's not just taking a nap, or all caught up in his reading."

"But how? The door is locked."

"Isn't there an extra key?"

"If there is, he's never told me where he keeps it. He's the only one with access to his precious books."

"The window," I said.

"It can't be opened. It is this triple pane of bulletproof glass, and——"

"And you couldn't budge it with a battering ram," I said. "He told me all about it. You can still see through it, though, can't you?"

"He's in there," I announced. "At least his feet are."

"His feet?"

"There's a big leather chair with its back to the window," I said, "and he's sitting in it. I can't see the rest of him, but I can see his feet."

"What are they doing?"

"They're sticking out in front of the chair," I said, "and they're wearing shoes, and that's about it. Feet aren't terribly expressive, are they?"

I made a fist and reached up to bang on the window. I don't know what I expected the feet to do in response, but they stayed right where they were.

"The police," Eva said. "I'd better call them."

"Not just yet," I said.

The Poulard is a terrific lock, no question about it. State-of-the-art and all that. But I don't know where they get off calling it pickproof. When I first came across the word in one of their ads I knew how Alexander felt when he heard about the Gordian knot. Pickproof, eh? We'll see about that!

The lock on the library door put up a good fight, but I'd brought the little set of picks and probes I never leave home without, and I put them (and my God-given talent) to the task.

And opened the door.

"Bernie," Eva said, gaping. "Where did you learn how to do that?"

"In the Boy Scouts," I said. "They give you a merit badge for it if you apply yourself. Karl? Karl, are you all right?"

He was in his chair, and now we could see more than his well-shod feet. His hands were in his lap, holding a book by William Campbell Gault. His head was back, his eyes closed. He looked for all the world like a man who'd dozed off over a book.

We stood looking at him, and I took a moment to sniff the air. I'd smelled something on my first visit to this remarkable room, but I couldn't catch a whiff of it now.

"Bernie——"

I looked down, scanned the floor, running my eyes over the maroon broadloom and the carpets that covered most of it. I dropped to one knee alongside one small Persian—a Tabriz, if I had to guess, but I know less than a good burglar should about the subject. I took a close look at this one and Eva asked me what I was doing.

"Just helping out," I said. "Didn't you drop a contact lens?"

"I don't wear contact lenses."

"My mistake," I said, and got to my feet. I went over to the big leather chair and went through the formality of laying a hand on Karl Bellermann's brow. It was predictably cool to the touch.

"Is he——"

I nodded. "You'd better call the cops," I said.

Elmer Crittenden, the officer in charge, was a stocky fellow in a khaki windbreaker. He kept glancing warily at the walls of books, as if he feared being called upon to sit down and read them one after the other. My guess is that he'd had less experience with them than with dead bodies.

"Most likely turn out to be his heart," he said of the deceased. "Usually is when they go like this. He complain any of chest pains? Shooting pains up and down his left arm? Any of that?"

Eva said he hadn't.

"Might have had 'em without saying anything," Crittenden said. "Or it could be he didn't get any advance warning. Way he's sitting and all, I'd say it was quick. Could be he closed his eyes for a little nap and died in his sleep."

"Just so he didn't suffer," Eva said.

Crittenden lifted Karl's eyelid, squinted, touched the corpse here and there. "What it almost looks like," he said, "is that he was smothered, but I don't suppose some great speckled bird flew in a window and held a pillow over his face. It'll turn out to be a heart attack, unless I miss my guess."

Could I just let it go? I looked at Crittenden, at Eva, at the sunburst pattern on the high ceiling up above, at the putative Tabriz carpet below. Then I looked at Karl, the consummate bibliophile, with FDR's *Fer-de-Lance* on the table beside his chair. He was my customer, and he'd died within arm's reach of the book I'd brought him. Should I let him *requiescat* in relative *pace*? Or did I have an active role to play?

"I think you were right," I told Crittenden. "I think he was smothered."

"What would make you say that, sir? You didn't even get a good look at his eyeballs."

"I'll trust your eyeballs," I said. "And I don't think it was a great speckled bird that did it, either."

"Oh?"

"It's classic," I said, "and it would have appealed to Karl, given his passion for crime fiction. If he had to die, he'd probably have wanted it to happen in a locked room. And not just any locked room, either, but one secured by a pick-proof Poulard, with steel-lined walls and windows that don't open."

"He was locked up tighter than Fort Knox," Crittenden said.

"He was," I said. "And, all the same, he was murdered."

"Smothered," I said. "When the lab checks him out, tell them to look for Halon gas. I think it'll show up, but not unless they're looking for it."

"I never heard of it," Crittenden said.

"Most people haven't," I said. "It was in the news a while ago when they installed it in subway toll booths. There'd been a few incendiary attacks on booth attendants—a spritz of something flammable and they got turned into crispy critters. The Halon gas was there to smother a fire before it got started."

"How's it work?"

"It displaces the oxygen in the room," I said. "I'm not enough of a scientist to know how it manages it, but the net effect is about the same as that great speckled bird you were talking about. The one with the pillows."

"That'd be consistent with the physical evidence," Crittenden said. "But how would you get this Halon in here?"

"It was already here," I said. I pointed to the jets on the walls and ceiling. "When I first saw them, I thought Bellermann had put in a conventional sprinkler system, and I couldn't believe it. Water's harder than fire on rare books, and a lot of libraries have been totalled when a sprinkler system went off by accident. I said something to that effect to Karl, and he just about bit my head off, making it clear he wouldn't expose his precious treasures to water damage.

"So I got the picture. The jets were designed to deliver gas, not liquid, and it went without saying that the gas would be Halon. I understand they're equipping the better research libraries with it these days, although Karl's the only person I know of who installed it in his personal library."

Crittenden was halfway up a ladder, having a look at one of the outlets. "Just like a sprinkler head," he said, "which is what I took it for. How's it know when to go off? Heat sensor?"

"That's right."

"You said murder. That'd mean somebody set it off."

"Yes."

"By starting a fire in here? Be a neater trick than sending in the great speckled bird."

"All you'd have to do," I said, "is heat the sensor enough to trigger the response."

"How?"

"When I was in here earlier," I said, "I caught a whiff of smoke. It was faint, but it was absolutely there. I think that's what made me ask Karl about fire in the first place."

"And?"

"When Mrs. Bellermann and I came in and discovered the body, the smell was gone. But there was a discoloured spot on the carpet that I'd noticed before, and I bent down for a closer look at it." I pointed to the Tabriz (which, now that I think about it, may very well have been an Isfahan). "Right there," I said.

Crittenden knelt where I pointed, rubbed two fingers on the spot, brought them to his nose. "Scorched," he reported. "But just the least bit. Take a whole lot more than that to set off a sensor way up there."

"I know. That was a test."

"A test?"

"Of the murder method. How do you raise the temperature of a room you can't enter? You can't unlock the door and you can't open the window. How can you get enough heat in to set off the gas?"

"How?"

I turned to Eva. "Tell him how you did it," I said.

"I don't know what you're talking about," she said. "You must be crazy."

"You wouldn't need a fire," I said. "You wouldn't even need a whole lot of heat. All you'd have to do is deliver enough heat directly to the sensor to trigger a response. If you could manage that in a highly localized fashion, you wouldn't even raise the overall room temperature appreciably."

"Keep talking," Crittenden said.

I picked up an ivory-handled magnifier, one of several placed strategically around the room. "When I was a Boy Scout," I said, "they didn't really teach me how to open locks. But they were big on starting fires. Flint and steel, fire by friction—and that old standby, focusing the sun's rays through a magnifying glass and delivering a concentrated pinpoint of intense heat onto something with a low kindling point."

"The window," Crittenden said.

I nodded. "It faces north," I said, "so the sun never comes in on its own. But you can stand a few feet from the window and catch the sunlight with a mirror, and you can tilt the mirror so the light is reflected through your magnifying glass and on through the window. And you can beam it onto an object in the room."

"The heat sensor, that'd be."

"Eventually," I said. "First, though, you'd want to make sure it would work. You couldn't try it out ahead of time on the sensor, because you wouldn't know it was working until you set it off. Until then, you couldn't be sure the thickness of the window glass wasn't disrupting the process. So you'd want to test it."

"That explains the scorched rug, doesn't it?" Crittenden stooped for another look at it, then glanced up at the window. "Soon as you saw a wisp of smoke or a trace of scorching, you'd know it was working. And you'd have an idea how long it would take to raise the temperature enough. If you could make it hot enough to scorch wool, you could set off a heat-sensitive alarm."

"My God," Eva cried, adjusting quickly to new realities. "I thought you must be crazy, but now I can see how it was done. But who could have done such a thing?"

"Oh, I don't know," I said. "I suppose it would have to be somebody who lived here, somebody who was familiar with the library and knew about the Halon, somebody who stood to gain financially by Karl Bellermann's death. Somebody, say, who felt neglected by a husband who treated her like a housekeeper, somebody who might see poetic justice in killing him while he was locked away with his precious books."

"You can't mean me, Bernie."

"Well, now that you mention it . . ."

"But I was with you! Karl was with us at lunch. Then he went into the library and I showed you to the guest room."

"You showed me, all right."

"And we were together," she said, lowering her eyes modestly. "It shames me to say it with my husband tragically dead, but we were in bed together until almost six o'clock, when we came down here to discover the body. You can testify to that, can't you, Bernie?"

"I can swear we went to bed together," I said, "And I can swear that *I* was there until six, unless I went sleepwalking. But I was out cold, Eva."

"So was I."

"I don't think so," I said. "You stayed away from the coffee, saying how it kept you awake. Well, it sure didn't keep *me* awake. I think there was something in it to make me sleep, and that's why you didn't want any. I think there was more of the same in the pot you gave Karl to bring in here with him, so he'd be dozing peacefully while you set off the Halon. You waited until I was asleep, went outside with a mirror and a magnifier, heated the sensor and set off the gas, and then came back to bed. The Halon would do its work in minutes, and without warning even if Karl wasn't sleeping all that soundly. Halon's odourless and colourless, and the air cleaning system would whisk it all away in less than an hour. But I think there'll be traces in his system, along with traces of the same sedative they'll find in the residue in both the coffee pots. And I think that'll be enough to put you away."

Crittenden thought so, too.

When I got back to the city there was a message on the machine to call Nizar Gulbenkian. It was late, but it sounded urgent.

"Bad news," I told him. "I had the book just about sold. Then he locked himself in his library to commune with the ghosts of Rex Stout and Franklin Delano Roosevelt, and next thing he knew they were all hanging out together."

"You don't mean he died?"

"His wife killed him," I said, and I went on to tell him the whole story. "So that's the bad news, though it's not as bad for us as it is for the Bellermanns. I've got the book back, and I'm sure I can find a customer for it."

"Ah," he said. "Well, Bernie, I'm sorry about Bellermann. He was a true bookman."

"He was that, all right."

"But otherwise your bad news is good news."

"It is?"

"Yes. Because I changed my mind about the book."

"You don't want to sell it?"

"I *can't* sell it," he said. "It would be like tearing out my soul. And now, thank God, I don't have to sell it."

"Oh?"

"More good news," he said. "A business transaction, a long shot with a handsome return. I won't bore you with the details, but the outcome was very good indeed. If you'd been successful in selling the book, I'd now be begging you to buy it back."

"I see."

"Bernie," he said, "I'm a collector, as passionate about the pursuit as poor Bellermann. I don't ever want to sell. I want to add to my holdings." He let out a sigh, clearly pleased at the prospect. "So I'll want the book back. But of course I'll pay you your commission all the same."

"I couldn't accept it."

"So you had all that work for nothing?"

"Not exactly," I said.

"Oh?"

"I guess Bellermann's library will go on the auction block eventually," I said. "Eva can't inherit, but there'll be some niece or nephew to wind up with a nice piece of change. And there'll be some wonderful books in that sale."

"There certainly will."

"But a few of the most desirable items won't be included," I said, "because they somehow found their way into my briefcase, along with *Fer-de-Lance*."

"You managed that, Bernie? With a dead

body in the room, and a murderer in custody, and a cop right there on the scene?"

"Bellermann had shown me his choicest treasures," I said, "so I knew just what to grab and where to find it. And Crittenden didn't care what I did with the books. I told him I needed something to read on the train and he waited patiently while I picked out eight or ten volumes. Well, it's a long train ride, and I guess he must think I'm a fast reader."

"Bring them over," he said. "Now."

"Nizar, I'm bushed," I said, "and you're all the way up in Riverdale. First thing in the morning, okay? And while I'm there you can teach me how to tell a Tabriz from an Isfahan."

"They're not at all alike, Bernie. How could anyone confuse them?"

"You'll clear it up for me tomorrow. Okay?"

"Well, all right," he said. "But I hate to wait."

Collectors! Don't you just love them?

THE KESTAR DIAMOND CASE
AUGUSTUS MUIR

UTTERLY FORGOTTEN TODAY, Charles Augustus Carlow Muir (1892–1989) had a burst of popularity in the 1920s and 1930s (his entire mystery-writing career spanned only 1925–1940, with fifteen books published), but then nothing in the genre appeared for nearly the last half century of his life.

Muir graduated from the University of Edinburgh and followed a career in letters, working as a novelist, historian, biographer, journalist, and editor. Following World War I, he became the editor of the *World* newspaper. He wrote a biography of Charles White, the anecdotal *Scotland's Road of Romance—Travels in the Footsteps of Prince Charlie* (1934), and several histories of industrial firms. In 1953, he edited *How to Choose and Enjoy Wine*. Muir had a brief try at screenwriting and was the coauthor with Joseph Krumgold of *The Phantom Submarine* (1940), which starred Bruce Bennett and Anita Louise.

Virtually all of Muir's mystery thrillers were set in Scotland. He received acclamation for his first book, *The Third Warning* (1925), lavishly praised by *G. K.'s Weekly* (edited by G. K. Chesterton), which also raved about his second book, *The Black Pavilion* (1926). He wrote two thrillers under the pseudonym Austin Moore: *Birds of the Night* (1930) and *The House of Lies* (1932), both of which were reissued as by Augustus Muir.

"The Kestar Diamond Case" was first published in *Raphael, M.D.* (London, Methuen, 1935).

THE KESTAR DIAMOND CASE

AUGUSTUS MUIR

"I THINK YOU'LL DO, Meredith," said the Harley Street specialist after he had questioned me for about twenty minutes. "You're young, you're keen, and I'm prepared to recommend you for the job." He smiled. "And now I expect you'll be wondering who your employer is to be!"

"You haven't mentioned his name yet, sir," I remarked.

"Perhaps you've heard of him. Perhaps not—for my friend Raphael hates publicity. And that reminds me. I must warn you. If Dr. Louis Raphael confirms your appointment as his personal secretary, you must never talk about your work outside his house. Not a hint of it to anyone! Understand?"

"I think you can count on my being discreet, sir," I said. "But who is Dr. Louis Raphael? I've heard the name, but I can't place him."

The specialist looked at me across his big glass-topped desk, and smiled again. "Who is Raphael? To be frank, I daresay you'll find him a rather strange man, but don't let that upset you. Every genius has his little eccentricities. A few years ago he threw up a good practice in the West End and retired to study forensic medicine in all its branches. He's probably the greatest living expert in the scientific aspect of crime. Unofficially, he's the adviser to Scotland Yard. And now, Meredith, perhaps you'll begin to see the need for secrecy. If you get this post, you'll hear and see things that you'll make haste to forget—if you're a wise young man."

I edged my chair a little nearer. "Perhaps you wouldn't mind telling me a little more about Dr. Raphael," I requested. "You see, sir, I'm dead keen to make good in this job."

The specialist nodded, and sat back in his chair. "As I've said, you may not find Louis Raphael an easy man to get on with. He has his moods. If he likes you, all will be well. If not . . ." He shrugged his shoulders. "If not, you'd better resign at once! I haven't known Raphael intimately for years without learning something about his ways. Listen!" He spoke for about ten minutes, and then rose to his feet.

"Well, I think I've told you all that's necessary, Meredith. He asked me to find a new secretary for him, and I hope I've done so. As for your work, that lies with you. I may say that Raphael is writing a big book on the scientific aspect of crime. When it's finished it will almost certainly be a standard work on the subject. I daresay you'll have some historical research to do in connection with it—he might even send you over to one or two of the Continental libraries for data, but that should be a pleasant change for you." He held out his hand. "Report to him to-night at seven o'clock; he can see you then for a few minutes. He lives in Temple House—it's that old house on the Embankment in the corner of the Temple gardens. You can't miss it—it's the place with stained-glass windows on the ground floor. Good-bye Meredith—and good luck."

I can still vividly remember my twinge of nervousness as I rang the bell at Dr. Raphael's residence on the Embankment that evening. There was no name-plate on the door; but as this was the only house that encroached upon the Temple gardens, I was fairly certain I had come to the right place.

"Yes, sir, this is Dr. Raphael's," said the white-haired manservant who appeared. "Perhaps you are Mr. Meredith? Please come in." He closed the door behind me. "Dr. Raphael will see you in his study."

Softly shaded lights burned in the panelled hall, and the man led me up a thickly carpeted staircase to a room with dark curtains draped across one end. A shaded lamp shone down upon the keyboard of a grand piano, and a big gramophone stood beside it. In the shadows I could see a music cabinet and a bookcase or two; and indeed the room struck me as more like the private den of a musician than a scientist's study.

Five minutes passed, and then I heard a slight cough behind me. I got to my feet with a start.

The curtains at the end of the room were parted, and I saw a man in a black silk dressing-gown.

"I've come to interview Dr. Raphael——" I began, and he nodded.

So this was Raphael himself! Though he was a man of about forty-five, as he stood there in the shadows he might have passed for a good twenty years younger. He was of medium height, slenderly built, with a pale and rather dark-skinned face, and shining black hair. His dark eyes looked tired, and there was a cigarette between his lips. He must have stared at me for nearly a minute before he spoke, and I found his gaze a trifle disconcerting.

"I'm sorry you've come to-night," he said in a quiet voice, and walked slowly forward. "To-morrow would have suited me better. I'm busy."

"I can come back to-morrow, sir," I told him.

He paced down the room and returned.

"Latimer tells me you're keen on the job," he said presently. As he resumed his walk across the carpet, some of the things which the Harley Street man had told me came back to my mind with a rush. I recalled the story of Dr. Raphael's unusual career, and the strange environment of his early days—how he had been educated at a monastery in North Africa before coming on to complete his studies at Cambridge—how he had inherited the fortune of his grandfather, the Victorian banker who had been a rival of the Rothschilds, although he had inherited none of the dead financier's interest in money for its own sake. He had got his half-blue at Cambridge for fencing, and this was now his only recreation: every afternoon between three o'clock and four, he spent with the foils, and there were few experts from Bertram's who could touch him. His dark skin and black eyes revealed the Latin strain in his blood, which perhaps explained something of the strange moods that the Harley Street man had already warned me about.

"If you come here, you won't find it easy, Mr. Meredith," he said over his shoulder. "The last man couldn't stand up to it—got nerves. You're a rugby-player, aren't you? You look as if your nerves were sound." He paused suddenly in his slow walk, and mentioned one or two things—such as my slight knowledge of analytical chemistry—which showed how complete had been his Harley Street friend's report about me. "You drive a car," he added. "Manage a big Centuria?"

"As it happens, I can," I was able to reply. And I need not explain that a sixty horse-power Centuria *does* take a bit of handling!

"Good. Come down to the library, Meredith."

A little puzzled at his abruptness, I followed him downstairs into a long narrow book-lined room. It was divided into two portions by an archway hung with crimson curtains, and there were many filing-cabinets around the walls. Raphael jerked out a drawer.

"Here's some of the material for the book I'm compiling. I work a lot at night. If you come here, you'll have to sleep when you get the chance, and I can't say you'll have much time to yourself."

At my eager response, his white teeth were revealed in a quick smile. He stood for a time with his eyes half-closed in thought. "I like you, Meredith," he said at last. "How soon could you start?"

"To-night if you like, sir."

"To-night? That will suit me admirably," he said, to my surprise. "I'll be glad of your help." He gave a quick nod. "Paine will see that your room is ready. Why not go now and bring what you require for the night? Be back here by nine o'clock, Meredith—I have a rather curious case on hand, and I want you to take some notes." He paused and shot a glance at me. "Will the sight of a dead body make you feel squeamish? I have to examine one to-night—the corpse of a murdered man."

For a moment I wondered if he was pulling my leg.

"I can't say I'm exactly familiar with corpses," I replied with a laugh, "but taking notes on a post-mortem will be quite a novel experience."

"A novelty that will soon wear off, Meredith! All pathology is dull—except criminal pathology. It is crime that is fascinating—the impulse to steal, to kill!" His dark eyes gleamed. "The oldest impulses in the world! They lurk in the heart of every man, of every saint. . . . Impulses that are curbed but not extinct." He looked at me through curling wreaths of cigarette smoke. "Ever heard of the Kestar diamond?"

"There was something about it in the morning newspapers," I replied. "Hasn't some Hatton Garden man bought it?"

Raphael nodded. "It came over from Paris this forenoon, and it was stolen—half an hour ago."

"Stolen! Fifty thousand pounds' worth——"

"Only one man knows who the thief is—and he's dead. Murdered in Jacob Bluthner's office in Hatton Garden. Bluthner was the dealer who'd bought the stone—a flawless blue-white of five hundred carats. . . . But we won't go into that now." He turned aside with a yawn. "I'm expecting Inspector Hanson from Scotland Yard

at nine o'clock. I'll look for you at that hour, Meredith. Until then, good-bye."

Dr. Raphael closed the front door behind me and I drove in a taxi-cab to my rooms in Marylebone, where I packed a suitcase for the night, and left the rest of my things ready to be moved on the morrow. As I looked around my old lodgings, I could scarcely believe my good fortune. After coming down from Oxford, I had fooled about in London for nearly a year enjoying myself and vaguely hoping to make my way in Literature, but in the end I had decided to take the first suitable job that came my way—and, thanks to my father's old friend, Latimer of Harley Street, this one had tumbled into my hands, a job that promised experiences of the most novel kind, to say nothing of my contacts with a most unusual man. I knew it wasn't going to be easy to work for Dr. Raphael, but it was going to be devilishly interesting!

As nine o'clock struck I was back at Temple House; and Paine, the manservant, led me straight upstairs to show me my bedroom.

"Dr. Raphael asked me to mention that he is waiting for you in the library, sir," he said; and handing over the key of my suitcase, I hurried downstairs at once.

Raphael was standing in front of the electric fire, his hands in the pockets of his dressing-gown. "You're punctual, Meredith," he said with a nod, "and I like punctuality above all things. I think Inspector Hanson is just arriving—you can set your watch by that man."

A motor had drawn up outside, there was a voice in the hall, and the library door opened.

"Any further news?" enquired Raphael at once.

"Nothing of much account, doctor," replied the newcomer, a short square-faced man with a black moustache. He had a slightly pompous manner, and he gave me a curt nod when Raphael introduced us. "We've brought along the body," he continued. "The police ambulance is at the side door. How long do you expect to be over the job, doctor?"

"Tell the ambulance to wait," said Raphael.

"We'll go through to the laboratory now. To save time, Mr. Meredith will take notes for me."

He led the way through the hall; and, throwing open a door, he switched on the lights. I found myself in a long wide chamber with powerful daylight lamps illuminating the rows of test-tubes, retorts, Bunsen burners, and other scientific apparatus on the benches. The walls were lined with shelves and cabinets, containing jars and bottles of many sizes and colours, and a big microscope stood in the corner.

Raphael opened the door on the left, and glanced into the room beyond. "They've already brought it in," he said, stripping off his dressing-gown and donning white overalls. "Come along, Meredith. This poor devil can't hurt anybody now."

On a metal table in the middle of the room there lay the body of a man. The white face was peaceful, the head was turned a little to one side, and on the forehead there was a trickle of congealed blood from a bruise on the temple.

"The work of the Lucian gang," said Inspector Hanson decisively.

"Think so?" Raphael was examining the pale hands through a magnifying glass. "Where's the divisional surgeon's report, Hanson?"

The Inspector pulled a sheet of paper from his pocket. "A deputy was on duty to-night. His report says this man Oakley died of shock following a blow on the head. That's simple enough. What isn't so simple is how the thief escaped. From the moment the diamond arrived in Jacob Bluthner's office at Hatton Garden, a plain-clothes man was detailed to keep watch——"

"Why was there a plain-clothes man on duty?" interrupted Raphael. "It isn't usual. Was there a special request for protection?"

"Request by Mr. Bluthner, head of the firm," nodded the Inspector. "But we had a reason of our own for keeping a look-out. We had word that the Lucian gang were after this stone. It's uncut, and can be broken up easily."

He went on to explain what had happened in the diamond-merchant's office. By six o'clock everyone had gone home except Oakley, the dead man, who had been Bluthner's confidential clerk. After six, nobody had entered the office, except the charwoman, and nobody had left it. The plain-clothes man, posted in the room beside the front door, was confident of this. At six-thirty he heard the telephone ring in Oakley's room.

"He knew Oakley was still there," continued the Inspector, "but the bell kept on ringing, and then our man found Oakley's door had been locked on the inside! He could get no reply, so he burst his way in. Oakley was dead in his chair. The safe in the corner was open—and the Kestar diamond gone."

"That's more or less what I was told by telephone," remarked Raphael absent-mindedly. He was peering closely into the dead man's eyes with a strong flash-light, and then he looked up. "I'm going to take a blood-film," he said. "Get me a glass slide, Meredith—you'll find one out there in the box beside the microscope."

"I fancy it's a waste of time, doctor. We know how Oakley met his death. What we don't know is how a member of the Lucian gang got into the place—and got away."

Raphael straightened up. "I doubt if the Lucian gang had the brains to pull off a job like that. They're gunmen pure and simple—not artists. This is more like the 'Baron's' work."

"Perhaps it is," admitted Hanson. "The 'Baron' was the smartest jewel-thief in England once. We didn't even know his identity, though we believe he once called himself William Baron, and we have his finger-prints at the Yard. But we've had no trouble from him for two years. They say he's left the country."

"I wonder," murmured Raphael, bending again over the body on the table. With the point of a lancet he made a tiny incision in the wrist, smeared a speck of blood upon the glass-slide I had brought him, and then he hurried through to the microscope. When he returned I could see in his eye an expression which I soon learned to recognise—a dreamy look which concealed intense activity of thought. He again picked up the tiny flash-lamp and examined the bloodless lips and nostrils, then he looked across to Hanson.

"This isn't so simple as it looks, Inspector," he said slowly. "Tell your ambulance-men to go away. This body must remain here for the night. I want to examine it more carefully."

Inspector Hanson nodded. "It did occur to me that some dope had been used. Our plain-clothes man heard no sound of a struggle. But I don't see that the point can help us much."

Raphael bit his lip. "What time did you arrange for me to meet Mr. Bluthner and the others at the office in Hatton Garden?"

"Ten o'clock. We haven't got much time in hand. I've to call back at the Yard first, so I'd better slip along. I'll come right back here, doctor."

"Good," said Raphael. "Meredith, you might take the Inspector to Scotland Yard in my car. I'll be ready when you return. Look, I'll show you the garage."

He opened a door on the other side of the ante-room, and I stepped out into an alley that ran down beside the house. The garage was half a dozen yards away, and I ran out to Dr. Raphael's big Centuria. The two men were talking about finger-prints, and with a final word the Inspector got into the car beside me.

I waited in the big dismal entrance-hall of Scotland Yard until he had completed his business, and he returned with a small attaché-case in his hand.

"I've brought the stuff," he said as Dr. Raphael stepped into the car beside us at the front door of Temple House; and as I drove along the Embankment and turned northward, I could hear from their talk that they were back on the subject of finger-prints. Under Hanson's directions, I drew up by the kerb in Hatton Garden, and followed the two men upstairs.

At the top of the building, a plain-clothes man let us in to the dingy offices of Jacob Bluthner, Diamond Merchant, and Inspector Hanson went along the passage.

"This is Oakley's room," he said. "Everything has been left as it was when the patrol burst in the door at half-past six and found Oakley dead and the diamond gone. As you know, doctor, it was locked on the inside—and nobody entered the office after six o'clock."

"Except the charwoman," added Raphael, his dark eyes making a slow survey of the room. In one corner, a big safe stood open, and the door of a smaller safe was ajar.

"I've seen the charwoman," declared Hanson. "We can count her out of it."

"We can count nobody out of it," said Raphael. "Not even Jacob Bluthner himself." He went over to the window and looked down to the street. "Four floors up," he murmured.

"No cat-burglar could have done this job, doctor!" And then Hanson's eyes followed Raphael's glance to the open ventilator in the glass partition that lit the next room. "I thought of that, doctor," he said quickly. "It's a mighty thin man who could wriggle through that hole."

"But it could be done. No finger-prints in the dust up there?"

"No marks at all," asserted Hanson. "This is the smartest thing the Lucian gang has ever pulled off. I don't generally admit I'm beaten, and I'm not admitting it just yet." He flung down his hat on the desk and mopped his forehead. "Hullo, that sounds like Bluthner."

There was a loud voice in the corridor, and a stout man pushed open the door. He had a heavy sallow face, and was breathing quickly. With a glance at Dr. Raphael and myself, he turned to Hanson. "Well, Inspector, any nearer to solving this damned business yet?"

"Leave that to us, Mr. Bluthner," said Hanson confidently. "We have it well in hand. We'll probably pull in some of the Lucian gang before morning—there's little doubt it was their job. This is Dr. Raphael, who is giving me the benefit of his help."

"It's a serious matter for me," said the diamond merchant.

"Just exactly *how* serious, Mr. Bluthner?" asked Raphael quickly. "Was the stone covered by insurance?"

Bluthner looked a little startled. "Oh, yes,"

he admitted. "I had it covered until ten o'clock to-morrow morning, when it was to be handed over to a client of mine."

"Then, in actual hard cash, you lose little or nothing by the theft?"

Bluthner shrugged his shoulders. "Put it that way if you like. I was thinking of the poor fellow who's lost his life. He was a good man, was Oakley—a man you could trust. He'll be difficult to replace."

Raphael sat down at the dead man's desk and stared moodily at the blotting-pad. "Apart from Oakley, who was the last to leave the office this evening?" he enquired of Bluthner.

"I was," said the other. "The junior clerk and Miss Symons went at their usual hour—half-past five. I brought the diamond in here and placed it in the safe. The combination? I wrote it down on a piece of paper, and Oakley put it between the leaves of a ledger in that other safe. Even if a thief knew that a note of the combination was in there, he'd have had a hard job to find it."

"You seem to have taken every precaution, Mr. Bluthner," said Raphael dryly, "and yet—the worst happened."

A few minutes later the junior clerk arrived, a lean little man of about thirty-five who stood uneasily fingering the rim of his hat. "You sent for me?" he said to Inspector Hanson. "I've already told you everything I know."

"Which wasn't much, Mr. Winch," nodded the Inspector.

"No, indeed. Practically nothing at all," agreed the clerk. "I only saw the stone for two minutes this forenoon. I——"

"You were on quite friendly terms with the dead man, Mr. Winch?" enquired Raphael.

Mr. Winch hesitated. "As a matter of fact, Oakley and I didn't exactly hit it off. . . . Not that I bore him any ill will," he added quickly. "I'm as sorry as everyone else. . . ."

"We all are," put in Mr. Bluthner. "We all are. It's a shocking business."

At the sound of a woman's voice outside, Inspector Hanson had stepped to the door.

"Come right in, Miss Symons. Now that we're all here, we can get down to business." He stood aside to let a young woman enter the room.

She was smartly dressed, and carried herself with confidence. For a moment she seemed surprised; then tucking her bronze curl into place with a neatly gloved hand, she turned her large brown eyes inquiringly towards Inspector Hanson. "You asked me to come here at ten o'clock," she said in a low voice. "I'm afraid I'm a little unpunctual."

"I'm sorry to bring you out at so late an hour, Miss Symons," replied the Inspector. "I think you can be of some further help to us. This is Dr. Raphael, who is helping in this case. We already have your statement, of course. But several points cropped up later. Please sit down. Go right ahead, Dr. Raphael."

Raphael sat back in his chair and lit one of his plump Egyptian cigarettes.

"Inspector Hanson spoke just now about the Lucian gang," he said thoughtfully. "As we all know, they have pulled off several big jewel-thefts in the last few years. I don't think I'm giving away any secret when I say that Scotland Yard knows one or two members of that gang by sight. But to know that a man's a criminal is a different thing from being able to prove it. Am I right, Inspector?"

"Quite right. But we'll rope in that whole crowd one day. . . . If luck's on our side, this will be their last job," declared the Inspector.

"You are still convinced it was the Lucian gang?" asked Raphael, letting the cigarette smoke trickle in tiny spirals from his lips.

"I certainly am," said Inspector Hanson confidently.

"And so am I," added Bluthner, dropping into an armchair at the window. "It's the general opinion in Hatton Garden."

"The opinion in Hatton Garden doesn't interest me," murmured Raphael, and then he shot a glance at the junior clerk. "But your opinion does, Mr. Winch! You've had time to think matters over. Have you come to any conclusion?"

Winch cleared his throat. "No, sir. I'm completely beaten. When a man's found dead, and the door locked on the inside . . ."

"Ever heard of a certain gentleman who used to be called the 'Baron'?"

"Oh, yes, sir. Who hasn't! But he faded out two years ago. Cleared out to the States, they say."

"So you know something of his career, eh?"

Winch gave a shrug. "Most people in Hatton Garden do. He was a bit of a terror hereabout at one time——"

"Listen, Mr. Winch. I wonder if this is news to you. The 'Baron' was employed in Hatton Garden——he mixed with the diamond people on friendly terms. That's how he got his inside information about all the big stones long before they came into this country. Is that news to you? Let me tell you something more. There was a blood-feud between him and the Lucian gang. He queered their pitch as often as he could, and they swore to finish him if they discovered his identity. Ever heard *that* before, Mr. Winch?"

The clerk moved back half a pace, his haggard eyes darting towards the figure of his employer in the arm-chair. "N-no, I hadn't heard that, sir."

"Is it true?" cut in Jacob Bluthner harshly.

"Quite true, Mr. Bluthner. The Inspector can bear me out. The 'Baron' and the Lucian gang were always deadly enemies. But I can correct Mr. Winch on one point. The 'Baron' did not clear out to the States. He remained quietly in Hatton Garden. Unless I'm very far wrong, he's in London to-night."

"You aren't suggesting, doctor——" began Hanson.

"Listen, Inspector! Do you honestly think that the Lucian gang had the brains to carry out this affair to-night? As I've said, they're mere gunmen. Shock-tactics—that's their line. The way the Kestar diamond was stolen from this office shows a different psychology. You've already admitted it has the 'Baron's' touch from beginning to end." Raphael had been addressing the Inspector, but his eyes were upon Winch, and now he spoke directly to him: "When you left this office at five-thirty, Mr. Winch, you saw nothing suspicious?"

"Nothing," said the clerk, moistening his thin lips.

"And you, Mr. Bluthner? You went home at six o'clock, leaving Oakley working at a ledger. There was nobody else in the office except the charwoman and the plain-clothes man. Did you actually see the charwoman?"

"No, but I heard her in Winch's room as I went out." He pointed towards the glass partition.

Raphael's dark eyes opened wide. "You had a diamond worth fifty thousand pounds in this office, and you weren't sufficiently interested to have a last look round, and make sure all was well!"

Jacob Bluthner scowled at his polished finger-nails. "There was a plain-clothes man on duty," he grunted. "Wasn't that sufficient?"

Dr. Louis Raphael sighed. "Let us turn to the question of finger-prints," he said slowly. "Naturally the police have taken photographs of every finger-print they could find in this room. Some of them will no doubt be yours, Miss Symons," he said, glancing at the typist.

"Naturally," she replied at once. "I handled several things here during the day."

"That glass, for instance?" Raphael inquired, pointing to a tumbler that stood beside the water-carafe on the mantelpiece.

The girl's eyes narrowed for the fraction of a second, then she shook her head quickly. "No, I don't think so—I had no reason . . ."

"No? Someone poured out a glass of water, as you can see, from the carafe. But the tumbler seems to have been carefully wiped out afterwards. A strange thing to have done, don't you think, Miss Symons?"

"Rather strange," she agreed; "but I don't know what you mean . . ."

"No matter," murmured Raphael. "All of you have probably touched different things in this room during the day, and the police would like to eliminate your finger-prints from those they have photographed. You have no objection, any of you, to Inspector Hanson taking a record of your finger-prints?"

Jacob Bluthner sat up in his chair. "Is it absolutely necessary?"

"Absolutely," said Raphael. "And you, Mr. Winch—you are agreeable?"

Winch gave a twisted smile, and shrugged his shoulders. Inspector Hanson had opened his attaché-case, which lay on the desk, and took out a small block of wood with a copper plate. Wetting a roller with thick ink, he passed it over the surface of the plate, then placed his thumb upon it, and made an impression on a sheet of paper. "You see, it's quite simple," he said; "I'd like both hands, please." He laid on the desk a bundle of printed forms, with a ruled square for each impression. The three records did not take many minutes to complete.

"Better push off to bed, Meredith," said Raphael, when we got back to his house on the Embankment. "There's nothing more you can do now. We'll resume our pleasant conversation with these three people at nine o'clock to-morrow morning. They've agreed to come here." He pulled off his coat as Paine came forward with his dressing-gown.

"Take up a decanter of sherry to the study, Paine, and a new box of cigarettes. Inspector Hanson may be back shortly, but I'll let him in myself. You can go to bed—and you too, Meredith. Good night to you both."

I made my way upstairs to my bedroom, which was at the back of the house; and pulling up the blind, I looked out over the laboratory roof to the dark Temple gardens, and the few lighted windows beyond. It had been one of the strangest evenings in my experience, and my mind was too full of what had happened for much sleep to come my way.

Again and again I went over the events of the evening, trying to penetrate to the heart of that ugly affair in Hatton Garden. What was the meaning of Raphael's cryptic reference to the empty tumbler on the mantelpiece? Did he believe that the dead man had been drugged before the theft of the diamond took place? But even if this were so, how had the thief got away under the very nose of the plain-clothes man on duty? . . .

It was a long time before I dozed off, and I woke up again an hour or two later. I could hear somebody playing a piano, and then I remembered what the Harley Street specialist had told me—how Raphael would sit for hours at night, playing softly to himself while he concentrated upon his problems.

My mind felt unusually clear, and after about twenty minutes had passed I felt a sudden desire for a cigarette. Lighting one, I went over to the window. The night was very still. I could hear the intermittent rumble of traffic over Waterloo Bridge—perhaps lorries for the Covent Garden market—and a tug-boat hooted on the river. Again my thoughts went back to the happenings of the evening, and I wondered what the conference at nine o'clock next morning would bring forth. But the next moment my heart missed a beat, and I peered forth into the darkness.

In the glass cupola on the roof of Dr. Raphael's laboratory, a dozen yards away, there was a sudden blink of light. It could not be Raphael himself, for I could still hear the music coming from the study. Who could be moving about down there at such an hour?

And then I saw that I had made a mistake. It wasn't in the laboratory I had seen the sudden gleam: it was in the skylight of the ante-room where the dead body of the murdered man lay.

I thought quickly. Whatever was happening, Raphael ought to know of it at once; and I rapidly hauled on some clothes, and hurried along the passage.

The study was in darkness, except for the shaded lamp at the piano. Raphael sat with a cigarette between his lips, his eyes half-closed, his fingers straying over the keyboard. He looked up with a frown of enquiry, and I explained what I had seen.

"The sooner we get downstairs, the better," he said quickly. "Just a moment."

With one hand still straying over the keyboard, he leaned back towards the open cabinet of gramophone records behind him. He pulled out a disc, and glanced at it. A few seconds later the gramophone was playing a piano-piece, and Raphael was hurrying across the study. "If the music had stopped, they might have smelt a rat downstairs," he whispered. "Come along, Meredith."

Across the hall and into the laboratory we tiptoed. I kept at Raphael's heels, moving cautiously in case I should blunder into some object and give away our presence. Raphael halted, and his fingers closed on my arm. The door leading into the ante-room was ajar, and I caught my breath.

The ray of an electric torch was shining upon the pallid face of the dead man on the table, and I could discern the vague outline of a dark figure bending over it. Then the light was switched off, and there was the quiet sound of retreating footsteps. A moment later, the door leading out into the alley was gently closed.

And then, to my utter surprise, Raphael spoke aloud in the darkness:

"Are you there, Sergeant?"

"Yes, sir," replied a voice, and a man moved quietly forward.

"Which of them was it?"

"I couldn't make out, sir. I was waiting to see what the game was."

"I know what the game is now, Sergeant. Somebody has been in to see that the way is clear—in a few minutes there's going to be an attempt to steal that body. Slip a bar across that door, and make sure nobody gets in again. Then ring up the Yard for two more men at once." Raphael paused, and from the open window of the study above I could still hear the music playing. "I think I can leave the matter in your hands, Sergeant. Don't disturb me unless I'm required."

Upstairs in the passage, Raphael gave a short laugh. "I had an idea it was the 'Baron' who stole the Kestar diamond," he said in the darkness. "Now I'm certain of it. Good night, Meredith."

I was awakened next morning with my breakfast on a tray, and it was in a very puzzled frame of mind that I went downstairs to the library at nine o'clock. When I entered the room, I found that Mr. Bluthner, Winch, and Miss Symons had already arrived.

They sat around the table, with Inspector Hanson at the head of it. The atmosphere was a trifle frigid, and nobody spoke; but there was a look of quiet satisfaction in the Inspector's eye which suggested that he was well pleased with the turn things had taken.

A couple of minutes later Dr. Raphael came in; and with a quick "Good morning," he got down at once to business.

"I must thank you all for coming here so early," he said, "and I don't think I need detain you for more than a few minutes. Since last night, the situation has altered—or rather developed, and in the direction I expected. Scotland Yard has now fairly complete evidence that it was not the Lucian gang who stole the Kestar diamond."

Mr. Jacob Bluthner leaned forward in his chair. "You sound confident, Dr. Raphael. Where is this evidence? I would like to know about it."

Raphael smiled. "Some of it is here in this room, Mr. Bluthner!"

The man Winch drew in his breath sharply; his pale eyes were fixed upon Raphael's face as the latter continued:

"You see, six years ago the Yard had an opportunity of taking the finger-prints of a certain gentleman I've already mentioned. I need not go into that, but it was the only slip the 'Baron' ever made—until last night when he made his second slip. And I think it will be the last."

In the brief silence that followed, Inspector Hanson cleared his throat loudly, and there was an odd glitter in his eye. I could not help noting that he occupied the chair nearest to the door.

"I have always been interested in the 'Baron's' activities," went on Raphael. "It used to be thought that he worked alone, but I sometimes wondered if he had assistance of a very clever woman. What happened last night has confirmed it." He took a cigarette from an open box on the table and lit it carefully. "An attempt was made last night to steal the body of Oakley from the ante-room of my laboratory. I believe that the attempt was organised by this woman, and it failed because we were ready for it. Sit down, Miss Symons!" he added sharply as she half-rose to her feet.

In a flash she had recovered her composure, and her red lips parted in a smile. "Well, Dr. Raphael?"

But he turned to Jacob Bluthner, who sat with his face drawn and his fingers gripping the edge of the table.

"It wasn't Scotland Yard that the 'Baron' was afraid of last night, Mr. Bluthner," said Raphael quietly. "It was the Lucian gang. Knowing about the old feud between them, I was forced to this conclusion. In making their plans to steal the Kestar diamond, they must have tumbled to the truth about the 'Baron's' identity. If the Lucian crowd had succeeded, they would have had the Kestar diamond now—and the 'Baron' would have had a bullet through his brain." Raphael rose from his chair. "But he was too clever for them, Mr. Bluthner. The 'Baron' got away last night with the stone. Perhaps you would all like to see it!"

From the pocket of his dressing-gown, he drew a small wad of cotton wool, which he opened and placed on the table. Before our eyes there gleamed a white clear stone.

Inspector Hanson moved back his chair. "Go ahead, doctor," he said abruptly.

Raphael nodded. "As for the 'Baron', I think his activities in Hatton Garden are at an end——" He was interrupted by Miss Symons. She had risen to her feet and was staring across the table at him with an insolent smile.

"Well, doctor," she said with a slight drawl, "I guess you've got the goods! And I guess you know who the 'Baron's' woman friend is. But I'll tell you this. You can bluff till your ink is dry,

but you've got no evidence against her. Not as much as would go on a threepenny piece!" With a laugh, she snapped her gloved fingers.

There was a glint of white teeth as Raphael smiled at her. "Do you know, my dear lady, I believe you're right. The 'Baron's' lady friend is at perfect liberty to walk out of this house. If you don't believe me, ask Inspector Hanson!" His eyes strayed to the white face of Winch, and then towards Bluthner. "You see, we've got the important one—the 'Baron' himself. His fingerprints prove it without an atom of doubt. He left the office in Hatton Garden last evening with the diamond in his possession—it was found in the hollowed heel of his shoe. That shoe is going into the Black Museum at Scotland Yard as a permanent relic of the Kestar diamond case! As for the 'Baron' himself, I fancy he will be a guest of His Majesty for several years to come——"

"If you ever find him!" cried Miss Symons, turning towards the door.

"He is in this room now," said Raphael, looking at her closely.

Bluthner gave a quick glance as Dr. Raphael took a few steps down the long narrow room and swept back the curtains which divided the library into two.

Standing erect was a square-shouldered man, and in an armchair beside him there lay a huddled figure with manacles on his wrists. His lips were white, and his sullen eyes were staring at the carpet.

With a sudden start, I recognised him. It was Oakley himself—the man I had seen last night in the ante-room of Dr. Raphael's laboratory, lying upon the table stiff and motionless.

"And now, Meredith," said Raphael an hour later, "let us get down to work on the historical section of my book. Yes, the case of the Kestar diamond might be worth mentioning in a later chapter. And yet I wonder! . . . It was an old, old game the 'Baron' played. He pulled off the same kind of thing ten years ago in New York before he began to work in England. To be carried away as dead, with fifty grains of a powerful derivative of the drug *Conium* in him—it took some nerve. If he had been put in the local mortuary, they'd have found the place empty in the morning—and that would have been the end of it. He had every symptom of death, Meredith," he continued. "If I'd been the police sergeon who examined him earlier in the evening, I'd have said he had died of shock following a blow on the head. When he was brought to my laboratory a few hours later, I was a little puzzled at getting a slight reflex from the pupils of his eyes, and when I took a blood-film I was still more puzzled. After we came back from Hatton Garden, and you went off to bed, I made a further examination. The body was certainly alive, and I told Hanson to put one of his men to watch the laboratory. Hanson showed up strongly at the end. It

was his idea to take the dead man's finger-prints, although I wasn't absolutely certain about his accomplice until Miss Symons gave herself away. . . . Incidentally, the effects of the drug lasted about twelve hours. I must look into the question of the *Conium* derivatives."

"The Lucian gang must be feeling pretty fed up," I remarked with a laugh.

"If it hadn't been for the Lucian gang," said Raphael deliberately, "the 'Baron' would have got right away with the loot. They had discovered who he was: they were out to get the Kestar diamond—and their revenge on the 'Baron' as well." And then a smile crept into his dark eyes. "To sum it up in a word, the 'Baron's' only chance of leaving Hatton Garden alive last night was to leave it—*dead*! And now, Meredith, to work. . . ."

THE ODOUR OF SANCTITY

KATE ELLIS

IT IS NO SIMPLE TASK to plot and write a good detective novel, but Kate Ellis (1953–) has managed to make it more difficult for herself (and more satisfying for readers) by intertwining her contemporary mysteries with crimes and other events of the past. Born in Liverpool, she came late to the literary world, having worked first as a teacher, an accountant, and a marketer before winning the North West Playwrights' competition and producing her first book, *The Merchant's House*, in 1999.

Fifteen of her novels feature Detective Sergeant Wesley Peterson, a policeman of Trinidadian descent who has a degree in archaeology, which comes in useful on more than one of his cases. He and his wife, a teacher, are newly arrived from London in the ancient coastal town of Tradmouth in rural South Devon when the first book begins, and this is where all his cases occur. Modern police procedures are the hallmark of these adventures, though they are always intruded upon and complicated by the discovery of some long-ago mystery. Ellis also has written two novels about Detective Inspector Joe Plantagenet, set in the North Yorkshire town of York (thinly disguised as Eborby), which are grittier than the Peterson series but also involve more than several plotlines that need to be first connected and then unraveled.

"The Odour of Sanctity" was first published in *The Mammoth Book of Locked-Room Mysteries and Impossible Crimes*, edited by Mike Ashley (London, Robinson, 2000).

THE ODOUR OF SANCTITY

KATE ELLIS

THE BRAKES HISSED with relief as the coach drew up in the car park at the back of Bickby Hall, and Vicky Vine—known as "Miss" on weekdays—climbed out onto the concrete first, clutching a clipboard protectively to her ample chest. Only two girls had been sick on the coach and one boy had bumped his head on the luggage rack. Three casualties: that was good going at this stage.

Vicky did a swift head count as her class emerged from the coach under the disapproving eye of the small, balding car park attendant. All there, every one of them: chattering; pushing; slouching; strutting; blazers shiny and misshapen, ties askew. 8C . . . the flower of Bickby Comprehensive: Vicky looked at them and sighed. She had done the history trip to Bickby Hall so many times: year after year; class after class; the bright and the dull; those interested in history and those who found the Elizabethan mansion, perched incongruously on the edge of a run down housing estate, less appealing than a double maths lesson.

Some girls began to giggle as they spotted their guide. Most of the boys stared, open mouthed, at the apparition.

"Is that the ghost, miss?" one wit asked as the dark haired woman emerged from the Hall's massive oak door in full Elizabethan costume; a huge-skirted creation in faded brocade with big padded sleeves, topped by a limp, yellowed ruff. The woman seemed to glide across the car park towards them, and when she reached Vicky she gave her a nervous smile.

"Hello, Muriel," said Vicky, trying to sound cheerful. "8C today. They shouldn't be much trouble but we'd better search them on the way out. After that unfortunate incident with the penguin on the zoo trip last year, I'm not taking any chances." She lowered her voice. "I was thinking about your Francesca last night. How is she?"

Muriel Pablos managed a weak smile. She looked strained and tired, older than her forty-eight years. "Still the same," she said quietly.

Vicky sighed. "Daughters are such a worry. It was always a pleasure to teach your Francesca . . . unlike some." She looked at her charges, whose volume was increasing with their restlessness. It was time to begin the tour before a minor riot broke out. "We'll get started then, Muriel. Ready?"

Muriel watched, straight backed and silent, as Vicky brought some order to 8C. After the din had died down—and all chewing gum had been collected efficiently in a paper bag—she led the way slowly towards the house with a ragged procession of pubescent youth trailing behind.

The excitement began, from 8C's point of view, when they were in the Great Hall. But it wasn't the magnificent hammer-beam roof that grabbed their undivided attention. It was the scream . . . a desperate, primeval cry. It came when Muriel Pablos was in full flow, giving a colourful, fleas and all, description of Elizabethan life. The unearthly sound made her stop in mid-sentence.

"Sounds like someone's being murdered, Miss," a precocious thirteen-year-old girl speculated knowingly.

"Someone's met the ghost, miss," the smallest boy, who looked no more than ten, added with relish.

Then two crop-haired boys skulking by the window turned towards Vicky, their faces ash pale. "We saw him, Miss," said one of them in an awed whisper. "He fell . . . like he was flying. He's there . . . in the courtyard. Do you think he's dead, Miss?"

Vicky and Muriel pushed their way through the crowd of children who were standing, still as startled rabbits. When they reached the leaded window which looked out onto the cobbled courtyard, Muriel knelt up on the window seat and her hand went to her mouth. "It's Jonathan. He was working up in the tower room. I've always said that window was dangerous. I'll have to call an ambulance . . . the police. The nearest phone's in the office upstairs." She scrambled to her feet, preparing for flight.

Vicky took a deep breath as she stood in the doorway watching Muriel hurry away up the great staircase. Then she turned to her class, who had fallen uncharacteristically silent. "There's been a terrible accident. As soon as Mrs. Pablos gets back from calling the police, I'll go out and see if there's anything I can do. In the meantime can everyone stay away from the window," she added firmly.

Surprisingly, 8C behaved with impeccable restraint until the police arrived.

"Suicide? Chucked himself from that open window up there?" Detective Inspector Anastasia Hardy looked up at the squat, square tower which glowered over the courtyard. "Not much mess, is there . . . considering?" She wrinkled her nose and turned away from the corpse of the fair haired, once handsome man who lay at her feet in an untidy fashion.

The young doctor who was kneeling on the cobbles examining the body glanced up at her. "Not suicide," he said casually. "He was already dead when he hit the ground. That's why there's not much blood about." He turned the body over gently. "Here's your cause of death . . . look. Knife wound straight to the heart. And he'd been dead at least half-an-hour before he fell. Sorry to add to your workload, Inspector."

Anastasia Hardy turned to the young uniformed constable standing a few feet away and gave him the benefit of her sweetest smile. She found charm worked wonders with subordinates. She herself had worked for a host of unpleasant superiors on her way up the career ladder and had always vowed never to follow in their footsteps.

"Constable Calthwaite, have you checked that window yet?"

"The door to the tower room's locked, ma'am, and the only key was in the possession of Mr. Pleasance . . . er . . . the deceased. I had a look through his pockets before the doc got here and I found it . . . a big old iron thing. With your permission, ma'am, I'd like to try it in the locked door . . . make sure it's the right one," said Joe Calthwaite, eager to make a good impression.

Anastasia nodded. She'd let Constable Calthwaite have his moment of glory . . . or disappointment. He was young and keen; his enthusiasm almost reminded her of her own when she had first joined the force . . . before paperwork and the exhaustion of combining police work with family life had set in.

Calthwaite chatted as he led the way up the winding stairs that led to the tower room. "Someone's already talked to the staff, ma'am. It seems nobody was near the tower when Mr. Pleasance fell. And everyone has someone to back up their story. There was a school party in the Great Hall and a couple of the kids actually saw him land in the courtyard. They heard a scream too. A costumed guide was with them . . . a Mrs. Muriel Pablos: she called the emergency services. And their teacher, Mrs. Vine . . . Actually," he said, blushing, "she used to teach me. I was in her class."

"Really?" Anastasia smiled to herself. "So you can vouch for her good character?"

"Oh yes. She's a brilliant history teacher. And I know Mrs. Pablos too, but not very well. Her daughter, Francesca, and I were in the same class at school. Francesca works at the museum now." A secret smile played on the constable's lips and Anastasia suspected that he'd once had a soft spot for Francesca Pablos.

"I think we'd better talk to the school party first then. They'll be causing a riot if they're shut up in that Great Hall for much longer."

"Actually ma'am, they're looking round the house. Mrs. Pablos asked me if she could show them the other wing . . . the parlour, the kitchen and a few of the bedrooms. I didn't think it could do any harm." He looked worried, as though he might have made some dreadful mistake.

"You did the right thing, Constable. As long as they don't go near the murder scene it'll keep them out of mischief."

"Here we are, ma'am . . . top of the tower."

"Good," said Anastasia. The climb had left her breathless. She told herself she should join a health club, take more exercise . . . if she could ever find the time.

PC Joe Calthwaite drew a large iron key from his pocket and placed it in the lock of the ancient door. It turned and the door opened smoothly.

The tower room was larger than Anastasia had expected; a square, spacious chamber lit by a huge window that stretched from floor to ceiling. A section of the window stood open, like a door inviting the unwary to step out into the air.

"Dangerous to leave that window open," Anastasia commented. "Anyone could fall out."

"Someone just has, ma'am."

"And the doctor said he'd been stabbed . . . he'd been dead at least half-an-hour when he fell. Which means somebody threw or pushed the body out . . . not difficult . . . the window reaches to the floor."

"But the door to this room was locked and the only key was in Pleasance's pocket. He was locked in here alone. How does a dead man throw himself from a window in full view of a pair of spotty schoolboys? And he screamed, ma'am. Don't forget they heard a scream."

They stood in the middle of the room, looking round, noting every item, usual and unusual. A massive oak table with sturdy, bulbous legs stood against the wall opposite the window. On it lay piles of leaflets advertising the delights of Bickby Hall and other local attractions. In contrast, a large modern work table stood in the middle of the room. A painting, a portrait of a man in eighteenth-century dress, lay at its centre surrounded by an assortment of trays containing cleaning fluids and materials.

The curator of Bickby Hall had already told one of Calthwaite's colleagues that the dead man cleaned and restored paintings. Jonathan Pleasance had divided his time and skills between the museum in the town centre and the various stately homes and art galleries round about. An evil smelling wad of cotton wool lay, marking the cheap plywood of the table: Pleasance must have been working, removing years of grime from the portrait, just before he died. Calthwaite sniffed the air. The chemical smell was strong. But there was something else as well.

Against the far wall stood a suit of armour, the kind found in stately homes and second rate ghost movies. As Calthwaite stared at it, it seemed to stare back. It leaned on a sword and the young constable's eyes travelled downwards to the tip of the blade. "Ma'am. That stain on the sword. Looks like blood."

Anastasia Hardy had been gazing at the open window. Now she swung round, taking a notebook from her capacious handbag. "So what have we got, Calthwaite? A man falls from a window and there's a scream as he falls. Everyone assumes it's an accident . . . or even suicide. Then the doctor ruins it all by saying he was already dead when he fell, killed by a stab wound. He didn't stagger round the room, injured, then tumble out of the open window. He was already well and truly dead. He was alone. The room was locked and the only key was on him when he fell so the killer couldn't have escaped and locked the door behind him. I assume that door is the only way in."

"Apparently, ma'am."

"And the stains on that sword certainly look like blood so that could be our murder weapon. I don't suppose . . ." The inspector and the constable exchanged looks. "The killer might still be in here . . . in the . . ." They both focused their eyes on the suit of armour.

"I'll check, ma'am." Gingerly, PC Calthwaite took the helmet in both hands and lifted it up. It was heavier than he had anticipated but it revealed no guilty face within. The armour was empty. But there was nowhere else to hide in the room. Calthwaite looked round again slowly and sniffed the air. There was a smell, something altogether more homely than the chemicals on the table, more in keeping with the surroundings. It would come to him in time.

A large, faded tapestry hung to the right of the armour, giving relief to the stark white of the walls. Anastasia examined it and lifted the edge carefully, as though she expected it to disintegrate at her touch. "Well, well. Look what I've found," she said triumphantly. Then she dropped the tapestry as though it had become red hot. "There's some kind of room behind here. The killer might still be in there," she mouthed.

"I'll have a look, ma'am," the constable whispered, suddenly nervous. The killer no longer had the murder weapon but Joe Calthwaite didn't relish the thought of coming face to face with a desperate murderer on a dull Wednesday morning.

Happily his fears were groundless. The tiny room concealed by the tapestry contained nothing more alarming than a pile of superfluous publicity material, a few lengths of red silken rope used to keep the public from wandering where they shouldn't, and a trio of wooden signs bearing bossily pointing fingers. But this room hadn't always been used as a storeroom. It had once had another, more dignified, function.

The altar was still there at the far end, draped in a dusty white cloth and topped by an elaborately framed painting of a plump Madonna and Child. Two sturdy, unused candles on high wrought iron stands stood at the side of the room and three more candles with white, unburned wicks had been placed on the altar. It was a small chapel and it had probably been used for its proper purpose in the not-too-distant past. Joe Calthwaite could still smell candles, the waxy odour of sanctity. He had smelt them in the tower room too, mingled with the stench of Jonathan Pleasance's chemical cleaners.

"There's nobody in here, ma'am," he said, turning to Anastasia who was standing behind him, her head bowed as though in prayer.

She looked up. "You'd better make a thorough search in case there's some hidden cupboard or priest hole or something. Dead men don't throw themselves out of windows. Someone or something was up here with him at nine forty when he fell."

Joe Calthwaite nodded. A priest hole, a secret passage: it was obvious. With renewed enthusiasm he began to search; tapping walls, lifting altar covers, looking behind paintings and seeking out suspicious floorboards. However, the priest hole theory rapidly lost its appeal: there was no hiding place either in the tower room or the tiny chapel. And yet the door had been locked and the only key had been found on the body. Joe Calthwaite frowned in concentration as he stared down at the tower room floor. Maybe the killer had escaped through some sort of trap door. But the shiny oak floorboards lay there, mockingly even and undisturbed. Then he spotted a tiny lump of some solid substance on the floor near the middle of the room, interrupting the rich gloss of the wood. He knelt down and touched it with his finger.

"Have you found something?" asked Anastasia, who had been staring out of the window down onto the courtyard in search of inspiration.

"No, ma'am. I don't think so," he replied uncertainly.

He followed her down the narrow stairs. When they reached the point where they met the elaborately carved main staircase, Anastasia turned to him and sighed. "I suppose we'd better ask some questions. Where shall we start?"

It was virtually unanimous. Jonathan Pleasance was a man to avoid. Not that he worked at Bickby Hall full-time: he was only there two mornings each week, which seemed to be more than enough for most of the staff.

The Hall's publicity office had once been an impressive bed chamber. Two people worked there: Jenny was a solemn dark haired young woman dressed in black as though in permanent mourning. Mark, in contrast, was an effeminate young man wearing a startling purple shirt. They were reluctant at first to speak ill of the newly dead. But gradually they grew more relaxed in Anastasia's motherly presence and began to voice their true opinions. Jonathan Pleasance was an unpleasant, spiteful man, full of his own importance. He had made barbed comments about Mark's sexual preferences and had made an arrogant pass at Jenny during the staff Christmas party. Mark and Jenny, seemingly united in their contempt for the dead man, provided alibis for each other. They had seen and heard nothing suspicious, and the first they knew of Pleasance's death was when Muriel Pablos had burst in, breathless, to call the police after the schoolboys had seen the body hurtle down into the courtyard. Mark and Jenny displayed no emotion, spouted none of the routine clichés of grief. It was almost as if Jonathan Pleasance's violent death didn't surprise or bother them in the least.

Anastasia decided to question the catering and cleaning staff next. None of them had had much to do with Jonathan Pleasance but the interviews weren't a complete waste of time. The chattiest of the cleaners was only too keen to reveal that the chapel was still used occasionally for special services: the last time had been a fortnight ago when the local vicar had christened the curator's baby son there. Most of the staff had been invited, apart from Jonathan Pleasance, who had complained about having to clear his

equipment from the tower room for the happy occasion. Joe Calthwaite sat behind the inspector with his notebook on his knee, pondering this interesting snippet of information. Could the aroma of burning church candles linger for a fortnight? He doubted it.

The inspector looked at her watch. It was time to speak to the top man, the curator himself. She liked to see witnesses on their own territory: the more relaxed they were the less they guarded their tongues.

If the curator's secretary, Mrs. Barker, had been wearing a starched uniform she would have resembled an old fashioned nanny. As Anastasia and Calthwaite entered her small, well ordered office, she was holding a tiny tape recorder aloft in triumph. "The dictating machine . . . I've been looking for it everywhere, and it's been hidden under the in-tray all the time."

Mrs. Barker smiled warmly at the newcomers and appeared to be enjoying the drama of the situation. "I've never had much to do with Mr. Pleasance . . . and I can't say I wanted to. I heard he was one for the ladies," she said meaningfully with a wink which bordered on the cheeky. "In fact," she said almost in a whisper, "he was . . . er . . . friendly with my boss's sister and he let her down rather badly by all accounts. But of course it's terrible that he's dead," she added as a righteous afterthought. "Was it an accident, do you think?"

Anastasia made no comment. "Where were you at nine this morning, Mrs. Barker?"

"Mr. Samuels and I were in here from half past eight working on an important report. Why?"

Before Anastasia could answer, a man emerged from the inner office. Petroc Samuels, curator of Bickby Hall, was a good looking man in his early forties. His body had lost the slender contours of youth and his dark hair was streaked with grey but his brown eyes sparkled with enthusiasm. He invited Anastasia and Calthwaite into his office and sat back in his swivel chair, relaxed, as the inspector began her questions in a deceptively gentle voice.

"I won't pretend I liked Pleasance. He was good at his job but he wasn't what you'd call a nice man. In fact I discovered what sort of person he was when my sister got involved with him about a year ago. But if we all murdered people we didn't like, the population would halve overnight," Samuels said with a nervous laugh.

"Where were you at nine forty when the body was found?"

"Here with my secretary."

"We think he died about half an hour before that. Where were you then?"

"Here in the office. Mrs. Barker and I came in early to work on a report."

"Did you hear the scream when Jonathan Pleasance fell?"

"I heard nothing. I'm rather confused, Inspector. How could he have fallen from the window if he was already dead?"

"That's what we're trying to establish, sir. Did he always lock the tower room door when he was working?"

"Yes. Always. He gets . . . er, got . . . extremely annoyed when he was disturbed. The chapel's used for storage and from time to time people needed to go in there."

"Who stores things in the chapel?"

"Mark and Jenny from publicity; the guides; myself and my secretary. At first he would let people in very grudgingly, but a couple of months ago he decided that he was sick of interruptions so he locked himself in and refused to open the door at all. But as he only worked here two mornings a week it wasn't a major problem."

"Did anyone go up there this morning?"

"If anyone had attempted to knock at that door, Inspector, someone would have heard Pleasance hurling his usual quota of abuse. People learned to steer well clear on the mornings he was in."

"Did Pleasance keep the key to the tower room?"

"No. There's only one key and it's kept in the cupboard by the staff entrance. Pleasance always picked it up on his way in. He'll have

been locked in that room alone, Inspector," said Samuels convincingly.

"Pleasance died at around nine o'clock. What time do your staff arrive?"

"Most of them come in at eight forty-five but the guides arrive a little later, about quarter-past nine. All the staff sign in: you can check if you like."

"And Pleasance?"

"He usually came in just before nine o'clock. And before you ask, I didn't see him this morning."

"Was the key in its cupboard when you arrived at eight-thirty?"

"I'm sorry, I've no idea."

Anastasia Hardy stood up and slung her handbag over her shoulder. "Thank you for your help, sir."

After Petroc Samuels had seen them to the door, all cooperation, the good citizen anxious to help the police, Anastasia marched swiftly away from his office and down the magnificent staircase, thinking fleetingly how satisfying it would be to sweep down those stairs in an elegant period costume. She turned to Calthwaite who was trailing behind, deep in thought. "I think it's time we spoke to those children, Calthwaite. Do you know where they are?"

"They should be back in the Great Hall by now." He hesitated. "Er . . . do you mind if I go and have a word with the car park attendant, ma'am. I noticed him outside when we arrived. It's just an idea I've got."

"In that case I'll have to tackle 8C on my own," she said, hugging her handbag defensively to her chest. "Don't be long will you."

As Anastasia reached the bottom of the stairs, the noise which oozed from the Great Hall sounded like the relentless buzz of bees in a particularly busy hive. She had found 8C.

She took a deep breath before she entered the Hall. She had faced murderers and armed robbers in her time but the prospect of facing thirty exuberant adolescents played havoc with her nerves. As she walked in she could tell that 8C were in high spirits, chattering merrily; the newly broken voices of some of the boys echoing up to the great hammer-beam roof. Anastasia made straight for their teacher who was standing by the massive stone fireplace talking to a middle-aged woman in Elizabethan costume.

"Mrs. Vine? I'm so sorry you've had to wait," Anastasia said with a disarming smile. "I'll get one of my constables to take names and addresses then you'll be able to go." Vicky Vine looked relieved as she glanced at her restless charges.

The costumed woman standing beside her fiddled nervously with the jewel which hung around her neck. "Muriel Pablos?" asked Anastasia. The woman nodded. "I'm afraid we need a statement from you. We're interviewing all the staff: it's nothing to worry about."

PC Joe Calthwaite chose that moment to march into the hall and the children fell silent for a few short moments at the sight of a uniformed police officer.

Anastasia watched Vicky Vine greet the constable like an old friend. "Joe. You do look smart," she said, touching his blue serge sleeve. "Enjoying the police force are you? It's what you've always wanted to do isn't it . . . ever since you discovered who started that fire in the school chemistry lab. Joe was one of my prize pupils, Inspector," she told Anastasia with professional pride as the young constable blushed.

Joe grinned modestly and turned to Muriel Pablos. "Hello again, Mrs. Pablos. I didn't have a chance to ask you earlier. How's Francesca?" Muriel Pablos smiled weakly but didn't answer.

Anastasia's attention began to wander and her sharp eyes spotted a huddle of conspiratorial boys standing near the window. They were up to something. And it wasn't long before she found out what it was.

"Miss," said a whining female voice from the centre of the room. "Darren's got matches, miss . . . and a candle."

"I found them, miss," Darren cried in his defence. "I found them in that window seat. I wasn't going to keep them, miss."

Vicky Vine confiscated the objects of desire

with a weary sigh and handed them to Muriel Pablos; a small box of matches and a chubby, half-burned church candle with a blackened wick . . .

Joe leaned towards Anastasia and whispered in her ear. "Ma'am, can I have a quick word outside?"

Watched by thirty pairs of curious eyes, Anastasia followed the constable into the entrance hall, intrigued. "Ma'am," he said as they stood beneath a pair of watching statues. "I've just spoken to the car park attendant . . . he told me something interesting." He paused. "I think I know who killed Jonathan Pleasance. And now I think I know how they did it."

Anastasia stared at him. "Well I'm baffled. A man dies at nine o'clock in a locked room then jumps or falls from the window half an hour later with the only key still in his pocket. But come on, Sherlock. Was the suit of armour computer operated? Or was the murder committed by the resident ghost? Let's hear your brilliant theory."

He looked at Anastasia Hardy and saw a sceptical smile on her lips. "I'll have to ask you to do something for me first, ma'am. Something that would be . . . er . . . better coming from a woman."

"What is it?" she asked, warily.

When Calthwaite told her she raised her eyebrows. "Are you sure that's necessary?"

"Oh yes, ma'am."

"Right, Calthwaite, you lead the way. And let's just hope this doesn't lead to questions being asked in high places."

They re-entered the hall. This time the children seemed quieter, more subdued.

"Mrs. Pablos, could we have a word outside in the entrance hall, please?" said Anastasia sweetly. Muriel Pablos glanced at Vicky Vine and followed Anastasia from the room, her long skirts rustling against the stone floor. "If you'd be good enough to lift your skirts up," she said when they were outside.

Muriel looked at her in horror. "This is outrageous . . ."

"I'm not suggesting a strip search, Mrs. Pablos. Just lift your skirts up. It'll only take a moment. Constable," she said firmly to Joe. "Stand by the door and make sure no one comes in."

Muriel Pablos looked round in helpless terror. Then she slowly raised her skirts to her knees showing a shapely pair of suntanned legs.

"A little higher, please, Mrs. Pablos."

Muriel Pablos was about to refuse. Then, as though she knew she was defeated, she lifted the skirts higher to reveal a length of red silken rope, coiled about her body.

"Untie the rope, please Mrs. Pablos."

Muriel Pablos slowly uncoiled the rope and it fell to the ground. It was in two sections, each with a burned end. Anastasia summoned PC Joe Calthwaite back and he stood, staring at the rope as though the sight amazed him.

"Well, Constable," said Anastasia. "Are you going to tell us how it was done?"

Calthwaite took his notebook from his top pocket and pulled himself up to his full height. "Well, ma'am, I first became suspicious of Mrs. Pablos when the car park attendant told me that her car was already in the visitor's car park when he arrived this morning at eight forty. He said he saw it later in its usual place in the staff car park, and I found that she'd signed in for work as normal at quarter-past nine. We were told by Mr. Samuels, the curator, that Jonathan Pleasance locked himself in the tower room when he was working and didn't let anyone in, so then I began to think. If nobody was let in then the killer must already have been there, probably hidden in the chapel. Pleasance arrived before nine o'clock so his killer must have been there earlier, already hidden. The key was only used by Pleasance—nobody else bothered locking the room—so it was easy. All the killer had to do was wait, kill Pleasance with the sword, lock the door as he or she left, drive round into the staff car park and then arrive for work as normal."

"But the key was found on the body . . ."

"I'll be coming to that, ma'am. Next I tried to work out exactly how it was done; how it was made to look as though Jonathan Pleasance had fallen from the window. Then I saw the lengths of rope stored in the chapel and an odd number of candles on the altar . . . three . . . so it was possible that one was missing. I found some candle wax on the floorboards in the middle of the tower room and I started to think. What if the body had been held by the open window with a length of rope secured to, say, that heavy oak side table: then if a lighted candle was placed under the rope so that it burned through slowly to give the murderer plenty of time to establish an alibi. Then the murderer would need some excuse to get away in order to hide the rope and candle once the body had fallen. That's where the miniature tape recorder came in. The curator uses one to dictate letters and his secretary said that she'd mislaid it for a while. I think the killer borrowed it and recorded a bloodcurdling scream to be played at the appropriate moment in front of a full audience to provide the perfect alibi. Nobody else in the building heard it because the tape was only played in the great hall. Then the killer ran upstairs to call the police. But first she made a detour and unlocked the tower room to deal with the incriminating evidence; she hid the burned candle and matches in those big padded sleeves where she'd hidden the tape recorder. Then she put them in the window seat until they could be disposed of properly. It's a pity 8C had to find them and give the game away isn't it, Mrs. Pablos? And the rope . . . well what better place to hide it than underneath a huge Elizabethan skirt. Am I right so far, Mrs. Pablos?"

Muriel Pablos looked at him, pleading. "You knew my Francesca at school, Joe. You know what a lovely girl she is. She met this older man at work in the museum: she was besotted with him, completely infatuated, but she wouldn't tell me his name . . . I never guessed it was Jonathan Pleasance. Then one day he saw me alone and he started to talk about their relationship. The things he said . . . the way he talked about Francesca. He was just using her and he said he intended to end their affair soon because she was getting too possessive . . . too clinging. He said that if she made things awkward for him, he'd make sure she lost her job at the museum: he was going to tell lies about her . . . say she was incompetent. I couldn't just stand by and watch him ruining her career . . . her life. I did it for my daughter."

Anastasia nodded, wondering how she would have felt if such a thing had happened to her own daughter. Then she dismissed the thought and reminded herself of her profession. "Is there anything else you want to say before I arrest you, Mrs. Pablos?" she asked sympathetically before reciting the familiar official words.

"I came in at eight this morning and parked in the public car park at the back so none of the staff would see me," Muriel began quietly. "The tower room wasn't locked—only Pleasance ever locked it—so I hid myself in the chapel. When he came in just before nine I killed him. Then I rigged up the rope and the candle, locked the door behind me, got into my car and arrived for work as usual. I had taken pieces of rope home and experimented so that I could time his fall for when I was showing Vicky's class round. When I went upstairs to call the police I made a detour to the tower room like Joe said. I wiped the tape on my way up and put the recorder back on Mrs. Barker's desk when I went in to tell her what had happened."

"But the room was locked and the only key was found on the body. According to everyone's statements you never went out into the courtyard . . . never went near the body," said Anasta-sia, puzzled. Muriel Pablos stood silent. She was saying nothing.

As Muriel was led to a waiting police car, PC Joe Calthwaite walked round to the back of the house where 8C were boarding their coach. He waited patiently until their teacher had counted them on before he spoke to her.

"You were always fond of Francesca weren't you, Mrs. Vine," he began gently. "Francesca was brilliant at history, your star pupil. You must have been delighted when she got that job at the museum. I think Mrs. Pablos told you about Pleasance and Francesca. I think you helped her. When she came downstairs again you left her looking after your class while you went to check the body for signs of life before the ambulance arrived. I think she'd locked the tower room door behind her and then she passed you the key. While you were bending over the body you put the key in his pocket. Is that right, Mrs. Vine?"

Vicky Vine smiled and shook her head. "I couldn't stand by and watch that man hurt Francesca. I had to help somehow." She took a deep breath. "What gave us away?"

"Do you remember when the chemistry lab burned down? I smelled petrol on the culprits' clothes."

"How could I forget."

"Well this time it was candles . . . I kept smelling candles. I've always had a good sense of smell."

As Joe Calthwaite put an arresting hand on her shoulder, his old teacher looked into his eyes and smiled.

THE PROBLEM OF THE OLD OAK TREE

EDWARD D. HOCH

THERE CAN BE NO DISPUTE that the master of the impossible-crime puzzle is John Dickson Carr; both under his own name and as Carter Dickson, he tirelessly published in this most difficult genre from 1931 to 1972. There can also be no argument that the closest in reputation and achievement is Edward Dentinger Hoch (1930–2008), who wrote nearly as many of these brain twisters during a career that spanned more than a half century (1955–2008). Most detective story writers shied away from this type of tale after Carr established himself as the lord of the locked-room mystery, conceding that just about every possible variation had been employed. Hoch not only accepted the challenge but created a series character, Dr. Sam Hawthorne, whose every mystery featured an impossible crime. His first case was "The Problem of the Covered Bridge" in the December 1974 issue of *Ellery Queen's Mystery Magazine.*

Hawthorne is a retired old (he was born in 1896) country doctor who practiced in a small town from the 1920s through the 1940s and reminisces about the improbable murders that occurred during the years in which he tended to the townspeople.

Hoch's most famous stories, not about Hawthorne, are the frequently anthologized "The Oblong Room" (1967), for which he won the Edgar Award, and "The Long Way Down" (1965), in which a man goes out the window of a skyscraper but doesn't land for two hours; it was the basis for a two-hour episode of the television series *McMillan and Wife* titled "Freefall to Terror," which aired on November 11, 1973. Hoch was named a Grand Master for lifetime achievement by the Mystery Writers of America in 2001.

"The Problem of the Old Oak Tree" was first published in the July 1978 issue of *Ellery Queen's Mystery Magazine*; it was first collected in *Diagnosis: Impossible* (Norfolk, Virginia, Crippen & Landru, 1996).

THE PROBLEM OF THE OLD OAK TREE

EDWARD D. HOCH

DR. SAM HAWTHORNE poured a little brandy from the decanter and settled back in his chair. "September of '27 is a time I 'specially remember, because that's when the folks came to make a talking picture in Northmont. And that's also when a man was apparently strangled to death by an oak tree. But I'm getting ahead of my story. First I should tell you something about the movies in those days, and 'specially about talking pictures."

We didn't get to see many movies around Northmont in those days (Dr. Sam continued) because there weren't any theaters. Viewing the popular silent films of the day meant a drive into Springfield or Hartford, or even all the way to Boston. A few people had made the trip the year before to see John Barrymore in *Don Juan*, the first film with synchronized sound effects, and people were already talking about *The Jazz Singer* with Al Jolson. Its New York opening was only a few weeks away that September, and the advance publicity promised Vitaphoned songs and some stretches of dialogue in sound for the first time.

So it wasn't surprising that movie-makers around the country were jumping on the talkie bandwagon. Nor was it surprising that some of them wanted to make movies about aviators. The silent film *Wings* had opened in August to critical and popular acclaim, and would go on to capture the first Academy Award for best picture of the year. And Lindbergh's triumph was still very much in the news.

That was why Granger Newmark came to Northmont—to make the first talking picture about fliers. Not the World War I aces of *Wings*, but the barnstorming pilots who turned up at county fairs and rural weekends to risk their lives for a few dollars' pay. Granger Newmark was very much a product of Hollywood, where motion-picture studios were beginning to congregate after their early years in New Jersey. He arrived in my office that first afternoon wearing riding britches and leather boots, with a zipper jacket topped by a white silk scarf around his throat. And I'll admit I didn't know quite what to make of him at first.

"What seems to be the trouble?" I asked, showing him to my office chair. "Sore throat?"

"Hardly! I've come here because they tell me you're the only doctor in this burg."

"That's correct."

"I'm producing and directing the barnstorming film being shot near here. You probably recognized my name."

I'd heard of the film but that was about all. "I've been too busy this week to read the papers, Mr. Newmark. You'll have to forgive me."

"I see." He sighed and took out a slim black cigar. "Well, I can see I'll have to educate you. I'm filming the first sound motion picture about barnstorming pilots. We needed a country set-

559

ting for some of the outdoor scenes and we chose Northmont."

"Why's that?" I asked, genuinely curious.

"I drove through here last year and liked the area. That big open field north of town is ideal for a small landing strip, and I obtained permission from the owner to use it."

"What field would that be?"

"Gates House Farm. Fellow named Hi Gates leased me the use of the land. It's a perfect setting for *Wings of Glory*."

I nodded. Hi Gates was the shiftless son of a moderately successful farmer who'd died a few years back. Hi, with a broken marriage and a drinking problem behind him, was on the lookout for any money-making scheme which would be labor-free on his part. The idea of filming a movie in one of his idle fields would appeal to him.

"What do you need me for?" I asked.

"Some of the stunt work in the picture's going to be dangerous. A parachute jump and a plane nosing over on takeoff. I want a doctor standing by and we didn't bring one with us."

"Look here, I've got my own patients to tend to. I can't neglect them to watch you making a movie."

"I'd only need you for a few days, during the stunt shooting, and I'd pay you well. They could come get you if there was an emergency."

I had to admit that the past week's business had quieted down to the birth of two babies to farm wives. There was no real reason why I couldn't accept his offer, especially since I knew my nurse April could hold down the office and notify me if I was needed. "All right," I decided finally. "But I couldn't spare more than three days."

"Good! I'll need you Wednesday morning, out at the Gates House Farm. Nine o'clock sharp!"

Granger Newmark was gone before I realized that he hadn't mentioned how much he'd be paying me. But by that time I knew I was hooked.

On Wednesday morning I left April in charge of the office, with instructions for reaching me, and drove my six-year-old Pierce-Arrow Runabout over the rutted roads to Hi Gates's farm. Even before nine o'clock the place was alive with activity. And sure enough—there was a flying machine at one end of the long field.

Newmark greeted me with enthusiasm and explained that the aircraft was a D. H. 60 Moth, a biplane with two open cockpits and a single engine. Though it looked just like the planes I remembered from the Great War, he told me it had been developed only two years earlier by Captain Geoffrey de Havilland, a British officer.

"It's perfect for the picture," he said enthusiastically. "Looks like those wartime crates all the barnstormers fly, but it's safer and it has a new sixty-horsepower Cirrus engine inside. Best of all, we can tow it along the road with its wings folded, so it's easy to move from place to place during shooting."

Gazing down the grassy runway toward the distant woods I was reminded of one landscape feature worth noting. "The haunted oak," I said aloud.

"What?"

"That old oak tree—the one that's partly dead. Some folks around here say it's haunted. Supposed to have been planted over the grave of a Revolutionary War traitor back a hundred and fifty years ago. I doubt if it's really that old, though."

Granger Newmark studied the distant tree, which stood alone some distance from the woods. "Ugly-looking thing," he agreed. "Can't think of a way we could work it into the script, though. Has it ever killed anyone?"

Though the question was asked in jest, I had a serious reply. "Boy fell from it a few years back and broke his neck. For folks around here that was enough to revive all the old superstitions."

A tall handsome man in a pilot's costume joined us then. I recognized him even before the introductions as a silent-screen favorite, Robert Raines. Newmark performed the introductions and Raines shook my hand firmly. "I hope I won't be needing your services, Doc."

"Hear that voice?" the director asked, aglow with pleasure. "When the women of America hear it, we're going to have ourselves a big *big* star! Half the silent actors will be out of work once the public hears their squeaky little voices!"

Raines grinned boyishly at the compliment. "It's just the voice that God gave me. I do the best I can with it."

"Are you going to be jumping?" I asked, noticing the parachute strapped to his back.

"We're using a double for the actual jump," Newmark explained. "Can't risk our big star on anything like that."

"Don't know as you should risk anyone," I said. "There's not much treatment I can give if his chute doesn't open."

"Don't be silly!" Newmark sputtered. "People were parachuting before there were airplanes! It's perfectly safe."

His statement seemed like such a downright impossibility that I admit I laughed at it. Later when I looked it up I found out he was right—there had been parachute jumps from hot-air balloons before the year 1800. I learned quickly that Granger Newmark rarely made mistakes.

About then we were joined by a young man dressed exactly like the star. "This is our double," Newmark said. "Charlie Bone."

Bone's rough, angular face bore little resemblance to the star's handsome features, but I could see they shared a similar height and build. The camera's eye on a distant falling figure would see them as one. "How are you?" Bone asked me, not expecting an answer. His interest was already elsewhere. "See those clouds rollin' in? Could be trouble."

"My cameras are ready to roll," the director said. "We'll need a shot of you two climbing into the plane, and then the takeoff. You jump out as soon as you can, Charlie, and Raines will bring the plane in."

"You can fly this thing?" I asked the star.

"Oh, sure. I'm a lot more comfortable flying it than being a passenger. We've got some stunt footage we'll stick in later, though. I don't do stunts."

I watched the two men go off, side by side, as

Granger Newmark explained the scene. "In the film Bone plays the pilot and Raines is his barnstorming partner. Raines is going up for a parachute jump even though a doctor has warned him the thin air could cause him to black out." He smiled apologetically. "Sorry we've shot the doctor scene already or we could have used you, Doc."

"Acting's a bit out of my line." The fliers had reached the biplane now and been joined by a dark-haired young woman in a long flowered dress. "Who's the girl?"

"Angela Rhodes. Our leading lady. This is her first picture, actually, but I think she's going to be a big star."

I watched her adjust the star's scarf, just as a princess might have done before her knight rode off to joust. Then both men were into the plane with a wave and the director shouted, "Camera! Action! Take one!" Raines waved from the front cockpit.

The cameraman followed the plane as it taxied into position and then took off. For the first time I noticed that Hi Gates had been watching too, standing just a bit behind me. "Hello, Doc," he said when I turned to him. "Never thought they'd be shootin' a movin' picture on my farm."

"I hope you're getting a good price for it, Hi," I told him. "These movie companies got piles of money."

"Don't you worry, Doc." He spat some tobacco juice at the ground. "They don't outfox ol' Hi. My daddy taught me a thing or two 'bout business afore he passed on."

I doubted if anybody had ever taught Hi Gates much of anything, but I didn't disagree with him. "How you been making out here by yourself, Hi?" I asked. Overhead, the plane was circling back after its takeoff.

"Good as can be expected. I keep hopin' Dorie'll come back, but I guess there's not much hope of that." Dorie was the wife who'd left him when he started to drink heavily. The last anyone had heard she was living up in Maine with her sister.

"Maybe she'll read about them shootin' this film at your farm," I said.

"Yeah. Maybe."

Nearby, Granger Newmark was standing at the cameraman's side. "Keep focused on the plane! Don't miss a thing! He'll jump now when they come over the field again."

The biplane with its two open cockpits had become a mere speck in the sky as it climbed high enough for the parachute jump. As I watched from the ground, glad that I wasn't up there, Angela Rhodes came over to join our group. "Isn't it dangerous?" she asked Newmark.

"No more dangerous than falling out of bed."

I saw a tiny speck detach itself from the plane and start to fall. Then a cloud of white billowed up behind it as the parachute was released. The falling figure was caught beneath a gently falling mushroom and began drifting slowly toward us. "Perfect!" Newmark shouted. "He should land right on the field in front of the camera!"

But the clouds that had gathered on the horizon were moving in now, and the wind was picking up. As the parachute neared the ground we could see it was drifting farther off course, toward the old oak tree at the edge of the field.

"Why doesn't he steer himself?" Angela asked. "He's going to hit that tree!"

"Charlie!" the director shouted, but his voice must have been lost in the gathering wind. The parachute came down in the upper branches of the tree, snagged by some of the dead limbs that stretched toward heaven. And beneath it, hanging from his harness some ten feet from the ground, was the limp body of the stunt man, Charlie Bone.

"Let's get him out of there!" I shouted, leading the others toward the tree. Just then I didn't care if I was ruining the scene. There was something about that limp body, swaying at the end of the parachute harness, that had galvanized me into action. "Somebody get a ladder," I called to them, reaching the tree before the others.

Hi Gates ran off toward the barn as I tried to boost myself onto a lower limb of the tree. Already I could see the blue of Bone's face, and the tongue half out of his mouth. I managed to climb high enough to feel for a pulse, but there was none.

"What is it?" Granger Newmark called from the ground. "What's wrong?"

I climbed a bit higher in the tree, reaching out toward the white scarf around his neck. But then I felt something else, and drew my hand away. I came down from the tree just as Hi Gates returned carrying a ladder. "Cut him down carefully," I instructed. "And then leave him here on the ground. I have to call Sheriff Lens."

"My God, do you mean he's dead?"

"Yes, Mr. Newmark, he's dead. And there's a piece of wire knotted around his scarf. He's been murdered."

I phoned Sheriff Lens from the Gates farmhouse and then walked back to the body. The cast and crew were gathered around in a circle, watching while Newmark worked to unknot the wire from Charlie Bone's neck. "You'd better leave that for the sheriff to see," I advised. "It won't do Bone any good now."

"But—but how could it have happened?"

I stared up at the old oak tree. "Damned if I know."

The biplane was circling the field and finally Newmark waved it in for a landing. I think we were all wondering what Robert Raines would say when he saw the body. Because we knew we had witnessed a murder with only one possible explanation. Charlie Bone had been strangled in the plane before he jumped—there was no other way. And Robert Raines was the only person up there with him.

We watched as Raines came running over to the circle, pushing his way through to stare at the body. "What happened to him?" he asked.

"He's dead," I said. "Strangled by a wire around his neck."

"Strangled! Here on the ground?"

"Before he reached the ground. His chute snagged in the tree and when I climbed up to free him he was already dead."

He stared at me with unbelieving eyes. "But

he was alive when he jumped! He had to be, to pull the rip cord!"

"That's right," Granger Newmark agreed. "I hadn't thought of that."

I saw Sheriff Lens arriving in his car, and I decided I could wind this thing up quickly. "You could have strangled him with the wire and dumped him out of the plane—and used a second wire or a string to pull open the rip cord when the body was free of the plane."

Raines strode up to me, hands on hips. Close up like that, he was intimidating. "You think so, Doc? I was in the front cockpit, remember? You tell me how I could have strangled someone sitting in the *rear* cockpit, several feet behind me, while the plane was in the air, then attached a string to his rip cord and dumped the body out of the plane. Go ahead, tell me!"

I'd forgotten about the cockpits, but now I remembered that he spoke the truth. I remembered him waving from that front cockpit as the plane took off. He was right—he couldn't have strangled Charlie Bone.

But no one else could have, either.

It was an impossible crime.

Sheriff Lens was not to be put off so easily. "You're telling me the damn tree killed him, Doc?"

"No, I'm not telling you the tree killed him. Trees don't strangle people with pieces of wire—not even haunted trees."

"All right, then—who did? He sure didn't commit suicide."

"No," I agreed. "People can shoot or stab or poison themselves, but it's impossible to strangle oneself to death. You'd pass out before you finished the job."

"Unless you hanged yourself. How about this, Doc—the wire was attached to the chute and when it opened the wire was pulled tight and choked him to death."

"A nice theory, except that the wire's not attached to the chute now. Besides, I've just examined the neck under that scarf and there's no evidence that the pressure came from above. Something like you suggest would have almost torn the head from his body. There'd be evidence of it."

"So how was it done, Doc? You're the expert on these impossible crimes."

"But I've never seen one quite as impossible as this."

There was something gnawing at my memory, though, and I went in search of Granger Newmark. Sheriff Lens could content himself with prowling around the oak tree till I returned. I found the director with his star, Angela, and I suppose you could say he was comforting her. He took his hand off her shoulder as I approached and frowned at me. "What is it now, Dr. Hawthorne? A bill for your services?"

"My services aren't finished yet. I was wondering about that plane Raines and Bone were in."

Newmark gazed out at the field where the Moth biplane stood. "What about it? We won't be reshooting the scene, if that's what you're wondering."

"I'm wondering if the plane has one of those automatic pilot gadgets I been reading about."

This brought a smile to the director's face. "So my star could have set it and climbed back along the fuselage to strangle Bone? Not a chance! There's no autopilot on it, and Raines would be scared to death to try a trick like that anyway."

I learned later that although the automatic pilot had been invented in 1910, it was not widely used on planes till after 1930. Newmark was telling the truth—there was no autopilot on the Moth. It was another good idea gone awry.

"Why are you so interested in who killed him?" Angela Rhodes asked me. "It's no business of yours."

"I was hired to minister to the ill and injured. I failed in that, quite badly."

Newmark smiled. "We won't hold it against you."

"What about the film you shot? Can you get it developed? It might give us a clue."

"The film has to go down to New York for processing. It'll be days before we see anything. You think we carry a darkroom along with us?"

I could see they had turned against me, as if somehow the impossible death of Charles Bone was my fault. And maybe it was—I did seem to attract murder with increasing frequency in those years.

Sheriff Lens was busy questioning Hi Gates, digging into a possible motive for the crime, and I decided that was the smart thing to do. Worrying about the how of it would get me nowhere. Maybe the why would prove more profitable.

"He was stayin' here at your farmhouse, wasn't he?" Sheriff Lens asked. They were in the tool shed near the barn.

Hi Gates nodded. I could smell his breath and I realized he'd been drinking again. For all I knew, maybe he never stopped. "Sure, I got three bedrooms upstairs just goin' to waste. I wait for Dorie to come home an' that'll be never, so I rented them out to some o' the cast and crew. Bone and that cameraman, Zeedler. And one of the extras."

"Any trouble between him an' the others?" the sheriff asked.

"No trouble I could see."

"No fights, drinking?"

"Hell, they'd only just got here this week." Gates looked sly, though, as if he wasn't telling us everything.

"Let's go up to the house," I suggested, "and take a look at Bone's room."

With the sheriff walking a little bit ahead of us, Hi Gates lowered his voice. "I got somethin' you'd want to see. Don't want Sheriff Lens to spot it, though."

When we entered the house I told the sheriff to go over Bone's things while I lingered behind. What Hi Gates produced was a tattered scrapbook full of clippings and credits which had obviously belonged to the dead man. "See this? I got it from his room."

"You stole it?"

His face fell a bit. "I found it when I was cleanin' up this mornin'. But I knew old Lens would say I stole it. Look at it!"

Charlie Bone had worked in silent films during most of the twenties, according to the clippings, appearing frequently in popular two-reel comedies and thrillers. He'd played the part of the old man in Poe's *The Tell-Tale Heart*, and of Edward Stapleton in *The Premature Burial*. There were clippings of his work as a stunt man and double too, and a gravure photograph of him standing with Robert Raines. They were wearing identical pirate costumes for a scene in *Captain Blood,* the 1925 swashbuckler.

"Interesting, but I don't see—"

Hi Gates reached over my shoulder and pulled something loose from under the *Captain Blood* photo. It was a fuzzy picture of a man and woman, naked, in a bed. "Dirty pictures," he announced triumphantly. "Look at the other side."

There were words written on the back that had been crossed out hurriedly. *"Remember this? If you don't want me to—"*

Hi Gates was pulling more pictures free from their hiding places in the album. They were much the same, or at least they seemed to show the same couple in various poses. All were too fuzzy and underexposed for clear identification, and none of these had writing on the back.

Charlie Bone had been blackmailing someone. But who?

The man in the picture could have been Robert Raines.

Or it could have been his double.

The girl just might have been Angela Rhodes, but her face did not show clearly in any of the scenes.

"You comin' up, Doc?" Sheriff Lens called down the stairs.

"Be right there!" I pocketed some of the pictures and told Gates to put the album away in a safe place. Then I went up to join the sheriff.

Charlie Bone's room was bare except for a bed and dresser and chair. He seemed to have unpacked little, and most of his clothes still rested in an open suitcase on the chair. "Nothin' much here," Sheriff Lens said. "Have a look." I glanced hastily through the suitcase and the dresser drawers, but found nothing of interest.

Hi Gates had no doubt been through it already, and thinking about that I wondered when he'd had the time. While we were waiting for the sheriff's arrival?

Or had he known of Bone's death even before that? Had he somehow tampered with his clothing, looped the wire around his scarf?

But for what motive? Charlie Bone certainly wasn't blackmailing Hi Gates.

I was on my way downstairs when I encountered the cameraman, Zeedler, on his way up to the room next to the dead man's. I suppose he was a suspect too, but I had to trust someone. "Got a minute? Let me show you something." We went into his bedroom and I brought out the photographs Hi Gates had discovered.

Zeedler grunted and scratched his balding head. "Fuzzy. They look like frame blowups from movie film. There's a lot of this blue stuff around—stag movies. They rent 'em to men's clubs and bachelor parties."

"Recognize the stars?"

He squinted at the blurred figures. "No, can't say I do."

"The man could be Robert Raines."

"Raines? Hell, no! He's too big a star for this sort of thing."

"He wasn't always a star."

"Doesn't look like him to me," Zeedler said, returning the photos. "Where'd you get these?"

"Found them," I answered vaguely. "Thanks for your help."

"Figured out how Bone was killed yet?"

"I'm working on it."

I went back outside and headed over toward the old oak tree. The body was gone and most of the others had drifted off. Zeedler's movie camera sat on its tripod pointed at the sky. A couple of kids from a neighboring farm were playing by the plane and nobody was chasing them away. The cast and crew had simply abandoned their stage and gone off somewhere to ponder the strange passing of Charlie Bone.

I saw something on the ground beneath the oak tree and I stooped to pick it up. It was a hard rubber ball and I wondered if it belonged to one of the children near the plane. I started to toss it in their direction, then changed my mind and dropped it into my pocket. I could see Angela Rhodes heading in my direction.

"Hello, Dr. Hawthorne," she said. "We haven't had a chance to get properly acquainted."

"And I'm afraid we won't have. If Granger Newmark continues with the picture he'll certainly want another doctor on the set now."

"Why? You didn't cause Charlie's death, did you?"

"I certainly didn't save his life. Tell me something—how long did you know Charlie Bone?"

"I just met him last month, when Granger was casting for the movie. But Robert's known him for years. Charlie doubled for him in the *Captain Blood* stunts."

"Who do you think killed him?"

She didn't answer right away. She stared up at the tree, and then off at the plane where the neighbor kids were climbing on a wing. "It had to be someone up there, before he jumped."

"Raines was the only one up there."

"I know."

But was he?

I had a sudden thought and ran off toward the plane, leaving Angela Rhodes standing there alone. "Come on, boys—off the aircraft," I shouted, chasing them away. Then I climbed up to the rear cockpit where Bone had been seated when the plane took off. Was it possible that someone small could have been concealed in the cockpit with him—someone who strangled him and pitched his body over the side? The idea was far-fetched to begin with, and as soon as I seated myself in the cockpit I saw that it was physically impossible as well. Not even a midget could have shared the cockpit with Bone. My legs were cramped and he was a bigger man than me.

But as I lifted myself out of the plane I saw Angela again, off in the distance, touching a finger to her smooth throat. I remembered the gesture from before. She'd touched someone else, adjusted a scarf just before the plane took off. Remembering now, it seemed it had been Raines's scarf. But it could have been Bone's.

Memories, memories. They play such damned tricks on you!

"Dr. Sam!"

I turned and saw April, my nurse, hurrying across the field toward me. "What is it, April—one of my patients?"

"No, Dr. Sam. But they've got the body in town and they need you to sign the death certificate. They couldn't get through on the phone."

"All right. I'll come along. Nothing much to do here, anyway." I told Newmark I'd be leaving and he waved me away. There was no point in asking for my pay. I certainly hadn't earned it.

They'd taken the body to the local funeral parlor, where Jud Miller was waiting to do what passed in those days for an autopsy. "Can't cut into him till you sign the paper, Doc."

I glanced at the corpse on the embalming table and turned away. "What about next of kin?"

"They say he didn't have any. Going to bury him here, I suppose."

"There's no doubt he was strangled?"

"Oh, I'll check his insides, all right. But it looks like a strangling to me. No other marks on him except a bruise on his temple. Probably got that when they were taking him down from the tree."

"Yeah," I agreed. I walked over and looked at it. "Except that dead men don't bruise like this. He was still alive when this happened."

"Maybe when he landed in the tree."

I started talking, to Jud Miller but mostly to myself. "He had to be strangled either before he jumped or while he was coming down or after he landed. Those are the only possibilities. Before he jumped Raines couldn't have reached him, and no one could have hidden in the cockpit. While he was coming down no one could have done it, and a device attached to the parachute wouldn't have worked in this way if it worked at all. That leaves only one possibility: he was strangled after he landed in the old oak tree."

Jud Miller chuckled as he got out his embalming equipment. "'Tweren't no haunted

tree strangled him. More likely the first person to reach him did it before the others arrived. I read a story like that once."

"Only trouble with that is, it was me who reached him first."

"Oh."

I signed the death certificate and went back to my office, feeling depressed. I felt right on the verge of figuring it out, but somehow it wouldn't quite come together in my mind. The only thing I knew for sure was that no oak tree had strangled Charlie Bone. The killer was quite human, and so was the motive.

April hadn't yet returned and I was alone in the office. I sat down at my desk and reached into my pocket to have another look at those pictures. My fingers encountered the hard rubber ball I'd picked up earlier.

Could that be the answer?

Had I made the one mistake no doctor should ever make?

I got to my feet just as the outer door opened and Granger Newmark came in. "I've been looking for you, Doc."

"Glad you're here. I just earned my money. I know how Charlie Bone was killed."

"You do?"

"I did a terrible thing this morning, Mr. Newmark."

"And what was that?"

"I pronounced a man dead when he was still alive."

Granger Newmark smiled slightly and slipped a small revolver from his pocket. "You're a smarter man than I thought. Now give me the pictures you took from Hi Gates."

I raised my hands slightly but made no effort to hand him the pictures. As soon as he had those I knew I'd be a dead man. "Can't we talk about this? The pictures are in a safe enough place."

"I don't have time for games, Doc. This whole thing is coming apart." He motioned with the gun.

"Because of Hi Gates? I suppose you didn't

figure on his going through the dead man's belongings and finding those pictures before you got to them. Charlie Bone was blackmailing you, wasn't he? Reminding you of the stag films you produced before you became a big Hollywood name. That sort of publicity could ruin you right now, on the brink of your success in the talkies. And Charlie knew all about it because he'd been your male star in those stag films. So you killed him, in a most ingenious manner. But when you went after the frame blowups he'd made from the stag movie, you found that Hi Gates had discovered them first."

"And even given some to you," Newmark said.

"Did you kill Gates?"

"Not yet. He gave me the rest of the pictures without knowing quite what was going on. But you're a different story, Doc. You know too much."

"You needed a dumb country doctor to work your scheme. That's why you didn't bring one along from the city. Charlie Bone was alive when he landed in that tree. He was simply playing the role of a dead man, as he had before, in two-reelers like *The Premature Burial* and *The Tell-Tale Heart*. I suppose it was a specialty of his. He gave his face a bluish tinge with a bit of makeup before he jumped, and tied that wire around his neck. The scarf kept it from doing any real damage.

"He used a hard rubber ball pressed into his armpit to cut off his pulse. Maybe he had one in each armpit for all I know. Then he let his tongue protrude a bit and acted like a man who'd been strangled to death.

"It was a break for you that the parachute went into the oak tree, because I had to examine him while balanced on a tree limb. Then when I ran in to phone the sheriff, you helped take him down from the tree. A quick blow to the temple knocked him out, and then you strangled him in full view of us all while seeming to unfasten the wire from his neck. Everyone thought Bone was already dead, of course, so even if they noticed you accidentally knock his temple they thought nothing of it."

"That's very good," Newmark said. "Now give me the pictures."

I ignored his request for the moment. "My only question is how you persuaded Bone to act as an accessory to his own murder. I suppose you told him it was a publicity stunt for the movie. 'Stunt man pronounced dead revives ten minutes later.' That sort of thing would get a few headlines, or so you could have convinced Bone. With the cast and crew around he thought he was safe."

"Right again!" He raised the revolver. "But we've had enough talk."

"Once I put the rubber ball together with Bone's movie roles as dead men, I knew how it was done. Maybe his role in *The Premature Burial* even gave you the whole idea. And knowing how it was done, I knew you had to be the killer. Only the producer-director of the film could persuade Bone to pull that stunt. And then I remembered you bent over his body, tugging at the wire around his neck—"

The door behind Newmark opened and April entered with a cheery "Hello there!" It was what I'd been stalling for. Newmark half turned toward her and instantly I threw myself at him, knocking his gun hand to one side.

It was as simple as that.

"Well," Dr. Sam Hawthorne concluded, "that was my one fling at movie-making. Newmark pleaded guilty and served a long term in prison. And *Wings of Glory* was never made. The old oak tree? It was struck by lightning the following year and just toppled over.

"If you'll come again soon, I'll tell you about what happened when a child evangelist came to Northmont and started curing my patients at an old-fashioned revival meeting in a tent. And about how I became the prime suspect in what happened next. Another—ah—libation before you go? One for the road?"

THE INVISIBLE WEAPON

NICHOLAS OLDE

IT IS UNLIKELY that you have ever heard of Nicholas Olde, less likely that you have read his only mystery book, the very scarce short-story collection *The Incredible Adventures of Rowland Hern*, and a veritable certainty that you know nothing about him—a true man of mystery. An exhaustive search through my substantial reference library and an exhausting search of the Internet revealed not a single word about him other than his authorship of that elusive volume of detective stories.

The indefatigable researcher into the world of mystery fiction, Allen J. Hubin, uncovered the fact that Nicholas Olde was the pseudonym of Amian Lister Champneys (1879–1951), which encompasses the entire known universe of information about the author. Examination of the text of his book reveals a bit more about his detective hero, Rowland Hern. In the manner of Sherlock Holmes (whose adventures were emulated by countless authors during Arthur Conan Doyle's lifetime), Hern is a genius private detective with a sidekick who is amazed at his friend's brilliance and narrates the stories in first person. The stories are not very violent and, in fact, seldom deal with murder, focusing instead on crimes and capers, often in a light and breezy manner that has been compared with many of G. K. Chesterton's tales. The murder in the present story does not break new ground, but was not yet the cliché that it became after its publication. While he is certainly a minor writer, Olde's relatively brief tales may be read with pleasure if the reader is not overly insistent on realism.

"The Invisible Weapon" was first published in *The Incredible Adventures of Rowland Hern* (London, Heinemann, 1928).

THE INVISIBLE WEAPON

NICHOLAS OLDE

BEFORE THE SNOW had time to melt the great frost was upon us; and, in a few days, every pond and dyke was covered with half a foot of ice.

Hern and I were spending a week in a village in Lincolnshire, and, at the sight of the frozen fen, we sent to Peterborough for skates in keen anticipation of some happy days upon the ice.

"And now," said Hern, "as our skates will not be here until to-morrow, we had better take this opportunity of going to see Grumby Castle. I had not intended to go until later in the week, but, as neither of us wants to lose a day's skating, let us take advantage of Lord Grumby's permission immediately. The castle, as I told you, is being thoroughly overhauled to be ready for his occupation in the spring."

Thus it was that, that same morning, we turned our backs upon the fen and trudged through the powdery snow into the undulating country towards the west until at last we came within sight of that historic pile and passed through the lodge gates and up the stately avenue. When we reached the great entrance door Hern took out Lord Grumby's letter to show to the caretaker—but it was not a caretaker that opened to our knock. It was a policeman.

The policeman looked at the letter and shook his head.

"I'll ask the inspector anyhow," he said, and disappeared with the letter in his hand.

The inspector arrived on the doorstep a minute later.

"You are not Mr. Rowland Hern, the detective, are you?" he asked.

"The same, inspector," said Hern. "I didn't know that I was known so far afield."

"Good gracious, yes!" said the inspector. "We've all heard of you. There's nothing strange in that. But that you should be here this morning is a very strange coincidence indeed."

"Why so?" asked Hern.

"Because," said the inspector, "there is a problem to be solved in this castle that is just after your own heart. A most mysterious thing has happened here. Please come inside."

We followed him through a vestibule littered with builders' paraphernalia and he led us up the wide stairway.

"A murder has been committed in this castle—not two hours since," said the inspector. "There is only one man who could have done it—and he could not have done it."

"It certainly does seem to be a bit of a puzzle when put like that," said Hern. "Are you sure that it is not a riddle, like 'When is a door not a door?'"

We had reached the top of the stairs.

"I will tell you the whole story from start to—well, to the present moment," said the inspector. "You see this door on the left? It is the door of the ante-room to the great ballroom; and the ante-room is vital to this mystery for two reasons. In the first place, it is, for the time being, absolutely the only way by which the ballroom can be entered. The door at the other end has

569

been bricked up in accordance with his lordship's scheme of reconstruction, and the proposed new doorway has not yet been knocked through the wall: (that is one occasion when a door is not a door)," he added with a smile; "and even the fireplaces have been removed and the chimneys blocked since a new heating system has rendered them superfluous. In the second place," he continued, "the work in the ballroom itself being practically finished, this ante-room has been, for the time being, appropriated as an office by the contractors. Consequently it is occupied all day by draughtsmen and clerks and others, and no one can enter or leave the ballroom during office hours unseen.

"Among other alterations and improvements that have been carried out is, as I have said, the installation of a heating apparatus; and there appears to have been a good deal of trouble over this.

"It has been installed by a local engineer named Henry Whelk, and the working of it under tests has been so unsatisfactory that his lordship insisted, some time since, on calling in a consulting engineer, a man named Blanco Persimmon.

"Henry Whelk has, from the first, very much resented the 'interference,' as he calls it, of this man; and the relations between the two have been, for some weeks, strained almost to the breaking-point.

"A few days ago the contractor received a letter from Mr. Persimmon saying that he would be here this morning and would make a further test of the apparatus. He asked them to inform Whelk and to see to the firing of the boiler.

"Persimmon arrived first and went into the ballroom to inspect the radiators. He was there, talking to one of the clerks, when Whelk arrived and the clerk returned at once to the ante-room and shut the ballroom door behind him.

"Five minutes later Whelk came out and told the clerks to have the cock turned on that allows the hot water to circulate in that branch of the system, and to see that the ballroom door was not opened until Mr. Persimmon came out, as

he was going to test the temperature. He spoke with his usual resentment of the consultant and told the clerks that the latter had imagined that he could see a crack in one of the radiators which he thought would leak under pressure, and that that was his real reason for having the ballroom branch of the heating system connected up.

"In the meantime he took a seat in the ante-room with the intention of waiting there to hear Persimmon's report when he came out. Mr. Hern," said the inspector gravely, "Persimmon never did come out."

"Do you mean that he is still there?" asked Hern.

"He is still there," said the inspector. "He will be there until the ambulance comes to take him to the mortuary."

"Has a doctor seen the body?" asked Hern.

"Yes," said the inspector. "He left five minutes before you came. He went by a field path, so you did not meet him in the avenue.

"Persimmon died of a fracture at the base of the skull caused by a violent blow delivered with some very heavy weapon. But we cannot find any weapon at all.

"Of course the clerks detained Whelk when, Persimmon failing to appear, they discovered the body. They kept Whelk here until our arrival, and he is now detained at the police-station. We have searched him, at his own suggestion; but nothing heavier than a cigarette-holder was found upon his person."

"What about his boots?" asked Hern.

"Well, he has shoes on," said the inspector, "and very light shoes too—unusually light for snowy weather. They could not possibly have struck the terrible blow that broke poor Persimmon's skull and smashed the flesh to a pulp. Whelk had an attaché-case too. I have it here still, and it contains nothing but papers."

"I suppose," said Hern, "that you have made sure that there is no weapon concealed about the body of Persimmon?"

"Yes," said the inspector. "I considered that possibility and have made quite sure."

"Could not a weapon have been thrown out of one of the windows?" asked Hern.

"It could have been," answered the inspector, "but it wasn't. That is certain because no one could open them without leaving finger-marks. The insides of the sashes have only just been painted, and the paint is still wet; while the hooks for lifting them have not yet been fixed.

"I have examined every inch of every sash systematically and thoroughly, and no finger has touched them. They are very heavy sashes too, and it would require considerable force to raise them without the hooks. No. It is a puzzle. And, although I feel that I must detain him, I cannot believe that Whelk can be the culprit. Would a guilty man wait there, actually abusing his victim before witnesses, until his crime was discovered? Impossible! Again, could he have inflicted that ghastly wound with a cigarette-holder? Quite impossible! But then the whole thing is quite impossible from beginning to end."

"May I go into the ballroom?" said Hern.

"Certainly," said the inspector.

He led the way through the ante-room, where three or four scared clerks were simulating industry at desks and drawing-boards, and we entered the great ballroom.

"Here is poor Persimmon's body," said the inspector; and we saw the sprawling corpse, with its terribly battered skull, face down, upon the floor near one of the radiators.

"So the radiator did leak after all," said Hern, pointing to a pool of water beside it.

"Yes," said the inspector. "But it does not seem to have leaked since I had the apparatus disconnected. The room was like an oven when I came in."

Hern went all round the great bare hall examining everything—floor, walls, and windows. Then he looked closely at the radiators.

"There is no part of these that he could detach?" he asked. "No pipes or valves?"

"Certainly not, unless he had a wrench," said the inspector; "and he hadn't got a wrench."

"Could anyone have come through the windows from outside?" asked Horn.

"They could be reached by a ladder," said the inspector; "but the snow beneath them is untrodden."

"Well," said Hern; "there doesn't seem to be anything here to help us. May I have a look at Whelk's case and papers?"

"Certainly," said the inspector. "Come into the ante-room. I've locked them in a cupboard."

We followed him and he fetched a fair-sized attaché-case, laid it on a table and opened it.

Hern took out the papers and examined the inside of the case.

"A botanical specimen!" he exclaimed, picking up a tiny blade of grass. "Did he carry botanical specimens about in his case? It seems a bit damp inside," he added; "especially at the side furthest fron the handle. But let's have a look at the papers. Hullo! What's this?"

"It seems to be nothing but some notes for his business diary," said the inspector.

'Feb. 12. Letter from Jones. Mr. Filbert called
    re estimate.
'Feb. 13. Office closed.
'Feb. 14. Letter from Perkins & Fisher re
    Grumby Castle.
'Feb. 15. Letter from Smith & Co. Wrote
    Messrs. Caraway re repairs to boiler. Visit
    Grumby Castle and meet Persimmon
    10:30 a.m.'

"February the 15th is to-day."

"Yes," said Hern. "The ink seems to have run a bit, doesn't it? Whereabouts does Whelk live?"

"He lives in Market Grumby," said the inspector. "His house is not far from where he is now—the police-station. Market Grumby lies over there—north of the castle. That foot-path that goes off at right angles from the avenue leads to the Market Grumby road."

Hern put everything back carefully into the case—even the blade of grass—and handed it back to the inspector.

"When do you expect the ambulance?" he asked.

"It should be here in a few minutes," said the inspector. "I must wait, of course, until it comes."

"Well," said Hern. "I suppose, when the body has gone, there will be no harm in mopping up that mess in there? There is a certain amount of blood as well as that pool of water."

"No harm at all," said the inspector.

"Well then," said Hern. "Please have it done. And, if it is not asking too much, could you oblige me by having the hot water turned on once more and waiting until I come back. I shall not be away for long; and I think that it may help in the solution of your problem."

"Certainly," said the inspector.

Hern and I went out again into the snowy drive and found, without difficulty, the path that led towards Market Grumby, for, in spite of the covering snow, it was clearly marked by footprints.

We walked along until we saw the opening into the road. A cottage stood on one side of the path, close to the road; and on the other side was a pond.

This was covered, like every pond, with a thick covering of ice, but in one spot, opposite the cottage, the ice had been broken with a pick and here an old man was dipping a bucket.

The water in the hole looked black against the gleaming ice and the sun glinted on the edges of the fragments loosened and thrown aside by the pick.

"Took a bit of trouble to break it, I expect," said Hern to the old man.

"Took me half an hour," grumbled the old fellow; "it's that thick."

"Is that the way to Market Grumby?" asked Hern, pointing to the road.

"That's it," said the other, and went into the cottage with his bucket.

The snow in the few yards between the cottage and the hole in the ice was trodden hard by the hobnailed boots of the old man, but Hern pointed out to me that another set of footprints, of a much less bucolic type, could be seen beside them.

"Let us go back," he said, "and see how the inspector is getting on with the heating apparatus."

"I've had it on for half an hour now," said the inspector when we got back to the ante-room. "The ambulance came soon after you went out."

"Well," said Hern. "Let us see how that leak is going on"; and he opened the door of the ballroom.

"Good heavens," cried the inspector. "It's not leaking now."

"It never did leak," said Hern.

"What is the meaning of it all?" asked the inspector.

"You remember," said Hern, "that you came to the conclusion that if Whelk had been guilty he would have got away before his crime had been discovered.

"Well, my conclusion is different. In fact, I think that, if he had been innocent, he would not have waited."

"Why so?" asked the inspector.

"I will tell you," said Hern. "Whelk had to stay or he would certainly have been hanged. He hated Persimmon and had every reason for taking his life. If he had gone away you would have said that he had hidden the weapon that killed Persimmon.

"Don't you see that his only chance was to stay until you had searched him and found that he had no weapon? Was not that a clear proof of his innocence?"

"But there must have been some weapon," exclaimed the worried inspector. "Where is the weapon?"

"There was a weapon," said Hern, "and you and I saw it lying beside the corpse."

"I saw no weapon," said the inspector.

"Do you remember," said Hern, "that your first account of the problem made me think of a certain old riddle? Well, the answer to this problem is the answer to a new riddle: 'When is a weapon not a weapon?'"

"I give it up," said the inspector promptly.

"The answer to that riddle," said Hern, "is 'when it melts.'"

The inspector gasped.

"I will tell you," said Hern, "what happened. There is a pond close to the Market Grumby road, and Whelk passed this as he was coming here this morning to meet his enemy. The thick ice on that pond has been broken so that a bucket may be dipped, and chunks of broken ice lie all around the hole. Whelk saw these, and a terrible thought came into his wicked head. Everything fitted perfectly. He had found a weapon that would do its foul work and disappear. He picked up the biggest block of ice that would go inside his case. I dare say that it weighed twenty pounds. He waited until his enemy stooped to examine a radiator, and then he opened his case and brought down his twenty-pound sledgehammer on the victim's skull.

"Then he put his weapon against the radiator, had the heat turned on, told his story about a leak, and waited calmly until a search should prove his innocence.

"But by the very quality for which he chose his weapon, that weapon has betrayed him in the end. For that jagged chunk of ice began to melt before its time—very slightly, it is true, but just enough to damp the side of the case on which it rested, to make the ink run on his papers and to set loose one tiny blade of grass that had frozen onto it as it lay beside the pond. A very tiny blade but big enough to slay the murderer.

"If you will go to the pond, inspector, you will find footsteps leading to it which are not the cottager's footsteps; and, if you compare them with the shoes that Henry Whelk is wearing, you will find that they tally.

"And, if they do not tally, then you may ask your friends a new riddle."

"What is that?" asked the officer.

"'When is a detective not a detective?'" replied my friend; "and the answer will be 'When he is Rowland Hern.'"

THE CONFESSION OF ROSA VITELLI

RAY CUMMINGS

ALTHOUGH HE WROTE prolifically in several genres, mainly for the pulp magazines in the years between the two World Wars, it was his prodigious body of work in the science fiction and fantasy field that caused Raymond King Cummings (1887–1957) to be described as the American H. G. Wells and one of the founders of the science fiction pulp story.

Born in New York City to wealthy parents, he attended Princeton University and is reputed to have mastered the entire three-year undergraduate physics curriculum in three months. The only job he ever held was as a technical writer and editor for Thomas A. Edison from 1914 to 1919, after which he resigned to become a full-time writer. His first story, "The Girl in the Golden Atom," was published in 1919 and was spectacularly successful, finding its way into book form in 1922, a prestigious occurrence for any American writer of science fiction of the era. It introduced what soon became a cliché of the genre, likening atoms to tiny suns and planets that are the homes of minuscule life forms, sometimes primitive, sometimes far advanced. Over the course of his career he produced about seven hundred fifty short stories, novellas, and novels; some sources credit him with more than a thousand works. His obscure detective series about the Scientific Crime Club was discovered in an elegant English magazine, *The Sketch*, all twelve stories being published in 1925 (July 8 to September 23). If they were previously published in an American pulp magazine, as would be expected of an American pulp writer, it has yet to be reported.

"The Confession of Rosa Vitelli" was first published in the August 19, 1925, issue of *The Sketch*; its first book appearance was in *Tales from the Scientific Crime Club* (London, Ferret, 1979), in an edition of only one hundred copies.

THE CONFESSION OF ROSA VITELLI

RAY CUMMINGS

"YOU SAY THIS Rosa Vitelli has confessed to the murder," exclaimed the Banker. "There's no mystery when you have a——"

The Doctor nodded. "Quite so. But, gentlemen, though she admits having killed the girl Angelina, she will not tell how she did it. There is considerable mystery about that." The Doctor gazed around the small private Clubroom, with its group of interested members; and then indicated the two visitors beside him. He added: "Mr. Green and Sergeant Marberry here are puzzled. More than that——"

"Suppose you give us an outline of the case," the Chemist interrupted. "If you think we can be of any help——"

"I will. As I told you, Sergeant Marberry—a good friend of mine—has been assigned to this Vitelli affair. His knowledge of Italian—he is very frequently given such cases. And Mr. Green, one of the Assistant District Attorneys, has the case in his office for prosecution."

The Banker raised his hand impatiently. "The murder, Frank——"

"Quite so," smiled the Doctor. "Briefly, the circumstances are these. Some three weeks ago—on the early morning of Jan. 10 to be exact—a young Italian girl was found dead. She lived in the Italian section south of Greenwich Village. Name, Angelina Torno. Age, twenty-three. Unmarried. An extremely pretty girl—a factory worker. With another girl roommate, she occupied a small flat on the third floor of a tene-ment building. This other girl does not enter the case—she had been on Staten Island with a sick mother for several weeks, leaving Angelina alone in the flat.

"On the early morning of Jan. 10, one of the fourth-floor tenants came downstairs, and in the dim, badly ventilated third-floor hall-way, smelled gas. There is no electric light in this building—only gas. Angelina did not answer thumps upon her door. It was later broken in. Her flat was found flooded with gas, and the girl in bed—dead."

"Suicide!" murmured the Banker. "You said murder——"

The Doctor smiled grimly. "Wait, George. It was murder, not suicide. The night of Jan. 9 and 10 was extremely cold—you all remember that three-day cold spell we had. Angelina slept that night with all her windows closed, even the transom over her door to the public hall was closed. All the doors and windows closed, and locked on the inside. The outside temperature was down to zero that night. It was perfectly natural for an Italian girl to shut herself up without fresh air and go to bed.

"But it was murder, not suicide, for though the small flat was full of gas, and the girl dead of asphyxiation, every gas-cock in the flat was turned off securely. That was not suicide, gentlemen. You don't kill yourself by turning on the gas, and then get up and turn it off."

The Astronomer murmured: "But how——"

"Exactly so." The Doctor glanced at his watch. "I must hasten. . . . Jack, are you and Professor Walton ready with everything?"

The Very Young Man nodded eagerly. "Yes, Sir. Everything's ready."

"Good. . . . Gentlemen, this Rosa Vitelli is in custody. Mr. Green has ordered her to be brought here to-night—they will have her here any moment. In a word, the Vitellis occupy the third floor flat across the hall from Angelina. A young, rather well-educated Italian-American couple. Rosa, eighteen; and Giorgio, twenty-six. Married just over a year. No children.

"Sergeant Marberry here was assigned to the case. Marberry established at once that young Vitelli had been paying undue attention to the Torno girl—so much so that he and his wife had had violent quarrels over it. After the murder, when the Vitellis were about to be arrested, Rosa gave way under Mr. Green's questioning and confessed. Jealousy was her motive. She was afraid she would lose her husband to the other girl. And doubtless she had good reason to suppose it.

"All that is clear enough. The queer part is that Rosa absolutely refuses to tell how she committed the murder. Nothing can break down that refusal. If by some unknown method she got into Angelina's flat, turned on the gas, and then turned it off and got out again—how she could leave the doors and windows locked on the inside, with a key on the inside lock of the hall door—all this she refuses to explain."

"Why won't she explain?" the Alienist demanded.

"There you have it! Why won't she? That also we do not know. But she will not. Her husband possibly could tell how she did it, but he maintains only a stubborn, sullen silence, and says he does not know."

Sergeant Marberry—a slender, dark-haired man, nearing forty—said abruptly: "You have not told them, Dr. Adams, that we think we know how the crime was committed. This Rosa Vitelli——"

The Doctor interrupted. "Sergeant Mar-

berry has unearthed a few other facts which might be used against the Vitelli girl to break her down. But it is only theory—not proof—and the difficulty is that if he and Mr. Green used them, and Rosa did not break down—nothing could ever be accomplished."

"I don't understand," the Banker exclaimed. "This girl has confessed to a murder. Why not go ahead and sentence her? Why bother with *how* she did it?"

"You'll see in a moment, George. It is a problem Mr. Green has several times had to face—particularly in dealing with Italians. Let me go on. Three significant facts were brought to light. One: A fourth-floor tenant over the Vitelli flat noticed that night a peculiar smell coming up. Something burning—a stench——"

"Burning a body!" the Banker ejaculated.

"George, don't be absurd. Angelina's body was found peacefully in bed—asphyxiated. The second fact, gentlemen. Whenever a peculiar, novel, and yet simple crime is committed, other criminals imitate it. You remember the 'poison needle' craze that swept over the country some years ago? And when bichloride of mercury once got publicity as a comfortable means of suicide, it was used widely."

"You mean that someone has already imitated this crime?" the Banker demanded.

"I do not. I mean that Sergeant Marberry felt at once that this crime might be in imitation of a previous one. Where would Rosa Vitelli get the ingenuity to plan it—to originate it? Sergeant Marberry guessed that she did not. Purely a guess, but on the chance, he searched all the New York newspapers of the previous few days. He found what he was looking for. On Jan. 7, in the Bronx, an attempted murder almost asphyxiated a whole family. Understand me, I don't mean to imply that this had any connection with the Vitellis—except to give Rosa the inspiration as to how she might murder Angelina. This Bronx affair concerned obscure people—and since no one was injured it occupied very little news space. None of you gentlemen noticed it, perhaps. But Sergeant Marberry did. And he saw in it a possible explanation of this murder of Angelina Torno."

Several of the Club members interrupted with questions, but the Doctor ignored them. "If Rosa Vitelli read that little news item—and possibly she did, as it was also run in the Italian paper which the Vitellis are in the habit of buying—then we can assume that she might easily have been prompted to imitate it. The circumstances were the same, and——"

"What circumstances?" demanded the Chemist. "You don't mean the motives?"

"No; I mean the method by which the murder was committed." The Doctor took a newspaper clipping from his pocket. "Here it is, read it. And then I'll tell you a surprising suspicion which Mr. Green and Sergeant Marberry feel is close to the real truth."

A knock sounded on the Clubroom door. The Doctor hastily disposed of his clipping. "No more now, gentlemen. You'll have to wait. Just sit quietly and watch. They're here, Sergeant Marberry."

The door had opened. Two policemen and a blonde, stocky man in civilian clothes entered with the girl Rosa Vitelli. And with them another young man—tall, slim, and dark—Giorgio Vitelli, husband of Rosa. The blonde young man—from the Assistant District Attorney's office—greeted his superior, and with a low command seated Rosa in a chair facing the Doctor. Her husband sat near her; the two policemen retired unobtrusively to the other side of the room and sat down, staring around curiously.

Very briefly the Doctor introduced the newcomers, and then, standing over Rosa, he demanded, "We want to know how you killed Angelina—will you tell us now?"

"No," she said sullenly, with her gaze on the floor. She was a small, dark-haired girl, typically Italian-American. Pretty in a pale, bedraggled fashion. She sat hunched in her chair, staring stolidly at the floor by the Doctor's feet.

"You won't?" he reiterated sharply.

No answer.

"Rosa, look up here."

Her gaze came reluctantly up to his face.

"Rosa, why won't you?"

Still no answer. The Doctor shifted his question; his tone became less harsh. "Why did you kill Angelina? You'll tell these gentlemen *that*, won't you?"

"Yes," she said. Her dark eyes flashed, colour flooded into her pale cheeks. She burst out passionately: "Angelina steal my Giorgio. You know that! Everybody knows it. And so I kill her."

"Gad!" murmured the Astronomer to the man beside him, "she may have had good reason, from her view-point, to kill that other girl. The sympathetic type. It's lucky she confessed—you'd never get a jury to convict a girl like that. And where are you going to get a judge to sentence her very heavily?"

The Assistant District Attorney heard the comments and flashed a warning glance. The Doctor was persisting: "Yes, Rosa; we understand that. But you know it's wrong to kill, don't you?" Her gaze again had fallen. "Don't you?"

She burst out: "No! That Angelina do wrong—she steal my husband. I tell her to let him alone."

"How did you kill her, Rosa? You planned it ahead of time, didn't you? . . . I say you planned it very carefully, didn't you?"

Silence.

"You won't tell?"

"No."

"Why not?"

Still no answer. And abruptly the girl looked up with a glance almost of appeal.

"Why won't you tell, Rosa?"

The Astronomer leaned towards the Assistant District Attorney. "She's been advised against it. Knows you are trying to establish premeditation."

"Yes, of course. But that doesn't apply to the first moment of her confession. She was almost hysterical—and she isn't clever enough to think of a thing like that. Sh!"

"We're going to make you tell," the Doctor was saying gruffly. "That's why we brought you here." It startled the girl. She gripped the sides of her chair with her small white hands.

Giorgio exclaimed, "You let my Rosa alone! I will get her lawyer." He started to his feet toward a telephone across the room, but the Doctor waved him back.

"Sit down, Vitelli. Your lawyer wouldn't have time to get here now. Besides, I think we won't question Rosa any further." He added abruptly: "Gentlemen, I want you all to listen to me very carefully. And you two also, Rosa and Giorgio. You, Rosa! You think we know nothing about this except what you've told us, don't you? Well, you're mistaken—we know a great deal about it." A grim smile pulled at the Doctor's lips. "This is the New York Scientific Club—you know that. You were both born in New York, you're both intelligent enough to know what science is—what it can do. We brought you here, Rosa Vitelli, to *show you* with your own eyes how you killed Angelina Torno. We guessed how you did it—Sergeant Marberry guessed it—but it was only a guess. Not proof. Then, last week, we of the Scientific Club, using apparatus which you will see working in a moment, *proved* it. Ah, that interests you, Rosa, doesn't it? Well, you watch and you will see." His tone grew ironical. "If we show you anything wrong, you can tell us." He whirled on Giorgio. "You, Vitelli, you'd better watch closely also. You'll want to repeat it all to your wife's lawyer. . . . By the way, gentlemen, I have not yet told you that Rosa's father is a fairly wealthy contractor down on Staten Island. He has retained quite able counsel to defend his daughter."

The Vitellis sat silent under this swift tirade. Several of the Club members were murmuring to each other, and the Doctor raised his hand for silence.

"You gentlemen will be interested in this demonstration. It involves a well-known scientific principle which only recently has been brought to its present practical perfection. Professor Walton here"—the Doctor indicated a frail, grey-haired man who sat apart with the excited Very Young Man—"Professor Walton has perfected an apparatus which he and Jack Bruce are shortly to operate for us, and which

will show Rosa Vitelli in the very act of murdering Angelina Torno. . . . Sit down, Rosa—we're not going to hurt you. . . . No, Vitelli, you don't need the lawyer—you can tell him all about it." The Doctor gazed over the room, and when he resumed his tone was quieter.

"Gentlemen, the scientific principle involved is that of light-rays. Light, as you know, is a vibration—of the ether, let us say for convenience. A vibration which travels at the rate of one hundred and eighty-six thousand three hundred and twenty-four miles a second. A small boy once asked me a very naïve question which I am going to ask you gentlemen. He demanded of me, 'Dr. Adams, where does light go when it goes *out*?' You need not smile—I am quite serious." The Doctor was watching Rosa closely without appearing to do so. A few of the Club members had smiled, but Rosa and her husband sat stolid—the young Italian listening intently and with apparent intelligence to the Doctor's words, and Rosa staring sullenly at the floor.

"I repeat that, gentlemen. Where does light go when it goes out? Let me show you something." He signalled to the Very Young Man, who produced a candle and placed it upright on the centre table. Rosa turned to face it, staring fascinated while the Very Young Man lighted it.

"Now, Jack."

The Very Young Man switched off the centre electrolier; the room was plunged into gloom—flickering yellow candlelight which disclosed little more than the table-top and the Doctor's standing figure. The Doctor went on: "Light-rays from this candle are bringing the image of it to your eyes at the rate of one hundred eighty-six thousand miles a second. An inconceivable velocity measured over so short a distance. You see my hand reaching toward the candle? I touch it with my finger—so. You gentlemen understand me, you did not see me touch that candle at the *exact* instant I actually touched it. There was a tiny interval of time in between—the time it took those light-rays to carry the image ten or fifteen feet.

"Is that clear? I assure you it has a bearing

upon the murder of Angelina Torno! I perform an act in this candlelight; I touch the candle—so. And a tiny fraction *after* I touch it, you see me touch it. A very tiny fraction of a second over such a short distance. But suppose you are ten times as far away, it will then be a tenfold greater interval of time. Then assume that you are on the moon, with a telescope powerful enough to observe me. I put a finger on the candle, and it is well over a second later that you see me do it. On the sun, some eight or nine minutes would have elapsed. On the nearest of the stars you would not see my action until more than four years after I performed it. And, observing me from one of the more distant stars, you would have to wait several hundred years!

"To go back to the child's question—watch my hand now, snuffing out the candle." The Doctor pinched out the wick; the room was black. Amid a shuffling of feet and a startled cry from Rosa, the Doctor's voice cried, "Lights, Jack!"

The lights flashed on. The Doctor resumed quietly, "You saw me snuff the candle. Those light-rays brought the image to you at that tremendous velocity. They went on past you. Where? Out! Quite so. But not obliterated, gentlemen. Not lost. Mark you that, for it is important. We are accustomed to a mode of reasoning which says that my act of snuffing that candle is *in the past,* dead and irrevocably gone. Not so! If you were watching me from the sun, at this present moment you would observe the candle still lighted and several minutes yet to wait before you would see me snuff it! To an observer on the sun, therefore, that particular act *has not yet been performed.* It is not in the past, but in the future.

"Do I make myself entirely clear? What I'm getting at, specifically, is this. The visual representation of every act ever performed is in existence at this present moment. Light does not go out, in the sense of being destroyed. It goes away. The light rays which shone upon the white sands of San Salvador when Columbus knelt there have not yet reached some of the distant stars. If you were on one of those stars, mechanically equipped to receive that image upon the retina of your eye, you could watch tonight and see Columbus discovering America!

"Thus no act can be termed accurately *of the past,* without reference to the equipment of the observer. Let me be still more specific. We think of the murder of Angelina Torno as an act of the past. It is not, if we could equip ourselves to receive the light-rays carrying it. I said light-rays did not go out, but away. They do that—but they also come back. Reflected light. . . . Rosa, are you listening to all this?"

The girl raised her eyes from the floor. "Yes," she said sullenly. "I kill Angelina. Why you bother about me? I kill her, I tol' you."

"Yes," agreed the Doctor. "But I want you to listen, and in a moment watch closely what we're going to show you." He flashed a look at the young husband. "You're listening too, Vitelli?"

"Yes, I listen; but——"

"But you don't make much out of it?"

"No. Rosa's lawyer, he——"

"You can tell him," the Doctor interrupted. "You'll have a lot to tell him before we're finished. . . . I was speaking of reflected light, gentlemen. It is reflected everywhere. Sunlight goes to the moon, and is reflected back to the earth. Our own light—itself mainly sunlight—goes to the moon, and comes back to us again, and we call it moonlight. And here on earth light is everywhere reflected back and forth, from the ceiling to the floor of this very room—from each of its walls to the other. Reflected constantly back and forth, like the reverberating echoes of sound."

The Doctor paused momentarily, then resumed. "I come now to the crux of the whole matter. Light-rays, you must realise, are never lost. Their velocity never changes. Nor do they in their entirety necessarily leave the neighbourhood of their source. The sound of my voice—also vibrations which travel at the rate of something more than a thousand feet a second—will echo back and forth across this room for, theoretically, a limitless period. Growing dimmer—yes. Almost instantly, far below the very narrow range of our human hearing.

"And so it is with light-vibrations. The light-vibrations that candle sent out are still reverberating across this room. Altered in form. Dimmer—yes. Almost instantly far below the narrow range of our human sight. But, gentlemen, they are still here. And we could still see the candle being snuffed if we could isolate those light-vibrations and again make them visible."

There was no one who spoke when the Doctor halted. Rosa still kept her gaze on the floor. But, though the girl's mentality could not follow the Doctor's reasoning, Giorgio quite evidently understood to what this scientific analysis might lead. He gazed at his wife with an obvious, growing fear, and then back to the Doctor, as though fascinated.

The Doctor continued: "In principle, gentlemen, I have told you it all. Some of you, even, are familiar with the detailed workings of Professor Walton's apparatus. To the rest of you I need only add that he has succeeded—crudely, still with much to perfect—in isolating and magnifying, let me say, otherwise invisible light-vibrations. The modern radio does something of the kind with otherwise inaudible vibrations of sound. To use popular language, Professor Walton 'tunes back' amid the mingled vibrations of light until he has isolated those he is seeking. They become crudely visible. The past, in so far as that particular scene is concerned, becomes the present."

The Doctor's voice rose to sudden vehemence. "In that tenement building where Angelina Torno lived, there are still vibrations of light carrying the scene of the murder. Professor Walton's apparatus is connected at this moment with that building. Gentlemen, you are about to witness—not a representation of the murder—but the actual murder itself!"

As though his words were a signal, the Very Young Man, without warning, switched off the electrolier. The room went black. For a second or two only, then a purple beam of light sprang from an unnoticed orifice in the wall. It bathed the room in a deep, lurid glare. The thing was startling. Rosa screamed. Giorgio was on his feet, but the Detective pulled him back to his chair. Over the confusion the Doctor's voice sounded—

"Quiet, gentlemen! We did not mean to startle you."

The Very Young Man, sprung suddenly into action, was lowering a cord. Professor Walton hurried past him—and, unnoticed in the purple glare, went through a side door and out of the room. The cord which the Very Young Man was operating lowered from the ceiling a shimmering veil—a rectangle some ten feet wide and eight feet high. It hung from the ceiling almost to the floor. The occupants of the room all turned to face it. The purple beam of light from the wall orifice struck it from behind. It glowed—purple, then dissolving into scarlet: a blood-red veil, still quivering from the movement of its descent.

The Doctor's voice said: "The fabric of that veil is finely woven wire. The light is from Professor Walton's apparatus in the adjoining room. Vitelli, I want you to watch closely. Your lawyer will be interested in this. You, Rosa! You hear me? You watch this! I am going to show you yourself, in the very act of murdering Angelina Torno!"

A silence fell over the room. The club members, the Vitellis, the Detective, the Assistant District Attorney, and the two policemen—all staring with a silent, awed fascination. The veil, blood-red, was creeping and crawling with colour. Spots of shadow seemed forming upon it. Vague, distorted, formless blurs of movement, shifting slowly as a cloud-bank—shapes dissolving formlessly one into the other. A hum now filled the room, low at first, then louder—a penetrating, electrical hum. The Doctor raised his voice above it.

"Those blurs which you see are scenes in the third-floor hall-way of the tenement building in question. Professor Walton's observation station is erected there. To the left is the door to the Vitelli flat. Angelina's door is directly across the hall to the right. Formless blurs, gentlemen, as yet. But wait a moment. Professor Walton is 'tuning back,' so to speak. Back through the mingled light-vibrations until he reaches those of the murder scene. Watch, Rosa! Soon you will see."

No need for his admonition. In the glare of red light the girl's figure showed as she sat in her chair, staring at the blood-red veil. The shadows there grew denser. Moving shapes—condensing, taking form. The hum in the room went up an ascending scale, then struck a level. Like an accelerating dynamo, reaching its pitch and holding it. The Doctor spoke louder.

"Now! You see? We are back to the morning after the murder."

The blurred outlines of a tenement hall-way became visible. To the left, a wooden door—old-fashioned, dingy, with a glass transom above it. To the right, a similar door. A dingy flight of stairs in the background, leading upward. In the centre, depending from the low ceiling, a ramshackle chandelier. On the floor, worn, ragged oilcloth. People—half-a-dozen men in uniform, Detective Marberry—moved about the scene, opened Angelina's door to the right, entered, and emerged. The whole a deep crimson. Blurred, occasionally grotesquely distorted; then again clearly distinguishable.

"The morning after the murder," the Doctor repeated. "Imperfect—as imperfect an apparatus as were our first, unimproved radios. . . . And now—look, Rosa! Now we are going back to the murder itself!"

The crimson scene blurred again into formless crawling patches of light and shade. The hum slid upward to a still higher pitch, held even, and the blurs clarified. The hall-way again. Empty and dark—so dark that only the stairs and the dim outlines of the doors left and right were visible. An empty, motionless scene. Sinister, expectant. And then, very slowly, the left-hand door was opening. There was no light behind it; only a dark rectangle of shadow there. Then a flare. A pencil-point of light showed—moved—came out of the doorway, resolved itself

into a human hand holding a lighted candle. For a moment nothing else in the blood-red gloom was visible. The hand with the candle advanced slowly into the centre of the hall-way. And now a dim blur of human shape beside it seemed almost distinguishable.

The hand with the candle stopped. The candle-light seemed unnaturally to disclose nothing. Then the other hand appeared—a hand reaching upward, holding a long rubber pipe of the sort used to connect small gas-heaters. The hand slipped the rubber pipe over the hallway gas-jet, fumbled there, then moved away, carrying the pipe to the transom above Angelina's door, pushing the transom open cautiously, sticking the pipe-end through, and closing the transom close upon it.

All blurred, dark-red, and barely distinguishable. Swiftly done; a few seconds only. And then abruptly the scene brightened and clarified further. The outlines of the figure adjusting the pipe, turning on the gas, suddenly became plainly visible. Not a woman's figure! Not Rosa Vitelli! The figure of a tall, slender, dark-haired man. Giorgio Vitelli! Unmistakable!

It was so abruptly disclosed that a gasp ran over the room. The hum ceased. The bloodlight went out. From the black darkness of the Club-room came the sounds of scuffling feet; an outcry from Rosa—her terrified, despairing moan in Italian: "They know I did not do it! Giorgio! Beloved! Run—run!" Her wild burst of sobbing; pattering footsteps; the clatter of a chair overturned; a thump; a body falling; an oath from the Very Young Man, and then his voice rising above the tumult—

"Light the lights! I've got him! Light the lights, someone! I tell you I've got him!"

The lights flashed on. Rosa sat in her chair, sobbing. On the floor by the door lay the struggling form of Giorgio Vitelli, with the muscular Very Young Man upon him. The Detective leaped to Rosa, gripping her by the shoulders, shaking her. "You saw that, Rosa! Why did you tell us you killed Angelina? You didn't kill her!"

"No! No!"

Still shaking her—"Why did you say you did? Why?"

"My Giorgio—he—he tol' me to say I did it."

She was sobbing, oblivious to what was going on around her. The Assistant District Attorney rushed up to them. The Detective shook the girl again. "He told you to confess? Why—why did you do it?"

"He tol' me to say I did it—because I'm a girl. I get off. He tol' me that. And you—you try always to make me say how I kill Angelina." She broke into a hysterical flood of Italian. The Detective released her. He said swiftly—

"As we thought. Says she never knew how or why her husband killed Angelina. She didn't know how it was done, so, of course, she couldn't tell us. It's obvious that he was afraid to let her know—afraid she might be clumsy and say something that would arouse our suspicions—incriminate him. Is *he* talking? Now's the psychological moment—we must *make* him talk!"

But the Very Young Man had already made Vitelli talk. Cuffed him on the head, choked him—until the Doctor and others pulled them apart. And in the confusion, hearing Rosa blurt out the truth, and before he could gather his wits, Vitelli had confessed.

When the room had quieted, with the two policemen in charge of Vitelli, and Rosa still sobbing softly to herself, the Doctor spoke—

"We have been successful, gentlemen—and I think that you probably understand almost everything which has transpired. Professor Walton would have me tell you that in fundamental principle every theory of light which I gave you is quite correct. Indeed, it is a hope of his that some day an apparatus such as I have described will be perfected. But for our ignorant present we had to use a motion picture. That was what you saw, gentlemen—a purposely crude and jumbled motion picture tinted red, made a few days ago with a young Italian actor playing the part of Vitelli. The scene so blurred and dark it was easy to catch the likeness.

"For the crime itself: Sergeant Marberry unearthed that newspaper clipping. I chanced to see it myself the day it was published. A rubber tube was discovered in a hall-way—a tube leading gas from the hall-way jet through a transom into a flat. A whole family narrowly escaped asphyxiation. No motive, no criminal was located—and the thing went by the board. But it gave Vitelli his inspiration—and, reading it, Marberry saw at once that the Torno girl could have been murdered in similar fashion.

"Other facts which Marberry brought to light made that assumption still more probable. The gas-jet in the hall-way on the Vitelli-Torno floor was *lighted* the night before; and in the morning the janitor found it turned out. Also, on the oil-cloth floor of the hall-way Marberry found drippings of red wax. They suggested that a candle had been used by the criminal to furnish light. Red wax. Perhaps one of those small Christmas candles of which Italians are so fond. And it was only a few weeks after Christmas. . . . As a matter of fact, the stump of a red-wax Christmas candle was found in the Vitelli kitchen.

"Another fact. Above the Vitellis, the tenants smelled a peculiar burning smell that night. Burning rubber! They recognised it at once. We knew then that the gas tube had probably been burned in the Vitelli grate—and now Rosa tells us this moment that her husband did burn something in the grate that night and would not let her know what it was. This grate, by the way, is a unique feature of the Vitelli flat—the only grate in the building.

"All this indicated to us that either one of the Vitellis was guilty, or perhaps both. Especially in view of their turbulent relations with Angelina. Then, before any of the evidence had been used against them, Rosa confessed. It is obvious now that Giorgio soon realised that one or both of them would be arrested. And so he made her confess, to save himself.

"To us, even then, it seemed a dubious confession for two reasons. First, Rosa would not tell how she committed the murder. Her lawyer soon counselled silence; but in the first hysteria when she confessed we were convinced she had had no such counsel. And her response to questions was such that we felt right along she had no knowledge of how gas was introduced into that flat. We made several cautious tests. For instance, to the sudden smell of burning rubber Rosa reacted much more innocently than did her husband.

"Our second reason for doubting the truth of Rosa's confession: The murdered girl was to become a mother. That changed the whole complexion of the affair, gentlemen! The probability was that Rosa did not know of this—but that Giorgio did. It supplied a very strong motive for him to kill this other girl who had suddenly become a millstone about his neck. Especially since, only two days before the murder, Rosa's father, thinking to straighten out his daughter's marital difficulties, offered Giorgio an excellent position in his contracting business, and insisted that the young couple move to Staten Island near him. Giorgio accepted. But Angelina had undoubtedly become a menace—and so he killed her.

"All this we could reason out. But with Rosa confessing to the murder—and in the hands of able counsel—what could Mr. Green do? Nothing but what we did here to-night.

"Rosa's motive for the confession? Self-sacrifice, gentlemen. She loved her husband—still does. And he told her to confess. Doubtless pictured how Angelina had ensnared him—how, if caught, *he* would go to the electric chair. And assured her that a young, pretty wife, murdering a rival for jealousy, would get a very light sentence, if any. And true enough. Especially in Italian cases. Courts are very sympathetic with the perfectly natural trait of violent, passionate jealousy in a pretty, young Italian girl. And most especially if she can prove she had cause to be jealous, and confesses at once to her crime. The District Attorney has had that sort of thing to fight before. It made this case extremely awkward. And Vitelli—guilty, undoubtedly, of first degree murder—would go scot-free."

The Doctor paused, and on an impulse went to the still sobbing Rosa and bent over her. "Your father will be very pleased, Rosa," he said gently. "You see—though you don't realise it now—your Giorgio isn't worth all these tears." He patted her shoulder and turned back to the room. "Poor little child! Only eighteen—and to have had a start in life like this!"

THE LOCKED ROOM TO END LOCKED ROOMS
STEPHEN BARR

AFTER WORKING as a commercial artist and architectural draftsman for much of his life, Stephen Barr (1904–1989) became a full-time writer in 1955, contributing numerous articles and short stories to such top-paying periodicals as *Vogue*, *Playboy*, *Mademoiselle*, *Harper's Bazaar*, and *The Atlantic Monthly*. He was also a repeated contributor to numerous science fiction and mystery magazines, notably *Ellery Queen's Mystery Magazine*, where many of his frequently anthologized stories were first published.

Born in England to American parents, he was educated in England but spent most of his life in the United States. He had avocational interests in composing music and creating puzzles. The latter resulted in Barr publishing several successful volumes on the subject: *Experiments in Topology* (1964); *A Miscellany of Puzzles, Mathematical and Otherwise* (1965; reprinted as *Intriguing Puzzles in Math and Logic*, 1994); *Second Miscellany of Puzzles, Mathematical and Otherwise* (1969; reprinted as *Mathematical Brain Benders: 2nd Miscellany of Puzzles*, 1982); and *Puzzlequiz: Wit Twisters, Brain Teasers, Riddles, Puzzles, and Tough Questions* (1978).

"The Locked Room to End Locked Rooms" was first published in the August 1965 issue of *Ellery Queen's Mystery Magazine*; it was reprinted as "The Locked House" in *Best Detective Stories of the Year* (New York, Dutton, 1966).

THE LOCKED ROOM
TO END LOCKED ROOMS

STEPHEN BARR

THE REGENT'S is possibly the small-est club in London, but it is undoubtedly the most argumentative. Any statement made in the Regent's, no matter how uncontroversial, will instantly be challenged. It is a bad place to be dogmatic. I was talking to two other members one evening, one of them a logician and the other a novelist, and the subject of detective stories came up.

"There are really only two kinds of mystery," the novelist said, rather recklessly.

"Nonsense," said the logician. "What are they?"

"Why, the whodunit," replied the novelist, "and the locked-room problem. The whodunit is—"

"I know what it is," interrupted the logician crossly, "but nine times out of ten it's unfair. The author omits to give all the pertinent facts. And if it does happen to be written fairly, the reader will be able to solve the mystery as quickly as the detective. As for the locked-room problem, it isn't a mystery at all: it's a self-contradiction."

"I don't see why—"

"Of course you don't," said the logician. "What the author asks the reader to believe is that a man is found murdered in a place from which the murderer could not have escaped, and yet the murderer is not there. Writers have var-ious ways of circumventing this. For example, the victim committed suicide in such a way as to resemble murder. Or the victim was dealt the fatal blow before he locked himself in: let's say, he was shot through the head, and contrary to popular belief, he did not die for some time. Or the murderer locked the door on the inside while he was still on the outside. Or he was still con-cealed in the room. Or he contrived the murder from the outside.

"The shoddiest solution of all is that he *did*, in fact, get out, and his escape appears impos-sible only because of the author's incomplete and therefore unfair description of the circum-stances. None of these faces squarely up to the real dilemma—that the murderer got out when he *could not*. That, by definition, is absurd."

"Rubbish," said a gentle voice behind the logician, who quickly turned around. I saw that it came from Dr. Sylvan Moore, our oldest member, and his usually calm face was deter-mined. "You are making the same mistake that I did once," he went on as we formed a circle to include him. "You are treating this as a prob-lem in topology, and humans as entities—like atoms."

"What the devil have atoms got to do with it?" said the logician, cross again.

"Nothing. That's my point. Did you ever hear of Petrus Dander, the explorer?"

"Certainly not," said the logician. "Why should I?"

———

585

If you read the newspapers (Dr. Moore said), you would have seen his obituary some years ago; but what was not told was that he was murdered, and almost certainly by his own son.

The circumstances were somewhat baroque, but because of a confidential mission he'd been on for Whitehall it was hushed up. The son's disappearance was also glossed over; they merely said he'd gone abroad.

Petrus Dander was one of the most charming men I ever met—and one of the most satanic. He inherited a fortune and a town house in Manchester Square from his father, and proceeded to marry Lily Maynard. It is on my conscience that I had introduced them to each other.

Their only child, Jonathan, was born during World War I while his father was with Allenby in the Near East. Dander made a brilliant war record but he never came home on any of his leaves, preferring each time to volunteer for extra duty that gave him in the end a reputation second only to that of Lawrence of Arabia. Lily was bewildered and crushed, but she pretended to believe it was patriotism rather than callousness. Dander arrived in Manchester Square during May of 1919 as though he had just come back from a stroll, and succeeded in fascinating his wife all over again. But this time it was more like the fascination of a serpent for a bird.

I don't think there was ever any physical violence; his bullying was far more subtle. Lily seemed to grow more and more transparent and less alive, so that those of us who knew her learned of her death without surprise—almost without shock. That was in 1931, and Dander was in the Gobi Desert. It very nearly finished off Jonathan then and there—I almost wish it had. He and his mother had become too close—much too close; and Jonathan was convinced that his father had caused Lily's death, in which he was right. The antipathy was returned—Dander despised his son as a milksop and a mother's boy.

My wife and I had Jonathan down to our place in Sussex after Lily's funeral to see if we could straighten him out a bit—but he was like a lost soul. Then Dander came home, and I had

my first taste of his temper, if it can be called that. He turned up unannounced one morning, and with a charming smile he proceeded to lay down the law.

"Hello, Mrs. Moore. Now look here, Sylvan"—he ignored Jonathan—"what the devil d'you mean by bringing my son here?" We were too nonplused to answer him. "If you think you can use the pretext of old acquaintance to interfere in my private affairs you're mistaken. Pack your gear, Jonathan."

My wife recovered herself first.

"But Jonathan *needs* to get away from London. He was all alone—"

"He's not alone now, and I'll decide his needs."

"Look here, Dander," I began, but he interrupted me.

"Jonathan's my son, more's the pity, and I'll not have him subjected to your second-rate middle-class sentimentality." He turned to Jonathan for the first time. "Didn't you hear what I said? Get your gear. You're going with me, and then you're going to a tutor's and then to Sandhurst."

"But Father, I don't want to go into the Army!"

"Shut your mouth, you young swine! You'll do as I tell you."

I looked at Jonathan and for the first time I saw a resemblance to his father, but his father looking out from behind bars, murderous yet helpless. They left a few minutes later.

Some time later I heard a rumor that Jonathan, after some sort of tussle with his father, had gone on a protracted hunger strike, but was sent to the tutor in spite of it. I heard nothing more of either of them for some years, and the Manchester Square house remained closed because Dander had gone abroad. Then Jonathan was sacked from Sandhurst under rather peculiar circumstances, and his father came back. I saw him in this room for a few minutes just before he was to meet Jonathan, and judging from the look in his eye I didn't envy the boy.

Dander acted toward me as though nothing

had ever happened between us, and in some mysterious way he made me accept it.

"Tell me, old man," he said to me, "can you recommend a really sound psychiatrist? I'm worried about Jonathan."

I am a psychiatrist, as he well knew, and as there were two members within earshot I was not exactly pleased. I believe I mentioned Gideon, the worst faker on Harley Street, and Dander left me with a flashing smile.

The first I heard of his death was a very solemn call from Blake-Smith of the Foreign Office. "Would you come up? Petrus Dander is dead, and you were his closest friend."

"Closest friend!" I said. "I hated the man. How did he die?"

"Well, at any rate you knew him better than anyone else, or at all events longer. Something's come up, but I can't discuss it on the telephone."

When I got to Whitehall I found three other men with Blake-Smith: Paul Gavin the criminologist, ex-Inspector Dowd, and, to my astonishment, the Foreign Secretary, Viscount Maturin. Everything was hedged about with protocol and hush-hush, but it was only that they were all at sea, and no wonder. When one of your most distinguished foreign agents is found murdered in his own house under circumstances that absolutely defy logic, you keep it quiet—that is, you do if you are the British Government.

"You knew him and his family, and you are a psychiatrist," said Viscount Maturin heavily. "That is why we have asked you to come here. We would like you to tell us about the son."

"Why?" I asked.

"Because he couldn't possibly have done it."

The facts as they were explained to me (Dr. Moore continued) were as follows: Dander had arrived on a P. & O. liner at the beginning of March and went to the Wanderers Club, where he spent the night. The next day was the day I saw him here, during which he arranged to have the Manchester Square house opened, and called up Sandhurst to get the details of Jonathan's escapade.

The headmaster had little to say: to him the

outré was un-English and therefore unspeakable. It appeared that during class Jonathan had unexpectedly gone mad. The history master had mentioned Dander Senior's fine war record, as a possible incentive to improve study on the part of the son, and Jonathan had rushed at him.

That in itself was bad enough, particularly as the history master's beard was nearly torn out by the roots. But worse was to follow.

Jonathan escaped from some kind of impoundment later, only to be discovered fingering a Winchester in the rifle room. Dander went and got him that evening.

The way in which the house in Manchester Square was opened up is important. Dander had cabled his lawyers from Aden to hire cleaners and so on to make the house ready for him, and then to clear out. This is not so remarkable as it might seem when I tell you that he had had the place renovated—at least, on the inside, to the most complete modernism. I don't mean the decor, but everything from central heating to heat-resistant windows, from a water-cooled roof to an incinerator in the cellar. Dander had what he called a machine for living. Also he had put in metal-sash windows and foolproof locks.

A young woman was engaged to come in the mornings to wash things and make the beds, but nothing else. She turned up the first morning and left immediately, terrified by the "dreadful shouting from the two gentlemen upstairs." She never returned.

The next thing we heard was that Dander cut every appointment he had made—at his club, at his lawyer's, and, what was more important, at the Foreign Office. Then the milk bottles began to arrange themselves in sour ranks in the areaway, and the postman could no longer stuff anything into the overfilled mailbox on the front door. The London policeman is not too eager to break into the house of a rich man, and the lawyers had had a taste of his fury at any interference. But this case was different.

The search of the premises was instigated by Whitehall. To break in, they smashed a basement window—the doors were metal-lined, and you will have to take my word for it that nothing was overlooked, and that every precaution was taken. Every possible exit that a man could use was locked on the inside; all front and basement doors were barred on the inside, and in such a way that it could not have been done from the outside. No one got out after the investigators entered, and no one was found in the house except Petrus Dander.

They found him face down on his bed upstairs, in two portions as it were. On the pillow his head, and a little farther away, the rest of him. The house was searched, and no clue turned up except the heavy Crusader's ax which had cut off Dander's head, and the ax was found in the cellar, stained brown and flecked with his iron-gray hair. Perhaps I should mention the empty bottle of sleeping pills, but that was something Dander had taken for years. Still, it was a possible clue— but to what? What was needed wasn't clues but logic—and there was none.

Now you may wonder why the authorities made such a careful entrance. It was fear—fear of repercussions on the part of the Police, and fear of entanglements on the part of the Foreign Office. They had not expected to be faced with the impossible—and yet a man was dead in a place from which his murderer could not have left, and yet the murderer was no longer there.

I have a little hobby, which is topology, and I had recently published an article on the Jordan curve theorem in the magazine *Situs*. Thinking to liven up my piece, I made the analogy of a man in a maze with no openings; but here was a case that seemed to make nonsense of what I wrote. Suicide was out of the question, and decapitation had been the sole cause of death.

So I wrote a letter to *Situs* saying I had somehow made a mistake, although I did not yet understand precisely what it was. And yet implicit in my mistake was the solution.

Rid your mind of any idea that the searching party made any slips: let me just assure you that when I was taken to the Manchester Square house I convinced myself that the facts were exactly as I have told them to you; and subse-quent findings have proved them to be true— absolutely true.

When I wrote my recantation to *Situs* they managed to get it into the next issue, which was on sale by the next Monday morning. The result was electrifying. Viscount Maturin was waiting for me at his office, to which I had been summoned in the early afternoon, and there was a cabinet minister with him.

"We asked you not to speak of it," Maturin said coldly. "Why did you write that letter in *Situs*?"

"But I said nothing to connect it with the case!" I said. "Besides, who reads the magazine?"

"The War Office reads it, and the connection was obvious. The point is that to the Power that engineered the murder—"

"If I may interrupt," interrupted the cabinet minister, "we do not actually know whether it was done by a Foreign Power."

"My dear Charles," Maturin said, "what we know is neither here nor there. But we must have some reasonable public excuse for believing that the son did it. Otherwise there'll be a bloody mess."

They both looked at me accusingly and expectantly.

"I don't see why," I said finally, "it should be any easier for a nation than for an individual to do the impossible."

"Look at the Pyramids," said the cabinet minister.

I said, "Anyway, what has to be done is to revise our concept of the impossible."

"Is that all you have to offer?" said Maturin.

"Well, somewhere in my subconscious is the recognition of a design, and that design includes the son."

"I trust, Doctor, that you will be able to bring it out into the conscious."

"I must have the answers to some questions," I said, "and then I will have to go over the Man-chester Square house again—with you, and preferably at once."

To get the answers to my questions we had to

go through a lot of records, but I learned nothing that I did not already know. At Dander's house the three of us started at the top, and my examination of the attic ceiling astonished Maturin. "This has been gone over a thousand times, my dear Moore! No one could possibly have got out, so what are you looking for?"

I shrugged—the truth is, I didn't know. In Dander's bedroom I stood staring at the ceiling again. "There's no sign of anything having hung there," I said, half to myself.

"If you mean the ax," Maturin said, "if you're thinking of some kind of booby trap, how did the ax get to the cellar? That's where it was found."

"I don't know," I said lamely. "Let's take another look at it."

In the cellar the ax had been pushed to one side, but its original position was marked in chalk on the cement floor. I looked at the childishly drawn outline—a possible scrawl on a pavement came to my mind, *Jonathan hates Petrus* . . . My eyes began to go over the floor.

"If you're thinking about tunnels," said Maturin, "we have already—"

"I am not thinking about tunnels," I said. "I usually look at the floor when I'm thinking. I did it as a child whenever—" I stopped, and realized suddenly that I knew the answer.

"It was suicide," I said.

Maturin looked at me as though I had gone mad, and sat down on the cellar stairs. "How can a man behead himself and then—" He stopped.

"There's only one possible place for it," I said, and went to the incinerator and opened it.

"Place for *what*?" Maturin snapped, and then came over with a flashlight, which he shone into the dark interior. "All the doors and windows were locked or barred on the inside, so it makes no difference *what* Jonathan burned up!"

"That's what I thought," I said, "before I wrote the letter to *Situs*."

There was a long silence while I pieced together my thoughts. Then I told them this:

"There was a man who could not bear to be thought small and of no account. He knew he was exceptional, but eventually he found that

another was standing in his way, and the woman he loved was more drawn to this other, and by links she did not know nor would have liked to recognize. He pretended rage to himself at this, but underneath this rage was guilt—for the hate he felt made him guilty. Guilt drives a man to a lower hell than hate.

"He had tried to conquer this, but he was fighting the invincible, and he made, over and over again, the futile gesture of running away—of removing himself from this impossible triangle. Then the woman died, and although the triangle no longer existed, he was still trapped—and he must kill his adversary to escape. I do not think he consciously planned what he did, but in the depths of his mind it must have been there all the time.

"He was brought here to this house, by a bullying overbearance which made things worse than ever. They reviled each other all night, and he followed his father up to the bedroom. I am talking of Jonathan, of course—in love with his mother, murderously hating his hateful father, and crawling with a guilt so strong that he had attempted suicide, as we know, at least twice. Once by hunger strike and then, after his attack on the bearded history master by rifle—for the history master was to him a symbol of his father's authority.

"Petrus Dander lay face down on the bed, exhausted by argument and alcohol, but before lying down he took his usual dose of the sleeping pills. Knowing him, I can imagine one last and unbearable taunt coming muffled by the pillow—a taunt perhaps referring to Jonathan and his mother. And Jonathan looked at him . . . You cannot move a black mark on paper, but you can erase a black mark.

"Jonathan went down to the library and picked out the most suitable of its military relics—one that may have looked to him like an executioner's ax. No doubt he felt very noble until the spasmodic contraction of the body separated it from the head. Then he saw the bottle of sleeping pills, and took them all—like a little boy taking medicine as a punishment. And then he realized that only one of his adversaries had been removed, that the nasty medicine was not enough.

"Jonathan cast away the empty bottle, and trailing the ax came down here to the cellar, as the sleeping pills began to cut off, bit by bit, his sensory system.

"Later, when you searched, you all looked for the murderer—a man. And you say he could not have got out of the house. That was your mistake—not realizing that you were absolutely right."

Maturin stared at me. "You say we were *right*?"

"Yes," I said. "Right in saying he could not have got out—but wrong in thinking that *because a man was no longer in a place he must have got out.*"

I reached into the incinerator. Then I turned, and held out a handful of ashes, which Maturin and the cabinet minister looked at uncomprehendingly.

"Jonathan timed it precisely. Just before he succumbed to the sleeping pills, he turned on this very up-to-date incinerator, and climbed into it. He was totally unconscious before it began to heat up, and dead long before it consumed his body and turned itself off.

"You see, you were looking for a man—not for his ashes."

SHOOT IF YOU MUST

It may not be terribly original, but shooting someone tends to be pretty effective.

NOTHING IS IMPOSSIBLE

CLAYTON RAWSON

ONE OF AMERICA'S most famous illusionists, Clayton Rawson (1906–1971) was a member of the American Society of Magicians and wrote on the subject frequently. Born in Elyria, Ohio, he graduated from Ohio State University and worked as an illustrator for advertising agencies and magazines before turning to writing. He used his extensive knowledge of stage magic to create elaborate locked-room and impossible-crime novels and short stories. Under his own name, all his fiction featured the Great Merlini, a professional magician and amateur detective who opens a magic shop in New York City's Times Square. There, he often is visited by his friendly rival, Inspector Homer Gavigan of the NYPD, when Gavigan is utterly baffled by a seemingly impossible crime. Merlini's adventures are recounted by freelance writer Ross Harte. There are only four Merlini novels, two of which have been adapted for motion pictures. *Miracles for Sale* (1939) was based on Rawson's first novel, *Death from a Top Hat* (1938). In this film, the protagonist is named Mike Morgan, played by Robert Young; it was directed by Tod Browning. The popular Mike Shayne series used Rawson's fourth book, *No Coffin for the Corpse* (1942), as the basis for *The Man Who Wouldn't Die* (1942), with Lloyd Nolan starring as Shayne, who consults a professional magician for help. The other Merlini books are *The Footprints on the Ceiling* (1939), *The Headless Lady* (1940), and *The Great Merlini* (1979), a complete collection of Merlini stories. Under the pseudonym Stuart Towne, Rawson wrote four pulp novellas as Don Diavolo. The author was one of the four founding members of the Mystery Writers of America and created its motto: "Crime Does Not Pay—Enough."

"Nothing Is Impossible" was first published in the July 1958 issue of *Ellery Queen's Mystery Magazine*; it was first collected in *The Great Merlini* (Boston, Gregg Press, 1979).

NOTHING IS IMPOSSIBLE

CLAYTON RAWSON

ALBERT NORTH had looked forward to retirement. An early pioneer in aviation design and the founder of Northair Corporation, he had promoted himself to Chairman of the Board and turned the active management of the company over to his son-in-law, Charles Kane.

A week later he was bored, irritable, and unhappy. He had been much too active for too long. He turned a small room off the study in his Fifth Avenue apartment into a workshop and, for a while, made airplane models. This was better than lying in the sun at Miami but it still didn't satisfy him.

Then he found a hobby that ran away with him. It was a curious hobby, and a magazine editor whom I queried agreed that there was a story in it. At first I intended to give it the light touch, but after listening to North talk for a couple of hours I wasn't so sure. I didn't know if he was pulling my leg or fooling himself, or if I had stumbled on the biggest story in the history of journalism.

I decided to get some expert professional advice. And I knew just where to go to find out if any deception was involved—a place that sold the very best grade in quantity lots. I walked into The Great Merlini's Magic Shop just at closing time.

The proprietor was totaling the day's receipts and he was not in a good mood. He had covered several sheets of paper with mathematics and had failed to find out why he had $3.17 more

cash on hand than the register total showed. In view of the fact that he designed, performed, and sold miracles, his annoyance at this situation was understandable.

"Obviously," he growled, giving the cash register a dark look, "that machine needs overhauling."

Since the shiny gadget he referred to was the latest IBM model, installed only the week before, I thought this conclusion somewhat unlikely. Not being an electronics engineer, however, I didn't say so. "What," I asked instead, "do you know about flying saucers?" I didn't really expect to surprise him with that; he's a hard man to surprise. But I certainly didn't expect the answer I got.

"Would you like to see our de luxe model—the one with invisible, double-action suspension and guaranteed floating power?" His straight face and deadpan delivery didn't fool me; I'd met that technique before.

I shook my head. "I know. You sell rising cards and floating ladies, and the Levitation section of your catalogue offers a couple of dozen methods of defying gravity, but don't tell me—"

The Great Merlini pointed to the neatly lettered business slogan on the wall behind the counter: *Nothing Is Impossible*. "You should know by now, Mr. Harte," he said, "that anything can happen here. Come with me."

He led me into the back room that serves as workshop and shipping department. I threaded my way through a maze of milk cans (for escaping from), walked around a guillotine (guaranteed to be harmless), and saw Merlini pick up a tin pie plate from the workbench.

"This is just a test model," he said. "But it works."

He scaled the plate across the room. Instead of falling to the floor with a clatter, the spinning disk acted as if it had a built-in boomerang. Maintaining a constant five-foot altitude, it curved through a 180-degree turn and sailed back toward Merlini. He grinned, stepped aside, and let it go past. I ducked, it skimmed over my head outward-bound again, and continued to circle the room, spinning steadily and utterly ignoring everything Sir Isaac Newton had ever said about gravitation.

"There's nothing very new or original about this," Merlini explained as he reached out and caught it. "If you ever saw the Riding Hannefords in the circus ring, you saw Poodles Hanneford do exactly the same thing with his derby hat. The secret—"

"Don't tell me," I objected. "It's probably so simple I'd feel like a dope for not having seen it instantly. But who ordered a flying saucer? Are you doing a mail order business with Mars?"

"Television," Merlini said. "When a TV space opera script calls for something that baffles the combined efforts of the special effects department and electronic cameras, then they call on me."

"I can see I came to the right place. You have just been appointed Chief Investigator for the Flying Saucer Division of the Ross Harte Research Laboratories, Inc."

Merlini placed the pie plate on thin air, gave it a quick spin, and left it there, whirling mysteriously on nothing. "And how," he asked, "did you get into that business?"

"Articles on the Great Flying Saucer Mystery sell magazines. I'm ghost-writing one. *Visitors From Space* by Albert North."

"He's solved the mystery?"

"That's what I want to know. He's set himself up as an unofficial clearing house for sau-

cer information. Whenever someone reports mysterious lights in the sky, North looks into it. He's had to hire a fulltime secretary to handle the mail and he has filled four large filing cabinets with reports. Did you know that since flying saucers first hit the headlines in 1947 there have been several thousand reported sightings?"

"A celestial traffic jam," the Great Merlini observed. "But I thought the Air Force issued a report which said that people had been seeing weather balloons, temperature inversion mirages, and spots before their eyes."

"Then you didn't read all of it," I replied. "They explained eighty percent that way, but they had to label the remaining twenty percent as 'Unknown.' That could add up to quite a lot of saucers. And just one bona-fide vehicle from outer space would be the biggest story since the invention of the wheel."

Merlini nodded. "I'll agree to that. And North thinks he has good solid evidence that will stand up in court?"

"He's convinced that where there's so much smoke there has to be a fire. He doesn't swallow everything he's told either. When some elderly lady in Bad Axe, Minnesota, reports that a doughnut-shaped object landed in her back yard and a horde of small green men with purple spots trampled her zinnia bed, he files it under H for Hysteria. It's the sober detailed reports of sightings by university professors, airplane pilots, and such people that have North convinced—and me confused."

"Has North figured out why saucer pilots have been content for so many years to flit about among the clouds, mostly at night, merely viewing the scenery? Are they shy? Or not very curious? Or what?"

"If you mean why haven't they landed, North's reply is: 'How do we know they haven't?' What's more, he believes that someone, or something, is watching him. He says that twice within the last week he has been followed."

"From flying saucers," Merlini murmured, "to persecution complex. That figures."

"It would," I said, "except for one thing. I

just came from North's apartment—and I was followed, too."

Merlini, who had started to light a cigarette, stopped, the match still burning in his fingers.

"Aliens from another world? Little green men with eyes on stalks, and tentacles coming out of them?"

"No, but it makes just about as much sense. There were two of them and I think I've seen one before. Down at Centre Street. Why would a couple of city dicks be tailing North and anyone who happens to be visiting him?"

That did it. Merlini's interest in flying saucer pilots was lukewarm, but an unexplained interest on the part of the Police Department aroused his curiosity. We had dinner together and he accompanied me uptown to continue my interview with North. No one, as far as we could see, tailed us.

A young man with broad shoulders, a crew cut, and an intense, somewhat worried look in his dark eyes let us in and introduced himself as Charles Kane, North's son-in-law.

"The old man's in the study with that well-stacked secretary of his. Dictating another batch of letters to his crackpot correspondents. At least, that was the official bulletin she released when she let me in a few minutes ago. All secretaries should be homely and flat-chested. It's much more efficient." He lifted the highball he held. "What can I get you to drink?"

As he filled our orders, Merlini said, "Apparently you and North disagree as to flying saucers."

Kane squirted soda water into our glasses. "That's putting it politely. We disagree about other things, too. Like the Chairman of the Board of Northair Corporation signing his name to magazine articles about flying saucers. This is *not* the kind of publicity that helps get new business."

"North," I said, "believes it will get him more saucer reports."

"Sure it will. An article in a national magazine about pixies would get him reports from people who'd swear they had gone to school with them."

"I'm told," Merlini said, "that North sifts his evidence pretty carefully."

Kane didn't actually snort, but he came close. "If he'd let me sift it for him I can assure you there wouldn't be enough left to write articles about. He's an enthusiast. Which is all right if you can control it. But every now and then he goes overboard. A few years ago he sank a couple of hundred thousand in an experimental aerofoil design that was to revolutionize aerodynamics. He thought it would prove that the Wright brothers started the whole science off on the wrong foot. Only it was a complete bust. Now he wants to find out what makes flying saucers fly. If he starts building saucer motors and if you own any Northair stock, you'd better sell quick."

Behind us a voice with a sharp cutting edge said, "My son-in-law is not a bad plant manager, but he lacks vision."

Albert North walked toward us from the study door—a short, stocky man with a pirate's face, a quarterdeck manner, and fire in his eye.

"Charles," he growled, "when you phoned this afternoon I told you I had an engagement with Mr. Harte this evening. Why are you here?"

Charles may have lacked vision, but he didn't seem to be afraid of talking back to the boss. He turned to the bar and added whiskey to his drink. "If you hadn't hung up in the middle of the call—as you do about half the time—you'd know why." Kane lifted a brief case that lay on the bar. "I need your signature on these government contract bids. They have to be in Washington tomorrow morning. If you'd give me the authority to sign . . ."

"And why," North growled, "weren't they ready yesterday? No, don't tell me now. Bring them into the study." He looked at me. "I'm sorry. This won't take long."

He turned abruptly and marched toward the study as a young lady who answered Kane's description quite accurately came through the door. As secretary in charge of flying saucers, she was quite a dish. I could see how her effect on the efficiency of a business office might not be all that a dedicated personnel manager could wish. And I suspect she knew it. In contrast to her face and figure, her voice was cool and impersonal, her manner brisk and businesslike. The tailored suit she wore tried hard to leave a similar impression but it definitely fought a losing battle.

"Will you need me for this?" she asked.

"No, Anne," North replied. "You may go now."

"Unless," Charles added, "you want to wait for *me*."

She gave him a smile and a fast no. "I've got a date with a man from Mars. He has two heads."

Albert North stopped and turned. "Are you making flying saucer jokes now, too?"

Anne shook her head. "No. But Charles is married to your daughter. I just wanted him to know that a two-headed date would be preferable."

North moved on. Kane followed, turning as he closed the door to eye Anne. "All that," he said, grinning, "and brains, too."

Miss O'Hara picked up a purse and gloves from a chair by the outer door. Then she saw our drinks. "Would there be any more of that?" she asked. "After today I could use a quick one."

She didn't have to ask twice; I was already at the bar.

"Tell me," Merlini asked, "do saucer pilots usually have two heads?"

She sat on the edge of an armchair. "They come in assorted sizes and shapes. So far, one head apiece seems to be standard equipment, but I wouldn't predict what might turn up in tomorrow's mail."

"You've seen all of North's evidence. Does any of it convince you that we are actually being visited by ships from space?"

Miss O'Hara sipped her drink first. "I wish I knew. Ninety-five percent of the reports are from people who could use a good psychiatrist. But every now and then there's a witness who is awfully hard to doubt—a professor like Dr. Price, for instance. And lately I've been waking up at three A.M. in a cold sweat after a nightmare about nine-foot Martians. I'm beginning to think that typing business letters about shipments of coffee and tea might be a welcome change."

"Nine-footers?" I asked.

"That's the record catch—a report from Arizona last week. Four people swear they saw a green disk in the sky traveling at the usual eighteen thousand miles per hour, and shortly after, a woman claims she found a nine-foot-high man—or something similar—in her bedroom. When she screamed he walked out—right through the wall."

"And who," Merlini asked, "is Dr. Price?"

"Professor of Archeology at U.C.L.A. He'll be here tonight."

"What is his evidence?"

Anne frowned. "You'd better ask him. He doesn't want publicity."

"North briefed me on Price," I said, "but I have to get the doctor's okay before using it. One of his graduate students was doing field work in the Navajo country last summer. A few days after a saucer sighting in the area, the boy found and photographed some very queer markings on the side of a cliff face. They seemed to have been burned into the rock. They look to me like something a beginning shorthand student might write after five martinis. But they gave Doctor Price a jolt. He'd seen the same sort of script once before—in a Yucatan jungle."

"Don't tell me," Merlini said, "that the Martians are going to turn out to be Mayans."

"It's worse than that. Price thinks this may be the clue to a major archeological mystery. Two years ago he was excavating a Mayan pyramid dating about A.D. 600 and found an inscription that had absolutely nothing in common with the Mayan hieroglyphs. When his student brought in another sample of the same thing—several symbols are identical—and when this new sample had a possible connection with saucers, Price remembered one phrase in the Mayan inscriptions found at the same site which he had thought was merely allegorical. Now he thinks the Mayans meant it literally. It was a reference to 'ships from the sky.'"

"And not long after," Anne added, "the Mayans, for some mysterious reason, completely abandoned all the cities of the Old Empire."

"Hmm," Merlini said. "That's certainly a Stop Press bulletin for the archeological journals. So Price brought his alien inscriptions to North?"

Anne nodded. "He'd read that North was collecting saucer information and he hoped more of the script might have turned up. He thinks that with enough of it he may be able to break it down and get a translation."

"Translation?" Merlini blinked. "The men who finally solved the Mayan writing succeeded only because they knew something of the Mayan culture. But Price is tackling a script of what he thinks is an extra-terrestrial culture. What he needs is a new Rosetta stone."

"Which," I said, "is what he hopes to find if he can get funds to finish excavating that Mayan pyramid. He—"

I stopped short. Merlini got slowly to his feet. We all stared at the closed study door.

Anne said, "What was that?"

"It sounded," Merlini and I replied almost together, "like a shot."

I was nearest the door and reached it first. I turned the knob and pushed.

The door was locked.

I rapped on the door—hard. "North!" I called. "Kane!"

There was no answer.

Merlini asked, "Is there another way in?"

Anne's voice was a whisper. "No."

I knocked again and got the same result—nothing.

Magicians who can't open doors for friends without keys have to take a lot of ribbing and on this account Merlini always carries an assortment of lockpicks. He had the leather case that held them in his hands now.

"I'll go to work on the lock," he said, kneeling before the door. "You phone. We want a squad car and an ambulance."

I agreed completely. The silence beyond that door was much too ominous. I found the phone on a writing desk and dialed.

And at that moment the buzzer of the door to the hall buzzed.

I snapped the address to Headquarters, and added, "Get a squad car and a doctor up here—fast."

A quiet voice said, "You're calling the police?" Anne had opened the door and a thin, dapper little man stood just inside, his rimless glasses glinting in the light. "Why the police?"

Anne, not nearly as cool and collected now, told him, her voice trembling a bit. "It's Mr. North and Charles, Dr. Price. In the study. We heard a shot—and they don't answer."

In the hall outside I heard an elevator door open and the sound of voices.

Merlini said, "Come in and close that door. We don't want sight-seers at this time."

But Price turned toward the hall. "There's a physician's office on the first floor. I think, under the circumstances . . ."

Merlini's voice suddenly took on an official tone. "We've ordered a doctor. And I may need you here. Come in and close that door!"

Price obviously wasn't used to taking orders. He took a step toward the hall. "It'll be quicker if I—"

Merlini cut in, "Ross, yank him in here. Hurry!"

I started for the professor on the double. Price scowled, hesitated, then decided not to argue the matter. He stepped inside again and closed the door. Then, stuffily, he asked, "Miss O'Hara, who are these men?"

Anne told him as I joined Merlini. He was probing the lock's interior with a slender blade of steel whose careful tentative movements were tantalizing in their slow deliberation.

There was still no sound from beyond the study door.

Then, at last, I heard a metallic click. Merlini stood up, turned the knob, and the door moved open.

Several framed enlargements of flying saucer photographs hung on the opposite wall. Below them, in a circle of light that dropped from the ceiling, was North's desk. He sat in the chair behind it, his body slumped forward, his head resting on the green blotter.

On the floor in front of the desk lay a man's coat.

The door opened wider. Against the left-hand wall was a secretary's desk and four filing cabinets. Close by the cabinets Kane's body lay face down on the floor, and near it, his over-turned highball glass, a wet stain spreading out from it across the beige carpet.

"The rest of you stay put," Merlini commanded. He stepped inside, strode swiftly to the open workshop door on the right, and looked inside. Then he turned and eyed Kane, scowling. I was still trying to believe what I saw.

Kane's trousers and shoes were on the floor near his coat.

And Kane's body was completely nude.

Merlini moved to the desk and bent above North. As he did so, Kane moaned and his body moved. His eyes opened and he began, in slow motion, to push himself up off the floor.

Merlini moved toward him. "What," he demanded, "happened to you?"

Kane regarded him blankly, lowered his head, and rubbed the back of it with one hand. Then slowly, as if it hurt him to speak, he said, "Where the hell . . . are my . . . clothes?"

His eyes lifted as he spoke and he saw North at the desk. "Is he . . . all right? What the—"

Merlini said, "North is dead. What happened in here?"

Kane stared a moment, then his eyes closed and his hand again massaged the back of his skull. "I gave North the papers. He sat at the desk, started to read them. I . . . I heard something move—behind me. I started to turn and something hit me on the back of the head . . . Will someone, for Pete's sake, get me some clothes?"

Anne, behind me, said, "Here." I took the bathrobe she had found in a bedroom, stepped forward and held it out as Kane got unsteadily to his feet and put it on. He lurched to an armchair beside the desk and sank heavily into it. "I've got one beaut of a headache."

He wasn't the only one. My head was beginning to spin. I took a quick glance into the workshop. It looked just as it had when I had seen it earlier—a workbench along one wall, tools neatly arranged above it on a pegboard, a stool, a small supply cabinet. The vise held a saucer-shaped disk of wood modeled after one of the photographs in the other room.

There was no place in either room where anyone could hide. Kane seemed to be having the same thought.

He asked Merlini, "You were in the living room all the time?"

Merlini nodded. "We were."

"Then you saw whoever it was that knocked me out. He'd have had to leave that way."

Dr. Price spoke suddenly, his voice not at all steady. "Anne, how long has that been there?"

He was pointing at the wall near the workshop door. About two feet from the floor several dark marks defaced the green-painted plaster—cursive, meaningless scrawls that a child might have made.

Anne's eyes were round—and frightened. "It wasn't there when I left the room."

I knew what it was; I had seen Price's photographs. He had wanted to find more of the alien script, but now he didn't seem happy about his unexpected success.

I crossed to the wall, stooped, and ran a finger across the marks. They had been burned into the plaster.

Kane pulled himself from his chair and faced Merlini. "Who came out of this room? Who did you—"

It was Anne who answered. "Nobody, Charles. No one came out—no one at all."

Kane stared at her. "But someone *must* have—"

"Only nobody did," Merlini said. "And it's high time we had some brass around here. Ross, there's a phone on the desk. See if you can get Gavigan before the squad car boys arrive."

Outside the door buzzer sounded.

"There they are now," I said.

"Start dialing!" Merlini ordered and moved

swiftly to the doorway in which Anne and Dr. Price still stood. "Anne, are the living room and study phones separate, or is one an extension?"

"Extension."

"Good. You answer the door. And tell the cops to listen in on the call we make." Quickly, before either could object, he slammed the door in their faces and locked us in.

Putting the three-way phone conversation that followed on paper is a job I'm going to dust off lightly. It was much too scrambled. Some of it occurred simultaneously and parts of it made no sense because two of the parties didn't know what the other was talking about.

I got through to Gavigan just as a heavy fist began pounding on the study door. Then, when the Inspector said, "Hello!" a cop at the living room phone bellowed, "Open that door! And be quick about it!" Gavigan said, "What door?" and the cop told him not to be funny.

At the same time I was trying to tell him, "Gavigan, it's Ross Harte." He said, "Who?" and the cop swore, and Merlini calmly advised me to tell Gavigan to tell the cop to shut up. This didn't work very well because the cop wasn't taking orders from just anyone on the phone who claimed to be an Inspector, and Gavigan wasn't very helpful because he had somehow got the idea that our end of the conversation was coming from a tavern.

"Merlini," I said, "you take it before Gavigan hangs up. And sound sober."

He had somewhat better luck, but it was involved. He got the cop to give his precinct number and asked Gavigan for the name of the captain of that precinct. When Gavigan knew it, the cop became suddenly more cautious and less noisy.

Rapidly Merlini said, "Call his captain, Gavigan, and have him call this number and tell the cop who answers to relax until you get here."

Gavigan still didn't like it. "What number? Where am I going? Why—"

Merlini gave him the telephone number and the address, then added, "Ross and I are locked in a murder room with the victim. And I don't want any garden variety of cop traipsing around

all over some of the damnedest clues you ever saw until you've seen them. Stop asking questions and get going!" And he hung up fast.

It worked. The phone rang a few moments later. I eavesdropped and heard the captain telling our impetuous friend outside to stand pat. Remembering the language he'd just used to an Inspector I understood why his "Yessir!" sounded a bit hollow.

"Gavigan," I told Merlini, "seemed to think I was tight. When he gets here and discovers that we are looking for a refugee from a flying saucer . . ."

Merlini wasn't listening. He was on his knees on the floor examining Kane's clothes.

When Gavigan arrived with Lieutenant Doran of Homicide West and Doc Peabody from the M.E.'s office, he was not in a good mood. He barked at Merlini, "You've certainly got a high-handed way of taking over a homicide investigation. Start talking."

Merlini didn't look happy either. "I don't know whether to break it gently or tell you all at once."

Gavigan stood in front of the desk scowling down at North's body. "I don't care how I get it, but I want it fast!"

That's how he got it. "The victim," Merlini said, "seems to have been killed by some unknown means by something about two feet high that left by walking through the wall."

This was too much for anyone to digest all at once. Gavigan didn't try. "Unknown means?" he asked. "That girl outside says you heard a shot."

"We did. But I don't see any blood nor any bullet wound. I hope Doc Peabody will be able to tell us what killed him."

Peabody moved toward the body. "You don't sound very confident."

"I'm not," Merlini told him. "That's one thing I'm fresh out of—confidence."

Peabody went to work and Merlini gave the Inspector and Doran the whole story from the beginning. They listened without interrupting. Even after Merlini had finished neither of them spoke.

Gavigan shook his head as if to rid it of a bad dream. Then he asked, "This walking through the wall stuff. Why that?"

"Several reasons," Merlini said. "One: Miss O'Hara reports that some flying saucer pilots can do that. Two: while we waited for you I looked in all the places a two-foot high something might hide and didn't find a single possibility. Three: take a look at the very curious condition of Kane's clothes."

Doran knelt by the coat. "What's so curious?"

"Turn it over."

Doran did. Curious was the word, all right. Kane's shirt was inside the coat, neatly buttoned, the Countess Mara tie still in place, still tied in a neat Windsor knot.

"And his undershirt is inside the shirt," Merlini said. "His shorts are inside the trousers, his socks inside the shoes—everything still buttoned up, tied, and zipped. Kane says his clothes were removed while he was unconscious. They would appear to have passed *through* his body in the process."

Gavigan didn't explode as I expected, but it was a near thing. "Why," he growled, "do you always have to pick the fanciest interpretation?" He turned and faced Kane. "It's about time you said something. Start with the clothes. After you took them off, you buttoned everything up again. Why? Are you setting up an insanity defense?"

Kane, staring at the clothing, didn't seem to hear. Then he looked up and shook his head slowly. "I'm sorry. I can't add a thing to what Merlini has told you. I came in here with North. I stood there in front of the filing cabinets. I—heard a movement behind me. Something hit me a crack on the head. Hard. When I came out of it, North was dead. I was naked. And that's it. That's all I know. I can't add one solitary—"

Behind us Doc Peabody said suddenly, "If you'd like to see what killed this man . . ."

We turned to the desk. Peabody poked with a slender pair of tweezers at a small metallic object that lay on a sheet of letter paper.

"It was in his head," Peabody said. "And the point of entry wasn't easy to find because it went in through his right ear."

Gavigan bent over the object. "That," he said, "takes care of the little man from Mars. It's a common, ordinary .32 caliber slug."

"It's a relief," Merlini said, "just to hear words like common and ordinary. But I wonder why we haven't yet seen anything of a gun—a common, ordinary .32, for example."

"We'll find it," Doran said flatly. "And then Mr. Kane goes downtown and gets booked."

Gavigan told Peabody, "See that Ballistics gets the slug, and I want a quick report. Doran, get your boys in and take this place apart." He turned to Kane. "And you, take off that bathrobe."

Kane blinked. "But . . ."

"Take it off! I want you out of here and I'm going to be damned sure you don't take a gun out."

Kane stood up. "If it'll convince you that I don't have and never did have a gun I'll walk all the way down to headquarters in my skin." He slipped the robe off and handed it to Gavigan. The Inspector turned the pockets inside out and found nothing. Then he held the robe up and let it fall to the floor. If it had contained a gun we would have heard it. We didn't.

Kane put the robe on again and Gavigan walked with him to the door, where he told a detective to find Kane some clothes and to keep an eye on him. "He's being held as a material witness."

Gavigan closed the door and came back. "The psychiatrists are going to have a field day with him. If he really thinks the New York Police Department is going to start tracking down a little green man from Mars . . ."

"But you aren't booking him?" Merlini asked.

"I will as soon as I have the gun. It didn't go out with him, and you say no one else left this room since you heard the shot. So it's here and we'll find it."

"I wish you luck," Merlini said gloomily. "But even if you do find it, don't book him too fast. You still may not be able to make it stick.

When I searched the room I found something I haven't yet mentioned." He turned to face the filing cabinets. "Cleaning women sometimes neglect to dust surfaces that are above eye level . . ."

Gavigan yanked Miss O'Hara's chair away from her desk, stood on it, and looked down at the top of the cabinets.

He froze.

He was still speechless when I looked a moment later. The steel surface was covered with a thin, gray film of dust across which something had walked, leaving three dark imprints.

They were the prints of naked feet.

The feet had only three toes.

And each print was not more than four inches in length.

The discussion that followed could have been engraved easily on the head of a pin. Gavigan obviously didn't want to think about the implications of those prints, and he avoided thinking by going into action. Assisted by Doran and two other detectives, he began a grimly determined and painstaking search for the gun. Merlini settled down in the armchair and appeared to fall asleep. I made a trip to the bar and poured myself a good stiff helping of Scotch. I am aware that this is not the recommended antidote for little men who leave three-toed footprints, but I needed it.

I have seen police searches before, but this one easily took the prize for thoroughness. Gavigan's final chore was to examine every one of some five hundred books on the shelves of one wall, looking for a hollowed-out recess that might contain a gun. He found no recess, and no gun.

Then he phoned Ballistics. I was quite prepared to hear them report that the slug which killed North was made of some unknown composition and probably fired from a .45 Intergalactic Special.

Gavigan listened a moment, then slammed the phone receiver down on the cradle. "It's a .32. Diameter of lands, grooves, and pitch of rifling indicate a Smith & Wesson. And they want to know when they can have the gun for comparison tests."

He looked at Merlini, who was still in a state of suspended animation.

"Did you hear me?" Gavigan roared.

Merlini opened one eye. "I thought for a minute it was an air raid siren. Yes, I heard you."

"That gun," Gavigan said, still rumbling like a volcano on the edge of blowing its top, "is not here. You're in charge of the Miracle Department. What happened to it? I want an answer—fast!"

"So do I," Merlini said. "But we've got problems. For one thing, the usual police routine is quite inadequate. The evidence says the gun was taken from the scene of the crime by the murderer. But you can't set up road blocks to stop a flying saucer, license number unknown, which is capable of speeds around eighteen thousand miles per hour. And if you broadcast a pickup order for a barefoot midget with three toes on each foot, sex, shape, and color unknown, people will think the teletype machines need repairing."

Gavigan glowered. "If you think any of this is funny . . ."

Merlini shook his head. "It's anything but that. I was merely pointing out that the gun is not our only problem."

"You give me an answer on the gun, then we'll worry about other problems. Do you have any idea on the subject, or are you completely up a tree?"

"One small idea," Merlini said, "but it's going to have to grow a lot."

"Let's hear it."

"If the vanishing gun is some extra-terrestrial hocus-pocus we'll never find it, but if it's the common garden-variety of trickery we at least have a starting point. An audience, watching magic, gets impossible answers because the magician so arranges things that the spectators ask themselves the wrong questions. That may be what we're doing. If we can figure out the right questions . . ."

As a progress report, this was not to the

Inspector's liking. He muttered something that didn't sound printable, then stopped short as the door from the living room opened and Doran came in with Captain Healy of the Pickpocket and Confidence Squad.

"I think," Healy said, "I might have a lead for you, Inspector."

"This case," Gavigan grunted, "doesn't have leads. But let's hear it."

"Who is the dapper old boy outside with the glasses?"

"Dr. Price? He's an archeologist who believes that flying saucers landed in Central America six hundred years ago. Why?"

Healy blinked. "He believes what?"

"I refuse," Gavigan said flatly, "to say it again."

"Well, whatever he says, don't buy any of it. One of my boys spotted him on the street a few days ago and we've been keeping an eye on him, wondering if he might be up to something his parole officer wouldn't like. The report says he's visited this apartment several times, so when I heard you've got a homicide here—"

Gavigan broke in. "Who is he?"

"A con man," Healy replied. "One of the best. Most con men work the same old games, but not this character. Some of the swindles he has dreamed up—"

"Who," Gavigan asked again, "is he?"

"The Harvard Kid. He got that monicker because when he's not working he always has his nose in a book. Egghead-type stuff, too. In one oil-well swindle he passed himself off on some pretty sharp businessmen as an expert geologist. And he once sold a trunkful of phony paintings for a quarter of a million dollars by posing as a Belgian art expert. Another time—"

"That," Merlini broke in, "explains why he tried to backtrack out of here the moment he discovered there had been a shooting. He's naturally cop-shy."

"And his pitch this time," Gavigan said, "was to get North to put up the dough for an archeological expedition. Then, instead of leaving for the jungles of Yucatan, The Kid would invest it in horses at Miami or the dice tables at Las Vegas. Let's hear what he says about that." Gavigan marched out into the living room followed by Doran and Healy.

"And the galactic script burned into the wall," Merlini said in a disappointed tone, "doesn't get translated after all. It's a great loss to science."

"We can also," I put in, "now forget all about flying saucers and invisible men."

"Can we?" Merlini asked. "I wonder. I have an uncomfortable feeling that our unfriendly refugee from the stars may pay us another visit."

But he didn't look uncomfortable; he was smiling faintly. So I didn't take him seriously. I said, "Oh, yeah," and went out to the bar for a refill. That was my mistake.

The living room, by now, was crawling with city officials. An Assistant D.A. and a police stenographer had set up shop in a bedroom and were getting a statement from Anne O'Hara. In the kitchen Gavigan and Healy were having a heart-to-heart talk with Dr. Orville Price. Doran took a photographer and a fingerprint man into the study and put them to work. Later, two men from the Morgue came for North's body.

As they were leaving I heard Merlini ask, "Lieutenant, I hope that search you made for the gun included the body?"

"It did," Doran answered. "If you think the gun is going out with him, the answer is no."

Ten minutes later it happened. From beyond the closed study door came the unmistakable sound of a shot.

Time, for a brief moment, stood still. Then a detective near the door sprang at it and pushed it open. I got there a second later and stared over his shoulder.

I saw Doran turn the knob of the workshop door and fail to open it. Then he banged on the door with his fist.

"Merlini!" he called. "Open up!"

There was no answer.

A heavy hand clamped on my shoulder and shoved me to one side. Gavigan went past in a hurry.

Then, suddenly, Doran's gun was in his hand, aimed at the slowly opening workshop door.

Merlini's voice said, "Don't shoot, Lieutenant. It's me."

He came out and faced Gavigan. "Inspector," he said gravely, "I'd like to have you meet our elusive little man from Mars."

Gavigan, who was still moving toward him, stopped. Then, seeing the look on Doran's face as the latter stared at something inside the room, he rushed forward.

"He's not easy to see," Merlini added, "because he's invisible. But there, on the floor, in that sprinkling of sawdust below the vise . . ."

I couldn't see it from where I stood, but I did later.

It was another nice, neat, tiny, and incredible three-toed footprint.

"And," Merlini went on, "you can search this room until Doomsday—you won't find a gun."

"Good," Gavigan said. "So you've figured out how to make a gun vanish into thin air. Doran, give him yours. This I want to see."

"Would you like," Merlini asked, "to get a confession at the same time?"

"Do I need one? If you know what happened to that gun—"

"I know what happened, but the evidence we need isn't going to be easy to find. There's a chance that when our man sees his very cleverly conceived murder coming apart at the seams, he may crack. But we should hit him hard while he's still wondering what that shot he just heard means."

The Inspector scowled at the footprint on the floor, then turned to Doran. "Get Kane in here."

Merlini took an electric soldering iron from North's bench, carried it into the study, spoke for a moment with the fingerprint man, then sat down behind North's desk.

Charles Kane was placed in a chair opposite Merlini. There was tension in the room, quite a lot of it, but none of it seemed to come from Kane. He waited, relaxed and quiet.

After a moment Merlini said calmly, "We have discovered one or two things you may want to comment on. Earlier you said that flying saucers were nonsense. Is that still your opinion?"

Kane shrugged. "After what's happened, I think I'll reserve judgment."

"Perhaps this will help you make up your mind. We have found that Dr. Price is not an archeologist but a con man who was trying to swindle your father-in-law. This means that the flying saucer script he says was found in Arizona is meaningless and his photographs faked. Since the script on the wall here contains some of the same characters, it is also spurious." Merlini lifted the soldering iron. "And it could have been burned into the wall with this."

Kane nodded. "Makes sense. Does that cancel out the flying saucer pilot too?"

"Not quite," Merlini answered, "but this might. Were you living in Rochester, New York, in 1936?"

Kane stared at him blankly. We all did.

"The police can find out easily enough," Merlini added. "So you might as well answer."

Kane thought about it. Then he nodded slowly. "I was born there. But what has that to do with anything?"

"There's something on the floor of the workshop that may answer that for you. Take a look."

Kane scowled, got slowly to his feet, and walked to the door. He stood there a moment looking in, then turned and came back. His face was blank, his voice flat. "Sorry. I don't get it."

"We found three more such prints," Merlini explained, "on top of the filing cabinets in this room, made by a two-foot, three-toed something-or-other from another world. But similar prints have turned up before in a sprinkling of flour on the floor of a séance room. Those prints had the customary five toes, and the inference was that they were made by astral visitors summoned from the spirit world."

Merlini gazed thoughtfully at Kane, then continued: "The convincer was the fact that the prints seemed to be those of child spooks, all much too small to have been made by the medium. But in Rochester one night some skeptic smuggled in a flashlight and turned it on unexpectedly. The newspaper account of that séance has a special place in my files because it is the only mention of this particular dodge I've ever found."

Merlini took a sheet of notepaper from a drawer of the desk and nodded at the fingerprint man to whom he had spoken earlier. The latter stepped forward and placed a glass plate bearing a film of ink before the magician.

"The medium made the prints," Merlini said. "But not with her feet."

He made a fist of his right hand and then rolled the edge of the hand opposite the thumb across the inked plate. He repeated the action on the notepaper. The edge of his hand and the side of his curled little finger left an irregularly shaped impression whose conformation and creases bore an astonishing resemblance to those made by the sole of a bare foot. Then he added toeprints using a thumb and forefinger, and the similarity was complete.

"You can, of course, give the print as many or as few toes as you like."

Doran said, "And when we compare the toe-prints we found with Kane's fingerprints—"

Merlini shook his head. "No. He knew those footprints would get a close examination. He moved his finger slightly on each impression so that the ridge markings are sufficiently smudged to prevent identification."

He looked at Kane as if waiting for confirmation. He didn't get it.

"You'll have to do better than that," Kane said. "Those prints may have been there for days. Anybody could have made them. Even if you could prove I made them it still wouldn't mean that I killed North."

"Perhaps not," Merlini said, "but it saves the Police Department having to track down a suspect through outer space. You didn't really expect them to swallow a two-foot high, three-toed Martian anyway. That was simply misdirection. As long as those footprints remained unexplained we had something to worry about that helped obscure the real problem. We thought we had to solve the mystery of a vanish-ing gun—a question whose answer is relatively unimportant because it is the wrong question."

"Now wait!" Gavigan exploded. "You said you knew what happened to the gun."

"No. I merely said I knew what happened. Suppose we start at the beginning." Merlini turned to Kane. "When you came in here with North, the first thing you did was knock him out. Most offices are equipped with an impromptu sandbag that leaves no marks—the telephone directory. Then you put the footprints on the filing cabinets, and burned the script in the wall with the soldering iron. Next, you undressed."

Kane grinned skeptically. "And rebuttoned my clothes so a crew of homicide detectives would believe they had passed through some fourth-dimensional hyperspace. Am I crazy?"

Merlini nodded. "Like a fox. Your real reason for stripping was to make it obvious immediately and beyond any doubt that there was no gun on your person. And you knew that when we failed to find one anywhere, no jury would convict you, and even your arrest was unlikely . . . Then you shot North."

"And what did happen to the gun?"

"As I said, that's the wrong question. The real problem is not how did a gun vanish into thin air, *but how did you shoot North—without using a gun!*"

For a long moment the silence was complete.

Merlini picked up the soldering iron. "You used this. The powder in a cartridge is usually exploded by percussion, but heat will do just as well. I tried it. I borrowed a cartridge from Doran, put it in the vise on North's workbench, and touched the base of the cartridge with the point of the hot iron. That was the shot you heard."

Doran scowled. "The slug that killed North had rifling marks on it. Made by a .32 Smith & Wesson."

Merlini nodded. "Of course. Kane had to supply rifling marks. Otherwise Ballistics would have known at once that a gun had not been used. But supplying rifling marks is not difficult."

"A slug that had been fired before," Gavigan said slowly. "And he refitted it with a new cartridge case and new powder load."

"I see," Kane said, "that I'm being framed by experts. And how do you answer this one? I'm no ballistics man, but I am an engineer. The function of a gun barrel is to contain the gases long enough for them to exert propelling force on the bullet and give it velocity and penetrating power. The firing method you've dreamed up wouldn't give the bullet enough punch to get it through a paper bag."

"That's right," Merlini admitted. "I had a little talk with Ballistics on the phone and got the same objection. But the slug that killed North was held close against him—it was fired into his ear. A barrel only an inch or so long would be ample."

Merlini got up, went into the workshop, and came back carrying a drawer from North's supply cabinet. "This contains odds and ends of hardware—nuts, bolts, washers, screws, angle irons, a hinge or two—and this."

He took from the drawer a two-inch length of brass pipe. "It's just the right size. A .32 cartridge fits into it neatly."

"Showing," Kane said a bit grimly, "how I might have killed North doesn't prove that's what I did. And you haven't one iota of concrete evidence that does."

"One is all we need," Merlini said. "A small one we haven't yet looked for—the cartridge case. Add that to the slug and the brass pipe and we have a complete weapon. The cartridge case will also show whether it was exploded by the hammer of a gun or with the soldering iron."

Kane said, "Perhaps you'd better start looking for it."

"You don't think we'll find it?"

"I didn't shoot North with a soldering iron and a piece of brass pipe, so there can't be any cartridge case that says I did."

"You could also be gambling on the fact that such a small object would, if carefully hidden, be hard to find. Now, however, we know just what we're looking for." Merlini stood up, walked around the desk and sat on its edge, facing Kane. "Have you any idea how thorough a competent police search can be? We'll take North's workshop apart piece by piece. His tools will be examined for hollow handles. We'll look inside cans of paint, tubes of glue. The workbench and woodwork will be gone over inch by inch in case you drilled a hole, inserted the case, and sealed it in with plastic wood.

"This room will get the same treatment. The upholstery on the furniture will be removed, the filing cabinets emptied. Miss O'Hara's typewriter will be taken apart. Even the telephone. Every single object larger than a cartridge case will be examined inside and out. We couldn't possibly miss it."

Kane's grin wasn't a happy one, but still he grinned. "Good. Apparently that's the only way I'll ever convince you you're wrong."

"And you'll be searched again," Merlini went on. "Including an x-ray examination because a cartridge case is small enough to swallow. The living room will also get the full treatment. Also Miss O'Hara and Dr. Price, in case you passed it to one of them."

I knew now what Merlini was trying to do. There is a mind-reading effect in which the magician asks his audience to hide some small object, usually a pin, while he is out of the room. When the magician returns he finds it, apparently by mind reading, but actually because the spectators' attitudes, as they watch him hunt, tell him when he is hot or cold. They give him what the psychologist calls unconscious cues.

Since even persons who are not emotionally involved cannot repress such cues, Kane, if guilty, would certainly react if Merlini, listing the possible hiding places, hit upon the right one.

But it obviously wasn't working.

Kane was still relaxed, smiling.

Merlini looked at Gavigan unhappily. "It'll have to be done, but I'm beginning to think you won't find it. Kane seems to be telling the truth."

Gavigan stared at him. "He's—what?"

"He knows," Merlini said, "that if we find it

he's done for. And since he's so sure we won't find it here, apparently it's not here."

"I'll believe that," Gavigan growled, "after we've looked."

Slowly, talking to himself, Merlini added, "If it isn't here, then obviously it must be somewhere else."

"Sure," Gavigan said skeptically, "only it couldn't have left this room."

Suddenly Merlini smiled. "I'm not so sure." Then, watching Kane, he said, "Doran, phone the Morgue. I want to talk to Peabody."

That did it.

The smile was still on Kane's face, but it was suddenly forced—the self-confidence behind it had drained away. When Merlini spoke again, the smile collapsed.

"One thing was taken out of this apartment— North's body. On it somewhere, in his clothes or in something he carried . . ."

The search was almost unnecessary. The look on Kane's face was that of a man already convicted.

Then, explosively, he moved. Suddenly he was on his feet, lunging toward Merlini, snarling.

Doran moved equally fast. His foot shot out, hooked Kane's ankle, and the man fell, his arms still reaching out toward Merlini. He smashed solidly at full length against the floor, and then Doran was on him, his knee planted firmly in Kane's back.

Peabody found the cartridge case inside the cap of North's fountain pen.

WHERE HAVE YOU GONE, SAM SPADE?

BILL PRONZINI

CHOOSING THE RIGHT NAME for a series hero is a tricky business and many authors have spent a great deal of time and energy coming up with just the right one, but when William John Pronzini (1943–) created his popular and long-running San Francisco private detective he decided to give him no name at all; the "Nameless Detective" series began in 1971 with *The Snatch* and continues to the present day, having appeared in more than thirty novels and scores of short stories. The lack of a name, combined with a less-than-flashy appearance and lifestyle (he's middle-aged and overweight, and a happy evening is drinking a cold beer and reading one of the pulp magazines from his extensive collection) make him the true Everyman mystery protagonist.

Born in Petaluma, California, where he still lives, Pronzini worked such odd jobs as salesman, sports reporter, and civilian guard with the U.S. Marshal's office before becoming a full-time writer in 1969. He has had a prodigious output, under both his own name and many pseudonyms, including Jack Foxx, William Jeffrey, Alex Saxon, and Robert Hart Davis. He has written literally hundreds of detective, suspense, and western short stories, yet somehow managed to find the time to edit scores of anthologies as well, mainly in the mystery genre, but also collections of horror, western, and military fiction. Among his outstanding nonfiction titles are *1001 Midnights* (1986, written with his wife, mystery writer Marcia Muller), reviews of 1001 volumes of detective fiction; *Gun in Cheek* (1982), a hilarious history of the worst writing in mystery fiction; its sequel, *Son of Gun in Cheek* (1987); and *Six-Gun in Cheek* (1997), an overview of the worst western fiction—all of which are produced with obvious affection for the authors and books that have been skewered. He was named a Grand Master by Mystery Writers of America in 2008.

"Where Have You Gone, Sam Spade?" was first published in the January 30, 1980, issue of *Alfred Hitchcock's Mystery Magazine*; it was first collected in *Case File* (New York, St. Martin's, 1983).

WHERE HAVE YOU GONE, SAM SPADE?

BILL PRONZINI

I.

THE BRINKMAN COMPANY, Specialty Imports, was located just off the Embarcadero, across from Pier Twenty-six in the shadow of the San Francisco–Oakland Bay Bridge. It was a good-sized building, made out of wood with a brick facade; it didn't look like much from the outside. I had no idea what was on the inside, because Arthur Brinkman, the owner, hadn't told me on the phone what sort of "specialty imports" he dealt in. He hadn't told me why he wanted to hire a private detective either. All he'd said was that the job would take a full week, my fee for which he would guarantee, and would I come over and talk to him? I would. I charged two hundred dollars a day, and when you multiplied that by seven it made for a nice piece of change.

It was a little after ten a.m. when I got there. The day was misty and cold, whipped by a stiff wind that had the sharp smell of salt in it—typical early-March weather in San Francisco. Drawn up at the rear of the building were three big trucks from a waterfront drayage company, and several men were busily engaged in unloading crates and boxes and wheeling them inside the warehouse on dollies and hand trucks. I parked my car up toward the front, next to a new Plymouth station wagon, and went across to the office entrance.

Inside, there was a small anteroom with a desk along the left-hand wall and two closed doors along the right-hand wall. A glass-fronted cabinet stood between the doors, displaying the kinds of things you see on knick-knack shelves in some people's houses. Opposite the entrance, in the rear wall, was another closed door; that one led to the warehouse, because I could hear the sounds the workmen made filtering in through it. And behind the desk was a buxom redhead rattling away on an electric typewriter.

She gave me a bright professional smile, finished what she was typing and said, "Yes, may I help you?" in a bright professional voice as she rolled the sheet out.

Along with a professional smile of my own, I gave her my name.

"Oh, yes," she said, "Mr. Brinkman is expecting you." She stood and came around from behind the desk. She had nice hips and pretty good legs; chubby calves, though. "My name is Fran Robbins, by the way. I'm the receptionist, secretary, and about six other things here. A Jill-of-all-trades, I guess you could say."

The last sentence was one she'd used before, probably to just about everyone who came in; you could tell that by the way she said it, the faint expectancy in her voice. She wanted me to appreciate both the line and her cleverness, so I said obligingly, "That's pretty good—Jill-of-all-trades. I like that."

She smiled again, much less impersonally this time; I'd made points with her, at least.

"I'll tell Mr. Brinkman you're here," she said, and went over and knocked on one of the doors in the right-hand wall and then disappeared through it.

The anteroom was not all that warm, despite the fact that a wall heater glowed near Miss Robbins's desk. Instead of sitting in the one visitor's chair, I took a couple of turns around the room to keep my circulation going. I was just starting a third turn when the left-hand door opened and Miss Robbins came back out.

With her was a wiry little man in his mid-forties, with colorless hair and features so bland they would have, I thought, the odd reverse effect of making you remember him. He looked as if a good wind would blow him apart and away, like the fluff of a dandelion. But he had quick, canny eyes and restless hands that kept plucking at the air, as if he were creating invisible things with them.

He used one of the hands to pat Miss Robbins on the shoulder; the smile she gave him in return was anything but professional—doe-eyed and warm enough to melt butter. I wondered if maybe the two of them had something going and decided it was a pretty good bet that they had. My old private eyes were still good at detecting things like that, if not much else.

Brinkman came over to me, gave me his name and one of his nervous hands, and then ushered me into his office. It wasn't much of an office—desk, a couple of low metal file cabinets, some boxes stacked along one wall and an old wooden visitor's chair that looked as if it would collapse if you sat in it. That chair was what I got invited to occupy, and it didn't collapse when I lowered myself into it; but I was afraid to move around much, just the same.

Sitting in his own chair, Brinkman lit a cigarette and left it hanging from one corner of his mouth. "You saw the trucks outside when you got here?" he asked.

I nodded. "You must be busy these days."

"Very busy. They're bringing in a shipment of goods that arrived by freighter from Europe a few days ago. Murano glass from Italy, Hummel figurines from West Germany, items like that."

"Are they the sort of things you generally import?"

"Among a number of other items, yes. This particular shipment is the largest I've ever bought; I just couldn't pass it up at the bulk price that was offered to me. Deals like that only come along once in ten years."

"The shipment is valuable, then?"

"Extremely valuable," Brinkman said. "When those trucks deliver the last of it later today, I'll have more than three hundred thousand dollars' worth of goods in my warehouse."

"That's a lot of money, all right," I agreed.

He bobbed his head in a jerky way, crushed out his cigarette and promptly lit another one. Chain-smoker, I thought. Poor bastard. I'd been a heavy smoker myself up until a couple of years ago, when a lesion on one lung made me quit cold turkey. The lesion had been benign, but it could just as easily have gone the other way. For Brinkman's sake, I hoped he had the sense to quit one of these days, before it was too late.

"The goods will be here in about a week," he said. "It will take that long to inventory them and arrange for the bulk of the items to be shipped out to my customers."

"I see."

"That's where you come in. I want you to guard them for me during that time. At night, when no one else is around."

So that was it. He was afraid somebody might come skulking around after dark to steal or vandalize his merchandise, and what he wanted was a nightwatchman. Not that I minded; nobody had wanted me to do any private skulking of my own in recent days, and there was that guarantee of wages for a full week.

I said, "I'm your man, Mr. Brinkman."

"Good. You'll start right away tonight."

I nodded. "When should I be here?"

"Six o'clock. That's our closing time."

"What time do you open in the morning?"

"Eight-thirty. But I'm usually here by seven."

"So you want me on the job about thirteen hours."

"That's right," Brinkman said. "I realize that's a much longer day than you normally work; I'm willing to compensate you for the extra time. Would two hundred and fifty a day be all right?"

It was just fine, and I said so.

He put out his second cigarette. "I'll show you around now," he said, "get you familiarized with the building and where everything is. When you come back tonight I'll show you what I want you to do on your rounds—"

There was a knock on the door. Brinkman was half out of his chair already; he stood all the way up as the door opened and a heavyset guy around my age, early fifties, with a drinker's nose and the thick, gnarled hands of a longshoreman, poked his head inside.

"See you a minute, Art?" the guy said.

"Sure. Come in, Orin; I want you to meet the man I've hired to guard the new shipment."

The heavyset guy came in, and we shook hands as Brinkman introduced us. His name was Orin McIntyre, and he was the firm's bookkeeper. Which was something of a small surprise; even though he was wearing a white shirt open at the throat and a pair of slacks, I had taken him, foolishly enough, for a warehouseman or a truck driver because of his physical appearance. He could have gone on the old "What's My Line?" television show and nobody would have guessed his occupation. So much for stereotypes.

"If you don't mind my saying so," McIntyre said to me, "I think Art is wasting his money hiring a nightwatchman. This place is built like a fortress; when it's locked up tight nobody can get in."

Brinkman gave him an irritated look. "You don't know that for certain, Orin. Neither do I."

"Well, the place has never been broken into, has it?"

"Not yet. But there's a first time for everything."

McIntyre said to me, "This building used to belong to an import-export outfit that dealt in high-priced artwork. They installed a number of safeguards: steel shutters over the windows on the outside, iron gates that you can padlock across the doors and windows on the inside. How can anybody get in through all of that?"

"It doesn't sound as if anybody can," I said. "But then, it didn't seem anybody could get into the Bank of England, either, and yet somebody did."

"Exactly," Brinkman agreed. He lit another cigarette; his hands plucked and fidgeted in the air, like a magician doing conjuring tricks behind a screen of smoke. He was one of the most nervous people I had ever encountered; he made *me* nervous just watching him. "I don't want to take any chances, that's all. This shipment is important to us all—"

"I know that as well as you do," McIntyre said. "Probably better, in fact."

Brinkman gave him another irritated look. There was some sort of friction between these two; I wondered what it was. And why Brinkman, the boss, put up with it.

I said, "I've been a cop of one kind or another for thirty years; if there's one thing I've learned in all that time, it's that there's no such thing as too much precaution against crime. The more prepared you are, the less likely you'll get taken by surprise."

"That sounds like a self-serving statement," McIntyre said.

"No, sir, it's not. It's a statement of fact, that's all."

"Uh-huh. Well, if you ask me—"

"That's enough, Orin," Brinkman said. "You've got better things to do than stand around here questioning my judgment or this man's integrity. So have I. Now, what did you want to see me about?"

"One of the bills of lading on the shipment is screwed up." McIntyre sounded faintly miffed, as if he didn't like having been put in his place. It was what he'd tried to do to me, but the "Do unto others" rule was one some men never learned; he knew how to dish it out, but he couldn't take it worth a damn. "You want to talk here, in front of him"—he gestured in my direction—"or in my office?"

"Your office." Brinkman looked at me. "This won't take long. Then I'll show you around."

"Fine," I said.

The three of us went out into the anteroom,

and Brinkman and McIntyre disappeared into McIntyre's office. Miss Robbins was busy at her desk, so I went over and stood quietly in front of the wall heater. From there I noticed that, as McIntyre had said, there was an iron-barred folding gate drawn back beside the front door. When it was extended and bolted into a locking plate on the other side of the door, it would provide an extra seal against intruders.

Brinkman was back in five minutes, alone. He fired another cigarette, hung it on his lower lip, did the conjuring trick with his hands and then led me off on the guided tour.

II.

The warehouse door off the anteroom led into a short corridor, beyond which was a section partitioned off with wall board: bathroom on the right, L-shaped shipping counter on the left. And beyond there was the warehouse itself, a wide, spacious area with rafters crisscrossing under a high roof, a concrete floor and white-painted walls. A cleared aisleway ran straight down its geometrical center to the open rear doors where the warehousemen were unloading the drayage trucks. Built into the joining of the right-side and rear walls, ten feet above the floor, was a thirty-foot-square loft; a set of stairs led up to it and its jumble of boxes and storage items.

To the right of the aisle, down to the loft stairs, were perpendicular rows of platform shelving, with narrow little aisles between them; some of the shelves were filled with merchandise both packed and unpacked, the unpacked boxes showing gouts of either straw packing or excelsior. To the left of the aisle was open floor space jammed with stacked crates, pallets, dollies, bins full of more straw packing, and carts with metal wheels—all arranged in such a mazelike way that you could, if you were careful, move among them without knocking or falling over something.

Brinkman led me through the clutter to the nearest window. An iron-barred gate was drawn across it, firmly padlocked to an iron hasp, and through the windowpane I could see that the outside shutter was in place. When I'd had my look at the window, he took me to the rear doors and showed me that they had double locks and their own set of iron-barred gates. He also mentioned the fact that the walls and roof were reinforced with steel rods.

The place was a minifortress, all right. About the only way anybody was going to break in there was with blasting caps or chain saws.

After we finished examining the security, Brinkman showed me some of the items in the big shipment from Europe and explained what the rest were. In addition to the Hummel figurines and the Murano glass, there were special flamenco dolls from Spain, crystal from Sweden and Denmark, pewter from Norway, Delft porcelain miniatures from Holland, intricate dollhouse accessories from France.

Looking at all of that, I thought that this was going to be a pretty easy job. I could understand how Brinkman felt, why he was so nervous about the possibility of theft, but the plain fact was, he had very little cause for alarm. In the first place, there was the fortresslike makeup of the building. And in the second place, his merchandise may have been valuable, but it was not the kind that would tempt thieves, professional or otherwise. There are people around who will steal anything, of course, but not very many who were likely to get hot and bothered over Italian glass candy dishes or Delft miniatures. And where would you fence stolen flamenco dolls or French dollhouse accessories?

I mentioned those facts to Brinkman, just for the record, but it didn't make him think twice about hiring me; he was bound and determined to have a nightwatchman on the premises for the coming week, as an added precaution, and nothing and nobody were going to make him change his mind. Nor did what I said reassure him much. He was a worrier, and there's never anything you can say that will reassure one of that breed. The more you tell them everything is going to be all right, the more fretful they get.

Through all of the tour, the warehousemen continued to unload the trucks and wheel crates inside and stack them here and there. There were four of them, three part-timers and Brinkman's full-time "warehouse supervisor," a guy named Frank Judkins. Brinkman intercepted Judkins on his way in with a hand truck loaded with boxes and introduced him to me.

He was a brawny guy in his forties, tough-looking—the kind you used to see, and probably still could, in longshoremen's bars along the waterfront. He had lank black hair that grew as thickly on his arms, and no doubt on the rest of him, as it did on his head; he also had vacuous eyes and a wart the size of a dime on his chin.

He said, "How's it going, pal?" as he caught hold of my hand and made an effort to crush the bones in it, either by accident or to show me how strong he was.

I've got a pretty good grip myself; I tightened it to match his and looked him square in the eye. "Pretty good, pal," I said. "How about yourself?"

Judkins liked that; he laughed noisily. Some of his teeth were missing, and what remained were either yellow or black with cavities. He let go of my hand and stood there grinning at me like a Neanderthal.

Brinkman said to him, "Everything going all right out here, Frank?"

"Yeah. Almost done with the first load."

"They'll bring the rest of the merchandise after lunch?"

"Yeah."

"Good." Brinkman told him I would be coming in at six to assume my nightwatchman's duties. "You'll have everything off-loaded and inside by then, won't you?"

"Yeah."

"See to it that you do. I don't want this place open after dark."

"Yeah," Judkins said. It seemed to be his favorite word, probably because it had only one syllable and required no mental effort to utter.

Judkins grinned at me again and looked at my hand as if he wanted to shake it some more, to see if my grip was really as strong as it seemed. But I didn't have to put up with any more attempts at bone crushing; Brinkman told him to get back to work and steered me away through the shipping area and into the office anteroom.

Fran Robbins was on the phone when we came in. She said, "One moment, please," into the receiver, took it away from her ear and put her hand over the mouthpiece, and tilted her head toward Brinkman. "It's the Consolidated chain," she said. "I think you'd better talk to them, Arth—uh, Mr. Brinkman. There's some problem about their order."

"Damn," Brinkman said. "Okay, tell them just a second and put 'em on hold."

She gave him her butter-melting smile. They had something going, all right; I could see it in her eyes. I wondered what those eyes saw in him. But then, *de gustibus non est disputandam.* Which was a Latin phrase I'd read somewhere that meant there was no accounting for taste. In this world, there was somebody for everyone; and Brinkman was obviously Miss Robbins's somebody.

He turned to me as she spoke again into the telephone. "I think we've covered just about everything for now," he said. "Unless you have any more questions?"

"No, I can't think of any."

"I'll see you at six, then."

"Right. Six sharp."

"Your check will be ready when you get here," he said, and hurried into his office to take his call.

I said good-bye to the Jill-of-all-trades, went out to my car, and drove downtown to my office on Taylor Street. I checked my new answering machine first; there hadn't been any calls. Then I prepared one of my standard contract forms for Brinkman to sign, stipulating the payment we had agreed upon. And then, because I had no other work to attend to, and because I was going to be up all night, I went home to my flat in Pacific Heights and took myself a nap.

At five o'clock I was up and dressed and ready to go, and at ten minutes to six I was back at the

Brinkman Company, Specialty Imports. The drayage trucks were gone and the warehouse was closed. Miss Robbins and Orin McIntyre and the warehousemen were gone, too; Brinkman was there alone. I gave him the contract form to sign, exchanged a countersigned copy for my retainer check. After we got that taken care of, he took me out into the warehouse again and showed me what he wanted me to do "on my rounds." Which amounted to checking the doors and windows periodically, and making sure none of the straw packing and excelsior caught fire, because they were highly combustible materials. He also warned me not to let anyone in, under any circumstances; there was no reason for anyone to come around, he said, and if anyone did come around, it had to mean they were there to steal something.

I assured him, with more patience than I felt, that I would do what he'd asked of me and that I was competent at my job. He said, "Yes, I'm sure you are," and fluttered his hands at me. "It's just that I worry. I'll call you later, before I go to bed, to check in. So it's all right for you to answer the phone when it rings." He paused. "You don't mind if I call, do you?"

"No," I said, "I don't mind."

"Good. It's just that I worry, you know?"

He went away pretty soon and left me alone with his $300,000 worth of knick-knacks.

It was some night.

The warehouse was unheated, and Brinkman's office, where I spent most of my time, tended to be chilly even with the wall heater turned on. Time crawled, as it always does on a job like this; there was nothing to do except to read the handful of pulp magazines I'd brought with me, eat a late supper, and drink coffee from the thermos I'd also brought, and listen to foghorns moaning out on the Bay. Nobody tried to break in. Nobody called except Brinkman at a little before midnight. And the only real night-watching I did was of the clock on the wall.

Ah, the exciting life of a private eye. Danger, intrigue, adventure, beautiful women, feats of derring-do.

Thirteen hours of boredom and a half-frozen rear end.

Where have you gone, Sam Spade?

III.

I got home at seven-thirty, gritty-eyed and grumpy, and slept until two o'clock. When I got up I packed another cold supper, made fresh coffee for the thermos and put everything into a paper sack with some issues of *Detective Tales* and *Dime Mystery* from my collection of pulp magazines. Then I drove down to my office to find out if anybody else was interested in hiring me.

Nobody was. The only message on my answering machine was from somebody who wanted to convert me to his religion; he was reading from some sort of Biblical tract in a persuasively ministerial voice, when the message tape ran out and ended his pitch. I did a little paperwork and then sat around until five-thirty, in case a prospective client decided to walk in. It was a decision nobody made. And the phone didn't ring either.

I pulled into the Brinkman Company lot and parked my car next to Brinkman's station wagon at two minutes to six. The weather was colder and foggier than it had been yesterday; the wind off the Bay made wailing noises and slashed at me as I hurried to the office entrance with my paper sack.

The door was locked, as it had been last night; I rapped on the glass, and Brinkman came out and opened up for me. "I'm glad you're on time," he said. "I have an engagement at seven-thirty and I've got to rush."

"Everything locked up, Mr. Brinkman?"

"Yes, I think so. But you'd better double-check, make sure the windows and doors are secure."

"Right."

The door to Orin McIntyre's office opened and McIntyre came out, carrying a briefcase in each hand. He seemed upset; he was scowling and his face was heavy and dark, like a sky full of thunderclouds.

I said automatically, "How are you tonight, Mr. McIntyre?"

"Lousy," he said.

"Something wrong?"

He looked past me at Brinkman—a look that almost crackled with animosity. "Ask him."

"Don't make a scene, Orin," Brinkman said.

"Why the hell shouldn't I make a scene?"

"It won't do you any good."

"Is that a fact?"

Brinkman sighed, made one of his nervous gestures. "I'm sorry, Orin; I told you that. I wish you'd understand that my decision is nothing personal; it's just a simple matter of economics—"

"Oh, I understand, all right," McIntyre said angrily. "I understand that you're a fourteen-carat bastard, that's what I understand."

"Orin—"

"The hell with you." McIntyre glared at him and then switched the glare to me. "And the hell with *you*," he said, and went to the door and slammed out into the windy dusk.

Through the glass I watched him walk across the lot to his car. When I turned back Brinkman said, "I suppose I can't blame him for being angry."

"What happened?"

"I had to let him go. His work wasn't all it should be, and I really can't afford his salary. Besides, I've been thinking of promoting Miss Robbins, turning the bookkeeping job over to her. She's had accountant's training, and she can handle it along with her other duties."

Uh-huh, I thought. The firing of McIntyre may have been for economic reasons, but I doubted there was nothing personal involved; I had a feeling Brinkman's relationship with Fran Robbins had had more than a little to do with it. But then, Brinkman's private life was really none of my concern. Nor, for that matter, were his business decisions, except as they pertained to me.

So I just nodded, let a couple of seconds pass and then asked him, "Everyone else gone, Mr. Brinkman?"

"Yes." He shot the cuff of his gray sports jacket and looked at his watch. "And I've got to be gone, too, or I'll be late for my appointment. I'll call you later, as usual. Around midnight."

"Whatever you say."

I followed him to the door and we exchanged good nights. When he'd gone out I closed and locked the door, using the latchkey he had given me. I made it a double seal by swinging the barred gate shut across the door and padlocking it. And there I was, sealed in all nice and cozy until seven a.m. tomorrow.

The next order of business was to shut off the ceiling lights, which I did and which left the anteroom dark except for the desk lamp glowing beyond the half-open door to Brinkman's office. I went in there and put my paper sack down on the desk, came out again and crossed to the door that led back into the warehouse.

A dull, yellowish bulb burned above the shipping counter, casting just enough light to bleach the shadows past the partitions. None of the overheads was on in the warehouse proper; it was like a wall of black velvet back there with all the windows shuttered against the fading daylight. I located the bank of electrical switches and flipped each in turn. The rafter bulbs were not much brighter than the one over the counter, but there were enough of them to herd most of the shadows into corners or behind the stacks of shelving and crates.

I made my way through the clutter on the right side of the aisleway, to the nearest of the windows. The barred gate was as firmly pad-locked as it had been last night. There was a second window several feet beyond, to the rear; I had a look at that one next. Secure. Then I moved over to the shelving, down one of the cross aisles past several hundred unpacked crystal candleholders that caught and reflected the light like so many prisms. The single window on that side, too, was both shuttered and barred up tight.

That left the rear doors. I went down there and rattled the gate and padlock, as I'd done at the windows, and peered through the bars at the double locks on the doors themselves. Secure. A team of commandos, I thought, would be hard-pressed to breach this place.

To pass some time, I prowled around for fifteen minutes or so, shining my flashlight into dark corners, examining glass vases and tiny pieces of dollhouse furniture, poking through what few purchase orders there were on the shipping counter. Lethargy was already starting to set in; I caught myself yawning twice. But it was as much a lack of sleep as it was boredom. I had never been able to sleep very well in the daytime, and I hadn't had enough rest during the past two days; by the end of the week I would probably be ready for about fifteen hours of uninterrupted sack time. I could have curled up in a nest of straw right here and taken a nap, of course, but my conscience wouldn't allow it. I had never cheated a client in any fashion and I was not about to start now by sleeping on the job.

So I shut off the overheads and went back to Brinkman's office, leaving the warehouse door open. It was almost as cold in there as it was in the warehouse, which was probably just as well; the chill would help keep me awake. I got my thermos bottle out of the paper sack and poured myself a cup of hot coffee. Sat back with it and one of the pulps I'd brought, bundled up in my coat, feet propped on a low metal file cabinet to one side of the desk.

And I was ready to begin another long night in my brief career as a nightwatchman.

IV.

The minute hand dragged itself around the clock on the office wall. In the pulp—the December 1936 issue of *Detective Tales*—I read "Satan Covers the Waterfront" by Tom Roan and "The Case of the Whispering Terror" by George Bruce. Outside, the velocity of the wind increased; I could hear it rattling a loose drain gutter on the roof as I read "Malachi Gunn and the Vanishing Heiress" by Franklin H. Martin.

Eight-forty.

I poured another cup of coffee. None of the other stories in the issue of *Detective Tales* looked interesting; I put it down and picked up the May 1935 *Dime Mystery*. And read "House of the Restless Dead" by Hugh B. Cave and "Mistress of Terror" by Wyatt Blassingame. The wind slackened again, and the only background noises I had to listen to then were creaking joints and the distant moan of foghorns on the bay.

Ten-oh-five.

I read "The Man Who Was Dead" by John Dixon Carr, which was a nice little ghost story set in England. The "Dixon" was no doubt a misspelling and the author was John Dickson Carr, the master of the locked-room mystery; I'd read somewhere that Carr had published a few stories in mid-1930s pulps, one other of which I'd read in the third or fourth issue of *Detective Tales*.

My eyes were beginning to feel heavy-lidded and sore from all the reading; I rubbed at them with my knuckles, closed the magazine, yawned noisily, and looked at the thermos and the three salami-and-cheese sandwiches and two apples inside the sack. But I wasn't hungry just yet, and the coffee had to last me the rest of the night. I got to my feet, stretching; glanced at the clock again in spite of myself.

Ten thirty-three.

And something made a noise out in the warehouse—a dull thud like a heavy weight falling against another object.

The hair poked up on my neck; I stood frozen, listening, for three or four seconds. The silence seemed suddenly eerie. Sounds in the night seldom bother me, but this was different. This was a building in which I was alone and sealed up, and yet I was sure the thudding noise had come from *inside* the warehouse.

I grabbed my flashlight off the desk, switched it on and ran into the anteroom. Just as I reached the open warehouse door, I had an almost subliminal glimpse of a streak of light winking out beyond the night-lit shipping counter. Somebody else with a flash? I threw my own beam down the corridor, went through the doorway after it.

In the clotted darkness ahead, there was a faint thumping sound.

Without slowing I veered past the shipping counter and over to the bank of light switches. The flash beam illuminated the near third of the main aisleway, but its diffused glare showed me nothing except inanimate objects.

Another thump. And then a kind of clicking or popping. Both noises seemed to come from somewhere diagonally to my left.

I threw all the switches at once, slapping upward with the palm of my free hand. When I hurried ahead into the aisle, the pale rafter lights let me see the same tableau as earlier—nothing altered, nothing subtracted, nothing added. Except for one thing.

There was a dead man lying a few feet to the left of the aisle, half-draped across one of the wooden crates.

I saw him when I was no more than twenty feet into the warehouse, and I knew right away he was dead. He was facing toward me, twisted onto his side, features half-hidden behind an upflung arm; there was blood all over the leather jacket and blue turtleneck sweater he wore, and the one eye I could see was wide open. Hesitantly, gawping a little, I moved to where he was and bent over him.

Sam Judkins, the warehouseman.

He'd been shot once in the left side, under the breastbone, at point-blank range with a small-caliber gun: scorch and powder marks were visible around the hole, and there was no exit wound.

His jacket and trousers were wet in front. And they smelled of . . . wood alcohol?

Ripples of cold flowed over my back. The eerie silence, the dead man, the bullet wound, the wood-alcohol smell all combined to give me a feeling of surreality, as though I were asleep and dreaming all of this. I backed away from the body, shaking my head. He couldn't have got in

here, but here he was. He couldn't have been murdered in here, but here he was. It was murder, all right; there was no gun near him, which had to mean that whoever had shot him still had it. And what had happened to *him*? Where did *he* go?

Still in here somewhere, hiding?

I stopped moving and made myself stand still for thirty seconds. No movement anywhere. No sounds anywhere. Over to my left, lying on a metal-wheeled cart, was one of those curved iron bars used for prying lids off wooden crates; I caught it up and held it cocked against my shoulder, wishing that I hadn't decided I would not need a handgun for this job.

But nothing happened as I paced back into the aisle, along it through the shipping area. Nor was there anything more to see or hear.

In Brinkman's office, I dialed the number of the Hall of Justice. Eberhardt, my sober-sided cop friend, was on night duty this week, and I got through to him with no problem. He grumbled and did some swearing, told me to stay where I was and not to do anything stupid, and hung up while I was reminding him I used to be a police officer myself.

I went back into the anteroom and took another look through the door leading to the warehouse. But if whoever had killed Judkins was still here, why hadn't he come after me by now? It didn't make sense that he would let me call the cops and then hang around to wait for them.

The front door seemed to be as secure as before; that was the first thing I checked. Nobody could possibly have come in through there when I was in Brinkman's office earlier, or gone out through there after I heard those noises. I walked back into the warehouse again, taking the pry bar with me just in case. Not touching anything, I checked the gates and padlocks on all the windows and the rear doors. And each of them was also as secure as before.

So how had Judkins and whoever killed him got in?

And how had the killer got out?

V.

When the banging started at the front entrance I was back in Brinkman's office, just hanging up the telephone for the third time. I hurried out and unlocked the gate and swung it aside; unlocked the door and opened it.

"What the hell are you guarding in there?" Eberhardt asked sourly. "Gold bullion?"

There were a half-dozen other cops with him: an inspector I knew named Klein, two guys from the police lab outfitted with field kits, a photographer and a brace of patrolmen. I moved aside without saying anything and let all of them crowd past me into the anteroom. Then I shut the door again to cut off the icy blasts of wind.

Eberhardt made a gnawing sound on the stem of his pipe and glowered at me. The glower didn't mean anything; like the pipe— one of twenty or thirty battered old briars he owned—it was a permanent fixture, part of his professional persona. The only times he smiled or relaxed were when he was off duty.

He asked me, "Where's the victim?"

"Warehouse area, in back."

I led him and the others out there. The two lab guys and the photographer headed straight for the body; Eberhardt told Klein and one of the patrolmen—the other had stayed in the anteroom—to have a look around, and then made it a foursome around the dead man. The alcohol smell coming off Judkins's clothes was strong on the cold air; I retreated from it, across the center aisle, and stood waiting against one of the platform shelves.

Nine or ten minutes passed. I watched Klein and the patrolman poking around, peering at the windows and doors, checking for possible hiding places. The patrolman climbed up into the loft and shone his flashlight among the boxes and things. More light flashed over near the body as the photographer began taking his Polaroid shots.

Klein came back from the rear doors just as an assistant coroner bustled in from the ante-room; the two of them joined Eberhardt for a brief consultation, after which Klein disappeared up front, the coroner's man moved to the corpse and Eb came over to where I was.

"You got anything to add to what you told me on the phone?" he asked.

"Not much," I said. "There's nothing missing from among the merchandise in here, at least as far as I can tell, and the place is still sealed up tight. I tried calling Brinkman after I talked to you, but there was no answer."

"Any idea where he might be?"

"He said he had an engagement at seven-thirty. I figured it might be with the receptionist, Fran Robbins, because it looks like they've got a thing going. But there's nobody home at her place either; I found her number in Brinkman's address book and tried it."

"Dead man worked here, too, that right?"

I nodded. "He was the warehouseman."

"Was he around when you got here tonight?"

"No."

"How many other employees?"

"Just one. Bookkeeper named Orin McIntyre. But he's an ex-employee as of today."

"Oh? Quit or fired?"

"Fired," I said. "Brinkman told me his work wasn't up to par and that he couldn't afford McIntyre's salary. McIntyre left just after I got here; he didn't look any too happy."

"You think there might be a connection between that and the murder?"

"I don't know. I tried McIntyre's number, too, just before you came. Third straight no-answer."

"All right. Let's go over your story again, in detail this time. Don't leave anything out."

I gave him a complete rundown of the night's events as I knew them. And the more I talked, the more he glowered. What we had here was a mystery, and mysteries annoyed the hell out of him.

Klein returned just as I finished. He said to Eberhardt, "I looked around outside. Nothing in the parking lot or anywhere else in the vicinity."

"You check the doors and windows?"

"Yep. All secured with inside-locking shutters."

"You're certain they're locked?"

"Positive."

"Same thing in here, too, huh? With the gates?"

"Afraid so, Eb."

Eberhardt muttered something under his breath—and up front, in the anteroom, the telephone began to ring. I glanced at my watch. Almost midnight.

"That'll be Brinkman," I said. "He said he'd call about this time to check in."

"You get it," Eberhardt said to Klein. "Wherever he is, tell him to come here right away."

"Right."

When Klein had gone again Eb said to me, "What is it with you? Every time I turn around you're mixed up in some kind of screwball case."

I said wryly, "Where have you gone, Sam Spade?"

"How's that?"

"Just something I was thinking earlier today."

"Yeah, well, from now on try to keep it simple, will you? No more homicides. Do skip-traces or find somebody's missing cousin like other private eyes."

"At least I don't go around getting hit on the head."

"It wouldn't hurt you much if you did," he said.

The assistant coroner called to him before I could say anything else, and he went over for another short conference. Just after they broke it up, Klein reappeared from the anteroom. He and Eberhardt converged on me again.

Eb said, "Was that Brinkman?"

"Uh-huh. He'll be right down."

"Where was he calling from?"

"The apartment of one of his employees," Klein said, "a woman named Fran Robbins. He says he's just given her a promotion and they've been celebrating all evening—at her place for dinner, then out for a couple of drinks around ten. They just got back. He sounded pretty upset when I told him what'd happened here."

"Wouldn't you be?" Eberhardt got a leather pouch out of his coat pocket and began thumbing shag-cut tobacco into the bowl of his pipe, scowling all the while.

Klein asked him, "Coroner's man have anything to say yet?"

"Confirmed the obvious, that's all. Shot once at close range, death instantaneous or close to it. Small-caliber weapon, looks like; we'll know what size and make when the coroner digs out the bullet and Ballistics gets hold of it."

I said speculatively, "Maybe a twenty-two with a silencer."

"Why a silencer?"

"Because I didn't hear the shot."

"The gun could have been muffled with something else. Heavy cloth, cushion of some kind—anything along those lines."

"Sure. But it was pitch-dark in here except for the killer's flashlight; it'd be kind of awkward to hold a flash on somebody and muffle and fire a gun all at the same time."

"Well, a silencer seems just as doubtful," Eberhardt said. "They don't leave powder and scorch marks like the ones on Judkins."

"Then why didn't I hear the shot?"

None of us had a ready answer for that. Klein said, "What about the alcohol smell?"

"Wood alcohol, evidently," Eberhardt told him. "Judkins had a bottle of it zipped inside his jacket pocket; the bullet shattered the bottle on its way into him."

"Was he drinking it, you suppose?"

"He was crazy if he was; that stuff will destroy your insides. No way to be sure yet, though. There's a strong alcohol odor around the mouth, but it could be gin."

I said, "Was there anything else on the body?"

"Usual stuff people carry in their pockets."

"How much money in his wallet?"

"Fifty-eight dollars. You thinking robbery?"

"It's a possibility."

"Yeah, but not of Judkins so much as by him and somebody else. Of what's in this warehouse, I mean. That would explain what he and whoever killed him were doing here tonight."

"It would," I said, "except that it doesn't add up. Nothing seems to be missing; so if two guys come to a place to rob it, why would one of them shoot the other *before* the robbery?"

"And how did they get in and out in the first place?" Klein added.

Eberhardt jabbed his pipe in my direction. "Listen, are you sure you were alone when you locked up after Brinkman left?"

"Pretty sure," I said. "I came out here first thing and checked the windows and doors. Then I wandered around for a while, looking things over. I didn't see or hear anything."

"But somebody—Judkins, say—*could* have been hiding in here just the same."

"It's possible, I guess. Up in the loft, maybe; I didn't go up there. But Brinkman told me Judkins had gone for the day, and it just isn't reasonable that he could've slipped back in without somebody seeing him. And I still think I'd have felt something. You know when you're alone and when you're not alone, at least most of the time. You get what the kids nowadays call vibes."

"Yeah," Eberhardt said. "Vibes."

Klein said, "Even if Judkins was hiding in here, what was the point in it? To steal something? Hell, he worked here; he could have committed theft during business hours. And it doesn't explain how the killer got in and out either."

"There's one explanation that'll cover all of that," I said. "But I don't like it much; it's pretty farfetched."

"Go ahead."

"Nobody got in and out of here because there's no killer. Judkins committed suicide."

Eberhardt made a growling noise. "Suicide," he said, as if it were a dirty word. "If he shot himself, where the hell is the gun?"

"He could've dropped it somewhere and staggered down here and fallen where he is now. A thorough search would turn it up."

"Why would he pick a place like this to knock himself off in?"

"He wasn't too bright, Eb. Suppose he hated Brinkman for some reason and figured the publicity would damage the business. Suppose he

wanted familiar surroundings when he pulled the trigger. . . ." I spread my hands because Eberhardt was shaking his head in a disgusted way. "Well, I told you it was pretty farfetched," I said.

"The other possibilities are just as improbable," Klein said. "One person, or even two, could have been hiding in here tonight without you realizing it; but there's nobody hiding in here now. Which means Judkins' killer had to get out, if not in—and how could he do that when all the doors and windows are double- or triple-sealed?"

"Maybe he's a magician or a ghost," Eberhardt said with heavy sarcasm. "Maybe he walked through the damned wall."

The patrolman who had been searching the warehouse came up and reported that he hadn't found anything of significance, unless you wanted to count an empty gin bottle tucked under some rags in the loft. Then a couple of white-coated interns entered with a stretcher and a body bag, and Eberhardt moved over to talk to the assistant coroner again before he gave them permission to remove the body. Klein, at Eb's instructions, returned to the anteroom to try again to get in touch with Orin McIntyre.

And I went into Brinkman's office, where it was quiet, to drink another cup of coffee from my thermos and do some thinking.

VI.

It was twelve thirty-five when Brinkman showed up. He came sailing in with Fran Robbins on one arm, looking more agitated than ever; his hands fluttered here and there, creating more of those invisible things out of the air. Robbins looked bewildered, nervous and a little frightened. She kept brushing a lock of her red hair out of one eye and casting glances around the anteroom as though she'd never seen it before.

Brinkman veered over to where I was standing in the doorway to his office. He gave me an accusing glare, as if he thought I had betrayed him somehow, and breathed stale tobacco and whiskey fumes at me; the heavy sweetness of enough cologne for a regiment was almost as unpleasant.

"What's been going on here tonight?" he demanded. "The officer on the phone told me Frank Judkins is dead, murdered."

"I'm afraid so, Mr. Brinkman."

"But how? By whom?"

"He was shot," I said. "The police don't know who did it yet. They think maybe you can help them."

"How can I help them? I don't even know what's going on." He fumbled a package of cigarettes from the pocket of his brown suit coat, got one into his mouth and fired it. "Is anything missing, stolen? Could it have been robbery?"

"Nothing stolen as far as I could tell," I said. "You'll be able to judge that a lot better yourself after you've talked to Lieutenant Eberhardt."

"Is he the man in charge?"

"Yes. He's out in the warehouse."

Brinkman nodded, started to turn away and then faced me again. "Orin McIntyre," he said, as if he were making some sort of revelation. "Maybe *he* had something to do with this. You heard what he said to me tonight. He's always struck me as the vindictive sort."

"The police got him on the phone a little while ago," I said. "McIntyre claims he spent the evening barhopping alone, drowning his anger at being fired, and didn't get home until just before midnight."

Brinkman's cigarette bobbed and weaved in his restless fingers. "Do the police believe that?"

"They're reserving judgment until they check out his story. Lieutenant Eberhardt sent a patrol car for him; he'll be here pretty soon."

Brinkman hung his cigarette on his lower lip, said, "I'll go talk to the lieutenant," and headed through the warehouse doorway trailing smoke. Fran Robbins hesitated, glancing at me and biting her lip, and then went after him; the patrolman by the door watched the movement of her hips with the intensity and admiration of a confirmed ladies' man.

I shut the office door and returned to Brinkman's desk and poured the last of the coffee into my cup. It was quiet in the room—but not at all quiet inside my head. Things had begun to go clickety-click in there, like a sturdy old engine warming up and about to run smoothly.

I sat on a corner of the desk, sipping coffee and concentrating. Vague ideas sharpened and took on weight and shape; bits and pieces of information slotted themselves neatly into place. And finally—

"Sure," I said aloud. "Hell, yes."

I went into the anteroom, through the warehouse door and past the shipping counter. Ahead, near where Judkins's body had lain, Eberhardt and Klein were talking to Brinkman and Fran Robbins. And to Orin McIntyre. It surprised me that McIntyre was there; I hadn't heard him being brought in. But when I looked at my watch I saw that it was one o'clock. A good twenty minutes had passed since the arrival of Brinkman and Robbins; I had been so deep in thought that I had lost track of both the time and my surroundings.

McIntyre, I saw as I came up, looked rumpled and bleary-eyed and upset. He was talking to Eberhardt but glaring at Brinkman as he spoke. "I didn't have a damned thing to do with what happened to Judkins. I told you, I was out drinking all evening."

"You haven't told us where," Eberhardt said.

"I don't remember where." McIntyre's voice was still a little slurred; he rubbed at his slack mouth. "A bunch of bars out in Noe Valley. Listen—"

"You never did get along with Judkins," Brinkman interrupted. "You were always arguing with him."

"That was because he was a half-wit. And you're a bastard, Brinkman—a lousy bastard."

"I don't have to take that from you," Brinkman said indignantly. "For all I know, you *did* murder poor Judkins—"

I said, "No, McIntyre didn't do it."

All eyes flicked toward me. Eberhardt took the pipe out of his mouth and waved it in my direction. "How do you know that?"

"Because," I said, "Brinkman did it."

VII.

Fran Robbins made a little gasping sound. Surprise opened up Brinkman's face for an instant: guilt flickered there like a film clip on a screen. Then it was gone and his stare was full of shocked indignation.

"You're crazy," he said. He turned and appealed to Eberhardt. "He's crazy."

Eb said, "Maybe," and narrowed his eyes at me. "Well?"

"He did it, all right."

"You got proof to back that up?"

"Enough," I said, which was not quite the truth. All I had were solid deductions based on circumstantial evidence and plain logic. But I knew I was right. There was only one person who could have killed Judkins and only one way the whole thing made sense; it was a simple matter of eliminating the impossible, so that whatever you had left had to be the answer. So I was pretty sure I could prove, at least to Eberhardt's satisfaction, that Brinkman *had* to be the murderer. After that it would be up to Eberhardt to make a homicide charge stick.

McIntyre said, "I might have known it," in a satisfied voice. His eyes were still on Brinkman, and they were wolfish now.

Brinkman drew himself up, all bluff and bluster, and ripped at the air with his hands. "This accusation is ridiculous," he said to Eberhardt. "I had nothing to do with what happened here tonight. I spent the entire evening with Fran; I've already told you that."

"So you have. Is that your story, too, miss?"

Robbins looked at Brinkman, wet her lips and said, "Yes." But the word came out almost as a question. She sounded anxious and uncertain.

I said, "You're sure about that, Miss Robbins? Being an accessory to insurance fraud is a minor offense; being an accessory to murder gets you a lot of years in prison."

That sharpened the anxiety and confusion in her eyes. She put a hand on Brinkman's arm. "Arthur?"

"It's all right, Fran. He doesn't know what the hell he's talking about."

Eberhardt asked me, "What's this about insurance fraud?"

"That was the idea from the beginning," I told him. "This outfit isn't as profitable as Brinkman wants people to believe; I think he's been operating in the red and doesn't have enough capital to pay off on the merchandise that just came in from Europe, or enough buyers to take it all off his hands." I looked at McIntyre. "Am I right, Mr. McIntyre?"

"Damn right," he said. "I warned Brinkman about making the deal; I told him it was liable to put the company under. He told me to mind my own business and went ahead with it anyway. But how did you know?"

"Some inferences you made yesterday, for one thing. He also let it slip tonight that one of the reasons he fired you was that he couldn't afford your salary. And there are only a small number of purchase orders on the shipping counter, not enough to account for more than a third of the total shipment."

"So what are you suggesting?" Eberhardt said.

"That the same bright idea occurred to Brinkman that's occurred to too many small businessmen these days," I said. "Burn the place down and collect the insurance."

I watched Brinkman as I spoke. Still all bluff and bluster, still plucking away at the air; the shrewd eyes weren't admitting anything.

"Only he was smart enough to realize arson would be suspected and there'd be a thorough investigation," I went on. "So he decided to set up a neat bit of camouflage. Hire a private detective with a good reputation to act as night-watchman, arrange an alibi for himself and then have a fire started right under the detective's nose. I wasn't supposed to get hurt; I was supposed to testify later that I was alone in a completely impenetrable building when the fire broke out. Nobody could have set it except me, and I'd be exonerated because of my record. The cause would go down as spontaneous combustion, which wouldn't be hard to believe with all the straw packing and excelsior lying around in here; he'd already planted the seed by warning me to watch out for fire during my rounds. The insurance company would have no recourse except to pay off on the claim."

"You're making sense so far," Eberhardt said. "Now where does Judkins come into it? The hired torch?"

I nodded. "He had to be. It explains the wood alcohol he had in his pocket. That stuff is inflammable as hell; you can use it to start a dandy fire."

"But then why would Brinkman kill Judkins before he could torch the building?"

"It doesn't figure to be a premeditated homicide; murder was never part of the original plan. Judkins died because of something that happened between him and Brinkman tonight, something that made Brinkman come down here around ten o'clock—"

"I don't have to listen to any more of this," Brinkman said. His expression still showed defiance, but a muscle had begun to jump under his left eye so that he seemed to be winking spasmodically. He lit another cigarette. "I wasn't anywhere near here at ten o'clock, I tell you. I was with Fran—"

I said, "You went straight to her apartment when you left here at six?"

"That's right."

"And had dinner and then went out for a few drinks afterward?"

"Yes."

"Then why did you change clothes?"

"What?"

"You were wearing a gray sports jacket when you left here; now you're wearing a brown suit. Why the change? And when and where? Unless maybe you got the gray jacket wet and bloody when you shot Judkins, and went home to change before you went *back* to Miss Robbins's apartment. And why splash yourself with so much cologne? You weren't wearing any earlier tonight, and now you reek of it. Unless it was to cover up the smell of wood alcohol; it was all

over Judkins's body, and if it got all over you, too, you wouldn't be able to get rid of the odor just by taking a shower."

The muscle kept on jumping under Brinkman's eye. He looked over at Fran Robbins; she had long since let go of his arm and backed off a couple of steps. She would not look at him now; there was a dark flush on both cheeks. She was just starting to admit to herself that he really was a murderer, and once she accepted the truth she would turn on him. That would be all Eberhardt needed.

"Keep talking," Eb said to me. "Something happened between Brinkman and Judkins tonight?"

"Right. An argument of some kind, probably over how much Judkins was to be paid. Maybe he tried to shake Brinkman down for a bigger payoff before he did the job. In any case, they met here, and one of them brought a gun, and Judkins ended up getting shot dead."

"Are you saying the shooting took place outside or inside?"

"Outside. That's why I didn't hear the shot; the wind muffled it."

"Then why put the body in here?"

"Because it probably seemed like the best alternative at the time. If Brinkman left it outside for somebody to find, the arson scheme would be spoiled and the police investigation might implicate him. And taking the body away somewhere was too risky. Both he and Judkins had to have come here on foot, because they wouldn't have wanted to alert me by driving into the lot; he couldn't carry the dead man all the way to wherever he'd left his car, and he couldn't bring the car onto the grounds for that same fear of alerting me.

"But if he took the body inside and started the fire himself, there was a chance the corpse would be burned badly enough to conceal the fact that Judkins had died from a gunshot wound. Which wouldn't have happened, forensic medicine being what it is today; but he had to have been rattled and desperate, and it looked to him like his only way out. And afterward he could claim that Judkins had set the fire on his own, for his own reasons, and been caught in it and died as a result. The insurance company, at least as he saw it, would still have to pay off.

"Only that plan backfired, too. He's a small guy and Judkins was a big guy; he got the body in here all right, but he lost control of it as he was setting it down. It landed on top of a crate and made that loud thudding noise I heard. Brinkman knew I'd come to investigate, and he was afraid I'd see him and recognize him; he panicked, shut off the flashlight he'd been using and got out."

Brinkman was standing ramrod stiff, both hands bunched together at his waist, his head wreathed in cigarette smoke. The only change in the way he looked was in the color of his face: it had gone paper-white.

"Now we come to the sixty-four-dollar question," Eberhardt said. "This place was sealed inside and out, like a damned tomb; it still is. How was Judkins supposed to get inside in the first place, and how did Brinkman get inside with the body?"

I said, "You told me the answer to that yourself a little while ago, Eb."

"*I* told you?"

"You said something sarcastic about the killer maybe walking through a wall. But you were right; that's just what Brinkman did."

"Don't give me double-talk, damn it. Say what you mean."

"He came in through the window," I said.

"Window? What window?"

I pointed to the nearest of the two in the left-hand wall, the one closest to where I had found Judkins's body. "That window."

"Nuts," Eberhardt said. "The gate is padlocked; I can see that from here. And the outside shutter is locked down—"

"Now it is," I said.

"What?"

"Eb, the beauty of Brinkman's little plan is that it's simple and it's obvious—so simple and so obvious that everybody overlooked it." I went to the window and demonstrated as I talked. "Like this: I come in here on my rounds and I test the padlock on the gate; it's firmly in place. I glance through the bars, and what do I see in this dim light? The window is closed and the shutter is lowered outside. So I automatically assume, just as anybody would, that both the window catch and the shutter catch are locked, because I *expect* them to be and because I *know* the gate is locked. For that same reason I don't bother to reach through and check either one.

"But the fact is, neither the window nor the shutter was locked at that time; just closed far enough to make me think they were. And the only person who could have rigged them that way is Brinkman. He was the one who locked up tonight. He even asked me to double-check him; he figured his little trick was foolproof, and he wanted my testimony that the building was sealed when the fire broke out.

"What he did after he shot Judkins was to lift the shutter from outside, then the window sash—slow and quiet so I wouldn't hear anything—and then reach through the bars, open the gate padlock with his key and swing the gate to one side. On his way out after he dropped the body, he closed the gate and relocked the padlock. Then he lowered the window—a little too hard in his haste, which explains the thumping sound I heard. But he couldn't have secured the window latch from the outside. . . ."

I reached through the bars, caught hold of the sash and tugged. It glided upward a few inches in well-oiled slots. "And he didn't. The clicking noise I heard just before putting on the lights was him closing the shutter hard enough to make its latch catch at the bottom—something he *could* do from the outside."

"And with all the inside gates and outside shutters in place," Klein said, "who'd think to try one of the windows sandwiched between them? Or attach the right significance to it if they did." He shook his head. "I see what you mean by simple and obvious."

Brinkman saw, too. He saw the expression on Fran Robbins's face: anger and fear and a congealing hatred. He saw the expression on McIntyre's face, and on the faces of the law. All the bluff went out of him at once, and along with it whatever inner force had been holding him together; the cigarette fell out of his mouth and he sat down hard on one of the crates, like a doll with sand-stuffed legs, and covered up his own face with both hands.

They never learn, I thought. The clever ones especially—they just never learn. . . .

VIII.

"The way it happened with Judkins," Eberhardt said, "was pretty much as you called it. He telephoned Brinkman at Fran Robbins's apartment and told him he'd been thinking things over and didn't want to go ahead with the torch job for the five hundred dollars Brinkman was paying him; he wanted another five hundred, and he wanted it right away. Brinkman tried to tell him he didn't have that much cash available, but Judkins wouldn't listen. Either Brinkman delivered the money immediately or not only wouldn't he set the fire, he'd blow the whistle to the insurance company."

"I told you Judkins wasn't very smart," I said.

"Yeah." Eberhardt fired up the tobacco in his pipe. It was the following afternoon and we were sitting in a tavern on Union Street, having a companionable beer—his treat—before he headed down to the Hall of Justice for his evening tour of duty. "Anyhow, Brinkman didn't have any choice; he agreed to meet Judkins and did, just outside the company grounds. All he had on him was fifty bucks, but he promised Judkins the rest as soon as he could get it."

"Only Judkins wasn't having any of that, right?"

"Right. He was half-drunk on gin, Brinkman says, and in a belligerent mood; and he'd brought a gun with him. He started waving it around, making threats, and Brinkman got scared and ran into the lot toward the building. He says he was going to call to you for help. But Judkins caught up with him; there was a struggle, and the gun went off. End of Judkins. Brinkman threw the gun—a twenty-five-caliber Browning—away later, into a trash bin a couple

of blocks from there. He led us right to it. Cooperating to beat the band, which probably means he'll cop a plea later on."

"Uh-huh. What did he tell Robbins when he got back to her place?"

"Fed her a line about some hardcases being the ones who wanted to burn down his company for the insurance; said he had to go along with them or they'd muscle him around—that kind of thing. So would she say he was with her all evening? She went along with it; she's not too bright either. After he called the company and talked to Klein, he told her it must have been the hardcases who'd killed Judkins. She went along with that, too, until you laid everything out in the warehouse. Now she can't wait to testify against him."

"Good for her."

"One other thing, in case you're wondering: Brinkman giving McIntyre the sack doesn't fit into it, except as a ploy to throw off the insurance investigators even more. Would a businessman about to burn down his own company fire one employee on the day of the blaze, and promote another? Like that."

"Cute. And when things got tough, he tried to steer the blame for Judkins's death onto McIntyre—the old vendetta motive."

"Some smart guy, that Brinkman."

"Some *dumb* guy," I said. "Judkins may not have been very bright, and Fran Robbins may not be either. But Brinkman's the dumbest of the three."

"Yeah. I wish they were all like that—all the damned criminals." Eberhardt picked up his beer. "Here's to crime," he said.

"I'll drink to that," I said, and we did.

Late that afternoon I drove across the Golden Gate Bridge for an early dinner in Sausalito. I got a window table in one of the restaurants built out into the Bay; the weather had cleared, and it was near sunset, and from there I had a fine view of the San Francisco skyline across the water.

It was a beautiful city when you saw it like

this—all the buildings shining gold in the dying sunlight, the bridges and the islands and the dazzling water and the East Bay and Marin hills surrounding it. It was only when you got down into its bowels, when you came in contact with the people—the few bad ones spoiling things for the rest—that it became something else. A jungle. A breeding ground for evil, a place of tragedy and unhappiness.

I loved that city; I had been born there and I

had spent half a century there and you couldn't have paid me enough to make me move anywhere else. But sometimes, my job being what it was, it made me angry and sad. Sometimes, in a lot of ways, it made me afraid.

The waitress had brought me a beer and I lifted my glass. Here's to crime, I thought, but I didn't drink to it this time.

I drank to the city instead.
And I drank to the victims.

G. D. H. COLE
AND M. I. COLE

AMONG THE LEADERS of socialist thought and activity in England for many years, the husband and wife team of George Douglas Howard (1889–1959) and Margaret Isabel Postgate (1893–1980) Cole were also extremely popular mystery writers during the Golden Age of fair-play detective stories, producing more than thirty novels between 1923 and 1942. G. D. H. (generally known as Douglas) Cole also produced more than eighty books about socialism, often focused on economics. His best-known work in the field was the five-volume *A History of Socialist Thought* (1953). M. I. Cole was the sister of the mystery writer Raymond Postgate.

Even during the years in which they were actively engaged in socialism, Fabianism, and the Labour Party, the Coles wrote prolifically in the detective genre, which they claimed they did for recreation. The first book, *The Brooklyn Murders* (1923), the only one written exclusively by Douglas Cole, introduced Superintendent Henry Wilson, a dedicated Scotland Yard investigator of great integrity. His outstanding detective work once proved an ex–home secretary guilty of a crime, costing him his job when political pressure forced him to resign. He quickly became one of England's foremost private detectives until the political climate changed and he resumed his former position. He is featured in most of the Coles' books.

"In a Telephone Cabinet" was first published in *Superintendent Wilson's Holiday* (London, Collins, 1928).

IN A TELEPHONE CABINET

G. D. H. COLE AND M. I. COLE

I

"IT WAS AN INGENIOUS murder," Wilson used to say of it on the rare occasions when he would consent to discuss his cases; "but from my point of view the chief interest was the speed at which I had to act. From the moment when I began to suspect that a careful designer had been at work, I had a conviction that if I delayed a few hours the trail would be not merely cold but non-existent. So in detaining the murderer I had to take a risk which might have proved entirely unjustified, *and* I had to complete the case against him within the time during which we could reasonably detain him on absolutely unproved suspicion. It was a race against time, and of course that doesn't make for good work. One gets careless and slipshod, allows preconceived theories to mislead one and misses the essential indications." Here one or two of his hearers smiled, wondering how often the ordinary man would have convicted Wilson of carelessness; but he went on unmoved.

"It is perfectly true. One ought not to be hurried over a case. One ought to have time to think out alternative hypotheses, and to test each one as one goes along. One ought not to have to go nap on a single series of deductions. Now, in this case that we are talking about, I fully deserved that my hypothesis should break down under me and the Department get into a very awkward row. It was a stroke of luck that it turned out all right. Of course, if it hadn't been for Michael I couldn't have brought it off at all."

"You are rather good at deriving assistance from the brute creation, then," Michael Prendergast laughed. "I should say I was about as much help as a hibernating tortoise. I didn't do anything, and what you were up to I hadn't the slightest idea."

"I was alluding to your substantial and inescapable presence, my dear Michael," Wilson retorted, "and to your excellent medical degree. But as a matter of fact you were standing at my elbow practically the whole time and could have followed all the steps in my conclusions."

"So could a tortoise, no doubt," said Prendergast, "if it was standing at the elbow of a man who was just preparing to convert it into tortoiseshell. For all I knew, you were going to order *my* arrest any moment."

"You forgot, then," Wilson said, "that *I* was the principal witness to your alibi, and that up to the present I have generally—though probably without warrant—considered myself a reliable witness. Also, if you will forgive my saying so, the crime was entirely beyond your powers. Your ingenuity doesn't lie in that direction."

At this point several of the company demanded that the two friends should cease talking in riddles and should explain what the case was which presented such remarkable features; and by dint of much cross-questioning—

neither of the two having any pretensions to narrative powers—they succeeded in getting out of them the following story.

The Downshire Hill Murder (to give it its newspaper name) was discovered about half-past nine on a Sunday morning of May, 1920, one of those lovely mornings with which our climate tries to pretend that it really knows how to make a summer. Superintendent Henry Wilson of New Scotland Yard was walking along Downshire Hill, Hampstead, in company with his friend Dr. Michael Prendergast. It was long before the sensational death of Radlett, the millionaire,* which, as everyone will remember, covered England and America with placards, and drove Wilson, who had committed the unpardonable sin of detecting an ex–Home Secretary in shady courses, into the exile of private practice. He was still a C.I.D. man, liable at any moment to be called from bed and board to attend to public affairs, and it was not without some misgivings that he had obeyed the commands of his sister, with whom he was staying, to put himself for one day at least beyond reach of the telephone. However, it was a wonderful morning; and Michael Prendergast, one of his few intimate friends, who had spent the Saturday evening and night with him, had added his entreaties; and the result was that the two men, in flannels and tennis shirts, were now walking briskly down the road to the North London Station, where they intended to catch a train for Richmond.

"You'd almost think you were in the country here," Prendergast said appreciatively, noting the trees which filled the little front gardens and the young green of the Heath which closed the end of the road. "There was an owl hooting outside my window all night."

"They do come close to the houses here," Wilson replied, "but I never heard of one actually nesting in the wall of a house before."

* See *The Death of a Millionaire*, by G. D. H. and Margaret Cole.

"Nor I. Why?" For answer Wilson pointed to the ivy-clad wall of a little house about a hundred yards farther down, which was only just visible through a mass of lilac and young chestnut. "Something flew in and out of the ivy just there, between those boughs," he said.

Prendergast stared at him. "You have sharp eyes. I was looking at the lilac, and I didn't see anything. How do you know it was an owl, anyway, at this distance?"

"I don't," Wilson said. "It may not have been. I couldn't see it at all clearly. But it was too big for any other bird. Anyway, somebody else appears to have seen it too." They were now approaching the ivy-clad house, which, though hidden from view on the west, was quite open in front, and standing by its gate on the pavement was a man to whom it appeared to be an object of enormous interest. As the two friends passed, he looked up at them with a dubious air, which suggested that he was wondering whether to open a conversation; and Prendergast, who never could resist conversing with all and sundry, responded promptly to the suggestion.

"Have you seen the owl, too?" he asked.

"Owl!" said the man. "I ain't seen no owl. But I've seen a man go in there," he pointed to the house. "What's he want to go in for, that's what I want to know."

"Perhaps it's his house," Prendergast suggested.

"Ho!" said the man. "Then what's he want to go in by the window for, that's what I want to know. Banging on the door fit to wake the dead, he was. When he sees me, he says, 'Something wrong here,' he says. 'Can't get no answer,' and he outs with a knife and gets in at the window. And what's he want to bang for, if it's his house, and what's wrong in there, that's what I want to know." He spat suspiciously.

In a moment his question was answered in a sufficiently dramatic manner. There was a sound of feet within the house; the front door, which was only a matter of twenty yards from the gate, opened suddenly, and a little man, pale and frightened in appearance, looked out and yelled in a voice of surprising power to come from a person of his physique, "Murder!"

All three started; and indeed the cry had sounded as if it must reach Camden Town at least. On seeing their astonished faces the man at the door looked rather confused, and coming down to the gate, said in a considerably lower tone, "Will you fetch the police, please, gentlemen? Mr. Carluke's been murdered."

He then closed the gate, and made as if to return to the house; but Prendergast, with a nod from Wilson, followed him up the path. "Can I do anything?" he said pleasantly. "I'm a doctor."

"'Tisn't a doctor he wants, poor fellow," said the little man. "He's as cold as a fish. He must have died hours ago." He stopped with his hand on the hall door. "If you'll fetch the police, sir, I'll stay with him. I don't think the house ought to be left alone. And there's nobody there."

"That's all right." Wilson, who had stopped to speak to the man at the gate, now came up to them. "I am from Scotland Yard. Here's my card." He produced one from his cigarette case, and Michael looked on with amusement, wondering what use he had intended to make of his official dignity at Richmond. The little man took it gingerly, as if it had been a spider, and looked with obvious distaste at the owner's clothes. Quite clearly he thought that policemen ought to dress as policemen and not stroll about in flannel trousers.

"I've sent that man to the Rosslyn Hill station with a message," Wilson went on. "They'll be here in a few minutes. But, as you say, the place oughtn't to be left alone. So, if you'll show me where the body is, I can start making the preliminary investigations, and my friend here can see how he was murdered. You're certain he was, Mr.——?"

"Barton," said the little man. "Edward Barton. He was murdered all right, sir. Shot right through the head. His brains are all over the floor, poor fellow. This way, sir." He seemed a trifle hurt at the doubt thrown on his diagnosis.

"Well, well, we'll see," Wilson said soothingly. "Where is he?"

"Telephone cabinet," said Mr. Barton, pointing. "By the stairs on the right. That glass door. It's his foot that's holding it open. I haven't touched him. I just made sure he was dead, poor fellow."

II

It was not a pleasant sight which greeted them when Wilson pulled open the door of the little dark telephone cabinet; and it thoroughly justified Mr. Barton's confidence in his own verdict. On the floor, crumpled up, with one foot half across the sill of the door, lay what once must have been a hale man of between fifty and sixty years of age. His body had fallen in a heap, facing the telephone, and the fingers of both hands were curved as if he had died gripping something which he had subsequently dropped. But the cause of death was plain enough; for the whole front of his face and part of his head had been pierced in a number of places, and the blood and brains which had oozed out from the wounds had covered the floor. Michael Prendergast had been through the war, and thought himself used to death; but the sight of the old man lying shattered in that gloomy, musty shambles stirred emotions in him which he believed wholly conquered, and he had to struggle with a violent feeling of nausea before he dared step across the threshold.

"Go carefully, Michael," Wilson warned; and Prendergast noted with shame and annoyance that he seemed wholly unmoved by the sight. "Don't tread in more than you can help. We'll want all the clues we can get." He surveyed with displeasure some unmistakable footprints in the blood that covered the floor. "You've been in here, Mr. Barton?"

"Of course I have," said Mr. Barton in injured tones. "I went to see if I could do anything for him, naturally. When I found I couldn't, I looked round to see if there was a revolver or anything anywhere. In case he shot himself, you see—in case it was suicide."

"Turn on the light, will you?" came Prendergast's voice from where he was bending over the body. "I can't see anything in this coal-hole."

"It's broken," said Mr. Barton. "I tried it when I came in." He was, however, obediently reaching his hand to the switch, a porcelain one of the old pattern, when Wilson forestalled him. With a handkerchief wrapped round his hand he turned the switch backwards and forwards several times, but without result.

"It's broken all right," he said. "Probably the bulb's gone. You must make shift with my torch, Michael. But be as quick as you can. It's pretty obvious that we can't do anything for this poor fellow now, except to find his murderer, and I want to get on with that as soon as possible." While Prendergast finished his examination he stood still in the doorway, staring at the little room as if memorizing its contents, at the telephone, which stood unperturbed on a rather high shelf at the far end, at a shelf above containing two or three old directories, and at a baize curtain which fell from the telephone shelf to the ground.

"What's behind that curtain, do you know?" he asked Barton.

"Boots—and some old rubbish, I think," the latter replied. "Mr. Carluke used to shove any stuff he didn't want there."

"You knew him quite well, then?"

"So-so," said Mr. Barton. "As well as anyone did, I daresay. He hadn't a great many friends; he was a bit of a queer old cuss, and didn't mind how much he was alone."

Prendergast straightened himself. "That's all I can do here," he said. "The poor chap's dead, of course—been dead about twelve hours, I should say, off-hand. He can't have lived more than a few seconds after he was shot."

"Shot from close quarters?" Wilson asked.

"Very close. Not more than a few inches, I should say. And—he was shot by a blunderbuss."

"Blunderbuss!" exclaimed the other two.

"Blunderbuss or something with an enormous charge of soft-nosed slugs in it. Beastly little things. Here are two I picked off the floor, and there are some more in his head. There must have been dozens in the charge."

"Extraordinary!" said Mr. Barton, with a kind of irritable incredulity. "Why should anyone want to shoot poor Carluke with a blunderbuss?"

"That's what we have to find out," said Wilson. "Perhaps, as you know the house, Mr. Barton, you'd take us into a room where we can talk."

The little man led the way into a small room which was obviously a sort of study or morning-room, and motioned Wilson and his companion to chairs. In broad daylight, Prendergast studied him with some interest, but found little to repay his scrutiny. He looked a very ordinary type of middle-class clerk or shopkeeper, about forty-five or fifty years old, with a bald crown fringed with grayish hair that had once been ginger, a ragged ginger moustache, and face and features of no particular shape. He appeared considerably upset and distressed by the position in which he found himself, rather more so than Prendergast would have expected, though, of course, it must be very trying for any friend of the murdered man. For all his agitation, though, he answered Wilson's questions clearly enough.

"Can you tell me Mr. Carluke's full name, and how you came to be a friend of his?" Wilson began.

"Harold Carluke," Mr. Burton replied. "Only we weren't exactly friends, as I told you, more kind of acquaintances. We came together through working in the same place, and we used to play chess a bit and go for a walk together now and then and so on."

"What place was that?"

"Capital and Counties Bank. Hampstead branch. Mr. Carluke is the cashier, and I'm head counter clerk."

"Had he any relations, do you know? Was he married?"

No, he wasn't married, Mr. Barton said. And he didn't think he'd any relatives. He'd once or twice spoken of a nephew, rather a wild young fellow, who seemed to give him some trouble. But that was all. Mr. Carluke wasn't the man to talk about his family, nor the kind you could put questions to. Not the sort many knew anything about.

"How comes it," Wilson asked, "that he is apparently alone in the house? Didn't he keep any servants?"

Barton explained that he did not. Mr. Carluke, it would appear, was something of a fussy old maid, and did not like to see servants about the house. So he employed only a daily woman who came in after he had left for business in the morning to clean and leave his supper laid for him, and departed before he returned. On Sundays she did not come at all. "You never saw anyone in such a bait as he was," Mr. Barton added, "if he found her in the house any time after he'd come home."

"What if he were ill?" Michael Prendergast's profession suggested to him. But it appeared that the question had not arisen. Mr. Carluke's health was excellent; he had never been known to miss a day at the bank.

"This charwoman, she must have had a key?" Wilson asked.

"I suppose she must have. But she doesn't come in on a Sunday. Besides, the door was bolted and chained when I got in."

"The front door, you mean?"

"Yes; but the back door was locked and bolted too."

"Oh!" Wilson took this in. "You had a look round, then, before giving the alarm?"

"Only the ground floor," Barton licked his lips and looked at him with a kind of frightened appeal. "I couldn't see anything I could do for *him*. So I thought I might just see—if there was anyone else about."

"And was there?"

Barton shook his head. "No. Not a sign. But I wasn't long at it. Then I opened the door."

"I see," said Wilson. "How did you get in yourself?"

"Through that window"—pointing. Wilson crossed and looked at the window, whose catch had plainly been forced back.

"Why did you break in?"

"Couldn't get any answer. I'd called to go for a walk with Mr. Carluke as we'd arranged. Then I knocked and rang and couldn't make anyone hear. And I was a good bit behind my time, too, so I got a bit anxious—I thought he might be ill, perhaps. So I got in."

"I see. When did you last see him?"

"Last night."

"What time?"

"About—about nine o'clock," said Mr. Barton, licking his lips again and looking considerably distressed. Prendergast gave a start of surprise; then, remembering that he was in effect representing the law, pulled himself together and tried to look as impassive as Wilson. No wonder the little man was showing signs of alarm. His own position was certainly dubious.

"Could you tell us what happened?" Wilson inquired. Mr. Barton could, and did, not without a good many nervous glances at Wilson's face. He had gone round at Mr. Carluke's invitation for high tea and a game of chess. He had had to leave about nine o'clock because he had promised to fetch his wife home from an evening party at some neighbours' in Hendon; but the two men had arranged to go for a country walk on the Sunday. Barton had then left, arranging to call at nine o'clock in the morning to fetch his friend, and Carluke had seen him out of the house and walked with him as far as the corner of Willow Road, where they had parted. Then Barton had gone on to fetch his wife; but they had stayed very much longer at the party than they had intended and had not got back to their home in Hendon until nearly one. As soon as he knew they were going to be late, he had tried to telephone Mr. Carluke to suggest a less early start in the morning; but though he had tried twice, once from his friend's house and once from his own when he returned, he had got no answer. "I supposed he was out," Barton said. "Though it was a bit odd, though, because he said he was going straight to bed when he left me. He liked to keep early hours. So I tried again; but there was still no answer, so I supposed he was asleep. So I came round this morning as early as I could, as he'd be waiting."

"I see," said Wilson again. "You didn't meet anyone as you left, did you? When you were with Mr. Carluke, I mean."

"Not *meet,* exactly," said Mr. Barton, looking very nervous. "There were a lot of people about—it was a fine evening—but we didn't meet anyone. But we stood outside the Dog and Duck, at the bottom there, a minute or two. The landlord was in the doorway—I saw him—and he might have noticed us. He knows Mr. Carluke quite well. Look here," he burst out suddenly. "I know what you're getting at, and I know what it looks like! If he went straight back and locked up when he left me I was the last to see him alive. But he *was* alive and perfectly all right when I left him—I'll swear he was!" He half rose in his seat, and sat down again, looking fearfully at the others.

"Quite, quite," said Wilson soothingly. "I'm not trying to cast any suspicion on you, Mr. Barton. But we must find out what happened, you know. Now, if you two will excuse me, I'll start having a look at the place. The police ought to be here in a minute or two, and then I want you, Mr. Barton, to go along with them to the station, if you will, and tell the officer in charge what you've just told me." He rose to his feet. "By the way, Michael, did you find any signs of a struggle on the body?"

"None whatever," Prendergast promptly replied. "I should say he was shot before he knew what was happening."

"That was my impression, too." Wilson nodded, and disappeared into the hall. Prendergast would have dearly liked to accompany him and see how a Scotland Yard man handled the scene of a murder (his association with Wilson having hitherto been entirely unprofessional); but he was distinctly in awe of his friend's official position, and felt sure that if he had been wanted he would have received an invitation. So he sat with

what patience he could muster in the uncomfortable little study, while Mr. Barton, on the other side of the fireplace, huddled in his chair and uneasily bit his nails.

They had not long to wait, for in less than three minutes there was a sound as of heavy feet on the path, and a loud official knock rang through the house. Barton and Prendergast both sprang to their feet, but Wilson was before them; and as they went into the hall they heard him giving a rapid account of the circumstances to an awestruck sergeant.

"Constable Wren's got your bag, sir," the sergeant explained. "I sent him round to Fitzjohn's Avenue for it as soon as I got your note. Lord, sir!" By this time they had reached the door of the telephone cabinet. "Well, he stopped one then, and no mistake, poor chap!" the sergeant said. "What was it, sir? Looks almost like a charge of grape-shot."

"Dr. Prendergast says it was a blunderbuss," said Wilson. "But you'd best get him along to the station at once. Is the ambulance here? Good. Get your man in and tell the divisional surgeon to examine him as quickly as possible. They can take Mr. Barton along with them too, and get his statement down. Is Inspector Catling there?"

"Just coming, sir," the sergeant said. "We rang him up, and he'll be along by the time the men get back."

"Good. Then they might as well be getting on. You stay with me, and we'll go over the house. Put a constable to watch the door. I'm sorry, Michael"—he turned to Prendergast—"but I'm afraid poor Carluke has rather put a stop to our expedition. Will you go without me, or would you rather stay?"

"I'd rather stay, if I can be of any use," said Prendergast, as eager as a schoolboy; and Wilson smiled a little, and nodded. "I'd like you to go to the station with the constables if you will, Mr. Barton," he said to the morose little figure that hovered in the background, "and give your account to the inspector. But first there are one or two more things I want to know. Did Mr. Carluke ever have charge of money or valuables in his house, do you know? For the bank, I mean?"

"Not that I know of," Barton said. "But he wouldn't have told me if he had. He was as close as an oyster on bank business."

"Thank you. Now, this nephew that you spoke of. Do you know his name, or address, or anything about him?"

Barton thought. "Edgar Carluke, his name is. I think he's a ship's purser, and I *believe* he's ashore just now. But I don't know his address."

"He didn't stay here, then, when he was ashore."

"He did once," Barton said. "But they had a row about money, and he wasn't asked again. That's how I happen to know about the once, because I came to call in the middle of it."

"How do you mean—about money?"

"Oh, Edgar Carluke wanted some; and his uncle wouldn't let him have it. I don't know—I didn't hear any more than that. But perhaps Mr. Carluke would have something about him in his papers, if you want to know."

"Do you know where he kept his papers?"

"Upstairs, in a safe in his bedroom. It's the room above this."

"Thank you. What is the bank manager's name—the branch manager?"

"Mr. Warren. He lives in Belsize Park, but he's away."

"Thank you. By the way, we shall want a light in that telephone cabinet, and the bulb appears to be broken. Do you happen to know where Mr. Carluke kept his spares?"

"Yes, in a cupboard in the kitchen, left of the gas-stove."

"Would you mind finding me one, as you know where they are? Medium strength, please." Wilson went to the door of the kitchen, and stood waiting while Mr. Barton groped in a cupboard and extracted an electric bulb.

"This do?" he said, unwrapping it. "It's a forty."

"Thank you." Wilson took it from him. "Now, sergeant, call your men in and tell them to disturb things as little as possible in getting

him out. Constable!" He called to the man standing on guard at the hall door. "Take Mr. Barton up to Inspector Catling at once and let him make his statement. Tell the inspector the sergeant and I are going over the house and will let him know as soon as possible how things are going. And, constable," he drew the man aside a little, and the conversation dropped to a whisper. Meanwhile the ambulance men had come in and were taking out their melancholy burden. Prendergast, who shuddered afresh as the remains of Mr. Carluke came out of the telephone cabinet, could not but marvel at the cool calm with which the police officers did their business. When it was finished, Wilson dismissed the other constable, who strode firmly off, a dejected Mr. Barton following in his wake.

III

"This is a shocking affair, sir," the sergeant began as the door closed on them.

"Shocking," Wilson agreed, beginning to open the case which the constable had brought, and which appeared to contain principally a number of little bottles of various kinds. "Did you know this Mr. Carluke, sergeant? Any idea why he should be murdered?"

"Not an earthly, sir," the sergeant said. "As quiet-spoken and nice an old gentleman as you could wish. Bit unsociable, they said, but nothing to matter. I shouldn't have said he'd an enemy in the world."

"So Mr. Barton seemed to think," said Wilson, extracting a thin pair of gloves and putting them on. "Well, we'd better get on. I've a feeling that we've no time to lose in this affair, if we want to catch the murderer. Will you go round the house, sergeant, and look at the doors and windows and see if you can find how he got away? Michael, could you look in that cupboard and see if you can find me a sixty lamp? I think I won't use this one after all." He laid it on a shelf as he spoke; and the sergeant looked up suddenly as if he were going to speak, but apparently thought better of it. Prendergast found the required lamp without much difficulty, and was taking it into the telephone cabinet to replace the old one, when Wilson stopped him. "Let me do that," he said; and unscrewed the old lamp carefully from the top with his gloved hands. The sergeant gave a chuckle.

"Looking for finger-prints, sir?" he said. "The murderer's not very likely to have held on to the lamp, is he? Especially as it was broken."

"Oh, you never know," said Wilson. "Come in, Michael, and tell me what you think of it. You needn't mind treading there now. I looked at the footprints carefully before the men came in. Tell me how you think the man died." As he spoke, he was dusting the broken lamp and a card which he held in his hands with powder from his little bottles.

Prendergast stared round the little cabinet, which measured about seven feet by three. "He was shot here," he said. "He couldn't have moved after he had been hit, and he couldn't have bled like that if he'd been carried from anywhere else."

"That's so. And where was he shot from? Where did his murderer stand?"

"There, at the far end of the cabinet. You can see by the direction of the slugs. There's one gone into the wall facing the telephone."

"And Carluke was standing—where?"

"Just by the telephone, I should think, from the way he fell. At the far end, anyway."

"Then where was the man who shot him standing? There doesn't appear to be any room for him. And do you suggest Carluke walked up to a blunderbuss and stood right in front of it?"

"It was dark. The light was broken."

"True, O Michael. But when it's on in the hall there is plenty light enough to see anyone inside the cabinet. I don't suppose Mr. Carluke kept his house in complete darkness. Try it yourself."

Prendergast went out into the hall to make the experiment, which resulted as Wilson had said. When he returned he found his friend blowing powder over the telephone. "He must have been behind the curtain," Prendergast said.

"Behind the curtain! My dear fellow, there isn't room! It's full of boots, and even if he'd removed the boots, the whole shelf is only a foot wide. A man couldn't get underneath it. You try. No, not this minute. Come and look at the telephone. This is rather interesting."

"Are those finger-prints?" asked Prendergast, looking at the instrument, to which little bits of yellow powder were adhering. "They don't look to me like anything."

"No, they aren't. The telephone's been rubbed clean. That's rather interesting in itself. People's charwomen aren't usually so particular. But that wasn't what I meant. Look at the shelf just by it."

"There's a bloodstain on it," said Prendergast. "I suppose it's Carluke's. But why shouldn't there be?"

"Because," said Wilson, "that bloodstain was right *under* the telephone."

"What! Then he was actually telephoning when he was killed, and managed to put the telephone back! I shouldn't have thought he would have been able to."

"Neither should I," said Wilson. "What's more, I don't think he did."

"Then his murderer did. Jove, that was pretty cool. By the way, Harry, at that rate, couldn't you fix the time of his death, anyway? The telephone people keep records of calls, don't they? If you asked for the last call he had that would fix the time almost exactly."

"Perhaps," said Wilson. "*If* he was telephoning. But we don't know that he was, yet. And you haven't told me where the murderer stood."

"Well, damn it!" Prendergast cried after a pause, which Wilson utilised to powder the electric light switch. "If he wasn't behind the curtain, I don't know where he stood! Could he have been at the other end of the cabinet—no, that's impossible, the shots are all the wrong way. I suppose he must have sneaked in while Carluke was telephoning and come right up to him and shot him from just by his ear. But it seems an insane thing to do."

"It does," said Wilson. "Quite insane."

"Well, do *you* know where he stood? And why he used a blunderbuss? It seems an extraordinary sort of weapon. Why not a revolver? They're plentiful enough."

"I think I've an idea where he stood—or rather, where he *didn't* stand," Wilson replied, "though it's only an idea; and at present I haven't the ghost of a notion how to prove it. And I'm pretty sure I know why he used a blunderbuss. Think of the specific characteristics of blunderbusses, and you'll be able to answer that question for yourself. Hullo, what's this?" He was standing close by the telephone, peering at the shelf above it. "God be praised, the charwoman isn't as thorough as might have been gathered from the telephone. Look there." Prendergast stared at the shelf, which was fairly thick with an accumulation of London dust. At one end, the end to which Wilson was pointing, there was a round depression in the dust about six inches across. "Something round has stood there," he said; and felt he was being a little obvious.

"It has," said Wilson. "And it has only recently been taken down, and it hadn't been standing there long. The dust on the mark is practically as thick as that on the rest of the shelf—it's only been compressed. Now look around, Michael, and tell me what made that mark."

"The telephone," Prendergast said promptly. Indeed it was the only possible object in sight.

"So it would appear. But we'd better make sure," said Wilson, proceeding carefully to measure the diameter of both telephone and mark. "Now perhaps you can tell me why the late Mr. Carluke kept his telephone in so inconvenient a position? I can hardly reach it, and I should say I'm as tall as he was."

"Taller," said the man of science mechanically; and racked his brains to think why the telephone should have been removed to that distant shelf. To make room for the murderer, seemed the only possible answer; yet what could it possibly avail a murderer to have the telephone cleared out of the way? Prendergast's mind, as he told Wilson, could only conjure up the vision of a murderous gnome the size of a telephone, sitting on the shelf with a blunderbuss in his arms. He was rather surprised that Wilson smiled at him encouragingly.

"That's better," Wilson said. "You're beginning to use your brains."

"If the only result of using them is to produce hobgoblins," Prendergast grumbled, "I think they might as well be unused." At that moment he nearly jumped out of his skin, for the bell of the telephone shrilled suddenly through the silent house.

"Somebody ringing up Mr. Carluke?" he said, as Wilson lifted the receiver.

"No, it's the station," the latter said. "Yes, inspector. Yes. Wilson speaking. . . ." Prendergast wandered out into the hall, where the sergeant was just coming downstairs after a careful official search of the house.

"Well, whoever did that poor fellow in's got wings," he said. "There's nowhere for him to have got out at. Back door's locked and bolted; windows all fastened and the snibs as tight as anything with this weather. You couldn't possibly push any of them back from outside. There's one window open on the top floor, but no signs of anyone getting in or out. And the window's too small to climb through without leaving marks."

"What about the chimneys?" Prendergast suggested. "I suppose a murderer could climb up a chimney?"

"Not up a gas-flue he couldn't, doctor," said the sergeant. "It's gas all over the house, and the flues quite tightly fastened in. No, he flew, that's what he did. Unless he chopped himself up and put himself away in pieces. I've looked everywhere a man could possibly hide himself in this house, and there's no one there."

At this point the telephone bell tinkled to indicate the end of the conversation, and Wilson came out into the hall. "You've some very efficient men at your station, sergeant," he said; and the sergeant blushed with pleasure. "They've checked Barton's statements already. His story's all right. The landlord of the Dog and Duck remembers him and Carluke passing the door last night, and actually watched Carluke back to his own house. Then they've got onto his hosts at Hendon, who say he arrived at nine-thirty and didn't leave till nearly one, and his wife and son say he came straight home."

"Sounds all right," said the sergeant. "Unless he came back after one."

"That would make it nearly two when he got back," said Wilson. "Buses and tubes would have stopped running by then, and he hasn't got a car."

He looked at Prendergast with a question in his eyes.

"I don't think so," the latter answered. "I'm pretty sure he was dead long before midnight. Of course, one can't tell to an hour or so—but I'm pretty certain. Did you think Barton's alibi was wrong then?"

"No," said Wilson, "I didn't. But we had to check it."

"And in any case," said the sergeant, "if he did come back, how'd he get out again?" He explained to Wilson the difficulties. "What are we to do now, sir?"

"Search the house thoroughly," Wilson said. "And his papers. I've got his keys. I'll help you. Only we must be quick."

"Anything you're looking for particular, sir?"

"Oh, as for papers—anything bearing on the crime—or suggesting that anybody else has been at 'em. And for the rest—the weapon."

"Blunderbuss, sir?"

"That, or something like it. But it may have been taken to pieces. Look for anything that could conceivably be part of a blunderbuss. It ought to be somewhere in the house, I'm pretty certain, but I've no idea where."

"It's my belief, doctor," the sergeant said admiringly, as they began their search, "that Mr. Wilson's got the whole thing solved already."

"Only half solved, sergeant," said Wilson, turning a rather anxious face on him. "I haven't got the motive, and I haven't got the weapon. And if we don't find one of them quickly I'm afraid I shan't get the murderer either."

IV

It was a long and depressing search that they conducted through the dead man's effects, while the minutes wore on, and Wilson's face got more and more tense. Prendergast felt that he had never till that morning known what a careful search really was. Wilson made them grope in every crevice, shake out every cushion and every piece of fabric; he felt along the seams of mattresses and chair seats; he made them turn out the dustbin and the sink and look under the traps; they even went into the little garden and searched the gravel path that encircled the house, and all its adjoining flower beds; but all in vain. There was no blunderbuss, nor any less unusual firearm to be seen; there was not even anything that might have been part of a blunderbuss. At length, after more than two hours' searching, they came to the safe, which Wilson unlocked with the dead man's keys.

"Doesn't look as if there was much to be found here, sir," said the sergeant, looking at the neat bundles of documents.

"Well, we can but try," said Wilson, beginning to examine the first packet.

"You know," he said after a few minutes, "I'm inclined to think that somebody's been through these papers before us. They're just a little bit out of order—as if somebody had tried to put them back tidily who didn't really know what the order was. Like one's library after someone's been dusting it. But for the life of me I can't make out what the somebody was after. Whatever it was, if he took it away it's left no traces. What on earth could he have wanted? There's not much sign of the mysterious nephew, anyway. Mr. Carluke seems to have been in the habit of destroying his private papers."

"You didn't," Prendergast, having no answer to the last question, suggested, "you didn't think anything of my idea that the telephone people might be able to give you the time of his death? That would settle people's alibis, anyway."

"I know," said Wilson. "The difficulty is, that

I'm pretty certain he wasn't telephoning when he died."

"But he was!" Prendergast cried. "You're forgetting his hands—his fingers, I mean. Don't you remember the way they were curved? I can just see them. They were exactly at the angle one uses to hold a telephone"—he illustrated with his own hands—"only a bit wider—as if it had been dragged out of them, and the rigor had fixed them in that position. I remember noticing at the time, and wondering what he could possibly have been holding. I thought it might have been the blunderbuss—but if it had been, of course, he'd be holding it still. But the telephone's much more likely." He stopped with a feeling of triumph, for Wilson had dropped the papers and was looking at him with real respect.

"By George, Michael, I believe you've got it!" he said. "I'd quite forgotten his hands, fool that I am. Sergeant, do you happen to know if the Post Office have lost an instrument lately?"

"An instrument? I'm afraid I don't, sir," the sergeant chuckled, while Prendergast gaped at this unexpected result of his suggestion. "The Post Office attend to their own lost property."

"Then ring them up and find out, as quick as you can," was the reply. "Hurry up, man, the whole thing may depend on it."

"Why ever should you think they've lost a telephone?" Prendergast asked.

"It's only a guess," Wilson answered. "But if it's right, it makes the thing pretty certain."

The sergeant was away a long time, while Wilson and Prendergast patiently searched through a quiet old gentleman's most uninteresting private papers. When he came back, he gazed at Wilson with an expression almost of reverence on his face.

"How *did* you know, sir?" he said. "They *have* lost one. There was one pinched out of an empty flat in Golders Green within the last week or two; but they can't say exactly when, and they've no idea who took it. How did you know?"

"Well, it was a fairly obvious conclusion, wasn't it?" said Wilson. "I wish it was as obvious where it had got to. Come, we *must* find this

thing. It can't have left the house; there wasn't time. And there's nowhere he can have dropped it—Good Lord!" He sprang to his feet, and made for the door. "The owl!"

"What's the matter?" Prendergast said, following him breathlessly as he rushed down the stairs.

"What a fool! The owl, of course!" was all the answer he got. "No, wait a moment. I'll be back directly."

Prendergast and the sergeant stood at the hall door, gaping, while Wilson ran out into the road and about a hundred yards up the hill. There he stood for five seconds or so, staring up at the trees which all but screened the house from view; and then he returned at the same pace. "It's the bathroom window, I think," he said as he regained the house; and shot up the stairs, the other two following. Arrived at the bathroom he flung wide the window, which was the same that the sergeant had already found open, and leaned out as far as possible to the left, groping with his hand in the thick ivy that covered the wall. After two or three seconds' searching he gave an exclamation of triumph.

"Got it!" he said. "At least, I think so. Will you both please look carefully? I want to have a witness to this." He brought his hand back, with a fat envelope in it marked Capital and Counties Bank. This he handed to the sergeant. "The weapon, sir?" the latter said, puzzled. "There's more coming," said Wilson; and dived again into the ivy.

"This wants careful handling," he said as he returned for the second time. In his hand was what at first sight looked like an ordinary telephone receiver. But on looking closely, it was apparent that the mouthpiece and the top of the telephone had been removed, and in their place was a fat muzzle of metal. Prendergast came close to it and stared down the black mouth of the thing.

"My God, it's the blunderbuss!" he said.

"It seems to be," said Wilson. "We'll have to take it to pieces to find out how it worked. But it seems quite clear what the murderer did. The inside of this instrument has been taken out to make room for the charge, and the hook for the earpiece is fastened to the trigger. A man going to answer a telephone ring in the dark—remember that broken light, sergeant, which was probably broken by the murderer—would take hold of the earpiece and let the gun off. You see now the point of having a blunderbuss—and a blunderbuss, as Dr. Prendergast noticed, charged with a peculiarly nasty type of expanding slug, like soft-nosed bullets. You can't make quite certain where a man's head will be when he's answering the telephone, and the blunderbuss was pretty safe to hit him wherever he was. There are some finger-prints on both the receiver and the earpiece"—he had been dusting it with powder as he spoke—"I'm pretty certain they are Carluke's, but we can compare them downstairs for certain. I took his prints on a card before he was taken away. *Now*, Michael, I think I can answer the question I asked you a while back—where did the murderer stand when he killed his victim? The answer is—at a private telephone in Hendon. Sergeant, will you send down to the station and tell them to detain Edward Barton on suspicion of being concerned in the murder of Harold Carluke? I think you'll find he's still there."

"Good God, sir," the sergeant said. "What a diabolical thing! Do you mean he fixed up this affair and then went off and left the poor old boy to be shot next time he went to the telephone?"

"And then rang him up to make sure he did go," said Wilson. "Twice, you remember, in case he should have been out the first time. The telephone people will be able to trace those abortive calls for us. But, of course, he was dead long before the second one was made."

"Good God!" said the sergeant again. "The cold-blooded devil! Why did he murder him, sir?" He spoke as though he regarded Wilson as an eye-witness of the whole thing.

"I don't know that yet," said Wilson. "But I shouldn't be surprised if the envelope you have in your hand throws some light on it." He tore it open, and a small bundle of cheques drawn on the Capital and Counties Bank fell out. Drawing a lens from his pocket, he made a rapid examination of the signatures.

"Of course, I don't know the Hampstead clients of the Capital and Counties Bank," he said. "But I should say there's no doubt that some of these are forgeries. Look at the waviness of that line in the glass. That's no true signature." He handed cheque and glass to the sergeant, who nodded agreement. "I presume friend Barton had either written them or helped to pass them through; and that Carluke had found it out. If we get into touch with the bank manager, we'll probably get the whole story. But you'd better go and make sure of your prisoner. I doubt whether Catling's finding it easy to detain him."

V

"You gave my eyesight better credit than it deserved. What I took for an owl was Barton's hand putting the papers away," said Wilson. "My only excuse is that I wasn't looking at the place at all. I only got a faint impression at the edge of the retina, and when I focussed on it, it was gone. There is only one spot in the road from which that particular bit of ivy is visible at all—and that spot's not visible from the window. Barton must have thought himself quite unobserved. But I nearly lost the clue, all the same, through not following up my impression quickly enough."

"What I don't see," Prendergast said, "is why you were looking for a weapon at all—why you thought it hadn't been taken away." They were discussing the case again after Barton's execution. Faced with the forged cheques and the incriminating telephone, his nerve had gone and he had confessed everything—incidentally giving away the actual forgers of the cheques which he had paid over the counter. The bank manager on his return had supplied the information that investigations had been taking place into one of the forged cheques, which had been detected, and that the dead man had asked him for an interview as soon as he came back on that very subject. Hence the necessity for his murder. The rest of the crime was as Wilson had indicated— even to the stealing of the telephone from the empty flat in Golders Green and the careful breaking of the electric light bulb.

"Well," Wilson said. "I didn't see what else he could have done with it. He had only been in the house a few minutes, the man at the gate said—no time to take it anywhere else. Of course, he might have had it on him; but I didn't think he'd risk that, as he knew he would have to go to the police station. If I hadn't found it in the house, I was going to have him searched, as a last resort. But I didn't want to do that, because we should have had to let him go, after his complete alibi; and that would have given him plenty of time to find and destroy his weapon, or to leave the country."

"Then you knew all along he was guilty?" Prendergast asked. "How?"

"Well, I began to suspect him as soon as I'd had a look at the telephone cabinet. You see, it was so obvious, from the dimensions of the cabinet and the direction of the shots, that the murderer hadn't been in the cabinet at all. You saw that yourself, only you were convinced that he must have been. But there was no room for him to have been, and no signs of his departure. There were only Barton's footprints visible, and no one could have got out across the body and across that pool of blood without stepping in it. I tried myself. That suggested that the man was alone when he was killed, and that he was killed by some mechanical means or other; and the fact that the bulb—a practically new one, as I daresay you noticed—was broken, was suspiciously convenient for a trap. I got Barton to put his finger-prints on another bulb for me so as to have a record of them, and later I discovered that the broken one bore prints of the same hand. Of course, that wasn't conclusive; but it was suggestive. The bulb's well out of Barton's reach; he wouldn't have been changing it in the ordinary course of events. That was his principal slip, by the way; he wiped everything else clean—the real telephone rather suspiciously so—but he forgot the bulb.

"Well, if the man was alone when he met his death, obviously his murderer could have a cast-iron alibi, so that any alibis could be left out of account in the preliminary investigations. Actually, it made Mr. Barton's own alibi a little suspicious—it almost suggested careful preparation. So when I'd got all I wanted out of him, I left you to look after him and went back to make a further study. Then I found, as I showed you, that there was blood *under* the telephone, showing that it had been put down after the crime. Carluke himself couldn't possibly have put it back, as you said; he must have fallen as soon as he was hit; and as additional evidence of that, I found, when I examined the telephone, that Carluke had apparently never touched it at all. That meant that somebody else must have put it back after his death, and cleaned it after moving. But, so far as we knew, only Mr. Barton had been in the cabinet after his death. So I tried a little more investigation of Mr. Barton's movements; and when I found, first that the telephone had apparently stood very recently for a few hours on an exceedingly inaccessible shelf, and secondly, prints of somebody's bloodstained toe-tips just below the place where it had stood, and a smudge on the shelf below which looked uncommonly like the mark of a knee resting there, I was pretty certain that it was he who had moved it—and moved it back again when he 'discovered' the corpse.

"But why? As you very pertinently said, to make room for the murderer. At this point, I must admit, I was criminally slow. I ought to have thought of the dummy telephone at once. But I was still looking for an ordinary blunderbuss— probably fixed to the upper shelf, and fired by some mechanical arrangement—when your lucky recollection of the corpse's hands gave me the clue. Then it was plain sailing; we had only to find the dummy."

"Why didn't he wait a little longer, and take the thing to pieces, instead of giving the alarm at once?" Prendergast wondered.

"Probably because he didn't dare delay for fear of exciting the suspicion of the man at the gate," Wilson said. "Of course he didn't expect to find us there too. He thought he would be able to send the man to the police station, and have a quiet twenty minutes to clear up. Our turning up was just a bit of bad luck for him. So was that tiny gap in the trees. Otherwise, except for the oversight in regard to the bulb, which might very easily never have been found, I think he showed remarkable intelligence. His acting of innocent apprehensiveness was very natural indeed, and his alibi, if I hadn't suspected him already, was just right, and not too circumstantial."

"Did you deduce the motive, too?" Prendergast inquired.

"Not really. I only noted that, as both men worked in a bank, there was one obvious possibility. But there might have been a hundred others. And you see, of course, the paramount necessity of haste. If we had stayed to look for the motive, we should never have got the man."

DEATH OUT OF THIN AIR
STUART TOWNE

THE GREAT MERLINI was not the only magician-detective created by the versatile Clayton Rawson (1906–1971). Under the Stuart Towne pseudonym, he produced four novelettes in 1940 about Don Diavolo, who sometimes performs as the Spanish Sorcerer, other times as the Scarlet Wizard. He tells a few friends that his real name is Nicola Alexander DeKolta, and they call him Nick but suspect that's not his real name either since it is made up of the names of three great illusionists of the past.

These stories were produced for a short-lived pulp magazine, *Red Star Mystery Magazine*, which ran for only four issues (June, August, October, and December 1940). The first two adventures, "Death from the Past" (originally published as "Ghost of the Undead") and "Death from the Unseen" (originally "Death Out of Thin Air"), were published in book form as *Death Out of Thin Air* (1941). The second two, published as "Act I" (originally "The Claws of Satan") and "Act II" (originally "The Enchanted Dagger"), were collected in a rare paperback volume, *Death from Nowhere* (1949). All four novellas and several additional short stories were collected in *The Magical Mysteries of Don Diavolo* (2005).

In addition to being a professional magician, illustrator, and writer, Rawson was an accomplished editor, serving as the editor of *True Detective Magazine*, Unicorn Books, Simon & Schuster's Inner Sanctum mystery imprint, and *Ellery Queen's Mystery Magazine* from 1963 until his death.

"Death Out of Thin Air" was first published in the August 1940 issue of *Red Star Mystery Magazine*; it was first collected in book form as "Death from the Unseen" in *Death Out of Thin Air* (New York, Coward-McCann, 1941).

DEATH OUT OF THIN AIR

STUART TOWNE

Chapter I

The Crime at Centre Street

LESTER HEALY walked slowly, reluctantly up the steps of the famous and dingy gray-stone building on Centre Street in which the New York City Police Department's Headquarters is located. Had you been there watching him you would have wondered why he was entering that building without handcuffs on his wrists and a cop on either side.

You would have spotted Lester Healy on first sight as being a crook and you would have been quite wrong. People were always making that mistake, and a good percentage of them suddenly found themselves getting their mail at Sing Sing on account of it.

Healy's slouchy posture, his cynical squint, the hard lean face with its ever present drooping cigarette, the underworld argot that was in his speech made him look the way you thought a gangster should look and gave you a jolt when you discovered—in court—that he was a sergeant of detectives.

At the moment, Healy was working on a special assignment for the Bureau of Missing Persons.

Shortly after Dr. Palgar had disappeared, Healy had picked up a rumor on the underworld grapevine that looked like a promising lead. Inspector Church had agreed that it could bear investigation and Healy had gone to work on it.

For the past week he had been a member of New York City's underworld. He had successfully tracked the rumor to its source and what he had discovered gave him a distinctly uneasy feeling in the pit of his stomach. He had just witnessed something that he was positive was utterly impossible, but which had happened just the same—something which he knew spelled trouble in big, nasty-tasting doses.

Sergeant Healy was more than a match for the average crook and for a lot that rated considerably above average. His experience had taught him just about all the answers; he knew what made the underworld and its members tick.

But this time he was up against something strange and unprecedented. This time he didn't have an answer because he'd never met anything like it before, and deep down within him he hoped he'd never meet anything like it again. If a man stopped to think about it, the criminal possibilities were enormous, utterly unpredictable and very possibly unbeatable.

He had decided that the smart thing for him to do was to turn in his facts and let some of the hot shots at headquarters do the worrying. He only hoped he could get them to believe he hadn't simply developed a case of delirium tremens or taken to using narcotics.

Healy, you see, had, under bright lights, just watched a man vanish into thin air. He had seen him fade slowly and completely into nothing at all. But it was even worse than that. He had been faced with clearly unmistakable evidence that the man who disappeared was still there under those bright lights—still there but quite invisible!

Inspector Church, Healy knew very well, wasn't going to accept a report like that without a good healthy argument. Church was an efficient, hard-hitting, no-nonsense cop who heartily disliked fairy stories in any shape or form, especially when they turned up in official reports.

Only a few weeks ago he had been involved in a curious case that the newspapers had referred to as The Vampire Murder. Church was still growling about it and a smart dick was careful not to make the slightest reference to it anywhere within a couple of hundred yards of the Inspector.

And now Healy had to take him a story like this!

Healy unlocked the door of his office, went in, threw his hat at the coat rack in the corner and seated himself at his desk. He put his hand on the phone and then sat there for a moment considering what would be the gentlest way of breaking his news to Inspector Church. He finally took a deep breath like a man about to dive into ice-cold water and started to lift the phone receiver.

At that moment his door opened abruptly and an excited man burst in and nearly overwhelmed Sergeant Healy. He jumped across the room, leaned over the desk, grabbed the startled Sergeant's hand and pumped it effusively.

He had a thick Italian accent. "You finda my leetle *bambina*. We are so happy! Maria, she is coming down to thank you herself. She was so afraid for Angelina and then you bring her back. I don't know how to tell you how happy—"

Healy slid back in his chair and disengaged his hand. The man seemed to be about to kiss him on both cheeks. "Wait a minute," Healy said. "I haven't found any little girls lately. Who were you looking for?"

The happy father bent forward looking closely at the sergeant. "You—you are not Lieutenant Farello? I am so sorry. My eyes—" He gestured toward the round tinted spectacles he wore.

"No," Healy said. "I'm not the lieutenant. You'll find him three doors down the hall."

Healy's visitor, flustered, apologized in Italian and backed out into the corridor, closing the door after him. Healy frowned as the thought passed through his mind that the man didn't look particularly Italian. But he had weightier matters bothering him and he turned again to the phone.

That was where he made his mistake. His last one. . . .

He asked the operator to connect him with Inspector Church, and when that gentleman's booming "Hello" came over the wire he said, "Sergeant Healy speaking. I've got a report to make in the Dr. Palgar case. I think I'd better give it to you verbally and do the written report later. It needs action immediately."

"Did you get any trace of Palgar?" the Inspector wanted to know.

"No, not yet. But I found that machine of his and something else. Something that looks like a big headache. Can I come up now and give it to you?"

"No. I'm on the way out. The boys just fished one of Dutch Kutzman's gunmen out of the East River. He was weighted down with machine-gun slugs. I've got to go take a look. I'll stop by your office on the way and you can give me a quick once over. See you in half a minute."

Healy said, "Yes sir," and replaced the phone receiver.

Inspector Church's office was on the floor above and it wasn't much more than a minute later when he walked down the stairs and along the corridor toward Healy's office. The Inspector, in his years of service, had never done the sort of undercover work that Healy did. He looked too much like a dick; a movie director would never have cast him as anything else.

He had the heavy, broad shouldered build, the flat feet that came from his long apprenticeship of pavement-pounding on the uniformed force, and the brusque, cocksure, suspicious manner of a policeman. His jutting, square-cut jaw had a determined forcefulness about it that a good many lawbreakers had discovered was the real thing.

But now, halfway down the corridor toward Healy's door, his jaw suddenly dropped and the determined look was replaced by one of amazement. The Inspector's quick walk abruptly became a wild dash.

He had heard behind Healy's closed door the familiar heavy crack of a gunshot.

Church's own gun was in his hand by the time he reached the door. As he grasped the doorknob, he heard a sound that made him throw his full weight against the door in a frantic smash. He was too late. The door was locked and the sound he had heard was the metallic click of the bolt sliding over.

Someone inside that room had locked the door. There was no other exit except for the window five stories above Centre Street. Church pounded on the door and shouted, "Healy! What the hell is going on in there?"

He got no answer whatever. Quickly, then, he put his gun to the door's lock, fired twice, and threw himself against the door again. The lock still held. Church fired once more, stepped back and this time really hit the door a hard smash. It gave suddenly.

The Inspector, falling inward, took a quick step, recovered his balance and stared at what he saw, the smoking gun in his hand lifted and ready but finding no target. Sergeant Lester Healy lay slumped forward in his chair, a streaming flow of blood moving down across his face and making a widening pool on the green desk blotter.

Sergeant Healy was there, the chair he sat in, a desk, a hat rack, and on the Inspector's right, behind the door, a table that bore a single-drawer filing cabinet. There was a tin wastebasket and one other chair. But that was all. Except for the Inspector himself, there was nothing and no one else in that room.

Church, a baffled angry look in his eye, looked quickly behind the door, under the table and the desk, found nothing, and made for the window. That was closed and locked on the inside.

Church stared at it with unbelief. Then he grabbed at the phone. As he did so, he heard a quick taunting voice behind him say, "*See you later, Inspector.*"

He whirled like a top and saw the door through which he had come swinging shut! He had turned in time to catch a glimpse of it end-on, and for a moment he saw both the inner and outer sides of it at once. The door was apparently closing of its own volition!

This uncanny sight made the Inspector hang fire for nearly a full second. Then, as the door slammed against the jamb, he sprang for it and yanked it open. There were men in the corridor outside, running toward him. Two detectives coming from the left; Inspector McShean, a uniformed cop and a secretary from the right. Church goggled at them.

"Who," he bellowed, "came out of this door just now?"

He got blank looks all around as the reinforcements reached him.

"No one at all, Church," McShean said. "What the—"

Inspector Church didn't answer. He turned back into the room, took a quick close look for the first time at Sergeant Healy.

"He's still alive," he said grabbing at the phone. Savagely he pounded an impatient tattoo on the receiver rest. "Operator, operator, dammit why doesn't . . ." His voice trailed off as he became aware that the phone cord was dangling uselessly over the side of the desk, its cut end attached to nothing at all.

Church put the phone down slowly. McShean rapped, "Kramer, get Pepper." Kramer left on the double quick.

McShean's bright quick eyes moved around the room. Suddenly he reached out and took the gun which Inspector Church still held. Church was thinking fast and furiously of something else. He let it go, then suddenly realizing what was happening, he blurted, "Hey, what's the idea of that?"

McShean was examining Church's revolver with an intent interest.

"Three shots fired," he said. "I heard four. But I don't see any other gun." He lifted Healy's body slightly and reached beneath the man's coat. He took a revolver from the holster there and examined it. "Full," he said. "It has to be suicide, but—"

"But," Church cut in, "it can't be suicide. "It—Brophy, get on a phone. Hurry like hell! See that men are stationed down stairs at every exit to this building at once! No one goes in or out until I say so." He turned to McShean. "Someone—or—or something locked that door from the inside just as I reached it—*after the first shot*! Healy couldn't have done it—not with that wound. It's murder. It has to be and yet—"

McShean didn't like the nervous glitter in Inspector Church's eyes, nor the jerky excited way he talked and acted. A suspicion was beginning to form in his mind that perhaps Church had been working too hard, that possibly he was sliding off in a nervous breakdown with hallucinations.

"And yet what?" McShean asked watching Church carefully, a clinical eye peeled for further symptoms.

"And yet," Church answered, "it can't be murder unless the murderer is invisible!" As Church said the word he knew that there could be no other answer.

Just as Dr. Pepper hurried into the room, Sergeant Healy's body made a slight convulsive motion and a moment later the doctor pronounced him dead.

Sergeant Healy had convinced Sergeant Church that there might be such a thing as an invisible man after all.

Chapter II

Invitation to a Burglary

Don Diavolo, The Scarlet Wizard, looked out across the footlights at the applauding audience that filled the great Manhattan Music Hall. His dark eyes beneath the scarlet half-mask held an engaging, devilish twinkle and his lips bore a mysterious half smile. His lithe, athletic figure bowed formally from the waist and the spotlight that centered on him made the red of his faultlessly tailored evening clothes glow like flame.

Diavolo had just finished his suavely deceptive routine of streamlined sorcery in which impossibilities crowded onto the stage with smooth rapidity, each one a little more astounding than the last.

Now, slowly, he turned and made a nonchalant gesture that took the great curtain behind him up out of sight to expose, in the exact center of the great bare stage, a small cabinet curtained with deep ultramarine drapes scattered with silver stars. A blue spotlight bathed it in a mysterious light; the orchestra played softly an exotic melody that had been born in the magic East.

Don Diavolo approached the cabinet. Its floor was three feet above the stage, supported on slender legs that permitted an unobstructed view beneath. The magician walked once around it, his hands weaving slow mystic passes in the air. Then, as the tempo of the music began to accelerate and grow louder he clapped his hands once, sharply. The curtains at the cabinet's front parted slightly and a dancer in the fluffy skirted traditional costume of the Imperial ballet stepped through and danced lightly, on her toes, down the short flight of glass steps that descended to the stage.

A spotlight picked her up as she pirouetted daintily. Then a second dancer came forth, and was caught by another bright circle of moving light as she followed the first. A third, fourth, and fifth followed. And in a few moments a dozen dancers moved slowly and gracefully on the stage. But the audience no longer saw them. All eyes were fastened on the opening in the curtain through which the girls emerged.

The cabinet, four and one half feet at the most, had already been emptied of more girls than it could possibly hold—and they continued to come. Now and again there was a slight pause as if the girl who had just come out were the last—but each time the music only grew more excited and more girls streamed forth. Eighteen, nineteen, twenty, twenty-one . . .

The audience was sure now that each one must be the last. Then Don Diavolo clapped his hands once more as the dancers formed a line on either side of him stretching across the stage.

He moved to the cabinet, hesitated briefly as he threw his enigmatic smile at the audience and then quickly flung the curtains aside. The audience looked intently, hoping to penetrate the secret of the inexhaustible cabinet. Instead of emptiness, the space within was filled with dancers, nine more who descended to the stage and joined the others. As the music suddenly changed and the whole chorus began to move through one of the beautifully synchronized precision routines for which they are famous, the audience looked around for the magician only to find that, having produced thirty chorus girls from a space which could have held no more than nine, he had himself vanished.

Chan Chandar Manchu, Don Diavolo's dresser and general boy-of-all-work waited in the wings and walked with Diavolo toward the elevator that would take them to the dressing room upstairs. He carried a valise, one of whose ends was fitted with a wire netting and inside which were the six white rabbits Diavolo had earlier produced from a silk hat.

"Those two card kings still at it?" Don asked.

Chan smiled, his almond eyes laughing. "Yes," he answered in his impeccable Oxford accent. "They are trying poker deals on each other now. They have me shuffle the deck and nobody ever gets anything less than four aces. I think that perhaps poker is not a good game for heathen Chinee to risk his money on."

Don chuckled. "Wily Oriental catches wise quick. Playing poker with those two guys allee same like imparting hard-earned cash to Four Winds of Heaven."

"Game of fan-tan might have different outcome," Chan said somewhat wistfully. "But they wouldn't play."

As Don pushed in the door of his dressing room he said, "Hello, Horseshoe. Hello, Larry. Chan says you won't take him on at fan-tan."

The Horseshoe Kid, an open-faced, guileless-looking gentleman shuffled a deck of cards with one hand and said, "What does he think we are, chumps? I make a living off guys who don't know no better than to place bets on the other man's game. Fan-tan! I'd probably lose my back teeth."

Larry Keeler said, "I've got an idea. What about a game—poker, bridge, blackjack, anything you like—with no holds barred? First man whose sleight-of-hand slips is out of the game and his chips go into the pot. How about it, Horseshoe?"

The Horseshoe Kid, otherwise known as Melvin Skinner, John B. Crooks, H. C. Orville and numerous other names, none of them his own, growled, "You've got big ideas, shorty. You're a magician, not a gambler. That stuff of yours would look swell on a stage, but across a card table it is phony as hell. Even a lop-eared fink would rumble those fancy shuffles of yours."

Keeler replied, "Says you," and calmly cut the deck that the Horseshoe Kid had just shuffled. He turned up the Ace of Hearts.

The Horseshoe Kid said, "That's nothing. Look." He lifted off the ace and threw it face down on the table. He gave the deck a quick shuffle and said, "I can cut to the Ace of Heavens even when it's not in the deck." He promptly did so. Chan reached out and flipped over the face down card only to discover that it was now the joker.

Keeler didn't care for it. "Your throwdown is antiquated," he criticized. "You're way back in the Dark Ages, still using the Erdnase method. Watch this."

The cardplayers in the audience outside would have blinked dazedly at this competition in dirty work. And though both the Horseshoe Kid and Larry Keeler were pretty evenly matched, Larry would probably have raised the most eyebrows. Horseshoe on the other hand would have taken away their shirts in a game.

He was a professional gambler whose trickery with cards was necessarily accomplished with a minimum of suspicion that it was anything of the sort. Larry was a magician who let his audiences know that he was using trickery and dared them to catch him at it. His card manipulations were more amazing to the lay audience than those of many of his competitors because the average person mistakenly supposes that sleight-of-hand consists mainly in the ability to palm cards.

Larry left them gaping because it was obvious from the start that he couldn't hope to palm a card of the regular size. His hands were several sizes too small. Larry is a cocky little man, known along Broadway as "Half Pint the Great" though few people have ever dared to call him that to his face. He is a dwarf, four feet tall at the outside, and sensitive as the devil about it.

His lack of stature has always prevented his debut on the legitimate stage as a serious magician because a conjurer of that size is more humorous than mysterious. Instead he plays circus sideshows and museums billed as "*Wizzo, the World's Smallest Prestidigitator.*"

Don Diavolo went on into the inner dressing room and started to change. "You boys will get conjurer's cramp or break an arm one of these days trying to out-maneuver each other."

Larry had just finished his trick and the Horseshoe Kid had taken the cards and started to try and top it when Woody Haines arrived. He nodded to the card players and went on in to where Don was seated before his dressing table removing the makeup from his face.

Woody had the build of an All-American back, which he had been, the amiable and ingenious brashness of a small boy crashing a circus, which he had done, and the breezy morale of a newspaper columnist, which he was. Running his *Behind the Scenes* stuff in the New York *Press* was his job. Tagging Don Diavolo like a large and persistent sheepdog puppy was his hobby.

Don Diavolo always made news. Besides, Woody liked the guy.

Don saw him in the mirror and greeted him. "Hello, Woody. How's the keyhole business? You look as if you had just corralled a front page story that'll need an eight column head."

"Eight column head," Woody exclaimed excitedly. "Hellfire, yes. And 72 point caps printed in four colors—or the city desk is nuts. Listen, Don. Last night Detective-sergeant Lester Healy was murdered in his office down at headquarters, and *you've* got to tell me how."

"In his office at headquarters?" Don asked in surprise. "That's hitting close to home isn't it? And why are you so late with it? I thought you were always Johnny-on-the spot?"

"I'm the only reporter in town who knows about it yet," Woody answered. "I've got me a nice pipeline right into Inspector Church's office, but even that almost failed me. The birdie who whispers things my way almost let me down altogether. He was afraid he'd be thrown out on his ear. I never saw a lid clamped down so tight as the one that's on at Headquarters today.

"D.A. is so burned up he steams, and Inspector Church nearly put me in the jug for saying good morning in a cheery tone of voice. That's what made me suspicious that something was up. So I put the thumbscrews on."

"Yes," Don said, "I can see why they'd be touchy about it. Who are the main suspects?"

"Most of the dicks say the only person that could have possibly killed Healy is Inspector Church!"

"What!" Don nearly exploded. The Horseshoe Kid and Larry Keeler crowded into the doorway, their eyes popping.

"You heard me," Woody added. "And Inspector Church says that Healy was killed by an invisible man!"

The Horseshoe Kid grunted, "And he's the cop who always says my alibis limp. Boy, wait until I tell him what I think of that one."

Don Diavolo was astonished, but he didn't appear to think it was funny. He was scowling. "Woody," he said slowly. "Let's have the story. All of it."

Woody pushed his hat back on his tawny head and obliged. "Church went down to Healy's office last night shortly before five o'clock. He heard a shot inside, someone locked the door in his face, he shot the lock off and broke in. Nobody there but Healy with a slug in his head. Then a voice came out of thin air and said, 'See you later, Inspector,' and the door closed.

"Church swears he saw it closing all by itself. A flock of dicks, in the corridor outside, swear that nobody came out the door. They couldn't find a gun. And that's that. Except for this."

Woody threw a five-by-seven sheet of paper down on the dressing table before Don. "Photostat," he said, "of a note that Inspector Church found an hour or so later. He and McShean chewed the rag in Healy's office for half an hour and watched the fingerprint men mess the place up. Then they went out for a few minutes to interview some men that had been stationed to guard the exits from headquarters immediately after the shooting. They all swear no one got by them.

"Then, when Church got back to Healy's office he started to pick up his hat. He had left it lying on Healy's desk. That note was lying on the crown of his hat."

Don read it aloud.

Inspector Church and as many friends as he cares to bring are cordially invited to attend the theft of the Madras Siva from The Museum of Indian Art at precisely 11 a.m. on Wednesday. Sorry about Sergeant Healy, but what he had to tell you would have been inconvenient.

Sincerely yours,
THE INVISIBLE MAN.

"Tomorrow at four," Don said. "Chan. The Madras Siva. What is it?"

Chan frowned. "The Madras Siva is a statue of Siva, The Destroyer, posed as Nataraja, Lord of the Dance. It is a nearly priceless sculpture

assigned to the tenth century, and I should say that its theft was impossible under any conditions."

"Why?" Woody asked.

"Because the statue is bronze, seven feet high and Siva has usual four arms extended in all directions like an octopus. Very unhandy object to pilfer."

Larry Keeler said, "It can't be done. The guy's a loony."

Don Diavolo looked at the note again. "He certainly seems sure of himself."

"After what happened to Healy," Woody said, "he has a right to be. He's got the whole Metropolitan Police Force standing on its ear right now. I'm breaking the story in the next edition and I want you to tell me—"

"This fingerprint that shows on the notepaper, Woody. Explain that."

"The lab gave the note the once over with their iodine fumes and developed that print. One thumbprint with a half inch scar across it. But it's not in the files either here or in Washington. Now what sort of hocus pocus is this Invisible bloke using? You're the expert on that subject. I want a signed interview."

Don was only half listening to Woody's request. He was more interested, and considerably startled by the curious expression that he saw on Patricia Collins's face.

Pat, his blond young lady assistant who gets sawed in two, burned alive, and generally mistreated at each performance only to come up smiling again at the next, had entered the room in time to hear most of Woody's story.

When she saw the reproduction of the note her face had gone completely white. Her hand as she reached and took the paper for a closer look trembled.

Chapter III

$10,000 an Hour

Don pretended not to notice Pat's trembling reaction and he turned quickly to Woody. "At the auto show a week ago," he said, "The Lord Motor Company displayed their new V-12 and a Dr. Valeski Palgar trained an electrical gadget of his invention on it six times a day. He called it an Invisibility Inducer.

"The Lord car promptly, in full view and under bright lights, faded out of sight except for the chassis and the running motor. When the doctor threw his switches into reverse the Fisher body slowly materialized again. The night before I had intended to go take a look at it someone burgled the Grand Central Palace and walked off with the doctor's machine.

"The next morning it was discovered that Dr. Palgar too had vanished. The papers were full of it. And now, I don't need to be a mind-reader to know darned well that you're going to tell me next that Sergeant Healy was working on the doctor's disappearance. Right?"

"Right," Woody replied at once. "That's what puts the finishing touch on the story. If it wasn't for that vanishing ray the D.A. would have had Inspector Church laced in a strait-jacket before now. It's the only thing that gives him an out."

"Palgar's invisibility gimmick was an advertising stunt, wasn't it?" Horseshoe asked. "Why don't you ask the Lord Company's advertising department what the gaff was? I should think they'd—"

"But they don't," Woody answered. "I got onto them right away. They've had cops in their hair ever since last night, and they couldn't tell any of us one blamed thing. They were pretty pleased about the publicity when their invisible ray vanished as if it had backfired, but now, with a murder tacked on, they don't like it.

"Palgar spent a couple of days before the show opened setting up his gadget, but he wasn't giving out any secrets. He worked behind closed doors and he yelled bloody murder every time anyone even tried to poke his nose into the place. He—"

Chan, who had gone to answer the phone in the other room, returned and announced, "A Mr. J. D. Belmont downstairs asking to see you."

Woody blinked. "J. D. Belmont. Holy cats! You do move in society, don't you, Don? What causes this?"

"Without looking in my crystal ball," Don said, "I wouldn't know. I've never set eyes on the man before. Have him sent up, Chan."

"Who," Horseshoe asked, "is J. D. Belmont?"

Woody stared at him. "So," he said, pretending to be greatly offended, "you don't read my column. Or maybe you just don't read. Try it sometime. J. D. Belmont is a millionaire about six times over—or is it sixty? I always get lost at that altitude. He is a sort of invisible man himself—the unseen mastermind behind a couple of dozen corporations and scads of holding companies. He spends his ill-gotten gains on his art collection. He's gathered in half the Old Masterpieces of Europe, his jewel collection has never been equalled, his library of Shakespeare First Folios, Gutenberg Bibles, and illuminated manuscripts is—"

The Horseshoe Kid, obviously interested, asked, "Does he play poker?"

"He does," Woody said. "But when he plays the stakes are so high you wouldn't be able to buy into the game unless you got a finance company to back you."

"Hmm," Horseshoe replied. "I'll have to give that some thought. I haven't met the sucker yet that I couldn't—"

As he heard the door to the corridor open Don got up. "You folks sit tight," he said. He went out and started to close the door behind him.

But Woody Haines slipped through after him, piloting his hefty frame with amazing agility. "No, you don't," he whispered. "I'm cutting myself in on this. It looks like a story."

J. D. Belmont stood in the center of the room. A stony-eyed gentleman who was obviously a private detective stuck close to his side and a uniformed chauffeur stood in the doorway, blocking it. They both had their right hands in coat pockets that bulged suspiciously.

The chauffeur was nervous. He kept looking back over his shoulders. Both of them acted as if they had itchy trigger fingers.

Mr. Belmont seemed a bit nervous himself; his short, gruff manner was even a little grouchier than usual. He was a large, heavily built man with bushy jutting eyebrows and a vast frown. He chewed irritably at a long cigar whose gold band bore his own initials. He emitted smoke like a Chinese dragon and there were sulphurous sparks in his deep voice.

"Mr. Diavolo?" he grunted.

Don nodded and introduced Woody as J. Haywood Haines without mentioning that he was a newspaper columnist. J. D. Belmont had a reputation for throwing things at reporters.

"Sit down, won't you?" Don asked.

"No," Belmont said. "Can't stay. Much too busy. I've got a job for you. Don't have confidence in the police force in this town. Bunch of nincompoops. Hmmmph!" The Finance King, like a destroyer trying to hide from a submarine, exhaled another cloud of smoke.

"But I have a job," Don started to object. "I—"

J. D. said, "I know. Damn good act too. Fooled *me* completely." He said it as if that was the first time anything like that had ever happened. "That trick of yours where you put the girl in the box, slide steel plates through her neck and hips, and then show us her head and her legs with nothing at all between. How do you do it? Mirrors, I suppose?"

"I'm afraid I can't tell you that, Mr. Belmont," Don replied. "You see I've never been able to figure it out myself. It isn't mirrors though, I'm sure about that. First thing I thought of too. I looked. There aren't any."

The financier almost produced a grin, but the heavy black eyebrows and his brusque, pugnacious manner killed it, half formed. "Yes. Of course. Quite right. About this job. It'll last about an hour. I'll pay you five thousand dollars. Be at my home at Oyster Bay at ten-thirty tomorrow night. Do you have a pen?"

Don said, "I do a show tomorrow night at eleven o'clock. I don't think—"

Belmont broke in. "Look here, young man. Are you trying to hold me up? Hmmmph. I'll make it ten thousand. Now stop arguing." He took a checkbook from his pocket, seated himself and opened it across his knee. He held out his hand. "Pen please, young man. I'm in a hurry."

Before Don could reply, Woody Haines produced a pen and gave it to Belmont. He said, "Hmmmph" again instead of "Thanks" and started writing. Woody made motions at Don behind the financier's back, and his mouth silently formed the words, "Take it, you dope." Woody's keen brown eyes obviously saw another big story staring him in the face and he wasn't going to let it get away if he could help it.

Don said, "Could you tell me what it is you want ten thousand dollars' worth of, Mr. Belmont?"

"Protection," the man growled, waving the check briskly. "Here. I got that in my mail this morning. Thought it was a crackpot until I saw the headlines in the *Press* an hour or so ago. Showed the note to District-attorney Cleever. He nearly had apoplexy when he saw it. Tells me the note writer murdered a detective last night. Cleever says he expects an arrest any moment. Means he doesn't know anything about it. I want you out there when it happens. I'll expect you at ten-thirty."

J. D. Belmont turned and sailed out of the room, leaving the check and a haze of smoke. His chauffeur went before him and the dick, scowling heavily, followed after.

Woody Haines snatched the note from Don's hand, took one look at it and made for the phone. "Boy, oh boy!" he exclaimed, dialing. "When it rains it pours. Rewrite desk, darling, and shake a leg."

He looked back toward Diavolo, who was scowling at the door that had slammed behind J. D. Belmont. "What's the matter with *you*? Don't you realize that even that check wouldn't begin to pay for the publicity you're going to—Hello, Mike. Here's a new front page for you! . . . War? Which war? Oh, stick it on the Sports page. Listen. Invisible man duels magician! J. D. Belmont, financial wizard, pays Don Diavolo, Scarlet Wizard, ten thousand smackers to outwit unseen menace. The little man who isn't there sent J. D. a note this morning. Quote: *'I want the Antoinette necklace. You won't miss it. Kindly have it ready for me when I call at eleven o'clock Wednesday night. You may inform the police. Best regards. The Invisible Man.'* Unquote.

"Don Diavolo replies as follows. Quote: *'Dear Invisible Man: Go take a running jump in the East River. Love and Kisses. Don Diavolo.'* Unquote. Start working on that. I'll be over with more right aw—"

"Hey!" Don shouted, suddenly coming out of his own brown study. "What goes on here? Blast you, Woody. You can't—" He started toward the big reporter, but Woody was too near the door. Woody dropped the phone and before Don Diavolo could collar him he was gone.

"See you later," his voice floated back. "I'm a busy man. Hmmmph!"

Don looked at the others who had come crowding into the room when Belmont left. "Pat," he said, "that little pet elephant of yours gets me into the damnedest messes. I don't have the slightest idea what makes the invisible man invisible and now—"

Pat hadn't as yet recovered from the shock that something about that note had given her. "Don," she said, her voice wavering. "I want to see you for a minute—alone." She started back into the inner dressing room.

The Horseshoe Kid said, "Larry and I are leaving, Pat. We're going down to Lindy's and have a drink and I'm going to call his bluff on that no-holds-barred card game. Come on, half-pint. We'll make it blackjack."

Larry got his hat and cracked back. "Okay, butterfingers. It's your funeral."

When they had gone, Don turned to Pat and waved graceful fingers at the photostat that she was still tightly clutching. "What do you know about that note, sweetheart?" he asked. "Better tell me," he said, more gently.

Her blue eyes were worried. "Don—I—I know whose thumbprint this is," she said slowly. "At least I'm—I'm afraid I do."

Don took the 'stat and glanced at it swiftly. "The scar?" he guessed, his dark eyes narrowing.

She nodded. "Yes. It's exactly like one on Glenn's hand. And I'm afraid. . . ."

"Your brother?" Don asked in surprise. "I thought he was in Hollywood."

She shook her blond head. "He came back a month ago, Don. The studio didn't renew his contract. He fell in love with Myra Shaw and she threw him over for some producer. It hit him pretty hard and he started drinking. He reported on the set several times so tight he couldn't act. That, coming on top of the flop his last picture made—it was a corny script—put him on the skids. But that's not all.

"He dropped every cent he had on roulette and horses. He wouldn't ask anyone for money, but Woody found out about it somehow—he always does—and I've been helping Glenn out. He hates that and he's just desperate enough to do something like this—only I don't understand. . . ."

"How he makes himself invisible?"

Pat nodded. "Yes. It's a trick of some sort, isn't it, Don?"

"I don't know. If it is, it's a honey." Don scowled. "And I'm going to get to the bottom of it. We could use something like that in the act. Where's Glenn staying, Pat?"

"Actor's hotel on East Fortieth. The Drury Lane."

"Good. Chan, you put on your hat and go get him. Tell him Pat wants to see him. Don't tell him why, but say that it's important. And bring him back if you have to knock him out."

Chan grinned. "My jiu-jitsu is somewhat rusty. This may be an excellent opportunity for practice. Don't worry, Miss Pat. I'll bring him in A No. 1 condition."

Chan hurried out and Pat stood by the window looking down onto 50th Street. After a moment she said, "But there's something wrong somewhere Don. Glenn wouldn't have murdered that detective."

Don's voice had a queer inflection in it as he answered, an incredulous note of amazement. Pat turned toward him quickly.

"There are a lot of things wrong everywhere, Pat. I'm beginning to think I don't much like our invisible friend, whoever he is. Look at this."

Pat looked where Don's finger pointed. Woody's hat, which its owner had been in too great a hurry to take, lay on the divan. A small white card rested on its crown. "That," Don added, "must have been put there *since* Woody came into the room."

Without touching it, Pat leaned forward to read the pencilled words.

Keep away from Belmont unless you want trouble.

—THE INVISIBLE MAN

"Not as polite as usual," Don said, scowling at the words.

Pat looked around nervously. A small shiver crept along her back. She couldn't rid herself of the feeling that had been growing within her, a curious feeling that was to affect a good many people in the next few days.

It seemed to her that if her eyes could only stare just a bit harder, she might almost manage to see the figure she had begun to fear was there in the room with them, invisibly listening—and watching every move.

Chapter IV

The Queen's Necklace

Chan Chandar Manchu had once hunted tiger in the Indian jungles. But finding Glenn Collins in Manhattan turned out to be more of a job.

There wasn't any trail to follow. At the Drury Lane Hotel, Chan was informed that Mr. Collins had checked out three days ago and had not left a forwarding address. Chan called Don Diavolo and asked for further orders.

"Booking agents, Chan," Don suggested. "Producers' offices, theatrical boarding houses, and hotels. Try them. Pat says he was looking for a job. You might find someone who has his new address. I'm going on for the last show in a few minutes, then home. Report back there."

Chan got two dollars' worth of nickels, tore the pages that contained the numbers of the theatrical agents and hotels from the Classified book, and disappeared into a phone booth.

The hour being as late as it was, his percentage of completed calls was small. Three of the agents he reached gave him Glenn's address, but they each said: "The Drury Lane." None of the hotels had anyone registered by that name.

Chan called Don again at the Fox Street house in the Village. Karl Hartz, Diavolo's private mechanical wizard, answered the phone. He listened to Chan's discouraged report, relayed it to Diavolo and then said, "Don says to try Sardi's and Lindy's. If you don't strike pay dirt there, come on in."

The headwaiters at both restaurants knew Glenn Collins by sight; neither had seen him for the last three days. Glenn seemed to have vanished from all his usual haunts quite completely.

Chan took the subway to Christopher Street and walked the two blocks over to 77 Fox Street, the house which was Don Diavolo's headquarters when he was playing New York City and which the newspapers always referred to as The House of Magic. It had more gadgets, all devised and installed by Hartz, than the Fun house at Coney Island. Dan Diavolo could, to all intents and purposes, walk through its walls with the greatest of ease. It was as impregnable as a fortress, but to Don and his friends it was, even when surrounded by policemen—as it had been at least once—no more effective a prison than a bag of wet tissue paper.

Don Diavolo, Patricia Collins, and Karl

Hartz were in the library when Chan came in. Karl was talking on the phone. "No, Inspector Church. Don Diavolo is not here at the moment. . . . No, I don't know when he'll be in. . . . Yes I'll tell him."

Karl hung up and said, "Somehow I get the impression that the Inspector wants to look at your fingerprints, Don."

Don nodded, "I was expecting that. Just because my magic annoys him, every time anything happens that looks both criminal and impossible he wants my blood." Don tossed a book onto the pile stacked on the floor by his chair. He looked at the gloomy expression on Chan's face and asked, "No luck, Hawkshaw?"

Chan said, "No. Mr. Collins has vanished like boy in Indian basket trick."

Diavolo frowned. Patricia Collins, who sat in a chair across the room, smoking nervously, said, "If we could only find him before eleven tomorrow, we might be able to stop . . ." Her voice trailed off, hopelessly.

Karl Hartz brought another book he had just taken from the shelves that encircled the room and gave it to Don. "Here. This is the one I was looking for. *The Fateful Diamonds* by Jocelyn Rhys. It says that Madame Lamotte pried the stones from their settings. Her husband took some to London and Vilette some to Amsterdam, and sold them."

Don took the book and looked at it. "None of the other authorities take the trouble to mention the fate of the necklace. And this writer doesn't give her sources. It sounds logical enough though."

"May I ask," Chan inquired, "what this Antoinette necklace is?"

"You may," Don answered. "It's the necklace that had all Europe dithering back in 1758. Count Alessandro Cagliostro, the last of the great sorcerers, was accused of having stolen it from Mme. Lamotte when she was arrested on a charge of having gotten it from Boehmer, the jeweler, by fraud. Boehmer had put all his cap-

ital into the necklace, a fantastically improbable affair of diamonds worth sixty-four thousand pounds in those days and a lot more now. That's around $320,000.

"Boehmer made the necklace, hoping to sell it to Marie Antoinette, and then discovered that she didn't want the thing. He hawked it around all the courts of Europe for nearly ten years and couldn't find any monarch rich enough or extravagant enough to buy it.

"Then the Comtesse Lamotte-Valois, a beautiful, wily, and unscrupulous adventuress had herself an idea. She had been handing His Eminence, the Cardinal de Rohan, Grand Almoner of France, quite a line. He was trying to gain the favor of Marie Antoinette, and Lamotte pretended to help him by posing as an intimate of the Queen's. She even arranged a date for him with the Queen and rang in an impersonator, the 'Baroness d'Olivia,' and got away with it.

"Hearing about the necklace, she told Rohan that the Queen wanted to buy it and would pay Boehmer 1,600,000 livres in four installments. If the Cardinal would help arrange this little matter, the Queen would be most happy. Rohan, like a dope, jumped at the chance, particularly after Lamotte fed him some notes in the Queen's handwriting which she had had forged.

"The Cardinal gave the jeweler a note from Antoinette promising to pay, and Boehmer handed over the necklace. De Rohan gave it to Lamotte. And that's the last anyone ever saw of it. Six months later, when the first installment didn't show up, Monsieur Boehmer spilled the beans to the Queen. Marie promptly threw the Cardinal, Madame Lamotte, the phony Baroness, Vilette the forger, and some others into the Bastille.

"Madame Lamotte accused Cagliostro of having stolen the necklace, and he and his wife were jugged too. At the trial, his alibis looked good and he was released. Lamotte was imprisoned in the Saltpêtrière from which she later escaped and made her way to London.

"If Belmont has that necklace, then our invisible man is certainly out after big game. There are over five hundred diamonds in it—many big ones."

Karl scowled. "I smell mice," he said. "I'd like to know how long Belmont had had the necklace and why I've never seen any mention of its sale in the papers. The sale of a thing like that would make news."

"Collectors," Don replied, "are odd fish. Sometimes they spend thousands of dollars on an item and want it kept a secret. Some of them are fanatic enough to pay fancy prices for pictures that have been stolen from great museums—pictures that they know they'll have to keep out of sight, under lock and key. Don't ask me why."

"Whether it's the real necklace or not," Pat said, "Belmont must have something valuable if he's willing to pay you $10,000 to keep it from being stolen."

"Yes." Don looked thoughtfully at his lighted cigarette, placed it in one hand, and squeezed it slowly into nothing. "Of course he may only *think* he's got the real thing." Don stood up. "But there's nothing we can do until the Invisible Man keeps his first appointment at eleven tomorrow. I'm going to bed and sleep on it. You see that this place is well locked up tonight, Karl. The Invisible Man, since he left that note in my dressing room tonight, must know we've got a finger in the pie."

Pat, Chan, and Diavolo went upstairs to bed. Karl Hartz made his rounds and saw that all his burglar alarms were in good operating order. "Though I don't know what good these'll do," he grumbled somewhat uneasily to himself, "if the Invisible Man's already come in."

Something touched lightly against Karl's ankle and he jumped a good three feet. Two yellowish, slitted green eyes stared up at him from the darkness. Karl's first startled thought was that it was the invisible man and that he was an almond-eyed Chinese midget.

Then Karl said, "Blast!" and reached down to pick up the Diavolo household's *poltergeist*, Satan, a large black cat. Karl put him outside the back door and then sought his own bed.

Chapter V

Siva the Destroyer

At nine next morning the traffic cops at 55th Street and Fifth Avenue began having their troubles. Traffic started to tangle and the sidewalk in front of the Museum of Indian Art on 55th just off the Avenue began to collect a crowd.

At ten o'clock several riot cars arrived. The north side of the street was roped off and cleared of everyone except Inspector Church, a couple of dozen detectives and a platoon of uniformed cops. Even the newspaper photographers and reporters were unceremoniously told to "get on the other side of the street and stay there, dammit!" They growled, but obeyed, joining their colleagues, the newsreel cameramen, whose sound trucks were lined up along the opposite curb.

Inspector Church stationed a solid line of cops across the entrance to the museum and sent others to the roof. He stood in the Museum doorway and scowled across at the newsreel men who were busily aiming their cameras at the crowd, the Museum, and the Inspector. One of them shouted, "Action, please. Give us a smile, Inspector."

Church gave him instead a dirty look. "If that blank-blank notewriter really is invisible, what the blazing fury do those guys think they are going to get a picture of?"

"An inspector of police having a fit, maybe," a laughing voice said, close by Church's side. "Better watch your language, Inspector. You'll have the Hays office on your neck."

"You!" Church whirled. "What are *you* doing here? How did you get past my men?"

Don Diavolo grinned. "I didn't, Inspector," he answered. "I've been here for some time. Chan introduced me to the curator, an old friend of his, and I've been inside looking over the layout."

Church turned to a detective nearby. "Brophy," he commanded. "Go and see if that statue is still there. If *this* guy's been nosing around it . . ."

Brophy departed hastily, looking worried. Church said, "I'm watching you."

"You can search me, Inspector," Don returned. "And you won't find any seven foot, four-armed bronze statues on my person. Say, you don't suppose that is why the Invisible Man gave you notice that he was going to snitch a statue of Siva the Destroyer, do you?"

"I don't suppose that is why . . . ? I don't suppose *what* is why?" The Inspector was upset.

"Well Siva is four-armed; and forewarned is also fore-armed!"

Don Diavolo's tact this fine morning was negligible. Inspector Church was in no mood for puns and he said as much in elaborate and colorful terms. His words glowed as if they had been lettered across the sky in neon tubing. Then he ordered, "Schultz and Gianelli. You two keep your eyes on this monkey. He doesn't leave here until I say so, and he doesn't go into the room where that accursed statue is on any account. Got that?"

They said, "Yessir!" simultaneously.

Inspector Church turned on his heel and went into the building. The curator, a lean, dark-skinned little man, Mr. I. J. Kamasutra, smiled politely at him, but it did no good. Church growled irritably and went on into the Court of the Gods.

The walls of this room were covered with ancient and priceless hangings whose intricate patterns told, in esoteric symbols, the story of the prophet Buddha, and pictured the many strangely shaped forms of the angels and demons of the Brahman hierarchy.

The Inspector, who hated magic and all things unexplainable, was here surrounded by just that on every side. Demon masks, their faces twisted with an inhuman ferocity, leered down at him, while several lesser statues of five-headed devils and hybrid elephant gods watched him suspiciously from the dark corners of the room.

"Get some light in this place," he commanded.

Two of the half dozen detectives who stood around the great bronze statue in the center of the room hurried out and returned with an extension cord and a portable light. They set it up and turned its 200-watt glare full on the posturing figure of Siva the Destroyer.

Lying prostrate on a heavy lotus pedestal was the small kicking figure of a dwarf whose back supported the right foot of the mighty Siva figure that balanced above, majestically, gracefully, caught by the sculptor in the midst of the symbolical movement of the Dance of Siva— graceful and yet, with his wide spread four arms, monstrous. The dark gold-green of the old bronze shone dully in the harsh white light.

Church glowered at the statue. "What the devil would anyone want with that pipe-dream? Now I know I'm dealing with a crackpot." He reached out, touched its metal surface experimentally, and shook his head. "Anybody'd need a derrick, a gang of expert piano movers, and a truck to lift that."

Church lifted his arm and looked at his wrist watch. The hands stood at five minutes to eleven.

Don Diavolo, standing at ease just outside the single doorway, his guards on either side of him, asked, "Well, Inspector?"

Church looked at him. "You make me nervous," he said. "Schultz, take him into the curator's office and put him on ice. I don't think anything is going to happen, but if it does, I don't want him around. But I want to know where he is."

Inspector Church, as it turned out, was right on both counts. Nothing happened; yet it did. And that came about in this way.

On the other side of 55th Street, directly opposite the Museum, there was a shop whose window bore the words: *Nathan Ziegler, Ltd.*, lettered in a conservative, dignified gold-leaf. Mr. Ziegler didn't bother to inform the passerby what sort of a shop it was. The man in the street wasn't a customer of his, and everyone who might conceivably be a prospective client knew about Mr. Ziegler.

They all knew that he was one of the three really important art dealers on this side of the Atlantic. They knew that if they wanted an El Greco or a jeweled medieval reliquary Ziegler, if anyone, could get it if it was to be had at all. They also knew that Ziegler was an art expert whose opinion of the authenticity of an artistic rarity had seldom been questioned.

At the moment when the Inspector looked at his watch, Nathan Ziegler stood at the door of his shop, his back stooped in its characteristic attitude, his small dark eyes peering out at the densely packed, waiting crowd along the street.

By his side another man stood, a dark-complexioned, straight-backed man whose blue eyes were quick and bright behind the pince-nez with its broad black ribbon. He wore a fashionably tailored overcoat over sedately correct morning clothes. He pointed toward the show window. "That Medici goblet and the T'ang vases are in danger. If the crowd should push too heavily against your window . . ."

Ziegler saw the risk. He motioned quickly to the two clerks who were nearby also watching the scene outside. "Clear the window out, quickly." Then he turned to his companion. "It is preposterous. Some publicity stunt, I suppose. It would take more than one man, invisible or not, to remove the Siva statue from that museum, even though it were quite unguarded. Do you care to look at more of the miniatures, Mr. Gates? It is nearly eleven and since you have so little time . . ."

Gates shook his head. "Not just yet." He gestured toward the crowd outside that had now grown silent and intent, all eyes on the museum doorway. "This interests me greatly. You know, I'm not so sure that it is a hoax. There was something about the way those letters were written that sounded devilishly serious. I half believe that somehow, in spite of that crowd and those policemen, the note writer, invisible or not, may get what he is after."

"But what would he do with that statue if he did get it?" Ziegler asked.

Gates shook his head. "That's the mystery. That is what makes the whole affair so intriguing."

Behind the two men, in the rear of the shop, a clock began to strike the hour. Nathan Ziegler, who had never been more completely wrong in his life, said, "Nothing will happen."

As the last stroke died away, the crowd outside stirred uneasily. They watched intently now, hoping for some incident that would give them an indication of what was going on inside the museum. But the closely formed line of patrolmen at attention before the doorway remained stolid and immovable.

Ten minutes later the scene was still the same. Gates looked at his watch. "Perhaps you are right, Mr. Ziegler. Either the Invisible Man is late or it is a hoax of some sort. Shall we look at the miniatures again? I would like to see the documents certifying the authenticity of that Coswell portrait of the Prince Regent."

Ziegler led the way back through the little rear door into the display room. He started toward the great safe on the left whose door was partly ajar as Ziegler had left it. Gates, who had gone across to a display case along the rear wall suddenly exclaimed, "Ziegler! This Caxton *Book of the Hours*! My copy has an earlier date, and you have this listed as his earliest piece of liturgical printing."

Ziegler turned immediately, and went to join Gates. "No," he said, obviously perturbed by Gates's statement. "That couldn't be true. It is a very well authenticated fact that William Caxton—"

Footsteps crossed the floor behind the two men.

"Mr. Gates?" a voice asked.

Gates turned. "Yes?"

A Western Union special messenger held out a pad and pencil. "Sign here, please." When Gates had done so, he handed over an envelope, took the tip Gates gave him and walked quickly out.

Gates ripped the message open. "From my New York office," he said. "I told them I was going to stop here." He read quickly and then frowned. "I must return to the office before catching that noon plane. I shall have to leave immediately."

He stuffed the message in his pocket, crossed the room and quickly gathered up his hat, cane, and gloves. "Send me photostats of the Coswell documents," he said. "If they are satisfactory, I shall send you a check for the portrait." He stooped to lift the large pigskin travelling case by the door.

"Wait," Ziegler said. "Let my clerk help you with that. Butterfield! Come and carry Mr. Gates's bag out for him. If you can force your way through that crowd, you should be able to get a cab on Fifth Avenue."

"Thank you," Gates said as the clerk came in. "I shall see you again when I am in town. If you should locate another of the Florentine pamphlets, let me know immediately. Goodbye."

Ziegler saw him to the door, and, after watching the still expectant crowd for a few moments, returned to the display room and started to return the miniatures he had laid out for inspection to their places within the safe.

At that moment, Don Diavolo, standing in the window of the curator's office, was looking down upon the upturned faces of the crowd. Woody Haines, below, who had been watching that window like a hawk ever since Don had appeared in it, saw him shake his head. Quickly Woody slipped away and headed for a phone.

That was how Woody, for once in his life, missed the excitement. Just at the moment when he was telling a rewrite man that the Invisible Man had failed to keep his promise, things began happening on 55th Street.

The first thing was the clerk who ran white-faced from Nathan Ziegler's shop, pushed through the crowd and hurried, as if Siva the Destroyer was at his heels, across toward the Museum. Four cops jumped on him at once. The newsreel cameramen's long faces brightened and their cameras swung into action.

The crowd saw the clerk gesturing frantically. They saw a detective leave the group around him and dash into the Museum.

A moment later Inspector Church, at the head of a running squad of men emerged, gathered the clerk in passing, and charged across the street like a football backfield going over for the final touchdown. They ploughed through the waiting mob and vanished into the little shop. Reporters converged on the scene of activity piled up against the shop's doors like a wave against a breakwater. More cops arrived and began pushing the crowd back.

One of the reporters buttonholed a detective who owed him money from last night's poker game. "All right, Joe," he threatened. "Talk, or else."

The detective whispered a few words in his ear and the reporter, his eyes popping, whirled and vanished. He made the drugstore phone booth down the street just as Woody Haines was coming out. The reporter saw him and slowed to a walk at once. "Hi, Woody," he said. "Can I use the phone? The wife's having a baby and I ought to call the hospital."

Woody nodded, stepped aside and then as the door closed, turned, scowled after his colleague, muttered, "Damn, that guy only got married last week!" When that realization exploded under his hat Woody legged it for the street at a pace that would have made Seabiscuit envious.

The reporter in the phone booth, half a minute later, was getting one of the biggest nickel's worth of phone service the telephone company had ever sold.

"The Invisible Man," he shouted, talking in headlines, "double-crosses police! Takes fortune in precious stones from Nathan Ziegler while New York's Finest are barking up wrong tree!"

The rewrite man on the other end of the wire dug savagely into a sheet of copy paper with his pencil, broke the point off short, swore and grabbed for another. A few minutes later tele-type machines in a hundred cities were chattering madly.

And a few blocks away Patricia Collins leaned forward breathlessly on the seat of a taxicab that moved down Fifth Avenue close behind another cab in which Mr. L. C. Gates sat with a satisfied smile on his face and a large pigskin bag between his feet.

Chapter VI

The Mysterious Mr. Gates

When Inspector Church burst like a raging cyclone into Nathan Ziegler's shop he found its proprietor in a hysterical and incoherent state. In answer to Church's torrent of questions he held out a shaking hand and gave the Inspector a small card whose size and shape were now all too familiar.

It was another impudent, taunting note from the invisible correspondent.

My apologies for having misled you. And be careful. I intend to do it again. Better luck tonight. Best regards.

—THE INVISIBLE MAN

A coldly determined, vindictive expression settled on the Inspector's red face as he read those words and his frosty blue eyes were like twin volcanoes spouting fire. He was really mad now.

He turned from Ziegler, whom shock had left nearly speechless, and went to work on the clerk, an elderly little man who sputtered with excite-ment, but who was still able to answer questions with some degree of coherence.

He told about Gates's visit and said that when he and his employer had started to return the miniatures to the big safe in the corner of the display room, they discovered at once that of the twenty which had been laid out, three were

missing; and those, according to the clerk, were the pick of the lot.

Ziegler spoke up now. "I sent him to get you, Inspector. And then I went to the open safe. . . ." Ziegler moved toward it now and stood looking in at the objects that shone gold and crystal in the light. "All the rarest pieces have been taken," he went on haltingly. "The Oviedo rock crystal cross which the Duchess of Savoy presented to the Infanta Isabella; Charles VII's gold locket that bore his name and the Imperial crown on its face in diamonds; a XVI century reliquary of enameled gold containing a piece of the True Cross; the Jacopo de Farnese jade cup; the only perfectly matched string of black pearls in the world; a Gribelin watch; a set of six Jacobite wine glasses . . ."

Ziegler moved from the safe to a display cab-inet nearby. "An Aldus choir book," he added hopelessly, "and two holograph Keats letters."

"They sound valuable," Church said.

Ziegler groaned. "They were priceless!"

"This bird Gates. Maybe he took the stuff out under his coat."

Ziegler shook his head wearily. "Impossible, Inspector. The jade cup was a foot high. The choir book weighed twenty pounds. The wine glasses . . ."

"Who is Gates?"

"I . . . he was a new customer, Inspector. Gave his address as Seattle. Lumber million-aire. Said he had just recently become interested in collecting miniatures and he ordered one of those that I showed him."

"Okay. Brophy, get someone started on a checkup. Find out if that's who he really is. Get the airport and—"

At that moment the clerk who had helped Mr. Gates to a taxi returned. Church pounced on him. "You didn't mention this man, Ziegler. Why has he been outside?"

"He carried Mr. Gates's bag to a taxi."

"Mr. Gates's bag?"

"Yes. A large pigskin travelling case. He was on his way to catch a plane at LaGuardia Field. He—"

"Brophy!" Church broke in. "Get busy. Check the airport. And put someone to work on Gates. Find out if that's who he really is. That's where your stuff went, Mr. Ziegler. It went out in that pigskin bag! You!" He turned to the clerk, "What's your name?"

"B-Butterfield, sir," the young man replied, stuttering nervously under the Inspector's accusing glare.

"What was the license number of that cab?"

"I . . . I d-didn't notice, s-sir."

"Naturally. Nobody ever does, dammit! Did you by any chance happen to notice what direction it left in?"

"Yes, of c-course, sir. Downtown."

Nathan Ziegler interrupted. "Inspector. The things could not have gone out in Gates's suitcase. That is impossible!"

"Why?" Church growled, turning on him.

"Simply because I was with Gates every moment of the time he was here. He had no opportunity, and everything was quite in order when he and I left this display room and went to look at the crowd in the street outside, just before eleven."

"Well, so what? One of your clerks loaded the bag for him."

Ziegler shook his head more decisively than ever. "They were both with us in the front room."

Church glanced at the Invisible Man's card which he still held in his hand. His face grew darker than ever, even if a minute before that had not seemed possible.

"Robbins," he growled, turning to another of his detectives. "Get this down to the lab and phone me a report." The Inspector then took off his overcoat and got down to business.

He spent the next two hours going over the premises of Nathan Ziegler, Ltd., looking for clues and interrogating Ziegler and his two clerks. He accumulated nearly enough information about the private lives of all three men to have written three full-length biographies. But he didn't find any clues—nothing but a strange insistence on Ziegler's part that J. D. Belmont

was the Invisible Man. He was sure it was Belmont because the financier had wanted to buy some of the very objects that had vanished.

Church didn't like the suggestion on two counts. "Belmont's got money to burn. He wouldn't need to steal them. Besides I've just talked to the D.A. on the phone. Belmont was in his office at eleven o'clock."

If the Inspector, however, had been with Patricia Collins in her taxi his face wouldn't have been so long. She was having rather more success. The taxi she had followed had circled around until it headed, not toward LaGuardia Field, where the occupant had, in Butterfield's hearing, originally told the driver to go, but in a diametrically opposite direction.

Once, the man she followed left his taxi, walked a block or two and then took another. He was doing that, Pat knew, so that if the cops should find the cabdriver who had picked up a fare at 50th and Fifth they'd not discover anything concerning his real destination. A few minutes later, at a red light, Pat took the opportunity to make a change herself, from a yellow cab to a checker.

The cab ahead, still going uptown, suddenly turned right, through the park. On Lexington it turned north again and Gates got out at the corner of 104th.

Pat passed him and waited at the next corner. Gates came toward her and she sat tight. He walked another block and turned left onto 106th. Pat made the corner just as he ducked into a house halfway down the block. She paid off her driver, dashed for the phone in a nearby drugstore and dialed the number of the Manhattan Music Hall.

When she had been connected with Don Diavolo's dressing room and heard Chan's calm matter-of-fact voice over the wire, she spoke and tried hard to keep the hopeless feeling that hung heavily on her from showing in her voice.

"Pat speaking. Is Don there?"

"He just went on stage, Miss Pat. Where are

you? We have been worried. Miss Mickey had to fill your spot and Don had to leave out The Great Transposition mys—"[1]

"Chan," Pat said hurriedly. "Listen. I want help. I'm on 106th Street. Drugstore, corner of Lexington. I—I think I've found Glenn!"

Chapter VII

Appointment with the Unseen

As Don Diavolo came off stage into the wings and busied himself making a lightning change of costume, Chan popped up beside him.

"Miss Pat's on the phone," he reported rapidly. "She was at the corner of Fifth and 50th where you had her stationed, when she saw a man she thinks was her brother in disguise get into a cab. He came from Ziegler's shop and he carried a large pigskin bag. She followed him."

Don threw the red opera cape around his shoulders, his eyes gleaming. "That's a fine place to stop for breath, Chan. Get on with it."

"She trailed him to a place on 106th Street. She's waiting there now. What do I do?"

As the music of the orchestra before the footlights rose in a crescendo, Don said, "Get the Horseshoe Kid and send him up to take over. And see if you can locate Larry Keeler and get him down here. Scram!"

Don Diavolo whirled and ran out onto the stage just barely making his cue.

The rest of that afternoon was hectic. Between appearances Don listened to Pat's story, conferred with Larry Keeler, and heard the Horseshoe Kid report several times at hourly intervals that Mr. Gates was still holed up.

A glum-faced Woody Haines stopped in once to report that Inspector Church was being as tight-mouthed as two clams, but that the best authenticated rumors had it that Nathan Ziegler was poorer to the tune of some two hundred grand.

Also, his informant in Church's office had given him a photostatic copy of the note that had been left in Ziegler's shop. The lab had found a thumbprint on this one too, though, unlike the first, this one bore no scar.

Once, between shows, Don made a hurried trip to 106th Street, looked the ground over and conferred with Horseshoe.

The latter had news. "We've hit a jackpot," he reported. "I just saw St. Louis Louie go in the joint."

"And who is St. Louis Louie?" Don Diavolo asked.

"A cheap gunman who used to play with the Blue Streak gang until it folded after Jake the Orphan got a twenty year jolt for getting in Hoover's way. Louie's a Chinese needle-worker who shoots first and thinks afterward—only he never thinks much.[2] If Pat's right about the guy being Glenn, I don't like the company he keeps."

Don Diavolo frowned. "Looks like trouble ahead. You sit tight, Horseshoe, I want to know where Mr. Gates and friend Louis are tonight when the fireworks display goes off out at Belmont's place. We'll play those two cards close to our vest until then. Keep the phone line working."

Diavolo returned to the Music Hall, did his eight o'clock show and then made arrangements to keep his $10,000 appointment with J. D. Belmont, Inspector Church, and the Invisible Man.

The financier's Oyster Bay estate on the shore of Long Island Sound was a tourists' landmark. But they never saw it except from a distance. High walls surrounded the entire estate except on the water side, and that was constantly patrolled by Belmont's private police department.

On a hill above the water, his turreted cas-

---

1 Mickey Collins was Pat's twin sister, a young lady who looked so much like her that it was a standing joke as to whether or not the twins themselves knew for sure which was which. Mickey, because Don would rather not have it known that he employed a pair of twins, wore a black wig over her own blond hair in public.

2 Chinese needle-worker: Narcotic addict.

tle stood out against the sky like the stronghold of some medieval robber baron. Some people called him that as it was. In England, for instance, there was an association of antiquarians named the "Save Our National Relics from J. D. Belmont" Society.

Belmont was without question the world's ace collector. Money from his pyramided companies and interlocking corporations apparently poured in on him so fast that he needed four overworked secretaries to help him spend it.

At just ten-thirty Don Diavolo braked his long scarlet Packard before the towering medieval gate that had once, centuries ago, withstood the onslaught of the Barbarian hordes and which Belmont had had brought across the Atlantic piece by piece and reassembled.

To Pat, beside him, Don said, "This is bad. I don't see a door knocker and we forgot to bring a battering ram."

As he spoke, from a lookout above the gate, a powerful searchlight swept down upon them.

"Larry," Don said quickly, "duck!"

Larry Keeler, the miniature magician who was in the seat behind, dropped quickly to the floor—and vanished. He had been standing in a large open valise which Don, reaching over, had snapped shut as Larry doubled up within it.

Lieutenant Brophy came toward them from the shadows of the gate.

"You'll have to leave the car here," he said. "The big gate isn't to be opened. The Inspector's orders. Come with me."

Pat and Don descended from the car and Don lifted the suitcase that held Larry Keeler's ninety pounds. They followed the detective and, moving closely one behind the other, they entered through a small door that was opened just enough to allow them to slip in.

The detective indicated the high, fortress-like walls that stretched away on either side. "If that invisible loony gets in here tonight, he's good. The top of that wall is electrified and the shore down there has a cordon of men along it that a mouse couldn't slip through. We won't see any invisible man tonight."

"If he warns us he's going to do one thing and then does something else as he did this morning, perhaps we won't," Diavolo said. "On the other hand, in spite of walls and guards an invisible man is a difficult visitor to avoid."

Don was thinking that if he could sneak Larry Keeler in past all these precautions, then a completely invisible man shouldn't have too much trouble. The reason for Larry's secret presence was that Diavolo had decided to have one watcher that no one else knew was present.

That morning at the Museum, the Invisible Man had successfully misdirected several thousand people in an expert manner that got Don's admiration. But Don, as a magician, knew one fact that might prove to be the monkey wrench in the machinery if the Invisible Man should try the same methods tonight. He knew that it is extremely difficult to misdirect someone that you do not know is there. The Invisible Man would naturally concentrate on misdirecting Diavolo, Belmont, the Inspector and his men. If he did not know that another pair of sharp magician's eyes were watching, his misdirection might not be complete.

A police car sped them along the winding road that led up to the great mansion. Diavolo noticed that the grounds were alive with cops and that the house itself was surrounded as if the Inspector were expecting the Goths and Vandals to descend upon him in all their armed force. It was apparent that he was taking no chances this time around.

As they went in with Brophy, the butler met them and tried to relieve Don Diavolo of the suitcase. The magician shook his head.

Brophy asked curiously, "What are you lugging around in that suitcase? Do you expect to stay the night?"

"Brought along a few gadgets that may help us trip up our invisible visitor," Don said. "Where's the party going to be held?"

"Library," Brophy answered, moving down the hall and opening a door on the right.

Don Diavolo put the suitcase on the floor ten feet or so from the door, leaned over it for a moment, unsnapped the catch and, slipping his hand in, came out with a common tin flour-sifter and a paper sack whose side bore the inscription *Silver Medal Flour*. He also took the opportunity to whisper, "Okay, Larry. Keep your eyes peeled. I'll leave the catch free so you can get out and snoop. But *watch that door!*"

Larry, curled uncomfortably inside, whispered, "Aye, aye, sir." When Don, Pat, and Brophy went on into the room and the butler had disappeared, the Invisible Man, if he were in the hall and watching closely, could have seen a narrow slitted peephole appear in the end of the suitcase that faced the library door.

Larry, watching through it, smiled grimly and waited.

As the newcomers entered the vaulted library, Inspector Church standing before the massive Gothic fireplace nodded glumly toward Don and spoke to Belmont who paced the floor nervously nearby. "You don't make it any easier for me, inviting a magician out here," he growled. "I don't trust him even when I'm looking at him."

Don pretended to look hurt. "But, Inspector, you know that I was in the curator's office this morning with Schultz watching me like a hawk. I couldn't have been robbing Mr. Ziegler at the same time."

"Maybe and maybe not," Church replied unconvinced. "What about that funny business in your act where the audience watches you just as hard as Schultz did and, suddenly, when you take off that damned mask of yours, you turn out to be your assistant and your assistant who's been helping with the props turns out to be you? When you make a living doing things like that, how can you expect me to—"

J. D. Belmont exhaled a cloud of smoke and asked a question. "Diavolo, have you figured out a way to prevent this theft?"

"I've got a precaution or two I'd like to take," Don answered. He glanced around the room.

"Grills on the windows," he said. "Good. Three doors. I suggest we lock all but one."

"I've done that already," Church said. "What are you going to do with that flour sifter?"

"Even an invisible man has to leave footprints," Don explained. "Unless he's a ghost. If we see any footprints being made, we'll know where he is and can take steps accordingly."

Church said, "Hmmmpf!" unconsciously giving such a good imitation of Belmont that the latter scowled at the Inspector, wondering if he was being kidded.

"Very practical scheme," the financier said then. "An invisible man could slip between a couple of cops. But I don't see how he could get across a flour-covered floor without leaving traces."

Diavolo opened his sack, filled the sifter and spread a wide twelve-foot strip of white flour across the floor before each door and window. "Any secret sliding panels or trapdoors in this room?" he asked.

Belmont nodded. "One. The book case on the right of the fireplace swings out."

Don proceeded to create a miniature snowstorm there, and then said. "Okay. Let him come. What's the time? Judging from this morning's performance, our friend is a punctual chap."

"We've a few minutes yet," Church answered. "Belmont, let's see that necklace. I want it where I can watch it."

The financier grasped the frame of an El Greco on the wall and swung it outward to reveal the face of a large safe set into the wall. He worked at the dial for a moment and then, when the heavy door had been opened, brought out a flat ebony case whose cover was inlaid with blue enamel and semi-precious stones.

He placed it on a table in the center of the room and the others all gathered around as he lifted the lid.

On a bed of black velvet lay an unbelievable display of diamonds whose scintillant, dazzling brilliance shone and sparkled in the light with living fire.

Belmont picked them up and the white light dripped from his fingers in shimmering silver cascades as if sunlight were falling on the tumbling icy waters of a foaming mountain stream.

"Five hundred and sixty diamonds," Belmont said. "Boehmer, the Parisian jeweler, put every cent of his capital into it." He turned, placed the necklace around Pat's neck, and snapped the gold clasp behind.

Seventeen perfect stones, each at least a half inch across, closely encircled her neck. From this glittering collar, festoons of smaller diamonds looped down carrying pendant rosettes—even larger stones encircled by small ones. Over the shoulders and down across the breast, two broad rows of medium size stones descended, joined and ended in tassels of diamonds caught by small tied bows of chased silver. Two further triple rows fell from the collar in back to more diamond tassels.

"It's beautiful," Pat gasped. "And ugly!"

"Yes," Belmont agreed. "The stones are perfect; the design is tasteless. Boehmer was no artist and the florid, ungraceful lines of the thing are probably one reason why he wasn't able to sell it to Antoinette. She advised him to break it up and realize on his frozen capital in that way. He refused. He didn't want to take the loss he'd been put to in assembling the matched stones. Because he was pigheaded, he lost the necklace itself."

Don Diavolo said quietly: "I understood that Madame Lamotte broke up the necklace as soon as she got her hands on it and that her husband, and Vilette, the forger, sold the stones in Amsterdam and London."

"Sure." Belmont nodded, puffing smoke and surveying the glittering impossibility that Pat wore. "That's what lots of people think. Hmmpf! Next time some so-called authority writes a book about Cagliostro, Lamotte, and the Antoinette necklace, I wish he'd check up his sources. I can show you dozens of books on the affair, and every damned author cribs whole sections from the previous book. The first writer makes a mistake and they all follow like so many blasted sheep. Bah! I've got Lamotte's husband's diary.

"He was the only member of the swindling gang who escaped arrest. Even the nitwitted authorities all agree on that. He fled to London and his diary tells how he took the necklace with him still intact. But he didn't have it long. Some thieves broke in to his lodgings one night. Beat him up and left with the necklace. The gendarmes were after him and all France was up in arms about the scandal so he couldn't very well report it. The necklace has been unheard of from that day to this."

"How'd you come on it?" Church asked.

"I didn't," Belmont answered. "One of Ziegler's buyers ferreted it out in England, along with the diary. Got it from a Duke. Can't tell you his name because he doesn't want it known that it was his ancestor who hired the thugs that lifted the necklace from Lamotte. There'd be a second scandal if I did."

"And Ziegler offered it to you secretly?"

"Sure. He knew I was the only collector who could afford to grab it because of its historical interest. But there isn't one of them could pay the price. That necklace was worth $320,000 when Boehmer made it. Now—well I paid a good bit more than that."

"I see," Diavolo said. "How many people knew that you had purchased it from Ziegler?"

Belmont said "Hmmmpf!" again and scowled at Don. "I don't know. Number of people in the trade perhaps. Ziegler, his buyer, the Duke, a few others."

"How do you suppose the Invisible Man knew you had it?"

"That," Belmont said gruffly, "would seem to depend on who the Invisible Man is."

Diavolo looked at his watch. "Pat," he said, "perhaps you'd better climb out of it. The bogeyman is due any minute now and if he takes the necklace, it might be just as well you weren't in it at the time."

Don unclasped the collar and gave it to Belmont who started to place it again in its velvet case.

"Leave it right there," Church said. "I'm not going to take my eyes off it from now on."

The Inspector, saying that, promised too much.

At that moment, behind them, a voice which the Inspector had heard once before said, *"Oh I see. Flour. That makes it difficult. I'll be back."*

The group standing around the necklace whirled together like marionettes pulled by a single set of strings.

The one unlocked door that had been closed now stood open perhaps a foot and the voice came from beyond, apparently from someone standing just outside on the threshold, looking in. The trouble was that from where they stood, they all had a clear view out into the dim hall— and there was no one there.

They saw that much and then the door swung quickly to, slamming in its frame. No hand had touched the doorknob.

Inspector Church, Sergeant Brophy, and Belmont dashed headlong for the door, across the intervening strip of floor and out the door.

Don, as they ran, shouted, "Wait!" but they didn't hear him. He said, "Damn and blast! Now they've done it."

Church commanded, "Watch that door, Brophy!" Then he ran down the hall toward the outer door. Don, scowling, followed them into the hall, knelt by the suitcase, and pretended to open it and take out a small automatic. Actually what he really did was to go through the motions and produce a gun that he had palmed in his hand. He also whispered to Larry, "What did you see?"

And Larry answered, "Not a single damn thing, Don! And I don't like it here. If that bird should get hep—"

"You stay on the job," Diavolo ordered. "You may get an eyeful yet." Don got up and quickly returned to the library. His lean and handsome face bore a dark, threatening scowl. His eyes

glistened brightly, anger and excitement mingling in them.

Belmont, looking nervously from side to side, went into the library with him. The money king's prognathous jaw jutted unpleasantly.

And then Pat pointed. "Don!" she cried. "The necklace case. It's been moved!"

Don and Belmont both raced toward it. The case had been turned so that its uplifted lid concealed its interior.

Pat got there first and when she looked within her eyes were round.

Marie Antoinette's diamond necklace was gone. The black velvet bed on which the hard bright stones had flashed was bare and empty.

Chapter VIII

The Problem of the Missing Combination

Belmont's jaw dropped. "But—but how—?" Don turned and went back toward the door. He stood there looking down at the white covering of flour and the trampled path of footprints that led across it.

Inspector Church charged in at the door and left more footprints across the space. "Nobody saw a cursed thing!" he exploded angrily.

Then he saw Belmont, holding the empty jewel-case. His eyes popped. "Brophy!" he roared. "Get in here and close that door. He's here, in this room!"

Don said, "He moves fast, Inspector. I wouldn't be too sure."

"But how—" Belmont growled, "how did he get across that—"

Sergeant Brophy pointed to the trail of footprints. "As soon as we ran out, he ducked through and walked in our footprints!"

Don Diavolo lit a cigarette and said with understandable exasperation, "I fix the room so nobody but a bird could get in unnoticed, and then three big flatfooted walruses barge across my telltale flour. I yelled at you to wait, but you were too busy chasing something you couldn't see. That was just what he wanted. Sometimes, Inspector, I wonder how you got the job. Of all the—"

Church blew up. "Brophy," he commanded coldly. "Search that guy!" He pointed a broad forefinger at Diavolo. "There isn't any invisible man. I know it now. Diavolo slammed that door by pulling a string or some such hocus pocus, and he threw his voice to make it sound like it came from the door. He's a ventriloquist. When we ran to the door he grabbed the necklace!"

Don Diavolo shrugged and held up his arms. Brophy gave him a thorough once over. "Nothing, Inspector," he reported.

Church turned on Pat then. "So!" he said, "You. Sergeant, one of the maids downstairs is a policewoman. I planted her here yesterday. Get her. She'll search Miss Collins."

A half hour later, Inspector Church was on the point of giving up. The diamonds had not been found on Pat, nor anywhere else in the room. Church had gone over it with as fine-toothed a comb as had ever been made. He sat at the table before the empty jewel-case and listened to reports from the men that had been posted through the grounds and along the shore and the wall.

"Nothing, nothing, nothing," he said. "I still don't believe it."

J. D. Belmont swore. "All the cops in Manhattan *and* a magician. This—this criminal walks in and takes what he wants in spite of you. Bah! Wait until the D.A. hears about this mess!"

"Oh yeah," Church glowered back at him. "You flatfooted it across that flour too, you know. So stop howling. I'll get your blasted diamonds back or know why!"

Meekly, Don Diavolo asked, "Inspector, now that Miss Collins and I are in the clear, may we go?"

"In the clear? What makes you think that?"

"We don't have the diamonds and you can't make an arrest unless—"

Suddenly Detective Sergeant Brophy exploded, "Inspector, I've got it. Diavolo's suitcase! After we ran out into the hall, he came out and took a gun from it. I'll bet he put the necklace inside!"

"Suitcase!" Church leaped to his feet. "Why the hell haven't I heard about—" He was across the room and through the door. When he came back with the case, he was grinning. "Feels as if he has the necklace *and* all the silverware in the house in it. I guess this settles your hash, Mr. Dia—"

He pulled the case open and stepped back in amazement as Larry Keeler stood up, stretched, looked up at the Inspector and said, "Thanks. I was beginning to think I'd been forgotten."

Church, recovering, reached out, grasped the back of Larry's collar in a big fist and lifted the dwarf out of the suitcase. He dropped him outside and bent to examine the case.

"Nothing," he said once more, and then turned on Diavolo. "What—what is the meaning of this?" he demanded, pointing at Larry.

It took Diavolo several minutes of fast talking to explain, but he finally managed to get his point across. Inspector Church was still not at all sure he believed a word Diavolo said. As long as he couldn't find the diamonds, however, there wasn't a lot he could do about it.

"Keeler," he snapped. "You were watching that door every minute?"

Larry nodded.

"You heard the voice and saw the door slam?"

Larry nodded again.

"And what did you see?"

The little magician flipped a coin on the palm of his small hand, and made a pass above it with his other. The coin vanished.

"Nothing," he said. "Nobody at all."

Church snorted. "Brophy," he ordered, "Get these magicians out of here! They give me a pain."

Diavolo jerked a thumb at his two companions. "Come on. Before he changes his mind. Mr. Belmont, I'll return your check since I don't seem to have been successful in preventing the theft."

Belmont waved his hand. "Forget it," he said. "It wasn't your fault. If the Inspector hadn't trampled up that—"

Church said, "And you clear out too, Belmont! I'm sick of the sight of you. Brophy, I'll start on the servants now."

Don grinned. "I'll send the check to the Police Benefit Fund for Retired Inspectors," he said as he went out.

To Pat and Larry as they drove away from the Belmont estate, he said, "I feel sorry for the Inspector. He's really up against something this time."

Larry answered "Any theories, Don? I'll admit I'm buffaloed."

Don nodded. His face in the moonlight was hard and tight. "I'm beginning to get one, Larry. And I don't like it."

Pat stared straight ahead, saying nothing. She was wondering where her brother had been during the last hour. Don Diavolo wanted very much to know that also. He pressed heavily on the gas and the powerful red car roared through the night, streaking back toward Manhattan.

When they hurried into the house on Fox Street, Don called, "Chan! Any word from Horseshoe?"

From the living room, the Horseshoe Kid's voice answered them. "Yes. Cuss words, all of them."

Horseshoe was lying on the divan, an icebag on his head and a tall glass of straight Scotch in his hand. "I'm a lousy dick," he said. "I was casing the 106th Street joint when some fink sneaked up behind and conked me one. I don't know just how long I was out, but it was long enough. I got a locksmith down the street. Told him I'd been knocked out and rolled for my dough. Took him back to the house I'd been watching and he got the door open for me. I went through the house. Nobody home. I'm sorry."

"What time was this?" Don snapped.

"About fifteen minutes after I phoned you the last time, just before you headed for Belmont's.

I tried to phone out there and get you, but some copper had taken over the switchboard and he wanted my name, address, occupation, and a dozen references, so I hung up on him."

"This," Don said heavily, "is too much." He turned to Pat. "Try not to worry, Pat. Maybe it isn't as bad—" He broke off and swore. "I'm going to town on this case starting now. You get to bed, Pat. Tomorrow's going to be a darned lively day. And I'll need your help. That's an order. Go on, Chan! Put something in a cocktail shaker and bring it in here. We need it."

But the cocktail didn't help a lot. Don was still scowling thoughtfully when Horseshoe and Larry left a short while later.

He still wore the same scowl the next morning when he went to the theater. And he saw another scowl just like his own on the face of the man who waited for him there. The man was pacing nervously back and forth at the stage door. His face brightened as he caught sight of Don.

"Mr. Diavolo," he said quickly. "May I see you a moment, please? It is extremely urgent."

He shoved a white square of cardboard at Diavolo. It bore the name *Julian Dumont* and across it was written, *"This will introduce my secretary Victor Perry."*

There was one detail about the card that Diavolo didn't care for. The ink that formed the printed name, Julian Dumont, was not quite dry. When Don rubbed a surreptitious finger across it, the name smeared.

He took a closer look at the man before him. Mr. Perry was a slender, open-faced individual with a disarming smile and quick, sharp gray eyes. He was smartly dressed and he talked with a confident, business-like air. The only other thing aside from the card that bothered Diavolo was the faintly feminine intonation and gesture which Mr. Victor Perry used. It wasn't quite what he would have expected from a secretary employed by a man like Dumont.

"My employer needs your assistance," Perry said. "A matter of the utmost importance. We have had a most distressing morning. Mr. Dumont finally thought of you."

"Dumont," Diavolo asked. "The president of the Dumont Chemical company?"

"Yes," Mr. Perry said. "And he needs your assistance, very badly. A matter of the utmost importance. Perhaps if we could talk privately?" Perry looked around at the elderly stage door-man who eyed them across the top of a morning paper. Its headlines in enormous type read:

INVISIBLE MAN SCORES AGAIN
BAFFLES MAGICIAN AND POLICE
Historic $320,000 Necklace
Stolen in Impossible Theft

Diavolo nodded. "My dressing room," he said.

Mr. Perry said nothing further until they were behind Don's closed door. Then he talked rapidly.

"I have here a blank check payable to you," he stated, taking a blue slip from his billfold. "I am authorized to fill it out for any reasonable amount that you name if you can come to Mr. Dumont's assistance immediately."

Diavolo raised an eyebrow. Two financiers waving checks at him in as many days! Perhaps he was wasting his time in the theater after all.

"Sounds interesting," he said. "Just how can I help your employer?"

"By opening his safe," Perry said. "Mr. Dumont is, as you may have heard, a rather eccentric man. Last night he changed the combination on his private safe. He unfortunately did so without informing me. He also neglected to make a note of the new combination. He prides himself on his memory, which I am sorry to say is not nearly as good as he likes to think. And this morning, finally, he is having to admit as much himself."

"He forgot the combination, Mr. Perry?" Don asked, his glance sharpening.

"Exactly." Mr. Perry smiled slightly. "I am almost pleased. Perhaps it will teach the old gentleman a lesson and so make my own job less irksome. His eccentricities are a bit annoying at times."

"Yes, I can see they might be if this sort of thing happens very often. But why me? Tell him to get Courtney. If anybody can open your employer's safe, he's the man."

"We thought of that, Mr. Diavolo. But we found that Mr. Courtney is out of town and will not be back until tomorrow. The safe contains some very important business contracts which must be signed and delivered without fail before noon. Mr. Dumont knows of your remarkable escape work and it occurred to him that opening the safe would be a small matter for The Great Diavolo."

Don thought, "Oh oh. Flattery too." Aloud he asked, "What make of safe?"

"A Holmes & Watson. Their No. I Double Dial Bank Lock."

Don did a few rapid mental calculations. He liked the story even less than he liked Mr. Perry and Mr. Dumont's freshly inked card. Don had come to the theater early to make some adjust-ments in a piece of apparatus that had not worked too smoothly during the last show the day before. Chan and Pat weren't due for another hour.

"Yes," he said after a moment, "I'll come. If you'll wait one moment." Quickly Don went into his dressing room and closed the door. He hurriedly threw off his business suit and slid into the scarlet evening clothes he wore in his act. He also took a quick look at a phone book. Then he returned to Mr. Perry.

Don grinned inside as he noticed Perry's face fall perceptibly on seeing the costume.

"I thought I had better change now," Don explained. "My first show is at one twenty and opening a safe of the type you mention is no cinch. I might be pressed for time on my return." This story was as thin as Perry's but Don knew the man couldn't very well contradict him.

"What is Mr. Dumont's address?" Don asked then, taking a sheet of notepaper from the desk. "I'll leave a note for my assistants in case they should need to reach me."

"Eight-eighty-four Riverside Drive," Mr. Perry replied, smiling once more.

But Diavolo didn't bother to mention that address in the note that he addressed to Chan. "Get Woody, Horseshoe, Larry, and Karl. Stand by for further orders. I'll send the cab-driver back for you. I'm wearing the red evening clothes so the trail from there on should be easy. Ask Horseshoe if he ever met a bird whose name is probably not Victor Perry. He uses Cirou's *Rose d'Amour* perfume."

Don didn't include the Riverside address because the phone book had told him that Julian Dumont lived on East 62nd Street!

He sealed the envelope, wrote Chan's name across its face and left it on the desk. Then he stood up, picked a glowing cigarette from midair with an expert gesture, opened the door to the corridor and said, "After you, Mr. Perry."

Chapter IX

The Synthetic Millionaire

When the taxi drew up before an apartment house on Riverside Drive, Don Diavolo looked at the address and the corners of his mouth curled in a faint smile. It was not only not Dumont's address; it wasn't even the address to which Perry had told him they were going.

Don smiled because, palmed in his right hand with a folded five dollar bill was a note which he had written, unknown to Mr. Perry, at the same time he wrote the message for Chan. This second note read, *"Driver: Return at once to Music Hall. Ask for Miss Collins or my assistant Chan. Tell them to what address you took me. They'll give you another five spot. It's a matter of life or death. Thanks."*

As Perry paid the driver and started to lead the way up to the door, Don flipped his note into the driver's lap, gave him a wink, and immediately engaged Perry's attention with a question.

"I thought you said Eight-eighty-four Riverside? This doesn't seem to be—"

Perry looked at him with skillfully raised eyebrows. "Eight-eighty-four? Oh no, you misunderstood. I said eight-forty-eight."

"Oh," Diavolo said. "My mistake." He spoke as if it were of no importance, but now, suddenly, he was beginning to realize just how important this little change of address really was. His quick eyes had caught sight of a familiar figure standing at the bus stop on the corner—one of the Inspector's men. And, as they passed through the lobby, he saw still another writing a letter at a desk in the lounge. That was when Don remembered where he had seen the address 848 Riverside Drive before—in yesterday's papers, given as the home address of Nathan Ziegler!

Perry put a key in the door of Apartment 12 E. A butler came toward them as they entered, a large man whose otherwise immaculate uniform was a trifle short in the sleeves and whose right hip pocket bulged interestingly.

Diavolo took off his hat, handed it to the man, getting as he did so a quick glimpse at the small mirror which he carried fixed to the inside of the crown. This was a useful conjurer's gimmick of his own invention that often supplied him, as it did now, with interesting bits of information. He distinctly saw Mr. Victor Perry, behind his back, give the butler an almost unnoticeable nod.

Don Diavolo was as certain as he had ever been of anything that his interview with Mr. Julian Dumont was going to be something to remember. He felt a warning, wholly instinctive tension tug at his spine, and the skin on the back of his neck went suddenly cold.

Mr. Dumont was a distinguished looking, gray-haired man with nose-glasses and a small VanDyke. He looked a lot like the pictures of the wealthy chemical-company president that Don had seen now and then in the papers, but, by this time, Don was inclined to be suspicious. He thought he detected one or two minor flaws. But his apparently relaxed body gave no indication that he was prepared to send it into instant action. That sort of inner tautness covered by the deceptive appearance of ease was part of Diavolo's stock in trade.

Dumont nodded at him across the top of the broad desk in his study. "I'm delighted to meet you, Don Diavolo," he said. "I've seen your act often. I particularly like your marvelous handcuff and straitjacket escapes. They are really uncanny. I've a little problem here." He waved his hand toward the large safe that stood in a small alcove off the study. "Mr. Perry has explained our dilemma?"

Diavolo bowed. "Yes. He tells me that it is locked and that you seem to have mislaid the combination." Don approached the safe and pretended to examine it. He squinted at the shiny dial so that the light from the window fell on it obliquely. And he saw what he had hoped might be there. Fingerprints—one of which was a thumbprint cut diagonally by the now-familiar line of a scar!

Then Diavolo turned and, as his eyes quickly surveyed the room, he saw one other thing. A cigarette box on a side-table, a small black rosewood affair whose cover bore the inlaid initials: N. Z. So, Diavolo thought, that's that. Ziegler's apartment. The question would seem to be: Where is Nathan?

Dumont said, "Well, Mr. Diavolo. Do you think you can open it for us? I must get those documents out by noon, without fail. That gives you half an hour."

Don was thinking that it would be just about that before Chan and the others could possibly arrive. He decided he'd better do a bit of stalling. Just to see what would happen, he threw a bomb.

"I'm afraid it will be difficult to open it that soon," he said. "Mr. Perry told me that this was a Holmes & Watson No. 1 Double Dial Bank Lock. But I find that it is their 1930 model. I assumed you'd have one of the more recent ones. I'll need a few instruments that I didn't bring. If I may phone my assistant."

He moved toward the phone, but Dumont swiftly raised his hand. Perry took a swift step forward as Dumont said: "Our phone is not working. It's been an extremely unfortunate day. Mr. Perry can go down to the lobby and make the call for you if you think it is necessary. But

I'm afraid your assistant would not be able to get here in time—"

"No, perhaps not," Diavolo said, afraid of just that. He knew it was useless to send Perry down. He doubted if the man would phone at all. Don turned again toward the safe. "Well," he said slowly, "I'll have a go at it, but I won't promise—"

Somewhere close by there was a sudden rapid, frantic pounding on a closed door and a girl's voice screamed, "Let me out, you—"

Diavolo heard the butler's quick footsteps in the hall, he heard a door open and the sound of a quick scuffle. The girl's voice stopped abruptly.

He saw Perry frown and he heard Dumont say:

"My daughter, Mr. Diavolo. Since her mother died a few years ago, she has developed psychopathic symptoms to such an extent that she cannot be allowed out of her room. Paranoic delusions of persecution. Perry, perhaps you had better phone Dr. Llyons. She seems to be worse this morning."

"I'll have him come at once." Perry nodded quickly, and left the room.

Don Diavolo turned to the safe, conscious that Dumont's eyes were boring a hole in his back. These boys were first-class actors and fast thinkers. The act was almost good enough—but not quite. Yesterday's newspapers, Don remembered, had stated that Nathan Ziegler had a daughter with whom he lived. The picture behind the false front that Dumont, Perry, and the butler were putting up was beginning to emerge. It was an unpleasant picture tinged with distinct overtones of peril.

Don didn't care for any part of it. He particularly disliked the fact that Julian Dumont had never once raised his right hand above the top of the desk behind which he sat. Don was sure that he didn't need X-Ray Vision to know that that hand was holding a gun. He had a healthy suspicion, too, that the butler was just outside the door holding another of the same in his hand. Don also had a gun, but he realized that getting the drop on these men was growing to be rather like trying to catch a train that has left the station ten minutes before.

Diavolo turned the big dial of the safe thoughtfully. Since this had something to do with Nathan Ziegler, it also concerned the Invisible Man. That being true, the game these boys were up to was big-time stuff, and they would very probably shoot at the first false move.

It might be a good idea not to make any just yet. Don could see only one thing to do at the moment—stall, if possible, until reinforcements arrived, or until he got something that was half way like a break.

Don's hand went to his pocket. Dumont's arm at once raised perceptibly. Don, watching for it out of the corner of his eye, suppressed a grim smile as he produced a metal screw clamp, a length of string, and a chamois watchcase. The latter held an ordinary watch which, after Karl Hartz had worked on it, now served an unusual purpose. It no longer told the time, but instead was capable of giving information of quite another sort. Karl had removed the mainspring and attached a small projecting arm to the main wheel. The slightest touch on this arm caused the second hand to vibrate wildly. It was sensitive to deviations of less than one-thousandth of an inch—one-tenth the thickness of a sheet of paper.

A rubber suction cup was also affixed to the back of the watch case so that the watch could be attached instantly to any smooth surface—such as the face of a safe. Don screwed the metal clamp on to the knob that threw the bolt within the lock once the combination had been dialed. From its outer end, by means of the string, he hung a heavy brass poker which he found by the fireplace.

Then he put the watch-micrometer in position on the face of the safe so that the weight pulled the outer end of the clamp down against and just touching the smaller projecting arm that issued from the watch.

Then, slowly, drawing out the process as much as possible, Don Diavolo began to turn the safe dial so that the inner combination wheels revolved one at a time. It is mechanically impossible to make these wheels so exactly alike in

diameter that such a safe-opening micrometer is not able to detect some difference.

As each wheel revolved, Diavolo, his eyes on the watch dial, waited for the tell-tale quiver which would tell him that the slot of one wheel had lined up with the bolt. Then the ultra-sensitive hand twitched as he turned the third inner wheel. Looking at the dial, he saw that it read seven and knew that this was the third number in the combination for which the lock was set.

Then, he began again, rotating each inner wheel in turn except the third, and watching until his micrometer should tell him when another wheel had lined up. He took his time, and his eyes fell now and then to the more ordinary watch on his wrist that counted off seconds rather than fractions of an inch. Fifteen minutes more of stalling would be necessary before he could expect Chan.

Don got another quiver, this time on dial number five. The fifth number on the combination was twenty-four.[3]

At that moment, Don, listening intently to every sound in the room behind his back, heard footsteps followed by Perry's voice. It wasn't quite the same voice. The polite smiling tones had gone from it completely and left a harsh, hard residue.

"This guy's pulling our legs," it said. "He's wise. He gave Louie this note."

Chapter X

Memory Is Murdered

Don Diavolo felt as if a bucket of ice water had been poured suddenly down his back. His hands dropped from the safe dial and he turned on his heel slowly.

3   This method of discovering a safe combination was used by James S. Sargent, inventor of the present-day time locks, in picking the locks manufactured by his lock making competitors. See the *New York Times* for Oct. 14, 1869 for an account of the challenge match in which Sargent collected the twelve hundred dollars offered by Linus Yale to anyone who could pick his double dial bank lock.

The taxi driver stood beside Perry, an automatic in his hand, his small, piglike eyes as cold and emotionless as glaciers. The muzzle of the gun, from where Don viewed it, was a perfectly round black hole. It was utterly motionless.

Dumont looked at the note that Perry gave him, read it aloud and then growled at Perry. "He rumbled you on the way up. I hope you can explain it to the boss. He isn't going to like—"

"I'll take care of him later!" The voice was in the room; there was no doubt of that. It was low-pitched—too low to have come from outside. Don had been waiting for this. It was the voice of the Invisible Man!

Perry's face was two shades whiter. The taxi driver licked his lips nervously, but it would have taken Don's sensitive micrometer to detect any motion in the hand that held his gun.

The voice spoke again. *"Dumont, put your gun on the desk!"*

Dumont's hidden hand came up and placed an automatic on the blotter. Dumont got to his feet and moved hastily to one side.

Except for St. Louis Louie, all eyes were on the gun. And then, like a movie scene dubbed in by one of Hollywood's trick photographers, the gun slowly tilted upward to a vertical position. The movement continued; the gun rose in mid-air, its nose pointing at Don Diavolo. Two feet above the desk it stopped and hung there, not as steady as the gun in Louie's hand, but, because the man who held it was invisible, twice as menacing.

"All right, Diavolo," the voice said then. "Get busy. Your friends, you see, won't be coming. You don't need to stall any longer. Open that safe."

Don's eyes had a light of understanding in them now. He was beginning to understand the Invisible Man's methods. But he wasn't in any position to make use of the knowledge.

"And I wouldn't advise you," the voice went on grimly, "to try to destroy the interesting apparatus you have set up. I am an excellent shot. And St. Louis Louie is a perfect one. You may have ten minutes. Time him, Dumont."

"And if the safe isn't open by then?" Don asked, his eyes watching for the break it didn't look as if he was going to get. The chill had spread from the back of his neck, reaching its icy fingers to his whole body.

"A good shot practices constantly. Neither Louie nor myself have done so yet today. If the safe isn't open . . ."

"Never mind," Don said shortly. "I get it. You don't need to talk like a bad play."

Diavolo turned to the safe and again began his careful turning of the dial. "And you don't need," he added, "to continue calling Glenn Collins Dumont. A man with a scar on his thumb should always wear gloves."

He heard Dumont, behind him, gasp. The Invisible Man said, "You'll work faster if you don't talk. Perry, make ready to clear out of here."

Don was working on the last combination wheel, when Dumont said, "You've got one more minute."

His voice, Don noticed, was unsteady and it no longer sounded like Dumont's. The Invisible Man apparently noticed it too. "All right, Dumont," he said. "Take your gun. Go outside and get ready to put on your act for that dick downstairs as soon as the others come out."

Don looked over his shoulder and opened his mouth to speak. He said, "Glenn—" and then St. Louis Louie cut him off.

"Okay, big boy." His words came flat and expressionless from between his teeth. "If you want what I got, go right on gabbing."

The Invisible Man's voice came again. "Half that minute is gone."

The second-hand on the micrometer moved the last time. Don Diavolo knew that once that safe was open, his usefulness would be ended. But he still wondered what was in it that they wanted so badly.

Hurriedly he took the watch from the safe face, set the big dial at zero and began. Four turns to the left, eighteen to the right, seven to the left, twenty-six to the right . . .

Don felt the intent eyes on his back. The dial stopped at the final number, and Don held his breath as he turned the knob to which the clamp was still fixed. He felt the bolt move over. He started to pull the safe door outward.

Perry's voice said, "Okay. Move over."

Don moved and Louie's gun followed him as if it was a piece of steel seeking a magnet.

The butler, standing in the door, came forward as Perry opened the safe. He carried two suitcases which he laid open on the floor. Perry began taking out the contents of the safe and transferring them to the grips. Don's eyes widened.

He saw a rock crystal cross whose face bore religious emblems in wrought gold and translucent blue enamel. He saw a shell-shaped, green jade cup set upon the carved figure of centaur, and several cases containing miniatures. There were other objects too—paintings, books with ancient bindings, jeweled watches, several pieces of Sèvres porcelain, a small tapestry—but the cross and the cup Don thought he recognized. They answered the descriptions of the ones stolen from Ziegler's shop!

Diavolo couldn't understand why those things should be in Ziegler's safe but he had no time to puzzle that out just then. The cold voice of the Invisible Man hung again in the room, its tone triumphant now—and inflexible.

"The magician knows too much. Louie—"

Don's hand jerked as it began the swift move toward his gun. He wasn't going to stand there and take the blast from the gunman's gun without any back talk at all.

His hand never reached his gun.

The butler's hand, blackjack raised, had started its downward motion first. A thousand fiery points of light whirled before Don's eyes, scattered, and dropped swiftly into blackness.

The magician's body crumpled and dropped.

The disembodied voice gave one more command. *"Throw him into the safe. Lock it. And get going!"*

The butler hesitated a brief moment, then lifted the limp, scarlet-costumed figure and dumped it inside the dark interior of the safe. Perry was thorough. He changed the combination, slammed the heavy, foot-thick door, threw the bolt and whirled the dial. Then he smashed the micrometer.

Had Don Diavolo been conscious and able to use the controlled breathing methods that he used in some of his underwater feats, the air within the safe would be breathable for as much as two hours. But he was unconscious and breathing at a normal rate. Under these conditions the air would last a half hour at the most.

The best safe-blower in the country couldn't get that door open in under an hour. Even if he did, the blast would be fatal to the man inside. The only practical existing way to get into the safe now was through a knowledge of the new combination, something that was itself locked within the head of one man—Perry.

Then, in the lobby downstairs, a hitch occurred. Dumont was not successful in holding the attention of the waiting detective. St. Louis Louie had to use his heater. But the detective, as he fell, managed one shot in reply. He missed Louie. His bullet entered Perry's head just below the right eye, tunnelled upward through the mental filing system of nervous tissue and made its exit just behind and above the left ear.

A certain series of eight numbers in a certain sequence, the combination of Nathan Ziegler's safe, was as utterly lost as if it had never been.

Chapter XI

Into Thin Air

Colonel Ernest Kaselmeyer, manager of the Manhattan Music Hall, was sputtering colored fire and throwing off streams of sparks like a two dollar Fourth of July pinwheel.

"Diavolo!" he thundered. "I've got his name in lights clear across the front of this theater! Letters six feet high! Last night he does not give his last show. I had to return four hundred admissions! He should go on in five minutes—

and none of you have the slightest idea where he is! Maybe I should go back to managing a flea circus! Magicians! Bah!"

Pat, Mickey, and Karl listened to his fulminations without paying attention to the words. They all turned expectantly each time there were footsteps in the corridor outside. Their faces all fell together each time as the steps went on past.

Karl was at the window, his eyes, behind their thick lensed glasses, fixed on the flow of traffic before the stage door in the street below. "I knew something like this would happen sooner or later," he frowned. "That driver should have been back ages ago. I'll wait another ten minutes, then I'm going to get Church after Belmont."

"Belmont?" Mickey asked. "Why him?"

"Because Don had me examine that check Belmont gave him. I found his fingerprints. His right thumb matches the thumbprints on the note the Invisible Man left at Ziegler's!"

"I'm going to phone the Inspector now," Pat said. "He might be able to pick up a clue at the house on 106th Street. If Glenn—" Her voice broke on his name, but her chin was firm as she went toward the phone.

Chan Chandar Manchu, who had just replaced the receiver after vainly trying to locate Horseshoe, Larry, and Woody, said, "I'll get him for you, Miss Pat."

But he failed there too. Inspector Church was, at that moment, roaring up Riverside Drive in a police car whose screaming siren was loud and angry. The report of a gun battle in the lobby of the hotel at 848 West End Avenue had just come in.

Chan had not been able to reach Woody Haines because that gentleman was talking to the detective stationed outside the hotel on Riverside Drive. He had gone there to get an interview with Nathan Ziegler, seen the dick and stopped to question him. The detective was telling him that the art dealer had asked for police protection after the robbery, afraid that the Invisible Man might not be satisfied with the

haul at his shop, but would attempt also to steal certain valuable art objects from Ziegler's own private collection.

Woody was listening to this when they heard the shots from inside. As the detective drew his gun and sped toward the lobby, Woody noticed something that the dick missed. He saw a taxi come around the nearest corner on two wheels and slide to a grinding stop before the building. "A getaway car," Woody murmured. "Maybe, just in case—" He turned quickly and signaled a cruising taxi down the street.

A moment later, St. Louis Louie, the butler, and Dumont, the latter white-faced and shaken, ran out and piled into the cab.

Woody leaned forward in his seat. "Follow that cab, Mac," he commanded. "If you lose it, I'll have your scalp."

"Lissen, buddy," the driver said. "Why should I stick my neck out? Those mobsters mean business. If they see us tailin' 'em . . ."

"What they'll do won't be half as bad as what I'll do if you don't," Woody cut in. "Keep your lip buttoned, your chin up, and step on that gas!"

The driver looked back over his shoulder straight into the nose of the .32 Colt that Woody held in one big paw. He carefully noted Woody's bulky shoulders and All-American arms.

"Okay, boss," he said, his eyes round, "Play like I didn't mention it." The taxi leaped forward with a grinding clash of gears.

The two detectives were being loaded into an ambulance when Church's car skidded to a stop before the hotel. The Inspector and Sergeant Brophy hit the pavement, running. They collected a frightened hotel desk clerk as they sailed through the lobby and an elevator shot upward, carrying them toward the Ziegler apartment.

The clerk opened the door with a master key and the two detectives rushed in. Their search at first was fruitless. The hall, living room, and study were quite empty. Church, in passing, gave the big safe a suspicious glance, noticed that it seemed undisturbed and securely locked, dismissed it from his mind and went on.

It was Sergeant Brophy who found the body.

"Bathroom door's locked," he called. "Get that clerk in here."

When the clerk's key had thrown the bolt and Brophy, gun ready, had pushed back the door, they saw Nathan Ziegler's body, stiff with rigor, lying on the cold tiles. There were three bullet holes in his chest.

"Sergeant," Church started, "Get headquarters and—"

It was then that he heard the muffled thumping sound. He turned toward the two bedroom doors. One was locked.

The clerk's shaking hand fumbled with his key. Church shoved him aside to unlock the door himself.

A girl lay on the bed, her feet kicking desperately against the footboard. Her ankles and wrists were tied with adhesive; a towel was pulled tight across her mouth and knotted behind her head. Her wide black eyes were filled with horror until Church drew a knife and began to cut the towel. Then they flooded with tears of relief and her taut body relaxed.

Sergeant Brophy turned to the clerk, "Get the house doctor!" The clerk left at a run and Brophy dashed for the phone in the study.

Inspector Church removed the gag from the girl's mouth, cut the tape that held her wrists, and then stiffened. He dropped his knife and ran.

Brophy's voice had come back to him from the study, saying, "Fancy meeting you here! Put your hands up, Diavolo!"

As Church galloped into the study, Brophy said, "He must have been hiding in here, Inspector. And he opened the safe while we were in the bedroom. Another minute and he'd have been gone."

The safe door was wide and Don Diavolo was supporting himself with difficulty, leaning heavily on his hands on the desk. He was drawing fresh air into his lungs in great draughts.

"Handcuffs, Brophy!" Church ordered. "And watch him. If he tries to go invisible on us, shoot!"

Diavolo shook his head and gave them half a smile. He inhaled another long breath of oxygen and said, "I wasn't trying to get *into* the safe, Inspector. I just got out. Look at the door."

Church looked. "What the hell!" he exclaimed.

The plate on the inner side of the safe door that covers the locking mechanism had been removed, exposing the combination wheels inside. The plate, its screws, and a knife with a broken point lay on the safe floor.

Don Diavolo rubbed the bump on the back of his head gingerly. "They knocked me out, Inspector, and locked me in. I pulled out of it just in time, broke off the point of my knife and used it as a screwdriver. Once the plate was off I could manipulate the wheels with my hands. It's much easier to get out of a safe than into one— provided you aren't unconscious. The air in that place nearly put me under again before I got the bolt to slide over."

Church looked at Don and then back at the safe. He scowled undecidedly. Then he shook his head. "Clever as usual. But I'm not so sure. This could be some more of your blasted misdirection."

"Inspector," Diavolo said wearily. "Please! You think of the damnedest—Who is that?"

Don motioned toward the doorway where the girl stood, the cut adhesive still dangling from her wrists and ankles.

The girl, staring at Don Diavolo, said, "And he murdered my father. *I saw him!*"

Don gasped at her. "I—I murdered your father? When did that happen?"

"Last night," the girl said, trembling with emotion. "Dad had just changed the combination of the safe and he was locking it. You came in with two other men. One of them grabbed me; you and the other went into the study. You were wearing those red clothes and a red mask. I—I heard you tell my father to put his hands up, and then I heard him slam the door of the safe. You swore, and then—"

The girl could go no further. She sank into a chair and covered her face with her hands, sobbing.

"Church," Diavolo said, "Ask her what time last night."

But the girl was hysterical now, and beyond questioning. The desk clerk hurried in with a doctor and they led Rose Ziegler to a bedroom.

Church said, "Yeah, I know. You're ready with some phony alibi, but it won't go down. I've got too much now. An eyewitness. You can't get around that."

Don looked at him for a moment and then said slowly, "You think that I'm the Invisible Man?"

"I know you are," Church shot back. "And the chair up at Sing Sing is one little gadget that you won't be able to squirm out of. Brophy—"

Don moved slightly away from the desk.

"Stay where you are!" Brophy ordered, coming toward him.

Don shook his head. "But I'm not the Invisi—"

The voice that cut him off affected both Church and Brophy like a powerful electric charge. They jerked, stood stock still, and stared at the automatic that floated slowly up in midair from behind the desk.

The cold familiar voice rang in their ears. *"No, he's not the Invisible Man, Inspector. And he did not kill—"*

Church's and Brophy's guns spit fire together. The gun that pointed at them from midair dropped suddenly.

The Inspector and the Sergeant rounded the desk from opposite sides and pounced—on nothing. The gun lay there on the rug, but they could not feel the prone body they had hoped to find beneath their hands.

Church reached out and picked up the gun. As his fingers touched it, his jaw dropped, hung there a moment, and then instantly, he was on his feet whirling to face Don Diavolo.

But Don Diavolo had become as invisible as the phantom that had held the gun! Where Diavolo had been, Inspector Church saw exactly nothing at all!

Chapter XII

The Little Man Who Wasn't There

When the Inspector and Sergeant Brophy had fired and jumped toward the gun behind the desk, Don Diavolo had made a swift and silent pounce for the door. He heard them pounding down the corridor after him as the elevator started its descent and he saw the frantic signals of the red light on the control board. The colored boy who ran the car took one look at Don's face and decided to make a non-stop trip.

Outside, Don signaled a taxi and, as he swung aboard, ordered, "The nearest phone, and step on it."

Three blocks over in a drugstore booth, Diavolo dropped a nickel in the slot and dialed the Music Hall. "Chan," he said, talking rapidly, "I'm in dutch with the police force again. I'm going down to Fox Street, but they'll have the place surrounded before I can get there. Did you reach Karl? . . . He's there. Good. . . . Have him bring the VanLio costume and cut cross town in a cab. I'll meet him at 50th and 11th Avenue. . . . Kaselmeyer? . . . Tell him that if I come in for the next show, it would be the first step toward Sing Sing and he'd have to refund admissions from now on. Get Karl started."

A half hour later two clerics descended from a cab before a red brick house at 79 Fox Street. One was a tall young man with a handsome bronzed face and black eyes that twinkled as he saw the detectives stationed on the stoop next door. His companion was an elderly little man with a great shock of white hair and thick-lensed spectacles. They were both dressed in sober black and their collars were on backward.

The short man carried a briefcase that might have contained sermons or missionary reports.

Actually it held the famous scarlet evening clothes which the police, at No. 77, were watching for.

Above the doorbell at No. 79 was a small dignified inscription that read "*Parish House*, Rev. O. O. VanLio, D.D."[4] As the two ministers went up the steps the taller one said, "That actor next door must be in trouble again. Detectives everywhere. It's scandalous! Tsk! Tsk! I fear our parish house is not located in the best of neighborhoods, my dear Bishop."

The Bishop scowled. His words came from the corner of his mouth. "They're going to rumble this gaff one of these days. The Inspector isn't as dumb as he acts sometimes."

"When he does," the Reverend answered, "we'll think up something else."

Inside, the Reverend VanLio went at once to a tall glass panel that was set into the wall. He looked through into the living room of the house next door.[5] What he saw made him grin. The Horseshoe Kid was there, faced by a Lieutenant and two detectives of the Homicide Squad who were radiating questions. The Horseshoe Kid had answers for them—he always did. But he looked just a wee bit uncomfortable just the same.

The Reverend's finger touched an instrument shaped like a telegrapher's key and tapped at it sharply. One of a pair of skull bookends within the Diavolo living room moved its jaw, its white teeth clicking. The detectives, startled, turned toward it, and Horseshoe, recognizing the signal, edged backward toward the paneled wall.

When the detectives looked around again the Horseshoe Kid was gone. The wall behind him had opened silently and he had come through into the house next door.

"Thanks, Don," he said. "It was getting a bit

4 An anagram for Don Diavolo.
5 This glass was what is known as a one-way window. On its other side it appeared to be a mirror set above the fireplace.

warm in there. I came to report good news and then those gorillas—"

"Good news?" the Reverend said, his voice changing from that of the stiff-backed minister to the lighter tones of Don Diavolo. "I haven't heard anything that answers to that description all morning. Let's have it."

"I got a lead," Horseshoe said. "Met an old pal this morning, Joe the Whiz. His cannon mob works the soup-and-fish customers at the Met. He tells me there's a *Help Wanted* call out on the grapevine. He got it straight from St. Louis Louie who says there's a few jobs open for the right sort of guys. Considering its source I thought you might be interested."

"I am," Don replied. "How do we apply for those jobs?"

"Joe gave me the address," Horseshoe said. "On East 26th Street. There's a meeting there this afternoon. I thought you might want to look in so Joe said he'd call Louie and duke us in."

Don Diavolo was already removing the clerical collar. "Who am I?"

"Scarface Mike, from Cicero," Horseshoe said. Don pulled a wardrobe rack from the wall. "Hmm. Disguise No. 18, I guess. The George Raft one."

Diavolo stopped once during his change of costume and put through a phone call to the house next door. He watched the Lieutenant through the glass as the latter answered it.

"Inspector Church speaking," Don said, his voice gruff and filled with authority. "We just collared that magician. You can remove your men from the house. Report back to Centre Street." Don replaced the receiver and said, "That will clear the coast."

A short time later Scarface Mike and the Horseshoe Kid ascended the steps of a house on East 26th Street. Karl Hartz watched them from his post in a doorway across the street. Don's friend, the butler, met them at the door. He didn't recognize the magician under his turned-down hat, his Latin coating of tan, and his scarred face.

Besides, he hardly expected to see Don Diavolo alive again. He had gotten a glowing report from Joe the Whiz of Scarface's criminal activities and he greeted Mike with respect.

He barred the door behind them and led the way to an inner room.

"Slapsie Monahan," Horseshoe whispered. "He's just back from a ten-year jolt at the Ossining college."

Slapsie ushered them into a room where half a dozen men waited. Don, looking them over, crossed his fingers, hoping that his disguise would hold up under the strain. He and Horseshoe were surrounded by a choice collection of characters all of whom had reputations as shady as the interior of a mine.

St. Louis Louie was there and the Horseshoe Kid recognized one or two others, men whose activities had given more than one desk-sergeant copy for his official blotter.

Don Diavolo looked for Julian Dumont but did not find him. Then his attention was caught and held by the curious machine in the center of the room.

A cylindrical lens-mount projected from a spherical chromium housing whose instrument panel was covered with unlikely looking switches and rheostat dials.

The apparatus was aimed at a small recessed alcove in the end of the room, some seven feet high by five feet square. Two shining glass insulators projected from the ceiling and terminated at about the height of a man's head in large copper electrodes.

Don Diavolo recognized the contrivance from the pictures that had been reproduced in the newspapers at the time of the opening of the Auto Show.

"Dr. Palgar's Invisibility Ray projector," he whispered to Horseshoe. "Keep your eyes peeled. It'll be a good show."

"And keep your rod handy," the Horseshoe Kid replied. "I don't like the looks of this crowd. Tough eggs, all of 'em and something's wrong. They're all nervous as hell."

"I don't know that I blame them," Don said.

"Somebody's been using some pretty good psychology on them. It's—"

A voice behind them cut across the room, *"Good evening, gentlemen."*

The hush that fell upon the room was complete except for the movement of feet as they all turned to face the doorway. The door stood half open. The voice came again. *"Be seated, please."* And the door slowly closed, apparently of its own volition.

The voice was that of the Invisible Man.

The chairs in the room faced a desk on the left of the alcove. One of the chairs moved across the floor to a position behind the desk, made a half turn and was still. An invisible hand moved several papers on the desk. A cigarette that someone had left on the edge of an ashtray on the desk, rose like the gun Don had seen float in midair earlier. Near it, suddenly, a stream of smoke issued from empty space as from the mouth of an invisible smoker. A lone chill chased down Don Diavolo's back.

The Invisible Man was a real showman; he had imagination. The lean, hard faces of the others watched this phenomenon with scowling intentness.

The cigarette returned to the tray and the voice spoke again. *"Please keep your seats."*

A moment later, Don saw a switch pull itself over on the Invisibility machine's instrument panel. A green circle of light glowed beside it, and then, as a rheostat turned, a long pulsating violet ray issued from the lens and its round circle bathed the small alcove in a bright hot light.

"Monahan," the phantom voice commanded. *"I'll take my place now. You will throw the operating switch as usual."* There was an interval of a few seconds and the voice, from within the alcove now, said, "Ready!"

The butler who had taken his position by the machine pulled a three point switch. Long purple flashes of spitting light jumped from the contact points to meet it. A deep whirring hum within the machine sent tingling vibrations radiating out across the floor. The vibrant smell of ozone crackled in the air.

Then, just below the two round shining electrodes within the cabinet a shape began to form. It was vague and transparent at first, a disconnected ghostly glimmer of highlights on a face and on two hands that grasped the electrodes.

Gradually the space beneath began to fill with a darker mass that steadily lost its wraith-like transparency and became solid. The Invisible Man stood there now, a young man wearing a gray business suit and a black mask.

Sparks streamed from his fingers as he took his hands from the electrodes. Monahan reversed his switch; the electric crackle of the machine died out and the violet beam faded.

The masked man stepped from his place and seated himself behind the desk.

Slowly his eyes, behind the mask, surveyed the group before him. Then his voice, a shade deeper now as if the change to visibility had altered it slightly, said, "Bring him in, Monahan."

The butler stepped to the door and opened it. Under his breath, Don said, "Damn!"

Karl Hartz came through the door followed by a low-browed individual with a gun. They came forward and stopped before the desk.

The masked man got to his feet. "So," he said. "You. I see."

"He was casing the joint outside," Slapsie reported. "I thought we'd better pick him up. He don't look like a dick though."

"He isn't. I know him. Take him out. I'll attend to him later."

As they left, the masked man's eyes sought Don's. "The two new members will step forward."

Don, rising, knew that there was trouble ahead. He went forward with Horseshoe to stand before the desk. Palmed in his right hand was his small flesh-colored automatic. The safety catch was off.

Don tried not to think about the half dozen other guns that he knew must be in the group at his back.

Then the masked man did a curious thing. He leaned forward across the desk, peering into Diavolo's face. His lips moved softly and Don barely caught his quick whisper. "If you fire, you won't have a chance. Follow my lead. When I shoot, play dead. I'll try to get you out." Out loud he said, "Your disguise is excellent, Diavolo. If we had not noticed your assistant outside, I might not have penetrated it. Monahan, search them!"

Don and Horseshoe stood quietly as the man's hands slapped at their pockets. He found Horseshoe's gun, but missed Diavolo's. Don decided to hang on to that just in case.

He knew who the masked man was. But could he trust that whispered offer of assistance? Would he and Horseshoe actually get a chance to play dead? Would the shots, when they came, be blanks as the masked man wanted to make him believe? Was it just another doublecross?

The masked man took an automatic from his pocket and raised it slowly until it pointed at Don Diavolo's chest.

Don was still trying to decide whether to fire first or take a chance. He knew that the man who stood before him was Pat's and Mickey's brother, Glenn Collins. If Don pressed his trigger first, he and Horseshoe would undoubtedly get a barrage from behind. If he let Glenn fire, he might get a blank—and he might not. . . .

But the gun whose report filled the room was neither Diavolo's nor Glenn's. It came from a smoking forty-five in the hands of Inspector Church as the corridor door slammed open and spilled detectives into the room.

The masked man fell. Slapsie Monahan fired once with the gun he had taken from Horseshoe. He got three shots in reply. The others, seeing him fall, stood pat.

Don saw Woody Haines barge through the door, grinning. Inspector Church approached the masked man who was sitting on the floor, holding a bloody shoulder. "Vanish on me will you, Don Dia—"

Church, jerking aside the mask, stopped, staring at Glenn Collins. Then he turned to Horseshoe. "What—where is that—"

Scarface Mike, realizing that he was still in the Inspector's black books and that capture, under the present circumstances, was going to be no help at all had moved like lightning.

Church whirled and saw him standing within the alcove, his hands reaching for the copper electrodes. Caught off guard, the Inspector stared with round eyes as the orange sparks leaped toward Don's fingers and then as the magician's body began to fade, Church shot from the hip.

His bullet had a strange effect. The scene within the alcove seemed to splinter into a thousand pieces. There was a glassy crash and Diavolo's body, half transparent, instead of falling, vanished instantly!

Chapter XIII

Death of an Invisible Man

On the other side of the alcove's wall there was another room. J. D. Belmont was opening a stairway door when a panel in the wall behind him slid aside and Don Diavolo stepped out, his gun raised.

"Not so fast, please," he said. "Get your hands up!"

Belmont only moved faster. Diavolo put a shot into the door three inches to the right of the man's head. Belmont changed his mind, his face gray. His hands came up, dropping the suitcase that he carried.

"That's more like it," Don said, his eyes surveying the room with a quick searching glance. "Get away from that door!"

Diavolo called back through the open panel behind him. "Inspector! This way! I've go something for you."

Church came through after a moment with Woody Haines and Brophy at his heels. Don said, "One of you keep a gun on Belmont. This is going to be interesting."

"I'll keep one on you too," Church said. "What the blazes are you trying to pull off now?"

"A solution to the case, Inspector. We've got most of the pieces now and if we put them together properly . . ."

"I've got all the pieces," Church said. "And I know how they fit."

"Yes?" Don asked. "Do you know where Belmont fits?"

"I've got a good idea. He's the other nigger in the woodpile."

"Yes." Don nodded. "That's right enough. But who else are you voting for? Me?"

"Why not?" Church asked, scowling. "I've got a witness that saw you shoot Ziegler. And you were the guy who levitated that gun at Ziegler's apartment this morning. It was a phony made of papier mâché and hung on a black thread strung across the room. When you stepped away from the desk, you had an end of the thread in your hand. When you took up the slack the gun floated. And you used ventriloquism for the voice we heard."

"Not bad, Inspector," Diavolo said. "That's the one time I *was* the Invisible Man. But if you had been there half an hour before you'd have heard a voice coming out of thin air ordering Monahan to throw me into that safe. *That* certainly wasn't me throwing my voice. I'm not committing suicide just yet and, when I do, it won't be that way.

"What's more, Rose Ziegler did not see me shoot her father. She saw two men, one in a red dress suit and red mask, go into the study with her father. She heard some shots. I suggest that you check St. Louis Louie's gun with the bullets in Ziegler's body."

Inspector Church said quickly, "Somebody impersonated you. That your story?"

"You know very well it is, Inspector. Because at the time the phony Scarlet Wizard appeared at the Ziegler apartment, you and I were worrying about a diamond necklace out on Long Island at Belmont's place. Ask Glenn Collins who impersonated me."

"Okay," Church nodded. "I'll take that. You were at Belmont's all right. I just wanted to know who was helping you at this end. The Belmont hocus pocus was more of your damned misdirection, wasn't it? Just a gag to get me out there while your assistants got after Ziegler. And I know who swiped the necklace now."

Church turned to Belmont. "You did. Diavolo threw his voice so that it seemed to come from the doorway just as you were about to put the necklace back in its case. You dropped it in your pocket instead!"

Belmont watched the Inspector narrowly. "You can't prove that, Inspector."

Don Diavolo smiled. "You're doing better by the minute, Inspector. You've got that pretty straight except for the ventriloquism. Answer me this one. If I'm the Invisible Man, how did I get that stuff out of Ziegler's shop when you had me guarded in the museum across the street?"

"Mr. Gates," Church answered. "That was Collins doing another impersonation. The swag went out in his bag."

"Right, Inspector. But who loaded the bag? Ziegler said he had Gates under his eye all the time."

"Well—I . . . Dammit, have I got to study to be a magician in order to get you behind bars? I don't know how you did it. It was another of your magic tricks. And when the D.A. handpicks a jury of men who have all seen your act, they won't let a little thing like that keep them from putting you on the hot seat."

"I suppose it was a conjuring trick that killed Sergeant Healy?" Don asked skeptically. "You've just seen the Invisibility apparatus in the next room. You ruined it with that shot of yours. You know it's only an illusion. Pepper's Ghost brought up to date with some scientific trimmings.[6] Dr. Palgar's Invisible Ray Projec-

tor, its shiny switches and weird violet light, is so much eyewash. Good showmanship, good advertising, but eyewash just the same. The illusion is all worked from the alcove."

Don pointed to a machine nearby from which a large disk projected. "Static machine," he said. "That furnished the sparks that jumped from my fingers when I touched the electrodes. Pressure on the right hand electrode makes the lights change which starts the illusion operating. But it's still only an illusion. You can *appear* to fade into invisibility in that cabinet, but you can't step out of it still in that condition."

"But—but . . ." Church started to interrupt.

"Quiet, please," Diavolo insisted. "The audience can ask the lecturer questions after class. There *is* an Invisible Man, but he's a different sort than you expect."

"Collins," Church broke in. "He—"

Don raised his hand. "Inspector," he threatened, "if you don't pipe down, I'll say a few magic words and vanish right now. And then you never will solve this case."

Church hesitated, then said, "Okay, talk, but I won't like it even if it's good. You can hand out the damnedest line I ever—"

Don's hand started a mystic pass and Church stopped abruptly, half afraid that perhaps the magician could make good on his threat to disappear.

"Glenn Collins," Don said quickly, "needed a job. He got one. He played the part of the Italian who barged into Healy's office just before he was shot. He was also Mr. Gates, Julian Dumont, and the Dr. Palgar that you've been trying to find. He didn't know he was taking on a job that included murder, but when that's what happened and when Glenn discovered that his employer had seen to it that his thumbprint was on the note left in your office, there wasn't much

6 A French conjurer, Henri Robbin, in his book *L'Histoire des Spectres Vivants et Impalpables* claims to have exhibited this very famous illustration as easly as 1847. Prof. John Henry Pepper, however, patented the idea in 1863 and exhibited it at the London Polytechnic Institute in 1879 with great success. Harry Kellar subsequently brought it to the United States under the name The Blue Room. This last version,

in which a man standing within a coffin changes visibly to a skeleton and back again, is still seen in carnivals and at fairs. See Henry Ridgely Evans: *History of Conjuring and Magic* and Ottokar Fischer's *Illustrated Magic*.

he could do but go through with it. He was in a hell of a spot. That right, Belmont?"

The financier shook his head. "I'm not talking."

"You will," Diavolo predicted. "There was a fingerprint on the third note that the Invisible Man wrote, the one that was left at Ziegler's shop. It was yours. Karl checked that. It matched a few prints you left on the check you gave me."

Belmont's face was dark. "Why that little—"

The noise of the shot that punctuated his sentence was loud in the small room. Belmont pitched forward on the floor, wounded only, but pretending death in order to avoid a second shot.

Church, Woody Haines, and two other detectives who had come in while Don was talking looked around hunting for the source of the shot. Their fingers itched on their triggers. And they saw nothing at which to aim.

Church said, "But—but that shot came from in here! It—"

"Yes," Diavolo answered. "The Invisible Man is present. And it's not me. If there's any more shooting you can try that suitcase Belmont dropped. I—"

There was one more shot, but Church and the others did not reply to it. They were staring at the hole that appeared in the side of the suitcase and the slow trickle of blood that was oozing out.

After a moment Inspector Church crossed the room and opened the grip.

When he looked up, he had a dazed expression of comprehension on his face.

"Larry Keeler," Don said, "is a dwarf. That gives him a headstart at invisibility. He's also a magician—Wizzo, The World's Smallest Prestidigitator. And *that* made the rest easy!"

Chapter XIV

Hocus Pocus

Inspector Church wasn't too sure he was satisfied. He still eyed Don Diavolo with a jaundiced eye. It wasn't until Glenn Collins had told his story that Church finally let Don and The Horseshoe Kid leave.

With Karl Hartz and Woody Haines, they sped in a taxi toward the Manhattan Music Hall.

"I took a look at the gun Glenn was going to knock us off with," Horseshoe said. "It was loaded with blanks. He was trying to give us an out, after all."

"Yes," Don said. "He had to do it that way because Keeler was watching him from beyond the wall. There's a peephole behind that illusion alcove. Driver"—Don leaned forward—"step on it, will you? Kaselmeyer is probably having kittens one right after the other. Litters and litters of them. I've got to stop helping Inspector Church and tend to some of my own knitting."

"He'll calm down after my story hits the papers," Woody said. "Invisible Man Loses in Magician's Duel! Kaselmeyer can paint himself a permanent S.R.O. sign in his lobby. But I want more details. Glenn Collins only hit the high spots before they popped him into the ambulance. Why did he barge into Healy's office, impersonate an Italian, and hand out that line about thanking him for finding his daughter?"

"He had to say something," Don answered. "He and Keeler had been following Healy. They'd just discovered that Healy, posing as a crook, had joined the gang the same way we did. They wanted to get him before he reported that he'd found Palgar's machine and told about the use to which it was being put. They trailed him to his office trying to get a chance to jump him.

"Then they became desperate and used drastic measures. Glenn broke in on Healy excitedly, jumped across the office and shouted his thanks in Healy's face so that Healy wouldn't see Keeler sneaking in at the door behind Glenn. I'd guess that Larry crawled across the floor and when Glenn left, stayed hidden down below the level of the desk top. Glenn, as he just told Church, didn't realize that Keeler was going to murder Healy. Keeler had said he was only going to hypnotize Healy and make him forget what he had seen.

"Glenn swallowed that one because he knew that Larry was a magician. He didn't know that hypnotism won't work on people who don't want to be hypnotized—not the first time around anyway.

"Keeler then shot Healy and when he heard Church coming, locked the door so he'd have a moment's time to cut the phone cord and to hide."

"Hide?" Woody asked. "But I've been in Healy's office. There isn't any place—"

"You sure?" Don replied. "What is in it?"

"Desk, two chairs, a table, wastebasket, a single-drawer filing cabinet, a hall tree."

"Where was the filing cabinet? A buck says it was on the table behind the door."

Woody's eyebrows went up under his hat. "Yeah. It is, but—"

"Keeler folded himself up in that," Don said. "Left it open, maybe three inches or so, and when Church came in and was staring at the body, Keeler, behind him, reached out, gave the door a push and said, '*See you later, Inspector.*' When Church whirled around all he saw was the door swinging to. And when he dashed out into the hall, Larry closed his filing cabinet the rest of the way like a turtle drawing into its shell. Simple as that."

"Oh yeah?" Woody said skeptically. "The filing cabinet wasn't empty. It had letters and memos in it."

"Larry could have taken them out, hid them in the wastebasket under some waste paper, and later, when he left, put them back."

"Well—" Woody said doubtfully. Then he shook his head. "No. Too much is too much. Keeler may have been a dwarf, but he wasn't a blooming midget. He was four feet tall and he weighed a good ninety pounds. No filing cabinet, even an empty—"

"Filing cabinets," Karl Hartz cut in, "are mostly about 12x12x24. That's 3456 cubic inches. I could almost squeeze into that space myself. It's just a matter of knowing the proper way to fold up. I built a trick for Thurston once in which we got a five-foot-six assistant into a 14x14x24 box. The audience saw it all the time, but it looked way too small to hold a man and they didn't give it a thought. They are still wondering where the man disappeared to. That was the whole secret of the trick. That guy weighed 137 pounds. That's 3900 cubic inches of man fitting into 4704 cubic inches of space. He was a wee bit cramped, but after I taught him how to fold, he did it twice a day. Keeler, in the filing cabinet, would have even more space to spare than—"

"Haven't you been around to see the new illusion in this week's stage show?" Don Diavolo asked. "Thirty girls from a cabinet the audience thinks is only big enough to hold nine."

Woody saw that Karl was making a diagram on the back of an envelope. "Okay," he said quickly. "I give in. But no more mathematics and no diagrams please. I'll take your word for it. You should know. So Half-pint stayed filed in the cabinet—under M, I suppose, for Monkey-shines and Magicians—until the room was clear. Then he hops out, leaves his first note about the Siva statue on the Inspector's hat and scrams."

"How did he get out of headquarters? Every exit was covered. Why didn't the cops notice an outsize little shrimp like him? They don't have dwarfs running in and out of headquarters every day. They were looking for something odd. He was."

"They didn't see him," Don replied, "because he did make himself invisible—or as close to it as possible. He was wearing a Western Union messenger's uniform. I found it in the room back there just now. And Western Union boys do run in and out of headquarters every day. So much so, nobody ever notices them. They're as good as invisible—like mailmen, doormen, milkmen, waiters, conductors—"

The Horseshoe Kid spoke up. "That explains how the Ziegler loot got into Gates's suitcase. Collins, playing the Gates role, carried Larry into the shop in the suitcase. The threat to steal the Siva statue from the museum across the street was a low down trick to get everyone's attention—especially that of Ziegler and his clerks—glued on the wrong spot.[7]

"Then Keeler pops out of the suitcase like a damned jack-in-the-box, cleans the safe and puts the loot in the grip. He was wearing his uniform. He hides behind the door. Ziegler and Gates return. Gates gets Ziegler's attention again, and Keeler steps out from behind the door, pretending to have just come through it. He hands Gates a wire, and walks out. If the clerks outside notice him they don't even think twice about it. It's sorta neat."

Don Diavolo leaned forward, lifted the taxi-driver's cap, and took from under it a lighted cigarette. Then he growled in mock dismay. "I thought *I* was going to get asked to explain this case! I can't get a word in edgewise! Maybe you know-it-alls can tell me why Keeler and Gates took the sort of stuff they did from Ziegler's safe. Rare, priceless pieces of art, but a fence would give you more for old papers. Every single item was so well known it would have been as hot as six kinds of hell. And you can't take a jade cup or a rare book apart to prevent identification as you can with a diamond necklace."

"That's easy," Horseshoe replied. "You gave us that answer yourself, yesterday. You said that some collectors were so bats they'd buy stolen rarities, knowing they'd always have to keep them under cover. Belmont was that way. Great

jumpin' catamounts! Of course—*he* was the bird who's behind the whole thing! He hired Keeler to swipe the stuff for him!"

"Yes," Don said disgustedly. "And darned if I know why I bothered to figure it out with you masterminds on the job. Who solved this case anyway? Blast it!"

"I suppose you knew all along that Belmont was one of the niggers in the woodpile?" Woody gave Don an incredulous look.

"I did just as soon as that necklace vanished under our noses," Don insisted. "Belmont was the only guy who could have taken it—and the only person Church didn't search!"

Woody wasn't listening. He snapped his fingers. "I've got it now. The reason for all this Invisibility business. It's as transparent as—as—"

"As an Invisible Man!" Don suggested glumly. "Well what? Let me in on it. I can't wait!"

"Ziegler," Woody said, "had some things that Belmont wanted, but wouldn't sell him. So Belmont propositioned Keeler—hired him to swipe them. Keeler agreed, but he had to have help. A sawed-off half-pint like him couldn't head a gang of crooks. They'd have handed him an all day sucker and told him to climb back into his baby carriage.

"So he started by picking up Glenn who was down on his luck. Told him he had a job of acting, but didn't tell him what it was all about. Glenn played the Dr. Palgar part first, and got some nice publicity through the auto show for the Invisibility Machine that Keeler cooked up from an old magic illusion he knew about.

"Then Glenn stepped out of the Palgar part and vanished with the machine. It hit the papers. Big mystery. That's when Keeler recruited his gang. They thought they had an invisible man for a leader instead of a half-pint dwarf that they'd have laughed at. Psychology. The way he worked it, he put across the idea that he was visible only for a short time—during the meetings when he dished out orders.

"He worked behind Glenn's skirts there too.

---

7   While writing the present account of the case of The Invisible Man I visited the Museum of Indian Art to see the statue of Siva. The curator pointed out to me an extremely odd thing which the newspaper accounts and all the other writers who have dwelt upon the case seem to have failed to note. The dancing figure of Siva the Destroyer, as I described it in the foregoing text, stands upon the symbolical prostrate figure of a *dwarf*. One would think that Larry Keeler must have been mad if he purposely chose to center everyone's attention on this statue so that his twisted sense of humor could enjoy yet another quiet laugh. And yet was he? The fact remains that no one, during the case, noticed this strangely prophetic figure that had another symbolism beyond the Brahmanical one the original sculptor intended.—Stuart Towne.

The rest of the time he was invisible and, for all they knew, watching every move they made. They didn't dare disobey any orders he gave out."

"Inferiority complex," Karl put in. "Larry's lack of height has always kept him from getting top-drawer bookings as a magician. He's always had a feeling that everyone laughs at him behind his back. He figured he'd have himself a quiet laugh at everyone else by outwitting all the cops in town, all the newspaper readers in the country, and make a monkey of the Great Diavolo to boot."[8]

"And—" Don began, vainly, trying to put in his oar. But The Horseshoe Kid talked louder.

"That was the reason for the Great Necklace Robbery, then—to get the laugh on Don. But why did Belmont play along with him on that? Why'd Belmont swipe his own necklace? Don't make sense to me."

Don Diavolo shrugged. "How would *I* know? You boys are doing the explaining."

They were, too. "I can give a guess," Woody grinned. "Belmont figured Ziegler would suspect him. But if he too were a victim of the Invisible Man, it would be a nice fat red herring across the trail. But say—" He turned to Don. "Larry did put it over on you just a bit, you know. You're the guy who sneaked the Invisible Man into Belmont's place in your suitcase, hoping *he'd* get an eyeful of something that would tell you who the Invisible Man was!"

8 One ironic note which needs mention is that Larry Keeler, jealous of Don Diavolo to the point of trying to frame him for Ziegler's murder by having Collins appear there in red evening clothes and mask, nevertheless was forced to ask Don's help. When Collins and St. Louis Louie tried to hold up Ziegler, the latter quickly locked the safe on which he had just changed the combination. Louie, who wasn't overly bright about such things, shot him. And Keeler himself, although a magician, couldn't pick the lock because, familiar as he was with locks and escape feats in theory, his physique had prevented his actual practice of that type of magic. Thus, Perry had to be sent to Don Diavolo, in an attempt to get him to open the safe.

Don grinned. "That's what he thought too. Belmont had intended to hide him in the house before the cops came; but when I suggested the suitcase stunt to Larry, he thought it was a swell joke on me. Trouble was, his joke backfired.

"It told me that he was The Invisible Man. A magician must never make a trick look too blamed impossible—his audience won't believe it. That was Larry's mistake. When we heard the voice and saw the door close. I knew Larry was the *only* person at Belmont's who could possibly have worked it. He was planted smack outside the door! It was as obvious as the Empire State Building.

"He got out of the suitcase, listened to our conversation and, at the psychological moment, pushed the door open, spoke his little piece and then pulled the door to with a length of black thread. He was probably standing in the suitcase again by then.

"As soon as the door slammed, he ducked down and when Church got there, the hall was empty. Swell trick—but too impossible—*unless Keeler was the Invisible Man himself!* And now, you guys are so all-fired smart, tell me this: why were some of the objects that the gang found in Ziegler's safe exact duplicates of those that were taken from his store?"

"They what—?" Woody exclaimed. "I don't get that." The Horseshoe Kid and Karl both shook their heads.

"Gee thanks, fellows," Diavolo said. "Nice of you to give me a chance. Ziegler was a collector like Belmont. He couldn't bear to sell some of the rare art objects he bought. But he had to make expenses so he made duplicates. He sold those and kept the originals. When Belmont's expert took a look at the Ziegler haul, Belmont discovered that some of the stuff was phony.

"So Larry got orders to have Glenn and the boys make a second try, at Ziegler's apartment this time—and he had them do the job while the Inspector and I were out watching the little show at Belmont's. More of Keeler's magician's misdirection. He was a good conjurer and he came within inches of being a first class criminal.

Only, like a lot of amateur magicians and criminals, he put in a shade too much fancy work."

"Whoa, there!" Woody exclaimed. "That doesn't hold water. Forgers fake paintings, books, autographed letters and such, but not jade cups, rock crystal crosses and medieval enameled reliquaries. It's too blamed much work and there are too many ways to get tripped up."

"You forget who Ziegler was, Woody. The hot shot art expert. The guy whose business it was to know all the fine points of detecting forgeries. Collectors brought their things to him for an opinion. When he said they were authentic, that was the last word.

"The curator at the Indian Museum this morning told me that there was only one other expert in this country who has the rep that Ziegler has. He's a man who works for Belmont. That was why Ziegler didn't dare sell any of his forgeries to Belmont. That was the one place he might get caught out."

"Um," Woody said, thinking it over. "I'll take it. I guess that explains the works."

"Not quite," Horseshoe added. "Where was Keeler hiding out at Ziegler's place when they dumped you in the safe, Don?"

"In the desk. One of the lower drawers is a deep one—as large as the filing cabinet. He'd taken out the partitions. Collins was the only one of the gang who really knew who the Invisible Man was. And he worked the floating gun with the thread the same way I repeated it later for Inspector Church."

Horseshoe said, "Concealed mikes around the room made his voice seem to come from different places just before that Invisible Machine exhibition just now, I suppose. Threads on the chair and another to float the cigarette. But what about the smoke that came from nothing? You don't manage that with threads—or mirrors or trapdoors."

"He had two atomizers built into the top desk drawer," Don said. "They pointed upward at a converging angle. One held hydrochloric acid, the other ammonia. They operated by a connection into the next room and when the invis-

ible fumes shot upward and met in midair they formed smoke—sal ammoniac. That's one way any high school chemistry student knows."

The taxi stopped before the Music Hall. Don Diavolo, Karl, and the Horseshoe Kid got out. Woody Haines told the driver, "The New York *Press* building, my boy, and don't stop for red lights!"

Upstairs, Col. Ernest Kaselmeyer was still boiling. "If that blankety blank, blank-blank magician isn't here in just two blank minutes, he's through. I'll see that every blank booking office in town—"

The Colonel's arms suddenly shot skyward. Don Diavolo, still disguised as Scarface Mike, was standing in the doorway, a gun in his hand. "Don Diavolo's a pal of mine, buddy. Yuh got dat? I don't wanna hear no more cracks like dem youse was just makin'. Unnerstan'?"

The Colonel eyed the gun nervously, gulped and nodded. Pat, Mickey, and Chan blinked.

"Good," Don said in his own voice. "Try to remember it." He tossed the gun aside and went toward Pat and Mickey. "We got the Invisible Man," he said. "It wasn't Glenn. He's in the hospital. Church winged him, but he'll be all right. I'm getting a lawyer for him and we'll spring him if he promises to keep out of trouble. He can put up a good defense on the grounds that Keeler framed him for a murder and forced him to follow through. You two can go see him after this show. Now get on stage—in your places."

Don blinked as he got two kisses, one on each cheek. Then he grinned and ran for his dressing table. "Karl," he called as he wiped away Scarface Mike's greasepaint, "go down and take a look at the skip on that center stage lift. It jammed a bit last night. Horseshoe, get Kaselmeyer out of here! He's blocking the doorway and I'm going to be using it. He loves blackjack. Take him away and give him a game. Deal him aces when he needs them. I'll foot your losses. Chan, get those rabbits down in the wings ready to go on!"

Not much more than five minutes later, Don

Diavolo, the Scarlet Wizard, took his entrance bow on the great stage and began producing rabbits from his red top hat.

At the same moment, Inspector Church and half a dozen detectives entered his dressing room upstairs. "All right boys," he ordered.

"Tear this place apart! Keeler was the Invisible Man behind Collins. Belmont was behind him and I *still* think Diavolo was the master mind! He hypnotized Belmont and Collins so they won't talk! I'm going to get the goods on him sooner or later! He can't fool me!"

THE DREAM
AGATHA CHRISTIE

THE MOST POPULAR WRITER of detective fiction who ever lived (her sales in all languages are reported to have surpassed four billion copies), Agatha Mary Clarissa Miller Christie's (1890–1976) remarkably proficient first book, *The Mysterious Affair at Styles* (1920), is generally given credit as the landmark volume that initiated what has been called the Golden Age of mystery fiction. This era, bracketed by the two world wars, saw the rise of the fair-play puzzle story and the series detective, whether an official member of the police department (such as Freeman Wills Croft's Inspector French), a private detective (like Christie's Hercule Poirot, who made his debut in her first novel and stars in "The Dream"), or an amateur sleuth (like Anthony Berkeley's Roger Sheringham, Dorothy L. Sayers's Lord Peter Wimsey, and E. C. Bentley's Philip Trent). But it was Christie who towered above the others, outselling, out-producing, and outliving the rest. Perhaps surprisingly, the manuscript of her first novel had been rejected by several publishing houses, and John Lane, the eventual publisher, held it for more than a year before deciding to offer only one hundred twenty-five dollars for it. Encouraged by the sale, Christie went on to write more than a hundred books and plays. The shy and reclusive author wrote the longest continuously running play of all time, *The Mousetrap* (since it opened in 1952, there have been more than twenty-five thousand performances—with no closing in sight), as well as one of the best, *Witness for the Prosecution* (less successful but infinitely superior, it opened in 1953, winning the Edgar, and was adapted for the brilliant motion picture starring Charles Laughton, Tyrone Power, and Marlene Dietrich).

"The Dream" was first published in *The Regatta Mystery and Other Stories* (New York, Dodd, Mead, 1939). It was first published in England in *The Adventure of the Christmas Pudding and a Selection of Entrees* (London, Collins, 1960). It was adapted as a 1989 episode of the London Weekend Television series *Agatha Christie's Poirot*, starring David Suchet.

THE DREAM

AGATHA CHRISTIE

HERCULE POIROT gave the house a steady appraising glance. His eyes wandered a moment to its surroundings, the shops, the big factory building on the right, the blocks of cheap mansion flats opposite.

Then once more his eyes returned to Northway House, relic of an earlier age—an age of space and leisure, when green fields had surrounded its well-bred arrogance. Now it was an anachronism, submerged and forgotten in the hectic sea of modern London, and not one man in fifty could have told you where it stood.

Furthermore, very few people could have told you to whom it belonged, though its owner's name would have been recognized as one of the world's richest men. But money can quench publicity as well as flaunt it. Benedict Farley, that eccentric millionaire, chose not to advertise his choice of residence. He himself was rarely seen, seldom making a public appearance. From time to time, he appeared at board meetings, his lean figure, beaked nose, and rasping voice easily dominating the assembled directors. Apart from that, he was just a well-known figure of legend. There were his strange meannesses, his incredible generosities, as well as more personal details—his famous patchwork dressing-gown, now reputed to be twenty-eight years old, his invariable diet of cabbage soup and caviare, his hatred of cats. All these things the public knew.

Hercule Poirot knew them also. It was all he did know of the man he was about to visit. The letter which was in his coat pocket told him little more.

After surveying this melancholy landmark of a past age for a minute or two in silence, he walked up the steps to the front door and pressed the bell, glancing as he did so at the neat wrist-watch which had at last replaced an old favourite—the large turnip-faced watch of earlier days. Yes, it was exactly nine-thirty. As ever, Hercule Poirot was exact to the minute.

The door opened after just the right interval. A perfect specimen of the genus butler stood outlined against the lighted hall.

"Mr. Benedict Farley?" asked Hercule Poirot.

The impersonal glance surveyed him from head to foot, inoffensively but effectively.

En gros et en détail, thought Hercule Poirot to himself with appreciation.

"You have an appointment, sir?" asked the suave voice.

"Yes."

"Your name, sir?"

"Monsieur Hercule Poirot."

The butler bowed and drew back. Hercule Poirot entered the house. The butler closed the door behind him.

But there was yet one more formality before the deft hands took hat and stick from the visitor.

"You will excuse me, sir. I was to ask for a letter."

With deliberation Poirot took from his pocket

the folded letter and handed it to the butler. The latter gave it a mere glance, then returned it with a bow. Hercule Poirot returned it to his pocket. Its contents were simple.

Northway House, W.8.

M. Hercule Poirot.

Dear Sir,

Mr. Benedict Farley would like to have the benefit of your advice. If convenient to yourself he would be glad if you would call upon him at the above address at 9:30 to-morrow (Thursday) evening.

Yours truly,
Hugo Cornworthy

(Secretary)

P.S. Please bring this letter with you.

Deftly the butler relieved Poirot of hat, stick and overcoat. He said:

"Will you please come up to Mr. Cornworthy's room?"

He led the way up the broad staircase. Poirot followed him, looking with appreciation at such *objets d'art* as were of an opulent and florid nature! His taste in art was always somewhat bourgeois.

On the first floor the butler knocked on a door.

Hercule Poirot's eyebrows rose very slightly. It was the first jarring note. For the best butlers do not knock at doors—and yet indubitably this was a first-class butler!

It was, so to speak, the first intimation of contact with the eccentricity of a millionaire.

A voice from within called out something. The butler threw open the door. He announced (and again Poirot sensed the deliberate departure from orthodoxy):

"The gentleman you are expecting, sir."

Poirot passed into the room. It was a fair-sized room, very plainly furnished in a workmanlike fashion. Filing cabinets, books of reference, a couple of easy chairs, and a large and imposing desk covered with neatly docketed papers. The corners of the room were dim, for the only light came from a big green-shaded reading lamp which stood on a small table by the arm of one of the easy chairs. It was placed so as to cast its full light on anyone approaching from the door. Hercule Poirot blinked a little, realising that the lamp bulb was at least 150 watts. In the arm-chair sat a thin figure in a patchwork dressing-gown—Benedict Farley. His head was stuck forward in a characteristic attitude, his beaked nose projecting like that of a bird. A crest of white hair like that of a cockatoo rose above his forehead. His eyes glittered behind thick lenses as he peered suspiciously at his visitor.

"Hey," he said at last—and his voice was shrill and harsh, with a rasping note in it. "So you're Hercule Poirot, hey?"

"At your service," said Poirot politely and bowed, one hand on the back of the chair.

"Sit down—sit down," said the old man testily.

Hercule Poirot sat down—in the full glare of the lamp. From behind it the old man seemed to be studying him attentively.

"How do I know you're Hercule Poirot—hey?" he demanded fretfully. "Tell me that—hey?"

Once more Poirot drew the letter from his pocket and handed it to Farley.

"Yes," admitted the millionaire grudgingly. "That's it. That's what I got Cornworthy to write." He folded it up and tossed it back. "So you're the fellow, are you?"

With a little wave of his hand Poirot said:

"I assure you there is no deception!"

Benedict Farley chuckled suddenly.

"That's what the conjurer says before he takes the goldfish out of the hat! Saying that is part of the trick, you know!"

Poirot did not reply. Farley said suddenly:

"Think I'm a suspicious old man, hey? So

I am. Don't trust anybody! That's my motto. Can't trust anybody when you're rich. No, no, it doesn't do."

"You wished," Poirot hinted gently, "to consult me?"

The old man nodded.

"That's right. Always buy the best. That's my motto. Go to the expert and don't count the cost. You'll notice, M. Poirot, I haven't asked you your fee. I'm not going to! Send me in the bill later—*I* shan't cut up rough over it. Damned fools at the dairy thought they could charge me two and nine for eggs when two and seven's the market price—lot of swindlers! I won't be swindled. But the man at the top's different. He's worth the money. I'm at the top myself—I know."

Hercule Poirot made no reply. He listened attentively, his head poised a little on one side.

Behind his impassive exterior he was conscious of a feeling of disappointment. He could not exactly put his finger on it. So far Benedict Farley had run true to type—that is, he had conformed to the popular idea of himself; and yet—Poirot was disappointed.

"The man," he said disgustedly to himself, "is a mountebank—nothing but a mountebank!"

He had known other millionaires, eccentric men too, but in nearly every case he had been conscious of a certain force, an inner energy that had commanded his respect. If they had worn a patchwork dressing-gown, it would have been because they liked wearing such a dressing-gown. But the dressing-gown of Benedict Farley, or so it seemed to Poirot, was essentially a stage property. And the man himself was essentially stagy. Every word he spoke was uttered, so Poirot felt assured, sheerly for effect.

He repeated again unemotionally, "You wished to consult me, Mr. Farley?"

Abruptly the millionaire's manner changed.

He leaned forward. His voice dropped to a croak.

"Yes. Yes . . . I want to hear what you've got to say—what you think. . . . Go to the top! That's my way! The best doctor—the best detective—it's between the two of them."

"As yet, Monsieur, I do not understand."

"Naturally," snapped Farley. "I haven't begun to tell you."

He leaned forward once more and shot out an abrupt question.

"What do you know, M. Poirot, about dreams?"

The little man's eyebrows rose. Whatever he had expected, it was not this.

"For that, M. Farley, I should recommend Napoleon's *Book of Dreams*—or the latest practising psychologist from Harley Street."

Benedict Farley said soberly, "I've tried both. . . ."

There was a pause, then the millionaire spoke, at first almost in a whisper, then with a voice growing higher and higher.

"It's the same dream—night after night. And I'm afraid, I tell you—I'm afraid. . . . It's always the same. I'm sitting in my room next door to this. Sitting at my desk, writing. There's a clock there and I glance at it and see the time—exactly twenty-eight minutes past three. Always the same time, you understand.

"*And when I see the time, M. Poirot, I know I've got to do it.* I don't want to do it—I loathe doing it—but I've got to. . . ."

His voice had risen shrilly.

Unperturbed, Poirot said, "And what is it that you have to do?"

"At twenty-eight minutes past three," Benedict Farley said hoarsely, "I open the second drawer down on the right of my desk, take out the revolver that I keep there, load it and walk over to the window. And then—and then——"

"Yes?"

Benedict Farley said in a whisper:

"*Then I shoot myself. . . .*"

There was silence.

Then Poirot said, "That is your dream?"

"Yes."

"The same every night?"

"Yes."

"What happens after you shoot yourself?"

"I wake up."

Poirot nodded his head slowly and thoughtfully. "As a matter of interest, do you keep a revolver in that particular drawer?"

"Yes."

"Why?"

"I have always done so. It is as well to be prepared."

"Prepared for what?"

Farley said irritably, "A man in my position has to be on his guard. All rich men have enemies."

Poirot did not pursue the subject. He remained silent for a moment or two, then he said:

"Why exactly did you send for me?"

"I will tell you. First of all I consulted a doctor—three doctors to be exact."

"Yes?"

"The first told me it was all a question of diet. He was an elderly man. The second was a young man of the modern school. He assured me that it all hinged on a certain event that took place in infancy at that particular time of day—three twenty-eight. I am so determined, he says, not to remember the event, that I symbolize it by destroying myself. That is his explanation."

"And the third doctor?" asked Poirot.

Benedict Farley's voice rose in shrill anger.

"He's a young man too. He has a preposterous theory! He asserts that I, myself, am tired of life, that my life is so unbearable to me that I deliberately want to end it! But since to acknowledge that fact would be to acknowledge that essentially I am a failure, I refuse in my waking moments to face the truth. But when I am asleep, all inhibitions are removed, and I proceed to do that *which I really wish to do*. I put an end to myself."

"His view is that you really wish, unknown to yourself, to commit suicide?" said Poirot.

Benedict Farley cried shrilly:

"And that's impossible—impossible! I'm perfectly happy! I've got everything I want—everything money can buy! It's fantastic—unbelievable even to suggest a thing like that!"

Poirot looked at him with interest. Perhaps something in the shaking hands, the trembling shrillness of the voice, warned him that the denial was *too* vehement, that its very insistence was in itself suspect. He contented himself with saying:

"And where do I come in, Monsieur?"

Benedict Farley calmed down suddenly. He tapped with an emphatic finger on the table beside him.

"There's another possibility. And if it's right, you're the man to know about it! You're famous, you've had hundreds of cases—fantastic, improbable cases! You'd know if anyone does."

"Know what?"

Farley's voice dropped to a whisper.

"Supposing someone wants to kill me. . . . Could they do it this way? Could they make me dream that dream night after night?"

"Hypnotism, you mean?"

"Yes."

Hercule Poirot considered the question.

"It would be possible, I suppose," he said at last. "It is more a question for a doctor."

"You don't know of such a case in your experience?"

"Not precisely on those lines, no."

"You see what I'm driving at? I'm made to dream the same dream, night after night, night after night—and then—one day the suggestion is too much for me—*and I act upon it*. I do what I've dreamed of so often—kill myself!"

Slowly Hercule Poirot shook his head.

"You don't think that is possible?" asked Farley.

"*Possible?*" Poirot shook his head. "That is not a word I care to meddle with."

"But you think it improbable?"

"Most improbable."

Benedict Farley murmured. "The doctor said so too. . . ." Then his voice rising shrilly again, he cried out, "But why do I have this dream? Why? Why?"

Hercule Poirot shook his head. Benedict Farley said abruptly, "You're sure you've never come across anything like this in your experience?"

"Never."

"That's what I wanted to know."

Delicately, Poirot cleared his throat.

"You permit," he said, "a question?"

"What is it? What is it? Say what you like."

"Who is it you suspect of wanting to kill you?"

Farley snapped out, "Nobody. Nobody at all."

"But the idea presented itself to your mind?" Poirot persisted.

"I wanted to know—if it was a possibility."

"Speaking from my own experience, I should say no. Have you ever been hypnotized, by the way?"

"Of course not. D'you think I'd lend myself to such tomfoolery?"

"Then I think one can say that your theory is definitely improbable."

"But the dream, you fool, the dream."

"The dream is certainly remarkable," said Poirot thoughtfully. He paused and then went on. "I should like to see the scene of this drama—the table, the clock, and the revolver."

"Of course, I'll take you next door."

Wrapping the folds of his dressing-gown round him, the old man half-rose from his chair. Then suddenly, as though a thought had struck him, he resumed his seat.

"No," he said. "There's nothing to see there. I've told you all there is to tell."

"But I should like to see for myself——"

"There's no need," Farley snapped. "You've given me your opinion. That's the end."

Poirot shrugged his shoulders. "As you please." He rose to his feet. "I am sorry, Mr. Farley, that I have not been able to be of assistance to you."

Benedict Farley was staring straight ahead of him.

"Don't want a lot of hanky-pankying around," he growled out. "I've told you the facts—you can't make anything of them. That closes the matter. You can send me a bill for the consultation fee."

"I shall not fail to do so," said the detective drily. He walked towards the door.

"Stop a minute." The millionaire called him back. "That letter—I want it."

"The letter from your secretary?"

"Yes."

Poirot's eyebrows rose. He put his hand into his pocket, drew out a folded sheet, and handed it to the old man. The latter scrutinized it, then put it down on the table beside him with a nod.

Once more Hercule Poirot walked to the door. He was puzzled. His busy mind was going over and over the story he had been told. Yet in the midst of his mental preoccupation, a nagging sense of something wrong obtruded itself. And that something had to do with himself—not with Benedict Farley.

With his hand on the door knob, his mind cleared. He, Hercule Poirot, had been guilty of an error! He turned back into the room once more.

"A thousand pardons! In the interest of your problem I have committed a folly! That letter I handed to you—by mischance I put my hand into my right-hand pocket instead of the left——"

"What's all this? What's all this?"

"The letter that I handed you just now—an apology from my laundress concerning the treatment of my collars." Poirot was smiling, apologetic. He dipped into his left-hand pocket. "This is *your* letter."

Benedict Farley snatched at it—grunted: "Why the devil can't you mind what you're doing?"

Poirot retrieved his laundress's communication, apologized gracefully once more, and left the room.

He paused for a moment outside on the landing. It was a spacious one. Directly facing him was a big old oak settle with a refectory table in front of it. On the table were magazines. There were also two arm-chairs and a table with flowers. It reminded him a little of a dentist's waiting-room.

The butler was in the hall below waiting to let him out.

"Can I get you a taxi, sir?"

"No, I thank you. The night is fine. I will walk."

Hercule Poirot paused a moment on the pavement waiting for a lull in the traffic before crossing the busy street.

A frown creased his forehead.

"No," he said to himself. "I do not understand at all. Nothing makes sense. Regrettable to have to admit it, but I, Hercule Poirot, am completely baffled."

That was what might be termed the first act of the drama. The second act followed a week later. It opened with a telephone call from one John Stillingfleet, M.D.

He said with a remarkable lack of medical decorum:

"That you, Poirot, old horse? Stillingfleet here."

"Yes, my friend. What is it?"

"I'm speaking from Northway House—Benedict Farley's."

"Ah, yes?" Poirot's voice quickened with interest. "What of—Mr. Farley?"

"Farley's dead. Shot himself this afternoon."

There was a pause, then Poirot said:

"Yes . . ."

"I notice you're not overcome with surprise. Know something about it, old horse?"

"Why should you think that?"

"Well, it isn't brilliant deduction or telepathy or anything like that. We found a note from Farley to you making an appointment about a week ago."

"I see."

"We've got a tame police inspector here—got to be careful, you know, when one of these millionaire blokes bumps himself off. Wondered whether you could throw any light on the case. If so, perhaps you'd come round?"

"I will come immediately."

"Good for you, old boy. Some dirty work at the crossroads—eh?"

Poirot merely repeated that he would set forth immediately.

"Don't want to spill the beans over the telephone? Quite right. So long."

A quarter of an hour later Poirot was sitting in the library, a low long room at the back of Northway House on the ground floor. There were five other persons in the room. Inspector Barnett, Dr. Stillingfleet, Mrs. Farley, the widow of the millionaire, Joanna Farley, his only daughter, and Hugo Cornworthy, his private secretary.

Of these, Inspector Barnett was a discreet soldierly-looking man. Dr. Stillingfleet, whose professional manner was entirely different from his telephonic style, was a tall, long-faced young man of thirty. Mrs. Farley was obviously very much younger than her husband. She was a handsome dark-haired woman. Her mouth was hard and her black eyes gave absolutely no clue to her emotions. She appeared perfectly self-possessed. Joanna Farley had fair hair and a freckled face. The prominence of her nose and chin was clearly inherited from her father. Her eyes were intelligent and shrewd. Hugo Cornworthy was a good-looking young fellow, very correctly dressed. He seemed intelligent and efficient.

After greetings and introductions, Poirot narrated simply and clearly the circumstances of his visit and the story told him by Benedict Farley. He could not complain of any lack of interest.

"Most extraordinary story I've ever heard!" said the inspector. "A dream, eh? Did you know anything about this, Mrs. Farley?"

She bowed her head.

"My husband mentioned it to me. It upset him very much. I—I told him it was indigestion—his diet, you know, was very peculiar—and suggested his calling in Dr. Stillingfleet."

The young man shook his head.

"He didn't consult me. From M. Poirot's story, I gather he went to Harley Street."

"I would like your advice on that point, Doctor," said Poirot. "Mr. Farley told me that he consulted three specialists. What do you think of the theories they advanced?"

Stillingfleet frowned.

"It's difficult to say. You've got to take into

account that what he passed on to you wasn't exactly what had been said to him. It was a layman's interpretation."

"You mean he had got the phraseology wrong?"

"Not exactly. I mean they would put a thing to him in professional terms, he'd get the meaning a little distorted, and then recast it in his own language."

"So that what he told me was not really what the doctors said."

"That's what it amounts to. He's just got it all a little wrong, if you know what I mean."

Poirot nodded thoughtfully. "Is it known whom he consulted?" he asked.

Mrs. Farley shook her head, and Joanna Farley remarked:

"None of us had any idea he had consulted anyone."

"Did he speak to *you* about his dream?" asked Poirot.

The girl shook her head.

"And you, Mr. Cornworthy?"

"No, he said nothing at all. I took down a letter to you at his dictation, but I had no idea why he wished to consult you. I thought it might possibly have something to do with some business irregularity."

Poirot asked: "And now as to the actual facts of Mr. Farley's death?"

Inspector Barnett looked interrogatively at Mrs. Farley and at Dr. Stillingfleet, and then took upon himself the role of spokesman.

"Mr. Farley was in the habit of working in his own room on the first floor every afternoon. I understand that there was a big amalgamation of business in prospect——"

He looked at Hugo Cornworthy who said, "Consolidated Coachlines."

"In connection with that," continued Inspector Barnett, "Mr. Farley had agreed to give an interview to two members of the Press. He very seldom did anything of the kind—only about once in five years, I understand. Accordingly two reporters, one from the Associated Newsgroups, and one from Amalgamated Press-sheets,

arrived at a quarter past three by appointment. They waited on the first floor outside Mr. Farley's door—which was the customary place for people to wait who had an appointment with Mr. Farley. At twenty past three a messenger arrived from the office of Consolidated Coachlines with some urgent papers. He was shown into Mr. Farley's room where he handed over the documents. Mr. Farley accompanied him to the door, and from there spoke to the two members of the Press. He said:

"'I'm sorry, gentlemen, to have to keep you waiting, but I have some urgent business to attend to. I will be as quick as I can.'

"The two gentlemen, Mr. Adams and Mr. Stoddart, assured Mr. Farley that they would await his convenience. He went back into his room, shut the door—and was never seen alive again!"

"Continue," said Poirot.

"At a little after four o'clock," went on the inspector, "Mr. Cornworthy here came out of his room which is next door to Mr. Farley's and was surprised to see the two reporters still waiting. He wanted Mr. Farley's signature to some letters and thought he had also better remind him that these two gentlemen were waiting. He accordingly went into Mr. Farley's room. To his surprise he could not at first see Mr. Farley and thought the room was empty. Then he caught sight of a boot sticking out behind the desk (which is placed in front of the window). He went quickly across and discovered Mr. Farley lying there dead, with a revolver beside him.

"Mr. Cornworthy hurried out of the room and directed the butler to ring up Dr. Stillingfleet. By the latter's advice, Mr. Cornworthy also informed the police."

"Was the shot heard?" asked Poirot.

"No. The traffic is very noisy here, the landing window was open. What with lorries and motor horns it would be most unlikely if it had been noticed."

Poirot nodded thoughtfully. "What time is it supposed he died?" he asked.

Stillingfleet said:

"I examined the body as soon as I got here—that is, at thirty-two minutes past four. Mr. Farley had been dead at least an hour."

Poirot's face was very grave.

"So then, it seems possible that his death could have occurred at the time he mentioned to me—that is, at twenty-eight minutes past three."

"Exactly," said Stillingfleet.

"Any fingermarks on the revolver?"

"Yes, his own."

"And the revolver itself?"

The inspector took up the tale.

"Was one which he kept in the second right-hand drawer of his desk, just as he told you. Mrs. Farley has identified it positively. Moreover, you understand, there is only one entrance to the room, the door giving onto the landing. The two reporters were sitting exactly opposite that door and they swear that no one entered the room from the time Mr. Farley spoke to them, until Mr. Cornworthy entered it at a little after four o'clock."

"So that there is every reason to suppose that Mr. Farley committed suicide."

Inspector Barnett smiled a little.

"There would have been no doubt at all but for one point."

"And that?"

"The letter written to you."

Poirot smiled too.

"I see! Where Hercule Poirot is concerned—immediately the suspicion of murder arises!"

"Precisely," said the inspector drily. "However, after your clearing up of the situation——"

Poirot interrupted him. "One little minute." He turned to Mrs. Farley. "Had your husband ever been hypnotized?"

"Never."

"Had he studied the question of hypnotism? Was he interested in the subject?"

She shook her head. "I don't think so."

Suddenly her self-control seemed to break down. "That horrible dream! It's uncanny! That he should have dreamed that—night after night—and then—it's as though he were—*hounded* to death!"

Poirot remembered Benedict Farley saying—"*I proceed to do that which I really wish to do. I put an end to myself.*"

He said, "Had it ever occurred to you that your husband might be tempted to do away with himself?"

"No—at least—sometimes he was very queer. . . ."

Joanna Farley's voice broke in clear and scornful. "Father would never have killed himself. He was far too careful of himself."

Dr. Stillingfleet said, "It isn't the people who threaten to commit suicide who usually do it, you know, Miss Farley. That's why suicides sometimes seem unaccountable."

Poirot rose to his feet. "Is it permitted," he asked, "that I see the room where the tragedy occurred?"

"Certainly. Dr. Stillingfleet——"

The doctor accompanied Poirot upstairs.

Benedict Farley's room was a much larger one than the secretary's next door. It was luxuriously furnished with deep leather-covered armchairs, a thick pile carpet, and a superb outsize writing-desk.

Poirot passed behind the latter to where a dark stain on the carpet showed just before the window. He remembered the millionaire saying, "*At twenty-eight minutes past three I open the second drawer on the right of my desk, take out the revolver that I keep there, load it, and walk over to the window. And then—and then I shoot myself.*"

He nodded slowly. Then he said:

"The window was open like this?"

"Yes. But nobody could have got in that way."

Poirot put his head out. There was no sill or parapet and no pipes near. Not even a cat could have gained access that way. Opposite rose the blank wall of the factory, a dead wall with no windows in it.

Stillingfleet said, "Funny room for a rich man to choose as his own sanctum, with that outlook. It's like looking out onto a prison wall."

"Yes," said Poirot. He drew his head in and

stared at the expanse of solid brick. "I think," he said, "that that wall is important."

Stillingfleet looked at him curiously. "You mean—psychologically?"

Poirot had moved to the desk. Idly, or so it seemed, he picked up a pair of what are usually called lazy-tongs. He pressed the handles; the tongs shot out to their full length. Delicately, Poirot picked up a burnt match stump with them from beside a chair some feet away and conveyed it carefully to the wastepaper basket.

"When you've finished playing with those things . . ." said Stillingfleet irritably.

Hercule Poirot murmured, "An ingenious invention," and replaced the tongs neatly on the writing-table. Then he asked:

"Where were Mrs. Farley and Miss Farley at the time of the—death?"

"Mrs. Farley was resting in her room on the floor above this. Miss Farley was painting in her studio at the top of the house."

Hercule Poirot drummed idly with his fingers on the table for a minute or two. Then he said:

"I should like to see Miss Farley. Do you think you could ask her to come here for a minute or two?"

"If you like."

Stillingfleet glanced at him curiously, then left the room. In another minute or two the door opened and Joanna Farley came in.

"You do not mind, Mademoiselle, if I ask you a few questions?"

She returned his glance coolly. "Please ask anything you choose."

"Did you know that your father kept a revolver in his desk?"

"No."

"Where were you and your mother—that is to say your stepmother—that is right?"

"Yes, Louise is my father's second wife. She is only eight years older than I am. You were about to say——?"

"Where were you and she on Thursday of last week? That is to say, on Thursday night."

She reflected for a minute or two.

"Thursday? Let me see. Oh, yes, we had gone to the theatre. To see *Little Dog Laughed*."

"Your father did not suggest accompanying you?"

"He never went out to theatres."

"What did he usually do in the evenings?"

"He sat in here and read."

"He was not a very sociable man?"

The girl looked at him directly. "My father," she said, "had a singularly unpleasant personality. No one who lived in close association with him could possibly be fond of him."

"That, Mademoiselle, is a very candid statement."

"I am saving you time, M. Poirot. I realise quite well what you are getting at. My stepmother married my father for his money. I live here because I have no money to live elsewhere. There is a man I wish to marry—a poor man; my father saw to it that he lost his job. He wanted me, you see, to marry well—an easy matter since I was to be his heiress!"

"Your father's fortune passes to you?"

"Yes. That is, he left Louise, my stepmother, a quarter of a million free of tax, and there are other legacies, but the residue goes to me." She smiled suddenly. "So you see, M. Poirot, I had every reason to desire my father's death!"

"I see, Mademoiselle, that you have inherited your father's intelligence."

She said thoughtfully, "Father was clever. . . . One felt that with him—that he had force—driving power—but it had all turned sour—bitter—there was no humanity left. . . ."

Hercule Poirot said softly, "*Grand Dieu,* but what an imbecile I am. . . ."

Joanna Farley turned towards the door. "Is there anything more?"

"Two little questions. These tongs here," he picked up the lazy-tongs, "were they always on the table?"

"Yes. Father used them for picking up things. He didn't like stooping."

"One other question. Was your father's eyesight good?"

She stared at him.

"Oh, no—he couldn't see at all—I mean he couldn't see without his glasses. His sight had always been bad from a boy."

"But with his glasses?"

"Oh, he could see all right then, of course."

"He could read newspapers and fine print?"

"Oh, yes."

"That is all, Mademoiselle."

She went out of the room.

Poirot murmured, "I was stupid. It was there, all the time, under my nose. And because it was so near I could not see it."

He leaned out of the window once more. Down below, in the narrow way between the house and the factory, he saw a small dark object.

Hercule Poirot nodded, satisfied, and went downstairs again.

The others were still in the library. Poirot addressed himself to the secretary:

"I want you, Mr. Cornworthy, to recount to me in detail the exact circumstances of Mr. Farley's summons to me. When, for instance, did Mr. Farley dictate that letter?"

"On Wednesday afternoon—at five-thirty, as far as I can remember."

"Were there any special directions about posting it?"

"He told me to post it myself."

"And you did so?"

"Yes."

"Did he give any special instructions to the butler about admitting me?"

"Yes. He told me to tell Holmes (Holmes is the butler) that a gentleman would be calling at nine-thirty. He was to ask the gentleman's name. He was also to ask to see the letter."

"Rather peculiar precautions to take, don't you think?"

Cornworthy shrugged his shoulders.

"Mr. Farley," he said carefully, "was rather a peculiar man."

"Any other instructions?"

"Yes. He told me to take the evening off."

"Did you do so?"

"Yes, immediately after dinner I went to the cinema."

"When did you return?"

"I let myself in about a quarter past eleven."

"Did you see Mr. Farley again that evening?"

"No."

"And he did not mention the matter the next morning?"

"No."

Poirot paused a moment, then resumed, "When I arrived I was not shown into Mr. Farley's own room."

"No. He told me that I was to tell Holmes to show you into my room."

"Why was that? Do you know?"

Cornworthy shook his head. "I never questioned any of Mr. Farley's orders," he said drily. "He would have resented it if I had."

"Did he usually receive visitors in his own room?"

"Usually, but not always. Sometimes he saw them in my room."

"Was there any reason for that?"

Hugo Cornworthy considered.

"No—I hardly think so—I've never really thought about it."

Turning to Mrs. Farley, Poirot asked:

"You permit that I ring for your butler?"

"Certainly, M. Poirot."

Very correct, very urbane, Holmes answered the bell.

"You rang, madam?"

Mrs. Farley indicated Poirot with a gesture. Holmes turned politely. "Yes, sir?"

"What were your instructions, Holmes, on the Thursday night when I came here?"

Holmes cleared his throat, then said:

"After dinner Mr. Cornworthy told me that Mr. Farley expected a Mr. Hercule Poirot at nine-thirty. I was to ascertain the gentleman's name, and I was to verify the information by glancing at a letter. Then I was to show him up to Mr. Cornworthy's room."

"Were you also told to knock on the door?"

An expression of distaste crossed the butler's countenance.

"That was one of Mr. Farley's orders. I was

always to knock when introducing visitors—business visitors, that is," he added.

"Ah, that puzzled me! Were you given any other instructions concerning me?"

"No, sir. When Mr. Cornworthy had told me what I have just repeated to you he went out."

"What time was that?"

"Ten minutes to nine, sir."

"Did you see Mr. Farley after that?"

"Yes, sir, I took him up a glass of hot water as usual at nine o'clock."

"Was he then in his own room or in Mr. Cornworthy's?"

"He was in his own room, sir."

"You noticed nothing unusual about that room?"

"Unusual? No, sir."

"Where were Mrs. Farley and Miss Farley?"

"They had gone to the theatre, sir."

"Thank you, Holmes, that will do."

Holmes bowed and left the room. Poirot turned to the millionaire's widow.

"One more question, Mrs. Farley. Had your husband good sight?"

"No. Not without his glasses."

"He was very short-sighted?"

"Oh, yes, he was quite helpless without his spectacles."

"He had several pairs of glasses?"

"Yes."

"Ah," said Poirot. He leaned back. "I think that that concludes the case. . . ."

There was silence in the room. They were all looking at the little man who sat there complacently stroking his moustache. On the inspector's face was perplexity, Dr. Stillingfleet was frowning, Cornworthy merely stared uncomprehendingly, Mrs. Farley gazed in blank astonishment, Joanna Farley looked eager.

Mrs. Farley broke the silence.

"I don't understand, M. Poirot." Her voice was fretful. "The dream——"

"Yes," said Poirot. "That dream was very important."

Mrs. Farley shivered. She said:

"I've never believed in anything supernatural before—but now—to dream it night after night beforehand——"

"It's extraordinary," said Stillingfleet. "Extraordinary! If we hadn't got your word for it, Poirot, and if you hadn't had it straight from the horse's mouth——" he coughed in embarrassment, and readopting his professional manner, "I beg your pardon, Mrs. Farley. If Mr. Farley himself had not told that story——"

"Exactly," said Poirot. His eyes, which had been half-closed, opened suddenly. They were very green. *"If Benedict Farley hadn't told me——"*

He paused a minute, looking round at a circle of blank faces.

"There are certain things, you comprehend, that happened that evening which I was quite at a loss to explain. First, why make such a point of my bringing that letter with me?"

"Identification," suggested Cornworthy.

"No, no, my dear young man. Really that idea is too ridiculous. There must be some much more valid reason. For not only did Mr. Farley require to see that letter produced, but he definitely demanded that I should leave it behind me. And moreover even then he did not destroy it! It was found among his papers this afternoon. *Why did he keep it?"*

Joanna Farley's voice broke in. "He wanted, in case anything happened to him, that the facts of his strange dream should be made known."

Poirot nodded approvingly.

"You are astute, Mademoiselle. That must be—that can only be—the point of the keeping of the letter. When Mr. Farley was dead, the story of that strange dream was to be told! That dream was very important. That dream, Mademoiselle, was *vital*!"

"I will come now," he went on, "to the second point. After hearing his story I ask Mr. Farley to show me the desk and the revolver. He seems about to get up to do so, then suddenly refuses. Why did he refuse?"

This time no one advanced an answer.

"I will put that question differently. *What*

was there in that next room that Mr. Farley did not want me to see?"

There was still silence.

"Yes," said Poirot, "it is difficult, that. And yet there was some reason—some *urgent* reason why Mr. Farley received me in his secretary's room and refused point blank to take me into his own room. *There was something in that room he could not afford to have me see.*

"And now I come to the third inexplicable thing that happened on that evening. Mr. Farley, just as I was leaving, requested me to hand him the letter I had received. By inadvertence I handed him a communication from my laundress. He glanced at it and laid it down beside him. Just before I left the room I discovered my error—and rectified it! After that I left the house and—I admit it—I was completely at sea! The whole affair and especially that last incident seemed to me quite inexplicable."

He looked round from one to the other.

"You do not see?"

Stillingfleet said, "I don't really see how your laundress comes into it, Poirot."

"My laundress," said Poirot, "was very important. That miserable woman who ruins my collars, was, for the first time in her life, useful to somebody. Surely you see—it is so obvious. Mr. Farley glanced at that communication—*one glance* would have told him that it was the wrong letter—and yet he knew nothing. Why? *Because he could not see it properly!*"

Inspector Barnett said sharply, "Didn't he have his glasses on?"

Hercule Poirot smiled. "Yes," he said. "He had his glasses on. That is what makes it so very interesting."

He leaned forward.

"Mr. Farley's dream was very important. He dreamed, you see, that he committed suicide. And a little later on, he did commit suicide. That is to say he was alone in a room and was found there with a revolver by him, and no one entered or left the room at the time that he was shot. What does that mean? It means, does it not, that it *must* be suicide!"

"Yes," said Stillingfleet.

Hercule Poirot shook his head.

"On the contrary," he said. "It was murder. An unusual and a very cleverly planned murder."

Again he leaned forward, tapping the table, his eyes green and shining.

"Why did Mr. Farley not allow me to go into his own room that evening? What was there in there that I must not be allowed to see? I think, my friends, that there was—Benedict Farley himself!"

He smiled at the blank faces.

"Yes, yes, it is not nonsense what I say. Why could the Mr. Farley to whom I had been talking not realise the difference between two totally dissimilar letters? Because, *mes amis,* he was a man of *normal sight* wearing a pair of very powerful glasses. Those glasses would render a man of normal eyesight practically blind. Isn't that so, Doctor?"

Stillingfleet murmured, "That's so—of course."

"Why did I feel that in talking to Mr. Farley I was talking to a *mountebank,* to an actor playing a part! Consider the setting. The dim room, the green-shaded light turned blindingly away from the figure in the chair. What did I see—the famous patchwork dressing-gown, the beaked nose (faked with that useful substance, nose putty) the white crest of hair, the powerful lenses concealing the eyes. What evidence is there that Mr. Farley ever had a dream? Only the story I was told and the evidence of *Mrs. Farley.* What evidence is there that Benedict Farley kept a revolver in his desk? Again only the story told me and the word of Mrs. Farley. Two people carried this fraud through—Mrs. Farley and Hugo Cornworthy. Cornworthy wrote the letter to me, gave instructions to the butler, went out ostensibly to the cinema, but let himself in again immediately with a key, went to his room, made himself up, and played the part of Benedict Farley.

"And so we come to this afternoon. The opportunity for which Mr. Cornworthy has been waiting arrives. There are two witnesses on the landing to swear that no one goes in or out of Benedict Farley's room. Cornworthy waits until a particularly heavy batch of traffic is about to pass. Then he leans out of his window, and with the lazy-tongs which he has purloined from the desk next door he holds an object against the window of that room. Benedict Farley comes to the window. Cornworthy snatches back the tongs and as Farley leans out, and the lorries are passing outside, Cornworthy shoots him with the revolver that he has ready. There is a blank wall opposite, remember. There can be no witness of the crime. Cornworthy waits for over half an hour, then gathers up some papers, conceals the lazy-tongs and the revolver between them and goes out onto the landing and into the next room. He replaces the tongs on the desk, lays down the revolver after pressing the dead man's fingers on it, and hurries out with the news of Mr. Farley's 'suicide.'

"He arranges that the letter to me shall be found and that I shall arrive with my story—the story I heard *from Mr. Farley's own lips*—of his extraordinary 'dream'—the strange compulsion he felt to kill himself! A few credulous people will discuss the hypnotism theory—but the main result will be to confirm without a doubt that the actual hand that held the revolver was Benedict Farley's own."

Hercule Poirot's eyes went to the widow's face—he noted with satisfaction the dismay—the ashy pallor—the blind fear. . . .

"And in due course," he finished gently, "the happy ending would have been achieved. A quarter of a million and two hearts that beat as one. . . ."

John Stillingfleet, M.D., and Hercule Poirot walked along the side of Northway House. On their right was the towering wall of the factory. Above them, on their left, were the windows of Benedict Farley's and Hugo Cornworthy's rooms. Hercule Poirot stopped and picked up a small object—a black stuffed cat.

"*Voilà*," he said. "That is what Cornworthy held in the lazy-tongs against Farley's window. You remember, he hated cats? Naturally he rushed to the window."

"Why on earth didn't Cornworthy come out and pick it up after he'd dropped it?"

"How could he? To do so would have been definitely suspicious. After all, if this object were found what would anyone think—that some child had wandered round here and dropped it."

"Yes," said Stillingfleet with a sigh. "That's probably what the ordinary person *would* have thought. But not good old Hercule! D'you know, old horse, up to the very last minute I thought you were leading up to some subtle theory of highfalutin psychological 'suggested' murder? I bet those two thought so too! Nasty bit of goods, the Farley. Goodness, how she cracked! Cornworthy might have got away with it if she hadn't had hysterics and tried to spoil your beauty by going for you with her nails. I only got her off you just in time."

He paused a minute and then said:

"I rather like the girl. Grit, you know, and brains. I suppose I'd be thought to be a fortune hunter if I had a shot at her . . . ?"

"You are too late, my friend. There is already someone *sur le tapis*. Her father's death has opened the way to happiness."

"Take it all round, *she* had a pretty good motive for bumping off the unpleasant parent."

"Motive and opportunity are not enough," said Poirot. "There must also be the criminal temperament!"

"I wonder if you'll ever commit a crime, Poirot?" said Stillingfleet. "I bet you could get away with it all right. As a matter of fact, it would be *too* easy for you—I mean the thing would be off as definitely too unsporting."

"That," said Poirot, "is a typical English idea."

THE BORDER-LINE CASE
MARGERY ALLINGHAM

IT IS NOT SURPRISING THAT, coming from a family prominent in English literary circles, Margery Allingham (1904–1966) took to writing at an early age, beginning at age seven and publishing her first book, *Black'erchief Dick* (1923), an adventure novel about piracy and smuggling on the Essex salt marshes, while still a teenager. Her career as a mystery writer began soon after her marriage to Youngman Carter, an artist and editor of *The Tatler* magazine. The same age as his wife, the teenager designed the cover of her first book and became her lifelong literary advisor and unofficial collaborator. While her earliest mysteries are fast-moving adventure stories with considerable physical activity, her series character, Albert Campion, becomes involved in more cerebral cases as his busy career as an amateur sleuth progresses. Early on, he is described as "a silly ass" and says of himself that he is a con man who will do anything for a price, provided it is not vulgar or sordid, though this does not appear to be true as there is no evidence that he has ever done anything illegal. His eternally brave valet, the Cockney Magersfontein Lugg, is a former burglar and Borstal inmate who has cleaned up his act and is a loyal and invaluable aide in solving crimes and helping thwart espionage plots against England. Allingham wrote more than two dozen books about Campion, the last of which, *Cargo of Eagles* (1968), was completed by Carter, who went on to write two additional novels about the intrepid detective. The most famous books about Campion are *Death of a Ghost* (1934) and *The Tiger in the Smoke* (1952), which was filmed in 1956 by the Rank Organisation, though the character does not appear in the film.

"The Border-Line Case" was first published in *Mr. Campion: Criminologist* (Garden City, New York, Doubleday, 1937).

THE BORDER-LINE CASE

MARGERY ALLINGHAM

IT WAS SO HOT in London that night that we slept with the wide skylight in our city studio open and let the sootblacks fall in on us willingly, so long as they brought with them a single stirring breath to move the stifling air. Heat hung on the dark horizons and beneath our particular bowl of sky the city fidgeted, breathless and uncomfortable.

The early editions of the evening papers carried the story of the murder. I read it when they came along about three o'clock on the following afternoon. My mind took in the details lazily, for my eyelids were sticky and the printed words seemed remote and unrelated to reality.

It was a straightforward little incident, or so I thought it, and when I had read the guarded half-column I threw the paper over to Albert Campion, who had drifted in to lunch and stayed to sit quietly in a corner, blinking behind his spectacles, existing merely, in the sweltering day.

The newspapers called the murder "The Coal Court Shooting Case," and the facts were simple.

At one o'clock in the morning, when Vacation Street, N.E., had been a deserted lane of odoriferous heat, a policeman on the beat had seen a man stumble and fall to the pavement. The intense discomfort of the night being uppermost in his mind, he had not unnaturally diagnosed a case of ordinary collapse and, after loosening the stranger's collar, had summoned the ambulance. When the authorities arrived, however, the man was pronounced to be dead and the body was taken to the mortuary, where it was discovered that death had been due to a bullet wound neatly placed between the shoulder blades. The bullet had made a small blue hole and, after perforating the left lung, had furrowed the heart itself, finally coming to rest in the bony structure of the chest.

Since this was so, and the fact that the police constable had heard no untoward sound, it had been reasonable to believe that the shot had been fired at some little distance from a gun with a silencer.

Mr. Campion was only politely interested. The afternoon certainly was hot and the story as it then appeared was hardly original or exciting. He sat on the floor reading it patiently, his long thin legs stretched out in front of him.

"Someone died at any rate," he remarked at last and added after a pause: "Poor chap! Out of the frying pan . . . Dear me, I suppose it's the locality which predisposes one to think of that. Ever seen Vacation Street, Margery?"

I did not answer him. I was thinking how odd it was that a general irritant like the heat should make the dozens of situations arising all round one in the great city seem suddenly almost personal. I found I was desperately sorry for the man who had been shot, whoever he was.

It was Stanislaus Oates who told us the real story behind the half-column in the evening paper. He came in just after four looking for

Campion. He was a detective inspector in those days and had just begun to develop the habit of chatting over his problems with the pale young man in the horn-rimmed spectacles. Theirs was an odd relationship. It was certainly not a case of the clever amateur and the humble policeman: rather the irritable and pugnacious policeman taking it out of the inoffensive, friendly representative of the general public.

On this occasion Oates was rattled.

"It's a case right down your street," he said briefly to Campion as he sat down. "Seems to be a miracle, for one thing."

He explained after a while, having salved his conscience by pointing out that he had no business to discuss the case and excusing himself most illogically on grounds of the heat.

"It's 'low-class' crime," he went on briskly. "Practically gang shooting. And probably quite uninteresting to all of you, who like romance in your crimes. However, it's got me right down on two counts: the first because the man who shot the fellow who died couldn't possibly have done so, and second because I was wrong about the girl. They're so true to type, these girls, that you can't even rely on the proverbial exception."

He sighed as if the discovery had really grieved him.

We heard the story of Josephine as we sat round in the paralysingly hot studio and, although I never saw the girl then or afterwards, I shall not forget the scene; the two of us listening, breathing rather heavily, while the inspector talked.

She had been Donovan's girl, so Oates said, and he painted a picture of her for us: slender and flat-chested, with black hair and eyes like a Russian madonna's in a transparent face. She wore blouses, he said, with lace on them and gold ornaments, little chains and crosses and frail brooches whose security was reinforced by gilt safety pins. She was only twenty, Oates said, and added enigmatically that he would have betted on her but that it served him right and showed him there was no fool like an old one.

He went on to talk about Donovan, who, it seemed, was thirty-five and had spent ten years of his life in jail. The inspector did not seem to think any the less of him for that. The fact seemed to put the man in a definite category in his mind and that was all.

"Robbery with violence and the R.O. boys," he said with a wave of his hand and smiled contentedly as though he had made everything clear. "She was sixteen when he found her and he's given her hell ever since."

While he still held our interest he mentioned Johnny Gilchick. Johnny Gilchick was the man who was dead.

Oates, who was never more sentimental than was strictly reasonable in the circumstances, let himself go about Josephine and Johnny Gilchick. It was love, he said—love, sudden, painful and ludicrous; and he admitted that he liked to see it.

"I had an aunt once who used to talk about the Real Thing," he explained, "and embarrassingly silly the old lady sounded, but after seeing those two youngsters meet and flame and go on until they were a single fiery entity—youngsters who were pretty ordinary tawdry material without it—I find myself sympathising with her if not condoning the phrase."

He hesitated and his smooth grey face cracked into a depreciating smile.

"Well, we were both wrong, anyway," he murmured, "my aunt and I. Josephine let her Johnny down just as you'd expect her to and after he got what was coming to him and was lying in the mortuary he was born to lie in she upped and perjured her immortal soul to swear his murderer an alibi. Not that her testimony is of much value as evidence. That's beside the point. The fact remains that she's certainly done her best. You may think me sentimental, but it depresses me. I thought that girl was genuine and my judgment was out."

Mr. Campion stirred.

"Could we have the details?" he asked politely. "We've only seen the evening paper. It wasn't very helpful."

Oates glared at him balefully.

"Frankly, the facts are exasperating," he said. "There's a little catch in them somewhere. It must be something so simple that I missed it altogether. That's really why I've come to look for you. I thought you might care to come along and take a glance at the place. What about it?"

There was no general movement. It was too hot to stir. Finally the inspector took up a piece of chalk and sketched a rough diagram on the bare boards of the model's throne.

"This is Vacation Street," he said, edging the chalk along a crack. "It's the best part of a mile long. Up this end, here by the chair, it's nearly all wholesale houses. This sand bin I'm sketching in now marks the boundary of two police divisions. We'll take that as the starting point. Well, here, ten yards to the left, is the entrance to Coal Court, which is a cul-de-sac composed of two blank backs of warehouse buildings and a café at the far end. The café is open all night. It serves the printers from the two big presses further down the road. That's its legitimate trade. But it is also a sort of unofficial headquarters for Donovan's mob. Josephine sits at the desk downstairs and keeps an eye on the door. God knows what hours she keeps. She always seems to be there."

He paused and there came into my mind a recollection of the breathless night through which we had all passed, and I could imagine the girl sitting there in the stuffy shop with her thin chest and her great black eyes.

The inspector was still speaking.

"Now," he said, "there's an upstairs room in the café. It's on the second floor. That's where our friend Donovan spent most of his evening. I expect he had a good few friends with him and we shall locate them all in time."

He bent over the diagram.

"Johnny Gilchick died here," he said, drawing a circle about a foot beyond the square which indicated the sand bin. "Although the bobby was right down the road, he saw him pause under the lamppost, stagger and fall. He called the constable from the other division and they got the ambulance. All that is plain sailing. There's

just one difficulty. Where was Donovan when he fired the shot? There were two policemen in the street at the time, remember. At the moment of the actual shooting one of them, the Never Street man, was making a round of a warehouse yard, but the other, the Phyllis Court chap, was there on the spot, not forty yards away, and it was he who actually saw Johnny Gilchick fall, although he heard no shot. Now I tell you, Campion, there's not an ounce of cover in the whole of that street. How did Donovan get out of the café, where did he stand to shoot Johnny neatly through the back, and how did he get back again without being seen? The side walls of the cul-de-sac are solid concrete backs of warehouses, there is no way round from the back of the café, nor could he possibly have gone over the roofs. The warehouses tower over the café like liners over a tug. Had he come out down the road one or other of the bobbies must have been certain to have seen him. How did he do it?"

"Perhaps Donovan didn't do it," I ventured and received a pitying glance for my temerity.

"That's the one fact," said the inspector heavily. "That's the only thing I do know. I know Donovan. He's one of the few English mob boys who carry guns. He served five years with the gangs in New York before Repeal and he has the misfortune to take his liquor in bouts. After each bout he has a period of black depression, during which he may do anything. Johnny Gilchick used to be one of Donovan's mob and when Johnny fell for the girl he turned in the gang, which was adding insult to injury where Donovan was concerned."

He paused and smiled.

"Donovan was bound to get Johnny in the end," he said. "It was never anything but a question of time. The whole mob expected it. The neighbourhood was waiting for it. Donovan had said openly that the next time Johnny dropped into the café would be his final appearance there. Johnny called last night, was ordered out of the place by the terrified girl, and finally walked out of the cul-de-sac. He turned the corner and strolled down the road. Then he was shot by

Donovan. There's no way round it, Campion. The doctors say that death was as near instantaneous as may be. Johnny Gilchick could not have walked three paces with that bullet in his back. As for the gun, that was pretty obviously Donovan's too. We haven't actually picked it up yet, but we know he had one of the type we are after. It's a clear case, a straightforward case, if only we knew where Donovan stood when he fired the shot."

Mr. Campion looked up. His eyes were thoughtful behind his spectacles.

"The girl gave Donovan an alibi?" he enquired.

Oates shrugged his shoulders. "Rather," he said. "She was passionate about it. He was there the whole time, every minute of the time, never left the upper room once in the whole evening. I could kill her and she would not alter her story; she'd take her dying oath on it and so on and so on. It didn't mean anything either way. Still, I was sorry to see her doing it, with her boy friend barely cold. She was sucking up to the mob, of course; probably had excellent reasons for doing so. Yet, as I say, I was sorry to hear her volunteering the alibi before she was asked."

"Ah! She volunteered it, did she?" Campion was interested.

Oates nodded and his small grey eyes widened expressively.

"Forced it on us. Came roaring round to the police station with it. Threw it off her chest as if she were doing something fine. I'm not usually squeamish about that sort of thing but it gave me a distinct sense of distaste, I don't mind telling you. Frankly, I gave her a piece of my mind. Told her to go and look at the body, for one thing."

"Not kind of you," observed Mr. Campion mildly. "And what did she do?"

"Oh, blubbered herself sick, like the rest of 'em." Oates was still disgruntled. "Still, that's not of interest. What girls like Josephine do or don't do doesn't really matter. She was saving her own skin. If she hadn't been so enthusiastic about it I'd have forgiven her. It's Donovan who is important. Where was Donovan when he fired?"

The shrill chatter of the telephone answered him and he glanced at me apologetically.

"I'm afraid that's mine," he said. "You didn't mind, did you? I left the number with the sergeant."

He took off the receiver and as he bent his head to listen his face changed. We watched him with an interest it was far too hot to dissemble.

"Oh," he said flatly after a long pause. "Really? Well, it doesn't matter either way, does it? . . . Still, what did she do it for? . . . What? . . . I suppose so. . . . Yes? . . . Really?"

He seemed suddenly astounded as his informant at the other end of the wire evidently came out with a second piece of information more important than the first.

"You can't be certain . . . you are? . . . What?"

The faraway voice explained busily. We could hear its steady drone. Inspector Oates's exasperation grew.

"Oh all right, all right," he said at last. "I'm crackers . . . we're all crackers . . . have it your own damned way!"

With which vulgar outburst he rang off.

"Alibi sustained?" enquired Mr. Campion.

"Yes." The inspector grunted out the word. "A couple of printers who were in the downstairs room swear he did not go through the shop all the evening. They're sound fellows. Make good witnesses. Yet Donovan shot Johnny. I'm certain of it. He shot him clean through the concrete angle of a piano warehouse as far as I can see." He turned to Campion almost angrily. "Explain that, can you?"

Mr. Campion coughed. He seemed a little embarrassed.

"I say, you know," he ventured, "there are just two things that occur to me."

"Then out with them, son." The inspector lit a cigarette and wiped his face. "Out with them. I'm not proud."

Mr. Campion coughed. "Well, the—er—heat, for one thing, don't you know," he said with profound uneasiness. "The heat, and one of your concrete walls."

The inspector swore a little and apologised.

"If anyone could forget this heat he's welcome," he said. "What's the matter with the wall too?"

Mr. Campion bent over the diagram on the boards of the throne. He was very apologetic.

"Here is the angle of the warehouse," he said, "and here is the sand bin. Here to the left is the lamppost where Johnny Gilchick was found. Further on to the left is the P.C. from Never Street examining a courtyard and temporarily off the scene, while to the right, on the other side of the entrance to Coal Court, is another constable, P.C. someone-or-other, of Phyllis Court. One is apt to—er—think of the problem as though it were contained in four solid walls, two concrete walls, two policemen."

He hesitated and glanced timidly at the inspector.

"When is a policeman not a concrete wall, Oates? In—er—well, in just such heat . . . do you think, or don't you?"

Oates was staring at him, his eyes narrowed.

"Damn it!" he said explosively. "Damn it, Campion, I believe you're right. I knew it was something so simple that it was staring me in the face."

They stood together looking down at the diagram. Oates stooped to put a chalk cross at the entrance to the cul-de-sac.

"It was *that* lamppost," he said. "Give me that telephone. Wait till I get hold of that fellow."

While he was carrying on an excited conversation we demanded an explanation from Mr. Campion and he gave it to us at last, mild and apologetic as usual.

"Well, you see," he said, "there's the sand bin. The sand bin marks the boundary of two police divisions. Policeman A, very hot and tired, sees a man collapse from the heat under a lamppost on his own territory. The man is a little fellow and it occurs to Policeman A that it would be a simple matter to move him to the next lamppost on the other side of the sand bin, where he would automatically become the responsibility of Policeman B, who is even now approaching. Policeman A achieves the change and is bending over the prostrate figure when his colleague comes up. Since he knows nothing of the bullet wound, the entrance to the cul-de-sac, with its clear view to the café second-floor room, has no significance in his mind. Today, when its full importance must have dawned upon him, he evidently thinks it best to hold his tongue."

Oates came back from the phone triumphant.

"The first bobby went on leave this morning," he said. "He was an old hand. He must have spotted the chap was dead, took it for granted it was the heat, and didn't want to be held up here by the inquest. Funny I didn't see that in the beginning."

We were all silent for some moments.

"Then—the girl?" I began at last.

The inspector frowned and made a little grimace of regret.

"A pity about the girl," he said. "Of course it was probably an accident. Our man who saw it happen said he couldn't be sure."

I stared at him and he explained, albeit a little hurriedly.

"Didn't I tell you? When my sergeant phoned about the alibi he told me. As Josephine crossed the road after visiting the mortuary this morning she stepped under a bus. . . . Oh yes, instantly."

He shook his head. He seemed uncomfortable.

"She thought she was making a gesture when she came down to the station, don't you see? The mob must have told her to swear that no one had been in the upstairs room; that must have been their first story until they saw how the luck lay. So when she came beetling down to us she must have thought she was risking her life to give her Johnny's murderer away, while instead of that she was simply giving the fellow an alibi. . . . Funny the way things happen, isn't it?"

He glanced at Campion affectionately.

"It's because you don't get your mind cluttered up with the human element that you see these things so quickly," he said. "You see everything in terms of A and B. It makes all the difference."

Mr. Campion, the most gentle of men, made no comment at all.

THE BRADMOOR MURDER
MELVILLE DAVISSON POST

THE QUINTESSENTIALLY American mystery writer Melville Davisson Post (1869–1930), born in West Virginia and a graduate of West Virginia University, who went on to practice law and engage in Democratic politics, surprisingly set many of his stories in England. Sir Henry Marquis, chief of the Criminal Investigation Department of Scotland Yard, appears in *The Sleuth of St. James's Square* (1920) and *The Bradmoor Murder* (1929). A middle-aged Englishman who seems more like an outdoorsman than a policeman, he is a Londoner who directs secret service operations in many faraway places, including Asia and the United States.

The first mysteries by the inventive Post feature Randolph Mason, an unscrupulous lawyer whose last name was given to an honest one by Erle Stanley Gardner when he created Perry Mason. Post's brilliant innovation gave a fresh look to crime stories. In the past, crooks had been concerned mainly with eluding capture but, in the hands of Randolph Mason, the focus is on avoiding punishment. Since the law is quite specific about what it defines as a crime, Mason finds tiny exceptions and gets his client off. Since Mason's cases are all based on actual legal loopholes, moralists feared that Post's stories would serve as handbooks for the villainous. For example, in "The Corpus Delecti," the first story in the first Mason collection, *The Strange Schemes of Randolph Mason* (1896), Mason tells his client that the only solution to his problem is for him to kill his wife. The story, and others that followed, spurred much-needed changes in criminal prosecution.

"The Bradmoor Murder" was first published as a three-part serial in *The Pictorial Review* in 1922; it was first collected in *The Bradmoor Murder* (New York, Sears, 1929); it was titled *The Garden in Asia* in England.

THE BRADMOOR MURDER

MELVILLE DAVISSON POST

"His right hand shall be his enemy. And the son of another shall sit in his seat. I will encourage his right hand to destroy him. And I will bring the unborn through the Gate of Life. And they shall lean upon me. And I will enrich them, and guide their feet and strengthen their hearts. And they shall laugh in his gardens, and sit down in his pleasant palaces."

I

THE NOTE

WE GOT SOME great men from England in the old day. They don't permit us to forget it. . . . Well, we can counter on them. They got Robert Harmscourt, the present Duke of Bradmoor, from us. And he is to-day beyond question, the ablest man in the British Empire. They can say that this American family is only the English branch, and cite their court decision giving it the title, should the English line become extinct. But it won't do! The man's an American. And he would have remained an American but for the will of a god. No, the expression is correctly written: not the will of God as we are accustomed to say it—the will of a god! Keep the distinction in mind.

And it wasn't Lady Joan! True, she sent for him at once, after old Bradmoor's death, and assembled at her table the three remarkable men concerned with the mystery. But it wasn't Lady Joan that transformed this American into a peer of England. She'd have gone to America with

Harmscourt—she'd already promised. . . . You can't doubt it. It wasn't Lady Joan: *it was the will of a god!*

You can read what Harmscourt says about it. It's the very strangest thing that was ever printed.

THE NARRATIVE

The very dining room was extraordinary.

The walls were of bare stone, and the floor had originally been the tamped earthen floor of the cottage. There was a wide, smoked fireplace, and an ancient beamed ceiling.

But the room had been made over by a deft hand.

It was a transformation with a slight expenditure of material; but it was that tremendous transformation which an excellent taste is able to accomplish with even primitive material. The ceiling had been permitted to remain; but the walls had been covered with a blue-gray wash—some dye, I imagine, with a calcimine. An iron grate had been set in the fireplace, and a board floor laid. It was a floor scarcely better than the wood platform of a tent; but one saw little of it,

709

for it was covered with old rugs—ancient, price-less rugs.

There was an immense mahogany table, a long mahogany sideboard against the wall, with silver knobs, their exterior presenting laurel wreaths inclosing a coat-of-arms carved in relief. The chairs were carved rosewood. There was no cloth on this table; but there was a gorgeous piece of brocade laid right across it, in the center of which was an immense bowl filled with roses. The silver, the glass, every article on the table was exquisite. It was the contrast between these superb furnishings and the crude room that impressed one, as though one should find a jewel mounted in the hull of an acorn.

For a moment the small-talk drifted vaguely by me. I was looking at the empty chair beyond, across the table. It was drawn back, and half-turned away, precisely as the girl had left it when she got up and went out, leaving me to her extraordinary guests, and their strange mission.

Extraordinary is not a word inapplicable to them. I think if one had looked over all England, he could not have selected three men to whom that word would more appropriately apply.

To my right was Henry Marquis, Chief of the Criminal Investigation Department of Scotland Yard. When one says that long, awkward sentence—with "Scotland Yard" at the end of it—one brings up the image of a conventional character in the penny-dreadfuls, or the hatchet-faced detective of Baker Street, with his hypo-dermic needle; a thin, lemon-colored person, with dreamy eyes, and the like. But—one would not look to see Henry Marquis.

A middle-aged Englishman, with short-cropped gray hair, and the typical figure in the hunting field. There was nothing peculiar about him except his rather long, pale face, and the strong formation of the jaw. One felt that it would be difficult to prevent this man from carrying out any plan upon which he had once determined. But—one would not associate him with mysteries.

If one had been selecting a character to illus-trate a personality concerned with mysteries, he would have selected Sir Godfrey Simon, who was sitting farther along to the right of the chair now empty. He was a big, old man. His head was entirely bald; there was not even a faint sugges-tion of a fringe of hair around the bald head.

The head was immense.

He had a large, crooked nose; shaggy eye-brows; eyes that seemed never open—they were always slits—narrow, like a cat's eyes; and a big, firm-lipped mouth. He looked like a sphinx. He was the greatest alienist in England. He spoke just then:

"The man was under a curse," he said; "that's what killed him!"

I realized suddenly that the conversation had drifted into the thing that these men had been asked here to explain to me. It had begun, and I had missed a little of it. I moved in the chair, and brought my attention swiftly back from the girl who had gone out.

The third man, seated at my left, had half turned to the fire. He had poured out another glass of whisky. When I try to describe this man, I am always embarrassed. Nature took an unrea-sonable advantage of him. He was the Thirteenth Earl of Dunn, and he looked like a bookmaker at Ascot, in the paddock with the sporting set.

No clothes could disguise it.

He was in the best evening clothes that one could buy in Bond Street; but he was the book-maker from Ascot, awkwardly put into them. He was one of the most charming men in England; but there he was, with his coarse shock of hair, his red face, his heavy jaw, his large, harsh voice, and his abrupt, physical vigor. He was a big-game hunter, and one of the most noted explor-ers in the world. . . . He used to say: "There's six million square miles of the earth's surface that nobody knows anything about"—then would come his harsh laugh—"except me."

He was replying now to the oracular pro-nouncement of Sir Godfrey Simon.

"A curse, eh! What?" he said. "It was charac-teristic of you, Simon, to sit perfectly still, like a joss, blink your eyes, and say the man was killed by a curse, when the thing happened. It would have been reasonable if you had meant that the outraged divinity, or hell-factor, or whatever you wish to call it, that old Bradmoor looted, had found a way to turn on him; but that was not what you meant."

Sir Godfrey *did* blink his eyes. They batted an instant. He added another sentence:

"I meant, of course, precisely what I said."

Henry Marquis took the conversation up then. He realized that I did not understand it, that it would have to be presented from the beginning. He touched the polished mahogany table with his fingers, as though they were smoothing out a cloth.

"I think," he said, "that you will get a more accurate understanding of this thing if we give it to you precisely as it impressed us at the time it happened: the facts, and then what we thought about them—what we still think about them. . . . You will probably have to imagine what Sir Godfrey Simon means, if he means anything."

He laughed, and his firm, capable hand continued to smooth out the invisible cloth on the table. There came a slight, facetious note in his voice.

"I suppose, in fact, it is not essential that an alienist should mean anything. It is the pose that counts in his profession. 'The man was killed by a curse!' Sir Godfrey does not need to mean anything, provided he goes no farther. . . . It is a fine, creepy explanation, and it precisely suits the average Briton with the Early Victorian novel in his mind. The lord of the manor was always under a curse, when the beautiful milkmaid got into trouble, in those stories. . . . Is there a family in England that has not a curse on it?"

The big man by the vacant chair spoke again: "This family has a curse on it."

Lord Dunn turned toward me. He made an abrupt gesture, precisely like a bookmaker sweeping aside a betting offer:

"There you have it," he said. "Set a madman to catch a madman; Simon is in the right profession; old Bradmoor was killed by a curse!"

The massive face did not change, but the mouth opened as though worked by a wire: "He was," he said.

Henry Marquis made a vague, abrupt gesture:

"Before we go again into our old quarrel," he said, "our friend here must understand the thing. It is mysterious enough, God knows—the whole awful business—when you understand as much as there is to understand about it."

He turned toward me.

"This is what we found," he said. "It was in the afternoon. It had been very dry—that long, unprecedented drought in England. Then there had been rains in the north; the streams had come up. Fishermen were beginning to get out their tackle; the water would be 'right' that evening. So the thing that old Bradmoor had been concerned with at the moment of his death was precisely what one would have expected. He was a keen sportsman, and next to Dunn, he was the best all-round explorer in the world."

The Earl of Dunn made another of his abrupt, bookmaker gestures:

"Bar nobody," he said, "old Bradmoor was the best explorer in the world, and he was a good man with a rod, none better; but he could not ride a horse. He was a damned poor hunter; he had sense enough to give it up. And he was not a first-class shot. He could handle a heavy gun—a big double express; but he was no good with a magazine rifle. . . . I don't know what killed him, unless it was that damned Baal from the plateau of the Lybian Desert. It's like Dunsany's story of the Gods of the Mountain—green stone Johnnies who finally came in to avenge their imitators. It might be the explanation here. How do we know? A thing does not cease to exist because some one says it isn't so. Would the Old Bailey cease to exist because a little sneak thief in Margate did not believe in it?"

Henry Marquis came back to his narrative:

"What we found," he said, "was this: Old Bradmoor was dead. He had been shot through the chest. It was a shot at the heart, but it had missed it. It was four inches to the right, and a hand's-width high; but the bullet was so big that the man was instantly killed. The bullet had gone through the back of the chair and lodged in the wainscoting. We cut it out, of course; but it was too battered up to say much about the sort of firearm it came out of.

"Old Bradmoor was sitting in the middle of the room.

"He was at least seven feet from the wall in any direction. He was facing a narrow window; in fact, it was a narrow slit cut in the wall. You know the sort of slit they made in the old days for archers. It is perhaps a yard high, and nine inches wide. The stone sloped on either side of the slit on the outside of the wall so that the archers could shoot to the right or left. . . . You know how they are cut, and how the house stands out into the open sea."

He made a gesture toward the fireplace— toward the great house across the road to the south.

I nodded. I knew all about the house, and especially that wing of it. The sea had come sheer in against it. It had tunneled in a deep eddy, against the wall. The dead Duke of Brad- moor had been forced in his time to supple- ment the foundation by putting in another wall straight down to the rock bed of the shore. That stopped the sea current from chiseling out the foundation; but it bored in here against the wall, on its stone floor. There was a sheer wall of fifty feet from the room with the archer's slit, to the open sea.

I understood exactly the description Marquis was giving me. I could see precisely what they had found. He went on making every detail vis- ible.

"Bradmoor was facing this window; his chair was in the center of the room, almost precisely in the center of it. There was very little furni- ture in the room. It was more a sort of storage room where he kept the junk gathered up on his explorations. There were maps on the wall, and a lot of tin boxes about, a theodolite, a compass or two—in fact, the traps an explorer would carry about with him. Bradmoor kept his fishing gear in this room—all sorts of rods, flies and the like.

"As I have said, he was sitting in a chair in the middle of the room, facing this narrow slit

in the wall; he was exactly ten feet away from it, and he was almost an equal distance from the door and the walls in every other direction. He had a fishing rod in his hand—in his right hand. It was tightly clutched in his hand. It was a long, heavy rod, fitted with a reel and line. He had some flies in his left hand; the thumb and finger of his left hand were closed on a partic- ularly bright-colored fly. The man was in the act of attaching this fly to the line. His hat was on the floor beside him, with a number of flies hooked in it. There was a book of flies open on his knee.

"It was perfectly clear that the man had been killed suddenly, without warning, while he sat unconscious of any danger, engaged simply with the selection of a fly.

"The door to the room was locked, and it was bolted on the inside. All the windows in the room were closed, and had not been opened. Not one of them had been opened. We were able to tell this on account of the metal fixtures. They had been turned to hold the windows firmly closed, and they had rusted in that position. The win- dows could not have been opened unless they were turned, and if they had been turned, the rust would have been disturbed.

"We sent an expert down to make sure.

"He went over it very carefully with a glass. It was certain the windows had not been opened. Besides, when we did open them, we were able to do it only with difficulty, because they had remained so long closed.

"The markedly strange thing about the situa- tion, so far as Bradmoor was concerned, was that the door had been so carefully fastened on the inside. Of course, whatever it was that ejected Bradmoor out of life may thus have fastened the door. But if so, how did it get out of the room? The bolt does not connect with the lock. It is at least two feet above the lock. It is a heavy oak door. The hinges were sound—the door had not been tampered with; the lock was right, and solid. The door had simply been strongly secured on the inside, and that was all there was about it. The key was in the lock on the inside.

"There was no way to get into this room, or to get out of it.

"The walls were all solid. It is true that the walls were wainscoted, paneled in heavy oak; but there was no chance of a secret exit; we took the panels all out, and went over every inch of the floor and ceiling. We could not have been mistaken—there was not any way to get into that room, or out of it, that we could conceive of; and yet here in the center of the room, on this hot afternoon, sat Bradmoor in a chair, shot through the chest—with a fishing rod in one hand, and a bright-colored fly in the other.

"Of course, we took the rod to pieces.

"But it was an absurd thing to do. It was the usual big fishing rod, about twelve feet long, and rather heavy. There were not any secret rigama-jigs about the rod, nor about anything else connected with the dead man, that we could find. He had simply been preparing for an evening's sport, when something killed him!

"You will not have failed to notice that I keep saying 'something,' and I suppose we shall have to keep on saying 'some thing'—the curse of Sir Godfrey, over there, or Dunn's God of the Mountain out of the Dunsany story. . . . I don't know what it was!

"We had no clue to any assassin. Bradmoor had been pretty hard up, at the end—no one realized how hard up, until the complete collapse after his death. The servants had gone into the village. Of course, we looked them up—the cook, to visit her daughter who was ill, and the old butler to do the marketing. There was no one about the place, except the butler's mother, in a little cottage in the garden—an old woman, practically unable to move from her chair.

"She was the only witness we had to anything; and her evidence included two features only: she had heard a sound, which she thought was the back-fire of a motor car—that, of course, was the sound of the shot that killed Bradmoor; and she had heard something leap into the water.

"Of course, she had a theory.

"All old women of her type have theories to explain mysterious happenings: the Devil did

it! She heard him leap into the sea! Of course, she gradually supplied details, as such persons invariably do—details that could not possibly have had any basis in fact! The Devil climbed the wall, shot Bradmoor and leaped off into the sea. Well, no one but the Devil could have climbed it; it is a sheer, smooth wall, and descends fifty feet from the window to the water.

"Of course, we went over the wall. We scaffolded up from the bottom, and examined, carefully, every inch of it. There was not a mark on the wall! It is bare of vines, to begin with—and there is a thin green fungus over the whole of it. I do not mean a lichen. I mean the thin fungus that presently covers a damp stone. If there had been any attempt to scale this wall, we would have found the marks—and we did not find the marks; there was not a mark on it in any direction.

"We did not stop at the sill of the window. We went up to the roof. Nothing could have descended from above. There was a lot of dust on the roof—it had been long dry, and one could have made a mark on the tiles of the roof and on the gutters. We were minutely careful.

"There was not a mark or a scratch, either above or below that narrow slit of a window. No human creature could have climbed the wall and killed Bradmoor. The old woman's theory was as good as any—it must have been the Devil.

"But she was profoundly disappointed that we did not find seared hoofprints on the wall. They must be there. We had not looked close enough! She wished to be carried out in her chair, so that she could examine it herself. She stuck to her theory. Of course, she could be persuaded out of her details—her amplifications of the thing. But she held stoutly to one fact—she had heard the Devil leap off into the sea!

"I put some of the best men from the Criminal Investigation Department of Scotland Yard on it at once; and they gave it up. Of course, we tried to get at it by the usual method of elimination. One had to consider every theory and see how it fitted the facts. How could anyone have murdered Bradmoor when it was impossible to get out of the room after having done it, or to get into the room if Bradmoor had himself locked the door?

"And how could the man have taken his own life?

"There was no weapon to be found; his right hand was clutched around a fishing rod; and his left hand was full of flies—with a bright-colored one between the thumb and finger. These things must have been in his hand before his death, and at the time of his death, for they were still clutched in his convulsed fingers.

"The wound was hideous. The man must have died instantly. He could not have moved after the thing happened. Every nerve must have been paralyzed. It was clearly beyond reason to formulate any theory which would have depended upon any movement of the man after the wound was made. The surgeons simply laughed at the idea.

"He could not have moved after the bullet struck him; and there he sat with his fishing tackle gripped in his hands. There could not have been anything else in his hands; and as I have said, there was no weapon.

"I don't think we omitted anything in our efforts to get at a solution of the mystery.

"Everybody in the country about was put in inquisition. There had been no one in the neighborhood of the house on that afternoon. We knew the names of each person, and his mission, who traveled the road that afternoon. We knew every motor car that went over it, and every workman that walked along it. We knew where every man, woman, and child in the community was that afternoon. There was simply no clew to an assassin. . . . And there was no explanation."

Sir Godfrey Simon's eyes batted again.

"Except mine," he said.

Marquis laughed. "Or Dunn's—the Stone God stumping down out of the mountain; or the old woman's theory. The country accepted that. It was even more popular than the theory Sir Godfrey advances.

"We have had a variety of mysteries at Scotland Yard during my time as Chief of the Criminal Investigation Department, and from Mayne's time down; but the Mystery of the Letts, the Rising Sun postcard, or the affair of the Chinese Embassy were nothing to this.

"In every other mystery with which we have been concerned, there was always some possible explanation. One could make a hypothesis that did not outrage the human understanding; but one could not form a hypothesis in this case that did not outrage it.

"Now, that is an appalling thing when you stop to think about it! The human mind is very clever, very ingenious. When you present a mysterious case, it will furnish you with some solution; but it can't furnish a solution for this case.

"Arrange the facts before you, and try it!

"A man is found dead in a locked room; there is no weapon; the fingers of both of his hands are gripped about objects that could have had nothing to do with his death. There is no way into, or out of, the room. There is a great, ragged hole in his chest. The sound of the shot is heard; and there you are.

"If you can formulate an explanation, you will be cleverer than the whole of England. There is nothing that the British public loves like a mystery; and when the details of one are given to them, every individual in the kingdom sits down to formulate an explanation. You can't stop him—it's an obsession. It's like a puzzle. He goes on doggedly until he gets a solution. That's the reason why, when Scotland Yard wishes to remove a mystery from public notice, it gives out a solution. The whole interest of the country lies in solving the mystery; once solved, it is forgotten.

"But even our best experts could not give out an explanation in this case; we wished to do so because we wished to keep the thing quietly in our hands until we could work it out. But we could not put out a solution; there wasn't any!"

He paused in the narrative, and selected a cigarette from an open box on the table but did not at once light it.

"When it became certain," he went on, "that no assassin could be connected with this incomprehensible tragedy, we turned back upon the details of the only witness who was able to furnish us any fact whatsoever. But with every day's delay, and with each complication of the matter, the old woman's story had become more involved. It was so decked out with fanciful imaginings that it became difficult to realize that the whole extravaganza was pure fancy, outside of two evidences.

"These two evidences stood alone as the only concrete features in the case; one, that she had heard a sound, which could have been the explosion of a weapon; that she took it for the back-fire of a motor car at some distance away indicated that it was a loud explosive sound.

"This fact seemed to be unquestioned.

"Bradmoor had been killed by a shot, and the sound of the shot had been heard. Of this we were certain; but that something had leaped off into the water was an evidence more in doubt. We were convinced that the woman had heard the sound of the shot that killed the old Duke, but we were by no means convinced that she had heard a splash in the water. That element of her story seemed always too closely associated with her theory—that the whole tragedy was at the hand and instigation of the Devil. Around that idea she presently built up her fantastic explanation.

"With every interrogation of her, she became more elaborate, more profuse in her details, and more extravagant in her assurance. She had heard the Devil leap into the sea. It was not a heavy splash—such as the body of a man would make; it could not have been the body of a man. It was a thin, slight, sharp splash, precisely what the slender body of a Devil's imp would make as it leaped lightly from the edge of the window into the water—its pointed feet descending, its arm up."

Henry Marquis laughed!

"She had every detail of it now. It must have given her an immense interest in life. Imagine that startling melodrama cutting into the monotony of uneventful days in a padded chair by a window. And from being a neglected and forgotten derelict, she was presently the heroine of a vivid romance, a person of importance to the countryside. The cottage was crowded, and she had the glory of a story-teller of Baghdad.

"The result was, of course, that she presently became useless so far as any further inquiry was concerned. That was clear. She was of value to us for two facts only—and one of them in doubt. That she had heard the shot was certain. We felt we could depend on that; but the splash was likely fancy. And the more we considered that element of the case, the more we were convinced that this was one of the colored details requisite to her theory.

"There was no ledge to the window. There was no way in which an assassin could have climbed there in order to leap off into the sea after the crime had been committed. There was no place beyond that window from which the shot could have been fired. There was only the open sea lying beyond it.

"Of course, there were improbabilities suggested—one of them was that the shot had been fired from the high mast of a sailing ship; but there had been no sailing ship on that afternoon. The officials of the Coast Service were able to assure us of that; they kept a record of everything. No sailing ship had been on the open sea on that afternoon inside of this point.

"Of course, we considered everything.

"Some crank sent us an anonymous letter, saying that the shot had been fired from an airplane, or a seaplane; and we looked into that. But there had been no such craft in the neighborhood on that afternoon. So those possibilities were excluded. They were so unlikely that it seemed almost absurd to inquire into them. But when you stop to think about it, they were the only theories that in any way indicated a rational solution of the matter; and that they were not the solution, there was, as it happened, conclusive evidence. There had been no sailing ship, and no aircraft, near the place on that afternoon."

Marquis paused again. He lighted his cigarette at one of the candles on the table, drew the smoke through it an instant, and then came back to his narrative.

"I have been giving you this case in extended detail," he said, "because I am trying to make you realize the difficulties that it presented, and how carefully those difficulties were considered. I wish you to understand, as we presently came to understand, how incapable the thing was of any solution. We returned again and again to it, as I have returned here in my narrative again and again to it, because we were constantly assailed with the belief that we had overlooked something. There must be some evidences that had escaped us—a way into that room, or a way out of it, by which an assassin could have encompassed Bradmoor's death. But we got no further. There was no way into that room, nor any way out of it, and there was no way from above it in which an assassin could have killed Bradmoor; and yet there he was, shot to death in his chair!"

Henry Marquis laughed. It was an ironical chuckle of a laugh.

"The butler's mother was the only person with a theory, and by Heaven, there were evidences to support it. She assembled them and fitted them together. She convinced the countryside. The very impossible things we found connected with the irrational explanations of the matter, were the strongest evidences of her theory.

"One had to consider them, no matter how practical one was.

"The very fact that we were able to show that old Bradmoor could not have been killed by any human agency of which we had any knowledge, proved, as she pointed out, that he could have been killed by a supernatural agency only. Certainly only a Devil's imp could leave no marks on a wall, and could leap off, disappearing into the sea. Besides, Bradmoor had been afraid of the Devil!"

Henry Marquis hesitated a moment. He broke the cigarette in his fingers into fragments, crumbling them on the table.

"Now, there," he said, "one came upon a series of evidences that had to be admitted. Bradmoor had been noticed to act queerly for some time. It was only after his death that the various trivial instances were precisely recalled, and fitted together. But they had been beyond doubt observed, and, now when they were connected up, they took on an unquestioned significance.

"The man had been afraid of something!

"He would lock himself into his room at night; he never sat long in one position; he would not stand before a window, nor sit with his back to an open door. It was recalled that he had been clever with an explanation of these idiosyncrasies—extremely clever. It was a draft he avoided before an open door. Or his eyes were sensitive to the strong light of a window; or he was nervous—too many pipes—he must find a milder tobacco, and so forth.

"The explanations covered the peculiarities while the man was living, and there was nothing to create a suspicion of some unusual motive; but after his death they became signboards that all pointed in one direction—the morale of the man had been gradually breaking down under an increasing monomania of fear!

"These evidences were all bright-colored threads for the Devil theory. Bradmoor had been afraid of the Devil! And he had not been afraid without a reason! The butler's mother had a fine, lurid theory that pleased the countryside."

Henry Marquis suddenly smote the table with his hand.

"But it could not be considered by us. There is only one thing of which I am absolutely certain, and that is that the supernatural does not exist. This is a physical world. Every problem in it has an explanation. The Devil is a myth.

"There was one thing only to do now," he pursued, "and that was to go back over the man's life to see if it contained any adventure that might be in any way connected with the tragedy. We began to investigate his life."

The face of Sir Godfrey Simon beyond him at the table lifted unmoving, like a mask:

"There is where you made a mistake," he

said; "it was not enough to go back over Bradmoor's life; you had to go farther than that."

"Farther than Bradmoor's life?" Marquis interrogated. "How could we go farther than that? What was farther than his life?"

A faint smile appeared on Sir Godfrey Simon's face, but he made no reply.

Henry Marquis was annoyed.

"You mean the curse that killed Bradmoor!"

"Precisely that," replied Sir Godfrey, his face unmoving.

"If you had come to me, I could have predicted what would happen to Bradmoor. He could not escape it."

Marquis interrupted.

"Then you knew it was going to kill Bradmoor?"

"Surely," he said. "Had it not killed his father and his grandfather?"

"But his grandfather was drowned on the Northwest Coast," continued Marquis. "He was shooting brant, and the plug came out of the boat."

"Some one pulled the plug out," replied Sir Godfrey.

"And his father fell from the steeple of the chapel here."

Again that vague smile, like a bit of sun on a painted image's face.

"Did he fall?"

Henry Marquis swore under his breath. "Damn it, man," he said, "you are a companion for the butler's mother, only the old woman is more satisfactory; she gives an explanation with her theory, and you never give an explanation. If you know what killed old Bradmoor, why don't you tell us how it killed him?"

Sir Godfrey Simon looked calmly across the table at the Chief of the Criminal Investigation Department of Scotland Yard. The mask of his face had now the expression of a man of experience regarding the futile chatter of a child.

"Marquis," he said, "you sometimes profoundly annoy me. Because one understands one feature of a matter, does it also follow that one must understand equally every other feature of it? I have made this explanation until I am monotonously weary of it: I know what killed the old Duke; I do not know how it killed him. You do not see the interest in this case as I see it. The interest to me lies exclusively in the fact that it did kill him. I am not concerned about the means it took. I don't care. I am not interested. That is for you to find out, if you care."

He took up the glass of whisky beside him, tasted it, and put it down again. He acted to me like an amused man, at a quarrel among children.

"If you find out how the old Duke was killed, you will see that I am right—if you ever find out."

Marquis shrugged his shoulders. He turned again to me and said:

"We finally reached the dead point. There was no solution to the thing!"

II

Lord Dunn now took up the narrative. He had been silent in his chair, moved back from the table. He had lighted a cigar, and enjoyed it while Henry Marquis had been talking; but he enjoyed it like a bookmaker. It was tilted at a rakish angle in his mouth; and he blew the smoke about him like a stableboy. He now took the cigar out of his mouth, and threw it into the fireplace.

"But there *was* something in his life," he declared.

"It was the last exploration old Bradmoor undertook, the one that used up the remnant of his fortune. I mean that terrible push into the Lybian Desert. He was too old to undertake it, and he was too poor. It broke him down in every direction. The man came out a wreck—a worse wreck than we realized; one could see the physical evidences on him."

He made a big, awkward gesture with his hands, precisely like a bookmaker rejecting a bet.

"I don't ask anyone to believe it," he said. "I don't know that I believe it. I judge, in fact, that I don't believe it. Of course, it's a crazy notion;

but this whole business is full of crazy notions—nothing but damned crazy notions."

He paused to light another big cigar.

"Anyway, I know the facts, and what happened. I know them better than any other living person, because I considered that expedition before Bradmoor did. The German came to me first; then he went to the old Duke. I was not interested in the Lybian Desert just then. Deserts don't amuse me. Women go through them and write books about it. I was going into Yucatan, so I sent the German to Bradmoor.

"I could not determine whether he was a liar, building on some facts, or whether he had been with Rohlfs' expedition. You know about that—or has everything that happened before the Great Mad War been forgotten? Rohlfs persuaded Kaiser Wilhelm to fit him out with an expedition to explore the plateau of the Lybian Desert. Rohlfs had a theory that the country now desert had been once well watered—the theater of an immense civilization, antedating the later civilizations of which we have any knowledge. He got the professors to back him up. They prepared a monograph for him, and it was published everywhere.

"Rohlfs persuaded the Kaiser to send him in.

"Of course, we don't know how much bluff the Germans were putting up. It is possible that the Kaiser was merely taking a look at Egypt, and the English possessions beyond it, and that the expedition was a scouting party. That would be an explanation of the wide publicity given to the monograph the professors put out, and the money the German Government spent on the expedition. But I don't believe that was Rohlfs's motive. I think Rohlfs was really on the trail of a civilization, and that he was sincere about it.

"Anyhow, the expedition went in, and everybody knows what happened to it, and where it broke down. Rholfs went on with a fragment of what he could get together, and he found some evidences of what he expected to find—not a civilization like that of the Egyptian Nile, but something more like what I found in Yucatan. At least, that's the story the German came to me

with. I mean Slaggerman. He turned up here, a sort of roustabout on a North German Lloyd ship; and he hunted me up.

"I suppose he saw the name in the newspapers.

"I sent him to Bradmoor," Lord Dunn went on. "He had a drawing—very well done. He said Rohlfs made it. It showed a path along a stone ledge. There was one strange feature about the path that he pointed out. He would hold a glass over it, and then he would get excited, and fall into the German language. The path was sunk in the stone of the ledge, but it had not been cut there; it had been *worn* there. It must have been eight or ten inches deep, and wide enough for a man to pass along it.

"And it was worn into the ledge!

"'*Ach*,' he would say, 'it was feet, human feet that wore that path down. How long did it take—one thousand, two thousand, five thousand years? And how many feet—how many generations of feet—and why did they travel on that path, and where did they go?'

"He said that Rohlfs, after the expedition had gone to pieces, had escaped from the surveillance of the desert sheiks, and had gone on, with only Slaggerman, disguised as an Arab cook. They had pushed on for a fortnight before they were overtaken and brought back. He said they reached the peak of a mountain ascending out of the sand to the southwest.

"It was not a range that extended like a geological formation across the whole plateau. It stood up abruptly out of it, as though a peak of mountain had thrust up suddenly from below. He said that it was possible to travel around it, that the native tribes did, in fact, travel around it. There was no reason for anyone undertaking to ascend it, in the opinion of the desert tribes.

"It was evidently a peak of barren rocks, without water or vegetation. The stone was hard, and rose-colored. The sharp peaks at a distance, the German said, with the sun on them, looked like a beautiful rose-colored cathedral. There was a certain harmony in the outline at a distance. Rohlfs thought it was a mirage. Neither of the two men had any other idea until they finally arrived at its base. They had time enough to go entirely around it before they were overtaken.

"There was no way to ascend it; in fact, they did not think of the possibility of anyone going up until by chance Rohlfs discovered this path. They were amazed, but they had no opportunity to follow the thing up. They were overtaken by the desert tribes and hurried out of the region. Rohlfs made a drawing of the path that night, while the memory of it was fresh in his mind. It was correct, Slaggerman said. He helped him with the details."

Lord Dunn put his cigar on the fruit plate before him. It was half burned out; the long ash crumbled, and a thin line of smoke ascended, rippling at the top like a fantastic flower. He seemed to reflect on the story he was telling. His voice was firmer, less harsh.

"When you come to think about it," he said, "there could have been nothing that would so pique the curiosity as that bit of drawing. There was just enough of it. One's imagination winged off at once with every sort of extravaganza. In the waste places of the earth two things have an unfailing fascination for the lone explorer—a human footprint, and a path. If one finds a human footprint, or a path, one can never turn aside from it; one must find out whither it leads.

"I remember the effect on me when the German got out his drawing.

"I was not much interested before that. I was considering a method to dismiss him. But that fragment of drawing attached my interest. The whole picture at once came up in vivid detail, with its absorbing enigma!

"Well, as I have said, I sent him on to old Bradmoor. We know what happened. The old Duke went bankrupt on an expedition to go in; and he did go in. It took a lot of time, and endless negotiations. He had to get the permits from the English Government, and from the Egyptian authorities, and the rights to pass, from the sheiks of the desert tribes. The English Government was willing to help him. They wished to verify Rohlfs's narrative. The report had not been translated into English; but it was in the German language, in the bulletins issued by the learned societies at Berlin.

"It took a lot of money.

"In fact, as we know, it cleaned old Bradmoor out, and encumbered his estate as it now stands—on the verge of the bankrupt court. But the old Duke had the patience of every great explorer; once on the way, once taken with the big idea, he stopped at nothing.

"Of course, everybody knows what he found. It's in the monograph he furnished the Royal Society; but everybody does not know *all* that he found. Bradmoor talked it over with me when he returned. He came to see me. He was very much perplexed. He asked me what he ought to do. I told him to make a conventional report to the Royal Society, covering what the exploration discovered, and omit the remainder of it—keep it to himself.

"My reason for urging Bradmoor to this decision was not only in the interest, as I pointed out, of his own reputation, but it was in the interest of the reputation of all persons engaged in exploration. It was necessary to retain the public confidence in the accuracy of our explorers. Anything taken to be incredible, or improbable, or fantastic, would not only injure Bradmoor before the great English reading public, but it would injure every other man who undertook a like exploration.

"We talked it over.

"The result was that the old Duke's monograph contained only the journal of the expedition, and the general verification of what Rohlfs had reported—that is to say, no evidence of any ancient civilization on the plateau.

"He found precisely what one would have expected him to find in the desert.

"The only unusual thing which his monograph indicated was the peak of rose-colored stone which stood up out of the plateau; and this, under my suggestion, he described from the unimaginative view of the geologist.

"He tells us that he found this stone formation precisely where Rohlfs said it was, and with the physical characteristics set out in the German report. He had the same difficulty that confronted Rohlfs; the desert tribes would not permit him to make any very careful examination of it. It was only with extreme difficulty that he was permitted to approach it. He was not able to learn why they objected to this inspection. He was impressed that it was merely the accumulated suspicion which would attach to any expedition going into that region—only one or two white men had ever entered it.

"He reported also the death of Slaggerman on the way out. He had strayed from the expedition, and been killed. And that was all!"

Lord Dunn leaned over in his chair, got the half-burned cigar out of the plate, and relighted it.

"But that was not all: Rohlfs's drawing was genuine, and Slaggerman had told the truth. Bradmoor said that when the peak of stone began first to form itself before him, he was amazed beyond any words to express it. The thing *did* look like a cathedral, like an airy rose-colored Gothic thing in the sky. In spite of Slaggerman at his elbow, he was quite sure, as Rohlfs had been, that the thing was a mirage. It could not be anything else.

"It was too delicate, too artistically perfect to be anything real.

"It was a fairy mosque, raised by some enchantment—like a Baghdad story; and as they traveled toward it, it grew more clearly outlined. It was only at the very base of the thing that one lost the illusion; then it became the peak of a mountain thrusting up through the desert sand, composed of some hard, reddish stone.

"Bradmoor said they had only a day; the sheik of the desert tribes treated him precisely as he had treated Rohlfs—he gave him a day. But he was luckier than Rohlfs. He did not put in the time traveling around this stone formation. He set out with Slaggerman alone, leaving a guard in his camp.

"Bradmoor said that the German went at once to the path he and Rohlfs had discovered. It was there precisely as the drawing showed it.

"They at once set out on this path.

"It was narrow, worn into the stone, as Rohlfs's drawing showed. The wearing was uneven, as though the rock had been softer in places; but the path was at no point worn in the stone to a less depth than eight or ten inches. Bradmoor was able to go along it, but the big German traveled with extreme difficulty.

"Bradmoor thought the path had been made by persons of a smaller stature than the modern European.

"The path wound about among the peaks of stone until it reached a beetling ledge at the top."

Lord Dunn paused, ground out the lighted end of the cigar on the plate, and put it down.

"I forget the precise details," he said. "Bradmoor had them minutely. I suppose by the very accuracy of his detail he hoped to make the story so realistic that it could not be doubted. Anyway, what he found was a small chamber, cut out in the highest peak of stone, and an image on a sort of stone bench.

"Bradmoor said this image was carved out of blue ivory. Of course, there isn't any such thing as blue ivory, and there could have been no piece of ivory in the world large enough. The image was about four feet high, and in proportion.

"He said the thing profoundly puzzled him. He could not understand where a piece of ivory that size could have been found in any age of the world. And then, when he began to examine it carefully with a magnifying glass, he found that it was made of a number of pieces, fitted together so that they interlocked.

"He thought the ivory had been dyed. But it was a dye of which we have no knowledge, for it had entered the grain of the ivory, and soaked through it. Bradmoor thought it was blue all the way through—at any rate so far as he could determine by scratching it with any implement that he had. He said that the image sat on a sort of bench cut out of the red stone, with its hands together, the palms up, extended between its knees. He said that the features and the whole attitude of the figure, very closely resembled the Baal or Moloch of some of the early Sumerian tribes.

"There was an inscription cut on the face of the stone below the image. It was in the wedge characters of the old Sumerian priests; it was partly defaced—the opening lines had scaled. Bradmoor and I got his copy of the inscription deciphered. It ran like a verse of Isaiah.

"'His right hand shall be his enemy, and the son of another shall sit in his seat. I will encourage his right hand to destroy him. And I will bring the unborn through the Gate of Life. And they shall lean upon me. And I will enrich them, and guide their feet and strengthen their hearts. And they shall laugh in his gardens, and sit down in his pleasant palaces.'

"You see," Lord Dunn went on, "it was a threat against anyone who should disturb the god.

"Bradmoor said the expression on the face of the image was one of inconceivable menace, an expression of eternal calm—a vast Satanic serenity—laid down over features exquisitely cruel. The menace in it struck one as with the impact of a blow.

"It stopped even old Bradmoor and Slaggerman when they came to the top of the path before it, and sent their hands to their pistol holsters. The old Duke said he had to compose himself a bit before he could go in.

"Now, that was a good deal for Bradmoor to say. He was a cold-blooded, hard-hearted man on an expedition—not a person to be affected by an image.

"The thing must have been pretty bad.

"They found nothing in the cell with the image. The bench on which it sat had been cut out of the red stone, and there was nothing about in the place, except the partly defaced inscription and a hole in the bench of stone directly under the extended, open hands of the image, between its knees. The hole was circular—about

six inches in diameter, and smooth. It seemed to descend into the stone. Bradmoor said he was profoundly puzzled about what this opening could mean. They had nothing with which to explore it, and the whole chamber about them was entirely bare. He went outside where the path began to ascend, and with a small hammer broke off some fragments of stone, and dropped one into the opening. He heard it tumble against something at a short distance, as though it were a piece of parchment—there was a crackling as of paper.

"He bared his arm, and put it down into the opening.

"The hole was perfectly smooth, and descended for about two feet; then it made a slight turn toward the face of the image. Here his fingers came in contact with something that felt like a piece of parchment. He got hold of it with difficulty, and finally brought it up.

"It was a bladder, containing a handful of something that rattled like pebbles.

"It had been dropped into the opening, but had been too large to make the turn to the front as it descended. They cut the bladder open. It was partly full of rubies. They were magnificent rubies—big, pigeon-blood stones, such as are now only found in Burma; and there was a whole handful of them.

"The reason for the hole descending into the stone was now clear. It was a contribution box for the god. The position of the hands open between the knees of the image was also clear—anything placed in them dropped into his contribution box.

"Bradmoor tried it with fragments of stone. They fell out of the hand into the open hole below, and descended. He said he could hear the pieces of stone rattle for a long distance. He could not tell how far. He had no line, and no method of judging how far the hole descended; but it was evident that it was some sort of chute leading to a treasure house, and that it descended for a great distance.

"It had been only by accident that the rubies contained in the bladder had lodged at the turn where he had found them. There was nothing else to be found. The hole was as smooth as glass. Neither Bradmoor nor Slaggerman were able to make a drawing of anything. A rough map was the best the old Duke could ever do with a pencil, and the German knew nothing at all about drawing. They had no camera.

"They had experienced the same difficulty with respect to all implements that happens to every explorer in the desert—the natives always attach some sinister design to them, and they have to be abandoned. Rohlfs had to give up his implements, and Bradmoor had to cache his before he got very far in. A camera could not be used. Even the notebooks had to be written up at night in a tent. One was lucky to be able to take a modern weapon.

"The old Duke copied the inscription, and they put in the remainder of the day trying to get some clew to the treasure house. It must be somewhere below. He said that human understanding staggered when it began to think about what the treasure house might contain. It was evident that the cult of this god had been immense, covering a vast period of time.

"Slaggerman's conjecture was evidently correct. Human feet had worn down the path bringing offerings to this god; and these offerings had all descended into his contribution box beneath him. The enormous treasure thus assembled over an incredible period at the hands of innumerable worshipers was beyond any sane conjecture.

"Bradmoor said the conception was so overpowering that neither he nor Slaggerman thought very much of the handful of rubies at the time. He put them into his pocket, and the descending night found them hunting for the treasure house.

"But they never found it.

"In fact, they were never able to get out of the path by which they had ascended, and when night came they were compelled to return to their camp.

"There they found themselves practically prisoners. The desert sheik had followed with

his retainers—their permit of a day was up. They were unable to move the sheik; their solicitations only made the tribes more determined, more suspicious. So they had to go back.

"Now, that's what Bradmoor found. He told me all about it, as I have said, when he came to make up his monograph for the Royal Society. He told it with accurate and elaborate detail—much of which I have omitted; and then he asked me my opinion.

"And I advised him to leave it out.

"I saw clearly what the result would be. The critics favorable to him would regard the story as the imaginings of a man broken down by fever, or overwrought at the end of an immense journey and great hardships; the unfavorable critics would merely say that it was a fantastic lie! In either event the man's reputation would suffer; and as I have said, the reputation of everybody else who undertook to make a serious exploration would suffer also.

"There was another thing Bradmoor told me that I advised him to leave out. It could do no good to give the correct report of it, and it might do a great deal of harm. When Slaggerman deserted the expedition on its return march, he took two things with him that the old Duke does not mention in his monograph—the big double express rifle, and the rubies.

"The German knew where the rubies were. In fact, Bradmoor had made no effort to conceal them from him. When they had leisure to examine them, they were amazed at the size and beauty of these jewels. Bradmoor had never seen anything like them. The German said that they were equal to the Crown jewels, both in size and luster.

"The two men frequently discussed them. It was a fascinating subject, and they speculated as to where the treasure house was under that peak of red stone, and what it contained—if these jewels were samples.

"As the two men were the only persons in the expedition who had any knowledge of the jewels, Bradmoor carried them in the medicine box, rolled up as though they were a package of bandages. The double express was the only rifle the expedition now possessed.

"When the German disappeared, Bradmoor stopped and endeavored to find him. He did not at the time think that Slaggerman had undertaken to make away with the treasure they had found. When he discovered the loss of the rifle, he imagined that the German had set out on some hunting expedition. Then he discovered that the German had taken his camping equipment with him, and some of the personnel of the expedition—evidently bribed to accompany him.

"Bradmoor did the only sensible thing possible. He offered a reward to the sheik of the district to bring the German in. Two days later he did bring him in, dead. He had been shot through the chest with the double express.

"The Arabs were not very definite about how the German came to be killed. It was clear, of course, that they had located his camp, crept in on him and shot him with his own gun. But they did not admit that. The sheik knew too much to be involved with the death of a white man.

"They had a very good story. They said they found Slaggerman dead, shot through the chest with his own gun. It was an accident, they supposed. They did not know. It was the will of Allah!

"They brought the gun, and every item of equipment which Slaggerman had taken, but they did not bring in the rubies. Bradmoor himself carefully searched the body, and through every part of the equipment, but he could not find them. He searched the camping place where they had found Slaggerman, and his other camping places; but there was no trace of them.

"Bradmoor said there was no use to ask the sheik or any of his people. If they had them, they would, of course, not give them up; and if they did not have them, it would make only useless complications to advise them now that he had found such a treasure.

"Nevertheless Bradmoor did not go on. He remained in camp for several days, and he con-

tinued to search through the clothes and equipment the German had taken away. He said the thing got on his nerves. He got to thinking about the German and the menacing blue image in its cell of rose-colored stone!

"And then he would put the Arabs to inquisition again on the manner of Slaggerman's death. But he learned nothing further. He never found any trace of the rubies; and presently he set out on his return trip."

Lord Dunn stopped in his narrative. He made his characteristic gesture, putting out his hands like a bookmaker dismissing a worthless bet.

"Now," he said, "that is what happened to Bradmoor. Marquis thinks there was no adventure in his life connected with the mysterious character of his death. When you come to think about it, wasn't this adventure connected with it? Wasn't the old Duke shot through the chest precisely as the German Slaggerman was shot, and apparently with the same sort of weapon?

"Bradmoor said that he recovered the double express rifle. I never thought to ask him what he did with it; but he evidently brought it back with him, and put it into the gun case in the room where he was killed. It is not in the gun case there; it's gone, and I believe it's the weapon with which Bradmoor was killed.

"Now, here is a coincidence, if you look at it in one direction. Of course, if you look at it in a direction equally convincing and probably more sensible, it isn't a coincidence. The Arabs shot Slaggerman; and we don't know who shot Bradmoor. But isn't there another side to it— the appalling menace in that ivory image, and its threat cut beneath it on the stone bench!

"It had guarded its treasure over an incredible period of time. Of course, it is easy to laugh at the notion; but we don't know what sinister influences were at one time abroad in the world, or what control they were enabled to enforce over events. All the religious legends of every race are crowded with stories of it.

"You can't dismiss them with a gesture.

"Bradmoor did not feel altogether at ease

about it. He said he could not get the notion of the deadly menace of that strange blue image out of his head! There it sat in its eternal Satanic calm above its threat cut in the rose-colored stone:

"'His right hand shall be his enemy. And the son of another shall sit in his seat. I will encourage his right hand to destroy him. And I will bring the unborn through the Gate of Life. And they shall lean upon me. And I will enrich them, and guide their feet and strengthen their hearts. And they shall laugh in his gardens, and sit down in his pleasant palaces.'

"And what became of the rubies? The German was no fool. Everything he did was practical and well-planned. He got his counter-expedition together carefully and slowly, and he did not leave Bradmoor until he was sure he could get out. He took the only rifle the expedition had, and he took the rubies.

"Now, what became of the rubies?

"It was an immense treasure. Bradmoor said he and Slaggerman had estimated the value pretty carefully. The German knew what such stones were worth in Europe; they could not have had a less value than one hundred thousand pounds sterling.

"The German did not take any chance with such a treasure. Before he robbed Bradmoor's medicine chest, he had figured out how he intended to conceal these jewels, and where he intended to conceal them. There could have been no doubt about that. There was only one place where he could have concealed them, and that was somewhere about himself. He could not have cached them in the hope of returning for them; and he could not have risked them anywhere except near to his own hand. That is the reason Bradmoor had not found them when he searched the body.

"But there is another hypothesis: suppose the Arabs did not find them? And that touches upon another theory with respect to his death. How do we know that the sinister influence expressing itself so appallingly in the physical aspect of that blue ivory image and its deadly threat, did not, in some manner, concern itself with the death of this German, who had helped to outrage its treasure house?

"And when you get into that idea, does it not follow along to the death of Bradmoor? After all, he was the main offender. He instigated the outrage, and he carried it out. If the blue image got Slaggerman with the double express, may it not—let's venture on the idea, anyway—have got the old Duke with the double express?

"The gun is gone, and we find Bradmoor shot through the chest! Of course, I am not advancing any theory about it. My position is: I don't know. If I were as bold an adventurer into the fantastic as the butler's mother, I would say the blue image got Bradmoor, just as it got Slaggerman.

"Let's consider some of the evidences that the old woman attached to her theory, the items which we know to be correct. The old Duke was afraid of something, and that fear developed, and finally got to be a kind of monomania.

"Now, what was he afraid of?

"He was not the sort of man to be afraid. No one could have undertaken the things he undertook in explorations if he had been a timid person. Any natural menace would not have put old Bradmoor in fear.

"Was it an *unnatural* menace?

"I don't know. But when you can't think of anything else, when no other hypothesis gets us anywhere in any direction, are we not driven back against that sinister inscription?

"'His right hand shall be his enemy. And the son of another shall sit in his seat. And I will encourage his right hand to destroy him. And I will bring the unborn through the Gate of Life. And they shall lean upon me. And I will enrich them, and guide their feet and strengthen their hearts. And they shall laugh in his gardens, and sit down in his pleasant palaces.'

"Only," he added, "I don't understand the promise in it."

Now, this is the story as Lady Joan's guests related it to me on that night. There was some desultory talk after Lord Dunn had concluded; and then the party broke up. Sir Godfrey Simon, at the step of his motor, handed me a folded paper: "Read that," he said, "not now— to-morrow, when your head's cool."

I had noticed him writing, on a tiny pad, with a thin silver pencil, while Lord Dunn was in the body of his story. I thrust the paper into my pocket, and Sir Godfrey Simon's motor turned out into the highroad.

I retained the memory of his big, inscrutable sphinxlike face.

III

We went outside, Joan and I, when the discussion of the mystery of Bradmoor's death had been given over for the evening, and Lord Dunn, Sir Godfrey and Marquis had gone.

Joan slipped a light opera cloak over her evening dress. It was a heavenly night. There was a great white moon over the sea.

We walked through the formal gardens from the cottage, passed the great stone house, to the sheer rock where the current of the Atlantic ran in under the window—where the mystery of Bradmoor's death had been enacted.

The ancient house was sinister, with the white moonlight on the walls. It stood on the rock, sheer over the sea. The grounds about it had been laid out by a king's gardener, but it had fallen by neglect into a wild beauty. The hedges were uncut, the walks overgrown with grass, the shrubbery sprawled in great clusters. With the moon on it, it was like the deserted gardens of some dead city in a Baghdad tale.

The house had been taken over by the old Duke's creditors, in the financial wreck after his death. Joan had gone to live in the lodge cottage at the land end of the place. The beautiful things from the house—her own possessions left to her

by her mother at her death—had been transferred into it. It was the magnificence of these things that contrasted so markedly with the crudities of the cottage.

She was not the dead man's daughter. He had married, late in life, the widow of the Marquis of Westridge; he had no children. The girl was Westridge's daughter. But she had lived on here after her mother's death, and it was evident that a great love for the place was in her.

She had grown up in its magnificence—the magnificence of a fairy story—and in a belief that it would always remain. . . . She spoke softly, gently, affectionately about it, as we stood there in the white moonlight above the sea, looking down into the dark water that moved in against the black, smooth-worn cliff below the tragic window.

The moving of the water stimulated a subconscious query in me, and I uttered it aloud.

"I wonder," I said, "what would become of anything that leaped into the water here; would it be carried out into the sea, or would it be cast up somewhere?"

The girl replied that long ago, when she was a little child, a fisherman had been drowned in the sea under the window, and his body had been discovered later in the sand of an inlet some quarter of a mile farther along the cliff. She pointed to it. We could see a patch of white where the sand extended, in a brief arc of beach, to the water.

I don't know that I mentioned actually in words the suggestion that moved vaguely in me—the nebulous idea that the thing that had accomplished Bradmoor's death might have drowned in the sea here, and its body gone ashore like that of the dead fisherman. I don't think I even undertook to imagine what the thing might be. Perhaps it was only the will to walk on with the girl in this mystic fairyland into which the witchery of the moon had changed the world.

At any rate we went along the path through the neglected gardens, down the broken ledge, until we came out on the arc of sand. The girl sat down on a bit of wreckage, her hands clasped about her knees, looking at the sea; and I walked about in an indolent inspection of the inlet.

But the thing of particular and vital interest to me was this girl, silent here in the moonlight; her dark hair drawn back from the beautiful oval of her face, her great eyes fixed on the sea beyond her, her lips parted, her body motionless. I had not seen her for three years; and it seemed impossible that the thin, great-eyed girl—who had laughingly promised to go with me to America, when I should come again for her—had grown into this magnificent creature! And my mind ran back to the one time I had kissed her. I recalled it as an hour out of a fairy day.

It had been three years ago, on my visit to England. Joan was only a slender slip of a girl then. We had ridden to a distant village along a highway bedeviled with motor cars, and we had determined to come back across the moors above the sea.

I remember the narrow sheep path that led up from the valley onto the plateau of the moors, and the long, almost sheer descent falling away a thousand feet into the valley below—not a ledge of stone, but a smooth slope grassed over with turf.

But it was as deadly dangerous as though it had been spikes of stone; there was barely width for a horse, and a misstep would have sent horse and rider rolling into eternity. We came at the top into a fairy cove, golden soft in the sun, and looking out over the sea. We stopped and got down and stood a moment by the horses.

Joan began to fondle the silky muzzle of her horse. And all at once I realized the heavenly creature she would presently become.

"Joan," I said, "will you go with me to America when I come again?"

She did not reply. She pressed her face against the horse and looked out shyly at me.

And I caught her up into my arms, and kissed her.

For a moment she was relaxed, soft like an armful of blossoms, and then she tore away,

swung into her saddle and raced over the moor. . . . And ten days later, in the middle of the Atlantic, I got a wireless message of three letters: "Yes."

No name, no address, only that single word materializing out of an Arctic fog. . . .

For a long time there was no word between us now.

I stood looking down at the girl, flooded with the soft moonlight, the white sand stretching from her feet to the dark water, where the tide went slowly out. All the events in this complicated tragedy seemed to remove themselves, and to leave only the charm of this girl—alone here, as in an abandoned world.

Finally I spoke: "You will keep your promise to me now, Joan; you will go with me to America?"

Her voice, when she replied, was low, even, without emotion.

"No," she said, "that is precisely what I never can do, now."

I stood in a sort of hypnotic apathy, and she went on in that level, dead voice.

"You are not free," she said, "and so you cannot decide this. It is I, who am free, who must make the decision for us. It is not a pleasant thing to say, but the fact is, now, that you are not free to make a choice. . . . A bankrupt peer of England would be an intolerable thing. You must find a wife, now, who can bring a fortune."

I made an impatient gesture.

"But I do not intend to take this title," I said. "I shall return to America, to my profession, and you shall go with me."

She cried out in sharp protest:

"Oh, no. . . . England has desperate need of the sort of man you are, Robin. You are an Englishman; after all, you cannot abandon England. The curse of this land is an aristocracy that thinks only of amusing itself. It needs the energy, the vigor that men like you would bring to it. The law in America is not the narrow profession that it is in England. One goes to the head of affairs in it, in America, as you are going. One becomes there a directing intelligence of great affairs, a guiding factor in all the national events that enable a civilization to advance."

She paused a moment; then she went on in the same dead, even voice:

"You are going to the head of affairs in America; but you must give it up. You must come back to England. You must take the position which this title will give you, and you must bring your energy and vigor of intellect to the aid of the land that needs you. And—and you must marry some one with a fortune. . . . Our dreams are ended, Robin."

She stood up with a whimsical smile.

"Besides, there is the promise of the Blue Image—the promise to you, included with a threat against the dead man."

And she repeated the strange words vaguely, as one repeats something in a distant memory:

" 'His right hand shall be his enemy. And the son of another shall sit in his seat. I will encourage his right hand to destroy him. And I will bring the unborn through the Gate of Life. And they shall lean upon me. And I will enrich them, and guide their feet and strengthen their hearts. And they shall laugh in his gardens, and sit down in his pleasant palaces.' "

She went on, a little quaver in her voice, hard-held, I thought, but with a courage that would not fail:

"You see, Robin, you are to sit in his seat, for you are the son of another. There is no common blood in the two branches of this house, as everybody knows. This line was the pretender, as your grandfather's suit made clear. But it had the right of possession, and the conservative English law would not put it out.

"And so, Robin," the hard-held voice went on, "you must get a rich wife, and 'laugh in his gardens, and sit down in his pleasant palaces.' "

I came over a step nearer to her.

"Joan," I said, "this is all the veriest nonsense. I love you. Will you go with me to America?"

Her voice, when she replied, had returned to its vague, even note, to its quality of memory.

"You must sit in his seat," she said. "It has been foretold in this strange affair."

"Then," I cried, "I shall sit in his seat with *you.*"

I laughed and went on: "I put the thing up to the Blue Image. If he wishes his prophecy carried out, let him see to it. If he enriches us, and guides our feet, and strengthens our hearts, then I will sit in the dead man's seat, and we shall laugh in his gardens, and sit down in his pleasant palaces. If the great God of the Mountain is able to do this, let him do it, and if he is not able to do it, then you will go with me to America. Shall we declare it is a bargain with him?"

I stooped over, took her hands and drew her gently to her feet. But before I got her into my arms, she cried out, and pointed to the beach, where the water was creeping slowly out.

There was something emerging from the sand, like the end of an iron rod. We went down to it. In the clear moonlight I was able at once to see what it was.

It was the heavy barrels of a rifle.

I drew it out of the sand. It was the double express that had disappeared on the afternoon of Bradmoor's death.

A surge of interest in the mystery returned. One phase of it, at least, was explained; whoever had assassinated Bradmoor had thrown the gun into the sea, and it had washed ashore here. We took it back with us to the lodge in a breathless interest, for we had a clew to this mystery; and incoherent explanations began to present themselves.

We took it into the dining room, and put it down on the great table. We lighted the candles, and sat down to examine it. It was rusted from the sea water. It was difficult to work the mechanism of the rifle in order to throw open the breech; and we searched among the articles brought into the cottage for oil, and implements to clean the barrels, and a screw driver. I had to take the rifle apart in order to find if it was loaded. The double barrels contained two cartridges, I found: one of them had been fired; the other remained loaded.

It was a heavy gun, with a big, hard rubber butt plate like that to be found on the modern shotgun. I made a discovery when I took the weapon apart:

The catch on the triggers had been filed.

Now, as a matter of fact, the pull on these heavy rifles is usually some ten pounds; but the catch on the triggers on this rifle had been filed until they were practically hair-triggers.

This rifle could be fired with the slightest touch on the triggers.

This seemed incomprehensible to me. A rifle like this with a hair-trigger would be an impracticable and dangerous weapon. No big game hunter would have ever thought of so filing the triggers. It must have been done with a deliberate intention—for some particular reason.

It was clear that this was the weapon with which the old Duke had been killed, for one barrel had been discharged. It was, therefore, more than probable—it was, in fact, certain—that the rifle had been made thus to fire at a touch, for the express purpose of this tragedy.

But who could have wished it to fire at a touch?

Who filed it, and for what definite purpose? I put the rifle together again, and we stood beside it where it lay across the table, the butt toward the stone fireplace. We were both aflame with the possibilities of this discovery. I winged out on the first suggestion that came into my mind.

The triggers had been thus filed for a phantom finger, a finger with no power of this world in the crook of it; and the threat of that old forgotten god—on his bench of rose-colored stone—cut in the wedge writing of the Sumerian priests, came up before me.

We could dismiss ancient religion with a gesture. These sinister gods were impotent images. How could they influence events? But after all, when we looked at the matter fairly, how did we know? The sacred books of every religion in the world were crowded with examples—especially the sacred books of the Jews, upon which our modern religions were all basically founded. What sinister power over events had the magicians of Pharaoh, the witch of Endor, the dead prophets of Yahveh!

And I could see this hideous idol of blue ivory moving about the doomed man, invisibly.

But I could not see it as Lord Dunn imagined, stumping heavily down from its seat of rose-colored stone to destroy the man who had outraged its dignity and looted it of its treasure. It seemed a nimble, insidious thing like that Devil's imp around which the butler's mother had built up her fantastic theory. I could see an avenging agent, of this sinister image, like that. Taking the doomed man at the moment of his unconcern—with a trigger filed to its phantom finger—and then slipping through that narrow slit in the wall to leap off into the sea, casting away the rifle as it descended!

And then the accident happened that unlocked the mystery of Bradmoor's death, like a key turned in the lock of a closed door.

So many involved suggestions were moving in my mind, that, I fancy, I failed to remember the change that had been made in the mechanism of the rifle, and I no longer thought about it. The old established knowledge of such weapons must have taken the place of what I had just discovered, for in resting my hand on the table beside the rifle, I touched one of the triggers with my finger.

I had forgotten that the opening of the breech had thrown back the hammers.

There was an explosion. The big lead bullet flattened against the stone of the opposite wall, and the gun leaped back from the table, the butt striking the stone corner of the chimney.

Joan cried out, and I stood for a moment astonished.

Then I realized another thing that threw a ray of light into this mystery. The heavy recoil of this gun would carry it backward; and it carried it backward with enough violence to cause it to be thrown entirely off the table.

It was Joan who caught the meaning of this thing.

"Did you see that?" she cried. "How it leaped back of itself, without being touched?"

"Yes," I said. "These rifles all have a heavy recoil. They are apt to bruise the shoulder unless they are tightly held."

"But it leaped back," she cried. "It leaped back of itself!"

Then she came around the table to me.

"If that rifle had been lying in the narrow slit of the window, it would have leaped out into the sea—it would have leaped out of itself!"

She took hold of my arm.

"Think about it! What does it mean? What does it mean that the gun has been made to fire with a touch?"

What did it mean?

I began to think madly along the line her suggestion indicated—the gun in the loophole—in the slit in the window: it would leap out into the sea when it was fired—and it would have leaped out, as she said, without being touched, without the assistance of any human agency!

I caught at the suggestion.

"That is true," I said; "it would have leaped back out of the window of itself, without being touched by anybody."

"After it was fired," she said. "But it had to be fired first. . . . Now, what did it mean that the mechanism was so filed that a touch would fire it? And what touch fired it? Who was it that wished the rifle to disappear after it was fired?"

She went on, her eyes wide, her face white, the tips of her fingers straining against the edge of the table:

"Not an assassin, for he could have thrown the rifle into the sea; it must have been someone who could not have thrown it in. Who after the shot was fired had to depend on the recoil of the rifle itself to cause it to disappear?"

Again I winged out into fantastic regions.

That old sinister god at his work of vengeance would require a slighter materialization than I had imagined. The heavy double express would itself leap into the sea if it lay in the slit of the wall and the triggers were touched by a phantom finger. But it would require to be placed there and trained on the doomed man seated in his chair, concerned with the preparation of his fishing tackle.

How had the Blue Image managed it?

Granted that it could move invisibly about Bradmoor on that afternoon, could it also move this heavy weapon invisibly about? And if it could also do that, why require that the triggers should be filed for a phantom finger? If it, or its invisible agents, could thus handle the heavy double express, would a ten-pound pull disturb them?

But had they handled it? And a line of that sinister threat cut in the rose-colored stone returned to me:

"I will encourage his right hand to destroy him."

The threat was not that this old, dread, mysterious, forgotten god would do the deed himself.

"His right hand shall be his enemy. I will encourage his right hand to destroy him."

It was thus that the threat ran.

It was the doomed man's own hand that the Blue Image would set about this deadly work. It was his own hand that should carry out all these material preparations.

And then I saw the answer to Joan's query.

"Bradmoor!" I cried. "But how could he have fired the rifle?"

Joan looked at me a moment, her face tense in its abstraction.

"There was the fishing rod in his hand; he could—he could——"

And then I saw the whole thing as the old Duke had so carefully planned it.

He knew that the recoil of this heavy rifle would carry it out of this window into the sea after it was fired. He had filed the catch on the triggers until a touch would fire it; then he had placed the rifle carefully, adjusting its position so the bullet would strike him in the chest near the heart; and sitting down in the chair in the middle of the room, on that afternoon, he had touched the trigger with the end of the fishing rod. The great lead bullet had plowed its way into his chest; the gun had leaped into the sea; and Bradmoor's body had crumpled in its chair—some flies in his left hand, and the fishing rod gripped in the fingers of his other hand.

And he had left behind him a mystery that no man could solve!

The splash that the old woman had heard, sitting in her cottage, was caused by the heavy double express descending into the water!

And then I remembered the penciled note that old Sir Godfrey Simon had handed to me, when, after the dinner, he had got into his motor:

"To-morrow," he had said, "when your head is cool, read it."

I brought it out of my pocket now, and tore it open. There were a few lines in a clear, fine hand like copperplate.

"Bradmoor killed himself, of course," the note ran. "I don't know how he did it, but in some clever way. They have all gone out like that—his grandfather, who left his death on the West Coast to look like an accident, and his father, who pretended to fall from the steeple of the chapel. There has always been a monomania of fear preceding the act. It is a common symptom. I said they were all under a curse. A streak of insanity is a curse. It is the worst form of curse, because it cannot be prayed off in a meeting-house."

I read the note and put it down on the table before the girl. She moved her head slowly, her eyes wide, her face still in its tense abstraction.

"The Blue Image carried out his threat," she murmured. "It was the dead man's right hand that destroyed him; it was his right hand that was his enemy! How awful!"

But the Blue Image, as a directing factor in this tragedy, seemed all at once a remote, fantastic notion, like the devil theory of the old paralytic helpless in her chair.

Sir Godfrey Simon had been right—alone of all the theorists right. The curse on this family had extended itself to Bradmoor. Sir Godfrey had seen it on the way. He had marked the evidential signs of it, the monomania of fear that preceded it, and the care to give the act the distinguishing features of a criminal agent.

Bradmoor's father and his grandfather had staged their self-directed act for accident, the tragedy of chance. But the old Duke had gone a step beyond them, and with a stroke of genius had put his exit beyond a conjecture of self-direction.

It was the cunning of the unbalanced mind in a moment of inspiration.

And it had sent the keenest intelligence of England to fantastic theories. Henry Marquis and his hard-headed experts had stopped against a wall; the countryside had gone full cry after a devil theory; and men like the Earl of Dunn, accustomed to the somber realities of life, had seen no solution except through the supernatural agency of a Dunsany god on his bench of rose-colored stone.

And yet how snugly the whole thing ran in the grooves of this fantastic theory!

It held, it enveloped the girl, beyond me. And how lovely, how desirable a thing she was! And the bargain with the god, struck in that mood of half humor, on the arc of sand, under the moon, before the sea, returned to me.

If there was any virtue in the legend cut in the wedge characters of the ancient Sumerian priests on the bench of rose-colored stone below that sinister image, let it now appear. If it was the moving factor in this affair, let it go on. If it had, as its threat ran, encouraged Bradmoor's right hand to destroy him, let it carry out the remainder of that legend. And the words of it returned striding through my memory:

"His right hand shall be his enemy; and the son of another shall sit in his seat. I will encourage his right hand to destroy him. And I will bring the unborn through the Gate of Life. And they shall lean upon me. And I will enrich them, and guide their feet and strengthen their hearts. And they shall laugh in his gardens, and sit down in his pleasant palaces."

The thing was like the pronouncement of a fate. And Bradmoor's death awfully confirmed it.

But was that one fact merely a sinister coincidence—or would the thing go on? If it required faith, here was the faith of Joan, and here was the bargain I had struck.

But the beauty, the charm, the fascination of the girl overwhelmed me. She became in that moment above all things, in any world, desirable, and I said aloud what I had already determined in my heart:

"If the God of the Mountain is so great a god, then let him carry out the remainder of his prophecy, for I shall never give you up."

For a moment there was utter silence. The girl looked about her vaguely, like one in a dream, like one expecting a visitation; and the beauty and the charm of her seemed to extend itself, to fill the empty places of the room.

Then suddenly something on the stones by the hearth came within the sweep of my eye. It looked like a red bead.

I went over and picked up the heavy double express from the hearth. The hard rubber butt plate, striking against the stone corner of the fireplace, had been broken to pieces, and a stream of rubies poured out.

The explanation was clear.

Slaggerman, when he had robbed Bradmoor in the desert, had unscrewed the butt plate, hollowed out the stock, and concealed the treasure in it.

As in a sort of dream I gathered up the handful of great gleaming rubies, and put them on the table.

Then I turned toward the girl, standing with her arms hanging, her lips parted, her eyes wide with wonder.

She came with a little cry into my arms.

"You shall sit in his seat," she said. "The God of the Mountain has carried out his prophecy."

I drew her in against my heart.

"But not all of it," I said. "I hold him to the letter of that contract. 'I will bring the unborn through the Gate of Life.'"

But her face crimson with blushes was bedded into my shoulder, and her hand creeping up, covered my mouth.

THE MAN WHO LIKED TOYS
LESLIE CHARTERIS

ALTHOUGH HE OFTEN ACTS as a detective, Simon Templar, better known as the Saint, is an adventurer, a romantic hero who works outside the law and has grand fun doing it. Like so many crooks in literature, he is imbued with the spirit of Robin Hood, who suggests that it is perfectly all right to steal, so long as it is from someone with wealth. Most of the more than forty books about the Saint are collections of short stories or novellas and, in the majority of tales, he is on the shady side of the street while also functioning as a detective. Unconstricted by being an official policeman, he steps outside the law to retrieve money or treasure that may not have been procured in an honorable fashion, either to restore it to its proper owner or to enrich himself. "Maybe I am a crook," Templar says once, "but in between times I'm something more. In my simple way I am a kind of justice."

In addition to the many books about the Saint, there were ten films about him, mainly starring George Sanders or Louis Hayward, as well as a comic strip, several radio series that ran for much of the 1940s, and a television series starring Roger Moore that was an international success with one hundred eighteen episodes.

Leslie Charteris (1907–1993), the creator of the phenomenally successful and much-loved character, was born in Singapore, lived in England for many years, and became an American citizen in 1946.

"The Man Who Liked Toys" was first published in the September 1933 issue of *American Magazine*. It included neither Simon Templar nor Inspector Teal, however, and was rewritten for its first book publication in *Boodle* (London, Hodder & Stoughton, 1934); it was published in the United States as *The Saint Intervenes* (New York, Doubleday, 1934). The story was adapted for *The Saint* radio series on the Columbia Broadcasting System in 1945 with Brian Aherne as Templar. It also served as the basis for an episode of Moore's television series.

THE MAN WHO LIKED TOYS

LESLIE CHARTERIS

CHIEF INSPECTOR Claud Eustace Teal rested his pudgy elbows on the table and unfolded the pink wrapping from a fresh wafer of chewing gum.

"That's all there was to it," he said. "And that's the way it always is. You get an idea, you spread a net out among the stool pigeons, and you catch a man. Then you do a lot of dull routine work to build up the evidence. That's how a real detective does his job; and that's the way Sherlock Holmes would have had to do it if he'd worked at Scotland Yard."

Simon Templar grinned amiably, and beckoned a waiter for the bill. The orchestra yawned and went into another dance number; but the floor show had been over for half an hour, and Dora's Curfew was hurrying the drinks off the tables. It was two o'clock in the morning, and a fair proportion of the patrons of the Palace Royal had some work to think of before the next midnight.

"Maybe you're right, Claud," said the Saint mildly.

"I know I'm right," said Mr. Teal, in his drowsy voice. And then, as Simon pushed a fiver onto the plate, he chuckled. "But I know you like pulling our legs about it, too."

They steered their way round the tables and up the stairs to the hotel lobby. It was another of those rare occasions when Mr. Teal had been able to enjoy the Saint's company without any lurking uneasiness about the outcome. For some weeks his life had been comparatively peaceful. No hints of further Saintly lawlessness had come to his ears; and at such times he admitted to himself, with a trace of genuine surprise, that there were few things which entertained him more than a social evening with the gay buccaneer who had set Scotland Yard more mysteries than they would ever solve.

"Drop in and see me next time I'm working on a case, Saint," Teal said in the lobby, with a truly staggering generosity for which the wine must have been partly responsible. "You'll see for yourself how we really do it."

"I'd like to," said the Saint; and if there was the trace of a smile in his eyes when he said it, it was entirely without malice.

He settled his soft hat on his smooth dark head and glanced round the lobby with the vague aimlessness which ordinarily precedes a parting at that hour. A little group of three men had discharged themselves from a nearby lift and were moving boisterously and a trifle unsteadily towards the main entrance. Two of them were hatted and over-coated—a tallish man with a thin line of black moustache, and a tubby red-faced man with rimless spectacles. The third member of the party, who appeared to be the host, was a flabby flat-footed man of about fifty-five with a round bald head and a rather bulbous nose that would have persuaded any observant onlooker to expect that he would have drunk more than the others, which in fact he obviously had. All of them had the dishevelled and rather tragically ridiculous air of Captains of Industry who have gone off duty for the evening.

"That's Lewis Enstone—the chap with the nose," said Teal, who knew everyone. "He might have been one of the biggest men in the City if he could have kept off the bottle."

"And the other two?" asked the Saint incuriously, because he already knew.

"Just a couple of smaller men in the same game. Abe Costello—that's the tall one—and Jules Hammel." Mr. Teal chewed meditatively on his spearmint. "If anything ever happens to them, I shall want to know where you were at the time," he added warningly.

"I shan't know anything about it," said the Saint piously.

He lighted a cigarette and watched the trio of celebrators disinterestedly. Hammel and Costello he knew something about from the untimely reincarnation of Mr. Titus Oates; but the more sozzled member of the party was new to him.

"You do unnerstan', boys, don't you?" Enstone was articulating pathetically, with his arms spread around the shoulders of his guests in an affectionate manner which contributed helpfully towards his support. "It's jus' business. I'm not hard-hearted. I'm kind to my wife an' children an' everything, God bless 'em. An' any time I can do anything for either of you— why, you jus' lemme know."

"That's awfully good of you, old man," said Hammel, with the blurry-eyed solemnity of his condition.

"Less have lunch together on Tuesday," suggested Costello. "We might be able to talk about something that'd interest you."

"Right," said Enstone dimly. "Lush Tooshday. Hic."

"An' don't forget the kids," said Hammel confidentially.

Enstone giggled.

"I shouldn't forget that!" In obscurely elaborate pantomime, he closed his fist with his forefinger extended and his thumb cocked vertically upwards, and aimed the forefinger between Hammel's eyes. "Shtick 'em up!" he commanded gravely, and at once relapsed into further merriment, in which his guests joined somewhat hysterically.

The group separated at the entrance amid much handshaking and back-slapping and alcoholic laughter; and Lewis Enstone wended his way back with cautious and preoccupied steps towards the lift. Mr. Teal took a fresh bite on his gum and tightened his mouth disgustedly.

"Is he staying here?" asked the Saint.

"He lives here," said the detective. "He's lived here even when we knew for a fact that he hadn't got a penny to his name. Why, I remember once——"

He launched into a lengthy anecdote which had all the vitality of personal bitterness in the telling. Simon Templar, listening with the half of one well-trained ear that would prick up into instant attention if the story took any twist that might provide the germ of an adventure, but would remain intently passive if it didn't, smoked his cigarette and gazed abstractedly into space. His mind had that gift of complete division; and he had another job on hand to think about. Somewhere in the course of the story he gathered that Mr. Teal had once lost some money on the Stock Exchange over some shares in which Enstone was speculating; but there was nothing much about that misfortune to attract his interest, and the detective's mood of disparaging reminiscence was as good an opportunity as any other for him to plot out a few details of the campaign against his latest quarry.

". . . So I lost half my money, and I've kept the rest of it in gilt-edged stuff ever since," concluded Mr. Teal rancorously; and Simon took the last inhalation from his cigarette and dropped the stub into an ashtray.

"Thanks for the tip, Claud," he said lightly. "I gather that next time I murder somebody you'd like me to make it a financier."

Teal grunted, and hitched his coat round.

"I shouldn't like you to murder anybody," he said, from his heart. "Now I've got to go home—I have to get up in the morning."

They walked towards the street doors. On

their left they passed the information desk; and beside the desk had been standing a couple of bored and sleepy page-boys. Simon had observed them and their sleepiness as casually as he had observed the colour of the carpet, but all at once he realised that their sleepiness had vanished. He had a sudden queer sensitiveness of suppressed excitement; and then one of the boys said something loud enough to be overheard which stopped Teal in his tracks and turned him round abruptly.

"What's that?" he demanded.

"It's Mr. Enstone, sir. He just shot himself."

Mr. Teal scowled. To the newspapers it would be a surprise and a front-page sensation: to him it was a surprise and a potential menace to his night's rest if he butted into any responsibility. Then he shrugged.

"I'd better have a look," he said, and introduced himself.

There was a scurry to lead him towards the lift. Mr. Teal ambled bulkily into the nearest car, and quite brazenly the Saint followed him. He had, after all, been kindly invited to "drop in" the next time the plump detective was handling a case. . . . Teal put his hands in his pockets and stared in mountainous drowsiness at the downward-flying shaft. Simon studiously avoided his eye, and had a pleasant shock when the detective addressed him almost genially.

"I always thought there was something fishy about that fellow. Did he look as if he'd anything to shoot himself about, except the head that was waiting for him when he woke up?"

It was as if the decease of any financier, however caused, was a benison upon the earth for which Mr. Teal could not help being secretly and quite immorally grateful. That was the subtle impression he gave of his private feelings; but the rest of him was impenetrable stolidity and aloofness. He dismissed the escort of page-boys and strode to the door of the millionaire's suite. It was closed and silent. Teal knocked on it authoritatively, and after a moment it opened six inches and disclosed a pale agitated face. Teal introduced himself again and the door opened wider, enlarging the agitated face into the unmistakable full-length portrait of an assistant hotel manager. Simon followed the detective in, endeavouring to look equally official.

"This will be a terrible scandal, Inspector," said the assistant manager.

Teal looked at him woodenly.

"Were you here when it happened?"

"No. I was downstairs, in my office——"

Teal collected the information, and ploughed past him. On the right, another door opened off the generous lobby; and through it could be seen another elderly man whose equally pale face and air of suppressed agitation bore a certain general similarity and also a self-contained superiority to the first. Even without his sober black coat and striped trousers, grey side-whiskers and passive hands, he would have stamped himself as something more cosmic than the assistant manager of an hotel—the assistant manager of a man.

"Who are you?" asked Teal.

"I am Fowler, sir. Mr. Enstone's valet."

"Were you here?"

"Yes, sir."

"Where is Mr. Enstone?"

"In the bedroom, sir."

They moved back across the lobby, with the assistant manager assuming the lead. Teal stopped. "Will you be in your office if I want you?" he asked, with great politeness; and the assistant manager seemed to disappear from the scene even before the door of the suite closed behind him.

Lewis Enstone was dead. He lay on his back beside the bed, with his head half rolled over to one side, in such a way that both the entrance and the exit of the bullet which had killed him could be seen. It had been fired squarely into his right eye, leaving the ugly trail which only a heavy-calibre bullet fired at close range can leave. . . . The gun lay under the fingers of his right hand.

"Thumb on the trigger," Teal noted aloud.

He sat on the edge of the bed, pulling on a pair of gloves, pink-faced and unemotional. Simon observed the room. An ordinary, very tidy bedroom, barren of anything unusual except the subdued costliness of furnishing. Two windows, both shut and fastened. On a table in one corner, the only sign of disorder, the remains of a carelessly-opened parcel. Brown paper, ends of string, a plain cardboard box—empty. The millionaire had gone no further towards undressing than loosening his tie and undoing his collar.

"What happened?" asked Mr. Teal.

"Mr. Enstone had had friends to dinner, sir," explained Fowler. "A Mr. Costello——"

"I know that. What happened when he came back from seeing them off?"

"He went straight to bed, sir."

"Was this door open?"

"At first, sir. I asked Mr. Enstone about the morning, and he told me to call him at eight. I then asked him whether he wished me to assist him to undress, and he gave me to understand that he did not. He closed the door, and I went back to the sitting-room."

"Did you leave that door open?"

"Yes, sir. I was doing a little clearing up. Then I heard the shot, sir."

"Do you know any reason why Mr. Enstone should have shot himself?"

"On the contrary, sir—I understood that his recent speculations had been highly successful."

Teal nodded.

"Where is his wife?"

"Mrs. Enstone and the children have been in Madeira, sir. We are expecting them home tomorrow."

"What was in that parcel, Fowler?" ventured the Saint.

The valet glanced at the table.

"I don't know, sir. I believe it must have been left by one of Mr. Enstone's guests. I noticed it on the dining-table when I brought in their coats, and Mr. Enstone came back for it on his return and took it into the bedroom with him."

"You didn't hear anything said about it?"

"No, sir. I was not present after coffee had been served—I understood that the gentlemen had private business to discuss."

"What are you getting at?" Mr. Teal asked seriously.

The Saint smiled apologetically; and being

nearest the door, went out to open it as a second knocking disturbed the silence, and let in a grey-haired man with a black bag. While the police surgeon was making his preliminary examination, he drifted into the sitting-room. The relics of a convivial dinner were all there—cigar-butts in the coffee cups, stains of spilt wine on the cloth, crumbs and ash everywhere, the stale smell of food and smoke hanging in the air—but those things did not interest him. He was not quite sure what would have interested him; but he wandered rather vacantly round the room, gazing introspectively at the prints of character which a long tenancy leaves even on anything so characterless as an hotel apartment. There were pictures on the walls and the side tables, mostly enlarged snapshots revealing Lewis Enstone relaxing in the bosom of his family, which amused Simon for some time. On one of the side tables he found a curious object. It was a small wooden plate on which half a dozen wooden fowls stood in a circle. Their necks were pivoted at the base, and underneath the plate were six short strings joined to the necks and knotted together some distance further down where they were all attached at the same point to a wooden ball. It was these strings, and the weight of the ball at their lower ends, which kept the birds' heads raised; and Simon discovered that when he moved the plate so that the ball swung round in a circle underneath, thus tightening and slackening each string in turn, the fowls mounted on the plate pecked vigorously in rotation at an invisible and apparently inexhaustible supply of corn, in a most ingenious mechanical display of gluttony.

He was still playing thoughtfully with the toy when he discovered Mr. Teal standing beside him. The detective's round pink face wore a look of almost comical incredulity.

"Is that how you spend your spare time?" he demanded.

"I think it's rather clever," said the Saint soberly. He put the toy down, and blinked at Fowler. "Does it belong to one of the children?"

"Mr. Enstone brought it home with him this

evening, sir, to give to Miss Annabel tomorrow," said the valet. "He was always picking up things like that. He was a very devoted father, sir."

Mr. Teal chewed for a moment; and then he said: "Have you finished? I'm going home."

Simon nodded pacifically, and accompanied him to the lift. As they went down he asked: "Did you find anything?"

Teal blinked.

"What did you expect me to find?"

"I thought the police were always believed to have a Clue," murmured the Saint innocently.

"Enstone committed suicide," said Teal flatly. "What sort of clues do you want?"

"Why did he commit suicide?" asked the Saint, almost childishly.

Teal ruminated meditatively for a while, without answering. If anyone else had started such a discussion he would have been openly derisive. The same impulse was stirring him then; but he restrained himself. He knew Simon Templar's wicked sense of humour, but he also knew that sometimes the Saint was most worth listening to when he sounded most absurd.

"Call me up in the morning," said Mr. Teal at length, "and I may be able to tell you."

Simon Templar went home and slept fitfully. Lewis Enstone had shot himself—it seemed an obvious fact. The windows had been closed and fastened, and any complicated trick of fastening them from the outside and escaping up or down a rope ladder was ruled out by the bare two or three seconds that could have elapsed between the sound of the shot and the valet rushing in. But Fowler himself might. . . . Why not suicide, anyway? But the Saint could run over every word and gesture and expression of the leave-taking which he himself had witnessed in the hotel lobby, and none of it carried even a hint of suicide. The only oddity about it had been the queer inexplicable piece of pantomime—the fist clenched, with the forefinger extended and the thumb cocked up in crude symbolism of a gun—the abstruse joke which had dissolved Enstone into a fit of inanely delighted giggling, with the hearty approval of his guests. . . . The

psychological problem fascinated him. It muddled itself up with a litter of brown paper and a cardboard box, a wooden plate of pecking chickens, photographs . . . and the tangle kaleidoscoped through his dreams in a thousand different convolutions until morning.

At half-past twelve he found himself turning onto the Embankment with every expectation of being told that Mr. Teal was too busy to see him; but he was shown up a couple of minutes after he had sent in his name.

"Have you found out why Enstone committed suicide?" he asked.

"I haven't," said Teal, somewhat shortly. "His brokers say it's true that he'd been speculating successfully. Perhaps he had another account with a different firm which wasn't so lucky. We'll find out."

"Have you seen Costello or Hammel?"

"I've asked them to come and see me. They're due here about now."

Teal picked up a typewritten memorandum and studied it absorbedly. He would have liked to ask some questions in his turn, but he didn't. He had failed lamentably, so far, to establish any reason whatsoever why Enstone should have committed suicide; and he was annoyed. He felt a personal grievance against the Saint for raising the question without also taking steps to answer it, but pride forbade him to ask for enlightenment. Simon lighted a cigarette and smoked imperturbably until in a few minutes Costello and Hammel were announced. Teal stared at the Saint thoughtfully while the witnesses were seating themselves, but strangely enough he said nothing to intimate that police interviews were not open to outside audiences.

Presently he turned to the tall man with the thin black moustache.

"We're trying to find a reason for Enstone's suicide, Mr. Costello," he said. "How long have you known him?"

"About eight or nine years."

"Have you any idea why he should have shot himself?"

"None at all, Inspector. It was a great shock.

He had been making more money than most of us. When we were with him last night, he was in very high spirits—his family was on the way home, and he was always happy when he was looking forward to seeing them again."

"Did you ever lose money in any of his companies?"

"No."

"You know that we can investigate that?"

Costello smiled slightly.

"I don't know why you should take that attitude, Inspector, but my affairs are open to any examination."

"Have you been making money yourself lately?"

"No. As a matter of fact, I've lost a bit," said Costello frankly. "I'm interested in International Cotton, you know."

He took out a cigarette and a lighter, and Simon found his eyes riveted on the device. It was of an uncommon shape, and by some means or other it produced a glowing heat instead of a flame. Quite unconscious of his own temerity, the Saint said: "That's something new, isn't it? I've never seen a lighter like that before."

Mr. Teal sat back blankly and gave the Saint a look which would have shrivelled any other interrupter to a cinder; and Costello turned the lighter over and said: "It's an invention of my own—I made it myself."

"I wish I could do things like that," said the Saint admiringly. "I suppose you must have had a technical training."

Costello hesitated for a second. Then:

"I started in an electrical engineering workshop when I was a boy," he explained briefly, and turned back to Teal's desk.

After a considerable pause the detective turned to the tubby man with glasses, who had been sitting without any signs of life except the ceaseless switching of his eyes from one speaker to another.

"Are you in partnership with Mr. Costello, Mr. Hammel?" he asked.

"A working partnership—yes."

"Do you know any more about Enstone's affairs than Mr. Costello has been able to tell us?"

"I'm afraid not."

"What were you talking about at dinner last night?"

"It was about a merger. I'm in International Cotton, too. One of Enstone's concerns was Cosmopolitan Textiles. His shares were standing high and ours aren't doing too well, and we thought that if we could induce him to amalgamate it would help us."

"What did Enstone think about that?"

Hammel spread his hands.

"He didn't think there was enough in it for him. We had certain things to offer, but he decided they weren't sufficient."

"There wasn't any bad feeling about it?"

"Why, no. If all the business men who have refused to combine with each other at different times became enemies, there'd hardly be two men in the City on speaking terms."

Simon cleared his throat.

"What was your first important job, Mr. Hammel?" he queried.

Hammel turned his eyes without moving his head.

"I was chief salesman of a general manufacturer in the Midlands."

Teal concluded the interview soon afterwards without securing any further revelations, shook hands perfunctorily with the two men, and ushered them out. When he came back he looked down at the Saint like a cannibal inspecting the latest missionary.

"Why don't you join the force yourself?" he inquired heavily. "The new Police College is open now, and the Commissioner's supposed to be looking for men like you."

Simon took the sally like an armoured car taking a snowball. He was sitting up on the edge of his chair with his blue eyes glinting with excitement.

"You big sap," he retorted, "do you look as if the Police College could teach anyone to solve a murder?"

Teal gulped as if he couldn't believe his ears. He took hold of the arms of his chair and spoke with an apoplectic restraint, as if he were conscientiously determined to give the Saint every fair chance to recover his sanity before he rang down for the bugs wagon.

"What murder are you talking about?" he demanded. "Enstone shot himself."

"Yes, Enstone shot himself," said the Saint. "But it was murder just the same."

"Have you been drinking something?"

"No. But Enstone had."

Teal swallowed, and almost choked himself in the process.

"Are you trying to tell me," he exploded, "that any man ever got drunk enough to shoot himself while he was making money?"

Simon shook his head.

"They made him shoot himself."

"What do you mean—blackmail?"

"No."

The Saint pushed a hand through his hair. He had thought of things like that. He knew that Enstone had shot himself, because no one else could have done it. Except Fowler, the valet—but that was the man whom Teal would have suspected at once if he had suspected anyone, and it was too obvious, too insane. No man in his senses could have planned a murder with himself as the most obvious suspect. Blackmail, then? But the Lewis Enstone he had seen in the lobby had never looked like a man bidding farewell to blackmailers. And how could a man so openly devoted to his family have been led to provide the commoner materials of blackmail?

"No, Claud," said the Saint. "It wasn't that. They just made him do it."

Mr. Teal's spine tingled with the involuntary reflex chill that has its roots in man's immemorial fear of the supernatural. The Saint's conviction was so wild and yet real that for one fantastic moment the detective had a vision of Costello's intense black eyes fixed and dilating in a hypnotic stare, his slender sensitive hands moving in weird passes, his lips under the thin black moustache mouthing necromantic commands. . . . It changed into another equally fantastic vision of two courteous but inflexible gentlemen handing a weapon to a third, bowing and going away, like a deputation to an officer who has been found to be a traitor, offering the graceful alternative to a court-martial—for the Honour of High Finance. . . . Then it went sheer to derision.

"They just said: 'Lew, why don't you shoot yourself?' and he thought it was a great idea—is that it?" he gibed.

"It was something like that," Simon answered soberly. "You see, Enstone would do almost anything to amuse his children."

Teal's mouth opened, but no sounds came from it. His expression implied that a whole volcano of devastating sarcasm was boiling on the tip of his tongue, but that the Saint's lunacy had soared into realms of waffiness beyond the reach of repartee.

"Costello and Hammel had to do something," said the Saint. "International Cottons have been very bad for a long time—as you'd have known if you hadn't packed all your stuff away in a gilt-edged sock. On the other hand, Enstone's interest—Cosmopolitan Textiles—were good. Costello and Hammel could have pulled out in two ways: either by a merger, or else by having Enstone commit suicide so that Cosmopolitans would tumble down in the scare and they could buy them in—you'll probably find they've sold a bear in them all through the month, trying to break the price. And if you look at the papers this afternoon you'll see that all Enstone's securities have dropped through the bottom of the market—a bloke in his position can't commit suicide without starting a panic. Costello and Hammel went to dinner to try for the merger, but if Enstone turned it down they were ready for the other thing."

"Well?" said Teal obstinately; but for the first time there seemed to be a tremor in the foundations of his disbelief.

"They only made one big mistake. They didn't arrange for Lew to leave a letter."

"People have shot themselves without leaving letters."

"I know. But not often. That's what started me thinking."

"Well?" said the detective again.

Simon rumpled his hair into more profound disorder, and said: "You see, Claud, in my disreputable line of business you're always thinking: 'Now, what would A do?—and what would B do?—and what would C do?' You have to be able to get inside people's minds and know what they're going to do and how they're going to do it, so you can always be one jump ahead of 'em. You have to be a practical psychologist—just like the head salesman of a general manufacturer in the Midlands."

Teal's mouth opened, but for some reason which was beyond his conscious comprehension he said nothing. And Simon Templar went on, in the disjointed way that he sometimes fell into when he was trying to express something which he himself had not yet grasped in bare words:

"Sales psychology is just a study of human weaknesses. And that's a funny thing, you know. I remember the manager of one of the biggest novelty manufacturers in the world telling me that the soundest test of any idea for a new toy was whether it would appeal to a middle-aged business man. It's true, of course. It's so true that it's almost stopped being a joke—the father who plays with his little boy's birthday presents so energetically that the little boy has to shove off and smoke papa's pipe. Every middle-aged business man has that strain of childishness in him somewhere, because without it he would never want to spend his life gathering more paper millions than he can ever spend, and building up rickety castles of golden cards that are always ready to topple over and be built up again. It's just a glorified kid's game with a box of bricks. If all the mighty earth-shaking business men weren't like that they could never have built up an economic system in which the fate of nations, all the hunger and happiness and achievement of the world, was locked up in bars of yellow tooth-stopping." Simon raised his eyes suddenly—they were very bright and in some queer fashion sightless, as if his mind was separated from every physical awareness of his surroundings. "Lewis Enstone was just that kind of a man," he said.

"Are you still thinking of that toy you were playing with?" Teal asked restlessly.

"That—and other things we heard. And the photographs. Did you notice them?"

"No."

"One of them was Enstone playing with a clockwork train. In another of them he was under a rug, being a bear. In another he was working a big model merry-go-round. Most of the pictures were like that. The children came into them, of course, but you could see that Enstone was having the swellest time."

Teal, who had been fidgeting with a pencil, shrugged brusquely and sent it clattering across the desk.

"You still haven't shown me a murder," he stated.

"I had to find it myself," said the Saint gently. "You see, it was a kind of professional problem. Enstone was happily married, happy with his family, no more crooked than any other big-time financier, nothing on his conscience, rich and getting richer—how were they to make him commit suicide? If I'd been writing a story with him in it, for instance, how could I have made him commit suicide?"

"You'd have told him he had cancer," said Teal caustically, "and he'd have fallen for it."

Simon shook his head.

"No. If I'd been a doctor—perhaps. But if Costello or Hammel had suggested it, he'd have wanted confirmation. And did he look like a man who'd just been told that he might have cancer?"

"It's your murder," said Mr. Teal, with the beginnings of a drowsy tolerance that was transparently rooted in sheer resignation. "I'll let you solve it."

"There were lots of pieces missing at first," said the Saint. "I only had Enstone's character and weaknesses. And then it came out—Hammel was a psychologist. That was good, because I'm a bit of a psychologist myself, and his mind would work something like mine. And then Costello could invent mechanical gadgets and make them himself. He shouldn't have fetched out that lighter, Claud—it gave me another of the missing pieces. And then there was the box."

"Which box?"

"The cardboard box—on his table, with the brown paper. You know Fowler said that he thought either Hammel or Costello left it. Have you got it here?"

"I expect it's somewhere in the building."

"Could we have it up?"

With the gesture of a blasé hangman reaching for the noose, Teal took hold of the telephone on his desk.

"You can have the gun, too, if you like," he said.

"Thanks," said the Saint. "I wanted the gun."

Teal gave the order; and they sat and looked at each other in silence until the exhibits arrived. Teal's silence explained in fifty different ways that the Saint would be refused no facilities for nailing down his coffin in a manner that he would never be allowed to forget; but for some reason his facial register was not wholly convincing. When they were alone again, Simon went to the desk, picked up the gun, and put it in the box. It fitted very well.

"That's what happened, Claud," he said with quiet triumph. "They gave him the gun in the box."

"And he shot himself without knowing what he was doing," Teal said witheringly.

"That's just it," said the Saint, with a blue devil of mockery in his gaze. "He didn't know what he was doing."

Mr. Teal's molars clamped down cruelly on the inoffensive merchandise of the Wrigley Corporation.

"Well, what did he *think* he was doing—sitting under a rug pretending to be a bear?"

Simon sighed.

"That's what I'm trying to work out."

Teal's chair creaked as his full weight slumped back in it in hopeless exasperation.

"Is that what you've been taking up so much of my time about?" he asked wearily.

"But I've got an idea, Claud," said the Saint, getting up and stretching himself. "Come out and lunch with me, and let's give it a rest. You've been thinking for nearly an hour, and I don't want your brain to overheat. I know a new place—wait, I'll look up the address."

He looked it up in the telephone directory; and Mr. Teal got up and took down his bowler hat from its peg. His baby blue eyes were inscru-tably thoughtful, but he followed the Saint without thought. Whatever else the Saint wanted to say, however crazy he felt that it must be, it was something he had to hear or else fret over for the rest of his days. They drove in a taxi to Knights-bridge, with Mr. Teal chewing phlegmatically, in a superb affectation of bored unconcern. Presently the taxi stopped, and Simon climbed out. He led the way into an apartment building and into a lift, saying something to the operator which Teal did not catch.

"What is this?" he asked, as they shot upwards. "A new restaurant?"

"It's a new place," said the Saint vaguely.

The elevator stopped, and they got out. They went along the corridor, and Simon rang the bell of one of the doors. It was opened by a good-looking maid who might have been other things in her spare time.

"Scotland Yard," said the Saint brazenly, and squeezed past her. He found his way into the sitting-room before anyone could stop him: Chief Inspector Teal, recovering from the momentary paralysis of the shock, followed him: then came the maid.

"I'm sorry, sir—Mr. Costello is out."

Teal's bulk obscured her. All the boredom had smudged itself off his face, giving place to blank amazement and anger.

"What the devil's this joke?" he blared.

"It isn't a joke, Claud," said the Saint reck-lessly. "I just wanted to see if I could find something—you know what we were talking about——"

His keen gaze was quartering the room; and then it lighted on a big cheap kneehole desk whose well-worn shabbiness looked strangely out of keeping with the other furniture. On it was a litter of coils and wire and ebonite and dials—all the junk out of which amateur wireless sets are created. Simon reached the desk in his next stride, and began pulling open the drawers. Tools of all kinds, various gauges of wire and screws, odd wheels and sleeves and bolts and scraps of sheet-iron and brass, the completely typical hoard of any amateur mechanic's work-shop. Then he came to a drawer that was locked.

Without hesitation he caught up a large screwdriver and rammed it in above the lock: before anyone could grasp his intentions he had splintered the drawer open with a skilful twist.

Teal let out a shout and started across the room. Simon's hand dived into the drawer, came out with a nickel-plated revolver—it was exactly the same as the one with which Lewis Enstone had shot himself, but Teal wasn't noticing things like that. His impression was that the Saint really had gone raving mad after all, and the sight of the gun pulled him up for a moment as the sight of a gun in the hands of any other raving maniac would have pulled him up.

"Put that down, you fool!" he yelled, and then he let out another shout as he saw the Saint turn the muzzle of the gun close up to his right eye, with his thumb on the trigger, exactly as Enstone must have held it. Teal lurched forward and knocked the weapon aside with a sweep of his arm; then he grabbed Simon by the wrist. "That's enough of that," he said, without realising what a futile thing it was to say.

Simon looked at him and smiled.

"Thanks for saving my life, old beetroot," he murmured kindly. "But it really wasn't necessary. You see, Claud, that's the gun Enstone *thought* he was playing with!"

The maid was under the table letting out the opening note of a magnificent fit of hysterics. Teal let go the Saint, hauled her out, and shook her till she was quiet. There were more events cascading on him in those few seconds than he knew how to cope with, and he was not gentle.

"It's all right, miss," he growled. "I am from Scotland Yard. Just sit down somewhere, will you?" He turned back to Simon. "Now, what's all this about?"

"The gun, Claud. Enstone's toy."

The Saint raised it again—his smile was quite sane, and with the feeling that he himself was the madman, Teal let him do what he wanted. Simon put the gun to his eye and pulled the trigger—pulled it, released it, pulled it again, keeping up the rhythmic movement. Something inside the gun whirred smoothly, as if wheels were whizzing round under the working of the lever. Then he pointed the gun straight into Teal's face and did the same thing.

Teal stared frozenly down the barrel and saw the black hole leap into a circle of light. He was looking at a flickering cinematograph film of a boy shooting a masked burglar. It was tiny, puerile in subject, but perfect. It lasted about ten seconds, and then the barrel went dark again.

"Costello's present for Enstone's little boy," explained the Saint quietly. "He invented it and made it himself, of course—he always had a talent that way. Haven't you ever seen those electric flashlights that work without a battery? You keep on squeezing a lever, and it turns a miniature dynamo. Costello made a very small one, and fitted it into the hollow casting of a gun. Then he geared a tiny strip of film to it. It was a jolly good new toy, Claud Eustace, and he must have been proud of it. They took it along to Enstone's; and when he'd turned down their merger and there was nothing else for them to do, they let him play with it just enough to tickle his palate, at just the right hour of the evening. Then they took it away from him and put it back in its box and gave it to him. They had a real gun in another box ready to make the switch."

Chief Inspector Teal stood like a rock, his jaws clamping a wad of spearmint that he had at last forgotten to chew. Then he said: "How did they know he wouldn't shoot his own son?"

"That was Hammel. He knew that Enstone wasn't capable of keeping his hands off a toy like that; and just to make certain he reminded Enstone of it the last thing before they left. He was a practical psychologist—I suppose we can begin to speak of him in the past tense now." Simon Templar smiled again, and fished a cigarette out of his pocket. "But why I should bother to tell you all this when you could have got it out of a stool pigeon," he murmured, "is more than I can understand. I must be getting soft-hearted in my old age, Claud. After all, when you're so far ahead of Sherlock Holmes——"

Mr. Teal gulped pinkly, and picked up the telephone.

THE ASHCOMB POOR CASE

HULBERT FOOTNER

WILLIAM HULBERT FOOTNER (1879–1944) was born in Hamilton, Ontario. He went to school in New York City and began his journalism career there, then moved back to Canada to take a newspaper job in Alberta. He had brief careers as an actor, playwright, and screenwriter. His early fiction reflects his locale as he set his mystery-adventure novels in northwest Canada. He returned to the United States and wrote mainly detective stories, primarily about two utterly disparate characters. Amos Lee Mappin, a wealthy author and criminologist who functions as an amateur detective, resembles the Mr. Pickwick of Charles Dickens. He is the protagonist in ten novels, though he seldom actually solves the mysteries, leaving "the dirty work" to his friends. Footner used his friend Christopher Morley as a major character in the first Mappin book, *The Mystery of the Folded Paper* (1930). Morley reciprocated by writing a warm tribute to Footner's posthumously published *Orchids to Murder* (1945).

Quite different from Mappin is the breathtakingly gorgeous Madame Rosika Storey, who describes herself as "a practical psychologist—specializing in the feminine." She made her debut in *The Under Dogs* (1925) and appears in eight additional books, mostly short collections such as *Madame Story* (1926), *The Velvet Hand: New Madame Storey Mysteries* (1928), and *The Almost Perfect Murder: More Madame Storey Mysteries* (1933).

"The Ashcomb Poor Case" was first published in *Madame Storey* (New York, Doran, 1926).

THE ASHCOMB POOR CASE

HULBERT FOOTNER

I

MOST OF YOU will remember how the murder of Ashcomb Poor set the whole town agog. The victim's wealth and social position and the scandalous details of his private life that began to ooze out whetted the public appetite for sensation to the highest degree. For years Ashcomb Poor had been one of the most beparagraphed men in town, and now the manner of his taking off seemed like a tremendous climax to a thrilling tale.

The day it first came out in the papers Madame Storey did not arrive at the office until noon. She was very plainly dressed and wore a thick veil that partly obscured her features. By this time I was accustomed to these metamorphoses of costume. From a little bag she carried she took several articles and handed them over to me. These were (a) a hank of thin green string in a snarl, (b) a piece of iridescent chiffon, partly burned, (c) an envelope containing seven cigarette butts.

"Some scraps of evidence in the Ashcomb Poor case," she explained. "Put them in a safe place."

I had just been reading the newspaper report.

"What! Have we been engaged in that case already?" I exclaimed. Madame Storey encouraged me to speak of our business in the first person plural, and of course it flattered me to do so.

"No," she said, smiling, "but we may be. At

any rate, I have forearmed myself by taking a look over the ground."

In the rear of her room there was a smaller one that she used as a retiring- and dressing-room. She changed there now to a more suitable costume.

Two days later she remarked: "The signs tell me that we shall receive a call from the district attorney's office to-day."

Sure enough, Assistant District Attorney Barron turned up before the morning was over. Though he was a young man for the job, he was a capable one, and held over through several succeeding administrations. This was the first time I had seen him, though it turned out he was an old friend of Madame Storey's. A handsome, full-blooded fellow, his weakness was that he thought just a little too well of himself.

I showed him into the private office and returned to my desk. There is a dictagraph installed between Madame Storey's desk and mine, and when it is turned on I am supposed to listen and make a transcript of whatever conversation may be taking place. Sometimes, to my chagrin, she turns it off at the most exciting moment, but more often she leaves it on, I am sure, out of pure good nature, because she knows I am so keenly interested. Madame Storey is good enough to say that she likes me to be in possession of full information, so that she can talk things over with me.

The circuit was open now, and I heard him

say: "My God, Rose, you're more beautiful than ever!"

"Thanks, Walter," she dryly retorted. "The dictagraph is on, and my secretary can hear everything you say."

"For Heaven's sake, turn it off!"

"I can't now, or she'd imagine the worst. You'll have to stick to business. I suppose you've come to see me about the Ashcomb Poor case."

"What makes you jump to that conclusion?"

"Oh, you were about due."

"Humph! I suppose that's intended to be humorous. If you weren't quite so sure of yourself you'd be a great woman, Rose. But it's a weakness in you. You think you know everything."

"Well, what did you come to see me about?"

"As a matter of fact, it was the Ashcomb Poor case. But that was just a lucky shot on your part. I suppose you read that I had been assigned to the case."

"Walter, you're a good prosecutor, but you lack a sense of humour."

"Well, you're all right in your own line, feminine psychology and all that. I gladly hand it to you. But the trouble with you is, you want to tell me how to run my job too."

"No one could do that, Walter."

"What do you mean?"

"Never mind. How does the Poor case stand?"

"I suppose you've read the papers."

"Yes; they're no nearer the truth than usual. Give me an outline of the situation as you see it."

"Well, you know the Ashcomb Poors. Topnotchers; fine old family, money, and all that; leaders in the ultra-smart Prince's Valley set on Long Island. They have what they call a small house out at Grimstead, where they make believe to live in quiet style; it's the thing nowadays."

"In other words, the extravagantly simple life."

"Exactly. They have no children. The household consisted of Mr. and Mrs. Poor, Miss Philippa Dean, Mrs. Poor's secretary, Mrs. Batten, the housekeeper, a butler, and three maids; there were outside servants, too—chauffeur, gardener, and so on—but they don't come into the case. Ashcomb Poor was a handsome man and a free liver. Things about him have been coming out—well, you know. On the other hand, his wife was above scandal, a great beauty——"

"Vintage of 1904."

"Well, perhaps; but still in the running. These women know how to keep their looks. Very charitable woman and all that. Greatly looked up to. On Monday night Mrs. Poor took part in a big affair at the Pudding-Stone Country Club near their home. A pageant of all nations or something. Her husband, who did not care for such functions, stayed at home. So did Miss Dean and Mrs. Batten. Mrs. Poor took the other servants to see the show."

"There were only three left in the house, then?"

"Yes—Mr. Poor, Miss Dean, and Mrs. Batten."

"Go on."

"Mrs. Poor returned from the entertainment about midnight. Mrs. Batten let her in the front door. Standing there, the two women could see into the library, where Poor sat with his back to them. They were struck by something strange in his attitude, and started to investigate, Mrs. Batten in advance.

"She was the first to realise that something had happened, and tried to keep Mrs. Poor from approaching the body. They struggled. Mrs. Poor screamed. The girl, Philippa Dean, suddenly appeared, nobody can tell from where. A moment later the other servants, who had gone around to the back door, ran in.

"Well, there was the situation. He had been shot in the back. The pistol was there. The butler telephoned to friends of the family and to the police. Grimstead, as you know, is within the city limits, so it comes within our jurisdiction. I was notified of the affair within an hour and ordered to take personal charge of the case. Nothing had been disturbed. I ordered the arrest of the Dean girl, and she is still in custody."

"What do you want of me?" Madame Storey inquired.

"I want you to see the girl. Frankly, she baffles me. Under our questioning she broke down before morning and confessed to killing the man. But the next day she repudiated her confession, and has obstinately stuck to her repudiation in spite of all we could do. I want you to see her and get a regular confession."

"What about the girl's lawyer?"

"She has none as yet. Refused to see one."

"You're sure she did it?"

"Absolutely. It was immediately apparent that the murder had been committed by one of the inmates of the house."

"Why?"

"Because when Mr. Poor and the servants departed for the entertainment Mrs. Batten, who let them out, turned on the burglar-alarm, and it remained turned on until she let her mistress in again. One of the first things I did on arriving at the house was to make sure that the alarm was working properly. I also examined all the doors and windows. Everything was intact."

"Why couldn't the housekeeper have done it?"

"A simple, timid old soul! Impossible! No motive. Besides, if she had she would hardly have given me the principal piece of evidence against those in the house; I mean her testimony about the burglar-alarm."

"What motive could the girl have had?"

"The servants state that their master had been pestering her—forcing his attentions on her."

"Ah! But this is all presumptive evidence, of course. What else have you?"

"Ashcomb Poor was shot with an automatic pistol belonging to Miss Dean. The butler identified it. At first she denied that it was hers. She could not deny, though, that she had one like it, and when asked to produce it she could not. It was not among her effects."

"Where did you find the gun exactly?"

"In the dead man's hand."

"In his hand?"

"Under his hand, I should say. It had been shoved under in a clumsy attempt to make it appear like a suicide. But the hand was clenched

on top of the weapon. Moreover, the man was shot between the shoulders. He could not possibly have done it himself. The bullet passed completely through his body, and I found it lodged in the wall across the room."

"Did the housekeeper hear the shot?"

"She did not. She was in another wing of the house."

"Anything else against the girl?"

"Yes. When she appeared, attracted by Mrs. Poor's cry, though she was supposed to have retired some time before, she was fully dressed. Moreover, she knew what had happened before any one told her."

"Ah! How does she explain these suspicious circumstances?"

"She will explain nothing. Refuses to talk."

"What story did she tell when she confessed?"

"None. Merely cried out: 'I did it—I did it. Don't ask me any more!'"

There was a silence here, during which Madame Storey presumably ruminated on what she had been told. Finally she said: "I'll see the girl, but it must be upon my own conditions."

"What are those?"

"As an independent investigator. I hold no brief for the district attorney's office."

"Well, there's no harm in that."

"But you must understand what that implies. Neither you nor any of your men may be present while I am talking to her. And I do not bind myself to tell you everything she tells me."

"That's out of the question. What would the old man say if he knew that I turned her over to an outsider?"

"Well, that's up to you, of course." Madame Storey spoke indifferently. "You came to me, you know."

"Well—all right." This very sullenly. "I suppose if she confesses you'll let me know."

"Certainly. But I'm not at all sure this is going to turn out the way you expect."

"After all I've told you?"

"Your case against her is a little too good, Walter."

"Who else could have done it?"

"I don't know—yet. If she did it, why should she have stuck around the house until you arrested her?"

"She supposed it would be considered a suicide."

"But, according to you, a year-old child wouldn't have been deceived into thinking so."

"Well, you never can tell. They always do something foolish. Will you come down to the Tombs? I'll arrange for a room there."

"No, I must see the girl here."

"That's impossible."

"Sorry; it's my invariable rule, you know."

"But have a heart, Rose. I daren't let her out of my custody."

"You and your men can wait outside the door, then."

"It's most irregular."

"I am an irregular person," was the bland reply. "You should not have come to me."

"Well—I suppose you must have your own way."

"Always do, my dear. With the girl send a transcript of whatever statements have been taken down in the case."

"All right. Rose, turn off that confounded dictagraph, will you? I want to speak to you privately."

"It's off."

It wasn't though, for I continued to hear every word.

"Good God, Rose, why do you persist in trying to madden me?"

"Mercy, Walter! How?"

"You know—with your cold and scornful airs, your indifference. It's—it's only vanity. Your vanity is ridiculous!"

"Oh, if you're only going to call names, I'll turn on the dictagraph."

"No, don't, don't! I scarcely know what I'm saying, you provoke me so. Why won't you be decent to me, Rose? Why won't you take me? We were made for each other."

"So *you* say."

"Do you never feel anything, anything behind that scornful smile? Are you a breathing woman or a cold and heartless monster?"

"Bless me, I don't know."

"You need a master."

"Of course I do. Why don't you master me, Walter?"

"Don't taunt me. A man has his limits. You make me want to seize and hurt you."

"Don't do that. You'd spoil my pretty frock. Besides, Giannino would bite the back of your neck."

"Don't taunt me. You'd be helpless in my arms. You're always asking for a master."

"I meant a master of my soul, Walter."

"I don't understand you."

"Yes, you do. Look at me! You can't. My soul is stronger than yours, Walter, and in your heart you know it."

"You're talking nonsense."

"Don't mumble your words. That's my tragedy, if you only knew it. I have yet to meet a man bold enough to face me down. How could I surrender myself to one whose soul was secretly afraid of mine? So here I sit. You know that the madame I have hitched to my name is just to save my face. No one would believe that a woman as beautiful as I could be still unmarried—and respectable. But I am both, worse luck!"

"It's your own fault that you're alone. You think too well of yourself. You make believe to scorn all men."

"Well, if it's a bluff, why doesn't some man call it?"

"I will right now. I'm tired of this fooling. You've got to marry me."

"Look at me when you say that, Walter."

A silence.

"Ah!—you can't, you see."

"Ah, Rose, don't torture me this way! Can't you see I'm mad about you? You spoil my rest at night; you come between me and my work by day. I hunger and thirst for you like a man in a desert. Think what a team you and I would make, Rose. There'd be no stopping us short of the White House."

Here, to my chagrin, the dictagraph was

abruptly turned off, but when, a minute or two later, Mr. Barron burst out of the inner room purple with rage I guessed that no change had occurred in the situation. He flung across the floor and out of the door without a glance in my direction.

Madame Storey called to me to bring in my notebook. As I entered she was talking to the monkey.

"Giannino, you are better off than you know. Better be a dumb beast than a half-thinking animal."

The little thing wrinkled up his forehead and chirruped as he always did when she addressed him.

"You disagree with me? I tell you men would rather go to jail than put themselves to the trouble of thinking clearly."

II

Eddie, the hall-boy, and I had become at least outwardly friendly. In his heart I think Eddie always despised me as "a jane out of the storehouse"—one of his own expressions—but as he had the keenest curiosity about all that went on in our shop, he was obliged to be affable in order to tap such sources of information as I possessed. He adored Madame Storey, of course; all youths did, as well as older males. As for me, I couldn't help liking the amusing little wretch—he was so new.

Like most boys of his age his ruling passion was for airplanes and aviators. At this time his particular idol was the famous Lieutenant George Grantland, who had broken so many records. Grantland had just started on a three days' point-to-point flight from Camp Tasker, encircling the whole country east of the Mississippi, and Eddie, in order to follow him, was obliged to buy an extra every hour. Bursting with the subject and having no one else to talk to, he brought these up to my room. This was his style—of course I am only guessing at the figures.

"Here's the latest. Landed at New Orleans four-thirty this a.m., two hours ahead of time. Gee! If I could only get out to a bulletin-board! Slept four hours and went on. Four hundred and forty-two miles in under four hours. Wouldn't that expand your lungs? Say, that guy is a king of the air all right. Flies by night as well as day. They have lights to guide him where to land. Hasn't had to come down once for trouble. Here's a picture of his plane. It's the Bentley-Critchard type. They're just out. Good for a hundred and forty an hour. Six hundred horse. Do you get that? Think of driving six hundred plugs through the clouds. Some team!"

After two days of this I was almost as well acquainted with the exploits of Lieutenant Grantland as his admirer. Every hour or two Eddie would have a new picture of the dashing aviator to show me. Even after being snapshotted in the blazing sun and reproduced in a newspaper half-tone, he remained a handsome young fellow.

Eddie was in the thick of this when they brought Philippa Dean up from the Tombs, but as she was indubitably a "class one jane," his attention was momentarily won from his newspapers. The assistant district attorney did not accompany her. To be obliged to wait outside was, I suppose, too great a trial to his dignity. Miss Dean was under escort of two gigantic plain-clothes men, the slender little thing. I was glad, at any rate, that they had not handcuffed her.

My first impression was a favourable one; her eyes struck you at once. They were full, limpid, blue, very wide open under fine brows, giving her an expression of proud candour in which there was something really affecting—however, I had learned ere this from Madame Storey that you cannot read a woman's soul in her eyes; so I reserved judgment. Her hair was light-brown. She was dressed with that fine simplicity which is the despair of newly arrived women. At present she looked hard and wary, and her lips were compressed into a scarlet line—but that was small wonder in her situation.

Madame Storey came out when she heard them. What was her first impression of the girl I cannot say, for she never gave anything away in her face at such moments. She invited the two detectives to make themselves comfortable in the outer office, and we three women passed into the big room. She waved the girl to a seat.

"You may relax," she said smiling; "nobody is going to put you through the third degree here."

But the girl sat down bolt upright, with her hands clenched in her lap. It was painful to see that tightness. Madame Storey applied herself to the task of charming it away. She said to the ape:

"Giannino, take off your hat to Miss Dean, and tell her that we wish her well."

The little animal stood up on the table, jerked off his cap and gibbered in his own tongue. It was a performance that never failed to win a smile, but this girl's lips looked as if they had forgotten how.

"The assistant district attorney has asked me to examine you," Madame Storey began in friendly style. "Being a public prosecutor, he's bent on your conviction, having nobody else to accuse. But I may as well tell you that I don't share his feelings. Indeed, he's so cock-sure that it would give me pleasure to prove him wrong."

I knew that my employer was sincere in saying this, but I suppose the poor girl had learned to her cost that the devil himself can be sympathetic. At any rate, the speech had no effect on her.

"I hope you will believe that I have no object except to discover the truth," Madame Storey went on.

"That's what they all say," muttered the girl.

"Satisfy yourself in your own way as to whether you can trust me. Come, we have all afternoon."

"Am I obliged to answer your questions?" demanded the girl.

"By no means," was the prompt reply. "Why don't you question me first?"

The girl took her at her word. "Who are you?" she asked. "I have been told nothing."

"Madame Rosika Storey. They call me a practical psychologist. The district attorney's office sometimes does me the honour to consult me, particularly in the cases of women."

"You'll get no confession out of me."

"I don't expect to. I don't believe you did it. No sane woman would shoot a man between the shoulder-blades and expect to make out that it was a suicide. At any rate, Ashcomb Poor seems to have richly deserved his fate. Come now, frankly, did you do it?"

The girl's blue eyes flashed. "I did not."

"Good! Then tell me what happened that night."

The girl sullenly shook her head. "What's the use?"

"Why, to clear yourself, naturally."

"They haven't enough evidence to convict me. They *couldn't* convict me, because I didn't do it."

"That's a perilous line to take, my dear. I suspect you haven't had much experience with juries. The gentlemen of the jury would consider silence in a woman not only unnatural, but incriminating. Of course they might let you off, anyway, if you condescended to ogle them, but as I say, it's perilous. Why did you confess in the first place?"

"To get rid of them. They were driving me out of my mind with their questions."

"I can well understand that. Well then, what did happen, really?"

The girl set her lips. "I have made up my mind to say nothing, and I shall stick to it," she replied.

Madame Storey spread out her hands. "Very well, let's talk about something else. Dean is a good name here in New York. Are you of the New York family?"

"My people have lived here for four generations."

"I have read of a great beau in the sixties and seventies—Philip Dean. Are you related to him?"

"He was my grandfather."

"I might have guessed it from your first name.

How interesting! All the chronicles of those days are full of references to his wit and *savoir faire.* But he must have been a rich man. How does it come that you have to work for your living?"

"The usual story: the first two generations won the family fortune, and the next two lost it. I am of the fifth generation."

"Well, I suppose one cannot have a famous *bon vivant* in the family for nothing."

"Oh, no one could speak ill of my grandfather. He was a gallant gentleman. I knew him as a child. He spent his money in scientific experiments which only benefited others. My poor father was not to blame either. He lost the rest of the money trying to recoup his father's losses in Wall Street."

"And you were thrown on your own resources."

"Oh, I was never a pathetic figure. I could get work. There were always women, not very sure of themselves socially, who were glad to engage Philip Dean's granddaughter."

"That's how you came to go to Mrs. Poor?"

"No, that was different. Mrs. Poor didn't need anybody to tell her things. Her family was as good as my own. Her husband was travelling abroad and she was lonely. She engaged me as a sort of companion."

"When did her husband return?"

The girl frowned. "Now you think you're leading me up to it, don't you?"

Madame Storey laughed. "I suspect you're the kind of young lady that nobody can lead any farther than she is willing to go."

Miss Dean glanced suspiciously at me. "Is she taking down all I say?" she demanded.

"Not until I tell her to," Madame Storey replied.

"He returned two months ago."

"Do you mind describing their house at Grimstead for me?" asked Madame Storey. "There's no harm in that, is there?"

The girl shrugged. "No. It's a small house, considering their means, and it looks even smaller because of being built in the style of an English cottage, with low, overhanging eaves and

dormer windows. You enter through a vestibule under the stairs and issue into a square hall. This hall is two stories high and has a gallery running around three sides. On your left is the library; on your right the small reception-room; the living-room, a large room, is at the back of the hall, with the dining-room adjoining it. These two rooms look out over the garden and the brook below. Between reception and dining-room there is a passage leading away to the kitchen wing. Besides pantry, kitchen, and laundry, this wing has a housekeeper's room and a servants' dining-room."

"And upstairs?"

"Mr. and Mrs. Poor's own suite is at the back of the house over the living-room and dining-room. My room is over the library. There is a guest room over the reception-room. All the servants' rooms are in the kitchen wing. There is no third story."

Madame Storey affected to consult the notes on her desk. "Where was this burglar-alarm that there has been so much talk about?"

"Hidden in a cranny between the telephone-booth and the hall fireplace. The telephone-booth was let into the wall just beyond the library door, and the fireplace is adjoining."

"Hidden, you say. Was there anything secret about it?"

"No. Everybody in the house knew of it."

"What kind of switch was it?"

"It was just a little handle that lifted up and pulled down. When it was up it was off; when it was down it was on."

"Describe the servants, will you?"

"How is one to describe servants? The butler, Briggs—well, he was just a butler, smooth, deferential, fairly efficient. The maids were just typical maids. None of them had been there long. Servants don't stick nowadays."

"What about Mrs. Batten?"

In spite of herself the girl's face softened— yet at the same time a guarded tone crept into her voice. "Oh, she's different," she said.

Madame Storey did not miss the guarded tone. "How different?" she asked.

"I didn't look on Mrs. Batten as a servant but as a friend."

"Describe her for me."

The girl, looking down, paused before replying. Her softened face was wholly charming. "A simple kindly, motherly soul," she said with a half-smile. "Rather absurd, because she takes everything so seriously. But while you laugh at her you get more fond of her. She doesn't mind being laughed at."

"You have the knack of hitting off character," said Madame Storey. "I see her perfectly."

I began to appreciate Madame Storey's wizardry. Cautiously feeling her way with the girl, she had discovered that Philippa had a talent for description in which she took pride—perhaps the girl aspired to be a writer. At any rate, when she was asked to describe anything, her eyes became bright and abstracted, and she forgot her situation for the moment.

It seemed to me that we were on the verge of stumbling on something, but to my surprise Madame Storey dropped Mrs. Batten. "Describe Mrs. Poor for me," she asked.

"That is more difficult," the girl said unhesitatingly. "She is a complex character. We got along very well together. She was always kind, always most considerate. Indeed, she was an admirable woman, not in the least spoiled by the way people kowtowed to her. But I cannot say that I knew her very well, because she was always reserved—I mean with everybody. One felt sometimes that she would like to unbend, but had never learned how."

"And the master of the house?"

The girl shuddered slightly. But still preoccupied in conveying her impressions, she did not take alarm. "He was a rich man," she answered, "and the son of a rich man. That is to say, from babyhood he had never been denied anything. Yet he was an attractive man—when he got his own way; full of spirits and good nature. Everybody liked him—that is, nearly everybody."

"Didn't you like him?" asked Madame Storey.

"Yes, I did in a way—but——" She stopped.

"But what?"

She hung her head. "I'm talking too much," she muttered.

Madame Storey appeared to drop the whole matter with an air of relief. "Let's have tea," she said to me. "I can see from Giannino's sorrowful eyes that he is famishing."

I hastened into the next room for the things. Madame Storey, in the way that she has, started to rattle on about cakes as if they were the most important things in the world.

"Every afternoon at this hour Miss Brickley and Giannino and I regale ourselves. We have cakes sent in from the pastrycook's. Don't you love cakes with thick icing all over them? I'm childish on the subject. When I was a little girl I swore to myself that when I grew up I would stuff myself with iced cakes."

When I returned I saw that in spite of herself the girl had relaxed even further. Her eyes sparkled at the sight of the great silver plate of cakes. After all, she was a human girl, and I don't suppose she'd been able to indulge her sweet tooth in jail. Giannino set up an excited chattering. Upon being given his share he retired to his favourite perch on top of a big picture to make away with it.

While we ate and drank we talked of everything that women talk of: cakes, clothes, tenors, and what-not. One would never have guessed that the thought of murder was present in each of our minds. The girl relaxed completely. It was charming to watch the play of her expressive eyes.

Madame Storey, who, notwithstanding her boasted indulgence, was very abstemious, finished her cake and lighted the inevitable cigarette. Giannino stroked her cheek, begging piteously for more cake, but the plate had been put out of his way. Madame Storey, happening to lay down her cigarette, Giannino, ever on the watch for such a contingency, snatched it up and clambered with chatterings of derision up to the top of his picture. There he sat with half-closed eyes blowing clouds of smoke in the most abandoned manner. Philippa Dean laughed outright;

it was strange to hear that sound from her. I was obliged to climb on a chair to recover the cigarette. I spend half my time following up that little wretch. If I don't take the cigarette from him it makes him sick, yet he hasn't sense enough to leave them alone—just like a man.

"Well, shall we go on with our talk?" asked Madame Storey casually.

The girl spread out her hands. "You have me at a disadvantage," she said. "It is so hard to resist you."

"Don't try," suggested my employer, smiling. "You may take your notes now, Miss Brickley. You needn't be afraid," she added to the girl. "This is entirely between ourselves. No one else shall see them. You were saying that you liked Mr. Poor—with reservations."

"I meant that one could have enjoyed his company very much if he had been content to be natural. But he was one of those men who pride themselves on their—their—what shall I say——"

"Their masculinity?"

"Exactly. And of course with a man of that kind a girl is obliged constantly to be on her guard."

"The servants have stated that he pestered you with his attentions," Madame Storey remarked.

The girl lowered her eyes. "They misunderstood," she said. "Mr. Poor affected a very flowery, gallant style with all women alike; it didn't mean anything."

Madame Storey glanced at a paper on her desk. "The butler deposes that one evening he saw Mr. Poor seize you on the stairs and attempt to kiss you, and that you boxed his ears and fled to your room."

Miss Dean blushed painfully and made no reply.

Madame Storey, without insisting on one, went on: "What were the relations between Mr. and Mrs. Poor?"

"How can any outsider know that?" parried the girl.

"You can give me your opinion. You are a sharp observer. It will help me to understand the general situation."

"Well, they never quarrelled, if that's what you mean. They were always friendly and courteous toward each other. Not like people who are in love, of course. Mrs. Poor must have known what her husband's life was, but she was a religious woman, and any thought of separation or divorce was out of the question for her. My guess was that she had determined to take him as she found him, and make the best of it. Such a cold and self-contained woman naturally would not suffer as much as another."

"Have you knowledge of any incident in Mr. Poor's life that might throw light on his murder?"

"No. Nobody in that house knew anything of the details of his life. He was not with us much."

"Tell me about your movements on the night of the tragedy," Madame Storey urged coaxingly.

But the girl's face instantly hardened. "It is useless to ask me that," she said. "I do not mean to answer."

"But since you did not commit the crime why not help me to get you off?"

"I do not wish to speak of my private affairs which have nothing to do with this case."

My heart beat faster. Here we were plainly on the road to important disclosures. But to my disappointment Madame Storey abandoned the line.

"That is your right, of course," she said. "But consider: you are bound to be asked these very questions in court before a gaping crowd. Why not accustom yourself to the questions in advance by letting me ask them? You are not under oath here, you know. You may answer what you please."

This was certainly an unusual way of conducting an examination. Even the girl smiled wanly.

"You are clever," she said with a shrug. "Ask me what you please."

"What were you doing on the night of the tragedy?"

From this point forward the girl was constrained and wary again. She weighed every word of her replies before speaking. It was impossible to resist the suggestion that she was not always telling the truth.

"I was in my room."

"The whole time?"

"Yes, from dinner until Mrs. Poor returned."

"Why didn't you go to the pageant?"

"Those affairs bore me."

"Had you not intended to go?"

"No."

"Where was Mrs. Batten during the evening?"

"I don't know. In her room, I assume."

"In what part of the house was that?"

"Her sitting-room was downstairs in the kitchen wing."

"An old woman. Wasn't she timid about being all alone in that part of the house?"

"I don't know. It did not occur to me."

"You didn't see her at all during the evening?"

"No."

"Where was Mr. Poor?"

"In the library, I understood."

"All the time?"

"I'm sure I couldn't say."

"Did you see him or have speech with him during the evening?"

"No."

"There was nobody in the house but you three?"

"Nobody."

"You're sure of that?"

"Quite sure."

"The servants testified that when the alarm was raised you appeared fully dressed."

"That's nothing. It was only twelve o'clock. I was reading."

"What were you reading?"

"Kipling's *The Light That Failed*."

"What became of the book?"

"I put it down when Mrs. Poor cried out."

"Are you sure? It was not found in your room."

"Of course I'm not sure. I may have carried it downstairs. I may have dropped it anywhere in my excitement."

"Please describe the exact situation of your room."

"It was in the north-east corner of the house. It was over the library."

"Yet you heard no shot?"

"No."

"That's strange."

"The house is very well built—double floors and all that."

"But immediately overhead?"

"I can't help that. I heard nothing."

"You had no hint that anything was wrong until you heard Mrs. Poor's cry?"

"None whatever."

"When she cried out what did you do?"

"I ran around the gallery and downstairs."

"The gallery?"

"In order to reach the head of the stairs I had to encircle the gallery in the hall."

"How long did it take you to reach Mrs. Poor's side?"

"How can I say? I ran."

"How far?"

"Fifty or sixty feet; then the stairs."

"Half a minute?"

"Perhaps."

"What did you see when you got downstairs?"

"The stairs landed me at the library door. Just inside the door I saw Mrs. Batten clinging to Mrs. Poor. She was trying to keep Mrs. Poor from reaching her husband's side."

"Mrs. Poor is a tall, finely formed woman, isn't she?"

"Yes."

"Is Mrs. Batten a big woman?"

"No."

"Strong?"

"No."

"Yet you say she was able to keep her mistress back for half a minute?"

"You said half a minute."

"Well, until you got downstairs."

"So it seems."

"Didn't that strike you as odd?"

"I didn't think about it."

"Did you know what had happened?"

"Not right away. I soon did."

"They told you?"

"No."

"How did you guess, then?"

"From Mr. Poor's attitude, sprawling with his arms across the table, his head down—the pistol in his hand."

"In his hand?"

"Well, under his hand, I believe."

"Did you recognise it as your pistol?"

"I—I don't know."

"Eh?"

"I mean I don't know just when I realised that it was mine. Pistols are so much alike. I hadn't handled mine much."

"Well, how was it that it could be so positively identified as yours?"

"There were two little scratches on the barrel that somebody had put there before I got it. I had shown it to Mrs. Batten, and we had discussed what those two little marks might mean. Mrs. Batten must have spoken of it in the hearing of the servants. At any rate they knew about the marks."

"How do you explain the fact that your pistol was in the dead man's hand?"

"I cannot explain it."

"Where did you keep it?"

"In the bottom drawer of my bureau."

"Was the drawer locked?"

"No."

"When had you last seen it there?"

"Two days before, when I——" She stopped here.

"When you what?"

"When I put it away."

"You had it out then?"

"Yes."

"What for?"

"To have it fixed."

"What was wrong with it?"

"I couldn't describe it, because I don't understand the mechanism."

"Had you ever fired it?"

"No."

"Then how did you know it was out of order?"

"I—I——" She hesitated. "I won't answer that."

"Surely that's a harmless question."

"I don't care. I won't answer."

"Who fixed it?"

"The man it was bought from."

"Who was that?"

"I don't know."

"You mean you won't tell me?"

"No, it is the truth. I don't know. I never asked."

"Ah, it was a gift, then?"

The girl did not answer. She was becoming painfully agitated, twisting and untwisting her handkerchief in her lap. I was growing excited myself. I felt sure we were on the verge of an important disclosure.

Madame Storey feigned not to notice her perturbation. "How long had you had the pistol?" she asked.

"A few weeks—three or four."

"Was it in good order when you got it?"

"Yes."

"Well, if you had never shot it off how did it get out of order?"

No answer.

"Who had been firing it?"

Silence from Miss Dean.

"What kind of pistol was it?"

"They called it automatic."

"What calibre?"

"I don't know."

The next question came very softly. "Who gave it to you, Miss Dean?"

I couldn't help pitying the poor girl, her agitation was so extreme, and she was fighting so hard to control it.

"I won't answer that question."

"It will surely be asked in court."

"I won't answer it there."

"Your refusal will incriminate you."

"I don't care."

"Tell them you found it," Madame Storey

suggested with an enigmatic, kindly look. To my astonishment she arose, saying: "That's all, Miss Dean."

I couldn't understand it. The girl, who was deathly pale and breathing with difficulty, seemed on the point of breaking down and confessing the truth—yet she let her go. I confess I was annoyed with Madame Storey. In my mind I accused her of neglecting her duty. The girl was no less astonished than I. Out of her white face she stared at my employer as if she could not credit her ears.

Madame Storey took a cigarette. "Many thanks for answering my questions," she said. "I see quite clearly that you couldn't have done this thing. I shall tell the assistant district attorney so."

The girl showed no gratitude at this assurance, but continued to stare at Madame Storey with hard anxiety and suspicion. I stared too. It was perfectly clear to me that Philippa Dean had guilty knowledge of the murder.

"We'll have to hand you back to your watchdogs now," said Madame Storey. "Keep up a good heart."

The girl went out like one in a dream. When the plain-clothes men took her Madame Storey and I sat down again and looked at each other.

She laughed. "Bella, you look as if you were about to burst. Out with it!"

"I don't understand you," I cried.

"Didn't you think she was a charming girl?"

"Yes, I did. I was terribly sorry for the poor young thing, but——"

"But what?"

I took my courage in my hands and continued: "You mustn't let your compassion for her influence you. You have your professional reputation to think of."

"You are more jealous of my professional reputation than I am," she said teasingly.

"Why did you stop just when you did?"

"Because I had found out what I wanted to know."

"What had you found out that Mr. Barron had not already told you? She was just at the point of——"

"Of repeating her confession?"

"I'm sure of it."

"That is just what I wanted to forestall, Bella. Another confession would simply have complicated matters."

I simply stared at her.

"Because she didn't do it, you see, Bella."

"Then why should she confess?"

My employer merely shrugged.

"How can you be so sure she didn't do it? Anybody could see she was lying."

"Certainly she was lying."

"Well, then?"

"It was by her lies that I knew she was innocent."

"You are just teasing me," I said.

"Not at all. Read over your notes of her answers. It's all there, plain as a pikestaff."

I read over my notes, but saw no light. "That unmistakably guilty air," I said. "How do you explain that?"

"I wouldn't call it a guilty air."

"Well, anxious, terrified."

"That's more like it."

"Even if she didn't do it she knows who did."

"Possibly."

"Then why didn't you make her tell you?"

"Sometimes young girls have to be saved from themselves, Bella."

And that was all I could get out of her.

III

The moment Philippa Dean got back to headquarters Mr. Barron must have started for our office. He arrived within forty minutes. When I showed him into Madame Storey's room I followed, for since the violent interview of the morning she had instructed me to be present whenever he was there.

He was furious at what he regarded as my intrusion. He said nothing, but glared at me and I breathed a silent prayer that I might not fall into the clutches of the district attorney's office, at least as long as he was there. He sat down crossing and uncrossing his legs, slapping his knee with his gloves, and scowling sidewise at Madame Storey from under beetling brows. Giannino, who detested him, fled to the top of his picture, where he sat hurling down imprecations in the monkey language at the man's head, and looking vainly around for something more effective to throw.

Madame Storey was in her most impish mood. "Lovely afternoon, Walter," she remarked mellifluously.

He snorted.

"Will you have some tea? We've had ours."

"No, thank you."

"A cigarette, then?" She pushed the box toward him.

"You know I never use them."

"Well, you needn't be so virtuous about it." She took one herself. The graceful movement with which she stuck it in her mouth never failed to fascinate me—him, too.

He was silent. Madame Storey blew a cloud of smoke. He scowled at her in a sullen, hungry way. I was sorry for the man. Really, she used him dreadfully.

"Rose, how many of those do you use a day?" he abruptly demanded.

"Oh, not more than fifty," she drawled, with a wicked twinkle in my direction.

She may have spoiled half that many a day, but she never took more than a puff or two of each.

"You're ruining your complexion," he said.

"Mercy!" she cried in mock horror, snatching up the little gold-backed mirror that always lay on her table. She studied herself attentively. "It does show signs of wear. What can one expect? It's six hours old already."

From her little bag she produced rouge-stick, powder-puff, pencils, *et cetera*, and nonchalantly set about using them. I might remark that Madame Storey had developed the art of making-up to an extraordinary degree of perfection. In the beginning I had refused to believe that she used any artificial aids until the process took place before my eyes.

Absolutely indifferent to what people thought, she was likely to lug out the materials at any time, but particularly when she desired to be delicately insulting.

Mr. Barron became, if possible, angrier than before. For a moment or two he fumed in silence, then said:

"Please put those things away. I want to talk to you."

"You told me my complexion needed repair, Walter. Go ahead. Making-up is purely a subconscious operation. I'm listening."

They were a strong-willed pair. She would not stop making up, and he would not speak until she gave him her full attention. There was a long silence. It was rather difficult for me. I sat at my little table, making believe to busy myself with my papers. Madame Storey put aside the cigarette. That little scamp Giannino came sneaking down, but I got it first, and clapped it in the ash-jar with a cover that he cannot open. He retired, sulking, into a corner, and swore at me in his way.

Madame Storey finally put down the mirror. "Is that better, Walter?" she asked, with a wicked smile.

He puffed out his cheeks.

"I'm waiting to hear you," she said, putting away the make-up.

"It's a confidential matter," he rejoined, glancing at me.

"Miss Brickley knows all about the Poor case," she said carelessly. "You needn't mind her."

"Well, what happened?" he asked sullenly.

"Nothing much."

"Did you get a confession from the girl?"

"No; I managed to forestall it."

His jaw dropped. "What do you mean?"

"She was just on the point of making a confession when I sent her back to you."

"Will you be so good as to explain yourself?"

"A confession would simply have puffed you up, Walter, and obstructed the ends of justice. Because she didn't kill Ashcomb Poor."

"I suppose you had your secretary take notes of her examination," he said. "Please let her read them to me."

Madame Storey shook her head. "The girl talked to me in confidence, Walter."

"But surely I have the right——"

"We agreed beforehand, you know."

The assistant district attorney, very angry indeed, muttered something to the effect that he "would know better next time."

"That, of course, is up to you," she said sweetly. "Anyway, it wouldn't do any good to read you the notes, because I brought out no new facts of importance."

"Then how do you know she's innocent?" he demanded.

"By intuition," she said with her sweetest smile.

He flung up his hands. "Good Heaven! Can I go into court with your intuition?"

"I suppose not. But so much the worse for the court. I haven't much of an opinion of courts, as you know, for the very reason that they throw out intuition. They choose to found justice solely on reason, when, as every sensible person knows, reason is the most fallible of human faculties. You can prove anything by reason."

To this Mr. Barron hotly retorted:

"Yet I never saw a lying woman in court who, when she was caught, did not fall back on her so-called intuition."

"That may be. But because there are liars is not to say there is no truth. Intuition speaks with a still small voice that is not easy to hear."

"Does your intuition inform you who did kill Ashcomb Poor?" he asked sarcastically.

"I shall have to have more time for that," she parried.

"I thought your intuition was an instantaneous process."

"Since you force me to meet you on your own ground, I must have sufficient time to build up a reasonable case."

"Aha! Then you don't despise reason altogether."

"By no means. But my reasoning is better than yours because it is guided by the voice of intuition."

"Do you expect me to release this girl on the strength of your intuition?"

"By no means. She'd run away. And we may need her later."

"Run away! This paragon of innocence? Impossible!"

"There are a good many things that reasonable men do not understand," drawled Madame Storey. "Take it from me, though, in the end you will come off better in this affair if you simply hold the girl in the House of Detention as a material witness."

"Thanks," he said; "but I am going before the grand jury to-morrow to ask for an indictment for homicide."

"As you will! Men must be reasonable. According to your theory, she killed him in defending herself from his attentions, didn't she?"

"That's what I intimated."

"Well, as a reasonable man, how do you account for the fact that she was willing to stay in the house with him alone except for the old housekeeper?"

"The point is well taken," he admitted, but with a disagreeable smile that suggested he meant to humble her later.

Madame Storey continued: "Moreover, she must have put herself in the way of his attentions, for the tragedy occurred in the man's own library."

"I confess that stumped me at first," he said; "likewise the fact that he had apparently been shot unawares. But since this morning some new evidence has come to light."

He waited for her to betray curiosity, but she, who read him like a book, only blew smoke.

"Ashcomb Poor's will was read this morning."

"Yes?"

"He left Philippa Dean ten thousand dollars."

Madame Storey betrayed not the slightest concern.

"As a testimony to her sterling character, no doubt," she murmured.

"Character nothing!" was the retort. "Well, as far as that goes, Ashcomb Poor's motives do not concern me. The salient fact to me is that the girl knew she was down in his will."

"When was the will dated?"

"Three days before his death."

"Well, she didn't lose any time! How did she know she was named in it?"

"It appears that Ashcomb Poor in his cups talked about the different bequests to his butler, who witnessed the document. The butler told Mrs. Batten, and Mrs. Batten told the girl."

"Was Mrs. Batten mentioned in the will?"

"Yes, for five thousand."

"Perhaps she killed Ashcomb Poor."

"Ridiculous!"

IV

Madame Storey decided that we must interview all the material witnesses in this case.

My desk in the outer office was beside the window. Next morning while I was awaiting the arrival of my employer I saw an elegantly appointed town car draw up below, and a woman of exquisite grace and distinction got out. She was dressed and veiled in the deepest mourning, and I could not see her face, but, guessing who it was, I experienced a little thrill of anticipation. The door was presently thrown open by Eddie—it was only visitors of distinction that he condescended to announce. "Mrs. Poor to see Madame Storey."

I jumped up in a bit of fluster. What would you expect? The famous Mrs. Ashcomb Poor, of whom so much had been written; her beauty, her dresses, her jewels, her charities, and now her tragic bereavement! How I longed to see her face! She made no move to put aside her veil, though.

"Madame Storey not in?" she said in a disappointed voice.

"I am expecting her directly," I said. "She will be very much disappointed to miss you."

"I do not at all mind waiting," Mrs. Poor replied.

Her voice was as crisp and clear as glass bells. I brought a chair forward for her. I knew I ought to have shown her directly into the adjoining room, but I did want to get a good look at her. Her simple black dress had been draped by a master artist. I cudgelled my brain to think of some expedient to tempt her to put back her veil. I offered her a magazine, but she waved it aside, thanking me. My ingenuity failed me. It was hardly my place to start a conversation.

Madame Storey was not long in arriving. She was all in black too, I remember, but it was black with a difference; there was nothing of the mourner about her. And Giannino, who, poor wretch, had to dress to set off his mistress, was wearing a coat and cap of burnt orange.

My employer expressed her contrition at keeping Mrs. Poor waiting, and led that lady directly into the adjoining room. Alas! I was not bidden to follow. I would have given a good deal to be able to watch and listen to the conversation between those two extraordinary women.

I remained at my desk in the deepest disappointment. Suddenly I heard the dictagraph click. With what joy I snatched up the headpiece and pulled note-book and pencil toward me!

At least I was to hear.

Madame Storey was saying: "It was awfully good of you to consent to come to a strange woman's office. I should not have asked it had I not thought that my coming to you would only have been an embarrassment."

"I was very glad to come," Mrs. Poor replied in her bell-like voice. "You are not by any means unknown to me. On every side one hears of the wonderful powers of Madame Storey. I was very much pleased to hear that you had interested yourself in my unhappy affairs. One longs to know the truth and have done with it. One can rest then, perhaps."

"And are you willing to answer my questions?"

"Most willing."

"This is really good of you. For of course it's

bound to be painful, though I will spare you as far as I am able. If I trespass too far you must rebuke me."

"There is nothing you may not ask me, Madame Storey."

"Thanks. I'll be as brief as possible. No need for us to go over the whole story. I am already pretty well informed from the police and from my examination of Miss Dean yesterday."

"Ah, you have seen the girl?" put in Mrs. Poor.

"Yes."

"What did she say?"

"Nothing but what has been published."

"Poor, poor creature!"

"You do not feel unkindly toward her?"

"My feelings toward her are very mixed. I could not see her, of course. But I feel no bitterness. How do I know what reason she may have had? And to convict her will not restore my husband to life."

"You have known Miss Dean a long time?"

"Since she was a child. Her family and mine have been acquainted for several generations."

"Has Miss Dean a love affair?"

"No, nothing serious."

"You are sure?"

"Quite sure. I must have known it if she had. Several of the young men who frequented our house paid her attention—a pretty girl, you know—but not seriously."

"I should have thought——"

"I'm afraid young men are worldly-minded nowadays," said Mrs. Poor. "She had no money, you see."

"Now I come to a painful subject," said Madame Storey compassionately. "I am sorry to have to ask you, but I am anxious to establish the exact nature of the relations between your husband and Miss Dean."

"You need not consider me," murmured Mrs. Poor. "I have to face the thing."

"Some of the servants have given evidence tending to show that your husband was infatuated with her."

"I'm afraid it's true."

"What makes you think so?"

"One learns to read the man one lives with—his looks, the tones of his voice, his little unconscious actions."

"You have no positive evidence of his wrongdoing; you never surprised him, or intercepted notes?"

"That would not be my way," said Mrs. Poor proudly.

"Of course not. I beg your pardon."

Mrs. Poor went on bitterly: "If I had wanted evidence against him plenty of it was forced on me—I mean in other cases."

"Nothing that could be applied to this case?"

"No."

"Then we needn't go into that. How did the girl receive his overtures?"

"As an honest girl should. She repulsed him."

"How do you know?"

"I knew in the same way that I knew about him—from her actions day by day; her attitude toward him."

"What was that?"

"On guard."

"That might have been interpreted either way, might it not?"

"Oh, yes. But there was her attitude toward me—open, affectionate, unreserved."

"That might have been good acting," suggested Madame Storey.

"It might, but I prefer not to think so."

"You have a good heart, Mrs. Poor. How long had this been going on?"

"About a month."

"But if the girl was sincere, how do you account for the fact that she was willing to put up with this intolerable situation?"

"Very simply; she needed the money."

"But if she'd always been well employed why should she be so hard up?"

"She has responsibilities. She supports two old servants of her mother's, who are no longer able to work."

"Ah! But how could you tolerate the situation, Mrs. Poor?"

"You mean why didn't I send her away? How could I turn her off? Ever since I realised what was going on I have been trying to find her a situation with one of my friends, but they thought if I was willing to let her go there must be something undesirable about her."

"Naturally. Was that the only reason you kept her?"

Mrs. Poor's answer was so low it scarcely carried over the wire. "No: I wish to be perfectly frank with you; I confess, as long as she was there I knew in a way what was going on, but if she had gone away—you see——"

"Then you did have some doubt of her?"

"My husband was a man very attractive to women. He was accustomed to getting his way. I was thinking of her more than of myself. His fancies never lasted long."

"Did you know that he had put her in his will?"

"Not until the will was read yesterday."

"What do you suppose was his motive in doing that?"

"How can one say?"

"May it not have been merely for the purpose of annoying you?"

"Possibly. He was not above it."

"Now, Mrs. Poor, with the situation as it was, how could you bring yourself to leave the girl alone with him except for the housekeeper?"

"That was not my fault. It was sprung on me. I had no time to plan anything."

"What do you mean?"

"It had been understood up to the last moment that Mr. Poor was to accompany me to the entertainment. But at dinner he begged off. What could I do? I had to go myself because I was taking a prominent part."

"Then why didn't you ask her to go with you?"

"I did."

"And she wouldn't?"

"She wouldn't."

"Why?"

"She said she had no dress in order."

"Did you believe that?"

"No."

"You suspected that this staying home might have been prearranged?"

"Oh, I wouldn't go as far as that."

"But if it were not prearranged why should she have gone to the library?"

"Who can tell what happened? He might have sent for her on the pretext of dictating letters. He had done that before."

"You seek to excuse her. That doesn't explain why she chose to stay at home after she knew he was going to be there."

"Perhaps she was excited—thrilled by his infatuation; girls are like that. Perhaps she was curious to see how he would act—confident in her power to restrain him. And found out too late that she was up against elemental things, and was obliged to defend herself."

"But she must have had some inkling of what was likely to happen, since she took her pistol with her when she went to the library. Did you know that she possessed a pistol?"

"No."

"Now, Mrs. Poor, let us jump to your return home that night. Describe your homecoming as explicitly as possible."

"It was five minutes past midnight. I am sure of the time because I glanced at the clock as I was leaving the club. It was five minutes before the hour then. It took us about ten minutes to cover the three miles, for the road was thronged with returning motors."

"One minute!—the entertainment was held in the open air, wasn't it?"

"Yes, and we dressed in the club-house. We had the limousine. I rode with my own maid, Katy Birkett, beside me, and the cook and the housemaid opposite. The butler was outside with the chauffeur. When we reached home I got out alone at the front door. I told the others to drive along to the service door, because I thought it might annoy Mr. Poor to have them trooping through the house. The car waited there until the door was opened, because they didn't want to leave me standing there alone in the dark.

"Mrs. Batten opened the door. This surprised me, because she was usually in bed long before that hour. I had expected my husband to let me in. I had had the chauffeur sound his horn in the drive to give notice of our coming. I said to Mrs. Batten: 'Why aren't you in bed?' She answered that she thought she'd better wait up—or something like that. I asked her where Mr. Poor was, and she said he had fallen asleep in the library.

"A few steps from the inner door I could see into the library. The door was standing open, as it had been when I left. I could see my husband sitting at his writing-table in the centre of the room, his back to the door. His head was lying on his arms, and I, too, thought he was asleep. I noticed the fire had gone out."

"Oh, there had been a fire?"

"Yes, Mr. Poor liked to have a wood fire in the library except in the very hottest weather. As Mrs. Batten removed my cloak I called to him: 'Wake up, Ashcomb! You'll get stiff, sleeping like that.'

"He did not move. Mrs. Batten and I were simultaneously struck by the suspicion that something was the matter. We both started toward him. I had not taken two steps before I saw—oh!—a ghastly dark stain on the rug beneath his chair. I saw the pistol. An icy hand seemed to grip my throat. I stopped, unable to move. The room turned black before me."

"You fainted?"

"No. It was only for a second. I started forward again. Mrs. Batten turned and blocked my way. 'Don't go! Don't go!' she cried. Then something seemed to break inside me. I screamed. Then Miss Dean was there. I didn't see her come. I clung to her——"

"One moment. After you screamed how long was it before Miss Dean came?"

"No time at all. She was right there."

"You are sure?"

"Quite sure."

"Perhaps you had cried out before without knowing it."

"Impossible. With that icy grip on my throat."

"Well, go on, please."

"I—I broke down completely then. It was so awful a shock, and—and that dark, wet stain on the rug! The other servants ran in from the back of the house. The maids set up an insensate screaming. Somebody got them out again. The butler examined my—the—the body. He said he was quite dead—cold. I had sufficient presence of mind to order that nothing in the room be touched. I had the man telephone my brother, who lives near, and our doctor—just to be sure. The servants helped me upstairs; people began to come—the police. My recollection is not very clear after that."

"Were you present when the police examined the servants and Miss Dean?"

"No."

"When did you first begin to suspect her?"

"In the morning when I asked for her they told me she had been arrested. That was a fresh shock. I had supposed it was suicide. I only learned the facts little by little, because people didn't want to talk to me about it and I hadn't the strength to insist."

"Did you notice anything peculiar in Miss Dean's manner when she came to you?"

"Not at the time, of course. I was too distracted. But when I thought about it later, she was strangely agitated."

"Well, you all were, of course."

"She was different. Hers was not the impersonal horror and dismay of the servants; hers was a personal feeling. She seemed about to faint with terror; she could hardly speak. She was not surprised."

"What did she say to you?"

"She, too, tried to keep me back. She said: 'Don't go to him. It's all over.' At the moment I thought nothing of it. Afterward it occurred to me that none of us had been near him then. We didn't know he was dead until the butler came."

"That is very significant," said Madame Storey.

This ended Mrs. Poor's examination. After the exchange of some further civilities she came out of the inner room. Her veil was pushed aside and I had my wished for chance to see her face. Her voice over the wire had been so cool and collected that I was not prepared for what I saw. A truly beautiful woman with proud, chiselled features, the events of the last few days had worked havoc there. There were dark circles under her eyes, and deep lines of suffering from her nose to her mouth. I realised how profoundly humiliating the disclosures, following upon the murder, must have been to her proud soul. Seeing my eyes on her face, she quickly let the veil fall and went out without speaking.

As a result of the examination of Mrs. Poor I will not deny that I felt a certain satisfaction. Greatly as I admired my employer I was not sorry to see her proved wrong for once. It is not the easiest thing in the world to get along with a person who is always right. Madame Storey's insistence on Philippa Dean's innocence had provoked me just a little. Madame Storey made no reference to what had taken place between her and Mrs. Poor, and of course I did not gloat over her.

V

An hour after Mrs. Poor had departed I heard a timid tap on my door, and upon opening it beheld a round little body in a stiff black dress and a funny little hat with ostrich tips. She carried her gloved hands folded primly on the most protuberant part of her person, and from one arm hung a black satin reticule. She had cheeks like withered rosy apples, and short-sighted eyes peering through thick glasses. There was a wistful, childlike quality in her glance that immediately appealed to one. At present the little lady was scared and breathless.

"Does Madame Storey live here?" she gasped.

"This is her office," I said. "Come in."

"I am Mrs. Batten."

I looked at her with strong interest. "Madame Storey will be glad to see you," I said.

"I told her I'd come," she faltered; "but I'm so upset—so upset, I'm sure if she asks me the simplest questions my wits will fly away completely."

"You needn't be afraid of her," I said soothingly.

I knew whereof I spoke. The instant Madame Storey laid eyes on the trembling little body, she smiled and softened. She put away her worldly airs and was just simple like folks. I remained in the room. Madame Storey talked of indifferent matters until Mrs. Batten got her breath somewhat, and brought the matter very gradually around to the Poor case. At the first reference to Philippa Dean the tears started out of the old eyes and rolled down the withered cheeks.

"My poor, poor girl!" she mourned. "My poor girl!"

"You were very fond of her, then?" put in Madame Storey gently.

"Like a daughter she was to me, madame."

"Well, let's put our heads together and see what we can do. You can help me a lot. First of all, where were you all evening while Mrs. Poor was at the entertainment?"

With a great effort Mrs. Batten collected her forces and called in her tears. Her hands gripped the arms of her chair. "I was in my room," she said, "my sitting-room downstairs."

"All alone?"

"Why, of course!"

"Please tell me just where your room is."

"Well, the way to it from the front hall is through a door between the reception-room and the dining-room and along a passage. Half-way down this passage is my door on the right and the pantry door opposite. At the end of the passage another passage runs crosswise. That we call the back hall. It has a door on the drive——"

"That is the door by which the servants entered when they returned with Mrs. Poor?"

"Yes, madame. And at the other end of the back hall there's a door to the garden. The back stairs are in this hall. The kitchen and the servants' dining-room are beyond."

"I get the hang of it. Wasn't it unusual for you to remain up so late?"

"Yes, it was."

"How did it happen?"

"Well—I got interested in a book."

"What book?"

Mrs. Batten put a distracted hand to her brow. "Let me see—my poor wits! Oh, yes, it was called *The Light That Failed.*"

No muscle of Madame Storey's face changed. "Ah! An admirable story! I know it well. What I particularly admire is the opening chapter, where the young man steps out of the clock case and confronts the thief in the act of rifling the safe."

"I thought that a little overdrawn," said Mrs. Batten.

I gasped inwardly. I could scarcely believe my ears. Our dear, gentle little old lady was lying like a trooper, and Madame Storey had trapped her. For, of course, as everybody knows, there is no such scene in *The Light That Failed.*

Madame Storey went right on: "Please tell me exactly what happened when Mrs. Poor returned that night."

Mrs. Batten complied. Up to a certain point her story tallied exactly with that of her mistress, and there is no need for repeating it. Mrs. Batten corroborated Mrs. Poor's statement that Philippa Dean had appeared as soon as Mrs. Poor cried out.

Then Madame Storey said: "But Miss Dean testified that she had to run all the way around the upstairs gallery and downstairs."

Mrs. Batten gave her a frightened look. "Oh, well, I may be mistaken," she said quickly. "It was all so dreadful. Maybe it was a minute before she got there."

"What did Miss Dean say to Mrs. Poor when she got there?"

"She didn't say anything—that is, not anything regular. She put her arm around her and said: 'Be calm'—or 'Don't give way,' or something like that."

"Didn't Miss Dean say: 'Don't go to him. It's all over'?"

Mrs. Batten sat bolt upright in her chair, and the near-sighted eyes positively shot sparks. "She did not say that."

"Can you be sure?"

"I'll swear it."

"She might have said it without your hearing."

"I was there all the time. I had hold of Mrs. Poor, too."

"But Mrs. Poor has testified that Miss Dean said that."

The old woman obstinately primmed her lips. "I don't care."

"Wouldn't you believe your mistress?"

"Not if she said that. She was mistaken. She was half wild, anyway. She didn't know what anybody said to her. Why, nobody knew that Mr. Poor was dead then. Not till the butler came."

Mrs. Batten's anxiety on the girl's behalf was so obvious that her testimony in the girl's favour did not carry much weight.

Madame Storey continued: "Did you notice anything strange about Miss Dean's manner when she came?"

Mrs. Batten sparred for time. "What do you mean?" she asked.

"Was she unduly agitated?"

"Why, of course, we all were."

"I said unduly. Did she behave any differently from the others?"

The little old lady began to tremble.

"What are you trying to get me to say?" she stammered. "She didn't do it. She *couldn't* have done it. That sweet young girl, so gentle, so fastidious!" The old voice scaled up hysterically. "Nothing could ever make me believe she did it. Like a daughter to me, a daughter. She didn't do it. I will say it to my dying day."

Madame Storey smiled kindly. "Your feelings do you credit, Mrs. Batten; still I hope you won't show them so plainly before the jury."

"The jury!" whispered Mrs. Batten, scared and sobered.

"Because if you let them see how fond you are of Miss Dean they won't believe a word you say in her favour."

"The jury!" Mrs. Batten reiterated, staring before her as if she visualised the dreadful ordeal that awaited her. "I will have to sit up there in the witness chair and take my oath before them all—and everybody looking at me—thousands—and lawyers asking me this and that a-purpose to mix me up——" She suddenly cried out: "Oh, I couldn't. I couldn't. I know I couldn't. I'm too nervous. I'd kill myself sooner than face that."

The little woman's terror was so disproportionate to the thing she feared that the strange thought went through my mind, perhaps it was she who killed Ashcomb Poor, or maybe she and the girl had done it together. I attended to what followed with a breathless interest.

Meanwhile Madame Storey was trying to quiet her. "There now! There now! Mrs. Batten, don't distress yourself so. This is just an imaginary terror. It may never be necessary for you to go on the stand. Let's take a breathing spell to allow our nerves to quiet down. Have a cigarette?"

I stared at my employer, for at the moment this seemed like a very poor attempt at a joke. I ought to have known that Madame Storey never did anything at such moments without a purpose.

Mrs. Batten drew the remains of her dignity around her. "Thank you, I don't indulge," she said stiffly. She was pure mid-Victorian then.

Madame Storey said teasingly: "Come now, Mrs. Batten! Not even in the privacy of your room?"

"Never. I'm not saying that I blame them that do if they like it; but in my day it wasn't considered nice."

"Does Miss Dean smoke?" asked Madame Storey with an idle air.

"I'm sure she does not," answered Mrs. Batten earnestly. "I've been with her at all times and seasons, and I never saw her take one between her lips. There was no reason she should hide it from me. Besides, the maids never picked up any cigarette ends in her room. They're keen on such things."

"You have the reputation of being a very tidy person, haven't you, Mrs. Batten?" asked Madame Storey. "They tell me you are a regular New England housekeeper."

By this time I had guessed from Madame Storey's elaborately careless air that this apparently meaningless questioning was tending to a well-defined point. The old lady glanced at her in a bewildered way but she could see nothing behind this harmless remark.

"Why, yes," she said, "I suppose I do like to see things clean—real clean. And everything in its proper place."

"Who does up your room?" went on Madame Storey in the purring voice that always means danger—for somebody. My heart began to beat.

"I do it myself, always," answered the little woman unsuspectingly. "I don't like the maids messing among my things. I like my room just so. I always sweep and dust and put things in order myself, and I mean to do so until I take to my bed for the last time."

"Every day?" asked Madame Storey, flicking the ash off her cigarette.

"Every day, most certainly."

Madame Storey drawled in a voice as sweet as honey: "Well, then, Mrs. Batten, who was it that was smoking cigarettes in your room the night that Ashcomb Poor was killed?"

The little old woman's jaw dropped, the rosy cheeks grayed, her eyes were like a sick woman's. Presently the hanging lip began to tremble piteously. I could not bear to look at her.

"I—I don't know what you're talking about," she stuttered.

"You have not answered my question," Madame Storey said mildly.

"Nobody—nobody was smoking in my room."

Madame Storey turned to me. "Miss Brickley, please get me the exhibits in the Poor case that I asked you to put away."

Hastening into the next room I procured the things from the safe. When I returned neither of the two had changed position. From the envelope that I handed her Madame Storey shook the cigarette butts.

"These were found in your room early the next morning," she said to Mrs. Batten. "In the little brass bowl on the window-sill."

"All kinds of people were in the house that morning," stammered the little woman with a desperate air; "police, detectives, goodness knows who! How do I know who passed through my room?"

"It was scarcely one who passed through," said Madame Storey. "He or she must have lingered some time—long enough, that is, to smoke seven cigarettes. See!" She counted them before the old woman's fascinated eyes.

"I don't know how they came there. I don't know how they came there," wailed the latter.

Madame Storey spread the cigarette ends in a row. "They are plain tip cigarettes," she said, "so I assume they are a man's. Women prefer cork tips or straw tips, because lip rouge sticks and comes off on the paper. What gentleman visited you, Mrs. Batten?"

"There was nobody, nobody!" was the faint answer. "Why do you torment me?"

"There's no harm in having a visitor, surely. Your son, perhaps, a nephew, a brother—even a husband. Women do have them, Mrs. Batten."

"Everybody knows I have no family."

"A friend, then. Where's the harm?"

"There was nobody there."

Madame Storey examined the cigarette ends anew. "One of them is long enough to show the name of the brand," she said, "—Army and Navy. One might guess that they were smoked by a man in the service."

The harried little woman gave her a glance of fresh terror.

Delicately picking up one of the butts, Madame Storey smelled of the unburned end. "The tobacco is of a superior and expensive grade," she remarked. "Evidently an officer's cigarette. But of what branch of the service? That is the question." She fixed the trembling little soul with her compelling gaze and asked abruptly: "Was he an aviator, Mrs. Batten?"

A terrified cry escaped Mrs. Batten.

"I see he was," said Madame Storey.

Mrs. Batten was gazing at Madame Storey as if the evil one himself confronted her.

Answering that look of awed terror, my employer said quietly: "No, there is no magic in it, Mrs. Batten. As a matter of fact, later that morning I found, in the field across the brook at the foot of the garden, marks in the earth showing where an airplane had alighted and had later arisen again. I was only putting two and two together, you see."

The little woman, seemingly incapable of speech, sat there with her hands clasped as if imploring for mercy. It was very affecting.

Madame Storey went on: "Upon consulting an expert in aviation I learned that such tracks could have been made by none other than one of the new Bentley-Critchard machines, of which there are as yet only half-a-dozen in service, and those all at Camp Tasker, which is only fifteen miles from Grimstead—a few minutes' flight. All I lack is the name of the aviator who visited you. Who was he, Mrs. Batten?"

The little woman moistened her lips and whispered in a kind of dry cackle: "I don't know. No one came."

"You might as well tell me," Madame Storey said patiently. "It would not be difficult to find out at Camp Tasker, you know. There cannot be many officers accustomed to driving that new type."

A groan broke from the little old woman. She covered her face with her hands. "You are too much for me," she murmured. "It was Lieutenant George Grantland."

I got out of my chair and sat down again, staring at the woman like a zany. Grantland! Eddie's hero! The popular idol of the day!

Madame Storey was no less astonished than I. "Quick, Bella! The morning paper!"

I hastened and got it for her. There was his name on the front page, of course, as it had been in every edition during the past two days. Madame Storey read out the headlines:

GRANTLAND AT CHICAGO LAST NIGHT

Flew from New Orleans Yesterday

Expected to land at Camp Tasker this morning. Has circumnavigated the entire country east of the Mississippi in little more than three days. The bold young flier's endurance test a success in every particular. Great ovations tendered him at every landing.

Meanwhile the wretched little old lady was weeping bitterly and wailing over and over: "I promised not to tell. I promised not to tell."

"Promised whom?" asked Madame Storey.

"Philippa."

"Well, you needn't distress yourself so, Mrs. Batten. If you love this girl, bringing the man's name into the case isn't going to hurt her chances any."

Mrs. Batten had forgotten all caution now. "But if you convict him," she sobbed, "it will kill Philippa just the same."

"Aha!" murmured Madame Storey to herself; "so that's the way the wind lies." She looked at the old woman oddly. "So Grantland did it?"

Mrs. Batten flung up her arms. "I don't know," she burst out, and at least that cry rang true. "I haven't eaten. I haven't slept since it happened. I'm nearly out of my mind with thinking about it."

Madame Storey whispered privately to me to call up Camp Tasker. If I could succeed in getting a message to Lieutenant Grantland I was to ask him to come to her office on a matter of the greatest importance concerning Miss Philippa Dean.

Through the open door I could hear her asking Mrs. Batten to forgive her for tormenting her.

"But you know you came here determined not to tell me the truth," she said.

In a few minutes I was able to report that I had got a message to Lieutenant Grantland, who had but just landed from his plane, and that he had promised to be in Madame Storey's office within an hour.

Mrs. Batten was quiet again—quiet and wary. Poor little soul, now that one understood better, one couldn't but admire her gallantry in lying to save her friends.

"Tell us about Lieutenant Grantland's visit," Madame Storey said coaxingly.

"There's nothing much to tell," was the cautious answer.

"He came to see Miss Philippa?"

"Yes."

"He had been before?"

"Oh, yes; a number of times."

"Did Miss Philippa know he was coming that night?"

"Yes. He had telephoned just before dinner. It was to say good-bye before starting on the big flight."

"What time did he come?"

"About nine."

"Tell me about it in your own way."

Mrs. Batten shook her head. "You must question me," she said warily. "I don't know what it is you want to know."

Madame Storey and I smiled, the old soul's equivocation was so transparent.

"Did Lieutenant Grantland always come in his plane?" my employer asked.

"No, that was the first time by plane."

"Didn't the noise of his engine attract attention at the house?"

"No; he shut it off and came down without a sound."

"How could he see to land in the dark?"

"He came just before it got too dark to see."

"But couldn't you see him land from the house?"

"No. He came down at the top of the field which is hidden from the house by the trees along the brook."

"Then how could he get away in the dark?"

"He had the whole length of the field to rise from."

"But in starting his engine didn't it make a great noise?"

"I don't know. We didn't notice it."

"Did you go to meet him?"

"I—no."

"Miss Philippa went?"

"Yes."

"And brought him back to the house?"

"Yes."

"Right away?"

Mrs. Batten bridled. "I don't see what that——"

"Well, what time did they get to the house?"

"About half-past nine."

"How did they get in?"

"I turned off the burglar-alarm and let them in the garden door."

"What happened then?"

"Nothing," said Mrs. Batten with an air which said: "You're not going to get anything out of me."

"Well, where did they go in the house?"

"They came into my room. They always sat there."

"You left them there?"

"No, I stayed. Miss Philippa always had me there when he came. So that nobody could have any excuse to talk. That shows you the kind of girl she was."

"Very commendable. Go on."

"There isn't anything to tell. There we sat as cozy and friendly as could be in my little room. I don't remember anything particular that was said. I wouldn't tell it if I did, for it was just their own matters. At ten o'clock I brought out a little supper I had made ready. The lieutenant was always hungry—like a boy. That's all."

"What time did he leave?"

"At midnight."

"That is, when Mrs. Poor got home?"

"Yes."

"How did you get him out of the house?"

Mrs. Batten bridled again. "There wasn't any getting out about it. He walked out of the same door that he came in. When I went to the front door to answer the bell I left the passage door open. When I switched on the light in the hall that was to tell them the burglar-alarm was off.

Then Miss Philippa let the lieutenant out of the door from the back hall into the garden."

"What was the necessity for all this secrecy, Mrs. Batten? Miss Philippa was treated like a member of the family."

Mrs. Batten was very uncomfortable. "Well, there was no necessity for it, so to speak," she said. "But it seems natural for young lovers to wish to meet in secret, to avoid talk and all that."

"And a moment after the lieutenant had gone you and Mrs. Poor discovered the murder?"

"Yes, but that isn't to say——"

"Of course it isn't! Up to that moment you yourself had no suspicion that there had been a tragedy in the house?"

"No, indeed! No, indeed!"

"After Miss Philippa let him out she presumably returned through the passage. That would explain how she came to be so close at hand when Mrs. Poor cried out."

"I suppose so. But there's no harm in that."

"Certainly not. But why was there so much lying, Mrs. Batten? Why did she tell me she had been in her room all evening? Why did you tell me you were alone in your room?"

"I couldn't give it away that she had been entertaining him."

"Why not, if it was all regular and above board?"

"Well—well, I said I wouldn't tell."

My employer became thoughtful. Mrs. Batten, watching her, began to fidget again.

Suddenly Madame Storey said: "Mrs. Batten, did Lieutenant Grantland know that Ashcomb Poor had been pestering Miss Philippa?"

"No," answered Mrs. Batten breathlessly—but the terrified glance that accompanied it told its own tale.

"Now, Mrs. Batten, you're fibbing again. What's the use when your face is a mirror to your soul?"

The little body hung her head. "Yes, he knew," she murmured. "He had heard some gossip or something. He was furious when he came. Wanted to march right into the library and tax Mr. Poor with it—to 'knock his block off,' he said. We had a time quieting him down. The only thing that influenced him was when Miss Philippa said the scandal would injure her."

"But you did quiet him down?"

"Yes. We were all as happy and pleasant as possible together. Then we had our supper."

Madame Storey fell silent for a while. Her grave and thoughtful glance seemed to inspire the little old woman with a fresh terror. Mrs. Batten struggled to her feet.

"I must go now," she said tremulously. "I've been away too long. They won't know what's become of me."

"Sit down, Mrs. Batten," said Madame Storey quietly.

The other's voice began to scale up again. "I won't answer any more questions," she cried. "Not another one. I can't. I'm in no fit state. I don't know what I'm saying. It's not fair to keep at me, and keep at me."

"Sit down, Mrs. Batten," repeated the grave voice.

The old woman dropped into a chair, weeping bitterly.

"Did Miss Philippa leave the room at any time during your party?"

This was evidently the very question Mrs. Batten dreaded. "Oh, why do you plague me so?" she cried.

"You know the truth has got to come out. Better tell me than a roomful of men."

Mrs. Batten gave up. "Yes, she did," she wailed.

"How long was she gone?"

"I don't know. Just a little while. Not more than ten minutes."

"And did Lieutenant Grantland leave the room at any time?"

"Yes."

"How long was he gone?"

"He left after her, and got back just before her."

"Ah! What was the occasion of their leaving the room?"

"The bell rang in the pantry. I went to see what it was. The indicator showed a call from the library. It wasn't my place to answer the bell, but I did so because I was afraid if I didn't Mr. Poor might come back. He was at his writing-table. I thought he had been drinking a little."

"Why did you think so?"

"His face was flushed. He had a funny look. He said: 'Will you please ask Miss Dean if she will be good enough to help me out for a little while? I have two or three important letters to get off, and I have such a cramp in my hand I can't write them myself.'"

"Did you believe this, Mrs. Batten?"

"N-no, madame, not with that look—an ugly look to a woman."

"What did you do?"

"Well, of course I couldn't say anything to him. I just went away as if I was going to do what he wanted. I went back to my room. I was hoping maybe he'd forget. But they saw from my face that something had happened——"

"That open countenance!" murmured Madame Storey.

"And they gave me no rest until I told them what he wanted. The lieutenant flared up again and said she should not go. Said he'd go instead and write his letters on his face. But she persuaded him not to. She knew how to manage him. She said she must go in order to avoid trouble. She said nothing could happen to her as long as the lieutenant was there in the house to protect her. So she went."

"Alone?"

"Yes. But when she was gone he could not rest. In spite of all I could do to stop him, he went after her. I stayed there sitting in my room—helpless. Every minute I expected to hear a terrible quarrel—but all was quiet. I could scarcely stand it. I would have gone, too, to see; but my old legs were trembling so they would not carry me."

"You heard no sound while they were gone?"

"None whatever."

"But there were three heavy doors between you and the library."

"The library door stood open all evening."

"But it may have been closed then."

Mrs. Batten wrung her hands. "It can't be. It can't be," she cried. "That young pair—so proud, so beautiful, so loving——!"

"Well, murder is not always so detestable a crime," observed Madame Storey enigmatically. "Did they come back together?"

The old woman shook her head. "He came back first."

"How did he look?"

"Nothing out of the way. No different from when he left."

"You mean, his face was set and hard?"

"Yes, but he always looked like that when Mr. Poor's name was mentioned."

"What did he say?"

"He said: 'Where's Philippa?' I just shook my head. He turned around to go look for her, but met her coming in the door. They spoke to each other."

"What did they say?"

"It was in whispers. I could not hear."

Madame Storey fixed the little woman hard with her gaze. "Mrs. Batten!" she said warningly.

But this time the housekeeper was able to meet it. She spread out her hands in a gesture that was not without dignity. "I have told you everything, madame. You know as much as I do now."

"And nothing happened after that?"

"No, madame. We sat down to our supper. Mr. Poor's name was not mentioned again."

"Either one of them could have done it," remarked Madame Storey thoughtfully.

Mrs. Batten wiped away her fast-falling tears.

VI

Lieutenant Grantland was prompt to his engagement.

Why is it that aviators, or nearly all aviators, are such superb young men? I suppose the answer is obvious enough: it is the young men with the shining eyes and the springy bodies that are naturally attracted to the air. However that may be, the mere sight of an aviator is enough to take a girl's breath away.

As for George Grantland, he was simply the handsomest young man I ever saw. When he came in, how I longed to be comely just for one second, in order to win an interested glance from him. Alas! His eyes merely skated over me. In his close-fitting uniform and marvellously turned leggings he was as graceful as Mercury. At present, whether from fatigue or anxiety—or both—his cheeks were drawn and gray. But his blue eyes were resolute, and he kept his chin up.

You can imagine Eddie's feelings. He had brought the lieutenant upstairs all agog, and now stood just within the door, staring at his idol, and fairly panting with excitement. I was obliged to push the boy out into the hall by main strength and shut the door after him.

I took Lieutenant Grantland directly into Madame Storey's room. Her glance brightened at the sight of him, just as any woman's would. She had mercy on me and nodded to me to remain in the room. Mrs. Batten, I should state, was still with us. Madame Storey had put her in the back room to rest and compose herself.

"Thank you for coming so promptly," Madame Storey said, extending her hand.

The young man blushed painfully. "I cannot shake hands," he said bluntly.

Madame Storey's eyebrows went up. "Why?" she asked, smiling.

"You will not want to shake hands when you know."

Madame Storey shrugged and smiled at him with an expression I could not fathom—a quizzical expression. "Well, sit down," she said.

He would not unbend. "Thank you, I cannot stay."

"Well, anyway, allow me to congratulate you on your flight."

He bowed.

Madame Storey went on: "My secretary tells me she got a message to you just as you were landing. I assume that you heard nothing during your flight of what was happening here."

"Not a word," he said. "But Camp Tasker was buzzing with it. I heard everything there."

"Then we need not go into lengthy explanations," said Madame Storey. "I need only say that Assistant District Attorney Barron has done me the honour to consult me in regard to this matter. That is where I come in. As for my secretary, she is acquainted with all the details of the case, so you need have no hesitancy in speaking before her. I would like to ask you a few questions, if you please."

"There is no need," he said, standing very stiffly. "It was I who killed Ashcomb Poor."

My heart went down sickeningly—not that I blamed him at all, but at the thought of that splendid young fellow being subjected to the rigour of the law, his career spoiled, that proud head brought low in a prison cell. I don't know what Madame Storey felt upon hearing his avowal. Her glance betrayed nothing.

"I never dreamed that they would dare arrest her," the young man went on with a break in his voice, "or I should not have gone away. I can never forgive myself that."

"Well, sit down," said Madame Storey for the second time.

He shook his head. "I am on my way to police headquarters to give myself up."

"Oh, but not so fast!" objected my employer. "There are many things to be considered. Meet Mr. Barron here. You will be at a better advantage."

"I have no desire to make terms," he said indifferently.

"Then let me make them for you. Or lay it to a woman's vanity, if you like. I found you first. Let me hand you over to the district attorney's office."

"Just as you like," he said.

Turning to me Madame Storey said: "Please call up the district attorney's office and tell Mr. Barron that important new evidence has turned up in the Ashcomb Poor case. Ask him if he will bring Miss Dean up here."

At the words "bring Miss Dean" a spasm of pain passed over the young man's face.

"Do you think he will?" I murmured, thinking of Mr. Barron's former objections.

"What he did once he can do again," Madame Storey said lightly. "Curiosity is a strong, impelling force." She added in a lower tone: "Mrs. Poor is at the Madagascar Hotel. Ask her to come, too. Then we'll have all the material witnesses."

Then to the aviator: "If you came here the moment you landed you haven't had anything to eat."

"I don't require anything, thanks," he muttered.

"Nonsense! You have a severe ordeal before you. You must prepare for it in any way that you can."

To make a long story short I ordered in a meal. It arrived after I had finished my telephoning, and both Madame Storey and I saw to it that the young man did justice to the repast. Notwithstanding his situation he developed an excellent appetite. It struck me at the time that we were treating him more like a returned prodigal than a self-confessed murderer; but good looks such as his are like a magic talisman in the possessor's favour. What would any woman have cared what he had done? How delightful it was to see a better colour return to his cheeks! And how grateful he was for cigarettes!

Mr. Barron brought two plain-clothes men and Miss Dean in his own automobile. We received them in the outer office, and Madame Storey insisted on allowing the girl to enter her room alone. When the door was opened and Philippa saw who was waiting within, a dreadful low cry broke from her that wrung our very hearts. Madame Storey closed the door behind her, and no one ever knew what took place between those two unhappy young persons.

While we waited Mr. Barron besieged Madame Storey with questions which she smilingly refused to answer, merely saying:

"Wait and see."

They were not together long. Lieutenant Grantland opened the door. His face was stony.

In a chair behind him the girl was weeping bitterly. It looked as if they had quarrelled.

He said to Madame Storey: "We must not keep you out of your own room."

Madame Storey, Mr. Barron, and I went in. My employer, much against Mr. Barron's wishes, insisted that the plain-clothes men be required to wait in the outer office.

"I fancy there are enough of us here to frustrate any attempt at an escape," she said dryly.

Mrs. Batten was called in. She was in a great taking at the sight of Philippa and the young officer, but the former kissed her tenderly, and the young man shook hands with her.

When we all seated ourselves the place instantly took on the aspect of a court-room. I am sure I am quite safe in saying that every one of us—except possibly my inscrutable employer—was shaking with excitement. Our faces were pale and streaked with anxiety. Madame Storey sat at her table and I was in my usual place at her right. Mr. Barron sat at her left, while Miss Dean, Lieutenant Grantland, and Mrs. Batten faced us in that order.

Before anything was said there was a knock at the door, and upon being bidden to open it Eddie ushered in a heavily-shrouded figure that all knew for Mrs. Poor, though her face was invisible. I expect Eddie would have given some years of his youthful life to be allowed to remain, but a glance from Madame Storey sent him flying. Mr. Barron hastened to place a chair for Mrs. Poor next to Mrs. Batten. The young soldier arose and bowed stiffly. Philippa turned her head away from the newcomer with a painful blush.

Madame Storey said in a voice devoid of all emotion: "Lieutenant Grantland wishes to make a statement."

Grantland was still on his feet. He came to attention and said in a low, steady voice: "I wish to say that it was I who shot Ashcomb Poor."

The widow started violently. One could imagine the piercing gaze she must have bent on the speaker through her veil. Philippa Dean covered her face with her hands, and Mrs. Batten began to weep audibly. Mr. Barron's face was a study in astonishment and discomfiture, Madame Storey's a mask.

Madame Storey said: "Please tell us the circumstances."

"Wait a minute," stammered the assistant district attorney. "It is my duty to inform you that anything you say may be used against you."

"I quite understand that," said Grantland.

"I must have a record of his statement," went on Mr. Barron excitedly.

"Miss Brickley will take notes of everything that transpires," said Madame Storey. "Please proceed, lieutenant."

He spoke in a level, quiet voice, with eyes straight ahead, looking at none of us.

"I was calling on Miss Dean to whom I am—to whom I was engaged to be married. We were with Mrs. Batten in her sitting-room. Mr. Poor sent to Miss Dean to ask if she would write some letters for him. I had heard certain things—things that led me to suspect that this was merely a pretext. Anyway it was no part of her duties to look after his correspondence. I didn't want her to go. But she persuaded me that it would be better for her to go. And she went. But when she left the room I became very uneasy. I followed her—down a passage, and across the main hall of the house. The hall was dark.

"The man was in a room off the hall—a library, I suppose. The door stood open, and from the hall I could see all that took place. Mr. Poor, with many apologies, was repeating his request that Miss Dean write some letters for him. He made believe his hand was cramped. But he looked at her in a way—in a way that made my blood hot. I think he had been drinking. I could see that Miss Dean was frightened. I was at the point of interfering then, but I heard her ask him to excuse her while she got a handkerchief, and she came out and ran upstairs. She did not see me in the hall.

"Well, I remained there watching him. The expression on his face as he sat there waiting for her to return drove me wild. I——"

"But he was sitting with his back to the hall,"

interrupted Madame Storey. "How could you see his face?"

"There was a mirror over the fireplace hung at such an angle that his face was reflected in it."

"But if you could see him in it could he not see you?"

"No, I was standing too far back in the dark hall."

"Go on."

"The look on his face conveyed an insult no man could bear. I went in and shot him; that's all."

Philippa Dean struggled to her feet. From her lips broke a cry none of us will ever forget.

"It's not true. It was I who did it. He knows it was I. He's trying to shield me."

She could go no further, but stood, struggling to control the dry sobbing that tore her breast. None of the rest of us stirred.

Grantland did not look at her. One could see that he dared not. "She knows it was I," he said stonily.

With a great effort Philippa regained a measure of control.

"Listen! Listen!" she cried desperately. "I will tell the truth now. Mr. Poor sent for me. He asked me to take some letters. He looked at me in such a way I was afraid—afraid. I asked him to excuse me while I got a handkerchief. I went upstairs. But it was my pistol that I went for. I was so afraid they would meet—and fight. I got my pistol. I came downstairs again. I shot him. Lieutenant Grantland wasn't there at all."

"I *was* there," cried Grantland. "Ask Mrs. Batten. Mrs. Batten, didn't I follow her?"

"Oh! Oh! Oh!" wailed the little body. "Yes, you followed her."

"And if I was not there how could I have known about the handkerchief?" he demanded.

By this time Philippa had nerved herself. She faced him out fearlessly. Never have I seen anything like that look, so hard, so full of pain. "Well, if you were there you didn't wait till I got back. You weren't there when I got back, were you? Answer that."

"No," he admitted, "but——"

She wouldn't let him go on. "Why should I have wanted a handkerchief at such a moment? It was my pistol I went for, and I got it, and I came downstairs and shot him."

"Without warning?" Grantland demanded in his turn.

"No. I sat down and made ready to take his letters. But he had no letters to dictate, of course. He put his hand on my shoulder and I—I shot him."

"How could you shoot him in the back when you were sitting beside him?"

"I reached around behind him and shot him."

"Where did you have the pistol?"

"Hidden in the bosom of my waist."

"The waist you wore that night was closed in front."

"Pooh! What do you know about such things? You never notice what I have on. Mrs. Batten, wasn't the waist I wore that night buttoned in front?"

The little body was completely distracted. "Yes—no—I don't know, I can't remember," she wailed.

"Now answer *me*," cried Philippa to Grantland. "How could you get into the room when the man was sitting there watching in the mirror for my return?"

"I dropped to my knees out of range of his vision and crept in."

The girl's eyes flashed at him. "Do you mean to tell all these people that you, an officer in the uniform of the United States, crawled in on hands and knees like a thug and shot the man in the back?"

Grantland's head dropped on his breast; a dark flush overspread his face, he gritted his teeth until the muscles stood out in lumps on either side of his jaw.

"It is the truth," he muttered. "I looked on him as a kind of wild beast against whom any measures were justifiable."

The girl passionately appealed to the rest of us. "Look at him! Look at him!" she cried. "Anyone could see he is lying."

The spectacle of the two lovers cross-examining each other; facing each other down with hard, inimical glances; each desperately striving to pull down the other's tale, was the strangest and most dreadful scene I ever expect to witness.

The young man stubbornly raised his head, and his glance bore hers down. He had better command of himself than she.

"Your story could not be true," he said firmly. "You were not more than half a minute behind me in returning to Mrs. Batten's room."

"Half a minute was long enough to pull the trigger," she retorted.

A new thought struck Grantland. "You could not have returned that way at all," he said. "You must have come down the back stairs. I remember now that as you came into the room you appeared from the rear of the house."

"Too bad you didn't think of that before!" she rejoined scornfully. "Your tardy recollection will not deceive Madame Storey or this gentleman. This is all wasting time anyway. You have not explained the most important thing of all."

"What's that?" he asked sullenly.

"How did you get hold of my pistol?"

She thought she had him there, but he instantly retorted: "You gave it to me yourself a week before to have it fixed. I had had it fixed, and I was bringing it back to you that night."

"Now I have caught you," cried the girl with wildly shining eyes. "You had returned my pistol to me two days before that night, and Mrs. Batten was present when you handed it to me." She whirled around. "Mrs. Batten, didn't you see him return my pistol to me two days before that night?"

The little woman, unable to speak, nodded her head.

"Now, who's lying?" cried Philippa.

The young aviator never flinched. "That wasn't your pistol I gave you two days before," he said coolly. "That was a pistol I borrowed from the dealer while yours was being repaired. I got it for you because I believed after what I'd heard that you ought not to be without the means to defend yourself."

"Why didn't you tell me all this at the time?" she demanded.

"Because I would have had to explain why I got you the pistol, and I didn't want to alarm you unnecessarily."

"Fine tale!" she said with curling lip—but her assurance was failing her. "How about the two little marks on the barrel that identified the pistol as mine?"

"That is the dealer's private mark to protect himself. It appears on all the weapons that he handles."

"Well, if it was really my pistol that you say you shot the man with, why did you leave it there to incriminate me?"

"I thought you had only to produce the one you had in order to clear yourself."

"It's not true. No other was found. There was no other. What did you want to leave the pistol there for anyway to make trouble?"

"I thought it would be regarded as a suicide."

Philippa had regained her assurance.

"Do you expect these people to believe that with your knowledge of weapons you thought you could shoot the man through the back and have anybody think he did it himself?"

Grantland showed some confusion. "Well, I was excited," he said sullenly. "One can't think of everything."

The girl smiled scornfully. "I've no more to say," she said abruptly. "These people will not need any help in deciding who is telling the truth." She sat down.

What the others thought of this confession and counter-confession I cannot say. I believed Philippa was telling the truth.

My employer's face was like a tinted ivory mask. "Have you anything more to say?" she asked Grantland.

He shook his head.

"Mr. Barron, do you wish to put any questions?"

"I think not," he answered, with a casual air that did not conceal his triumph. "I see no reason to alter my original opinion. Lieutenant Grantland's motives do him credit, but his story simply does not hold water. Leaving aside all other considerations, it is preposterous to suppose that after shooting the man in the way he describes he could fly away and leave the two women to their fate."

Philippa looked gratefully toward him. What a strange, topsy-turvy situation that she should actually thank him for expressing his belief in her guilt!

My employer said in the silky tones that always portended danger: "I must differ with you, Mr. Barron. Lieutenant Grantland has explained how he thought he had ensured Miss Dean's safety. On the other hand it is incredible to suppose that a gently reared girl, after having killed a man, could sit down and sup with her two friends as if nothing had happened. A man might, a soldier, but this girl, never! And afterward allow him, her only protector, to leave her without a word!"

"I had to let him go," sobbed Philippa. "His reputation was staked on that flight."

I noticed at this point that Mrs. Poor's foot was nervously tapping the floor. In my concern for the two young people, it had not occurred to me what a harrowing business all this must have been for the widow.

"No," said Madame Storey to Mr. Barron, "you have done me the honour to consult me in this case. I must ask you to put Lieutenant Grantland under arrest. I pledge myself to justify it directly."

Grantland fairly beamed on my employer. I wondered mightily what she was up to. Poor Philippa seemed on the verge of a collapse.

"But how—why—on what grounds?" demanded the puzzled prosecutor.

Madame Storey's next words fell like icy drops: "At the proper moment—I will produce an eyewitness to the affair—who will swear—that Lieutenant Grantland shot Ashcomb Poor."

"*You lie.*"

This scream—for scream it was—from a new direction, almost completed the demoralisation of our nerves. Every eye turned toward Mrs. Poor. She had leaped to her feet and had thrown her veil back. The pale, proud face was working with intense emotion, her hands were dragging at her bodice, she had lost every vestige of control—a dreadful sight.

"It's a conspiracy," she cried shrilly, "to railroad him—with his consent. They staged it here together. Can't you all see? That's why we were brought here."

Madame Storey turned to the hysterical woman with seeming surprise. "Why, Mrs. Poor, what do you know about it?"

Under that cold glance the woman suddenly collapsed in her chair. Her eyes sickened with terror. The strident voice declined to a whisper. "Of course—of course I don't know," she stuttered. "I am simply overwrought. All this—all this has been too much for me. I am simply overwrought. I beg your pardon. I will retire—if some one will help me to my car."

Mr. Barron made a move to go to her, but Madame Storey laid hand on his arm and looked at him significantly.

He fell back in his chair, muttering: "My God!"

At Madame Storey's mention of a new witness Philippa had sagged down in her chair. Little Mrs. Batten had flown to her, and now knelt beside her with an arm around the girl. Grantland was staring at Mrs. Poor with a strange, perplexed frown.

"Don't go, Mrs. Poor," said Madame Storey softly. "Help us to throw a little light on this baffling matter."

Mrs. Poor made an attempt to draw her accustomed garments of pride and aloofness about her, but they would no longer serve. She shivered under our glances like a naked woman.

Madame Storey proceeded: "How long have you known Lieutenant Grantland?"

"About two years," was the reply.

"Ah, that is longer than Miss Dean has known him, isn't it?"

"Yes."

"Miss Dean met Lieutenant Grantland in your house?"

"Yes."

"Formerly you took a great interest in Lieutenant Grantland?"

"I liked him, if that is what you mean. We were friends."

"Great friends?"

"That is such a vague phrase. I advised him as I could out of my greater experience."

"Like an elder sister?"

"If you like."

"Did you notice any change in him after he met Miss Dean?"

"No."

"But he stopped coming to see you."

"Well, yes. I saw him less often."

"But he was still coming to the house?"

"So it seems."

"Did you know they were engaged?"

"Yes."

"How?"

"Gossip, rumour."

"He did not tell you?"

"No."

Madame Storey turned unexpectedly to Mrs. Batten. "Mrs. Batten," she said, "why did Lieutenant Grantland come to see Miss Dean secretly? Quick, the truth!"

The little body could not resist that sharp command. She glanced in a scared way at her mistress, and the truth came tumbling out involuntarily. "She—she had taken a fancy to him. They did not wish to anger her."

"That is sufficient," said Madame Storey.

Mrs. Poor struggled to her feet. "Servants' gossip!" she cried. "This is outrageous. I will not stay to be insulted."

Madame Storey rose too, and said in a tone oddly compounded of scorn and pity: "What's the use, Mrs. Poor? You have passed the limit of a woman's endurance. Tell the assistant district attorney who killed your husband."

The other woman with a last effort threw her head back, and tried to face Madame Storey down—meanwhile her ashy cheeks and trembling lips told their own tale.

"How should I know?" she cried. "How dare you take such a tone to me? Do you presume to accuse *me*? Oh, this is too funny!" Her laugh had a mocking ring. "You know very well I was performing at the club when it happened. Hundreds saw me there. I returned home with my servants. Ask them."

"I know all this," said Madame Storey with a bored air, "but that's only the beginning of the story. Sit down and I'll tell the rest."

Mrs. Poor obeyed—simply because her legs would not support her. As Madame Storey proceeded the other woman let her veil fall over her face. Her hands convulsively gripped the arms of her chair.

Madame Storey sat down and drew from the drawer of her table the several bits of evidence in connection with the case. She had in addition a programme of the pageant given at the Pudding Stone Club. Consulting this, she said:

"You made your first appearance in the second tableau as Starving Russia," she said. "This was at nine-fifteen. Upon leaving the stage your maid dressed you for your second appearance. This consumed about twenty-five minutes. You then went out into the audience to view the performance. Your maid joined the other servants in the part of the grounds reserved for them. You had told her you would not need her again.

"While everybody was looking at a tableau you slipped into the shrubbery surrounding the open-air theatre and made your way to your car. You are an expert chauffeur, as everybody knows. You drove it home. You did not turn in at the main gate but at the lower entrance leading to the service door. You did not drive up to the house, but left the car just inside the gate and walked to the house. The tracks made by the car were found where you had run it just inside the gate and later backed it out into the road again. It was identified as your car by certain peculiarities in the tyres.

"You went to one of the French windows of the library—to be exact, it was the second window from the front door. In order to reach the sill you had to make one step in the soft mould of the flower bed. You turned around on the sill, and stooping over, with your hand you brushed loose earth over the print of your foot. But a slight depression was left there, and by carefully brushing the loose dirt away again I was able to lay bare the deep print made by your slipper.

"I assume that you tapped on the window, and that your husband, seeing you, turned off the burglar-alarm and let you in. This would be about ten o'clock, or just as the other three persons in the house were sitting down to supper in Mrs. Batten's room. Perhaps you glanced through the window of that room as you passed by on the drive. What you said to your husband, of course, I do not know. My guess is that you accounted for your unexpected return by saying that an unforeseen request for a contribution had been made on you. At any rate he sat down at his writing-table and drew out his cheque-book. As he dated the stub you shot him in the back with Miss Dean's pistol which you had previously stolen from her bureau."

A convulsive shudder passed through the frame of the woman in black.

Madame Storey continued in her sure, quiet voice: "You had wrapped your right arm and the hand holding the pistol in many folds of a chiffon scarf. This was for the double purpose of concealing the weapon and of muffling the report. After the deed you tore off these wrappings and, crumpling the scarf into a ball, threw it on the fire which the servants have testified was burning in the room. But it must have opened up as it burned. At any rate a small piece fell outside the embers and was not consumed. Here it is. The characteristic odour of gunpowder still clings to it faintly.

"My principal difficulty was to establish how you got out of the house. I suspected that you must have contrived some means of setting the burglar-alarm behind you. The string box on Mr. Poor's desk furnished me with my clue. It was empty. When the last piece of string comes out of such a box, a man's instinctive act is to put a fresh ball in at once—if he has one. There were several spare balls in Mr. Poor's desk. Yet the box was empty. I may say that I subsequently found the length of string that you pulled out of that box in a tangled skein beside the road where you threw it on your way back to the club. Here it is.

"When I examined the burglar-alarm all was clear. A tiny staple had been driven into the floor under the switch. It was still there at nine o'clock of the morning after the murder when you had had no opportunity to remove it. You tied the string in a slip-knot to the handle of the switch, passed the other end through the staple in the floor—this gave you the necessary downward pull on the handle. You then ran the string across the floor and passed it through the keyhole of the front door. This door locks with a spring lock, and the original keyhole is not used.

"You went out closing the door behind you. Your first light pull on the string set the alarm—the handle of the switch moved easily. A second and harder pull slipped the knot, and you drew the string through the keyhole. You returned to the club, arriving there in ample time for your second appearance as Victory at ten-fifty."

An absolute silence filled the room. We glanced at one another in a dazed way, wondering if we dared credit what our ears had heard. Then suddenly joy flamed up in the faces of the two young people—the loveliest thing I have ever seen. But I turned away my head. We all did. We heard them cry each other's names.

"Philippa!"

"George!"

Presently Madame Storey said: "Mrs. Poor, are the facts not as I have stated?"

The wretched woman sat huddled in her chair like a demented person. I was glad her face was hidden. Suddenly she straightened up and cried out:

"Yes, it's true. It's true. I killed him. I shot him just as you say. Thank God, I've told it! I can sleep now."

Once the bonds upon speech were broken she could not stop herself. "Yes, I killed him. I killed him," she repeated over and over. "I couldn't stand it any longer. I'm not sorry for it. Who's going to blame me? What kind of a life did I lead? What kind of a wife was I? An object of scorn to my own servants! No one will ever know what I put up with. . . . Oh, I know what they said: 'The proud, cold Mrs. Poor, she doesn't feel anything.' Proud! Cold! Oh, my God! When I was burning up! When I died a thousand deaths daily! What do gabbling women know of what such a woman as I can suffer?"

This was unspeakably painful for us to listen to. Madame Storey looked significantly at Mr. Barron. He, whose attitude toward Mrs. Poor had undergone a great change during the past few minutes, now stepped forward and touched her arm.

She drew away from him with a sharp, new cry of terror: "No! No! Not that! Not that!" Throwing aside her veil again, she turned to Grantland with outstretched arms. "George, don't let them take me away!" she cried. "George, help me! Help me!"

The young man walked to the window. Mrs. Poor was led out, still crying pitifully upon his name.

Madame Storey turned quickly to Mrs. Batten. "Will you go with her? She needs a woman near."

The good little body hurried after.

Grantland went back to Philippa. Drawing her hand under his arm he brought her up to Madame Storey's table. After their terrible ordeal they were gravely happy; it seemed not to be necessary for these to speak to each other: the look in their eyes told all.

The young man said to my employer: "How can we ever thank you?"

Madame Storey put on a brisk air to hide the fact that she was moved, too. "Nonsense! You owe me nothing. I got my reward in taking the wind out of the assistant district attorney's sails."

"What a wonderful woman you are!" murmured the girl.

"That's what people always say," said Madame Storey ruefully. "It makes me feel like a side-show."

Philippa looked at her lieutenant. "What a fool I was to believe he could have done it!"

He looked back. "I was the bigger fool."

"Wonderful liars, both of you!" said Madame Storey dryly. "You had me guessing more than once. Like all really good liars, you stuck close to the truth. His story was true up to the point where he said he crawled into the library on hands and knees. That was just a little overdone, lieutenant. As a matter of fact when Philippa didn't come back, you returned to the housekeeper's room to look for her. By the way, that touch about the second revolver was masterly."

Grantland blushed.

Madame Storey turned to Philippa. "You told the truth up to the point where you said you got your pistol out of the drawer. It wasn't there, of course. After searching frantically for it, you were afraid to return to the library without it, and you stole down the back stairs, knowing you would be safe with your young man anyhow."

They bade her a grateful farewell and went out. They made an uncommonly handsome pair.

Mr. Barron returned to the room. He had a highly self-conscious air that betrayed him.

"Oh, I thought you'd gone," said Madame Storey.

"No, I sent Mrs. Poor down-town in her own car with my men. I'll follow directly. I want to speak to you."

"Go ahead," said Madame Storey.

"It's a private matter," he said, with a venomous glance in my direction.

Madame Storey, with a whimsical twinkle in her eye, signified that I might leave. I knew she was going to turn on the dictagraph. She had no mercy on that man.

I heard him say: "Well, Rose, I take off my hat to you. In this case you certainly beat me to it. I confess it. I couldn't say fairer than that, could I?"

"It's not necessary to say anything, Walter."

"But I want you to know the kind of fellow I am. I'm a generous-minded man, Rosie. The trouble is you provoke me so I fly in a rage when I'm with you, and you don't get the right idea of me. I'm gentle as a lamb if you take me right."

"Well, I'm glad to hear that, Walter."

"Take me for good, Rosie. You and I need each other. Your intuition is all right. With your intuition and my logic we'll make an unbeatable pair. I'll tell you all my cases, Rosie, and let you advise me. Honest, I will. Give me a smile, Rosie. I don't mean that kind of smile. From the heart. You cut the ground from under my feet with that wicked little smile. Smile kindly on me, Rosie——"

It was indecent to listen to a man making such a fool of himself. I took the headpiece off and laid it down. The next minute Mr. Barron, very red about the gills, banged out of Madame Storey's room, stamped across my office and downstairs.

Madame Storey rang for me. She was imperturbably lighting a cigarette.

"I'm ready to take up the Cornwall case," she said. "Bring me the papers from the file."

THE LITTLE HOUSE AT CROIX-ROUSSE

GEORGES SIMENON

WHILE IT IS CERTAINLY TRUE that the Belgian author Georges Joseph Christian Simenon (1903–1989) was prolific, estimates of the number of works he produced have been exaggerated, some alleged scholars of crime fiction putting the figure at five hundred or more. In fact, his output was less than half that—still a remarkable achievement. His series about the Paris policeman Jules Maigret totals about eighty novels and a modest number of short stories, beginning with *The Death of Monsieur Gallet* (1932). The work he considered more serious than the Maigret series may be categorized as psychological crime and has been counted as one hundred twenty-six books. He also produced lesser work under various pseudonyms, including Christian Brulls, Jean du Perry, and Georges Sim. Although the Maigret series has been more successful in England and the United States, in France Simenon's reputation soared with his crime novels. Andre Gide proclaimed him "perhaps the greatest and most truly 'novelistic' novelist in France today." Many of Simenon's books have been filmed, mainly in France but also in England and the United States, including the highly regarded RKO motion picture *The Man on the Eiffel Tower* (1949), which starred Charles Laughton as Maigret, Franchot Tone, and Burgess Meredith, who also directed. Among the non-Maigret works adapted for the screen in English are *Temptation Harbor* (1947), based on *Affairs of Destiny* (1942); *Midnight Episode* (1950), based on *Monsieur La Souris* (1938); *The Man Who Watched the Trains Go By* (1952; American title: *Paris Express*), based on *The Man Who Watched the Trains Go By* (1938); and *The Bottom of the Bottle* (1956), based on the 1954 novel of the same title. Mystery Writers of America presented Simenon with the Grand Master award in 1966.

"The Little House at Croix-Rousse" was translated by Anthony Boucher and first published in English in the November 1947 issue of *Ellery Queen's Mystery Magazine*; an earlier translation was published in *Esquire* in 1935 under the title "The Case of Dr. Ceccioni."

THE LITTLE HOUSE
AT CROIX-ROUSSE

GEORGES SIMENON

I HAD NEVER SEEN Joseph Leborgne at work before. I received something of a shock when I entered his room that day.

His blond hair, usually plastered down, was in complete disorder. The individual hairs, stiffened by brilliantine, stuck out all over his head. His face was pale and worn. Nervous twitches distorted his features.

He threw a grudging glare at me which almost drove me from the room. But since I could see that he was hunched over a diagram, my curiosity was stronger than my sensitivity. I advanced into the room and took off my hat and coat.

"A fine time you've picked!" he grumbled.

This was hardly encouraging. I stammered, "A tricky case?"

"That's putting it mildly. Look at that paper."

"It's the plan of a house? A small house?"

"The subtlety of your mind! A child of four could guess that. You know the Croix-Rousse district in Lyons?"

"I've passed through there."

"Good! This little house lies in one of the most deserted sections of the district—not a district, I might add, which is distinguished by its liveliness."

"What do these black crosses mean, in the garden and on the street?"

"Policemen."

"Good Lord! And the crosses mark where they've been killed?"

"Who said anything about dead policemen? The crosses indicate policemen who were on duty at these several spots on the night of the eighth-to-ninth. The cross that's heavier than the others is Corporal Manchard."

I dared not utter a word or move a muscle. I felt it wisest not to interrupt Leborgne, who was favoring the plan with the same furious glares which he had bestowed upon me.

"Well? Aren't you going to ask me *why* policemen were stationed there—six of them, no less—on the night of the eighth-to-ninth? Or maybe you're going to pretend that you've figured it out?"

I said nothing.

"They were there because the Lyons police had received, the day before, the following letter:

"Dr. Luigi Ceccioni will be murdered, at his home, on the night of the eighth-to-ninth instant."

"And the doctor had been warned?" I asked at last.

"No! Since Ceccioni was an Italian exile and it seemed more than likely that the affair had political aspects, the police preferred to take their precautions without warning the party involved."

"And he was murdered anyway?"

"Patience! Dr. Ceccioni, fifty years of age, lived alone in this wretched little hovel. He kept house for himself and ate his evening meal every day in an Italian restaurant nearby. On the eighth he left home at seven o'clock, as usual, for the restaurant. And Corporal Manchard, one of the best police officers in France and a pupil, to boot, of the great Lyons criminologist Dr. Eugène Locard, searched the house from basement to attic. He proved to himself that no one was hidden there and that it was impossible to get in by any other means than the ordinary doors and windows visible from the outside. No subterranean passages nor any such hocus-pocus. Nothing out of a mystery novel . . . You understand?"

I was careful to say nothing, but Leborgne's vindictive tone seemed to accuse me of willfully interpolating hocus-pocus.

"No one in the house! Nothing to watch but two doors and three windows! A lesser man than Corporal Manchard would have been content to set up the watch with only himself and one policeman. But Manchard requisitioned five, one for each entrance, with himself to watch the watchers. At nine p.m. the shadow of the doctor appeared in the street. He re-entered his house, *absolutely alone.* His room was upstairs; a light went on in there promptly. And then the police vigil began. Not one of them dozed! Not one of them deserted his post! Not one of them lost sight of the precise point which he had been delegated to watch!

"Every fifteen minutes Manchard made the round of the group. Around three a.m. the petroleum lamp upstairs went out slowly, as though it had run out of fuel. The corporal hesitated. At last he decided to use his lock-picking gadget and go in. Upstairs, in the bedroom, seated—or rather half lying—on the edge of the bed was Dr. Luigi Ceccioni. His hands were clutched to his chest and he was dead. He was completely dressed, even to the cape which still hung over his shoulders. His hat had fallen to the floor. His underclothing and suit were saturated with blood and his hands were soaked in it. One bullet from a six-millimeter Browning had penetrated less than a centimeter above his heart."

I gazed at Joseph Leborgne with awe. I saw his lip tremble.

"No one had entered the house! No one had left!" he groaned. "I'll swear to that as though

I'd stood guard myself: I know my Corporal Manchard. And don't go thinking that they found the revolver in the house. *There wasn't any revolver!* Not in sight and not hidden. Not in the fireplace, or even in the roof gutter. Not in the garden—not anywhere at all! In other words, a bullet was fired in a place where there was no one save the victim himself and where there was no firearm!

"As for the windows, they were closed and undamaged; a bullet fired from outside would have shattered the panes. Besides, a revolver doesn't carry far enough to have been fired from outside the range covered by the cordon of policemen. Look at the plan! Eat it up with your eyes! And you may restore some hope of life to poor Corporal Manchard, who has given up sleeping and looks upon himself virtually as a murderer."

I timidly ventured, "What do you know about Ceccioni?"

"That he used to be rich. That he's hardly practiced medicine at all, but rather devoted himself to politics—which made it healthier for him to leave Italy."

"Married? Bachelor?"

"Widower. One child, a son, at present studying in Argentina."

"What did he live on in Lyons?"

"A little of everything and nothing. Indefinite subsidies from his political colleagues. Occasional consultations, but those chiefly *gratis* among the poor of the Italian colony."

"Was anything stolen from the house?"

"Not a trace of any larcenous entry or of anything stolen."

I don't know why, but at this moment I wanted to laugh. It suddenly seemed to me that some master of mystification had amused himself by presenting Joseph Leborgne with a totally impossible problem, simply to give him a needed lesson in modesty.

He noticed the broadening of my lips. Seizing the plan, he crossed the room to plunge himself angrily into his armchair.

"Let me know when you've solved it!" he snapped.

"I can certainly solve nothing before you," I said tactfully.

"Thanks," he observed.

I began to fill my pipe. I lit it, disregarding my companion's rage which was reaching the point of paroxysm.

"All I ask of you is that you sit quietly," he pronounced. "And don't breathe so loudly," he added.

Ten minutes passed as unpleasantly as possible. Despite myself, I called up the image of the plan, with the six black crosses marking the policemen.

And the impossibility of this story, which had at first so amused me, began to seem curiously disquieting.

After all, this was not a matter of psychology or of detective *flair*, but of pure geometry.

"This Manchard," I asked suddenly. "Has he ever served as a subject for hypnotism?"

Joseph Leborgne did not even deign to answer that one.

"Did Ceccioni have many political enemies in Lyons?"

Leborgne shrugged.

"And it's been proved that the son *is* in Argentina?"

This time he merely took the pipe out of my mouth and tossed it on the mantelpiece.

"You have the names of all the policemen?"

He handed me a sheet of paper:

Jérôme Pallois, 28, married
Jean-Joseph Stockman, 31, single
Armand Dubois, 26, married
Hubert Trajanu, 43, divorced
Germain Garros, 32, married

I reread these lines three times. The names were in the order in which the men had been stationed around the building, starting from the left.

I was ready to accept the craziest notions. Desperately I exclaimed at last, "It *is* impossible!"

And I looked at Joseph Leborgne. A moment before his face had been pale, his eyes encircled,

his lips bitter. Now, to my astonishment, I saw him smilingly head for a pot of jam.

As he passed a mirror he noticed himself and seemed scandalized by the incongruous contortions of his hair. He combed it meticulously. He adjusted the knot of his cravat.

Once again Joseph Leborgne was his habitual self. As he looked for a spoon with which to consume his horrible jam of leaves-of-God-knows-what, he favored me with a sarcastic smile.

"How simple it would always be to reach the truth if preconceived ideas did not falsify our judgment!" he sighed. "You have just said, 'It *is* impossible!' So therefore . . ."

I waited for him to contradict me. I'm used to that.

"So therefore," he went on, "it *is* impossible. Just so. And all that we needed to do from the very beginning was simply to admit that fact. There was no revolver in the house, no murderer hidden there. Very well: then there was no shot fired there."

"But then . . . ?"

"Then, very simply, Luigi Ceccioni arrived *with the bullet already in his chest*. I've every reason to believe that he fired the bullet himself. He was a doctor; he knew just where to aim— 'less than a centimeter above the heart,' you'll recall—so that the wound would not be *instantly* fatal, but would allow him to move about for a short time."

Joseph Leborgne closed his eyes.

"Imagine this poor hopeless man. He has only one son. The boy is studying abroad, but the father no longer has any money to send him. Ceccioni insures his life with the boy as beneficiary. His next step is to die—but somehow to die with no suspicion of suicide, or the insurance company will refuse to pay.

"By means of an anonymous letter he summons the police themselves as witnesses. They see him enter his house where there is no weapon and they find him dead several hours later.

"It was enough, once he was seated on his bed, to massage his chest, forcing the bullet to penetrate more deeply, at last to touch the heart . . ."

I let out an involuntary cry of pain. But Leborgne did not stir. He was no longer concerned with me.

It was not until a week later that he showed me a telegram from Corporal Manchard:

AUTOPSY REVEALS ECCHYMOSIS AROUND WOUNDS AND TRACES FINGER PRESSURE STOP

DOCTOR AND SELF PUZZLED POSSIBLE CAUSE STOP REQUEST YOUR ADVICE IMMEDIATELY

"You answered?"

He looked at me reproachfully. "It requires both great courage and great imagination to massage oneself to death. Why should the poor man have done that in vain? The insurance company has a capital of four hundred million . . ."

STOLEN SWEETS ARE BEST

How does a thief remove valuables from a closely guarded room? It seems impossible, but . . .

ERLE STANLEY GARDNER

IN ADDITION TO HIS unprecedented popularity, it is numbers that are so impressive when considering Erle Stanley Gardner (1889–1970). He created the most famous lawyer in literature, Perry Mason, when he published *The Case of the Velvet Claws* on March 1, 1933. He went on to produce eighty Mason novels that, in all editions, sold more than three hundred million copies.

The novels were the ultimate in formulaic genre fiction, with the defense attorney taking on the role of detective to prove his client innocent at trial, then turning to point a finger at the real culprit, who generally broke down and confessed. The television series based on the character, starring Raymond Burr, was enormously successful for nine years, running from September 21, 1957, to May 22, 1966, and has been available in reruns pretty much ever since.

Before Perry Mason, however, there was Ken Corning, an equally hardhitting, fearless, and incorruptible defense attorney, who made his debut in *Black Mask* magazine in November 1932. Had he been named Perry Mason, and his secretary named Della Street instead of Helen Vail, it would be impossible to tell the difference between the two. Gardner created numerous other series characters working on both sides of the law, the most famous being the Bertha Cool and Donald Lam stories written as A. A. Fair, Doug Selby in the *D.A.* novels, and the crook Lester Leith.

Gardner began his lengthy writing career in the pulps in *Breezy Stories* in 1921, eventually producing hundreds of short stories, countless articles, more than a hundred novels, numerous nonfiction books on the law and, as a noted outdoorsman, on travel and environmental issues. At the time of his death, he was the bestselling writer in history.

"The Bird in the Hand" was first published in the April 9, 1932, issue of *Detective Fiction Weekly*; it was first collected in *The Amazing Adventures of Lester Leith* (New York, Davis, 1980) and *The Bird in the Hand* (New York, Black, 1980).

THE BIRD IN THE HAND

ERLE STANLEY GARDNER

CHAPTER I

The Missing Jewel Trunk

LESTER LEITH surveyed his valet through a film of blue cigarette smoke. His thought-slitted eyes were brittle hard with interest.

"Found him dead, eh, Scuttle?"

The valet nodded his ponderous head in vehement affirmation.

"Dead as a doornail, sir," he said.

Lester Leith's eyes became speculative. He inhaled a deep drag of smoke which made the end of the cigarette glow like a coal in the half darkness beyond the floor lamp.

There followed a silence, broken only by the crackling of the flames in the fireplace. The valet, poised on the balls of his feet, like a man about to strike a knockout blow, surveyed his master as a cat might stare at a mouse. And the flickering flames made little red reflections which danced in the staring eyes.

But Leith's eyes were focused upon the twisting spiral of cigarette smoke which eddied upward from the end of the cigarette.

"Dead, eh?" he mused.

"Yes, sir."

"Murdered, of course, Scuttle?"

The valet wet his thick lips with the tip of a nervous tongue.

"Why do you say 'of course'?" he asked.

Lester Leith made a deprecatory gesture with the hand which held the cigarette, and the motion sent the blue smoke column tumbling about in wavy fragments of drifting haze.

"According to your statement, the man was an international gem thief. He'd arrived on the boat with a big shipment of stolen gems, or there's every reason to believe he had them.

"The customs had a spy planted on the boat, a man who acted as room steward. He'd found out that a small steamer trunk, made along the lines of a miniature wardrobe trunk, had been cleverly designed with a false side that would slip out when one unscrewed the lock. And the smuggler evidently realized the steward had made the discovery, for he lured him down into a passage back of the baggage room, knocked him unconscious, bound and gagged him.

"Then the smuggler landed, got his ingenious trunk through customs and went to the Palace Hotel. You tell me that the steward regained consciousness, managed to free himself and telephoned the police and the customs authorities. They rushed to the Palace Hotel and found their man dead. It's a natural assumption that he had been murdered."

The valet nodded his head in oily and emphatic agreement.

"Well, sir, whether it's the natural assumption or not, the man was murdered. There was a knife driven right through his heart."

Lester Leith blew a contemplative smoke ring, watched it as it drifted upward and disintegrated.

"Humph," he said at last, "any sign of a struggle?"

The valet's voice lowered, as though he was about to impart a secret.

"Now we're coming to the strange part of it, sir. The man had been tied in a chair, bound hand and foot, and gagged, and then he'd been stabbed, straight through the heart."

Lester Leith's eyes became level-lidded with concentration.

"Yes?" he said, his voice like that of a chess player who is concentrating on the board, "and the trunk?"

The spy's voice became a dramatic whisper.

"The trunk, sir—was gone!"

And the last two words, coming at the end of an impressive pause, were hurled forth like a denunciation.

Lester Leith's eyes lost their look of glittering concentration, became lazy-lidded with mirth.

"Come, come, Scuttle, there's no need to be so dramatic about it. You're like an amateur elocutionist at a charity entertainment, reciting 'The Shooting of Dan McGrew.' Of course the trunk was gone. Obviously, the man was murdered by some one who wanted the jewels."

The spy wagged his head solemnly.

"No, sir, you don't understand. The police were right on the man's heels. He hadn't been in the hotel fifteen minutes when the police arrived."

Lester Leith let his forehead crease in a frown of annoyance.

"Well, what of it? Obviously, fifteen minutes was time enough for a murder. It should have been time enough for a robbery as well. Hang it, Scuttle, what's the big idea? You're as mysterious about this as an old hen with a choice morsel of gossip. Why the devil shouldn't the trunk have gone?"

The valet answered with the faintest touch of triumph in his voice.

"Because, sir, every piece of baggage that's checked in to the Palace Hotel is listed on their records, and there's never a piece of baggage that goes out that isn't checked against that list. They had too much trouble with baggage thieves and with guests who slipped their baggage out of the back door. So they installed a baggage checker.

"Now that trunk of Cogley's was distinctive. It was striped so it could be easily identified in customs. The baggage checker remembers it being taken into the hotel, and he's positive it didn't go out. And the bell boys and the freight elevator man are all certain it didn't go out. The Palace Hotel is run on a system, and it's easier to get money out of the safe than to get baggage out without a proper check!"

Leith yawned.

"Very possibly, Scuttle. The Palace Hotel has several hundred rooms. It's obvious that the murderer simply took the trunk into a vacant room where he could work on it at his leisure."

The valet snorted.

"You must think the police are fools, sir!" he exclaimed, and there was a trace of bitterness in his voice. "All of that was checked by the police. They realized that possibility within five minutes, and made a complete check of the place. It was done without any confusion or ostentation, of course, but it was done. A bell boy or a house detective or a police officer, under one excuse or another entered every single room in the hotel within twenty minutes of the time the murder was discovered. What's more, every nook and cranny of the hotel was searched.

"And the trunk vanished. It simply evaporated into thin air. It went in, but it didn't stay in. Yet it didn't go out. There isn't a single clew to the murderer, nor to the trunk!"

And the spy smirked at Lester Leith with that exaltation shown on the face of a pupil when he asks a question which baffles the teacher.

Lester Leith shrugged his shoulders.

"Oh, well, there's an explanation somewhere. Trunks don't vanish into thin air, you know. But why bother me with it? I'm not interested."

"I know, but you're always interested in unusual crimes."

"Was, Scuttle, was. Don't say that I am. I admit that I formerly took a more or less academic interest in crimes. But that was before Sergeant Ackley got the idea I was beating the police to the solution of the crime and robbing the robber."

The valet's voice was insinuating.

"But this is such a very, very interesting crime, sir. After all, there'd be no harm in thinking out a theoretical solution, would there?"

Lester Leith did not answer the question directly.

"What other clews were there, Scuttle? How did the police decide that the murderer had entered?"

"Up the fire escape and through the window."

"The fire escape?"

"Yes, sir. The room was locked on the inside, the key was in the lock. The window opened on the fire escape and it had been jimmied. The marks of the jimmy showed plainly in the wood, and there were traces of prints on the fire escape, rubber heels."

Lester Leith blinked his eyes rapidly, twice.

"Rubber heels!"

"Yes, sir."

Lester Leith tossed away the stub of the cigarette, took out his cigarette case, absently abstracted another cigarette and tapped it upon the silver side of the container.

"Funny that the murderer could have worked so quickly, and it's strange that of all the rooms in the hotel the man would have secured one that opened on the fire escape. Of course, though, that solves the mystery of the trunk. The man took it down the fire escape with him—the murderer I mean."

Long before Lester Leith finished, the valet was wagging his head in negation.

"No, sir, no, sir. If you'll only take enough interest in the case to listen to me, I'll explain it all. In the first place, it was the most natural thing in the world for Cogley to have a room which opened on the fire escape. The murderer

had made all the arrangements. In the second place the missing trunk couldn't possibly have gone through the window. The window is small, and the trunk, although smaller than the average wardrobe trunk, is, nevertheless, too big to . . ."

Lester Leith, hitching himself to an upright position in the reclining chair where he had been lounging, interrupted his valet.

"The murderer made arrangements for the room!"

"Yes, sir. You see, a Mr. Frank Millsap telephoned the hotel and said that he wanted two rooms, that they had to be adjoining and on the fourth floor. He seemed quite familiar with the hotel and suggested rooms four hundred five and seven. He said the name of the party who would occupy four hundred and seven was Cogley.

"Of course, it's all apparent now. He wanted to get this man, Cogley, in a room which had the fire escape opening from it. But the request didn't seem unusual then. When Cogley arrived from the boat and registered he was shown at once to the room. The clerk didn't ask him about the reservation, he was so certain that . . ."

Suddenly Lester Leith chuckled.

"That would be the police theory," he said.

"That *is* the police theory," said the spy with dignity.

Lester Leith raised an eyebrow.

"Indeed!" he muttered. "You seem remarkably well posted."

"I only read it in the newspaper!" said the spy hastily.

"I see," murmured Lester Leith, "and who was this Frank Millsap?"

"Probably a fence, a man who deals in stolen jewels on a large scale."

CHAPTER II

The Bloodhound of the Air

Lester Leith lit the cigarette, inhaled deeply, then extinguished the match with a smoky breath and smiled. There was something indulgent about that smile.

"The loot, Scuttle?"

"There were at the very least five magnificent diamonds. The customs detective was certain of that. And then there were some odds and ends of miscellaneous thefts, amounting in all to rather a goodly sum, but the most valuable part of the loot consisted of the diamonds."

Leith nodded, a meditative, speculative nod.

"Are you interested, sir?" asked the spy anxiously.

Lester Leith sighed.

"In spite of myself I'm becoming interested."

"Ah-h-h-h!" breathed the spy, and his tone contained the satisfaction of a salesman who has just secured the name of the customer on the dotted line.

"Yes," resumed Lester Leith, "I can almost think of a possible solution, Scuttle. That is, you understand, an academic solution. And I say 'almost,' because I am afraid to let my mind complete the thought and actually secure a solution.

"This confounded Sergeant Ackley is so obsessed of the idea that I beat the police to the solution of crimes, simply by reading of them in the newspaper . . . bah! The overzealous, pigheaded boor!"

Lester Leith took the cigarette from his mouth to snort his contempt, then added, scornfully:

"As though a man could sit on the sidelines, read of crime in a newspaper and then beat the police to a solution, in spite of all the advantages the police have. If I were a policeman, Scuttle, I'd hang my head in shame if I were ever driven to make any such confession of incompetency."

The valet followed the conversational lead.

"But you yourself have admitted that it's sometimes possible for one to reach what you refer to as an 'academic solution' through a study of the newspaper reports of crime."

"Certainly," acquiesced Lester Leith. "Many times the facts necessary to solve a crime are all in the hands of the police, and in the hands of

the newspaper reporters. They simply don't fit those facts together—don't seem capable of fitting them together.

"It's like one of these jig-saw puzzles. There may be all the parts in one's hands, but fitting each part so it dovetails with the corresponding part to make a complete picture is something else.

"What I was commenting on, Scuttle, was the attitude of the police. I would be ashamed to admit such a degree of incompetency as the sergeant admits when he accuses me of doing what he thinks I have been doing."

The valet nodded, impatiently.

"Yes, sir. But *I've* always admired your academic solutions immensely. And you can confide in me quite safely. I'd sooner lose my life than breathe a word of anything you say, sir—so, if you have any ideas about a solution—er—an academic solution of the present crime, sir, I should like to hear them."

Lester Leith yawned.

"You've given me all the facts, Scuttle?"

"Yes, sir. All the facts the newspapers have published."

"Let me see the papers."

"Yes, sir."

The valet passed over the newspapers. Lester Leith read them through. His eyes were clouded with thought, his forehead furrowed in concentration.

"So the police have been watching every one that checked out of the Palace Hotel since the crime, eh?"

"Yes. That is, the police have felt that there might have been an inside accomplice, due to the disappearance of the trunk. If that were the case, it would undoubtedly be some transient guest, some one who checked into the hotel merely in order to help in the commission of the murder. And so they've been keeping an eye on those who checked out. Nothing offensive, but just a check-up to see who they are and what they do for a living."

Leith nodded again. His eyes were narrowed now.

"Very interesting about the woman, Scuttle."

"What woman, sir?"

"The kleptomaniac. Didn't you read about her? The one who can't remain away from department stores and who always tried to pick the pockets of gentlemen friends?"

The valet moved his massive shoulders in a gesture of impatience.

"Bah!" he exclaimed. "That's just an ordinary case. She can't be interested in this murder mystery. That's what *we're* interested in. That's where the missing loot is!"

Lester Leith raised sternly disapproving eyes.

"Scuttle! Are you insinuating that you'd like to solve this murder case and find the missing loot?"

"Just an academic solution," muttered the spy.

Lester Leith let his lips expand into a grin.

"Well, if I were getting an *academic* solution, and, mind you, it would have to be academic, I'd get the kleptomaniac and a bloodhound-canary and after that there'd be nothing to it."

The spy blinked twice, as a man blinks who has received a heavy blow on the head, and hasn't enough sense left to know exactly what has occurred.

"A bloodhound-canary!" he said.

Lester Leith nodded, casually.

"In a big cage, Scuttle. And I should say that the cage should be kept covered with canvas or a very heavy twill."

The sigh of the police spy was much like a gasp.

"And the kleptomaniac. Whatever would she have to do with a solution of the case?"

Lester Leith arched his brows in well simulated surprise.

"But she's a thief!"

"Well?" demanded the spy.

"And," proclaimed Lester Leith, "there's an axiom to the effect that it takes a thief to catch a thief. And one can't disregard axioms, Scuttle. You know that as well as I do—or should."

The valet shook his head as though he had taken a long dive through very cold waters and was seeking to catch his breath as well as to clear his vision.

"A kleptomaniac and a bloodhound-canary," he said. "I never heard of any such thing."

Lester Leith nodded.

"You'll get accustomed to the idea after a while. It's really very logical, Scuttle."

The valet grunted.

"The thief to catch the thief," he said. "But what in heaven's name is a bloodhound-canary?"

Lester Leith lowered his voice.

"The bloodhound of the air, Scuttle."

"Huh?" said the valet.

Lester Leith nodded.

"It's the rarest breed of bird in the world, Scuttle," he said. "I'm not at all surprised you've never heard of it. In fact, there's only one specimen in this country. It belongs to a friend of mine who lives in the city—he brought it back from a dangerous trip to the tropics.

"The chief trait of a bloodhound-canary is that it can trail things through the air—other birds, or airplanes, or falling bodies—anything that goes through the air. That's due to its wonderful ability to recognize scents. We have canine bloodhounds to trail things across the ground. The rare bloodhound-canary does the same thing in the air a bloodhound does on the ground."

The valet looked thunderstruck, but for a moment he was speechless. Lester resumed.

"And since this trunk vanished into thin air," he said. "I'd say a man would need the help of my friend's valuable bloodhound-canary to trail them—"

The valet, his face purple now, whirled on his heel.

"Very well," he gritted. "You've had your little joke. I tried to give you the facts you wanted because I thought you'd be interested, and this is all the thanks I get? Being made the butt of a joke! And rather a poor joke—if you will pardon me for saying so, sir!"

And he strode toward the door which led from the room.

Lester Leith watched the man with laughing eyes. The spy was huge, some six feet odd of hulking strength, and he moved with a ponderous stealth, like a stalking elephant. Lester Leith, on the other hand, was closely knit, feline, well formed, quick in his motions.

"Scuttle," he called.

The spy paused, his hand on the door.

"I wasn't making sport of you," drawled Lester Leith. "And, since you seem inclined to doubt my statement, I've decided to show you just how a theoretical solution *could* be worked out with the aid of this wonderful canary and a kleptomaniac.

"Would you mind getting a cab, going to a bird store and getting me a bird cage? I shall want a perfectly huge cage, Scuttle, one that has a diameter of at least four feet. And I'll want a cover for it. Have the cover tailored to fit smoothly—something made of dark cloth so that the canary will get lots of rest. It's very delicate, you know.

"I'll attend to getting the kleptomaniac myself, Scuttle. And I'll see my friend and borrow his flying bloodhound. And you may start now. Of course you won't breathe a word of this to Sergeant Ackley."

And Lester Leith arose, flipped the cigarette into the fireplace and strode toward his bedroom, leaving a gaping spy standing awkwardly, one hand on the door knob.

"But," stammered the spy, "I don't understand."

"No one asked you to, Scuttle," said Lester Leith, and slammed the bedroom door.

CHAPTER III

The Kleptomaniac

Bessie Bigelow glanced up at the man who sat in the taxicab, faultlessly tailored, wearing his evening clothes with an air of distinction.

"The bail," she said, "was five grand."

Lester Leith nodded, as though five thousand dollars was distinctly a minor matter.

"Plus about a thousand to pay the department store," went on Bessie Bigelow.

Lester Leith nodded again.

Bessie reached over and placed a hand on his coat sleeve.

"Now listen, guy," she pleaded. "I'm a good scout but I'm a shoplifter and a pickpocket, and I ain't nothing else. Don't get me wrong. You come along and play Santa Claus for me, but that ain't going to get you no place.

"I'm a crook, all right. I've worked the department stores and pulled the pickpocket stuff for a long time. I ain't no kleptomaniac. Kleptomaniac, my eye! That's a line of hooey the lawyer thought up for the judge, and the newspaper boys glommed onto it and made a big splurge about the beautiful woman who was in jail because she just couldn't keep her hands to home."

Lester Leith lit a cigarette. He hadn't even glanced at the blonde who was rattling off the conversation at his side.

"Listen," insisted the blonde, "if you're playin' Santa Claus with the idea that you're gettin' a blond lady friend you got another guess comin'. And if you're one of those settlement workers that always come around givin' the girls a chance to reform, you got two more guesses comin'.

"I ain't goin' to be a sweetie, and I ain't goin' to reform. I'm spillin' it to you straight because you got a chance to go back an' glom the coin you put up for bail and to reimburse the department store. I've done lots o' things in my life, but I ain't never obtained no money from a gent under false pretenses. I'm a girl that shoots right straight from the shoulder, that's me."

Lester Leith nodded.

"Very commendable, your frankness," he muttered.

The girl snorted.

"Listen, guy, what do you want?"

Lester Leith turned to face her.

"I want your help."

"In what?"

"In convincing the police that I am innocent of certain crimes they try to pin on me."

The girl's blue eyes widened until they seemed like China saucers.

"Now that," she said judicially, "is a new one!"

Leith nodded.

"And what do I do?" she asked.

"You go to a hotel with me, and we get rooms, separate rooms, but rooms which adjoin," said Lester Leith.

The girl yawned.

"Pardon me," she said wearily.

"For yawning?" asked Lester Leith.

"Naw," she drawled, "for thinking your line was a new one. From there on, big boy, I know it by heart."

Lester Leith shook his head.

"No," he said, "I'm afraid you don't."

She shrugged her shoulders, shook her head, the smell of the jail disinfectant still clinging to her hair.

"Well, go on," she said, "and don't hesitate in the rough places. Spill it and get it over with. Exactly what is it you want?"

"I want you to occupy this room, probably as my sister or niece," said Lester Leith, "and I want you to come and go as you please. You will probably be followed by police, but that's a minor matter. And I want you to curb your illicit activities as much as possible. Use a certain amount of discretion as to the pockets you pick. That's all."

The girl's eyes were narrow and hard.

"Listen," she said, "I hate a damned mealy-mouthed hypocrite. Now you been pretty decent to me. So come clean. If that's all, say so, and if it ain't, say so."

"That," said Lester Leith, "is all."

She sighed.

"Well," she said, "I sure gotta hand it to you. If that's all, you're sure a new one."

"Nevertheless, that *is* all," said Lester Leith. "Only I want to warn you that the police will be watching you. If you do exactly as I say they

can't convict you of anything. If you fail to follow instructions you may get yourself into rather a tight fix."

Bessie Bigelow nodded.

"Guy," she proclaimed, "I like you, and I like the way you came across with the bail money. I'm going to do it."

Lester Leith's nod was rather impersonal.

"Thanks, Bessie," he said.

The cab rumbled on in silence.

"Well," said Bessie, rather ruefully, "if we're going to be pals, I may as well start shooting square by giving you back your things."

Her hand disappeared down the front of her dress, came out with something that glittered in the reflected street lights.

"Your watch," she said.

Lester Leith took it unsmilingly.

"Thank you, Bessie."

She regarded him with a puzzled expression.

"Didja know when I lifted it?" she asked.

He shook his head.

"Within ten seconds after I got in the cab," she said. "I sized you up as a settlement worker that was goin' to pull a lot o' hooey and wind up by having to be slapped to sleep, so I made up my mind I'd get mine while the gettin' was good."

Lester Leith returned the watch to his pocket.

"I don't blame you," he said.

Her next sigh was almost a groan.

"And your wallet," she said. "It sure feels fat."

She passed him over his wallet.

"Take that after the watch?" asked Lester Leith with a note of respect in his voice.

"Naw," she said. "I took that while you was talking with the bail clerk, right after you put up the six grand . . . listen, guy, you ain't lost nothing but a thousand bucks, that's what the department store took to square up the charge account. The rest of the money is simply bail, and they can't make that shoplifting charge stick. They can't identify the goods. I'll stick right around and demand trial, and they'll dismiss the case. Then your five grand comes back."

Lester Leith muttered a word of thanks.

"And if you let me work that hotel we're goin' to, I'll have your thousand back for you inside of a couple of weeks."

Lester Leith shook his head.

"No, Bessie. While you're with me, your play is to be the sad, penitent kleptomaniac who is taking medical treatments from a psychiatrist, having, however, occasional symptoms."

"Okay," she said. "You shoot square with me and I'll shoot square with you. Where we headed for now?"

"The Palace Hotel," said Lester Leith.

"The Palace, eh?"

"Yes. Ever been in trouble there?"

The young woman knitted thoughtful brows.

"I don't think so," she said. "There was a rap there a coupla years ago, but I beat it."

"That's fine," said Lester Leith. "I'd hate to cause the hotel any embarrassment. Why don't you reform and go straight, Bessie?"

She stared at him as though he had made some astoundingly new suggestion.

"Now, *that's* an idea!" she said. "The only trouble with it is that I've heard it somewhere before!"

And then she laughed, a low, purring laugh.

"Why don't you?" insisted Lester Leith.

"Baloney," she said. "Why should I? It's a crooked world. I'm enjoying myself, le'me alone. You promised you weren't going to try and reform me. Gimme one of those cigarettes. The Palace, eh? That place gives me a pain. They try to put on lots of dog so they can stick you on the bill."

The cab drew up in front of the hotel.

Lester Leith assisted the girl to the ground. He indicated some three bags to the doorman, stalked into the lobby. The clerk bowed obsequiously and spun the register, handed him the desk pen.

"I believe," said Lester Leith, with dignity, "that you have a reservation for me?"

"Yes?" asked the clerk. "What was it?"

"The name," said Lester Leith, "is Frank Millsap. I wired about rooms. I was to have 407 reserved for me, and 405 for a friend of mine."

And Lester Leith scrawled a signature across the hotel register.

"Frank Millsap," he wrote.

Had he slapped the clerk in the face with a wet towel, that individual could not have shown greater astonishment or dismay.

"Mill . . . Millsap . . . Frank Mill-sap . . . 405!" he stammered, then ceased speaking to gasp for air, no sound whatever coming from his pale lips.

"Yes," snapped Lester Leith, "Millsap, and I fail to see any reason for excitement or comment. I made the reservation over the telephone several days ago."

The clerk took a deep breath, gripped the sides of the counter.

"But Mr. Cogley came here . . ."

"*Mister* Cogley!" snapped Lester Leith. "Who the devil said anything about a Mister Cogley? The room was reserved for Miss Cogley, my niece. And I want to warn you that she's suffering from a certain type of nervous disorder and any commotion is quite likely to raise the devil with her nerves. Now get busy and assign us to those rooms."

The clerk was gaping.

"You mean to say . . ."

"I mean to say," snapped Lester Leith, "that I have come here to secure treatment for my niece, that she's highly nervous, and that I wanted rooms on the fourth floor because she prefers the fourth floor, and that I wanted rooms back from the street to be away from the noise. I secured the assurance of the manager that 405 and 407 would be reserved, and I want those rooms."

The clerk nodded.

"Just one moment," he said. "I'll have to consult the manager!"

"Very well. Consult him then!" snapped Lester Leith. "While you're doing that I'll bring in the rest of my baggage, a very valuable bloodhound-canary, and I don't want him subjected to any undue jar or noise. He's very delicate. In fact I'll carry the cage myself!"

He stalked to the door, where a second taxicab had drawn to the curb. Inside that cab was an enormous cage tightly covered with a black cloth which had been tailored to fit over the bars like a glove.

Lester Leith pushed aside the curious doorman, the eager bell boys, gently lifted the big cage from the cab, raised it to his shoulder, carried it into the hotel.

From the interior sounded little fluttering noises.

CHAPTER IV

Scuttle Warns the Sergeant

Sergeant Arthur Ackley, bull-necked, grim-jawed, sat at the battered desk at headquarters which had been the scene of many a stormy interview.

The side of the desk bore scratches made with the nails of police shoes where they had been elevated from time to time in moments of relaxation. The surface was grooved with various charred lines, marking the places where cigarettes had been parked and forgotten.

Across this desk, facing the sergeant, was Edward H. Beaver, the man who worked under cover as valet for Lester Leith, and upon whom Leith had bestowed the nickname of Scuttle.

"I know a canary *has* got something to do with it," Beaver was saying. "It sounds goofy, and it *is* goofy. A bloodhound-canary! But when you stop to think it over, it ain't so goofy after all. He's always getting some fool thing that don't make sense, and then using it to . . ."

He broke off as the telephone shrilled its summons.

Sergeant Ackley grunted as his vest pressed against his diaphragm in the process of leaning over the desk, then scooped the telephone to him, raised the receiver and grunted an inarticulate sound into the instrument.

He twisted the cigar to one side of his mouth, sighed wearily.

"Yeah," he grunted.

There was a moment of silence, then a metallic, rasping sound from the receiver.

"Yeah!" growled Sergeant Ackley. "Him talkin' right now. Spill it!"

The receiver rattled like a tin can tied to the tail of a fleeing canine. Sergeant Ackley gradually hitched himself bolt upright. His eyes popped wide open. The sagging lips caused the end of the cigar to droop.

"Huh?" said Sergeant Arthur Ackley.

The receiver rattled in repetition of its almost hysterical sounds.

Sergeant Ackley cleared his throat, by a conscious effort tightened his lips and raised the cigar back to its former angle of belligerency.

"Okay. Now get this straight. Play right into his hands. Let him get away with it, with anything. And rush ten of the boys right down there. Let 'em register as guests. Stick a dick on the elevator. Put one of our men at the desk. But keep the whole thing under cover. Don't let him think there's a plain-clothes man in the place. Get me? Let him think he ain't tailed.

"But keep a watch on his door, and keep a watch on that fire escape. Don't let him make a move that ain't reported. And if he ever tries to leave that hotel have one of the boys pretend to be a sucker from the sticks that's had his pockets picked. See?

"Let him make a squawk and there'll be a man in uniform always within call. Let them hang the pickpocket rap on this guy for a hurry up search. Get me? This is once I ain't taking no chances.

"Now get busy!"

Sergeant Ackley slammed the receiver back on the hook, banged the telephone down on the desk and glowered at his undercover man.

"The crust of the damned fool!" he exploded.

"What's he done now?" asked Beaver.

"Gone to the Palace Hotel and claimed he was the Millsap that telephoned in the reservation for Millsap and Cogley, and that the broad he's got with him is his niece."

Beaver wet his lips.

"You mean the kleptomaniac?"

"That's the baby. He put up the bail and squared the department store charge account for a thousand bucks, cash money. Then he shows up at the hotel and says her name's Cogley and that she's suffering from a nervous trouble.

"The clerk stalled him along while he telephoned in, and now I'm going to get enough men on the job to cover the case right. I ain't going to let that damned, supercilious, smirking . . ."

Beaver interrupted.

"Has he got the canary?" he asked.

"He sure as hell has. He's got the thing all wrapped up in a cage that's big enough for an eagle."

Beaver furrowed his brows.

"What the devil does he want with a canary? And why does he insist it's a 'bloodhound-canary'?"

Sergeant Ackley waved his hand, the gesture of one who brushes aside an unimportant detail.

"Forget it. He's just got that canary to kid us along. He wants to sidetrack us. Concentrate your attention on the main problem, Beaver. We gotta find out what he's doing in that hotel . . . Not that we don't know. It's simple as hell. What I mean is that we gotta do like the Japs do with their pelicans."

Beaver's eyes widened.

"What's that got to do with it?"

Sergeant Ackley laughed.

"Plenty. They starve the birds and then take 'em out on their boats. They clamp a ring around their necks to keep 'em from swallowing. The bird sees a school of fish and flies over, swoops down and scoops up a whole beakful of 'em, an' a pelican's beak holds a lot. Then the bird tries to swallow 'em, but the ring keeps the fish right where they belong. The Jap pries the bird's bill open, spills out the fish, and sends him away after more fish.

"Now this guy, Leith, has been lucky. I ain't giving him credit for any great amount of brains, but for a lot o'luck. He's managed to dope out the solution of a few crimes from having the facts told to him, and he's always thrown us off the trail by kidding us along with a lot o' hooey.

"This time he ain't going to kid nobody except himself. He's got the hiding place of those diamonds figured out, and he's going there to cop 'em off. Well, I'm going to just stick the ring around his neck, and let him cop. Then when he tries to swallow, he'll find that we'll just pry his jaw open an' make 'm spill the goods.

"See? He'll be just like the trained pelican. He'll go get the stuff for us, then we'll shake him down and take all the credit for solving the case. After that we'll cinch the stolen goods rap on this guy, Leith, and fry the murderer. And if we can't find the murderer, we'll just hang the whole works on Leith, frame him for the murder, and fry *him*."

Beaver sighed.

"It sure sounds nice the way you tell it, Sarge, but I wish you'd find out what he's goin' to do with that there canary before we get into this thing too deep. Somehow or other I got a hunch that canary is goin' to be the big thing in this case . . ."

Sergeant Ackley's face turned red.

"That'll do, Beaver. You go ahead and obey orders, and don't ball things all up trying to get intellectual. You leave the thinkin' to me. You do the leg work.

"That's where you've always gummed the works before. You let this guy drag some red herring across the trail, and you go yapping off on that side trail while Leith gets his stuff across and ditches the swag.

"Now I don't want to offend you, but I'm in charge of this case, and I'll do the thinking. You beat it on back to Leith's apartment, and telephone me in a report whenever anything breaks. I'm going to play this hotel end of it my way."

The undercover man started to say something, thought better of it.

"Yes, sir," he said, saluted, turned on his heel and walked out.

CHAPTER V

Leith Finishes Arrangements

Lester Leith stared around him at the hotel rooms.

There was nothing to indicate that one of these rooms had been the scene of a grewsome murder. Hotels have press agents who thrust forward certain favorable facts and keep others very much in the background when it becomes necessary.

The newspaper accounts of the Cogley murder had only mentioned the location of the crime as having been in a "downtown hotel." They had been indefinite as to the name and location of this hotel and none of the accounts had so much as mentioned the floor on which the room had been situated, let alone the number of that room.

People have a superstitious dread of sleeping in a bed in which a murder has been committed, and some persons shun a hotel merely because a crime of violence has been committed under its roof.

The girl stared at Lester Leith with uncordial eyes.

"You're leavin' that connecting door unlocked?"

"Yes. I want to get into this room without going down the hallway."

She sneered.

"Well, don't walk in your sleep."

Lester Leith bowed.

"I am a sound sleeper. When you are in the room you can lock the door. But when you are absent I want to be free to come and go."

"And you want me to do my stuff?" asked the girl.

"Meaning?" inquired Lester Leith.

"Copping watches and that sort of stuff?"

He nodded.

"But you don't want me to do anything with 'em, hock 'em or anything like that?"

Lester Leith shook his head vehemently.

"No. I want you to give everything you take to me."

The girl sighed, half turned, slid the hem of her dress up along the silken contour of a shapely limb.

"Hell," she said, bitterly, "somebody's always taking the joy outta life. Here it is!"

And she tossed a hard object to the hotel dresser, an object that rattled, that rolled and sent forth sparkles of scintillating fire.

Lester Leith stared at it.

"Where did that come from?"

"The hotel clerk's necktie, of course," she said. "You didn't think I'd pass up anything like that, did you?"

Lester Leith stared at her in appreciative appraisal.

"Good work! Did you get anything else?"

She shook her head.

"I lifted the bell hop's watch, but it was a threshing machine movement, so I slipped it back again."

Lester Leith smiled, crossed the room to the telephone.

"Can you shed any tears?" he asked the young woman.

She shook her head.

"Never shed a sob in my life. I never regretted anything I did bad enough. All I ever regretted was gettin' caught, an' that was somethin' somebody else did."

"Can you look meek and regretful?"

"Maybe."

"Okay. Get gloomy then, because I'm getting the clerk up here."

Lester Leith took down the telephone receiver.

"The room clerk," he said.

There was a pause, then the click of a connection.

"A most unfortunate occurrence," muttered Lester Leith apologetically into the transmitter. "Please come up right away to room 407. I'll explain when you get here. Come at once."

He hung up the telephone, turned to the girl.

"Pull out the handkerchief and droop the eyes," he said.

She sat down on the edge of the bed, hung her head.

"Okay, but don't put it on too thick, or I'll giggle."

There was a knock at the door.

The clerk, white faced, wide-eyed, stood on the threshold. Back of him was a lantern jawed individual with pig eyes. Out in the corridor, two men were engaged in a casual conversation of greeting, exclaiming that it was a small world after all, shaking hands with a fervor that was too audibly exclamatory to be entirely genuine.

The clerk stepped into the room.

"Meet Mr. Moses," he said, nervously.

Lester Leith bowed.

"The house detective, I take it?"

The clerk cleared his throad nervously, but the big form of the man with the lantern jaw barged forward.

"Yeah," he growled, "I'm the house detective, if that means anything."

Lester Leith was suavely apologetic.

"So glad you came, so glad we can have this little conference. I'm so sorry it all happened, but so glad we can discuss it privately.

"You see my niece is suffering from a nervous disorder. In short, gentlemen, she's a kleptomaniac. Her hands simply will not let other people's property alone. She's particularly hard on department stores."

The house detective glowered at the girl who sat on the edge of the bed, head hung in shame, her hands clenched.

"Klepto—hell!" he exclaimed. "What you mean is that she's a shoplifter. I've heard of lots of these here cases of nervous troubles, but they're all the same. They used to be just plain sneak thieves until some slick lawyer hired a crooked doctor, and then they all became kleptomaniacs. Now, don't you try to pull nothing in this hotel, because . . ."

"No, no!" exclaimed Lester Leith. "You don't understand. The girl has everything she could wish for, everything that money can buy. She simply has an irresistible impulse to steal. Now what I wish to do is to assure you that if there is anything taken from any of the guests of the hotel I will be financially responsible. I will make good the loss."

The house detective sneered.

"Daddy, eh!" he said.

Lester Leith paid no attention to the interpolation.

"I had intended to have my niece examined by the best brain specialist in the city. But unfortunate symptoms have developed which make me realize that there is an acute attack developing, and I cannot reach the brain specialist. I think, perhaps, your house physician would be able to handle the situation until we could secure a specialist."

The clerk fidgeted, looked at the house detective.

The house detective yawned, visibly and audibly.

"Bushwa!" he said. Then, after an interval, added: "Baloney!"

Lester Leith extended his hand toward the clerk.

"Permit me," he said.

He opened the hand.

"Good God!" exclaimed the clerk, his hand darting to the knot of his tie, drifting down the glistening silk, "That's my stickpin!"

Lester Leith was smilingly suave.

"Exactly," he said.

The detective got his feet in under him, half raised his body from the chair he had been occupying, then settled back. The clerk clutched at the diamond pin.

"Now," purred Lester Leith, "perhaps you will be so good as to call the house physician."

The clerk and the detective looked at each other.

The house detective carefully twisted his head to one side and closed a surreptitious eyelid.

"I think," he said, "I got a friend who's a specialist on this sort of a case. I'd better get him. The house sawbones ain't no good for anything except liquor prescriptions . . . And," he added, ruefully, "he ain't no good for those anymore. His book's used up."

Lester Leith arose, bowed politely.

"As you say, gentlemen. I will endeavor to keep my niece under restraint until the physician arrives. I hope I don't have to confine her in an institution.

"In the meantime, remember that I will be responsible for any loss which occurs in the house. And perhaps it would be advisable to notify the occupants of the adjoining rooms that there is an . . . er . . . unfortunate case located here. They could be asked to report promptly on anything they might find . . . er . . . mislaid."

The clerk sniffed.

"And spread it all over the hotel that we got a criminal stuck in one of the rooms! Not much. We'll go get this brain specialist, and then you get out!"

The house detective yawned, stretched, and as he stretched, managed to move his leg so that his toe gently kicked the shin of the indignant hotel clerk.

"Now don't go talkin' that way," he soothed. "People can't help it when they get that kleptomania, any more than they can help sleepwalkin' or coke-snuffin'."

Leith flashed him a grateful glance.

"I'm certain," he muttered politely and deferentially, "that you're an expert in your line, Mr. Moses."

"You said it," said Moses, and nodded his head to the clerk.

"C'mon," he said.

They shuffled out. The door closed. The girl raised an unpenitent face and grinned.

"Now what?" she asked.

Lester Leith regarded her gravely.

"If you had to build an ironclad, copper-riveted alibi, what would you do?"

She puckered her lips, narrowed her eyes in thought.

"Absolutely ironclad?" she asked.

Leith nodded.

The girl grinned.

"Well," she said, "I've pulled a stunt once along that line that ain't never been improved on. I let a cop who was pretty well up in the big time date me up. He was married. It would have been a swell alibi if I'd had to use it; only I didn't have to use it."

Leith took out a wallet.

"I think," he observed, "it would be a fine time to start building an alibi."

She took the bill he handed to her, let her eyes widen, whistled, thrust the money down the top of her stocking, and grinned.

"I like," she said. "You'd rate a good-by kiss if I hadn't just smeared my mouth all up pretty for the clerk. As it is, you're a good guy. G'by."

"Good-by," said Lester Leith.

The girl turned to go.

CHAPTER VI

The Hiding Place

She went out the door, as graceful as a slipping shadow. The hallway seemed to be unduly active. Three men were strolling along. A fourth man was arguing with a porter about the cost of transporting a trunk.

Lester Leith smiled.

He locked the door, walked through room 407 to room 405, took a small leather packet from his pocket, extracted a tiny drill. With this drill he bored a very small hole in the panel of the communicating doorway which led to room 403.

When this hole was completed, Lester Leith applied his eye, saw that the room was dark and vacant, nodded sagely, and took additional tools from the leather case.

After some ten seconds the bolt twisted and the communicating door swung open.

The room showed that it had been occupied for some time. The furnishings were those of the stock hotel bedroom, but there were individual touches, photographs on the walls, a pennant or two, a sofa cushion, and a special reading lamp.

Lester Leith noted them, noted also that the

clothing had been unpacked from the suitcases and trunk and placed in the closet of the room, the drawers of the bureau. The massive trunk was presumably empty, but it was tightly locked.

Lester Leith nodded, as though he was finding exactly what he had expected, and set to work. He dragged the bulky trunk into room 405, then across the floor into room 407. He pulled the clothes out of the bureau drawers, took the suitcases, then reading lamp, the sofa cushion, even the photographs on the walls. He denuded the room of every single item of individual furniture.

Then he retired once more to room 405, locked the communicating door, applied his eye to the peep hole he had gimleted in the panel, and waited.

He had something over an hour to wait.

His room was dark, save for such light as came through the windows, light which ebbed and flowed with the regularity of clockwork, marking the clicking on and off of some of the intermittent electric signs which were on the roofs of adjoining buildings. The noise of the side street came to his ears in a confused roar. The blare of automobile horns, impatiently trying to move traffic more expeditiously, the muttered undertone which marks the restless motion and conversation of hustling throngs, all blended into an undertone of sound.

Lester Leith remained at his post, silently observant.

His vigil was at last rewarded.

A key clicked in the lock of 403. The door swung open, showing light from the corridor, the silhouette of a chunky man. The door closed. The bolt clicked, and the light switched on.

Lester Leith could see the look of stunned amazement on the face of the man in the adjoining room as his horrified vision appraised him of what had happened.

The man was in the early forties, alert, broad shouldered, self-sufficiently aggressive. But now his self-sufficiency melted away from him. His face writhed with conflicting emotions. He glanced back of him at the door through which

he had just entered, then at the doorway where Leith watched.

For some ten seconds he stood motionless, apparently adjusting himself. Then his hand slipped beneath the armpit of his coat, abstracted a snub nosed automatic, and he tiptoed toward the door behind which Lester Leith crouched.

Softly, silently, he twisted the knob of that door, and found that the door was locked. Then he stepped back, letting light once more come through the small hole Leith had bored.

The man walked on the balls of his feet to the telephone in the corner of the room, took down the receiver.

"Room clerk," he rasped, and his voice sounded with the strain of his feelings.

That voice was rising in a vibrant emotion which was akin to nervous hysteria as he recounted his troubles to the hotel clerk. Lester Leith could not catch all the words, but he could hear the tone, and gather the import of the conversation.

Then the man in the adjoining room hung up the telephone, crossed swiftly to the window, pulled down the shade, went to the door, made certain it was locked, looked at the transom, making sure it was closed.

Then he secured a chair, stood on it, and unscrewed the brass screws from one of the wall lighting fixtures. The fixture lifted out, disclosing a cunningly designed hiding place. In that hollowed out hiding place, at one side of the spliced electric wires which conveyed current to the wall fixture, was a chamois bag.

The man opened this bag with fingers that quivered.

Then he gave an exclamation of relief. For several seconds his greedy eyes stared down at the bag, and the contents of the bag, sending scintillating shafts of light upward, were, in turn, mirrored in the man's eyes, until the reflections seemed to turn the eyes to cold fire.

Then the man hastily closed the bag, pushed

it back into its hiding place, paused for a moment's consideration, and then replaced the screws in the wall fixture. He got down from the chair, moved it so that its back was against the wall, unlocked the outer door, stepped into the corridor, and closed the door, locking it from the outside.

Lester Leith worked with swift rapidity.

He opened the communicating door, glided into the opposite room, pulled the chair back to the place directly underneath the wall fixture, untwisted the screws with a rapidly geared screwdriver, opened the chamois bag.

There were many gems in that bag, gems that sparkled and glittered. But Leith was careful to take only a certain limited number, a very few, but those few the best. Then he closed the bag, pushed it back into its recess in the wall, screwed back the light fixture, replaced the chair and slipped from the room into his own room, number four hundred and five.

He thrust a cautious head out of the window.

The fire escape stretched down the side of the building like a black ribbon. Three men were seated in the alley underneath that fire escape, shooting craps. Another man sprawled on the seat of a truck that was parked a few feet to one side.

Leith abandoned the window.

He tiptoed to the door of his room, pulled up a chair, climbed on the chair, stared out through a crack in the transom.

He could see a section of the hallway.

Two men, wearing the uniform of bell-hops, yet seeming strangely mature for bell boys, were walking up and down, their manner that of sentries on duty. A burly porter, who would have never been taken as a porter save for the cap he wore, was seated on a trunk. A well dressed man with alert eyes was standing well down at one end of the corridor.

There was no possibility of escape from that room, undetected.

And, as Leith stared, three purposeful men emerged from the elevator and moved toward his room. They were the clerk, the house detective, and the self-sufficiently belligerent man who occupied 403.

Even as Leith stood there, they started to knock on the door, and, as they knocked, the two mature bell boys crowded forward, the porter jumped down from his seat on the trunk, and the gimlet eyed man at the end of the hall moved forward on rubber soled feet.

Lester Leith stepped from the chair, moved into swiftly purposeful action.

What had been a polite knock was repeated with more noise. Then it was repeated again with two fisted emphasis.

"What is it?" called Lester Leith in the blurred tones of one who has been aroused from slumber.

"Open this door," said the hoarse voice of the house detective. "We want to talk with you. This is Sam Moses, the house man."

"Oh," said Lester Leith. "Just a minute."

And he jumped on the bed to give a creaking noise to the springs, then let his feet thud to the floor.

Yet it was several seconds later that he opened the door.

His hair was tousled. His eyes were blinking. His collar was wrinkled and his coat was off. There was an air of dazed perplexity about him.

". . . lay down for a minute," he explained sheepishly. "Must've dropped off."

He sucked in a prodigious yawn.

Sam Moses lowered his broad shoulders and pushed past Lester Leith into the room. Directly behind the detective, walking with a certain cat-footed belligerency of manner, his right hand hovering near the lapel of his coat, his eyes narrowed, anxiously alert, came the occupant of 403. The clerk was a tardy third in procession.

One of the mature bell boys cleared his throat suggestively.

The house detective turned, called over his shoulder:

"Come in here, Joe."

The bell boy pushed eagerly forward, forcing the clerk into a quicker step.

Lester Leith seemed more awake now.

"What's the matter?" he asked anxiously.

The house detective switched on the light, looked the room over.

"Where's the broad?" he asked.

"You mean my niece?" asked Lester Leith.

The house detective sneered.

"To hell with that line," he said. "You know who I mean. I asked where the broad was. She went out. Did she come back?"

It was the bell boy who answered.

"Naw," he said, "she didn't come back."

"Certain?" asked the house detective.

"Sure," said the bell boy.

Lester Leith let his eyes widen.

"Why," he exclaimed with a simulation of ingenuous innocence and surprise, "you're a detective!"

The man who was dressed as a bell boy snorted.

"Go sit on a tack!" he invited. "Let's take a look around."

They moved forward, a compact knot, save for the squat man who occupied room 403. He gravitated slightly to one side.

"All the personal belongings from my room," he said, "have been stolen."

Lester Leith let his jaw sag.

"Good heavens!" he said.

The detectives strode through the connecting bathroom, walked into 407.

"This the stuff?" asked the man who had posed as a bell hop.

The occupant of room 403 stared at the assortment.

"Good Lord, yes!" he exclaimed. "How did it get *here*?"

Lester Leith joined in the exclamation, his tone one of dismay.

"Good heavens!" he groaned. "She's had an attack!"

"Yeah," sneered the detective. "Ain't that too bad!"

Lester Leith turned to the occupant of room 403.

"But I'm responsible," he said. "I'm finan-

cially responsible. Only I want to know for just what I am responsible. Here, in the presence of these officers, we will open this baggage and list the contents."

There was a sudden swirl of motion behind Lester Leith. Two hands clamped down on his arms. Glittering bracelets of steel clicked around his wrists.

"Yeah," sneered the man who had posed as bell hop, "and we'll just keep you out of mischief while we're making the examination."

CHAPTER VII

Handcuffs for Leith

Lester Leith stiffened. His face mirrored dismay.

"Listen, officer," he said. "I can't explain, but you'll ruin some very precious plans I have if you do not remove those handcuffs. I demand that you release me. I have important plans."

The detectives joined in a guffaw.

"Ruining plans of crooks is one of the best things I do," said the detective.

"No, no. You don't understand. Call Sergeant Ackley. Get him here at once. I demand that this baggage be opened. And I want Sergeant Ackley here . . ."

The squat occupant of room 403 moved easily toward the door.

"I'll open it fast enough," he promised. "But I've got to go to my room to get my keys."

He took swift steps toward the door.

"No, no!" yelled Lester Leith. "Stop him. Get Ackley! Get Ackley. I dare not make an accusation while that baggage is unopened, but I want Sergeant . . ."

The detective swung his right fist.

The blow contacted Lester Leith on the jaw. Leith slumped to the floor, inert.

"Hell," said the detective. "I didn't hit him hard. He must be playing possum. I didn't want any more of his damned bawling. Where's the sarge?"

"Coming," said a voice from the corridor.

A compact body of men moved into the room.

"Better frisk him," said some one.

"He'll keep," chuckled one of the detectives. "Let's look around."

"Maybe we went a little too fast, Joe," cautioned one of the men. "Orders was to give him enough rope to spring his stuff, and then clamp down on him."

"Well," countered the individual addressed as Joe, "he had enough rope, and he was pulling his stuff, or I miss my guess."

Hands went through Lester Leith's clothing.

"Nothing here," said a voice.

"Look the room over," ordered some one else. "Close that damned door. We don't want a crowd in on this. Where the hell's the sarge? He was sticking around for a while. Then he said he had a sick friend he had to see, and left a telephone number where we could call him if anything broke."

"You call him?" asked the clerk.

"Yeah. Soon as the guy from four-oh-three made the squawk. Say, where is *that* bird?"

"Gone to get his keys."

"Well, we better go down there, and . . . here's the sarge now."

There were purposeful steps, the banging of the door as it slammed open, then shivered on its hinges, then the voice of Sergeant Ackley.

"Well," he exclaimed, "what's up! See you got the bracelets on him. Did you catch him with the goods?"

"We caught 'm right enough," said the voice of the man called Joe. "I don't know just what he was pulling, but . . ."

Lester Leith stirred, moved his eyes, groaned.

"Open the man's trunk," he said, and then slumped back into silence.

"What happened to him?" asked Sergeant Ackley.

"Oh, he was squawking, and I cracked him an easy one an' he wilted. Don't know what got into 'm."

Sergeant Ackley grunted.

"Better be careful. He's a smooth one. And he keeps a good lawyer. If we haven't got the goods on him . . ."

"We got the goods on 'm right enough," said Joe.

"Open the trunk anyway," said Sergeant Ackley.

"Guy's gone for the keys," said Joe.

There was a period of shuffling silence. Some one scraped a match and lit a cigarette. Then some one coughed.

"Say, where the hell *is* that guy?" asked some one.

Lester Leith moaned, twisted.

"Don't let him get away," he pleaded in a groaning whisper. "I tried to get you, sergeant . . ."

Sergeant Ackley suddenly exploded into action.

"Go grab that bird, Joe. Bill, get that trunk open. This looks like a job that's been bungled. That guy in 403 . . . Get started!"

There came a scurrying motion, swift voices, shouted comments. Then a report was called down the hallway. "Went down the stairs. Thought you sent him, Joe. He said you did!"

Profanity spouted from Sergeant Ackley's lips.

"Get that guy! He's the murderer and gem thief. Hurry up. Throw out the dragnet. Give the signal. Close the block!"

And he ran to the window, flung it open, raised a police whistle to his lips, blew a shrill blast.

Lester Leith sat up.

For a man who had been knocked out, he seemed to be in serene possession of his senses.

"I warned you, sergeant," he said. "Will some one please give me a cigarette?"

Sergeant Ackley flung back from the window, glowered at the handcuffed figure on the floor.

"Hell!" he said.

Lester Leith talked fluently.

"We've had our differences, sergeant, but I thought I could patch them up by putting a feather in your cap. I figured the trunk the murdered man had held the gems, but that the trunk had proven obstinate. The murderer, however, would never have carried the whole trunk with him unless something had happened to make that the only course possible.

"He'd killed the gem thief, and was opening the trunk when something happened to alarm him. That something must have been the arrival of the officers. That meant the murderer was trapped in the room when the officers were demanding an entrance.

"He'd previously forced the window over the fire escape to make it seem like an outside job. But he couldn't have escaped through that window because it's obvious that he took the trunk with him.

"Therefore there was only one escape he had, through the communicating room, and into his own room. If my theory was correct, the murderer had been at work on the trunk when the officers banged on the door. He didn't want to leave his loot, so he shouldered the trunk, slipped into 405 and through it into his own room and locked the door.

"Then he had to do something with the trunk. He realized there'd probably be a search for it. So he did the obvious. He simply put the stolen trunk, which was small, inside his own trunk, which was large.

"That meant he had to wait for a later time to tackle the secret combination. It also meant that he had to be an old resident of the hotel, both for the purpose of avoiding suspicion, as well as to have been sufficiently familiar with the hotel to know that the rooms he wanted for his victim, which would adjoin his room, would have an opening on the fire escape.

"He knew Cogley was coming here, and he planned to get Cogley in his power by setting a trap, reserving a room for him. Cogley walked into that trap . . ."

Lester Leith was interrupted by a man bursting into the room.

"There's a secret hiding place in 403 back of a wall fixture. A guy jerked it out by the roots, and . . ."

And that man, in turn, was interrupted by the rattle of gunfire from the street, revolver shots which stabbed the night with exploding pulsations.

There were more than a dozen of them, exploding in rapid succession. Then the wail of a siren, the sound of shouts, a police whistle blowing frantically.

A woman screamed, and the scream came up through the window.

"They've got him!" exclaimed Joe.

The men rushed toward the window.

"Go see what happened, Joe!" rasped Sergeant Ackley.

Men piled from the room.

CHAPTER VIII

The Bird in the Hand

Left behind, Sergeant Ackley glowered at the handcuffed figure.

"I think I've got you this time!" he said.

Lester Leith sighed.

"I did *so* want to give you an olive branch by letting you take the credit for capturing the murderer. And then you had to spoil it all. And one of your men struck me, when I was handcuffed! An unprovoked, brutal, police assault."

Sergeant Ackley grinned.

"Tell it to the jury," he said.

Lester Leith shook his head.

"No," he said, "I shall tell it to the newspapers!"

Sergeant Ackley looked worried.

He surveyed the room with glittering, suspicious eyes, strode to the covered birdcage, ripped off the cover. A startled canary hopped about the cage, chirped indignantly. Ackley cursed the bird, kicked the cage.

A man rushed into the room.

"Bagged him!" he exclaimed. "He was shot

half a dozen times. They closed in on him and he tried to smoke his way out. Dead now, but he had enough life left when they got to him to tell them that he did the job. And he had the loot with him."

There was disappointment in Sergeant Ackley's voice.

"Had the loot with him!"

"Yep, in a small chamois bag that he'd kept hidden in the space back of the wall light. He told 'em how he did the job. Knew Cogley was coming here to the Palace. Knew he was going to keep an appointment with a fence. So this bird reserved the room he wanted, trapped Cogley, and tipped off the fence the bulls were hep. That kept the fence away.

"The guy sneaked into Cogley's room when he was washing up, cracked him on the dome, tied and gagged him, intended to get the stuff and beat it. But Cogley came to, recognized him, so he croaked Cogley, then started after the trunk when he heard the officers coming.

"He dragged the trunk into his own room, and . . ."

"Never mind all that," snapped Sergeant Ackley. "I had deduced that much myself. I would have arrested this man only I wanted to use him to bait a trap for this man Leith. But did the police recover *all* the gems?"

"The whole sack!" gloated the detective.

"Hell!" said Sergeant Ackley.

Lester Leith smiled.

"Now can I have a cigarette?" he asked.

Sergeant Ackley walked to the door, slammed it shut.

"Listen, this guy never had the chance to check all the jewels. There were a lot of diamonds in that haul. Maybe some of 'em got away. Let's search this room and the two adjoining. And I mean search 'em. No maybe about it. Take 'em to pieces. Rip out the wall fixtures, X-ray the furniture. This bird is too smooth to have let anything like that slip through his fingers."

The detective stared at Sergeant Ackley.

"Well," he said dubiously, "we can do it. This guy couldn't have hid nothing, though. The fire

escape was watched, and the hall was watched, and there wasn't a chance, not a single chance."

Sergeant Ackley grunted.

"This guy don't need a chance. He only needs a half a chance, and sometimes not even that. Get busy and search!"

They got busy and searched, and the net result of that search was to uncover nothing at all. Never had rooms been subjected to such a complete search, and Lester Leith, himself, was one to make the search more complete. Whenever the police seemed to be overlooking a single cranny or corner, Lester Leith would point it out.

"The brass in the bed is hollow, sergeant," he suggested. And: "There might have been a hole bored in the curtain pole in the closet."

Those suggestions were received in sullen silence, but acted upon with alacrity. The morning was sending its chill fingers through the air when the officers finished. A clock struck two somewhere, and Sergeant Ackley ran doubtful fingers through his matted hair and surveyed the wreckage.

"Well," he said, "they ain't here."

Lester Leith grinned.

Sergeant Ackley scowled at him.

"But you still got some explaining to do. I've half a mind to throw you in on suspicion and let you explain how you happened to be trailing this crook around. You *intended* to hijack him, even if we did beat you to it!"

Lester Leith looked hurt.

"Tut, tut, sergeant! I was doing you a favor. My solution was only academic. I could even bring evidence to show that it was suggested by Scuttle, my valet. I really *had* finished with these *academic* crime solutions, but Scuttle egged me on. He'd have to admit that—if he were questioned."

And because Sergeant Ackley knew that this was true, knew also that any further investigation would result in the real capacity of the undercover operative being brought to light, he sighed, turned away.

"All right, boys," he said wearily. "Let 'm go."

One of the detectives had a bright idea.

"The woman accomplice," he said, "the one that posed as his niece. She was away . . ."

Sergeant Ackley hastily interposed an interruption.

"Let her out," he growled. "She's got an ironclad alibi, one that don't need to enter into the case, but one that's good. I checked it up myself. That's what delayed me getting here."

The detective's voice held a trace of admiration.

"Gee, sergeant, you sure work fast!"

Sergeant Ackley nodded.

"That's the way to work!" he said. Then his eye fell on the canary in the huge cage.

"Say," he demanded, "what the hell's the idea of that bird?"

"A very valuable bird," said Lester Leith. "A Peruvian bloodhound-canary. I was hoping to try him out."

Sergeant Ackley stared at the cage.

"False bottom, maybe," he said.

The detectives shook their heads.

"Nothing doing, sergeant," said Joe. "Every inch of it has been checked."

Sergeant Ackley fixed his moody eyes upon the canary.

"Birds have craws, boys, and maybe there's a fine stone stuffed down this bird's craw. Wring his neck and let's have a look!"

Lester Leith's voice suddenly became ominous.

"Sergeant, I've let you ride roughshod over my rights long enough. If you take the life of that canary, I'll have you arrested for cruelty to animals, and, by God, I'll spend a hundred thousand dollars prosecuting the charge! That's a very rare species of canary, and very delicate. It's worth thousands!"

Sergeant Ackley's face broke into a smile.

"Now," he gloated, "we're getting close to home. Pull that damned bird out here and let's see what he's got inside of him."

One of the detectives was more humane.

"We've got the house physician's X-ray machine," he said. "We can use that just as well, and then this guy won't have any squawk."

"Okay," said Sergeant Ackley, too weary for further argument. "Give 'm the once over."

The bird was held under the X-ray. The result was as the search had been, negative.

Lester Leith made a facetious comment.

"The bird in the hand," he said.

"That'll do!" bellowed Ackley.

Leter Leith continued to smile.

"All right. We've solved the Cogley murder. That's a good night's work. Let's get home, boys," said Sergeant Ackley. "It's getting along—"

He fished mechanical fingers in his watch pocket, then let his jaw sag, his voice trail into silence as those searching fingers encountered nothing.

"My watch!" he said.

The men stared at him.

His hand darted to his necktie.

"And my pin! Good heavens! What'll my wife . . ."

He paused.

In the moment of tense silence which followed, Lester Leith's drawling voice carried a cryptic comment.

"I'm *so* glad the young lady has an alibi," he said.

Sergeant Ackley's face purpled.

"Shut up!" he bellowed. "I remember now, I left my pin and my watch on my dresser at home. Let's go, boys. Get out of here. Leave the damned slicker and his canary!"

And Sergeant Ackley pushed his men out into the hall, showing a sudden haste to terminate the entire affair.

Edward H. Beaver, undercover operative of the police department, detailed to act as valet to Lester Leith, suspected hijacker of stolen jewels, held up a grayish feather between his thumb and forefinger, and stared reproachfully at Ackley.

"I told you, sergeant, that he never did anything without a reason. That canary, now . . ."

Sergeant Ackley banged his feet down from the desk. His face was distorted with rage.

"Beaver, you're detailed on that suspect. You live with him, hear everything he says, know everything he does, and yet the guy keeps pulling things right under your nose. It's an evidence of criminal incompetency on your part."

"But," interpolated the spy, "I suggested this about the canary before, sir. I suggested that the solution of the whole affair might be . . ."

Sergeant Ackley raised his voice.

"You're all wet, Beaver. I even X-rayed the damned canary. He couldn't have had a thing to do with it!"

"Yes, sergeant," said the spy, meekly, a little too meekly, perhaps; "but I found this feather in the bottom of the cage."

"Well, what of it?"

"It's not the color of the canary, sir. It's not a canary feather."

Sergeant Ackley stared, his eyes slowly widening.

"Well, what sort of a feather is it?"

"I had it classified at the zoölogical gardens. It's a feather from a pigeon, one of the sort known as a homing pigeon. It's barely possible that covered cage contained half a dozen homing pigeons, beside the canary, trained to go to a certain particular spot immediately upon being released.

"And then Lester Leith could have picked out a dozen of the most valuable stones, slipped them into sacks that were already attached to the birds' legs, tossed the birds out of the window, and then later on, gone to the place where they had flown and picked up the diamonds. After all,

we have no assurance that the cage contained *only* a canary except what Leith said. The cage was always covered. It may have contained homing pigeons, and . . ."

Sergeant Ackley glowered, bellowed his comment.

"Well, that was your business! You're a hell of a spy if you can't tip us off to what's going on!"

"I warned you, sergeant, that this canary was the key to the crime. But you overlooked the bird in the hand to go chasing off after . . ."

Sergeant Ackley's chair scraped back along the floor as the big bulk of the sergeant got to its feet, as the sergeant's face glowered down upon his subordinate.

"That'll do, Beaver! Your suspicions are absurd, your statements incorrect, and your deductions too late. This department is interested in getting results, not in diagnosing failures. Get out!"

"Yes, sergeant," said Edward H. Beaver.

"And keep your mouth shut, Beaver!" warned the sergeant as the spy's hand was on the doorknob.

The retort was a grunt, inarticulate, undistinguishable, but hardly respectful.

Then the door banged.

Sergeant Ackley raised a hand to his necktie. His fingers caressed the smooth expanse of silk where his diamond stickpin had formerly glistened. That spot was now bare, unornamented.

Sergeant Ackley's face was twisted into an expression which was neither prepossessing nor pleasant.

"Damn!" he said.

THE GULVERBURY DIAMONDS
DAVID DURHAM

WILLIAM EDWARD VICKERS (1889–1965) had a successful publishing career in England, which did not carry across the Atlantic until Ellery Queen discovered his work. Vickers produced books and stories under the pseudonyms David Durham, Sefton Kyle, John Spencer, and the best-known Roy Vickers. Among his most popular works are the "inverted" detective stories that appeared in several collections, most notably *The Department of Dead Ends* (1947; the expanded British edition of 1949 has mainly different contents). In this challenging type of detective story, the reader witnesses the crime, is present when the incriminating clue is finally discovered, and follows the police methods leading to arrest. Queen found one of these stories, "The Rubber Trumpet," in an old English magazine, liked it, and reprinted it in *Ellery Queen's Mystery Magazine*, leading to several of Vickers's books being published in the United States.

The other enduring character created by Vickers, under the Durham pseudonym, was Fidelity Dove, an angelic-looking young woman who is one of the most inventive and successful of all fictional crooks. Her ethereal beauty has made slaves of most of the men who meet her, especially her "gang," which consists of a lawyer, a scientist, a businessman, and others whose specialized knowledge assist in her nefarious undertakings. Her frustrated adversary is Detective Inspector Rason, who has greater success when he heads the Department of Dead Ends.

"The Gulverbury Diamonds" was first published in *The Exploits of Fidelity Dove* (London, Hodder, 1924); it is one of the rarest mystery books published in the twentieth century. The short-story collection was reissued in 1935 with the same title but under the Roy Vickers name.

THE GULVERBURY DIAMONDS

DAVID DURHAM

THERE IS ONE MAN alive who once inflicted a terrible hurt upon Fidelity Dove. He never claims that distinction for reasons that you will guess—but it is ten to one that you will guess them wrongly.

Before his retirement, you used to read pretty regularly about the Marquis of Gulverbury as a shining light of the House of Lords, as a patron of the Turf and of the Ring. He was the only member of the aristocracy who was a typical aristocrat of the old school, with a grave, courtly manner and an altogether charming belief in the grandeur of his caste. Fidelity Dove cultivated his acquaintance just about the time of his retirement. You have heard of the Gulverbury diamonds, and so had Fidelity.

Almost, one could write that the Marquis of Gulverbury was too much for Fidelity. For instance, he was too upright a man to be ensnared by her beauty, so she used her brains. She studied heraldry, one of his hobbies, and in their long chats together Fidelity tasted the sweets of an artistic friendship. She came to respect and admire him quite a lot, and that wasn't very good for business.

One day when he was strangely listless, she forced herself to mention the Gulverbury diamonds.

There broke from him a laugh that made Fidelity suddenly conscious of his age. That startled her. His next words startled her more.

"Did you happen to read in your paper this morning, Miss Dove, amongst the less impor-

tant news of the day, that a young man named John Hilliard drove a motorcar over the cliffs at Rottingdean yesterday and was killed? It was assumed that he ran off the road in a mist. He did not. He ran off the road deliberately. And his name was not John Hilliard, though no one will ever know that but you. He was, to be precise, Lord Paynton. He was my son."

"Oh!" gasped Fidelity. "How great of you to tell me like that! I will not hurt you with platitudes! I will go." She was trembling—she knew she had paled. This emotion that was sweeping her—this aching pity—frightened her by its intensity. It was so long since she had been moved. . . . "I will go," she repeated.

"You asked about the diamonds that belong to our family," continued Lord Gulverbury as if he had not heard her. "They are in the possession of Miss Lola Marron of the chorus of the Olympic Theatre. She is the one other who knows the truth about my son. He stole the diamonds from me to give to her. He left a letter, a broken-hearted letter, confessing to me what he had done and what he intended to do. This morning my agents have offered double the intrinsic value of those diamonds and have been refused. The lady is under the impression that the possession of the Gulverbury diamonds will be the foundation of her career."

The thin lips twisted bitterly; the white head was erect, but the eyes were those of a man whom ill-fortune has beaten at last.

"I have told you thus much, and I must, if

you will allow me, tell you more—for I would not have you think ill of my son. He was wounded twice in a frontier war and received the Victoria Cross. One of his wounds was in the head and he was never the same man. He had fits of violent emotionalism. This woman maddened him with her coquetry. When she had obtained the diamonds she flaunted a rival. That, I think, must have unbalanced him."

Fidelity no longer struggled with her longing to give comfort; she let herself be swept away. She told herself that just for once she could afford to do so. She was no longer the amazing Miss Dove; she was a girl in grey who grieved with her friend. She put out a hand and laid it on the clenched fist of the old man.

"To me there is an added grief in this lamentable history. If I may speak of such a subject to you, Miss Dove, the woman gave him nothing. It would have been easier to bear if he had had the pleasure of such kindness as she could give him. But he played the infatuated fool and for the destruction of his life and honour he once kissed her finger-tips."

There was another silence. Fidelity was softly caressing the withered hand.

"That is my personal bereavement. There is a loss that goes through me, beyond myself. I am of those, Miss Dove, who are not ashamed to own to a pride of family. My family was ennobled by Richard Cœur de Lion. Since then we have stood for service. We have fought corruption, and as for our women—those diamonds have symbolized their crystal purity. Successive generations of women have been proud to wear them. And now their work is to enhance the reputation of a courtesan. I don't grudge the woman their worth. But I would rather they were at the bottom of the sea than that they should serve such a purpose. And as for my poor boy—I will not bore you with the tale of his gallantry when he was himself——"

"Tell me about the V.C.," whispered Fidelity.

"You would like to hear?" The father's eyes brightened. "It was on the eve of the battle proper. His company . . ."

For an hour Fidelity listened. Then she stole from the room, leaving the old man sitting in his chair staring dreamily at the visions of the past.

Fidelity left the house in Portman Square for the green peace of Regent's Park. She walked there for an hour or more, battling with her conflicting desires. Then she took a taxi and drove home.

In the vast hall of her house in Bayswater a letter was waiting for her. It had been delivered by express messenger and it bore Lord Gulverbury's crest—Lord Gulverbury's handwriting.

"Dear Miss Dove," she read.

"A few minutes after you had left a gentleman called on me who I believe is known to you—Detective-Inspector Rason of New Scotland Yard. To your attempted injury, need you have added the cruel insult of allowing me to talk about my son? You have at least given me the satisfaction of knowing that I have amused you—Gulverbury."

Fidelity stood very still. The grand old man had talked with Rason—and now classed her beside Lola Marron. Fidelity made her way upstairs very slowly.

She noted the sombre beauty of her house as though she were a stranger; the grim Holbeins on the wall, the carvings, the stained glass, the forbidding beauty of the long corridors. It was a house that would have utterly repelled many a young girl, but she—she had created it eagerly yet carefully, had chosen the gruesome prints and the massive tapestries.

"I do not look as though I had been hurt," she thought, as she looked at herself in the triple mirrors of her dressing-room. "Perhaps that is because I never cry. But then I was not meant to cry. I was meant—to fight."

The fierce fighting pride drove her hurt inwards. When she entered the drawing-room, exquisite in cloth of silver, none of them knew there was aught amiss with her. Appleby, who could never shake off his professorial habits, was giving his colleagues an informal lecture on meteorology, one of his special hobbies.

"He's been telling us what the weather's like ninety thousand feet up," explained Varley, the jeweller.

Fidelity forced herself into the simulation of interest.

"Ninety thousand feet!" she echoed. She gave Appleby an angelic smile. "Much learning, my friend, has made you inconsistent. A little while ago you told me that mortal man had risen no more than twenty-five thousand feet above the terrestrial sphere and lived. I fear your weather reports of the upper air were written by a novelist."

"You don't, Princess," said Appleby with mock severity. "You believe every word I tell you, always."

"Self-flattery is born of self-deception," said Fidelity. "Here comes our news-gatherer."

"You've been wasting your time with the Marquis of Gulverbury, Fidelity," said Gorse. Fidelity winced. "The diamonds have passed into the hands of the fair Lola Marron. I don't know exactly how, but I can find out later."

"Why should we concern ourselves with inessentials?" asked Fidelity reprovingly. "That is mere curiosity, and as such cannot be excused."

Gorse was the only one of the gang who could not accept with equanimity Fidelity's pose of puritanical aloofness; he made an effort to keep his temper, however, and succeeded.

"Lola Marron lives in a suite at the Parnassus on the third floor," he continued. "It costs her fifty pounds a week. Her official salary at the Olympic is just enough to tip the servants. I've got the plans of the Parnassus, so my work's done, unless you want me on the main stunt, if you've decided what it is. Personally, I think hotels are the devil."

"The devil has been exorcised by science," announced Fidelity. She hesitated a moment, head bent. Then—"Friends, for my own reasons, I am disinclined to concern myself with this matter. If the—reward seems to you of sufficiently easy attainment, make the necessary plans and tell me my part in them."

A week later Fidelity was told that the time was ripe. Appleby, she found, had been placed in charge.

"And what are your plans, dear friend?" she asked.

"My plan is to find out whether my self-flattery proceeds from self-deception," said Appleby. "I have told myself that you will carry out my directions without question."

He handed her an aluminum cylinder some eight inches in length by three in diameter.

"That will go in your bag, Fidelity."

Fidelity nodded. She had regained her old serenity. Her eyes were lustrous, her lips slightly parted with the happy expectancy of a child who is given a magic wand. . . .

"We've got an electric bell under the hearth-rug in Miss Marron's sitting-room, but, of course, every time anyone steps on it it rings. You'll have to ring in code. When you make the signal the lights will go out. You will then place the diamonds in this cylinder——"

Fidelity smiled the smile of an angel.

"Having done so, you press the steel catch, and then, by means of this metal ring, slip it onto a hook which you will find just inside the chimney of the sitting-room at a point I'll show you on this chart."

Fidelity had opened her big grey velvet bag that might have contained a fleecy shawl, a piece of altar embroidery and, perhaps, a charitable dole or two. For the present, apparently, it was to contain an aluminum cylinder fitted with a steel catch and a metal ring.

There were men at Scotland Yard who dreamed of that grey bag.

Two days later, at a quarter to six, Fidelity called at the private office of Sir Frank Wrawton, her solicitor. She waited while he reached for his hat and then took him down to her car.

"It is very good of you to come with me, Sir Frank," she said, as they sped in the direction of the Parnassus.

No one had ever been able to discover the real attitude of Sir Frank Wrawton to his client

Fidelity Dove. Fidelity herself did not know, and she had the wisdom never to find out. It is probable—for Sir Frank had an enormous circle of acquaintances—that he was fully informed of Fidelity's activities and was under no misapprehension as to their nature. And it was, after all, his affair. For Fidelity's purpose, it was enough that his manner to her was courtesy itself, and that he grasped fully the futility of ever offering her advice, legal or otherwise.

"I am only too delighted—but I'm afraid I don't yet understand what you wish me to do, Miss Dove," said Sir Frank with a laugh. "Do I understand that you merely wish me to be present during an interview with Miss Lola Marron at the Parnassus?"

"Miss Marron very kindly consented to let me interview her and to show me her diamonds, which once belonged to the Gulverbury family, for my book, *The Historic Gems of England*," explained Fidelity, her saint-like face very grave above her wonderful grey furs. "I felt a little nervous, because somehow I always seem to bring bad luck to persons who own jewellery." Sir Frank removed his gaze to the ceiling of the car. "Also, Sir Frank, I—er—that is, I know nothing about the lady except that she is a musical comedy actress and I—I—as you know, the sect whose faith I cherish has a—possibly unfair— prejudice against the stage and its votaries——"

"Quite so, quite so, Miss Dove," said Sir Frank with creditable vagueness. "You did very wisely, and it's a great pleasure to me to come."

"The evenings are beginning to draw out nicely," said Fidelity. "We shall soon have spring with us."

Sir Frank mumbled appropriately as the car turned into the courtyard of the Parnassus. Three minutes later they were being ushered into Miss Marron's sitting-room; its quiet opulence had been disturbed by the chorus girl's own litter of gaudy gew-gaws. The evening light was failing and the page who had taken them up switched on the lights as he left the room.

Lola Marron's beauty was of the most flamboyant type, and from the moment she entered, Fidelity found herself wondering how the son of Lord Gulverbury could ever have been attracted. There was a very noticeable twang in her voice as she greeted Fidelity, and she looked at Sir Frank with a certain pleased insolence in her dark eyes.

"Sir Frank Wrawton," murmured Fidelity. "Sir Frank is my solicitor, Miss Marron, and I have asked him to accompany me——"

"Pleased to make your acquaintance, Sir Frank. Come and sit over here and make yourself comfortable," invited Lola Marron.

When Sir Frank had assured her that he was comfortable, thanked her, and refused her offer of a cocktail, Lola Marron turned to Fidelity.

"Well, now, I couldn't quite get the hang of that letter you wrote me, Miss—er—Dove," said Lola. "You want to see my jools, don't you, to put in your book?"

"That is so, if you will be so kind," said Fidelity with humility. "My book is nearly completed. I have had interviews with three duchesses, four marchionesses, and nine viscountesses." Fidelity glanced at Sir Frank, but he was staring at his boots. "Of course, my book deals only with gems that have a history."

"Well, all I can say is you've come to the right shop," said Lola Marron, good-tempered at the idea of appearing in a galaxy of women of the aristocracy. "My joolry, as I daresay you know, used to belong to Lord Paynton. They belonged to his mother, and he came by them when he was twenty-one. He was one of my best pals——"

Fidelity's eyes hardened until their violet gleam became a gleam of steel; but her attitude of interested attention did not falter.

"—the poor boy was dying for me to marry him. I turned him down—I simply had to. Then he said, 'Lola,' he said, 'if you won't wear those jewels my mother left me, no one shall,' he says, 'will you accept them as a gift?' he says. I says, 'Don't be silly,' and he says, 'I mean it,' he says. So I says, 'I'll take them if you like, but I'm going to pay for them, as it wouldn't be right otherwise, being as I can't marry you.' In the end I gave him twenty thou. for them. But don't put that bit in your book. I hate anything to do with money—it always seems sordid to me somehow. Now I'll show them you if you like."

Fidelity murmured pious appreciation of the favour, and Lola Marron rang for her maid.

"Fetch my joolry out of the safe and bring it here," she ordered, and when the girl returned with the jewel cases and hovered: "All right, I'll ring when I want you."

Fidelity was allowed to admire in turn a diamond necklace, a pendant, two bracelets, two buckles, and a wonderful crescent for the hair. She fingered the necklace rapturously.

"Oh, how fortunate you are!" she exclaimed. "These stones are wonderful. I can almost claim to be an expert and I have rarely seen stones to equal these. And they have a history. You know their history, Miss Marron? No? You must let me tell you the story—let me see, how does it begin?" She closed her eyes and her silvery tones were hushed.

"One day—many hundreds of years ago—a stately lady had a private audience of Queen Elizabeth. 'Madam,' whispered the Queen, 'you know that I fear you, but for all that I have sent your husband to the Tower.' And the Marchioness of Gulverbury replied—replied——"

Fidelity's memory was evidently growing a little blurred, but it revivified when she took the pendant in her hand beside the necklace.

"'Your Majesty has three ships at sea,' replied the Marchioness of Gulverbury . . ."

The breathless little anecdote of Court intrigue was being built up piece by piece as Fidelity piece by piece gathered the Gulverbury jewels into her hand. She touched the last piece and talked on. Her heel tapped rhythmically on the hearth-rug, but no one noticed that. When her heel had finished tapping, the lights went out. Sir Frank stifled an exclamation.

"Ow!" gasped Lola Marron and snatched at her jewels. But the jewels were not where they were when the lights went out. They were inside an aluminum cylinder. Some five seconds later, the cylinder was fixed onto a hook just inside the chimney. Fidelity's heel tapped again in rhythm.

The lights went up. Sir Frank had risen and was looking hard at Fidelity.

"My joolry!" shrieked Lola Marron. "You had it in your hand, all of it! Where is it?"

"I don't know," said Fidelity diffidently. "You snatched it from me as the lights went out."

"You've robbed me, you little—Help! Burglars! Burglars! Help!" Lola Marron's shrieks rang through the room. She made for the door.

Fidelity turned with a helpless little gesture to Sir Frank Wrawton.

"Oh, Sir Frank, you see what has happened! How terribly thankful I am that you are here! Oh, dear, who is this?"

As Lola reached the door it was flung open—by Detective-Inspector Rason.

"It's all right, madam," said Rason reassuringly.

"I've been robbed," shouted Lola. Sir Frank was still eyeing Fidelity, but he had drawn her hand through his arm and was patting it—he simply couldn't help it.

"And I know who's robbed you," Rason was saying. "Your jewels are either in the chimney itself now—or they've been taken through the wall into the next room by a crook. We were warned this afternoon that the fire-place had been tampered with and we stood by. There's one of our fellows watching the window of the next-door room from the street below and there are two entering it at this moment. I'll just see if the goods are still here."

Self-flattery is born of self-deception, ran in Fidelity's brain. She leant quite heavily upon Sir Frank's arm as she waited while Detective-Inspector Rason examined the chimney. He flashed an electric light inside. Nothing happened.

"Sir Frank," said Fidelity with a timid, upward glance. He was too absorbed in the detective's growing bewilderment to hear her. "Sir Frank," she repeated. "I think that you and I had both better remain in this room until the police have found Miss Marron's jewellery or are convinced that neither you nor I know anything about its disappearance. In the circumstances we must not blame Miss Marron and this gentleman for distrusting us."

A man stood in the doorway.

"Well?" snapped Rason, abandoning his search in the chimney.

"Nothing doing, sir. The fire-place has certainly been loosened, but the bricks are quite intact and there's no communication that I can see."

"But——"

"Yes, sir. We've detained the man who was in the room; he's submitted to search, and we're going through the room itself. The window was latched when we went in, and there's no ventilator, and he couldn't have passed them out of the window—nor through the door, because we were outside."

"Phone for a female searcher," ordered Rason. "You get onto the roof and I'll be with you in a few minutes. Your name, sir?"

"Wrawton."

"Sir Frank Wrawton is my solicitor," murmured Fidelity. Rason looked at her with something approaching awe. Then, at Sir Frank Wrawton's request, he searched him. Needless to say, the diamonds were not forthcoming.

"I was sitting over there," volunteered Sir Frank amusedly, "so that really, however nefarious my intentions——"

At the end of an hour Fidelity had been searched; the police had satisfied themselves that no one had been on the roof—that neither were the jewels in the chimneys nor had they been removed through the chimney to another room—that they were not in the carpets or the upholstery of the room. In fact, the only discovery they made was that of a metal disc in the floor connected with a wire.

"That's where the signal was given to put the lights out," said Rason. "Track out where that wire runs."

They succeeded in tracking out where the wire ran; it ran to where the floor mains had been tapped. But further they discovered nothing. Or, rather, they discovered beyond doubt that neither by door, by window, by concealment in the walls or the furniture, could the jewels be accounted for.

They proved, in fact, that the jewels could not have left the room.

Which, as Euclid used to say, was absurd.

"Were you afraid, Princess, when you sat in that room and the police came and searched the chimney—and told you all about the fire-place in the next room?" asked Appleby three hours later. "Or was my self-deception founded on reality?"

Gorse grinned. He had had the task of creating a diversion with the fire-place.

"Where are the diamonds?" asked Fidelity, demurely.

"I again flatter myself that you will believe me, Princess, when I tell you that neither I nor any of us know. Am I right?"

Fidelity's smile answered that he was.

She asked him the same question again a week later and received the same answer. A week after that, just as they were going to sit down to lunch, Appleby handed her the Gulverbury jewels.

"Now you have teased me, tell me," begged Fidelity. She could see by the others' faces that there was a huge joke on and she was willing to play up to it. She loved them all, but not in the sense that each of them separately wished her to love him.

"You handed in the opinion, Fidelity," said Appleby with ponderous good-humour, "that the—er—weather reports of the atmosphere at a height of ninety thousand feet were written by a novelist. In point of fact, they are written by little instruments that record such dull things as pressures and so forth with complete accuracy. Do you wish to know who takes the little instruments up there?"

"Yes, please," said Fidelity, meekly.

"No one takes them up there," said Appleby. "They are sent. They are attached to small balloons, not very much larger than a child's balloon. So little as ten cubic feet of hydrogen will lift, roughly, one pound weight. These little balloons go on ascending until they reach an enormous height and then they burst. Attached to these scientific instruments is a parachute and a float—and a label offering a reward to anyone who forwards them to the authorities."

"Oh!" said Fidelity, as light broke upon her. "How did you prevent these being sent to the authorities?"

"We didn't. They *were* sent to the authorities—the authorities of the International Meteorological and Aviation Observance Society, of which Varley was last week elected president—er—by the unanimous vote of the society, which consisted of Gorse, Garfield, Maines and myself. Our offices are in Cockspur Street—or, rather, they were. The society has gone into liquidation, after paying the reward."

Fidelity clapped her hands in congratulation.

"But wait a minute," she interrupted herself. "The wire in the chimney was attached to a balloon. Where was the balloon?"

"The wire ran up the chimney—and from the chimney through the window into the room I occupied on the top floor. The balloon, by the way, was not a balloon as you understand the word. It was twelve balloons, each the shape of those sort of super-German-sausages you sometimes see in Bond Street. They were, of course, tied together, and their lifting power was as great as a single balloon that just could not get through the doorway—still less the window. As Maines flicked up the lights in reply to your O.K. signal, I simply let my super-sausages out of the window. Some five seconds later they were hauling your cylinder to the upper air. Above that hook to which you fixed the cylinder, was a complete outfit as used by the real Meteorological Society."

For a moment Fidelity was silent. There came into her eyes the look that had been there—an hour after she had left Lord Gulverbury.

"Appleby, you have not restored my faith, for it had never waned. But I have learned in all humility to guard my tongue from careless speech. I feel a certain affection for these stones that have been the means of admonishing me. I would like to buy them from the firm. Will you value them, Varley?"

"I will not, Fidelity."

"It is your birthday, Princess," said Appleby with amazing gentleness.

Fidelity started. She had genuinely forgotten the fact. Though none of them knew Fidelity's age, all of them knew her birthday. For a moment she hesitated, then she gathered up the jewels and slipped them into the big grey bag.

"You are all so good to me," she said, and her voice was like the croon of a bird at eve. "These stones, what are they?—pretty toys that may corrupt, or be destroyed, or taken from me; but the spirit in which you have given them to me will be mine forever."

Gorse groaned. His career held no regrets for him, but he could have dispensed with the "sermonettes." Fidelity glanced at him indulgently. She detained him after lunch when he would have left with the others.

"Gorse, my news-gatherer who despises me, I seek a favour of you," said Fidelity.

"It is the same as a command," said Gorse dully.

"Then bring to me here—by any means other than that of physical force—the Marquis of Gulverbury."

Gorse brought him by artifice. The Marquis did not even know that he was coming to see Fidelity. The house gave him no hint. When the door of the study closed behind him and he faced the grey-clad form and dream-like face, he was for a moment incapable of speech.

"Lord Gulverbury, you wrote to me recently saying that I intended to steal your diamonds. You were quite right. I have succeeded. Here they are."

The bag was on her wrist. From it she drew handfuls of crystal fire. She let them slip through her fingers and clatter down upon the polished table.

"You stole them!" gasped Lord Gulverbury.

"Yes—I have stolen them—but not in the same manner in which Lola Marron stole them.

I am not a moral philosopher, Lord Gulverbury, but one of my friends is, and I have no doubt that he could prove to you that I have a great deal more right to them than Miss Lola Marron."

"I can guess the purpose of your having sent for me," said Lord Gulverbury. "I betrayed to you the fact that I value those diamonds for their association. My agents offered Miss Lola Marron twenty thousand pounds for them. I will pay you the same."

"My price is higher than that," said Fidelity, her eyes pools of contemplation.

Lord Gulverbury winced.

"Forty thousand. It is all that I can afford," he said haltingly.

"It is far, far more than that, Lord Gulverbury. My price is that you accept those stones from me as a gift."

They looked at one another. Then—

"I understand," said Lord Gulverbury. "In profound humility, I apologize."

Fidelity extended her hand.

"Madame, I am proud to accept your gift," said Lord Gulverbury, that gallant of the old school. He stooped over her hand, and, like the *grand seigneur* he was, touched her fingers with his lips.

THE FIFTH TUBE
FREDERICK IRVING ANDERSON

LARGELY, IF INEXPLICABLY, forgotten today, the Infallible Godahl may well be the greatest criminal in the history of mystery fiction. Unlike such better-known thieves as A. J. Raffles, Arsène Lupin, and Simon Templar (the Saint), who rely on their wit, charm, intuition, and good luck to pull off a caper, Godahl has a purely scientific approach to jobs. His computer-like mind assesses every possibility in terms of logic and probabilities; his successes are triumphs of pure reason—the inevitable victory of superior intellect. As a result of his infallibility, he has never even been suspected of a crime, much less caught.

The exploits of Godahl are the product of one of America's most underrated mystery writers, Frederick Irving Anderson (1877–1947), who also created the only slightly better-known jewel thief, Sophie Lang. The pretty young woman's adventures are recounted in *The Notorious Sophie Lang* (1925) and further immortalized in three films: *The Notorious Sophie Lang* (1934), *The Return of Sophie Lang* (1936), and *Sophie Lang Goes West* (1937); all were produced by Paramount and starred Gertrude Michael.

Born in Aurora, Illinois, Anderson moved east and became a star reporter for the *New York World* from 1898 to 1908 and then became a successful and highly paid fiction writer for the top American and English magazines, notably *The Saturday Evening Post*, in which most of his mystery stories, and all six of his Godahl stories, were first published. Anderson's only other volume of mystery fiction was *The Book of Murder* (1930), selected by Ellery Queen as one of the 106 greatest collections of mystery stories ever published.

"The Fifth Tube" was first collected in *The Adventures of the Infallible Godahl* (New York, Crowell, 1914).

THE FIFTH TUBE

FREDERICK IRVING ANDERSON

I

"IT WILL BE observed," noted the pharmacopœia, "that the size of the drops of different liquids bears no relation to their density; sulphuric acid is stated by Durand to yield ninety drops to the fluid drachm, while water yields but forty-five, and oil of anise, according to Professor Procter, eighty-five. It follows, then, that the weight of the drop varies with most liquids; but few experiments on this subject have been recorded, the oldest being contained in Mohr's Pharmacopœia Universalis of 1845. More accessible to the American and English student are the results of Bernoulli"—and so on.

Godahl—the Infallible Godahl—did not have the printed page before him, but he had visualized it in one glance only a few hours before and the imprint was still fresh on his memory. Reduced to elementals, a drop of liquid varies in size from one-third to one and one-half minims. Godahl split the difference and called a drop and a minim synonymous for his purpose. Later, if he were so minded, he might arrive at precise results by means of atomic weights. He began a lightning mental calculation as he sat idly stirring his beer of Pilsen with a tiny thermometer, which the proprieter of this Hanover Square resort served with each stein of beer.

"It should be fifty-two degrees Fahrenheit, my friend," said the master of the house, who in passing saw that Godahl was seemingly intent on the thermometer. Godahl was not intent at all on the tiny thread of mercury; rather he was studying the drops of golden brown liquid rolling off the pointed end of the glass instrument. However, it was as much as one's life was worth to dispute the proper temperature of beer at this eating place, and Godahl smiled childish acquiescence and explained that he was awaiting with impatience the rise of half a degree of temperature before he indulged his thirst.

"It should be just such a color," he mused—"possibly a little more inclined to orange—and a little sirupy when stone cold." And, with his head thrown back and his eyes shut, he completed his calculation: there should be sixty-one thousand, four hundred and forty such drops to the gallon—at ten cents a drop!

"Tut, tut!" he exclaimed to himself, conscious of feeling exceedingly foolish; it was so simple, so insolently obvious, like all great inventions and discoveries once they have been uncovered.

This was one of the three tasks he had dreamed of, each worthy to be the adventure of a lifetime—three tasks he had dreamed of, as a poet dreams of a sonnet that shall some day flow from his pen with liquid cadence; as an author dreams of his masterpiece, the untold story; as an artist dreams of a picture with an atmosphere beyond the limits of known pigments.

One was the Julius Tower, where at the bottom of a well lay thirty millions in coined golden eagles, hoarded by an emperor more medieval than modern, against the time when he must resume the siege of Paris. The second was the fabled chain of the Incas, one hundred fathoms of yellow gold, beaten into links; it lies purple with age in the depths of a bottomless lake ten thousand feet in the clouds of the Peruvian Andes. And the third—it was this nectar of the gods, more potent, more precious than the rarest of collected vintages. The Julius Tower and the fabled chain were remote—the one guarded by an alien army, the other guarded by superstition—but this nectar lay within a stone's throw of where Godahl sat now studying, with the fascination of a great discovery, the tiny drops of liquid falling from the tip of the glass thermometer, each drop shaping itself into a perfect sphere under stress of the same immutable laws that govern the suns.

"Ach!" cried a voice of truculence behind him, and his precious mug of beer was unceremoniously snatched away from the hand of Godahl by Herr Schmalz. In his abstraction the master rogue had violated a rule of the house— the temperature of the brew had climbed to sixty. Godahl, with an amused smile, watched the testy old host adjust the temperature of a fresh mug to a nicety, and when the mug was returned to him he drank deep at the other's insistent command.

"Every man to his own religion," thought Godahl. "His is fifty-two degrees Fahrenheit; mine is gold!"

Godahl, swinging his cane with a merry lilt, picked his way up the crooked street under the Elevated to Wall Street. To the east the Street was lined with grimy warehouses; to the west it was lined with marble. To the west was the heart of gold. Godahl turned west. Every window concealed a nest of aristocratic pirates plotting and scheming for more gold. In the street the *hoi polloi* were running errands for them, enviously cognizant of the shiny silk hats and limousines of their employers. Gold bought everything the heart could desire; gold attracted everything with invisible lines of force radiating on all sides.

An express wagon was backed up to the curb and curious pedestrians were peering over each other's shoulders, attracted and held spellbound by no more rare a sight than a pyramid of rough pine boxes, each as big as a shoebox, piled on the pavement. The boxes contained gold—ingots of gold. If the guards, who stood on each side of the sweating porters carrying the boxes inside, had not looked so capable it is more than likely that many individuals in the crowd would have remembered that they had been born thieves thousands of years ago, and fought madly for the possession of this yellow stuff.

"It should obey the laws of gravity and be subject to the stress of vacuum," mused Godahl, still delighted with the obvious idea he had discovered over his beer in Hanover Square. "I think," he wandered on ruminatively—"I think I shall reduce it to its absolute atom and beat it into a frieze for the walls of my study. Sixty-one thousand drops to the gallon! It should make a frieze at least four inches wide. And why not?" he thought abruptly, as though some sprite in him had snickered at the grotesque idea. It was in this way that the dead and buried races of the Andes prized the yellow metal—not as a vulgar medium of trade and exchange, but as a symbol of kingship, a thing to be possessed only by a king. They decorated the walls of their royal palaces with bands of beaten gold. It must have been very satisfactory, thought Godahl, pursuing his whimsical idea; at least—he added as an afterthought—for the kings!

He paused at the curb and his esthetic eye sought not the boxes of gold that lay on the pavement, but the exquisite lines of the little structure of which the barred door stood open to receive the treasure. The building was no bigger than a penthouse on the roof of any of the surrounding skyscrapers; yet, with its pure lines and its stones mellowed with the wash of time, it was a polished gem in a raw setting. It stands, as any one may see, like a little Quaker lady drawing her shawl timidly about her to shut out the noise and clamor of the world crowding in on all sides. On one side rises a blank wall twenty or more stories in height; on the other, the cold gray pile of the Subtreasury stands guard as stolid and sullen as the Great Pyramid itself.

The windows were barred, so that even a bird might not enter; the door was steel-studded; the very stones seemed to cluster together as if to hide their seams from prying eyes. The cornices were ample for a flood and the tiles of the roof were as capacious as saucers. Before the days when electrolytic chemistry came to the aid of the crude agencies of earth, air, fire, and water, the very smoke that emerged from the blackened chimneys was well worth gathering, to be melted down in a crucible to yield its button of gold. The whole represented the ideal of a strong-house of a past age. It was the Assay Office of the United States that Godahl regarded.

"If," thought Godahl delightedly, as his eye caressed the picture—"if it were painted on china I am afraid, friend Godahl, you would not sleep until the plate was secure in your possession."

The hour of one was suddenly, stridently ushered in by a crash of steam riveting hammers, like the rattle of machine guns. Little apes of men, high in the air back of the little building, were driving home the last of the roof girders of a tiny chimney-like skyscraper, which in several months' time was to absorb the functions, with ultramodern methods, so long and so honorably exercised by the beautiful little house in the street—the old Assay Office.

Godahl passed on and shortly was in his lodgings. There was mellow contentment here—something he prized above all things; and he sighed to think that he would not know this comfort again for weeks. That same day, as an expert electrician named Dahlog—with a pronounced Danish accent—he presented his union card and obtained employment at sixty cents an hour. Things worth doing were worth doing well in his philosophy; and, though he hated soiled fingers and callous hands and walking delegates, he must regard the verities.

II

The spic-and-span new Assay Office of the United States is sometimes described as the House Without a Front Door. Indeed, it has no front door; but it has two back doors, and gets along very well at that. In reality it occupies two back yards, balancing itself nicely on the party line between a parcel of land fronting on Wall Street and another on Pine. The Wall Street entrance is effected through the dingy halls of the now tenantless Assay Office of the olden time; on the Pine Street side a tall iron paling suggests to the passer-by that something more precious than bricks and mortar is contained within. There is a wicket gate of ornamental iron in the fence, wide enough to admit two men abreast, or to allow the passage of the hand trucks laden with boxes of gold and silver bullion. A long wooden ramp, uncovered—a temporary structure—connects the street with a window in the second story of the new building, which for the time is serving the purpose of a door.

Some day the precious parcel of land standing between the gaunt face of the new building and the street will be occupied by a pretentious façade, and then the magnificent plant that turns out pure gold day and night at the rate of some forty million dollars a year will be lost to view entirely. Now, to the street passenger it suggests nothing of its functions—suggests less, in fact, to the imagination than the pine boxes laden with bullion, whose appearance daily is always calculated to draw a breathless audience.

The walls are sheer, without architectural embellishment of any kind; it is, in fact, nothing more than the rear of a skyscraper, some day to be given a face.

It was four o'clock in the afternoon of a June day. The upper windows of the Assay Office stood open, and through the apertures there emerged a fine sustained hum, like the note of some far-away violin. It told the passer-by that the motor generators of the electrolytic plant within were churning at their eternal task of separating gold from dross.

A party of four men were in the act of leaving the place on the Pine Street side. One was the superintendent of the plant and another the master refiner, the two men responsible for the wealth within—two men whose books were balanced each year on a set of scales that will weigh a long ton or a lead-pencil mark with equal nicety.

A third man of the party was a Canadian government official who had come down from Ottawa to inspect this latest monument to the science of electrolytic chemistry. He was not interested in the Assay Office as a stronghouse—it had long ago passed into tradition that the Mint of the United States, with its accessories, is inviolable; and to ask whether this latest plant of its kind in the world were burglar-proof would be to laugh.

The fourth member of the party was the chief of a division of the United States Secret Service, who in passing through the city had run down to find out whether Guinea gold owed its peculiar color to a unique atomic structure or to the presence of a trace of silver. On the answer hung the fate of two rascals he had laid by the heels.

"No; you haven't the idea yet," the master refiner was saying to the Canadian official. "We superimpose a low frequency alternating current on the direct current for the purpose of shaking out the bubbles of gas that otherwise would prove very troublesome."

"It is due to a small percentage of silver," the superintendent was explaining to the secret agent; and the latter was gnawing his mustache in chagrin, for the answer meant that he had barked a 'coon up the wrong tree.

At this point an incident occurred, seemingly trivial in itself, the significance of which, however, struck the four with the force of a thunderbolt a few hours later on that momentous evening. It had to do with the secret agent's enforced moderation in the matter of tobacco. His physician had ordered him to cut his nicotine allowance down to three cigars a day; and now, in the first throes of his abstention, he was as cross as a bear with a sore toe. The whiff of an Irishman's cutty-pipe smote his nostrils as the little party passed through the gate.

Now there is something about the exotic fragrance of a well-seasoned cutty-pipe that induces in those who happen to be in its immediate neighborhood an almost supranormal desire for a puff of the weed. Whether it was the intensive quality of the tobacco itself, the ripeness of the clay cutty-pipe, or the fact that the cutty-pipe is subjected to a forced draft by reason of the extreme abbreviation of its stem—whichever of these elementary causes it might have been—the psychological effect was the same.

The secret agent stared vacantly about him. A mud rat—so the brown-jeaned scavengers whose business it is to scoop mud out of catch-basins are known—was igniting a fresh charge of tobacco in the lee of his mud cart, a watertight affair of sheet steel. The tempted one drew a cigar from his pocket and regarded it with a scowl.

"It's the vile pipe that scavenger is hitting up as though it were a blast furnace!" explained the secret agent guiltily as he bit off the end of the cigar. "This is my after-dinner pill; here goes!"

He searched his pockets for a match, forgetting that he had adopted the practice of traveling matchless to make life easier. He appealed to his three companions, but they could not scare up a match among them.

"What!" ejaculated the secret agent incredulously. "Do you mean to say there are three able-bodied men in one bunch who turn up their noses at tobacco! I have heard," he went on, with infinite sarcasm, "of isolated instances—of individuals—like our friend, Doctor Pease, for example; but three men in one spot—I am amazed!"

It was true nevertheless.

"Will you honor me with a light?" said the secret agent, stepping over to the mud rat and touching him on the shoulder, interrupting that worthy in the act of dumping a scoopful of subterranean mud into the capacious bottom of his cart. "You seem to be the only man in my class around here," he added facetiously. "We have a vice or two in common. My friends," he said, airily indicating the three beside him, "are pale angels."

The mud rat surveyed the four with an air of vague curiosity. He went through the pockets of his jeans, but his hands came away empty; so, with the free-masonry of smokers, he offered the other the live coal in his cutty-pipe for a light, which the agent accepted gracefully.

"A most remarkable mud rat!" commented the secret agent. "Did you notice that he wore rubber gloves? I shouldn't be surprised to learn that he patronized a manicure on holidays!"

As a matter of fact, this particular mud rat did not confine his patronage of manicures to holidays. He had the finest set of fingers in Greater New York.

"Also," noted the professional thief-chaser mechanically, "his horse, which is a little curbed on the nigh side, has the number 2-4-6 burned in its hoofs."

"Yours must be a very interesting life," commented the bland Canadian, who had never before had the good fortune to dally with a real secret agent.

"It has its drawbacks at times," said the other, smiling over his cigar. "A man gets into this stupid habit of noting details, until at the end of the day his head is so muddled with facts for cataloguing that he can't sleep."

An hour passed; and still Pine Street, in front of the back window that is used as a door, gave no hint of the history then in the making to mark this day in the annals of crime. At the stroke of five the tall buildings vomited forth their hives of workers. The Wall Street District empties itself swiftly at this period of the year, when there are still several hours of daylight for sports afield before dinner for the army of clerks. Fifteen minutes later only a thin stream remained of the flood that had overflowed the sidewalks.

A pushcart man, catering to messenger boys and the open-air brokers of the curb, was resting on his cart taking stock of his day's business. The mud rat who worked at his unsavory calling with the aid of rubber gloves was still industriously burrowing in the depths of the manhole; a white-suited street-sweeper, a son of sunny Italy, with his naturalization papers in his pocket, was

pursuing his task to the tune of the Miserere, with an insistent accenting of the grace-note at the antepenult.

A policeman or two swung along the curb. A truck, with wheels as big as a merry-go-round, drawn by ten spans of horses, bearing a sixty-ton girder for the new Equitable Building round the corner, rolled past the scene like a Juggernaut.

One—even one with the sharp eyes of a secret agent—might have photographed the scene at this moment and still overlooked the obvious clew to the situation. The drama was in full swing. It was nearing the hour of six when the curtain came down on the big act—marked, as is usual, by the gentle tinkling of a bell.

On the seventh floor of the Assay Office a man was seen to stop his task suddenly at the sound of the bell, and to look at the switchboard standing on the west side of the room. He crossed the room hurriedly, disappearing; he reappeared at the window, staring blankly and rubbing his eyes.

Two miles away, one minute later, a liveried page, silver salver in hand, passed through the corridors and parlors of the Holland House, droning wearily:

"Mister Hamilton! Mister Hamilton!"

"They are paging you," said the open-eared secret agent to the young master refiner. "Here, boy!"

"Telephone, sir—number sixteen!" And he led the master refiner to the indicated booth.

"Yes; this is Hamilton. Who is this? Jackson, you say? It doesn't sound like your voice. What's that? Say that again. Come close to the phone, man—I can't make out what you are trying—— Empty, you say?"

The young scientist looked blankly at the narrow walls of the booth that held him. Then with a peremptory note in his voice:

"Who is this? Where are you? What is this tomfoolery anyway?"

He pressed the receiver to his ear, his heart thumping.

"Empty! The tank is empty? You are—crazy—man!"

Evidently the voice at the other end of the wire had become incoherent.

"Jackson," cried Hamilton sharply, "you are lying! You are seeing things! Can you understand me?"

He waited for the answer, which did not come—only a suppressed gasp through the telephone. "Jackson!" he cried. "Listen to me! Turn round and walk to the tank; then come back and tell me what you see! . . . Boy!" he shouted through the half-open door of the booth. A dozen pages rushed for the door. "Tell Mr. Whitaker to come to me at once. He is the man with the red mustache who is sitting on the ottoman in the smoking-room."

When Whitaker, the secret agent, thrust his head in at the door he was met by Hamilton bounding out. Hamilton's face told the agent that something big was afoot, and as the other dashed out he followed. Hamilton picked up Banks, the superintendent, on the way out.

They left the Canadian gasping and alone. The nice little dinner for four that had been planned for the evening was off. The three officials were half a dozen blocks down-town in a taxicab before the Canadian guest of honor woke up to the fact that, as the whitefaced refiner had stated bluntly, something was afoot that was not his affair.

The street scene that met the eyes of the three, as they tumbled out of their cab in Pine Street and ran up the long ramp leading to the door, was much the same as when they had passed out a short time before—the same actors in different persons, that was all. It was not until three days later that the story leaked out, and crowds surrounded the block, gazing at the gaunt Assay Office as they were wont in lesser numbers to gaze at the rough pine boxes laden with gold.

While the dumpcart driver and the driver of a steel truck were disputing the right-of-way at the Nassau Street corner, a little group of dumfounded men stood about a huge porcelain tank on the seventh floor of the building. From their awed silence the tank might have been a coffin. The tank was empty!

Forty gallons of gold, held suspended in an acid solution of the consistency of good beer at just the right temperature, had evaporated into thin air—forty gallons—sixty-one thousand drops to the gallon—at ten cents a drop! Of it now there remained only a few dirty pools settling in the unevenness of the lining.

Hanging suspended like washing on the line were two parallel rows of golden shingles. On one line they were covered with canvas, black with the scum of dross; on the other, the precious metal, still wet and steaming, had formed itself into beautiful branching crystals. But the nectar—the nectar of the gods—through which the dense electric currents worked in their eternal process of purifying, selecting, rejecting— the nectar of the gods was gone!

III

The three officials looked at each other foolishly. Each in his own way, according to his lights and his training, was doing his utmost to grasp the idea that presented itself with the force of a sledgehammer blow.

According to the testimony of the switchboard, between the hours of four and six o'clock on this June afternoon, in the year of grace nineteen hundred and thirteen, forty gallons of piping-hot gold-plating solution, valued at ten cents the drop, six thousand dollars the gallon, a quarter of a million dollars the bulk, had been surreptitiously removed by a thief— undoubtedly a thief—so much was obvious— from the inviolable precincts of the New York Assay Office, adjunct to the United States Mint. Jackson, the assistant refiner on night duty, warned of the interrupted electric current by the bell on the switchboard, was the first to give the alarm.

At first blush it would seem that a ton of hay, wrapped up in one package, would be far easier loot as to bulk. Counting two grains of gold to a drop of liquor, the very weight of the stuff would have been over ten thousand troy ounces—over eight hundred pounds; and its bulk, counting seven gallons to the cubic foot, would have been nearly six cubic feet—the size of a very respectable block of granite. Yet eight hundred pounds, six cubic feet, of the stuff, a quarter of a million dollars, had unquestionably departed without leaving a trace of its path.

As has been said, the Assay Office possesses two perfectly serviceable means of exit and ingress—back doors, it is true; but still doors. The structure possesses possibly fifty windows. Whitaker raised a window and peered out. The walls were as sheer as the polished sides of an upright piano. That the intruder might have entered by a window was a childish suggestion, quickly dismissed.

The doors were at all times of day and night guarded by intricate mechanical contrivances, of which no one man knew all the secrets. In addition there were the human guards, with their army six-shooters of the peculiarly businesslike aspect that tempts one to refer to them as guns.

The three officials all tried to say something after a time; but the thing was beyond words so soon after the impact. The secret agent, trained for such occasions, was the first to collect his wits. He began examining the rifled tank. He had not gone far before he began to swear softly to himself. The tank was composed of porcelain in a steel retainer. He pointed to the two rods that ran parallel lengthwise of the empty receptacle. These two rods were covered with a saddle of yellow metal throughout their extent.

Suspended from the rods were hooks roughly cut out of the same sheet of metal. Suspended from the hooks on one rod were some fifty canvas sacks, each the size of a man's sock. They contained crude bullion, from which the plating solution extracted its pure gold. On the other rod, suspended from similar hooks, were yellow plates ten or twelve inches long, varying from one-eighth to an inch thick, covered with a fine incrustation of yellow crystals, clustering together like grains of damp sugar.

"What is all this stuff?" he asked bluntly, turning to his companions who had sprung to his side when he exclaimed: "Is it gold?"

The two men nodded assent. It was solid gold, pure gold—even to the roughly hewn hooks. The very electrical connections were of gold.

"What's it worth?" demanded Whitaker.

"I could tell you in a second from my books—" began the superintendent.

"Never mind your books! A million?"

The superintendent shook his head. He could not yet grasp details.

"Half a million?"

"Easily!" responded the refiner. "Yes; quite that, I should say."

Whitaker lifted one of the incrusted plates, still wet from the solution in which it had been immersed so short a time before. He swung it on his finger by means of its golden hook.

"Doesn't it strike you as a bit strange," he said, "that a thief with wit enough to make away with six hundred pounds of your precious juice should have left behind half a million dollars in raw gold, lying loose in the middle of a room?"

This was a nut that for the time being resisted cracking. The secret agent said, "Humph!" and fingered his vest pocket for the interdicted cigar, which was not there.

"In emergencies," he said absent-mindedly, "it is justifiable." He turned to Banks and added: "See that no one leaves the building until I return. The first thing to do—it's foolish, but it must be done—is to round up all your employees and bring them here. I suppose all of them knocked off for the day with a clean shower?"

Yes; all the men had passed through the changing room, emerging therefrom after a shower bath, a fresh suit of clothes and an inspection. Such is the daily routine.

Whitaker walked thoughtfully down the ramp to the street and sought out a shop where he might procure fuel for thought—cigars; long, strong, and black. Then he felt better. As he turned into Pine Street from Nassau he noted a small boy, of the free tribe of street urchins, holding up one dirty foot and howling with pain.

Whitaker's methodical mind noted that the foot was of a singularly blotched appearance, as though from a burn; but he had weightier things on hand than rescuing small boys in distress.

The details of the start of the investigation were soon put through when he reëntered the office. Every employee of the institution was rounded up, though it was ten o'clock before the last startled porter was led protesting before the stern officials and put to the question. The trail was blank.

"It's a blessed thing we have got you with us," said Banks, who had been biting his finger-nails since the opening of the drama. "It kind of takes off the curse."

He looked at Whitaker, truly thankful that so broad a pair of shoulders was there to take the burden.

"Humph!" said Whitaker, who was studying the toes of his shoes as though they contained the answer to the riddle. "It is quite evident," he began, "that eight hundred pounds of gold, especially in a fluid state, did not get up and walk off without help. I think," he said, rising, "that before we go farther I will take lessons in electrolytic chemistry. We haven't lost much time on this case and we can afford to waste a few minutes getting at fundamentals."

They retired to the seventh floor, the floor of the yawning porcelain tank; and in a short time Whitaker was in possession of the facts. It was a simple system, when all is said and done, this system of refining gold, which had been worked out by the greatest students of the time. The secret agent was put through the elementals of the process of transmuting gold from the alloy by means of the electric current.

"Very clever indeed!" remarked Whitaker. "Also, gentlemen, let me add that it is very clever indeed to lock up gold bars downstairs in safes that cost a fortune, and leave a tankful of the stuff standing in the center of an unprotected room like this."

"But who could come seven stories up in the air and get away with stuff of this bulk?" querulously interjected Hamilton. "The thing is preposterous!"

"The preposterous thing," said Whitaker, with his drawl, "has occurred—apparently under your very noses; and, from the looks of things, the fact that the liquor was steaming hot did not interfere with the plans of the thief in the least. What is that collection of pipes?"

He indicated a nest of black-varnished iron pipes running along the outside of the tank.

"Those are the conduits to carry the electric wires," explained the master refiner.

No sooner were the words out of his mouth than he exclaimed aloud and leaped into the empty tank, running his fingers with feverish haste over the conduit outlets.

"By Gad! I have got it!" he cried, his voice a high falsetto under stress of his excitement. "Hand me a portable light—quick!"

With an electric bulb at the end of a portable cord, he inspected every inch of the tank, more especially the outlet boxes of the electric wires. Four tubes were required to carry the electric current.

There were five. The fifth was empty of wires. So cunningly concealed it lay behind an elbow-joint that only eyes sharpened by an idea born of genius could have detected it. With a cry of triumph, the refiner dashed to the door and down the stone stairs. He was at the panel of the switchboard in the converting-room, where the electric current is properly tuned for its task of assaying. There were only four conduits leading from the upper floor—the fifth had lost itself somewhere among the studdings and joists of concrete and steel.

The astonished Whitaker, finding his recently acquired knowledge insufficient to follow the leaping mind of Hamilton, finally seized that individual and cornered him.

"What is it?" he cried.

"It's as plain as the nose on a man's face!" cried Hamilton. "That fifth tube! Good Heavens! man, are you so stupid? That fifth tube could drain that tank of its last drop by siphoning it out!" He broke away, cheering. "They have taken our gold out of the tank, but they haven't got it away from the building yet. Find out where that fifth tube runs to and there you will find our gold!"

Through the simple means of a siphon their

forty gallons of precious liquor could have been removed through an aperture scarcely larger than a pinhole. The dawn was beginning to break. Whitaker's mind, clogged by its abnormal meal of technical details, was beginning to run cleanly again.

"Stop!" cried Whitaker. "I am in charge of this affair. I want you to answer my questions. In the first place," he cried, seizing the refiner by the arm and twisting his hand above his head, "what is the matter with your hands?"

Hamilton's hands, where he had been pawing about in the electrolytic tank, were stained brown, as though from cautery. They were drawn with pain, though in his excitement, up to this moment he had not noticed it.

"Cyanide of potassium!"

"Where did it come from? Quick!"

"Oh, you fool! The tank—the tank, of course. The process—I went all through it with you. The tank contained chloride of gold dissolved in cyanide of potassium!"

"Does it hurt?" inquired Whitaker, with an irritating slowness.

"Hurt! Do you think you can take a bath in red-hot acid and—— Help me trace that extra tube. How the deuce do you suppose that tube ever got there?"

Instantly the picture of a small burned foot came before Whitaker—an inspiration. He held the struggling Hamilton as in a vise.

"If you will sit still three minutes," said Whitaker, his eye gleaming and a forbidden cigar cocked fiercely, "I will guarantee to lead you to the place where your precious gold is—or was; I won't promise which. Or, here—come along with me!" he said as an afterthought; and the pair started for the street on the run.

Whitaker came to a stop on the corner where he had seen the barefooted boy yelling with pain.

"What's that?" he asked, pointing to a wet spot on the pavement where a liquid had collected in the ruck about a sewer opening. Hamilton dug his hands in the dirt and sprang up with a cry. In the mud were tiny needles of an orange yellow color.

"There it is! There's our gold!" he cried ecstatically; and then, with a despairing gesture: "In the sewer!"

Whitaker was taking advantage of the refiner's desolation to quiz an interested policeman. Yes; it was a fact that a steel dumpcart and a steel derrick wagon had brushed hubs at this corner about six o'clock, and that the shock had washed as much as a bucketful of mud out of the dumpcart.

Did the policeman happen to have the names of the drivers? He did, because there had ensued quite a flow of language over the accident, but no arrests. The derrick wagon belonged to the Degnon Company; and the dumpcart was one of the wagons of the General Light and Power Company. Whitaker broke into an easy laugh.

Half an hour later the foreman of the stables of the General Company was on the carpet before the fierce cigar. Could he produce Dumpcart Number Thirty-six, to which—Whitaker blew rings about his head—was attached a horse with a slight curb on its nigh hind leg? The horse—Number 2-4-6—was driven by a man who wore rubber gloves. Thus the expert thief-catcher.

"Simple as falling off a log!" Whitaker's gesture seemed to say as he put the question to the stable boss. Then he said:

"It all goes to show that the average thief loses in the long run in the battle of wits, because he leaves some apparently inconsequential clew on his trail—some tiny clew that is as broad as a state road to a trained intelligence. If, for instance," he said, forgetting for the moment the man standing before him twirling his hat in his hands—"If, for instance, that mud rat had not played on my one weakness, by blowing the smoke from his infernal cutty into my face, the chances are that he would have given me a long chase."

"The mud rat!" exclaimed the two officials in unison.

The trained intelligence accepted their implied and wondering admiration of his powers of divination with a nod, and turned again to the stable boss.

"Now, my man!" he said. "I want Dumpcart Number Thirty-six, the man who was driving it this afternoon, and the horse here at the gate in fifteen minutes. I will send one of my men with you."

"If you can tell me where to lay hands on it, sor," said the stable boss, still rotating his hat, "I would be much obliged to you, sor. Dumpcart Thirty-six was stolen from the stables this noon, and we had just sent out a general alarm for it through the police when your man nabbed me."

At this point in the prosecution of the investigation of the looting of the Assay Office of its liquid assets the irresistible force of the trained intelligence in charge met with an immovable post. It never got much farther. The missing wagon was found—abandoned in the Newark meadows—the humane driver having provided the horse liberally with grain and hay before departing.

Curiously enough, the interior of the wagon had been coated with some acid-proof varnish. In the bottom, crystallized by the cold, was a handful of needles of gold, to show that Dumpcart Number Thirty-six was indeed the receptacle in which the thief had carted off forty gallons of gold worth ten cents a drop.

It was a simple matter to trace the mysterious pipe from the gold tank through the junction boxes of the electric system to the electrical manhole in the street. Evidences were numerous that this extra conduit had been installed by the far-thinking thief at some time during the period when the building was in process of erection. In the bottom of the manhole were found a few pints of the precious stuff that had been siphoned down through seven floors to the street by the adroit expedient of breaking open a concealed plug.

"I must confess I am not much of a scientist," said Whitaker a week later; "and before we turn the page on this subject I want to find out one thing: Admitting that our dumpcart friend got away with a quarter of a million dollars' worth of gold in the form of mud, what value would it be to him? How could he get the gold out of it?"

An indulgent smile curled Hamilton's lips.

"The process of extracting gold from mud is one of the simplest in chemistry and mechanics. And the joke is," he went on, screwing up the corners of his mouth, "that when that crafty mud rat has manufactured it into bullion again he will probably have the supreme gall of bringing it here and asking us to buy it. The devil of it is that we shall have to buy it too!"

At this remote date the Assay Office officials are still in doubt whether they have repurchased their stolen treasure. It is worthwhile to say in passing that the surety companies responsible for the men responsible for the treasure of the Government Assay Office are still engaged in suing each other and the various contractors responsible for fitting and inspecting the interior of the new building.

The robbery undoubtedly had been planned and the properties arranged months ahead of time; but, aside from the fact that an expert electrician named Dahlog, who had been employed on the premises at odd times—a man with a pronounced Danish accent—turned up hopelessly missing, the case has not progressed. It promises in time to become as celebrated in court annals as the antique litigation of Jarndyce versus Jarndyce.

Whitaker seldom confessed his failures; but several months later, over cigars in the library of his friend Godahl the exquisite, he related the story—unabridged—of the most remarkable bit of thievery in his experience. It was his secret hope that the acute mind of this celebrated dilettante, who had many times pointed his researches with astounding analyses, might help to the solution. Godahl laughed.

"Let us go below the surface," said Godahl. "Abolish the lure of gold and the world will be born good again. Your mud rat is the apotheosis of the pickpocket. How much better they managed the whole thing ten thousand years ago!

To the remote races of the Andes gold was not a vulgar medium of trade and exchange. It was a symbol of kingship—a thing to be possessed only by kings.

"In my small way," said Godahl deprecatingly, with a wave of his fine hands, "I have erected a monument to the Incas in this room. My frieze—have you noticed it? A poor thing! Where I have used grains of gold, they used pounds. But to me it symbolizes the same poetic idea. Will you join me in a fresh cigar? Ah! I beg your pardon! One's physician is a tyrant!"

THE STRANGE CASE OF STEINKELWINTZ

MACKINLAY KANTOR

MACKINLAY KANTOR (1904–1977) is best known for his mainstream novels, such as the sentimental dog story *The Voice of Bugle Ann* (1935), filmed the following year; the long narrative poem *Glory for Me* (1945), filmed as *The Best Years of Our Lives* (1946), which won the Academy Award for Best Picture; and the outstanding Civil War novel about the notorious Confederate prisoner-of-war camp, *Andersonville* (1955), for which he won the Pulitzer Prize.

Already a journalist at seventeen, he began selling hard-boiled mystery stories to various pulp magazines at almost the same time, quickly followed by several novels in the genre, such as *Diversey* (1928), about Chicago gangsters, and *Signal Thirty-Two* (1950), an excellent police procedural, given verisimilitude by virtue of Kantor's having received permission from the acting police commissioner of New York to accompany the police on their activities to gather background information. His most famous crime novel is *Midnight Lace* (1948), the suspenseful tale of a young woman terrorized by an anonymous telephone caller; a film was released twelve years later, starring Doris Day and Rex Harrison.

His most famous crime short story is "Gun Crazy," published in *The Saturday Evening Post* in 1940, which served as the basis for the noir cult film of the same title, for which Kantor wrote the screenplay. Released in 1950, it was directed by Joseph H. Lewis. The film, an excellent though more violent expansion of the story, features a clean-cut gun nut, played by John Dall, who meets a good-looking sharpshooter, played by Peggy Cummins, and their subsequent spree of bank robberies and shootings.

"The Strange Case of Steinkelwintz" was first published in the *Chicago Daily News Midweek* in 1929; it was first collected in *It's About Crime* (New York, Signet, 1960).

THE STRANGE CASE OF STEINKELWINTZ

MACKINLAY KANTOR

THE PHONE BELL blatted in the darkness, insistent, exasperated, like the second cousin of a two-dollar alarm clock.

Maxwell Grame pushed the wrong electric light switch so that only a parchment-shaded corner lamp was illuminated, and he skinned his ankle against the leg of a chair as he staggered through the half glow of the living room to the telephone stand.

"Yes, yes!" with that unamiable severity which young men exude when roused from their honest slumbers at three o'clock in the morning.

"Max! Hello, Max!" The voice was strained like a taut rubber band. "Max, for God's sake come down here right away——"

Grame growled to himself before he addressed the transmitter. "You might tell me who you are, calling at this hour."

"Larry Greening, Max! This is Larry——"

"Yes."

"Can you come down here to our apartment right away, old man? There's hell to pay——"

"That's all right if you've got the money." Slumber was sliding away from Grame's brain and he began to feel more natural.

"Max, don't kid like that. This is serious. I mean it. Maud will lose her mind unless something is done!"

Grame sighed. For the ten years of their acquaintance, Larry's unstrung impetuosity had dogged him. "What's the trouble? Have you discovered a banshee in the flat?"

"Come down, come down!" chanted Larry with frenzy. "I won't call the police or do a thing until you get here——"

"All right. I'll dress and get a cab." Grame hung up the receiver. He chuckled to himself, but grew more serious as he pondered on the possibilities of Larry's wild call. What on earth had happened, anyway? Maud and Larry didn't possess any valuable jewels or securities insofar as he knew. Nothing important could have been stolen. . . . Was it a mysterious threat which they had received?

In his role as amateur detective, Grame was often called upon by his friends to search out a stray dog or discover the writer of an anonymous note. Now came the Greenings, at three o'clock of a cold morning, to swell his list of nonpaying clients. And he had to be at the office—his workaday bread-and-butter law office—at nine o'clock.

"Why did I ever get this detective notion?" he muttered, and drew on his trousers.

Half an hour later he entered the lobby of a gaudy, none-too-exclusive apartment hotel on Sheridan Road in the 40s, and was slowly lifted to the second floor by an automatic elevator. He rang the bell at Larry's door, and the door flew open immediately to disclose Larry, pale-faced and disheveled in an old bathrobe and the trousers of his tuxedo, with his wife hovering behind him. Maud was even paler than Larry, and her fingers twitched as they held her dressing gown together.

"It's gone!" howled Larry.

831

Max shook his head and scowled. "Will you please get hold of yourself and talk sanely? What's gone?"

"Look, look!" Larry dragged him into the living room of the small apartment and motioned dramatically toward the farther end of the room.

Nothing seemed very wrong. It was a neat room with Coxwell chairs and bridge lamps, taupe rug, and a Windsor desk. "Looks all right to me," said Grame. "I don't see anything missing."

"The *pee-an-oh*!" his friend shrieked. "Gone!"

Grame sat down, removing his topcoat and nodding agreeably at the gibbering Larry and anguished Maud. "That's so. You did have a piano."

"Did have a piano?" Maud was wailing now. "Listen to him, Larry. I said to call the police. . . ."

Larry's faith was shaken but he remained loyal. "Wait a minute, Maud. . . . Maybe I am too excited, Max, but I tell you, it gave us a shock to walk in here from Consalti's party and find that seven-hundred-and-fifty-dollar baby grand gone!"

With dogged patience Grame managed to pry the story out of them. The piano—a Christmas gift from her beloved Larry, at which Maud sat and warbled heroically to the neglect of the dishes—was sitting in its usual corner, scarf-draped and serene, when they went out to a party given by Consalti, the opera singer, at nine p.m. Five hours later they arrived home to find the embroidered scarf and stacks of music neatly piled on a divan, and the piano missing.

Maud was in hysterics. Larry had dashed madly through the building, summoning janitor, clerk, and manager. All swore that no one had gone near the Greening apartment that evening; the lock was of the most improved, complicated type, and Larry's key reposed safely at the desk where he had left it. The porter who operated the freight elevator was above reproach; he had been employed for many years by the manage-ment, in this and in other buildings owned by the same firm, and when he declared that no one had operated the freight elevator during the evening, nobody could doubt his honesty.

Reluctantly the baffled manager acceded to Larry's demands, and glanced into every apartment in the building, a task occupying an hour and resulting in the threat of broken leases. The piano was not in the building. Larry himself had accompanied the searching party.

"What I want to know is, what'll we do without that baby grand?" wailed Larry. "Maud adores it—she worships it like a child. We can't afford to buy another this year. What will Maud do for accompaniment when she sings? Max, you've heard Maud sing, haven't you?"

Yes, Max had heard Maud sing. He would not be apt to forget the experience for a long time.

He got up and scanned the room carefully, noting that the woodwork near the door bore no scars or telltale scratches such as might have resulted had the instrument been drawn through the front doorway in haste. The windows. . . .

"Larry, were your windows open when you went to the party?"

Greening looked at the windows. "Sure. Of course they were. We always keep the apartment aired well, the radiators are red-hot most of the time."

"Your piano went out of the window," said Max.

Maud began to laugh inelegantly. "Banana oil! You couldn't get that piano through any of those windows. Anyway, it's a two-story drop to the ground, and there isn't a fire escape on this side of the building. Larry, as a detective Max Grame is a good equity lawyer. Call the police!"

Grame shook his head at her. "That would be silly. If you told a policeman the story you've told me, he would try to arrest you for a fraudulent operation against your insurance company. Of course the piano was insured?"

"Insured nothing," Larry lamented. "Maud said that in her home they had a piano for twenty-one years and nothing ever happened to it. Why should we bother with insurance? She spent the amount of the premium on new music instead."

Max came back from a tour of exploration into the dinette. "Let us look at this thing coldly," he argued. "The piano has gone. That is established. We are reasonably certain that it is not in the building. We are well satisfied, through the testimony of employees as reported by you, that it is not in the building. We are well satisfied, through the testimony of employees as reported by you, that it wasn't taken out of the front door and down the stairways or elevators. Now, is there a back door?"

"No such thing," Greening replied. "There's a little hole that the janitor takes the garbage through. No ice; there's an electric machine. Absolutely no back door and no need for one."

"Well, it went through the window, then. It didn't slide down the drainpipe in the bathroom."

"Foolishness!" Maud choked again tearfully, and flung herself on the chaise longue in despair.

Grame rolled up his sleeves. "I," he said, "shall look for clues."

"Go to it, old man," urged Larry without much faith.

The apartment occupied by the Greenings was at a corner of the building; living room and dinette windows faced an alley on the west, and bedroom windows faced an airshaft on the north. Max went into the bedroom and poked his head out into the dimness.

He found that the airshaft was in reality a narrow court, open toward the alley on the west, with the blank wall of a building next door forming the north side. There were no fire escapes, pipelines or other means by which access could be gained to the Greening apartment, although that floor was not a full two stories above the alley level. . . . Leaning farther from the window, Max struck a match and examined the bricks directly beneath him. Scanning the surface closely, he saw what appeared to be two small scratches or bruises, rubbed on the bricks a few inches below the concrete sill and about

eighteen inches apart. But of other signs there were none.

Something in his subconscious brain was tantalizing him as he joined Larry and Maud in the living room. . . . Something elusive and intriguing—some clue that seemed to be all about him, and yet which he could not identify. Nothing which he had seen, nothing which he had heard. . . .

The Greenings sat, sullen and weary. Larry lit a cigarette.

"Larry!" cried Grame. "Put out that cigarette!"

Larry stared at him. "Huh?"

For reply Grame jumped to his side, grasped the cigarette, and pounded its sparks against the bottom of an ashtray.

"It's an odor!" he exclaimed with exultation. "An odor! I don't want you smelling up this apartment with cigarettes. . . . Now tell me, can't you discern some sort of an unusual odor in this room?"

Larry sniffed ambitiously. "Incense?" he asked.

"No, fool. It's more like—like the hotel at South Raub, Indiana." Maud's theory was indefinite, but she clung to it stubbornly.

"There *is* an odor," she repeated. "I noticed it when we came home, though I was so upset about the dear piano. . . . But, Max Grame, you can't arrest an odor! I suppose you think that an odor stole my piano?"

"Nonsense!" said Max. "If I can identify that haunting, elusive odor that's in here. . . . I've smelled it often, but not for a long time. It . . . makes me think of my grandmother."

Maud arose with a jerk. "Grandmother, bah! Larry, I'm going to bed. And in the morning, we'll have a real detective come."

Greening also got up. "I'll open the daybed for you here, old man. No, we won't hear of your chasing out north again tonight. And maybe, sleeping here . . . it'll bring some clues to your mind or something."

Fifteen minutes later the Greenings had retired, Max Grame was stretched on the daybed, and the apartment was in darkness. Being very weary, the "great detective" went to sleep immediately. But his subconscious mind and his conscious nostrils were working overtime. Shortly before daylight he sat up with a jolt.

"Fried onions!" he repeated to himself, over and over. "No, that's not it. . . . *Cheese! Cheese!* By God, I've got it now. . . ."

He sprang from the couch, turned on a light, and began examining the floor on his hands and knees. Near the vacant corner where the baby grand had stood, he found a small smudge of grease. He sniffed at this tiny, soiled patch of rug and chuckled with satisfaction.

While Maud was preparing breakfast and Larry was shaving, Grame went into the alley for a tour of inspection.

The early sun was steaming the frost on roofs and sheds, but the alley was still deep in shadow. Secure amid the backyard bustle of milkmen and incoming servant girls, Max wandered close to the fences which abutted properties on the west side of the alley. He gazed carefully into each successive yard as he passed it, perusing the homely porches and rear areaways with a peculiar intensity.

Directly opposite the hotel where the Greenings lived was an unusual backyard. All the others were barren nooks sacred to tin cans and matted papers, but this lawn, serene between well-kept fences, bespoke an oasis of the sort not often found in the city's spare ugliness. There were a couple of plum trees, two birdhouses, and a frost-bitten hedge of autumn flowers. As Max Grame looked into this yard he saw something else that gave him a glow of victory.

Walking to the end of the alley, he turned down Thole Street and back along Kenmore. Several sets of the ordinary three- or four-story flats. Then . . . the building with the backyard.

You could tell by looking at it that it would have a backyard. The old porch was scrubbed and painted, there were bridal wreath bushes near the walk, and even a bird bath. Obviously

the place was one of those narrow, high-stepped, three-story-single apartment houses put up late in the nineteenth century. Boldly enough, Grame marched up to the front door and entered the small vestibule where he examined three mailboxes with their cards.

3. B. F. EDDY
2. GRACE COOK
1. C. STEINKELWINTZ

"Maud," said Grame, when he entered the apartment four minutes later, "you'll have your piano back tonight or tomorrow. I will let you know immediately after dinner, and will then make out my bill. . . . No, no, good people, do not question me! Genius requires a cloak of mystery."

At seven o'clock that evening, Max Grame walked into the three-story-single apartment house on Kenmore Avenue and pressed a bell button opposite the name STEINKELWINTZ.

After a moment's delay the inside door, and then the vestibule door, were opened by a little gray-haired woman with a black shawl about her bent shoulders.

"Could I see Mr. Steinkelwintz?" asked Max.

"Yah," said the little old lady, and she called back into the dark hall behind her, "Carl!" She watched Grame with beady, black eyes as her husband came shuffling out.

He was also short and bent, but his shoulders were broad and his muscular arms sturdy, although his mustache was well-mixed with white. He peered up at Grame through thick, gold-rimmed glasses.

"Mr. Steinkelwintz," said the great detective, "I'm Mr. Johnson from around the corner on Thole Street. My little girl's kitten climbed up into that high tree in front of our place and can't get down. One of the neighbors said that you had a long ladder. May I borrow it?"

For an instant there was a flash of suspicion in the glance that the old German gave him, but the face of Max Grame was guileless. Then the old man grinned kindly.

"Jildren und gittens dey is awful bodder," he beamed. "I got idt nice ladder by der backyart. Come along, I show you."

He led the way through a dimly lighted, strong-smelling apartment to the rear porch. As they passed through the kitchen, two sturdy young men looked up from their newspapers and stared at the stranger.

The backyard was well illuminated by lights which streamed from windows of the opposite apartment hotel. Old Steinkelwintz fumbled his way down the rear steps, groped beneath the porch, and began to draw out a long ladder. It seemed endless; indeed, one end protruded far beyond the edge of the wide porch, as Grame had seen it protruding when he passed that way in the morning.

He grasped a rung and helped the old man pull it out.

"Very goot ladder," said Steinkelwintz proudly. "By der backyart I geep it to drim drees und built houses for der birds. Gittens up in drees you can also coax down so easy."

"Mr. Steinkelwintz," Max inquired easily, "what did you do with Mrs. Greening's piano?"

The old man dropped the ladder, and suddenly became a frail little gnome trembling in the darkness. "I—ach—I . . ."

"Nobody's going to hurt you, my man," Grame went on soothingly. "Just tell me all about it. I'm a detective."

Steinkelwintz swayed and put his hand tightly to his breast. "Ach, Mister Getacktiff, is idt to brison me und my boys must go?"

"I hope not," said Max. "Sit down here on the back steps and tell me all about it."

The little man collapsed on the steps and hugged his crooked knees. Through the darkness his thick lenses glittered with watery sorrow.

"Almost a year ve stood idt. Sudge singing und blaying I neffer knew. In der mornings alvays goming acrossdt der alley like a bandt— 'Do-re-mi-fa-sol. . . .' Ach! Und in der eve-nings ven home ve gome, by us idt is torment. 'Wah—hoo—ah—hoo. . . .' Sudge a noise dat voman can make! Mister Getacktiff," he added pleadingly, "should you hear sudge singing und blaying you vould know!"

"I have heard it," said Grame in a husky voice.

"By us idt is vork all day in der factory uff Bryan und Heany, makers uff bianos und instrumendts. Myself und der jildren, Carl und Emil. Fordty years I vork dere, und der jildren vork ten. By us idt is all day der vork uff bianos—ve hear der sound uff vire und bianos alvays. Und still idt is good music dat ve love. . . . But at night, each night, effery night. . . ." He threw out his arms in a defeated gesture.

"Home ve gome, und acrossdt der alley gomes der sound uff dat voman blaying. My Lena say ve all go madt. I go madt. Carl und Emil go madt. Is idt ve can move from here? No. Idt is our home, our abartment house. Is idt ve can gomplain to people in der hotel? No. By dem is der right to blay und sing.

"So last night, dat voman und her husband are gone. Dey go for hours ve know, und not to return for hours, for often ve vatch dere lights. Carl und Emil und I take der ladder und into der alley at vunce, und all is quiet. By der ladder ve enter at der vindow—like scoundrels, like burglars even. At vunce on der biano ve take off der legs. Ve go to vork to take idt oudt in bieces, as so often by der factory. Hours ve toil by der biano——"

Grame interrupted. "Did you have a lunch with you?"

"Even bottles uff beer under der bread und jeeze. So hard do ve vork! Und oudt uff der bedroom vindow, down in der alley by ropes do ve take all der bieces uff der biano. No vun does see, no vun does hear. Like burglars ve go to brison if caught. But no vun. Ve are safe. So ve take der biano in darkness into our yart und inside der abartment. Dere now ve have idt."

Steinkelwintz arose sadly and stood with bowed head. "Now by der brison ve go, maybe."

"No," said Grame, "I shan't arrest you and

I don't think that the Greenings will prosecute. Re-assemble the piano and ship it over there by some transfer company tomorrow."

The old man regarded him incredulously through the gloom. "Not—not to brison? Carl und Emil und I? No policemens . . . no courts . . . ?"

"No. Just send the piano back to the Greenings. G-r-e-e-n-i-n-g. Greening. That's the name." He left old Steinkelwintz standing in a bewildered fog as he walked across the backyard, through the neat gate, and into the alley.

Up to this point, all had been easy. The ladder marks against the wall, then the odor of Limburger cheese, bringing its memories of his maternal grandmother and her kitchen. The motive for the theft was easy to find: no musically inclined neighbors could for many months hear the singing and playing of Maud without going insane. A ladder; the odor of cheese; a neighbor; the nearby German backyard; Steinkelwintz. It was all appallingly simple—until now.

He didn't know what he could say to the Greenings. Better tell them that the piano was found, and plead for leniency in the strange case of Steinkelwintz. . . .

Grame entered the cross street at the end of the alley, turned a corner, and walked south toward the hotel. As he reached the front entrance, Larry himself crossed the street through traffic and, briefcase under his arm, accosted Max from the curb: "Hello, old man. Are you here to report no clues? Lucky I was delayed downtown, would have missed you——"

"Larry," Max hesitated. Then . . . well, he might as well tell the whole story. "The piano will be returned tomorrow morning."

Greening stood rooted to the sidewalk. "*What?* You *found* it?"

"Yes. An old man across the alley had stolen it. Took it out in sections, with the help of his sons. But . . . Larry, don't be too hard on the old fellow. He——"

Larry's voice was very far away, deep in the caverns of his throat. "You found. You found it. . . ."

"Certainly I found it," said Max with irritation. "What's the matter with you anyway? I thought you'd at least thank me. Last night you——"

"Oh, yes." Greening's face was set in an impotent snarl. "Yes. Last night I put up a very good piece of acting. But—my God—did I ever think you'd find it? You or anybody else? I did not! And now the cursed thing will be back, and Maud will start pounding it and caterwauling again. Just my luck! I thought you were a rotten detective, so I called on you. Damn it all! I don't think I ever want to see you again!"

And he strode savagely toward the entrance of the hotel.

MAURICE LEBLANC

PERHAPS THE GREATEST HERO of French mystery fiction is the fun-loving criminal Arsène Lupin, created by Maurice Marie Emile Leblanc (1864–1941) for a new magazine in 1905. Born in Rouen, Leblanc studied in France, Germany, and England before becoming a police reporter and hack writer. The Lupin stories immediately became wildly popular and Leblanc achieved wealth and worldwide fame, and was made a member of the French Legion of Honour. Although the concoctions are fast-paced, the amount and degree of action borders on the burlesque with situations and coincidences often too far-fetched to be taken seriously.

Lupin, known as the Prince of Thieves, is a street urchin–type of young man who thumbs his nose—literally—at the police. He steals more for the fun of it than for personal gain or noble motives. He is such a master of disguise that he is able to take the identity of the chief of the Sûreté and direct police investigations into his own activities for four years. After several years as a successful criminal, Lupin decides to turn to the side of the law for personal reasons and assists the police, usually without their knowledge. He is not, however, a first-rate crime-fighter because he cannot resist jokes, women, and the derring-do of his free-lance life as a crook.

"Arsène Lupin in Prison" was first published in *Arsène Lupin, Gentleman-Cambrioleur* in Paris in 1907. The first English-language edition was *The Exploits of Arsène Lupin* (New York, Harper, 1907); it was reissued as *The Seven of Hearts* (London, Cassell, 1908) and as *The Extraordinary Adventures of Arsène Lupin, Gentleman Burglar* (Chicago, Donohue, 1910). The book served as the basis for two silent films, *Lupin the Gentleman Burglar* (1914) and *The Gentleman Burglar* (1915).

ARSÈNE LUPIN IN PRISON

MAURICE LEBLANC

THERE IS NO tourist worthy of the name who does not know the banks of the Seine, and has not noticed, in passing, the little feudal castle of the Malaquis, built upon a rock in the centre of the river. An arched bridge connects it with the shore. All around it, the calm waters of the great river play peacefully amongst the reeds, and the wagtails flutter over the moist crests of the stones.

The history of the Malaquis castle is stormy like its name, harsh like its outlines. It has passed through a long series of combats, sieges, assaults, rapines, and massacres. A recital of the crimes that have been committed there would cause the stoutest heart to tremble. There are many mysterious legends connected with the castle, and they tell us of a famous subterranean tunnel that formerly led to the abbey of Jumieges and to the manor of Agnes Sorel, mistress of Charles VII.

In that ancient habitation of heroes and brigands, the Baron Nathan Cahorn now lived; or Baron Satan as he was formerly called on the Bourse, where he had acquired a fortune with incredible rapidity. The lords of Malaquis, absolutely ruined, had been obliged to sell the ancient castle at a great sacrifice. It contained an admirable collection of furniture, pictures, wood carvings, and faience. The Baron lived there alone, attended by three old servants. No one ever enters the place. No one had ever beheld the three Rubens that he possessed, his two Watteau, his Jean Goujon pulpit, and the many other treasures that he had acquired by a vast expenditure of money at public sales.

Baron Satan lived in constant fear, not for himself, but for the treasures that he had accumulated with such an earnest devotion and with so much perspicacity that the shrewdest merchant could not say that the Baron had ever erred in his taste or judgment. He loved them—his bibelots. He loved them intensely, like a miser; jealously, like a lover. Every day, at sunset, the iron gates at either end of the bridge and at the entrance to the court of honor are closed and barred. At the least touch on these gates, electric bells will ring throughout the castle.

One Thursday in September, a letter-carrier presented himself at the gate at the head of the bridge, and, as usual, it was the Baron himself who partially opened the heavy portal. He scrutinized the man as minutely as if he were a stranger, although the honest face and twinkling eyes of the postman had been familiar to the Baron for many years. The man laughed, as he said:

"It is only I, Monsieur le Baron. It is not another man wearing my cap and blouse."

"One can never tell," muttered the Baron.

The man handed him a number of newspapers, and then said:

"And now, Monsieur le Baron, here is something new."

"Something new?"

"Yes, a letter. A registered letter."

Living as a recluse, without friends or busi-

838

ness relations, the baron never received any letters, and the one now presented to him immediately aroused within him a feeling of suspicion and distrust. It was like an evil omen. Who was this mysterious correspondent that dared to disturb the tranquillity of his retreat?

"You must sign for it, Monsieur le Baron."

He signed; then took the letter, waited until the postman had disappeared beyond the bend in the road, and, after walking nervously to and fro for a few minutes, he leaned against the parapet of the bridge and opened the envelope. It contained a sheet of paper, bearing this heading: Prison de la Santé, Paris. He looked at the signature: *Arsène Lupin.* Then he read:

"*Monsieur le Baron:*

"*There is, in the gallery in your castle, a picture of Philippe de Champaigne, of exquisite finish, which pleases me beyond measure. Your Rubens are also to my taste, as well as your smallest Watteau. In the salon to the right, I have noticed the Louis XIII cadence-table, the tapestries of Beauvais, the Empire gueridon signed 'Jacob,' and the Renaissance chest. In the salon to the left, all the cabinet full of jewels and miniatures.*

"*For the present, I will content myself with those articles that can be conveniently removed. I will therefore ask you to pack them carefully and ship them to me, charges prepaid, to the station at Batignolles, within eight days, otherwise I shall be obliged to remove them myself during the night of 27 September; but, under those circumstances, I shall not content myself with the articles above mentioned.*

"*Accept my apologies for any inconvenience I may cause you, and believe me to be your humble servant,*

"*Arsène Lupin.*"

"*P. S.—Please do not send the largest Watteau. Although you paid thirty thousand francs for it, it is only a copy, the original*

having been burned, under the Directoire by Barras, during a night of debauchery. Consult the memoirs of Garat.

"*I do not care for the Louis XV châtelaine, as I doubt its authenticity.*"

That letter completely upset the baron. Had it borne any other signature, he would have been greatly alarmed—but signed by Arsène Lupin!

As an habitual reader of the newspapers, he was versed in the history of recent crimes, and was therefore well acquainted with the exploits of the mysterious burglar. Of course, he knew that Lupin had been arrested in America by his enemy Ganimard and was at present incarcerated in the Prison de la Santé. But he knew also that any miracle might be expected from Arsène Lupin. Moreover, that exact knowledge of the castle, the location of the pictures and furniture, gave the affair an alarming aspect. How could he have acquired that information concerning things that no one had ever seen?

The baron raised his eyes and contemplated the stern outlines of the castle, its steep rocky pedestal, the depth of the surrounding water, and shrugged his shoulders. Certainly, there was no danger. No one in the world could force an entrance to the sanctuary that contained his priceless treasures.

No one, perhaps, but Arsène Lupin! For him, gates, walls, and drawbridges did not exist. What use were the most formidable obstacles or the most careful precautions, if Arsène Lupin had decided to effect an entrance?

That evening, he wrote to the Procurer of the Republique at Rouen. He enclosed the threatening letter and solicited aid and protection.

The reply came at once to the effect that Arsène Lupin was in custody in the Prison de la Santé, under close surveillance, with no opportunity to write such a letter, which was, no doubt, the work of some impostor. But, as an act of precaution, the Procurer had submitted the letter to an expert in handwriting, who declared that, in spite of certain resemblances, the writing was not that of the prisoner.

But the words "in spite of certain resemblances" caught the attention of the baron; in them, he read the possibility of a doubt which appeared to him quite sufficient to warrant the intervention of the law. His fears increased. He read Lupin's letter over and over again. "I shall be obliged to remove them myself." And then there was the fixed date: the night of 27 September.

To confide in his servants was a proceeding repugnant to his nature; but now, for the first time in many years, he experienced the necessity of seeking counsel with some one. Abandoned by the legal official of his own district, and feeling unable to defend himself with his own resources, he was on the point of going to Paris to engage the services of a detective.

Two days passed; on the third day, he was filled with hope and joy as he read the following item in the *Réveil de Caudebec*, a newspaper published in a neighboring town:

> *"We have the pleasure of entertaining in our city, at the present time, the veteran detective Mon. Ganimard who acquired a world-wide reputation by his clever capture of Arsène Lupin. He has come here for rest and recreation, and, being an enthusiastic fisherman, he threatens to capture all the fish in our river."*

Ganimard! Ah, here is the assistance desired by Baron Cahorn! Who could baffle the schemes of Arsène Lupin better than Ganimard, the patient and astute detective? He was the man for the place.

The baron did not hesitate. The town of Caudebec was only six kilometres from the castle, a short distance to a man whose step was accelerated by the hope of safety.

After several fruitless attempts to ascertain the detective's address, the baron visited the office of the *Réveil*, situated on the quai. There he found the writer of the article who, approaching the window, exclaimed:

"Ganimard? Why, you are sure to see him somewhere on the quai with his fishing-pole. I met him there and chanced to read his name engraved on his rod. Ah, there he is now, under the trees."

"That little man, wearing a straw hat?"

"Exactly. He is a gruff fellow, with little to say."

Five minutes later, the baron approached the celebrated Ganimard, introduced himself, and sought to commence a conversation, but that was a failure. Then he broached the real object of his interview, and briefly stated his case. The other listened, motionless, with his attention riveted on his fishing-rod. When the baron had finished his story, the fisherman turned, with an air of profound pity, and said:

"Monsieur, it is not customary for thieves to warn people they are about to rob. Arsène Lupin, especially, would not commit such a folly."

"But——"

"Monsieur, if I had the least doubt, believe me, the pleasure of again capturing Arsène Lupin would place me at your disposal. But, unfortunately, that young man is already under lock and key."

"He may have escaped."

"No one ever escaped from the Santé."

"But, he——"

"He, no more than any other."

"Yet——"

"Well, if he escapes, so much the better. I will catch him again. Meanwhile, you go home and sleep soundly. That will do for the present. You frighten the fish."

The conversation was ended. The baron returned to the castle, reassured to some extent by Ganimard's indifference. He examined the bolts, watched the servants, and, during the next forty-eight hours, he became almost persuaded that his fears were groundless. Certainly, as Ganimard had said, thieves do not warn people they are about to rob.

The fateful day was close at hand. It was now the twenty-sixth of September and nothing had happened. But at three o'clock the bell rang. A boy brought this telegram:

"No goods at Batignolles station. Prepare everything for to-morrow night. Arsène."

This telegram threw the baron into such a state of excitement that he even considered the advisability of yielding to Lupin's demands.

However, he hastened to Caudebec. Ganimard was fishing at the same place, seated on a campstool. Without a word, he handed him the telegram.

"Well, what of it?" said the detective.

"What of it? But it is to-morrow."

"What is to-morrow?"

"The robbery! The pillage of my collections!"

Ganimard laid down his fishing-rod, turned to the baron, and exclaimed, in a tone of impatience:

"Ah! Do you think I am going to bother myself about such a silly story as that!"

"How much do you ask to pass to-morrow night in the castle?"

"Not a sou. Now, leave me alone."

"Name your own price. I am rich and can pay it."

This offer disconcerted Ganimard, who replied, calmly:

"I am here on a vacation. I have no right to undertake such work."

"No one will know. I promise to keep it secret."

"Oh! nothing will happen."

"Come! three thousand francs. Will that be enough?"

The detective, after a moment's reflection, said:

"Very well. But I must warn you that you are throwing your money out of the window."

"I do not care."

"In that case . . . but, after all, what do we know about this devil Lupin! He may have quite a numerous band of robbers with him. Are you sure of your servants?"

"My faith——"

"Better not count on them. I will telegraph for two of my men to help me. And now, go! It is better for us not to be seen together. To-morrow evening about nine o'clock."

The following day—the date fixed by Arsène Lupin—Baron Cahorn arranged all his panoply of war, furbished his weapons, and, like a sentinel, paced to and fro in front of the castle. He saw nothing, heard nothing. At half-past eight o'clock in the evening, he dismissed his servants. They occupied rooms in a wing of the building, in a retired spot, well removed from the main portion of the castle. Shortly thereafter, the baron heard the sound of approaching footsteps. It was Ganimard and his two assistants—great, powerful fellows with immense hands, and necks like bulls. After asking a few questions relating to the location of the various entrances and rooms, Ganimard carefully closed and barricaded all the doors and windows through which one could gain access to the threatened rooms. He inspected the walls, raised the tapestries, and finally installed his assistants in the central gallery which was located between the two salons.

"No nonsense! We are not here to sleep. At the slightest sound, open the windows of the court and call me. Pay attention also to the water-side. Ten metres of perpendicular rock is no obstacle to those devils."

Ganimard locked his assistants in the gallery, carried away the keys, and said to the baron:

"And now, to our post."

He had chosen for himself a small room located in the thick outer wall, between the two principal doors, and which, in former years, had been the watchman's quarters. A peep-hole opened upon the bridge; another on the court. In one corner, there was an opening to a tunnel.

"I believe you told me, Monsieur le Baron, that this tunnel is the only subterranean entrance to the castle and that it has been closed up from time immemorial?"

"Yes."

"Then, unless there is some other entrance, known only to Arsène Lupin, we are quite safe."

He placed three chairs together, stretched himself upon them, lighted his pipe and sighed:

"Really, Monsieur le Baron, I feel ashamed to

accept your money for such a sinecure as this. I will tell the story to my friend Lupin. He will enjoy it immensely."

The baron did not laugh. He was anxiously listening, but heard nothing save the beating of his own heart. From time to time, he leaned over the tunnel and cast a fearful eye into its depths. He heard the clock strike eleven, twelve, one.

Suddenly, he seized Ganimard's arm. The latter leaped up, awakened from his sleep.

"Do you hear?" asked the baron, in a whisper.

"Yes."

"What is it?"

"I was snoring, I suppose."

"No, no, listen."

"Ah! yes, it is the horn of an automobile."

"Well?"

"Well! it is very improbable that Lupin would use an automobile like a battering-ram to demolish your castle. Come, Monsieur le Baron, return to your post. I am going to sleep. Good-night."

That was the only alarm. Ganimard resumed his interrupted slumbers, and the baron heard nothing except the regular snoring of his companion. At break of day, they left the room. The castle was enveloped in a profound calm; it was a peaceful dawn on the bosom of a tranquil river. They mounted the stairs, Cahorn radiant with joy, Ganimard calm as usual. They heard no sound; they saw nothing to arouse suspicion.

"What did I tell you, Monsieur le Baron? Really, I should not have accepted your offer. I am ashamed."

He unlocked the door and entered the gallery. Upon two chairs, with drooping heads and pendent arms, the detective's two assistants were asleep.

"Tonnerre de nom d'un chien!" exclaimed Ganimard. At the same moment, the baron cried out:

"The pictures! The credence!"

He stammered, choked, with arms outstretched toward the empty places, toward the denuded walls where naught remained but the useless nails and cords. The Watteau, disappeared! The Rubens, carried away! The tapestries taken down! The cabinets, despoiled of their jewels!

"And my Louis XVI candelabra! And the Regent chandelier! . . . And my twelfth-century Virgin!"

He ran from one spot to another in wildest despair. He recalled the purchase price of each article, added up the figures, counted his losses, pell-mell, in confused words and unfinished phrases. He stamped with rage; he groaned with grief. He acted like a ruined man whose only hope is suicide.

If anything could have consoled him, it would have been the stupefaction displayed by Ganimard. The famous detective did not move. He appeared to be petrified; he examined the room in a listless manner. The windows? . . . closed. The locks on the doors? . . . intact. Not a break in the ceiling; not a hole in the floor. Everything was in perfect order. The theft had been carried out methodically, according to a logical and inexorable plan.

"Arsène Lupin . . . Arsène Lupin," he muttered.

Suddenly, as if moved by anger, he rushed upon his two assistants and shook them violently. They did not awaken.

"The devil!" he cried. "Can it be possible?"

He leaned over them and, in turn, examined them closely. They were asleep; but their repose was unnatural.

"They have been drugged," he said to the baron.

"By whom?"

"By him, of course, or his men under his direction. The work bears his stamp."

"In that case, I am lost—nothing can be done."

"Nothing," assented Ganimard.

"It is dreadful; it is monstrous."

"Lodge a complaint."

"What good will that do?"

"Oh; it is well to try it. The law has some resources."

"The law! Bah! it is useless. You represent the

law, and, at this moment, when you should be looking for a clue and trying to discover something, you do not even stir."

"Discover something with Arsène Lupin! Why, my dear monsieur, Arsène Lupin never leaves any clue behind him. He leaves nothing to chance. Sometimes I think he put himself in my way and simply allowed me to arrest him in America."

"Then, I must renounce my pictures! He has taken the gems of my collection. I would give a fortune to recover them. If there is no other way, let him name his own price."

Ganimard regarded the baron attentively, as he said:

"Now, that is sensible. Will you stick to it?"

"Yes, yes. But why?"

"An idea that I have."

"What is it?"

"We will discuss it later—if the official examination does not succeed. But, not one word about me, if you wish my assistance."

He added, between his teeth:

"It is true I have nothing to boast of in this affair."

The two assistants were gradually regaining consciousness with the bewildered air of people who come out of an hypnotic sleep. They opened their eyes and looked about them in astonishment. Ganimard questioned them; they remembered nothing.

"But you must have seen some one?"

"No."

"Can't you remember?"

"No, no."

"Did you drink anything?"

They considered a moment, and then one of them replied:

"Yes, I drank a little water."

"Out of that carafe?"

"Yes."

"So did I," declared the other.

Ganimard smelled and tasted it. It had no particular taste and no odor.

"Come," he said, "we are wasting time here. One can't decide an Arsène Lupin problem in

five minutes. But, morbleu! I swear I will catch him again."

The same day, a charge of burglary was duly preferred by Baron Cahorn against Arsène Lupin, a prisoner in the Prison de la Santé.

The baron afterwards regretted making the charge against Lupin when he saw his castle delivered over to the gendarmes, the procureur, the judge d'instruction, the newspaper reporters and photographers, and a throng of idle curiosity-seekers.

The affair soon became a topic of general discussion, and the name of Arsène Lupin excited the public imagination to such an extent that the newspapers filled their columns with the most fantastic stories of his exploits which found ready credence amongst their readers.

But the letter of Arsène Lupin that was published in the *Echo de France* (no one ever knew how the newspaper obtained it), that letter in which Baron Cahorn was impudently warned of the coming theft, caused considerable excitement. The most fabulous theories were advanced. Some recalled the existence of the famous subterranean tunnels, and that was the line of research pursued by the officers of the law, who searched the house from top to bottom, questioned every stone, studied the wainscoting and the chimneys, the window-frames and the girders in the ceilings. By the light of torches, they examined the immense cellars where the lords of Malaquis were wont to store their munitions and provisions. They sounded the rocky foundation to its very centre. But it was all in vain. They discovered no trace of a subterranean tunnel. No secret passage existed.

But the eager public declared that the pictures and furniture could not vanish like so many ghosts. They are substantial, material things and require doors and windows for their exits and their entrances, and so do the people that remove them. Who were those people? How did they gain access to the castle? And how did they leave it?

The police officers of Rouen, convinced of

their own impotence, solicited the assistance of the Parisian detective force. Mon. Dudouis, chief of the Sûreté, sent the best sleuths of the iron brigade. He himself spent forty-eight hours at the castle, but met with no success. Then he sent for Ganimard, whose past services had proved so useful when all else failed.

Ganimard listened, in silence, to the instructions of his superior; then, shaking his head, he said:

"In my opinion, it is useless to ransack the castle. The solution of the problem lies elsewhere."

"Where, then?"

"With Arsène Lupin."

"With Arsène Lupin! To support that theory, we must admit his intervention."

"I do admit it. In fact, I consider it quite certain."

"Come, Ganimard, that is absurd. Arsène Lupin is in prison."

"I grant you that Arsène Lupin is in prison, closely guarded; but he must have fetters on his feet, manacles on his wrists, and a gag in his mouth before I change my opinion."

"Why so obstinate, Ganimard?"

"Because Arsène Lupin is the only man in France of sufficient calibre to invent and carry out a scheme of that magnitude."

"Mere words, Ganimard."

"But true ones. Look! What are they doing? Searching for subterranean passages, stones swinging on pivots, and other nonsense of that kind. But Lupin doesn't employ such old-fashioned methods. He is a modern cracksman, right up to date."

"And how would you proceed?"

"I should ask your permission to spend an hour with him."

"In his cell?"

"Yes. During the return trip from America we became very friendly, and I venture to say that if he can give me any information without compromising himself he will not hesitate to save me from incurring useless trouble."

It was shortly after noon when Ganimard entered the cell of Arsène Lupin. The latter, who was lying on his bed, raised his head and uttered a cry of apparent joy.

"Ah! This is a real surprise. My dear Ganimard, here!"

"Ganimard himself."

"In my chosen retreat, I have felt a desire for many things, but my fondest wish was to receive you here."

"Very kind of you, I am sure."

"Not at all. You know I hold you in the highest regard."

"I am proud of it."

"I have always said: Ganimard is our best detective. He is almost—you see how candid I am!—he is almost as clever as Sherlock Holmes. But I am sorry that I cannot offer you anything better than this hard stool. And no refreshments! Not even a glass of beer! Of course, you will excuse me, as I am here only temporarily."

Ganimard smiled, and accepted the proffered seat. Then the prisoner continued:

"Mon Dieu, how pleased I am to see the face of an honest man. I am so tired of those devils of spies who come here ten times a day to ransack my pockets and my cell to satisfy themselves that I am not preparing to escape. The government is very solicitous on my account."

"It is quite right."

"Why so? I should be quite contented if they would allow me to live in my own quiet way."

"On other people's money."

"Quite so. That would be so simple. But here, I am joking, and you are, no doubt, in a hurry. So let us come to business, Ganimard. To what do I owe the honor of this visit?"

"The Cahorn affair," declared Ganimard, frankly.

"Ah! Wait, one moment. You see I have had so many affairs! First, let me fix in my mind the circumstances of this particular case. . . . Ah! yes, now I have it. The Cahorn affair, Malaquis castle, Seine-Inférieure . . . Two Rubens, a Watteau, and a few trifling articles."

"Trifling!"

"Oh! ma foi, all that is of slight importance.

But it suffices to know that the affair interests you. How can I serve you, Ganimard?"

"Must I explain to you what steps the authorities have taken in the matter?"

"Not at all. I have read the newspapers and I will frankly state that you have made very little progress."

"And that is the reason I have come to see you."

"I am entirely at your service."

"In the first place, the Cahorn affair was managed by you?"

"From A to Z."

"The letter of warning? the telegram?"

"All mine. I ought to have the receipts somewhere."

Arsène opened the drawer of a small table of plain white wood which, with the bed and stool, constituted all the furniture in his cell, and took therefrom two scraps of paper which he handed to Ganimard.

"Ah!" exclaimed the detective, in surprise. "I thought you were closely guarded and searched, and I find that you read the newspapers and collect postal receipts."

"Bah! these people are so stupid! They open the lining of my vest, they examine the soles of my shoes, they sound the walls of my cell, but they never imagine that Arsène Lupin would be foolish enough to choose such a simple hiding-place."

Ganimard laughed, as he said:

"What a droll fellow you are! Really, you bewilder me. But, come now, tell me about the Cahorn affair."

"Oh! oh! not quite so fast! You would rob me of all my secrets; expose all my little tricks. That is a very serious matter."

"Was I wrong to count on your complaisance?"

"No, Ganimard, and since you insist——"

Arsène Lupin paced his cell two or three times, then, stopping before Ganimard, he asked:

"What do you think of my letter to the baron?"

"I think you were amusing yourself by playing to the gallery."

"Ah! playing to the gallery! Come, Ganimard, I thought you knew me better. Do I, Arsène Lupin, ever waste my time on such puerilities? Would I have written that letter if I could have robbed the baron without writing to him? I want you to understand that that letter was indispensable; it was the motor that set the whole machine in motion. Now, let us discuss together a scheme for the robbery of the Malaquis castle. Are you willing?"

"Yes, proceed."

"Well, let us suppose a castle carefully closed and barricaded like that of the Baron Cahorn. Am I to abandon my scheme and renounce the treasures that I covet, upon the pretext that the castle which holds them is inaccessible?"

"Evidently not."

"Should I make an assault upon the castle at the head of a band of adventurers as they did in ancient times?"

"That would be foolish."

"Can I gain admittance by stealth or cunning?"

"Impossible."

"Then there is only one way open to me. I must have the owner of the castle invite me to it."

"That is surely an original method."

"And how easy! Let us suppose that one day the owner receives a letter warning him that a notorious burglar known as Arsène Lupin is plotting to rob him. What will he do?"

"Send a letter to the Procureur."

"Who will laugh at him, *because the said Arsène Lupin is actually in prison*. Then, in his anxiety and fear, the simple man will ask the assistance of the first-comer, will he not?"

"Very likely."

"And if he happens to read in a country newspaper that a celebrated detective is spending his vacation in a neighboring town——"

"He will seek that detective."

"Of course. But, on the other hand, let us presume that, having foreseen that state of affairs, the said Arsène Lupin has requested one of his friends to visit Caudebec, make the acquaintance of the editor of the *Réveil, a newspaper to which the baron is a subscriber,* and let said editor understand that such person is the celebrated detective—then, what will happen?"

"The editor will announce in the *Réveil* the presence in Caudebec of said detective."

"Exactly; and one of two things will happen: either the fish—I mean Cahorn—will not bite, and nothing will happen; or, what is more likely, he will run and greedily swallow the bait. Thus, behold my Baron Cahorn imploring the assistance of one of my friends against me."

"Original, indeed!"

"Of course, the pseudo-detective at first refuses to give any assistance. On top of that comes the telegram from Arsène Lupin. The frightened baron rushes once more to my friend and offers him a definite sum of money for his services. My friend accepts, summons two members of our band, who, during the night, whilst Cahorn is under the watchful eye of his protector, remove certain articles by way of the window and lower them with ropes into a nice little launch chartered for the occasion. Simple, isn't it?"

"Marvelous! Marvelous!" exclaimed Ganimard. "The boldness of the scheme and the ingenuity of all its details are beyond criticism. But who is the detective whose name and fame served as a magnet to attract the baron and draw him into your net?"

"There is only one name could do it—only one."

"And that is?"

"Arsène Lupin's personal enemy—the most illustrious Ganimard."

"I?"

"Yourself, Ganimard. And, really, it is very funny. If you go there, and the baron decides to talk, you will find that it will be your duty to arrest yourself, just as you arrested me in America. Hein! the revenge is really amusing: I cause Ganimard to arrest Ganimard."

Arsène Lupin laughed heartily. The detective, greatly vexed, bit his lips; to him the joke was quite devoid of humor. The arrival of a prison-guard gave Ganimard an opportunity to recover himself. The man brought Arsène Lupin's luncheon, furnished by a neighboring restaurant. After depositing the tray upon the table, the guard retired. Lupin broke his bread, ate a few morsels, and continued:

"But, rest easy, my dear Ganimard, you will not go to Malaquis. I can tell you something that will astonish you: the Cahorn affair is on the point of being settled."

"Excuse me; I have just seen the Chief of the Sureté."

"What of that? Does Mon. Dudouis know my business better than I do myself? You will learn that Ganimard—excuse me—that the pseudo-Ganimard still remains on very good terms with the baron. The latter has authorized him to negotiate a very delicate transaction with me, and, at the present moment, in consideration of a certain sum, it is probable that the baron has recovered possession of his pictures and other treasures. And on their return, he will withdraw his complaint. Thus, there is no longer any theft, and the law must abandon the case."

Ganimard regarded the prisoner with a bewildered air.

"And how do you know all that?"

"I have just received the telegram I was expecting."

"You have just received a telegram?"

"This very moment, my dear friend. Out of politeness, I did not wish to read it in your presence. But if you will permit me——"

"You are joking, Lupin."

"My dear friend, if you will be so kind as to break that egg, you will learn for yourself that I am not joking."

Mechanically, Ganimard obeyed, and cracked the egg-shell with the blade of a knife. He uttered a cry of surprise. The shell contained nothing but a small piece of blue paper. At the request of Arsène he unfolded it. It was a telegram, or rather a portion of a telegram from which the post-marks had been removed. It read as follows:

"Contract closed. Hundred thousand balls delivered. All well."

"One hundred thousand balls?" said Ganimard.

"Yes, one hundred thousand francs. Very little, but then, you know, these are hard times. . . . And I have some heavy bills to meet. If you only knew my budget . . . living in the city comes very high."

Ganimard arose. His ill humor had disappeared. He reflected for a moment, glancing over the whole affair in an effort to discover a weak point; then, in a tone and manner that betrayed his admiration of the prisoner, he said:

"Fortunately, we do not have a dozen such as you to deal with; if we did, we would have to close up shop."

Arsène Lupin assumed a modest air, as he replied:

"Bah! a person must have some diversion to occupy his leisure hours, especially when he is in prison."

"What!" exclaimed Ganimard, "your trial, your defense, the examination—isn't that sufficient to occupy your mind?"

"No, because I have decided not to be present at my trial."

"Oh! oh!"

Arsène Lupin repeated, positively:

"I shall not be present at my trial."

"Really!"

"Ah! my dear monsieur, do you suppose I am going to rot upon the wet straw? You insult me. Arsène Lupin remains in prison just as long as it pleases him, and not one minute more."

"Perhaps it would have been more prudent if you had avoided getting there," said the detective, ironically.

"Ah! monsieur jests? Monsieur must remember that he had the honor to effect my arrest. Know then, my worthy friend, that no one, not even you, could have placed a hand upon me if a much more important event had not occupied my attention at that critical moment."

"You astonish me."

"A woman was looking at me, Ganimard, and I loved her. Do you fully understand what that means: to be under the eyes of a woman that one loves? I cared for nothing in the world but that. And that is why I am here."

"Permit me to say: you have been here a long time."

"In the first place, I wished to forget. Do not laugh; it was a delightful adventure and it is still a tender memory. Besides, I have been suffering from neurasthenia. Life is so feverish these days that it is necessary to take the 'rest cure' occasionally, and I find this spot a sovereign remedy for my tired nerves."

"Arsène Lupin, you are not a bad fellow, after all."

"Thank you," said Lupin. "Ganimard, this is Friday. On Wednesday next, at four o'clock in the afternoon, I will smoke my cigar at your house in the rue Pergolese."

"Arsène Lupin, I will expect you."

They shook hands like two old friends who valued each other at their true worth; then the detective stepped to the door.

"Ganimard!"

"What is it?" asked Ganimard, as he turned back.

"You have forgotten your watch."

"My watch?"

"Yes, it strayed into my pocket."

He returned the watch, excusing himself:

"Pardon me . . . a bad habit. Because they have taken mine is no reason why I should take yours. Besides, I have a chronometer here that satisfies me fairly well."

He took from the drawer a large gold watch and heavy chain.

"From whose pocket did that come?" asked Ganimard.

Arsène Lupin gave a hasty glance at the initials engraved on the watch.

"J. B. . . . Who the devil can that be? . . . Ah! yes, I remember. Jules Bouvier, the judge who conducted my examination. A charming fellow! . . . "

THE MYSTERY OF THE STRONG ROOM

L. T. MEADE
AND ROBERT EUSTACE

USING THE NOM DE PLUME Lillie Thomas Meade, Elizabeth Thomasina Meade Smith (1854–1914) not only wrote more than two hundred fifty books for young adult girls, but also wrote numerous volumes of detective fiction, several of which are historically important. *Stories from the Diary of a Doctor* (1894; second series 1896), written in collaboration with Dr. Edgar Beaumont (under the pseudonym Dr. Clifford Halifax), is the first series of medical mysteries published in England. *The Brotherhood of the Seven Kings* (1899), written in collaboration with Robert Eustace, is the first series of stories about a female crook. The thoroughly evil leader of an Italian criminal organization, Madame Koluchy, matches wits with Norman Head, a reclusive philosopher. Other memorable books by Meade include *A Master of Mysteries* (1898), *The Gold Star Line* (1899), *The Sanctuary Club* (1900), which features an unusual health club in which a series of murders is committed by apparently supernatural means, all written in collaboration with Eustace, and *The Sorceress of the Strand* (1903), in which Madame Sarah, an even more sinister villainess than Madame Koluchy, specializes in murder.

Robert Eustace is the pseudonym of Dr. Eustace Robert Barton (1863–1948). He is known mainly for his collaborations with other writers. In addition to working with Meade, he cowrote stories with Edgar Jepson; a novel with the once-popular mystery writer Gertrude Warden, *The Stolen Pearl: A Romance of London* (1903); and, most famously, with Dorothy L. Sayers on a novel, *The Documents in the Case* (1930).

"The Mystery of the Strong Room" was first published in *The Brotherhood of the Seven Kings* (London, Ward, Lock, 1899).

THE MYSTERY OF THE STRONG ROOM

L. T. MEADE AND ROBERT EUSTACE

LATE IN THE AUTUMN of that same year Mme. Koluchy was once more back in town. There was a warrant out for the arrest of Lockhart, who had evidently fled the country; but Madame, still secure in her own invincible cunning, was at large. The firm conviction that she was even now preparing a mine for our destruction was the reverse of comforting, and Dufrayer and I spent many gloomy moments as we thought over the possibilities of our future.

On a certain evening towards the latter end of October I went to dine with my friend. I found him busy arranging his table, which was tastefully decorated, and laid for three.

"An unexpected guest is coming to dine," he said, as I entered the room. "I must speak to you alone before he arrives. Come into the smoking-room; he may be here at any moment."

I followed Dufrayer, who closed the door behind us.

"I must tell you everything and quickly," he began, "and I must also ask you to be guided by me. I have consulted with Tyler, and he says it is our best course."

"Well?" I interrupted.

"The name of the man who is coming here to-night is Maurice Carlton," continued Dufrayer. "His mother was a Greek, but on the father's side he comes of a good old English stock. He inherited a place in Norfolk, Cor Castle, from his father; but the late owner lost heavily on the turf, and in consequence the present man has endeavoured to retrieve his fortunes as a diamond merchant. I met him some years ago in Athens. He has been wonderfully successful, and is now, I believe—or, at least, so he says—one of the richest men in Europe. He called upon me with regard to some legal business, and in the course of conversation referred incidentally to Mme. Koluchy. I drew him out, and found that he knew a good deal about her, but what their actual relations are I cannot say. I was very careful not to commit myself, and after consideration decided to ask him to dine here to-night in order that we both might see him together. I have thought over everything carefully, and am quite sure our only course now is not to mention anything we know about Madame. We may only give ourselves away in doing so. By keeping quiet we shall have a far better chance of seeing what she is up to. You agree with me, don't you?"

"Surely we ought to acquaint Carlton with her true character?" I replied.

Dufrayer shrugged his shoulders impatiently.

"No," he said, "we have played that game too often, and you know what the result has been. Believe me, we shall serve both his interests and ours best by remaining quiet. Carlton is living now at his own place, but comes up to London constantly. About two years ago he married a young English lady, who was herself the widow of an Italian. I believe they have a son, but am not quite sure. He seems an uncommonly nice fellow himself, and I should say his wife was fortunate in her husband; but, there, I hear his ring—let us go into the next room."

We did so, and the next moment Carlton appeared. Dufrayer introduced him to me, and soon afterwards we went into the dining-room. Carlton was a handsome man, built on a some-what massive scale. His face was of the Greek type, but his physique that of an Englishman. He had dark eyes, somewhat long and narrow, and apt, except when aroused, to wear a sleepy expression. It needed but a glance to show that in his blood was a mixture of the fiery East, with the nonchalance and suppression of all feel-ing which characterize John Bull. As I watched him, without appearing to do so, I came to the conclusion that I had seldom seen more perfect self-possession, or stronger indications of sup-pressed power.

As the meal proceeded, conversation grew brisk and brilliant. Carlton talked well, and, led on by Dufrayer, gave a short *résumé* of his life since they had last met.

"Yes," he said, "I am uncommonly lucky, and have done pretty well on the whole. Diamond dealing, as perhaps you know, is one of the most risky things that any man can take up, but my early training gave me a sound knowledge of the business, and I think I know what I am about. There is no trade to which the art of swindling has been more applied than to mine; but, there, I have had luck, immense luck, such as does not come to more than one man in a hundred."

"I suppose you have had some pretty exciting moments," I remarked.

"No, curiously enough," he replied; "I have personally never had any very exciting times. Big deals, of course, are often anxious moments, but beyond the natural anxiety to carry a large thing through, my career has been fairly simple. Some of my acquaintances, however, have not been so lucky, and one in particular is just going through a rare experience."

"Indeed," I answered; "are you at liberty to tell us what it is?"

He glanced from one of us to the other.

"I think so," he said. "Perhaps you have already heard of the great Rocheville diamond?"

"No," I remarked; "tell us about it, if you will."

Dinner being over, he leant back in his chair and helped himself to a cigar.

"It is curious how few people know about this diamond," he said, "although it is one of the most beautiful stones in the world. For actual weight, of course, many of the well-known stones can beat it. It weighs exactly eighty-two carats, and is an egg-shaped stone with a big indented hollow at the smaller end; but for lus-tre and brilliance I have never seen its equal. It has had a curious history. For centuries it was in the possession of an Indian Maharajah—it was bought from him by an American millionaire, and passed through my hands some ten years ago. I would have given anything to have kept it, but my finances were not so prosperous as they are now, and I had to let it go. A Russian baron bought it and took it to Naples, where it was stolen. This diamond was lost to the world till a couple of months ago, when it turned up in this country."

When Carlton mentioned Naples, the happy hunting-ground of the Brotherhood, Dufrayer glanced at me.

"But there is a fatality about its ownership," he continued; "it has again disappeared."

"How?" I cried.

"I wish I could tell you," he answered. "The circumstances of its loss are as follows: A month ago my wife and I were staying with an old friend, a relation of my mother's, a merchant named Michael Röden, of Röden Frères, Corn-hill, the great dealers. Röden said he had a sur-prise for me, and he showed me the Rocheville diamond. He told me that he had bought it from a Cingalese dealer in London, and for a compar-atively small price."

"What is its actual value?" interrupted Dufrayer.

"Roughly, I should think about fifteen thou-sand pounds, but I believe Röden secured it for ten. Well, poor chap, he has now lost both the stone and his money. My firm belief is that what he bought was an imitation, though how a man of his experience could have done such a thing is past knowledge. This is exactly what happened. Mrs. Carlton and I, as I have said, were staying down at his place in Staffordshire, and he had the diamond with him. At my wife's request, for she possesses a most intelligent interest in precious stones, he took us down to his strong room, and showed it to us. He meant to have it set for his own wife, who is a very beautiful woman. The next morning he took the diamond up to town, and Mrs. Carlton and I returned to Cor Castle. I got a wire from Röden that same afternoon, begging me to come up at once. I found him in a state of despair. He showed me the stone, to all appearance identically the same as the one we had looked at on the previous evening, and declared that it had just been proved to be an imitation. He said it was the most skilful imitation he had ever seen. We put it to every known test, and there was no doubt whatever that it was not a diamond. The specific gravity test was final on this point. The problem now is: Did he buy the real diamond which has since been stolen or an imitation? He swears that the Rocheville diamond was in his hands, that he tested it carefully at the time; he also says that since it came into his possession it was absolutely impossible for any one to steal it, and yet that the theft has been committed there is very little doubt. At least one thing is clear, the stone which he now possesses is not a diamond at all."

"Has anything been discovered since?" I asked.

"Nothing," replied Carlton, rising as he spoke, "and never will be, I expect. Of one thing there is little doubt. The shape and peculiar appearance of the Rocheville diamond are a matter of history to all diamond dealers, and the maker of the imitation must have had the stone in his possession for some considerable time. The facsimile is absolutely and incredibly perfect."

"Is it possible," said Dufrayer suddenly, "that the strong room in Röden's house could have been tampered with?"

"You would scarcely say so if you knew the peculiar make of that special strong room," replied Carlton. "I think I can trust you and your

friend with a somewhat important secret. Two strong rooms have been built, one for me at Cor Castle, and one for my friend Röden at his place in Staffordshire. These rooms are constructed on such a peculiar plan that the moment any key is inserted in the lock electric bells are set ringing within. These bells are connected in each case with the bedroom of the respective owners. Thus you will see for yourselves that no one could tamper with the lock without immediately giving such an alarm as would make any theft impossible. My friend Röden and I invented these special safes, and got them carried out on plans of our own. We both believe that our most valuable stones are safer in our own houses than in our places of business in town. But stay, gentlemen, you shall see for yourselves. Why should you not both come down to my place for a few days' shooting? I shall then have the greatest possible pleasure in showing you my strong room. You may be interested, too, in seeing some of my collection—I flatter myself, a unique one. The weather is perfect just now for shooting, and I have plenty of pheasants, also room enough and to spare. We are a big, cheerful party, and the lioness of the season is with us, Mme. Koluchy."

As he said the last words both Dufrayer and I could not refrain from starting. Luckily it was not noticed—my heart beat fast.

"It is very kind of you," I said. "I shall be charmed to come."

Dufrayer glanced at me, caught my eye, and said quietly:

"Yes, I think I can get away. I will come, with pleasure."

"That is right. I will expect you both next Monday, and will send to Durbrook Station to meet you, by any train you like to name."

We promised to let him know at what time we should be likely to arrive, and soon afterwards he left us. When he did so we drew our chairs near the fire.

"Well, we are in for it now," said Dufrayer. "Face to face at last—what a novel experience it will be! Who would believe that we were living in the dreary nineteenth century? But, of course, she may not stay when she hears we are coming."

"I expect she will," I answered; "she has no fear. Halloa! who can this be now?" I added, as the electric bell of the front door suddenly rang.

"Perhaps it is Carlton back again," said Dufrayer; "I am not expecting any one."

The next moment the door was opened, and our principal agent, Mr. Tyler himself, walked in.

"Good evening, gentlemen," he said. "I must apologize for this intrusion, but important news has just reached me, and the very last you would expect to hear." He chuckled as he spoke. "Mme. Koluchy's house in Welbeck Street was broken into a month ago. I am told that the place was regularly sacked. She was away in her yacht at the time, after the attempt on your life, Mr. Head; and it is supposed that the place was unguarded. Whatever the reason, she has never reported the burglary, and Ford at Scotland Yard has only just got wind of it. He suspects that it was done by the same gang that broke into the jeweller's in Piccadilly some months ago. It is a very curious case."

"Do you think it is one of her own gang that has rounded on her?" I asked.

"Hardly," he replied; "I do not believe any of them would dare to. No, it is an outside job, but Ford is watching the matter for the official force."

"Mr. Dufrayer and I happen to know where Madame Koluchy is at the present moment," I said.

I then gave Tyler a brief *résumé* of our interview with Carlton, and told him that it was our intention to meet Madame face to face early in the following week.

"What a splendid piece of luck!" he cried, rubbing his hands with ill-suppressed excitement. "With your acumen, Mr. Head, you will be certain to find out something, and we shall have her at last. I only wish the chance were mine."

"Well, have yourself in readiness," said Dufrayer; "we may have to telegraph to you at a moment's notice. Be sure we shall not leave a

stone unturned to get Madame to commit herself. For my part," he added, "although it seems scarcely credible, I strongly suspect that she is at the bottom of the diamond mystery."

It was late in the afternoon on the following Monday, and almost dark, when we arrived at Cor Castle. Carlton himself met us at the nearest railway station, and drove us to the house, which was a fine old pile, with a castellated roof and a large Elizabethan wing. The place had been extensively altered and restored, and was replete with every modern comfort.

Carlton led us straight into the centre hall, calling out in a cheerful tone to his wife as he did so.

A slender, very fair, and girlish-looking figure approached. She held out her hand, gave us each a hearty greeting, and invited us to come into the centre of a circle of young people who were gathered round a huge, old-fashioned hearth, on which logs of wood blazed and crackled cheerily. Mrs. Carlton introduced us to one or two of the principal guests, and then resumed her place at a table on which a silver tea-service was placed. It needed but a brief glance to show us that amongst the party was Mme. Koluchy. She was standing near her hostess, and just as my eye caught hers she bent and said a word in her ear. Mrs. Carlton coloured almost painfully, looked from her to me, and then once more rising from her seat came forward one or two steps.

"Mr. Head," she said, "may I introduce you to my great friend, Mme. Koluchy? By the way, she tells me that you are old acquaintances."

"Very old acquaintances, am I not right?" said Mme. Koluchy, in her clear, perfectly well-bred voice. She bowed to me and then held out her hand. I ignored the proffered hand and bowed coldly. She smiled in return.

"Come and sit near me, Mr. Head," she said; "it is a pleasure to meet you again; you have treated me very badly of late. You have never come once to see me."

"Did you expect me to come?" I replied quietly. There was something in my tone which caused the blood to mount to her face. She raised her eyes, gave me a bold, full glance of open defiance, and then said, in a soft voice, which scarcely rose above a whisper:

"No, you are too English."

Then she turned to our hostess, who was seated not a yard away.

"You forget your duties, Leonora. Mr. Head is waiting for his tea."

"Oh, I beg a thousand pardons," said Mrs. Carlton. "I did not know I had forgotten you, Mr. Head." She gave me a cup at once, but as she did so her hand shook so much that the small, gold-mounted and jewelled spoon rattled in the saucer.

"You are tired, Nora," said Mme. Koluchy; "may I not relieve you of your duties?"

"No, no, I am all right," was the reply, uttered almost pettishly. "Do not take any notice just now, I beg of you."

Madame turned to me.

"Come and talk to me," she said, in the imperious tone of a sovereign addressing a subject. She walked to the nearest window, and I followed her.

"Yes," she said, at once, "you are too English to play your part well. Cannot you recognize the common courtesies of warfare? Are you not sensible to the gallant attentions of the duellist? You are too crude. If our great interests clash, there is every reason why we should be doubly polite when we do meet."

"You are right, Madame, in speaking of us as duellists," I whispered back, "and the duel is not over yet."

"No, it is not," she answered.

"I have the pertinacity of my countrymen," I continued. "It is hard to rouse us, but when we are roused, it is a fight to grim death."

She said nothing further. At that moment a young man of the party approached. She called out to him in a playful tone to approach her side, and I withdrew.

At dinner that night Madame's brilliancy came into full play. There was no subject on which she could not talk—she was at once fantastic, irresponsible, and witty. Without the slightest difficulty she led the conversation, turning it into any channel she chose. Our host hung upon her words as if fascinated; indeed, I do not think there was a man of the party who had eyes or ears for any one else.

I had gone down to dinner with Mrs. Carlton, and in the intervals of watching Mme. Koluchy I could not help observing her. She belonged to the fair-haired and Saxon type, and when very young must have been extremely pretty—she was pretty still, but not to the close observer. Her face was too thin and too anxious, the colour in her cheeks was almost fixed; her hair, too, showed signs of receding from the temples, although the fashionable arrangement of the present day prevented this being specially noticed.

While she talked to me I could not help observing that her attention wandered, that her eyes on more than one occasion met those of Madame, and that when this encounter took place the younger woman trembled quite perceptibly. It was easy to draw my own conclusions. The usual thing had happened. Madame was not spending her time at Cor Castle for nothing—our hostess was in her power. Carlton himself evidently knew nothing of this. With such an alliance, mischief of the usual intangible nature was brewing. Could Dufrayer and I stop it? Beyond doubt there was more going on than met the eye.

As these thoughts flashed through my brain, I held myself in readiness, every nerve tense and taut. To play my part as an Englishman should I must have, above all things, self-possession. So I threw myself into the conversation. I answered Madame back in her own coin, and presently, in an argument which she conducted with rare brilliance, we had the conversation to ourselves. But all the time, as I talked and argued, and differed from the brilliant Italian, my glance was on Mrs. Carlton. I noticed that a growing restlessness had seized her, that she was listening to us with feverish and intense eagerness, and that her eyes began to wear a hunted expression. She ceased to play her part as hostess, and looked from me to Mme. Koluchy as one under a spell.

Just before we retired for the night Mrs. Carlton came up and took a seat near me in the drawing-room. Madame was not in the room, having gone with Dufrayer, Carlton, and several other members of the party to the billiard-room. Mrs. Carlton looked eagerly and nervously round her. Her manner was decidedly embarrassed. She made one or two short remarks, ending them abruptly, as if she wished to say something else but did not dare. I resolved to help her.

"Have you known Mme. Koluchy long?" I asked.

"For a short time, a year or two," she replied. "Have you, Mr. Head?"

"For more than ten years," I answered. I stooped a little lower and let my voice drop in her ear.

"Mme. Koluchy is my greatest enemy," I said.

"Oh, good heavens!" she cried. She half started to her feet, then controlled herself and sat down again.

"She is also my greatest enemy, she is my direst foe—she is a devil, not a woman," said the poor lady, bringing out her words with the most tense and passionate force. "Oh, may I, may I speak to you and alone?"

"If your confidence relates to Mme. Koluchy, I shall be only too glad to hear what you have got to say," I replied.

"They are coming back—I hear them," she said. "I will find an opportunity to-morrow. She must not know that I am taking you into my confidence."

She left me, to talk eagerly, with flushed cheeks, and eyes bright with ill-suppressed terror, to a merry girl who had just come in from the billiard-room.

The party soon afterwards broke up for the night, and I had no opportunity of saying a word to Dufrayer, who slept in a wing at the other end of the house.

The next morning after breakfast Carl-ton took Dufrayer and myself down to see his strong room. The ingenuity and cleverness of the arrangement by which the electric bells were sounded the moment the key was put into the lock struck me with amazement. The safe was of the strongest pattern; the levers and bolts, as well as the arrangement of the lock, making it practically impregnable.

"Röden's safe resembles mine in every particular," said Carlton, as he turned the key in the lock and readjusted the different bolts in their respective places. "You can see for yourselves that no one could rob such a safe without detection."

"It would certainly be black magic if he did," was my response.

"We have arranged for a shooting party this morning," continued Carlton; "let us forget diamonds and their attendant anxieties, and enjoy ourselves out of doors. The birds are plentiful, and I trust we shall have a good time."

He took us upstairs, and we started a few moments later on our expedition.

It was arranged that the ladies should meet us for lunch at one of the keepers' cottages. We spent a thoroughly pleasant morning, the sport was good, and I had seldom enjoyed myself better. The thought of Mme. Koluchy, however, intruded itself upon my memory from time to time; what, too, was the matter with Mrs. Carlton? It needed but to glance at Carlton to see that he was not in her secret. In the open air, and acting the part of host, which he did to perfection, I had seldom seen a more genial fellow.

When we sat down to lunch I could not help owning to a sense of relief when I perceived that Mme. Koluchy had not joined us.

Mrs. Carlton was waiting for us in the keeper's cottage, and several other ladies were with her. She came up to my side immediately.

"May I walk with you after lunch, Mr. Head?" she said. "I have often gone out with the guns before now, and I don't believe you will find me in the way."

"I shall be delighted to have your company," I replied.

"Madame is ill," continued Mrs. Carlton, dropping her voice a trifle; "she had a severe headache, and was obliged to go to her room. This is my opportunity," she added, "and I mean to seize it."

I noticed that she played with her food, and soon announcing that I had had quite enough, I rose. Mrs. Carlton and I did not wait for the rest of the party, but walked quickly away together. Soon the shooting was resumed, and we could hear the sound of the beaters, and also an occasional shot fired ahead of us.

At first my companion was very silent. She walked quickly, and seemed anxious to detach herself altogether from the shooting party. Her agitation was very marked, but I saw that she was afraid to come to the point. Again I resolved to help her.

"You are in trouble," I said; "and Mme. Koluchy has caused it. Now, tell me everything. Be assured that if I can help you I will. Be also assured of my sympathy. I know Mme. Koluchy. Before now I have been enabled to get her victims out of her clutches."

"Have you, indeed?" she answered. She looked at me with a momentary sparkle of hope in her eyes; then it died out.

"But in my case that is impossible," she continued. "Still, I will confide in you; I will tell you everything. To know that some one else shares my terrible secret will be an untold relief."

She paused for a moment, then continued, speaking quickly:

"I am in the most awful trouble. Life has become almost unbearable to me. My trouble is of such a nature that my husband is the very last person in the world to whom I can confide it."

I waited in silence.

"You doubtless wonder at my last words," she continued, "but you will see what I mean when I tell you the truth. Of course, you will regard what I say as an absolute secret?"

"I will not reveal a word you are going to tell me without your permission," I answered.

"Thank you; that is all that I need. This is my early history. You must know it in order to understand what follows. When I was very young, not more than seventeen, I was married to an Italian of the name of Count Porcelli. My people were poor, and he was supposed to be rich. He was considered a good match. He was a handsome man, but many years my senior. Almost immediately after the marriage my mother died, and I had no near relations or friends in England. The Count took me to Naples, and I was not long there before I made some terrible discoveries. My husband was a leading member of a political secret society, whose name I never heard. I need not enter into particulars of that awful time. Suffice it to say that he subjected me to almost every cruelty.

"In the autumn of 1893, while we were in Rome, Count Porcelli was stabbed one night in the Forum. He had parted from me in a fury at some trifling act of disobedience to his intolerable wishes, and I never saw him again, either alive or dead. His death was an immense relief to me. I returned home, and two years afterwards, in 1895, I married Mr. Carlton, and everything was bright and happy. A year after the marriage we had a little son. I have not shown you my boy, for he is away from home at present. He is the heir to my husband's extensive estates, and is a beautiful child. My husband was, and is, devotedly attached to me—indeed, he is the soul of honour, chivalry, and kindness. I began to forget those fearful days in Naples and Rome; but, Mr. Head, a year ago everything changed. I went to see that fiend in human guise, Mme. Koluchy. You know she poses as a doctor. It was the fashion to consult her. I was suffering from a trifling malady, and my husband begged me to go to her. I went, and we quickly discovered that we both possessed ties, awful ties, to the dismal past. Mme. Koluchy knew my first husband, Count Porcelli, well. She told me that he was alive and in England, and that my marriage to Mr. Carlton was void.

"You may imagine my agony. If this were indeed true, what was to become of my child, and what would Mr. Carlton's feelings be? The shock was so tremendous that I became ill, and was almost delirious for a week. During that time Madame herself insisted on nursing me. She was outwardly kind, and told me that my sorrow was hers, and that she certainly would not betray me. But she said that Count Porcelli had heard of my marriage, and would not keep my secret if I did not make it worth his while. From that moment the most awful blackmailing began. From time to time I had to part with large sums of money. Mr. Carlton is so rich and generous that he would give me anything without question. This state of things has gone on for a year. I have kept the awful danger at bay at the point of the sword."

"But how can you tell that Count Porcelli is alive?" I asked. "Remember that there are few more unscrupulous people than Mme. Koluchy. How do you know that this may not be a fabrication on her part in order to wring money from you?"

"I have not seen Count Porcelli," replied my companion; "but all the same, the proof is incontestable, for Madame has brought me letters from him. He promises to leave me in peace if I will provide him with money; but at the same time he assures me that he will declare himself at any moment if I fail to listen to his demands."

"Nevertheless, my impression is," I replied, "that Count Porcelli is not in existence, and that Madame is playing a risky game; but you have more to tell?"

"I have. You have by no means heard the worst yet. My present difficulty is one to scare the stoutest heart. A month ago Madame came to our house in town, and sitting down opposite to me, made a most terrible proposal. She took a jewel-case from her pocket, and, touching a spring, revealed within the largest diamond that I had ever seen. She laid it in my hand—it was egg-shaped, and had an indentation at one end. While I was gazing at it, and admiring it, she suddenly told me that it was only an imitation. I stared at her in amazement.

"'Now, listen attentively,' she said. 'All your future depends on whether you have brains, wit, and tact for a great emergency. The stone you hold in your hand is an imitation, a perfect one. I had it made from my knowledge of the original. It would take in the greatest expert in the diamond market who did not apply tests to it. The real stone is at the house of Monsieur Röden. You and your husband, I happen to know, are going to stay at the Rödens' place in the country to-morrow. The real stone, the great Rocheville diamond, was stolen from my house in Welbeck Street six weeks ago. It was purchased by Monsieur Röden from a Cingalese employed by the gang who stole it, at a very large figure, but also at only a third of its real value. For reasons which I need not explain, I was unable to expose the burglary, and in consequence it was easy to get rid of the stone for a large sum—but those who think that I will tamely submit to such a gigantic loss little know me. I am determined that the stone shall once more come into my possession, either by fair means or foul. Now, you are the only person who can help me, for you will be unsuspected, and can work where I should not have a chance. It is to be your task to substitute the imitation for the real stone.'

"'How can I?' I asked.

"'Easily, if you will follow my guidance. When you are at the Rödens', you must lead the conversation to the subject of diamonds, or rather you must get your husband to do so, for he would be even less suspected than you. He will ask Monsieur Röden to show you both his strong room where his valuable jewels are kept. You must make an excuse to be in the room a moment by yourself. You must substitute the real for the unreal as quickly, as deftly as if you were possessed of legerdemain. Take your opportunity to do this as best you can—all I ask of you is to succeed—otherwise'—her eyes blazed into mine—they were brighter than diamonds themselves.

"'Otherwise?' I repeated faintly.

"'Count Porcelli is close at hand—he shall claim his wife. Think of Mr. Carlton's feelings, think of your son's doom.' She paused, raising her brows with a gesture peculiarly her own. 'I need not say anything further,' she added.

"Well, Mr. Head, I struggled against her awful proposal. At first I refused to have anything to do with it, but she piled on the agony, showing me only too plainly what my position would be did I not accede to her wishes. She traded on my weakness; on my passionate love for the child and for his father. Yes, in the end I yielded to her.

"The next day we went to the Rödens'. Despair rendered me cunning; I introduced the subject of the jewels to my husband, and begged of him to ask Monsieur Röden to show us his safe and its contents. Monsieur Röden was only too glad to do so. It is one of his fads, and that fad is also shared by my husband, to keep his most valuable stones in a safe peculiarly constructed in the vaults of his own house. My husband has a similar strong room. We went into the vaults, and Monsieur Röden allowed me to take the Rocheville diamond in my hand for a moment. When I had it in my possession I stepped backward, made a clumsy movement by intention, knocked against a chair, slipped, and the diamond fell from my fingers. I saw it flash and roll away. Quicker almost than thought I put my foot on it, and before any one could detect me had substituted the imitation for the real. The real stone was in my pocket and the imitation in Monsieur Röden's case without any one being in the least wiser.

"With the great Rocheville diamond feeling heavier than lead in my pocket, I went away the next morning with my husband. I had valuable jewels of my own, and have a jewel-case of unique pattern. It is kept in the strong room at the Castle. I obtained the key of the strong room from my husband, went down to the vaults, and under the pretence of putting some diamonds and sapphires away, locked up the Rocheville diamond in my own private jewel-case. It is impossible to steal it from there, owing to the peculiar construction of the lock of the case, which starts electric bells ringing the moment the key is put inside. Now listen, Mr. Head. Madame knows all about the strong room, for she has wormed its secrets from me. She knows

that with all her cleverness she cannot pick that lock. She has, therefore, told me that unless I give her the Rocheville diamond to-night she will expose me. She declares that no entreaties will turn her from her purpose. She is adamant, she has no heart at all. Her sweetness and graciousness, her pretended sympathy, are all on the surface. It is useless appealing to anything in her but her avarice. Fear!—she does not know the meaning of the word. Oh, what am I to do? I will not let her have the diamond, but how mad I was ever to yield to her!"

I gazed at my companion for a few moments without speaking. The full meaning of her extraordinary story was at last made abundantly plain. The theft which had so completely puzzled Monsieur Röden was explained at last. What Carlton's feelings would be when he knew the truth, it was impossible to realize; but know the truth he must, and as soon as possible. I was more than ever certain that Count Porcelli's death was a reality, and that Madame was blackmailing the unfortunate young wife for her own purposes. But although I believed that such was assuredly the case, and that Mrs. Carlton had no real cause to dread dishonour to herself and her child, I had no means of proving my own belief. The moment had come to act, and to act promptly. Mrs. Carlton was overcome by the most terrible nervous fear, and had already got herself into the gravest danger by her theft of the diamond. She looked at me intently, and at last said, in a whisper:

"Whatever you may think of me, speak. I know you believe that I am one of the most guilty wretches in existence, but you can scarcely realize what my temptation has been."

"I sympathize with you, of course," I said then; "but there is only one thing to be done. Now, may I speak quite plainly? I believe that Count Porcelli is dead. Madame is quite clever enough to forge letters which you would believe to be *bonâ-fide*. Remember that I know this woman well. She possesses consummate genius, and never yet owned to a scruple of any sort. It is only too plain that she reaps an enormous advantage by playing on your fears. You can never put things right, therefore, until you confide in your husband. Remember how enormous the danger is to him. He will not leave a stone unturned to come face to face with the Count. Madame will have to show her hand, and you will be saved. Will you take my advice: will you go to him immediately?"

"I dare not, I dare not."

"Very well; you have another thing to consider. Monsieur Röden is determined to recover the stolen diamond. The cleverest members of the detective force are working day and night in his behalf. They are quite clever enough to trace the theft to you. You will be forced to open your jewel-case in their presence—just think of your feelings. Yes, Mrs. Carlton, believe me I am right: your husband must know all, the diamond must be returned to its rightful owner immediately."

She wrung her hands in agony.

"I cannot tell my husband," she replied. "I will find out some other means of getting rid of the diamond—even Madame had better have it than this. Think of the wreck of my complete life, think of the dishonour to my child. Mr. Head, I know you are kind, and I know your advice is really wise, but I cannot act on it. Madame has faithfully sworn to me that when she gets the Rocheville diamond she will leave the country forever, and that I shall never hear of her again. Count Porcelli will accompany her."

"Do you believe this?" I asked.

"In this special case I am inclined to believe her. I know that Madame has grown very anxious of late, and I am sure she feels that she is in extreme danger—she has dropped hints to that effect. She must have been sure that her position was a most unstable one when she refused to communicate the burglary in Welbeck Street to the police. But, hark! I hear footsteps. Who is coming?"

Mrs. Carlton bent forward and peered through the brushwood.

"I possess the most deadly fear of that woman," she continued; "even now she may be watching us—that headache may have been all a pretence. God knows what will become of me if she discovers that I have confided in you. Don't let it seem that we have been talking about anything special. Go on with your shooting. We are getting too far away from the others."

She had scarcely said the words before I saw in the distance Mme. Koluchy approaching. She was walking slowly, with that graceful motion which invariably characterized her steps. Her eyes were fixed on the ground, her face looked thoughtful.

"What are we to do?" said Mrs. Carlton.

"You have nothing to do at the present moment," I replied, "but to keep up your courage. As to what you are to do in the immediate future, I must see you again. What you have told me requires immediate action. I swear I will save you and get you out of this scrape at any cost."

"Oh, how good you are," she answered; "but do go on with your shooting. Madame can read any one through, and my face bears signs of agitation."

Just at that moment a great cock pheasant came beating through the boughs overhead. I glanced at Mrs. Carlton, noticed her extreme pallor, and then almost recklessly raised my gun and fired. This was the first time I had used the gun since luncheon. What was the matter? I had an instant, just one brief instant, to realize that there was something wrong—there was a deafening roar—a flash as if a thousand sparks came before my eyes—I reeled and fell, and a great darkness closed over me.

Out of an oblivion that might have been eternity a dawning sense of consciousness came to me. I opened my eyes. The face of Dufrayer was bending over me.

"Hush!" he said, "keep quiet, Head. Doctor," he added, "he has come to himself at last."

A young man, with a bright, intelligent face, approached my side. "Ah! you feel better?" he said. "That is right, but you must keep quiet. Drink this."

He raised a glass to my lips. I drank thirstily. I

noticed now that my left hand and arm were in a splint, bandaged to my side.

"What can have happened?" I exclaimed. I had scarcely uttered the words before memory came back to me in a flash.

"You have had a bad accident," said Dufrayer; "your gun burst."

"Burst!" I cried. "Impossible."

"It is only too true; you have had a marvellous escape of your life, and your left hand and arm are injured."

"Dufrayer," I said at once, and eagerly, "I must see you alone. Will you ask the doctor to leave us?"

"I will be within call, Mr. Dufrayer," said the medical man. He went into the ante-room. I was feverish, and I knew it, but my one effort was to keep full consciousness until I had spoken to Dufrayer.

"I must get up at once," I cried. "I feel all right, only a little queer about the head, but that is nothing. Is my hand much damaged?"

"No. Luckily it is only a flesh wound," replied Dufrayer.

"But how could the gun have burst?" I continued. "It was one of Riley's make, and worth seventy guineas."

I had scarcely said the last words before a hideous thought flashed across me. Dufrayer spoke instantly, answering my surmise.

"I have examined your gun carefully—at least, what was left of it," he said, "and there is not the slightest doubt that the explosion was not caused by an ordinary cartridge. The stock and barrels are blown to fragments. The marvel is that you were not killed on the spot."

"It is easy to guess who has done the mischief," I replied.

"At least one fact is abundantly clear," said Dufrayer: "your gun was tampered with, probably during the luncheon interval. I have been making inquiries, and believe that one of the beaters knows something, only I have not got him yet to confess. I have also made a close examination of the ground where you stood, and have picked up a small piece of the brasswork of a cartridge. Matters are so grave that I have

wired to Tyler and Ford, and they will both be here in the morning. My impression is that we shall soon have got sufficient evidence to arrest Madame. It goes without saying that this is her work. This is the second time she has tried to get rid of you; and, happen what may, the thing must be stopped. But I must not worry you any further at present, for the shock you have sustained has been fearful."

"Am I badly hurt?" I asked.

"Fortunately you are only cut a little about the face, and your eyes have altogether escaped. Dynamite always expends its force downwards."

"It is lucky my eyes escaped," I answered. "Now, Dufrayer, I have just received some important information from Mrs. Carlton. It was told to me under a seal of the deepest secrecy, and even now I must not tell you what she has confided to me without her permission. Would it be possible to get her to come to see me for a moment?"

"I am sure she will come, and gladly. She seems to be in a terrible state of nervous prostration. You know she was on the scene when the accident happened. When I appeared I found her in a half-fainting condition, supported, of course, by Mme. Koluchy, whom she seemed to shrink from in the most unmistakable manner. Yes, I will send her to you, but I do not think the doctor will allow you to talk long."

"Never mind about the doctor or any one else," I replied; "let me see Mrs. Carlton—there is not an instant to lose."

Dufrayer saw by my manner that I was frightfully excited. He left the room at once, and in a few moments Mrs. Carlton came in. Even in the midst of my own pain I could not but remark with consternation the look of agony on her face. She was trembling so excessively that she could scarcely stand.

"Will you do something for me?" I said, in a whisper. I was getting rapidly weaker, and even my powers of speech were failing me.

"Anything in my power," she said, "except——"

"But I want no exceptions," I said. "I have nearly lost my life. I am speaking to you now almost with the solemnity of a dying man. I want you to go straight to your husband and tell him all."

"No, no, no!" She turned away. Her face was whiter than the white dress which she was wearing.

"Then if you will not confide in him, tell all that you have just told me to my friend Dufrayer. He is a lawyer, well accustomed to hearing stories of distress and horror. He will advise you. Will you at least do that?"

"I cannot." Her voice was hoarse with emotion, then she said, in a whisper:

"I am more terrified than ever, for I cannot find the key of my jewel-case."

"This makes matters still graver, although I believe that even Mme. Koluchy cannot tamper with the strong room. You will tell your husband or Dufrayer—promise me that, and I shall rest happy."

"I cannot, Mr. Head; and you, on your part, have promised not to reveal my secret."

"You put me in a most cruel dilemma," I replied.

Just then the doctor came into the room, accompanied by Carlton.

"Come, come," said the medical man, "Mr. Head, you are exciting yourself. I am afraid, Mrs. Carlton, I must ask you to leave my patient. Absolute quiet is essential. Fortunately the injuries to the face are trivial, but the shock to the system has been considerable, and fever may set in unless quiet is enforced."

"Come, Nora," said her husband; "you ought to rest yourself, my dear, for you look very bad."

As they were leaving the room I motioned Dufrayer to my side.

"Go to Mrs. Carlton," I said; "she has something to say of the utmost importance. Tell her that you know she possesses a secret, that I have not told you what it is, but that I have implored her to take you into her confidence."

"I will do so," he replied.

Late that evening he came back to me.

"Well?" I cried eagerly.

"Mrs. Carlton is too ill to be pressed any further, Head; she has been obliged to go to her room, and the doctor has been with her. He prescribed a soothing draught. Her husband is very much puzzled at her condition. You look anything but fit yourself, old man," he continued. "You must go to sleep now. Whatever part Madame has played in this tragedy, she is keeping up appearances with her usual *aplomb*. There was not a more brilliant member of the dinner party to-night than she. She has been inquiring with apparent sympathy for you, and offered to come and see you if that would mend matters. Of course, I told her that the doctor would not allow any visitors. Now you must take your sleeping draught, and trust for the best. I am following up the clue of the gun, and believe that it only requires a little persuasion to get some really important evidence from one of the beaters; but more of this to-morrow. You must sleep now, Head, you must sleep."

The shock I had undergone, and the intense pain in my arm which began about this time to come on, told even upon my strong frame. Dufrayer poured out a sleeping draught which the doctor had sent round—I drank it off, and soon afterwards he left me.

An hour or two passed; at the end of that time the draught began to take effect, drowsiness stole over me, the pain grew less, and I fell into an uneasy sleep, broken with hideous and grotesque dreams. From one of these I awoke with a start, struck a match, and looked at my watch. It was half-past three. The house had of course long ago retired to rest, and everything was intensely still. I could hear in the distance the monotonous ticking of the great clock in the hall, but no other sound reached my ears. My feverish brain, however, was actively working. The phantasmagoria of my dream seemed to take life and shape. Fantastic forms seemed to hover round my bed, and faces sinister with evil appeared to me—each one bore a likeness to Mme. Koluchy. I became more and more feverish, and now a deadly fear that even at this moment something awful was happening began to assail me. It rose to a conviction. Madame, with her almost superhuman knowledge, must guess that she was in danger. Surely, she would not allow the night to go by without acting? Surely, while we were supposed to sleep, she would steal the Rocheville diamond, and escape?

The horror of this thought was so over-powering that I could stay still no longer. I flung off the bed-clothes and sprang from the bed. A delirious excitement was consuming me. Putting on my dressing-gown, I crept out onto the landing, then I silently went down the great staircase, crossed the hall, and, turning to the left, went down another passage to the door of the stone stairs leading to the vault in which was Carlton's strong room. I had no sooner reached this door than my terrors and nervous fears became certainties.

A gleam of light broke the darkness. I drew back into a recess in the stonework. Yes, I was right. My terrors and convictions of coming peril had not visited me without cause, for standing before the iron door of the strong room was Mme. Koluchy herself. There was a lighted taper in her hand. My bare feet had made no noise, and she was unaware of my presence. What was she doing? I waited in silence—my temples were hot and throbbing with over-mastering horror. I listened for the bells which would give the alarm directly when she inserted the key in the iron door. She was doing something to the safe—I could tell this by the noise she was making—still no bells rang.

The next instant the heavy door slipped back on its hinges, and Madame entered. The moment I saw this I could remain quiet no longer. I sprang forward, striking my wounded arm against something in the darkness. She turned and saw me—I made a frantic effort to seize her—then my brain swam and every atom of strength left me. I found myself falling upon something hard. I had entered the strong room. For a moment I lay on the floor half stunned, then I sprang to my feet, but I was too late. The iron door closed upon me with a muffled clang. Madame had by some miraculous means opened the safe without a key, had taken the diamond from Mrs. Carlton's jewel-case which stood open on a shelf, and had locked me a prisoner within. Half delirious and stunned, I had

fallen an easy victim. I shouted loudly, but the closeness of my prison muffled and stifled my voice.

How long I remained in captivity I cannot tell. The pain in my arm, much increased by my sudden fall on the hard floor, rendered me, I believe, partly delirious—I was feeling faint and chilled to the bone when the door of the strong room at last was opened, and Carlton and Dufrayer entered. I noticed immediately that there was daylight outside; the night was over.

"We have been looking for you everywhere," said Dufrayer. "What in the name of fortune has happened? How did you get in here?"

"In pursuit of Madame," I replied. "But where is she? For Heaven's sake, tell me quickly."

"Bolted, of course," answered Dufrayer, in a gloomy voice; "but tell us what this means, Head. You shall hear what we have to say afterwards."

I told my story in a few words.

"But how, in the name of all that's wonderful, did she manage to open the safe without a key?" cried Carlton. "This is black art with a vengeance."

"You must have left the strong room open," I said.

"That I will swear I did not," he replied. "I locked the safe as usual, after showing it to you and Dufrayer yesterday. Here is the key."

"Let me see it," I said.

He handed it to me. I took it over to the light.

"Look here," I cried, with sudden excitement, "this cannot be your original key—it must have been changed. You think you locked the safe with this key. Carlton, you have been tricked by that arch-fiend. Did you ever before see a key like this?"

I held the wards between my finger and thumb, and turned the barrel from left to right. The barrel revolved in the wards in a ratchet concealed in the shoulder.

"You could unlock the safe with this key, but not lock it again," I exclaimed. "See here."

I inserted the key in the keyhole as I spoke. It instantly started the bells ringing.

"The barrel turns, but the wards which are

buried in the keyhole do not turn with it, and the resistance of the ratchet gives exactly the impression as if you were locking the safe. Thus, yesterday morning, you thought you locked the safe with this key, but in reality you left it open. No one but that woman could have conceived such a scheme. In some way she must have substituted this for your key."

"Well, come to your room now, Head," cried Dufrayer, "or Madame will have achieved the darling wish of her heart, and your life will be the forfeit."

I accompanied Carlton upstairs, dressed, and though still feeling terribly ill and shaken, presently joined the rest of the household in one of the sitting-rooms. The utmost excitement was apparent on every face. Mrs. Carlton was standing near an open window. There were traces of tears on her cheeks, and yet her eyes, to my astonishment, betokened both joy and relief. She beckoned me to her side.

"Come out with me for a moment, Mr. Head."

When we got into the open air she turned to me.

"Dreadful as the loss of the diamond is," she exclaimed, "there are few happier women in England than I am at the present moment. My maid brought me a letter from Mme. Koluchy this morning which has assuaged my worst fears. In it she owns that Count Porcelli has been long in his grave, and that she only blackmailed me in order to secure large sums of money."

I was just about to reply to Mrs. Carlton when Dufrayer hurried up.

"The detectives have arrived, and we want you at once," he exclaimed.

I accompanied him into Carlton's study. Tyler and Ford were both present. They had just been examining the strong room, and had seen the false key. Their excitement was unbounded.

"She has bolted, but we will have her now," cried Ford. "We have got the evidence we want at last. It is true she has the start of us by three or four hours; but at last—yes, at last—we can loose the hounds in full pursuit."

NO WAY OUT

DENNIS LYNDS

BETTER KNOWN AS MICHAEL COLLINS, one of his eight pseudonyms, Dennis Lynds (1924–2005) began his writing career producing literary fiction for such highly regarded publications as *Prairie Schooner* and *New World Writing*. Five of his stories have been selected for the prestigious *Best American Short Stories* series; some of these mainstream stories were later collected in *Why Girls Ride Sidesaddle* (1980). He was born in St. Louis, Missouri, and worked as a chemist; when World War II broke out, he served in France and received a Bronze Star, a Purple Heart, and three battle stars.

Lynds began to write detective fiction in the early 1960s: first short stories, then eight novels about the Shadow, and finally the novel *Act of Fear* (1967), under the name Michael Collins, for which he received the Edgar Award for Best First Novel. It featured the one-armed Dan Fortune, his most successful character, though there also were numerous admirers of "Slot-Machine" Kelly, another one-armed private eye who liked to gamble on those slot machines known as "one-armed bandits." He got the idea for these characters from a real-life detective who hired only disabled process servers, believing that those being served would refrain from physical retaliation against the server. Lynds also wrote about industrial espionage as William Arden, created a high-class private eye as Mark Sadler, and set a series in Buena Costa, California, as John Crowe. He received a Lifetime Achievement Award from the Private Eye Writers of America in 1988.

"No Way Out" was first published in the February 1964 issue of *Mike Shayne Mystery Magazine*. It was first published in book form in *Best Detective Stories of the Year* (New York, Dutton, 1965).

NO WAY OUT

DENNIS LYNDS

NEXT TO WINE, women, and whisky, Slot-Machine Kelly's favorite kick was reading those real puzzle type mysteries. You know, the kind where the victim gets on top of a flagpole and they can't find the weapon because it was an icicle and melted away.

"There was this one I liked special," Slot-Machine said to Joe Harris. "Guy was knocked off in an attic room. The guy was alone, there was a cop right outside the door, and another cop was down in the street watching the one window. The guy got shot twice—once from far, once from real close. Oh, yes—and there were powder burns on him. The cops got into the room in one second flat, and there was no one there except the stiff. How about that, baby?"

"I'm crazy with suspense," Joe said as he mopped the bar with his specially dirty rag.

"Simple," Slot explained. "The killer shot from another attic across the street; that was the first shot. Then he tossed the gun across, through the window, and it hit the floor. It had a hair trigger, and it just happened to hit the victim again!"

"You're kidding," Joe said. "You mean someone wants you to believe odds like that?"

"It's possible," Slot said.

"So's snow in July," Joe said. "The guy who wrote that one drinks cheaper booze than you do."

"Don't just promise, pour," Slot-Machine said.

Slot-Machine liked these wild stories because things like that never happened in his world. When he got a murder it was ninety-nine percent sure to be something about as exotic as a drunk belting his broad with a beer bottle in front of forty-two talkative witnesses at high noon.

"Did you know that ninety percent of all murders are committed by guys with criminal records," Slot went on informatively. "The victim usually has a record, too, and they usually know each other? A lot of them take place in bars. It's near midnight, and both guys are swinging on the gargle."

"And the bartender gets hauled in for serving whisky to drunks," Joe said.

"Life is dull," Slot sighed.

Which was why this time Slot-Machine Kelly was not even aware that he had a puzzler until it happened. Things like this just didn't happen in Slot-Machine's world. When they did there had to be a logical explanation and a reason. In the real world a man has to figure the odds and forget about guns with improbable hair-triggers. Only no matter how you sliced it, there was no reason for the guard to be dead, no way the rubies could have been stolen, and no way out of that tenth story room. It was one hundred percent impossible. But it had happened.

It all started with the usual routine. Mr. Jason Moomer, of Moomer, Moomer, and McNamara, Jewel Merchants, came to Slot's dusty office one bright morning with a job offer. The morning was bright, but Slot-Machine wasn't. He was nursing a fine hangover from a bottle of Lafite-Rothschild '53 he had found in Nussbaum's Liquor Store. The price had been right, and Slot had killed the bottle happily over a plebeian steak.

"It was the brandy afterwards," Slot explained to Moomer. "Speak soft, my skull's wide open."

"For this job you stay sober," Moomer said.

"Don't ask for miracles," Slot said.

"You did a good job for us before," Moomer said. "My partners think you're not reliable, but I vouched for you."

"You're a brave man," Slot said.

"You know the set-up," Moomer said. "We're displaying the rubies in a suite at the North American Hotel. They're on display all day for three days, and they're locked in the safe at night. Twenty-four-hour watch on all doors, at the safe, with the jewels when they're out. We're hiring three shifts of Burns guards, five men to a shift to cover the three doors, the safe, and the elevators, just in case. We're hiring a private detective to work with each shift, to keep his eyes and ears open."

"You got more protection than a South American Dictator," Slot-Machine said.

"There are five rubies, a matched set. They're worth perhaps a quarter of a million dollars."

"Maybe you need the Army," Slot-Machine said.

"You'll change shifts each day," Moomer went on, ignoring Slot's witicism. "I'm hiring Ed Green and Manny Lewis for the other shifts. You'll all wear uniforms, so you'll look like ordinary guards."

"A tight set-up," Slot said.

Slot-Machine disliked regular work, and he particularly disliked uniformed-guard work. But, as usual, his bank account looked like a tip for a hashhouse waitress, and Joe's current employer was already beginning to count the shots in the Irish whisky bottle every time Slot appeared in Joe's bar.

"You got a deal," Slot said. "I have a little free time. You're lucky."

"Well," Moomer said, "if you're so busy, you won't need any money in advance."

"You're dreaming again," Slot said.

Moomer grinned, paid $50 in advance, and left. Slot counted the money four times. He sighed unhappily. It always came out to $50. He hated clients who could count. At least, he decided, it would be easy work except for the wear and tear on his feet.

He was wrong. Before it was over, he had a dead man, five missing rubies, a very unfriendly Jason Moomer, a suspicious Captain Gazzo, and a room from which there was no way out except for a bird.

For two days all the trouble Slot-Machine had was tired feet. The suite in the North American was crowded with ruby-lovers, and jewelry dealers who loved only money, for the whole two days. The uniformed guards, and the three private detectives, earned their pay.

During the day the guard at the elevator checked credentials. Slot-Machine knew that this was necessary, but it was not a very valuable precaution. Moomer, Moomer, and McNamara wanted to see their rubies sold, and almost anyone could get an invitation.

There were three doors to the suite. Two were locked on both sides, but a uniformed guard was stationed at each door anyway, as an additional security measure. The third door was the only entrance and exit to the suite. The Burns man there kept his pistol in plain sight. There was no need for guards on the windows, for the suite was ten floors up without a fire escape.

The fifth Burns guard stood like an eagle-eyed statue right behind the display case. It would have taken an invisible man with wings to steal the rubies during the day. Which did not stop the Messrs. Moomer and McNamara from prowling like frightened hyenas.

"If you see anything suspicious, get to the alarm fast," Jason Moomer explained to the guard at the display case. "The alarm is wired in to the case itself, but there's the extra switch, just in case."

"You're in charge of your shift, Kelly," Maximillian Moomer said. "Just stay sober!"

Old Maximillian did not like Slot-Machine. That came from the fee Slot had charged for finding a stolen diamond tiara a few years ago. Maximillian was a skin-flint, and he had always suspected Slot of stealing the tiara and returning it for the handsome fee. Slot hadn't, but he had thought it a good idea.

"Bringing in detectives is ridiculous anyway," Maximillian Moomer said. "The uniformed guards are enough."

"I think we should have had the showing in our own strong room," Angus McNamara said. The tall Scotsman seemed the most nervous of the three owners.

But nothing happened for the first two days, and at night everything was quiet. The Burns men remained on guard at all the doors, the elevator remained under watch, and the man inside the suite camped in front of the safe.

Day or night, Slot-Machine Kelly, Ed Green, and Manny Lewis kept a roving eye on everything as they wandered through the rooms and halls in their uniforms. The detectives could not be told from the other Burns guards. For two days Slot-Machine cat-footed through the four rooms, eyeing the rubies and the guests, and sneaking some of the free liquor when no one was looking. The only incident occurred on the second day when Slot was off duty.

Ed Green was on duty at the time. It happened just as the day-shift was going off. The swing-shift guards had taken their stations, and Ed Green was talking to Manny Lewis outside the room, when the alarm went off like a scared air-raid siren.

People started to mill and shout. Manny Lewis ran to check the other doors. Ed Green and the uniformed guards poured into the main room and surrounded the display case. The guard at the case already had his gun out.

"What is it!" Green had snapped.

A very nervous and embarrassed young woman stood near the alarm switch. "I turned it," she said. "I'm sorry. I thought it was for the waiter."

Green swore angrily, and the Moomer brothers insisted that the attractive offender be taken to the police. The young woman did not seem to mind too much. She checked out nice and clean; she was the legitimate secretary of a small merchant named Julius Honder.

"The dame was just curious," Green said to Slot-Machine. "At least we got sort of a drill."

The guard system had worked fine. No one on the doors had left his post, and the Moomers and McNamara seemed happier. The final precaution, the electronic scanner that was set up to cover the elevators during the day, and the single exit from the lobby of the hotel at night, was working perfectly.

"It's a vacation with pay," Slot told Joe before he went on duty on the third day. "A cockroach couldn't get into that room, and a germ couldn't get out."

It happened on the third day.

Slot-Machine had the lobster shift on the third day—midnight to eight o'clock in the weary morning. He had stopped for a couple of quick whiskies at Joe's tavern, and when he arrived he had to hurry into his uniform. The five Burns men of his shift were ready and waiting.

Ed Green greeted Slot-Machine. After the shift had been changed, and Slot's men were in their places at the locked doors and in front of the safe, Green and Slot had a cigarette just outside the main door to the suite. The Burns men of Green's shift relaxed in the hallway.

The two shots exploded the silence a second or two before the alarm went off.

The shots were inside the suite. The alarm clanged like a wounded elephant.

"Come on!" Green shouted.

The Burns guards poured into the suite. They all rushed into the room where the safe was.

"Stay alert!" Slot snapped to his Burns man who was on the front door.

He watched his man pull his gun and stand alert, and then he hurried inside the suite and into the room where the safe was. The first thing he saw was the open safe. The second thing he saw was the body of the guard lying in front of the safe with Ed Green bending over it.

"Twice, right through the heart!" Green said.

"Search the place!" Slot snapped. "Tear it apart."

Slot-Machine and Green checked the safe. It was clean as a whistle. It had been neatly and expertly burned open. The torch was still on the floor. The safe was a small one, and it had not taken much burning.

Ed Green called the police. Slot-Machine called the Burns men on the single night exit from the hotel downstairs, and told them to start the scanner and let no one out of the hotel without checking them. By this time all the Burns guards had torn the apartment apart, and had found nothing at all.

By the time Captain Gazzo of Homicide arrived, in company with Sergeant Jonas and Lieutenant Mingo of Safe and Loft, the Moomers and McNamara were also there. Maximillian Moomer was almost hysterical.

"Search them all! Search Kelly! No one could have gotten in or out of this room!" Maximillian wailed.

"He's got a point," Captain Gazzo said to Slot-Machine.

"Green and I were together," Slot said.

"I wouldn't trust Green too far, either," Sergeant Jonas said.

Lieutenant Mingo had finished his examination of the suite. Now he broke in on the hysterical owners of the rubies.

"Here it is, Captain. Safe was torched—an easy job. All windows are locked inside. A caterpillar couldn't have come up or down those walls outside anyway. The torch is still here. We searched all the guards, nothing on them. The Burns men on the doors never left their posts."

Gazzo turned to the Burns man who had remained at the front door of the suite the whole time.

"No one came out?"

"No, sir," the Burns man said. "I never budged. The guy at the elevators never moved, and no one came out except Green, Kelly, and the other guards."

"In other words," Gazzo said. "No one went in, no one came out. Only—we've got a dead man and we don't have five rubies worth a quarter of a million in real cold money."

In the room everyone looked at everyone else. The Moomers and McNamara were ready to cry like babies.

It was an hour later, and Gazzo and Mingo had been over and over the situation fifty times with Slot-Machine Kelly and Ed Green. The morgue wagon had come, and the white-suited attendants were packing the body in its final basket.

"The Burns boys from my shift want to go home," Green said. "We've searched every part of them except their appendix."

"Okay," Gazzo said. "But you'd better check them through that scanner downstairs, just in case."

"That's some machine," Lieutenant Mingo said admiringly. "You just dab the rubies with a little radioactive material, and the scanner spots them forty feet away."

"It also spots radium watch dials and false teeth," Gazzo pointed out. "Let's get back to our little puzzle, okay? First how did anyone get into the room?"

Everyone looked blank. Slot-Machine rubbed the stump of his missing arm. It was an old habit he had when he was thinking.

"It's impossible," Slot-Machine said, "so there has to be an answer. Look at the odds. It's a million to one against the guy being invisible. It's two million to one against him having wings. It's a couple of hundred to one against that guard having shot himself."

"Very funny, Kelly," Gazzo said.

"Wait," Slot-Machine said. "I'm serious. We

got to rule out science-fiction, weird tales, and magic. So how did he get *into* the room past all of Green's guards? Be simple. There's only one way—he was already in the room."

"Kelly's shootin' the vein again," Jonas said.

Even the morgue attendants turned to look at Slot-Machine. They had the body by head and feet, and they paused with it in mid-air, their mouths open. Gazzo looked disgusted. But Ed Green and Lieutenant Mingo did not.

"He's right," Ed Green said. "We never searched, never thought of it."

"It's not an uncommon MO," Lieutenant Mingo agreed. "Now that I think of it, the suite is full of closets piled with junk. It wouldn't have been hard as long as the guy knew the guards didn't search."

Captain Gazzo morosely watched the morgue attendants close their basket and carry it out. The Captain did not seem very pleased about the whole matter.

"Which means the joint was cased," Gazzo said. "Okay, it figures. Our ghost has to be a pro. He got in by hiding here for about five hours. Now how did he get out?"

"Yeh," Sergeant Jonas said. "You guys didn't search the place because a snake couldn't have sneaked out of this suite."

"You had twelve guards around and in the suite, damn it," Gazzo said. "Twelve! A worm couldn't have crawled out!"

Slot-Machine seemed to be watching something very interesting in the center of the far wall. His one good hand was busily rubbing away at the stump of his left arm. Now he began to talk without taking his eyes away from the blank wall.

"Let's talk it out," Slot said. "He didn't fly out, he didn't crawl out, he didn't dig out, he . . ."

"Trap door?" Sergeant Jonas said.

Lieutenant Mingo shook his head.

"First thing I checked. The floors are solid. Checked the rooms below, too," Mingo added.

"Secret doors in the walls?" Gazzo suggested.

"Hell, Captain," Ed Green said, "we know a little about our work. We went over the walls with a microscope."

Slot rubbed his stump and nodded. "Keep it up, we're ruling out. Look, the guy was a pro, he was in the room, he had to have his plan to get out. It had to be workable. It had to be simple."

"Maybe he's still inside the room!" Green said.

"Negative," Mingo replied. "I combed the place."

"What do we have," Slot-Machine said. "He's in here, and there are eleven guards outside and one inside with him. He shoots the guard, torches the safe, and . . . Hold on! That's not right. He burned that safe fast, but not fast enough to do it between the time of the shots and all of us busting in.

"So he must have torched the safe *first*—then shot the guard and set off the alarm! He couldn't have torched the safe with the guard still awake, so it follows that he must have knocked the guard out. But why did he kill the guard later? He knew the shots would bring us running. He must have *wanted* the shots to bring us in just when it happened! Why did he pull the job at the exact moment when there were twelve guards instead of six? He timed it for the shift change!"

There was a long silence in the room. Sergeant Jonas looked blank. Ed Green was obviously trying to think. Mingo shook his head. Only Gazzo seemed to see what Slot-Machine was seeing on the blank wall.

"No one came out," Gazzo said softly. "There was no way out. Only a killer got out with five rubies. So, like Kelly says, we rule out magic, and somehow a guy walked out."

Gazzo turned to the Burns guard who had been on the main door.

"Do you know *all* the guards who work with you?" Gazzo asked.

"Sure, Captain," the Burns man said. "Well, I mean, I know most of them to look at. I know the boys in my shift, and—"

"Yeh," Gazzo cut him short. "There it is. So damned simple. He just walked out in the confusion. Right, Kelly? He was probably behind the front door waiting. He probably even helped search the suite with all of you. He was just . . ."

"Wearing a Burns uniform," Slot-Machine said. "He simply mingled in with us. That's why he timed it for two shifts to be here. He mingled with us, and walked out through the front door!"

The swearing in the room would have done credit to a Foreign Legion barrack. Everyone began to move at once. Mingo called in to alert the Safe and Loft Squad to start watching all fences in the city. Ed Green went to check with the guard on the elevator. Jonas called downstairs to the single exit door. Gazzo just swore. Ed Green came back.

"Burns man on the elevator says he did see a Burns man go for the stairs!" Green said. "God, he was lucky! How could he know we wouldn't search him? I mean, we searched all the guards mighty quick. He couldn't be sure he could get away so fast! He took a hell of a risk!"

Sergeant Jonas hung up the telephone in anger.

"Green's shift of Burns men passed out twenty minutes ago," Jonas said, "and they were all clean. That scanner didn't find anything on them."

"How many men?" Gazzo said.

"Six," Jonas said.

Gazzo cursed. "He's out!"

"But the rubies aren't," Green said. "He must have stashed them somewhere inside. That means he plans to come back for them."

Slot-Machine shook his head. "I don't know. He planned this mighty careful. We could have searched him right here in the room like Green says."

"All right, genius," Gazzo said. "You've figured how he got into the suite, and how he got out. Now tell us how he plans to get the stones out if he didn't stash them. No one's gone out of this hotel since it happened, except through that front door where the scanner is!"

"He just had to know about the scanner," Slot-Machine said. "This was a fool-proof plan.

So he must have figured a way around that scanner."

"Great," Gazzo said. "Only no one got out of here without being checked."

Slot-Machine stood up suddenly.

"One person did! Gazzo, come on!"

Slot-Machine led them all from the suite in a fast dash for the first elevator.

The night was dark on the city. The streets were bare and cold in the night. Traffic moved in small, tight groups down Sixth Avenue as the lights changed like small packs of animals. The late night revelers staggered their weary way home. In the all-night delicatessens the clerks yawned behind their counters through the gaudy plate-glass windows.

In Gazzo's unmarked car, the five sat alert and waiting. Gazzo swore softly, and Ed Green smoked hard on his cigarette. Slot-Machine leaned forward tensely and watched the car-exit from below the towering glass and steel of the North American Hotel. Suddenly, Slot leaned over and touched Jonas who was behind the wheel.

The morgue wagon came out from under the hotel and turned left down Sixth Avenue. Jonas eased the car away from the curb and followed the morgue wagon.

They drove down Sixth Avenue, turned across town toward the west, and the morgue wagon moved steadily on its way a half a block away. The silent procession turned again on Ninth Avenue and continued on downtown toward the Morgue.

Suddenly, as the morgue wagon slowed at a traffic light that was just changing from red to green on the staggered light system of Ninth Avenue, the back door of the wagon opened. A man jumped out. The man hit the pavement, stumbled, and then began to run fast toward the west.

The man wore the uniform of a Burns guard.

The morgue wagon continued on its grim journey. Jonas swung the police car in a squealing turn and gunned the motor down the side street. The running man was forty feet ahead. Jonas roared after him. The man heard the motor, looked back, and then dashed toward a fence. In a flash he was over the fence and gone.

Slot-Machine and Gazzo were out of the police car before Jonas had brought it to a halt. Mingo and Green were close behind them. Slot-Machine was the first of the three over the fence with a powerful pull of his single arm.

The man in the Burns uniform was scrambling over a second fence just ahead.

The chase went on down the rows of back yards and fences in the silent darkness of the night. At each fence Slot-Machine gained on the uniformed runner. As he went over the last fence before a looming, dark building ended the row of back yards, the uniformed man turned and shot.

Slot-Machine ducked, but didn't stop. He went over the last fence in a mad leap and dive. Another shot hit just below him, and wood splinters cut his cheek. In the next second, Slot-Machine was on the uniformed man who was trying frantically to get off one more shot.

The man in uniform never made it. Slot-Machine drove him back against the brick wall of the building with the force of his rush. His pivoting body slammed into the wall, his gun went flying, and he came off the wall like a rebounding cue ball on a lively pool table.

Slot's one good hand caught the uniformed man across the throat. He collapsed with a single choking squawk like the dying gurgle of a beheaded chicken.

By the time Gazzo, Green, and Mingo had caught up with Slot and his victim, Slot was holding the rubies in his hand. In the beam of light from Mingo's flashlight, the deep red stones shone like wet blood.

Slot-Machine handed the pistol to Gazzo.

"This'll be the murder weapon," he said. "It's a regulation Burns pistol, he was a meticulous type."

Mingo was bending over the supine man who had not even begun to wake up. The Lieutenant looked up at Gazzo and shook his head.

"No one I recognize," Mingo said. "Chances are he's not a known jewel thief."

"That figures," Slot said. "I think you'll find his name is Julius Honder, a legitimate jewel merchant."

"Why Honder?" Ed Green said.

"He had to have cased the job," Slot said. "He knew we'd all go running into the suite. Remember that woman? The one who thought the alarm was a waiter's button? She was Honder's secretary. I expect we'll find her waiting at Honder's office for the boss to bring home the loot."

From the dark, Sergeant Jonas came up. The Homicide Sergeant looked down at the sleeping killer and thief.

"So he made another change," Jonas said, "and played one of the morgue boys?"

Slot-Machine shook his head.

"Too risky," Slot-Machine said. "Gazzo said no one had gotten out of the building through the front door. You don't take a stiff out the front way, right? He knew that. The stiff went out through the basement. What tipped me was what I said myself—why did he kill the guard *after* he'd opened the safe and got the stones? To get us into the room, I said.

"Only the *alarm* alone would have done that. There had to be another reason. All at once it came to me. He killed the guard just to have a way of hiding the stones on the body and getting them out!"

They all looked down at the uniformed man who was just beginning to groan as he came awake. There was a certain admiration in the eyes of the police.

"He knew we wouldn't search the dead man until you got him to the morgue," Slot-Machine said. "So he had to get the stones from the body before it reached the slab. It was quite simple. He just hid in the wagon. Who would think to look for him there?"

Later, in the tavern where Joe Harris was working, Ed Green leaned on the bar beside Slot-Machine Kelly and bought Slot a fourth expensive Irish whisky. Green was still admiring Slot.

"You just got to think logical," Slot-Machine

explained. "Figure the odds. Miracles are out, so there has to be a simple explanation. The more complicated it looks in real life, the simpler it has to be when you figure it out."

"You make it sound easy," Green said. "Have another shot."

"Twist his arm," Joe said as he poured. "The thinker. So it turned out it was Julius Honder, right?"

"Yeh," Slot said as he tasted his Irish whisky happily. "He needed cash. Too bad he needed a corpse. He'll fry crisp as bacon."

THE EPISODE OF THE CODEX' CURSE

C. DALY KING

HIS SLIM OUTPUT prevents Charles Daly King (1895–1963) from being ranked at the top rung of detective fiction writers, but he has produced some masterly works, notably in *The Curious Mr. Tarrant*, selected by Ellery Queen for his *Queen's Quorum* as one of the 106 most important volumes of mystery short stories of all time, where it was described as containing "the most imaginative detective short stories of our time."

Born in New York City, King graduated from Yale University, received his master's degree in psychology from Columbia University, and a PhD from Yale for an electromagnetic study of sleep. He was a practicing psychologist who wrote several books on the subject, including *Beyond Behaviorism* (1927), *The Psychology of Consciousness* (1932), and the posthumously published *States of Human Consciousness* (1963). In the 1930s, King divided his time between Summit, New Jersey, and Bermuda, where he wrote his detective novels. With the advent of World War II, he stopped writing mysteries and devoted the rest of his life to his work in psychology. As a mystery writer, King is an enigmatic figure, at times writing brilliantly with the verve and assurance of a master; at other times he is as frustrating as the club bore who tells the same stories over and over again. He once inserted a fifteen-page treatise on economic theory into a detective novel for absolutely no reason.

"The Episode of the Codex' Curse" was first published in *The Curious Mr. Tarrant* (London, Collins, 1935).

THE EPISODE
OF THE CODEX' CURSE

C. DALY KING

Characters of the Episode

JERRY PHELAN, the narrator

JAMES BLAKE, Curator of Central American
Antiquities

MARIUS HARTMANN, a collector

ROGER THORPE, a Director of the
Metropolitan Museum

MURCHISON, a Museum guard

TREVIS TARRANT, interested in the bizarre

KATOH, Tarrant's butler-valet

I HAD NOT wanted to spend the night in the
Museum in the first place. It had been a foolish
business, as I realised thoroughly now that the
lights had gone out. A blown fuse, of course; but
what could blow a fuse at this time of night? Still,
it must be something of that nature, perhaps
a short in the circuit somewhere. Murchison,
the guard in the corridor outside, had gone off
to investigate. Before leaving he had stepped in
and made his intention clear; then he had closed
the door, whose handle he had shaken vigorously
to assure both of us that it was locked. The lock
had had to be turned from the outside, for the
door was without means of being secured from
within. I was alone.

The room was in the basement. It was comparatively narrow and about fifty feet long; but,
since it was situated at one of the corners of the
great building, its shape was that of an L, with
the result that, from where I sat near its only

door, no more than half of the room could be
seen. Of the three barred windows near its ceiling, the one in my half of the room was already
becoming dimly visible as a slightly lighter
oblong in the darkness.

The darkness had given me quite a jolt. Earlier, at half-past ten, when I had propped my
chair back against the wall and settled down
to read my way through the hours ahead with
the latest book on tennis strategy, it had been
very quiet; I had seen to it that the three windows were all closed and fastened, so that even
the distant purr of the cars across Central Park
had been inaudible. Murchison, from outside,
had reported every hour, but of course he had
other duties than patrolling this one corridor,
although he was giving it most of his attention
to-night. We had considered it better, when he
was called away, to leave the door locked and this
he had done on each occasion. At first he had
unlocked it and either come in or lounged in the
doorway when reporting, but lately he had been
contenting himself with calling to me through
the closed entrance.

The silence, which to begin with had been
complete, seemed somehow to have gotten
steadily more and more profound. Impercepti-
bly but steadily. Oppressive was the word probably, for by two a.m. I had the distinct feeling that
it would have been possible to cut off a chunk of
it and weigh it on a scale.

I am a person who is essentially fond of games

and outdoor life generally; being cooped up like this was uncongenial as well as unusual. As the silence grew deeper and deeper and Murchison's visits farther and farther apart, the whole thing commenced to get on my nerves. Inside, I undoubtedly began to fidget. There was no possibility of backing out now, however. The diagrams showing just how one followed the ball to the net for volley (the proper time to do so being explicitly set forth in the text) made less claim upon my attention as the hours drew past. I had finally ended by closing the book and dropping it impatiently to the floor beside me.

Could there possibly be anything in this Curse business? Absurd! I stared across at the Codex lying on the little table near the closed door. What power for either good or evil could be possessed by some unknown Aztec, dead hundreds of years ago? It was an indication of my unaccustomed nerviness that I found it of comfort to reflect that I was in a world-famous Museum in the centre of modern New York, to be specific on upper Fifth Avenue; there must be a score of guards in the Museum itself, a precinct station was but a few blocks away, the forces of civilisation that never sleep surrounded me on all sides. I glanced at the Codex again and gave something of a start. Had it moved ever so slightly since I had looked at it before? Hell, this was ridiculous. Then the lights went out.

The effect in any case is startling and in the present instance it was doubly so. Nothing could have been more unexpected. Unconsciously, I suppose, one becomes accustomed to hearing the click of a button or a switch when lights are extinguished; even in a roomful of people, unexpected darkness descending suddenly causes uneasiness. And I was not in a roomful of people by any means. The unbroken silence preceding and following made a sort of continuity that ought to have prevented any abrupt change. Darkness, silently instantaneous, for a moment was unbelievable.

Murchison's voice through the door a minute later was, I admit, a bit of a relief. He opened the door, flashed his light about for a moment, then locked it again and hurried away.

The guard's light had shown the Codex quietly in its place on the table. Well, naturally; how could it have moved, since I had not been near it and no one else was in the room? A Curse from the dark past of Aztlan. The third night. Nonsense. Here was merely a matter of a short circuit. It suddenly occurred to me that that, too, might not be unimportant. Where there are short circuits, there are sometimes fires. The door was locked on the outside. I could break any of the windows, of course, if they couldn't be unfastened, but what then? All of them were guarded by sturdy iron bars set in the stonework of the building. It was plain enough that in any emergency I couldn't get out by myself.

I simply couldn't help thinking how often these coincidences seemed to happen. An ancient warning and a modern calamity. It was a silly notion; it persisted in running through my head. In that inanimate manuscript written by dead Aztec hands there couldn't possibly be anything——

When I had come into town that morning, nothing had been further from my mind than spending the night in the Metropolitan Museum. At most I had anticipated no more than calling there for a few minutes around noon to take Jim Blake out to lunch. Blake is considerably older than I am, being in fact a friend of one of my aunts; our common interest, however, is not the aunt but the game of golf, as to which we are both enthusiasts. Thus, having some business in town, I thought I might run up and compare notes with him about a recently opened course in New Jersey which we had both played, though not together. Blake had been with the Museum for years and, I understand, is now the Keeper, or whatever they call it, of their Central American antiquities.

When I found him in his basement office, however, I discovered Marius Hartmann already with him, a fellow about my own age whom I knew slightly at college and never liked very much. A quiet, studious chap, though I suppose that's nothing against him. What I really disliked was his contempt for all sports, a matter he took little trouble to conceal. I had not seen him since graduation but had heard that he had come into a large inheritance and taken up collecting. This interest, I suppose, had brought him and Blake together but, not knowing of their acquaintance, I was considerably surprised to find him in the office.

He shook hands with me pleasantly enough but it was evident that his interest had been excited and was wholly taken up by the subject he had been discussing with Blake.

"Why, a Codex like that is priceless, literally priceless!" he exclaimed, as soon as the greetings were over. "Such a find isn't reported once in a century. And when it is, it's usually spurious."

Blake, leaning back in his chair with his feet resting on a corner of his desk, grunted acquiescence. "Fortunately there's no question of authenticity this time," he asserted. "Our own man found it, sealed away in a small stone wall-vault in the *teocalli*. More by chance than anything else, he says himself. The place where it was must have been rather like a safe; they never did find out how it was properly opened. It was partly broken open during the excavation work and when they saw that some sort of storage chamber had been struck, they finished it up with a pick. As I say, it was only a small receptacle, a few feet each way, I understand."

"I suppose that accounts for its preservation," Hartmann reflected. "Over seven hundred years, you say? It's a long time, that, but if this temple safe was sealed up—— Of course, we do know of manuscripts as old as seven hundred years. The oldest Codex I have is about four hundred," he added.

I thought it was high time to find out what a Codex is, so I asked.

"A Codex, Jerry," replied Blake with half a smile, "is a manuscript book. Strictly speaking, the thing we're talking about is not a Codex; it's written on stuff resembling papyrus and it is rolled rather than being separated into leaves and bound. But so many of these Central American records *are* Codices written by Spaniards or Spanish-speaking Aztecs after the conquest,

that we have been calling this record a Codex, too."

"But seven hundred years?" I was puzzled.

"Oh, yes, it far antedates the conquest. In fact, it purports to have been inscribed by the Chief Priest of the nation at Chapultepec on the occasion of the end of one Great Cycle and the beginning of the next. 'Tying up the bundles of bundles of years,' they called it; a bundle, or cycle, being fifty-two years and a bundle of bundles being fifty-two cycles, or twenty-seven hundred and four years. The end of the particular Great Cycle in question has been pretty well identified with our own date, 1195 A.D."

Hartmann's eyes were glistening as he leaned forward. "What a treasure!"

"You knew of it some time ago, I believe?" Blake asked him.

"Yes. Yes, I did. Roger Thorpe, one of your directors, told me. I offered the Museum forty thousand dollars for it, through him, before it ever got here. Turned down, of course . . . But I had only the vaguest idea about the contents. It appears to be even more valuable than I realised; undoubtedly it contains an historical record of the whole preceding Great Cycle."

"More than that," Blake chuckled, "more than that. When this is published, it is going to make a sensation, you can be sure . . . I don't mind telling you in confidence that the Codex contains the historical high spots of the preceding five Great Cycles, including place names and important dates of the entire Aztec migration. In some way we have not been able to ascertain as yet, the occasion of its writing was even more impressive than the end of a Great Cycle; apparently it was the ending of an especially significant number of Great Cycles in their dating system. Possibly thirteen; we're not sure."

Frankly the subject wasn't of much interest to me. I couldn't work up the excitement that Hartmann obviously felt, and Blake, too, to a lesser degree. But I didn't want to mope in a corner about the thing. More to stay in the conversation than for any other reason, I asked what sort of writing was employed in the manuscript.

"Eh, what sort of writing? Why, picture writing, naturally. Much more developed than the American Indian, though; more like the Egyptian hieroglyphs. Some ideographs; Chapultepec, for example, which means 'grasshopper-hill,' is represented by a grasshopper on a hill. But there is a lot of phonetic transcription also, in which the symbols stand for their sounds rather than the objects pictured. The curious thing is that this Codex, by far the earliest Aztec manuscript we know of, uses a much more highly developed script than the later writings just preceding the conquest. It certainly makes the Popol-Vuh look just like what some of us have always suspected— the ignorant translation by a Spanish priest of traditions that had already been badly mangled and half forgotten by the natives themselves."

Marius Hartmann had been doing some rapid calculation. He said: "But if this covers five Great Cycles, it goes back thirteen thousand five hundred years or more from 1195. Thirteen thousand five hundred years! Why, that's— why——"

"Oh, yes," acknowledged Blake with an understanding grin. "It is indeed. You know the controversies concerning the origin of the Aztecs, the location of the original Aztlan from which they traditionally migrated. I've only had a chance for one look at the Codex myself but it appears to me to be a highly circumstantial history without any embroidery at all. The writer states definitely that Aztlan is nothing else than the Atlantis mentioned by Plato. He even gives the clear location of the ancestors of the Aztecs in one of the western, coastal provinces of the continent. After the catastrophe the survivors found themselves on the North American coast, apparently in the vicinity of what have now become the Virginia capes. From there, after the passage of thousands of years and through the operation of a good many different causes, their migrations finally carried them into central Mexico."

Hartmann's mouth was partly open and his eyes, I thought, would soon be popping out. "You—you believe this is an authentic record?" he stammered.

"I can only tell you this, but I really mean it. I've been here a good many years now, Hartmann, and so far as my own experience goes, it's the most authentic document that I have ever come across. I'd be perfectly willing to stake my reputation on it."

There could be no doubt about it; the man's eyes would pop out in another minute. That would never do.

I said, "How about getting some lunch? I'm empty as a football, for one."

The lunch was highly unsatisfactory from my point of view at any rate. Highly so. I had no opportunity to discuss the new course with Blake, or anything else about golf, for that matter. Marius Hartmann came with us; he stuck to Blake like a leech and there was no getting rid of him. Worse, they both continued to discuss the matter of the Codex with undiminished zeal. Most of the time I ate in silence and by the approach of the end of the meal I was pretty thoroughly fed up on everything connected with Aztecs.

It was during lunch that the question of the Curse came up. It appeared that the Codex really comprised two separate parts, although both were written on the same manuscript. The second part was the historical section already mentioned, while the first dealt with a religious ritual or training of some kind. "Curious," Blake observed, "very curious. The title of the first part is almost identical with the actual title of the Egyptian Book of the Dead, *Pert em Hru*, 'Coming into Light.' The Aztec title is *Light Emergence*, but the contents are certainly not concerned with a burial ritual or anything like it."

Preceding this part of the Codex and introducing the entire manuscript, a species of warning had been placed. Blake quoted some of it. "Beware," it ran, "lest vengeance follow sacrilege. Who would read the Sacred Words, let him be instructed, for ignorance conducteth disaster. Quetzalcoatl, the Reminder, (goeth) in dread splendour. The desecration of Light-Words is an heavy thing; in an unholy resting-place the third night bringeth the Empty." And considerably more to the same general effect.

"It doesn't sound much like the Codex Chimalpopoca, does it?" ventured Hartmann.

"Not a bit. No, we have to do with something along different lines here. The Chimalpopoca is not much more than folklore at best, written some time after the conquest, even if it is in the native language. Our Codex is a genuine article; the man who wrote it was quite certainly the religious head and he had no doubts as to what he was writing about. Not only is the form of expression quite different but the content is, too; even the language is far more evolved. The author isn't guessing, in other words; he gives the strongest impression both of accuracy and of knowledge."

"How do you mean, Blake? Are you hinting that you take the opening Curse seriously?"

"Well, no. I didn't mean that exactly. I was referring more to the historical section and even to the ritual part itself. That seems to be a good bit more explicit, in parts at least, than most such compilations; from what I had a chance to read, one section appears to lead up to and introduce the following one, quite otherwise than in the usual haphazard collections. It gave me rather a strange feeling, just glancing through it. . . . As a matter of fact I've heard that you take such passages as the prefatory Curse more seriously than most of us."

Hartmann looked up from his salad. "As a matter of fact, I do. When I meet the real thing. Of course there was a lot of pseudo-magic in Greek times that couldn't affect a child. I mean the real thing," he repeated. "I can assure you that I'm much more sceptical about the dictum of a modern scientist than I am about that of a High Priest of, say, the Fourth Dynasty."

Blake smiled at our companion's earnestness. "Can't say I feel your way entirely. However, if that's your opinion, to-night is your night."

"Why? How is that?"

"'In an unholy resting-place the third night bringeth the Empty.' We've finally gotten the Codex to its permanent resting-place and I've no doubt at all that the writer would consider it unholy. To complete the point, to-night is the third one." He paused and smiled again. "If I took it literally, I'd expect the Codex to vanish or undergo spontaneous combustion or something of the kind before morning. I shouldn't feel any too pleasant myself, either, for I happen to be its custodian now."

"Oh, you're all right. It doesn't say anything about the custodian," Hartmann answered. I was surprised, I must admit, at the entire seriousness of his words, which were accompanied by no hint of a smile. "About reading it, that's another matter; I don't know whether I'd be prepared to try it or not, 'uninstructed.' But its custody, especially in an official capacity, will surely be harmless. It's not as if you had stolen it or even been the one to dig it up."

Blake looked a touch astonished himself, though not as much as I was. He explained to me later that enthusiasts often get these notions. He had known a man once who had been determined to obtain an Egyptian mummy and had finally procured one which he kept in his library as his most prized possession; but he had assured Blake that were he ever prevented from doing a proper obeisance—"purification ceremony," he called it—night and morning upon entering the room, he would get rid of the mummy the same day. I, however, had not met this man and Hartmann's sentiments, I confess, were strengthening my disposition to consider him something of an ass. Too much learning—some old fellow said once, I think—is worse than not enough.

But he was continuing. "About to-night, though, that's a different thing. *If* it will really be the third night and *if* it was set forth literally in the warning just as you said, I should be frankly anxious, in your place. What precautions have you taken?"

"It's really the third night," Blake acknowledged. "And the threat, or whatever you want to call it, is not ambiguous; it is simply and literally that the third night will bring 'the Empty.'

But, thank heaven, I haven't your idea about it and I'm not anxious at all. My word, if I worried about those things, I'd have been out of my mind long ago; I'm surrounded every working day by more curses and threats from the past than I can count. I just don't bother about 'em. To tell you the truth, I haven't taken any precautions," he finished, "and I don't intend to."

"Surely you've got it locked up somewhere?"

"Oh, surely. Your friend Thorpe, by the way, is of your mind; he seems quite worried over the matter. You ought to talk to him about it . . . Yes, it's down in one of the extra rooms in the basement, locked up naturally. No one could get at it down there. In the first place, a thief wouldn't know where to look for it, in the second, although the room isn't a bank vault by any means, it *is* locked; and in the third place, the usual patrols will be on duty near it anyhow. That's safe enough from my point of view."

"Oh, thieves." Hartmann snorted contemptuously. "I wouldn't be concerned about modern sneak-thieves; no market for such a thing, anyhow. I'm thinking of something quite different than that, I assure you."

"So is Thorpe apparently. I can't make him out this time. He has insisted upon putting the Codex into the same room every night with his precious statue from Palestine, until we are ready to put it on exhibition in the main halls. *I* believe he has some superstition about that statue; thinks it will be a guardian angel or something. He surprised me, really. You do too, if you're serious. What do you imagine could happen, thieves ruled out?"

The other man shrugged. "Nothing— possibly. These warnings don't materialise sometimes but in my opinion that is because we don't know enough to interpret them correctly. Neither you nor I have any definite knowledge as to what 'the Empty' means. Maybe your Codex will disappear to-night, although a thief would be the last thing I should look for in such a case. I don't know; but I am certain of this, that something, and something more or less unpleasant, will happen on the third night that that bit of

ancient wisdom rests in a museum. . . . After all, a museum is simply an exhibition house for the ignorantly curious, or vice versa."

Blake grinned his appreciation. "No reflections, I take it? A lot of us have to earn our bread and butter, you know. . . . Well, why don't you sit up with it to-night and see what happens? I'll get you permission."

"Not a chance! I'm going to a ball at the Waldorf to-night; but if I had nothing to do, you can take it I wouldn't do that. I don't want to be anywhere near your Codex on the third night."

"I believe you're more than half in earnest," said Blake, regarding our companion with an estimating glance. "It's tosh, you know."

Hartmann suggested, "Ask Jerry. He has heard both sides." Turning to me. "What's your idea, old man; will anything happen, or won't it?"

It was an opportunity I couldn't resist. I said briefly, probably all too briefly, "*Nuts!*"

He leaned back, smiling as he lit a cigarette. "Nuts, eh? . . . Well, Jerry, I'll give you a thousand you won't stay up with the Codex and, further, if you do, that something will happen and you won't be able to prevent it . . . On?"

Doubtless I looked as bewildered as I felt at the offer. Before I could pull my wits together and reply, Blake volunteered: "Wish I could take you myself. As a matter of fact, though, I'm taking Jerry's aunt to the opera to-night and I don't intend to miss out on that. You might tell her sometime, Jerry, that I paid one grand, extra, for the pleasure of seeing her this evening."

"Sure, glad to." My impatience with the whole business had reached a crucial point and I was feeling fairly irked. Not a word about golf the entire time and in another minute or so I should have to leave. "Look here," I said, "I can't afford to take you for a thousand but you're on for a hundred. I'll spend the night with your damned Codex and nothing will happen to it at all or about it at all. So what?"

"So there's a hundred for me," came the exasperating answer.

"Nuts again. Draw your cheque."

Suddenly he was serious. "You mean this? You really intend to go through with it?"

"Naturally."

"All right. Now listen to me. A hundred isn't enough to make me want to have you take a risk. And you'll be taking one, no matter what you think about it. I'm sorry now that I made the proposition. I'd much rather call it off. Shall we?"

Let him crawl out like that? "Nothing doing, my lad. It was your suggestion. It's on now; I'm chaperoning the Codex to-night and collecting in the morning." If there's one thing I can't stand, it's these fellows who know more than every one else about everything. Except golf, of course.

"As you will." He shrugged, as who remarks that sagacity is wasted on any but sages. "Do you mind, Jerry, if I call you up once or twice during the night? I'd feel a little easier."

"Call away. All you want."

"It can be arranged, Blake, can't it?"

"Easily. I'll have the phone in the room plugged through before I leave." He smiled broadly, with more pleasure than I could muster over the tedious performance. "I don't think, though, that I'll stay up fretting over Jerry," he added.

"No?" The tone had just that accent of the sceptical tinged with the supercilious that is appropriate, I suppose, to these occasions.

The waiter was bringing our check.

Late that afternoon Blake showed me the room. As I have said it was L-shaped. There was a roll-top desk in it and a flat one, both obviously unused. Several piles of bundles, pamphlets no doubt or some of the monographs the museum is frequently publishing, were stacked against the long back wall. There were also a few small boxes, various odds and ends that accumulate in a disused apartment. The statue, still in its skeleton crate whose sides were covered with sacking, stood at the farther end of the room beyond the flat desk on which rested the telephone instrument. Life-size, apparently, to judge from the

crate. "Thorpe's sweetheart," said Blake in a dry voice. "He won't even let us see it. It's a particularly nifty one of Astarte, I understand. Came in ten days ago from the Palestine expedition and he insists on unpacking it himself. Hasn't gotten around to it yet."

He laid the Codex on the small table in the other half of the room, near the entrance door. It was contained in a cylinder of wood, black with age, on one side of which two symbols, or letters, had been skilfully inlaid in white shell. "Sacred very-very," Blake translated them, explaining that the Codex was in its original package, as found. He had taken it carelessly from one of the drawers of his own desk.

As we turned to the door, he said: "Here's a note I've written for you to Murchison, the guard who will be on duty down here to-night. He's not here yet. And I'll introduce you to the supervisor as we go out, so there will be no trouble when you come in after dinner."

On the way up to the main entrance I surprised an unwonted expression on Blake's face. He said abruptly, "Of course, Jerry, I don't really know much about that Codex or its origin. Something might happen—I suppose. Watch your step. And if anything does begin to break, get out."

I stared at him in plain amazement. Through the big doors the sunlight was slanting cheerfully across Fifth Avenue. "Forget it. I'm making the easiest hundred bucks I've ever found. . . . Remember me to Aunt Doris."

There wasn't any sunlight now. I sat back on my chair, staring into black murk. I couldn't fool myself into believing that I was relaxed; I realised in fact, that my muscles were tensed as if for a spring. Not that I had any idea where to spring or for what purpose.

Funny, how thick the darkness seemed to be. One's eyes usually become accustomed to lack of light within a relatively short time, but the window continued as dim as at first, minute after minute. I couldn't see the table, only a few feet away. This darkness was like the silence—it had weight—it *pressed*. The cigarettes I had been smoking all evening, perhaps? That was a comforting thought and I clung to it as long as I could. Still, cigarette smoke doesn't show a preference, in a closed room, for one part rather than for another. I became more and more certain that the gloom was deeper in the corner where the Codex rested than anywhere else. Where the mischief was Murchison? How long *did* it take him to plug in a new fuse, anyhow?

A little rustle! Little enough, it would not even have been perceptible ordinarily; in the silence of the room it was not only perceptible but it just couldn't be put down to imagination. Thank God it didn't come from the direction of the table. It was only momentary and the silence resumed, as leaden as ever. *Had* I imagined it? As I strained my ears for a repetition, Blake's words occurred to me—"If anything breaks, get out." It also occurred to me that the Codex was between me and the door. The fact that the door was locked, if I remember correctly, didn't occur to me till later.

Why hadn't I brought a flashlight? I hadn't brought a thing, actually. A gun would have helped a lot, too. I'm a good shot with an automatic; but a good shot without an automatic is about as useful as a fine yachtsman in the subway. I couldn't blame myself for that, however. When I had left home in the morning I hadn't foreseen a night of conflict with the nebulous menace of a piece of manuscript.

I suppose your eardrums, if you are listening intently, become supersensitised. Something about "sets," I think. At any rate the noise that broke out was terrific; it seemed as if fifty devils had started screaming simultaneously. I don't know whether I yelled or not (probably did) but I gave such a jump that I upset the chair and found myself sprawling on the floor, supported by one foot, one knee and one hand. As I scrambled to my feet, still instinctively crouching, I was too scared to do any thinking. It was only when the noise stopped and then began again, that I realised the telephone was ringing.

I was relieved. For the moment I just straightened up and felt like singing the first song that came into my head. Then I became annoyed, suddenly, at the infernal din the thing was making. I started toward the bend in the room and the instrument beyond it; and of course knocked a couple of bundles off the pile at the corner. With a hearty "Damnation!" I took up the receiver.

"Hallo."

"Hartmann speaking from the Waldorf. Jerry, is everything O.K. so far?"

That fellow certainly wouldn't find out how uncomfortable I was, if I could help it. I felt grateful to him, though, for the steadying effect of his silly voice. But I wasn't prepared yet for much talking. "Certainly. Why not?"

"You're sure? Nothing a bit out of the way has happened?"

"Well, the lights seem to be out for the moment."

"What? . . . My God! . . . "

I waited but there wasn't any more.

"What do you mean, my God?"

The quiet over the wire continued for so long that I began considering the possibility that he had left the phone. Then his voice came through excitedly.

"Jerry, get out of that room! Listen, Jerry, please, *please* will you get out? I'll pay you the hundred, I'll——. Get out now! Before it happens. Now!"

I'll admit I had a hard time answering that one, but I did. I said, "I won't get out at all. Anyhow, I can't; the door's locked——"

"Oh my God! You say the door's *locked*?" Hartmann's voice rose into a kind of wail that, under the circumstances, wasn't the pleasantest sound I could have thought of. "Jerry, Jerry! Listen to me; listen carefully. If you can't get out, you must do this. You must; understand, you must! Don't go near the Codex. Get as far away from it as you can, even if only across the room. And lie down on the floor. Do you hear me, Jerry? You must lie down on the floor; get as——"

Click.

And there I was, inanely banging the hook of the telephone up and down. It was dark as pitch in the room. There was silence over the wire. There isn't much that is deader than a dead telephone line, but somehow the silence over the wire didn't seem half as dead as the silence in the room.

I couldn't go one way, nor could I go the other. I stood there, with the telephone receiver still in my hand. The telephone had gone now, too. The lights had gone, the guard had gone, the telephone had gone; what price those "forces of civilisation"? What is unavailable, it was being borne in upon me, might just as well not exist. . . . What could he possibly mean, about lying down? Why lie down? It didn't——

The lights came on.

Instantaneously. Just as they had gone off.

Light is truly a blessed thing. I only realised that I had been trembling when I stopped, after the first dazzle was over. There were the blank walls, the two black windows, the piles of bundles, the crated statue. All motionless, with the stolidity of the prosaic. It was all right; it was all right, I repeated, it was all right. I drew a deep breath of the heavy air and expelled it in a long "whew." Automatically I put the receiver on the phone. I started back to my chair in the other part of the room.

Right then I got the biggest shock of my life. The table was absolutely bare. The Codex had vanished!

I jumped to the door and shook it; it was locked as tightly as ever. I turned and stood stock still, staring down at the table, disbelieving my eyes.

From somewhere I heard an unmistakable chuckle.

I whirled around. And saw him.

There he stood, leaning negligently against the corner of the wall where the room turned, and regarding me with amusement in his grey eyes. A tall, lean man in an ordinary tweed suit. A sensitive face, ending in a long, strong jaw.

A number of thoughts chased themselves through my head in the space of that first second. Amazement was one of them. How had he gotten in? And if he had (which was impossible, unless he could walk through locked doors), how had he managed to get behind me? He hadn't been in the other half of the room when I had put down the telephone receiver; and during my trip from the flat desk to the door, he could not have passed me, for the lights had been on then. Hostility was another of the thoughts. Had I not been overwrought by what had gone before, I might have reflected that, once in, he certainly couldn't get out again until the guard returned, and I might have acted differently. But as it was, I would probably have flung myself upon anything in the room that moved or betrayed an appearance of animation.

I flung myself upon the man at the corner, glad that he no more resembled an Aztec bird-god in armour than did any one else to be met with on Broadway in the daytime. Here was some one I could deal with adequately, at any rate.

It soon turned out that I was wrong in that, however. Unexpectedly as my sudden attack must have been, he slipped back in a quick turn and landed a powerful blow against my shoulder. I got in with a few then on my own account, while he contented himself with little more than parrying. Within a short time, however, he appeared to have come to the conclusion that I meant business. He stepped closer; just as I was launching a smash toward his chin, he ducked with an agility that caught me unprepared, grasped my arm in a grip like a vice, and twisted.

The arm was bent back behind me. My face was forced suddenly forward and collided smartly with a bony knee that moved into its path at the proper instant. Then the knee moved on and I was forced to the floor with my opponent kneeling over me. Pain shot along my arm from the wrist and began spreading over the shoulder. I grunted with it and tried in vain to twist away; all I accomplished was to rub my face along the floor until it was turned once more in the direction of the doorway.

I had just achieved this position, surely no improvement upon its predecessor, when the door opened. Murchison stood in the entrance, his mouth partly open in amazement. But not for long. Like the other museum guards, he was a special officer and the gun that came up in his hand was business-like and steady. Although it was pointing too near my own head for comfort, I have seldom been more pleased with the sight of any weapon.

"Get up outta that," commanded Murchison. "Stand away."

They were the first words, except my short replies to Hartmann, that had been spoken in the room since he had left.

"Who is the man?" Murchison demanded.

I said: "I don't know. I never saw him before." I had gotten to my feet now and crossed over to the guard beside the doorway. Opposite us the fellow stood nonchalantly in the centre of the room, his hands in his coat pockets, and regarded us quizzically but with evident good humour. Murchison still had him covered.

"Don't worry, he's got the Codex," I went on grimly. "It was here when you left to see to the lights. When they came on, it was gone and he had gotten into the room somehow."

"Search him. . . . Up with your hands, my man."

I made the search, to which he acceded willingly enough, with that amused half-smile still on his lips. Most of it I conducted with the left hand, for my right arm was growing no less painful and was now beginning to swell. There was no sign of the Codex; and since it was a good two and a half feet long and a number of inches in diameter, it could scarcely have been concealed on his person. I found a bunch of keys and took from his coat pocket (where his own hand had so recently been) a wicked little automatic. I realised abruptly that he could easily have shot down Murchison, and myself too, a few seconds before. I looked at him perplexedly; this was certainly a funny sort of chap.

I tried his keys on the door immediately. None of them fitted and I tossed the bunch back to him. There was no other key on him. He said, "Thanks, old man," and pocketed them.

"Now," he went on, "you'll want to search the room. You have my word that I won't interfere, nor will I attempt to get away. Let's get it over with."

The easy sincerity in his voice impressed me, but Murchison, I noticed, continued to keep a wary eye on him. We began at the door and went completely through the room. Every bundle was moved, every box was opened, the desks were thoroughly searched and also moved about. No sign whatsoever of the Codex could we find.

When we came at last to the crated statue at the end of the room, there was a long slit down one side of the sacking. Before I could say anything, our prisoner remarked conversationally, "Yes, that's where I was. Of course. The lady with me looks hot but feels cold. If you have to lean against her for a few hours."

I hadn't an idea what he meant until I enlarged the slit somewhat and peered inside the crate. I recalled vaguely that Astarte was never considered as a symbol of the virginal and this conception, chiselled some thousands of years ago in Palestine, even from the small glimpse I could get, was sizzling. It struck me as a side thought that the basement was probably destined to be her permanent home at the Metropolitan.

The crate yielded nothing either. And that was the end. Definitely, the Codex had vanished from this locked room.

Our companion suggested calmly: "It's getting late and I should like to leave presently. Will you please call up Mr. Roger Thorpe on that telephone? The number is Butterfield 7-8344."

For want of anything better to do, the truth being that my mind was filled with bewilderment, I followed the suggestion. But I decided not to be too naïve about it. First I called Information and verified that the number was that of Roger Thorpe.

After a minute's ringing Thorpe himself answered the phone; and since he was already acquainted with the situation, it took little time to tell him what had happened. He received the news with rumbles of excitement. "Let me speak to Tarrant at once," he snorted through the receiver.

I placed the receiver against my side and turned about. "What is your name?" I asked the man across the room.

He was bending forward, lighting a cigarette. When he had finished, he said: "My name is Trevis Tarrant. Thorpe wants to speak with me?"

I handed the instrument over to him and heard him confirming the information I had just given. . . . "And kindly speak to this guard here, so I can go home. . . . Oh, forget it, Roger; and stop that snorting. You'll have it back by noon to-morrow, one o'clock at the latest. . . . Yes, I give you my guarantee."

More bewildered than ever, I hardly caught the end of Murchison's words through the instrument. The upshot, however, was a complete change in the guard's attitude. He now treated Tarrant with the utmost respect and seemed prepared to follow any directions the latter might give.

"Well," said Tarrant, "first of all I'll take back my little gun. And then I shall bid you good-night, if you will be so good as to show me the way out. How is your arm, young man?"

I winced with pain as he touched it and his concern was apparent at once. "That's a bad wrench," he ejaculated. "Worse than I meant. See here, you must come along with me and spend the night. No, I insist. I can fix that arm up for you; I owe you that much at the very least. Yes, yes, it's decided; let us be getting along."

I was too tired and in too much pain to argue. I merely went with him.

———

We picked up a cab opposite the Museum and in a few minutes were set down before a modern apartment house in the East Thirties. As Tarrant opened the door of his apartment a little Jap butler-valet, spick-and-span in a white coat, came hurrying into the entrance hallway, despite the lateness of the hour.

"Katoh," Tarrant advised him, "this is Mr. Jerry Phelan. He will spend the rest of the night with us. Let us have two stiff whiskies for a nightcap, please."

In the lounge-like room, pleasant and semi-modernistic, which we entered, the butler was already coming forward with a tray of bottles, glasses, and siphon. The drinks were quickly mixed.

"Bless," said Tarrant raising his glass. He took a long pull. "Mr. Phelan is suffering from a severe ju-jitsu wrench in his right arm. See what you can do for him, Katoh."

Once again the man hastened away, to return in a moment with a small bottle of ointment. He indicated a couch upon which he invited me to rest and helped me out of my coat and shirt. The arm was now throbbing with pain and was almost unbearable when he first touched it. His fingers were deft, strong—and gentle; and within a short time the peculiar massage he administered began to have a soothing effect.

To distract my attention, Tarrant was talking. "Katoh is as well educated a man as either you or I," he was saying. "He is a doctor in his own country in fact. Over here he is a Japanese spy. I found that out some time ago."

Katoh, busy with the muscles of my shoulder, looked up and grinned impishly. "Yiss." He poured out more ointment. "Not to mention, pless. Not everybody so broad-minded."

"Oh, I don't mind a bit," my host assured me. "If he wants to draw maps of New York when he could buy much better ones from Rand McNally for fifty cents, it's entirely all right. . . . I heartily approve of spy systems that permit me to hire one of my equals as a butler. . . . A hobby of mine, as you saw to-night, is investigating strange or bizarre occurrences and he's sometimes invaluable to me there also. No; I'm not only amused by the spy custom but I am actually a beneficiary of it."

My arm was now so greatly improved that I was becoming aware of a tremendous fatigue. I sat up, mumbling my thanks, and finished off my drink. Tarrant said: "I think you'll sleep very well. Show him where to do it, Katoh."

I hardly saw the room to which the little Jap conducted me and where he assisted me out of my clothes and into a pair of silk pyjamas. The events of the evening had worn me out completely; I remember seeing the bed before me, but I don't remember getting into it.

At quarter of ten the next morning Katoh came into the room just as I was preparing to open one eye. As he advanced toward me, he grinned cheerfully and observed, "Stiff, yiss?"

In a moment I was sufficiently awake to perceive the justice of the remark. My whole arm and shoulder were incapable of movement and as I inadvertently rolled over on my side, I gave a grunt of pain.

"Pless."

The butler very gently removed my pyjama top and got to work with the same bottle of ointment. His ability was amazing; it could have been no more than a minute before the arm was limbering up. Within five minutes the pain had gone completely.

"All right now. You rub to-night, then all finish. Your shower ready, sair."

Tarrant was waiting for me in the lounge, beside a table upon which two breakfast places had been laid out. As soon as we had greeted each other I lost no time in attacking the ice-cold grapefruit before my place. I was hungrier, in fact, than I can ever remember being.

During an excellent repast, of which I evidenced my appreciation in the most practical way, little was said. But when we had finished the last cup of coffee and were leaning back enjoying that first, and best, cigarette of the day, Tarrant remarked: "I see you know Marius Hartmann."

This was surprising. I was sure I had not mentioned Hartmann to him during our brief acquaintance.

He smiled at my puzzled expression. "No," he remonstrated, "I am not trying to emulate Holmes and bewilder a Dr. Watson. His card dropped out of your pocket last night when Katoh helped you out of your coat. There it is, over on the smoking stand."

"Oh, I see. Yes, I know him, worse luck. And by golly I shall have to step round and see him this morning." I explained how I had come to be in the Museum the night before and related the matter of the wager. "So there it stands," I finished. "I'm out a hundred dollars I certainly never expected to lose."

"Bad luck," my host observed. "Still, it was a foolish bet to have made. As I believe I mentioned last night, I interest myself in the sort of peculiar affairs with which we had to do; and whatever else may be said about them, they always come out unexpectedly. Very poor subjects for wagers. I should never risk anything on them myself."

"I am altogether in the dark," I confessed. "I can't imagine what happened to the Codex. You—you don't think it's possible that that Aztlan Curse thing really worked, do you?" With the sunlight streaming in brightly I was viewing the matter quite differently than a few hours before. And yet, what could have happened?

"If you are asking whether I take a seven-hundred-year-old Mexican threat literally, I can tell you I don't. I have seen older warnings than that take a miss; very much older. You heard me talking to Thorpe over the phone; he was afraid something would happen and, at my suggestion, he smuggled me into the room in the basement to discover what it might be."

I grinned. "So I'm not the only one out of luck this morning."

"I'm afraid you are," Tarrant stated calmly. "In spite of your own unexpected presence which kept me much closer to the charmingly immoral Astarte than I had intended, I know exactly what occurred, and why."

"Well——"

"Yes, I think you are entitled to an explanation, but I should rather let you have it a little later. Before the morning is out, I'll be glad to tell you. Meantime, if you intend calling on Marius Hartmann, I should like to go with you, provided you have no objection. It happens that I should like to meet him and this will be a good opportunity, if you are sure you don't mind."

I expressed my entire willingness; indeed I was finding my new friend a pleasant companion. And presently we alighted in front of Hartmann's sumptuous apartment on upper Fifth Avenue, somewhat above the Museum.

His rooms were ornate, with the stuffiness of classic furnishing, and filled with *objets*, as I am sure he called them. We had little time to notice them, however, for he made an immediate appearance. His smile was just what I had expected, as he greeted me. "I take it you have come to make a little settlement? You're very prompt, Jerry."

With the best grace I could summon I admitted his victory; and seeing a spindly kind of desk against one wall, I sat down and wrote out a cheque for him without more ado.

As I got up and waved the paper in the air to dry it (the desk had a sand trough instead of a blotter), I remembered Tarrant with sudden embarrassment. Hartmann had so exasperated me that I had forgotten my manners. I stammered some apologies and made the introduction.

They shook hands and Tarrant appropriated the only decent chair in the room. "By the way, Mr. Hartmann," he asked, "how did you know so soon what happened at the Museum last night?"

"Eh? Oh, I telephoned Roger Thorpe first thing this morning and he told me all about it. I felt pretty sure something unusual would occur; the ancients possessed strange powers on this continent as well as in the East. But this is more remarkable than I imagined. Really inexplicable."

"Why, I wouldn't say that exactly." Tarrant crossed one long leg over the other, as he lounged back comfortably. "I was there myself last night during the—phenomenon and a rather simple explanation occurs to me."

"Is that so? You have discovered what type of power is in the Codex?" Hartmann leaned forward with every appearance of interest.

"There is undoubtedly a certain force in the Codex," my companion agreed, "though not quite the sort you are thinking of. The recent phenomenon, however, was modern, very modern. And in a way estimable; scheduled simplicity is always a characteristic of the best phenomena. I almost regret that it didn't come off."

"How do you mean? I thought——"

"Oh, surely, the Codex vanished. But I have the strongest reasons to believe that it will return before one o'clock this afternoon. If you know what I mean?"

"But I don't know at all. I can't imagine. You suppose that in some way it became invisible last night and will materialise again to-day?"

"No, Mr. Hartmann," said Tarrant softly, "I do not look for anything so astonishing. The Codex will reappear in a much more prosaic manner, I expect. It would not surprise me, for instance, if it should be handed in at the entrance of the Museum by a messenger, addressed to the Curator of Central American Antiquities. Of course, it might be delivered otherwise, but that, I should think, would be perhaps the best way."

"You surprise me," Hartmann declared. "Why should such a thing happen?"

"Chiefly because a certain Deputy Inspector Brown is a great friend of mine. He is a very busy man, handling cases turned over to him by the District Attorney, signing search warrants, but I am sure he would be glad to take a few minutes any time to see me. Ours is a very close friendship; he has actually sent two of his men with me this morning, simply on the chance that I might have some unexpected use for them. . . . Yes, that, I think, is the real reason why the Codex may be expected to reappear before my time limit runs out. It would embarrass me somewhat if the prediction I made to Roger Thorpe should fail in any particular."

Hartmann had plainly been giving the words his serious attention. He said, "I see."

Tarrant got unconcernedly out of his chair and, on his feet, extended his right hand. "It has been a pleasure to make your acquaintance, Mr. Hartmann, I should be glad of your opinion about my little prediction. Of course, I can come back later—I should be delighted to see you again—but in that case I fear it will be too late to justify *all* my claims as prophet."

The other apparently failed to observe Tarrant's hand. He said, "I should really prefer not to interfere further with your day. Pleasant as your visit has been, I feel that we might not get on if we saw too much of each other. On the other hand, I may say I feel certain that so *brilliant* a man as you cannot be mistaken, especially when he has gone so far as to confide his expectations to one of the Museum Directors."

It was evidently our cue to leave and I followed Tarrant across the room puzzled by the enigmatic fencing with words to which I had been a witness. At the doorway he turned.

"Oh, I'm afraid I nearly forgot something, Mr. Hartmann. Experiments of the kind we engaged in last night naturally carry no other penalty than failure. There is, however, a small fine of one hundred dollars, to cover the necessary experimental expenses and I have arranged that my friend Phelan should be empowered to deal with it rather than my other friend, Inspector Brown. To save every one's time and trouble. Brown, as I said, is so busy he has doubtless forgotten all about it by now and it would be a shame to impose on his time unnecessarily."

Marius Hartmann did a most surprising thing. He said, "I fear I shall be forced to agree with you again. Fortunately the matter is simple, as you have arranged it."

He took from his pocket the cheque I had given him and, tearing it into small bits, dropped them into a tall vase.

In the taxi, on the way downtown, I turned to Tarrant. "But what—how—what *is* this all about?"

Tarrant's expression was one of amusement. "Surely you realise that Hartmann has the Codex?"

"Well, yes; I suppose so. I couldn't make head or tail of most of the conversation, but when he tore up my cheque, I realised he must be on a spot somehow. But I don't see how he *can* have gotten hold of it. He was at the Waldorf telephoning me just before it disappeared. . . . Or was that a fake? Wasn't he at the Waldorf at all?"

"Oh, no," said Tarrant, "I'm sure he was at the Waldorf; and almost certainly had a friend with him at the telephone booth, to make sure of his alibi. His accomplice took the Codex, of course, and delivered it to him later."

"His accomplice?"

"Murchison, the guard. That is the only way it could have happened. The affair was run off on a time schedule. Murchison turned the lights off at an arranged time. A few minutes later Hartmann phoned, calling you into the other part of the room, and while you were talking to him, the guard quietly opened the door, secured the Codex in the dark and locked the door again. His cue to do so was the ringing of the telephone bell. I've no doubt Hartmann did everything he could to upset you while the lights were out so that you would be too nervous to connect anything you might hear with an ordinary opening of the door."

"Yes, he certainly did. He pretended to be frightened half out of his wits about me. Told me I must get as far away from the Codex as I could. But look here, Hartmann was the one to suggest that I be there, in the first place. Surely he wouldn't have done that, if——"

"A brilliant idea; he is really a smart chap. He didn't know I was going to be there; didn't know anything about me. But if no one was present, it is obvious the guard would be suspected, as the only person to have a key, and be grilled unmercifully. He might break down. But this way, here was some one else, present at Hartmann's own suggestion, who would give evidence that the door had not been opened at the crucial time. Provided everything worked out as planned. No, that was a clever notion of his."

"How could you figure all this out, when you were inside that crate, if I'm right, during the theft?"

"Why, it's the only way it *could* have happened. Although I didn't see it, I was there in the room and knew just what the conditions were. If you attack the problem simply with reason—dismiss the smoke screen, an Aztec Curse this time—there cannot be any other solution."

I thought that over. After a few moments I said: "That might do for Murchison. But how did you know who had bribed him?"

"Oh, that. Well, it was a longer shot. But Thorpe had some suspicions of him, to begin with. Hartmann had suggested the possibility of something supernatural about the Codex when his offer was turned down. And when he heard about the opening warning, he mentioned it again. He slipped there. Thorpe felt sure, though, that Hartmann wouldn't plan an ordinary theft; that was why he fell in with the idea that I should be smuggled in. I wasn't entirely

certain, until he made that other slip, giving away his knowledge of what had happened, when he first saw you just now. I talked with Thorpe this morning myself and asked especially whether Hartmann had called him. He hadn't."

"The man's no better than a common thief. It will be a good thing to have him arrested." By golly, I never had liked that man; and for the first time I was beginning to feel my animosity justified.

"Wouldn't think of having him arrested," was Tarrant's calm comment.

"Why not? He's a thief," I repeated.

"Nonsense. The episode was more in the nature of good entertainment than theft. The Codex will be back unharmed within an hour, which in itself is a very mitigating circumstance. All that talk of mine about Inspector Brown was pure bluff. Arrest one of the future benefactors of the Museum? He'll be on the Board some day. Don't be silly.

"As for me," Tarrant concluded, "I should dislike greatly seeing him arrested. There are far too few such clever fellows at large as it is. With Hartmann confined there would be just one less chance for my own amusement."

ONE MAN'S POISON, SIGNOR, IS ANOTHER'S MEAT

Often described as a woman's murder weapon,
poison doesn't really care who administers it.

THE POISONED DOW '08

DOROTHY L. SAYERS

REMEMBERED TODAY MAINLY AS the creator of the great aristocratic detective Lord Peter Wimsey, Dorothy Leigh Sayers (1893–1957) was a
renowned intellectual who produced numerous books on other, more rarified,
subjects during a full, rich career. The only child of the headmaster of Christ
Church Cathedral Choir Church, Oxford, she learned Latin by the age of seven
and spoke fluent French as a child. A brilliant scholar at Somerville College,
Oxford, she received her degree in 1915—one of the first English women to
do so. Volumes of her poetry were published in 1916 and 1918, and she began a
lifelong interest in religious literature at that time. Needing more remunerative
employment than poetry or religious research could offer, she took a job as a
copywriter at an advertising agency and, in 1920, conceived the foppish detective who was to make her fortune. In Wimsey's first case, *Whose Body?* (1923),
the amateur detective is about to attend a sale of rare books when his mother
asks him to help a friend who has inconveniently discovered a corpse in his bath-
tub. Her second mystery, *Clouds of Witness* (1926), established her as a major
figure in the Golden Age of detective fiction, those years between the world wars
that featured the fair-play school of pure detection, exemplified by such authors
as Agatha Christie, Ellery Queen, John Dickson Carr, Christianna Brand, and
S. S. Van Dine. After only fourteen novels and some short stories, she stopped
writing mysteries; her last novel was *Busman's Honeymoon* in 1937. Apart from a
few short stories, her literary efforts from that point produced mainly religious
articles and books, as well as a highly praised translation of Dante's *The Divine
Comedy.*

    "The Poisoned Dow '08" (also published as "The Poisoned Port") was orig-
inally published in the February 25, 1933, issue of the *The Passing Show*; it was
first collected in *Hangman's Holiday* (London, Gollancz, 1933).

THE POISONED DOW '08

DOROTHY L. SAYERS

"GOOD MORNING, miss," said Mr. Montague Egg, removing his smart trilby with something of a flourish as the front door opened. "Here I am again, you see. Not forgotten me, have you? That's right, because I couldn't forget a young lady like you, not in a hundred years. How's his lordship to-day? Think he'd be willing to see me for a minute or two?"

He smiled pleasantly, bearing in mind Maxim Number Ten of the *Salesman's Handbook,* "The goodwill of the maid is nine-tenths of the trade."

The parlourmaid, however, seemed nervous and embarrassed.

"I don't—oh, yes—come in, please. His lordship—that is to say—I'm afraid—"

Mr. Egg stepped in promptly, sample case in hand, and, to his great surprise, found himself confronted by a policeman, who, in somewhat gruff tones, demanded his name and business.

"Travelling representative of Plummet & Rose, Wines and Spirits, Piccadilly," said Mr. Egg, with the air of one who has nothing to conceal. "Here's my card. What's up, sergeant?"

"Plummet & Rose?" said the policeman. "Ah, well, just sit down a moment, will you? The inspector'll want to have a word with you, I shouldn't wonder."

More and more astonished, Mr. Egg obediently took a seat, and in a few minutes' time found himself ushered into a small sitting-room which was occupied by a uniformed police inspector and another policeman with a note-book.

"Ah!" said the inspector. "Take a seat, will you, Mr.—ha, hum—Egg. Perhaps you can give us a little light on this affair. Do you know anything about a case of port wine that was sold to Lord Borrodale last spring?"

"Certainly I do," replied Mr. Egg, "if you mean the Dow '08. I made the sale myself. Six dozen at 192s. a dozen. Ordered from me, personally, March 3rd. Dispatched from our head office March 8th. Receipt acknowledged March 10th, with cheque in settlement. All in order our end. Nothing wrong with it, I hope? We've had no complaint. In fact, I've just called to ask his lordship how he liked it and to ask if he'd care to place a further order."

"I see," said the inspector. "You just happened to call to-day in the course of your usual round? No special reason?"

Mr. Egg, now convinced that something was very wrong indeed, replied by placing his order-book and road schedule at the inspector's disposal.

"Yes," said the inspector, when he had glanced through them. "That seems to be all right. Well, now, Mr. Egg, I'm sorry to say that Lord Borrodale was found dead in his study this morning under circumstances strongly suggestive of his having taken poison. And what's more, it looks very much as if the poison had been administered to him in a glass of this port wine of yours."

"You don't say!" said Mr. Egg incredulously.

"I'm very sorry to hear that. It won't do us any good, either. Not but what the wine was wholesome enough when we sent it out. Naturally, it wouldn't pay us to go putting anything funny into our wines; I needn't tell you that. But it's not the sort of publicity we care for. What makes you think it was the port, anyway?"

For answer, the inspector pushed over to him a glass decanter which stood upon the table.

"See what you think yourself. It's all right— we've tested it for finger-prints already. Here's a glass if you want one, but I shouldn't advise you to swallow anything—not unless you're fed up with life."

Mr. Egg took a cautious sniff at the decanter and frowned. He poured out a thimbleful of the wine, sniffed and frowned again. Then he took an experimental drop upon his tongue, and immediately expectorated, with the utmost possible delicacy, into a convenient flower-pot.

"Oh, dear, oh, dear," said Mr. Montague Egg. His rosy face was puckered with distress. "Tastes to me as though the old gentleman had been dropping his cigar-ends into it."

The inspector exchanged a glance with the policeman.

"You're not far out," he said. "The doctor hasn't quite finished his post-mortem, but he says it looks to him like nicotine poisoning. Now, here's the problem. Lord Borrodale was accustomed to drink a couple of glasses of port in his study every night after dinner. Last night the wine was taken in to him as usual at nine o'clock. It was a new bottle, and Craven—that's the butler—brought it straight up from the cellar in a basket arrangement—"

"A cradle," interjected Mr. Egg.

"—a cradle, if that's what you call it. James the footman followed him, carrying the decanter and a wineglass on a tray. Lord Borrodale inspected the bottle, which still bore the original seal, and then Craven drew the cork and decanted the wine in full view of Lord Borrodale and the footman. Then both servants left the room and retired to the kitchen quarters, and as they went, they heard Lord Borrodale lock the study door after them."

"What did he do that for?"

"It seems he usually did. He was writing his memoirs—he was a famous judge, you know— and as some of the papers he was using were highly confidential, he preferred to make himself safe against sudden intruders. At eleven o'clock, when the household went to bed, James noticed that the light was still on in the study. In the morning it was discovered that Lord Borrodale had not been to bed. The study door was still locked and, when it was broken open, they found him lying dead on the floor. It looked as though he had been taken ill, had tried to reach the bell, and had collapsed on the way. The doctor says he must have died at about ten o'clock."

"Suicide?" suggested Mr. Egg.

"Well, there are difficulties about that. The position of the body, for one thing. Also, we've carefully searched the room and found no traces of any bottle or anything that he could have kept the poison in. Besides, he seems to have enjoyed his life. He had no financial or domestic worries, and in spite of his advanced age his health was excellent. Why should he commit suicide?"

"But if he didn't," objected Mr. Egg, "how was it he didn't notice the bad taste and smell of the wine?"

"Well, he seems to have been smoking a pretty powerful cigar at the time," said the inspector (Mr. Egg shook a reproachful head), "and I'm told he was suffering from a slight cold, so that his taste and smell may not have been in full working order. There are no finger-prints on the decanter or the glass except his own and those of the butler and the footman—though, of course, that wouldn't prevent anybody dropping poison into either of them, if only the door hadn't been locked. The windows were both fastened on the inside, too, with burglar-proof catches."

"How about the decanter?" asked Mr. Egg, jealous for the reputation of his firm. "Was it clean when it came in?"

"Yes, it was. James washed it out immediately before it went into the study; the cook swears she saw him do it. He used water from the tap and then swilled it round with a drop of brandy."

"Quite right," said Mr. Egg approvingly.

"And there's nothing wrong with the brandy, either, for Craven took a glass of it himself afterwards—to settle his palpitations, so he says." The inspector sniffed meaningly. "The glass was wiped out by James when he put it on the tray, and then the whole thing was carried along to the study. Nothing was put down or left for a moment between leaving the pantry and entering the study, but Craven recollects that as he was crossing the hall Miss Waynfleet stopped him and spoke to him for a moment about some arrangements for the following day."

"Miss Waynfleet? That's the niece, isn't it? I saw her on my last visit. A very charming young lady."

"Lord Borrodale's heiress," remarked the inspector meaningly.

"A very *nice* young lady," said Mr. Egg, with emphasis. "And I understand you to say that Craven was carrying only the cradle, not the decanter or the glass."

"That's so."

"Well, then, I don't see that she could have put anything into what James was carrying." Mr. Egg paused. "The seal on the cork, now—you say Lord Borrodale saw it?"

"Yes, and so did Craven and James. You can see it for yourself, if you like—what's left of it."

The inspector produced an ash-tray, which held a few fragments of dark blue sealing-wax, together with a small quantity of cigar-ash. Mr. Egg inspected them carefully.

"That's our wax and our seal, all right," he pronounced. "The top of the cork has been sliced off cleanly with a sharp knife and the mark's intact. 'Plummet & Rose. Dow 1908.' Nothing wrong with that. How about the strainer?"

"Washed out that same afternoon in boiling water by the kitchenmaid. Wiped immediately before using by James, who brought it in on the tray with the decanter and the glass. Taken out with the bottle and washed again at once,

unfortunately—otherwise, of course, it might have told us something about when the nicotine got into the port wine."

"Well," said Mr. Egg obstinately, "it didn't get in at our place, that's a certainty. What's more, I don't believe it ever was in the bottle at all. How could it be? Where *is* the bottle, by the way?"

"It's just been packed up to go to the analyst, I think," said the inspector, "but as you're here, you'd better have a look at it. Podgers, let's have that bottle again. There are no finger-prints on it except Craven's, by the way, so it doesn't look as if it had been tampered with."

The policeman produced a brown paper parcel, from which he extracted a port-bottle, its mouth plugged with a clean cork. Some of the original dust of the cellar still clung to it, mingled with finger-print powder. Mr. Egg removed the cork and took a long, strong sniff at the contents. Then his face changed.

"Where did you get this bottle from?" he demanded sharply.

"From Craven. Naturally, it was one of the first things we asked to see. He took us along to the cellar and pointed it out."

"Was it standing by itself or with a lot of other bottles?"

"It was standing on the cellar floor at the end of a row of empties, all belonging to the same bin; he explained that he put them on the floor in the order in which they were used, till the time came for them to be collected and taken away."

Mr. Egg thoughtfully tilted the bottle; a few drops of thick red liquid, turbid with disturbed crust, escaped into his wineglass. He smelt them again and tasted them. His snub nose looked pugnacious.

"Well?" asked the inspector.

"No nicotine there, at all events," said Mr. Egg, "unless my nose deceives me, which, you will understand, inspector, isn't likely, my nose being my livelihood, so to speak. No. You'll have to send it to be analysed of course; I quite understand that, but I'd be ready to bet quite a little bit of money you'll find that bottle innocent.

And that, I needn't tell you, will be a great relief to our minds. And I'm sure, speaking for myself, I very much appreciate the kind way you've put the matter before me."

"That's all right; your expert knowledge is of value. We can probably now exclude the bottle straight away and concentrate on the decanter."

"Just so," replied Mr. Egg. "Ye-es. Do you happen to know how many of the six dozen bottles had been used?"

"No, but Craven can tell us, if you really want to know."

"Just for my own satisfaction," said Mr. Egg. "Just to be sure that this *is* the right bottle, you know. I shouldn't like to feel I might have misled you in any way."

The inspector rang the bell, and the butler promptly appeared—an elderly man of intensely respectable appearance.

"Craven," said the inspector, "this is Mr. Egg of Plummet & Rose's."

"I am already acquainted with Mr. Egg."

"Quite. He is naturally interested in the history of the port wine. He would like to know— what is it, exactly, Mr. Egg?"

"This bottle," said Monty, rapping it lightly with his finger-nail, "it's the one you opened last night?"

"Yes, sir."

"Sure of that?"

"Yes, sir."

"How many dozen have you got left?"

"I couldn't say off-hand, sir, without the cellarbook."

"And that's in the cellar, eh? I'd like to have a look at your cellars—I'm told they're very fine. All in apple-pie order, I'm sure. Right temperature and all that?"

"Undoubtedly, sir."

"We'll all go and look at the cellar," suggested the inspector, who in spite of his expressed confidence seemed to have doubts about leaving Mr. Egg alone with the butler.

Craven bowed and led the way, pausing only to fetch the keys from his pantry.

"This nicotine, now," prattled Mr. Egg, as

they proceeded down a long corridor, "is it very deadly? I mean, would you require a great quantity of it to poison a person?"

"I understand from the doctor," replied the inspector, "that a few drops of the pure extract, or whatever they call it, would produce death in anything from twenty minutes to seven or eight hours."

"Dear, dear!" said Mr. Egg. "And how much of the port had the poor old gentleman taken? The full two glasses?"

"Yes, sir; to judge by the decanter, he had. Lord Borrodale had the habit of drinking his port straight off. He did not sip it, sir."

Mr. Egg was distressed.

"Not the right thing at all," he said mournfully. "No, no. Smell, sip, and savour to bring out the flavour—that's the rule for wine, you know. Is there such a thing as a pond or stream in the garden, Mr. Craven?"

"No, sir," said the butler, a little surprised.

"Ah! I was just wondering. Somebody must have brought the nicotine along in something or other, you know. What would they do afterwards with the little bottle or whatever it was?"

"Easy enough to throw it in among the bushes or bury it, surely," said Craven. "There's six acres of garden, not counting the meadow or the courtyard. Or there are the water-butts, of course, and the well."

"How stupid of me," confessed Mr. Egg. "I never thought of that. Ah! this is the cellar, is it? Splendid—a real slap-up outfit, I call this. Nice, even temperature, too. Same summer and winter, eh? Well away from the house-furnace?"

"Oh, yes, indeed, sir. That's the other side of the house. Be careful of the last step, gentlemen; it's a little broken away. Here is where the Dow '08 stood, sir. No. 17 bin—one, two, three and a half dozen remaining, sir."

Mr. Egg nodded and, holding his electric torch close to the protruding necks of the bottles, made a careful examination of the seals.

"Yes," he said, "here they are. Three and a half dozen, as you say. Sad to think that the throat they should have gone down lies, as you might say, closed up by Death. I often think, as I make my rounds, what a pity it is we don't all grow mellower and softer in our old age, same as this wine. A fine old gentleman, Lord Borrodale, or so I'm told, but something of a tough nut, if that's not disrespectful."

"He was hard, sir," agreed the butler, "but just. A very just master."

"Quite," said Mr. Egg. "And these, I take it, are the empties. Twelve, twenty-four, twenty-nine—and one is thirty—and three and a half dozen is forty-two—seventy-two—six dozen—that's O.K. by me." He lifted the empty bottles one by one. "They say dead men tell no tales, but they talk to little Monty Egg all right. This one, for instance. If this ever held Plummet & Rose's Dow '08 you can take Monty Egg and scramble him. Wrong smell, wrong crust, and that splash of white-wash was never put on by our cellar-man. Very easy to mix up one empty bottle with another. Twelve, twenty-four, twenty-eight and one is twenty-nine. I wonder what's become of the thirtieth bottle."

"I'm sure I never took one away," said the butler.

"The pantry keys—on a nail inside the door—very accessible," said Monty.

"Just a moment," interrupted the inspector. "Do you say that that bottle doesn't belong to the same bunch of port wine?"

"No, it doesn't—but no doubt Lord Borrodale sometimes went in for a change of vintage." Mr. Egg inverted the bottle and shook it sharply. "Quite dry. Curious. Had a dead spider at the bottom of it. You'd be surprised how long a spider can exist without food. Curious that this empty bottle, which comes in the middle of the row, should be drier than the one at the beginning of the row, and should contain a dead spider. We see a deal of curious things in our calling, inspector—we're encouraged to notice things, as you might say. 'The salesman with the open eye sees commissions mount up high.' You might call this bottle a curious thing. And here's another. That other bottle, the one you said was opened last night, Craven—how did you come

to make a mistake like that? If my nose is to be trusted, not to mention my palate, that bottle's been open a week at least."

"Has it indeed, sir? I'm sure it's the one as I put here at the end of this row. Somebody must have been and changed it."

"But—" said the inspector. He stopped in mid-speech, as though struck by a sudden thought. "I think you'd better let me have those cellar keys of yours, Craven, and we'll get this cellar properly examined. That'll do for the moment. If you'll just step upstairs with me, Mr. Egg, I'd like a word with you."

"Always happy to oblige," said Monty agreeably. They returned to the upper air.

"I don't know if you realise, Mr. Egg," observed the inspector, "the bearing, or, as I might say, the inference of what you said just now. Supposing you're right about this bottle not being the right one, somebody's changed it on purpose, and the right one's missing. And, what's more, the person that changed the bottle left no finger-prints behind him—or her."

"I see what you mean," said Mr. Egg, who had indeed drawn this inference some time ago, "and what's more, it looks as if the poison had been in the bottle after all, doesn't it? And that—you're going to say—is a serious look-out for Plummet & Rose, seeing there's no doubt our seal was on the bottle when it was brought into Lord Borrodale's room. I don't deny it, inspector. It's useless to bluster and say 'No, no,' when it's perfectly clear that the facts are so. That's a very useful motto for a man that wants to get on in our line of business."

"Well, Mr. Egg," said the inspector, laughing, "what will you say to the next inference? Since nobody but you had any interest in changing that bottle over, it looks as though I ought to clap the handcuffs on you."

"Now, that's a disagreeable sort of an inference," protested Mr. Egg, "and I hope you won't follow it up. I shouldn't like anything of that sort to happen, and my employers wouldn't fancy it either. Don't you think that, before we do anything we might have cause to regret, it would be a good idea to have a look in the furnace-room?"

"Why the furnace-room?"

"Because," said Mr. Egg, "it's the place that Craven particularly didn't mention when we were asking him where anybody might have put a thing he wanted to get rid of."

The inspector appeared to be struck by this line of reasoning. He enlisted the aid of a couple of constables, and very soon the ashes of the furnace that supplied the central heating were being assiduously raked over. The first find was a thick mass of semi-molten glass, which looked as though it might once have been part of a wine bottle.

"Looks as though you might be right," said the inspector, "but I don't see how we're to prove anything. We're not likely to get any nicotine out of this."

"I suppose not," agreed Mr. Egg sadly. "But"—his face brightened—"how about this?"

From the sieve in which the constable was sifting the ashes he picked out a thin piece of warped and twisted metal, to which a lump of charred bone still clung.

"What on earth's that?"

"It doesn't look like much, but I think it might once have been a corkscrew," suggested Mr. Egg mildly. "There's something homely and familiar about it. And, if you'll look here, I think you'll see that the metal part of it is hollow. And I shouldn't be surprised if the thick bone handle was hollow, too. It's very badly charred, of course, but if you were to split it open, and if you were to find a hollow inside it, and possibly a little melted rubber—well, that might explain a lot."

The inspector smacked his thigh.

"By Jove, Mr. Egg!" he exclaimed, "I believe I see what you're getting at. You mean that if this corkscrew had been made hollow, and contained a rubber reservoir, inside, like a fountain-pen, filled with poison, the poison might be made to flow down the hollow shaft by pressure on some sort of plunger arrangement."

"That's it," said Mr. Egg. "It would have to be screwed into the cork very carefully, of course, so as not to damage the tube, and it would have to be made long enough to project beyond the bottom of the cork, but still, it might be done. What's more, it has been done, or why should there be this little hole in the metal, about a quarter of an inch from the tip? Ordinary corkscrews never have holes in them—not in my experience, and I've been, as you might say, brought up on corkscrews."

"But who, in that case—?"

"Well, the man who drew the cork, don't you think? The man whose finger-prints were on the bottle."

"Craven? But where's his motive?"

"I don't know," said Mr. Egg, "but Lord Borrodale was a judge, and a hard judge too. If you were to have Craven's finger-prints sent up to Scotland Yard, they might recognise them. I don't know. It's possible, isn't it? Or maybe Miss Waynfleet might know something about him. Or he might just possibly be mentioned in Lord Borrodale's memoirs that he was writing."

The inspector lost no time in following up this suggestion. Neither Scotland Yard nor Miss Waynfleet had anything to say against the butler, who had been two years in his situation and had always been quite satisfactory, but a reference to the records of Lord Borrodale's judicial career showed that, a good many years before, he had inflicted a savage sentence of penal servitude on a young man called Craven, who was by trade a skilled metal-worker and had apparently been involved in a fraud upon his employer. A little further investigation showed that this young man had been released from prison six months previously.

"Craven's son, of course," said the inspector. "And he had the manual skill to make the corkscrew in exact imitation of the one ordinarily used in the household. Wonder where they got the nicotine from? Well, we shall soon be able to check that up. I believe it's not difficult to obtain it for use in the garden. I'm very much obliged to you for your expert assistance, Mr. Egg. It would have taken us a long time to get to the rights and wrongs of those bottles. I suppose, when you found that Craven had given you the wrong one, you began to suspect him?"

"Oh, no," said Mr. Egg, with modest pride, "I knew it was Craven the minute he came into the room."

"No, did you? You're a regular Sherlock, aren't you? But why?"

"He called me 'sir,'" explained Mr. Egg, coughing delicately. "Last time I called he addressed me as 'young fellow' and told me that tradesmen must go round to the back door. A bad error of policy. 'Whether you're wrong or whether you're right, it's always better to be polite,' as it says in the *Salesman's Handbook*."

A TRAVELLER'S TALE

MARGARET FRAZER

IN COLLABORATION WITH Mary Monica Pulver Kuhfeld (1943–), an established mystery writer, Gail Lynn Frazer (1946–2013) created the joint pseudonym Margaret Frazer to produce six medieval detective novels about a Benedictine nun, Dame Frevisse. After the writing partners amicably separated, Gail Frazer continued the adventures, which now number seventeen novels, on her own. The successful series has been nominated for two Edgar Awards, one for *The Servant's Tale* (1993) and the other for *The Prioress's Tale* (1997). Born in Kewanee, Illinois, Frazer worked as a librarian, secretary, gift shop manager, and assistant matron at an English girls' school before beginning her writing career.

Sister Frevisse, a nun at St. Friedswide's Abbey and the granddaughter of Geoffrey Chaucer, made her first appearance in *The Novice's Tale* (1992), which offered accurate historical insights into such far-ranging subjects as medieval medicine, the Hundred Years War, and the attitude of the English people toward Joan of Arc. The series has been lavishly praised for the careful attention the author has placed on research to ensure that the portrayals of large historical events, as well as the tiniest details of daily life, are authentically described. It should be noted that the author deliberately named the vehicle in the following story inaccurately. In medieval England it would have been called a chariot but Frazer was willing to sacrifice authenticity in favor of clarity for the modern reader.

"A Traveller's Tale" was first published in *The Mammoth Book of Locked-Room Mysteries and Impossible Crimes*, edited by Mike Ashley (London, Robinson, 2000).

A TRAVELLER'S TALE

MARGARET FRAZER

When that April with his showers sweet
The drought of March has pierced to the
*   root . . .*
Then long folk to go on pilgrimages . . .

D A M N . He hated that verse.

Not hated, Thomas amended. Was only brutally tired of it, having heard it a few too many times in his life to want it wandering through his head at odd moments. Besides, this wasn't April and he was on no pilgrimage: it was definitely January and he was simply going home after rather too long a time at Westminster, where he'd only gone because he was needed to make a little peace between his cousins Hal and Gloucester, and if ever there was a thankless task in the world, that was it because the only peace either of them wanted was the other one out of his way—forever and in every way, for choice.

Ah, well. He had done what he could for now. They wouldn't kill each other this month, likely, and he'd be home by supper if the weather held and nobody's horse threw a shoe on the ice-set road.

Thomas eyed the grey, lowering sky and judged there was good chance the snow would hold off for the few hours more of riding he needed. January's trouble was that the days were so short. And cold. He huddled his cloak more snugly around his shoulders and was glad of his fur-lined boots and that he had given pairs for New Year's gifts to Giles and Ralph. They were

riding behind him now without the displeasure that servants as good as they seemed able to make known without sound or gesture, when they did not approve of whatever their master had dragged them into—such as the long ride from London into Oxfordshire in a cold January with snow threatening—when there was no real need except that Thomas wanted to be home and with his books and family. And although whether those in service to him liked him or not, came second to whether or not they served him well, for choice he preferred to have people around him whom he liked and who, though he could live without it, at least somewhat liked him, too. Hal—otherwise my Lord Bishop of Winchester and son of a royal duke—had been known to tease him that such concern came from his somewhat low-born blood, to which Thomas invariably answered in return that it came from his good common sense and Hal ought to try it some time, thank you very much. Then they would laugh together.

Why was it he could talk and laugh and enjoy Hal's company, and talk and laugh and enjoy Gloucester's company, and all that Hal and Gloucester could do with each other was hate their respective guts? It was tedious of them and more tedious that they needed him to sort them out. Maud would say so over and over when he reached home, until he had given her kisses enough and her present from London—a pretty gold and enameled brooch this time—to make her feel she had been missed while he was gone, and then she would begin to tell him all that had happened the week and a half he'd been away and everything would be back to where it had been before he had left.

The road slacked downward and curved left and he knew that around the curve, beyond this out-thrust of trees, the Chiltern Hills fell steeply away to the lowlands that reached westward for miles upon miles, an open vastness that on a clear summer's day at this hour would be filled with westering sunlight like a bowl full of gold, but today would be all dull shades of lead and grey. But Thomas had seen it from here in every season and weather and loved it every time and way, and besides, from here there were not many miles left to home, though it was further than it seemed because the steep, long drop from the Chilterns had to be managed first and . . .

With a slight sinking of spirits Thomas saw trouble ahead. A carriage stopped right at the crest above the first long downward drop of the road; and by the scurrying of three men around it and the woman standing to one side, wringing her hands and wailing, it was halted for more than the necessary checking of harness and wheels before the start of the treacherous way down.

With wanhope that it was not as bad as it looked, Thomas raised a gloved hand out of the sheltering folds of his cloak and gestured Giles to go forward and ask what the trouble was and if they might be of help, little though he wanted to be; and while Giles heeled his horse into a jog past him, Thomas put his hand back under his cloak, loosened dagger and sword in their sheaths, and then, as he and Ralph drew nearer the carriage, pushed back his cloak to leave his sword-arm free, on the chance this was after all a waylaying rather than simply someone else's trouble.

Just for a moment then the possibility of robbery took stronger hold as Giles, after a brief word with the men there, drew his horse rapidly around and headed back with more haste than a carriage's breakdown warranted, shouting well

before he was back to Thomas's side. "There's some people dead here!"

Suddenly not minded to go closer, drawing rein and putting hand to sword-hilt openly, as Ralph moved closer up on his flank, Thomas asked, "I beg your pardon?"

"There's people dead," Giles repeated, stopping beside him. "You know William Shellaston? A merchant from Abingdon?"

"By name." Thomas urged his horse forward. "It's him?"

"And his wife and son, looks like."

"All of them dead? How?"

"There's none of that lot knows. It's only just happened. Or they only just noticed. It's odd, like."

Thomas supposed it was, if three people were dead and their servants had "only just noticed." But he was to them now, clustered beside the carriage, the woman still sobbing for the world to hear.

"I told them who you are," Giles whispered at Thomas's side. "That you're a coroner and all."

"In London," Thomas pointed out, annoyed. For no reason anyone could explain, the office of Chief Butler to the King included the office of Coroner of London, and by that, yes, he was a coroner but, "I've no jurisdiction here."

"They don't need to know that," Giles replied. "What they need is someone to settle them and tell them what to do."

And here he was and had to do it, Thomas supposed, and summoned up what he had heard of William Shellaston. A wine merchant whose wines were never of the best, a bad-humoured man, heavy-handed, not given to fair-dealing if he could help it, with a mind to join the landed gentry and the purchase of a manor lately near Henley to help his ambition along. Exactly the sort of man Thomas avoided like the plague because the only interest that sort had in his acquaintance was how much he could do for them.

Well, there wasn't much to be done for him now, if he was dead, Thomas thought, dismounting beside the servants and the carriage that was of the common kind—long-bodied, with low wooden sides, closed in by canvas stretched over metal half-hoops, and high-wheeled to keep it clear of muddy roads. The richer sort were painted, sides and canvas both, but this was all brown wood and bare canvas, nothing to make it remarkable except, Thomas noted, it was solidly built, the only expense spared seeming to have been to decorate it for the eye.

The servants had all begun to talk as soon as his feet were on the ground. "Be quiet," he said, so used to being obeyed it did not surprise him when they fell silent; then said to the man he had singled out as babbling the least at him, "What's in hand here?"

"They're dead. All three of them! We stopped to tell Master Shellaston we were about to start down. He hates to be surprised by the sudden drop and we've orders to always stop to tell him. Only when I called in, no one answered and when I looked in to see why, they were all . . ." He swallowed as if holding down his gorge. ". . . dead."

"That's all you know?"

The man nodded, tight-lipped over apparent gut-sickness.

"That's all any of you know?"

More nods all around.

"No outcry? Nothing? No sign of how they're dead?"

"Nothing," the woman answered, her voice rising shrilly. "They're just dead and it's awful and . . ."

"I'll see for myself," Thomas said curtly, less because he wanted to see anything and more to stop her carrying on. He moved to the carriage's rear, the usual way in. The chain meant to go across the gap to make falling out less easy had been unfastened at one end and looped aside, the last link dropped into the hook on the other side, and the heavy canvas curtain meant to keep draughts out strapped aside, out of the way, giving him a clear view of the long tunnel of the carriage's inside. He stepped up on a chest that had been taken out and set down on the ground for a step—its usual use, to judge by

its dried-muddy bottom and the footmarks on its top—and ducked inside. Or as clear a view as the shadows and grey light allowed him; the flaps over the window on each side of the carriage, meant for air and light and a sight of the countryside in better weather, were closed and it took a few moments for his eyes to get used to the gloom.

His sense of smell worked faster. There was a reek to the place that said death, and he pulled a fold of his cloak over his mouth and nose before he ventured further in, able to see well enough now not to tread on . . . anything . . . before he reached the windows. Thomas held his breath while dropping his cloak's fold long enough to roll up and tie the window flaps out of the way to give better light and eventually, he hoped, better air.

In the meanwhile, pressing his cloak over his nose and mouth again, he looked around and saw he had been right: there was nothing here he wanted to see, though it interested him that the inside of the carriage was nothing like its outside. Close-woven green wool lined the canvas cover for colour and comfort, there was well-stuffed padding on the wooden side-walls and woven carpets covered as much of the floor as he could see, for the high-piled cushions of all sizes, meant to make for comfortable sitting against the jounce and lurch of travel, with willow-woven hampers, lidded and strapped to the carriage sides near the entrance, the only other furnishing because anything of wood would be an invitation to bruising in this small carriage.

It was what else the carriage contained he did not want to see, but he looked, God help him, because he was a coroner and there, at the man and woman he presumed were Master and Mistress Shellaston, slumped on their backs among the piled cushions in the middle of the carriage. Their clothing and jewelled rings went finely with the carriage's furnishings and, living, they would probably have claimed they'd rather die than be seen in their present unclean disarray, lying with heads cast back, eyes shut but mouths gaping, arms and legs sprawled, and the place stenching with what their bowels and bladders had loosed in death.

Where was their son?

Stepping carefully, Thomas found him beyond his parents, near the carriage's front. A solid bulk of a child, maybe twelve years old, burrowed into a pile of cushions and curled tightly in on himself like a small hedgehog into its nest. Or he had been tightly curled before his body went slack in—Thomas pressed fingertips against the side of the throat and found, as he expected, no pulse—death.

They were all, as he had been told, dead. Father, mother, son.

How?

As he made his way back to the carriage entrance, Thomas considered the possibilities. Not by a weapon, surely, though the bodies would have to be brought out into better light and looked at to be certain there were no wounds; but if there had been violence of any kind among them, there would have been some sort of struggle, enough to leave some evidence of it, and there was none, nor apparently any outcry the servants riding on either side or behind had heard.

A person could smother on charcoal fumes, always a winter danger, but even if Master Shellaston had dared to have a brazier among so much cloth—and Thomas had noticed none—a canvas-covered carriage with its constant draughts was nowhere anyone was likely to suffocate except by making deliberate effort.

Poison then? A possibility, Thomas granted but doubtfully. From what he'd heard of poisons, most tended to go about their business with a deal of pain, and people did not tend to suffer quietly, so if it had been poison, why, again, had no one cried out?

He ducked thankfully out of the carriage into the open air, stepped down onto the waiting box and from there began giving necessary orders. Since there was now no hope of him reaching home today and no point to staying where they were, growing colder, he said, "There's a village and inn a half mile back. We'll return there and do what needs doing."

No one argued with him and while they went through the awkward business of turning the carriage around, Thomas learned a little more, beginning with the servants' names—Bartel, who claimed to be Master Shellaston's body servant and in charge of the others; Jack, whose size had probably recommended him as a guard on the journey because it surely hadn't been his wits out of which he was presently badly frighted; Godard, the carriage driver who just now had no time for anything but his horses; and Mary, a squawking chicken of a female who seemed more in horror than in grief, saying she was—had been, oh, God save her, what would happen now?—Mistress Shellaston's waiting woman and sobbing harshly to Thomas's question of why she had not been in the carriage, too, "Master Shellaston didn't like to be crowded, didn't like servants breathing down his neck and cluttering his way, he said. He made me always ride pillion behind Bartel and cold it is, too, this time of year and . . ." And probably hard on Bartel, Thomas did not say, dismissing her.

He learned something more from looking at the Shellastons' horses. The servants' mounts were all third-rate beasts of doubtful worth and dull coats, much like the servants themselves, now he thought of it, while the three pulling the carriage tandem, although a plain lot, shaggy with unclipped winter coats and their harness nothing to boast of—no dyed leather, brass trim, or bells to make the journeying more bright— were nonetheless, like the carriage, solid-built and not likely to break down. It seemed Master Shellaston had not been given to show, Thomas thought: he'd spent his money only on his own close-kept comforts and let the world think what it liked.

Did that evidence solid common sense, Thomas wondered. Or merely a contempt for anyone not him?

He was readying to talk to Bartel while watching Godard and Jack work the carriage and its horses around, when the clop of shod hooves on the frozen road warned that more riders were coming. Beside him, Bartel said with what might be disgust or maybe worry, even before the new-comers were in sight, "This'll likely be Master Hugh. Thought he'd be along soon."

"Master Hugh?"

"Master Shellaston's cousin. He's Master Shellaston himself, come to that, but to call him Master Hugh has kept things simpler over the years," Bartel said broodingly and added, as three riders came round the same curve of the road that Thomas had, "Aye, that's him."

He looked to be a man of early middle years, well-wrapped in an ample cloak, riding a shin-ingly groomed, handsome bay, with two well-turned out servants behind him on lesser but no less well-kept mounts. They all drew rein for the time it took to understand what they were see-ing, then Master Hugh came forward at a can-ter, raising his voice to ask as he came, "Bartel, what's toward?"

There were explanations to be made all over again, Thomas keeping aside, leaving it to the servants, with Master Hugh saying angrily, part way through, "You're making no sense. They can't all be simply dead. I want to see them."

At his order, Godard paused the horses and Master Hugh went into the carriage as Thomas had, though not for so long, and came out to go aside to the verge and dryly heave before, more pale than he had been, he came back to demand past Bartel to Thomas, "Who are you and what are you doing here?"

"I was on my way home when I overtook all this. I'm Master Thomas Chaucer of Ewelme."

He watched Master Hugh recognize his name and inwardly back off into respect. Doubt-ing he'd have trouble from him now, Thomas asked in his own turn, "How do you come to be here?" peremptory enough that Master Hugh accepted it was no light question.

His look slightly darkening, he answered, "I was following them."

"Why?"

"Because William—my cousin Master Shellaston—told me to. He'd ordered me to come see him at his manor and we'd quarrelled,

as always, over a piece of land he'd taken out of an inheritance of mine, and he finally said he wanted to be done with me once and for all, that if I'd go back with him to Abingdon, he'd hand over the deed I wanted and there'd be an end."

"So why weren't you riding with him?"

"Because, as always, my cousin wanted me no more around him than need be. He ordered me to keep well behind him. What business of yours is it to be asking all this?"

"I am a coroner," Thomas said.

Master Hugh's lips moved as if he might have been silently swearing but aloud he only said, jerking his head toward the carriage, fully turned now. "That's your doing, too?"

"We're going back the half-mile to the inn," Thomas said for answer. "You'll of course come with us?" He made it more invitation than order, though he would change that if need be, but Master Hugh merely nodded in agreement.

On his own part, Thomas regretted the need to go back. It would necessitate telling over yet again, to new folk, what was already certain—that the Shellastons were dead—when what he wanted was an answer as to why. He was already hearing among the servants a mutter-ing of, "Devil come for his own," and he knew that once the Devil or "God's will" was brought into a thing folk were too often satisfied not to bother looking further. For himself, profound though his belief in God and the Devil might be, Thomas had never found either one dabbled so directly in the world as this: these deaths were devil's work, right enough, but a man's hand had done it, and as the carriage creaked forward, he rode away from Master Hugh and over beside Godard riding the middle of the three carriage horses, guiding them by reins and voice and a short-tailed whip. The man cast him a shrewd sideways look and said, before Thomas could ask it, "Aye, I'm near as anyone but I didn't hear aught to make me think there was trouble."

"What *did* you hear?"

"Naught but the usual and that was never much once we were under way. They always did their bitch-and-bellow before we started, then settled down to drink themselves into comfort. The lurch and jounce"—he twitched his head back to the carriage lumbering behind—"unsettled their stomachs."

"Why didn't they ride, then?"

"Because he'd bought the carriage, damn it, and damn it, they were going to use it, damn it," Godard said without heat, apparently giving Master Shellaston's words and feelings in the matter rather than his own. "Besides, he didn't like to be seen lifting the bottle as much as he did, and a carriage is better than horseback for hiding that."

"He drank then?"

"Then and anytime. And she did, too, come to that, though maybe not so much."

"And the boy?"

"Made him throw up."

"Riding in the carriage?"

"No. The wine they favoured for drink. It made him throw up. Cider, that's what he had to have."

That would have made poisoning them all at once more difficult, with two drinks to deal with rather than one. If it had been poison. Thomas thanked him and swung his horse away and found Giles riding close behind and to his side. Surprised to find him there, Thomas raised eyebrows at him and Giles said, "The Hugh fellow was looking to ease in and hear what you were saying, so I eased in instead."

Thomas nodded his thanks. "I doubt anything was said he doesn't already know about his cousin, but I'd rather he not know how much I know." Or don't know, he did not add aloud. He and Giles were as alone as they were likely to be this while, riding aside from the carriage, with the three Shellaston servants riding behind the carriage, Master Hugh and his men gone on ahead, and Thomas's Ralph bringing up the rear on Thomas's quiet order to make sure they lost no one along the way, Thomas took the chance of going un-overheard to say, "He looks as likely a possibility as anyone for wanting Master Shellaston dead. But why the woman and boy, too?"

"Because he'll for certain have it all, now they're dead," Giles answered. "There's none others to the family."

"Servant-talk?" Thomas asked, and when Giles had nodded that it was, asked, "How much is all?"

"The business in Abingdon and a good-sized manor Master Shellaston bought a few years back, and the land they'd been quarrelling over these past five years, too, but they'd nearly settled over that anyway, it seems."

"How much does this Master Hugh have on his own?"

"He's not hurting, as they say. He was Master Shellaston's apprentice a while back, with it understood there'd be partnership when all was said and done, but they fell out and he set up on his own in Henley. Looked likely to rival Master Shellaston soon, by what this lot says."

"But no love lost between them?"

"Not a drop."

"Ride here and keep an eye ahead. I'm going back to see what they'll tell me."

"Just about anything you ask," Giles said. "They're starting to warm to the thought they're done with Master Shellaston and his wife."

With that to encourage him, Thomas slowed his horse to the side of the road, letting the carriage lumber on past him, and joined the Shellaston servants. Since he doubted anyone was thinking of anything except what had happened, he forebore subtlety, starting in immediately to them all, with a nod ahead, "So Master Shellaston and his cousin didn't get on together?"

"Not for above the time it takes to spit," Bartel readily agreed.

"Ordered him to ride behind, did he? The way Master Hugh said?"

"Did indeed. You always knew where you stood with Master Shellaston."

"Usually in the bad," said Jack. "Grudged a man the air he breathed and double-grudged Master Hugh any breath at all."

Mary crossed herself. "You shouldn't speak ill of the dead and them not even cold yet."

"They're cold and getting colder and so are we," Bartel said bluntly.

"We should lay them out decently before they stiffen too much," she sniffed. "It's not good, them lying there like that."

She was right, but Thomas wanted someone besides themselves for witness before anything else was done in the carriage, and asked, to divert her, "Had you served Mistress Shellaston long?"

"Three years last Martinmas."

"A good mistress?"

"Not very. Nor not too bad, neither," she hurried to add. "Just . . . a little too quick with her hands sometimes."

"And sharper than ever, now she was childing again," Jack said. "No pleasing her ever."

"She was with child?"

"About five months along," Mary said. "Glad of it, mind you, but it didn't sweeten her any."

Four deaths instead of three then to the credit of whoever had done this thing, Thomas thought grimly, but asked aloud, "Travelling didn't agree with her, from what the driver says."

"Nor did it," Mary said. "She wasn't happy with travelling or happy at Master Shellaston suddenly deciding they'd go back to Abingdon."

"It was sudden?"

"Sudden enough. He and Master Hugh had been yelling at each other off and on since yesterday and then, late this morning, it's up and on the road, let's have this over with, says Master Shellaston, and here we are. Liked keeping folk off balance, he did. Whether he'd have given over the deed once we were home, that's another matter."

"Did Mistress Shellaston quarrel with him over it? The deed or leaving so suddenly?"

"Bit snippy at first but nothing untoward."

"They didn't outright quarrel?"

"Nay. They weren't much for quarrelling with each other. Saved all their ire for other folk."

Thomas fell silent, considering what he had and asking nothing more until they had reached the inn yard, and while Master Hugh saw to telling the innkeeper what was the trouble, he went aside to his own men and, first, gave Ralph order to find someone to go to whoever was the coroner for this end of the county and bring him here, and added, seeing his look at the snow-heavy sky, "No need to hurry or risk yourself

about it. The weather is cold enough, they'll keep. All I want to know is he's on his way." And turned to Giles to say, "This place is big enough, there should be an herbwife somewhere. Find her for me."

He would have preferred an apothecary, but a knowledgeable herbwife—and, please God, this one would be—would do as well; and while he waited, he would have preferred to go inside the inn and be comfortable, the way Mary was gone, bustled away on a burst of the innwife's sympathy and curiosity, and Master Hugh whose men and Godard were seeing to the horses while Bartel and Jack were still to hand, kept by a look and gesture from Thomas while he had sent Giles and Ralph about his business, because he had meant to set them as guard on the carriage. But he had also had a hope the cold and ending day would keep people indoors but that was gone along with hope of setting Bartel and Jack to guard. They were already at the centre of a spreading cluster of folk and eagerly telling all they knew—or didn't know, Thomas amended, hearing Bartel saying, "Aye, there they lie, dead as dead and not a mark on them and never a cry. It had to have been the Devil, look you, come for Master Shellaston because he was a hellish master, sure enough."

By tomorrow there'd likely be a band of demons added to the telling, dancing in the road around the carriage with shrieks and the reek of sulphur, Thomas thought and said, "The Devil maybe came for Master Shellaston, but why for his wife and son, too?"

"They were just there," someone among the listeners said, eager to help the story along, "and so Old Nick took 'em, too."

"I've never heard it works that way," Thomas said dryly. "That the Devil can seize innocent souls just because they happen to be nigh a sinner."

"Well," Bartel put in, "she was only half a step not so bad as he was. They were a pair and no mistake."

"But the boy," Thomas said.

"Died of fright," Jack promptly offered.

Bartel, openly enjoying himself, added, full of scorn, "Huh. Likely the Devil decided to save time by coming only once for all of them. They were a matched lot. Young William was shaping to go the same way as his sire and dam and no mistake."

"Here now," Master Hugh protested, come up unnoticed from the inn with a steaming mug of something warm between his hands. "Little Will was a good lad."

"Praying your pardon, sir." Though it was fairly plain Bartel didn't care if he had it or not. "You spoiled him some and got on fine with him because you never crossed him. Some of us weren't so lucky." As if aside but not lowering his voice, he added to Thomas, "And it set Master Shellaston's back up to see how well along they got."

Dragging the talk back to where he needed it to be, Thomas asked, "Today, from the carriage, are you certain there was never any outcry at all?" because he could not believe three people had died without a sound.

"Well . . ." Bartel said.

He and Jack cast quick, doubtful looks at each other, and more forcefully, impatient, Thomas asked, "You heard something. What?"

"We heard . . . I heard and Jack with me, so Mary must have, too, we heard young William give a cry," Bartel admitted unwillingly. "Just once and it wasn't like we hadn't heard such other times. See, Master Shellaston had a heavy hand and was ready with it, especially when he was drinking, which was mostly."

"She could lay one along a man's ear, too, when she wanted, come to that," said Jack bitterly.

"When did you hear this cry?" Thomas asked and added, to their blank looks, "Before or after you passed through here?"

"Ah," said Bartel, understanding. "Before. Wasn't it, Jack?"

"Aye," Jack agreed. "Quite a while before, maybe."

And maybe it had been and maybe it had not, or maybe they were mistook or maybe they were lying—Thomas could think of several reasons, not all guilty ones, why they might be—because the more both men were coming to enjoy this, the less confidence he had in their answers.

"By your leave, sir, she's here," Giles said behind him, and Thomas turned away from the men and their eager listeners to find Giles standing with a firm-built woman, neatly aproned, wimpled and cloaked, her sharply judging eyes meeting his as she curtsyed and said, "Esmayne Wayn at your service, Master Chaucer. I'm herb-wife and midwife here. Your man says there's three folk dead and you want me to see."

More happy with her directness than with anything else he'd encountered these past two hours, Thomas said, "Mistress Wayn, thank you for coming. Yes, if you'd be so good as to look and tell me what you think about their deaths . . ."

Master Hugh started what might have been a protest, but a glance from Thomas made him think better of it and he subsided. Meanwhile Bartel at Thomas's nod went to pull the carriage's end curtain aside and tie it back, and Jack hauled out the chest and set it down for a step. "Some better light would help, too," Thomas said to Jack because the day was drawing in toward dark, then he offered Mistress Wayn a hand up.

He felt no need to ready her for what was there. As the village healer and midwife, she had surely seen enough of death in various forms and degrees of unpleasantness for this to be no worse. Besides, the cold was doing its work; the smell was none so bad as it had been, and Mistress Wayn went forward without hesitation, making room for him to follow her as she bent first over Master Shellaston, then over his wife, apparently able to see enough for now by the light from the opened window-flaps. The further jouncing of the carriage seemed not to have moved the bodies, already jostled into settled places between when they had died and when they were found, Thomas supposed. "The child is further on," he said quietly.

Mistress Wayn nodded but took Mistress Shellaston by the chin, moved her head slightly back and forth, then prodded at her stomach and leaned close over her face, seemingly sniffing. None of that was anything Thomas would have cared to do and he heard murmurs from the watchers outside and wished the door-curtain could be closed, but Mistress Wayn, ignoring everyone and him, repeated with Master Shellaston what she had done with his wife, before she straightened as much as the low curve of the ceiling allowed her, to look to Thomas and ask, "How long have they been dead?"

"No one is certain. At least three hours at a guess. It's been maybe two since I first saw them and the bodies were cooling by then."

"Best I straighten them, if I may? Much longer and we'll have to wait until they unstiffen again."

"If it will make no difference to what we might learn about how they died . . ."

"You've noted how they're lying and can say so if asked? And that their eyes be closed. Nobody did that, did they?"

Thomas far outranked her in life but she had a greater skill than he at this, and they both accepted the equality that gave them. So her interruption did not matter and he said simply, "I've noted, and no, nobody closed their eyes."

"That's enough then. Cleaning them can come later," and briskly, firmly, she straightened both bodies out of their sprawl, then moved on to young William, still curled into his nest of cushions. "You've noted him, too?" she asked.

"Yes."

"Good." She straightened the boy and rolled him onto his back, moved and prodded and did with him much as she had with his parents, before sitting back on her heels and saying up at Thomas, "His eyes be open, you see. That's the usual way with dead folk that didn't die easy."

"You're saying his parents died easily and he didn't? That they didn't all three die the same way?"

"Aye. Him and her, they died the same as each other, surely." Mistress Wayn nodded to the elder Shellastons. "The boy, he went otherwise. I can smell it on him. He took dwale would

be my guess, only I'm not much guessing. It's good for some things, carefully used, but only outwardly. Taken inwardly, it takes not much to kill."

"Poison," Thomas said. "You're saying the boy was poisoned. What about his parents? They had to have been poisoned, too."

"You'd think it," Mistress Wayn said. "It would seem the most likely but they're chancey things, poisons." She sounded almost regretful over it. "What kills one person only makes another sick and there's no way to know beforehand which way it will be. That I can still smell on him—" She nodded at young William. "—tells me he had enough to be almost certain of killing him, being a child. Why he didn't taste it as he started to drink it down, that's a question I don't have answer to. As for his parents and what they drank . . ." She shrugged.

"You don't think it was the same thing?"

"There's no smell of it and it would have to have been more than the amount that killed the boy to kill them quick and quietly. No, whatever they drank down was different, I'd say. I don't know what. It's that they made no outcry and show no sign of suffering I don't understand. Poisons hurt. I'd guess by the way the boy was curled in on himself he was hurting when he died, but with them it's more like they fell to sleep and died without waking up."

"There are potions that do that. Bring on a sleep so deep it turns into death."

"Aye." She still sounded unsatisfied. "But why one kind for them and another for the boy? Why weren't they drinking all the same?"

"Wine made the boy sick," Thomas said absently.

"So two different bottles had to be poisoned." She pushed a half-full, stoppered one lying near young William with her foot. "But still, why two different poisons? And he didn't just fall to sleep, neither," she added with a nod at the boy.

Thomas noticed there was no nonsense about the Devil from her. To her it was plain that poison had killed these three and, like him, she had no doubt that poison was a thing that came from a human hand.

Or poison*s*, it must have been, according to her.

Different poisons by different hands?

Three murders planned—Master and Mistress Shellaston's separate from their son's—by two different people with two different poisons, with it only being chance they happened together?

Or . . .

A sudden, ugly guess rose up in Thomas's mind.

Something of it must have shown in his face because Mistress Wayn asked sharply, "What?"

He shook his head. "I need more questions answered first, before I say."

But at least now he had a better thought of what the questions were.

An hour later, as the day drew in to grey twilight, when he had asked some of those questions and had answers, he gathered in a sideroom of the inn bespoken from the innkeeper for the sake of privacy with Master Hugh, Giles, the other servants, and Mistress Wayn, along with the innkeeper and a few village men for witness. Thomas had not put it that way but had merely asked the innkeeper if there were a few worthy men in the village who might care to join them for hot, spiced cider and talk this cold evening. That he meant to guide the talk he did not say.

After Mistress Wayn had overseen the moving of the bodies respectfully to her house for cleaning and shrouding, he and Giles, without asking Master Hugh's leave—and by his expression he would not have given it if asked—had searched through the carriage, generally seeking, finding specifically, and now asking, "Bartel, the wine Master and Mistress Shellaston were drinking, where did it come from?"

"It was his own. Being a wine merchant, he could lay hands on good stuff when he wanted."

"Was it a new bottle he had . . ."

"Bottles," said Bartel. "Three at least."

That accorded with what Thomas had found in a hamper in the carriage. Safely cushioned among various wrapped food bundles, there had been an empty bottle, a mostly empty bottle, and a full, tightly corked one.

"Could anyone have been at those bottles before they were put into the carriage?"

"Been at them? I filled them from a cask at the manor if that's what you mean, and put them in the hamper and put it into the carriage." Bartel straightened with sudden suspicion. "Hoi, hold up there. You're not saying I put something in them, are you? There were folk around all the time can say I never had chance to."

"Nor do I think you did. I just wanted to know that no one else had chance at them either."

Bartel subsided, not fully happy.

"There was a bottle that had held cider beside young William and then there are these." Thomas held up two pottery vials, slight enough to have fit in a belt pouch. "Do any of you know these?"

No one did, but Bartel's suspicion had been catching. All the Shellaston servants looked wary now and Master Hugh was frowning.

Thomas held one of them higher. "This one held poppy syrup sweetened with sugar, Mistress Wayn tells me. Master Shellaston favoured sweet wine, I gather?" Heads agreed he had, and indeed it had been malmsey in the bottles. Thomas held up the other small bottle. "This one held dwale, otherwise called nightshade, enough of it to kill if drunk straight down. And young William must have, because there was half the cider left in the bottle and no dwale in it."

Thomas regarded the empty vial sadly for a moment, then handed it with the other to Giles to keep. "We found it under young William. The other one was in the bottom of the box used for a step into the carriage. The box that has what's needed to keep the carriage in good order on the road." Spare parts for mending wheels and harness, grease for axles, tools and other odds and ends that might be useful. "It was Mistress Wayn who noticed and showed me the black grease smear on the back of young William's hand that he had mostly wiped off—black grease he could have come by in the carriage nowhere else but in that box. From one of the rags probably, when he hid the other vial there, the one with poppy syrup, after his parents were unconscious. Or after he'd killed them. Before he drank the potion of dwale in the other vial, a potion strong enough it brought him to death almost immediately."

"He killed his parents and then himself?" Master Hugh asked. "Is that what you're saying? He'd have to be off his wits to do any of that!"

"Off his wits or misled," Thomas said levelly. "But to go back to his parents. Let us guess he found a way to put the poppy syrup into one of the bottles of wine. It wouldn't have been hard. They were packed in a hamper with food. He only had to pretend he was taking overlong getting out what he wanted to eat, while pouring the syrup into the wine. After that, he only had to wait until his parents guzzled it down, as it seems was their way with wine. Now, poppy syrup, if you give enough, brings on sleep and if too much is given, it can kill. There was never enough in that vial to kill two people but there was enough to make them both sleep so heavily, helped on by the wine, that they didn't wake even when their son—and it had to have been him, there was no one else there to do it—pressed a pillow over the face of first one of them and then the other. He was a large, solid child, with weight enough to hold a pillow down and smother someone if they were heavily unconscious, the way his mother and father were. And then he closed their dead eyes, to keep them from staring at him."

"But why would he go and do it? Kill them, I mean," protested one of the village men. "It's not natural."

"I'd guess he did it for hatred. From everything I've heard, there was little love lost between him and them. Today, when he cried out in the carriage, probably from the unexpected pain of the dwale working in him, he was heard but no one thought anything about it but that he'd been struck by his mother or father, and that was too

usual to take much heed of. Besides, I'd guess he thought—or maybe someone put it in his head—that if he were orphaned, rid of his parents and no one able to say how they died—he'd be given in ward to Master Hugh Shellaston, who got on with him far better than his parents did."

"But then why would he kill himself?" Bartel asked.

"I don't think he did. I think his death was Master Hugh's doing."

Master Hugh jerked up straight in his chair, his stare furious at Thomas before he gathered his thoughts and exclaimed, "That's mad! I was nowhere near any of them when they died. You said yourself my cousin and his bitch-wife were smothered. I was never in the carriage or anywhere near it. And you said the boy drank that poison of his own will and died of it."

"I said he drank it of his own will and died of it, yes. I didn't say he *meant* to die of it. Why bother to hide the vial he'd poisoned his parents with if he was going to kill himself afterwards? He probably thought that what he drank was some light potion that would make him merely sleep and that when he and his dead parents were found he could claim all ignorance of their deaths and simply be weepingly thankful he was spared whatever had killed them. My guess is that you gave him the poppy syrup and dwale, told him the dwale was harmless, maybe even warned him there might be some pain and to keep from being caught he must fight against crying out, which he mostly did. He must have been a brave boy in his way. But he never meant to kill himself. You're the one who's guilty of his death. As guilty as if you'd poured the poison down his throat yourself."

Master Hugh did not give way yet. Instead—with what he probably meant to be the outrage of innocence—he fell back on, "You can't prove any of this!"

"Not at this moment," Thomas said coldly. "But I'll warrant that if question is made among apothecaries and every herbwife anywhere near where you've been of late, we'll learn of rather many requests for poppy syrup and dwale potion from them."

"No one is going to admit to making him a killing potion," Mistress Wayn said quietly.

"No, and probably none did. But I daresay several will be found who'll admit to making a non-killing potion. Dwale is after all good for some poultices. But put several lots together and they'd kill, yes?" Thomas asked at Master Hugh.

Boldly surly, the man tried, "My shit of a cousin had more enemies than me who'd probably like him dead. And how likely is it I've been wandering around talking to herbwives and apothecaries? I've a life to lead and people who notice where I go and why."

"We'll find out if other enemies had chance to give young William the poisons. We'll see if anyone had as much to gain from their deaths as

you do as the only heir. We'll see who's been asking for poppy syrup and dwale, and we'll find, I'll lay odds, that if not you, then some several of your servants have been, sent here and there without knowing what they were doing."

With one of his men already looking at him with widening eyes and dawning alarm, Master Hugh suffused a slow, deep red, rose to his feet and looked around the room for a way out.

"The window is shuttered," Thomas said mildly, "and my man is ordered to stop you going out the door by whatever means are needed. Nor do I think you'll find anyone here, even your own men, ready to help you."

That much Master Hugh had already read in the faces around him; and heavily he dropped back into his chair and said, from the heart, "Damn."

DEATH AT THE EXCELSIOR
P. G. WODEHOUSE

GENERALLY UNREMEMBERED TODAY is that one of the world's most popular and beloved humorists, Sir Pelham "Plum" Grenville Wodehouse (1881–1975), began his literary career by writing other kinds of fiction as well, including straight detective stories, of which "Murder at the Excelsior" is a good example. Several of his later stories and novels involve mystery or crime but are generally nonsensical, such as *Hot Water* (1932), *Pigs Have Wings* (1952), and *Do Butlers Burgle Banks* (1968).

Born in Guildford, he became a banker after graduating from Dulwich College, but, by the time he was twenty-two, he was earning more as a writer than as a banker and resigned to become a full-time writer, which he did with enormous success for the next half century. His first novel was *The Pothunters* (1902), but his greatest creations, the Honorable Bertie Wooster and his friend and valet, Jeeves, did not make their appearance until *The Saturday Evening Post* published "Extricating Young Gussie" in 1915. Wooster is a not-exceptionally-brilliant young man who ceaselessly finds himself in difficulties with his aunt, a girl, or the law, relying on Jeeves to get him out of trouble. Wodehouse's high earnings from magazines impelled him to visit the United States several times before World War I and, for much of his life, he spent half his time in America and half in England, becoming a U.S. citizen in 1955. He wrote screenplays for MGM, beginning in 1930, and provided the book and lyrics for numerous musicals. During World War II, his English home was taken over by Nazis who treated him well, as Wodehouse told the world in broadcasts from Berlin, severely upsetting the British. He was dubbed a traitor for a time before his countrymen accepted the notion that he hadn't really understood the ramifications of his naïve act. Shortly before his death, he was given a knighthood as Commander of the Order of the British Empire by Queen Elizabeth II.

"Death at the Excelsior" was first published in the December 1914 issue of *Pearson's Magazine*; it was first collected in *Plum Stones—The Hidden P. G. Wodehouse* (London, Galahad, 1993).

DEATH AT THE EXCELSIOR

P. G. WODEHOUSE

THE ROOM WAS the typical bedroom of the typical boarding-house, furnished, insofar as it could be said to be furnished at all, with a severe simplicity. It contained two beds, a pine chest of drawers, a strip of faded carpet, and a wash basin. But there was that on the floor which set this room apart from a thousand rooms of the same kind. Flat on his back, with his hands tightly clenched and one leg twisted oddly under him and with his teeth gleaming through his gray beard in a horrible grin, Captain John Gunner stared up at the ceiling with eyes that saw nothing.

Until a moment before, he had had the little room all to himself. But now two people were standing just inside the door, looking down at him. One was a large policeman, who twisted his helmet nervously in his hands. The other was a tall gaunt old woman in a rusty black dress, who gazed with pale eyes at the dead man. Her face was quite expressionless.

The woman was Mrs. Pickett, owner of the Excelsior boarding-house. The policeman's name was Grogan. He was a genial giant, a terror to the riotous element of the waterfront, but obviously ill at ease in the presence of death. He drew in his breath, wiped his forehead, and whispered, "Look at his eyes, ma'am!"

Mrs. Pickett had not spoken a word since she had brought the policeman into the room, and she did not do so now. Constable Grogan looked at her quickly. He was afraid of Mother Pickett,

as was everybody else along the waterfront. Her silence, her pale eyes, and the quiet decisiveness of her personality cowed even the tough old salts who patronized the Excelsior. She was a formidable influence in that little community of sailormen.

"That's just how I found him," said Mrs. Pickett. She did not speak loudly, but her voice made the policeman start.

He wiped his forehead again. "It might have been apoplexy," he hazarded.

Mrs. Pickett said nothing. There was a sound of footsteps outside, and a young man entered, carrying a black bag.

"Good morning, Mrs. Pickett. I was told that—good Lord!" The young doctor dropped to his knees beside the body and raised one of the arms. After a moment he lowered it gently to the floor and shook his head in grim resignation.

"He's been dead for hours," he announced. "When did you find him?"

"Twenty minutes back," replied the old woman. "I guess he died last night. He never would be called in the morning. Said he liked to sleep on. Well, he's got his wish."

"What did he die of, sir?" asked the policeman.

"It's impossible to say without an examination," the doctor answered. "It looks like a stroke, but I'm pretty sure it isn't. It might be a coronary attack, but I happen to know his blood pressure was normal, and his heart sound. He

913

called in to see me only a week ago and I examined him thoroughly. But sometimes you can be deceived. The inquest will tell us."

He eyed the body almost resentfully. "I can't understand it. The man had no right to drop dead like this. He was a tough old sailor who ought to have been good for another twenty years. If you want my honest opinion—though I can't possibly be certain until after the inquest—I should say he had been poisoned."

"How would he be poisoned?" asked Mrs. Pickett quietly.

"That's more than I can tell you. There's no glass about that he could have drunk it from. He might have got it in capsule form. But why should he have done it? He was always a pretty cheerful sort of man, wasn't he?"

"Yes, sir," said the constable. "He had the name of being a joker in these parts. Kind of sarcastic, they tell me, though he never tried it on me."

"He must have died quite early last night," said the doctor. He turned to Mrs. Pickett. "What's become of Captain Muller? If he shares this room he ought to be able to tell us something."

"Captain Muller spent the night with some friends at Portsmouth," said Mrs. Pickett. "He left right after supper, and hasn't returned."

The doctor stared thoughtfully about the room, frowning.

"I don't like it. I can't understand it. If this had happened in India I should have said the man had died from some form of snake bite. I was out there two years, and I've seen a hundred cases of it. The poor devils all looked just like this. But the thing's ridiculous. How could a man be bitten by a snake in a Southampton waterfront boardinghouse? Was the door locked when you found him, Mrs. Pickett?"

Mrs. Pickett nodded. "I opened it with my own key. I had been calling to him and he didn't answer, so I guessed something was wrong."

The constable spoke, "You ain't touched anything, ma'am? They're always very particular about that. If the doctor's right and there's

been anything up, that's the first thing they'll ask."

"Everything's just as I found it."

"What's that on the floor beside him?" the doctor asked.

"Only his harmonica. He liked to play it of an evening in his room. I've had some complaints about it from some of the gentlemen, but I never saw any harm, so long as he didn't play it too late."

"Seems as if he was playing it when—it happened," Constable Grogan said. "That don't look much like suicide, sir."

"I didn't say it was suicide."

Grogan whistled. "You don't think—"

"I'm not thinking anything—until after the inquest. All I say is that it's queer."

Another aspect of the matter seemed to strike the policeman. "I guess this ain't going to do the Excelsior any good, ma'am," he said sympathetically.

Mrs. Pickett shrugged.

"I suppose I had better go and notify the coroner," said the doctor.

He went out, and after a momentary pause the policeman followed. Constable Grogan was not greatly troubled with nerves, but he felt a decided desire to be where he could not see the dead man's staring eyes.

Mrs. Pickett remained where she was, looking down at the still form on the floor. Her face was expressionless, but inwardly she was tormented and alarmed. It was the first time such a thing as this had happened at the Excelsior, and, as Constable Grogan had suggested, it was not likely to increase the attractiveness of the house in the eyes of possible boarders. It was not the threatened pecuniary loss which was troubling her. As far as money was concerned, she could have lived comfortably on her savings, for she was richer than most of her friends supposed. It was the blot on the escutcheon of the Excelsior, the stain on its reputation, which was tormenting her.

The Excelsior was her life. Starting many years before, beyond the memory of the oldest boarder, she had built up a model establishment. Men spoke of it as a place where you were fed well, cleanly housed, and where petty robbery was unknown.

Such was the chorus of praise that it is not likely that much harm could come to the Excelsior from a single mysterious death, but Mother Pickett was not consoling herself with that.

She looked at the dead man with pale grim eyes. Out in the hallway the doctor's voice further increased her despair. He was talking to the police on the telephone, and she could distinctly hear his every word.

The offices of Mr. Paul Snyder's Detective Agency in New Oxford Street had grown in the course of a dozen years from a single room to an impressive suite bright with polished wood, clicking typewriters, and other evidences of success. Where once Mr. Snyder had sat and waited for clients and attended to them himself, he now sat in his private office and directed eight assistants.

He had just accepted a case—a case that might be nothing at all or something exceedingly big. It was on the latter possibility that he had gambled. The fee offered was, judged by his present standards of prosperity, small. But the bizarre facts, coupled with something in the personality of the client, had won him over. He briskly touched the bell and requested that Mr. Oakes should be sent in to him.

Elliott Oakes was a young man who both amused and interested Mr. Snyder, for though he had only recently joined the staff, he made no secret of his intention of revolutionizing the methods of the agency. Mr. Snyder himself, in common with most of his assistants, relied for results on hard work and common sense. He had never been a detective of the showy type. Results had justified his methods, but he was perfectly aware that young Mr. Oakes looked on him as a dull old man who had been miraculously favored by luck.

Mr. Snyder had selected Oakes for the case in hand principally because it was one where inexperience could do no harm, and where the brilliant guesswork which Oakes preferred to call his inductive reasoning might achieve an unexpected success.

Another motive actuated Mr. Snyder. He had a strong suspicion that the conduct of this case was going to have the beneficial result of lowering Oakes's self-esteem. If failure achieved this end, Mr. Snyder felt that failure, though it would not help the agency, would not be an unmixed ill.

The door opened and Oakes entered tensely. He did everything tensely, partly from a natural nervous energy, and partly as a pose. He was a lean young man, with dark eyes and a thin-lipped mouth, and he looked quite as much like a typical detective as Mr. Snyder looked like a comfortable and prosperous stockbroker.

"Sit down, Oakes," said Mr. Snyder. "I've got a job for you."

Oakes sank into a chair like a crouching leopard and placed the tips of his fingers together. He nodded curtly. It was part of his pose to be keen and silent.

"I want you to go to this address"—Mr. Snyder handed him an envelope—"and look around. The address is of a sailors' boardinghouse down in Southampton. You know the sort of place—retired sea captains and so on live there. All most respectable. In all its history nothing more sensational has ever happened than a case of suspected cheating at halfpenny nap. Well, a man has died there."

"Murdered?" Oakes asked.

"I don't know. That's for you to find out. The coroner left it open. 'Death by Misadventure' was the verdict, and I don't blame him. I don't see how it could have been murder. The door was locked on the inside, so nobody could have got in."

"The window?"

"The window was open, granted. But the room is on the second floor. Anyway, you may dismiss the window. I remember the old lady saying there were bars across it, and that nobody could have squeezed through."

Oakes's eyes glistened. "What was the cause of death?" he asked.

Mr. Snyder coughed. "Snake bite," he said.

Oakes's careful calm deserted him. He uttered a cry of astonishment. "Why, that's incredible!"

"It's the literal truth. The medical examination proved that the fellow had been killed by snake poison—cobra, to be exact, which is found principally in India."

"Cobra!"

"Just so. In a Southampton boardinghouse, in a room with a door locked on the inside, this man was stung by a cobra. To add a little mystification to the limpid simplicity of the affair, when the door was opened there was no sign of any cobra. It couldn't have got out through the door, because the door was locked. It couldn't have got out of the window, because the window was too high up, and snakes can't jump. And it couldn't have got up the chimney, because there was no chimney. So there you have it."

He looked at Oakes with a certain quiet satisfaction. It had come to his ears that Oakes had been heard to complain of the infantile nature of the last two cases to which he had been assigned. He had even said that he hoped some day to be given a problem which should be beyond the reasoning powers of a child of six. It seemed to Mr. Snyder that Oakes was about to get his wish.

"I should like further details," said Oakes, a little breathlessly.

"You had better apply to Mrs. Pickett, who owns the boardinghouse," Mr. Snyder said. "It was she who put the case in my hands. She is convinced that it is murder. But if we exclude ghosts, I don't see how any third party could have taken a hand in the thing at all. However, she wanted a man from this agency, and was prepared to pay for him, so I promised her I would send one. It is not our policy to turn business away."

He smiled wryly. "In pursuance of that policy I want you to go and put up at Mrs. Pickett's boardinghouse and do your best to enhance the reputation of our agency. I would suggest that you pose as a ship's chandler or something of

that sort. You will have to be something maritime or they'll be suspicious of you. And if your visit produces no other results, it will, at least, enable you to make the acquaintance of a very remarkable woman. I commend Mrs. Pickett to your notice. By the way, she says she will help you in your investigations."

Oakes laughed shortly. The idea amused him.

"It's a mistake to scoff at amateur assistance, my boy," said Mr. Snyder in the benevolently paternal manner which had made a score of criminals refuse to believe him a detective until the moment when the handcuffs snapped on their wrists. "Crime investigation isn't an exact science. Success or failure depends in a large measure on applied common sense and the possession of a great deal of special information. Mrs. Pickett knows certain things which neither you nor I know, and it's just possible that she may have some stray piece of information which will provide the key to the entire mystery."

Oakes laughed again. "It is very kind of Mrs. Pickett," he said, "but I prefer to trust to my own methods." Oakes rose, his face purposeful. "I'd better be starting at once," he said. "I'll send you reports from time to time."

"Good. The more detailed the better," said Mr. Snyder genially. "I hope your visit to the Excelsior will be pleasant. And cultivate Mrs. Pickett. She's worthwhile."

The door closed, and Mr. Snyder lighted a fresh cigar. Dashed young fool, he thought and turned his mind to other matters.

A day later Mr. Snyder sat in his office reading a typewritten report. It appeared to be of a humorous nature, for, as he read, chuckles escaped him. Finishing the last sheet he threw his head back and laughed heartily. The manuscript had not been intended by its author for a humorous effect. What Mr. Snyder had been reading was the first of Elliott Oakes' reports from the Excelsior. It read as follows:

"I am sorry to be unable to report any real progress. I have formed several theories which I will put forward later, but at present I cannot say that I am hopeful.

"Directly I arrived I sought out Mrs. Pickett, explained who I was, and requested her to furnish me with any further information which might be of service to me. She is a strange silent woman, who impressed me as having very little intelligence. Your suggestion that I should avail myself of her assistance seems more curious than ever, now that I have seen her.

"The whole affair seems to me at the moment of writing quite inexplicable. Assuming that this Captain Gunner was murdered, there appears to have been no motive for the crime whatsoever. I have made careful inquiries about him, and find that he was a man of 55; had spent nearly 40 years of his life at sea, the last dozen in command of his own ship; was of a somewhat overbearing disposition, though with a fund of rough humour; he had travelled all over the world, and had been a resident of the Excelsior for about ten months. He had a small annuity, and no other money at all, which disposes of money as the motive for the crime.

"In my character of James Burton, a retired ship's chandler, I have mixed with the other boarders, and have heard all they have to say about the affair. I gather that the deceased was by no means popular. He appears to have had a bitter tongue, and I have not met one man who seems to regret his death. On the other hand, I have heard nothing which would suggest that he had any active and violent enemies. He was simply the unpopular boarder—there is always one in every boardinghouse—but nothing more.

"I have seen a good deal of the man who shared his room—another sea captain named Muller. He is a big silent person, and it is not easy to get him to talk. As regards the death of Captain Gunner he can tell me nothing. It seems that on the night of the tragedy he was away at Portsmouth with some friends. All I have got from him is some information as to Captain Gunner's habits, which leads nowhere.

"The dead man seldom drank, except at night when he would take some whisky. His head was not strong, and a little of the spirit was enough to make him semi-intoxicated, when he would be hilarious and often insulting. I gather that Muller found him a difficult roommate, but he is one of those placid persons who can put up with anything. He and Gunner were in the habit of playing draughts together every night in their room, and Gunner had a harmonica which he played frequently. Apparently he was playing it very soon before he died, which is significant, as seeming to dispose of any idea of suicide.

"As I say, I have one or two theories, but they are in a very nebulous state. The most plausible is that on one of his visits to India—I have ascertained that he made several voyages there—Captain Gunner may in some way have fallen foul of the natives. The fact that he certainly died of the poison of an Indian snake supports this theory. I am making inquiries as to the movements of several Indian sailors who were here in their ships at the time of the tragedy.

"I have another theory. Does Mrs. Pickett know more about this affair than she appears to? I may be wrong in my estimate of her mental qualities. Her apparent stupidity may be cunning. But here again, the absence of motive brings me up against a dead wall. I must confess that at present I do not see my way clearly. However, I will write again shortly."

Mr. Snyder derived the utmost enjoyment from the report. He liked the substance of it, and above all, he was tickled by the bitter tone of frustration which characterized it. Oakes was baffled, and his knowledge of Oakes told him that the sensation of being baffled was gall and wormwood to that high-spirited young man. Whatever might be the result of this investigation, it would teach him the virtue of patience.

He wrote his assistant a short note:

"Dear Oakes,

"Your report received. You certainly seem to have got the hard case which, I hear, you were pining for. Don't build too much on plausible motives in a case of this sort. Fauntleroy, the London murderer, killed a

woman for no other reason than that she had thick ankles. Many years ago I myself was on a case where a man murdered an intimate friend because of a dispute about a bet. My experience is that five murderers out of ten act on the whim of the moment, without anything which, properly speaking, you could call a motive at all.

> *Yours very cordially,*
> *Paul Snyder*

P.S. I don't think much of your Pickett theory. However, you're in charge. I wish you luck."

Young Mr. Oakes was not enjoying himself. For the first time in his life the self-confidence which characterized all his actions seemed to be failing him. The change had taken place almost overnight. The fact that the case had the appearance of presenting the unusual had merely stimulated him at first. But then doubts had crept in and the problem had begun to appear insoluble.

True, he had only just taken it up, but something told him that, for all the progress he was likely to make, he might just as well have been working on it steadily for a month. He was completely baffled. And every moment which he spent in the Excelsior boardinghouse made it clearer to him that that infernal old woman with the pale eyes thought him an incompetent fool. It was that, more than anything, which made him acutely conscious of his lack of success. His nerves were being sorely troubled by the quiet scorn of Mrs. Pickett's gaze. He began to think that perhaps he had been a shade too self-confident and abrupt in the short interview which he had had with her on his arrival.

As might have been expected, his first act, after his brief interview with Mrs. Pickett, was to examine the room where the tragedy had taken place. The body was gone, but otherwise nothing had been moved.

Oakes belonged to the magnifying-glass school of detection. The first thing he did on entering the room was to make a careful examination of the floor, the walls, the furniture, and the window sill. He would have hotly denied the assertion that he did this because it looked well, but he would have been hard put to it to advance any other reason.

If he discovered anything, his discoveries were entirely negative and served only to deepen the mystery. As Mr. Snyder had said, there was no chimney, and nobody could have entered through the locked door.

There remained the window. It was small, and apprehensiveness, perhaps, of the possibility of burglars had caused the proprietress to make it doubly secure with two iron bars. No human being could have squeezed his way through.

It was late that night that he wrote and dispatched to headquarters the report which had amused Mr. Snyder.

Two days later Mr. Snyder sat at his desk, staring with wide unbelieving eyes at a telegram he had just received. It read as follows:

HAVE SOLVED GUNNER MYSTERY.
RETURNING. OAKES.

Mr. Snyder narrowed his eyes and rang the bell.

"Send Mr. Oakes to me directly he arrives," he said.

He was pained to find that his chief emotion was one of bitter annoyance. The swift solution of such an apparently insoluble problem would reflect the highest credit of the agency, and there were picturesque circumstances connected with the case which would make it popular with the newspapers and lead to its being given a great deal of publicity.

Yet, in spite of all this, Mr. Snyder was annoyed. He realized now how large a part the desire to reduce Oakes's self-esteem had played with him. He further realized, looking at the thing honestly, that he had been firmly convinced that the young man would not come within a mile of a reasonable solution of the mystery. He had desired only that his failure would prove a valuable educational experience for him. For he believed that failure at this particular point in his career would make Oakes a more valuable asset to the agency.

But now here Oakes was, within a ridiculously short space of time, returning to the fold, not humble and defeated, but triumphant. Mr. Snyder looked forward with apprehension to the young man's probable demeanor under the intoxicating influence of victory.

His apprehensions were well grounded. He had barely finished the third of the series of cigars which, like milestones, marked the progress of his afternoon, when the door opened and young Oakes entered. Mr. Snyder could not repress a faint moan at the sight of him. One glance was enough to tell him that his worst fears were realized.

"I got your telegram," said Mr. Snyder.

Oakes nodded. "It surprised you, eh?" he asked.

Mr. Snyder resented the patronizing tone of the question, but he had resigned himself to be patronized, and keep his anger in check.

"Yes," he replied, "I must say it did surprise me. I didn't gather from your report that you had even found a clue. Was it the Indian theory that turned the trick?"

Oakes laughed tolerantly. "Oh, I never really believed that preposterous theory for one moment. I just put it in to round out my report. I hadn't begun to think about the case then—not really think."

Mr. Snyder, nearly exploding with wrath, extended his cigar case. "Light up and tell me all about it," he said, controlling his anger.

"Well, I won't say I haven't earned this," said Oakes, puffing away. He let the ash of his cigar fall delicately to the floor—another action which seemed significant to his employer. As a rule his assistants, unless particularly pleased with themselves, used the ashtray.

"My first act on arriving," Oakes said, "was to have a talk with Mrs. Pickett. A very dull old woman."

"Curious. She struck me as rather intelligent."

"Not on your life. She gave me no assistance whatever. I then examined the room where the death had taken place. It was exactly as you described it. There was no chimney, the door had been locked on the inside, and the one window was too high up. At first sight it looked extremely unpromising. Then I had a chat with some of the other boarders. They had nothing of any importance to contribute. Most of them simply gibbered. I then gave up trying to get help from the outside and resolved to rely on my own intelligence."

He smiled triumphantly. "It is a theory of mine, Mr. Snyder, which I have found valuable that, in nine cases out of ten, remarkable things don't happen."

"I don't quite follow you there," Mr. Snyder interrupted.

"I will put it another way, if you like. What I mean is that the simplest explanation is nearly always the right one. Consider this case. It seemed impossible that there should have been any reasonable explanation of the man's death. Most men would have worn themselves out guessing at wild theories. If I had started to do that, I should have been guessing now. As it is— here I am. I trusted to my belief that nothing remarkable ever happens, and I won out."

Mr. Snyder sighed softly. Oakes was entitled to a certain amount of gloating, but there could be no doubt that his way of telling a story was downright infuriating.

"I believe in the logical sequence of events. I refuse to accept effects unless they are preceded by causes. In other words, with all due respect to your possibly contrary opinions, Mr. Snyder, I simply decline to believe in a murder unless there was a motive for it. The first thing I set myself to ascertain was—what was the motive for the murder of Captain Gunner? And after thinking it over and making every possible inquiry, I decided that there was no motive. Therefore, there was no murder."

Mr. Snyder's mouth opened, and he obviously was about to protest. But he appeared to think better of it and Oakes proceeded: "I then tested the suicide theory. What motive was there for suicide? There was no motive. Therefore, there was no suicide."

This time Mr. Snyder spoke. "You haven't been spending the last few days in the wrong house by any chance, have you? You will be telling me next that there wasn't any dead man."

Oakes smiled. "Not at all. Captain John Gunner was dead, all right. As the medical evidence proved, he died of the bite of a cobra. It was a small cobra which came from Java."

Mr. Snyder stared at him. "How do you know?"

"I do know, beyond any possibility of doubt."

"Did you see the snake?"

Oakes shook his head.

"Then, how in heaven's name—"

"I have enough evidence to make a jury convict Mr. Snake without leaving the box."

"Then suppose you tell me this. How did your cobra from Java get out of the room?"

"By the window," replied Oakes impassively.

"How can you possibly explain that? You say yourself that the window was too high up."

"Nevertheless, it got out by the window. The logical sequence of events is proof enough that it was in the room. It killed Captain Gunner there and left traces of its presence outside. Therefore, as the window was the only exit, it must have escaped by that route. Somehow it got out of that window."

"What do you mean—it left traces of its presence outside?"

"It killed a dog in the back yard behind the house," Oakes said. "The window of Captain Gunner's room projects out over it. It is full of boxes and litter and there are a few stunted shrubs scattered about. In fact, there is enough cover to hide any small object like the body of a dog. That's why it was not discovered at first. The maid at the Excelsior came on it the morning after I sent you my report while she was emptying a box of ashes in the yard. It was just an ordinary stray dog without collar or license. The analyst examined the body and found that the dog had died of the bite of a cobra."

"But you didn't find the snake?"

"No. We cleaned out that yard till you could have eaten your breakfast there, but the snake had gone. It must have escaped through the door of the yard, which was standing ajar. That was a couple of days ago, and there has been no further tragedy. In all likelihood it is dead. The nights are pretty cold now, and it would probably have died of exposure."

"But I just don't understand how a cobra got to Southampton," said the amazed Mr. Snyder.

"Can't you guess it? I told you it came from Java."

"How did you know it did?"

"Captain Muller told me. Not directly, but I pieced it together from what he said. It seems that an old shipmate of Captain Gunner's was living in Java. They corresponded, and occasionally this man would send the captain a present as a mark of his esteem. The last present he sent was a crate of bananas. Unfortunately, the snake must have got in unnoticed. That's why I told you the cobra was a small one. Well, that's my case against Mr. Snake, and short of catching him with the goods, I don't see how I could have made out a stronger one. Don't you agree?"

It went against the grain for Mr. Snyder to acknowledge defeat, but he was a fair-minded man, and he was forced to admit that Oakes did certainly seem to have solved the impossible.

"I congratulate you, my boy," he said as heartily as he could. "To be completely frank, when you started out, I didn't think you could do it. By the way, I suppose Mrs. Pickett was pleased?"

"If she was, she didn't show it. I'm pretty well convinced she hasn't enough sense to be pleased at anything. However, she has invited me to dinner with her tonight. I imagine she'll be as boring as usual, but she made such a point of it, I had to accept."

For some time after Oakes had gone, Mr. Snyder sat smoking and thinking, in embittered meditation. Suddenly there was brought the card of Mrs. Pickett, who would be grateful if he could spare her a few moments. Mr. Snyder was glad to see Mrs. Pickett. He was a student of character, and she had interested him at their first meeting. There was something about her which had seemed to him unique, and he welcomed this second chance of studying her at close range.

She came in and sat down stiffly, balancing herself on the extreme edge of the chair in which a short while before young Oakes had lounged so luxuriously.

"How are you, Mrs. Pickett?" said Mr. Snyder genially. "I'm very glad that you could find time to pay me a visit. Well, so it wasn't murder after all."

"Sir?"

"I've been talking to Mr. Oakes, whom you met as James Burton," said the detective. "He has told me all about it."

"He told *me* all about it," said Mrs. Pickett dryly.

Mr. Snyder looked at her inquiringly. Her manner seemed more suggestive than her words.

"A conceited, headstrong young fool," said Mrs. Pickett.

It was no new picture of his assistant that she had drawn. Mr. Snyder had often drawn it himself, but at the present juncture it surprised him. Oakes, in his hour of triumph, surely did not deserve this sweeping condemnation.

"Did not Mr. Oakes's solution of the mystery satisfy you, Mrs. Pickett?"

"No."

"It struck me as logical and convincing," Mr. Snyder said.

"You may call it all the fancy names you please, Mr. Snyder. But Mr. Oakes's solution was not the right one."

"Have you an alternative to offer?"

Mrs. Pickett tightened her lips.

"If you have, I should like to hear it."

"You will—at the proper time."

"What makes you so certain that Mr. Oakes is wrong?"

"He starts out with an impossible explanation and rests his whole case on it. There couldn't have been a snake in that room because

it couldn't have gotten out. The window was too high."

"But surely the evidence of the dead dog?"

Mrs. Pickett looked at him as if he had disappointed her. "I had always heard *you* spoken of as a man with common sense, Mr. Snyder."

"I have always tried to use common sense."

"Then why are you trying now to make yourself believe that something happened which could not possibly have happened just because it fits in with something which isn't easy to explain?"

"You mean that there is another explanation of the dead dog?" Mr. Snyder asked.

"Not *another*. What Mr. Oakes takes for granted is not an explanation. But there is a common-sense explanation, and if he had not been so headstrong and conceited he might have found it."

"You speak as if you had found it," said Mr. Snyder.

"I have." Mrs. Pickett leaned forward as she spoke, and stared at him defiantly.

Mr. Snyder started. "*You* have?"

"Yes."

"What is it?"

"You will know before tomorrow. In the meantime try and think it out for yourself. A successful and prosperous detective agency like yours, Mr. Snyder, ought to do something in return for a fee."

There was something in her manner so reminiscent of the school-teacher reprimanding a recalcitrant pupil that Mr. Snyder's sense of humor came to his rescue. "We do our best, Mrs. Pickett," he said. "But you mustn't forget that we are only human and cannot guarantee results."

Mrs. Pickett did not pursue the subject. Instead, she proceeded to astonish Mr. Snyder by asking him to swear out a warrant for the arrest of a man known to them both on a charge of murder.

Mr. Snyder's breath was not often taken away in his own office. As a rule he received his clients' communications calmly, strange as they often were. But at her words he gasped. The thought crossed his mind that Mrs. Pickett might be mentally unbalanced.

Mrs. Pickett was regarding him with an unfaltering stare. To all outward appearances she was the opposite of unbalanced.

"But you can't swear out a warrant without evidence," he told her.

"I have evidence," she replied firmly.

"Precisely what kind of evidence?" he demanded.

"If I told you now you would think that I was out of my mind."

"But, Mrs. Pickett, do you realize what you are asking me to do? I cannot make this agency responsible for the arbitrary arrest of a man on the strength of a single individual's suspicions. It might ruin me. At the least it would make me a laughingstock."

"Mr. Snyder, you may use your own judgment whether or not to swear out that warrant. You will listen to what I have to say, and you will see for yourself how the crime was committed. If after that you feel that you cannot make the arrest I will accept your decision. I know who killed Captain Gunner," she said. "I knew it from the beginning. But I had no proof. Now things have come to light and everything is clear."

Against his judgment Mr. Snyder was impressed. This woman had the magnetism which makes for persuasiveness.

"It—it sounds incredible." Even as he spoke, he remembered that it had long been a professional maxim of his that nothing was incredible, and he weakened still further.

"Mr. Snyder, I ask you to swear out that warrant."

The detective gave in. "Very well," he said.

Mrs. Pickett rose. "If you will come and dine at my house tonight I think I can prove to you that it will be needed. Will you come?"

"I'll come," promised Mr. Snyder.

Mr. Snyder arrived at the Excelsior and shortly after he was shown into the little private sitting room where he found Oakes, the third guest of the evening unexpectedly arrived.

Mr. Snyder looked curiously at the newcomer. Captain Muller had a peculiar fascination for him. It was not Mr. Snyder's habit to trust overmuch to appearances. But he could not help admitting that there was something about this man's aspect, something odd—an unnatural aspect of gloom. He bore himself like one carrying a heavy burden. His eyes were dull, his face haggard. The next moment the detective was reproaching himself with allowing his imagination to run away with his calmer judgment.

The door opened and Mrs. Pickett came in. She made no apology for her lateness.

To Mr. Snyder one of the most remarkable points about the dinner was the peculiar metamorphosis of Mrs. Pickett from the brooding silent woman he had known to the gracious and considerate hostess.

Oakes appeared also to be overcome with surprise, so much so that he was unable to keep his astonishment to himself. He had come prepared to endure a dull evening absorbed in grim silence, and he found himself instead opposite a bottle of champagne of a brand and year which commanded his utmost respect. What was even more incredible, his hostess had transformed herself into a pleasant old lady whose only aim seemed to be to make him feel at home.

Beside each of the guest's plates was a neat paper parcel. Oakes picked his up, and stared at it in wonderment. "Why, this is more than a party souvenir, Mrs. Pickett," he said. "It's the kind of mechanical marvel I've always wanted to have on my desk."

"I'm glad you like it, Mr. Oakes," Mrs. Pickett said, smiling. "You must not think of me simply as a tired old woman whom age has completely defeated. I am an ambitious hostess. When I give these little parties, I like to make them a success. I want each of you to remember this dinner."

"I'm sure I will."

Mrs. Pickett smiled again. "I think you all

will. You, Mr. Snyder." She paused. "And you, Captain Muller."

To Mr. Snyder there was so much meaning in her voice as she said this that he was amazed that it conveyed no warning to Muller. Captain Muller, however, was already drinking heavily. He looked up when addressed and uttered a sound which might have been taken for an expression of polite acquiescence. Then he filled his glass again.

Mr. Snyder's parcel revealed a watch charm fashioned in the shape of a tiny candid-eye camera. "That," said Mrs. Pickett, "is a compliment to your profession." She leaned toward the captain. "Mr. Snyder is a detective, Captain Muller."

He looked up. It seemed to Mr. Snyder that a look of fear lit up his heavy eyes for an instant. It came and went, if indeed it came at all, so swiftly that he could not be certain.

"So?" said Captain Muller. He spoke quite evenly, with just the amount of interest which such an announcement would naturally produce.

"Now for yours, Captain," said Oakes. "I guess it's something special. It's twice the size of mine, anyway."

It may have been something in the old woman's expression as she watched Captain Muller slowly tearing the paper that sent a thrill of excitement through Mr. Snyder. Something seemed to warn him of the approach of a psychological moment. He bent forward eagerly.

There was a strangled gasp, a thump, and onto the table from the captain's hands there fell a little harmonica. There was no mistaking the look on Muller's face now. His cheeks were like wax, and his eyes, so dull till then, blazed with a panic and horror which he could not repress. The glasses on the table rocked as he clutched at the cloth.

Mrs. Pickett spoke. "Why, Captain Muller, has it upset you? I thought that, as his best friend, the man who shared his room, you would value a memento of Captain Gunner. How fond you must have been of him for the sight of his harmonica to be such a shock."

The captain did not speak. He was staring fascinated at the thing on the table. Mrs. Pickett turned to Mr. Snyder. Her eyes, as they met his, held him entranced.

"Mr. Snyder, as a detective, you will be interested in a curious and very tragic affair which happened in this house a few days ago. One of my boarders, Captain Gunner, was found dead in his room. It was the room which he shared with Mr. Muller. I am very proud of the reputation of my house, Mr. Snyder, and it was a blow to me that this should have happened. I applied to an agency for a detective, and they sent me a stupid boy, with nothing to recommend him except his belief in himself. He said that Captain Gunner had died by accident, killed by a snake which had come out of a crate of bananas. I knew better. I knew that Captain Gunner had been murdered. Are you listening, Captain Muller? This will interest you, as you were such a friend of his."

The captain did not answer. He was staring straight before him, as if he saw something invisible in eyes forever closed in death.

"Yesterday we found the body of a dog. It had been killed, as Captain Gunner had been, by the poison of a snake. The boy from the agency said that this was conclusive. He said that the snake had escaped from the room after killing Captain Gunner and had in turn killed the dog. I knew that to be impossible, for, if there had been a snake in that room it could not have made its escape."

Her eyes flashed and became remorselessly accusing. "It was not a snake that killed Captain Gunner. It was a cat. Captain Gunner had a friend who hated him. One day, in opening a crate of bananas, this friend found a snake. He killed it, and extracted the poison. He knew Captain Gunner's habits. He knew that he played a harmonica. This man also had a cat. He knew that cats hated the sound of a harmonica. He had often seen this particular cat fly at Captain Gunner and scratch him when he played. He took the cat and covered its claws with the poison. And then he left the cat in the room with Captain Gunner. He knew what would happen."

Oakes and Mr. Snyder were on their feet. Captain Muller had not moved. He sat there, his fingers gripping the cloth. Mrs. Pickett rose and went to a closet. She unlocked the door. "Kitty!" she called. "Kitty! Kitty!"

A black cat ran swiftly out into the room. With a clatter and a crash of crockery and a ringing of glass the table heaved, rocked, and overturned as Muller staggered to his feet. He threw up his hands as if to ward something off. A choking cry came from his lips. "Gott! Gott!"

Mrs. Pickett's voice rang through the room, cold and biting. "Captain Muller, you murdered Captain Gunner!"

The captain shuddered. Then mechanically he replied, "Gott! Yes, I killed him."

"You heard, Mr. Snyder," said Mrs. Pickett. "He has confessed before witnesses."

Muller allowed himself to be moved toward the door. His arm in Mr. Snyder's grip felt limp. Mrs. Pickett stopped and took something from the debris on the floor. She rose, holding the harmonica.

"You are forgetting your souvenir, Captain Muller," she said.

OUR FINAL HOPE
IS FLAT DESPAIR

Some stories simply can't be categorized.

MARTIN EDWARDS

DUE TO HIS CAREER as a solicitor, the writing career of Kenneth Martin Edwards (1955–) began with such thrilling volumes as *Understanding Computer Contracts* (1983) and *Managing Redundancies* (1986). Fortunately, his affection for crime fiction led to his writing *All the Lonely People* (1991), which introduced Liverpool lawyer Harry Devlin, who is the protagonist of seven additional novels. That effort was nominated for the John Creasey Dagger by the (British) Crime Writers' Association for best first novel. In addition to the Devlin novels, Edwards has written several novels about Detective Chief Inspector Hannah Scarlett and historian Daniel Kind that are set in the Lake District. He has also written *Take My Breath Away* (2002), a novel of psychological suspense, and *Dancing for the Hangman* (2008), a fictionalized version of the life of Hawley Harvey Crippen, the American physician hanged in a London prison in 1910 for murdering his wife. Edwards is an exceptional short-story writer, with more than forty to his credit, including "Test Drive," nominated for a Dagger in 2005, and "The Bookbinder's Apprentice," which won a Dagger in 2008. Additionally, he has edited more than thirty mystery anthologies, reviewed crime fiction since 1987, and contributed to mystery fiction reference works. He was elected in 2008 to the prestigious Detection Club, the membership of which is reserved for the most distinguished mystery writers in the United Kingdom.

"Waiting for Godstow" was first published in *The Mammoth Book of Locked-Room Mysteries and Impossible Crimes*, edited by Mike Ashley (London, Robinson, 2000).

WAITING FOR GODSTOW

MARTIN EDWARDS

CLAIRE DOHERTY practised her grief-stricken expression in the mirror. Quivering lip, excellent. Lowered lashes, very suitable. All that she needed to do now was to make sure she kept the glint of triumph out of her eyes and everything would be fine.

She glanced at the living room clock for the thousandth time. Time passed slowly when you were waiting for bad news. The call could not come soon enough, that call which would bring the message that her husband was dead. Then she would have to prepare herself for her new role as a heartbroken widow. It would be a challenge, but she was determined to meet it head on. More than that, she would positively relish playing the part.

If only she didn't have to rely on Zack doing what he had to do. Zack was gorgeous and he did things for her that previously she had only read about in magazines, while having her hair done. But he was young and careless and there was so much that could yet go wrong. No wonder that she kept checking the clock, shaking her watch to see if it had stopped when it seemed that time was standing still. She readily admitted to friends that patience wasn't one of her virtues. Besides, she would add, vices are so much more interesting anyway. Above all, she liked to be in control, hated being dependent on others. It was hard being reduced to counting the minutes until freedom finally came her way.

The phone trilled and she snatched up the receiver. "Yes?" she demanded breathlessly.

"Is that Mrs. Doherty?" The voice belonged to a woman. Late twenties, at a guess. She sounded anxious.

"Yes, what is it?" If it was a wrong number, she would scream.

"I'm sorry to bother you, really I am."

"No problem." It was all she could do not to hiss: get off the line, don't you realize I'm waiting for someone to tell me my husband is dead?

"My name is Bailey. Jennifer Bailey from Bradford."

Oh, for God's sake. Karl's latest floosie. Suppressing the urge to give the woman a mouthful, Claire said coldly, "Can I help you?"

"It's just that your husband left a few minutes ago. I'm afraid I kept him longer than expected. He was rather concerned, because he said he would be late home and his mobile didn't seem to be working. So I offered to give you a ring to let you know he is on his way. He said he should be with you in about an hour-and-a-half if the road was clear. You live on the far side of Manchester, I gather?"

"That's right." Claire thought for a moment. "Thank you. It's good of you to let me know."

"My pleasure," Jennifer Bailey said.

She said it as though she meant it. Indeed, she sounded so timid that it was hard to believe that she had probably spent the last couple of hours *in flagrante* with Karl. Perhaps he'd tired of the bimbos and was now taking an interest in the submissive type. Someone as different from herself, Claire thought grimly after she put down the phone, as he could manage to find.

Would the delay have caused a problem? Something else for her to worry about. Zack had refused to tell her precisely how and when he proposed to do what was necessary. He said it was better that way. Claire knew he could never resist a melodramatic flourish. She blamed it on all the videos he watched. It amused her, though, all the same. She'd gathered that he would be keeping his eye on Jennifer Bailey's house, with a view to dealing with Karl when he emerged. So he would have had to wait for a while. Surely that wouldn't have been too much of a challenge. She was having to wait. Was it so much to ask that her lover should also have to bide his time?

The phone rang again. Claire made an effort not to sound too wound-up. "Yes?"

"It's done." Zack sounded pleased with himself, relaxed. He liked to come across as cool, as comfortable with violence as a character from a Tarantino movie. "No worries."

"Wonderful," she said. The tension went out of her; she felt giddy with the sense of release.

"I know I am," he said roguishly.

"How . . . ?"

"Hit and run. Stolen Fiesta. No witnesses."

"You're sure about that?"

"Bradford's pretty quiet at night, you know."

"And he's definitely . . . ?"

"Believe me," he said with a snigger. "I reversed back the way I'd come, just to make sure. The job's a good 'un."

How could she ever have doubted him? After saying goodbye, she hugged herself with delight. He might only be a boy, but he'd kept his word. He'd promised to free her and that was exactly what he had done. She uttered a silent prayer of thanks that she'd agreed to let him ring her, to prevent the suspense becoming unbearable. He'd said he would nick a mobile from somewhere and call her on it before throwing it away. She'd worried that the call might be traced, but he said the police would never check and, even if they did, so what? She had an alibi and besides, he meant to make sure Karl's death looked like

an accident. She should stop fretting and leave it all to him.

She'd gambled on him and her faith had been repaid. She could hardly believe it. Part of her wanted to crack open a bottle of champagne. Never mind waiting for it to be safe for Zack to come here and share in the celebrations. But it wasn't safe. There was no telling when the police might turn up at her door with the tidings of Karl's demise. She made do with a cup of tea. She would need to have all her wits about her, so that no-one would ever suspect there might be more to the death than met the eye.

Poor Karl. She wasn't so heartless as to deny him a thought. At least it had been a quick end. Besides, he didn't have too many grounds for complaint. He had died happy. Jennifer Bailey didn't give the impression of being a ball of fire, but perhaps she'd simply been daunted by the need to speak to her lover's wife on the phone. She'd certainly kept him occupied for most of the evening.

She smiled indulgently, remembering how Karl had downplayed his trip to see Jennifer. "I really tried every trick in the book," he'd said. Protesting rather too much, she had thought. "I was desperate to cancel the appointment. I mean, you know what it's like. A one-legger is hopeless, a complete waste of time."

Karl was a salesman. It didn't matter much to him what he sold. Kitchens, carpets, computers. He was good at it. Persuasive. No wonder he had charmed her into marrying him. He could talk for England. Trouble was, he wasn't so hot when it came to performance. But that never seemed to bother him. Currently he was working for a firm that specialized in bespoke loft conversions. The commission was good, provided you made the sale—and that was the rub. No one with any nous ever wanted to bother with a one-legger. The object of a home sales visit was to get the punters to sign up on the dotted line. But people would do anything to avoid making a commitment to buy. When you were dealing with a married couple, it was vital to have them both there, listening to the pitch. If you had to contend with a one-legger, it was too easy for the decision to be dependent on the okay of the absent spouse. If that happened, then nine times out of ten, the sale would never be made. It was all about human nature, as Karl often said. He fancied himself as an amateur psychologist. In fact, Claire thought, he fancied himself, full stop. That was true of Zack too, of course. But with rather more reason.

"She's married, then, this Mrs. Bailey?" Claire had asked, a picture of innocence.

"Oh yeah. Husband's away a lot, she says."

I bet, Claire thought. "What sort of age is she?"

Karl pursed his lips, considering. "Middle-aged, I'd say. Yeah, that's it. Fat, fair, and forty."

Lying bastard. The woman on the phone had been much younger than that. Oh well. It didn't matter now. Zack had done the necessary. Now all she had to think about was whether she still looked good in black. It was a young colour, she thought, and you needed the figure to carry it off. But she had a few years left in her yet, that was for sure. And with the benefit of the pay-out on Karl's life insurance, she meant to make the most of them.

Suppose it didn't work out with Zack. She dipped into a box of After Eights and told herself she had to be realistic. He was a hunk, and he'd carried out his task more efficiently than she had dared hope, but he wasn't necessarily the ideal lifetime soulmate. No-one so keen on motorbikes and football could be. Not to worry. She could play the field, look around for someone handsome who could help her to get over her tragic loss.

The doorbell sounded. Suddenly her mouth was dry, her stomach churning. This was the test, the moment when she would need to call up all the skills from her days in amateur theatre. She'd tended to be typecast as a dumb blonde, but now she must be shattered by bereavement. She took a deep breath.

The doorbell rang again, long and loud. She checked the mirror. Eyebrows raised, lips slightly parted. Understandable puzzlement at such a late call. A faint touch of apprehension. Perfect.

She remembered to keep the door on the chain. An important detail. These things mattered. The police must not think that she had been expecting them to turn up. In fact, they had moved quickly. Impressive efficiency. She had not thought they would be here so soon.

The door opened and she saw her husband Karl on the step. He was breathing heavily. Yes, despite Zack's claim to have killed him, he was definitely still breathing.

Five minutes later, she was telling herself that it was a good thing that Karl was so obviously— and uncharacteristically—flustered. Flustered and, more typically, self-centred, concerned only with himself. He had not noticed how his arrival had shocked her.

"Here you are." Her hands were trembling as she passed him the tumbler of whisky he had asked for. She poured one for herself. Both of them needed to calm down.

"Thanks, darling." He swallowed the drink in a gulp. "Christ, I needed that."

"Uh-huh." She wasn't going to panic, whatever the temptation. Faced with a husband who had died and achieved resurrection within the space of half-an-hour, the best course was to say as little as possible. He was obviously panic-stricken. And he needed her help. These days he only called her darling when he wanted something.

"Listen," he said hoarsely. His tie was at half mast and his hair, normally immaculate, was a tousled mess. "I have—a bit of a problem."

"What sort of problem?"

"I'm not going to bullshit you," he said, in precisely the sincere tone he adopted when lying to her about his trysts with clients or young girls at work. "I'm in a spot of bother. If any questions are asked, I need you to say that I spent the evening here."

"What?" She was baffled. "Who will be asking questions? Why do you need me to lie for you?"

He caught her wrist, and looked into her eyes, treating her to his soulful expression. "Darling, I'm asking you to trust me."

"But why? I mean, none of this makes sense."

"It—it's not something I can talk about right now. Okay?"

No, she wanted to say, *it's bloody well not okay.* But she chose her words with care and spoke more gently than she might have done. "It's just that, if I don't have a clue what has happened, I might just put my foot in it unintentionally. If it's trust we're talking about, don't you think you should trust me enough to tell me what's going on?"

He buried his head in his hands. Claire had never seen him in such a state. If she didn't despise him so much, if she didn't loathe him for not being dead when he was supposed to be, she might almost have felt sorry for him.

"I can't!" It was almost a wail.

"You must," she said, a touch of steel entering her voice.

"But . . ."

She folded her arms. "It's up to you."

He looked up at her. Distressed he might be, but Claire recognized the familiar glint of calculation in his eyes. After a few moments he came to a decision.

"I don't want to say much about it," he said. "But I suppose I do owe you some sort of explanation."

"Yes, you do."

He blinked hard. "It's like this. I had a row with this girl—you know, it's Lynette, who used to work in our office. We were going to go for a drink at this pub in Stockport. Oh, I know it sounds bad, especially after I swore that our little—flirtation—was a thing of the past. But I can explain. Our meeting up was innocent enough, but something happened. There was—an accident. She hit her head. When I tried to bring her round, I realized she was dead."

Claire stared at him, unable to comprehend what he was saying. "You killed Lynette?"

"Oh, don't say it like that. We were in this alleyway near the pub and we started arguing. I gave her a push—a tap, really. She fell over and smashed her head on a jagged stone, simple as that. It was all so sudden. She must have had a thin skull or something. Oh God, I didn't mean this to happen."

"In Stockport, you said? When was this?"

He shrugged, as if irritated by the irrelevance of the question. "Does it matter? Twenty minutes ago, I guess. If that. I broke every speed limit in the book on my way back over here."

"But—your meeting with Jennifer Bailey . . ."

He waved his hand dismissively. "Forget about it. The police mustn't hear about it. I was here at home with you. Watching the box all evening. Okay?"

"I don't understand," she said and it was no more than the truth.

"Oh God," he said again. Tears were trickling down his cheeks. "It just happened. I can't explain any better than that. Not right now."

But he hadn't given any sort of an explanation, so far as Claire was concerned. It wasn't so much the mystery of why he had killed that silly little girl Lynette. Last year's fling had evidently started up again, even though he'd promised he would never see her again after she left the company. No, what Claire could not get her head around was the sheer impossibility of it. How had her husband managed to murder someone in nearby Stockport, when according to Jennifer Bailey he was at one and the same time in Bradford on the other side of the Pennines, and Zack was convinced he'd been run over by a stolen Fiesta?

She wasn't able to contact Zack until the middle of the next morning. Karl didn't work nine-to-five hours and he didn't have any calls to make first thing. But after a night of tossing and turning, he decided to visit the office and file his weekly report. He had managed to regain a semblance of composure and he thought it would be a good idea to be seen to act normally.

On his way out, he kissed her for perhaps the first time in a month. "I just wanted to say— thanks. You've been fantastic. I won't forget that."

Claire gave him a weak smile. It seemed the safest response.

"And you'll remember, won't you? If the police come, we were together all night. You never let me out of your sight for more than a couple of minutes."

"But how do you expect to get away with it?" she asked. "You were with Lynette. Won't someone have seen you?"

He shook his head. "We never made it to the pub. The streets were dead quiet. We both arrived in separate cars. There's nothing to link me with that place. No-one saw us, I'm sure of it."

"I still don't follow," she said. Already she regretted agreeing to help him out. He'd caught her at a bad time the previous night, when she was so shocked by his reappearance that he could have talked her into anything. "I mean, what about Jennifer Bailey? Why not get her to do your dirty work for you?"

His expression was one of genuine horror. "She was a customer. I told you. How could I ask her to give me an alibi? You don't think we were having an affair, do you?"

"Well, I . . ."

"You did! Oh, Claire." He took her hand in his. A romantic gesture; no doubt he employed it with all his conquests. "Listen to me. I realize things haven't been great between us for a while. But we can try again, can't we? I've come to my senses, honestly. You're a wife in a million, I see that now. Will you give me another chance?"

She withdrew her hand. "You're saying you haven't got a thing going with Jennifer Bailey?"

"I told you. She's a middle-aged frump. Last night, I was on my way over to Bradford and I suddenly decided it was a complete waste of time. You know what one-leggers are like. I don't know what got into my head, but I decided to give Lynette a ring. See how she was getting on, for old times' sake, that's all. There was

nothing in it. Zilch. She suggested meeting for a quick drink. But when we met, she made it clear she wanted us to get together again. I told her there was nothing doing, that I wanted to make a go of things with you. She became angry, hysterical. I didn't know how to deal with it. She lunged at me and—and that's when I pushed her."

His voice was breaking. He had missed his true vocation, she thought. He was better at acting than she was; he might have made a fortune on the stage. Because he wasn't telling her the truth, of that she was sure. His story didn't begin to explain why his client, the frump, the one-legger, had called her to say that he was on his way home when he was out pubbing with his floosie. She thought about confronting him, telling him about the message from Jennifer Bailey, but decided against it. He obviously knew nothing about the call. She would keep that morsel of information to herself until she had more of a clue as to what he had really been up to.

As she made herself a snack lunch, Claire asked herself if it was possible that the whole story about killing Lynette was some sort of elaborate charade. She wouldn't put it past him. Like most serial adulterers, Karl possessed a vivid imagination and a gift for telling fairy stories that the Brothers Grimm might have envied. Suppose he planned to resume his affair with the girl. The prospect of divorce held no appeal for him, she was well aware of that. Too expensive. Perhaps he had decided to concoct this extraordinary story of killing the girl by accident so that Claire would think she had him in her power and relax. If she thought Lynette was dead, she wouldn't suspect him of continuing to sleep with her, would she?

No. It was too bizarre. Ridiculous, even by Karl's standards of excessively ingenious subterfuge. There had to be some other explanation. She would need to undertake a bit of detective work. But first, she must find out what had gone wrong at Zack's end. She had tried to phone him as soon as Karl had stepped out of the door, but there was no answer on his mobile. She pressed redial, but as the number began to ring, she heard footsteps coming up the path to the front door. Hurrying into the dining room, she saw through the window that a lean young man was standing on the step, pressing the bell. Quickly, she cancelled her call. Zack would have to wait a few minutes.

Her immediate impression when she answered the door was that the young man was almost as gorgeous as Zack. He didn't have the same dark and dangerous eyes, or the muscular shoulders and chest. But he was smart to the point of elegance and his neatly scrubbed face was boyish and appealing. Very nice. Wholesome, you might say. It made a change.

"Mrs. Doherty?"

She stared at him with only the slightest nod.

"My name's Godstow. Sergeant Paul Godstow. I'm with the police." He showed her his I.D. "May I come in?"

"Certainly, sergeant." When in doubt, ooze charm. She treated him to a brilliant smile which she hoped would disguise her nervousness. What now? "Can I offer you a drink?"

"Thanks, but no." He followed her into the living room. "You see, Mrs. Doherty, it's like this. I just need to ask you one or two questions about last night."

He was checking up on Karl. They had already got wind of her husband's past relationship with Lynette. She swallowed and launched into the tale that she had agreed with her husband. He'd been with her since coming home from a call at half past five. They had eaten together, watched a little television, discussed the need to redecorate the hall and first floor landing. She'd ironed a couple of shirts, he'd done a bit of tidying in the loft. They had retired to bed at about eleven o'clock to sleep, she strongly implied, the sleep of the just.

The policeman frowned. "So you were together all the time?"

"That's right, sergeant." She smiled again. He was dishy, there was no denying it. "Not a

very interesting evening, but that's married life for you. The excitement doesn't last."

He looked straight at her. "Depends on who you're married to, I suppose."

"That's true," she murmured. "Will—will that be all?"

"For the moment, Mrs. Doherty. It's just possible I may need to come back to ask you one or two more questions."

"Any time, any time at all," she breathed and was secretly entertained when his face turned beetroot red. "Actually, I was preparing lunch when you arrived. Nothing special, just a salad. I don't suppose you'd care to join me?"

"Thanks, but no," he said. "There's a lot to do in connection with the enquiry."

"Oh, well, another time perhaps."

He handed her a card. "This is my number. If anything springs to mind, I'd be glad to hear from you."

"Sorry I haven't been able to help. Perhaps I ought to return the compliment anyway." She found a slip of paper and wrote the number of the house and her own mobile in her flamboyant script. "Don't hesitate to call me."

He considered her carefully. "Thanks, Mrs. Doherty."

"Please call me Claire."

"Thanks, Claire. I'm sure we'll talk again."

"Zack? God, I've been trying to get hold of you all day. What went wrong?"

"Nothing," he replied. His voice sounded dreamy, as though he were living out a fantasy. "I went out for a ride on my Harley, that's all. And I felt free as a bird. It's amazing, you know, darling? You can snuff out a life just like that"— she heard him click his fingers—"and guess what? You carry on, same as before. You haven't changed. You're still you. You've murdered someone, but it's not the end of the world. Not for you, at any rate."

"Not for your victim, either," she said grimly.

"What do you mean?"

"Karl's still alive."

She could hear his intake of breath. "This your idea of a joke? Don't tell me you can't cope with what we've done. You told me you were sick of him. I did it for you."

"You didn't do it at all," she said curtly. Rapidly, she told him what had happened. The awestruck silence at the other end was eloquent. "Are you still there?" she demanded.

"I don't get it. There must be some mistake."

"Yes, and it looks like you made it."

"But it all went according to plan."

"Something went wrong with the plan, then."

"No, no, you don't understand."

"That's true, Zack. I don't bloody understand a thing. I suppose it's too much to hope that you can cast any light on this whole God-awful mess?"

"No, I . . ."

He was stammering, sounding like an overgrown schoolkid. He was so much less mature than the sergeant, she thought. Now there was a young man who was going places. Quiet, assured, effective. Everything that Zack was not.

"So tell me what really happened. Did you by any chance run over a bit of sacking that you mistook for my husband? An easy mistake to make in the dark, I suppose. A shop window dummy that seemed to have a bit of life? Or at least more of a brain than you?"

"No, honest. I did the business. He came out of the house, just like you said he would. I mean, I didn't see his face under the streetlight, so it wasn't easy to compare him to that photo you gave me. But he was a big bloke, muscular, walked with a bit of a swagger. It had to be your old man."

Claire groaned. Zack coughed and kept on talking. She thought he was trying to convince himself, rather than her, that he hadn't made the ultimate in fatal errors. "He'd been in there since before I turned up. I couldn't see where he'd parked. I thought it was probably out of sight so the people next door wouldn't twig that something was going on. I was following him down the road and then the pavement came to

an end. I'd staked the spot out in the afternoon. Double-checked the address you gave me, the photograph of your old feller. Everything was planned down to the last detail."

"Go on," she said bleakly.

"He was forced to cross over. No choice. And that's when I did it. Put my foot down and went for him. Tossed him up in the air like a pancake and then, when he hit the deck, reversed back over him just to make sure. I'm telling you, no-one could have survived that. I even saw the blood making a pool on the roadside before I drove away. Believe me, he was dead all right. The car was in a right state when I dumped it."

"You're sure about this?"

"I swear to you. On my mother's life."

"There's only one more question, then."

"What's that?" He sounded bewildered. He'd been expecting her undying gratitude and now it had all gone wrong. "Hurry up, there's someone at the door. They're leaning on the buzzer. What's your question?"

"Who exactly was it that you did kill?"

That was it, Claire said to herself as she pulled down the ladder that led up to the loft. Zack was finished, as far as she was concerned. She should have remembered her late father's favourite saying. If you want a job done properly, do it yourself. How could she ever have believed that he would do what she wanted without a slip-up? She blamed herself, even though it wasn't her habit. All her life, it seemed, she'd been seduced by men talking big. They always acted small. That nice sergeant would be different, she thought. He hadn't worn a wedding ring: she noticed these things. If only . . .

She reached up to switch on the loft light. It was a large loft, running the length of the house, but so dusty that it made her want to sneeze. Telling the sergeant that Karl had been up here tidying the previous night was probably the biggest lie of all. Her husband thought that life was too short for tidying and he never bothered with their attic. Taking a job with Slickloft had not made the slightest difference. His argument was that if he'd wanted a fourth bedroom he'd have bought a bigger house on day one. Besides, he said that nine out of ten loft conversions were only any use for midgets who liked walking down the middle of a room, and he was six feet three. The loft was, therefore, an admirable hiding place so far as Claire was concerned and she often made good use of it. Amongst the bits and pieces she kept here was the note she had made of Jennifer Bailey's name, address, and telephone number: information she had needed for Zack's briefing and which she'd managed to copy surreptitiously from Karl's personal organizer.

In fact, there were two numbers. Home and work, presumably? The codes were different. She recognized one immediately; it was the code for Bradford, she had a cousin who lived there. Next to the other were the initials "AA" and a couple of exclamation marks. Karl had a tedious sense of humour and she could not imagine what had been in his mind. Alcoholics Anonymous? Automobile Association? Agony Aunt? Nothing seemed to make sense at the moment. However, she had more important things to worry about.

She hurried downstairs and dialled the Bradford number, having taken care to withhold her own. "Yes?" The woman sounded subdued, very different from the night before.

"Mrs. Bailey? You may not remember, but you rang me last . . ."

"This isn't Mrs. Bailey," the woman interrupted. Of course not: she was elderly by the sound of her, probably a pensioner. "My name's Dora Prince, I'm her next door neighbour. I'm sorry, but she's not able to come to the phone right now. I'm afraid she's still in shock. You know what's happened, do you?"

I wish, Claire thought. "No . . ."

"It's a terrible tragedy," the woman said, lowering her voice. "Her husband went out last night to pick up some fish and chips and he was run over as he was crossing the road. The driver didn't stop. The policewoman's here now. She hasn't even got round to asking me anything.

She's too busy comforting Jennifer, of course. You can imagine."

Yes, Claire could imagine. "Oh dear," she said.

"Awful, isn't it? Such a lovely chap. And a dab hand at do-it-yourself, too. He'll never finish that pergola now, poor fellow. Shall I tell Jennifer you rang?"

"Oh, it's all right. Don't bother. We—we hardly know each other. I don't want to intrude."

As she put the phone down, Claire's heart was pounding. She had solved one mystery, only to be confronted with others. What on earth had possessed Jennifer Bailey to telephone her the previous night? Come to think of it, why had she lied about having seen Karl? And why had Karl said she was a one-legger when her husband— her late husband, thanks to bloody Zack, a real case of collateral damage, poor sod—had apparently been at home with her throughout the evening?

She sighed and looked for Jennifer Bailey's second number, the one which Karl had marked with the initials "AA." The code seemed familiar. Wasn't it Crewe? Curiouser and curiouser. Why would a woman who lived in Bradford have a work number in south Cheshire? Well, it was possible, but it seemed strange. She was seized by the urge to find out what "AA" stood for. She rang the number.

"Hello?" The woman who answered sounded familiar.

"Who is that?"

"Who's calling?" Definitely evasive.

The penny dropped. This was the woman who had rung the previous evening. Jennifer Bailey. Or rather, someone purporting to be Jennifer Bailey.

"Is that AA?" Claire asked in a hopeful tone.

"Yes." The woman sounded less guarded. "How may I help you?"

"Well, I just wondered . . ."

"You're interested in our services?" The woman seemed to recognize Claire's hesitancy, and to regard it as natural enough.

Claire pondered. Was she calling some kind

of brothel? She wouldn't put much past Karl. "Could you give me some details?"

"Of course." The woman became business-like. "It's very simple. The Alibi Agency's name speaks for itself. We provide excuses for people who need them. Most of our business comes by way of word-of-mouth recommendation, but you may have seen that feature article about us in *The Sun*. You want to be in one place when you're supposed to be in another? We can help. Our rates are very reasonable and . . ."

"That's all right, thanks," Claire said faintly. "I've changed my mind."

Well, well, well. She made herself a coffee after her evening meal and congratulated herself once again on solving the conundrum. Perhaps she had missed her way in life. She should have been a private detective. It was all so simple. Karl had never intended to visit Jennifer Bailey. She was a blind; he'd mentioned all that stuff about the one-legger simply to throw Claire off the track, lend a touch of verisimilitude to his tall story. He'd arranged to see Lynette and hired the Alibi Agency to impersonate his customer, so that Claire was none the wiser. He knew that their marriage, already on the rocks, could not survive if Claire found out that Lynette was still around. But he'd fallen out with Lynette—perhaps she had wanted him to get a divorce and move in with her and he'd fought shy of making the commitment. Something like that would be typical. Whatever. He'd lost his temper and she'd lost her balance and hit her head on something hard. End of Lynette. Claire smirked to herself. She'd always loathed Lynette.

It occurred to her that she might yet be able to kill two birds with one stone. Suppose she told the police that Karl had threatened her with violence so that she would back up his story? She might say that her conscience would not allow her to live a lie, that she'd decided Karl must pay for his crime. True, she was going to miss out on the life insurance, but she would at least be rid of her husband. And it would serve him right.

She rang the number that the nice sergeant had left with her and was quickly put through.

"This is Claire again. You remember our conversation?" she asked. Just the faintest seductive hint at this stage. Then see how he responded.

"I certainly do," he said. Was it her imagination or was there a faint leer in his voice? She hoped so.

"I won't beat about the bush. I lied to you about my husband. He was out last night, but he threatened what he would do to me if I didn't back him up."

"Ah."

"I hope you won't think too badly of me," she said in her meekest voice. "I felt as though I was under duress."

She told him the story, making no mention of the Alibi Agency. She didn't want to draw attention to the existence of the recently bereaved Mrs. Bailey. The policeman listened intently, murmuring his agreement every now and then when she insisted that life with Karl was hellish and that her only wish now was to do the right thing. He was sympathetic, a very good listener.

"I thought," she said tentatively, "that you might like to come back here and take a statement from me. A detailed statement."

"Yes, I'd love to do that."

"You would?"

"Oh yes," he said softly. "And perhaps when we've finished talking about your husband . . ."

"Yes?" she breathed.

". . . I can introduce you to a couple of colleagues of mine from Bradford CID. They've just finished interviewing a young man called Zack Kennedy."

She swallowed. "Oh yes?"

"It's in connection with a death in their patch. A Mr. Eric Bailey was killed in a hit and run incident last night. The vehicle was a Fiesta that was later dumped. What's interesting is that they found a photograph in the car. It had slipped between the driver's and passenger's seats. A picture of a man standing proudly next to a Slickloft van, apparently parked outside his own house. Right next to the street name, the name of the street where you live, actually. On the back of the photograph was your husband's name and a brief description. The handwriting is distinctive. As soon as it was shown to me, I recognized it from the note you gave me of your phone number." He paused. "All rather puzzling. Mind you, once it turned out that Mr. Kennedy's fingerprints were on the photograph, things started to become clearer. He has a criminal record. Nothing big league, just a few burglaries and car thefts. Possibly you didn't know that?"

Claire made a noise that was half-way between a sigh and a sob.

"No? Ah, well. By the way, the Baileys' neighbour, Mrs. Prince, saw the Fiesta yesterday afternoon. The driver was behaving suspiciously, and she gave a description which bears an uncanny resemblance to Mr. Kennedy. He's been arrested. The charge will be murder, I guess, but his lack of competence is equally criminal, wouldn't you say? We can chat about it later. I'll be with you in a quarter of an hour."

Slowly, as if in a trance, Claire put the receiver back on the cradle. She couldn't help glancing at the clock. She'd always been impatient, always hated having to hang around. The next fifteen minutes would, she knew, be the longest of her life as she sat helplessly on the sofa and waited for Godstow.

PERMISSIONS ACKNOWLEDGMENTS

Reprinted by permission of Curtis Brown Group Ltd., London, on behalf of the Estate of Lord Dunsany.

"Waiting for Godstow" by Martin Edwards. Originally published in *The Mammoth Book of Locked-Room Mysteries* (London, Robinson, 2000). Copyright 2000 by Martin Edwards. Reprinted by permission of the author.

"The Twelfth Statue" by Stanley Ellin. Originally published in *Ellery Queen's Mystery Magazine*, February 1967. Copyright 1967 by Stanley Ellin; renewed 1995. Reprinted by permission of Curtis Brown, Ltd.

"The Odour of Sanctity" by Kate Ellis. Originally published in *The Mammoth Book of Locked-Room Mysteries* (London, Robinson, 2000). Copyright 2000 by Kate Ellis. Reprinted by permission of the author and the author's agent, A. M. Heath.

"A Traveller's Tale" by Margaret Frazer. Originally published in *The Mammoth Book of Locked-Room Mysteries* (London, Robinson, 2000). Copyright 2000 by Gail Frazer. Reprinted by permission of the author.

"The Bird in the Hand" by Erle Stanley Gardner. Originally published in *Detective Fiction Weekly*, April 9, 1932. Copyright 1932 by Erle Stanley Gardner; renewed. Reprinted by permission of Queen Literary Agency.

"The Flung-Back Lid" by Peter Godfrey. Originally published in *John Creasey's Crime Selection 1979* (London, Gollancz, 1979). Copyright 1979 by Peter Godfrey. Reprinted by permission of Ronald Godfrey.

"Mike, Alex, or Rufus" by Dashiell Hammett. Originally published in *Black Mask* magazine, January 1925. Copyright 1925 by Dashiell Hammett; renewed. Reprinted by permission of the Dashiell Hammett Literary Property Trust.

"The Man from Nowhere" by Edward D. Hoch. Originally published in *Famous Detective Stories*, June 1956. Copyright 1956 by Edward D. Hoch. "The Theft of the Bermuda Penny" by Edward D. Hoch. Originally published in *Ellery Queen's Mystery Magazine*, June 1975. Copyright 1975 by Edward D. Hoch. "The Problem of the Old Oak Tree" by Edward D. Hoch. Originally published in *Ellery Queen's Mystery Magazine*, July 1978. Copyright 1978 by Edward D. Hoch. Reprinted by permission of Patricia M. Hoch.

"The Sands of Thyme" by Michael Innes. Originally published in *Appleby Talking* (London, Gollancz, 1954). Copyright 1954 by J. I. M. Stewart. Reprinted by permission of Coolabi PLC.

"All at Once, No Alice" by William Irish. Originally published in *Argosy* magazine, March 2, 1940. Copyright 1940 by Cornell Woolrich; renewed 1967. Reprinted by permission of JP Morgan Chase as Trustee for the Claire Woolrich Memorial Scholarship Fund.

"The Strange Case of Steinkelwintz" by MacKinlay Kantor. Originally published in *Chicago Daily News Midweek*, 1929. Copyright 1929 by MacKinlay Kantor. Reprinted by permission of the Donald Maass Literary Agency on behalf of the Estate of MacKinlay Kantor.

"The Locked Bathroom" by H. R. F. Keating. Originally published in *Ellery Queen's Mystery Magazine*, June 2, 1980. Copyright 1980 by H. R. F. Keating. Reprinted by permission of Sheila Mitchell Keating.

"The Crewel Needle" by Gerald Kersh. Originally published in *Lilliput* magazine, May/June 1953. Copyright 1953 by Gerald Kersh. Reprinted by permission of New World Authors on behalf of the Estate of Gerald Kersh. "The Episode of the Codex' Curse" by C. Daly King. Originally published in *The Curious Mr. Tarrant* (London, Collins, 1935). Copyright 1935 by C. Daly King. "The Episode of the *Torment IV*" by C. Daly King. Originally published in *The Curious Mr. Tarrant* (London, Collins, 1935). Copyright 1935 by C. Daly King. Reprinted by permission of Valerie King Beatts.